Mother Blues

a novel

Owen Thomas

Text copyright © 2021 OTF Literary, Anchorage, Alaska
Author Website: http://www.owenthomasliterary.com

ISBN 13: 978-1-7346303-3-6
ISBN 10: 1-73463-033-7
LCCN: 2021916531

To all the old, blue masters, for knowing how to set a soul to music when nothing else could.

"When you are through with the blues, you've got nothing to rest on."

— Mahalia Jackson

"Blues means what milk does to a baby. Blues is what the spirit is to the minister. We sing the blues because our hearts have been hurt, our souls have been disturbed."

— Alberta Hunter

"It's a long old road…"

— Bessie Smith

Chapter 1

It is a plain dusted thrasher of some kind. Or a thrush. Sheldon is not sure which. It alights upon the broken blue door lying in the road.

Too big for a sparrow.

It grooms its brown feathers and twitches. One way then another.

Oblivious to what is coming.

Quiet out here on the midday road, cutting through the arid Texan scrub like an old scar. A carpet of hot sound registers as a buzzing from every direction. A sonic pastiche of insect, foul, reptile and rodent woven together into a single vibration as easy to ignore as the air itself.

The earth, too, grinds on its axis. But we do not hear that either. We tune it out, listening only for the sounds on top of that sound.

Sounds of the pertinent.

Sounds of the new and the different and the deadly, letting the background – all of the constancy of the world –drop away into the oblivion of irrelevance.

And then we listen.

All is quiet.

Except that the black metal belly of the thing he had been pursuing, pops and hisses its dying soliloquy.

There is a slow dripping, too, which Sheldon knows cannot be good.

And then … *fa-woomph.*

Fire.

It seems to stab up from the hot asphalt, as if up through a fissure, a puncture wound in the mantel that taps down into the molten core.

Only seconds left now. The bird, no longer oblivious, is gone. Back into the cosmic vibration.

He grabs both of her wrists. Squeezes his hands closed. Pulls her across the glass-strewn ceiling of the burning Civic.

Her boot catches on a contortion of mangled frame. He curses. Yanks. Her left arm pops. Sickeningly. As if it were merely a rope of putty.

1

Yanks again. It lengthens in his grip.

He pulls her, now bootless, through the passenger window and out onto the road. Her dark hair hangs. Drags. Smears red across the yellow line. The left side of her face is a mess.

He does not perceive the Jeep decelerating in a waft of dust, nor its driver fumbling for his phone.

He breathes. Tries not to see the blood. Pulls hard.

He drags her in one unbroken effort for the ditch behind his own car, a sleek silver splinter glinting in the sun.

The man is out of the Jeep now. Running. He yells into his phone.

A sudden rending of air shreds the peace, scattering it like birds, dissolving the solid flock into a panic.

Sheldon reacts without thinking. Covers Olivia's body with his own.

Chapter 2

The realtor is a cloud now. An atomized essence. Buddy's friend, reduced to a stubborn trace of citrus. The scent collects in the back of his throat. He tries to spit it out in the sink. Opens the bottle. Drinks.

The cloud has expanded since she left. It fills the entire place now. Into rooms she had never entered. Wafts up against the ceiling. Clings to the drapes she had pulled back from the kitchen windows, showing him the postage-stamp patio affixed to the envelope of dirt stretching away from the house. The boundary is marked by a barren ditch. A broken, black PVC pipe jutting up into the air like a newly excavated dinosaur shank.

Beyond that there is nothing much. A mottled swath of desert. A slash of sun-bleached road. A strip of cattle fencing. A dead, bony spray of ocotillo claws at an empty blue sky.

So it doesn't get any better than the fake prehistoric tibia.

Davis turns from the window. Leans back against the sink.

Her business card is still on the counter. *Trina Lopez.* The *T* and *L* are made to look like spongy, cartoonish cacti. A coyote pup rests happily, tongue flopping, in the shade of the '*z*'. In the pinkish, cottony sky she has scrawled her home telephone number. Circled it. Underlined it. Added an exclamation mark.

Just in case his cute came with a side of stupid.

Buddy had been right about her. *"She'll set you up with the house, but Trina'll be all over you like a sunburn. Just like her mother. Don't encourage her."*

Buddy was right. Buddy was always right.

The business card is clipped to a stack of colorful, single-page *Welcome to Corbin* brochures. He picks up the sheaf. Takes a swig from the bottle. Flips the top page.

A leaf-green map of Corbin, Texas.

Flips.

Sienna-shaded maps of Crockett, Val Verde, Terrell and Pecos counties with dusty red cactus flowers scattered along the lattice of green stem roadways to

3

mark human concentrations. Iraan. Sheffield. Ozona. Carta Valley. Langtry. Comstock. Del Rio. Sanderson. Dryden. Fort Stockton.

Flips.

A turquoise sheet entitled *"A Brief History of Corbin, Texas."* He swigs. Reads.

> *Named after Scottish railroad magnate, Corbin Draego, the community of Corbin Texas was founded in 1881.* Draego, an Ohioan, was one of several original owners of the Galveston, Harrisburg and San Antonio Railway *along with Thomas W. Pierce. Pierce ultimately bought out the interests of his partners in what was thereafter commonly called the* Pierce Line *as it stretched its way to San Antonio in early 1877. Draego, enamored by the Southwestern frontier, left the railroading business and kept moving deeper into Texas, settling just west of what is now Corbin proper. There, Draego used his fortune to start one of the largest and most successful sheep ranching operations in the four hundred mile stretch between San Angelo and El Paso. In 1890, Draego suffered the tragic ...*

Flips.

A pearlescent, oyster-colored sheet entitled *"The Corbin Moon Garden Festival."* Swigs. Reads.

> *Every October, the citizens of Corbin, and people from throughout south Texas, come together for the annual Corbin Moon Garden Festival. A celebration of music, flowers and food, the Moon Garden Festival has been a tradition since 1945 with the dedication of the* Fuente de la Luna *("Fountain of the Moon") in the Corbin Town Square. As legend has it...*

He tosses the packet back on the counter. Finishes the bottle. Sets it in the sink. Pulls another out of the case and twists off the cap. Drinks.

He leaves the kitchen. Walks down the hall to the spare bedroom. Kicks at the box nearest the door. He pushes it down the hall with the side of his boot. The box scrapes against the warped wooden floor like it is strewn with gravel and bits of glass.

The box is not heavy so much as inconvenient. Bending and lifting takes more energy than he cares to muster. That, and he's holding a bottle. Nothing new there.

But just ginger ale now. Fifty-nine days. Tomorrow is sixty.

Davis half-sits, half-falls, back into the only chair worth a damn. Irony is that it's not his chair. Or it hadn't been. It had come with the place. Which meant it had been abandoned. Too big to fit the new home of whomever had lived here last. That, or *screaming geranium* did not have a place in the new color scheme.

4

Anyway, it was his chair now.

He takes a drink of ginger ale and props his feet up on the box. Like that had been the whole point of kick-sliding the thing down the hall.

But that wasn't the point. The point was *one-box-a-day*. No more, no less. Every day he forced himself to dislodge one box from the pyramid of boxes stuffed into the spare room and unpack it. He could not go to bed until that was done. That was the rule. A box a day. Life was all about rules now.

Box a day.

Will not take long at that rate. He does not own much. Floods hate a pack rat. Two years post Harvey had filled just over a dozen boxes. Not that he wants all of it.

But it's his.

He'd considered not unpacking anything. Just living out of the boxes for awhile before moving back to Houston. He would not be here long. *Temporary,* Buddy had said. *"Long enough to clean yourself up. Dry yourself out. Long enough for it to stick this time."*

Davis looks over at his old, beat up, mushroom couch squatting across the room beneath the window, still littered with moving day detritus. The screaming geranium chair is kicking its ass in the personality department. But the couch gets points for loyalty. No question there. It had been with him through some of the worst of it and had the stains to prove it.

Out the front window is a stand of three large poplars, like folded-up umbrellas waiting for the rain that never comes. He'd known trees like those. Back when he was a boy. Back before everything went to hell.

Those kinds of boxes –the memory boxes –unpacked themselves.

Beyond the poplars, across the street, is a house that looks almost exactly like his. Even the little porch off the front door with its sad little steps. Except that house is painted the color of a robin's egg, instead of an armadillo like his house and all of the others.

Inside the robin's egg there is no baby robin trying to peck its way out. Instead there sits an old woman with white straw for hair. On moving day she stood at the window for the better part of an hour, gripping the slats of her blinds like the bars of a cell and watching Davis and the movers unload the truck. Sizing him up. Looking for tattoos. Waiting for the motorcycle to make an appearance. And the marijuana cigarettes and the naked floozies and the screaming pregnant girlfriends and the weaponry and all the rest of it.

But there was nothing else. There was only Davis Payne and all of his stuff, packed in identical, unmarked, perfectly square boxes. That was it.

Well. There was a motorcycle.

Davis takes another swig of his ginger ale. Sets the bottle on the floor next to the chair. Pulls the box closer.

It's a game of roulette, this thing with the boxes. Never know which one is next. Most of them are harmless. Not all of them.

He leans forward and pulls up one of the cardboard flaps.

It's the writing box. Five accordion folders are wedged inside. He pulls one out. It seems to breathe, expanding in his hands like a paper squeezebox. He inserts two fingers into one of the slots and extracts a sheaf of pages.

He reads. Laughs to himself. Shakes his head.

It is the second edition of *Voices*. Maybe the third. He flips through the pages. Scanning. Spot reading here and there.

There were three interviews in that piece, which is entitled simply "*The Road*": a long-haul truck driver ("*Traveling the Road*"), a district court judge ("*Rules of the Road*"), and the owner of a mortuary ("*The End of the Road*"). As Davis recalls, *The Road* was the piece that had finally convinced Buddy Lincoln to make *Voices* a permanent feature of the *Ocotillo Review*.

'I see what you're gettin' at there, Davis," Buddy had boomed. Other diners had looked up. Stopped chewing for a second. "I get it now. Pieces of somethin' bigger."

Davis had nodded and taken another bite of his burger. Buddy had slipped the last page face down on the table beneath his black felt Cattleman with the others.

"*Voices*. Like voices in a choir."

Buddy Lincoln was big enough and black enough already. He didn't need a black felt Cattleman on his head. Not that anyone dared tell Buddy such a thing. But it was true.

Davis had nodded. Buddy had swatted the table, rattling the silverware.

"Okay then. I'll keep it. I'll run it every quarter. Don't let me down, kid. You gon' eat all them fries?"

Davis had been letting Buddy down ever since. Not so much with *Voices*, which was about the only thing that Davis had gotten right over the years. His readership had grown steadily. *The Ocotillo Review* had taken to marketing him as a literary mainstay. But with just about everything else, Davis had tested Buddy's patience. Tested his loyalty. Somehow, through it all, fries or no fries, Buddy was still backing him up.

Of course, Buddy Lincoln had more than enough cattle under that hat. He was an avid reader of Texas newspapers. He knew the whole ugly story of Davis T. Payne. So he'd taken an interest from the beginning. And Buddy was one of those men who, much as he might want to, couldn't abandon a wild animal he'd taken in and named.

So the move out to Corbin had been Buddy Lincoln's idea.

"You can write '*Voices*' anywhere, Davis. You need to get your punk ass outta Houston. Nothin' but a soggy graveyard of bad decisions out here. Get yourself a place in Corbin."

"Corbin?"

"Watch yourself, boy. I grew up in Corbin. Good people. Hell, Dallas Letti lives out that way."

"Go on. She's still alive? *Letti Blue?* In Corbin?"

"What I hear. You should go find out. Interview her. Work her in somehow."

"Yeah, right."

"Goals are important, Davis."

Davis had shrugged. Buddy poked him in the chest with a giant finger.

"Get... the fuck... outta Houston. Hard to get into trouble in Corbin. All kinda' houses to rent. I checked. Nothin's sellin' so all kinda' shit for rent. You pick the house, I'll split the rent. You can work it off."

What could he say to that? Standing there on the sidewalk outside the Harris County Detention center. Sun splintering over the peaks of Buddy's Cattleman like Davis had been standing in the shadow of the Matterhorn. When Buddy Lincoln said *frog*, you jumped. Nothing to do but nod.

"And you go to the *got-damned* meetings, you hear me Davis? I gotta name and number for you to call. Elvis Broussard. Good man. And you can bet I'll be checking up. You hear?"

Davis had heard. He'd go to the *got-damned* meetings. He would.

Just as soon as he *got* moved in. One box at a time.

He slips the pages back into the accordion file and closes the folder. Drops it on the floor next to the box. He removes the other four folders and does the same. From inside the now empty box comes a soft *slap*.

The empty box is not empty. A lone manila folder lays flat.

Davis reaches in. Pulls it out. Opens it. Recognizes it. Closes his eyes.

Shit, he thinks. Because he hates the feeling in his chest. Old and terrible.

He needs to throw it out, once and for all. Or at least label the damn folder. Put it in something neon. Something with a combination lock. Anything to slow him down. Warn him. Shouldn't always be such a gut-punch surprise.

Dr. Bees would say that this is no surprise at all. Dr. Bees would say that he knows exactly what he is doing. That he *wants* to keep finding this folder. That some part of him is always *looking* for this folder. Because once the folder is in his hands, he is powerless to keep from reading the words inside.

The forwarding note from Dr. Bees is on top, binder clipped to an all too familiar packet. Even the irregular, unreliable shape of the scrawl is a kind of poison that he feels instantly in his gut.

Davis. Now that Houston has drained itself of Hurricane Harvey and I have found you (which took some doing) I am sending this letter back to you. It was never really for me in the first place. Hate me all you want if that helps. You need to stay in touch with these feelings if you want them to recede. One of your mother's lifelines came from Bessie Smith. "It's a long old road, but I know I'm gonna to find the end." You are welcome to call me any time, Davis. In the meantime, just keep walking. Yours, Fredrick Bees.

He folds back the note, uncovering the letter beneath. Reads.

And that is not an easy thing. Reading those words. *His* words. Dumping him unceremoniously back into the summer of his seventeenth year. All of those feelings are still there waiting for him. All of them. Perfectly preserved and coiled up into his awkward cursive script like a Texas diamondback waiting for him to return.

Dear Dr. Bees:

You asked me to write it all down. The whole story. From wherever I think it begins to wherever I think it ends. It has taken me a long time. You probably thought I was hiding from it. You always say I'm hiding from it. I wasn't hiding. It was just hard to find the time. I have school and practice and work. I tried to work on it for a few minutes each night before bed. I have not been hiding. I did what you asked. I trusted you that this would help.

Like I have told you a million times, I don't like thinking about any of this. It makes me feel terrible. I still have an ulcer. I don't eat much. I still have nightmares. Thinking about her doesn't help. And writing about her makes everything worse. I knew it would. I tried to tell you. I wish you had listened to me. You accuse me of hiding. I'm not a coward. I wish I had never agreed to see you. This has not helped me. You have not helped me.

But you wanted it, so here it is. I know you are trying to help. I know my mother trusted you. But she would have wanted me to be happy. To be free of this. I don't want to see you any more. I can't. Please leave me alone.

Sincerely,

Davis

He should have sued Dr. Bees is what he should have done. His mother would not have liked that. But there it was, just the same.

Dr. Bees, from his leather throne. Twisting his ring. "You need to write all of this down, Davis. You need to get all of these feelings out of your head and down onto paper. Into a journal. Start from the beginning. Wherever you think all of this begins. And then write it out to the end, wherever you think it all ends."

"No. Why should I?"

"So you can see all of this more objectively. So you can see that it wasn't your fault. Just like your mother …"

"Told you I'm not talking about that any more."

"I apologize. We won't talk about your mother. We'll stay focused on this. *This* was not your fault either, Davis."

"Right. Tell that to the police. The newspapers."

"This is what I mean. The police, the newspapers… they all got the wrong idea. Okay?"

Dr. Bees had looked at him over his glasses in that familiar way. Tone saturated with professional-grade condescension. Davis had heard it as sympathy.

"But the police believe you now. And the papers have moved on, Davis. The only thing left is for you to forgive yourself. You're the one who needs convincing. Not the police. Not the newspapers. Think about it."

Davis had thought about it. It seemed like a terrible idea. All he wanted to do was to get away from the feelings. Away. Away. Far away. He would not spend more time trapped inside her burning memory. He would not shape his emotions into words. It was masochism. Reckless. He didn't want to write anything down. Didn't want to talk.

He had wanted to curl up and die.

As long as he was suing people, he might also have sued *The Houston Writer*. In the glow of his father's ambition for him, he had subscribed. *The Houston Writer* had selected that month, of all months, to devote an entire issue to the benefits of journaling. All the best, great dead writers, suddenly, out of nowhere, had been big into journaling. Woolf, Emerson, Thoreau, Kafka, Dostoevsky, Cheever. All of them. Who knew?

Davis had taken it as a sign. Not that he had been one of those folks who looked for signs in the world. But his mother had always been one of those folks. She would have encouraged him to take it as a sign. So he had. He had written everything down, just as Dr. Bees had suggested. From the beginning of things to end of things. It was supposed to help.

It didn't.

It was supposed to *process* his feelings. Neutralize them.

It didn't.

It was supposed to free him from her, Abby, forever.

It didn't.

He opens the journal. Takes a deep breath. The Texas diamondback stirs.

He reads all over again.

I met Abby Palmer, two summers ago, at the Texas State Fair. I was sixteen. She was twenty-seven. She read my open hand inside a purple tent. Behind a curtain of glass beads. Fat Jack and Skinny Kenny stood outside snorting and trying to listen.

The air around her smelled of jasmine incense. And her perfume. Her eyes were large and clear with dark brown chocolate pools at their centers.

She said I had a pure heart. She said I was "stalwart soul."

She said I would save her life.

Chapter 3

Abby and Davis

She said I had a pure heart. She said I was "stalwart soul."

She said I would save her life.

It had taken me all day to screw up the courage to go inside that tent. I am not the most outgoing person. I guess you know that already. I'd seen her before. We all had, standing at the entrance by the hand-lettered sign: "Palm Readings." Watching people come and go. But that day I really saw her –I mean *SAW* her – for the first time.

She was so pale. Vampire pale. Like she'd never been outside in the daylight before. The sun lit her up like the moon. Her hair was a thicket of brown ringlets down to her shoulders. Her fingernails were painted black, maybe to match the bruised color of her lips and eye shadow. She wore a thin, purplish tunic, just about the same color as the tent behind her.

She smiled as we passed, pulling her hand through the curtain of red and gold glass beads hanging around her shoulders. Combing her fingers through them like strands of hair.

My heart stalled for several beats and then raced to catch up. Something about her look. The shape of her eyes. Her lips. And something else I can't describe. In that moment, suddenly, I found her beautiful. You have that clipping from the newspaper, the one we always talk about. But I never thought that photo in the newspaper did her justice.

The picture I have in my head will always be the sight of her that Saturday. Standing in front of her tent, holding those glass beads in the sun next to her face. It was like a bolt of lightning.

I'm not a nut, even though you probably think I am. I didn't think she was actually smiling just at me. I thought she was smiling at all three of us. We were walking shoulder-to-shoulder through the throngs of gabbling fair-goers, covering the maybe quarter mile or so from the livestock pavilion to the carnival rides. We were still close enough to the main entrance to hear Big Tex doing his thing over and over and over. *Hoooowwwdeee, fooollllllks!* I'm sure you know.

It was hot for late September. Mid-nineties. But every so often a breeze blew in over the fairgrounds that felt like a wave sliding up onto a burning beach. The air smelled like sugar and fat and dust. And whenever that wave of air came in from a slightly different direction, you got a good whiff of steer shit too. Broken bits of live country music drifted by from different parts of the fairgrounds. Kids running everywhere. Yelling and screaming. Begging their parents for more of everything. More baby strollers than we could count. Levis and Stetsons and shit-kickers everywhere you turned. Even on the babies.

It was the rides we were after that afternoon. *The Tornado. The Octopus. The Scrambler.* We were all about the rides. Even Kenny who, among the three of us, was famous for having gotten sick two years in a row on *The Scrambler.*

Fat Jack, Skinny Kenny and me, Davis, the one with a name that did not conveniently rhyme with some physical weirdness. I was taller than either of them. More developed in my shoulders. I had been called good-looking, even back then. But my oddities are the invisible kind. Timid as a little field mouse. Still am. Shrank from every challenge. Still do. I had no faith in myself. Still don't. So two years hasn't changed me much. Not for the better anyway. So much for therapy. Sorry but its true.

The three of us have been friends from the early days of our freshman year. Skulking the halls of Davy Crockett High, trying not to be noticed. Don't know if we would have even liked each other in any other context. But we bonded in our antisocialism, if that's the right word. Insecure, distrusting loners. Beat down by life. Abused by our peers. Abandoned in some form or another by our families. Death or divorce or neglect. That was the glue that stuck us together.

There was no reason for Abby to separate one of us out from the others. We were a unit that day. Jack and Kenny and me. Just like always. We stuck together.

But, still. It *seemed* like she had smiled at *me.* Maybe because I was the only one of the three of us that was looking back at her. I couldn't help but see that smile as kind of message. A personal invitation. And I was stupid enough to share that with the guys. Kenny dared me and then Jack jumped on board. They called me chicken shit and bet me money.

I'd have done the same, I guess. That's just how we were.

It was not enough to just go in and have my palm read. Too easy, they said. I had to tell her I loved her. Or that I wanted to marry her. Or that I wanted to have raunchy sex with her. Not just sex. *Raunchy sex.* That was the dare. That was the bet. Ten bucks.

None of us had a girlfriend. None of us had *ever* had a girlfriend. But sex was close to all we ever talked about. Picking a woman out of a crowd and boasting about how she was the one. Claiming her, defending her, guessing her name.

That was as close to dating or sex as we ever got. So we did it all the time, making pretend lovers of strangers.

After every carnival ride we passed back by the palm-reading tent even though it was way out of our way. Something about the rides convinced me that I could do it. That it would be easy. If you could survive *The Octopus* or *The Tornado*, how hard could it be to lie to a grown woman and tell her you loved her? It would probably make her day and what harm could come of it in the end?

Well, the opposite. The harm would come from *not* telling her. Even if I said nothing about raunchy sex. Even if I just told her that I loved her. If I didn't do at least that, I'd never live it down. I'd always be chicken shit to Jack and Kenny. I was tired of all of us talking the talk. Tired of being timid. Someone had to walk the walk.

And so after every ride we would all charge dizzily off across the fairgrounds, shoulder-to-shoulder, me in the middle, headed back for the purple tent. Like declaring love to the palm reader was some sort of life-or-death mission.

When she did not have a customer inside the tent with her, she kept the curtain of glass beads tied open. We could see her in there at her table, sometimes laying out cards. Sometimes doing nothing but staring at her own hands. I almost went inside so many times, coming right up to the entrance. And then without fail, some gal would choose that very moment to slip in ahead of me pulling some guy behind her by the wrist, usually sporting a mullet and shit-kickers, and eating a corndog or a cotton candy. Kenny and Jack would laugh and spit whenever that happened, making it out like I had planned it that way all along, and then we would all run off for another ride.

But then, one time, toward the end of the day, I just did it.

I stood there near the entrance silently telling myself to *Cowboy Up*. Kenny and Jack were maybe fifty feet away burning holes in my back with their eyes. Not too far away at one of the bandstands, just on the other side of the people selling Kettle Corn, someone with a high, thin twang was checking the mics. You know: *Check. Check. One, two, three. Check. Check. One, two...*

I took a breath and stepped inside. I bowed my head a little as I entered, the way I had seen so many adults do. I was the tallest of my friends, but there was still plenty of room to spare in the doorway.

But I bowed my head anyway. Like I'd entered a church.

She looked up at me from her table. One of her hands was holding the other, palm up. I stood there, saying nothing. Terrified of her and of what I had to do. I could hear my friends skidding into a pile on the side of the tent.

She released her hand, folding her fingers over her palms as if closing a diary that she did not want me to see. She stood. Smiled. Her almond eyes turned up at the corners when she did this, making the smile personal. My heart was like something wild, twitching in a dream, running for its life.

She moved past me without a word. Just the smile.

I could smell perfume. Cosmetics. A hint of sweat.

She was only a little taller than me. Brass bangles on her wrists brushed against the folds of her tunic as she passed. I kept my head lowered, eyes wide. She wore gold sandals. Her feet were pale and delicate and beautiful, like something aquatic. I couldn't move. I was frozen. Immobilized by fear and awe. She was so close to me I could feel the entire length of her body along the ache of my left side.

I still can. Even today. I can still feel it. I'm sure you have some fancy phrase for it. All I know is that sometimes when I think of that day it feels like she is still right next to me. Even as I write these words.

She slipped behind me, unhooking the loop of fabric that held open the curtain of glass beads, and closed the entrance. The flame of daylight at my feet that lit up the patchy grass and the Persian rug beneath the table and that burned up the sides of the tent suddenly broke into moving balls of red and gold. Indirect light filtered in through the large air vents in the top of the tent.

We were both still and quiet for several long seconds. Neither of us moved. Neither of us spoke. I could feel her standing behind me. I could smell her. I could not speak the words, but I could smell them.

Desire. Fear. Love. Fair to say that those were the words.

"Do you have a name?" she asked over my shoulder. I wasn't prepared for the British accent.

"Davis," I said, too softly. My voice sounded alien, like someone else had entered the tent and was speaking for me.

"Davis," she repeated. Like she was tasting the sound of it. "Davis. I like that. That's a sensitive name. Would you like to have your palm read, Davis?"

"I guess so," I said.

"You guess so?" I felt her hands on my shoulders. She turned me so that our faces were only inches apart. She was so beautiful. I wanted to cry. I wanted to kiss her mouth. I wanted to run.

"Yes," I corrected myself. "Yes, please."

She stood, silent. Looking at me. I didn't know what to think. She held out a hand. I thought she wanted me to shake it. She laughed at me. It sounded like music.

"No," she said. "It costs five dollars for a reading."

I shoved my hands into my pockets, with too much pent up energy, searching for money. I pulled out a wad of bills. Four ones and a ten. Torn ride tickets. Several coins dropped from between my fingers to the grass. I handed her the ten.

"You can keep it," I said.

"Quite a tip," she said with a tone of respect. I didn't know what to say so I didn't say anything. I stood there and blushed.

"My name's Abby," she said, moving past me to the table. "Come sit down, Davis."

I did as I was told, following her and then sitting in the folding metal chair as she lit two coils of incense in tiny brass kettles. She placed the kettles on opposite sides of the table. Between them she unrolled a plush velvet runner the color of ripe eggplant like mom used to buy. It was like a purple bridge spanning the sea of white tablecloth. Thin wisps of gray smoke rose out of the kettles like snakes from a basket. The scent was thick and hard to take at first.

"What are those for?" I asked, pretending to be relaxed. Abby sat down and smiled, pointing alternately to one kettle and then the other.

"That one is myrrh. That one is dragon's blood. Natural resins. They've been used for centuries."

"Why?"

"All kinds of things, I suppose. Medicine. Religious purification. To make spells more potent."

"Spells? You mean like witchcraft?"

"Yes. Like witchcraft."

"Do you believe in witchcraft?" I asked.

She laughed a little.

"No. I don't believe in witchcraft."

I blushed at the thought that maybe she thought *I* believed in witchcraft.

"But I believe in destiny," she said. "I believe we can see destiny. We can read it. Our own destiny. The destiny of others. It's recorded on our bodies. Our palms. The soles of our feet. We can read it, Davis. You just have to know how."

"And you do?"

"Yes. I do."

"You're not from here," I said. It sounded like an accusation.

"No," she said. "I'm from London. Will that be quite all right with you, Guvnor?"

"I... I didn't mean it like that. I just... I like your accent. We don't hear that much around here."

There was a snort and a soft thudding. Abby moved her gaze to a place past me, over my left shoulder.

"Those your friends out there?"

I turned. There was a dark shadow, like a boulder or a shrub on the side of the tent. The shadow shifted and swayed. It grew an arm and then reabsorbed it.

"Yes," I said, embarrassed.

"Are they interested in my accent too?" She was smirking.

I stood up and punched the side of the tent, dead center of the shadow. There was a sputtering of laughs. The shadow broke into two pieces and scattered.

"You come in here on a dare or something?"

15

"No," I lied, sitting back down at the table.

"How old are you?"

"Almost seventeen," I lied again. Abby nodded.

People always think I'm older than I really am. It's not just my size. My mother said I have mature features. I have my father's jaw line. You even said I carry myself like I have grown-up concerns. You said I have a mature way of expressing myself.

But even if you are a shrink, what the hell do you know?

"Will you give me your hand, Davis?"

Her directness, the sound of my name from her lips, the look from those deep brown eyes. These were like steel arrows, Dr. Bees, *one-two-three*, right into my chest. She extended her open hands across the table. I swallowed. I placed my right hand upside down into hers.

My hand was dirty and the knuckles were ragged. It was larger than hers, which were small and soft and clean. I might have been ashamed. But there was no room for shame. Abby cradled the back of my hand in her left. Using only the very tips of her fingers, she slowly stroked my palm. I felt shivers.

"You have a pure heart, Davis," she said. "These are strong lines. Indeed, a rather stalwart soul, I should think."

I swallowed, too overcome by the feeling of her skin moving against mine to respond. I couldn't help thinking about sex. It was the first thing I thought about. Sex. *Raunchy* sex. But it was so much more than that. There was something caring, something reassuring in the way she held this one part of my body and caressed it with the tips of her fingers.

It's all going to be okay. That's what her fingers seemed to say to me as I imagined her naked. As I lusted for her. *It's all going to be okay.*

It had been a long time since I had felt that anyone really cared whether anything was ever going to be okay ever again. Jack and Kenny were good for some things, but not that. Dad kept a roof over my head but was too angry and too deep in the bottle for much else.

In the tips of Abby's fingers I felt not only what I wanted, but also what I had lost. It cut right through me. I had to fight back a rising lump in my throat.

She moistened the pad of her middle finger on the flat of her tongue, and then traced the lines on my palm, one after the other. Like she was spelling a word she did not want to speak.

The sounds of the fair around us seemed to fall away. I did not care if Kenny and Jack were still outside listening. I did not care if they were back on *The Scrambler* or if they had gone back home without me. Every thought and sensation was beneath the tip of that one delicate finger and its bright, glistening trail.

Abby suddenly lifted my hand so close to her face I thought she might kiss it.

Her eyebrows knitted, coarse and dark against her moon skin. Her face pinched in sudden concern, putting a deep groove right in the center of her forehead.

Then she closed her eyes. I could see them darting back and forth beneath her dark stained lids, like frightened animals beneath a tarp.

"What?" I asked. "What is it? What do you see? Something bad?"

She opened her eyes, fixed, burrowing into me.

"You're the one," she said with something like astonishment. "You're going to save my life."

The brass bangles slid from her wrist to her forearm.

Had I been looking at her wrist rather than searching her face, I might have noticed the scars. Never saw those until much later. After there was no turning back.

Although I honestly don't know whether seeing them sooner would have changed anything. I think it was too late from the very first time she said my name.

Chapter 4

The Watcher. His handlebar mustache is a follicular scowl. A furry frown. His wife-beater is too small. Gut is too big.

He is on the treadmill. He does not run. He stomps quickly. Slapping his feet at fleeing cockroaches. The machine, not built for such punishment, rattles and shakes.

Eight televisions are suspended in front of him. So he can chase the dream.

But *the Watcher* is not watching television. *The Watcher* is watching her. *She* is his dream for now.

She knows this, of course. History has honed her instincts. She can see him in the corner mirror across the club. Bald skin above his dingy headband like a wet beet. Like some angry new life is crowning out of the top of his head.

She dips the cloth into the bucket. Wipes down the black metal frame on the second-to-last spinner. When she is done with the bikes, she will need to get down on her hands and knees to clean the rubber mats next to the free-weights.

That'll give him a good view.

Olivia blocks him out. Shrugs him off. Keeps working.

Not that she likes this kind of attention. She is not Libby, after all.

She simply doesn't give two hoots one way or the other. Not any more.

It's always someone. Every shift some *Watcher* or another follows her with his eyes. Crowds her as she wipes down the equipment or scrubs the floors or cleans the mirrors or hauls a load of towels from the laundry room.

The *Longhorn Fitness* uniform does nothing to discourage the attention. Black shorts. A hot pink v-neck t-shirt for the women. A hat-waving cowboy is breaking the spirit of a longhorn bull that just happens to straddle the left breast.

But she does not regret the job. Pay is okay. Not near enough, but more than she'd make waiting tables over at *The Hay Barn* or *Cowboy Up* or *Silo Jack's*. More than she currently makes at *The Diamondback*. Hours are good. She works out every day for free, which has put her in the best shape of her life.

And people mostly leave her alone. She likes that in a job.

They watch her. That's true. Corral her with their eyes. But they rarely strike up conversation.

Which allows Olivia to think about things.

About the missing melody, mostly. Like a bird lost in the desert.

And about how all she needs is two or three hundred thousand dollars.

Enough to be free. Really free. Free to no longer need this world. Free enough to lose herself, find herself, in another world.

Those kinds of things.

For now she is on her own kind of treadmill. Her own kind of spinner. Tremendous effort going nowhere. Fleeing in place.

It's not like she has a rich uncle. Or parents that would give two nickels to save her life.

Best thing about *Longhorn Fitness* –the *real* reason she is there at all –is that the General Manager, Mr. Pete, one of Libby's regulars, lets her give massages. It's about the only work Olivia is actually qualified to do beyond serving drinks and cleaning the sweat off of things.

True, she does not have a proper license. Kicked out of the San Angelo Community College before that all-important embossed piece of paper had been printed and signed. The SACC did not tolerate violence against its faculty. She was lucky, the instructor had yelled through a wad of wet red gauze, that he did not file charges. "*I was just trying to be your fuckin' friend!*" Maybe so. But *he* was lucky, even if he didn't realize it, that "*the misunderstanding*" had occurred before Olivia had taken up with Libby Holder.

So she is not official.

But when it comes to soft tissue, she knows what she is doing. Working a sore muscle. She knows how to go deep. And Mr. Pete knows that no one is going to complain about Olivia DeLuna. Quite the contrary. The tips are impressive.

But anything is possible when it comes to people. So just in case, Libby provides her with some extra job security. Whenever Mr. Pete feels the urge, which is about once a month or so, he gets a special Liberty Cherish discount. A little more for a little less. And Libby always knew how to serve up a little more.

Not that Olivia feels good about this sacrifice for her benefit. But once Libby made up her mind, there was no changing it.

"*Last time I check, baby, this shit here ain't yo' bus'ness. I'ma keep doin' for Mr. Pete. An' if that mean Mr. Pete keep doin' for you? Then you best jus' let his white cowboy ass pay that shit fo'ward.*"

Mr. Pete. He calls her *Mocha*. Or *Latte*. Or *Caramel*. *Cara-meuhl*, like his mouth is full of marshmallow. There are others at *Longhorn* with the same skin tone. But they all get real names. He lets her keep a key to the massage room. Gives her an hour per shift to schedule appointments. No pay for that hour. All off the books. But she keeps the tips.

She has a list of regulars. Mostly men, but more than a few women.

For as small as she is, Olivia has a pair of hard, strong hands. Granite thumbs that can plow into a person's back like the edge of an iron hoe into soft loam. She's got a no-nonsense reputation. Olivia, they all say, can make it hurt, but in a good way. Deep tissue. Swedish. Shiatsu. Easy on the oil.

And no small talk. She suffocates questions and nervous prattle with a wry smile and a nod. Keeps her head down, mouth shut. Gets right down to it. One too many comments about the weather and Olivia will find the pain. One little twitch of her thumb and she can make you care a whole lot less about the heat or the wind.

Not that anyone understood what was really going on in that little room. The rhythm of kneading flesh. Like rocking in place. Or polishing a talisman. It stilled the world. It lit a dim path to a ragged hole. On the other side of the hole was the bright life she did not have.

But she could see it, that bright life. She could hear it.

Kneading flesh. Not altogether different than the repetitive monotony of polishing the rods and handles and seats of exercise equipment. Except that massaging paid her tips, smelled better, and the lights were dimmer. That and the country rock blasting through the rest of *Longhorn Fitness* was on the other side of a thick door, reduced to a low, dull thudding sensation.

Like she had dived into an ocean.

It was never a sexual thing for Olivia. Not that it couldn't be under the right circumstances. It just wasn't.

Too mindless to be sexual. Like washing a car. Or grouting the shower.

But also too mindful. Too meditative.

Not all of her clients felt the same, of course. But Olivia was not one for happy endings. Didn't believe in them. That was not her life. Never had been.

Whenever a man rolled over on the table, full at attention with that expectant look on his face, she knew what to do. Snap on the lights and walk out of the room is what she did. Massage over.

Sometimes she even left the door open.

Once, when the look was more aggressive than a mere hope, she had taken the man's clothes with her down the hall to Mr. Pete's office. Dropped them on his desk. Mr. Pete had looked down at the pile of clothes and the big brass '*Buckin' Best'* belt buckle and then looked back up at Olivia.

"*This one ain't ever gon' come back,*" she had said, wiping her oily hands on the pile of empty clothes.

And he didn't come back. Not ever. Banned for life from all San Angelo *Longhorn Fitness* locations. Mr. Pete had seen to it.

Devin Argood had been a little different. Brother of the owner, Jackson Argood, Mr. Pete's boss. Devin's ending had been almost happy.

Which made a stickier wicket for Mr. Pete.

Devin was a regular. Black sweats. Red muscle-tee. Liked the free weights. He was buff and *Mr. Clean* bald. Oddly handsome from the neck up. Oddly tattooed from the shoulders down, with indecipherable script and astrological symbols every which way.

Olivia had pulled her fingers over the soft page of his back like it was some kind of braille. Picked out a word.

"Queequeg. That like a riddle?"

"Key to understanding the world, darlin'," Devin had said.

"Which is what?" she had asked.

And so Devin Argood had rolled over. He had shown her his key to understanding the world. His world, anyway.

But if that was the key, then it was nothing new. She'd seen keys like that before. Devin had grabbed her hand. Shown her the grip he expected. Tried to get her started.

A moment. Weighing rage against consequence. Sleepwalking back into that old nightmare as time collapsed in on itself.

Two.

A creeping numbness. Peripheral vision constriction. Into the tunnel.

Three.

She had imagined that her family of cactus people was up on the shelf, even the little dog with the glued on ear, looking down on them. Trying to understand. Waiting.

Four.

She had squeezed. Hard. Dangerously hard. Devin Argood had let go of her hand. Shoved it away. Like he was trying to throw her hand across the room. Like it was a thing separate from her and her intention.

Then he had laughed off the pain. Rolled off the table and got dressed. Thanked her. Said he'd see her next week. Scattered bills on the stack of towels.

And then he was gone. Door open. Fluorescent light and *Friends in Low Places* flooding into the tiny room.

Olivia had complained. Held back hot, furious tears.

Him or me. Him or me. Him or me.

Mr. Pete was not the brightest star in the Texas sky. But he understood enough to know an unwinnable situation when it presented itself. There would be no talking Olivia DeLuna down and there would be no banning Devin Argood from the business owned by his older brother. So Mr. Pete had opted to let the situation play itself out. Hope the problem would solve itself.

It hadn't.

Devin put his name on Olivia's schedule. Olivia took his name off the schedule. The pattern repeated each day. Before the week was out Jackson Argood was on the phone from Austin. Told Mr. Pete to lighten the *Longhorn Fitness* payroll by one. Never mentioned his brother. Didn't have to.

Mr. Pete had to do what he had to do.

But before he did it, he had made the drive out to Corbin to see Liberty Cherish. Taken off all of his clothes. Eaten two of her penis-shaped cookies. And then he had told her everything.

Libby had dimmed the lights, put on a Bessie Smith record and done what she does so incomparably well. And then, after Mr. Pete had gone home to his family, Libby had picked up the telephone like it was a bow and arrow, aiming from the outskirts of Corbin, Texas, and letting that arrow fly three hundred some-odd miles to the center of Austin. Two minutes of talking was all it had taken. Easy duty for Liberty Cherish.

After all, Jackson Argood is a church-going, family man. And no dummy.

Baby brother, Devin, has since taken to working his abs across town.

Olivia wipes down the workout mats. Cleans the mirrors.

The Watcher is still there on the treadmill, slapping his size tens at the invisible roaches. He is now too physically exhausted to care for much more than a quick glance every twenty or thirty slaps.

He breathes in big wet wheezes.

She cleans up the women's locker room. Scrubs the toilets. Wipes down the showers. Restocks the shampoo. Helps Dooley Simms in the laundry room fold a load of hot towels.

Dooley invites her to a party. She doesn't like parties.

"Just a couple of friends. Good people. Really."

But she is done with friends. For a long time now. Done with people. And family. The little cactus people are her family. Aside from Libby, they are the only ones she can trust.

She is all about the melody now. A current. A creature. Swimming down there in the dark.

She walks over to the office. Clocks out. Mr. Pete looks up. She tips the hat she is not wearing and is out the door onto the blistering pavement by one o'clock.

The blue Civic is waiting where she left it.

She climbs in and slams the door so hard her the sound echoes across the street. The door has a mind of its own. It takes a helluva slam. Even then, every so often as she is flying down the highway, it pops open unexpectedly, forcing her to slam and drive at the same time. Nothing quite gets the same respect from her fellow motorists. Certainly not her horn, which also does not work so well.

She takes the cardboard out of the driver's-side window to let in the boiling air. Turns the key. It starts. She lurches forward from beneath the *Jack Rabbit's Furniture Warehouse* time-and-temperature sign, stuck on 103° for the past ten days. The rubber screeches against the hot pavement.

She pats her pocket for a cigarette and hits I-67 for Corbin like she's the only one on the road.

She hums a tune about the ocean. Her little blue car shrinks in the distance like an ice cube skidding across a hot skillet.

Chapter 5

He slips the silver car into the moon shadow beneath a rangy pecan, like the tip of a metal arrow just missing its mark. Turns out the headlights. Cranes this way and that, engine running, looking for signs of life.

There are no signs of life.

Well. Except the syrupy glow seeping through the shutters. The house waits quietly on the far side of a square of patchy turf.

He passes a moment in the dark, marveling at what daylight does for a place. What daylight does for a person. For her.

And for him.

There was a song. Wasn't there? About daylight and truth. About daylight revealing? About all that is lain bare 'neath the scouring noonday sun?

That's rich, he thinks. The daylight is a lying mask. A disguise in brilliance. Everything comes off at night. Everything comes out. Truth lives in the dark.

Christ. Just look at *him*.

He touches the key with a finger, but then thinks better of it. Backs out from beneath the tree. Turns the car around and then slips back in so that the tip of the silver arrow is now pointing forward at the invisible road that connects back with *Crowline* that connects with *Sawtooth* that, eventually, connects with I-67 and the world.

He cuts the engine.

Silence. Like he has been swallowed.

Then, crickets.

He pulls the briefcase over from the back seat. Opens it. Takes off the ring and drops it inside. Then his watch. Takes his wallet out of his back pocket. Extracts three crisp one hundred dollar bills. Tosses the wallet in after the ring and watch.

He pats his front pockets. Looks around the car.

He sees the lime green folder in the back seat. Stretches for it with his fingers. It goes into the briefcase. He closes it. Folds down the silver latches with two sharp clicks.

He grabs the key out of the ignition and climbs out. Stretches. He closes the door, opens the trunk, deposits the briefcase, and closes it again.

He pushes a button on his key fob. The silver arrow makes its little noise.

Sheldon Davis looks up through the branches of the pecan tree at the modest house sitting on the far side of the ragged patch of lawn. He takes a deep breath of dark air and steps forward, making his way to the front door of *Libby's Nuts* for the second time this day.

"Weh, now." She stands in the rectangle of warm yellow that falls from the door, painting the stoop. The inside air comes too, smelling of jasmine and spices. "Looky who out an' about t'night. Mmmmmmm-*Mmm*." She shakes her head.

All he can do is look at her. Again, the dissonance between the *look* of Liberty Cherish and *sound* of Liberty Cherish has left him confused and not knowing how to respond.

"How you, Mr. Davis?" She cocks her head, mocking sincerity.

His own name is slightly arresting. Like he has heard it in the hollow of his chest where the sound has been trapped and now panics like a frightened bird in a cage of ribs.

She knows my real name, he thinks. Stupidly.

Of course she knows his name. They had spoken right here for the better part of an hour only eight hours earlier. Back when he had no reason to be anybody else. Why did he think he could be anonymous now, simply because it suited him to be anonymous?

She is dressed differently now. Has traded her jeans and New Orleans Saints t-shirt for a thigh-length kimono the color of over-ripe mango. Open-toe stilettos, covered in black sequins.

So she is taller now.

She has painted each of her nails –hands and feet –baby pink.

Her face, too, is different. Lips. Cheeks. Eyes. Everything is more intense.

Only the black hair is the same. Like a long silky tongue hanging down the small of her back.

The kimono is sashed loosely at the waist. Not that it matters. Little has been left to imagination.

She can see his difficulty. Puts her hand on a hip.

"We gon' talk some more 'bout Cale Hargrove sellin' this land?"

Sheldon shakes his head.

"Mmmmmm-Hmm."

Liberty Cherish holds out a hand and smiles wolfishly. He looks at it for a moment. Like he does not know how to interpret this alien gesture.

He takes her petite hand in his. Holds it like a small lake trout.

She pushes the door closed with the heel of her shoe. Leads him inside. Past the no-nonsense mahogany living room where they had spoken earlier in the day about deeds and development and progress. Past where they had remembered Cale and Raimey Hargrove. Past where he had thanked her for her time and then left with more questions than answers.

She keeps moving. Her heels on the hardwood are little gunshots.

She leads him through a set of double doors into a room festooned with beads and boas. The air is scented. Rose-colored. A bed covered in faux leopard and beaded pillows. Opposite the bed is a velvet settee of a deep royal plum. A lamp on a wicker table is draped with a hot pink scarf. On the walls, in place of windows, are hung all sizes of ornately scrolled, gold-painted mirrors. There are masks with plumage and beads, paisley wallpaper showing through their hollow eyes like little ovular acid trips.

"You want you a Rio Lobo?" Liberty asks, turning to look up into his face. She sees his confusion. "That a *Char-do-nay*, baby."

She does not wait for an answer. Points.

"Oh hale yes you do too want some. You got that *bring-it-to-me-quick-quick-fo'-I-pass-out* look in yo' eyes. I be back wit' a glass a Rio Lobo an' a shuga-stick. Go on an get yosef comf'table, baby."

She moves past him, back toward the doors. Stops in mid-course. Reverses to the far end of the purple settee where there is an old record player on a draped table.

"I'ma put on some Ms. Willie Mae first. You like Big Mama Thornton, baby? 'Course you do. Ain't nobody don't like Mama."

She sets the needle in the groove. Pops and scratches punch through a high hiss. Buddy Guy leads the way into *Ball and Chain*. Mama follows with that voice of hers, moving in the heavy backbeat likes she's wearing iron boots.

Sheldon closes his eyes, remembering this place. This house. Cale Hargrove over there in his rocker with his bourbon. Listening to the radio. Listening to this music. The both of them covered in the nut dust that stuck to the sweat like a second skin. Waiting for the earth to cool and the crickets to come out singing so they could ride into town and see what was doing.

A voice. Cutting through time. Singing about what it's like to sit down by the window. Do nothing but look out at the rain.

She's right, he thinks. Ain't nobody don't like Big Mama.

Chapter 6

The blue Civic. It had come to Olivia second-hand from an edentulous old cuss in Plano. Called himself Buster. Buster told her he had to sell the car. Texas had revoked his license. Next time they'd lock him up.

Fascist Nation, he had kept repeating. *Fascist Nation.*

At least the fascists allowed Craigslist.

Buster said his daughter wanted the car for herself but he was goddamned if he was going to let that happen since it was her intent to put him in a home. He wasn't going gentle into that good night. Planned to fight senescence all the way to the Pearly Gates.

Buster had asked for fourteen hundred fifty dollars. Said he intended to use the money from the sale to run off to Atlanta. There was a woman there, he had said.

Then he had winked his eighty-three year old eye.

Olivia had not wanted to hear the rest. She had offered him nine hundred take it or leave it. Buster still had enough going on upstairs to know that she was ready to walk and that no one was standing in line behind her.

So he took it. She wished him luck.

Buster never told her about the door.

* * *

Fifteen. Sixteen. Seventeen.

She keeps count as she drives. Can't help it.

She is up to eighteen by the time she hits the halfway mark between her morning job and her afternoon job. Just past *The Silverado Indian Jewelry Emporium*. Seven possums. Four armadillos. One rattlesnake. One coyote. Five mystery mammals. Last night had been a rough one for getting to the other side. Not a single chicken to be counted among the dead.

The corrugated sheet she has removed from the window of Buster's blue Civic rattles violently in the back seat. Invasions of *Chihuahuan* air rampage through the car for signs of water. Olivia's hair whips at her face, stinging her eyes.

She puts on cheap sunglasses. Hums a song about the ocean. The melody is still altogether wrong, she thinks. *Too... too... what...*

Wistful. Disconsolate.

Romantic.

Something. She lights a cigarette. It helps. She can see the notes in her head. It's the only time she ever smokes. She tries to keep it to one a day.

Tuning the melody occupies her for the rest of the drive.

Nineteen. Twenty.

Twenty-one.

In Corbin, she has time for a quick stop at *Pepita's* for her usual *ensalada de pollo con jalapeños* and a Coke.

"*Hola*, Olivia." Eladio waves from the kitchen.

Still awkward after Miguel. Too polite. Too restrained. It is no longer possible for Eladio to joke about stealing her away. About him being the better man for her.

He is the better man. Or will be. For someone.

He will be taller than his brother, too, she thinks. He has a dancer's ease about him. An innocent relationship with gravity.

"*Hola*, Eladio," she says.

She sits on a stool at a pocked, wooden counter. In front of her is the heart carved into the bar around the name *Maric*. *Maric*, it says. Clearly *Maria* but for an inconveniently placed knot in the wood. It's where she always sits. Right at the heart.

Olivia wonders whether there is some lonely and forgotten cuss named *Maric* out there someplace that has ever sat down on this stool to eat. Seen his own highly unusual name in the middle of the heart. Left wondering at the source of such devotion.

Maric. Maric.

She imagines that it must make his day, this imagined man. Just thinking about it. Just wondering what the carver of that heart must be like.

And when he's driving home in the dark, window down, dry desert blowing through his long brown hair, the woman he doesn't know, but who carved a heart around his name, is probably all poor Maric thinks about.

And all because the name is wrong. Not *Maric. Maria.*

The wooden, pock marked, heart-carved counter looks out of a large, clean window that opens out onto a sidewalk. Sporadic traffic trundles dustily down *Broken River Road*. Mostly looky-loos this time of day. Taking a mid-day detour through quaint little Corbin. Wetting their whistles and buying an ice cream at the *Lick-n-Tipple* before finishing the blistering trek west to Odessa. Or maybe Tucson. Or east to Waco. Or Shreveport.

Cars with stir-crazy kids fighting in the back seat.

Cars with women who have a problem pulling over to squat in a ditch. Watering the rattlesnakes, they call it.

Most all of them are *coming from* somewhere else and *going to* somewhere else. As much as anything, Corbin owed their visit, however brief, to the unrelenting *Lick-n-Tipple Ice Cream and Spirits* signs stretching out ten miles in each direction along the long, straight scratch in the dirt that is I-67. Something about those lips on that white, creamy mound of coldness that was just too appealing to keep most folks from heeding that impulse. Hitting the turn signal. Turning the wheel for the Corbin exit. *Oh, what the hell.*

The *Lick-n-Tipple* is the only place for a hundred miles you can buy a scoop of chocolate pecan with buttered caramel and a bottle of rot-gut whiskey in a single transaction.

Maybe two hundred miles.

There is no confusing these ice cream and liquor prospectors for the locals. Even if they lived just up in San Angelo, not but eighty miles northeast, they may as well be from another planet. Fat, stooped, dull-eyed pasty things, with glowing phones for hands. They park and roll out of their seats and stand and stretch a little. Walk in a slow, incurious huddle from the pay-lot behind the *Coahuiltecan Trading Post,* across the street, venturing neither a step to the north, towards the Corbin Town Square and the Evangelina Huerta Memorial *Fuente de la Luna,* nor to the south, towards *Pepita's* and, at the end of the block, *Matilde of the Sacred Heart First Church of Christ.* They follow an arrow-straight line, precisely threading the hole in that old brickwork needle between the *Caddo Lone Star Laundry* and the *Leather Craft / Jewelry Works Showcase.* Disappear through the white wooden doors of the *Lick-n-Tipple,* beneath a cracked and faded, hand-painted rendering of those familiar burning lips.

As if the lips have sucked them right off the freeway.

Invariably, they reemerge in mere minutes. Same order of procession. Back to the gleaming vehicles from whence they came. Lobotomized expressions. Hands sticky with frozen sugar.

Eladio brings her food and a Coke.

"Gracias, Eladio."

"De nada." He hesitates. "How are things?"

She is already chewing.

"Oh. 'Bout as good as I can expect, I guess. Too damn hot."

"Yeah. It is." He turns to go. Turns back. "Miss having you around," he says. "Up at the house."

She swallows. Wipes her mouth. Drinks. Looks up at him. Tries to smile.

"Shit happens, Eladio. Don't you worry about it none. Tell your daddy I said hey." It's her turn to hesitate. "And as for your mama…"

She doesn't finish. Doesn't need to.

Eladio beams. Backs away, finger to his lips. "I never saw you."

She eats her lunch. Looks out the window.

The true Corbinites rolling up and down *Broken River Road* are hard to miss. Nut farmers and ranchers in dirty pick-ups mostly. Windows down. Mutts in the back, or sometimes wiry, brown shirtless boys yelling out at their friends. *KSPT –K-Spit radio* –blasting the *Tejano* out over the scrub.

Not a one of them holding ice cream.

To be a Corbinite, a person had to live in or around Corbin. And if you didn't actually live in Corbin, then you had to be born in Corbin, in which case you would be a Corbinite no matter where you laid your head. Olivia is both of these.

She sees Marky-B ride by in Miguel's white, rust-eaten Toyota. Rangers hat on backwards. Left arm draped so far out the window it looks like he is trying to pick pennies up off the street. She figures Don Dickson is still laid up with a broken leg and that Miguel is stuck wrangling the pickers. No way Marky-B scores a provisions run in Miguel's truck for any other reason.

Marky-B looks up just in time to see her in the window. Waves.

She thinks too long about waving back.

She finishes her lunch and slips some cash under the empty plate. Slaps the bar twice to tell Eladio she is leaving.

In thirty seconds she is back in the car, slamming the front door –once, twice –like she's trying to teach it a lesson.

She checks her watch. Puts the cigarette back in her mouth. Resists the lighter. Drives.

Twenty-seven. Twenty-eight. Twenty-nine.

The front door to the house opens as she pulls up the driveway. Yvonne Lawry pokes her head out. Points to her watch. Disappears, leaving the door open.

Wednesdays are Yvonne's opportunity to escape the life she has made. The excuse is a weekly three-hour art class at the SACC. Husband Brent, an engineer for a petrochemical company out of Houston, travels several times a month, leaving Yvonne alone with Kevin. Going on thirteen and severely dystrophic. The San Angelo Community College has a daycare program, but not one that can take on Kevin.

She finds him in his wheelchair, parked at the windows at the back of the house.

"Hey, Tiger," Olivia says. "Watchin' them birds again?"

He does not answer, of course. Except maybe in the way that he registers any stimulus, which is to curl bodily –fingers, hands, arms, neck, head, torso –around a fresh muscle spasm. Like he wants to keep the moment close. Keep it from leaving him. Olivia places an open palm on the back of Kevin's neck. Moves to the front of his wheelchair. Bends. Looks at him in the eyes.

"You and me again, partner." She grabs the napkin from his tray. Wipes his mouth. "Mama got to go paint her pretty pictures."

Olivia and Yvonne. They go all the way back to the SACC massage school. Back when Yvonne was eying a nursing degree. Different as night and day, these two. The twilight between them was always a fondness for hating men.

Not *hating*. Hating.

Just hating. The way they are. The things they say. The things they promise. The way they stride around the planet.

With their penises.

There had been the hint of attraction between them.

More than a hint. Fingertips on bare shoulders. A whisper. A palpable after-drink vibe that might have bloomed into something regrettable between them.

But Olivia had known better. Somewhere between the beer and the bourbon, Olivia had heard the flat note. The one buried inside an attraction borne of enmity. Even a shared enmity.

So she had chosen not to follow Yvonne's whiskey-soaked breadcrumbs. The moment had passed. Yvonne surrendered to the inevitability of someone like Brent and the realization that he was about as good as it was ever going to get. Not that it was all bad. She had plenty of money. And time.

Thirteen years later. Yvonne has a ring that no longer fits the plump of her finger. An absentee husband. A kid in a wheelchair. And enough frustrated ambition to fill her septic tank.

All of that and a repeating predicament on Wednesday afternoons.

Olivia can only help with the last of these problems. She'd offered Yvonne her services. Not so much out of friendship. Or pity. Or the hundred dollars of Brent's money that Yvonne agreed to pay her. Mostly it was for a few hours of unrestricted access to the baby grand piano in the living room.

Truth is, Olivia would have paid Yvonne.

Fortunately, the arrangement seems more than fine with Kevin.

She waits until Yvonne is gone. Rolls Kevin up next to the piano.

She can't smoke in Yvonne's home. So she talks to herself as she works, pencil in her teeth. Untangles melodies and harmonies like long strands of fishing line kept too long in a drawer. She mutters in a melodic burble like a crazy person, wrangling the cowlicks of recalcitrant lyrics. Asks Kevin questions about meter and rhyme that he cannot possibly answer.

Kevin, so used to being the odd one in the room, looks on between spasms as if a dancing bear has stopped by for a drink on the way to the circus.

Inevitably, she hits a wall, her creative force dissipating in a bog of dissatisfaction. As often as not, she wads up the sheets of paper on the top of the piano, stuffs them into her backpack and tumbles into something well beyond her reach. A soggy, shambling boogie-woogie. Drunken ghosts and twelve-bar memories. Little Willie Littlefield. Roosevelt Sykes.

Today it's Jelly Roll. Rolling in his grave.

Doesn't matter. It all hangs together in her head.

Kevin, clutching awkwardly at the arms of the chair, leans sharply forward, grimaces a smile as if thrusting his slick, snaggletooth face into a storm of blue butterflies.

When Yvonne returns, they are out on the back deck. Olivia is feeding Kevin bits of cheese as they watch the wrens in the feeders. There is no sign that she has been anywhere near the piano.

Such is Olivia's way.

"He hates cheese," Yvonne says, leaning in the doorframe. She holds a hundred dollar bill between two fingers. Her honey blonde hair works alone now. Even the blue eyes have given it up.

"He only eats cheese for you. Why is that?"

Olivia answers without looking.

"I told him it was absolutely forbidden. But my man Kev really digs rebellion. Don't you Kev?"

"You really shouldn't feed him cheese. His system..."

"Missed a deer earlier." Olivia points. "Tame as a dog. Went off past the shed."

"I ran into Miguel," says Yvonne.

Olivia rolls her eyes conspiratorially at Kevin. He clutches his own fingers. Throws himself forward. Back. Wrenches sideways. She glances back at Yvonne for the first time.

"You mean like, ran into him with the car, or...?"

"Funny, Liv. No, at SACC. He asked about you."

Olivia feeds Kevin the last bit of cheese. She thinks about what they have chosen to call each other: *Eve* and *Liv*. One the beginning of an ending. The other an aspiration.

"He's still really a nice guy, Liv. And so... *mmm-mmm*. If I weren't married..."

"Well, you are. Eve. You *are* married."

Yvonne absorbs it. Keeps on. Adds a little judgment of her own.

"You'd feel different if you had your own place. You need to get out from under Liberty Cherish's roof, is what."

"I'm sure you meant Libby Holder," says Olivia.

"Mmm." Yvonne looks away. "I'm sure I did."

They are silent. Yvonne tries again.

"He's just so handsome. You sure there's not still some... I don't know... Don't you ever want..."

"You're right." Olivia stands. "You really *don't* know. I gotta go, Eve. Manny's on tonight."

"Can you come by Friday? Same time? Only two hours. He wants us to try painting something from…"

"Yeah. Whatever. Sure."

She doesn't care about the reason. She stands. Musses Kevin's hair. Crosses the deck, pushes past Yvonne for the house, snatches the hundred dollars. Yvonne follows her inside.

"If not, I can call…"

"I said yes, Eve. Gotta go. Bye now." Raises her voice. "Bye Kevin."

Olivia climbs in the car. Slams the door. Again. Again. Skids out of the drive. The piece of cardboard behind her seat starts its rattle and her black hair flies in the hot breath of the road as she picks up speed. She puts the same cigarette in her mouth. Leaves the flamingo-pink lighter in the handle of the door.

It doesn't really need to be lit to do its job. It's more like an antenna.

She hums all the way back to Corbin proper.

By seven o'clock she's in the break room of *The Diamondback* pulling on a black skirt with one hand and sticking a card in the time clock with the other.

"Rye unda da wya, O," says Manny from the hallway looking at his watch. He calls her *O*. Just *O*. Like the rest of the syllables are unimportant.

He is a fireplug, Manny, with a flat nose and a pocked face and spectacularly good teeth. He co-manages the bar with Gary Pepper, first cousin to the owner, Lou Dimond. Lou lives up in San Angelo where he owns a swimming pool and another bar called *Diamond Lou's*.

Gary Pepper is Manny Soto's polar opposite. Tall. Flawless skin. Crooked teeth. Hates drama. Lets everything slide as long as no one gets hurt. Manny wears his *not-Garyness* like a crown.

He knows nothing of Liberty Cherish.

Well. Manny Soto undoubtedly *does* know about Liberty Cherish. Many Corbinites know about Liberty Cherish in some way or another. But Manny has no reason to consider Liberty Cherish and Olivia as part of the same thought.

Which is good for everyone.

"Rye unda da fuckin' wya, O," Manny says again, lifting his eyebrows.

Olivia lays on the accent. "Oh, da where I live, Manny Boy." She sways her neck. Swishes her finger in the air. "Chu know da. Rye unda da wya, Manny."

She tucks in her white *Diamondback,* rattler-emblazoned tee. Squeezes out of the door into the hall. Smiles at him too sweetly.

A dangerous attitude to take with Manny. Olivia knows this. But Manny himself does not know it at the moment. Not with her breasts almost at eye level as she passes. Manny is incapable of holding more than a couple of thoughts in his head at a time. So she leaves him with a left thought and a right thought and no room for concern over her insubordinate attitude.

She picks up a tray. Heads for the nearest table. Feels him still looking from down the hall. She knows that there is a thought in Manny's head that never seems to be very far away. Flickering back there in the dark. The thought is that she holds some interest for him. Or that she might be persuaded to hold some interest.

She has tried to extinguish that flicker. Tried depriving it of oxygen. She keeps her head down and works. Does not initiate. Does not engage. Borders on caustic. Dismissive. Even belittling. Doesn't matter. The flame in Manny's eyes gutters and sputters and spits back to life every time like a trick birthday candle.

Olivia fills the tray with empties. Wipes down the table. She takes everything to the bar. Slides it across. Nods to Ryan, who is busy cleaning glasses.

Sandy-blond curls on a pretty, boyish face. Inviting smile. Ryan has that all-American football-scholarship look to him. No doubt what his crazy racist girlfriend Aileen sees in him. Aileen works at the gas station, which she likes to call *Checkpoint Chevron*. She has a six-pack of brothers in El Paso, big into volunteer border patrol and paramilitary dress-up slumber parties.

Ryan looks up. Nods back at her. Goes back to what he was doing.

More than fine by Olivia. If only Manny Soto was so disinterested.

She puts the tray under her arm. Grabs two table settings and a fresh bowl of roasted nuts. Heads back out.

She blames herself for Manny's delusion. It was the ride home in his truck that had done it. Her broken blue Civic had been in one of its moods. The malfunctioning door had conspired with the engine while she had been working her shift. She had climbed out, slammed the door and then slammed it again. Kicked the lifeless thing in frustration. Looked around for a solution or at least some commiseration.

And there was Manny Soto, loitering in his newly-acquired, used black Ford pick-up. Ready with an answer to the question she had never asked.

"Why you drive da piece a shit, O? You need you a real ride. You need you a big ride. You know I'm rye, O."

She had ignored the suggestion within the suggestion. She had taken the ride. The bucket seats had been ripped out and replaced with a single black vinyl bench seat that must have come out of the back of an old Suburban. No seat belts. The only thing separating them was a grocery bag full of apples. Manny was big on apples. Most of the trip had been about his skill as a negotiator.

"He wan' fi'teen thousand. Fi'teen, O! An' I tell this puta madre he lucky to get him three. He say, three thousand? Fuck you three thousand. And I say suit yo'self yo. I say, this rig missin' bucket seats, missin' a runner on the driver' side an' it got shit for a stereo and it got shit for brakes an' ain' got no fucking horn. An he say it do too

got a horn an' I say a horn da don' work ain' no fuckin' horn yo! I walk off. Jus' lye da. I walk away. Puta madre call me da nye! Ten o'clock da fuckin' nye! Say he sell for three thousand. He beggin' me to buy."

"*No horn?*" she had asked. Manny had pounded the steering wheel, laughing, trying to make a sound that never came.

"*No fuckin' horn!*"

"*Why?*"

"*Fuck if I know why. It jus' don' work.*"

"No, I mean why would you buy a truck without a horn?"

"*Who need a fuckin' horn, O? In Corbin? No horn cost da puta madre twelve thousand dollars. I put in my cousin's stereo. I don't give a shit about no driver-side runner. An' I lye this bench seat, man. Lots of room, yo? An' who need a fuckin' horn? You got you a twelve thousand dollar horn in da blue piece a shit car you drive, O?*"

Her blue piece of shit car did not have a working driver's door or an engine. She was grateful for the ride. She let him believe he had impressed her.

"*Guess you know what in the hell you're doin' when it comes to buying trucks, Manny. No foolin' you, huh truck stud?*"

"*Goddamn rye, O. Goddamn rye.*"

She pulls a seven-hour shift. Works the entire floor by herself, slinging drinks and tortillas and beef sliders to a bunch of regulars looking to blow off some steam after a day of pulling things out of the ground or off the trees. Corralling livestock. Fixing fences. Wednesday shifts are always a hard pull because they include the last half of the *Double Happy-Hour Wednesdays*, from six to eight. They bring in a rowdier set looking to get drunk on the cheap. Tonight is no different.

Manny eventually leaves her alone. Switches his focus to riding the cook for using rancid oil.

"Wha da fuck, Kiko! You try to making people sick lye da? You *loco*? You can no smell da?"

There is a genuine fake vintage jukebox in the corner. Fire engine red metal trimmed out in fake glass and plastic chrome. White square buttons that correspond to an encased color-coded menu. It offers the predictable slate of bubble gum pop, new country, and classic rock favorites. Left to its own, the playlist is supposedly random and, given its Internet access, infinite.

Supposedly. It still plays the same thirty songs.

More shifts than not, Olivia finds occasion to kick the plug out of the wall and then plug it back in. There is a special process for rebooting.

She is diligent about reporting to Manny or Gary that *the damn box is on the fritz again,* just to clear herself as the culprit. Eventually they get around to investigating the origins of the problem, but it usually buys her thirty minutes to an hour of relative peace. Just the people-noise.

There is a lifetime limit to the number of times she can listen to *Get Off My Cloud* and *Dude Looks Like a Lady* and *Love Me Do*. Not to mention the over-sampled, atonal dreck that makes a hit record these days. Why Lou Dimond thought to purchase such a contraption without giving any thought to the music itself was beyond her. If she thought about it enough, it made her angry.

So she tries not to think about it. Contents herself with kicking the plug out of the wall.

"Damn box is on the fritz again, Manny."

Manny spins on the greasy tile floor. Turns his back on the beleaguered cook, Kiko. Spreads his arms in a *what next* exasperation.

"How many time I got to tell you, O?" Pokes himself in the temple with a stubby forefinger. "You dense? You got to put in da code an let da box reboot, yo!"

She wrinkles her forehead. Looks past him at Kiko. Looks back. "There's a code?"

It buys her another twenty minutes. When the thing finally reboots and flickers back to life, she keys in selection G-17 three times. There is, as yet, no lifetime limit to the number of times she can listen to Etta James sing *A Sunday Kind of Love*.

Two after twelve.

Olivia sticks her card in the time clock. Logs her tips. Changes out of her uniform. Heads out the back door stepping into dark, redolent desert air.

The world is cooler now. There is the slightest breeze. It carries in the ocean of desert scrub, through an oasis of more deliberate foliage that permeates the township. A rumpled blanket of bougainvillea, yellow rose, and purple sage that Corbin gathers up close against itself to keep from dying of exposure.

A sickle of lunar bone hangs in the dark above the *Fuente de la Luna*. The fountain is off now, quiet until sunrise.

Olivia crosses the parking lot. Slips behind the wheel. Slams the blue door with a vengeance. She leaves town, due west, night air pillaging the car. She hums as she drives. Finds the cigarette in the door handle. Moves it from one side of her mouth to another, looking for reception.

Then, suddenly, it is there. A song.

Not a song. Not yet.

A wisp of melody. A beginning. But still with her. Still in her head.

It has been there all night, a bird behind a tumbleweed on the side of the road, hiding from the traffic of living. Hiding from Manny Soto and the genuine fake vintage jukebox and the *Hey-Hey, You-You* and *Dude Looks Like a Lady* and rancid cooking oil and wiping tables and making change and a thousand petty concerns that all mesh together into the buzzing that is everywhere and nowhere.

The sound of oppression. The sound of nothing.

In twenty minutes she is parking under the giant pecan tree in the southwest corner of the grove.

Old Faithful, they call it. A hundred fifty years old and still producing, like a great wooden geyser pushing pecans out of the earth from an inexhaustible sea of nuts floating beneath this crust of the world.

A fair likeness of *Old Faithful,* an iconic silhouette dead-on for its lack of detail, adorns the smallish yellowing sign pounded into the dirt at the turn-off from the main road. Centered beneath this artistic rendering are two words in a simple font: *Libby's Nuts.*

Olivia's blue Civic is not the only car in the orchard tonight. There is also a sleek silver car. A BMW backed in at an angle and pointed at the road. As though whoever owns it thinks that having to back the car out before leaving might take too much time.

The silver Beamer means only one thing. It means Libby is busy. Means she's working. Third night in a row Olivia has come home and essentially had the place to herself. Or at least all of it but the room Libby liked to call *The Parlor,* off limits whenever the doors were closed.

She crosses the last bit of orchard, pecan trees like massive stanchions holding up the dark. Traverses the ragged square of lawn on which the white clapboard, two-story house sits. The upstairs windows are dark. Yellow light blazes through the cracks in the downstairs shutters. Like the light is liquid, spilling out of a house half-full.

Olivia opens the door.

Chapter 7

Sheldon opens his eyes. Sees that he is alone in the room.

The little gunshots of Liberty Cherish's heels on the hard floor recede to places unknown. Off to fetch him a drink.

He takes in everything. Gilded mirrors hold his face on every wall, portraits of wary excitement. Fear. Constipation.

And now there is a new sensation. A dreadful feeling rising up through the soles of his feet. Filling him like cold seawater.

He should not be here. He should not be here. He should not be here.

The carnal itch had survived, relentlessly pacing his nether regions through the heat of the day. Convincing him that this was something he needed. Something he deserved.

The itch had worked its magic for hours now, utterly persuading him that Christi –for whom sex had become a kind of seasonal maintenance chore somewhere between changing the water filter and swapping out the ant traps – could hardly complain about outsourcing. If he was willing to hire a professional, then so much the easier for her to cross that chore off of her list.

Of course, Christi would not hesitate to feign grievous emotional injury for her daddy's sake. She did not so much as sneeze without Grayson knowing whether Sheldon had had the decency to offer her a tissue.

But then, that was the Tates. Grayson and Christabelle. The southern tycoon and the cosseted trophy wife. Except that they are not married. Texas had laws about that sort of thing.

So, against his better judgment, Grayson had essentially outsourced the husband role to Sheldon. But Grayson was always right there. Holding him accountable for the family name.

It would be like the time Christabelle informed her father that Sheldon had nearly been arrested on a bench warrant for neglecting to pay a speeding ticket. On their way to a black tie benefit hosted by the Houston Realtors Association, a cop had pulled them over for a missed turn signal in the heart of downtown

Houston. It had taken Christabelle's long-legged, blue-eyed charm to convince the officer not to haul him off to jail. When she told her father why they were late, Grayson was instantly enraged. The very notion of his daughter –his beloved Belle –standing out in traffic negotiating with the police for her scofflaw husband's freedom. Grayson had refused to speak to or introduce Sheldon for the entire night.

So, no. His father-in-law would never take in stride any revelations about… *outsourcing the marital sex function.* Grayson would string him up by the nostrils.

But then, Grayson Tate was a man who would never tolerate a scandal in his relations. The real estate business, Grayson was fond of saying, was about trust. It was about integrity. *"You lose your integrity in this business, Shelly, and you will fail."* His prodigious wealth gave those words some gravity. He only drank the best bourbon and associated with straight shooters. He cared deeply about family. Cared deeply about community. Knew that what people thought about him mattered. Not just the people of Houston, but anywhere in Texas and, for that matter, anywhere in the universe of non-Texas.

Louisiana.

Florida.

Russia.

It mattered. So Grayson would surely have a keen interest in the sexual impulses of his son-in-law. He tried to imagine the moment of revelation on Grayson's face. Much worse than the speeding ticket debacle. It was daunting.

But the carnal itch had been ready for that sort of trepidation.

Grayson Tate, argued the itch, was not the one married to Christabelle Tate Davis. Her last name was *Davis.* Sheldon, for better or worse, was the one married to Christi. Which meant it was *Sheldon's* marriage and *Sheldon's* sexual extinction at issue. He would be a better husband if he just went ahead and got it out of his system. This was not a marital transgression. This was a marital necessity.

And besides, the itch had added, how would either Belle or Grayson ever find out in the first place? A brothel, masquerading as a nut farm, way out in the boonies past Corbin nearly four hundred miles away? Could it get any safer?

Sheldon had found the itch's logic rather compelling.

The thought of scratching the itch had not even occurred to him until only eight hours earlier. Libby Holder had set it off. The woman who calls herself Liberty Cherish. The woman living in Cale Hargrove's old home and who somehow owned every last acre of Cale Hargrove's pecan orchard. He had been fine through their entire conversation. Right up until she had leaned into the doorway and whispered her farewell.

"You want you a massage, baby, you jus come on back tonight. I give you one," she had said. *"Feel so good you fogetchy' own name."*

Sheldon, standing on the sun-scorched stoop with his briefcase in one hand

and the lime green folder in the other, hadn't known what to think. He could only give her a quizzical smile. Wave at her with his folder-holding hand. Walk off to his car.

He had driven away with her voice in his head and it had stayed with him the rest of the day. Like she was sitting in the passenger seat of his silver arrow repeating herself. *Feel so good you fogetchy' own name.*

By the time Sheldon had re-entered the Corbin city limits, he had stopped dismissing the idea out of hand. Started to consider it as an idle fantasy. Nothing serious. Just an entertaining thought to play with to pass the time.

But by the time he had rolled into San Angelo, idle fantasizing had given way to practical problem solving.

He would need a hotel for the night.

He would need some cash.

He would need an excuse. Something to explain why he would not be home until tomorrow. Something Christi would believe and that Grayson would not think to question if she told him. Which, of course, she would. In fact, he would need to call Grayson directly.

Because he was going to miss that barbeque.

He had spent the balance of the afternoon driving and walking and eating around San Angelo. Trying to calm his nerves and steel his resolve. The more he tried to stop thinking about what was coming, the more he obsessed over what was coming.

He bought a box of three condoms at a drug store. Put two of them in his pocket and threw the third one in the trash along with the little box and the bag and the receipt.

Mostly, he waited. He called Christi. He called Grayson. Neither of them knew he had come over to Corbin in the first place. They thought he had driven up to Dallas to pitch an ad campaign for *Texas Brand Beef.*

They thought this because that is what Sheldon had told them.

They each had the same questions for him. Like they shared a brain.

"Why not take a commuter flight?"

"I do my best creative thinking while I'm driving. I like the road."

"Then why not send Adam? Or Jill?"

"Adam's busy. And TBB wants a man. They won't ever listen to Jill."

"So you'll be back tonight? For the barbeque?"

"Tonight. Yes, tonight."

He had decided he did not want to tell anyone about Corbin. He was not quite sure why he had not wanted to tell anyone. He just didn't.

Something about the whole Corbin deal did not make any sense. The records did not match. Names were different. Maybe it was nothing. Probably *was* nothing. But still. No use in getting Grayson all spun up until he had a chance to look into things. The Corbin deal was too big and Grayson was too high-strung about it.

He might have told Christi. She would not have cared two wits.

But in six years of marriage, he knew enough not to say anything to Christabelle that he would not want Grayson to know about.

So he had said he was driving to Dallas and that he would be back that night. Yes, in time for the barbeque.

And he would have been.

But then, suddenly, there was Liberty Cherish. *Feel so good you fogetchy' own name.*

Sitting in the parking lot of the *San Angelo Double-J Market Fresh,* Sheldon had called up Grayson Tate. Said he was still in Dallas trying to wrangle a deal.

Wrangle. Like the contract was an obstinate steer.

He'd told Grayson he was going out for drinks with *Texas Brand Beef* after a long pitch session and he was trying to remember the name of the rodeo clown in Houston that stole all of that bull semen and put it up on EBay. He said he thought Grayson might remember.

Grayson had not remembered. Instead, Grayson had asked whether Sheldon was driving back to Houston tonight.

"You still gonna make it?"

"Doesn't look like it. No."

The tone in Grayson's voice had changed, the molasses cooling quickly. He had asked whether Sheldon would still be able to meet with the River Walk folks tomorrow morning for a status check on the Corbin project. There was a lot of talking to do. Marketing talk. Sheldon should *god damn* be there. That had been the whole *god damn* point of the barbeque.

Sheldon had expressed his regret. It would be too late to drive back to Houston. The *Texas Brand Beef* people were insisting on drinks. He would set out early tomorrow morning. He could fit in a River Walk discussion tomorrow afternoon if they were still in town.

The change of plan had not sat well. He could tell by the silence on the phone. Grayson Tate wore disappointment like a cat wears the rain. He was a man of his word and he expected the same of others. He especially did not like disappointing the River Walk people. But what could he do?

"Should'a flown, Shel."

"Yep. Yep. You're right, Grayson. Should'a flown."

Then he had called Christabelle. Told her basically the same thing. She had seemed secretly pleased but, for the record, very annoyed. He figured she would hang up and call her daddy. Grayson would say he already knew. They'd complain about his decision to drive. *Why the hell didn't he fly? I don't know daddy. Says he likes the time to think. To think? It's what he said. Well I'll tell you what I think; I think it's goddamned inconvenient.*

Grayson would arrange to pick her up for the barbeque he was hosting for the River Walk folks. Christi would then resume obsessing over what to wear to the pig roast. All thought of her husband would then sink like a stone to the bottom of her well.

Then it was fully dark. Sheldon had finished his final idle loop through San Angelo. Made his way back toward Corbin. Resolute. Remorseless.

Truth was, he had felt a kind of excited, terror-tinged gladness in his heart. *Alive.* Never done anything like this before. He had managed to keep the tingly feeling alive all the way up to the front door of *Libby's Nuts.*

But now…

"Here, baby," Liberty says, closing the double doors of the Parlor behind her. She sets her own glass of wine on the bedside table. Slinks his way, extending a hand. "This yo' Rio Lobo."

Sheldon takes the glass and drinks. Winces. Liberty reacts.

"Don't you pull no face." Shakes her head. "Mmm-mmm, baby."

She extends her other hand, revealing two sparkling brown cookies. He mistakes the shape for that of rolling cannons.

"Go on have you wunna these."

But the barrels have distinctive tips.

So then he gets it.

"No. No. Thanks," he says. He takes another drink of the Rio Lobo, which now seems like the better alternative.

Liberty pulls her head back, furrowing the smooth skin of her brow. She strokes her hair. Tries to comprehend.

"No thanks? Baby, you outchu mind? These here is Liberty's *shuga… stick… cookies.* I'm right near famous for this shit. Take you one bite an *tell* me you don't want you some more. Go on now."

She holds the head of the glittery baked penis up to his mouth. He hesitates. Bites off the tip. She waits, expectantly.

"Mmmmmm-hmm?" she asks. "Mmmmmm-hmm?"

It's delicious. It's nutty and sweet and chewy. He can taste the pecans. Nutmeg. Cinnamon. There are other flavors he cannot identify. Like little silver fishes swimming in the muck of a lake.

"Very… Mmm. That *is* good," he says.

"Go on then," she says, smiling. "Take 'em both." She puts the cookies in his hand. He takes another bite. She watches him chew.

Off in the corner, Big Mama moans about the rain.

"Les go sit," she says, making her way to the purple settee. "C'mon, baby."

He follows. Sits. Rio Lobo in one hand, baked genitalia in the other. Mouth half-full, he watches her warily.

Liberty crosses her legs, splitting the kimono up the center. She bends slowly forward, gripping one shoe, then the other, unsheathing her naked feet and their perfect pink nails.

"Whatchu got for me, Mr. Davis?" she purrs.

Sheldon stares. His heart panics. *She knows his name.*

A gray sequined mask on the wall above the bed is bleeding magenta feathers. It stares at him with paisley eyes.

He should not be here.

"Baby?"

He finishes chewing. Swallows. Washes the cookie back with a slug of Rio Lobo.

"I don't... I don't..."

"Now, baby... you a smart man. You *know* Liberty don't be pourin' no Rio Lobo and handin' out no shuga-stick cookies fo' *free*. You know *that* shit, huh?"

A moment. Two.

Then, suddenly, her meaning is clear. He acts without thinking. He is too nervous. Thinking is a luxury. It's all reflex and training now. We must pay what we owe.

He holds the remaining confected penis in his teeth and stuffs his free hand into his pocket. In the extraction, all three Franklins appear at once, slipping from his fingers. Liberty collects the money all too slowly from his lap. Drops the bills into the pocket of her kimono.

She un-sashes the garment and pulls it fully open. Her skin is like a pale, clear stream flowing over the purple settee. Breasts fuller than he would have imagined. There is a small, downy black bush to mark the diverging tributaries of her limbs. She bends her knees. Folds her naked legs and feet beneath her. Reaches over to him with both hands.

She pulls his frozen money-hand to the flat of her belly, moving it in slow circles. Reaches for his face. Breaks free the testicles of dough hanging over his chin. Puts them in her mouth.

"Chew, baby," she mumbles.

He chews.

She chews.

They stare as they chew. She moves his hand up and down the length of her torso. He is trembling. He swallows.

"I'm married," he says. His voice is small and hoarse.

"You is?"

Sheldon nods.

She holds up his hand. "Where you ring at? You was wearin' it today when the sun was shinin'."

"I... I..."

"It wunna them *daytime* rings, huh?"

"No... I..."

"You think you less married if you leave it out in the car? Or you leave it in the car 'cause you afraid Liberty gon steal that shit?"

"No... no... of course not. I..."

"You wife as nice as that ring?"

"..."

"That okay, baby. Liberty ain't gon' judge. We all done made our mistakes. Ain't like bein' married is murder. You ever done a killin'?"

"Me? No."

"Okay then. Yain't got to worry. Fo'give yo'self fo' bein' married." She wiggles her fingers in front of his face like she is sprinkling magic fairy dust in the air. "I forgive you. Les get them shoes off."

"No... I..."

But she is already out of the kimono, kneeling naked on the floor before him, pulling off his shoes and socks.

The grey mask has a small red slit for a mouth. It's partly open, showing a paisley throat. Like it's trying to say his name.

"Oooo, you got you some soft, white dawgs. I seen some ugly ass feet in my day. Yo' feet belong on a giant-ass baby. So smooth. So soft. Mmm."

"I can't do this," he says. He stands. Which is a mistake. It brings the precise middle of his body to her face.

"Mistake? Don't know 'bout no mistake, Mista Davis. Look to me like you *can* do this. Look to me liiiiike... *parta* you can do this. Look to me like *parta* you in a damn hurry. *Parta* you ready right... *now*. Maybe you only part-way married, baby."

She reaches out, feeling him through his pants. His blood is in torrents. His head is not right. He closes his eyes. She keeps at it. "Maybe this here part ain't so married."

He steps sideways, away from her, stumbling over his shoes, bracing himself against the arm of the settee.

"No. No. I'm all the way married. I am. Really. All the way."

Liberty Cherish looks at him for a long moment. The air is thick with scent. Mama sings from the corner about having a heartache.

She sighs. Stands. Slips her feet back into her shoes.

Nothing else. Just the shoes.

"Why you here, baby?"

"I... I... a massage." He grips his own shoulder like he is trying to pick himself up. "Just a massage. A *massage*-massage."

"A *massage*-massage," she repeats. Sheldon nods.

There is a soft thud from beyond the double doors. Sheldon's eyes widen, listening. *Police*, he thinks. His heart shrieks. The unimpeachable evidence of his illicit intent will not subside. It refuses. It wants to testify.

Liberty smiles. Pats him on the face.

"Have you another drinka that Rio Lobo. I be right back."

He watches her go. Naked but for the shoes. Black hair swishing across her back in metronomic opposition to her hips. He looks away, ashamed of himself. Ashamed of his ringless finger. His adolescently overeager penis. His large clay feet. His face is on every wall. What was he thinking?

But there is another feeling. One he cannot explain. A softening of attention wholly at odds with his relentless hardening. An odd relaxation coalescing on the underside of his anxiety. A laugh, bubbling beneath the threat of panic.

"Come on out, baby," he hears Liberty say. He looks up. He can see her in the hall, near the foot of the stairs, right where Cale Hargrove once kept his daddy's grandfather clock so many years ago.

She beckons with both hands. "Come on. Good Lord in Heaven, baby, you so shy you like a little baby bird. Ain't no one gon' hurt you, baby bird."

Chapter 8

The double doors to *The Parlor* are closed, just as she had expected. The house smells of jasmine and jambalaya. *Jambalaya* because it is Wednesday. Libby usually makes her jambalaya on Wednesdays. *Jasmine* because there is a silver Beamer under the pecans.

There are voices from behind the double doors. Libby is laughing; cajoling in that singsong way of hers. The other voice, a man's voice, is explaining. Resisting.

Olivia can hear that Big Mama Thornton is in there with them, spinning on the record player. Crying all night long. Coming out of that dream, soaking wet to the soul. Not a nightmare, she sings. It's that lover she loves. Still gone.

Olivia kicks off her shoes. Walks quietly to the kitchen.

Opens the fridge.

Leftover Chinese.

A jar of olives.

Tabasco.

One can of Dr. Pepper.

Six bottles of *Rio Lobo* Chardonnay, down from seven bottles this morning.

A plate of *Sugar Sticks,* cookies modeled after male genitalia in varying states of arousal. The shapes tended to be vaguely reflective of Libby's mood and worldview at the time she makes the batter. When she stirs in all of the pot. And the Spanish Fly. And the Viagra. And other things.

"Call that my pixie dust, baby. My little love sprinkles."

The jambalaya is in a black pot on the stovetop. She tastes it with a spoon. Scoops some into a bowl and heads upstairs to her room with the last can of soda. She does not make it up to the second floor landing before she hears the doors to the Parlor open.

Olivia turns. Sees. Sits down on the top step and places the bowl down next to her. Opens the Dr. Pepper. Drinks. Waits.

Libby stands at the foot of the stairs. One foot up on the lowest step. Hand on her hip. She shakes her head slowly, like the very idea of Olivia sneaking up to her room is somehow pathetically optimistic.

She is completely naked, of course. Except for her pink nail polish and her sequined pumps, which still bring her to a height of only sixty-six inches. Her skin, body, long sleek hair, are all vaguely Asian.

But not the sound of her. Not the voice. That's straight up Louisiana bayou.

"O-Livia, baby," drawls Libby. "Yain't goin' up t' bed just yet now is you?"

Olivia smiles wanly. There is only one answer to this question.

Libby nods. "MmmHmm." Turns to the open parlor doors. "Come on out, baby. Come on." She coaxes with both hands. "Good Lord in Heaven, baby, you so shy you like a little baby bird. Ain't no one gon' hurt you, baby bird. Thas it. Thas it."

The man appears. He stands at the foot of the stairs next to the fearsome, stilettoed stick of naked flesh that is Liberty Cherish.

White. Clean. Late-fifties, early sixties. Completely out of his element. Hands stuffed into the pockets of his slacks. His feet are bare, pale flippers on the wood floor.

He looks up the stairs at her uncomfortably. Olivia raises the can of Dr. Pepper as in a toast. Drinks. The man looks away. But then looks back. Liberty wrenches his left hand out of his pocket, clasping it between her own. Points up the stairs.

"That there O-Livia DeLuna," she says with a flourish of emphasis.

Libby looks up again at Olivia. Pulls the man's captive hand up in a wave.

"O-Livia, baby. This here Sheldon. His ass *aaallll* the way married. He want him a *massage*-massage."

Chapter 9

Sheldon shuffles forward. Stuffs his hands in his pockets. Tries to soften the enthusiasm of his profile.

"Thas it. Thas it," says Liberty.

He stops next to her at the foot of the stairs. He is conscious of the front door. Conscious of the parlor. He has forgotten his socks and shoes. He is embarrassed. Ashamed. He wants to run. He wants to laugh. He is terrified. He is … is… *groovy.*

A woman sits on the top stair. Fully dressed but for bare feet. Looking down. She raises a can of Dr. Pepper in casual salute.

The impact might have been less had she fired a crossbow into his chest. He looks away. Looks back. She is attractive. More than attractive. But that is not it. *What then? What?*

She is time traveling. Or he is. Standing at the foot of this same staircase, grandfather clock knocking in his ear, decades ago. Decades. Looking up at her. Half-dressed. Tumescent. Enthralled. And she is looking down at him, decades ago, wrapped in a sheet, holding a can of Cale Hargrove's beer. Holding it out and down to him. Toasting. Drinking. Laughing that laugh.

Liberty yanks his left hand out of his pocket. His profile returns with a vengeance.

"That there O-Livia DeLuna." She looks up again at the woman with the soda.

Rose, he thinks. *Rose.*

"O-Livia, baby. This here Sheldon. His ass *aaallll* the way married. He want him a *massage*-massage."

His head is soft. There are heat waves lifting off the staircase. They blur everything. He blinks. Wants to laugh. He is so hard he hurts. It feels like he might split his pants open. *Rose.* He says the name to himself again. *Rose.*

The woman sighs. "Well. Come on, then." She picks up a bowl sitting next to her. Stands. Turns. Looks back over her shoulder. Waits.

Liberty pats him sharply on the rump. "G'on up, baby."

He takes a step up. Grips the handrail. He feels like he can float.

"Sheldon had him two shuga-sticks."

"*Two?*" Her voice is directly above him. Closer. Closer.

"Mmm-hmm. An' some Rio Lobo. Ain't you, baby?"

He doesn't answer. Another step. Another.

"That b'fo I know he want him a *massage*-massage."

He hears Liberty laugh. Part cackle, part moan. He pauses. Continues up. Then, suddenly, he is there. Like he has climbed a mountain. Floated a mountain.

"Let's go," she says. She turns and walks away down the hall, bare white soles flashing against the dark wood. Walks away from Cale's bedroom, to the room where Raimey Hargrove used to sleep. She disappears inside.

His head swims. He wants to call out after her.

He steps up into the hall. Follows her into the room.

Raimey's bed is gone. Instead there is a white padded table on black metal legs. She is unfolding a sheet as he arrives. She flutters it in the air. It settles like snow over a steppe.

She opens a wicker trunk in the corner. Extracts another folded white sheet. Plops it on the table. His throat is dry. Where is his Rio Lobo? He wants to laugh. His penis hurts.

"What kind?" she asks, unfolding the second sheet.

He cannot make sounds quickly enough for her.

"Swedish? Deep tissue? Shiatsu?"

"I... uh... no. I don't know." *Rose? It's me.*

Both hands on her hips, she looks at him from across the table. Narrows her eyes. Skin so much lighter. *But her eyes.*

"So, two cookies," she says. He thinks it's a question. He nods. Smiles. Gives her the peace sign.

"Right. Well, go on then. Get undressed. Put your clothes there on the chair. Cover yourself with this top sheet. Back in two shakes."

She is gone. He can hear her descending the stairs.

Sheldon takes off his shirt and tosses it in the general direction of the chair by the door, missing terribly. Unbuckles. Unzips. His pants fall around his ankles with a clunk of car keys. He steps out. Kicks the pants over towards the shirt. Removes his boxers with a sigh of relief. Marvels at the strength of the thing. Snickers in spite of himself. *What is so funny? What... is... so... damn... funny?*

He lifts the sheet. Slides beneath it on the padded table, face down.

The dreams come instantly. Almost before he closes his eyes. Cale Hargrove is gone. Gone to town. Gone to get Raimey out of jail again.

Rose is here.

Rose is sitting up on the top stair, wrapped in a white sheet.
She lifts her beer.
I love you, Sheldon Davis.

Chapter 10
Abby and Davis

I lied to my friends. They expected it of me. That's how the game is played.

Being a shrink I'm sure you know all kinds of reasons for why people lie. But there doesn't always have to be some big deep, dark reason. Sometimes the lie is just for fun. Sometimes the lie is expected and not lying would be a disappointment.

Jack and Kenny wanted details, so I held out until they figured nothing had happened. Then I stopped in the middle of the path back to the old locomotive where we had parked, looked at them for a second as people passed around us on all sides like water around a cluster of rocks in a stream, and then I lied. I said that I had looked Abby Palmer straight in her beautiful brown eyes and told her that I was interested in some sex. Raunchy sex.

They stood there quiet for a moment, looking at me and narrowing their eyes. Trying to figure out if I was for real. I demanded my ten dollars.

They didn't believe me, of course. Fat Jack was all over me with questions about how Abby had responded.

"Flattered," I told him. Then I kept lying. "But she said she was married."

Jack said I was bullshitting. He must have said some version of that word ten times as we stood there. Skinny Kenny tried to insist that he knew I was lying because they had been listening through a hole in the tent. But I knew that there was no way they could hear us. Not with the chaos of the fair all around them.

And there was no hole anyway.

So I told them to pay up and they told me to stick it, saying that I was trying to steal their money. We argued all the way back to Jack's truck, and then half way back to Kenny's house where we spent the rest of the afternoon and evening drinking his uncle's beer and playing video games. We never solved anything. None of us ever expected to. The more that I swore something happened in that tent, the more they held their ground and insisted that absolutely nothing had happened.

Which was exactly what I had wanted.

Because something *had* happened in that tent. Something completely unexpected. I fell in love with Abby Palmer.

I didn't know it at the time. I honestly had no idea what to think. But looking back, that's what is was. Love.

I hate talking about this with you. You call it 'infatuation' and 'a crush' and 'a little lust.' I think you want to make it smaller. I think you want to make it less important. Less real. That must be what it means to be a shrink. You like to *shrink* things. But you weren't there, Dr. Bees. You weren't in my head back then.

It was love. It was real. It was important.

I went back to the fair the very next day, without Jack and Kenny. I had to take the bus because, unlike Fat Jack, I didn't have an uncle with a beat-up pickup he never used. Nor did I have a driver's license.

Not that being only sixteen had ever stopped Jack from driving or us from riding with him. Not that being sixteen had ever given Jack's uncle any concern.

Not that Jack's Uncle Zeke was ever around enough to see anything that he might be concerned about.

What Jack and I have always had in common is a lack of sober supervision. Skinny Kenny's got an older sister that kind of looks after things, but Jack and I are basically on our own. Dad makes more of an effort than Jack's Uncle Zeke. He at least comes home every night. Evenings are okay. We take turns making dinner. We basically watch the same shows. He can hold his drink until after eight or so when we part company and he starts writing.

I can't say I like him much. But I don't hate him. I feel bad for him. Even when he tries he seems to come up short. He's always struggling to hold on to the damn bookstore, but *B. Dalton Books* has kicked his ass with a pointy boot every year since they moved into the *Swanson Spur Mall*. And he works on that novel of his like he's paddling a paper life raft. Like he thinks it will save him. It's mostly just another opportunity to park himself at the kitchen table, pour himself a drink and stare out the window.

The novel is not going to save him. Nothing will save him. Now that Mom's gone, nothing will. She was his last chance.

And I sure took care of that.

Anyway. When I went back to the fair that Sunday, I popped into Abby's tent mid-morning like we were old friends. When I look back on it, my over-eagerness is just flat embarrassing. True, she had asked me to come see her again. But she had not asked me to come see her again within the next eighteen hours. I should have waited a week. But that would have been impossible.

If she thought I was being over-eager she didn't show it. She was at her table, hunched over a scattering of smooth gray rocks with silver markings. She was whispering to them. That's what it seemed like.

She later explained to me all about the runes, but at the time I thought she was playing some sort of strange game. She looked up at me and smiled. She said my name. It sounded strange, wrapped in a British accent. It sounded new. Polished like those stones.

She stood and gave me a hug exactly like the hug I had taken home with me the previous day. The hug I had kept from Jack and Kenny and taken to bed with me. The hug that had kept me awake most of the night.

It lasted three or four seconds, but I tried to stretch it in my mind. I closed my eyes and buried my face in her thick brown curls, pulling the smell of her into me. I tried to appreciate in that moment everything that I had been too stunned to appreciate the day before. The warmth of her neck. The feel of her shoulder blades beneath my palms. The brush of her pelvis.

When she pushed me back to arms length it was like pulling my head out of a lake. All of the light and sounds and feelings of the normal world returned.

We made small talk about the fair and the weather and the music playing outside her tent, which must have been ridiculous and boring for her but, for me, just her voice was like a kind of music all its own, or a kind of expensive art, the way her mouth precisely shaped each sound and then broke it off like one of those glassblowers at the other end of the fair. My name sounded beautiful when she said it. *Davis.*

When I sensed we were running out of things to talk about, I pulled a five-dollar bill from my pocket and handed it to her. She smiled with her eyes, bowed slightly and gestured at the table.

We sat down just like we had the day before. I watched as she wrapped the smooth stones in a burgundy colored cloth and then put the bundle into a small silk bag. As she did this, guessing that I was curious, she explained the historical significance of runes and how they were used.

"Most people read them," she said. "Interpret them. Like hieroglyphics painted on a cave wall."

She reached across the table and took my right hand, brushing my palm with the tips of her fingers as she had before.

"Most people?" I asked.

"I don't use the runes that way," she said.

"Why? How do you use them?"

"I don't interpret them, really. I listen to them."

"Listen to them? They're *rocks*."

"They're not rocks, Davis. The stones just hold the symbol. Anything will do. Bits of wood. Ceramic tiles. Anything, although I prefer something elemental. Something natural, like stone. But it's the *symbols* that are important."

"Why?"

"The symbols are ancient. They focus energy into patterns. And if I put two runes on the table next to each other –or four, or ten, or whatever –then those patterns of energy interact. That interaction creates a new energy pattern. Unique. It's a kind of voice for me. And I know how to recognize that voice. I know how to hear it. Not with my ears, but in my head."

She was not looking at me as she explained. She was looking at her hand stroking my hand, sometimes so delicately that I could barely feel her fingers and at other times full on, palm to palm, like two bodies rubbing up against each other.

"What kind of things do the voices tell you?"

Abby looked up at me suddenly, hand still, I think to see if I was mocking her. I wasn't. I didn't know what to believe about the runes, but I didn't disbelieve her. I didn't believe that she was just making it all up.

"That's personal," she said. "I don't read the runes for other people. And I don't share what they tell me. That abuses the gift." She resumed stroking my palm. "That violates the rules."

"There are rules? Who's rules?"

She smiled. "There are always rules, Davis."

"What rules?"

She didn't answer my question. I knew she wasn't going to. She just looked at our hands on the table as if she were watching something through a window or from over a hedge. Something that pleased or intrigued her.

I wanted to ask her again what she had meant, the previous day, when she told me that I would save her life. But I knew she was not going to tell me that either. She would simply repeat the answer she had given three times before: "*You were meant to find me. You will be there when the time comes. And when the time does come, you will know what to do.*"

She gave me a crash course in palm reading, tracing my lines again with a moistened finger, switching from one hand to the other. She said I have water hands, which suggests that I am emotional and seek peace even to a fault. My 'head' line is curvy, suggesting creativity. My 'life' line is short and shallow, which she assured me had nothing to do with how long I would live.

I have a deep-set 'fate' line, which she said meant I was controlled by destiny.

My 'heart' line is long, starting between my first and third finger, intersecting my 'life' line and discontinuing in two places. She said that means I fall in love easily and have my heart broken easily. She said she saw great trauma. And a lot of guilt. She looked up at me with a worried, concerned expression. But she didn't ask.

I almost told her everything right then and there. You more than anyone know that I don't talk about Mom. Especially not back then. Not with Dad. Not even with you, until you crawled inside my head with all of your games and pictures and tricks of logic.

But here was this person that I barely knew and I was ready to tell her everything. The trauma and the guilt. Everything. She was just that way. I trusted her instantly. It was like she had the key to every locked door and knew where to find me hiding. There was no resisting Abby.

I'd probably have told her the whole horrible story if we hadn't been interrupted. Two teenaged girls and their mother walked in, not understanding the meaning of a closed curtain. They asked how long the wait would be. Abby told them to give us another minute or two. But when they left, they took the moment with them.

Without releasing my hand, Abby looked at me directly.

"Want to show me the fair?" she asked.

"Me? I mean, now?"

"No. Silly willy. About five. I can close down then for a couple of hours. I always have to *work* the fair so I never really get to *see* the fair. *Experience* it. You can show me your favorite parts."

I pretended to think about it.

"You can say no if you like," she said.

"No. No, I mean… I mean yes. Of course. I'll pick you up at five. I mean I'll be here at five."

"Brilliant," she said. She laughed, probably at me being awkward. "Just wait for me outside."

She stood, releasing me, and I left. I spent the next five hours and forty-five minutes walking the fairgrounds, a knot in my stomach the size of my fist. I was ecstatic and terrified at the same time. Part of me knew better than to think of it as an actual date. But to be honest, that fantasy had been the only thing in my head since the first time I walked into Abby's tent. I wanted to tell Jack and Kenny. I remembered the payphones at the bus station and thought several times about walking all the way back just to call one of them and tell them what was happening.

Not that they would have ever believed me. I started imagining that they had come to the fair without calling me, or maybe hoping to find me there. I searched the faces in the crowd and went to all of places that I knew they would go if they were there. I wanted them to be there so I could tell them.

I spent a long time at the rodeo. Kids in over-sized hats were roping calves and riding horses and spitting chew in competitions to see who could look most like a grown-up cowboy. It seemed a fitting way to spend my time as I waited for my pretend date with a woman twelve years older than me. So I could feel like a grown up man.

When five o'clock came, I was waiting in the pathway outside Abby's tent, trying my best to stay clear of the evening crowds. An endless supply of new arrivals came surging in from the main gates which were well beyond my sight but close enough that I could hear *Big Tex* welcoming them every five minutes: *Hoooowwwdeee, fooolllllks!*

Abby emerged a few minutes late with a small wave. I helped her unfasten the main tent flap and zipped it closed. She pulled a small padlock from her purse and handed it to me. I locked the zipper to a ring in the tent as she hung up a sign that said she would be back at seven o'clock.

Off we went into the crowd.

It turned out not to be a date after all. At least not in any kind of romantic or sexual way, which was the only way that Jack and Kenny and I ever really conceived of a date. If there was no chance of making it to any base, then it wasn't a date. It was just going to the movies or going out for a burger or going bowling. Abby and I just went to the fair.

But it was way more fun than I ever expected. We laughed a lot. We ate too much greasy fried food. We played nearly every game twice. I won a stuffed bull for scoring twelve out of fifteen in the *Duck Shoot*. I had wanted the rattlesnake bracelet, but Abby said she liked the bull. It was about the size of a Thanksgiving turkey with a fake brass ring through its nose and horns with yellow tips. I gave it to her because I thought that was kind of expected of the man, even if it wasn't a date.

An hour later she scored five out of five on the ring toss and won an identical bull, except that the horns had blue tips. There were no other choices. She gave her bull to me and told me we were even. I made some crack about the craziness of the coincidence. Abby said there were no coincidences.

Part of me was disappointed about the bull exchange. I didn't want things between us to be even. Jack and Kenny and I were always fighting over who had what, and whether it was fair that one of us had something the others didn't. But with Abby, I didn't want to keep score like regular friends. I wanted to be the man. I wanted to do things for her. Hold doors open for her. Flatter her. Make her laugh. I wanted to win a stuffed bull for her and then give it to her with other people watching. I didn't want a bull in return.

I tried to convince her to go on some of the rides but she wasn't having it. She said she got sick easily and that she would not be able to stand *The Scrambler* or *The Octopus* for more than thirty seconds. I made my best argument for the *Texas Star*, which was only a year old at the time. In case you have been too busy shrinking heads and telling people what to think to ever go to the state fair like a normal person, the *Texas Star* is the largest Ferris wheel in North America. It lifts you over two hundred feet off the ground and at night it's all lit up in purple and blue and during the day you can see forever. Not that I ever told Jack or Kenny, but I liked the *Texas Star* more than *The Scrambler* or *The Octopus*.

Since there is nothing especially wild about a Ferris wheel ride, I thought Abby would go for it.

"I'm kind of afraid of heights," she said.

"Nothing's gonna happen," I insisted.

"Bollocks," she said. "You don't know that." I could tell she was embarrassed. She blushed and fidgeted and tortured her stuffed bull. Her vulnerability made me feel heroic. "Just because it hasn't collapsed yet doesn't mean it won't collapse tonight."

"Nothing *can* happen to you, Abby," I said.

"Why is that?"

"Because I'll be sitting right next to you."

"So."

"So, if anything happens I'll save you. That's why I'm here. Remember?"

I had meant it as a joke, turning the thing she refused to talk about against her. If she believed I was supposed to save her life from some secret threat, then maybe that threat was a defective Ferris wheel. Why the hell not?

But Abby didn't think it was funny. Her expression deflated slowly from playful embarrassment to something far more serious and thoughtful.

"You're right," she said after a few long seconds. "You're completely right."

She suddenly laughed a little, almost like a cough, looked around at the people lining up at the slow-rolling *Texas Star*, looked at me and laughed again, like she was realizing something important for the first time.

"You're right, Davis. My...God. You are so... You are so right. I need to be higher up. That's why I can't hear. I'm too bloody low."

"Abby... What are you talking about? Hear what?"

"There's too much noise at ground level. That's why I'm afraid of heights! They *want* me to be afraid!"

I looked at her closely. Her eyes were wide with excitement and she was smiling like she had when she won the ring toss.

"Who wants you to be afraid?"

"Wait. I need to think. I need to think."

"Abby..."

"Wait, wait."

She closed her eyes for a moment, tucking her hair behind one ear, then the other. A large, cow-eyed woman with a pink cloud stuffed on top of a paper cone looked at us as she waddled by. Her t-shirt said *Texas Big and Ten-Gallon Crazy*. I watched her pass. Abby was oblivious, staring at the ground and muttering like she was trying to remember something. I waited.

"Okay," she said at last, eyes open with a new focus. She jabbed the yellow-tipped horns of her bull into my chest. "I will ride on your silly Ferris wheel. Tomorrow afternoon. It needs to be daylight."

"I have school tomorrow."

"Skip bloody school. This is more important."

"I barely passed last year. This year's barely started. If I start skip…"

She interrupted me sharply, as if I was being unreasonably difficult.

"Fine. When can you be here when the sun is up?"

"Saturday."

"That's the last weekend of the fair. Are you sure you can be here, Davis? Are you sure?"

I nodded. "Yeah. I guess so."

"You *guess* so? Davis, you have to be sure. Can you be here?"

"Yes."

"Do you promise? Cross your heart and hope to die?"

"Yes, yes. I can be here. What's all the… can you just tell me what's…"

"I have to get back. I have to make something."

"Make something? What are you making?"

But Abby had already turned and was marching off in the direction of the main bandstand, back the way we had come. I stood watching her, frozen in my lack of understanding, with the massive *Texas Star* grinding on its axle, rolling in place behind me. People shrieked from the top, like they were about to be pulverized, ground into the earth beneath its neon rims.

Abby stopped, turned, urged me forward with both arms. She called my name, smiling. I was helpless. I ran to catch up.

Like I said. There was no resisting Abby. I'd have done anything she asked.

But you already know that.

Chapter 11

She awakens in her bed to the movement of a body not her own. The pull of a sheet. The groan of the mattress. A weight slipping in somewhere behind her.

Olivia DeLuna cracks an eyelid. Realizes.

The digital clock on the antique nightstand says almost seven. The family of little Mexican cactus people are neatly arrayed behind the clock.

At least she likes to think of them as a family. Six of them, some proportionally children, and a dog with tiny pink flowers for ears. They look at her like they've been waiting for hours. Her little desert people. They cast their tiny shadows on the wall behind the nightstand, which has taken to a soft morning blush.

A small plane drones into the soundscape. It bores its way, she imagines, through a lone, hapless cloud.

The roosters next door are up. They remind her.

She disables the alarm before it can do its thing. Yawns. Rolls over.

"This here yo' wake up call, baby," says Libby. She is propped up on one elbow. Naked.

Olivia rubs her face with her hands. Yawns again. Stares up at the fan. It slowly stirs the morning air like the plane she heard had left the imagined cloud and silently crashed nose-first through the ceiling.

She closes her eyes again. Croaks.

"Too tired to get up. I don't want to go to work."

"Then don't," says Libby.

"Have to."

"Hell you do. Want me to call up that Mista Pete? Tell him you got you some food poison from some nasty-ass Texas Chinese?"

"No."

"Somma them *dim sum fuck dumplins* wit' the fro-up fish sauce?"

"No."

"And the *moo goo gotta go to the toilet gai pan* noodles?"

"Libby."

"An the fo'tune cookie that say Mista Pete gots him a teenie, tiny lil' egg roll fo' a pee pee?"

Olivia laughs. Swats sideways, missing.

"You go on an' laugh, baby. But I seen that lil' egg roll many a time. Many a time. Try to anyway. You got to really *look* fo' it." Libby starts to laugh in that full body way of hers, clutching her midriff like she is three-hundred pounds and not one-forty-two. She lets herself fall back onto the bed. "Got to call out the dogs an' horses an' go on a *hunt* fo' that lil' thing. Got to get out the *bye*-noclas and the telescopes. Like a grain a rice. *They it is! They it is!* Oh. No. That just a grub worm, baby. Gots to keep on lookin'."

They both laugh up toward the plane propeller in the ceiling, pushing around air that is already too hot. Olivia kicks at the sheet. Again, until it is off of her legs. Libby squeezes her hand.

"That Mista Pete do whatevah the hell I say, 'Livia. He *know* I got the goods. Fool ain't never got no money so he *always* wantin' it at a discount." She pushes herself up enough to look down at Olivia, offended. "Like I'm selling sofas on President's Day." She lies back again. "And you *know* he gon' want to keep that shit goin'. President's Day all year round."

"You wouldn't do that if it weren't for me, Libby. You really shouldn't."

"Hush. Mista Pete also got him a wife I reckon he want to keep. You recollect that punk ass boss' kid? What his name?"

"Devin Argood."

"Thas it. Devin punk ass Argood. Wantin' you to massage his dingly dang. I take care of that mess with one phone call to Mista Pete an' one phone call to Jackson Argood up in San Angelo. *Shazam.* Shit got done."

"I know. I know."

"Okay then. So you know I can deliver. You want you that day off?"

"No. It's my job. Need the money. I'm just being lazy."

"'Livia DeLuna, you the most unlazy person I know." Libby flicks her pink nails in the air one at a time. "*Longhorn Fitness*, five day a week." Flick. "*Diamondback*, five day a week." Flick. "*Papi's* every damn weekend." Flick. "Babysittin' for yo' bitchy lil' friend, Yvonne Dyke."

"Lawry."

"I know the bitch's name. Dyke is what she is, baby, ain't her name. Open yo' eyes to that woman. She afta the lady bits. Now stop interruptin'." Libby flicks the last finger up into the air. "An when you come *home*, to *my* house, where you *live*, you givin' *massage*-massages to chicken-shit white men who suddenly all-the-way married."

Olivia lolls her head. Looks.

"Because you told me to."

"Damn right I tol' you to. Rich man want a *massage*-massage, I'm gon' find him one. Not like *you* payin' me any rent."

It was true. But it was unlike Libby to bring it up. Olivia lifts herself.

"I wasn't complaining. I was just…"

"Hush, 'Livia. I'm just ringin' yo pretty 'lil bell. You go on to work if you want. But listen here." Libby bugs her eyes until Olivia's face acknowledges the moment. "You keep this here pace up an you be dead 'fo you fifty. You want you some breakfast?"

"Ain't hungry."

The morning storm of birdsong rises up out of the pecan trees in the orchard behind the house. Out the corner window, she can see the middle branches of Old Faithful holding the sunlight two hundred years above the ground. Libby perches on an elbow.

"Fess up, baby. You end up having relations with that funny little rich man last night?"

Olivia looks at her. Scolding disbelief.

"You know better."

"'Spose I do. But that was one long-ass *massage*-massage. And when he left – what, three 'clock or some such –he be like some doughy-white bullet. I'm comin' out the baf room and here come Sheldon-*massage*-massage-all-the-way-married, movin' like some jackrabbit under the gun, down the stairs an' out the damn door, belt in one hand, shoes in t'other. What you do to that poor boy?"

"Nothing. Gave him a massage. You had him so fuckin' doped up on your cookies he passed out and slept for a good forty-five minutes." Olivia looks at Liberty hard. "Two cookies, Libby? Really?"

Libby shrugs.

"Liberty Cherish here to please, baby. Man want him two shuga-sticks, I give him two." She covers her mouth. Pretends to stifle a laugh. "Batch *did* come out ass-kickin' strong this time."

"You don't say."

"'Cain't hep it, baby. Learnt that shit the hard way. Ain't no recipe for shuga-stick cookies. Every batch diff'rent."

"Well, you knocked him out. I left him alone, sleeping like a baby, went and took a shower. Ate some jambalaya. Did my dishes. I had to wake him up. Then he wanted to talk."

"*Talk*?" Libby hoists herself back on her elbows. Moves her shoulders up against the headboard so that her body is a smooth crescent of light brown flesh. She raises one foot, then the other, rotating each slowly in the air, to the left and then the right, admiring the pink polish on her toes. "What y'all talk about? You and chicken-shit *massage*-massage Sheldon."

Olivia thinks for a moment. Remembering.

"He thinks he's in love," she says.

"With you?"

Olivia shrugs.

"*Oooooo….*" Libby points accusingly. "Rich man like that? 'Livia done got her a shuga-daddy."

"He was stoned off his ass. Seein' double. Kept sayin' I reminded him of someone. I was afraid he was gonna start cryin'."

"Afraid? Why you afraid? Baby, that shit like gold. You ain't had no relations and he already cryin? He pay you any damn thing you want."

"I don't do that."

Libby pokes her in the arm.

"No you don't. But I do."

"I ain't judgin'."

"Hell you ain't. Go on see if I care any."

"I'm just sayin' that even if he did… you know… want to pay me for it…"

Libby laughs.

"Not fo' no relations, dummy. Jus' to see you. Jus' to lay his rich, married eyes on yo' pretty lil' face. He let you give him ten *massage*-massages a day. He sleep outside in his 'lil silver car 'til you ready. And Sheldon worth a lotta damn money."

"And just how do you know that?"

Libby rolls over again. "Look." Pokes herself in the chest. "We jus' done established me bein' the ho. This here *my* business. I knows money when I sees money. *All-the-way married* drives him a Mercedes coupe. He wearin' no jewelry. No watch. No rings. No wallet. He hide all that shit out in the car so we don't steal it." She pinches up her face. Indignant. Like she smells something rotten. "Like I'ma steal his shit. Baby please. *But…* that mean he worth something. See?"

"Whatever."

"Got to wear shoes, though. Can't hide the shoes in the trunk. Show up at my do' without no shoes I'ma think you crazy. An' I don't fuck no crazy people, don't care how much money you wavin' 'round. So there they was, right there on his cotton-soft feet."

"Shoes? So."

"Here to tell you them shoes worth mo' than the damn car."

"Well, that ain't …"

"Come on, girl. You saw them hands and feet. *Massage*-massage is groomed. He gettin' him mani-peddies every damn week."

Olivia nods. "Yep. Pretty groomed."

"*Sheeit.* Like a damned show pony. Now he a show pony in love. He be back, too. 'Fo the week is over, Sheldon be all up in here givin' you googly eyes."

"We'll see."

"Yes we will, too."

It might have ended there. Libby's penchant for idle morning chit-chat would keep her there until she got out of bed and left the room. Olivia looks again at nightstand. The clock flicks red seconds at her face.

The cactus people have their own opinions.

"He's actually... kind of... interesting," she says.

"*Mmm, hmm.* He int'restin' alright."

"We talked a lot about music."

"I put on Big Mamma fo' him. Could tell he like it, too. Ain't no one don't like Big Mama."

"He likes them all," says Olivia. "Sippie Wallace, Chippie Hill. Alberta Hunter. Ma Rainey. Mamie, Billie, Bessie, Koko. Man knows his shit."

"We talkin' 'bout the same pasty white rich boy? Sheldon? All-the-way-married-*massage*-massage Sheldon?"

"That's him."

"Damn, girl. You impressed, huh?"

"A little. Yeah. I guess a little."

"Bet I know somethin' 'bout the man that you don't."

"Like?"

"Like he spent all kinda time in this house a long-ass time ago."

Olivia sits upright. Leans back against the headboard.

"This house?"

"*Mmm, hmm.* Tol' me that when he come by yesterday afta'noon. He one of Cale Hargrove's pickers back in the day."

"Who's Cale Hargrove?"

"Hell, I never know the man. He dead 'fo Antoine an' me ever set foot in Texas. Antoine pay Cale's boy Raimey for the house an' the business. This house. All that land out back. All them trees. Raimey a drunk. When he won't sleepin' here in this very room he sleepin' in a cell over at the Sheriff's office in Corbin. An' Raimey in debt like a muthafuck. Antoine got this place for a song. Anyways, *massage*-massage was a picker for that fool's daddy. Cale."

"Where's Raimey now?"

"Dead. They all dead, baby. Raimey. Cale. Antoine. Not Sheldon. He ain't dead. He all-the-way-married. He the *livin'* dead." She laughs at that. "Sure you don't want you some eggs?"

"No."

"Ham?"

"So then he was over here before last night?"

"*Mmm hmm.* Come over in the afta'noon to find out if I own this place. I tell him hell yes I own this place and he want to know how I got it and I tell it none of his damn business but I tell him anyway when he tell me 'bout him pickin' for Cale Hargrove."

"Why'd he want to know? I mean… what the hell business is it of his?"

"He in advertisin'. Doin' a survey."

"What kind of survey?"

"Survey of prop'ty owners 'round Corbin. Findin' out who sold what to some jackasses who think they gon' turn Corbin into another river walk like they gots in San 'tonio."

"Oh, the river walk thing. Put little Corbin on the map. Just what we need is a bunch of tourists."

"Tourists. 'Livia, that a buncha shit is what that is."

"Why?"

Libby rolls sideways. Scrunches up her face again. Irritated.

"Ain't no damn river in Corbin, baby. How you have another river walk without no river?"

"They say there will be. Gonna take some from the Pecos."

"That some shit, baby. Trust me. What do Corbin got that people want to see anyway?"

"I don't know. The Moon Garden Festival."

Libby laughs.

"Moon Garden… Girl, you outchu mind. You been eatin' my shuga-sticks?"

Olivia doesn't answer. She pulls back the sheet. Stands. Stretches. Pads off down the hall to the bathroom. She brushes her teeth and showers. Dries her hair. She pulls it into a ponytail as she walks back in the bedroom.

Libby hasn't moved an inch.

"What you want me to do when all-the-way-married Sheldon come back askin' fo' you?" she asks.

"What? Nothing. He ain't coming back."

"Hell he ain't. An' you betta hope he do."

Olivia pulls on a pair of ratty jeans and a bra. She rummages through the drawers in the Mexican oak dresser for a halter. She finds it in the bottom drawer. The one so warped it sticks. She kicks at it with a bare foot.

"Hate this damned drawer."

"Well it ain't too fonda you neither. That dresser three times older than yo' skinny ass. That a Cale Hargrove dresser. But you can go on an' kick at if you want."

Libby gets up and sways her hips out of the bedroom, swatting Olivia on the rump as she goes.

"Wait. Why?" asks Olivia. "What do I care if he comes back?"

Libby pauses for a half-swish in the hall.

"'Cause *Papi's* only gon' be fo' the buyin' but so long. Then where you gon' be wit' all yo' dreamin' and schemin'? You wanchu some eggs? I make you some eggs, baby."

Olivia dresses and follows Libby downstairs. She eats her eggs. Like always. Libby sits at the table and watches. Not like some short-order cook looking out over the customers of some dusty Texan diner. More like a mother before the school bus comes. A mother about as idolatrous and unwholesome as Jezebele of Samaria on a hot day.

But a mother just the same.

Because in her own way, that is how Libby Holder thinks of Olivia.

Her baby.

Out beneath Old Faithful, Olivia slams the stubborn blue door. A speckled woodpecker and a turtle dove rocket sideways out of the tree, headed in opposite directions. Like they'd been caught up to no good in a no-tell motel.

It takes three times before the door finally sticks. She starts the car and skids out in a plume of brown dust for the corner and the I-67 beyond.

The sky is a reckless, nearly unnatural color. More beryl than blue. It reminds her of water, taunting the buzzing desert from above.

When she hits the freeway, hair lashing her face, she is humming again. A song about the sea. *Mother Sea. Mother Ocean.* Something like that. *Mother Ocean with your sorrow so deep. Your children have floated away.* Something like that.

She looks for a cigarette.

It's there in the door handle where she left it, next to the flamingo lighter. She doesn't need the lighter. She needs the antenna. She needs the signal. She needs the tune. It's the melody that she really needs. The words always come looking for the melody. The words will follow the melody like some lovesick schoolboy in the lunch line behind the new girl in town. Like some horny old cuss following the sound of thighs brushing together inside the frilly hoop of a skirt on a hot Saturday night. The melody is the only place the words can make sense of themselves.

Everyone needs a place to belong.

But the cigarette does not tune in the melody. If the words are out there looking for their place in a song, then they are wandering lost in the buzzing burnt brown scrub.

The only song her cigarette tunes in is the one where Sheldon-*massage*-massage-all-the-way-married sings about all of his money looking for a purpose in the world. It is a quick-tempo song. Double time. Triple time. Classic Jump Blues like something the Andrews Sisters chirped out in the forties.

The money in the song, green and crisp, dances. Struts. Walks on with a bounce in its step. The money, it seems to Olivia, is in a powerful hurry.

'Cause Papi's only gon' be fo' the buyin' but so long.

65

Chapter 12

Davis takes another drink. Tries not to react. Prickly-pear has never been his cup of tea. It's like drinking pure honey. Or iced maple syrup.

Calling it lemonade doesn't help.

He swallows. Twists his head once to the side and smiles.

As if a big pink glass of diabetes is just the thing on a hot morning.

Celia Morales beams. Then winces. Her cherubic cheeks narrow her eyes to thin almond slivers. She's worried.

"Is it too sweet?"

"This?" Davis looks at the glass sweating in his hand. Like he'd never really considered it. He shakes his head. "No. No. Delicious."

"I always add a little sugar."

"That's the way I like it. It's perfect."

She relaxes. Sighs. The fullness of her returns.

Davis nods across the modest stone patio. Over the pink bougainvillea that hems the threadbare hedge and toward the playground across the street. On the other side of a tall chain link fence, dozens of children laugh and shriek and chase each other.

"Do you ever mind living so close to where you work?", Davis asks. He bumps his head in the direction of the playground. "Ever need a break from that sound?"

Celia swivels in her chair, regarding the children. Shakes her head. Laughs.

Celia is always laughing. She can't help it. Her round body shakes beneath the shine of corvine hair.

"The children? Oh, no. That sound is music. Music to me, anyway. I could sit right here for hours and just watch them. Just listen to them."

She is quiet for a moment.

"I do that sometimes," she says. "Days like this when I'm off. Or sick. I just sit and watch and listen."

A large green saguaro stands in the corner of the yard. It towers above a dry ceramic fountain like a plump born-again Christian, hands up to Heaven. Praise Jesus.

A small speckled wren flits in and out of a softball-sized hole eaten right into the heart of the thing. There are babies inside.

There are at least a half-dozen other such cavities. Caves of shade mined into the leathery alligator hide. Mother Nature gives whatever she can. She is there for the taking.

She has to. There is no one else.

There are cubes of colored glass buried in the waterless white basin of the fountain, catching the morning light. Refracting it into shards.

"Do you have any children of your own?" He knows it is a risk. There is no sign of a man, let alone children. He asks anyway, letting the glass of cold syrup sweat a ring onto his notebook.

He keeps the notebook closed. Still too early in this process to take notes.

Celia smiles. It registers on her face the way the leaves of a plant betray a tremor before anyone can feel it. Another laugh. Her body jiggles. But she does not swivel back to look at him. She talks to the playground across the street.

"No. No kids."

Davis nods. Lets the silence do its work, pressurizing the conversation. The words will come. They always do.

"I was almost married. Long time ago. That sure didn't take." Celia laughs and nods vigorously like she has said something funny.

Silence.

"Tried to have a baby." Silence. "She didn't take either."

"I'm sorry," says Davis.

"Oh," Celia pretends. Swats the air. "Long time ago. I've got lots of children in my life. Always have."

"How long have you been teaching?"

"Near thirty years."

"All right here in Corbin?"

Celia nods. Laughs. Shakes. "Can you believe it?"

"That's a long time. You must know everybody."

"That's true. If I don't know 'em, I know *of* 'em. I knew Buddy Lincoln well when he was here. And his family. He's a good man."

"That's the God's own truth, Celia," he says. His father's phrase, *God's own truth.* Stuck in his head like an unknown thing buried in a pocket, a mystery shape he keeps pulling out to identify. Oh, *that.* "Buddy is a good man. The best."

"How's he doin', anyway?"

"Same ol' Buddy. Terrifying. Like a second father."

"You should have known his mother. Mavis." Celia laughs, remembering.

"I'll just bet," says Davis.

He almost adds that Buddy Lincoln has saved his sorry butt more times than he can count. But he holds all of that back. First rule of interviewing: *don't become the subject.*

"Buddy was always too big for Corbin," she says. "Houston fits him."

"So were your parents from around here?"

Celia nods. "I grew up about thirty miles south. Near Devils' Creek. *Caleta Diablo.* Me and my mother and my two sisters. We were very poor."

"What about your father?"

Celia shrugs and laughs. She looks back across the street.

"My mother raised us. Then *I* raised us."

Davis hesitates. Lets it go.

"You were the oldest?"

She nods. "Magdalena was five years younger. Amalia was seven years younger. She was slow. My mother was a drinker. Amalia had some issues. But she was a sweet girl. Maggie was just… wild. *Wild!*" Celia laughs. Shakes. "I lost control of her when she was fourteen. *Dios mio!* The fights we had. I was like their mother. Amalia listened to me. But not Maggie. She was not a girl who listened."

"Where are they now?"

"My mother went a little… *loco.*" Celia stops herself. Laughs. She holds her hands out wide like she is showing him the size of a fish. "*Mi madre fue* realmente *loco.*"

More shrieking from across the street. Davis looks up and back.

"Sounds bad."

"They arrested her for burning down a nearby farm. Killed two people. Amalia liked to spend time there. They had a goat. Mother felt threatened. They sent her away. She died in prison of cancer. Texas took custody of Amalia. Moved her to Dallas. They didn't think I could take care of her. I was young."

A woodpecker alights on the quiet fountain. They watch it stab at one of the glass squares. It tries to mine the colored light. Then it's gone again.

"My time with Amalia was too short. Sweet girl. Oh," Celia tenses. She grips the arms of her chair and starts to stand, staring intently. "Marcos…."

Across the street a boy is on his back, wailing beneath the swings. A girl in yellow approaches, nudging him with her foot. She stoops, grabbing his wrist. She drags him backwards through the dirt. The boy is suddenly up and dusting himself off. He shouts and gives chase. Celia relaxes back into her chair. She laughs.

"Gabriela," she says. "Tough love. She will teach him not to cry."

The wren disappears again into the body of the saguaro. Davis smiles. Indulgently. Patiently. Drinks his sugar. Waits. He still has the thread in his mind. He tugs at it.

"What about Magdalena? Maggie."

Celia nods. Like she was expecting it.

"She died. Sheriff found Maggie in a dry riverbed when she was seventeen. It had been some time since I'd seen her. Tracks in her arms. Heroine."

Davis sighs. They are quiet. Listening to the children.

He could tell her about his own mother. It might put her at ease. He could tell her about Abby. She is too much on his mind now. Again. Always.

No, he thinks. *First rule of interviewing.*

"You've had a hard time of it, Celia," he says finally. "In a way, you might say your *sisters* were your children."

She shrugs. Then the dissembling laugh. Then she nods. Davis tugs gently at the thread again.

"So now your *students* are your children. Is that how you think of them?"

"Sometimes. Yes. But it can also be hard to think of them that way."

"Why?"

"Because they're always leaving." Celia flutters her fingers like a bird. Like a cactus wren from a leathery green hole. "Always going away. Every year they go away. Every year I worry about them. I cannot help them when they leave."

Celia is not laughing now. Her smile is a thin ghost.

Davis furrows. Grips the thread that has become a rope. Pulls.

"Do they *need* help?"

"Some, yes. Others, maybe. I never know. Because they leave."

"Have you helped them? The ones who leave?"

"Yes. Some. One anyway. I helped one."

And there it is. The line. The story. The piece. One voice in a chorus of voices yet to be found. He didn't know the song. He never does at this stage. It always hits him sideways, a fraction of a melody spilling from the window of a speeding car. Call it intuition. A sixth sense. He couldn't begin to explain it. He just knows it when he hears it.

And now there it is, clear as a bell: *I helped one.*

"Who did you help, Celia? And how? Will you tell me? Will you share that with me?"

She looks at him. As if for the first time. New weather crests the rolling hills of her cheeks. Dark cumulus drifts, scudding low over the flood plains beneath her eyes. Uncertainty folding over worry folding over suspicion.

"Is that what you will write about, Mr. Payne? In Buddy's magazine?"

"Please, call me Davis. Maybe. The piece wouldn't really be just your story. Probably about two or three people. Usually three."

"What other people?"

"Don't know yet. I just got into town. You're the third person I've talked to. And only because Buddy said I should look you up. I don't really know anybody else. Not yet."

She is silent. Thinking.

"Pretty small town, Davis," she says. "Everybody knows everybody."

"I'd change all the names. People and places. Magazine is out of Houston anyway. No reason for anybody to think of Corbin."

"Will I be paid?"

"No. *I* barely get paid."

"Then why should I?"

He knew it would come to this sooner or later. Usually does. He borrows the rationale he has always hated from Dr. Bees.

"I don't know, Celia. To be heard. To hear yourself. Guess you're the only one who can answer that question. Sometimes it helps to see your story written out on the page. Then you can frame it. Or you can crumple it up. Or set it on fire."

"I don't even know you," she says.

"No. You don't. And I don't know you. But we both know Buddy. And if Buddy Lincoln says you're good people, then... well, then that's good enough for me."

Celia looks away again. Not at the children this time. Above the children. At the smear of blood orange fluff in the sky.

He can see in her face that she knows where this leads. This conversation. This interview. She knows it is a bad idea. She has no business telling him this story, whatever it is. Unpacking all of those little boxes of time. But he doesn't care. He leans forward, elbows to knees. Yanks the thread.

"Celcia?"

Silence.

"Paola," she says at last. "Almost lost my job for Paola. Almost lost my life for Paola. But I helped. I think I helped."

She looks down at her hands.

"I hope I did."

Chapter 13
Celia and Paola

It's not that the baby didn't take.

That's just how Celia has tried to think of it.

The baby was never really meant to *be* in the first place. Against God's plan.

It's what she told Father William. And he had blessed that particular explanation.

But then, he would.

At the time, undecided and in the heart of her anguish, Celia had made the trip from Dallas all the way out to Gatesville, where Texas keeps its bad women.

Where Texas kept her mother.

Yolanda had been in another fight. A front tooth missing. Wrist in a brace. And that was the least of it. She was changed in some fundamental way. A defiled portrait. A home gutted by fire. An emptiness behind the windows.

She'll die in here, Celia had realized. *She'll never see the outside again.* Turned out to be true, and sooner than she had imagined. Her mother's pancreas was an organ of mercy.

Yolanda had had a lot to say that dour morning. She'd reached across the gray metal table. Squeezed her daughter's wrist. One of her fingernails was completely gone, the rest bitten short, dirty and ragged like an old saw blade.

"You can't kill, Celia. It is a sin. You can't."

"*You* did. *Dos personas, mamá.*" She'd made a peace sign. "*Dos personas.*"

"That was different. That was to protect Amalia. You know that. And, anyway, I did not mean to kill anyone, Celia. It was an accident. But what you are thinking of... Oh, Celia. Can you really believe he will leave the church? He hasn't yet. *Hombre de Dios.* Ha. *Pendejo.*" Yolanda would have spit had the guard not been looking. She had bumped Celia's forehead with the heel of her hand. "You are not thinking clearly, Celia."

"He says he will. I believe him. He's just not ready. Not yet. But he will not accept as his own a child conceived in sin, *mamá.*" Celia had pressed both hands against her heart. "Conceived by my own carelessness."

"He has told you this? Told you to do this... thing?"

"No. Not directly. Of course not. But I know it, *mamá*. I *know* it."

"How does he even know about it?" Yolanda had gestured vaguely at something beneath the plane of the table. "You are not even showing."

"I confessed. He is so good, *mamá*. He can save me."

"He will only save himself. You are so young. You should have been more careful, Celia. You are not smart. Three daughters and you are the smartest but you are not smart. But listen. *Listen.*" Yolanda's eyes had popped in that way of hers as she squeezed Celia's hand. The brace clanked against the table. "You are walking around. Breathing. Thinking. Speaking. And so is Amalia. Amalia is with her new family, laughing. You know she is laughing. Amalia is always laughing. And that is because, Celia, *I* did not do what you are considering. All for this man. This priest asking you to sin."

Celia had grasped for something convincing. Pleaded.

"*Pero no me puedo permitir este bebé, mamá.*"

"Bah. Excuses. You think *I* could afford you? Any of you? I could not. And I regret nothing. Even Magdalena. I regret nothing."

Celia had thumped her own chest. It made a hollow sound.

"Yes, but *I* raised them, *mamá*. You did not. You could not. Your drinking and your…. I raised them and I failed. Amalia is gone. Maggie is dead. *¡Muerto!*"

Yolanda had examined her saw tooth fingernail. Shaken her head.

"She was wild, that one. Poor Magdalena."

"I am a failure as a mother and so are you."

Then Yolanda had looked up again. Directly into her daughter's eyes.

"Don't do this thing, Celia. It is a terrible thing."

But Celia had done it. Celia had done the terrible thing.

And then, the man she had done the terrible thing for had had not done what he said he would do. Just as Yolanda, her mother, had predicted.

He had continued to minister, of course. At the church. And at Celia's tiny Dallas apartment. Continued to pour his attention, God's attention, on the facts of her misfortune. The facts that had brought them together in the first place: her mother's incarceration for setting fire to a farmhouse; followed by the state of Texas wrenching young, slow Amalia out of Celia's arms and placing her with a family in Dallas; followed by Celia's desperate effort to relocate across the state in order to be near to her sister; followed by Celia's ill-conceived effort to snatch Amalia at recess; followed by the restraining order, supported by psychological reports that she posed a threat to Amalia's emotional wellbeing and development.

Followed by, followed by, followed by.

Then, like God's knife in the back, another *followed by*; this time word that Magdalena had turned up in a dry riverbed outside of Corbin. Needle tracks like ant trails over her arms and legs.

Followed by drunken night, after drunken night, after drunken night until Celia's grief and anguish had delivered her into the company of a man three bar stools away. He had been good for only one night.

But that's all it had taken.

All of those terrible links in a terrible chain had brought her to Father William. Had brought her to his little Dallas church.

And he had been so kind. Even upon learning that her mother was a killer and that she had tried to kidnap her own sister and that she was a slave to liquor and that she had not been to church or prayed to God in a very long time, William had been so kind.

Assuring. Understanding. Not just as a priest, but as a person. As a man.

After a time, he had made a point of coming to visit *her*. Of opening up to *her*. Priests were people too, it seemed. Even priests like Father William who was favored for a higher position in the diocese. His uncertainties were excruciating. She could listen to him. Touch him. His flesh was weak, just like hers. She could comfort him. She could hear *his* confession just as he had heard hers.

And that, in turn, had helped her. Just knowing that *she* was helping *him*.

So he had continued to visit with her. Had continued to confide in her. Had continued to confess. With no protection but God.

Truth was, Celia did not know which man was responsible for the baby inside. Could have been the Devil on a barstool with a bottle of whiskey. Probably was. Maybe.

But who really knew for sure? Certainly not Father William.

And so, contrary to Yolanda's counsel, Celia had done the unspeakable thing. She had taken his prayers. Had listened to his advice. Had folded herself around the shape of his promises. Had made the appointment. Put another terrible link in the terrible chain.

Father William, ultimately, had not changed anything. He had stayed the course with precision, continuing to visit her. Ministering in her tiny apartment. Confessing his weaknesses on the musty couch beneath the dirty window that overlooked the *Dallas Bowl & Brew*.

She had not visited Yolanda after it was done. Not ever again. Mothers see everything. Know everything in a single glance. Issue a new judgment with every blink. So Celia had written a letter instead.

I know you are concerned, mamá. So I am writing to tell you the news. It was all unnecessary worry. She didn't take. I am relieved. But I am also heartbroken. I am paying for my sin. I should never have imagined her. I

73

should never have named her. She was never meant to be. It was not God's will.

But it is done. And I am taking your advice about 'Bill.' You were right about him. He cannot save me.

She had eventually retreated back to little Corbin, the town near where she was raised and near where they had found Magdalena. Left William to his better calling. Left little Amalia to her better life and better family. It had been like gnawing herself free of her own arm and then leaving it in the dust. Walking away.

She had curled up in a ball in the desert. Drank.

In time she had uncurled. Dried out. Pity had given over to anger. Anger at the world had allowed her to stand back up. Brush herself off.

She'd gotten a job cleaning the floors and walls at the elementary school. Scouring away all of those little footprints and fingerprints. Until there was no trace left. Like she was burnishing her sin. Polishing and waxing the thing, the blasphemous act and the emptiness, that defined her. And still she had wanted more.

She applied to be the playground monitor. No standing on the swings. No hitting. Pigtails are not for pulling. Be nice. What would your mother say?

Then she enrolled in the San Angelo Community College for a teaching degree. Two years of long bus rides and late nights until she had an embossed certificate to hang on the tiny wall above her tiny sofa.

Even before the certificate was behind glass Celia had applied to the Crockett County School District for a position in or near Corbin. She had hoped for Corbin Elementary. Just because that was how she had imagined it would go when she'd first allowed the idea of teaching into her head.

But the only opening was at Corbin Middle, home of the *Fightin' Coyotes*.

So she'd gone where she was needed, mid-year, picking up where Mrs. Aldarollo, God rest her soul, had left off, teaching English and reading to a pack of twelve to fourteen-year old fightin' coyotes.

Even on that first day, Paola had impressed her with her differentness.

Her otherness.

Pretty. Shy. Attentive. Smart. Unlike the others in almost every way. She moved not among them, but through them, like a bubble of air through water. Self-contained. Alone. She spoke when called upon to do so, nothing more. Never laughing or smiling. None of those things we reserve for others. Paola had no others.

But she did have a reputation. It had been part of that first day orientation. *"Keep an eye on the music teacher's kid. Likes to fight. Just like his other kid. Lyle. He stopped comin' altogether. She ain't worth the trouble if you ask me. Most of the other kids know to just let her be. But every now and again someone wants to touch the rattle. Then ever'body's bleedin' and cryin' and off to see the Principal."*

Celia had taken the advice. Had given Paola a wide berth. Let her sit in the back of the class, head down, doodling in the margins, hair like a black curtain pulled over her face.

She had ventured to call on Paola only once that first week.

"Why do you think it was important to make the whale white? Paola?"

Paola had looked up. Shrugged. Looked down.

"Give it a try. What's the first thing that occurs to you?"

Again. Actual eye contact this time. "Whales ain't white. Not those kind."

"What kind of whale is white?"

She'd been looking for albino. She'd been looking for the loneliest, angriest thing in the ocean.

"A ghost whale," said Paola.

Laughs and whispers, like a fetid breeze. Paola had slipped away again, back behind her curtain.

At the end of the next day, on her way out to her car, Celia had seen Paola leaning up against the trunk one of the two large *palos verdes* that separated the front of the school from the street. Bright yellow torches of bloom set off against a shock of cloudless blue sky. Celia had stopped.

"I liked your answer. The ghost whale. I liked that."

Paola had looked up at her. Squinted in the stooping, oblique sun. Shrugged.

"Waitin' for your ride?" Celia asked.

Paola nodded. "Yes ma'am."

"Understand your father teaches music on Fridays."

"Yes ma'am."

"Well then I look forward to meeting him." A beat. Two. "I'm new. So I don't know many people at this school. Don't have many friends yet. Still trying to find people I like. Not so easy sometimes. Figuring out who to trust. Know what I mean? Paola?"

It was clumsy. Awkward. Transparent.

Paola had looked up again, squinting. Tucked her hair behind her ear with a finger. Nodded. Looked down again.

"That's easy," Paola said.

A horn honked from the street. Paola stood, sliding her back up against the tree. Walked away. Celia had watched her go. Started to turn.

But then she had felt the pull. Somewhere in her chest. It had been the first of many times. Like a briny rope pulling taught.

She followed along behind Paola to the waiting red station wagon. Stuck out her hand.

"You must be Garvin Cross," she said. "I'm Celia Morales. Just started here this week."

He was lean and rangy. Clean and pink in a scrubbed-hard-all-over sort of way. He had neatly combed baby-fine hair, almost yellow, and a broad smile that bared a set of dingy, crooked teeth. His fingers were long and clean and boney. They shook hands as Paola climbed into the back seat and closed the door.

They spoke superficially of the music program. Then of Principal Deazy.

"A good man, long as you mind your P's and Q's," said Garvin with a laugh and finger wag. "This here is my son, Lyle." Garvin jerked his head toward the passenger seat. "He can tell you all about Principal Deazy. Can't you Lyle?"

Celia had bent down. Looked. Smiled. Waved a tiny wave.

The boy was maybe seventeen. Bad skin. Hair like his father but long and dirty. He'd looked over and stretched a petulant expression into a mocking smile. Then looked away again.

"And Paola back there… she's a spitfire too," said Garvin. "But maybe you know that already."

"All I know is that she is very creative," Celia had said, looking carefully into the back seat. "And very smart."

Paola had been looking down at her hands, submerged in a deluge of dusty amber light pouring over her lap from the far window. Celia remembers it like something breaking inside. Coming loose.

Like something stirring where seconds ago there had been nothing.

It was her stillness. Her sadness. Her wounded, brooding perfection in that syrupy light. Her aloneness. Even here in an idling car with her father and brother. Paola was a thing apart.

She was *other.*

"Not so sure about the smarts sometimes," said Garvin. "But she's about the prettiest little she-devil that ever walked around on two legs, that's for sure. Well, listen." He smacked the steering wheel with his palm. "The wife's at home settin' up for people comin' over tonight so we best be gettin' back. I can smell the tamales from here. Real nice to meet you, Celia."

"Nice to meet you, Mr. Cross."

A long bony finger wagged in the air. "Ah. Ah. Garvin'll do just fine thank-you-very-much."

"Okay Garvin. See you Friday."

"See you Friday. God bless, now."

And off they'd rolled, bits of hot gravel crunching and popping under the tires. Garvin had driven to the end of the school property. Turned the station wagon around. Headed past her again going the other direction.

Paola had been framed perfectly in the window. Head down. Not looking. Not looking. Not looking. Hiding behind that silky black curtain of hair.

Until that last possible second.

Chapter 14

It's another three hours before Davis leaves the home of Celia Morales. His notebook is half-full. His head is completely full. Celia will make for a good piece. A good voice. Better than the rancher he had interviewed the day before. Or the part-time rodeo clown the day before that. He would need two more, but Celia's voice was something he could use. That feeling was never wrong.

He kicks awake his third-hand-piece-of-shit-estate-sale Harley that Buddy had given him and rattles up the road to the corner. The playground swings are still now. The children gone, back to learning their p's and q's.

So his is the only sound. The heat coming off the pavement is almost its own sound. A low horn. A slow nail grating up an E string. A burning moan.

He rides out into Corbin proper. Stops for a late lunch at a place called *Pepita's*. It's the *Help Wanted* sign that catches his eye but the aroma doesn't hurt any. He talks to the cook about the job and orders off the specials board. The cook is all of seventeen. Scrubby clean. Short hair. Black bandana around his forehead. Tiny stud in one lobe. He has a perpetual sideways grin. Like he is just on the verge of figuring things out. He hands Davis an application. Davis asks his name.

"Eladio."

"Davis."

They shake. Turns out he's not the cook. He's the manager. They need someone to wash dishes and take out the trash and keep the place clean. Davis says that's okay by him. Eladio nods. Says his father does the hiring.

Davis wants to ask about Eladio's history. His family. But then he doesn't. Celia Morales is still in his head. There isn't any room. Besides, this isn't the one. He can tell. Eladio is all about the girls. That's his whole world. Davis doesn't want to write about teenage girl trouble. He's done enough of that.

Two men in boots and hats scuff up behind him. Davis nods. Moves on.

He sits at a counter and watches the people on the road. He fills out the application until Eladio brings him his food. He eats his *carnitas* and drinks his tea to the old cantina music from the kitchen. He thinks about Celia Morales and the girl, Paola. When he is done he leaves his money and the application on the counter under the empty glass and steps out into the heat. He rides off down *Broken River Road* and then along *Evangelina Huerta Drive* like he knows where he is going.

At the Town Square he pulls his bike up next to the *Fuente de la Luna* and puts a boot up on the white stone. He dips his hand in the water and splashes the back of his neck.

He has to ask to find the church. When he does, it's the wrong church. He has to ask again. He rolls up ten minutes late.

Elvis Broussard is waiting for him in the parking lot. He is leaning up against his *Agro-Bell Fertilizers* pickup, white with a green logo that substitutes a rangy Mexican beechnut for the *'F'* in Fertilizers.

Elvis is a small, bent black man, grizzled gray around the jaw line, in a dingy white button-down and a green and white baseball cap. Same logo. He finishes his cigarette and steps on it with the tip of his boot.

"Mr. Broussard." Davis cuts the engine and swings his leg around off the seat. Elvis shakes his hand, squeezing.

"Young man, you call me Mr. Broussard again and I'll break your hand. I let you get away with it last week because it was a first introduction. You've been warned. Name's Elvis. I know it's a difficult name to remember but Buddy Lincoln thinks you're smart enough to write for his magazine so I'm guessin' you're smart enough to remember a man's first name."

Davis smiles. Nods.

"Okay. Elvis. I'm late. Got the wrong church. Sorry."

Elvis winks.

"These people wouldn't start a meetin' on time if their lives depended on it. But th'ain't gonna be any donuts left, you can count on that. You ready?"

Davis looks up at the sign by the door. *Matilde of the Sacred Heart First Church of Christ.* He runs his hands through his hair, which he knows is probably too long for this town.

"Don't like churches much," he says. "Used to meeting in the basement of an old boxing gym. Smelled like leather and sweat."

"All humility smells the same, boy. Long as it don't smell like bourbon. Let's go surrender ourselves to a higher power."

The meeting is down a flight of stairs at the end of a hall. All-Saints Hall, judging from the gilded portraits. Davis is conscious of the sound of his boots on the white tile. He doesn't like attention.

Doesn't like to be the story.

There are eleven others in the room eating donuts and drinking coffee. Three of them standing in a knot by a cluttered bulletin board are laughing about something when they enter. They look up, nod, look away. A thin woman in a grass green shirt and bird's nest hair is pushing metal folding chairs into a semi-circle. Her eyes swivel up quickly from within deep hollows, then down again like burrowing mice.

Davis remembers the holes in the saguaro outside Celia Morales' home. The body is just a shell, he thinks. A hollow log. A husk. We live inside and peer out at the world. Like the woman who lives across the street from his new home. One hand just barely pulling back the curtain. We grip the edge of our orbital bone and pull ourselves up by the fingers of our souls, hanging there behind our face, looking out of an eye socket at the people. *Who is that,* we ask. *How can they hurt us?*

"Come on in," she says, seemingly to the chair in her hands. "We're about ready."

Elvis makes a beeline for the folding table along the wall. He picks up the empty donut box with two fingers and shows it to Davis, who is loitering in the back. Davis shrugs his apology.

The people sit. The woman in green, Brenda is her name, sober three years, kicks things off. She talks about a recent close call. Had to break the glass to keep from drinking. She holds up a bandaged hand. People applaud. She goes on about the relativity of all pain.

"This here is nothing," she says to the bandage. "Lose your job. Lose your friends. Lose your man. Lose your kids. Lose your God. That's pain."

Davis listens. Not for wisdom. Or inspiration. He listens for material. He listens for that second voice. The one to accompany Celia Morales. If not Eladio, then maybe Brenda.

But then no. Not Brenda either.

"Who wants to jump in?" she asks.

There is a collective hesitation. They all want to give the new guy a chance. Elvis elbows him in the ribs.

"Go on, kid. Get in the water."

So he does.

"My name is Davis Payne. I'm an alcoholic."

"Hey Davis," they say together.

He tells his story. Not the whole story. Just a sliver. Just the bare facts about losing his mom, and about his dad being more of a drinker than a writer, and about having a rough time as a teenager and crawling inside the bottle on a regular basis before he was twenty. Just the facts. Just the headlines. He doesn't give them the hows and whys of any of it.

He drinks to forget, he tells them. Only partly true, but true enough. He tells them about being kicked out of bars and being scooped up off the streets of Houston like the city was scraping something nasty off its heel. Something excretory. He adds his Harvey story to the rest of them. Tells them about living in flood shelters for too long. He tells them about jail. They all nod. They've all been there.

Difference was, Davis had started early. He was on the accelerated program.

"I haven't had a drink for nearly three months," he says. They all applaud and he stares down at his boots. "I feel pretty good. I think so anyway. The city's got my number, so I moved out here for a change of scenery. Thought it might help to get a new lifestyle."

"What do you do, Davis?" asks Brenda. "Can I ask you that?"

"What do I do. Well, I'm looking for work right now. I'm a writer, but that won't pay the bills. I write a feature called *Voices* for a literary publication out of Houston. *The Ocotillo Review.*"

A few of them nod like they are familiar. But he knows they have no idea. He tells them he is looking for interviews. What kind of interviews? Any kind. People with stories to tell. Interesting people. Characters. He knows the right ones when he hears them. That's just the way it works.

They nod like they understand. They don't. He doesn't either. He says he'll put his card on the bulletin board. He pats his pockets. He doesn't have any cards. Next week, he tells them.

After the meeting, Davis sits side-saddle on his bike in the baking sun as Elvis talks to him from behind the wheel of the *Agro-Bell Fertilizers* truck. He is full of advice about how to stay out of trouble in Corbin, Texas.

"Stay out of the *Lick-n-Tipple*," he says pointing. "Don't you fall for that one. I'll save you the trouble: you'll tell yourself you want some ice cream, but brother, you ain't goin' for the lick. Feel me? You ain't ever goin' for the lick."

"I'm goin' for the tipple," says Davis.

"You goin' for the tipple. Damn right you are. Every time. Stay outta that place. You ever run into trouble, you call me. Day or night. Buddy Lincoln near saved my life once and I'll look after you like you're one of my own. But, boy, I can't save you from you if you don't dial my number. Got it?"

"Got it. Thanks."

"So tell me. How'd Danny Osgood work out for you?"

"Okay. I don't know. Kind of squirrelly. Not what I expected of a rodeo clown, I guess."

"What *did* you expect?"

"I have no idea."

"Suit yourself. Who's next?"

"Don't know. Still askin' around. Thought I'd go up to see Dallas Letti."

"Dallas Letti?" Elvis throws his head back and laughs. He takes off his cap and tosses it in the empty seat next to him. "*The* Dallas Letti? Don't you bullshit no bull-shitter, boy."

"Buddy thought I should try."

"Buddy think he's publishin' *Rollin' Stone*? Shit, oh dear. Dallas Letti. Miss Letti Blue 'bout as legend as Corbin Texas ever known."

"I'm not from Mars, Elvis. I know who Dallas Letti is. My mother had every record Letti Blue ever made." Davis opens his arms. "I clean up okay. What makes you think she won't talk to me?"

"No reason. 'Cept she hates people, she's mean as a snake and she don't give interviews. She's famous for that shit, boy. Do your research. And that's about the only thing she's famous for nowadays. *Argo-Bell* did a job up on her property oh, 'bout three years ago now, and my boys could not wait to haul ass outta there. Dallas Letti. *Sheeit*. Better off sticking to rodeo clowns."

"Worth a try. Worst thing she could do is say no."

"No. Worst thing she could do is shoot you in the face before you finish sayin' your name." Elvis snaps his fingers. "You know who you should interview?"

"Who?"

Elvis looks at him. Thinking. Replaying the thought in his head.

"Nah," he says. "Never mind. Bad idea. Buddy'd take my head off, sending you out there."

"Seriously. Who?"

Elvis sighs. He looks out the window up at the church. Then back.

"Okay. Woman by the name of Libby Holder. Owns a pecan farm, oh, 'bout twenty miles south called *Libby's Nuts*."

"Okay."

Elvis wags a finger, sharpening his eyes into thin, black points.

"But don't you go out there after sundown. Promise?"

"Why?"

"Promise me. I'm your sponsor. I'm responsible for you, boy."

"Okay. I promise. Why not after sundown? Vampire?"

"'Cause that's when Libby Holder turns into Liberty Cherish."

Davis shakes his head. "I don't..."

"Liberty Cherish is a madam."

"A madam. Like a ..."

Elvis nods. "Used to be anyway. She's a one-woman show these days. Crazier than a shithouse rat though. She'll sure enough give your little magazine some color." Elvis laughs and shakes his head to himself.

"Think she'll talk to me?"

"Boy, she'll talk your damn ear off. Question is whether you can understand a damn word she's sayin'."

"Okay. Thanks."

"Just don't eat her cookies. Don't let her give you anything to drink."

"Because?"

"'Cause you're an alcoholic, boy. Don't you forget it. Liberty will fuck you up six ways from Sunday in about fifteen seconds."

"Okay."

"Word is she poisoned her husband."

"Serious?"

"As a heart attack. Ask around. Dead as a doornail. She cut off his thing and threw it out to a pack of coyotes like a chew toy. Keeps his balls in the freezer for ice cubes."

Davis laughs, looking around the empty parking lot for confirmation. He looks back to Elvis.

Elvis hasn't moved. Elvis is not laughing.

He lights a cigarette. Starts the truck.

"You watch yourself, boy. You a long way from Houston."

Chapter 15

Sheldon decides to stand. It is the only way he can keep his eyes open.

A wise precaution, he figures. He is only moments from pitching forward. Bending at the waist like a trap door on a hinge. Slamming face-first into the remains of his breakfast and his empty Longhorns coffee mug.

He rises slowly from the table. Drops his napkin in his chair. Leans in as if to get a better view of the map. Adrian Hewitt's manicure is sweeping fluidly from one side of Corbin, Texas to the other.

"The first phase will impact the entire township," Adrian is saying.

Sheldon stifles a yawn. His eyes water, glistening in the spray of morning sun.

The charade is not fooling Christi. Her eyes roll quietly toward him like a couple of icy blue marbles. He doesn't engage. She looks over at her father. Wants to see if Grayson sees what she sees: Sheldon falling asleep in the middle of the meeting.

For all of her distraction over her husband, Christi's head –unnatural in its pancaked, honeyed perfection –never moves. Her physical presence at the table, a conspiracy of posture and expression, barely falters.

She genuinely appears to give a shit.

Grayson Tate, never one to be misunderstood, is less circumspect. The silver mustache flattens out beneath his nose, cowering from the small, uncompromising eyes. The irritation in his voice is hard to miss.

"Shelly, why don't you just grab yourself some more coffee there, partner. Maybe the fourth cup'll do the trick."

Sheldon smiles. Shakes his head in a light, discouraging tremor. He does not want to interrupt.

But Adrian Hewitt is already quiet and becoming still. His hands stop their fussing over the map. He looks up. Christi too purses her former Miss Houston lips and swivels her face up to Sheldon. Even Nicholas, off on the edge of the veranda adjusting his camera on its tripod to catch the pair of cardinals on the garden wall, has stopped and turned.

"Pardon my manners," says Adrian. "I am most sympathetic." He leans back in his chair, crossing his legs. His gray suit coat is off, sleeves rolled up. But his paisley tie, in tones of mauve and powdered blue and knotted in a tight Windsor, is perfectly in place. Face, smiling, without an actual smile to be found anywhere inside.

Unlike Nicholas Voss, Adrian is lean and willowy and graceful. Dark eyes and sharp, refined features. He has either a debonair handsomeness or an effeminate verve to his presence. Depends on whether one compares him to Christabelle Tate Davis on his right, or Grayson Tate III on his left.

"Mr. Davis has a lot of irons in the fire," he says. "His business has taken his sleep. And here I am eating his food, perched on his patio prattling on about property rights and desert flood plains. I think maybe its time Nicki and I were on our way. I never like cutting airline departures close."

"Oh, like Hell, Adrian. You boys got plenty of time." Grayson points at his son in law. "Shel, go throw some cold water in your face. Belle, go get your damn garden hose so we can wake this boy up."

It is good for a hearty group laugh, even from quiet Nicholas Voss. He drapes one of his chiseled marble arms over the top of the tripod-mounted camera like it was a fence post.

A quiet specimen, Nicholas. Clean blond hair down to his collar. Glowing, youthful skin stretched tautly over the body of a large gymnast. His eyes are cut from the same blue glass as Christi's, which appear to gleam at the comic prospect of taking a garden hose to her husband.

If there is any agreement among the four of them that Sheldon is to be sprayed with the hose, and not beaten with it, then it is not apparent.

A niggling detail. Harmless levity is the point.

"Not necessary," says Sheldon, hands in the air. "Not necessary. I am wide awake. Please continue, Adrian. I'm very interested in the progress."

Adrian nods sharply. He resumes his more active posture over the map. Continues.

"So again, most of this land here, in the northwest quadrant, has already been acquired by CDC. The same is true here, in the southwest quadrant. CDC is currently in negotiations with four or five development companies to purchase the land. That excludes the reserve to Grayson here, which if I recall is four percent on each corner of the township?"

Grayson nods, playing with a tip of his mustache. "Tate Realty and Development is reserving four percent of the Tier-One acreage in each of the southern corners and will reserve six percent of the Tier-One acreage in each of the northern corners."

"Smart man," says Adrian with a wink. "Quinco is reserving a total of sixteen percent of the acreage for itself. Some of that is Tier-One. Most of it is Tier-Two and Tier-Three so that we don't hog all of the Tier-One investment property close in to Corbin."

Apparently sensing the need, Adrian pivots towards Christi.

"There are, or will be, five tiers of properties available for investment. Tier-One property is this ring here, in a tight circle around Corbin. That is where the early and intense development will be. Tier-One will deliver very quick returns in the scheme of things. Tiers two through five radiate out, this way, like Corbin was a rock dropped in a pond. The higher the tier, the lower the price and the longer it will take to realize the returns. See?"

Christi smiles, which may or may not indicate comprehension.

"Anyway, some of those non-reserve sales have already gone through. The others are coming. The developers are itching to chop it up and sell it, but the various boards are waiting until the regulatory pieces fall into place."

"Regulatory pieces," Christi repeats. "What regulatory pieces?"

"The Pecos, doll baby," says Grayson with extra molasses to convey extra fatherly patience. "Want to make sure there's actually gon' be some water."

"Yes," says Adrian. "You see, there is a lot of government work at every level –local, state and federal –required to divert even a trickle from a major waterway. And, you may be surprised to learn, *that* is actually the part of all of this that concerns us, the CDC, the least. Why, you ask."

He looks up. Waits.

"Because everybody benefits from greening up a patch of desert." Adrian sweeps two of his fingers in an arc over the center of the map. "This land is doing nothing for anybody right now. Complete waste of space. But if we siphon a little bit off the Pecos River up here, near Grand Falls, run it about forty, fifty miles southeast this way, bring it down into Corbin and loop it around the backside, and then send it back to rejoin the Pecos down here, just south of the I-10, that will enhance this entire triangle of Texas." He traces a triangle on the map with his index finger and then taps one of the corners. "With little Corbin and its storied Moon Garden Festival as the crown jewel."

He glances up meaningfully at Christi, looking for a reaction. Grayson has explained the project to her a hundred times over the past five years, as has Sheldon. Each time is like the first.

"Think of what that does," Adrian says. "Think of the jobs involved in making that happen. Then think of what that will do to the property values..." He taps the map. "From here..." *Taps.* "To here..." *Taps.* "To here..." *Taps.* "Think of the commerce. Tourism. Look at San Antonio. Look at the River Walk. Win, win, win across the board."

Adrian leans back. Looks up at Sheldon.

"Sheldon, I was telling Grayson last night at the barbeque that the list of major retailers who have registered to receive the CDC Progress Bulletins has tripled in a month. *Tripled*," he intones. "In a *month*. We're talking *Neiman. Gucci. Apple. Saks*."

"*Neiman?*" asks Christi with genuine confusion. "In Corbin?"

Adrian pats her on the hand. "You're not getting it sweetheart. This project will completely transform little Corbin. The town won't resemble itself. All of the big names will all want a place along the new Corbin riverfront. *Neiman Marcus*, yes. *Tiffany's*, yes. *Coach*, yes. *Victoria's Secret*, yes."

Christi looks up, perfect mouth agape. From Sheldon to Grayson and finally over to Nicholas. She searches for some confirmation that *Victoria* might one day keep some secrets in little Corbin, Texas.

"But my point is that it takes time, you see. The lobbying work on this has already taken, what, three years?"

Grayson nods. "'Bout that. The house bill passed last year so, yeah, 'bout three years now."

"Right. The implementing legislation is now mostly in place. The governor is on board. Every politician who wants to get re-elected is signed up. But the regulatory piece is taking forever. The environmental groups don't have much to stand on, but they get their process. That takes time. The tributary will cross a state highway and an interstate, which brings in a lot of other complications at the state and federal level. Then you've actually got to do the work of siphoning the Pecos River and channeling the tributary. Not an easy task. Lots of planning there. And until we know the exact route of the tributary, it is difficult to divide up some of the parcels in the northwest, the entry point, and in the southwest, the exit point. It will all get done. It is *getting* done. But it will take time."

"And money," says Grayson.

"Yes." Adrian reaches for his last corner of toast and pops it into his mouth. "And money. A small tributary of water will take another much larger tributary of money."

He raises a finger, asking for time to swallow. Takes a drink of juice. Resumes.

"Fortunately, this is not Quinco's first rodeo as you say in these parts. We've managed large development projects all over the world. Spain. India. England. Africa. Russia. And several in this country. New York. Colorado. California. We know what we're doing. The banks know that. The serious investors know that. The construction companies *definitely* know that. The construction firms are falling all over themselves to give us a deal on the work in exchange for an investment interest. They're putting together a joint venture to do the work and Quinco will be negotiating a deal in the next few months. That's going to make the lenders happy. We'll need to sit down with the utilities too. All doable I think."

Adrian holds up both hands, palms out, as if to assure his listeners that he has not detached himself from reality.

"People are cautious, and appropriately so. Boards of directors are an inherently suspicious lot. I am not one to count my chickens before they have hatched. But we're already beyond our investment targets. I am quite confident —as is the rest of the Quinco board —that everyone will eventually want a piece of Corbin, Texas. We are not worried about the money."

"What *are* you worried about?" asks Christi. "Anything?"

Adrian crosses his legs. Looks out over the garden beyond the veranda. "Worried is the wrong word," he says. "But we need to make sure the CDC is not so busy on the big picture that it overlooks the local investment needs. The CDC needs…"

"I'm sorry," says Christi. "What is CDC? Are they the disease control people?"

To his credit, Adrian betrays not a hint of irritation.

"No. Perhaps we should have chosen a better acronym. CDC stands for the Corbin Development Corporation. That is the umbrella company that Quinco International established to… to…" Adrian rolls his eyes skyward for the word that is most likely to connect. "…to *wrangle* all of the various details on this particular venture. The CDC in turn, has its own subsidiaries and venture partners to handle everything from lobbying to litigation to title insurance to design and planning and construction to," he extends a hand towards Grayson, "brokering property transfers, to" he extends his other hand towards Sheldon, "advertising and marketing."

A hopeful silence as Adrian Hewitt watches Christi's face process the information. Grayson and Sheldon look on. Sheldon half-expects his wife to actually speak the question he suspects is coalescing in her beautiful head: *how did an umbrella company get mixed up in all this?*

But she does not ask. Instead she points to Grayson.

"So then daddy's business is not actually working for CDC or Quinco or whatever."

"No," says Adrian. "Your father's business is playing an important role in facilitating many of these various property transfers and in working some of the political issues, but it remains an independent business. Just as your husband's business is helping us to advertise these investment opportunities at the state and local level. Tate Realty and Houston Market Research are helping Quinco and CDC keep their feet on the ground right here in Texas."

"Keep the little guy in the game," says Grayson, knowingly.

"Right. Learned that one the hard way. You can't just have a bunch of outside investors swoop in and take over. We've got a list of investors from all over the world ready to buy in, but they don't know a thing about Corbin or even Texas. A high percentage of those investors will double their money and then go invest someplace else —the next big thing —whatever that is. So we need to be looking ahead at the next investment wave. We need a *local* investment presence right from the beginning. You need a *local* buy-in and a *local* information campaign to really make a venture like this a success. In the end, this whole thing has to be about Texas." Adrian pauses. Eyebrows raised dubiously at Christi. "Clear as mud?"

But Christabelle Tate Davis is no longer listening. Another cardinal has alighted on the branch of the magnolia. She extends a finger and bobs it up and down in the air. Like she is ringing a bell on the desk of a concierge.

"Nicholas," she whispers. "Nicholas."

They all turn. And then Nicholas Voss turns. Sees. Swivels the long lens. He gets his shot. Nods to her his silent gratitude.

"Nicholas got some spectacular photographs and video this week," says Adrian. "Didn't you, Nicki?"

Nicholas scrunches up his Slavic stoicism so that he appears to be pouting. Then nods, relaxing his features. Unscrews a lens. Sets it on the railing. Screws in another. "Sure. Yes. There will be good ones to use."

"He's being modest," says Adrian. "So much color and personality. It's a beautiful little town. Painted desert and all that. Nicki knows how to take a picture."

Christi beams. Nicholas shrugs.

"Wait 'til you see the investment brochure the marketing team is putting together. Gorgeous. We're mixing in a lot of San Antonio River Walk footage and some artist renderings of Corbin just to show the potential."

Adrian's enthusiasm seems to give him a second wind. He launches into an unnecessary sales pitch for the new Corbin. His slightly effeminate, manicured hands shape an oasis for the modern, desert-dwelling consumer; a sculpted, meandering, brick-lined canal draped in vines of bougainvillea. Gondolas. Riverside cafes. Strolling musicians. Bike paths. Shaded benches and tables with husbands pleasantly passing the time as wives indulge in upscale retail therapy. He lists them all again, inflecting. *Macy's. Cartier. Bergdorf. Apple. Coach. Victoria's Secret.*

Sheldon imagines that traveling the world making investment pitches in the homes and boardrooms of the well-to-do is Adrian's main mission in life. He wonders what Quinco International pays him to eat other people's food and *'wrangle details.'*

He wonders, too, about Nicholas Voss. Always so quietly in the background. Nodding his agreement. Taking pictures. Sketching. Carrying bags. Getting the car.

It is obvious to Sheldon that Christi is intrigued by Nicholas. *Nicki.* She is not a subtle person, even when she wants to be. He supposes that it is the very aloofness of Nicholas that has captured her imagination. She wants to be noticed.

Just as she had once wanted to be noticed by Sheldon.

Which had never been particularly difficult.

Breakfast at their house had been entirely Christi's idea. She had insisted on it. Convinced Grayson to cancel his reservations at the *Clubhouse on the Greens* and invite the two men to something more intimate on their last morning in Texas before heading back to New York. The arrangements had been made at seven that morning, just as Sheldon was arriving from a very long, very fast drive from Corbin.

"Daddy," Christi had lamented from her side of the bed, phone perched open on Sheldon's pillow.

"Belle, doll baby," Grayson had said, his authority filling the room, "we just had them to a Texas barbeque in my back yard. That ain't intimate enough for you? Clubhouse is nice."

"Daddy, Shelly and I want the chance to welcome them into our home. I think it would be nice."

"I can't get Shelly to come home long enough to even shake their damn hands."

"He just walked in." Her eyes had quickly brushed him from top to bottom and back up again. "And lookin' like somethin' I don't want to say warmed over. Say hey to Daddy, Shel."

"Hey, Grayson," Sheldon had said to the phone on the pillow.

"You close the deal with Texas Beef?"

"Still working on it," he had lied. "We're close I think. Still talking. May have to go back up to Dallas."

"Back?" Christi had whined.

"We'll see."

"Listen Shelly," Grayson, irritated. Looking to change the channel. "You want to meet the Russians at your house this morning? 'Stead of the club?"

The Russians. Sheldon had tried to roll his eyes but he had been too exhausted to complete the full roll. Instead, his eyes had detoured into a slow, prolonged blink. The danger was that they might not open back up, even standing in the doorway of his bedroom, car keys hanging from the crook of his finger.

Grayson called anyone and everyone associated with Quinco International *the Russians.* In the four or five meetings Grayson has had with the Quinco executives in charge of North American development —three in New York, one in London and one in Hamberg —he had managed to develop a kind of schoolgirl crush on a particularly charismatic and forceful vice president named Gregor Buchvarov. Mr. Buchvarov, Sheldon was to understand, was not only Russian, but *very* Russian. *Extremely* Russian. Accent. Clarity of purpose. Choice of libation. Temper. Everything. *Extremely Russian.* So now they were all *the Russians.*

The true answer was that no, in fact, Sheldon had not wanted to invite *the Russians* to their home for breakfast. Sheldon had wanted to collapse into his bed. Not move for another full day.

"C'mon, Daddy. Please? It'll be good. I want to learn more 'bout all this y'all are always talkin' about. Club's too noisy and the waiters and all. We'll just do somethin' nice right on our veranda. I'll call Antonia an' have her get her lazy behind outta bed and come cook us up somethin' eggy."

"Shelly?" Grayson asked.

Sheldon had looked at his wife, still in her sheer pleated pink baby-doll. Legs crossed at her delicate white ankles. Snowy shoulders propped up against the headboard. Eyes like round, blue children playing beneath a blonde waterfall. She had scowled at him, wrinkling her brow like she was trying to shoot darts across the bedroom from her forehead. *Yes*, she had mouthed emphatically. *Yes*.

Sheldon had known it was hopeless.

"Yeah. Sure. Whatever, Grayson."

"All right then," Grayson had said. "I'll cancel at the Club and call Adrian. Y'all get ready. Get Antonia's ass in gear. And Shelly, you still there?"

"I'm here."

"You need to be sharp. Hear me? Last night at that barbeque you missed, I told the Russians what I know of your advertising plans –the three prongs or levels or branches or whatever it is."

"Stages."

"Stages. Whatever. But they damn well need to hear it from you. I brought you into this deal and I don't want you makin' me look like I was just throwin' a bone to my son-in-law. Get what I'm sayin?"

"I understand."

"I know you got a business to run with other accounts, including Texas Beef, but none of those jackasses can hold a candle to this Corbin deal. I say fuck 'em all if it means keepin' the Russians happy."

"Daddy," Christi had scolded, frowning at the pillow that held her father's voice.

"Sorry Belle. I know it's early. Your mama used to box my ears if I cursed before noon. God rest her. But this shit here is goddamned important and I don't want it all fucked up because Shelly's out chasing Texas Beef."

From the doorway, Sheldon had given the phone the middle finger, walked into the bathroom and closed the door. He sat down on the toilet and listened to the conversation go on without him.

"Shelly?"

"He's gone, daddy. You don't need to talk to him that way."

"Well goddamnit, Belle. I'm sorry, but I think I do. He needs to be more of a go-getter on this goddamned thing."

"He's tired. He's been workin' real hard. Drivin' all night. He looks like hell."

"Tired? I don't care if he's tired. I don't care what the man looks like. I don't care what he *feels* like. The Russians will go get some other advertising firm. They don't need HMR. They took Shelly on my recommendation. And hell, they don't even need me or Tate Realty. They'll give the work to someone else in a heartbeat if we don't deliver."

"I know."

"You get him cleaned up and presentable and I'll try not to kick him in the ass in front of the Russians. I've sold 'em this silly idea that Texans are tough and can get the goddamned job done."

Sheldon had planted his elbows on his knees. Lowered his face into his palms. Yawned. Almost immediately, darkness had flooded his senses like a sweet black oil. The voices through the bathroom door had thinned and drifted away. In their place had come another voice.

Olivia's voice. And then her face.

No. Not Olivia. *Rose.*

Like a ghost. Like some rippling visage from the bottom of a cold lake. Like an old blues song, sweet and sad and ripe with so much that he had dreamed of as a young man, his life unfolding itself like a pair of wings, beating themselves dry in the hot evening of his youth.

Rose. Like an old ache.

He needed sleep. The wine and whatever had been in those cookies *–shuga… stick… cookies,* Liberty Cherish had called them –had lingered in his brain as a low-frequency buzz. Had vibrated him right to the border of consciousness. The drive home, most of it at nearly eighty miles an hour for five hours, half-stoned, half asleep, had finished him off. He'd been lucky to be sitting on a toilet seat in his very large marble bathroom and not scattered in bits and pieces across some eastbound section of Interstate 10.

So he had wanted to sleep. Right there on the toilet if necessary as Christi called up Antonia and ruined her morning and then busied herself primping and preparing for breakfast with the Russians.

But more than that –more than sleep, more than anything –what Sheldon Davis had wanted was to slip out of the bathroom, stumble out to the car, back out of the driveway, and aim his little silver Mercedes for the westbound I-10.

And then head right back to Corbin.

Chapter 16
Abby and Davis

The week after Abby and I had our "date" at the fair was torture on so many levels. School was only just getting started for the year and it had already turned stale. It all seemed the same. The teachers. The students. The routine. It was like the previous summer had lasted all of three days. My teachers went on about things I just didn't care about. All of the books seemed to be written in a foreign language.

I tried though. Mom always liked to tell me that I would only get out of life what I chose to put into it. So I tried.

But as hard as I tried, the only thing I could think about was the coming weekend. And Abby. The way she looked. The way she sounded when she said my name, or just about anything else. The way she smelled. The way she tucked her hair behind her ears. The brush of her fingertips over my palms. The way she hopped and clapped when she won the ring toss game. She was so adult in some ways and so young in others.

I hung around Jack and Kenny and a couple of other regulars, just like always. We played poker in the empty science lab every day during lunch. But they were like everything else: dull and old. I wanted to tell them about Abby. I almost did a thousand times. But something stopped me. It was like connecting those two worlds —ours and hers —would ruin her somehow. Like she'd disappear if I told anyone. It was like not wanting to talk to people about Santa Clause or the Tooth Fairy. I didn't want Jack and Kenny to tell me all of the ways that I was crazy for feeling the way I did. Hell, I didn't understand any of it myself.

So I kept quiet. I swallowed as much of my confusion and excitement and impatience as possible. I tried to move slowly, like I didn't care about the hours passing. That Thursday the three of us all went out to see a double feature at the multiplex. *Ferris Bueller's Day Off* and *Stand by Me*. It was such a relief because I didn't have to talk. I could just sit there and eat popcorn and stare up at the screen and think about Abby. I remember hardly anything about those movies.

You're probably not a movie guy anyway. Shrinks probably hate movies. Can't ask any questions and even if you did, people would tell you to shush. I should have thought of that.

When Saturday morning finally came I was up and out of the house before Dad woke up. He was sleeping on the couch again. His typewriter was at the kitchen table next to a stack of pages and a dirty glass. There was a mostly blank sheet in the roller with a sentence at the top of the page. I wish I hadn't read it. But I did. I read it so many times that now it's in my head forever. It read: "*I dreamt she was still down there, eyes open, looking up at the surface, and not moving, like it was the wet light holding her against the bottom.*"

It's creepy to me that he writes that book like it will bring her back, or like it will heal him in some way, and here I am writing you this —whatever *this* is — because you think it will heal me. Or help me. Or save me from myself I think you said. Why am I the only one who can see things for what they are? Why am I the only one who can accept a shitty hand of poker without having to write about it?

Anyway, I thought of waking him up. Making him some breakfast. Washing the glass. I just left. I got the hell out and sprinted for the bus stop.

The last Saturday of the Texas State Fair was so choked with people, like twice as many as the previous weekend, that it was nearly impossible to walk a straight line or to stand still without bumping into others. It was *The Rivalry* more than the fair that brought them all out.

I guess I can't imagine you are any more of a football person than a fair person or a movie person, and since you're a latecomer to Texas I probably need to explain that *The Rivalry* is short for the *Red River Rivalry*, which is the annual showdown between the Oklahoma Sooners and the Texas Longhorns, played right there at the Cotton Bowl Stadium. For a lot of Texas, *The Rivalry* is the most important game of the year. People would miss their own funerals to see that game. Uncle Zeke (that's Fat Jack's uncle) has gone every year since he was fifteen. Jack tried to get me to go with them that year but I begged off. I told them Dad had me cleaning out our back shed.

I made a beeline from the bus depot to Abby's tent. I kept my eyes open for Jack and Uncle Zeke, even though I doubted that they'd be spending any time at the fair before the game. People swarmed into the fairgrounds from all directions like clouds of cicadas having one last go at it. Red Longhorn hats, jerseys, flags, and those oversized foam *We're #1* hands were everywhere. The sky was a slow, lazy blue, hazy with heat and with only the slightest breeze, directly from the west, rolling in over the stockyard. It smelled like my granddaddy's farm out in Lubbock. I spent many a summer cleaning up after horses when I was a kid. It smelled good to me. It smelled like Texas.

Abby was in her tent but busy reading palms for nearly two hours before she could leave. There was a line of five or six people waiting. I excused myself to the front and stuck my head in so she could see that I was there. She said nothing, but nodded that she saw me. The sight of her nearly took my breath away. Soft, billowy peasant blouse and black denim skirt, naked legs stretching beneath the table into a pair of painted leather boots. Her hair was tied behind her head with a hot pink ribbon that matched the color of her lips.

She was holding the hand of a pot-bellied cowboy with dirty gray hair. They both looked at me in silence until I backed out of the tent.

I waited, wandering in loose circles through the park, all the way to the auto show and back, watching jugglers and listening to fiddle-players, checking in every fifteen or twenty minutes until I finally saw her outside, fixing the "*Will Return*" sign to the door of the tent.

As we walked off toward the rides, I looked at her closely for the first time that day. She seemed tired and keyed up at the same time, like she hadn't slept for days and was relying on caffeine and adrenalin to keep herself together. She seemed preoccupied with the people around us, like one of them might suddenly make a grab for her purse. She clutched the strap over her shoulder with both hands. She was unusually quiet and so it was mostly up to me to carry the conversation.

I say '*unusually quiet*'. I really didn't know what was usual with Abby. I had spent so much time thinking about her it was easy to think we had known each other for years. But I knew almost nothing about her. I knew she was from England, but I didn't know anything about why she was in the United States, let alone Texas. I didn't know if her parents were alive or dead or whether she had siblings. I didn't know if she was married or had a boyfriend or children or pets. I didn't know any of the big stuff, not to mention how she '*normally*' acted.

Still though. She was acting different.

"You're in high demand today," I said.

"All of them want me to predict the outcome of that stupid match," she said, looking at me briefly. "They're completely mental about it."

"You should charge extra for that," I said. "You'd make a killing."

"I can't predict a football match, Davis."

"Game. You have to stop calling it a match. People will think you're British."

She laughed at this and I could see her face light up a little for the first time that day.

"Game. Right. Sorry. Game. I can't predict games either. I'd get it wrong at least half the time."

"Oh, you'd definitely need to pack up and leave before the game was over. No question. You'd never work the state fair again."

"Well *then* what would I do?"

I stopped. She stopped.

"Let me see your hand," I said. She gave it to me, smirking. I brushed her palm with my fingers. I licked my index finger and traced her lifeline like I knew what I was doing. People looked at us as they passed.

"Hmmm."

"What are you on about?"

"Wow."

"Davis!" she laughed. I could feel the tension draining out of her body. "You've gone crackers! What?"

"Says here that you're going to have a career in television."

"Television? I'm to be a big star am I?"

"Yes. Weather forecasting. Looks like it's going to rain, by the way."

She snatched her hand away howling with laughter, hitting me about the shoulders. I cowered and darted away through the crowd with Abby close behind. I ran backwards and nearly fell into a man pushing a stroller. Abby laughed all the harder. Suddenly she was back to the person she had been seven days earlier. I decided her odd mood had been nothing but a bad case of nerves, her fear of heights filling her head with images of the *Texas Star* wheeling her twenty stories up off the ground.

We detoured to eat corndogs and fries at a table beneath a red umbrella. We lingered to watch a troupe of line dancers work their way through a bad Hank Williams medley. We stopped by the ring toss game to see if Abby could pull off another perfect score. She ended up one for six. She wanted to try again. I accused her of stalling. She pretended to be offended, but we both knew I was right.

We waited twenty minutes in line for the *Texas Star*. Behind us were three boys —one baseball hat, two mini-Stetsons —who looked to be in their early teens. From the sound of things, their adult supervision was already at the *Rivalry* game having left the kids to as many rides and hotdogs as they could stomach. They reminded me of me, Jack and Kenny barely more than a week earlier when we were scampering around the fairgrounds from one ride to the next, arguing with each other and making dares. But on that day, standing next to Abby with those kids behind me squabbling over sticks of beef jerky and telling fart jokes, I felt like I'd crossed some kind magic line in my sleep.

I felt like a man.

I felt like more of a man back then than I usually feel in your office now, two years later, talking about all of this stuff.

The ride attendant opened the door to our gondola and we stepped in and took a seat. Abby chattered nervously about having eaten too much and asked questions about the number of times you have to go around before they let you off. I did not think to ask the attendant if we could have the gondola to ourselves. Before I knew what was happening, all three of the boys behind us were taking their seats.

The wheel spun us backwards in a smooth, slow arc up over the fairgrounds. Abby clutched desperately to the side of the gondola, doing her best to keep looking forward out over the distance between us and the towers of the Dallas skyline, glinting in the sun. The sounds of thousands of people, music, and machinery rose up with us, broadening outward as we got higher up, as if we were pulling sound from every corner of the fair.

Every so often Abby would take a glance directly below us but then quickly looked away again. I clutched her shoulder and gave her a playful shake, just to show her that I was not the least bit concerned about crashing to the ground.

The boys across from us were talking loudly and pretty graphically about what it would be like if the bolts that kept the gondola attached to the wheel were to suddenly snap off. They each had their own idea about which exact spot on the rotation would be the most deadly for such a thing to happen.

"Here."

"No, here."

"No way. *Riiiiight*, here!"

And there were related questions, like how many other gondolas we would take out when we fell, and how many people on the ground would be flattened, and whether the whole *Texas Star* would come down on top of us. And so on.

I kept up my assurances. The best Abby could manage was a sickly, unconvincing smile.

As we were making our first descent, Abby opened her purse and pulled out a flat mesh of copper wire about eight inches long and four inches wide. She took off her various bangles, dropped them in her purse and bent the mesh around her right wrist like a wide bracelet.

"What's that?" I asked. She didn't answer. Instead she pulled out another one.

"Put this on," she said, handing it to me. "Left wrist."

I did as she instructed.

"You want to tell me what..."

She pulled two more out of her purse and handed one of them to me.

"Put this around your ankle. Left ankle. Bare skin. No sock."

"Abby..."

She wasn't listening. She had pulled her bare foot out of her boot and wrapped the copper mesh around her ankle. When she looked up, she could see that I was still holding the thing in my hand and staring at her completely confused.

"Oh criminy, Davis. Just ..."

She snatched the wire out of my hand, bent down and untied my shoe, pulling it from my foot. The boys across from us were suddenly quiet. They were watching her, kneeling on the floor of the gondola, one foot bare and her denim skirt hiked up to her hips. The scene had all the makings of something they were not supposed to see. They watched her strip off my sock and shove my pant leg up my calf. By the time we were once again nearing the top of the *Texas Star*, Abby was holding my bare foot in her hand and bending the copper band around my left ankle. Had I not been so confused, the self-consciousness might have killed me.

She returned to her seat just as the Ferris wheel slowed to a stop and we swayed a couple hundred feet above the concrete.

"Okay, I'm completely..."

"Shut up," she said. She tugged her skirt up her right leg so far that I could see a sliver of pink underwear. My heart pounded at the sight. There was a small gasp from across the gondola. Abby threw her right leg over my left, hooking her foot behind my ankle so that our naked legs intertwined and the copper anklets touched. She wrapped her right arm around my left, clasping my hand and interlacing our fingers, bracelet to bracelet.

"Abby..."

"Shhh." She put the tips of her fingers of her left hand to my lips. "I need to be high up. They're so much clearer up here."

"What's clearer? I don't..."

"Shhh. Close your eyes. Clear your mind."

"Abby..."

"Davis!"

I closed my eyes, but my mind was anything but clear.

"Tell me that you will save me, Davis," she whispered. I heard Abby's voice, cutting through the noise of the fair. Then it was the only thing I heard. "Tell me."

"I will save you, Abby," I whispered back. "I will save you."

I felt her hand pulling against my right shoulder, pulling me towards her. Her mouth on mine, warm and soft and wet, was better than the best dream I have ever had in my entire life. The smell of her, the taste of her filled my head. The sensation of the *Texas Star* turning again beneath me disappeared and for long moments on the way down I felt like I was floating. I'm sure those kids were gawking at us but I didn't care. They didn't even exist anymore. My entire body surged and soared. In the press of that kiss I felt my old life falling away like a gondola dropping from a broken bolt, freeing me from even the sorrow of my father and the guilt of my mother, giving birth to something new and glorious and mine.

Sometimes that's just how falling can feel.

Chapter 17

"Come on, *chica*. Is that what I look like to you? *Un niño pequeño? Un muchachito?* I'm not a little boy any more, yo? I can take it."

Eladio Rivera has found the sweet spot on the fence between earnestness and mockery. He can fall either way. But at least he has moved past awkward.

The kitchen hisses behind him. It sounds to her like a wave, slipping back down a beach. Retreating into the sand.

Eladio leans his featherweight frame against the counter, holding himself up on his elbows, silver tongs in his hand. Olivia chews, narrowing her eyes. She shakes her head. Drinks.

"Eladio," she says. She doesn't finish.

He laughs. "What? I can handle her." He drops to a whisper and claps the tongs together like an aluminum beak. "Just, you know…" He looks both left and right. "Put in a good word."

"No."

"Why? She trusts you, yo? You two are tight."

The silver beak snips closed again. Olivia bats it away.

"What would your father say?"

"Right of passage, yo?"

"Ernesto? Bullshit. What would your *mother* say?"

"My mother?" His eyes darken. He does not like her in this conversation. "*Olvídate de mi madre.* You're the one who lives there. Listening through the walls. What would *your* mother say about it? Living with her. Liberty Cherish. *Una puta. Una prostituta.*"

"My mother never gave a shit about anything. That's not the issue."

"You'd really tell *mi madre*? That's some cold shit, Olivia. You disappoint me."

He tries to hold a hurt scowl on his baby-smooth face. The pout is adorable. She knows he is not serious. And that he is completely serious.

"Eladio, you're cute enough to have three girlfriends, so go get one. She'd chew you up and spit you out like a pumpkin seed. You don't need to pay for it."

"Pay for it? No, no, no, *mi amiga.* That is why you're putting in a good word. See? That's how friends do. Just like I'm not charging you for that delicious *ensalada.*" He passes the tongs slowly back and forth like a wand, intoning. "*Pollo adicional. Jalepenos adicional.* Free refills."

She drinks. Crushes a cube of ice between her teeth.

"Eladio."

"*Sí.*"

"Are you listening?"

"*Sí.*"

"If I catch you within a thousand feet of Liberty Cherish I will tell your mother. Maybe I'll ask her if she knows why her baby boy is always so *arrecho.*"

"*Adio?! Arrecho?*" He is blushing now. Backing up. She almost feels sorry.

"*Sí,*" she mocks.

"Because I'm a man. All men are horny."

"No. All *boys* are horny." She nods at the back of a man carrying two bags of trash out the side door into a detonation of daylight. His third trip. She has been watching. The door slams behind him. "Who's the new guy?"

Eladio swivels away and back.

"Juan quit. Got a job fixing roads. Holdin' a flag in the hot sun. Olivia, you ain't gonna ask *mi madre* any such thing. You know I am just joking, yo?"

The boyish smile is back. Beatific. Innocent. Tongs wide open.

"I'll think about it," she says. "Behave yourself."

Eladio shakes his head. Smiling. Beaten. "Miguel was right about you. You're a cold, dangerous woman."

The side door opens again and the light spits the man back inside, empty handed. His hair is longish. Ponytail. His neck glistens. He disappears.

"Yeah, well, I guess your brother would know. Has he replaced me yet?"

Eladio looks away. Away and down. Smile fading. He is a good kid.

He nods.

"Three times," he says, like he wants to apologize.

She gives him something like a sideways smile. "That's Miguel."

A final drink and she is up off the stool. She slaps some money on the counter and with a backward wave to Eladio, kicks the door open with a boot and is back out under the sun scalding *Broken River Road.*

Miguel Rivera. He is in her head all the way to the car. She allows it like she has a choice. She wants to feel self-pity. She hates that. She wants to feel hate, which feels pitiful.

Three times, Eladio had said. She wants to feel glad. Relieved. She doesn't.

She draws the line at the car, kicking all thoughts of Miguel out onto the hot sidewalk. Leaves him to fry like an egg. Again.

She slams the blue door. Once. Twice. The third time with authority. Starts the engine. Pulls away

The wind yanks at the sheet of cardboard in the back seat. The sun bleaches a bloody hillock of coyote on the side of the road. She finds a cigarette on the way to Yvonne's. She lights this one. Savors the burn in her lungs.

She tries to find the melody in her head. That rolling give-and-take of the ocean. That rhythm of forgiveness. But she can't. He is there again, preventing it. As hard as she tries, she can't seem to banish him.

Not Miguel. Sheldon.

Massage-massage-all-the-way-married.

She cannot stop from wondering whether he is the answer. She has told herself *'no'* a thousand times already. But *'no'* is no good. Libby is there in her head to swat the word away. *'Cause Papi's only gon' be fo' the buyin' but so long.*

Yvonne is wired. Keyed up. Pacing the windows that overlook the driveway like a caged jackal. They look at each other through the glass as Olivia disembarks and slams the car door. Yvonne pantomimes her enthusiasm. Olivia lets the blue door swing back open. No sense in closing it here. She lets it swing. Goes inside.

"Bit sexy for an art class," says Olivia slinging her pack into a chair. Yvonne looks down at the bright silky, lacey, slinky mango-colored thing on her body. It's supposed to drape. It doesn't. It is also too young for her. Not that she can see any of this.

"I know. But I have to wear it sometime. It just hangs in my closet, mocking my life. I can either wear it inappropriately or not at all."

But it is not about the silky, lacey, slinky thing.

It's about the hair. The eyes. The toes. For an instant, Olivia is back to that night over drinks in San Angelo. Wonders if this is all for her.

"Brent buy that for you?" she asks.

Yvonne pretends not to hear, moving for the kitchen. Kevin is in his chair at his table. He throws himself forward and back when he sees Olivia, upsetting his orange slices. He makes his sounds.

"Hey, kiddo," says Olivia with a wink.

"Thanks for coming, Liv. I'm late so I've got to run. Please, please, please no cheese this time. It really doesn't agree with him."

Yvonne grabs her purse and phone from the counter, kisses Kevin on the forehead and is gone. The house is quiet. Abandoned.

Olivia goes to the refrigerator and grabs the cheese. She slices it into little French fry shaped sticks and makes a star design next to the oranges. Kevin is pleased to no end. Most people would never be able to tell. One spasm looks just like the next.

But she can tell.

After his snack, Olivia wheels him out of the kitchen to the piano. She plays. *Trouble in Mind.* Then *Goodbye Daddy Blues.* Then *Everything Gonna Be Alright.* Kevin lunges forward and sideways. His body does not know rhythm. But it wants to.

She plays to a large, polished Mexican pine credenza in the corner of the room. It towers over a lonely, suede leather chair, ivy tendrils spilling from the top of each end like green waterfalls. On the shelves are photos of the happy couple, and infant Kevin, strategically clustered with southwestern trinkets.

On the third shelf is a glass star with an engraved plaque in the center. Kudos from the Texas petrochemical establishment.

On the wall abutting the windows hangs one of Yvonne's experimental impressions framed in beech. The painting is large with angry, stabbing tongues of washed-out desert color. There is an emptiness in the middle the color of eggplant. Olivia doesn't know what it means. Only that she doesn't like it.

The piano beneath her fingers is an old Wurlitzer in need of tuning. The middle notes are flat. Yvonne doesn't play. Brent doesn't play. Brent's mother played. She wanted to keep it in the family.

So here it sits.

Olivia thinks of *Papi's*. Sees the ramshackle edifice in her head sitting in the pouring rain of notes. Notes streaming from the gutters and puddling on an Austin sidewalk. Suddenly, there is Sheldon. Right on cue. His face. His unconscious naked white body beneath a narrow fold of towel. Then he is awake and talking. Talking about music. Shaping the notes as he talks. Fingers in the air with their perfectly manicured nails. Expensive silver Mercedes waiting in the dark beneath Old Faithful.

She stops playing. Right in the middle of *Everything Gonna Be Alright.* Hands suspended in mid-air, fingers floating. Kevin slows his thrashing. Tries to look at her.

It has hit her like a board across the temple. Sheldon, is long gone. It's pointless. She will never see him again. It's just a fantasy. One of Libby's willful delusions.

She sighs. Heavy. Hopeless. Shakes her head. Picks up again with *Trouble in Mind.*

Forget *Sheldon-massage-massage.*

She thinks of asking Yvonne for a loan. How much? A hundred? Seventy-five? Fifty? Not a loan. An *investment.* A hundred gets you one twenty-five. One thirty. She'd watch Kevin for free.

She tries to do the math in her head.

It was preposterous. But it wouldn't hurt to ask.

She looks over at Kevin. He is looking back at her sideways, from inside his tilted face, like a critical bolt has gone missing from his neck. He is still clutching two sticks of cheese.

"Eat up, kiddo," says Olivia. And he does.

She stands and slides the piano bench out of the way. Rolls Kevin up to the keyboard. Stands behind his chair and reaches over, grabbing the backs of his pale, cheesy hands. It's awkward. One arm does not want to reach. She has to twist the chair.

It is a jangling, clamorous racket.

But it is music to Kevin. He rocks forward and back with a gleeful violence. The shaking shouts at her. *I did that! I did that!* That is what she imagines.

She laughs. Folds all of his fingers except the indexes into their respective palms. Curls his index fingers beneath her own. Together they tap out the melodic thread of *Sunny Side of the Street*. She whispers the words in his ear.

When they are done, Kevin is still.

For a few long seconds he is still. Hands suspended above the keyboard. She can feel him, between her arms, listening to the notes dance away from him in sequence, snaking off into the forest in his head. Until the vibration along the piano wire has completely stopped.

He is still. Listening to a memory of music. Just like her.

When Yvonne returns, they are outside watching the birds.

"He give you any trouble?" she asks.

"Never. How'd it go?"

Yvonne shrugs her shoulders, as if to convey some ambivalence or a waning enthusiasm. "Mostly just for a change of scenery," she says.

Olivia is unconvinced. Yvonne's enthusiasm is contained, not waning.

"When's Brent back?"

"Tonight. He'll be around for a few weeks this time. Then they're sending him out again. He says fracking is changing everything in the industry. He wants to move."

"Where?"

"North Dakota."

"Why don't you?"

"North Dakota? *Ick.* I don't want to move. I like it here. You're one to talk, Liv. You should move out of Libby's whore house and get yourself a real life."

She doesn't take the bait.

"Don't have the money to move," she says.

In her head is the question. She can feel the constituent components of that question make their way to the larynx where they cue up nervously and wait.

Papi's.

Investment.

A hundred gets you one twenty-five. Maybe one thirty.
"Money," says Yvonne. "That reminds me."
She slips a hand down into her purse. Pulls a hundred dollar bill out of her wallet. Then counts out seven twenties. Then a five. Then four ones. Kevin flails at the chickadee on the railing pecking at a seed. Beyond, the horizon throbs over the bloodstained scrublands as late afternoon clouds work to staunch the wound.
"Two and a half hours," says Yvonne, handing Olivia the stack of bills. Yvonne opens the coin purse, stabbing a finger inside. "I've got four quarters I think."
"Forget it," says Olivia, standing. She says it to herself again.
Just forget it.

She drives into Corbin, dying sun at her back, hissing into a distant sea. She kicks herself for not asking. Couldn't have hurt. But then she knows the answer all over again. She shakes her head in the wind.
"Fuck that," she says, looking for the cigarette.

Corbin is quiet. Not unusual for this time of day. Family time is just starting. Mothers and fathers and sisters and brothers reconvening before dinner. It will pick up again once the sun drops and the dishes are cleaned.
There is still an hour before she has to clock in at *The Diamondback* and deal with Manny Soto and the demonic jukebox.
She parks the car. Walks up the street to the *Fuente de La Luna*. She kicks off her boots and lies back on the hot stone lip of the fountain. Closes her eyes. Dips the back of a hand into the water. Listens.
The ocean. She is on a boat. Rocking.
She smells flowers. Like perfumed clouds wafting over the waves. She pretends the aroma is an old, landed memory.

Mother Ocean. Mother Ocean. Your sorrow so deep.
Your children have floated away.
Down in green coffers such mem'ries you keep
Are you sorry you sent them astray?

Shadow crosses her face. She imagines a gull. A lone albatross in a salty sky.
"Watch you don't fall into that fountain."
She opens her eyes. Papi smiles. "'Cause I can't swim for shit."
She is surprised to see him only because he has been on her mind. It is like she has summoned him with sheer longing. Suddenly, here he is. Crooked nose. Saggy lower lip. Kindly, baggy eyes. Dark, weathered face with hair graying at the temples. *Papi.* Bending over her, hands behind his back. Out of nowhere like some genie from a bottle.

It is not uncommon to see Papi at the fountain about this time, as dusk spreads its wings and flexes its talons and swoops low over the desert. Papi's daughter, Willa, lives in Corbin with her two children and her excuse for a husband. Papi makes the drive from Austin a couple of times a month to see his grandkids. Lecture his daughter and shame his son-in-law. Willa works as a clerk on the second floor of the Corbin town hall. Her office looks out on the fountain.

That's where Papi always waits.

"Hey, Papi," she says. She sits up. Swings around. Starts putting on her boots. "Meeting Willa?"

"Goin' for some grilled chicken over at *Coyote Slim's*. Come join us. On me."

She shakes her head. Looks at her watch. "Gotta work in a few minutes. Thanks though. Saw Willa and the kids coming out of the *Lick-n-Tipple* last Friday. How she doin'?"

"Still married to a fool is how she's doin'."

"Love is what love wants, Papi. Ain't no accountin' for it. May as well let that one go."

He turns and lowers himself slowly down onto the fountain next to her. Folds his large black hands over the lip of stone. He groans as he comes to rest.

"You okay?" she asks, hand on his shoulder.

"Old bones. Nothin' I can do about that either. Standing up is worse. Met with a lawyer today who looks about sixteen. Says he's crazy about ridin' bulls and skydiving. Fool thinks he's immortal. I remember that feeling though. Indestructible." He slips her a sideways look. Nods. "You're young. You probably still think that way too. But it passes. And when it does, you pine for it. I do. Ain't no going back though."

"Ain't never thought I was immortal," she says. "Plenty of times I think the end's right around the corner. That's the truth too."

He looks at her hard. "Shouldn't think that way. You're young. Strong. Looker like you? If I was a hundred years or so younger…" He doesn't finish the thought. "If anyone gets to be immortal, it should be you. Anyway, this is your time. Right now."

But she's not in the mood for that kind of conversation.

"Why you spending time with lawyers, Papi? Everything okay?"

"Ahh. Estate planning horseshit. There's some tax consequences to selling that place. And I got some liens to deal with. Need someone smarter than me to figure all that mess out."

She nods, heart hardening. "Got a buyer yet?"

Papi gives a grin. Elbows her in the arm.

"Waitin' on you, girl. Get with it. Make me an offer. You know you want it. And I know why."

He winks his old, bloodshot eye. He is joking with her. It has always been a distressingly playful subject.

"And you know I can't, Papi."

He nods. Looks out into space. Opens his mouth like he might respond. She doesn't let him.

"See, all of my millions are tied up in big time investments. Stocks and bonds and whatnot. My lawyers ain't a buncha kids jumpin' outta airplanes. They're older than sin and smart as the Devil."

Papi laughs from the belly as she stands.

"Gotta go clock in. Tell Willa I said hey."

"See you Saturday?"

"You know better than to ask, Papi."

"Alright then."

She leaves him at the fountain. Walks back up *Broken River Road* away from the Town Square. She's still early so she takes her time, looking into windows of the *Coahuiltecan Trading Post* like she's interested. A hand-woven horse blanket is spread over a water barrel. On the blanket is a collection of cactus people. They are larger than hers. Brighter. Painted and shellacked. Ersatz eyes and smiles drawn on with colored marker. Twig arms wave. Their enthusiasm is inauthentic.

She has to wait for two men in straw hats to clear the sidewalk. They're fresh from the *Lick-n-Tipple,* each with a case of beer under one arm and a soft spire of white ice cream in the other hand. She can feel them turning. Can feel their eyes. She keeps walking.

She passes her car on the street. Turns up the alley on the north side of the *Caddo Lone Star Laundry.* She can hear *The Diamondback* before she can see it. Garth Brooks is singing about his friends in low places. Next Aerosmith will sing about a dude looking like a lady.

But she isn't thinking about the jukebox.

Forget it, she tells herself for the hundredth time. *Let it go. Just forget it.*

Manny Soto is in a particularly foul mood. A bad day, she suspects, given the pettiness of the fights he is picking in the kitchen. She steers clear. Keeps to herself. Puts up with the jukebox without kicking the plug out of the wall. In the last thirty minutes she breaks a glass stacking too many empties while cleaning table nine. Manny unloads like he has been waiting all night.

She apologizes. Takes it. Says she needs to be more careful. Manny finds her acceptance unnerving. He expects her to say something. To get in his face. But she only looks back up at him as she sweeps the damage into a dustpan.

"Wha' wrong wichu, O?" he asks, hands on his hips, squinting down at her on the floor. He looks over his shoulder and then back. He says it again, softer this time, like he really wants to know. ""Wha'… is… wrong… wich…u, O?"

On the drive home the moon is out. Not full, but close enough. Everything is milky blue. The road is for ghosts. On the arrow-straight stretch between the old cattle gates and Pescante Gulch she snuffs out the headlights. Slips the car into neutral. Lets it coast as far as it will go until it rolls to a stop. She pulls over and cuts the engine. Gets out. Climbs up on the hood. Leans back against the windshield. Lights a cigarette. Listens.

There is nothing to hear.

That is, there is *nothingness* to here. And it has a sound.

She has to tune out the distant truck. And the popping beneath the hood. And the coyote miles away. And the sound of her own breath.

Beneath all of that… is *nothing*. And it has a sound. Something is buried within the nothing. A heartbeat. A scream. A moan of longing and ache. An ocean.

All of this was once an ocean.

She sits up, panning the miles of scrub through the thin, blue ink of the moon. The beds we make are sea beds. Ancient. Forgotten. Quilted with memory. It is hard not to feel abandoned.

Mother Ocean. Mother Ocean. Your sorrow so deep.

She reclines again, crossing her ankles, humming to herself until the cigarette is done. The distant truck is upon her now. It blows past like a whale.

She slides off the hood. Climbs back in. Slams the door. Once. Twice.

She drives the rest of the way in the dark, moving slow, wary of animals.

Old Faithful looms in the night even a half-mile away, a shadow towering among shadows. Olivia stops before she is there. Just after the final turn, where the entirety of the massive tree is visible and the farmhouse glows buttery yellow off in the periphery.

Not that she means to stop. It is the other car that triggers the reflex.

Quiet and glinting like a silver splinter stuck in the base of the trunk.

Chapter 18

He does not see her there. Standing in the entrance to the parlor.

For all he knows, the doors are still closed.

It is partly the music. Bessie Smith is in the room like a slow, blue hurricane moving over the gulf in the middle of the night. Nothing to see. All you can do is listen to her snap the trees and drown the neighbors, going on about that man. Corkscrew crooked and evil as a snake. Oh how she loved him. Oh how her heart did ache.

But it is also the *Rio Lobo* that has him occupied. And the cookie.

Cookies. Plural. Meaning both the one he has just finished and the one he is now attempting to fish out of Liberty Cherish's kimono-clad cleavage with his teeth.

It would be much easier if she would stop dancing. Wriggling.

Or if he could use his hands.

But Liberty, a supple tree in the slow, blue hurricane, will not stop dancing.

And as for his hands, they are bound behind his back with a purple nylon stocking. The stocking mate lays curled like a festive python over his empty pants, recklessly discarded over the back of the sofa.

It would be much easier, too, were he not wearing Liberty's leopard-skin panties. As a blindfold.

But he is.

"Come on, baby," Liberty sings out a shout over the music. Her hands are up over her head, moving counter-tempo to her hips. "You close. You so close. You can smell that shuga stick, caintcha, baby? You wantchu mouth aaaalllll over tha..."

Liberty stops. Cocks her head at the open doors. Smiles like her face might completely break open. Her expression speaks.

Can you even believe this here shit? He back, ain't he? Did I tell yo sorry ass or did... I... tell... yo... sorry ... ass that he would be back?

Liberty lowers one arm and palms the back of Sheldon's head. She pulls his face slowly forward, guiding it in towards the glittery baked phallus poking out over the top of her kimono.

Sheldon Davis bumps it with the tip of his nose. Smiles. Does a little dance with his backside. He takes as much of the cookie into his mouth as he can manage. Severs the shaft with a single triumphant bite.

He is, in his own way, exuberant. He is free now to dance to Hurricane Bessie. Hands tied. Eyes wrapped in leopard Lycra. He does his little dance.

Olivia bites her lower lip. Tries not to laugh. She slowly backs out of the threshold and makes to close the double doors.

But Libby is having none of that.

"Well!" she exclaims. She dislodges the remains of the cookie. Brushes away the crumbs. "Lookie here, *Mista cookie-man-massage-massage*. Oh Livia DeLuna finally come to pay us a visit."

Sheldon continues chewing, nodding his head and moving his mostly naked body to the music. In his leopard-spotted darkness, he has no sense of the room. The eyes of Mardi Gras watch him from every mask on every wall. He is nearing the corner, in danger of pitching over into the open steamer trunk, full of playful apparel. Toys. Restraints.

Libby's words are slow to sink in.

But then they do. Sheldon stops.

"What?" It is less a word than a sound.

"Here, baby. We got to get my draw's off yo' pretty face." With the crook of a finger, she restores his sight. He blinks. Chews. Looks down into the steamer. Turns.

Olivia gives a small, tentative salute from the doorway.

Sheldon wants to speak, but his mouth is full. Wants to return the greeting with a gesture, but his hands are tied. They watch him struggle for a moment in his open shirt and his tautly-tented boxers.

"No, baby," says Libby. "This is jus'… you know… this shit here jus' sad. Caint watch this no mo'. Turn 'round, baby. Let Liberty liberate them hands." She spins him around. Goes to work on the nylon knot. Shouts back to Olivia.

"We playin' the *find the cookie* game while we wait on you."

"You were waiting for me?"

"'Course we waitin'. Sheldon-all-the-way-married wants him a *massage-massage*. That mean you. I just keepin' him from gettin' hungry and thirsty and bored and lonely while he wait. You *see?*"

She spins him back around. Stuffs the purple nylon down between her breasts, fluffing out one end like a handkerchief splaying out of a pocket. "Ain't that right, baby?"

Sheldon nods, swallowing the last of the cookie. He sways on his feet like they are planted on the deck of a ship.

"So you've been playing the cookie game," says Olivia to Libby, her eyes louder than her voice.

"*MmmmmHmm*. Sheldon done good, too."

"How good? Exactly."

"He done two an' one-quarter-cookies good." She pats Sheldon Davis on the cheek. "You didn't dive quite deep enough fo' that last shuga stick, did you baby?"

"I… Well I…"

He doesn't finish. Abandons all language for his discarded pants. He bunches them up against the boxer tent.

Olivia shakes her head. "Okay then. Sheldon. Let's go. Follow me."

And he does. Like a little lost duck. Waits for her to kick off her boots at the front door. Then up the stairs.

"Bye, baby," Liberty calls.

But he is not listening to Liberty. Liberty no longer exists. *Rose*, he thinks. Her bare legs and feet only five, six creaking risers ahead of him, inches from his face. *Rose!*

Down the hall. He waits in the doorway as she unfolds the massage table. Snaps in the headrest attachment. Covers the whole thing with a clean white sheet. Hands him a big white towel.

He is ready to speak. Ready to say that he couldn't stay away. That he drove hundreds of miles because he had to see her again. With every turn of her body they connect briefly at the eyes. He can see her anticipation. They are both waiting for him to say *something*. His head is buzzing. Bessie is still laying waste to the parlor below.

He takes the towel. She smiles. *Those eyes! Those lips!*

"I'll take these," she says. Two fingers pull his waded pants slowly from his grasp. "And you get situated. Back in two shakes."

Sheldon listens to her descend the stairs, straining his ears against the music to hear the pad of her naked feet against the old wood. He is so engorged it almost hurts. Almost. His head. The buzzing is incessant. He should feel embarrassed. To have been discovered like that? Like *this*? He should feel mortified.

But he does not feel mortified. He feels… *fantastic*. Euphoric. He feels the opposite of mortified. He feels alive. He feels happier than he can remember feeling in a very, very long time.

There is something in the cookies. And maybe the wine. He knows this now. He is not stupid. He knew it before he had arrived because he remembers how he had felt the last time he was in this room. Only three days ago.

Definitely something in the cookies.

He had decided that there was something in the cookies on the drive back from Houston as the prospect of seeing her again had spooled out over the highway in front of him. He had tried to game it out. Imagined what he would say. Imagined how he would conduct himself. *Stay away from the cookies. There's something in those cookies.*

He had even imagined Christi and Grayson shaking their heads, in perfect tandem, in mutual disgust at his naiveté. *There was something in the cookies.* Adrian Hewitt and Nicholas Voss were in the background of this road-blind fantasy. They too thought he was an idiot.

And yet it had taken no arm-twisting to convince Sheldon to play the cookie game. A couple of glasses of Rio Lobo. Well. Three glasses. Plus some nerves. Plus some awkwardness. Plus a lot of time in a closed room with Liberty Cherish and Hurricane Bessie. The cookies, and whatever was in them, had been an easy sell. And now the buzzy, swimmy feeling in his head. The throbbing pressure between his legs. All confirming what Sheldon already knew.

There was something in those cookies.

And maybe something in the wine.

Something wonderful.

He does as Olivia had instructed. Takes off his open shirt. The white boxers. Dumps them in the corner chair. Lies face down. Flattens his enthusiasm as best he can against the table. Pulls the large towel over his rump.

Voices. From downstairs. Bessie. Liberty. *Olivia.* Sounds that are too far away to shape into words. He stops trying. He waits. Cheek flat on the sheet, hands along his sides. He breathes deeply. Smiles. He can feel himself relaxing. Drifting. Liberty… Rose… Olivia. Bessie. Bessie. Singing about that fire that never stops burning. Singing about mister devil down below and his pitchfork. That's where you're going, Bessie sings. *Do you understand?*

When he comes to, hands are working his shoulders. He smells the oil. Perfume. The overhead light is off. A shaded lamp in the corner glows in a low, burnt saffron beneath a yellowish scarf. Olivia's voice.

"Nice nap?"

It is a minute before he can clear his head enough to answer.

"Sorry," he says eventually. The sheet beneath his mouth is wet with drool. "Sorry. I must be… uh… tired. Long drive. How long have I been…"

"*Shhhh.*" She tuts at his concern. "People go to sleep on me all the time. Totally normal. I take it as a compliment. All of that driving is in your shoulders. Right here. And your neck. Right here. You're one stiff customer."

An innocent comment he assumes. But it reminds him. He takes a mental inventory. Four out of five appendages are soggy-noodle relaxed. Not the fifth.

"Must have a lot of business down here," she says. "In Corbin. Driving all that way. Twice."

She squeezes. He groans. He shapes the pain into sounds resembling words.

"Oh. Corbin. Lots of. Stuff. Happening in Corbin."

"Anything to do with that River Walk thing everyone won't shut up about?"
He tries to raise his head. He can't.

"Yes," he says, closing his eyes again. "You guessed it. The River. Walk. Thing." After a second he adds: "Not what it's called, but…"

"They really gonna steal some of the Pecos? Bring it to Corbin?"

He feels himself slipping away. Falling back into dream. He doesn't want that. He blinks hard.

"That's the plan. Yeah."

She begins pulling his right arm away from his body, like she is gently trying to lengthen it, one hand tugging at his wrist, the other stroking the length of his arm, from pit to palm. Sheldon opens his eyes as wide as he can. Yawns. Watches her stepping in and out of view. "Can I ask where you heard about it?"

"The River Walk thing? Hard not to hear about it." She slowly shakes out his arm. Kneads his hand, palpating his palm with her thumbs. Pulls and strokes each finger like she is getting the last bit of toothpaste out of the tube.

He wants to close his hand over hers. Wants to pull her to him. He doesn't.

"Gossip," she adds. "News. Read an article in the Houston Sun I think."

"That was us," he says. It feels like bragging. It feels desperate. He doesn't care. "We did that."

"Who did what?"

"I own Houston Market Research. Advertising. Chances are? If you heard anything about the Corbin Development Project in Houston, I'm behind it. Well, *my people* are behind it."

My people? It sounds so elitist. Sounds like Grayson. Like the person Christi wants him to be. He doesn't care. God he feels good. Yes, *my people.*

"We set up that whole series in the Sun. Lot more coming, too. It'll go national. Global."

She is quiet. He wants her to be impressed. Her face gives him nothing. She is focused. Working.

"That. Feels. Soooo. Good. How long. Have you. Been doing. This?"

She places his right arm carefully next to his side. Moves over to the other side of the table. Her hip stirs the air along the top of his head. She takes hold of his left hand. Begins working on the arm.

"Ten years maybe. Off and on, though. Never done it full time."

"You like it?" he asks.

"I guess."

She does not elaborate. She pulls and palpates and strokes every inch of his arm. Her smooth black hair falls over her face. Swishes. Like it's a kind of dark, dry water. She kneads the pale flesh of his underarm, pulling the rest of his arm alongside her body like she is playing an instrument or hoeing a field. His palm makes contact with her waist. Innocent but sustained.

They separate.

It happens again.

His heart surges, pressurizing the pipes. He lets his open palm rest on her hip. She does not move it. He wants to pull her to him. Wants to encircle her waist. Kiss the flat of her belly. He wants to inhale the smell of her.

He resists. His entire body aches. His head is mush.

The room spins slowly on its axis.

A thought comes to him, lazily, drunkenly, through the narcotic fog. A perception. She is different somehow. Tonight. Different than the last time. Quiet. Timid. She has not laughed once. There is a tension to her presence.

She's nervous, he thinks.

Nervous? Why is she nervous? Because she can feel it too, that's why. Because there is something undeniably powerful between them. Something just on the other side of the line that neither of them has yet found the courage to cross.

Liberty's words. The sound of them resurface in the swamp of his brain like little bubbles of air. *Pop. Pop. Pop.* He had written them off. It was only Liberty toying with him. Leading him on, just to convince him to stay.

"You heard me, baby. Invest. I ain't fibbin' either. She be home now any time. You can ask her y'own self. Now, ain't them britches uncomf'table?"

Then he had downed another glass of *Rio Lobo* and finished his first cookie and allowed what she had told him to be lost in the parlor hurricane.

But what if she had been telling him the truth? What if the tension he perceives in Olivia's fingertips is coming from… *that*? Or is it all just the cookies coaxing the britches off of his perception?

"I think there's something in those cookies," he says.

There is a pause in the palpation.

"Oh?" Olivia begins stroking her way down to his wrist.

"Not complaining. I feel great. I feel… *God* I feel good."

"Good." She replaces his arm. Moves behind him. Folds the towel up to reveal the crease on each leg that marks the upper outskirts of legdom. He can hear her oiling up. She grips his left thigh, plowing her thumbs down hard into the soil of his flesh. He groans.

"Too hard?"

"God no," he whispers. The back of her inside hand makes repeated, incidental contact. He can feel each lovely knuckle. It is so sensitive it almost hurts. The sensation is excruciating.

"Just let me know," she says.

He fights to redirect his own attention. Scans the strip of room in front of him. Anything will do. Anything to keep safe, non-sexual custody of his interest. Just for a couple of minutes. Just long enough for the fresh tide of excitement, more than he can control, to retreat.

But the room is mostly bare. She keeps it empty on purpose, he thinks. Impersonal. Hides herself in the emptiness. The scarf-draped lamp is on a small wooden table. It matches the carved dresser along the back wall from which she had extracted the sheet and the towel.

On the wall above the dresser is a painting in a gaudy gilt frame. An old whaling boat tossed upon the spuming lips of an angry sea. Again, the back of her hand grazes... *it*. Words, all in a single knot of sound, explode from him like a Champaign cork.

"Liberty tells me you're looking for an investor."

All movement behind him stops. As if in some silent but violent collision.

"What?"

He tries to turn his head. Tries to look back at her over his shoulder and see her expression. He can't. The very effort makes him dizzy.

"She said you were looking for an investor. Said you were looking to buy... some... business. I think. She thought I might be interested in helping."

He can feel her fingers moving again, then the heel of her hand sinking into the back of his thigh, harder than before.

"Ow."

"Sorry," she says, easing off the pressure. "She shouldn't have told you that."

"Oh, she didn't tell me... I mean, I have no idea what you're getting yourself into. She just... you know... she thought. I should. Ask you about it. She thinks you need a partner."

She does not speak. She works on his calf. His foot.

"So do you? Need a partner?"

Silence except the sound of skin on oil on skin and Bessie moaning up from downstairs. She does not answer him. She strokes the length of his leg like she had his arm.

"'Cause I've always got money for a good investment," he says. "Trick is making sure it's good. Lot of ways to take a bath out there. I've learned the hard way, believe me."

Silence. His words are like little birds. He watches them flapping off into the saffron dusk hanging low over the shaded lamp. He marvels that they have come from him. That he made them. If he could not *think* coherently –and he couldn't; his thoughts almost instantly lose any discernible integrity, colliding and merging with each other like raindrops on a windshield –then how could he *speak* coherently?

Maybe he hadn't. Maybe the little word-birds had all been in the wrong order. Maybe they weren't even words. But he keeps at it anyway.

"So if you just want some advice. Someone to look at the numbers. I can... I'm happy to help."

The smell of oil. Perfume. The silence makes him uncomfortable. He tries to fill it.

"I'm guessing massage studio. Am I right? I'd be willing to help you with that. I mean… if you wanted."

He doesn't know what he is saying. He doesn't care.

Silence.

He wants to look at her. Wants to move his arms and roll over and sit up and look at her. Wants to call her by the name ringing in his head. Wants to pull her on top of him and whisper in his ear that he still loves her. Whisper that somehow, impossibly, he has grown old and she is still young but that he still loves her as though he, too, is still young. And then… no… yes… *God yes*. Then he wants to pull away the towel.

He lies still. Listens. He can hear the fresh oil slicking her hands.

"Ain't a massage studio," she says, finally. She makes a long, firm pass up the length of his leg.

"Okay. Bad guess. What is it?"

"Can't say. It's private. It's personal."

"If it's a marketplace investment, it won't be private or personal for long." More birds! How is he making such meaningful sounds? Who is working his brain?

Silence.

"You can trust me. I won't tell a soul. Scout's honor."

She works his leg. Up and back. Like she is rolling dough. He lets her. Listens. Bessie is still downstairs in the parlor singing about how hard it is to find a good man. The song ends and she starts up again with the one about how the devil's gonna get him.

The sound of oil slicking over flesh.

And there is also the sound of Olivia thinking. That sound, apart from the pounding of the muscle in his chest, pushing the blood in wild torrents through his body, is the only thing Sheldon really hears. *Thinking*.

She tugs the bottom end of the towel toward her. Readjusts it over the back of his legs. She lifts the top end of the towel off his back, letting it hang like a curtain, the upper half of him on one side, his legs and Olivia on the other.

"You can turn over now," she says, turning her head away.

So he does. It takes a second or two for him to send enough strength into his arms to make it happen. But he does and then collapses down onto his back with a groan. The change in position sends the ceiling spinning like a warped record in slow, wobbling turns around the spindle of a dark, frosted globe.

He looks down along the length of his body. She is placing the towel over his midsection. Over his indefatigable erection.

He sees her face. Sees it register.

He strains against the weight of the towel. It aches. She approaches. Places her hands gently on either side of his neck. Her thumbs stroke the underside of his chin. The ceiling above her is still spinning. She looks directly into his eyes.

He wants to shout her name.

She is so beautiful he wants to cry. So he does. He *does* cry. He can feel each tear as it slips free. He can feel his nose starting to run.

Olivia smiles a little. He sees this. How can he *not* see it, directly beneath her like this? It is a nervous smile. But he makes his own meaning.

Gravity pulls at a thin chain of metal looped around her neck. On the chain is a pendant of hammered silver. The pendant appears and disappears, swinging in and out of her blouse, as she moves. He watches it come and go.

Her face. So close to his face. The face she is cradling. Caressing. A lift of inches and he could kiss her. He could. He could lift his mouth to hers. He could imagine it.

So he does. He imagines it.

And then he does it. He does it.

She is moving back. Suddenly. Moving up. Moving away. Her features darkening, closing, like a time-lapse movie of a desert flower as the sun sets, retracting its beauty. His head is sloshing in the spinning room. He is crying. Seeping. He reaches for her. Finds the back of her neck with his hand.

She keeps pulling away. "*No,*" she is saying. "*Stop it. Stop it.*" He pushes himself up from the table with the other hand. He wants to assure her.

"I'm not... I'm not..." He cannot speak. All the birds have left him. They have taken his words in their little beaks.

He is sitting now. The room is a carousel. She knocks his hand away from the back of her neck. His legs flail, looking for purchase atop the wobbling table in the revolving world. They find the edge and hang, stretching for mother earth.

The towel slides. He tries to catch it. He cannot spare a hand. He tries to hook it with his foot as it drops. He fails. Where is she? Where did she go? He stands, gripping the table from behind.

"I'm not... I'm not..."

He hears her coming around the table. She is in front of him and moving fast. Too close. He is leaning back against the table. But the table moves, tipping away, and the world shifts. He lashes out for balance with one hand. Finding nothing.

Nothing except hair. He clutches it like a rope. Pulls against gravity.

The room explodes. Three times. Sound. Pain. Light.

Sound. "No!" She says. "I said no!"

Pain. From his nose to the center of his brain. He can smell the blood. He can feel it run. He can taste it in the back of his mouth. He lets go the rope. Falls.

Light. A double sixty-watt supernova from above. He closes his eyes. He can hear her moving. Can hear her naked feet on the old wood floor just as he had so many years ago. He opens his eyes. She is leaving the room.

She has his clothes in her hands.

"Hey! I'm not… I'm not… Wait!" He wipes his face. His hand wet with red stickiness. He stumbles forward out into the hall. She is at the top of the stairs, throwing his clothes to the bottom.

"Hey!" he lurches forward, one hand on the wall, the other on his nose, pinching.

"Libby!" Olivia shouts down the stairs. Then to him. Like cold steel.

"Get. The fuck. Out. Don't come back."

She turns her back. Storms down the hall. Slips inside an open door and slams it closed.

"Hey! What… what…"

It is the pain, now, that keeps him upright. It is the only thing that is solid. The only thing that is real. He clutches his nose like it's a handle that will keep him from falling.

Movement from below. Sound.

"Oh, baby."

Liberty Cherish is in her open kimono at the bottom of the stairs, leaning up against the wall where Cale Hargrove's grandfather clock used to stand. She shakes her head in pity.

"You a mess, baby. You say you want you a *massage*-massage."

"I did!" He shouts into his nose-pinching hand.

She looks up at him like he has just claimed to be Abraham Lincoln.

"MmmHmm. *MmmHmm.* Well that not what it look like to me. All the way down here I can see you done forgot to tell yo little dingly dang that you is *aaalllll*-the-way-married. He up and lookin' around for the business. See? *Where she go? Where she go? Gimme some, gimme some, gimme some.*"

She slowly stoops to pick up his clothes.

"No! I didn't do anything! I just… I just…"

Liberty stops. Looks up. Arches her penciled eyebrows. Points.

"Uh, uh. You do *not* raise yo' voice at me, baby. Not in this house. I will lay you out and you will never get yo' doughy-white ass back up again. You understand that shit? Sheldon wit' the bloody nose? You get what I'm sayin'? I will bury you in six diff'rent places. Maybe seven."

Bessie. Rolling like a thick fog, on and on about mister devil and his pitchfork.

"But…"

Liberty has turned her back. She shimmies to Bessie. Hips left, *pump, pump.* Hips right, *pump, pump.* Moves for the front door.

"Come on, baby. You want you some clothes fo' the ride home? I just go put 'em right outside on the grass where you can find 'em."

That's where you're going, she sings. *To see mister devil.*

"Oh, mercy me. I almost forget. I go get yo' pretty lil' shoes too. Them some nice-ass shoes, baby." She pauses. Finds his hysterical eyes with hers. "Sheldon

Davis, advertisin' man from Houston who own Houston Market Research, an who *all-the-way-married* to Christabelle Tate Davis in they house on fo-teen, fo-teen Alamo Heights Lane."

Do you understand?

Chapter 19
Celia and Paola

Don't approach wildlife. Your intention counts for nothing. You just have to wait.

Celia had been much too eager in those first weeks. Genuine is not the same as smart. She'd reduced Corbin Middle School to a brick structure of opportunity, not for learning but for enticement. For bonding. Taming.

Not that Celia could explain it. That yearning for connection. But there it was. Not connection with just anybody. Connection with *her*. With Paola.

Paola was having none of it, of course. She could see Celia coming from a mile off. Offering conversation. Company in the lunchroom. Money for the vending machine. All that forced humor.

Each time, young Paola was either gone before Celia could close the distance or she had made it clear that she *wanted* to be gone.

Celia might have finally accepted the rejection. Might have reinvested that energy and attention into teaching others. Bonding with students more willing to engage.

But she had not accepted the rejection. She couldn't. There were no others. Without Paola, Corbin Middle School may as well have been completely empty. Like Corbin Elementary had been in the late evenings, smelling of solvent.

There was only Paola. Just the two of them. Celia and Paola.

So she could not accept the rejection. Each day she started again. Hand out, walking slowly toward the velvety, chocolate-eyed fawn in the woods. To Paola, it had to look like stalking.

It was stalking. In a certain light. The quiet reconnaissance. The deceptively casual conversation with other teachers. The not so coincidental intersections with Paola's father, Garvin Cross, every Friday in the music room. Excavating information like some paleontologist, extracting brittle fossilized bones, old fish skeletons, buried within the shallow, casual dialogue about Garvin's love of music.

And the Lord Jesus. And his wife's cooking.

Garvin talked with his hands, his long, boney, fret-reaching fingers shaping words in the air.

Cooking was what Maria Cross did best in life, Garvin had told her. It was her gift back to God. As if Jesus was coming back for the food.

"What's her best dish?" Celia had asked once in the teachers' lounge. "What's Paola's favorite?"

"Oh, I'd say Maria's best dish is prob'ly her *sopes* or *tamales,* Garvin had said. "Or her *huaraches*. Or… well shoot it's all good. Paola's not much of an eater though. Eats like a bird. Which is fine by Lyle, who pretty much cleans Paola's plate every night. Last year, November first, Maria made a dozen birthday cupcakes. Mexican chocolate with sprinkles. Lyle ate nine of 'em. Paola ate herself about one-half of one of her own cupcakes. Lyle's like a gosh-darn vacuum cleaner."

Well that was something, wasn't it? *November first.* Celia had carefully brushed off that fossil and slipped it into her pocket. The emotional significance was lost on her initially.

But not for long.

As the day approached, as October rolled out its pumpkins and the dead began to stir, November 1 did what it did every year: It pulled a cloak of meaning over its shoulders, covering its cold number with the warmth of deeper sentiment. *Día de los Inocentes*, like an eager child pulling at the hand of *Día de los Muertos*.

So the birthday had inevitably tangled itself with old grief. The birthday and the non-birthday —the born and the not born, the living and the dead —had found a secret, conspiratorial association in Celia's mind.

But not just *Day of the Dead*. Not just *Day of the Innocents*. Not just the daughter that had never come to be. For the association had lead to further, unintended entanglement: Magdalena was also down there in the mix. Each year, on October 25, Celia said a prayer for her poor, lost, dead sister.

Happy birthday, Maggie. God keep you, Maggie. I'm sorry, Maggie.

November 1. It meant that Magdalena and Paola were both Scorpios.

Water signs.

Brave, passionate.

Secretive, violent.

Not that astrology held anything for Celia. But it had once held something for Maggie. She had gone through a scorpion phase. She had accepted it as her totem. Had looked for them. Trapped them. Brought them into the house. If Maggie's aim had been to provoke Yolanda out of her stupor, then it had worked. It had been good for a lot of very specific unmotherly attention.

Maggie had increasingly asserted her independence. First from Yolanda. Then from Amalia. Then from Celia, her older sister, surrogate for a drunken mother.

Celia had tried to walk in Yolanda's shoes. Eventually Maggie just stopped coming back home.

Shoes. Every morning the sun had risen up past the roofline of the Clarkson's two-story farmhouse, casting a yellow-orange nimbus that presaged its felonious burning. Celia's youngest sister, little Amalia, made a ritual of checking every shoe in the house for scorpions. Turning them upside down. Knocking the heels against the wall. Like she was looking for signs of her absent sister. She never found any.

So. November 1. *They're both Scorpios. Little Paola and long lost Magdalena.*

That, in any event, had been the lick of lightning when Celia had spotted the silver scorpion bracelet. Dangling from the arm of a little wooden display cactus on the front counter of the *Coahuiltecan Trading Post.* She'd told herself it was an impulse purchase, nothing more.

On the morning of November first, Celia had come upon Paola Cross leaning up against the *palo verde* in front of the school, waiting as usual for the last bell to summon her into the building. She'd tried to be breezy about it. Stopped at the tree. Winked. Reached into her purse.

"Well, if it isn't my favorite Scorpio."

Paola had looked up. Said nothing. Her face was confused.

"Understand it's your birthday today." Big smile. Flying eyes. "Happy birthday!"

Paola had looked away. Nodded.

"Thanks."

"I got this for you." Celia had handed down the little box, wrapped in blue tissue. "Just kind of an impulse. I saw it and thought… I dunno. I don't know if you're into this sort of thing. Thought maybe you'd get a kick out of it."

Paola had turned back. Blinked. Reached up and taken the box uncertainly. Reluctantly. Like she had been handed an actual scorpion. Unwrapped it. Her gratitude was as thin as the tissue.

"Thanks, Ms. Morales," she'd said, putting on the bracelet and then taking it off again. "You didn't have to."

"I know, I know. Just kind of made me think of you. No big deal. Anyway. Happy birthday, Paola. See you inside."

She'd then strode off toward the building, pleased at her discipline. The light touch. The casual air. She'd imagined Paola back at the tree. Trying on the bracelet again in private. Allowing herself the secret pleasure of feeling special. Loved.

Loved? No. Too strong. Too early. Not loved. But something like it.

As the morning progressed, Celia's self-satisfaction had expanded. Like a gas, pressuring her mood. Energizing her. Blinding her.

Paola was in her fourth period class, just after lunch.

"Decision time, everyone. I asked all of you to think about this and now you have to choose. '*Sounder*,' by William Armstrong? Or '*The Adventures of Huckleberry Finn*,' by Mark Twain? Or maybe something else on your list? Let's go around the room. Tell me what you would like to read next. And let's start..." Arms wide. Ascending tone. "... with our birthday girl!"

Paola, always in the back of the room, had frozen in place at her desk. Head down. Curtain drawn. Two-dozen heads had pivoted, following the arrows of Celia's attention.

Then snorts. Dismissive grumbles. A stifled laugh. Another.

"Paola?"

She had finally looked up. Eyes no longer velvet. Or chocolate. Or bottomless. Eyes suddenly impenetrable chips of black schist. Glossy with hate, or something like it.

"I don't care," she'd said.

"Why don't you care?"

"Because I hate reading. I hate..."

A pause to choose among options. Everyone in the room had used the moment to fill in the empty space on their own. '*Books?*' '*Fiction?*' Paola had opened her palms. Encompassing everything. Encompassing everyone.

"*This.*"

Celia had felt profoundly shaken. Realizing her mistake. Knowing suddenly that this was a girl who had never wanted to assimilate. Never wanted to belong. Never offered the others the benefit of the doubt in exchange for their trust and acceptance. Paola trusted no one. No one.

And the mob had accepted those terms. The mob loves to hate the loner. They had all held her in a perpetual isolation, like spirited white blood cells surrounding and attacking the mysterious brown antigen.

So inviting their collective attention, suggesting that she was one of them, was the last thing Paola could have wanted.

Celia had had the sense to move on. To get Paola out of the spot light. But not before the others had laughed. Made their sounds. Not before the damage had been done.

She'd found the bracelet at the end of the day. On the floor in the corner. Twisted and bent.

After that she had not seen Paola for another two weeks. It was another month following her return before they had made actual eye contact. Celia had kept her distance. Watched. Wanted.

The fight happened in January. Just after the Christmas break, when the heatless *Chihuahua* felt the most abandoned. Agave, creosote, tarbush, all quietly yearning for the touch of mother sun, even at her most withering. Ocotillos at attention, casting long shadows, keeping the faith.

It happened in a biology class of all places. Mandy Klutch had taken the antagonist mission to a new low. It was never clear who had smeared the ketchup on Paola's chair. Or who had managed to tie the tampon to Paola's belt loop. But the trigger had been Mandy's singsong voice as Paola traversed the room to collect her test paper.

"Uh… guess it's that time of the month. Not really how tampons work, Paola."

Realization, comprehension, rolled under the class, like something tectonic. Row-by-row, adjusting posture, directing attention. Laughter had alighted merrily upon the bass notes of revulsion. Disgust.

It had all happened in slow motion for Mr. McKenzie. Sixty-one. Distracted in sorting out the test papers. Never particularly perceptive on his best days.

But Paola, at the front of the room, had put two and two together very quickly. Felt the wetness against her backside. Discovered the tampon. Her face had flushed with embarrassment and rage. Time had changed, the stream of moments angling sharply down into a lake of hot oil, detaching each second from the next.

Paola had closed her eyes for a beat. *Two. Three.*

Turned. Walked up to Mandy Klutch in her seat and stared down at her. *Four.*

Then backhanded her hard across the face.

Two-dozen heartbeats reset. Synchronized. Surged forward as a single pulse, racing to catch up to real time. The ketchup-smeared tampon was in Mandy's mouth before she could get to her feet. Her nose was bleeding before she could spit the thing out. Mandy, defensive, flailing, was all sound.

But Paola. Paola Cross was quiet, unrelenting fury.

Others had ultimately come to Mandy's defense, pulling Paola off of her with a tearing of fabric, pinning her backwards to a desk and then to the floor just as Old Man McKenzie was breaking his way into the circle of squeaky savages.

But the rage from thin little Paola had been daunting to the interveners. The depth of it. The purity of it. It had surprised everyone. Scared everyone.

The suspension lasted a full two weeks. But she had stayed away longer than that. Paola had not returned to school until late February. Rumors were that expulsion had been seriously discussed but rejected in favor of stern lectures and final warnings delivered by Principal Deazy, both to Paola and then separately to Garvin and Maria Cross.

Filing out of the Principal's office was the first time Celia had ever laid eyes on Maria Cross, Garvin's sorceress of Mexican cuisine. She'd never really wanted to meet Paola's mother. Nothing against the person. It was the *concept* she did not like. It was the *idea* of Paola's mother that Celia had steered around like a crumbling pothole in the road.

She had secretly preferred to think of Paola as motherless.

But then, hand-in-hand with Garvin, there she was in the flesh. Maria Cross. Celia had expected an adult likeness. Had expected Paola's almond eyes. Her lips. Hair. Her slightness.

But Paola was nowhere to be found in this woman. Maria Cross was a doughy, dirty blonde with pale skin. Protrudent eyes, round and small and yellowing, centered too close over a raw, button nose. Her features, so dramatically unlike Paola's, all floated like fleshy flotsam in a white, freckled sea.

Adoption had never even occurred to Celia. Not once.

Confirmation was surprisingly easy. It had been common knowledge among the teaching staff. Lyle was born a Cross. Paola was not.

But both children had been merged into the same anti-social and violently inclined reputation. They occupied the same thought. *The Cross kids.* It was difficult not to put the blame on bad parenting.

In private conversation, everybody seemed to do exactly that: blame bad parenting. Garvin and Maria were not well liked, Celia learned. Not for anything in particular. Garvin was nice enough. Decent enough music teacher. And it was rare that anyone encountered Maria beyond the occasional teacher's conference. Besides, just because a kid acts up doesn't mean the parents have done anything wrong.

True enough. But there was still a nearly uniform, visceral objection in place. They were *odd*, those Crosses. Weird. Somehow… *off.* Some worried about the unfairness of such assessments, and were always qualifying. Softening.

But not many.

If Paola was a kind of wildlife before the fight, then she was wounded wildlife after the fight. Celia had kept her distance. But she had never stopped watching. Caring. Wanting.

Two weeks after Paola's return, purely by happenstance, Celia had once watched from her car as Paola drifted out the door and around the back of the school building. Nothing wrong with that, exactly. Or unusual. It was one of many ways that Paola chose to escape during the day. Like she was a sea mammal, lungs to the point of bursting, coming up for air.

So. Not unusual. But it had been a cold, drizzling February morning, pressed from above by an unrelenting concrete sky. Paola's solitude, surrounded by such bleakness, had reached Celia like a dim wheelhouse light, appearing and disappearing behind dark, ocean swells.

Celia had waited as long as she could. But then she couldn't stand it. She had felt an inexplicable, rapidly expanding pressure. In her. Around her. Like she was being pushed out of the car.

When she rounded the back of the building, Paola was nowhere to be seen. Celia had wondered whether she had completed a full loop, or reentered through the side door and was already back inside. She had almost turned around.

A plume of white smoke rose up from the other side of the large green dumpsters. So she had plotted a course.

"Those things really aren't good for you, you know."

Paola had started, but kept her composure. Took an unapologetic drag. Blew the smoke out in a stream. Watched it become the sky. Said nothing.

Then they *both* said nothing.

"I'm sorry," said Celia eventually. "About your birthday. In November. I never told you that. I wasn't trying to embarrass you. But I should have known better. I won't make that mistake again. I promise."

Paola had been quiet. Unchanged. Like something ornamental set into a garden to give shape to the rain. She'd taken another slow pull on the cigarette. Celia continued.

"My sister was a Scorpio too. You remind me of her. In some ways. I miss her when late October rolls around."

Paola had turned her head just enough. Actually looked. Eyes narrowing, asking the question. Celia had answered as if the question had been spoken.

"Overdose. Magdalena was wild. Rebellious. A real handful. But she was sweet too, inside. Innocent. About your age. Well, no. A few years older, I guess. I always remember Maggie younger."

Paola had looked away again. Dragged. Blown smoke at the houses beyond the schoolyard fence. Watched the cloud rise and disappear.

But she was listening.

"She just kind of... I don't know. Drifted away from us. My mother wasn't... she wasn't a very good mom. Anyway. You let someone drift far enough and then one day... Well." A shrug. A sigh. "One day they just never come back. Maggie was alone."

To the east of the dumpsters, the blind side from where they were standing, was a patch of gravel that surrounded a weathered picnic table. There was no discernable purpose for the gravel. It constantly escaped its wooden railroad-tie containment. It had to be raked back in bounds every week. And replenished every year. It was a pointless nuisance serving an arbitrary aesthetic.

But it could capture the sound of a human footstep.

Two. Three. Four.

Unaccountable impulse. Instinct. Celia had shot her hand out towards Paola's face. Snapped the cigarette from her fingers. Pulled it into her lips. Inhaled.

Principal Deazy had been like a predator rising up out of the ground behind her. Celia could see him only in Paola's rapidly changing expression, its depth shallowing instantly into fear. Celia exhaled a cloud.

"Paola." His voice, deep, stern. "You need to get to class. *Immediately*. Ms. Morales."

Celia had already turned to face him. His glasses were streaked with drizzle.

Like he was inside a human-shaped building, glaring out at her through a window.

"You need. To put out. That. Cigarette. *Immediately.* My office."

Paola had opened her mouth. Perhaps in protest. Perhaps for oxygen.

But Celia had turned back quickly. Widened her eyes at the girl. Stubbed the cigarette against the dumpster. She had formed her lips, like she was preparing to blow a ring of smoke into the shape of a single, silent syllable.

Go.

Chapter 20

"Ain't no call to be angry, baby."

Olivia remains on her side, pillow bent over the back of her head. The little family of cactus people stare back at her, clustered on the nightstand. The boy is waving. He is always waving. How is it he doesn't have a name? All of these years and none of them have names. Not even the dog.

"Y'aint sleepin' neither," says Libby.

She was right about that much. Sleep had been a wild, skittish animal all night, gone well before sunrise. Olivia had been wide-awake when Libby had let herself in and slipped into the bed, still damp from the shower.

She could hear Lewis and Darnell talking as they walked beneath the window over snapping twigs and shattered nut husks on their way out to the back orchard. Something about a busted tree shaker. And then a sharp command to their spaniel.

"Buster! Damnit. Get outta there. Come on."

The cruel irony of it all is that today is the single day of the week on which Olivia does not have a morning shift to work at *Longhorn Fitness.* Either sleep or the call of duty might have been an excuse from this conversation and neither was available. She tries to breathe evenly.

Libby's hand finds her shoulder. Neck. Earlobe. She pulls. Olivia sighs. Rolls over on her back.

"Got every reason to be fuckin' angry, Libby. It's my secret. Not yours."

"Secret? What secret? You mean *Papi's*?"

Olivia rolls back toward the family of cactus people. They are happy to see her again so soon. The boy is waving. Libby pulls her back.

"Now how you gon' buy *Papi's* without no one knowin'?"

"Ain't the point. It's my decision who knows and who don't know. *Mine.*" She hits herself in the chest with the flat of her hand. "You had no right to tell him. Or anyone. Who else have you told?"

"Ain't tol' no one," says Libby. Defiant. Daring contradiction.

"You told *him*."

"Did not. I tol' Sheldon *massage*-massage-all-the-way-married that you lookin' to in-*vest*. I din' say invest in what."

"Well you shouldn't have even told him that much."

Libby squeezes her lips together. Narrows her eyes. Like she is trying to decode gibberish.

"I'm jus' looking to help, baby. Thas all. Lookin' to hook you up wit' what you need. You wants somethin', then I wants it for you. You wants *Papi's*, then I wants *Papi's* for you. You see how that shit is? Someone out to hurt you, then I'm the bitch gon' hurt them first."

"You don't need to have anything to do with *Papi's*."

"You just a baby in this world, 'Livia."

"You're not my mother and I ain't a baby."

"No I ain't yo' mama and yes you is too a baby. An' you *need* you a mamma to tan yo' hide with this kinda ungrateful ass attitude. I'm jus' tryin' to hook you up with a money man. Like you say you need."

She begins flailing her right arm up at the ceiling fan.

"*Oh, Libby, I wish I had me some money! Oh, Libby, I want to buy Papi's. Oh, Libby, what am I eva' gon' do?* What you gon' do? Girl, Sheldon massage-massage-all-the-way-married standin' two feet away lookin' at you all googly-eyed, dingly-dang in his one hand an' a fist full o' money in t'other. He ready to jump in wit' both feet. You want *Papi's*? They 'tis."

"He never said he'd buy me *Papi's*."

"What he say then?"

"He said he was always interested in a good investment."

"They you go. See? He ready to jump."

Olivia grimaces. "Not any more."

"Why? 'Cause I froed his clothes out on the grass? 'Cause you punch him in the face? He be back, baby."

"Don't think so."

"Won't I right the first time? He came back. He gon' *keep* comin' back."

"Not this time."

"Punch in the face ain't nothing' when it come to love, baby."

"Nope. And good riddance."

"What he do to you anyhow?"

"He tried to kiss me."

"That all? Shit. You fro him out the house fo' *that*? A *kiss*?"

"There was more coming. Believe me. He pulled my hair. He was goin' for it."

"So?"

"So?" Olivia turns her head to look at Libby in the eyes. "*So?*"

"Baby, it a *ho*-house. The man nekid, rock hard and feelin' the sexy drugs in a *ho*-house with Bessie Smith moanin' on the record player an' yo' hands all over his lily-white body. You think he Superman?"

"Libby, no offense, I don't do that. I'm not…"

Libby's face hardens into its invincible humor.

"You can say it, baby. Go head. I know what I do."

"Well I don't do that."

"Not even fo' *Papi's?*"

"Not even for *Papi's.*"

"'Cause *massage*-massage all-the-way-married ready to do whatever the hell you tell him to do. He ready to in-*vest.*"

"He ain't gonna do something like that, Libby."

"Baby, that man eat a chicken-shit pie you ask him to. He tol' you…"

"He didn't know what he was saying. He was stoned out of his mind on your stupid dick cookies, Libby."

Liberty laughs. It is a rolling, infectious sound twice the size of her body. Olivia locks her jaw. *It is not funny. It's not. It's not. Don't laugh.* She closes her eyes.

"*Hoooooooo!* Yes he was too. That boy took to them dingly-dang shuga sticks like a mouse to cheese. He go from *Oh, no thank you, I jus' sit here all quiet an' wait for my massage-massage,* legs crossed, arms crossed, all that shit, right to *I want to bury my face in yo' business an' feel around fo' the crumbs,* all in like… half a cookie. Well… an' three glasses of *Rio Lobo.* An' Bessie Smith."

Olivia opens her eyes, alert to something new.

"God…"

"What, baby."

"I hope he's okay," she says. "He was in no condition to drive. What if…"

Libby's face turns earnestly reassuring. She touches Olivia's shoulder with her fingertips. Admires her nails as she speaks.

"Baby, Sheldon all-the-way-married done slep' it off in his little silver bullet. He out there for two hours sleepin' an' holdin' his nose fo' he goes tearin' off, spewin' dust, madder'n a wet cat. Don't you worry none 'bout *massage*-massage. He doin' fine." She pauses. Looks off toward the window. "'Cept…"

"Except what?"

Libby looks back. Swallows.

Lewis and Darnell have fired up the leaf blowers to clean up beneath the trees. They have started at the far end of the sixteen acres and will work their way in towards the house. The dual droning sounds like a siren. Libby widens her eyes.

"Libby. What?"

"Baby. You *know* all-the-way-married still got him that certain… *condition.*"

Libby's mouth begins to quiver at the corners.

"It ain't funny, Libby."

"I know. I know. That shit ain't one bit funny."

"You could really hurt someone. Kill someone even."

"I know. He could close his thang in the car do'."

"Seriously."

"I know, baby. I know. Ain't no laughin' matter fo' a man to drive home from a ho-house an' haft to explain to his *wife*, who all worried an' cryin' over where he been all night, why his dingly dang look like a damn bus."

"Libby."

"No, baby. You right. You right. Shit ain't one bit funny."

Chapter 21

It cannot fairly be described as a large house, the dwelling at 1414 Alamo Heights Lane. Doesn't capture the essence of the thing.

It is a miniature colossus. That is, it is a colossus in miniature. A house of average size for its upper crust environs, but one that poses on its modest acreage with an architectural attitude that defies its actual footprint.

There are white iron gates at the base of the driveway. Only five feet high. A poor masquerade of security for all of the inconvenience. They take far too long to open, swinging slowly in toward the house with a labored grinding sound. They separate at the place where the noses of the two sheet metal horseheads should appear joined in an act of equine intimacy.

Except that the gates have settled. Shifted slightly over the years. So that now they are uneven. The mouth of the left horse seems fixed upon the nose of the right horse. Joining them, when the gates finally close, less in an act of equine intimacy than equine cannibalism.

Up the hill sits the house. The mini-manse. The columns arrayed in front are too many. Too close together. Three would have sufficed.

There are seven.

Christi had wanted seven columns, just like her father. So there are seven bone white, fluted Doric columns, stationed from one end of the home to the other. They support what is ultimately an unimpressive roof, lending the entire structure the look of a place where leisure is kept under strict house arrest.

But the driveway. Like an unspooled ribbon of black silk, it meanders luxuriously up toward the colonnaded portico. Disdainfully avoiding the direct route. There is enough plush green real estate between the cannibalizing horses and the mini-manse to allow for a kind of leisurely tour of the grounds. So it loops first to the west and then languorously east before straightening itself into the garage.

Sheldon pushes the button on the visor. Waits. Pulls the car into the garage. Cuts the engine. Pushes the button again. The door glides down behind him.

All is silent. Dim. Cool.

The space next to him is empty. It is the space that belongs to Christi's red Beemer. Her convertible parade car. Not *actually* a parade car, of course.

But it looks just like the real thing. He'd seen the photos.

He closes his eyes. Lays his head back. Breathes in the emptiness, exhaling relief. It is the one emotion he has experienced in the past eight hours that has not savaged his peace of mind and he is glad for it.

He had hoped she would be gone. Prayed.

On the long drive back to Houston, during the short breaks in which the savage emotions had waned with exhaustion, he had tried to call to mind his wife's social calendar. An impossibility, even under the best of circumstances. He knew that the Houston Pageant Board met on either the last Thursday morning of every month, or the last Friday morning of every month. But he could not remember which.

Not remembering, and thus contemplating that Christi might be home to greet him —see him, smell him —had been a weight of additional stress. The possibility had coiled atop his anger. His humiliation. Worry. Exhaustion. It had coiled atop his excruciating physical pain.

Like a kind of serpent deciding whether to strike.

But Christi is not home. She is away pageant planning. Administering Texan teen beauty and charm for the free world. Thank God.

He sits. Breathes in and out, eyes closed. The quiet, dark garage is like a bandage.

Five minutes. Ten.

He opens the car door. Crawls out. Goes inside. Navigates furniture. Climbs the stairs and collapses onto the bed. On his back, the only non-bloody part him left. His face hurts. His entire groin hurts. He is no longer priapic. But it hurts anyway. He is queasy. He feels like he could be sick.

Lies there. Breathes in and out. The icemaker downstairs makes its noise. Sleep. He wants to sleep.

Five minutes. Ten.

Sleep. Sleep. But the rage is back now, punching through the older, cooling emotion like new lava pushing through an old crusty vein. He can see them both in his aching head. Liberty Cherish. Olivia. *Bitches*, he thinks. *Whores.*

The epithets no longer satisfy him. He has worn them out over the last six hours. His anger wants more. Demands more.

But there is no more. He is angry with himself as much as anyone. Deep down. Where he does not want to explore. He was to blame as much as they were. He knows this. Deep down. He had been drugged within an inch of his consciousness, but he had asked for all of it.

And why? Why had he asked for it?

Because he wanted Olivia DeLuna to be someone she was not. Olivia was no more Rose than Fidel Castro was Rose. When he was not completely tripped out in a narco-sexual haze, the resemblance between Olivia and Rose was practically non-existent.

But he had *wanted* it to be true. Desperately. He had wanted whatever was in those cookies to help him believe.

So he, Sheldon Davis, had knocked over that first domino. Had he not wanted the *illusion*, he would never have indulged in the cookies. Or the wine. The *Rio Lobo*; he cannot call it wine. Without the cookies and the *Rio Lobo*, the misunderstanding on the massage table never would have happened. Olivia would never have punched him in the face. Liberty Cherish would never have tossed him bleeding and broken and naked and nearly mindless out onto the lawn.

He had caused all of this. *He* had set it all in motion. He knew this. Somewhere deep down.

Sleep. Five more. Ten more.

He wrenches himself off the bed. Strips off his clothes. His shirt is smeared with blood. The legs of his pants too, where his sticky red hands had rested as he had slumped sleeping in the front seat of his car beneath that enormous pecan tree.

He looks at his hands. Thinks. He will need to clean up the car.

He drags the clothes down the hall to the laundry room, sleeve in one hand, pant leg in the other. Pauses in the doorway. Looks at the large sink. Considers whether he wants to work on the blood himself.

No. He does not.

He stuffs the clothes into the dry cleaning bag. As far toward the bottom as he can reach. Christi will have no reason to root around in the dry cleaning bag and Antonia would never ask any questions even if she did see his clothes. Which was unlikely anyway since the dry cleaning chore required only that Antonia throw the bag into her car, drive to the dry cleaners, and then throw the bag at the kid behind the counter and wait for him to hand her a claim ticket.

But trying to clean up the shirt and pants himself? Wet clothes hanging from the rack? That would raise all kinds of alarms. From everybody.

He cinches up the bag. Plods back down the hall for the shower. Stops in front of the mirror.

He looks like he has a werewolf hangover. Like he has been biting into live deer. His right eye is darkening. He touches the bridge of his nose.

Fuck Almighty! Gently! Carefully!

Six hours of practice has taught him how much pressure is too much. *Should have* taught him. He winces. Curses under his breath. Gets in the shower. Ten minutes. He watches blood circle the drain.

The mirror tells him he looks much better. Nothing to do for the eye or the swollen, probably broken, nose. But the absence of blood smears has worked wonders.

He shaves. It is a delicate process. Stretching the skin of his face and twisting his mouth has surprising implications for nose cartilage.

He thinks of them again as he is drying his hair. Sees them in the mirror. *Bitches. Whores.*

The bathroom fan sounds like a kitchen coffee grinder. He turns it off.

It wasn't the fan. It was the coffee grinder. Down in the kitchen.

Well, shit.

He dresses. Looks for a tie Christi has given him. His head hurts. His nose hurts. His crotch hurts. He can feel the swelling in his eye. Blinking fucking hurts. He cannot find his watch. Or his ring. They are still in the trunk of the car.

Shit. Shit.

He mentally rehearses his story. Goes downstairs.

She is at the kitchen table in a red silk dress. Pantyhose. No shoes. Bent over her phone. She types with both thumbs. Her face is hidden in a tunnel of hanging blonde hair. She does not see him at first.

"Oh!" Christi snaps off the phone. Puts it smartly, screen down, on the table in front of her. "I didn't hear you, Sugar."

"Sorry," he says. He roots around in the pill drawer. Finds the aspirin. Pops two in his mouth. Opens the refrigerator. Grabs the orange juice. "Pageant meeting?"

She looks at him like she might a child or an octogenarian. He pours. Waits.

"That's tomorrow, Shel. I was at Mary Lou's. Remember?"

He looks at her blankly.

"She's designing a new garden? It's going to be..." She stops. Scrunches up her perfect features. "Sheldon... what the Sam Hill happened to your face?"

"I think I broke my nose."

"What?" She stands. Approaches. He steps back, holding out a hand to keep her from touching. "Meeting with *Texas Beef?*"

"No. Not meeting with *Texas Beef*. Walking to the car after the meeting. I tripped. Hit my face on the edge of the car door."

"Your eye?"

"My face. My nose."

"You're eye looks puffy."

"It's from the nose."

"Does it hurt?"

"Yes it hurts." Too sharp.

"You don't have to snap at me, Shel. *I* sure didn't break your nose."

"Sorry. I just. I'm tired. And I think my damn nose is broken. I'm going to the hospital."

"Well, let me, just..."

"No. Do not touch my nose. Do not..."

"Alright, alright. I was just going to look."

"I said it hurts."

"And I said all-*right*. Sheldon. I'm not touching anything. Good Lord."

She sits back down at the table. Glances at her phone. Lays it back on the table. Watches him drink his juice.

"Want some ice?"

"No. This is good."

"The nose, Shel. Not the juice. Do you want some ice on your nose?"

"No."

"Want me to take you to the hospital?"

Sheldon shakes his head. Finishes the glass. Swallows. "I can take myself. Thanks."

"Well did you at least get the account?"

"Huh?"

"Texas Beef."

"Said they'd be in touch."

"But what do you think?"

"I think they'll be in touch."

"I mean..."

"I know what you mean, Christi. But I don't know. They're lookin' to break in a new horse, but I'm not the only horse in the herd. They're talking to a lot of firms. And not just from Texas. So I don't know. Okay?"

They look at each other across the kitchen table. Man and wife. Christi breaks first. Looks at the back of the upside-down phone.

"You're in some mood this mornin'."

"I think I broke my nose."

The phone makes a rattling buzz against the hard table. Christi twitches sharply. Like the buzz was a bite. She flips the phone over. Reads. Lays it back down.

"Who's that?" he asks. He walks to the sink. Sets the glass down.

"No one."

"No one?"

"One of the gals. Sharon."

"What's she want?"

"Nothing."

"Nothing?"

"Gal stuff. Shopping. Daddy wants you to call him."

"I'll call him."

"Sheldon?"

"What?"

"Where is your wedding ring?"

He looks at his hand like he is surprised to see it there, attached to his wrist and secretly talking to his wife.

"Upstairs. Got blood on it. Had to wash it off. I took a shower and forgot to put it back on."

"Blood?"

"Broken noses bleed, Christi."

She is quiet. Thinking. Her eyes like little blue interrogation room mirrors. He can feel her on the other side. Watching.

"On the edge of the door?" she asks. She holds one hand up stiffly and runs a red, well-manicured nail from her wrist up along the side of her pinky. "Like right there on the *edge* of the car door?"

"What? Yeah, Christi. The edge of the door. Like I said."

The phone on the table buzzes. Christi flips it over. Reads.

"I'm going to get this looked at," he says quickly. Too quickly. He beelines it out of the kitchen. Hopes she does not follow.

She doesn't. He heads for the garage.

There are two cars in here now. Her car, spying on his car. Asking questions. Looking at that door.

He opens it. Pops the trunk latch. Walks around to the back of the car. Opens the trunk.

His briefcase is right where he had left it. He reaches in. Slides the buttons. The little brass tabs flip up; one, two. He opens the lid.

Stands. Stares. Listens to his heart stop.

Watch. Gone.

Wedding ring. Gone.

Wallet. Gone.

He pulls out all of the papers and files. He looks in every pocket and pouch. Gone.

Bitches! Those whores! Fucking thieves!

They had drugged him, taken his keys, opened up his trunk, opened up his briefcase, taken his valuables. And then, just to be perfectly cruel about it, broken his fucking nose.

He leans his forehead against the edge of the open trunk. Presses forward with the weight of his body. Tries to make it hurt. He feels the metal edge embedding in his flesh. There will be a new mark to explain.

He closes his eyes. Breathes. Wants to scream.

Wants to call the police. Wants to see them both in jail. How many others have they drugged, conned and robbed? How would they like to be cuffed and stuffed into the back of a squad car?

It is Liberty's voice that answers him on this point: *Sheldon Davis, advertisin' man from Houston who own Houston Market Research, an' who all-the-way-married to Christabelle Tate Davis in they house on fo-teen, fo-teen Alamo Heights Lane.*

Rage pushes too much blood up into his injured face. He can feel a warm trickle inside his left nostril. Reflexively he reaches for his nose. It ruptures in pain. *Fuck!* His fingers come back scarlet. Red drops splat sideways off the bumper. Spots bloom into the fabric of his slacks.

"*Damnit!*"

He slams the trunk ferociously without bothering to reload all of the papers back into his briefcase.

It does not occur to him that the lime green folder –the one that had brought him to Libby Holder's doorstep in the first place –is no longer among those papers. He is too consumed with pain and anger to think about lime green folders.

If there is any other thought in his head that can be isolated from the rage swirling like another thousand-year storm between his ears, it is only the thought of confronting those despicable women. In person. Righteous indignation in his eyes. The threat of violence, however implausible, hanging in the air. That is the only thought in his battered head.

The thought of reclaiming what is rightfully his.

The thought of going *back* to Corbin, Texas.

Chapter 22

Davis drapes his wrist over a low branch. Watches Libby Holder bend herself in half. She picks two pecans up off the ground. Three. Four. Five. Tosses one away. Picks up number six. Seven.

"So ten acres?" he asks. "You're the sole owner?"

She walks over into the shade where he is standing. Holds out her hand.

"See here, baby. These some quality nuts. Ain't half bad anyways. Look at them shells. An' it sixteen acres, not ten. An' yes I own eva las' one, even them back two which ain't worth a big pile a pig shit. Cain't grow nothin' back there. Little sticks pokin' out the ground. Don't ask me why. Lewis say it the soil. Don't make no kinda sense to me."

He watches her move, circling the tree as she talks, fingertips grazing the trunk, eyes sweeping the ground looking for more to show him. She is in black capris. Pink t-shirt emblazoned on the back with a line-drawn panda reaching for a sprig of bamboo. Her hair is braided into a single black rope that swings just beyond the panda's grasp. Baby blue dime-store sandals slap against the heels of her feet. Well-maintained. Hot pink nails polished to a high gloss.

As much as anything, Davis is mesmerized by the depth of sound coming from her small, curvaceous body. Like a backyard pond that turns out to be five hundred feet deep. Or hearing the voice of the ocean inside a tiny conch.

"How many employees do you have?"

"'Ployees?" Libby laughs. "Ain't no one workin' for me. Got someone clean my house for rent. That count?"

"Well, I'm assuming you don't harvest all sixteen acres yourself."

She makes the final turn around the trunk so that she is standing in front of him again. Drops another two pecans into his hand.

"Baby, I ain't got nothing to do with bringin' in no nuts. SNS do that shit."

"SNS?"

"Sloan brothers. Lewis and Darnell. *S an' S Pecans.*"

"Oh. Right. I saw the signs. So then…"

"SNS got all the 'quipment and know-how, but they only has them three acres. They pay me to get they hands on my crop an' they cut me in on the profit. In return, I stay the hell out the way. Keep my toes clean. See how that shit work?"

"Sounds like a good deal. How's the money?"

"It keep the lights on. You askin' a whole lot a questions, baby."

"Sorry. That's what I do. I ask questions."

"*MmmHmm.*" She puts her hands on her hips. "Well then I'ma ask *me* one."

"Okay."

"Why a Houston magazine... send a fine-looking, tight-jean-wearin', motorcycle-ridin' man... out past Corbin... in his shit-kickers an' his ponytail... to write a story 'bout lil' ol' Libby?"

"Didn't come out here just for you. I live near Corbin now. For awhile anyway. Got a restaurant job. And when I'm not cleaning dishes and taking out the trash, I'm interviewing lots of people."

"Lotsa people like who?"

Davis gives an apologetic smile. Shakes his head.

"Can't tell you that. Confidential."

"*MmmHmm.* Confidential. So then this shit here confidential too."

"Yes ma'am. It is."

"*Yes ma'am.*" Libby smiles and pats him on the chest. "Listen to you tryin' to butter me up. Les go inside, baby. Too hot even in the shade. Two-hundred muthafuck degrees. Like breathin' in fire."

She leads the way back to the house. He tells her about *The Ocotillo Review.* Tells her about *Voices.* He can't tell if she understands.

"So it a news magazine then," she says, holding the back door open with a foot. Sandal falls off. She forks it back on as he steps in.

"The magazine does have some more traditional news features, but it's mostly a literary review. Part fiction. Part poetry. Some journalism. I just write *Voices.*

"Which is..."

"Which is about people. It's... like... stories about people. It's the stories people tell about themselves. They print it once a quarter."

Libby furrows.

"Twenty-five cent? Say what?"

"No. A quarter. Once every three months. Longer recently. I've kinda been off awhile. Harvey really messed things up."

"Oh, Harvey a muthafuck, I tell you what. You want you a glass of sumpin'-sumpin', baby? Sumpin' wet?"

Davis thinks for half a beat as she bends into the cold glow of the refrigerator. He remembers Elvis. *Don't eat her cookies. Don't let her give you anything to drink.*

"No. I'm good."

"I'ma have me a *Rio Lobo*. Cool me right off. Cookie?"

"No. Thanks."

"Alright then. Suit yousef. Les go to the parla where we can sit. That the coolest place in the house, baby."

He follows behind as she swings her hips through the kitchen, floorboards creaking beneath her, into a bright, hot, surprisingly traditional dining room. Large mahogany table with four matching high-backed chairs. An arrangement of lilies in the center. Lace curtains are drawn across the flaring day.

Through the curtains, the road beyond the front lawn is like a scorch mark. A dirty match strike. The lace paints shade patterns on the table that look like smoke.

Like the window is an open door to a furnace.

Like the whole room is in the process of a slow burn.

Libby rounds the corner through a pair of double doors into the deep purple shade of a room that smells strongly of jasmine incense and perfume.

Jasmine.

The olfactory invitation is more than his memory can resist. The past hits him hard. He is stepping into Abby Palmer's orchid-colored tent.

His mind supplies the rest. The smell of the fairgrounds. Spun sugar. Roasted meat. The livestock. The soft turf beneath his boots. All of that, and the feeling of *woman.* Everywhere. Erotic. Forbidden.

Like a kind of narcotic fog, swamping adolescent senses.

His heart moves from trot to gallop. Mouth dries up. He even stoops a little as he enters the room, extending a hand to pull aside the curtain of glass beads not actually there.

Abby, he thinks. All of her is packed into that single illicit thought. *Abby.*

Libby illuminates the room in small pools of orange and violet light as she pulls the brass chains of scattered table lamps and floor lamps, each draped with some kind of scarf.

There is a large bed covered with an elaborately brocaded spread. A fan-back chair with scrolled armrests. A wide, antique settee, made up in purple, with tasseled, silk pillows and legs of burled wood.

On the walls are masks. Everywhere. Large and small. Beaded and feathered. Occasionally pinned with gargoyles or butterflies. On the floor in the corner, near a tall, brass ovular mirror, is a large steamer trunk. Sitting on the lid is a coiled purple boa and a stuffed pink pig with a curly tail.

Like the kind you might win at a state fair.

Libby pulls the brass chain on a wooden ceiling fan. The blades begin slowly stirring the light and the smells and the colors into a blended sensory soup. The feathers on the walls start to murmur.

Davis blinks hard. Forces himself back into the present.

"Damn," he says. Oscillates his head from left to right and back again. "Quite a room."

"Sit, baby," she says, moving to the settee. She kicks off her shoes and curls up at one end, wiggling her toes and cradling her wine glass with both hands. "Tell me why you want me fo' you lil' story thing."

Davis moves uncertainly through the room. Sits. Crosses his legs. Uncrosses.

"I think you have an interesting story," he says.

"You *think*?"

"I suspect."

"Why?" She narrows her eyes. "What you heard?"

Davis hesitates.

"Come on, baby. Les hear it."

"Well, uh… the rumor is that the nut farm is just a cover."

"Cover fo' what?"

"A brothel."

"I see. *Mmmhmm*. What else, baby?"

"That you're actually a fairly notorious… uh… madam… That you were. That you work alone now."

"Madam. Notorious too. Well now."

"They call you Liberty Cherish."

She takes a drink. Swallows. Nods.

"An'?"

"And that you… uh… murdered your husband and fed his… uh… penis… to the coyotes. As a chew toy."

She throws her head back. Laughs. Davis laughs too.

"Sure you don't want you some *Rio Lobo*, baby?" she asks, wiping a tear.

"No. Thanks. I don't drink," he says.

"Don't drink?"

"Not any more."

"Oh. You one'a them. Can't stop once you get started."

"'Bout sums it up. Yes ma'am. Better off without it. Let's just leave it at that."

"Leave it at that? You want to ask me if I fuck fo' a livin' an' kill people on the side an' feed the dangly bits to the wildlife an' you want to *leave it at that*? That shit sound fair to you?"

"No." Davis shakes his head. "It doesn't. I'm one of those who can't stop drinking once I start. You one of those who thinks life's fair?"

It is a slow, lasting smile she gives him.

"Alright then. Suit yousef. Mo' *Rio Lobo* fo' me an' none fo' you. So tell me… what you say yo' name is again?"

"Davis. Davis Payne."

"I like that name. *Davis. Davis.* That a *handsome* name. That a sexy, fuck-all-day-'til-you-all-wore-out kinda name."

She looks at him, appraisingly. Testing him. He sits still. Takes it. There is a price to pay for intrusive questions.

"So tell me Mista Davis fuck-all-day, you believe all that 'bout me? All that shit you hear?"

"Should I?"

"Don't you answer a question with no question. I'm askin' *you*."

The army of feathered sequined faces on the wall behind her lends its full support. Davis shakes his head.

"I wouldn't have," he says. "Didn't the first time I heard it."

"But?"

"But then I heard roughly the same story from three other people."

"I see. So you want to ask me questions fo' you magazine, that *Voices* thing, to see if it all true, huh?"

He shrugs.

"Maybe it's true. Maybe not. I just want to find out what your story is."

She takes another drink. Wrinkles her brow. Looks at him hard.

"Supposin' it all true... you gon' come visit me in prison? You gon' let me touch yo' pretty face through them bars?"

"Oh. No. I mean, true or not true I'd never use your real name. And there'd be no way for anyone to know where in Texas the story's coming from. *The Review* is published in Houston. I'd never mention Corbin. It's a big state."

"What my name be then?"

"What would you want it to be?"

"I get to pick?"

"Sure."

She drinks. Thinks.

"Big Mama Bessie," she says. "Bessie fo' short."

"Okay."

"How much you pay me?"

"Nothing."

She laughs. Drinks.

"Nothing? *Sheeeit*, boy. Why should I then?"

"Most people like telling their story. It's therapeutic. Cleansing. It's validating. Helps you step out of yourself and look back in. Confession is good for the soul."

He thinks of Dr. Bees. Then Abby. Then his mother. Pushes them all away.

"Con*fession*?"

Wrong word for her. He nods anyway. Smiles.

"Oh, baby. Now I *know* you ain't no priest."

He laughs. "Far from it."

"But people do like that, don't they? Tellin' they shit. Confessin'."

Davis nods. He feels the buzz in his chest. He almost has her.

"Yeah," he says. "They do. Especially to a stranger." He leans closer. "Especially to a stranger with a sexy fuck-all-day name."

Libby laughs. The sound weighs three hundred pounds and could break through walls. Davis laughs with her. She is his. He knows it.

There is movement, suddenly, in his peripheral vision. He can see Libby focus on the room behind him. He turns toward the door. Someone is there.

He has seen her before, he thinks. The eyes. Hair. Skin. Face. Head. Something. But he cannot place her. He can sense a hesitation in her look. Like she, too, is processing the past.

"'Livia, baby," booms Libby. "This here my new writer friend. He want me to confess my sins. Fo' a *mag*-a-zine. How 'bout that shit?"

"Hope it's got a lot of pages," she says. Libby laughs.

"Thas true huh! You gon' have to write you a book, baby!"

"Whatever it takes," says Davis. Not laughing. Looking.

The woman flashes a quick smile. Turns her attention back to Libby.

"I'm goin'," she says. "Won't be back 'til Saturday night."

"Okay then, baby," says Libby. "You watch yo'sef, now. Crazy-ass *massage*-massage-all-the-way-married lookin' fo' you like a man po-*ssessed*. He back today, too. Muthafuck beat on my do'."

"I'll be fine."

"You see him you tell him he gon' answer to me if he pull any mo' shit."

"He's all bark and no bite, Libby."

"He all *dog* anyway. An' he off his damn leash."

"I'll be fine. Bye."

She waves. Davis waves. Their eyes catch. Gone.

"Seems nice," he says, still staring at the door. He is slow to turn back to Libby.

"Oh she *real* nice. An' she off the damn menu too. Ain't tellin' you shit 'bout Olivia. She private as can be."

Davis nods. Pushes. "Sounds like someone is after her."

"Man by the name of *massage*-massage-all-the-way-married. He been here two days this week. Las' time he yellin' an' poundin' on the do'. *Goddamn this* an' *Goddamn that*. I jus' let him go 'til he get tired."

"What's he want?"

"Can you believe? Says we took his damn watch. But it ain't about that shit."

"No?"

"Uh-uh. *Massage*-massage in love."

"With you?"

"Oh *hale* no, baby. He scared to death of me. Should be, too. No, all-the-way-married in love wit' 'Livia."

"And what does she think about him?"

He knows he has gone too far. Libby's face hardens.

"Told you already, mista fuck-all-day-no-kinda'-priest. I ain't talkin' 'bout Olivia. You want to talk about me," she leans forward and lifts her eyebrows, "– an by *me* I mean Big Mama Bessie –or not?"

"Okay," he says. "Okay."

"Gon' cost you fifty bucks."

"I don't have fifty bucks."

"Well how much you got?"

He sighs. Pulls out his wallet. "Twenty."

"Twenty? You want to talk to me fo' one lil' raggedy-ass Jackson?"

"Thirty."

She holds out her hand. He slaps the money into her palm.

"This is totally against policy," he says. She stands and crosses the room to the nightstand by the bed. Sets down her glass and drops the bills by the lamp.

Strips off her hungry panda shirt.

"Whoa, there," says Davis. He half rises off the settee. Alarm in his voice. "Wait. I'm just… I don't want…"

She turns. Hand on her hip. Areolas like a new pair of eyes in the room.

"Baby, I ain't doin' no interview in my capris an' a panda tee. You as dumb as you is cute. Tellin' my story is a silky kimono kinda thing. So sit back down. Ain't gon' touch you an' yo' sexy lil' ponytail. Fo' thirty dollars? Shccit. Who you think I am, anyway?"

He sits. Watches.

"You like music?" she asks, stripping out of her capris.

"Sure."

"Not that bubblegum country shit. Real music. Blues music."

"Yeah," he says. "Always."

She leaves her clothes in a pile on the floor and crosses the room to a record player behind the steamer trunk. She kneels. Extracts a record from a sleeve in a stack. Looks at him over her shoulder. She puts the record on the spindle. Lowers the needle into a nest of snakes.

"Good. Who *this* then?"

He knows the answer in under five beats. Guitar gives it away.

He is seven. Eight. Sitting at the kitchen table working on the puzzle. The one with the tiny boat and the massive whale. His mother dancing from sink to stove, making dinner. She tousles his hair. Shouts to his father in the other room to turn it up. But he is already downstairs. Down for the night. The piece with the whale's eye is missing.

"Rosetta Tharpe," he says. "Didn't It Rain."

Libby looks at him, clearly impressed.

"Well I'll *be*! Mista sexy-name-fuck-all-day-no-kinda-priest know his *shit!* Sister Rosetta Tharp. Damn boy. How you know Sister Rosetta?"

"My mom had this record. She loved all those gals. Rosetta. Bessie. Ma Rainey."

"Big Mama?"

"Big Mama."

"No shit? Really?"

He nods. "She loved them."

"My mama too," she says. "We get all the good shit in the world from our mamas. Don't we, baby?"

Davis smiles. Nods. Tries not to stare at her nudity. A thought comes in sideways.

"And Dallas Letti," he says. "Mom was wild about Dallas Letti."

"Oh, Miss Letti know how to get it said. Well. She *did* know, anyway. She live out this way, you know."

"Dallas Letti lives in Corbin?"

"Twenty mile west. *MmmHmm.*"

"You know her?"

"Baby, eva'body know Dallas Letti enough to know to stay the fuck away from Dallas Letti. Bitch is crazy. And mean as a snake with a broken rattle. Livin' alone so long do that to a person I 'spose. Ain't never met the woman."

"Why does she live alone?"

"Well, fuck all. Ponytail-no-kinda-priest. You give me thirty dollars to talk 'bout Dallas fuckin' *Letti*? That shit cost you fifty."

She juts out a hand. Davis holds up his hands in surrender.

"Good," she says. "Damn."

She turns up the volume and opens the lid of the steamer trunk. The stuffed pig and the purple boa slip off the back into the darkness behind. Libby, now suddenly Liberty, extracts a silk, twilight-colored kimono from the trunk as Sister Rosetta lays down a solid metal groove through the rain of hand-clap percussion. The choir and the piano rise up behind her like a storm. And then out it comes, all that rain, Rosetta singing about all the folk banging on Noah's door. Brother Noah! Brother Noah! But God's got that key, yes he does, and the people will drown in their sin. Just listen to it rain, sings Sister Rosetta. Just listen.

The music and the nudity is all consuming. So there is no telling exactly how long the two uniformed representatives of the Crockett County Sheriff's Department have been in the doorway.

Libby sees them first. Davis sees them reflected on her face.

Although at first, before he turns, he thinks that maybe Olivia has returned. That thought —a *hope,* really, as he turns his head —is like a little flicker of lightning in the part of his mind that can see all the way back to the beginning.

Oh, just listen to that rain…

Chapter 23
Abby and Davis

Sometimes the hardest part of remembering all of this is knowing what to call her. More than just a friend. Obviously. But *girlfriend* never felt right either. And not the things everybody else has called her. Not the things you have called her.

So girlfriend, I guess. Even though she laughed at me the one time I ever called her that. She didn't laugh in a mean way. More of a *'ain't you cute'* way.

We were on her ratty yellow couch watching TV. I was sitting with my feet up on the table drinking a beer and Abby was curled up with her head on my leg. It was the middle of the afternoon. Phil Donahue was on talking about Catholic priests and alter boys. Someone in the audience said this kind of thing wouldn't happen if priests were allowed to marry.

"Could you do that, Davis?" she asked. Like she was revolted. "Could you bugger some poor little alter boy?"

"Nah. Got me a girlfriend." It was out before I knew what I was saying.

And she laughed at me in her *'ain't you cute'* way. I never called her that again. Not that I thought she minded it so much. It just felt kind of wrong. Like I was trying to walk around in another man's boots.

So I just mostly think of her as Abby. She'll always be Abby.

Even if that isn't her name.

I started going over to Abby's house the weekend the State Fair ended. The Sunday after our Ferris wheel ride I went back to the fairgrounds and helped her strike her tent and load her things into her pick up. We went out for burgers and then she drove me back to the fairgrounds where she thought I had a car waiting. I watched her drive off and then I headed for the bus depot.

Everyone likes to put the relationship on Abby. Especially you. Even as I am writing these words I can feel you shaking your head as you reach for that awful smelling tea. Or make your notes. I know you think she forced me in over my head.

But you're wrong. It was me who kept pushing. Maybe she knew I'd come back. But she never asked. Not once. I just kept showing up at her door. She'd smile when she saw me through the screen. She'd push open the screen door with two fingers and let me in, never asking why I was there. It was like she just accepted me in her life. Like it was meant to be. She never pushed or chased after me or anything like that. She never had to.

And maybe it *was* meant to be. It was almost too easy. Getting out to her house should have been impossible. I didn't have a driver's license or a car. Busses would have gotten me only within maybe five miles and it would have taken forever. I didn't have money for a taxi.

But it was like the cosmos just provided, which was something Abby always said. She was always going on about the cosmos. Like it was a person. The cosmos knows what we want and it provides. She said the cosmos delivered me to her. It knew what she needed and it provided. So maybe you should blame the cosmos.

She really believed it. She told me a thousand times about how we're all tiny bits of consciousness. And those tiny bits of consciousness are living inside a larger consciousness that could feel our every twitch. And that it could know our thoughts. To Abby, that was the cosmos. All-knowing and all-feeling.

I said some people call that God, and believe that God hears our thoughts and prayers. God provides what we need.

Abby laughed that one off. She didn't believe in God. God was a fairy tale for children and simple people. *Other people* believed in God. She believed in a universal consciousness.

She believed that certain people and things could act as antennas to gather energy. Focus it. Make meaning of it. She believed that the Universe was alive. The Universe was a crowded room, full of information, full of meaning that came in pulses of energy, across a whole range of frequencies. *Voices*, she called them. The Universe was one voice made of many voices. It had thoughts and intentions –good and bad. Those thoughts and intentions were ours to intercept. Ours to hear and interpret. She believed the Universe cared about what happens to us. For better or worse.

Better *and* worse. It wanted to save us. It wanted to kill us.

I didn't understand most of it. It may not have been religion to her, but it felt like religion to me. It felt like something to be accepted but never really understood.

I pretended to understand. I pretended to believe. Abby was so intense about this stuff she reminded me a little of Pastor Wilks back when Dad was making me and Mom go out with him every week to First Evangelist. Pastor Wilks preached like his life or his sanity depended on us believing him. Eyes wide. Sweat pouring off his big bald head. Pacing the stage, shaking his Bible at the ceiling. I said '*Amen*' along with everybody else just to help ease his suffering. But I didn't really believe any of it. *'Amen'* is such a small price to pay. It was the only thing I could do.

Being a shrink, I suspect you are not a church-going man, Dr. Bees. When my parents argued about you Dad always called you Godless and mom would defend you. Try to anyway. I figure you've got your own religion. You're always preaching to me to let go of my guilt. Before any of this happened, Pastor Wilks was always preaching that Jesus knows my guilt. He sees my sin. He knows I am wicked for what I have done and what I will do.

'Amen' I said. And I said it every time.

So I guess I gave Abby the same as an *Amen*. It was important to her that I understand. That I believe the cosmos knows what we need and that it provides. I did my best to keep an open mind. But inside, down in the dark where Pastor Wilks says Jesus sees our sin, I knew better.

But at the same time, I could not explain how, at the exact moment in my life when I was desperate for a way out to Abby's house in Fairfield, Fat Jack showed up on my doorstep with the keys to his uncle Zeke's truck.

"Zeke thinks it's stolen," he said, grinding his cigarette out on my stoop. "Don't say nothin.' And don't drive it unless you have to move it. I just need you to store it for awhile."

I looked at the keys and then at Jack suspiciously. I should have said no. I know trouble when I smell it. But the pieces were falling into place. The cosmos was providing.

"And don't ask any questions," he said, knowing that they were coming. "The less you know the better. It's just for awhile. A few months maybe. It just can't be seen around my house."

"You want me to be charged with possession of a stolen car?"

"No," he said, like I was stupid. "No one's gonna report it stolen. Hell, Davis, Zeke stole it first. Don't ask any questions about that either. Point is, Zeke will never report it stolen. He ain't gonna be lookin' for it anyway. It just can't be around my house. Okay? Will you do this for me?"

"What am I supposed to tell my dad?"

"Well I didn't park it in your driveway, did I? *Duh.*" Jack pointed up the road. "I parked it next to the empty lot. He won't even know you have anything to do with it."

The only thought in my head was Abby. Her face. Her voice. That kiss on the Ferris wheel. The impulse surfaced more than once to tell Jack about my new universe. But I had enough sense about me to swat the impulse away. I didn't want Jack, or any of my friends, coming inside that universe.

More than that, I wanted the truck.

"Ok. I guess. Whatever."

"Good," said Jack. "I gotta get back. You have bus money I can borrow?"

"Want me to drive you?"

"Davis, what did I just fuckin' say, man?"

"I could drop you at the Kroger. Not a far walk to your place."

"Two miles if it's a foot."

"I'll take you to your front door."

"Can't do that. Even Kroger's too close."

"Walking from Kroger's faster than the damn bus. But hey, do whatever, man."

I started to walk off as Jack was thinking. He grabbed my arm.

"Wait. Okay. But you have to bring the truck right back here. Don't drive it around. Wait. You don't even know how to drive, do you?"

"How hard could it be if you can do it?"

He made me promise twice more on the way to the store. But Abby was like a heartbeat in my head I couldn't ignore. No sooner had I dropped Fat Jack off at the store, I was rolling the black 1972 Ford F-100 down Interstate 45 for Fairfield. It was the first time I'd driven any kind of vehicle alone on a freeway. I'd be lying if I said that it didn't go to my head a little. That it didn't make me feel like I was suddenly a grown man headed out to see his woman.

But there were two things that kind of kept the lid on that feeling. The first was the steering wheel. Instead of the letters F O R D, the middle two letters had been popped out and in their place someone had used white paint to write the letters R E. Every time I looked down I saw F R E D, which just reminded me that I wasn't really a grown man in his truck riding out to see his woman, I was just a horny kid riding in a stolen truck owned by some poor sap named Fred.

The second thing that kept the lid on my mood was just being kind of terrified that I'd be pulled over for everything from speeding, to driving without a license, to being underage, to possession of a twice-stolen vehicle. Every time a trooper showed up in the rearview mirror I thought I'd be going to jail.

But every last one of those Troopers glided on by without so much as a second glance.

At first, I drove out to Abby's place no more than once or twice a week, between Friday and Sunday. It was hard taking the bus to school knowing that I had Jack's truck waiting not two hundred feet from my front door. Once you start driving, there really is no going back. But every time Jack saw me get off that bus, he was satisfied that I was leaving the truck alone and he stopped hounding me for promises that I wouldn't drive it anywhere.

As the weeks passed, my visits out to see Abby increased. I began dropping by after school, three or four days a week. I'd pick her up and we'd go get a bite to eat, or we'd go out to the speedway to see the *Go Karts*. Sometimes we'd drive in to Corsicana for something at the bakery and a cone at the *Dairy Queen*. Other times we just drove around, in her truck or Jack's truck, talking and wasting time.

Once we drove out to Lake Waco to the place where those three teenagers were tied up and stabbed to death a few years back. Abby said she had kind of followed the trial. I'm sure you read about this since I don't think I have ever been in your office without a copy of the *Dallas Morning News* sitting on your table. They had to call in dental specialists to identify bite marks. They said it was a case of mistaken identity. The killer was stalking some gal who was a dead ringer for someone he once dated. So he ended up killing the wrong person. The others were just in the wrong place at the wrong time.

Abby said that during the trial she dreamed that she had come upon the scene before anyone was dead and that she had untied the teenagers and tied up the killer and set him on fire. She said the killer in her dream offered no resistance because he knew he was already damned. Then she said she started having dreams that they never actually caught the real killer. That he was still out there and that he knew *she* knew.

Anyway, after telling me that whole story, Abby decided she wanted to show me where it all happened so we drove out to Waco. We walked around the old crime scene awhile. She said she could still feel the violence and pain in the energy signature. That was her name for it: the energy signature. She said that all living things have an aura and that she knew how to read auras. She said the aura of that place was still midnight black.

Afterwards we walked down to the lake holding hands like it was the most natural thing in the world. Abby was crying, sad because the horror of that day still hung from the branches of the trees. She apologized. I put my arm around her and she put her head on my shoulder.

"If something horrible like that was ever going to happen to me, would you rescue me, Davis? Would you find me and rescue me?"

I couldn't tell if it was a serious question. I answered as though it was.

"No one is going to hurt you, Abby. I'll be there. I'll burn their asses to cinder."

She kissed me softly on the neck. I felt about ten feet tall and every square inch of me burned for her. I resisted. Every urge that Abby had set in motion up on that Ferris wheel had been building up in me ever since. But I resisted.

We rode back to Fairfield in the dark, holding hands almost the whole way and saying almost nothing, my heart hammering away in my chest.

The week after that I was over at Abby's house at least five of the seven days. I skipped two classes. I avoided my friends. Practically abandoned my father, leaving him to his typewriter and his bourbon. Which I felt kind of bad about.

There were two shows me and my dad usually watched. Dumb network *who-done-its*. It was really our only time together aside from sharing dinners. Anyway, that week I skipped both shows. Like I said, I felt kind of bad about that. Even though he never said anything, I knew he was disappointed. But I couldn't help myself. I had to see her. Abby was like a drug. She was the only thing in my head. I lied and told him I was meeting friends to see a movie. I always had the name of a movie ready in case he asked. He never did.

I had probably been to Abby's home seven or eight times before I saw any more of it than the living room, kitchen and bathroom. It was a ranch-style house and when we stayed indoors, we stayed at one end. I didn't ask her about the other side of the house. Not because I wasn't curious, but because I was afraid she would think that all I really cared about was the bedroom.

I suppose it makes me a coward that I couldn't just tell her how I felt about her. Tell her that I wanted her to be my first experience. I tried. The words stuck together in my throat. I was terrified at what she'd say. I didn't want her to laugh me off or tell me that we were just friends or that I was too young for her. That kiss on the Ferris wheel was like a lighthouse in a storm of confusion, guiding me in and warning me away at the same time. It was easier and safer to just let her lead.

So I never asked to see the rest of the house. I just hoped quietly to myself that I would be invited. That never happened.

But you've seen pictures of the trailer. You and everybody else. She did show me the trailer.

It was parked on the back of her lot, glinting in the sun like silver boot box. One day we were standing in her kitchen opening beers.

"You read palms and stuff like that only at fairs?" I asked.

"I do it here and there," she said.

"People come all the way out here? To Fairfield?"

"Sometimes people come round. Mostly I go to them."

"Their houses?"

"Yes. Their houses. Businesses. Parking lots. Fairs. Wherever they want me to look at their hands. Or read the runes. Or auras."

"And you make a living doing that?"

I wasn't trying to be rude. It was an honest question that came out like I might be looking down on her. Her face showed a kind of disapproval. I felt myself blush.

"Having a laugh, Davis?"

"What? No. I mean. I just. I didn't think that many people would want ..."

"It's not *all* I do to make a living. It's what I *like* to do. There's a big difference you know."

"I'm sorry. I didn't mean..."

She laughed a little and stroked my temple with her fingertips, tugging gently at my hair. "There, there. No need to apologize. No harm done, luv, is there now?"

I relaxed and was ready to let the matter drop, taking a long pull on my beer.

The exchange had confirmed my concerns about the danger of asking questions.

"Well, aren't you going to ask me?" she said with a smile.

"Ask you what?"

"How I make my living?"

"No."

"Why not?"

"Not my business," I said, looking away.

"So I'm supposed to let you think that I do something terrible for my money, is that it? Am I a dodgy sort on the corner? A pickpocket? A common slag? Is that what you think, Davis?"

"No. I… what's a slag?"

She laughed.

"A working girl."

"A working girl?"

"A prostitute."

"No!"

"Alright then. I suppose you'd better ask, shouldn't you?"

"Okay, I give up. What do you do?"

She gave me a sideways smile, put her hands on my shoulders and turned me around so that I was facing the sink. Then she pointed out the dirty kitchen window at the silver trailer. Maybe twenty-five feet long, it was dingy and dented and had ten or eleven large antennas lined up on the roof like some sort of metal porcupine with concrete pillars for legs.

"That yours?" I asked. "What is that?"

"That's my shop," she said.

"Your shop? What kind of shop?"

"Come on, Curious George."

I followed her out the back screen door and across the dry scrub to the far end of the lot. The sun was slamming off the face of that silver wall so hot and intense it hurt to keep my eyes open. The door was blue, like a rectangular lake in the middle of a silver field. On either side of the door was a window, curtained from the inside. Abby fished a key out of her pocket and slipped it into the large round knob.

"What's with all the antennas?" I asked.

"Helps me focus," she said and stepped inside.

It was stuffy and dark inside, but not nearly as hot as I had expected. It smelled intensely of aromas I couldn't identify but that reminded me of the incense Abby had burned at the fair. She closed the door behind me. The space around us glowed a dim yellow. There were four windows, two in front of me and two behind, each of them covered with heavy green curtains.

To the right, against the far end, was a cot. It was neatly made with a light brown spread and a stack of three pillows. The spread was not long enough to reach the floor and I could see a chaotic clutter beneath the mattress that included empty bottles, a loose pile of books, a wadded up road map, and a large bag of peanuts. I could also see a spool of copper wire that I recognized from the bracelets she had wrapped around our wrists and ankles at the fair.

To the left was a chair and a small, round wooden table. The table was deeply scarred and covered in splotches of something waxy. A pair of scissors was on the table surrounded by bits of string. Behind the table against the far wall were lower and upper cabinets the color of a sickly pea green. One of the cabinet doors was missing and I could see shelves holding a jumble of junk. Large spoons and tin cups and rags and rows of white boxes full of little vials and a dozen or so spools of thick white twine.

Directly in front of me, along the far wall of the trailer, was a narrow countertop littered with aluminum cups, glass jars, rags, a pair of rubber gloves and an assortment of knives. In the center of the counter was a double Bunsen Burner like the kind we had in chemistry class. It was beneath a wire mesh platform that held a large silver kettle. The burners were connected to a black hose that snaked through a hole in the counter down to a green metal tank on the floor next to three large red metal coolers.

At the end of the counter, in the corner of the trailer where the counter met up with the cabinets, was a neatly arranged, six-level pyramid of four-inch cylindrical candles.

"Candles," I said. "You make candles?"

"It's called aromatherapy," she said. "It's been big in England for a long time. Commercially, I mean. Texas is just catching on. There's going to be big money in this."

"In scented candles?"

"Not just scented candles, Davis. *Aromatherapy. Essential oils.* They help the healing process. They open all of the chakras. It improves relaxation. Circulation. Memory. Lowers anxiety."

"Huh," I said, not really knowing what to think. Abby pointed at the red coolers on the floor. "Just 'cause of the smell?"

"Aroma. I keep all my wax in there. All of my oils and scents are in the cabinet. My wicks come on spools. Making the candles is easy but it takes knowing something about essential oils and what they do and how to combine them. Thyme. Peppermint. Lavender. Jasmine. They all do different things." Abby smile accusingly. "You think I'm mental."

"No. No I don't. Why isn't it roasting in here?"

She pointed to two rectangular vents near the ceiling.

"Generator clicks on every three hours to keep it cool."

I nodded toward the cot at the other end.

"You sleep here?"

She nodded. "Sometimes I work all night out here. It's peaceful. The metal walls and the antennas really help bring everything into focus. I listen to the cosmos out here. Good energy."

"They're not connected to anything, Abby," I said.

"They're connected to me," she replied. "Full stop."

She looked at me in a way that I had already come to understand as an invitation to challenge her beliefs. Like it was some kind of sport. But I had no interest in questioning her religion, or whatever it was. Even if I was not prepared to accept what she was telling me, I also had no ability to disprove it. So I let it go and kept looking at the small space around me.

"Hey, I know that guy." I pointed over to the bed. On the far side of the pillows, was the stuffed bull with golden yellow horns I'd won for her on that second day at the fair.

Abby smiled.

"She keeps me company, that one. I call her Goldie."

"*Goldie*? Why Goldie?"

Abby frowned.

"Don't know really. 'Cause of the horns, I suppose. Me mum was called Goldie. She had golden yellow hair, you see. So it's a lovely name."

"You realize that those horns make *Goldie* here a boy."

She laughed and blushed. She picked up the bull and pulled it to her chest like a child. "I don't care then. I think it's a sweet name. Like you're sweet."

"I'm sweet?"

She put Goldie aside and took a step towards me. She held my face between her hands. "Davis, Davis, Davis. You're oh so *very* sweet, indeed."

She closed her eyes and kissed me full on the mouth. It was warm and wet and went on forever. I felt heat surging through my chest and up into my face, as though my head might ignite right then and there, a human candle between her palms.

The closeness of Abby's body inside that tiny trailer was almost more than I could handle. The Ferris wheel had been out in the open air, surrounded in all directions by miles of day-lit space. As intense as that first kiss had been, all that was Abby Palmer had been diluted by the swirling madness of the Texas State Fair. My emotions had a thousand places to hide.

But the metal trailer trapped everything. There was no place to hide.

She undressed me without speaking. I watched, an alien in my own body. Then I undressed her. I remember doing it, but I do not remember *how* I did it. What I mean is, I don't remember thinking to myself, *now the top button, now the next button, now the pants, pull the zipper*. It was as if some other entity had taken over the movements of my fingers and did not know how to work them very well.

All I can remember was the paleness of her skin against my hands in the dim light and the brightness of her body, gathering like an open flame as I peeled away her clothes.

She touched me. First with one hand, then both. Gentle, but firm. She knelt. I couldn't move. I couldn't even close my eyes. I stared at the floor beneath her naked shoulders. Like a stupid kid.

She stood, turned and walked to the bed. The sudden separation was excruciating.

She said my name. I remember that. I will never forget her saying my name. The sound was like something wild in there with us, measuring the space. A coyote. A hawk.

I stepped over the clothes and followed her.

It was not at all what I had expected. Nothing like the movies or magazines. More tender. Less explicit. Quieter. Softer. Slower.

When it happened, you know, ended, I didn't know what to say. I only knew what I wanted to say. *I love you. I love you. I love you.*

So that's what came out.

When we were done, she curled up over my body, playing her fingers along my side. I could feel her heart beating against my chest. The world, all of a sudden, was a different place. Quieter. Softer. Slower.

We breathed next to each other.

I thought of Mom. Not on purpose. She was just suddenly in my head, like she always is when I am on the verge of being happy. Or when I have done something wrong. I didn't know which one this was.

"Can you hear that?" she asked.

"What?"

"In your mind. That voice."

"What voice?"

"More like a feeling than a voice. But a feeling you can hear. Or a sound you can feel."

"No," I said. "I can't."

"It takes practice. You have to tune your mind, Davis. It's like you have to find the frequency."

"I don't think I can do that."

"*Pish.* Anyone can do that. Anyone who cares. Anyone who tries."

"What do they say? The voices I mean."

"Well they don't all say the same thing, Davis. They're not a choir. It's like listening to people walking around at the fair."

"Okay, well then the one you just heard. Felt. Whatever."

"*Everything's going to be alright. You've found him. Everything's going to be alright.* That's how it felt. That was the sound of it."

I was silent. Uncomfortable. I didn't want to dislike any part of Abby. I didn't like these discussions.

"Do you think I'm mental, Davis?"

"No. No. Of course not. You're unusual maybe. But I like unusual."

"Ahh. *Unusual.* There it is then. *Unusual.*"

She brushed her palm against my cheek. It was so quiet in that trailer. Skin against skin makes a sound. An actual sound. There are so many sounds we never hear.

I clasped her wrist in my hand. My thumb found both ridges. I had forgotten. Abby stiffened. I was not going to ask. I did not want to embarrass her.

"Abby…"

"*Shhh.*"

It wasn't about the scars. She was listening.

"What?" I asked, preparing myself for more. "What is it?"

She put the tips of her fingers to my lips. I thought I saw fear in her face.

"*Shhh.* Simon's home."

Chapter 24

Ironic that it is Desmond Vaughn who makes the mistake.

For a lot of reasons.

He is not supposed to be at work today. He scheduled his annual *staycation* a month early. Wants to paint his house a pale desert green while his sons are back from college. Visiting their mother.

Ironic, too, because Desmond's reputation at *The Chacha* borders on obsessive-compulsive when it comes to editing. He color-codes his copy edits. Returns emails corrected for spelling and grammar.

And it is ironic because Desmond has so recently refused to continue in his role as Editor of *The Chacha* if he is also supposed to function as its General Manager. It is an annually renewed refusal. But it had felt real this time. It had felt like Cal Aronson, in his role of controlling owner of the paper, had actually been listening.

And yet, here he sits. Not painting his house with his sons. Editing *The Docket*. Editing *Community*. Editing *Living Arts*. Editing the whole goddamned paper. What's left of it anyway.

Which really isn't much.

There are worse newspapers in the world. There have to be. Maybe not in Texas. But the world? The whole world? Have to be. So many rags out there. Dailies. Weeklies. Monthlies. All of those tabloids. At least one of them has to make the *Chachalaca Gazette* look like a publication of measurable quality. A publication with some claim to journalistic integrity.

If nothing else, *The Chacha*, as it is called by its thirty-seven thousand Crockett County subscribers, should get some credit for sincerity of aspiration.

The Chacha started in the summer of 1948 as a birding circular, the half-cocked brainchild of Calvin J. Stewcamp. Having moved his family of seven from Savannah to San Antonio, the retired Army colonel and bird enthusiast had wanted to establish himself as an authority on the Southwestern avian populations. Stewcamp named the circular the *Chachalaca News* after a physically unimpressive bird, plentiful throughout the Rio Grande Valley, called the *Plain Chachalaca*.

The bird has a tiny head for its medium size. Long neck. Flat, greenish-grayish-brownish plumage. It is partial to tomatoes, cucumbers and tree fruit, so it is not only unremarkable in its appearance but also widely loathed by farmers as a pest.

And it's a skittish little thing, this *Plain Chachalaca*. Tends to run rather than fly from danger, which it perceives to be just about everywhere. The name of the bird is onomatopoeic. It comes from the grating, near hysterical, *cha-cha-LAW-ka* call it makes every sunrise and sunset. Like the coming of some fresh apocalypse.

No surprise, then, that the ubiquity of the bird, not to mention its alarmist and histrionic disposition, recommended it as a newspaper namesake. A birding circular called *The Chachalaca News* was begging to expand its charter beyond the kingdom of birds.

By the early 1970's the paper had garnered a reputation as a solid, if overly parochial, addition to the sources of printed news available to the denizens of Crockett County, Texas, covering topics of local, state and national interest. Its circulation spiked to forty-eight thousand and its advertising revenue was double what it had been only ten years earlier. Its subscribers were scattered through a trapezoidal area from Pecos and Midland counties to the west and Brown and Llano counties to the east, and all of the counties in between.

But by the early 1980's, the signs of competitive erosion were already visible. For as much good ink as *The Chacha* had been pumping out of its Corbin headquarters, the papers in San Antonio and Austin were faring much better. *The Chacha's* readership was loyal, but aging. Readers were dying, inevitably, and without enough replacement. The late Eighties had coalesced around a host of hostilities. Demographic trends, pulling would-be subscribes into the larger cities. Profit drain, wrought by technological retooling. The siren song of twenty-four hour cable news. The Internet. All conspiring to constrict the printed news market like a snake around the body of a desert ground bird.

And by now it's already an old story. Strangled, rural-bird newspapers, lifeless along the side of a road that spools off toward Digital City. Where the people communicate in ones and zeros. Trade in their attention span for video bandwidth.

It's nearly dead now. This particular desert bird paper. The *Chachalaca Gazette*. Staff reporters and editors leaking away, one by one, for years. There is a bitter and embattled remainder with less inspiration than they need and more to do than they can reasonably accomplish. Everybody multi-tasks. Advertising dollars are down. Way down.

The buzzards stopped circling some time ago. They're out of the air and on the ground now. Hopping in through the scrub.

The latest payroll defection is reporter Rick Stoddard. Square jaw. Watery gray eyes. Smooth baritone. He has recently traded the newspaper business altogether for a job with CBS in New York.

Rock loves the camera. The feeling is mutual.

It is Rick's last day at *The Chacha*. He has said his goodbyes and now whistles along through the hot afternoon in a Jeep, on his way out of Corbin to the airport. Up ahead, climbing off to the left over the scrub, is a thin pillar of black smoke. Like a snake out of the basket.

Not right, he thinks. *Not right.*

He pulls the wheel. Turns off of I-67 onto a spur. Accelerates.

The Civic is upside down. Its black belly burns orange through a thin blanket of smoke. A blue door, ripped off its hinges, lies in the middle of the road.

Rick slows, tentative at first. Then skids the Jeep to a stop.

A man is in the middle of the road. Hands and knees. He is reaching into the burning wreckage. He half-stands and then drags a young woman out over the asphalt. She is unconscious. Bleeding. He pulls her by her wrists. She sticks. He yanks. Her wet, red head is limp and bobs with each pull, threatening to scrape across the road and leave a skid of bloody scalp.

Rick grabs his phone. Alights. Runs for the burning car as he dials for help. The man —the hero, for *that* is unquestionably what he is, a hero, a fucking hero —makes it to the other side of the road. Pulls the woman into the ditch, behind a small, sleek, silver car. Throws his body over hers.

Like a big blue bomb, the little Civic explodes before Rick can reach them. He drops to the road and covers his head, waiting for flying metal to pierce some part of his body. In seconds he is up again. Runs for them still huddled in the ditch. Pats his shirt pocket for a pen.

Within three hours, Rick is back inside the building he thought he had left for the last time. *The Chacha* greets him in the usual way —the light choked with dust, the smell of the musty bullpen like a bone yard. He winds his way to the angrily cluttered desk of Desmond Vaughn.

Rick tells Desmond the whole story. Hands over his five sheets of scrawl.

"Can't you just type them up?" Desmond asks, slumping over the notes. "I've got a deadline. My fucking computer is down. I'm going to have to go to another desk."

But Rick Stoddard, man soon to be on the beat for CBS News, is unmoved.

"And I've got a plane to catch."

Like catching a plane is something only special people are allowed to do. Like he is Superman and by 'catch a plane' he means literally 'catching a plane.' He speaks so the neighbors can hear.

"Angie's already in New York moving into the new house. So I gotta go."

"I'm not asking you to move back to Texas," says Desmond.

Rick shrugs his prodigious shoulders.

"Sorry, Dez. I don't work here anymore. Take the by-line, man. Technically I'm already on contract for CBS."

"Fuck CBS, Rick. It's a goddamned traffic accident."

Rick winks.

"Dez, this is as simple as it gets. Okay? Heroic motorist saves very attractive woman from flaming death. Critical condition but doctors cautiously optimistic. Hero is from Houston. Modest, shy, just passing through. It's three inches of ink. Four inches tops."

Desmond sighs. Scans the notes.

"What caused it? I don't see anything in here about what caused it?"

"Don't know. She's unconscious. The hero, whatshisname, *Davis*, says he drove up on her already upside down."

Desmond reads on, temples pounding.

"Well *that's* not in your notes either, Rick. What fucking *else* is not in your notes?"

But Rick has already moved on. He's now ten feet away explaining to Sylvia Bloom in *Living Arts* why he is back so soon after saying goodbye.

"Thing just exploded," he says to Sylvia. "Right in front of me."

Desmond rereads the notes. Makes jagged red scribbles in the margins. He circles the name *DeLuna, Olivia*. Circles the name *Davis, Sheldon*. He circles the name of *Dr. Aaron Bligh*. He underlines the name of *Shannon Medical Center*, which Rick has misspelled as *Shanin Medicle Center*.

The phone rings. Alberto Flores. His sister Octavia has been deported. Tragic all the way around. Alberto is weeping over the phone. Someone in the background is outright wailing.

For Desmond the news brings the time-sucking tragedy of inconvenience. *Part Three* of the five-part immigration piece running in *The Docket* section is now incorrect. As currently written, the piece devotes fully three paragraphs to Octavia Flores' success in convincing immigration officials that she was *not* a candidate for deportation. The worm has turned.

It takes twenty minutes and six pages of notes to deal with Alberto. When he is finished he slams down the phone. "Fuck!"

The phone objects to the violence and rings again. Desmond picks it up.

"Fuck," he says again. "What."

"What'd I do?" Laurie Weaver asks.

She is working *The Docket* beat for Alan Taylor. Alan quit last week after a scream fest with Desmond over compensation. Laurie is at the San Angelo courthouse for the afternoon call-in on new court filings. Desmond closes his eyes. Takes a breath.

"Nothing. Sorry, Laurie. Bad day. Goddamned computer..." He searches for something to write on. "Okay. Let's have it."

"It's a lot today."

"A lot. Well, that's just great."

"You ready?"

He pushes aside his notes from Alberto. Grabs Rick Stoddard's notes about the accident. Flips over to the back page. Grabs his red pen. "Go."

Laurie rattles through a list of court filings, verdicts and arrests, county by county. Somewhere in the middle, Desmond is already out of writing room. He flips over the second-to-last page of Rick Stoddard's notes and keeps scribbling.

Laurie tells him that over in Corbin, the Crockett County Sheriff's office, acting on an anonymous tip, arrested one Libby Holder, Libby with a Y, Holder H-O-L-D-E-R, owner of *Libby's Nuts*, for running a brothel out of her pecan business. Also arrested was one Davis Payne, P-A-Y-N-E, on charges of soliciting a prostitute. Desmond circles the name *Libby Holder.*

Then he circles the name *Davis Payne*. Just as, elsewhere on the other side of the same page, he had circled the name *Davis, Sheldon*. Hero.

Laurie Weaver keeps talking. Desmond keeps scribbling.

And then Desmond Vaughn's day moves forward. It wobbles and lurches toward its deadline and a functioning computer on the other side of the pressroom next to the rattling air conditioner. There, he madly transcribes his angry red scrawl into something that is printable. Readable.

And wrong. Readable, but tragically, ironically incorrect.

In fact, completely backwards.

Chapter 25

Elvis Broussard is at a table in the back. Away from the street. Beneath the fan. He's the only one in the place except for two women at the front counter.

Girls really. Flirting with Eladio Rivera.

Davis steps out from the kitchen. Waves as he takes off his gloves and apron. Elvis nods. Takes off his green and white *Agro-Bell Fertilizers* hat and hangs it on the chair next to him. He wipes his forehead with the back of his wrist. He waits as Davis crosses *Pepitas*, navigating chairs, a large white cup in each hand.

"Iced tea," Davis says, sitting. "I took a guess."

"I'm a Dr. Pepper man," Elvis rasps.

Davis reaches. "Sorry. I'll drink it."

Elvis grabs the cup and pulls it back.

"Didn't say I wouldn't drink it. It's cold and wet. 'Bout to die in this heat. Just telling you for future reference. I'm a Dr. Pepper man."

"Okay. But soda'll kill you, Elvis. Nothing but sugar and chemicals."

"Says the drunk."

"Former drunk."

"Once a drunk, always a drunk, Davis."

"Not me."

"No?" Elvis' eyebrow arcs in amusement.

"I'm done," says Davis.

"Oh. Well then. Good to hear. You one of those one-vice-at-a-time people?"

"Huh?"

"You know. Into hookers now so you got no time for the booze? You give up the hoochie for the coochie?"

Davis smiles. Tries not to look surprised. He shouldn't be. He holds the cold cup to the side of his face.

"Buddy called you," he says finally. Elvis smiles. Nods.

"Yeah. He did."

"He called and told you that I'd been arrested for soliciting a prostitute. That

I had called him for help with bail and a lawyer. And now he's sittin' up there in Houston worried about whether I'm back in the bottle. So he's got you on my case to find out. I got that about right?"

Elvis shrugs. Fiddles with the brim of his hat. The women at the counter break into laughter, the sound of girls who do not yet know how to laugh like women. Eladio is telling a story about something tall and wide.

"So... are you?" Elvis asks. His mottled black face is like a kind of leopard skin. "Back in the bottle?"

"I said I was done. So I'm done."

"So then you weren't out there gettin' lit with Liberty Cherish? Like I warned you about?"

"No."

"No?"

"Not that she didn't offer. But no."

"So then you were just..."

"No. *Elvis.* I wasn't doing that either. Cops jumped to conclusions."

"Come on now, boy. I was born at night but I wasn't born *last* night. You can tell me."

"Seriously. Lawyer called me this morning. Said they're probably gonna drop the charges. I kept tellin' them to talk to Buddy. And they did. He told 'em I was writing a story, which is exactly what I told them. And probably what Libby told them. Lawyer said they don't want a First Amendment thing and they can't prove anything except that I was in the room when Libby was changing her clothes."

Elvis gives a kind of snort.

"Changin' her clothes. And you just happened to be in the room, huh?"

"Middle of the day. We were talking."

"About?"

"About whether she'd interview."

"*MmmHmm.* Told you to watch out for her."

"You told me I should *interview* her, which is what I was doing."

Elvis drinks his iced tea. Davis watches.

"You coming to the next meeting?" Elvis asks.

"I guess."

"Good. You got something to say, it will do yourself a world of good to stand up and just say it. Come clean."

"I am clean. Got a job. Doin' good."

Elvis takes a slow look around. Drinks.

"You like workin' here?"

"It's okay. Not enough pay though. I'm barely scraping by. I either need to trade or double up. I'm used to workin' three jobs. You need any help sellin' fertilizer?"

Elvis chuckles. Rolls his eyes.

"Lucky to keep my own job. They keep downsizing. People droppin' like flies out there. But…" He digs into the front pocket of his pants and extracts a folded piece of paper. He flips it across the table. "I thought you might be interested in this."

Davis unfolds the paper. Reads. He looks back at Elvis, baffled.

"And why, exactly, would I be interested in purchasing any of these fine *Agro-Bell Fertilizer* products?"

Elvis shakes his head. "Other side, Holmes."

He turns the sheet over. Strains to read the hand-written scrawl. Looks up. "You're shitting me."

Elvis shrugs. "Don't know what it pays. Don't even really know what the work is. Manual, I'm sure. Throwin' shit away. Cleaning. Clearing. Hauling. Hell, maybe something with the garden. Woman loves to garden. We take a yard and a half out there once a year. Yesterday she was going on about wantin' help. Non-Mexican help. Racist bitch. Anyway, I said you might be interested. Call that number."

"You say anything about…"

"About you getting' pinched for dippin' your wick out at Liberty Cherish's nut farm?"

"No. No. Not about that. About what I do."

Elvis reacts. Irritated. "Shit's none of my business to talk about. 'Course not. I just figured you'd be interested. I'm your sponsor. So I'm lookin' out for you. Drunks can't be idle. You need work."

Davis nods.

"Thanks, man. I appreciate it."

"I don't think you're gonna be thankin' me later. It'll be some kinda hell if you ask me. Workin' for her. But, there you go anyway. And I didn't say nothin' about where you choose to scratch your itch neither."

Elvis laughs at Davis not laughing.

"You seen the paper?" Elvis asks. "*The Chacha?*"

Davis shakes his head. "I don't get the paper."

"Well you made the news."

"What?" Alarm. Davis looks furtively over at Eladio, still holding court. Whispers. "You saying my name made the paper?"

Elvis nods.

"Shit. Unless the owner of this place believes me more than you do I really am going to have to find another job. He doesn't put up with…" He stops. "What? Why are you smiling?"

"Because *The Chacha* don't say what you think it does."

"What? Why? What's it say?"

"Says you're a hero."

"A hero?"

Elvis nods. "A hero."

"For what?"

"You tell me." Playful. Smug. "You a hero, Davis?"

Davis tries to figure out the joke. He can't. "No. I'm no hero."

"Didn't think so. I'd go get yourself a paper if I was you. Which I'm not. Which is too bad. Because if I could fuck Liberty Cherish, get arrested and get called a hero all in the same damned day, you can bet I would do it. Well. Probably wouldn't. But I'd think long and hard about it. Anyway, there's two articles in there you're going to want to read. Then it will all make sense." Elvis pushes himself up. Grabs his hat off the chair. Picks up the cup. "Okay, well I gotta get back at it."

"You just got here."

"I work for a livin' boy. I told Buddy I'd check in. I checked in. You seem okay to me." He points to the creased scrap of paper in Davis' hand. "And I wanted to give you that, which I did."

"Want something to go?"

"I gotta get back. Boss man thinks I'm off taking inventory. And not *twelve-step* inventory either. Fertilizer inventory. Keep your nose clean, Davis. You got my number so use it if you need it. And Dr. Pepper next time."

He watches Elvis shuffle out, one hand up to Eladio as he steps out into the bleaching sun. The white of his hat lights up like a struck match and he is gone.

Davis rereads the scrawl on the paper as he drinks his tea. He folds it and stuffs it in his pocket. Heads back to finish his shift.

When he is done working, he claps Eladio on the shoulder and starts to leave out the back door but thinks better of it and heads for the front. He leaves *Pepita's* and walks up *Broken River Road* for a newspaper.

A hero, he thinks. *A hero?*

The late afternoon heat is stale. Yesterday's leftover heat just warmed up. Reheated heat. Corbin needed a stiff breeze. If rain was out of the question, then it at least needed something to stir the air around a little. Just enough to feel like change.

A white, grime-streaked pick-up rattles past blaring *Tejano.* A dark-haired boy in the passenger side –ten, eleven –is hanging out the window. He is missing a tooth. He yells something in Spanish and waves his hands. Davis waves. Two other boys race past him up the road from behind, riding rusted-out bicycles, one without a seat and the other with plastic streamers flapping from the hollow end of the handlebars. They look back over brown shirtless shoulders and yell at the kid in the truck. Davis realizes the greeting, or whatever it was, had not been for him.

The Lick-n-Tipple across the street provides the nearest opportunity for a newspaper. He passes it. Imagines the column of cool air in front of the door. Keeps on walking toward the *Coahuiltecan Trading Post*.

The Lick-n-Tipple sold newspapers, true, but it also sold temptation. Rows of it, in clean, clear, cold bottles. He'd told Elvis he was done with all of that. Same thing he had told Buddy Lincoln on the phone from the Crockett County lock-up. *Done.*

And he *was* done. He was.

But still. He keeps walking.

There is no one at the *Coahuiltecan Trading Post* except the woman at the counter. She is young. Shy. Beautifully Mexican.

"*Hola*," she says, looking up from her book. Davis nods.

"Hey."

He buys a copy of *The Chacha* and some jerky, both right there at the front counter.

"Every day this week so far," she says. She smiles down at the till as she makes change. "Might have to start calling you a regular."

"Well," he says. "Guess I'd be honored. But maybe just call me Davis instead."

"Lucela," she says. She tips the coins into his palm. Covers them with a dollar. He gives her a smile.

"See you tomorrow, Lucela."

"*Hasta mañana*, Davis."

He walks the rest of the way up *Broken River* toward the *Fuente de la Luna* splashing and burbling away in the town square like something aortic. The very heart of Corbin's circulatory system.

He tries to read as he walks. On the front page is a photograph of a burning apartment building. Firemen are watching it go. Someone in quotation marks seems to think arson is possible.

Below the fold is a headline about Crockett County property values. Seems they are swelling on the news of major commercial real estate development. Someone in quotation marks is working with the Army Corps of Engineers. She is upbeat about approval of plans to divert a sliver of the Pecos River.

Davis flips through the pages as he walks. Sees nothing of interest. He drops the package of jerky. Stops. Retrieves it. Continues.

He gives up reading until he gets to the town square where he can sit on the wide stone edge of the fountain and go at it more methodically. He dips a hand in the water and runs his fingers through his hair. A small indigo bunting alights here and there, drinking. Flashing its feathers in the sun. It displaces a yellow kiskadee like a spark.

The fountain is a twenty-foot stalk of white stone, like a frozen miracle rising out of the desert. At the top of the stalk is an open flower, petals out, wide, curving around the sun, waiting to catch the rain that never comes.

It makes it own rain, this fountain. Water swells up out of pores hidden within its bloodless pistil. It slides off the petals in thin, clear sheets, down to a wreath of twelve stone, leaf-shaped platforms, like little lily pads jutting out from the central spire into the airspace above the pool of water below.

On the platforms sit large hot pink baskets of trailing bougainvillea. They are wild with color. Reckless. Like undisciplined children. Their stony, unforgiving mother keeps vigil above and prays to the sun for mercy. She has given them everything. Her color. Her lissomeness. Her fragrance. Until she has none.

The water slips from the twelve platforms in trickles and drips. An alien sound in the dry air.

Davis opens *The Chacha* over the rim of the fountain. He flips the pages, looking for his name. Skimming headlines. Then he stops. Reads.

Crockett County Sheriff's Department deputies arrested a man on Friday afternoon on charges of solicitation when they entered the premises of a pecan nut wholesaler on an anonymous tip that the establishment was a front for prostitution. Sheldon T. Davis of Houston was booked on one count of solicitation, a misdemeanor, and then released. Sheriff's deputies also arrested Libby Holder, the owner of the business, Libby's Nuts, on charges of prostitution, a misdemeanor. Libby's Nuts is located approximately twenty miles south of Corbin. Crockett County Sheriff Department policy prohibits public comment on misdemeanor arrests. Mr. Davis could not be located for comment. The Chachalaca News was able to contact Ms. Holder, who denied the allegations in language not suitable for publication.

Confusion. Davis rereads. And again. He flips the page. And again. And again. Skimming. Skimming. Stops. Reads.

Tragedy was narrowly averted Friday afternoon in a vehicle accident on Silo Road off of I-67 five miles south of Corbin. Crockett County resident Olivia DeLuna is currently in stable but critical condition at Shannon Medical Center in San Angelo after her 1975 Honda Civic skidded, left the roadway and flipped over, crushing the roof and pinning DeLuna inside. No information is currently available regarding the cause of the accident. A passing motorist, Davis Payne, came upon the wreckage just in time, freeing Ms. DeLuna and dragging her to safety mere seconds before her car exploded. Former Chachalaca Gazette reporter Rick Stoddard happened to come upon the scene just as Payne was pulling her clear.

"It was pretty incredible," said Stoddard. "The guy was on his hands and knees reaching into this flaming car. I was still too far away to help and I remember thinking, you know, oh God, this thing is going to blow. And it did, maybe three or four seconds after he had pulled her to safety into the ditch behind his car. He's a real hero if you ask me," said Stoddard. "He saved her life and he risked his own doing it. No doubt about it."

But Payne, who told Stoddard that he was just in Corbin for the day on business, does not care to think of himself as a hero, saying only that he was in the right place at the right time and that he hoped anybody else would have done the same. He said he hoped DeLuna's recovery was rapid and complete. Attending emergency room physician, Dr. Aaron Bligh, acknowledged that DeLuna is in critical condition but declined to elaborate on her injuries.

As the ambulance raced DeLuna to Shannon Medical Center, Davis Payne answered questions for Crockett County Sheriff's deputies on the scene and then continued on his way, declining further interviews. "His humility was astounding," said Stoddard. "The last thing this guy cared about was credit for saving her life. Just like a hero."

He sits for minutes. He should be happy at this incredibly fortunately mistake. Or at least amused. He is neither of these things. He cannot reach those feelings. He stares down at the paper. Rereads the entire article, his eyes tumbling down to that last line like a body pushed from a building.

"Just like a hero."

The words on the page decompose into tiny broken black twigs; shavings from something larger he cannot comprehend. He shuts his eyes. Slowly. Casually. Then tighter.

He tries to isolate the echo in his head. Tries to silence the sound of falling water. He inclines his face. Finds the sun. Feels the heat of it. The inferno.

Then he smells the blood. He feels it on his face. The feel has a sound. It sounds like dripping water.

"You stupid bloody fuck! You think you're a hero? Is that it?"

His eyes snap open like he has been shocked with an electric cattle prod. He looks around the nearly empty town square.

Simon, he thinks. His brain shutters. *Simon.*

He folds up the paper. Stands. Turns. Walks back up *Broken River Road* for the Harley. He feels sick now. He wants to lie down in the road.

He moves slowly. So slowly that each step has two distinct syllables. *Heel. Toe.*

Heel. Toe. Heel. Toe. His brain translates through the recollected smell of smoke and blood.

Si-mon.

Si-mon.

Si-mon.

Chapter 26

Waking. It is the same for her every time now. Emerging from darkness. Climbing out of a hole by pulling herself, hand over hand, up a ladder of pain.

Pulling herself *toward* the light, of course. It's how she is wired. It's how we're all wired. DNA likes the idea of hope. We have an instinct to pull against gravity. Toward the light. Even when the light itself feels like a hot blade. We have an instinct to pull ourselves up. Out of darkness. To keep waking up and facing the light. Feeling the pain as proof that we are still alive.

So she does. Several times a day now. Wakes up. Encounters the light. Like a thin spike to the temple.

The light is much sharper than the nurse. *Suzanne.* Almost two weeks now and she cannot seem to remember to dim the lights when she leaves.

So Olivia keeps her eyes closed. Well. Her eye. She couldn't open the other if she wanted to. Which she doesn't.

She wants to sleep. Wants to drift back down and away on a morphine dream. Sink back down into darkness. Like clutching a polished black stone.

But she cannot escape. She is chained now to the hard, bright noisy world. Pain is an insolent bully that keeps her awake, poking her with a stick. Laughing in stabs of illumination.

It pokes her in the face, mostly. And the left side of her head. Her eye. Her right leg.

Voices at the nurse's station. Dr. Holloran is having a birthday.

"He doesn't look fifty. Number 17B needs a catheter check. May as well wait until she's done with her lunch. Maria says Dr. Holloran hates his wife. No, seriously. Hates. *Hates.* She is so mean. Have you seen her? She comes in the other day and she's all like, where is Dr. Holloran? I need you to find Dr. Holloran. Like I'm her damn slave. Billie? Billie. *Billie.* 20A needs a sheet change. 20A. Sheet change. Thanks. So, yeah, he hates her. *Hates* her. Does he look fifty to you?"

Knuckles lightly on a metal doorframe.

"Liv? You awake?"

Olivia cracks opens the one lid just enough. Yvonne Lawry. Again.

"Hey," she croaks. "Will you turn off that god damned light?"

She does. It's like falling into cool water on a hot day.

"Thought you were gone."

Yvonne sits in the chair next to the bed. Like she'd never left.

She knows, finally, to whisper.

"I was just down in the cafeteria having lunch with Miguel."

Incomprehension pulls at the muscles in Olivia's face, which hurts.

"Miguel?"

"Rivera. He came by to see how you're feeling. Said Eladio came by too but you were still out of it. He's worried, Liv."

"Miguel?"

"I know. Isn't that sweet?"

"No. Eve. It ain't sweet."

"Oh, now, yes it is. *Yes it is.* He's a nice guy. Maybe you didn't like him as a boyfriend. I'm not saying anything about that, but he's a nice guy. He's concerned about you. I told him you were sleeping. Figured he's probably the last thing you want right now."

"Got that right," says Olivia. She swallows. Tries to. Her mouth is dry. She tries to sit up to reach the cup with a straw. But she hurts too much to move. She lets go of the effort. Tries to tune back into Yvonne.

"He bought me lunch though. And he says he's got a car you can use when you're well enough to drive again. Friend of a friend's car he said. Poor guy got deported a few months back so he's not using it."

Her face wants to split in two. There is not enough morphine in the world.

"Don't want his friend-of-a-friend's stupid car," she says.

"You're just feeling sorry for yourself. Understandable. I get it. But there's a free car out there for you to use when you change your attitude. I told him I'd tell you he came by."

She manages to swallow. Feels her orientation to reality start to return in tiny teaspoon increments. She will need to pee soon. But that will take Nurse Suzanne. Bright light. Climbing a mountain of pain. She'll wait.

"You tell him I look like a mummy?"

"Stop that, now." No longer a whisper. "You don't look like a mummy."

"Frankenstein."

"Stop."

"You haven't seen underneath..." she gestures weakly at her face, "all this." Reaches slowly for her head. Stops herself. "And they had to shave my head, Eve."

"Liv, stop it. It's just that one patch there."

Olivia widens the only eye not behind gauze. Blinks. It takes effort. She stares at Yvonne's blonde waterfall. At her rolling, dusty blue eyes. The moving, made-up lips.

"Christ, Liv. It'll…"

"Voice, Eve. You're killin' me."

"Sorry." She resumes in a whisper. "It'll grow back. You're lucky to be alive. You could be dead. You could still be in a coma. If that brain swelling hadn't stopped… Who cares about the damn hair? Did I mention that you're still alive? Miguel said he was really afraid you were a goner."

She wants her to go. Wants stillness. Silence. Or at least a different subject.

"What'd you do with Kevin?" she asks.

"Brent's home for a week. You picked a good time to almost die. Not sure I could have made it out here again so soon."

"Could have brought him with you."

"That's a big deal. Packing him up."

"And this way you can get some shopping done as long as you're in San Angelo. Right?"

Yvonne smiles. Pats Olivia on the arm. "It ain't Paris, Liv."

"Better'n Corbin if you're the shoppin' type. Which you are."

"True. Not for long if we get our own River Walk. Can you even imagine a Bergdorf's in Corbin?"

"Never been in a Bergdorf's. Don't really care to. Never happen anyway."

"San Antonio's got its own River Walk. Why not Corbin?"

"Gee, don't know, Liv. How about that there's no damn river?"

Yvonne makes a *pishing* sound. "Meantime, I've got to come all the way into San Angelo to get a decent shampoo and go to Dillard's. "

"And to visit your dying friend." Olivia closes her eye again. It doesn't help.

"You'll be out soon. Maybe you almost died, but you're not dying now."

"Dyin?" It is a loud, reckless voice from the doorway, punching a hole through the cloud of whispers over the bed. Yvonne jolts around like she has been whipped.

Libby Holder, in a nimbus of fluorescent backlighting, has one hand on her hip, the other stretching up to the doorframe.

"Ain't nobody dyin', baby. Like a damn coffin in here. You want you some light?"

"No!" Yvonne is on her feet, hand out to guard the light switch like it's the pin to a grenade. "No lights. No lights. It hurts her head. And you have to whisper."

Libby does not budge. Looks. Up and down. "You don't *look* like no kinda doctor to me."

"I'm not a doctor."

"Oh, then you the light switch police, huh?"

"I'm a friend."

"A friend? Baby, me too. I'm a friend."

"Yes, I know who you are. I'm not sure you're a friend she needs."

"Yvonne," croaks Olivia from the bed.

"Eva'body need friends, baby," instructs Libby.

"If she had been living somewhere else, none of this would have happened."

"Yvonne…"

"It was one of your… your *customers* that did this to her. One of your *Johns.* You do know that, don't you?"

"Yvonne…"

"I bet you need you a friend too," says Libby. "Bet you need you a replacement friend eva couple weeks."

Olivia opens her eye again. "Look. Y'all want to go fight, do it outside. Otherwise…"

"I was just leaving," says Yvonne, grabbing her purse from the chair. She pats Olivia on the forearm. Whispers. "Call me if you need me, Liv. I'm here for you. Well, it's a drive but you know what I'm sayin'. I'll come."

"Case you need the light switch po-po to come 'round."

"Libby…"

Yvonne stops at the door, purse on her shoulder, waiting for Libby to move her hand. Libby is easily a foot and a half shorter. She smiles up at Yvonne.

"'Cause she all over that shit, baby. *Mmmhmm.* Like lipstick on a dick. She gon' *suck* the light right out the room."

"Libby…"

"Like a superhero. Like *Light Switch Girl* or some shit."

"Libby… Go, Eve. Just go. I'll talk to you later."

"Look!" Libby points out to the nurse's station. "Light! Shit's eva-where! Go get it, Light Switch Girl!" She rotates out toward the blinding sterility. Raises her voice. "Here come the light brigade!"

Yvonne goes. Libby comes in. Closes the door. Sits. Her perfume hurts to smell. She whispers for the first time.

"How you feelin', baby?" she asks.

"I wish you wouldn't do that."

"I asked you… how… are…"

"I hurt. Okay? My head. My face. Like it's in a vice of nails. And my fuckin' leg."

"Get you some drugs. Ain't this thing workin?" She flicks at the hanging bag with a finger.

"That's just saline. They're giving me pain meds. They only help but so much."

"You need you a sip a sump'n wet? Here, baby."

Libby retrieves the cup of water. Holds the straw to Olivia's lips. Lets her drink.

"Oh God. Thank you."

"God ain't got nothin' to do wit' that shit, baby. Done that all by myself." Silence. She starts. "Libby." Stops. The silence rebuilds its pressure. Tries again. "Libby." Her voice, even in its careful whisper, breaks. "I'm going to have scars on my face. Bad ones."

Libby smiles. There is a sadness to it that Olivia can see. It makes her well up. "I can't cry," she says, weeping anyway. "Not s'posed to cry."

Libby leans in. Kisses her on the forehead. Brushes away the tear. She lays the flat of her hand ever-so-lightly along the white gauze bandage covering the entirety of the left side of her face. Olivia winces. Sniffs.

"Baby, you gon' be the most beautiful person with a scar anyone eva did see."

They are silent for a moment, listening to the sounds of health care administration. Libby leans back in her chair. Thinking. Whispers.

"My mama Mable had her a scar. Her daddy come at her with a shuckin' knife one day when she was but fo'teen. He drunk. Sayin' she been out fuckin' the shrimper again. Which she was too. He got her right up on the fo-head. I used to like to touch it back an' fro with my finger. Like a little white kinda rope over the eyebrow. An' mama Mable say to me *Libby, you ever get you a scar then you wear that shit with pride 'cause it mean life thought about it an' decided to keep you around. Scar mean the shit coulda gone t'other way and didn't.*"

Silence again. Just Libby stroking her forearm.

"You tell the police on that shithead?" Libby asks eventually.

"Who?"

"Who? *Who? Massage*-massage-all-the-way-married. That who. Man need to go to prison fo' this shit."

"No. They haven't been by yet. Well they have but I was in a coma, so… I don't want to get you in trouble. Who knows what Sheldon will say. They'll investigate."

Libby begins flicking out her pink-tipped fingers.

"One, fool damn near kill you." *Flick.* "Two, don't need you lookin' after me. I can take care of my own self." *Flick.* "Three, you too late anyway 'cause I already got popped."

"What?" It is enough to make her want to be more upright. She tries. Succeeds just a little. "Arrested? When?"

"'Bout the time yo' car blow up."

"Why didn't you tell me?"

"Ain't botherin' you with that mess. All broke up like a matchstick. You busy fightin' fo' y'own life up in here."

"Should have told me, Libby. What happened?"

"Deputies come walkin' on in easy as you please as I'm talkin' to fuck-all-day-no-kinda-priest."

"Who?"

"That my sexy new writer friend. He want to write a story 'bout me in his little magazine. Good lookin' man, too. You seen him. Got him a ponytail to hang onto. Like ridin' a bull."

She has to wait for Libby to stop whisper-laughing. Pantomiming.

"But you were just... talking?"

"Yeah, jus' talkin', baby. We wasn't fuckin'. I was just changin' into my robe. Deputies come in and seen the money he give me fo' the story he gon' write. Then they put two and two together an come up wit' five."

"Didn't I tell you it was only a matter of time?"

"Don't you worry 'bout any of this shit 'Livia."

"Why not? It's..."

"'Cause the lawyer say they can't make no kinda case. They dismissin' it."

"Well, why were they out there in the first place? Wait, don't answer. I'll tell you why. 'Cause everyone knows what you do, Libby. Ain't no secrets in that town."

"Naw, that ain't it. It 'cause of an anonymous chicken-shit tip."

"A tip?"

"That what the lawyer say. You wanna guess?

Olivia thinks. It only takes half a second. "Shit. Sheldon."

"You got that right, baby. *Massage*-massage-all-the-way-mother-fuck-married drop a dime. I bet my life it was him. He the one out looking to rent some pussy in the first place an' he gon' drop a dime on my ass? So he call the *po*-lice on me, and then, while they puttin' my ass in the car, he out there tryin' to run you off the damn road. The man need to be put down like a dog. He need to be a prison bitch fo' a long time."

"No," says Olivia. She tries to mean it. "Don't do anything stupid, Libby."

"Ex*cuse* me? You callin' me stupid?"

"No. I... just..."

That's when it hits her. The arrow of inspiration, slicing through the fog of pain and exhaustion. Opening a slit in the narcotic foam packed around her consciousness.

She pushes herself up a little more. Stares through Libby like she's vapor. Then she closes her one good eye. Thinks. Tries to imagine it.

Libby furrows. Leans in again. Whispers.

"What is it, baby? You in pain? You want some more water? You want me to call a doctor? You want..."

"What if I sued him?" Eye open. "That should be worth... something. Shouldn't it? He's got money. He ain't gonna want to go to court over this. Or jail."

Libby leans back in her chair. Thinks. Shakes her head.

"*Massage*-massage got him plenty of money for a lawyer. Do you?"

"No. Maybe I don't need any money."

"Free lawyer? Good luck, baby. You know what I got to do for legal services?" Olivia holds up a hand. The plastic tube yanks at the hanging bag.

"No. And I don't want to know."

"No you don't either, baby. But I can hook you up with my lawyer Clarence if you want. I pay the fee too. May's well. He already workin' fo' me on account of *massage*-massage-all-the-way-shithead. I just put you on my tab. Clarence don't care. Sex is sex, baby."

"No," says Olivia. She closes her eye again. Everything hurts. Her leg. Her entire face. Her right eye socket feels like it has been scraped to the bone with a metal file. "I don't want that."

"Ain't no thing, 'Livia. Clarence is quick. Ten minutes a time. *Bam*, an' he is done. He always make me put on my Blind Willie record. Every time. Blind Willie. Only got time to get through *Nobody Fault but Mine* an' he zippin' up and headin' out like he late for court."

"Ain't talkin' about a free lawyer, Libby. I'm talkin' about just, you know… making the threat. I mean… he caused the accident. I'm probably…" She breaks off. The words are too fat with the ugly truth to clear her throat. Libby leans in.

"What is it, baby?"

"I'm probably disfigured for life, Libby. For the rest of my *fucking* life."

Libby shakes her head. "*Uh-uh.* You gon' heal right up, baby."

"No, Libby. This ain't something that heals right up. Can't pay for plastic surgery. Me just bein' here in this room is already costin' a billion dollars I don't have. You think any of my jobs come with a lick of insurance? Answer is no, Libby. And my leg's gonna be all scarred up too and they're gonna have to put metal pins all in it. I'm gonna walk like some old one-legged sea captain from now on."

The emotion swells again. It pushes her fluids up against the inside of too many raw, tender wounds. The pain centers bleed into each other. She feels her leg in her face. Feels her eye in her knee. It's like stepping into open flame.

Libby strokes her arm again. They listen quietly to the hospital around them. When the swell subsides she tries again.

"Don't you think that just the *threat* might be worth something? No lawyers. No proceedings. Just… like a letter saying… you know, Dear Sheldon, here's the easy way and here's the hard way."

Liberty furrows the smooth skin above her eyes. Looks hard at Olivia. Then comes the smile. Not the sweet one that gets the men into the parlor. It's the wicked one that won't let them out. She crosses her arms.

"Fuck a duck," she says. "You ain't thinkin' 'bout the cost of no plastic surgery. Well, maybe you are, but that ain't all. You thinkin' 'bout *Papi's*."

"Libby, I…"

"Don't you *Libby*, me, baby. You layin' up in this bed like a mummy in the dark, all beat up an' bandaged an' hurtin' an' you still schemin' away on that piece-a-shit juke joint."

Olivia shrugs.

The inside edge of the gauze covering the left half of her face wrinkles. Right there at the corner of her mouth. Just a little.

Chapter 27

Morning had been the plan. It is too late for this now. Sun is too high.

Davis rolls on anyway, tracing a blackened seam over the earth like a lost ant looking for the colony. His hair is in the wind. He feels the sun focusing on the back of his neck. God is an idle bully with a magnifying glass.

He rides west, the air like a hot dust of pulverized bone caking the back of his throat. He misses the turn and has to double back. He misses it again. Doubles back again. The dirt road is there, small and unmarked. He would have missed it a third time. The bull snake slipping over the stack of white stones catches his eye.

Gateposts but no gate. He'd been looking for a gate.

He throttles up. The bike spits out a squirrel tail of bleached dust.

It is another mile before he can see the house. Single-level ranch style. It clings to the backside of a low, flat hillock covered with dark scrub. An improbable assemblage of desert willows line up to the north and the west. To the east and the south is a wall of rocks. An opening in the wall is flanked by large riddled saguaros.

He leaves his bike at the wall. Stretches. Looks around. Steps through the stone gate.

Stops. He assumes it is her. Kneeling in the dirt next to a green paper bag split up the middle, a wooden handle emerging from the white wound. A dozen other bags are stacked up against the house. He recognizes the logo.

Her back is to him as he approaches. But she knows he is there.

"You're trespassing," she says. It is a strong, rich voice. Coffee. Black loam.

"Sorry. I'm looking for Dallas Letti?" says Davis.

"You may be. But you're still trespassing."

"Ms. Letti?"

She sighs. Pushes herself up. Stands. Turns. Takes off her gloves and beats them against her leg. She is tall. Darkly complected. Mexico is in there someplace. She is well-preserved. Seventy-something with a stoop to her shoulders. Knobby knuckles, wrists and elbows. A hard, flat face with sharp eyes. Curly black hair escapes the band of her yellow gardening hat. She throws words at his face.

"What. Do. You. Want."

What does he want? He wants two things. There is a proper order to these things. He's just not sure what that order is. His gut decides.

"I'm very sorry to interrupt, Ms. Letti. My name is Davis Payne. I'm a writer for *The Ocotillo Review*. I'm here because I'd like to see if I could interview you for a feature that I write called *Voices*. I would have called but I…"

"What'd you say your name was?"

She is squinting at him. He can smell the alcohol.

"Davis. Davis Payne."

"*Mmm.*" She chews something small. Seeds. Or something left over. She finds it with her teeth. Crushes it. Spits. "So you the hero, then?"

It takes a second for him to get it. Then he does.

"Oh. Not really. I…"

"Good thing you did, Hero. Savin' that girl."

He knows it is his last chance to correct her. He knows he should. He almost does. He even opens his mouth.

But then there it is again. *The feeling.* Just like with Eladio. *Hey Homes! You like a hero now, eh? I know her, man! Olivia's in here all the time! She used to date my brother. You just, like, reach into the fucking fire and pull her out by the fucking hair? You got some stones, man. She'd be dead.*

The feeling. It had been like a firm hand clutching his larynx. He had not said a word to correct the misunderstanding.

And now here it was again. The feeling. The brain itch that keeps him up night after night. The skip in the rhythm of his heart that had taken him all the way into San Angelo and led him down the white labyrinthine corridors of a hospital, looking for someone he did not know. The inexplicable knot in his gut that had brought him to a standstill at the nurse's station outside the ICU.

The feeling had been the catch in his throat that had coughed up his name. *Davis Payne. Not family.* The nurse had written it down on a piece of paper; on the back of something that had some other purpose. *When she wakes up I'll tell her you were here.*

She had not said *If she wakes up.* But that was what she meant.

He had walked away, the feeling still inside his brain, his heart, his gut, his throat, kicking and clawing and keening like a wild, wounded animal.

And now here it was again. The feeling. Looking over the shoulder of another chance to be honest. She thinks he's a hero. He's not a hero. But what if it gets him what he wants.

"So you're from Houston then." Dallas Letti shifts her weight. Shoos off a fly.

Davis closes his mouth. Clears his throat. Kicks dust off his boots. Remembers the woman at that last AA meeting. *Addicts are liars. Everyone in this room is a liar.*

He nods.

"Uh, yeah. Originally from Houston. Livin' in Corbin for the time being. The magazine is based in Houston. I'd have called, Ms. Letti, but I didn't have your number."

She stares at him for a few seconds. Shakes her head. Turns. She sinks back down to her knees, unsteady in the dirt.

"I don't do interviews," she says, putting her gloves back on. "Ever. Not no more."

"It's not like an ordinary interview. It's not like that. It's for a literary magazine."

"Don't care, hero. Don't do interviews."

"It'd be a piece written on a theme, built around the experiences of two or three other people. You wouldn't be the only one."

"Ever." She stabbed a spade into the ground. "Not ever."

"I'd let you read the piece before I submitted it."

"Not ever."

"I wouldn't even be using your real name. No one would have to know it was you. Doesn't even have to be about your music."

She stops stabbing. Like she was not expecting that last part. Davis stares at her hunched shoulders. Watches her think. Decides to hit her again while she is unstable.

"You'd be totally anonymous. And if you don't approve the draft, I don't submit the draft."

She makes a slow, quarter turn. As if to see him.

She reverses. Stabs the spade back into the ground. Steel scraping rock.

"Not ever," she says. The richness of her voice seems to come from between her shoulder blades. "You be careful not to kick up the dust when you ride on outta here. Hero."

Davis takes off his hat. Runs this fingers through his hair. Gathers it in the back. Looks up at the sun.

"Okay," he says. "I respect that. 'Preciate your time, Ms. Letti."

He pretends to shuffle off. Stops. Turns back.

"Say, would you happen to know anyone around here looking to hire? Writing doesn't pay the rent. I'm tryin' to fill two, maybe three hours a day. Late afternoons, early evenings."

The spading stops. Dallas Letti rises, pushing up from her knees. Turns. Takes off her gloves. Spits. Smiles.

God adjusts the magnifying glass.

"Well now."

Chapter 28
Abby and Davis

We've never really talked about Simon. You've never asked.

My guess is that you were satisfied with what you read about him in the papers. I don't know how much of that stuff is true. All of it, maybe. Maybe none of it. I'm just a young, dumb Texas plug. How am I supposed to know any of that? What I do know is that Simon Dory scared the piss out of me.

He was not so big and burly or anything. You've seen the pictures. I'm as big as he is. I suppose it doesn't make me much of a man to confess my fear. But then, none of this makes me much of a man, does it?

So I'll add this to my pile of shame: Simon was scary. There was always something in his eyes. Not wild and crazy. Not what you'd expect. Something quiet. Something relentless. Like, no matter what he happened to be saying or doing, he was always looking for where things were wrong. Waiting for the right time to do something terrible. His eyes paced. Like animals in a cage.

I met him that afternoon, after my first experience in Abby's trailer. We lay there on that cot for most of an hour, waiting for him to leave the house. He listened to heavy metal music that busted out of that house and came all the way across the back lot and clawed at the trailer. We waited. He wasn't leaving.

Abby described him as a friend who travelled a lot and who stayed with her from time to time. I was instantly concerned that Simon was the husband or the ex-husband or the boyfriend or the ex-boyfriend that she had never told me about. That she had been lying to me all along. And there I was naked with her in her candle-shop trailer.

"My *husband?*" she said, laughing. But that laugh was not her normal laugh. It was a nervous laugh. Looking back, I know that Abby was scared too. "Is that what you think? That I'm married?"

"I don't know," I mumbled.

"Simon's a mate. Nothing else. A good guy."

"Then why are we hiding?"

"Is that what we're doing? Are we hiding? I rather thought we were canoodling in the afterglow."

That phrase lightened the mood. *Canoodling in the afterglow.* She made fun of me for not knowing the word *canoodling.* I insisted she had made it up. I loved making her laugh.

We dressed and walked across the lot to the house. The walls were shaking with raw electric sound. We went in through the back screen door, through the kitchen to the living room.

I could see the top of Simon's shaved head propped up on the near end of the couch. His black steel-toed boots were up on the other end. Abby snapped off the stereo. The house collapsed into nothingness.

I'd have expected Simon to leap up in surprise at the sudden silence. There was no way he could have heard us come in. But the head and the boots did not move an inch.

"You know how to make an entrance, Simon," said Abby.

"Who's this, then," said Simon. It wasn't a question.

The accent I remember almost more than the words. It made me think all over again that he was her husband. Brits married Brits. Brits in Texas did not have casual Brit friends. A boy Brit and a girl Brit in the same house were either married or related. I hoped for a second that maybe they were related. A brother. A cousin, maybe. That would have been a relief.

But I was not relieved. I came right back to married. Or at least sexual. That really was the thought that I couldn't get out of my head. Sex. Possession.

Five minutes post-canoodle and I was already possessive. Abby was mine. At the same time, I was terrified at what I had done. Because inside I knew she was not mine; she was Simon's. These thoughts near paralyzed me. I am ashamed that my first instinct was to think that Abby had been lying to me.

That shouldn't have been my first instinct.

Right behind the impression of Simon's accent were his actual words.

Who's this, then.

It sounded more like a command than a question. But what confused me is how he knew I was even in the room. I was standing ten feet behind him under cover of bone-rattling heavy metal. And I hadn't breathed a word. It was like he had eyes in the back of his head.

And if he knew I was there, then he also knew what I had been doing with Abby out in the shop. And if he knew that, then he knew how I felt about her. He not only had eyes in the back of his head, but those eyes could see directly into my mind and my heart. I remember wanting to run. Fighting panic.

I realized later that he could see my reflection in the front window. And that Fat Jack's truck was sitting out in the drive. Of course he knew she was with someone.

But that realization had come too late. He'd already become a dangerous mystery. Simon was someone I feared from the very beginning.

"This is my mate, Davis," said Abby. "He helped me this year at the fair."

Simon swung his legs off the couch, stood up and turned around. He had a beer in one hand. He was wearing baggy green fatigue pants and a dirty white Henley, torn above the left shoulder and smeared with greasy finger tracks. A bluish tattoo of some sort was snaking out of his shirt along the base of his neck. His head was square and too big for his body. His mouth flashed a set of white but crooked teeth inside thin, pale lips.

"Davis is it then?" His black, deep-set eyes slid slowly to Abby and then back to me. "And how old might you be? Davis."

"Comin' up on eighteen," I lied.

"Like the fair, do you?"

"Yeah. It's okay I guess. Too many people."

"Too many people. That's what I always say," he said, looking at Abby. "Don't like people much. Don't trust 'em, see."

Simon took a long drink, eyes open, looking at me.

"But you seem like a regular bloke. Davis. Fancy a beer?"

"No. No thanks. I should be going."

He rattled his can in the air.

"I'm empty. There's a cold one in the freezer. Be a mate, yeah?"

He and Abby were both looking at me. Waiting. Abby nodded. I turned and stepped into the kitchen. I opened the freezer door. The smell hit me before the cold. A blue can of Fosters sat wedged between a dozen clear bags of frozen, gray fish. Nothing else. Just the blue and the gray. I grabbed the can and closed the freezer and headed back. Neither of them had moved or said anything.

But it felt like they had been talking.

Abby looked back and pretended to smile. Simon set down the empty and held out his hands. I tossed him the Foster's.

"Good lad." Simon opened the can and drank. "What've you two been about then?"

I looked at Abby, wanting her to answer.

"Listening to the voices," she said.

"Ah, the voices. Right. Should have guessed that. You hear the voices then, Davis? Does the Universe go on about its day to you too?"

I shrugged, not knowing what to say.

"Did she show you her candles?"

I nodded. "Yes."

"And did she light one for you?"

"No."

"No? Pity. She really knows how to light a candle."

"Simon…" said Abby, warning in her voice.

I looked over at her. She was looking hard at Simon.

Looking at him look at me.

"I should be going," I repeated.

Abby looked at me and then nodded. I saw relief in her eyes. Like fear loosening its grip.

"Thank you, Davis," she said. "Wonderful surprise seeing you again. Don't be a stranger, love."

I left without another word. The screen door slapped closed behind me. I felt Simon looking at me as I walked across the dead scrub lawn to Fat Jack's stolen truck. I never turned around.

But I could sure feel Simon at that window.

I drove away wondering what Abby was telling him about me. Why was I there? What was our relationship? What did she want from me? What did I want from her?

It wasn't until I was halfway to Corsicana I realized that not even I knew the answers to those questions.

Chapter 29

"Don't know what's gotten into you lately, Shel. I really don't. I really…"

Christi shakes her head. Sadness. Pain. Incomprehension.

She is wearing too much jewelry for lunch. He, clearly, is not wearing enough.

Sheldon sits on the edge of the bed, face in his hands, listening to his wife bustle around the room pulling clothing on and off of her plastic body.

He almost doesn't perceive her. The envelope stuffed into his pocket is siphoning away all of his attention.

He tries to open it with is mind. Imagines a corner. Rips. Widens the gap. Dilates his mind's eye. Imagines the inside. But all is too dark.

He wants to go downstairs. Or into a bathroom and close the door.

Anywhere but here.

"It's your *weddin' ring,*" she is saying. "Shelly, are you even listening to me?"

"What?"

"Why do you even need to take it off your dang finger?"

"Honey…" But he doesn't have the energy to finish.

"*Honey* what, Shel? *Honey* what? You gon' tell me again 'bout how your finger swells up sometimes when you drive? 'Bout how…"

"…Yes. That's…"

"'Bout how you put it up on the dash and forgot about it?"

"That's what…"

"'Bout how you stopped to pick up the wine…"

"Honey…"

"…but didn't lock the car door and then when you got home you noticed it was gone? You still stickin' with that story, Shel?"

"It's not a story. It's what happened. I told you…"

"Yeah, you told me alright. Last time I asked you about that ring, you told me you got blood on it from your… your… broken nose and took it off in the shower and left it on the corner of the sink."

"Christi, that was… *weeks* ago."

She is mostly naked now. She throws a turquoise blouse on the bed. Disappears back into the closet wearing a sheer pink bra and panties. Reemerges stripping a poppy-colored sundress from a hanger.

"Exactly," she says, tossing the hanger. "And I haven't seen that ring since."

"Oh, yes you have too." He replies quickly. Calmly dismissive. Gives the lie a truth-like certainty. "I wear it every day."

"That is a load of puckey, Shel. I haven't seen that ring since."

"You're just not remembering. And what… what are you really saying here, Christi? Are you saying I'm… I'm…"

"I'm sayin' you haven't worn your weddin' ring in weeks. I'm tryin' to believe you just plum lost it. That you were *that* stupid. I'm tryin' to go with the whole *accidents happen* thing, Shel. I really am. But then when you lie like this, I just…"

"If it's not lost or stolen, why *wouldn't* I be wearing it?"

"Oh I don't doubt one bit it's lost. Not one bit. I'm just concerned 'bout how you lost it."

"I'm not lying, Christi. Christ Almighty."

"You don't need to start taking our Lord's name in vain," she snaps. She yanks the sundress down unevenly over her marmoreal, reinforced breasts. He wants to point out that he is not *starting* anything; that he has been taking the Lord's name in vain for a very long time now. Wants to ask her to take a nice long look at her own name. Wants to write it down on paper and underline it for her. *Christ-i.*

He bites his tongue. There is no better way to squirt kerosene onto the fire of his wife's tantrums than to ridicule her piety.

Funny though. He remembers, suddenly, their courtship days. Christi lashing out against every one of her father's expressions of piety like they were evil voodoo.

"Now, Christi, what would your mother say, up in the bosom of Jesus, as we look upon this bounteous Thanksgiving feast and not say a word of grace?"

"What would she say, Daddy? You want to know what Mama would say? She'd say don't be such a fuckin' hypocrite, Grayson. That's what she'd say. She'd say you've done enough goddamned bounteous feasting in all the wrong places. So pass the fuckin' potatoes. Please."

She was, back then, still well within the shadow of her mother's death. So angry with Grayson she could spit fire. As though *he* had killed Layla and not Layla's twenty-five year, pack-a-day affair with Phillip Morris. All Grayson had done to Layla was keep a mistress for the last six years of Layla's life.

He hadn't *actually* killed her. A technical distinction lost on Christi.

She had damned her father to Hell every time his name came up. Their eighteen-month estrangement had lasted from Layla's funeral to Christi's betrothal. Almost exactly.

Father and daughter had officially buried the hatchet in Christi's four-tiered wedding cake after a tearful speech by Grayson. He'd invoked the spirit of his late wife. Asked for his daughter's forgiveness. Swallowed a lot of pride.

Were it not to recover his daughter's good graces, Grayson Tate would never have approved of Sheldon Davis as a son-in-law. He didn't play football, for one thing. Didn't even like football. What kind of man didn't like football?

Maybe worse, Sheldon had some money, but no wealth. He owned a small advertising business, *Houston Market Research*. Six employees. That was it. Six. And that count included Sheldon.

He had no social pedigree. Didn't know people of power. People of influence. Didn't know people who knew people. Didn't come from people who knew people.

And he was not religious. No relationship with the *Man Upstairs* whatsoever. And —related but not the same —he did not go to church. So everybody *knew* good and well Sheldon had no relationship with the *Man Upstairs,* and no sense of how good business gets done in Texas.

He was not, in short, what Grayson had been carrying around in his head for his daughter. That, Sheldon had long suspected, was precisely why Christi had picked him in the first place. Why that first party had led to a date. And a second. A third. Why she was so eager to have him on her arm.

Grayson would grind his teeth at the very sight of them. That was why.

Christi's first husband, Tig Larson —his parents had named him *Tiger*, Christi affectionately named him *Tigger* —had been in place while Layla was alive. Tig had been a little closer to Grayson's vision of a son-in-law. Good Houston family. Loved God. And Church. And Texas football. Loved it. A little too much. Tig had lasted only two and a half years in the Tate family orbit before running off to Costa Rica with a cheerleader for the Dallas Cowboys.

Winnie-the-Pooh has remained a rage trigger for Christi. A volatile emotional accelerant. Piglet too. The whole gang. She had loved Tig.

Last time she would ever let *that* happen.

After Tig, and after Grayson had cheated Layla into an early grave, Christi had been primed to consider someone completely different than everyone else she had ever dated. Smart. Sensitive. Middle class. Easy enough on the eye. Not a movie star. Not a temptation to any of the Cowgirls. But attractive.

Which was Sheldon. She was ready for him. Or someone like him.

Of course, that Sheldon owed Christi's early affections mostly to Grayson Tate and Tig Larson was entirely lost on him at the time. Not that he could explain why a former Miss Houston Texas, daughter of one of the wealthiest developers in the state, was showing such interest.

But the truth was, he didn't *want* an explanation. He didn't *want* to question anything or do anything that might disturb the delicate universal balance that was delivering Christabelle Tate into his arms night after night.

So he had quietly held his breath. Tried not to second-guess fate. He had never been one of *those* guys. A winner. A head-turner. He had never been lucky at love. And then suddenly, in his mid-thirties, *bam*. There he was. Sheldon Davis: *one of those guys*. Miss Houston Texas on his arm. Having regular sex on piles of Daddy-Tate's money.

He had explained it by convincing himself that he really was an up-and-comer in the advertising world, the profession he had stumbled on just trying to pay the bills. He owned his own agency. Accounts had been steadily multiplying. His *Cow-Cow-Boogie* campaign for Texas Beef had paved the way to the Horizon Award from the Houston Advertisers Association. It was not unreasonable to believe his stock was rising.

The serendipity of striking up a conversation with Christabelle Tate at the open bar was difficult to ignore. It was immediately after the ceremony at which he had been presented with the Horizon Award. He had handed her the large gold medallion so that he could manage his wallet and pay the bartender. One drink in each hand, he had turned to face her. Gazed upon this otherwise unreachable beauty, beaming beneath her golden tresses and holding his golden symbol of business promise. It was easy enough to believe that the gods of good fortune were simply being efficient. They were giving him everything he could reasonably hope for, all in the same evening.

Hard to know back then just what that feeling really was. The feeling when he looked at her. Wasn't love. Somewhere he knew that much. He had known love. *This* was not *that*. Love felt horrible. Love was gut-wrenching agony. Love was rejection and pointless misery. But *this*… This was exhilarating. This was affirming. This was elevating.

This, by God, was *success*.

So he'd just went with it. Held his breath all the way to the wedding. Supported Christi in grieving the loss of mother Layla, in banishing the memory of husband Tig, and in hating the air inhaled by her father, Grayson. Sheldon had proudly carried the mantles of *Not-Grayson* and *Not-Tig*. He had done everything he needed to do. Said everything he needed to say. Went to football games and beauty pageants. Cared as passionately as he could about the outcomes. Went to church. Prayed to the gods of momentum that he would get the job.

And then he *did* get the job. He had pulled out his guitar one night after a romantic, torch-lit dinner and strummed out the song he had written for her. *My garden in the desert. My flower in the sand. My kingdom for your smile. My promise for your hand.* Then he had put the guitar down. Knocked over the wine. Taken her hands in his. Asked her the question.

And she had said yes.

Simply. Without hesitation. Christabell Tate had said yes.

Six months later, she had accepted his ring and he had accepted her ring. He had watched the mighty Grayson Tate lift his glass in front of two hundred people assembled on the rolling slopes of his back lawn. Watched him sing Sheldon's name in a song of contrition for his daughter's happiness. Sheldon felt as though he had finally arrived.

Lost in the bliss of that moment was what, exactly, it all meant. What it meant that Christi had consented to slipping back into Grayson's orbit. Reconciliation had been fast and lucrative. Among other things, Grayson had made a half-million dollar investment in Sheldon's business, showing that he was behind his daughter's choice in a husband *"one hundred and ten percent."*

Beyond that, Grayson had put his inestimable connections to work, demonstrating almost immediately that he was in a position to steer a lot of new business Sheldon's way. *HMR* grew from six employees to fifty-seven employees almost over night.

But reconciliation also meant that Christi would return to the fold. Back to being Daddy's girl. God's girl. She doted and prayed. Doted on her sixty-one year old father like he was twelve. Prayed to a judgmental God before reaching for the potatoes. Her disrespectful, accusing, irreligious mouth ceased to have any rebellious value. Grayson Tate reassumed his role as Lord of the Manor. Jesus Christ, King of the Pageants, triumphantly returned to her universe. The rings on their fingers were not just promises to each other. They were promises to God.

And now that promise had gone mysteriously missing from his finger.

Her tantrum is not really about the missing wedding ring. He knows it and she knows it. The missing wedding ring is just a proxy. A stand-in for the singular subject that has most recently animated their marriage: a small article, just a note really, in the crime blotter of *The Chachalaca Gazette.*

Christi is an avid reader. Of sorts. *Glamour. Cosmopolitan. Pageant Parade Monthly. Horse Fancy. Houston Fellowship in Christ Monthly.* She also enjoys romance novels, which she selects from the impulse racks in the check-out line at Kroger, weighing the promise of one libidinous antebellum cover tableau against another as she waits to purchase her Diet Cokes and her pizza-flavored rice cakes.

Christabelle Tate Davis is not, however, an avid reader of newspapers. She picks her way through the matrimonial, fashion, society and religion stories of the Houston Chronicle as she sips her morning coffee like a blonde crow pecking through trash to find digestible morsels.

She is an early riser. A four-mile walk through the neighborhood, then a shower, then dressing for the day, and then the paper and a cup of coffee. All before Sheldon is out of bed. She likes to sit at the table just off the kitchen, facing the mirrored wall that appears to double the size of the room. Her back to the windows. Birdsong washing up against the house like an ocean tide. The sun fracturing itself into pieces over the glass and chrome. That is where he usually first encounters her. Reading the newspaper. *Mornin' sleepyhead!*

But there certainly would not have been any reason for her to be reading *The Chachalaca Gazette*.

It had been Sheldon's rotten luck that a friend of Christi's on the Texas Pageant Association Board had whispered some concern during a break in the proceedings to elect new officers.

"How you holding up, Christi?"

That was how his wife had learned the news. From her best frenemy, the 2001 runner-up for *Miss Houston*, who had just happened to read in a second-rate, low-circulation rag based in Corbin, that Sheldon T. Davis had been arrested for soliciting a prostitute. Conveniently enough, the frenemy –whose mother lives in San Angelo –just happened to have the clipping in her purse.

Would've been better if Sheldon had seen it coming. Had he known the article was out there, he might have been better prepared.

But he hadn't known.

His first news of the article was when Christi had slapped it down in front of him on the counter as he was pouring himself a drink. She'd stomped off without saying a word, leaving him to read it alone, bourbon bottle hovering over empty tumbler.

No, no, no. Oh no. Oh … oh… fuck.

He'd found her upstairs in the bedroom. The place she most liked to fight. She was sitting in her chair, arms and legs crossed so tightly they were pushing all the blood in her body up into her beautiful blonde head.

"You better damn well tell me that ain't you, Shelly."

"I don't know who it is, Christi. It's not me."

But she wasn't ready to listen.

"You better damn well tell me that you did not break your damn nose in some skanky Corbin whorehouse. Or on the door of some sheriff's car as you were resisting arrest. Or in jail. My God, Shelly, what is Daddy gonna say?"

"Christi, take a breath. It's not me. It's a mistake. It's a different…"

"You know any *other* Sheldon T. Davis'? Do you?"

"No, but that doesn't mean…"

"Daddy is gonna hit the roof."

"I'll call the paper," he had said. "I'll look into it."

"Look into it? You're gon' *look into it?* No. Shelly. You're gon' sue the goddamned paper is what your gon' do." She had jabbed a red-tipped finger at the clipping still in his hand. "If this wasn't *you*, Shelly, if this *wasn't* you, then you're gon' sue those sons of bitches to clear the family name. And the first thing you're gon' do is call Daddy and tell him about this before he finds out on his own."

"I'll deal with Grayson ..."

"No. You won't *deal* with Daddy. You'll *call* him. On the *telephone*. Right now. And you will *tell him* about this."

"Yes. I will call him. I'll tell him. What's important to me now, Christi, is that you believe me when I tell you that this is not me. Do you believe me? Look at me. Christi?"

She had looked at him. Blue eyes sharpened into little daggers of ice.

"Well Adele thinks it's true!"

"Adele?"

"Adele Connor? Hello? Her mother lives in San Angelo, Shel. She's the one brought me the article. She obviously thinks it true. And Adele's got a mouth on her, boy. Everybody on the board knows by now. *Susan.* God, *Janelle.* And then she'll blab her fat ass to Charlene, like always."

"Well what does Adele know?" he had asked, angrily. "What do any of them know? And who cares anyway?" Sheldon had forced himself to take a breath. Perched himself carefully on the edge of the bed. Reached out for her little boney fists. "I care about what *you* think, Christi. Not Adele Connor."

It had taken him another half-hour to calm her down. Eventually her anger had congealed into an irrational loathing for all *whoring newspapers*, making their *damned profits* off the smoldering remains of *good reputations*.

He had, unwisely, felt it in his own non-litigious self-interest to give the paper the benefit of the doubt.

"But if there really *is* another Sheldon T. Davis who..."

Christi was not in the mood to be fair.

"Don't care, Shelly. *I. Don't. Care.* That *Chachalaca* bullshit pardon my French newspaper has to print something that says it was not the Sheldon Davis that lives at this address married to me and son-in-law to Grayson Tate. Hear me?"

"Yes, but if they accurately reported the name of..."

"I am callin' Daddy right this blessed cotton-pickin' minute."

"Christi..."

She had been out of the chair and on top of the phone before he could stop her. He had even reached for the receiver but she had snapped her sharp, delicate shoulders sideways, cutting him off like a slamming door.

"Daddy? You sittin' down? Well go grab yourself a seat. Yes. Yes. As a heart attack. Go sit down."

Sheldon had collapsed backwards on to the bed and listened to his wife relay the news. Her initial revelation seemed to bleed off some of the pressure and she had tried to assume the voice of reason through most of the conversation. Even so, she had shot him razor-thin glances every so often just to let him know that he was witnessing diplomacy on his behalf and not a display of her true feelings.

"Calm down, now," she had said into the phone, rolling her eyes. "I know. I know. How'd you think I feel? 'Course it's not him. Probly's got to be another Sheldon Davis. Daddy... now, Daddy, I told you how he broke his nose. That has nothin' whatever to do with this. Goodness sakes, Daddy. You know how many rings and earrings I've lost in my life? Dropped down the sink or God knows where? 'Course I do. He's my husband. How's the paper to know any better? What happens when they arrest a John Smith? Must be two hundred men get in trouble with their wives. I know. I know. I'm with you, Daddy. We're all good as long as they print a clarification. And not somethin' the size of a gnat's eyelash buried in the classifieds either. Front page. Yes, front page. Front page. Front page. And if they don't, then we need to sue for defamation of character. He's gon' talk with a lawyer in the mornin'."

She had turned then. Looked hard at him, chin down, brows raised. Like she was making the point over a pair of reading glasses.

"Oh he's hoppin' mad about it. And you know Shel. He doesn't get fired up much. Now? Yeah we're both here talking about this whole mess. Come on by. You can stay for supper."

It had been a long evening, careening through barely concealed accusations and threats headlong into long-winded lecturers about "a man's good name" and "the currency of reputation." For a silver-haired patrician, Grayson Tate paced a room like a dog when he was upset. He liked the sound of his boots on the hardwood. Liked to point with the same hand that held his amber highball.

"This is a small state, Shel. For gossip? Texas is 'bout the size of a goddamned middle school. Word like this gets around the business community? *My* business community? Then you're done, boy."

"Grayson..."

"Hear me? *Done.* 'Cause I won't have you."

"Look, Grayson..."

"We got a tiger by the tail, boy."

The memory of Tig Larson had been hiding in that word, *Tiger*, and it had pounced. Christi had involuntarily stiffened and Grayson involuntarily plotted an alternate route.

"I'm tellin' you this is a dinosaur of a deal. This Corbin River Walk deal? No room for this kind of nonsense. None. This is all about hearts and minds. To get this done? Hearts and minds. One whiff of corruption? Illegality? Immorality? The Russians'll drop us all in a New York minute like a steamin' lump-a-shit. Not because the Russians are so damn pure, but they're businessmen, Shel. *Biz-ness-men.* They don't want headlines like this. They want the other kind of headlines. The kind *they* are paying *you* to get for them. They're smart enough to know they're not in Moscow. Or Paris. They know they're in Texas. Dealing with Texas politicians. Texas voters. Texas money. Texas virtue. One whiff that this newspaper shit is true? That their own ad-man can't be trusted? They. Will. *Drop*. Us."

"Grayson…"

"And I'll goddamned drop you first. Son-in-law or not. I will drop you first before that happens. Hear me?"

"Grayson…"

"We need to clean this up. If the wrong word is already out there circulating, then we need to get the right word out there to stab the wrong word in the muther-fuckin' heart."

"Daddy…"

Sheldon had had no choice but to feign savage enthusiasm for a plan of aggressive saber rattling against *The Chachalaca Gazette*. The paper would either print a prominent clarification that cleared his name, or it would be defending itself in a lawsuit. That simple. *Yes*, he had nearly shouted, newspapers needed to take precautions to protect the innocent. *The Chacha* should have printed the address or some other uniquely identifying information about the person arrested –the *other* Sheldon T. Davis –to protect all of the other bastards unfortunate enough to share his name.

He had assured his wife and father-in-law that he knew just the lawyer to take the pound of flesh, if it ever came to that. He said he would jump on it first thing in the morning.

Grayson had seemed provisionally convinced. The follow-up would be all-important. With Christi's urging, he had unfurled the banner of supportive father-in-law and offered his help.

"Nope," Sheldon had said. "Thanks. I got this. I know just the lawyer, too. I'll jump on it first thing. First thing."

The truth was that Sheldon did not know any such lawyer. And he had not *jumped* on anything. He had not made any contact with the paper, although he had sleuthed out the name and phone number of its Editor-in-Chief. The truth was that he was highly ambivalent about exactly how to proceed. Argument and counter-argument had played seesaw in his head until he was paralyzed with indecision.

Back and forth. To and fro.

On the one hand, he was quite confident that he had *not* been arrested in a Corbin whorehouse for soliciting a prostitute. *The Chacha* was simply wrong. If he called the paper, they would investigate. Talk to the Sheriff's office. Realize their mistake. Problem solved.

On the other hand, why did they have his name in the first place? Was it because he had actually been inside that same whorehouse on multiple occasions? In Corbin wearing leopard panties on his face when his wife and father-in-law believed he was in Dallas wooing the purveyors of a different kind of meat? Did the paper have information that he was a customer? Had they simply mixed his name up with the person arrested? Neglect to take his name out of an earlier draft pending confirmation of his arrest? Were they coming for him next? Will raising a stink with the paper merely hasten that process?

True... he had not paid for or engaged in any kind of sexual act.

But... he *had* been assaulted by a prostitute while naked and covered in body oil. A prostitute who, if he is honest, he had tried to kiss.

Then again... he did not *actually* kiss her. At least he does not think he did. He would remember if he had. Wouldn't he?

But, then again... the reason he is so unclear on the underlying facts is that he was stoned out of his mind.

Yet... it was not as though he had any prior knowledge of the drugs in those cookies.

Although... when he had gone back to the whorehouse that *second* time, the first thing he had done was ask for some of *those* cookies.

Not that he had any *particular* knowledge of any *particular* drugs. Except maybe Viagra or one of those types of drugs. That much had been painfully clear.

But... that would not stop the prostitutes in question from lying. From saying that he had showed up high, paid them for sex, and tried to get rough with one of them upstairs.

But... none of that had *actually* happened. Why would they just lie about him?

Well. Because he had ratted them out to the Sheriff's office, that's why. He had gotten their whoring, thieving asses arrested. Of course they will lie about him. They wanted his head on the wall and his balls on a plate.

But... they had stolen his wedding ring. And his watch. And his wallet. They would not want to compound their misery by picking a fight with the person that could brand them as thieves. How would *that* be for their sex business?

On the other hand... one of those prostitutes had been hospitalized from a car accident that had occurred as he had been trying to persuade her to pull over and give him back his ring. Well. *Angrily persuade.* At high speed. The authorities had surely interrogated them. They were probably already accusing him of trying to kill her or run her off the road. Which was patently ridiculous. But still. The prostitutes probably no longer care much about the risks of stolen jewelry or any of the rest of it. Revenge was probably the only thing they cared about now. If *they* were going to jail, then *he* was going to jail. They would see to it. They had his driver's license. They had proof.

On the other hand... he had not actually been the *cause* of the accident. In fact, he had saved her. *Olivia.* The prostitute. He had saved the whore's life. She *should* be feeling gratitude. He should be the *hero* in all of this.

He had called the hospital. *Twice.* Hoping to find someone on duty who would not care that he wasn't a family member. Someone who would confirm that she was going to be okay.

"But I'm the one who saved her," he had said to the last one. Nurse Feffer or Fiffer or Pepper. *"I pulled her out of the burning car. I just want to make sure she's recovering."* Didn't matter. Not authorized to release medical information blah, blah, blah. *"Can't you just tell me if she is still alive?"* No. Rules are rules. Well, fine. He had resolved that he would just drive down to San Angelo and pay a personal visit.

That idea had lasted roughly eight seconds. *Rules were rules.* Being there in person did not make him family. He wouldn't find out anything more than he had on the phone. And he was in enough trouble already without making another secret road trip to south Texas.

All he knew was that if Olivia the prostitute was still alive, maybe she was well enough to have read the newspaper. And, if so, maybe the newspaper actually got something right and identified him, Sheldon T. Davis, as the one who saved her life. So maybe she felt some gratitude. Maybe she would not be so inclined to out him as a customer.

And yet... if his name turns up in the paper as a hero for saving a prostitute, then it will only serve to prove him a liar to Christi and Grayson. Would only show that he was actually in Corbin –home of prostitutes –and not up in Dallas –home of big clients –making love to *Texas Beef.* As far has he knew, the paper had run a story about the accident and then mixed it up with the story about the prostitution arrest, in which case the prostitute... Olivia... might have no idea he had saved her. Not likely, of course. But possible. *Possible.*

But... but, but, but –if *that* were the case, then he really *would* have a claim for defamation of character. Because he *had* saved her and he had *not* been arrested for solicitation.

But then *that* would mean... if he got tough with *The Chacha* and made them fix things, that would only put another newspaper story out there, a corrected story, circulating around, stuffed into the cluttered depths of frenemy purses, that placed him in Corbin, land of prostitutes and broken noses and missing wedding rings and multi-billion dollar land development deals involving his father-in-law. The correction would only confirm the original suspicion. The original lie.

Back and forth. To and fro.

The seesawing had continued for days. Forced Sheldon to lie all the more extravagantly to Christi and to Grayson. Lie that he was playing phone tag with the Editor of *The Chachalaca Gazette.* Lie that he had finally given up and had made his complaint with a junior editor who had said he would look into the matter and get back to him. Lie that he had reached out to a lawyer, Milton Barkley of the Dallas firm of Barkley & Chalmers, for representation. Lie that he was waiting to hear back from Milton. *Milt.* Lie that he had had a conversation with Milt Barkley who said that he would be following up with *The Chachalaca Gazette* directly once he was out of trial. Whenever that would be. Big trial. Big. Something about drilling rights.

None of this had been true, of course. The truth was simply beyond contemplation. So the lies had come easily. A new *status quo* had settled in: Sheldon and his lawyer –Milt Barkley –were working on the newspaper thing. No results yet. Wait and see. Sheldon had jumped on it. *Jumped…on…it!* He was *upset!* There would eventually be some kind of prominent, satisfying correction in the *Chacha*. In the meantime, there was nothing much else to say about the matter. Grayson had returned to his own business concerns. Christi had affected her grimly determined, *life-goes-on* chirpiness.

But Christi's anger over the *Chacha* article had not gone away. That was now readily apparent. The anger had merely congealed into a toxic, smoldering resentment, seeping just below the surface of her demeanor. No matter what she thought her husband was doing to "fix" things, Christabelle Tate Davis did not take kindly to having been made the subject of idle gossip. Adele Connor and the others, including the sanctimonious, buxom piece of work that was *Miss Corpus Christi 2012,* always seemed to have a lot to say to each other. Always just out of earshot. In hallways. Parking lots. Much if it humorous. Apparently.

No mystery, then, when Christi seized upon opportunities to bludgeon Sheldon over inconsequential things. Her little *Chacha* proxy dramas. The toilet seat. His tie left over the arm of the chair. His penchant for skipping past the "good" commercials. His unwillingness to dock Antonia's pay for, once again, missing the trash in the can out by the pool.

Christi's tone frequently found a measure of suspicion when she observed his comings and goings.

"Well *THAT* was sure a long time gone for a quick trip to the store." Or "Workin' on a Saturday are you? Some kinda irresistible work you got there, Shel."

And nothing, absolutely *nothing,* had provided greater opportunity for Christi to vent her barely sublimated anger and suspicion than noticing, over and over again, Sheldon's naked ring finger.

"It's not right," she says, shaking her head to herself in the mirrored alcove of the bedroom. She gives each profile its due. Picks at invisible things on her skirt. "Somethin' stinks to high Heaven 'bout that ring, Shel. I don't know what it is. But it's somethin'."

"It's gone," he says. "I've looked everywhere. Someone took it off the dash. It's the only explanation. I know it was a stupid move. Really stupid."

These conversations usually end with some concession that he is mentally defective. He has started volunteering the concession just in the hope of triggering a Pavlovian change of subject.

He sits on the very edge of the bed next to her. Watches her absorb the word *stupid* as his best self-assessment. As he watches, he can feel the envelope in his pocket. Burning.

This envelope is not like the last envelope. It is not flat. There is a lump in this one. A *circular* lump. The whores have mailed him back his ring. He wants to rip open the envelope and pull the ring out of his pocket in triumphant surprise. *Well looky here what I found! In my pocket the whole time!*

But he is smarter than that. He needs to plant the ring between the seats of his car. Maybe under the driver's-side floor mat. He needs to think of a way for Christi to find it. Accept some eye-rolling scorn for not having looked thoroughly enough. Then they could both be done with this.

Why, though? Why, exactly, were the whores mailing back his ring, and not his watch? Or his wallet? The question keeps inserting itself into the silent conversation in his head. He presses against his pocket with his palm. He cannot tell whether there is also a note in the envelope that might provide some explanation. He can only feel the circular lump.

"*Stupid* I can take," Christi is saying. "*Stupid* and me are old friends. It's *dishonesty* I can't tolerate."

If there were a note, then it would certainly be something for him to worry about. The note in the *last* envelope, which he had found tucked *just-so* beneath a wiper blade when he was leaving the office, had made it plain enough. They were not out to make amends. They were out to hurt him.

That note had read, simply: *Poor Sheldon.* What the note really meant was *We know who you are. We know where to find you.*

He had known instantly that there would be more to come.

And now here it was: a *second* envelope. Wedged into the crack of his front door where anyone, meaning Christi, might have found it.

He assumes that was the point. Return his wedding ring to his wife with a note. Ruin his marriage.

But, as luck would have it, *he* had found the envelope —the same shade of dusty light blue —and stuffed it into his pocket mere seconds before Christi had come up the walkway behind him. She had been carrying a pair of hedge clippers the gardener had left out on the lawn.

And he and Christi had been engaged in this ridiculous conversation ever since. He had not had any opportunity to scan the street for suspiciously parked cars, let alone open the envelope and examine its contents.

"At the end of the day, bein' stupid is no sin. Forgettin' things. Losin' things. That's what Christian forgiveness is all about. I'll turn the other cheek all day long for that kinda' thing. But lyin'? Cheatin'? Whorin' around... That's somethin' else entirely. Even if *I* could forgive you, Daddy never would. You'd be lucky to see the next sunrise."

Fortunately, his wife had failed to notice his change in watches. She also had been oblivious to the fact that he had spent a great deal of time over the past week cancelling his credit cards. Waiting in line at the Texas Department of Public Safety to get a new driver's license. Driving out to Macy's for a new wallet.

But that damned wedding ring. He palpates the envelope in his pocket.

"What are you doing?" Fuchsia Pump in one hand, jutted hipbone in the other.

"What?" He segues cleanly from palpating to scratching.

"You're not listening to a thing I'm saying?"

"Yes I am. I'm just… tired of it. Christi. Okay? I'm tired of it. This is a ridiculous conversation. They all are. Believe me or don't believe me. It's up to you. I'm going back downstairs."

She slips on her other shoe. Follows him to the top of the stairs.

"You have to admit, Shel," she says. "It's just a little… odd."

"No. I don't have to admit anything."

The envelope is emerging from his pocket even before the bathroom door is fully closed behind him. He rips off a short end. Dumps the contents out on the vanity.

No note.

But there is a ring.

Not a finger ring. Just a circle of metal. Too large for a finger. He can see that now. It's supposed to go with a key fob.

But there is no key fob. There is only a loop of thin, silver wire.

Connected, in turn, to a small silver rectangle.

Sheldon sits on the toilet lid, chest like a collapsing mine. Somehow he knows without knowing.

A thumb drive.

Chapter 30

Jesús Batista. Friend of a friend of a friend to Miguel Rivera.

Jesús. Gone now.

Like he was abducted in the night.

This is his car. A 1986 Ford Falcon. Dog-shit brown. Serious dent on the passenger side. A crater beneath silver scars. Jesus –Christ, not Batista –arms outstretched, is glued to the dash, between the scorch marks on the left and knife gashes on the right. The driver's seat has been gutted. You can see the springs. Bits and pieces of foam innards are here and there. They blow around on the floor when the windows are open and the thing hits the freeway.

But it runs. And the driver-side door closes. And it's free.

Olivia adjusts the couch cushion Jesús Batista had been using as a driver's seat. Jesús won't be needing the cushion any more than the car itself. Deportation is a kind of death. You can't take the car with you.

She lights a cigarette. Holds the smoke. Exhales.

Looks again in the rearview mirror. Sighs. She is almost used to them now. Finally recognizes the face in the reflection. So that's an improvement.

There are three of them, less angry than at first, but still show-stoppers. One of them forks like lightening, bisecting the left eye and also arcing around it.

Another is straight as an arrow. Just over an inch and a quarter. Cutting down her left cheek.

And then a third. Right where the neck bends out under the left jawline. That one is not so straight. A shallow, poorly-formed 'W'.

So there are three of them. One for each of the others. The older ones on her wrist. The old practice runs.

Sleeves and bracelets had been so easy. What does one do with the face?

She rotates in the mirror. Looking sideways. Pulls black tendrils of hair forward. Rotates. Someone standing to the right of her might never know.

She closes her eyes.

On the upside, *The Diamondback* has been more tolerable. Manny Soto hasn't given her a single word of grief since she has been back. It's not sympathy, like the others. For Manny it's something else. He looks away now. Let's her pass. She can stand him down from all the way across the bar.

Longhorn Fitness is the worst of them now. The lights are too bright. Too many mirrors. Nowhere to turn. Everyone looks. Heavy respiration all around like a kind of running, speculative commentary. Folding towels in the laundry room, not really her job, has become her favorite thing.

Second favorite thing. The massage time still tops the list. Almost alone in a dark, quiet room. Work never gets any better than that.

Yvonne is the opposite of Manny Soto and the sweaty mouth-breathers. Yvonne likes to pretend nothing is different. She is afraid of sympathy. Afraid of encouraging self-pity. She parses out compassion like it's an addictive opioid. Mustn't be an enabler.

Libby is the only one who has found the sweet spot. The only one waiting for her between sameness and difference. Between yesterday and tomorrow.

Olivia takes another drag. Leans her head back on the seat. Exhales.

Mother Ocean.

Mother Ocean.

Your sorrow so deep.

The melody is still there. Through it all. Swimming in her head like a blue lullaby. She hums to herself, searching for the rest of it. The drone of a leaf blower washes it away. Brings it back. Washes it away.

Then it stops. She opens her eyes.

There is movement, suddenly, across the street at 1414 Alamo Heights Lane. A woman, presumably Mrs. Sheldon Davis. Dressed as a flower for a garden party. She is at the top of the ridiculous driveway next to a red BMW convertible. She is pointing at the house behind its colonnade. A Mexican holding a leaf blower in one hand and a pair of large blue headphones in the other is nodding. The woman gives a wave. Slips down into the car like a dainty foot into an expensive shoe.

Olivia lays back the front seat as the misaligned metal horsehead gates begin to open. She can feel the woman waiting for the edge of the gates to clear her driveway. Looking at Jesús Batista's shit brown Ford across the street. Wondering if it belongs to the gardener. Making a mental note beneath all of that over-worked blonde hair to talk to someone about it when she gets home from wherever she is going. The spa. The country club.

Then she is gone. Red Beemer whispering off into the distance. Metal gates grinding back to a close. Until the teeth are back at the nose.

Olivia sits up. Plastic Jesus is looking down at her from the ravaged dash, all compassion and forgiveness. But he can only see the right side of her face.

She fingers the envelope. Considers her options.

Sheldon Davis. Her handwriting. She should have typed it. More intimidating if it is typed. She had not been thinking. She had grabbed one of Libby's envelopes, stuffed in the letter. Sealed it. Written his name across the front. All in one fluid motion. It was done and she was out the door, speeding her way over to Houston before she had even considered that she might have done something different.

Too late now.

She also could have simply mailed the letter to him. She had at least considered that option. It would have spared her the drive.

But the fantasies of encountering Sheldon. Confronting him –personally, on his own property. Seeing the look on his face as he recognized her and cringed in horror at her disfigurement. Feeling the letter slap against his open palm. All of that had counseled against using the postal service. She wanted the visceral sense of his fear and regret. A stamp could not buy that kind of satisfaction.

The letter was simple enough in laying out the facts. In a highly intoxicated state, he had attempted to coerce some sexual service, forcing her to defend herself. He had then stalked her. Tailed her in his car and attempted to run her off the road. Had he not been recklessly pursuing her at a high rate of speed, frightening her, unintelligibly shouting at her and waving his arms, blocking the passing lane, she would not have had to swerve. There would not have been any accident. Had a passing motorist not pulled her from the wreckage, she would be dead. She is now scarred for the balance of the life she is lucky to have. There are titanium pins and screws in her leg. She is in constant pain.

And, it continues, he may wish to know that since her release from the hospital she has been consulting lawyers. All of them are anxious to take her case. All of them are recommending that she pursue criminal charges in addition to civil litigation. She is inclined to accept this professional advice. But she is willing to consider a less adversarial approach. Give him the opportunity to take responsibility for what he has done.

How? By paying her two hundred and fifty thousand dollars. That's how. A fraction of what he will otherwise have to pay. No legal complications. No publicity. No risk of civil or criminal repercussions. She is willing to let him decide. If he is agreeable, he should mail her a check. If, for whatever reason, it was better for him to pay her in cash, she is willing to meet him in a public place of her choosing. He had two weeks to contact her or she will assume he is opting for legal process.

The letter was not entirely accurate, of course. She had not consulted any lawyers just yet. She did not have time or patience for the legal process. She couldn't afford to pay a lawyer. That meant anyone she hired would want to get paid out of the recovery. Which meant they would demand the moon of Sheldon Davis, as they should. But the moon would be worth fighting over. Her lawyers and Sheldon's lawyers would take to a slow grinding process with filings and arguments. And court dates. Judges and juries. All to fight over the moon.

But she didn't need the moon. She needed *enough*. And she needed it now. Or very soon, anyway. Getting the moon too late was worth a lot less to her than getting enough and getting it now.

Couldn't explain any of that, of course. Not to Sheldon *massage*-massage, as Libby called him. Could not tell him she was in a hurry. He'd see that as a weakness. He'd use it against her.

As for the prospects of his criminal prosecution, she really had no idea. She had spoken to the police. There was no sign that her car had actually collided with anything. There were no drugs in her system. They were perplexed.

She could have cleared everything up. But she had not wanted to foreclose any chance that Sheldon might pay her what she needed. So she had said that she was having difficulty remembering the events that led up to the accident. Dr. Bligh had confirmed for them that spotty recall was not uncommon. Not for her kind of coma-inducing head injuries. One of the officers had given her his card. If she remembered anything, she was supposed to call. She said she would.

And she might. Depending.

But first things first.

She stubs out the cigarette. Takes a breath. Pulls the door handle. Stops.

Up the hill, the garage door is opening. A car backs out into the sunlight.

Not a car. *The* car. The last car she remembers seeing before her ruination. Before waking up to the mind-splitting pain of light, and the bandages, and the new topography of her face.

Sheldon's car.

What to do? Block his exit? Follow him? Jump out and stick the envelope beneath his wipers?

He is down the hill to the gate before she can decide. She lies back in the seat as she had before. Waits. Listens.

Sits up. He is gone and the gates are closing.

Well… shit. She watches the silver splinter glint away in the distance.

She had specifically picked a Saturday. Had figured he was more likely to be home. More likely to see her limping up that driveway.

So now what? Wait for him to return? Wait for another day? Next weekend?

No. She was not waiting. She would wedge the envelope into the front door. Or give it to the gardener, *someone*, to give to him. Either way Sheldon Davis would know that she had been here. In person. He would know that the contents of the envelope meant more to her than the post office could deliver. He would know that she meant business.

She climbs out of the car. Slams the door with unnecessary force, remembering too late her old blue Civic. May it rest in pieces.

Crosses the road. Approaches the sheet metal horses. Pushes against the nose of one and pulls against the teeth of the other. Slips easily through. She hobbles up the hill. Slowly. Painfully. She does not follow the winding ribbon of concrete, but charts a straight path up the grass to the front door. Looks for the gardener. She can hear the hypnotic drone of his blower on the other side of the house.

She pushes the button to ring the bell. Listens. Waits.

Nothing.

Kisses the envelope. Wedges it into the seam of the large wooden door.

She looks at her watch. She needs to get moving if she is going to make *Papi's*. It will mark another unveiling of her new face. More people to startle.

She takes a last look at the envelope in the door. Turns. Slaps one of the white, faux marble columns and steps back onto the freshly mown grass.

Chapter 31
Celia and Paola

Principal Deazy. Long, rigid torso, cantilevered over the top of his desk. Made it seem so small. Like he was sitting at a child's desk. The chair had creaked forward in a succession of slow wooden snaps.

Hadn't asked for an explanation.

Hadn't been interested in listening to one.

He'd seen what he'd seen. Known what he'd known. His only interest had been to be understood. *Perfectly* understood. He had dried his glasses on his tie. Spoken.

"Do you understand, Ms. Morales, what I am telling you?"

Celia had nodded. Cleared her throat. "Yes sir."

He had leaned back again. Let the silence reestablish itself as he gathered up his warning to her. Then he'd broken the warning into manageable little twigs of sound and meaning. He'd spoken in kindling.

"If you must. Smoke. Cigarettes. Then you must do so. On your own time. And off. *Off.* School property. Now. I do not care. If Paola approached you. Or if you approached Paola. Does not matter. Does. Not. Matter. If I ever. Ever. See you. Smoking. On school property. In the presence of a student. Even just once. I will end your employment. Do you. Understand?"

Celia had understood.

Paola, too, had understood. Celia had taken the heat. Celia had risked.

Had sacrificed.

After weeks of conspicuous avoidance —the looking away, the sharp course corrections in the school hallways, the iron door demeanor —Paola was suddenly a receptive presence. Her eyes found Celia's eyes easily. Her face, a tracking sunflower, following Celia's transit from one end of the classroom to the other. She lingered. Asked unnecessary questions. Pretended to smile.

And Celia had noticed. She had been careful not to overplay her hand. Had learned her lesson about the fragility of trust. If her self-sacrifice had earned

Paola's faith, or even just piqued her interest, then Celia had not wanted to do anything, say anything, to discourage those feelings.

It was now Celia's turn to be still in the forest. To be approached. Stalked.

The enmity of Paola's classmates had been palpable. If she had been disliked and excluded before the fight with Mandy Klutch, then she had been a pariah after her return from suspension. The whisper abuse continued in full force. Efforts to intimidate Paola with displays of unity –of strength in numbers –were daily.

But by then they were afraid of her. All of them. Each of them. The mob had no leaders. No courage. The campaign went no further than strutting.

Paola had shown no sign that they even existed. The only person that existed, suddenly, was her English teacher.

Ms. Morales. Celia.

It was the wind that had finally brought them together. Blowing over the Chihuahuan plain like the breath of an approaching dragon, heralding the coming of summer. The end of the school year had leant a strange desperation to the moment.

Desperation for each of them.

On her way to the parking lot, slanting into the gusts, Celia had seen Paola, leaning up against her *palo verde*. Had seen Paola see her. Had seen her waiting for something. Open. Receptive. The tracking sunflower.

Celia had waved. Kept moving.

At the car, Celia's door had flung open in the wind. Violently, like a newly unbound sail. The stapled sheaf of summer school guidelines had become a renegade kite, rattling into the wind. Celia had tossed her purse into the front seat. Slammed the car door. Moved forward in pursuit. Stopped.

Paola, appearing from out of nowhere, like something else caught up in the gust, had chased down the fly away papers. Threaded parked cars. Pinned the fluttering, flapping thing to the pavement with her foot. She had shaken the pages free of dirt, brushing them with her hand, as she made her way back to the car.

Celia had stood still in the wind. Watching. Beholding Paola like a timid heart beholds approaching wildlife. She had reached out slowly to take the papers from Paola's outstretched hand.

A scar. Still pink. Not deep. But deep enough.

Celia had not reacted. Had done her best to resist sudden movements and exclamation. Had tried to unsee what she had seen.

"Thank you," she said. "You're a lot faster than I am."

Paola had nodded once. Dropped her arm. Looked away.

"Can I maybe… Could I get a ride home?" Looked back. "I was supposed to take the bus today." Looked away. "I forgot. I missed it. Garvin can't pick me up."

Looked back.

The lie had been obvious enough. Paola had not forgotten anything.

The *implications* of the lie had bloomed behind Celia's eyes. Paola had been waiting for her. Planning this. Maybe for weeks. The waning days of the school year had finally forced her out into the open.

"Uh, yeah. Sure. Of course. Hop on in."

Doors closed. Seatbelts.

As they rolled away from the school, there had followed a flurry of directions. Paola pointing. Celia nodding, confirming. Paola correcting. Celia reconfirming. It all wrongly suggested that Paola had been interested in talking. That she was receptive to some kind of shallow conversation.

But once Celia knew how to find the house, Paola had fallen into silence. Watched the desert outside her window slip past and drop away. Celia had let the quiet go as long as she could.

"So," she'd said at last. "Your folks must be off busy with other things today."

Paola had not moved. Not spoken. Shrugged without looking. Two beats. Three.

Four.

"Guess you mean Garvin and Maria."

"Is that what you call them?"

"That's their names ain't it?"

"I'm just asking."

"Off doin' their twice a year thing."

"What thing is that?"

Paola might have looked over at Celia. Might have drawn a deep breath. Changed her tone. Cleared her throat. Paused. Sighed. *Something.*

But she had done none of those things. She had just said it. And she'd said it with all of the emotional investment of watching a barren strip of desert blurring into oblivion outside the car window.

"Garvin beats her 'til her face swells all up and Maria..."

A jolt from behind the wheel. Celia had turned and looked, shock in her eyes. "What?"

"Maria calls her sister Arlene. Then Arlene drives down and takes her away in the middle of the night. Then two days later Garvin gets in the car to go get her. Arlene lives all the way up in Haskell."

"Paola that's... that's *terrible.* Are you being serious?"

A slow nod at the window.

"Happens like twice a year. Three times last year. Takes two or three days. They'll be back. Actin' like nothin' happened. All lovey-dovey. Breath of Christ in their lungs. Blood of Christ in their hearts."

They rode in silence long enough for Celia to find a place to pull the car over to the side of the road. The eighteen-wheel cattle truck behind them had blared angrily at the sudden deceleration. Both of them, Celia then Paola, had turned to watch it pass.

Inside the slatted silver trailer, large dark shapes were shifting uncertainly. An eye. The tawny tip of horn. Then just the back of the truck, shrinking in the dust. Celia had squared herself to Paola. Locked eyes.

"This is not okay, Paola. This is not... Do you feel safe? Has he ever hurt you? Or your brother? Has he ever hurt Lyle?"

There had been a long moment then. Looking. Waiting. Another truck passing behind, rocking her little green car. Paola had shaken her head.

"Garvin drinks. Takes it out on Maria. Never lays a hand on me. All he really cares about when he ain't drinkin' is teachin' music and teachin' the Bible. I get a lot of both of those things I guess. Garvin likes to teach. Give his little sermons. Lyle don't take to music _or_ the Bible. Maybe 'bout the only ways he don't take after his daddy. Anyway. Garvin's never hit me. Never really hits Lyle neither." Paola had turned away. Back flat against the seat, looking out at the road. Celia had wanted to reach out and stroke her hair. "Even when Lyle deserves it."

"Nobody deserves that, Paola. Not anybody." She had suddenly felt her words insufficiently affirming. Like she was already betraying Paola's trust in opening up. "But I know Lyle has had his problems. I know."

Paola had given a small, counterfeit laugh. Looked away out the window.

"Lyle's just bein' Lyle. That's what Maria loves to say. Like every damn day she says that. Lyle's just bein' Lyle. None of us can help bein' who we really are. It's how God made us. Sometimes Lyle just can't help but be Lyle."

"Well." Silence. What to say to that? "I guess we all have our little things we need help with. Things we need to work on. I know when I was about your age..."

"Ms. Morales, why do you like me?"

The question had come without any warning. Pinned Celia to the driver's seat like an arrow through the windshield.

She did not have an answer. Best she could do was stall.

"I... can't you just call me Celia?"

"Why do you like me, Ms. Celia? Why'd you take that cigarette? Would you've done that for anyone else at school?"

"I don't..."

Something had elbowed Celia from inside. An unexpected jolt that drew her up short. As if Yolanda, aim as good as ever, had sat up in her grave and thrown one of her shoes at the back of Celia's head.

She had cleared her throat. Started again.

"No. I wouldn't have done that for anyone else."

"Why?"

"Because… I think you're special, Paola."

"Special how? You don't know nothin' about me."

"Sometimes you just… *know things.* Paola. Sometimes you just have a feeling about another person. And I have a feeling that there's no one like you in the whole world. I think you're going to grow up to…"

Another shoe from the grave.

"To do…"

Another shoe.

"To be… a wonderful person."

The words had sounded horrible to Celia. Alien. False. She had no idea who Paola would grow up to be. She had no words to explain the attraction. She had only grasped for words with the right sound to them.

She had pulled the car back out on to the road hoping new movement would bring answers. Or at least better sounds.

"First time I met you I thought to myself, now here is someone truly special. This is someone I could be great friends with. Maybe someone I'll be friends with the whole rest of my life."

"'Cause I remind you of your sister. Maggy. Like you said before." The tone had been part confirmation, part accusation.

Celia nodded. "Probably part of it. But I like you for you, Paola. For who you are. It's not all about Maggie. Maggie just got us started. Made the introduction."

Silence.

The road passed beneath them like a narrow, grey river. Paola pointed.

"Up there. Slow down or you'll miss it."

Celia had slowed. Turned. Aimed up the dirt road that was not much more than a line drawn out into the desert by a big stick, threading saguaro and scrub.

"You get in trouble?" Paola had asked. "With the principal?"

Celia nodded. "Yes. A little. Not too bad. Look, Paola. I'm worried for you. I don't like what you told me. About what's going on in your family."

A shrug. A sigh.

"You got any kids, Ms. Celia?"

Another arrow to the chest. She thought of the lost children. Maggie. Little Amalia. And the one she had named but never delivered. The one Yolanda died believing just never took.

"No."

"Why not?"

"Because… I… I'm not even married."

"If you were married would you want kids?"

"If I was married? Yes. I would."

"Boy or a girl?"

"Healthy. That's all I…"

"No." Something in the voice. Celia had ventured a look. The side of Paola's face was wet. Eyes red and narrow. Jaw clenched, pulsing. "Boy... or girl?"

"Girl. I'd want a girl. Paola, if you need help, I can get you help. If you need someone to talk to... If you..."

Paola wiped her cheek with the back of her hand.

"Don't want to talk. Don't want help. Don't go tryin' to fix me. Shouldn't have told you anyhow."

Hurt. Confusion.

"But... why not?"

A man had appeared on the road. Maybe an eighth of a mile ahead. Not walking. Just standing. Hands in his pockets.

Not a man. A large boy.

Lyle Cross.

Black t-shirt like a distant rectangular hole in the light brown earth.

Paola had opened the door without warning. Celia slammed on the brakes, skidding the car. The wind carried the dust away from them in pale brown billows.

"Stop! Wait. Paola, what are you doing?"

"I can walk from here," she'd said.

"I'll drive you the whole way. Let's just... Let's talk some more. Who is that up there? Is that Lyle?"

Paola had leaned against the open door, squinting in the wind. Hair flying. Already unreachable.

"I like you, Ms. Celia. Don't exactly know why. But I guess I do. I thank you for the ride. But you need to turn on around. If you want me to talk to you again sometime, if you really want to be my friend forever and ever amen, then that's just what you'll do. Turn around."

"You've got nothing to be ashamed of, Paola. All families have problems. I know you're adopted. Is that... I mean are you upset that..."

"Ain't adopted." Voice calm. Resolute. "That's just something Garvin and Maria like to say to people."

"Paola, wait. I don't understand."

"No you don't. Nobody does."

Paola had pushed the passenger door closed. Turned. Walked on up the road as Celia was opening the window, speaking through the widening crack.

"Paola..."

But she had kept putting one foot in front of the other. Getting smaller with every step. Reclaimed by wind and sun and desert. Her last words, blown back over her shoulders, were barely audible over the rushing air and idling engine.

"Go on, now."

Chapter 32

He starts with the door. Good a place as any.

It is a narrow thing for a door. It's blue. Bluish. Beneath all of the dirt and grime. Given the size, he thinks it must have belonged to a small bathroom. It's not scorched like most of the rest of the wood. The knob still turns.

Davis drags it behind him, over and through the heap of broken church. He throws it clattering into the back of the truck. It is the only sound out here, except for that background buzz that humanity knows as silence. The mash of infinitesimal movement. The invisible mortar of vibration connecting all things into one thing.

Looks at his watch. Four ten. He's been at it fifteen minutes now. Already thinking about when he can stop. Four to six, they agreed. Every day until it is done. Could have picked two to four. *Pepita's* would have let him work a different shift. But he'd thought two to four might be too hot for this kind of work.

Dallas Letti sure didn't care. Fifty bucks a load. Cash. She'd pay him every day. He could pick the money up on the drive out. Or when he came back to swap her truck for his bike.

Irony is, the scrubland is hotter now than it was at two. Air is cooler, but the land is like a glowing coal. Just from taking the solar abuse hour after hour.

He turns. Leans back against the truck. Beats his gloves against his leg.

The church, if that is what it was, is a ruin of broken, blackened glass and burnt lumber. Roof is mostly gone. Windows shattered. Not from the fire so much as from the bullets of scrub rats, hunting rabbits and looking for any kind of satisfaction.

Beneath the broken skeleton of the place is the trash heap of the living. Furniture. Clothing. Cookware. A weather-eaten Bible. Rotten bedding.

Because the structure had been more than a church. And less.

Beneath all of that, Davis is quite certain, are the snakes.

The boat, by contrast, was in surprisingly good shape. Three times as long as a Greyhound and twice as wide.

Boat. Dallas, in her fog of bourbon-breath, had called it a boat. *That damn boat.* An ark is what it really is. A wooden ark.

It was a hundred feet or so from the main structure, which is how it had survived the fire. Vandals had gotten to it. Scrub rats had lived in it. The elements had taken their toll. Bullet holes everywhere.

But there it is. A boat. An ark. The inspired labor of a couple of out-of-work Mississippian boat builders who had come out west to try their hand at ranching and ended up in the congregation of the First South Texas Fellowship of Charismatic Nazarenes. The pastor had thought it a brilliant idea. A beacon of hope in the desert.

Davis reaches in through the window of the truck. Takes out a water bottle. Drinks. Wipes his mouth. Tosses the bottle back on the seat.

He walks out a ways so he can see the front of the thing, which faces away from the church. Nods to himself. He was wrong about the blue door coming from a bathroom. In the middle of the ark is a doorway where two half-doors were supposed to swing outward into the drowning world. There is a faint bluish caste to the sun-bleached wood. Only one of the doors is hanging in the doorway.

"Tear the muthafucker apart is what I want you to do. Plank-by-plank. Brick-by-brick. Stone by fuckin' stone, boy. Haul *all* that shit away. Tired of lookin' at it."

Which was funny. Odd funny. Because Dallas Letti couldn't see either the church or the ark unless she walked or drove a quarter mile or so around a little out-cropping of scrub and cactus that hid the ruins from her home. And even then it was still nearly a half-mile away and up a small rise. She'd need to go out of her way. Something Davis suspected she never did.

Why would she? Nothing else around for miles in any direction.

Davis suspected that what Dallas Letti meant was that she was tired of knowing it was all still out here. Just knowing was enough.

He walks back up to the church. House. Whatever. Grabs the aluminum shower curtain rod he uses for a staff. Resumes poking at things. Turning them over from a distance. Looking for diamondbacks.

When he feels good about a little patch of rubble, he leans the curtain rod against the wall and starts heaving things into the back of the truck. When he is done with that little patch, he picks up the curtain rod again.

On the third patch, probably his last for the day, he sticks the curtain rod into the cavity of a green, ceramic jardinière. The pot is still in one piece and small enough for him to lift up into the air with the pole. He wants to sling it sideways, right to left, into the back of the truck.

It is a medium-sized bullsnake that is inside the pot. Not a diamondback. Harmless. Doesn't matter. All snakes look the same in that first second.

Everything falls at once. Pot. Pole. Snake. Like a clump of wet rope onto the ground. Davis too. Landing in the dirt. Crabbing backwards frantically toward the truck. The snake slides off in the other direction, over the pole and the broken green shards of ceramic. Back to the nearest pile of rubble to begin setting up the next heart attack.

Davis picks himself up. Brushes off the dirt. Reclaims the curtain rod.

He picks up the triangular pieces of ceramic and begins tossing them into the bed of the truck. The last piece is the biggest. It still has some curve to it. He takes off his glove. Wipes it clean with his thumb.

The memory surprises him more than had the snake.

The ceramic of his memory is blue, not green. But it has that same smooth finish and those same jagged edges. It is broken just the same.

The ceramic of his memory is in the shape of a blue whale. Painted, smiling mouth. Tail curving up off the bookcase. Geranium sprigs sprouting from its back like sea spray.

His mother had been on the floor. Crying and picking up pieces of whale and handfuls of soil. Davis was still in his pajamas, sitting in the chair by the window, looking out at the place on the driveway where his father's truck should have been.

Why was he so mad? He felt he should have known the answer.

He had heard the whole fight, laying in his bed with a knot in his stomach the size of his head. He had heard it all, right up to the detonation of the whale against the wall and the slamming of the front door.

But he still didn't know.

"*Why was he so mad?*"

She'd sniffled. Wiped her nose. "*I don't know, Davis. He's not very happy sometimes. He gets frustrated with me.*"

"*But why?*"

"*I don't know.*"

It was a lie. Even Davis knew better.

"*Was he drunk?*"

"*Yes.*"

"*Where did he go?*"

"*I don't know, honey. Church maybe. Church helps him. His God brings him comfort when he is upset.*"

"*God is for everybody, mom.*"

"*Go back to bed, Davis. Or watch cartoons. Everything's okay. He'll be fine. He just needs some time alone. Away from me.*"

A kind of panic had taken him before he could dwell on those last words.

"*Will he be back in time to take me to the party? It's at two o'clock, mom. Will he be back by then? Mom, will dad be back by then?*"

"*I don't know, Davis.*"

"He said he'd take me to the party! Mom? Everyone will be there!"

She had looked up at him then, eyes red and horrible but doing their job. Discerning. Reading the landscape of his emotions.

"Davis, you know none of this is about you, don't you? You know we both love you. We weren't fighting about you."

"I'm supposed to be there at two o'clock. And we have to drive there first. Where is he? Where did he go? Should we go to the church and get him?"

She had looked. Blinked. Wiped.

"Bring me the trashcan. Help me throw this mess away."

It was a trick, of course. To bring him near.

He had trudged into the kitchen. Pulled the trashcan from beneath the sink. Dragged it out into the living room. Knelt. Picked up a shard of porcelain. He didn't know why he was crying. The night of screaming. Seeing his mother crying on the floor. The broken whale. The party suddenly in jeopardy. Everything.

But she knew. She had taken his hand.

"You know I love you, Davis. You know I would do anything for you. Right? You know that. Whatever happens today. I will be there for you. I'm not going anywhere."

"But we have to go! Everyone will be there, Mom. I'm supposed to go."

"I know, baby."

"I'm supposed to go. I'm supposed to go."

"I want you to know I'm not going anywhere."

But she had. She had gone somewhere.

The memory dissolves, atomizing. It recombines with fragments of time. Place. People. Events. All long gone but still in his brain like a scent on the breeze.

His crazy Aunt Tallulah. Disheveled gray hair. Broken front tooth. Scorching pink lipstick. Sitting on the bench outside the funeral home. Davis was in the chair against the railing. Wanting the world to stop. Wanting darkness. Wanting silence. He hadn't seen Tallulah in two years. She kept talking.

"Because she was supposed to go. It was her time, Davis. When it's your time, Hon, you just go. Don't matter how or who. Simple. You go. 'Cause you know it's what you have to do. Don't go blamin' yourself none."

His mother called her Tullah. And Tullah loved her little sister. So she was dressed up for the service as best as she could. It was a dress of sorts, like pink frosting with a slash of olive green to trim the bottom hem. Might have been dirt. Dried mud. Pig shit. She was a farmer's wife. Didn't have any church clothes. Not that she needed any. Back in Abilene where Tallulah and his Uncle Dizz lived they wouldn't let her back into the church for Sunday service. Tullah liked to stand up in the back and take issue with the sermon. *Shushing* her only made it worse.

"I know at the service they said she's with God. But she ain't with God, Davis. Is

no God. Not like they teach anyway. She ain't with no white-bearded man in the sky. She's a part of the Motherverse now. What I call it anyways. You know what that is? The Motherverse?"

He hadn't answered. He would have waited in the car, but it was locked.

"Boy?"

Davis sighed. Shook his head.

"It's energy. That's all it is. Energy all around us. Not electricity. Energy."

She had leaned forward on the bench. Elbows to knees. Her hands were rough and large and permanently dirty. Fingers always twitching in the air like two five-legged scrub critters looking for anything they could dig into, pulling at the leashes attached to Tallulah's shoulders. Davis could hear his father's voice inside the funeral home talking to someone. Tallulah had kept at it.

"But it's a maternal energy, see. You know what maternal is, Davis? Means mother. The God of the church is all about the father. Judgin'. Accusin'. Condemnin'. The universe is our mother. The Motherverse is love and sadness. It protects us. Looks out for us. Mourns us. It feels what we feel. It knows everything. Sees everything. Everything that happened and everything that will happen. May not happen for fifty years. A hundred years. A thousand. The Motherverse still already knows it. Has already seen it. We are each born from her, see. And when we die we each go back to her. Like Einstein said E equals MC or whatnot, only the E stands for energy and the M stands for mother and the C stands for children. We are all children of the Motherverse. You understand, Hon?"

She was trying to help. Trying in her way to cushion the blow. Make sense.

Davis had nodded. Not understanding anything. Not anything about anything any more ever again. Wanting blackness. Wanting silence. Cold dark water was everywhere in his mind. Sloshing. Reeking of death.

"People call me crazy. Maybe I am. But your mama and me were the same, Davis. Lizzy just knew how to play along, see. For your daddy. You know how upset he gets. Not his fault, I guess. He got his religion from his daddy and so on. People will go along with anything for love. That's why I kept my peace back at the church this morning. Preacher talkin' all 'bout the bosom of Lord Jesus. Lizzy would'a let all that nonsense go on by. Just because of your daddy. So I kept my peace. But we were the same, Lizzy and me."

He could hear his father's name from inside the funeral home. Condolences. Back slapping in the way men hug each other. Talk of the weather.

"When my mama died, your grandmother, Mama Mae, I was just twenty-nine. Your mama was near 'bout eighteen. Thought my life was over right then. Mama Mae and I was close. All of my man troubles? Lordy. Mama was 'bout my only friend in the world. Lizzy didn't care much for me back then. She was a bit wild and not at home. Daddy was a drinker. Your Uncle Gus was off with his girl. Anyway, I moped around for one month after another. Nothin' was right in my life. Nothin'.

Weren't worth a spit. One day I walked two miles up to the dry quarry and sat right down on the edge, danglin' my feet. I had made up my mind, see. I was done with it. All of it. I kicked off my shoes. Stripped off all my clothes. Watched them fall, one by one. Said all my goodbyes inside my head. Said a little prayer for my baby sister 'Lizabeth inside my head. You know what happened?"

Davis had looked up then. Tallulah was staring at him. He had no idea what happened. He only knew what didn't happen. Because there she was. Still talking.

"Little bird, one of them Chachalacas, come from outta nowhere behind me, making its god-awful noise. Just about startled me right off that cliff. Ziggin' this way and zaggin' that way. Like it knew it was about to be picked up into the hooks of some Mississippi Kite or a Red Tail. And then maybe 'bout a minute later here come the mama Chachalaca. Talkin' to it in the way they do. And wouldn't you know it, that little thing sat right down in the dirt and didn't move a feather. Mama bird come up, says a few things, and the two of them head off together. Straight line, calm as you please. Now... you ever known a calm, straight-walkin' Chachalaca in your whole life?"

Davis shook his head.

"No ma'am."

"Me neither. Realized right then that Mama Mae knew what I was up to and that she had arranged it so those two birds were right there... in that very spot... at that very moment. That's when I started believin' in the Motherverse. Mama Mae was out there somewhere that I couldn't go. But she could come to me, see. She could reach me. She wasn't gone. She was everywhere."

Tallulah had spread her arms so wide she smacked the wall of the funeral home behind her.

"Everywhere! So I got myself up off a that ledge and walked on back home, naked as the day I was born. People talk about how they's born again into the arms of Jesus? Well I was born again into the arms of the Motherverse."

His father had been there in the doorway of the funeral home. Arms crossed. Listening to the last of it. He never liked Aunt Tallulah.

No. That's not fair. He hated Tallulah.

"Gettin' late, Davis."

It is getting late. The eastern horizon has begun to brood. Begun to gather up the day. Bagging the light like shafts of cut straw piled in a darkening field.

A movement brings him back. A small desert hare, darting from one clump of rubble to the next. Ears like enormous sails catching the last gusts of sun. He twitches beneath a broken stool seat. Listens.

He blends perfectly. Camouflaged against the desert floor like a soft stone.

It is his softness that sets him apart. Gives him away amid all the hot, dry harshness. That's what will betray him in the end. Some of these piles of debris have eyes. They all see him coming.

Davis carries the piece of broken green ceramic to the back of the truck. In his peripheral vision the weathered ark is a hulking presence he cannot name.

A mountain. A silent crowd. A carcass of whale.

He tosses the piece into the truck. It breaks over a corner of the blue door that had started his afternoon. He picks up one of the smaller shards. Runs his thumb over it. The smooth curvature. The jagged edge. Puts it in his pocket.

Chapter 33

The desk has some curve to it. A ninety-degree bend right in the middle. Like a high-gloss boomerang lost its way in a Houston office park, wedging itself in the corner of a medium-sized room. Little higher and it might have smashed through the windows and kept on flying.

It looks out across a parking lot at the *Houston Dentistry* building.

Sheldon Davis sits right in the crook of the boomerang. Face to the windows. Taking refuge in the only glimmer of good dumb luck he has seen in a long time.

For he had been saved.

Saved by a fish. *Shiners* they're called. Little tiny, silvery things.

He had been saved in the way a cheating politician is saved by an even bigger headline. The people who might have cared, even violently, suddenly do not care at all because there are other more important things to care about. Assassination. Royal weddings. Stock market crashes. High rise infernos. Thousand year hurricanes.

The first two times, Grayson Tate had asked him politely. Casual curiosity. *Not-to-pry, but...* He wanted to know how Sheldon and his lawyer were coming in their discussions with the *Chachalaca Gazette*. How goes the fight to clear his good name? Sheldon had, so he thought, successfully placated his father-in-law with assurances that were long on vigor and short on detail.

But that third inquiry.

It had been stripped of any deferential pretension that Grayson was concerned about Sheldon. Or that the matter was really any of Grayson's business. It was a phone call. So he couldn't actually see Grayson poking himself in the chest. But he could feel it.

"It's *my* goddamned business and it's *my* goddamned daughter and it's *my* goddamned reputation and it's *my* goddamned deal and so help me God boy if you fuck up this deal for me –for us, for *us*, Shelly; for me and you and Christi – if you fuck up this deal because some third-rate rag and the Sheriff of Bumfuck Texas caught you in a Corbin whorehouse with your pants down, then... then..."

Grayson hadn't finished. He had breathed heavily into the phone. Sheldon had listened. Panicked. Heart climbing up into his throat. The tirade had slipped sideways out of a perfectly calm discussion about the new spate of Corbin River Walk press releases that Sheldon was overseeing. And then suddenly Grayson was on fire about the *Chacha* drama. As he listened, Sheldon had hurriedly arranged in his head more words of assurance. Words that might, as they had in the past, at least buy him some time.

He had tried. But the words of assurance never had a chance.

"I don't want to hear about all that, Shel. I'm tired of hearing you try to talk this away. I want you to set up a meeting. You, me and your goddamned lawyer. We need to kick this thing in the ass. Set it up and call me."

That right there might have been the beginning of the end. Sheldon had no lawyer. He had not contacted the editor of the *Chacha*. He had not sent so much as an angry letter.

But it was *not* the beginning of the end. He had been saved.

Saved, as it turns out, by a kind of fish.

"Goddamned little... little fuckin' things! Fuckin' fish! Endangered my ass!"

"Daddy, stop. You turnin' the air blue is not gon' solve the problem."

Christi had poured him a bourbon and put a plate of food in front of him. Neither had done much good.

Sheldon had busied himself in the kitchen, trying to stay as clear of Grayson as possible. As though his father in law was some kind of wasp hurling itself angrily into the walls and windows and furniture. Made no sense to to be in the vicinity when, inevitably, the wasp decided to go off about Corbin whores and then sink his stinger into someone's eyeball.

"Nothin' but nothin' is gonna solve the problem but kickin' New Mexico's ass out of the goddamned union. Those fuckers don't give a good goddamned about the fish. The only thing they care about is kickin' shit on our boots."

The fish in question was the Pecos Bluntnose Shiner. Little tiny things. Sleek, silver minnows, each about the size of an extended middle finger. Historically, they inhabited the 320-mile stretch of the Pecos River from Santa Rosa, New Mexico down to the Carlsbad area. More recently, their territory has shriveled to a mere 200 miles from Fort Sumner down to the Brantley Reservoir.

The Shiner population was under assault. Water diversion and impoundment. Habitat modification and destruction. Water pollutants. Inadequate protection of habitat and in-stream flow. As the United States Government saw things, such assaults put the Pecos Bluntnose Shiner on the list of threatened and endangered species.

Not something that would ordinarily spin Texans into a flurry of emotion.

Except that the waters in which the little Shiners reproduce flowed out of New Mexico and into Texas, burbling on its way to rejoin the Rio Grande.

Whatever concern may exist for the Pecos Bluntnose, everybody in the desert cares about the water.

Everybody. Especially Grayson Tate.

As patiently as his temper would allow, Grayson had laid out the historical context. Since 1948, he had explained, New Mexico and Texas have been signatories to an agreement, approved by Congress, called the Pecos River Compact, limiting the amount of water that New Mexico can divert from its journey into Texas. It also established a framework within which to resolve disputes, creating the Pecos River Commission, comprised of one commissioner from each of the two states and a nonvoting representative of the federal government. Christi hadn't understood.

"Well can't *our* people on the Commission just out-vote *their* people?"

"Baby doll." There had been a long, labored breath of patience. "We don't have *people* on the Commission. Texas has one *person*. New Mexico has one *person*."

"So then it's a tie. How do you break a tie vote?"

"You can't. You can't break a fuckin' tie. The feds can't vote but if they could they'd vote against us outta concern for the goddamned fish. But the whole thing is horseshit anyway, honey, pure horseshit, 'cause Texas does not −*DOES NOT* −need the Commission's approval for the diversion of water to Corbin because this is all happenin' in Texas territory. None of this is in New Mexico. It's all *Texas* water we're talkin' about. Commission has no say in this and New Mexico goddamned knows it. They just want to fuck us over a barrel because Texas has been blocking their project to divert water north of Lake Avalon."

"Well then why are we... blockin' their 'lil project or whatever?"

Because the Avalon thing is *OUR* goddamned business, even though it's in New Mexico, because in the long run it will deplete the water flow into Texas. But they're good and pissed about it because they want the water. The purpose of the Commission is to protect *Texas*, not goddamned New Mexico. Pecos flows down, not up. It flows *THIS* way," Grayson had pointed in a stabbing motion with his steak knife, "not *THAT* way."

"Well then they can't stop us. We can just go on about our business."

"Christi, you're sweet as a peach but it's like you don't listen to a goddamned thing I'm sayin'. They're takin' us to federal court to get an injunction."

"New Mexico is suing Texas? Can it do..."

"Not the state of New Mexico, darlin'. It's this goddamned environmental group, whatever the fuck it's called, Environmental Conservation Alliance or some such horseshit. But New Mexico is propping them up, see. Using this lawsuit as leverage to get our guy on the Commission to drop Texas' objection to their water diversion project up near Avalon. It's all horseshit. They're sayin' they found," and here Grayson, still holding his utensils, had tried to make dramatic air quotes around the phrase "potentially sustainable populations of minnow."

Sheldon, looking up from the bag of trash he was tying in the kitchen, had thought Grayson looked like a vengeful, mustachioed cat clawing his way in through a screen door. Like he was ready to savage whatever was on the other side of the screen, dismember it with a knife and a fork and commence eating.

"They found those... those minnow fish things in Texas?" Christi had asked.

"Yes, in Texas. South of Red Bluff Lake, before the Salt Creek inflow."

"Well, Daddy, is that even true?"

Grayson had looked at his daughter like she was speaking a foreign language with a southern accent. Sheldon had felt a twinge of sympathy for his wife, imagining what it must have been like, ponies and antebellum dollhouses aside, to grow up under the thumb of Grayson Tate.

"How the hell should I know if it's true? Christi? You seen me on my hands and knees up in goddamned Pecos, my head in the river lookin' for a goddamned fish the size of a goddamned pinky? I don't give a goddamned if it's true. I can't afford to have this project tied up in a courtroom over a goddamned fish. I told the Russians there was no way New Mexico could fuck us up. And here we are. This could drag on for years."

"Well... what are you gonna do?"

"What am I gonna do? Saddle up and work my contacts to put the squeeze on the friendlies in the goddamned New Mexico senate is what I'm gonna do. They either need to pull the plug on this nonsense or we need to give them what they want up in Avalon so that we can have what we want for this project."

"Which is what, exactly?"

"Goddammit Christi! Which is just a little goddamned trickle of Pecos River spit to loop around Corbin so that you can go shopping and eat lunch looking at gondolas and listening to live jazz in the middle of the goddamned desert! *That* is what we want! Goddamned river water at the goddamned Corbin Moon Garden Festival!"

Christi had stopped asking questions. She sat across from him at the table and watched him stab at his steak, shaking his head.

"Goddamned desert," he said more softly. "They don't have these problems in Florida. I'm gonna have to call the goddamned Russians tomorrow."

And so, suddenly, Sheldon's progress or lack thereof with the editors of the *Chachalaca Gazette* was the very last thing on Grayson Tate's mind. He had been saved, if only temporarily, by a fish in the desert.

Movement behind him. April March sticks her head in the door to Sheldon's office. Waits for him to make eye contact. He looks up. Swivels.

"Can't find it," she says

"Well it's here somewhere," he replies, looking up. "I know I've seen it."

"You've looked through all that stuff there?"

April points an accusing bright red fingernail to an uneven stack of paper on the corner of his polished boomerang desk. She is a sprightly twenty years younger than he is and she looks ten years younger than that. And yet her tone carries a scolding, slightly maternal quality, as if to say: *if I find the thing I have been looking for all mornin' right there on your desk, you are going to be in one big mess of trouble, young man.*

He finds this quality in her mildly annoying, deciding to blame her parents, Dale and Lydia March, friends of Christi's. It was for Dale and Lydia that he had hired April as an associate at Houston Market Research. Parents named *March* who decide to call their daughter *April* are, from the very beginning, burdening the world with a mild annoyance.

Sue would have been a better name, he thinks to himself. Short for Sousa.

"I've looked through that stack three times. It's not there."

"Well it's not in the file, Sheldon." One hand on her tiny hip. Head cocked in a *ball's-in-your-court-now* sort of way. Sheldon sighs.

"I told you, April, I took it out of the file and put it in one of those green folders. It's all in a lime green..."

He breaks off. Mouth open. Eyes fixed but unseeing.

"What?" she asks, tone cresting into condescension. "Are we remembering now? Where is it?"

He can see it now. In the trunk of the car.

Just as the briefcase lid is closing.

Beneath a very large pecan tree.

In Corbin.

He was certain he had brought the green folder back into the office from his car. Hadn't he? He plays the memory reel in his head. Watches himself, in slow motion, pulling the briefcase out of the trunk.

And the folder was in the briefcase. Right?

Or was the folder... *not...* in... the briefcase? *Shit.*

"No. I have no idea," he lies, shrugging. "Keep looking, I guess."

Shit.

April March spins and heads back into the hallway. Starts to close the door.

"April," he calls after her. Her head reappears with a face of *what-am-I-going-to-do-with-you* exasperation. "Forget it," he says. "I think I can mostly duplicate those documents. Go ahead and get back to something more productive. Thanks for looking."

It was not true, of course. He could not reproduce the documents. Not all of them anyway. The list of Corbin property owners was easy enough. But not his notes of his conversations with some of those property owners. Property owners who had told him that they had not, in fact, sold their property to the Corbin

Development Corporation. Property owners who had never even heard of the CDC. Who had no intention of selling anything.

Property owners like Libby Holder.

He watches the little glimmering fish in his head. The little Bluntnose Shiner. Swimming off into the blackness of his existence. He sees the self-delusion now for what it was: a diversion from bigger worries. Choosing to assure himself about the single piranha rather than the circling shark. Saved? He had *not* been saved. Not in the least.

Sure, Grayson Tate was off his back about the *Chachalaca* for a second or two, but so what? That was now the very least of his growing list of problems.

At the top of the list? Extortion. Blackmail. He, Sheldon Davis, was being blackmailed. The plain truth of that word still shocked him. *Blackmail.*

By a couple of cheap Corbin whores.

The images were indelible now. They are a kind of tattoo. A moving stain.

The moving stain is a clear –shockingly clear –video of a man, white, not quite pear-shaped, wearing only light blue boxers, waistband tucking up under the slightly protruding dough of his midsection, boxer fabric as taught and triangular as a sideways big-top tent.

The man's hands are behind his back, tied with long, purple stockings that swish across the backs of his blinding white legs.

The man is blindfolded with a pair of leopard-skin panties. A sagging leg hole is looped beneath his nose.

The man is… how to put it… *dancing* of a sort. Wiggling. Jutting. Thrusting. Swaying. Doing a circular, stirring thing with his waist. An invisible hula-hoop.

Also… the man is trying to eat a penis-shaped cookie from the cleavage of a kimono-draped bosom.

There is no soundtrack to the video. The moving stain. But no matter. Sheldon can hear it in his head, Bessie Smith weeping and moaning about her careless love, bringing in the wrong man and leaving the sins for which she must atone.

He can hear Bessie in his head because he, Sheldon Davis, husband of Christabelle Tate Davis, son-in-law of Grayson Tate, is that man. Not the man in the song. The man in the song was a woman; a black Asian whore named Liberty Cherish. He, *Sheldon,* is the man in the video bobbing for the penis cookie. Plain as day.

Smiling. Laughing. *Dancing.*

In the upper left corner of the video is a darkish blur. It never moves. Like someone's finger was partly over the lens.

But he knows it is not a finger. He knows it's a feather.

He remembered his initial disquiet in that parlor. In his head, he can see the feathered *Mardis Gras* masks on every wall and behind the bed. Scores of hollow black eyes and lip-lined crescents for mouths. Like little empty funhouse caverns.

Not so hollow and empty after all it seems. And not so fun.

Sheldon had eventually smashed the flash drive with a hammer on the floor of his garage with far more force than was necessary, plastic bits skittering off into the corners. The thing was dead. He'd swept it up in a dustpan and dumped it in the trash with the torn up envelope in which it had been delivered.

Didn't matter. It was all in his head now. Playing on a loop. No way to destroy *that* short of beating his head with a hammer. Which was tempting. He had not had a solid night's sleep since. He knew it was only a matter of time before they made a demand. Every day he waited and every night he did not sleep.

But there was no demand.

Days. Then weeks. A month. He had fought back the hope that the Corbin whores had lost interest. They were in prison. Or they were dead. Maybe they had overdosed on narcotic cookies. Or they had found Jesus and abandoned their criminal ways.

He had fought it mightily. The hope.

Should have known better. Hope is like water, seeping beneath the walls, down into the dry foundation. A trickle is all it takes. It weakened him. Could they be done? Could it be over? Flash drive smashed to bits and that was it. Right?

He had begun to believe.

And then, one day, one stupid sunny Saturday when the air smelled of honeysuckle and the bees were drunk in the garden, he had returned from the hardware store to find an envelope wedged into the crack of his front door.

An envelope like the others. Light blue. The color of his boxers.

A caldron of hot lead had emptied into his chest as he stood on his colonnaded porch and stared at the light blue envelope, utterly dumbfounded that the thing he had expected had finally... *actually...* happened.

It had been an incredibly good fortune that it was he, Sheldon, who had found the envelope and not Christi. Or Grayson. But that good fortune was nearly lost in that moment. Nothing in that moment felt like good fortune.

He had read it in the bathroom. Door closed. Toilet seat down. Fan on.

Dear Sheldon.

The sight of his own name was a punch in the face. It was like the word on the page was looking to break the nose that the Corbin whores had almost broken.

> *Dear Sheldon. I will assume this letter is coming as no surprise. I have spent
> a lot of time in a hospital bed thinking about what you have done to me.
> I have spent a lot of time thinking about how I want to respond.*

He has read it a dozen times. He knows the awful thing by heart now. It is a smartly written letter. It does not mention the video. Does not threaten its release. And why should it? The strategic, poison arrow release of the video, was implied. The collapse of his marriage, implied. The ruination of his business standing. All implied. Unless he gave them what they wanted, all of that, impliedly, would come to pass. They did not need to spell out the words "unlawful extortion".

And what did they want? Money. Of course. It was all about money. A quarter of a million dollars to be exact.

Quarter. Million.

But the whores had had the sense to make the letter more about injury than money. To the extent money was a part of the equation it was only about *"just compensation." "Fair recovery." "Far less than the anticipated damage award."*

On the face of the letter, money had nothing whatsoever to do with the fact that they had his marriage and career by the balls and that unless he obliged their demands they would begin to squeeze.

No, the letter was not explicitly about extortion. Olivia DeLuna had been injured in the accident. She had almost died. She had been in a coma. Now she walked with a limp. She has been disfigured. The hospital bills were astronomical.

"Just compensation." "Fair compensation." "Anticipated recovery of damages."

In fact, the quarter-million-dollar demand had been held out to him as a bargain; a generous gift, given that the *"anticipated damages"* had been estimated by Olivia DeLuna's *"lawyers"* to be closer to two to three million. She was having a bargain-basement sale just so that he might avoid the time and expense of defending a lawsuit he would lose anyway.

How thoughtful. It was a gift, really. Not extortion.

Problem was, the letter was not from a lawyer. The letter, hand written, was from Olivia DeLuna. And Olivia DeLuna was a whore. She did not have a lawyer. Whores did not have money to hire lawyers and whores did not recover money from Texas juries. It was all a bluff designed to cover up the fact that this was not about *"just compensation"* and the *"anticipated recovery of damages"* but about extortion plain and simple. He had two weeks to pay up or suffer the consequences.

Two weeks.

Not that Sheldon doubted Olivia DeLuna's misery. For a moment there, when her boot had wedged behind the steering wheel and the blood from her head was pooling on the roof of the overturned car, he had thought she was dead.

But while there was no doubt she had been badly injured –and maybe she *had* been in a coma, and maybe she *did* walk with a limp and maybe she *was* disfigured, all of which was truly terrible –the problem was that Sheldon Davis had not caused the accident.

He had *saved* her from certain flaming death.

Yes, he had been trying to get her attention on the road. Yes, he had been angry and she might have misunderstood his intentions. But his car had never touched her car. He had stayed cleanly within the passing lane. She was the one who had swerved inexplicably toward him and then for the shoulder. Her tires had left the pavement and she had over-corrected without cutting her speed, flipping her piece-of-crap Honda onto its back.

She did all of that. *She* did. Not him. Her injuries, however regrettable, were not his fault.

The Troopers had looked into the accident and then they had closed the investigation. *Closed.* Sheldon knew this because he had called the investigating officer –*Sgt. Stephen P. Karluck* –personally, to learn what he could about Olivia DeLuna's injuries. And Sgt. Stephen P. Karluck had informed him that he did not have that information and that even if he did have that information he was not authorized to release it and that the most he could tell Sheldon was that the investigation was officially closed. Officially…*closed.*

So, *the law* did not think he had done anything wrong. He knew it and Olivia DeLuna knew it. The letter was not about lawsuits. The letter was about extortion. It was about salacious videos. It was about his wife and his father-in-law and his business and his good name. It was about money. A quarter of a million dollars.

All of that was bad enough. And now there was one more thing. To the flaming pyre of shit burning in his head, in which glowed his wallet, his credit cards, his watch, his wedding ring, a newspaper article, and now *three* light blue envelopes from Corbin Texas whores –all of which were burning dangerously close to his reputation, his marriage, and his career, or at least the sizeable part of his career that was underwritten by Grayson Tate –he could add the lime green folder.

Shit.

He considered the papers inside the lime green folder. Watched them in his mind. Could see the pages blackening and curling into flame. Slowly scorching into a trail of smoke rising high enough in the sky for Grayson to see it all the way from Houston.

But why would they care? What use were those papers to Corbin whores? They were just notes. Lists of names and property descriptions. Circles, underlines, checkmarks. Marginalia scrawl indecipherable by anyone but him.

What would they want with any of that? Nothing maybe.

What else had been in that folder?

He closes his eyes. Tries to remember. What else? Nothing. Just the lists and his notes. Right?

No. Something else. There was something else. Because when he pulled out the lists and his notes there was still a rectangle of white remaining in the folder. He remembers white, not green. It was something he had read once and no longer needed to…

Sheldon opens his eyes. Remembering. *Shit.*

The *memo* was in the folder. The memo. Gregor Buchvarov's big-picture memo to the CDC Board of Directors laying out his vision of the ten-year Corbin Redevelopment Plan.

So the whores had Quinco International's aspirational blue prints for a wetter, greener, revitalized Corbin.

Sheldon considers this. So? Does he even care? The memo was probably four years old and there was nothing in it particularly sensitive or confidential. From the New York desk of Quinco Executive VP Gregor Buchvarov, down to the Corbin Development Corporation board, down to Adrian Hewitt and his team, down to the troops on the front lines in Texas like Grayson Tate and Sheldon Davis and the hard working staff of Houston Market Research. The memo had been disseminated to just about everybody. For a supposedly confidential document, it was very public. Far greater details of the Corbin Redevelopment Plan had been disseminated to the press on multiple occasions and in a variety of ways.

That, in fact, was Sheldon's job: *to get the information out there.* Houston Market Research had quite strategically injected that information out into the marketplace. Business interests had aligned. Political interests had coalesced. Property values had responded.

So why did he care if a couple of hookers had the original memo?

He didn't care.

Did he? No. He didn't.

But why would *they* care? What use would common prostitutes have for ten sheets of paper —a wide-vision think-piece sprinkled with hypothetical cost projections and outdated market assumptions —that they could not possibly understand? He does not know the answer to that question.

And that bothers him.

His head hurts. Worry, once a splinter in his brain, has become a jagged, bark-crusted spear that twists in place, goring his sanity. He needs sleep. He can't sleep. Not for many days, now. When sleep finds him, it is never for more than a couple of consecutive hours. His eyes are heavy and hot in their sockets. He can taste the acid in his stomach. There is no clear way forward.

The way forward is backward. Retreat. He longs to go back to his insanely hot postage stamp studio, years ago, where he sat alone day after day with a beat-up six-string and a third-hand keyboard, recording television and radio jingles for the cost of frozen dinners.

Most of the jingles had been awful. Unforgivable affronts to the tower of song, as Leonard Cohen might put it. How does one wrap a melody around *Texas Pete's Rodeo Supply?* Not the lyrics; the melody. And even if that were possible —and Sheldon had proven that it was, in fact, possible —how did one, supposedly an *artist,* look at oneself in the mirror?

226

And yet, in so many ways, that life had been preferable. Yes, he had been lonely. Yes, he had been poor. And frustrated. Sure. All of that. But he had also been his own man. And strangely optimistic. He had the optimism of a man with very little to lose in the world. Change was always right around the corner.

Texas Pete, he's our guy
He's the name in Rodeo Supply
Shoe that hoof and barrel that clown
Texas Pete is the hoss in town

Turned out to be an awfully long corner. But, eventually there it was. Change. Waiting. He met Christabelle Tate and then his life had almost instantly ceased to resemble itself. Point is that in those days, in that life, change always *could* be right around the corner. That was the thing; it *could* be. It *would* be. That was the optimism of those days. It *would* be. Wasn't the change itself he missed. It was the anticipation of it.

Break that bull and rope that filly
Come see Pete 'tween Polk and McGilly

Jingles had paid the bills, as they say. Or at least some of the bills. And that had given him some time to himself. Time to himself, *for* himself. Creative time. Time to write. Time to dream. Time to want.

So it was not only the optimism of that era that he remembered so fondly. It was the romance of it. The romance of yearning to render in music what could never be captured in life. What could never be owned. Back in the day, before writing jingles had turned into an advertising business, music and longing were lovers. In that creative dalliance, money had all the relevance of unicorns.

And for all of the destitution and loneliness, he had had no worries and nothing to lose. Unlike now. Now, for all of his wealth, and for the status of his associations, he had nothing to wake up to except the worry of what he had to lose.

Sheldon leans back in his chair. Pulls the letter out of his front pocket. He has moved it from one pair of pants to another, from front pocket to front pocket, since he found it wedged in the crack of his front door.

He opens it up on top of the boomerang desk. Flattens it out with his hands. He finds the number, pinning it with a finger to the polished wood. Reaches for the phone. Dials.

Hangs up. Sighs. Dials again.

He hangs up the phone. Slowly. Like it is a delicate piece of equipment. Like it might explode.

Two weeks, it said. Two weeks had expired yesterday.

Coward. Fucking coward.

"Numbers are in," chirps April March, suddenly in his door.

Sheldon starts. He turns to look at her. She is dangling a thin sheaf of papers by the corner with two fingers. "Our saturation levels in Dallas are spotty. We can do better. Want me to set up a call with Steadman? Map out another ad buy?"

"I'm going home," he says, reaching for his keys. "I can't shake this migraine. The numbers and Steadman will have to wait. Call Holly. See what she thinks."

He stands, pushes past April into the hall.

"Hope you feel better," she says, disappointed. She has furrowed her baby smooth brow to convey worry.

Sheldon stops. Turns. Retraces his steps back to the boomerang. He grabs the letter and folds it, returning it to his front pocket. *Idiot*, he thinks to himself.

"Thanks," he says, passing her again. "It'll all work out."

He drives directly for home. He wants to lie down. Wants to sleep. But he knows sleep will never come. *Coward. Fix this, goddammit!*

He imagines having called and accepted her proposal. Imagines meeting her to discuss his surrender. Imagines a time and place.

Where does he get that kind of money? He doesn't. It would have to come from the business. And it would have to be a cash deal. He couldn't risk a trail of bank transfers. Grayson has access to all of the business finances. *Shit.*

And where would he meet her? Corbin? No. He was not going back to Corbin. Maybe not ever. Houston? No. Too close to home.

And what was he to say to her, anyway? She would be expecting a quarter million dollars. What was he to say?

A quarter-million. Jesus. He did not have that kind of money just laying around. He couldn't get a quarter-million dollars if his life depended on it. Even from the business. Not without people noticing.

Not that he could risk telling her that. She would want to show him that Corbin whores meant business. That they wouldn't just go away with poor-mouth excuses. He needed to play along. He needed time.

Of course, if she thought that he was going to hand her a quarter-million dollars in cash, in person, then she would not be alone. Someone would be there with her. *For* her. Watching. Listening. Who? How many? With what instructions? Intimidate him? Take the money and rough him up? Whores knew such people. Lowlife desert rats looking to even the score on her behalf. Thuggish friends who think he ran her off the road.

Would he need protection? He did not even own a gun. He was not a *gun guy*.

Christi had a gun. Christi had *guns*. Two pistols and a rifle. All from Grayson.

Father-daughter target practice up at the Fair Oaks Shooting Club, every couple of months. Sheldon wasn't a shooter. Never had been. In case anyone ever forgot, Grayson was always there to remind.

Nah, Shelly don't shoot. That dog don't hunt.

But he could sure *hold* a gun. Or flash it from under a shirt. He could wave one around in the air if necessary.

Maybe the Wilson .38.

Or the Smith & Wesson 9mm.

Just in case. Just to have it. Just to show it if he had to. Ammunition? No. Bullets would not be necessary. No bullets. And no money. He wouldn't bring a goddamned dime.

But what, exactly, would he tell her? He with his empty gun and his empty pockets. What were the words? Words were the only thing he was ever any good at. What were the words? And where would they meet? Not Corbin. Not Houston. Where? Maybe he should take *some* money. Rather than nothing. *Some.* A show of good faith. How much?

He reemerges from his fugue, back into the real world in which he has not had the courage to even make the phone call. His head throbs violently, buckling under the weight of the insult, which he drags behind him for the rest of the drive.

Coward.

The gates grind open, misaligned horseheads parting. Sheldon serpentines his way up the hill to the garage. There is a car in the drive, a spotless silver Land Rover that he does not recognize. No doubt *Miss El Paso 1995*, showing off the latest jewelry from her husband. Clement. Plastic surgeon. He does all of her work.

Sheldon pushes open the front door.

The voices are coming from the kitchen. He fumbles his keys pulling them out of the door and they drop to the floor. *Shit.*

"Shelly?"

"It's me, Christi," he calls out.

"What are you doin' home? Two-thirty? Come on in the kitchen. Look who's back in town."

He does as he is told.

Nicholas Voss. Nordic specimen. Marble statue come to life. He raises his cup of coffee from the table. Smile so perfunctory it is almost invisible.

But the blue ice in his eyes gleams in reflected light.

Christi is turning, moving for the cabinets to get another cup. She always becomes the incomparable hostess when she is flustered.

"In't this a big 'ol surprise?"

Chapter 34

He is different today. Kevin Lawry.

Probably the same to anyone else. He rocks and leans dangerously in his chair like always. Making his noises. The right half of his torso still folds over to lash impatiently at the left side, right arm bent at the elbow, clawed hand clutching at his collar. He jerks with the same mysterious violence. Like he has been jabbed in the ribs with something hot or sharp. His rubber face bends, trickling its drool.

Same as ever.

But to Olivia he is different. She can tell.

It's his eyes mostly. The way he looks at her between spasms. He sees the scars, like forked lightening. Sees how she walks.

And he is sorry for what he sees. He is sorry for her.

Him. Sorry. For *her*.

And this breaks her heart.

They sit on the back deck watching the wrens flit about the feeders and wait for Yvonne to return. She is late. Thirty minutes late. Olivia gives Kevin a grape and another piece of cheese.

The morning sky is a pale, desert blue. So watery it's almost white. Almost sterile.

She has avoided the large, black thing in Yvonne's living room. Like it was an open, piano-shaped hole in the middle of the floor.

The music in her head has gone quiet. Since the accident the melody has dived to depths she cannot reach, surfacing only occasionally like some great blue whale. She thinks maybe Kevin can hear the silence in her head as much as he can see the scars on her face.

His whole life is interior. Makes sense that he can see inside others. That he can see the shape of feeling. See the song of whales.

A bird alights on the feeder. Kevin groans and thrashes.

"Mockingbird," says Olivia, matter-of-factly. "Female. Chicks are off in a nest somewhere, I bet. Waitin' for her to come back. Look how pretty she is." She nods her head in the direction of the feeder. "Beautiful, huh?"

Kevin lunges forward and back, pointing with his elbow and twisting his face away. She pats him on the shoulder.

"I know. Those chicks are depending on her. She's probably a good mom, don't you think?" She separates another grape from the stem. Holds it out to him. Kevin seizes it with the hand that is not clutching a stick of cheese.

"You know this whole desert used to be an ocean once. You know that? We're sittin' on the bottom of an old ocean. Lookin' at birds. Figure that."

She can hear the spasm next to her. She doesn't look. Doesn't need to. The mockingbird bolts off into the pale blue unknown.

"Sometimes I can feel it. All that wetness. All that water. Fish. Jungles of seaweed. Right here. Right where we're sittin'."

She looks at him seriously. Eats one of his grapes. Hands him another.

"Ever felt like you're stuck in a bubble? Like you're, I don't know. Surrounded by a different world? One you can't really be a part of?"

There is a long silence.

"Like inside your bubble is… is air… and sand and desert and burned-out scrub… and a few birds and nothin' else? No one else?"

Kevin is strangely still. Fighting the spasm. He floods his veins with steel, lending her his strength. Lets her cry.

"Screaming and screaming and beating your hands against the walls of this *fuckin'* bubble prison but no one can *fuckin'* hear you because no one *fuckin'* cares anyway?"

She wipes her nose and eyes with the back of her hand. Kevin clenches his entire body, holding on. Leans forward in his chair, pushing his shoulder toward her.

"And they all just fuckin'… just… just … swim around you in the water and you're stuck in the fuckin' desert bubble of fuckin' silence and sand and rotting road kill and all you *fuckin'* want is to be *fuckin'* heard? And it's like you can see… you can see in your dreams this beautiful kind of… kind of… *hope*… this white, glowing hope swimmin' around out there, in and out of the gloom. And you scream and you scream and you push for it but it's too far away?"

She sighs forcefully. Uses his napkin to clean her face. He relieves the pressure a little by leaning away and back, clutching only once at his collar, and then throwing himself back towards her. She sniffs.

"Until you realize it's all a fuckin' mirage, Kev. It ain't real."

The sound of the heavy front door closing stiffens her spine. She wipes her eyes and nose with the napkin and fans her face. Puts on something like a smile.

"Hey," says Yvonne.

"Hey. Beginnin' to wonder."

"Sorry I'm late. Art class went long."

Kevin surges forward and back, awash in the forces he has been restraining, paying the price for his own compassion.

"My goodness," says Yvonne. "Someone is happy I'm home. Did you miss me, sugar?" She tousles his hair from behind. "Olivia…" She reaches over her son's shoulder. Plucks the stick of cheese out of his hand. "You can't do this. I keep telling you that he can't have cheese and you keep giving it to him. He's got a lactose intolerance. Jesus."

"Sorry." Olivia stands. Limps around her chair. "I'll see you later."

"Well. What's wrong with you?"

"Nothing. You're late. I gotta go."

"Let me pay you."

"Don't worry about it, Eve. This one's on me. Let's call it a cheese penalty." Olivia squeezes Kevin's shoulder. Puts the cluster of grapes in his hand. "Later kiddo."

"Oh, come on," says Yvonne. She follows Olivia to the front door, slobbery stick of cheddar in her hand. "Look, Liv. You've got to pull yourself out of this depressive funk you've got going. The accident… I'm not minimizing. But you've got to pick yourself up and move on. You've got to stop… I mean feeling sorry for yourself is no way to live. You just end up taking it out on others. Like me."

"Right. Thanks. Good advice. I'm all better now."

And she is out. Gone. She does not mean to slam the door.

She limps down the drive to the street where she has parked the car. A white pick-up is just pulling in.

Miguel.

Fuck.

"Olivia." The window is sliding down. *Tejano* pours out like seawater. He turns off the music. "*Hola, chica.*"

"Hey," she says.

"How you feeling?"

"Fine." Her tone is too strong. Dismissive. She keeps limping for the street, trying to angle her face up and away. Trying to hide the wreckage. Hating herself.

"How's the car working out? Giving you any problems?"

He is the same, Miguel. Relaxed. Handsome. A more rugged, better-built version of his younger brother, Eladio. Less humor in his eyes, but more depth. Eladio, she thinks, will live in Miguel's shadow forever.

He is perfectly framed in the window of the pick-up, one arm out. Looking at her. Trying to smile. For an instant she is with him again. For an instant, she is sorry again. He never had a chance with her. Not really. Same as all the others. He had handed her the excuse. The out. And she'd taken it.

But she knows better. Always did.

"No. Runs great. 'Preciate the car. Thank your friend for me. Really."

"*De nada, de nada.* Not like he can use it. Poor fuck. Fucking ICE. He's back in Toluca driving for his uncle now. Scrap metal. Spare parts. Poor *Jesús.* Good guy, bad luck."

A long awkward beat. They both look away. Look back.

"How's the family?" she asks, because there is nothing else she can think of.

"Same." He smiles a little. Rolls his eyes. *Family.*

"I'm late," she lies. "Gotta go."

She opens the door of the 1986 shit-brown Ford Falcon. Stops. Realizes.

"Miguel… what are you even doing here?" she asks, gesturing in the general direction of the house.

He looks down to the passenger seat. Holds up Yvonne's purse.

"She forgot it."

A beat. Then another. It all suddenly clicks into place. *Art class ran long.*

"Ahh." Olivia nods. She slips into the front seat with a backwards wave. Slams another door she does not need to slam.

* * *

Thirteen. Fourteen. Fifteen.

Bodies like mileposts.

Thirty-seven. Thirty-eight.

Fifty-one.

The drive to Austin is like a two-hundred-fifty-mile blast crater, still smoldering and littered with dead civilians.

No surprise. She has taken the long way on purpose. The 67 to San Angelo. Then the 87 through Brady and Mason and Fredricksburg. Then the 290 through Johnson City. Then Dripping Springs. Then into Austin.

She prefers this route, where the traffic is less and the bodies —coyotes, rabbits, snakes, a falcon, and the ubiquitous unidentifiable —will lend a somber sense of community.

She smokes a cigarette. Listening to the desert hum. That flatline buzz. Searching for that melody in the ether. Trying to tune it in.

But there is nothing there. After Fredricksburg she smokes another. Listens. Nothing.

She is early. She checks into *Drifter Jack's.* She hates hostels, but she does not have the will to resist thirty bucks for a night. She considers sleeping in the car, but pays the man anyway. Last time she had the room to herself.

It is the only hope that she allows. A room to herself. That she will be alone.

All of the other hopes are still, bulbous blobs on the periphery of her consciousness. Even the hope that was once Sheldon *massage-massage-all-the-way-*

married and his bags of money. Even that hope was now one of the ubiquitous unidentifiables on the side of the road.

She had given him two weeks to contact her. Two weeks. The letter was clear. After two weeks, the wrath of legal process was to crush him into paste. She'd thought that was a generous amount of time. Long enough for him to figure out how to make it happen.

Today was day fifteen. Nothing.

Sheldon had not called her. He had called her bluff instead. Somehow he already knew what Libby's lawyer –a short, pasty grub worm of a man, his dirty tie constricting his neck to define his head –had told her: there was no case against Sheldon Davis. No physical evidence, no case. Closed police investigation, no case. Rich defendant, expensive lawsuit, but no case. Swearing match between a reputable, connected Texas businessman and a barmaid living in a whorehouse, but no fucking case.

And the clincher: no two-thousand dollar retainer, no lawyer.

She had not played the Liberty Cherish card. Libby had insisted –*"you tell Arvin Culpepper Esquire to send the bill to me. I guar-un-tee he will know what that shit mean, baby"* –but she couldn't bring herself to ask the question. Could not bring herself to lay the naked body of whatever Libby was to her –landlord, friend, surrogate mother –on the grub worm's paper-strewn desk.

No matter. He'd done it for her, little whitish tongue glistening his upper lip. "Since you're a friend of Libby, I reckon we can work something out for an up-front retainer of, oh, say, fifteen hundred."

So she had left the office without any legal representation. Her only hope now was the audacious bluff of that Arvin L. Culpepper, attorney-at-law, was standing by, ready to file a life-ruining complaint.

And now. Fifteen days gone. That bluff had been called. Sheldon *massage-massage* had cut the thread of spit and that last glimmering hope had landed with a lifeless thud on the side of the road.

Fifty-two. Fifty-three.

It is past five when she arrives. Johnny Flip is behind the bar. *Flipper.* Because of the way he laughs. The place is still mostly empty. That will change in another three hours. It will be hard to hear herself think.

Papi is in the back at his table. Doing his paperwork and drinking something gold. He looks up. Leans back in his chair. Waits.

"Don't you have an office?" she asks. She scrapes back a chair. Sits heavily with a sigh. Tries to ignore the deep ache in her leg. Nothing is aligned any more. Every part of her skeleton is compensating for some other part. Her back always hurts.

"I like to keep an eye on things," he says. "That office is like a coffin."

She is silent. Flipper laughs with the two at the bar. He looks up. Sees her. Waves. She nods. Papi watches.

"How you holding up?" he asks. "You look…"

"Don't finish that sentence," she says. "I know how I look."

"Was going to say *tired*."

"No. *You* look tired. *I* look like a train wreck."

She looks at him for the first time. He smiles sadly. Puts down his pen. Puts his big black hand on hers. Pats it.

"Didn't think you'd come," he says.

"Told you I would."

"Yes, you did. But you don't have to do this. I can make do…"

"No." Her eyes sharpen. Warning him. "No."

Papi smiles a little, tightening his saggy lip. He nods. Shows her a weathered palm.

"Okay then. Okay. Whatever you want."

She relaxes. Eyes soften.

"Sorry."

A group of three comes in through the front. The woman –big salon blowout 'do, bangles, boobs –is in the middle of a story. Seems someone –*the fucker*, she calls him –cut her off, gave her the finger, lost control, and then plowed straight into a parked police car. Seems she circled the block six times just to wave and smile.

The other two –maybe a husband and a brother –eat it up, washing the entire bar with new sound. Olivia looks back to Papi.

"You gonna fill the seats tonight?" she asks.

Papi nods. Knocks the ice cubes around in his glass.

"Did last week. These guys are pretty good. Just off the circuit in San Antonio. They're goin' places. Bass player's got a coke problem. They need to lose him. The sound is real tight though. 'Bout half way into the first set. When they find the groove. "

The threesome takes a table in the far corner. Stage left. Josie Salinas comes out of the kitchen with menus and a pitcher. She is all of five-foot-six in heels, seven months pregnant, sporting new braids.

"Josie looks likes she's gonna pop."

Papi nods. "Wants to keep workin'. Needs the money. Sonny lost his job at the dealership."

"Shit. *Really?*"

"Goin' out of business."

"When?"

"Last week."

"Last week? Some fucked-up timing. That's terrible."

Papi shrugs.

"I hired him as a bouncer. Pay is for shit. But it's what I can do."

Olivia smiles for the first time, stretching those scars. She clutches his forearm. "You're a good man, Papi. You're the best of men."

"Stop." He rubs his baggy brown eyes with his fingers. "I'm an old man, is what I am. An old man playin' a young man's game. Place is fallin' apart around me."

She looks around at the walls of the only memory she truly loves.

"No it ain't. Thought you were going to replace the floor though."

Papi pretends to laugh.

"Gotta put solid gold plating over the walls first. *Then* I aim to redo all the floors. Yes, indeed."

"I'm being serious here."

"Me too. These walls got to look *nice*."

Papi's face splits into a smile. He laughs softly into his glass.

"Seriously," she says. "Get rid of the checkerboard crap. It's too New Orleans ice cream parlor. Too busy. Go back to the wood." She stomps her good leg. "Still real wood under there. Never was clear on why you put in this crap floor anyway."

"Needed a change, I guess. Everything needed to be different. Not the same place it was."

"So change it again. Change it back."

He shakes his head.

"All I can do to make payroll. If the new owners want the old floor, then they can pay to tear up the new floor. If they want to sell gumbo ice cream then they can do that too."

There is a catch in her chest. Everything stops.

"New owners. You sold."

"Think so. We're talkin'."

"Who?"

"Can't say until it's done and public. They're all hush-hush. I signed a contract to keep my mouth shut. So I aim to. I don't need a lawsuit on my hands." He hesitates. Sees the anguish in her face. Sighs. "It's a group out of San Antonio."

"What are they gonna do with it?"

He gives his best *what-did-I-just-tell-you* look.

"I know." Irritation. Disappointment. "You can't say."

"Even if I could say, I don't know. They don't have to tell me their plans. I'm just the seller. It's all lawyer-to-lawyer talk anyway. I just wait until someone tells me what to sign and what information to turn over."

He reads her face. Takes another drink as he looks over at the new threesome in the corner. Puts down the glass.

"There's no going back, Olivia. Those days are gone. Forever. You can't go back. You got your whole life in front of you. Forget those days."

Olivia nods. Crosses her arms over her chest. Resists the urge to touch her fucking scars. Papi tries to redirect.

"How was the drive?"

"Same," she says, looking down at the checkerboard floor. "Forsaken."

"Forsaken?"

She is silent for a beat or two. Then nods.

"You know this whole fucking state used to be an ocean?"

By nine o'clock *Papi's* is in full swing. It smells of beer and sweat. Sweet cologne. Deep fried shrimp. Onion rings. All kinds are here. The regulars were here early to get the good seats. Balcony was full by seven. Someone somewhere is smoking a joint.

Papi goes home at nine-thirty, leaving Flipper and Mac in charge. The kitchen is a hissing inferno. Olivia and Josie Salinas and Josie Salinas' unborn baby work the floor alone until Kelli Donner gets off work at the Costco warehouse and shows up like the cavalry in her shit-kickers and cut-offs and her tits and her too-tight *Hey, big tipper* t-shirt. Sonny Salinas works the front door. By ten he is turning everyone away, shaking his head over and over.

"Fire code, man. Sorry. Fire code. Fire code. Full up. Fire code. Hey, homes. Full up, man. Fire code. Try us tomorrow. Gotta get here early, man. Sorry."

Papi is right about the band. *The Jambalaya Nut Shuckers.* The sound is a spicy zydeco washboard blues with the occasional sweetness of Smokey Mountain bluegrass on the slower numbers, of which there are precious few. The bassist is animated but good. Coke or no coke, he delivers. The lead vocals belong to a perfect, *cute-as-a-button* thirty-something pair who could pass as a brother-sister act. They sing with the exuberant confidence of unbroken children, celebrating the continued inevitability of their own fortune. They sing like they have the breath of the gods at their backs.

Voodoo mama in the kitchen, cookin' up a spell
Little baby play that fiddle, like he got a soul to sell
Voodoo mama tell the Devil, she'll give her soul away
If he come to bed and sleep with the dead
And just let her baby play.

But the slow songs are only technically good. Counterfeit heartbreak while everyone catches a breath and a drink of water. The woman sings the blues with a smile.

The respite never lasts for more than a song. Three minutes and *The Jambalaya Nut Shuckers* are back at it, whipping the crowd into a raucous frenzy. Olivia is content to disappear, swallowed whole into the belly of sound. She moves invisibly, easily lost in the crush of people. They look at her hands, not her face. She is only what she brings them and what she takes away. She is there and gone and mercifully forgotten.

It helps, too, not to have time to think. To not have the luxury of contemplating her surroundings. She cannot bear to look at the place. *Papi's.* These walls. That stage. The bar. Not now. It was like coming to the wedding of an old lover. The one who left in the middle of the night and never came back.

By two o'clock the place is closed and almost empty. Olivia collects her tip envelope from behind the bar. Stuffs it in her purse. Josie and Sonny and baby-makes-three are long gone. Flipper and Kelli invite her up to the balcony where Kelli is feeling generous with her weed.

If Kelli's invitation is sincere, Flipper's is not. Kelli and dope makes three a crowd. The sooner the place is empty, the sooner Flipper can get under that t-shirt.

Olivia looks up. Salutes. Keeps moving, passing slowly beneath them. The slower she moves, the less pronounced the limp. Her leg aches from being on her feet without any rest. And her back. And her shoulders. Her boots make a dull knocking against the floor. There are no people to absorb the sound. It finds all of the old walls. The sound bounces back to her with the news.

The whale is dead. It's belly is empty.

* * *

She thinks of sleeping in her car.

No. Not *her* car. *The* car. *Her* car is a blackened scrap metal corpse in some desert junk lot. Or it is already a scorched blue pancake.

So she thinks of sleeping in the car that once belonged to poor, deported Jesús Batista, friend of a friend of a friend of poor Miguel Rivera, who she had tossed away and who was now fucking poor Yvonne Lawry, who was married to poor cuckolded Brent Lawry, father to poor Kevin Lawry, who was the only person she knew who really knew what it was like to be alone in a world full of people.

The driver's seat of the shit-brown Ford slumps sharply toward the door when it is reclined. Like it wants to dump her out into the street. She adjusts the sofa cushion. Puts the seat up and lights a cigarette. Drives.

She does not have a room to herself at *Drifter Jack's*. Whoever it is —the head on the pillow belongs to a dark-haired woman —she is asleep and snoring. Olivia picks a bunk in the far corner by the window. Takes her boots off. Slips under the sheet, fully dressed.

Tires squeal in the distance.

Her anonymous roommate rolls over. The snoring stops.

She is exhausted but unlikely to sleep. She stares out into the dark, still room.

There is no bedside table. She misses her cactus people. Her little cactus family with its little cactus dog. Misses the way they look at her from their place next to the clock.

Family.

She tries not to think of her parents. The selfish calculation of her mother. Her shit-stain for a father. She tries to banish those thoughts. Those memories. But it is not possible to consider the cactus people family without considering the opposite. The old hate is still there. Still the same.

Her leg throbs its message from someplace much deeper. Blooms of heat from an undersea vent. A wound in the mantle, oozing magma.

She drops a hand toward the floor. Fishes through her purse for the plastic bottle with the last Vicodin. Her hand comes back up with her phone.

Flashing.

She opens it. Pokes the numbers. Listens.

"This message is for Olivia DeLuna. This is… well, you know who this is. Call me at this number." Silence. Palpable hesitation. "I want to meet in person."

Chapter 35

"My name is Davis Payne. I am an alcoholic."

"Hi Davis."

It is a dolorous chorus. Six men. Four women. Elvis Brussard is at the rickety table along the sidewall filling his cup. He says it late and alone.

"Hi Davis."

Elvis looks up at him when the pause goes on too long.

"Go on, boy," he says calmly. "Get it out."

Davis hates this.

"Been sober comin' on six months now. Doin' pretty good I guess. I just… when I drink… I mean when I *was* drinking, I did it to forget. I drink to forget. Forget who I am. What I did. What I didn't do."

Some of them are looking at him. Others have their elbows glued to their knees, looking at the floor. Holding their cups. Eventually they look up too.

They are open vessels, wanting more. So he keeps pouring.

"It was like… like I could be, you know, someone else. Sometimes for days. I'm a writer. Not really. But I think of myself as one. Close as anything else. Except being a fucked-up drunk. That's the bull's eye. Fucked-up drunk. Booze helped. Little too much and I could be a writer. A drunk writer with no life to remember. A drunk writer getting' punched in the face. A drunk writer gettin' tossed out into the street. Losin' a job. Livin' in a Harvey shelter for too long. Gettin' arrested. All of that felt better to me. Better than remembering. *Feels* better. Booze does that, I guess. Didn't feel so good after I sobered up. My twenties are kind of a blur. Anyways. I'm doing better now."

Silence washes in around his ankles. Rising. Rising. They wait.

"Go on, Davis. Out with it," says Elvis softly. They look at each other across the room. Elvis jerks his head.

"Right. Well, I got a letter last week."

He doesn't tell them everything. Almost nothing, really. But he tells them everything Elvis knows, which is more than he has ever told anyone about his father. He leaves his mother out of it. Can't even begin to talk about her. That's a whole other level.

This is supposed to make him feel better. More secure. Elvis insisted.

But Elvis is wrong. It feels terrible.

When he is done, the people applaud. Thank him. It sounds like the *Amen* after a prayer. They use his name. He blushes. Sits down. He listens to the others talk about why they are doing better. Why they are still lost. Why they will always be.

He meets Elvis outside, half way through a cigarette.

"That so bad?" he asks.

"Yes."

The sky is an ashcan haze. Like Elvis and God are having a smoke together. They walk out to the Harley. Elvis stubs out the cigarette as Davis throws his leg over the seat.

"It's good for you," he says.

"What. *That?*"

"Yeah. That. Confession's good for you."

"Yeah. Well. Confession makes me want to drink."

"No doubt." Elvis nods. "No doubt. But listen. Ain't no way to go around the shit that makes you want to drink, Davis. You can't heal by goin' *around* the shit. You got to go *through* it." His cigarette hand shoots out toward Davis like a sword. "Got to go through it. Feel me? And you got to go through it sober."

Davis nods, just wanting the lecture to be over. Wanting to not see the church in the background.

"And all that in there?" Elvis jerks his thumb over his shoulder at the steeple. "That's all part of goin' through the shit that makes you want to drink. 'Cause even though you got to go through the shit, you don't have to do it alone."

"Yes you do, Elvis," he says. "I do."

Elvis makes a face, like pointlessness has an odor.

"So when you gon' to meet with him then?"

"I'll ride up in the morning," Davis says. "Spend the day in Houston. Get my shit together. Drop in on Buddy. Guess I should tell Dallas Letti I won't be there tomorrow. That'll be fun."

Elvis chuckles. "*Hoo-wee!* She one cast-iron bitch, ain't she?"

They laugh at this, joining in the irony that it has taken Dallas Letti, of all people, to lighten the mood. Davis shakes his head.

"You know, I look at her, take her abuse, and it's hard to imagine that she can sing like that." He starts his bike. "You know?"

"Sing? *Sheee-it,* boy. Sing. You mean *yusta*-could. Miss Letti Blue *could* sing. No doubt. But Dallas Letti? Nowdays, she just a angry, washed-up drunk." Elvis swats him on the arm, shit-eating grin slipping sideways across his face. "But you tell her I said *hey*. And make it sound like I mean it. Woman scares the piss outta me."

Elvis pivots away towards his truck waiting on the other side of the lot. Stops. Turns back. Points.

"And you keep your shit together tomorrow night. Call me if you need me, hero."

Davis nods. Throttles up. Thunders away.

The word is a fraud. *Hero*. It is a hot, wooden thorn in his brain. He can feel it all the way to *Pepita's*.

Elvis knows the truth just like he does. Knows he is the opposite of a hero.

And yet there is a fraud within the fraud. A worm inside the Trojan thorn. Something that Elvis cannot see.

Every morning before the sun is up, as he lies in bed sleepless from a night of writing in his journal, or writing about Celia Morales, or writing about Libby Holder, the worm escapes the thorn. It burrows in just a little deeper. Feeds on the rich flesh of secret longing. The worm grows fatter on his wish that the lie were true. The wish that the lie had always been true.

Hero.

Each night, on the knife's edge of consciousness, he allows himself to imagine that the lie *is* true. Each night, he indulges this fraud. Leafs through its glossy pages like a filthy magazine. He pictures the hospital bed. Pictures himself sheltering her on the heat-scorched ground as the fireball behind them mushrooms into the bluebird Texas sky.

Pictures himself hauling her out of the lake up into the boat.

Sputtering and coughing. Drawing air.

Pictures the gratitude in her eyes. The love. Suddenly nothing to be forgiven.

Every night he feeds the Trojan thorn worm like a beloved pet. Feeds it from the palm of his secret self. And every day he feels the hangover of new shame layered upon the old.

At *Pepita's* he does his best to spar with Eladio Rivera in the way that they have come to do. Eladio spinning his yarns of improbable seduction, the ascendant Don Juan of Corbin, Texas. Davis shooting him down, all for the benefit of some customer-friend that Eladio is trying to charm.

"I am telling you, Davis, she wanted me before the song was even over. Right there on the dance floor. She was melting in my arms. The way I can dance for a woman? *Estaba indefensa!*"

"Oh, I'm sure she felt helpless, alright. She was looking for someone to rescue her from your horny little clutches, Eladio."

"Ha! Listen to you talk, Davis. You think because you are now a hero you could have saved her too? Saved her from her own desires? You think she would have left my arms for your arms? *Nunca, mi amigo. Nunca!*"

The two girls at the counter laugh over their burritos. Whispers. More laughing. Less innocent this time.

Davis does not have the energy for this. He does his best to stay back in the kitchen with the cook. Jorge does not speak English. Davis cleans things that do not need cleaning, just so he can try to be alone.

But none of that is possible.

His father, or the sense of him, will not leave him alone.

Elvis is right, of course. There is no going around the shit. You have to go right through the goddamned middle of it. So he will.

But he doesn't have to like it. And he doesn't. He dreads it.

He clocks out. The back door closes on his *adios* to Eladio. He rides out of town, heading west into the hot, drooping bag of fire. His father is behind him on the back of his bike, whispering the old poison into his ear. Davis throttles up, moving as fast as the old Harley can manage.

But there is no throwing the old man. Not ever. The hot wind cannot smother his words. They roll into him, one by one, like smoldering black marbles into his inner ears.

Worthless. Coward. Killer.

He turns up the narrow desert road that leads to the home of Dallas Letti. It fills him with a strange sort of relief. He has come to look forward to the demolition. It is hot, grueling work, dismantling the old broken structure. Throwing it away, piece-by-piece, into the back of Dallas' old truck and carting it off to the dump. Every plank, every nail, every fixture resists him, clinging to the shape of the past. The sun is always enraged at the audacity of the effort.

And then there are the snakes.

But he can be alone with himself out here. It is desolate enough to make little Corbin seem like Houston. Out here is neither of those places. He does not have to pretend. Not for anybody. Not for himself. It is a place of muscle and sweat. Exertion. Physical pain.

It is a kind of balm, this pain. The hurt in his muscles. It is a narrow beam of light that chases away the shadows in his head. He has come to like it.

He has come to need it.

When he needs to rest, he takes refuge from the sun inside the hold of the bleached wooden ark with its missing blue half-door. Drinks his bottled water. Looks out of the tiny paneless window at the desert. Imbibes emptiness.

It has become better than anything else he does now.

Davis dismounts, leaving the bike at the wall. He stands just inside the gate and calls out her name. Waits. Calls again. He is about to leave.

"Fuck you want? Hollerin' like that."

Dallas Letti needs the doorframe to help her stand upright. She wears a dirty white nightgown beneath a storm of black hair. Her eyes are pools of bloody milk.

"Usually you're here in the garden," he says. "Sorry. I didn't want... I didn't mean..."

"Whatchu' want me for? You know where the damn truck is. Go get it, fool." She flicks a hand at him. Turns and recedes into the house, moving slowly. The white of her nightgown begins to fade in the dark like a ghost. Davis shouts after her before she is gone.

"I wanted to tell you... I won't be here tomorrow."

The ghost floats back to the door.

"What say?"

"I have to go into Houston tomorrow. See my dad. I won't be here. I just wanted to..."

"Fuck I care 'bout yo' daddy?"

"Nothing. I just..."

"He dyin?"

"No. He's..."

"I pay you to work. Hero. You want this job or don't you?"

"I do. I..."

"Think I won't find somebody else come do this shit in half the time it take yo' raggedy white trash ass? Some Mexican do it faster and better than you."

He wants to protest. To defend himself. Wants to remind her of just how much broken wood and broken glass and rusty metal he has already hauled away without making much of a dent in the mountain of detritus that is left.

But he knows it is pointless.

He puts his hands on his hips and kicks at a rock with his boot.

"You out there in my truck writin' in yo' lil' magazine. Writin' 'bout how you save that girl. That *must* be what you been doin' all these days."

"No."

"'Cause you sure as *fuck* ain't been workin', boy."

"I've hauled out nine loads, Ms. Letti."

"Don't you *Miss Letti*, me. This all about getting' inside my head."

"No."

"You want to get close to Dallas Letti, ain't that it? You *playin'* at work just so you can get yo' interview."

"No."

"Oh... so you don't want an interview. That it?"

"I'd love an interview, but that's not..."

"Or maybe you want you a *piece*." She attempts a sardonic smile. She cannot control her mouth. She clutches at her chest, bunching her nightgown with the hand that is not holding the doorframe. She kneads old flesh. "You lookin' to tell yo' friends that you done fucked the one and only Miss Letti Blue?"

"No." Davis turns, shaking his head. Walks back through the gate. He heads around back for the truck. Dallas spits out into the yard.

"Y'ain't getting' nothin' from me, boy. Hear me? Nothin'. You not here tomorrow then don't you come back. Hear me? Hero?"

Chapter 36
Abby and Davis

It was almost three weeks before I saw her again.

It might have been the longest three weeks of my life.

Not one single hour passed that I did not want to jump in the truck and barrel out to Fairfield. I had almost constant daydreams about kicking open Abby's front door, picking her up light as a feather in my arms and carrying her away to a field or a hotel, anywhere we could be alone and make love for hours. A couple of times I fantasized about taking her out to Lake Waco and spreading a blanket by the water beneath the trees where she had laid her head on my shoulder and I had felt twenty feet tall promising that I would burn to cinders anyone who hurt her.

Lake Waco never worked very well as a fantasy. I couldn't keep those murders from intruding. Severed limbs and rotting corpses were always just on the other side of wherever I imagined spreading out that blanket as Abby took off her clothes. In time the body parts were bobbing up out of the water. Then they were under our blanket. Then on top. It's a sick game my stupid mind plays, making me think about the exact thing I don't want to think about. I'm sure you shrinks have some fancy six-syllable word for it. Doesn't matter.

I dreamed up other locations. Corn fields. A fancy penthouse suite in some high-rise. My bedroom. The football field at school. A beach on an island somewhere I couldn't name. These were always very detailed fantasies I built for myself. I could live in them for hours. They were partly about sex (well, they were a lot about sex) but they were also about love.

You will make your little frown at that, Dr. Bees. I can see it in my mind as I write these words. That frown and the way you tilt your head a little sideways when I say things you don't like. You think I am too young or stupid or manipulated or whatever to know love when I feel it. You can play whatever little head games with me you want, and we can pass a million billion words in your office, but my answer on this will never change. It was love. At least partly, it was love.

In my head I was always rescuing her. I was saving her from something or someone, although from what or who was never really clear. There was always some urgency to kicking in her door. Maybe that was why I came up with Lake Waco in the first place. That was the place where rescue was needed and never happened. I know it's stupid. I'm only trying to interpret the fantasies because I know that is what you will do when you read this. You over-read everything. You can't help yourself. More likely they mean nothing important. I loved her. She told me from the beginning I was her savior. My fantasies took it from there. You don't have to be a shrink to figure it out. But I know better than to try to stop you from coming up with some ridiculous theory about what it all means in my subconscious. Knock yourself out.

As much as I wanted to see Abby, I stayed in Houston. I am ashamed to say that it was mostly fear that kept me away. I was short of gas money for a while too, but I solved that problem soon enough. It was mostly fear.

Fear of what, you're probably asking. Fear of Simon Dory. I did not like the way he had looked at me. I did not like the smell of his breath or the tentacle of ink crawling out of the neck of his dirty t-shirt. And even though Abby had insisted that Simon was only a friend and that there was nothing romantic between them, part of me was unwilling to believe her. I felt like I was in his house, messing with his woman. I felt like a humiliated little kid and Simon was like this masculine hardness I could only pretend to be.

So I stayed away. I fantasized. Every day I told myself I was being silly. Everyday I told myself that today was the day I would head back out to Fairfield and see Abby. Kiss Abby. Make love to Abby. And every day I stayed away.

I managed the courage to call her four times on the phone. Two of those times Simon answered the phone and I hung up before he was done saying the word "hello." The other two times Abby answered. Hearing her voice was like something magic. Like being filled with honey and clover.

"Davis, love! How are you? What mischief have you got up to?"

We talked about innocent things. Like we were just friends catching up. I imagined Simon on the couch, bald head up on one end, dirty boots up on the other, listening in. If what she had told me was true, there should have been no reason to pretend we were just friends. To pretend that I did not love her and want to be with her. On top of her. Under her. In her. But I couldn't be honest on the phone. I kept it light and breezy, hoping she would invite me over. That is all it would have taken. *Davis, love. Come see me, will you? I miss you.*

But she never said that or anything else that I could fairly interpret as an invitation to come out to see her. She kept the conversations as light and breezy as I did. I took that as an unspoken request to stay away.

So I did. I went to school. I hung out with Jack and Kenny. I didn't tell them anything. Not only had I had sex, but I had had sex with a woman more than ten years older than me. It doesn't get better than that. And don't start up again about the law. That just made it better. You have no idea how much I wanted to drop that in front of Jack and Kenny. But I didn't. They'd never have believed me anyway.

We saw movies and went target shooting with Jack's twenty-two. We hung out at the go-cart track and went to a football game and watched our school get trounced. Fat Jack came by the house after school a couple of times, I think as much to make sure the truck was where it was supposed to be as to play video games. We went out to sit in the truck once because Jack wanted to smoke a cigarette and he knew my dad would not allow cigarettes in the house. It was just another excuse for Jack to check up on me. I let him sit in the driver's seat. He seemed satisfied.

Had Jack been just a little smarter person, he'd have checked the mileage.

I spent most evenings with dad who was kind of in a better mood because he felt like he was making better progress on his book. I could tell he wanted to talk about what he was writing. He found too many occasions to mention the book whenever we were talking about anything else.

But dad's book always had a way of shutting our conversations down, tiny and infrequent as they were. My dad wanting to talk about his book is just my dad wanting to talk about mom. I didn't want to talk about mom. I wanted to be happy. Happiness for me was not at the bottom of a lake or six feet under the grass or inside a bottle of bourbon or inside a book that only pretended to be about something other than meaningless tragedy. Or at least *our* meaningless tragedy.

Happiness for me was right up I-45 in Fairfield wearing nothing but a smile and smelling like jasmine.

I guess I should have felt encouraged that when dad tried to talk about his book he usually didn't have that look on his face. I've told you about it. Hell, you can probably draw it by now we've talked so much about that look. But it really didn't matter what his face was doing. That look is inside me now. He doesn't have to use it to make me feel like dying. It's already in my head. It's always there, like the arms and legs in the water and in the bushes and under the wet weeds out at Lake Waco. I was not trying to hurt him more than I already had. I just couldn't talk about it.

Well, I could have I guess. I should be honest, or what is the point of all of this? I could have talked about it. His book. Mom. I just didn't want to.

I wanted to be happy.

The call from Abby came early on a Saturday morning, pulling me out of a dream. It is instinct for me to dive for the phone in the mornings. If dad is not asleep, he's hung over and a ringing telephone is not welcome. I don't remember how I answered. I was disoriented and not ready to be awake. But I felt a jolt of adrenaline bring me upright as soon as I heard her voice.

"Davis. Is that you?"

I could tell instantly that something was wrong. She spoke in a hoarse whisper. The words came out unevenly, in gushes of sound, like they were lodging in her throat and had to be pushed out with great force.

"I need you, Davis. You must save me. You must hurry."

"Abby..."

"You must save me."

"Abby, what is it? What's wrong? Tell me. Are you hurt?"

"He's going to kill everyone. Davis, he's..."

"What? Who? Abby, what's going on? Have you called the police?"

"No."

"Do you want me to call the police?"

"No! You cannot, Davis. You cannot call the police. Don't trust the Bobbies. Promise me."

"Abby..."

"Promise me!"

"You have to tell me what's happening. Are you safe?"

"I don't know."

"Who's going to do the killing? Is it Simon? Is Simon there with you?"

"I don't know. Simon's gone."

"Gone where? Gone to kill someone?"

"I don't know."

"Is Simon going to kill someone?"

"I don't know. You must save me."

"How do you know someone is going to be killed?"

"Ijah said so. Davis..."

"*Ijah?* Who's Ijah? Abby? Abby?"

The line went dead. I stared at the phone in my hand for a full thirty seconds. I didn't know what to do. Part of me wanted to pound on the wall and yell for dad. I wanted him to take charge of the crisis. I felt like a child in an adult situation.

But I did not pound on the wall. I dialed 9-1-1. I reported an emergency at Abby's address and hung up the phone in ten seconds without any details. I threw on some clothes and bolted out of the house. I sprinted across the lawn and down the street for the truck. My hands were shaking so hard it took me three times to get the key in the lock.

I flew up I-45. I drove faster than I have ever driven anywhere in my life. It's a miracle I did not get pulled over or cause an accident. I was barely in control of that damn truck. Too much play in the steering wheel with the word *FRED* in the middle like a ship in a bad storm, always pitching forward and backward dunking either the *F* or the *D* under the waves. It made quick lane changing risky. I got angry honks from three or four cars I nearly sent into the ditch.

All I could think about was getting there. I didn't know what was waiting for me or how I would deal with it. I imagined Simon's bloody hands wrapped around Abby's white neck. I imagined Simon raping her in the kitchen. Or in the trailer. Or in the street. I imagined Simon's hand pushing her head into the bathtub. I didn't know what was coming. All I knew was that the woman I loved needed me and that I would be there to save her. I had promised. So I jammed that gas pedal and I flew. And it still took forever to get there.

There were no police when I arrived. I didn't know if that was good or bad. As I was climbing out of the truck, Abby exploded out of the front door in a nightgown and came barreling across the yard in her bare feet. For a second or two I thought she was happy to see me.

"Bloody hell! You promised not to call them! You promised!"

She swung at me, but I caught her arm.

"Who?"

"The bobbies! The police!"

"I did not promise! You told me people were going to die! You told me to save you! I'm here!"

She kept trying to swing at me. I kept holding her wrists and shouting at her.

"I'm here! Abby, I'm here! I came!"

Eventually, the sound of my voice punched through her rage. She looked at me in a frozen, wild-eyed stare. Her face was as pale and beautiful as ever, but she was someone I did not know. Her hair was a ragged mess. Her dark brown eyes were empty. I grabbed her shoulders and gave her a hard, sharp shake.

"Abby!"

She blinked. It was like she was seeing me for the first time. I did it again.

"Abby!"

She melted a little and started to cry. Behind her, two crows alit from the roof of her house, flashing black in the sun. She held my face between her hands.

"Davis. You've come. Of course you have. My dashing prince, Davis. Of course you have."

I loosened my grip. After a slow moment she turned and walked back across the yard, into the house. I watched her go, almost too stunned to move. The screen door slapped closed behind her.

I followed carefully, looking up the street in both directions. As far as I could tell, the entire display had gone unnoticed.

When I entered the house, she was on the couch, knees pulled tightly up to her chest. Her feet were tucked beneath the hem of her nightgown. She was rocking slowly back and forth, bouncing off the back cushion and staring out into empty space.

"Abby," I said as softly as I could, looking warily for Simon or anyone else that might pose a threat. "What's going on? Where's Simon? Who's Ijah?"

It was a long, confusing conversation that was mostly me pulling answers out of her that she either did not know how to put into words or, for whatever reason, did not want tell me.

And what she did tell me, I did not know how to make sense of.

Part of me (only a small part) wishes you had been there in the room. Just off in the corner somewhere listening with your bottomless cup of tea and your notepad. You probably would have been able to make more out of what she said than I did. To me it just sounded... It sounded crazy.

"He's out to kill me," she said to the wall in a weightless whisper. "He's going to kill everyone."

"Who? Ijah? Is Ijah going to kill someone?"

"You don't understand."

"Then help me understand."

"Ahab is the king, but Ijah is the *voice*. Ijah is the electric prophet. Ijah comes to me in the quiet."

"Who then, Abby? Who is going to kill you?"

"Everyone. He's going to kill everyone."

"Who? Abby."

She swallowed. Her hands trembled trying to shape her words in the air.

"Ahab is the king, but Ijah is the *voice*. The white whale... swims like a shark, devouring stars. He swims the universe devouring stars. He's going to kill everyone. He is all the bad energy. He knows I know. He knows I know. He knows I know. He knows I know. He knows I know. He knows..."

"Abby."

"Ijah has told me in the quiet that he is coming. Swimming with black eyes like a shark. Ijah has said it is up to you. I have found you. Don't you see? I've found you. You must save me, Davis. He's going to kill everyone. I shouldn't know that. I shouldn't. But I *do* know it. Because I can hear him plotting. I can hear and I can understand. I don't mean to, but I can. The voices come to me. And he knows I know. He knows I know."

"Who's plotting? The shark?"

"*Whale!* Davis, not a shark! It's not a fish! It's not a fish! It's not a..."

"*Abby!* I don't understand. A whale is plotting?"

"No. Ball. Ball. Ball. Ball sends the whale! Ahab is king and Ball sends the whale."

"Ball?"

"No! Not ball like a soccer ball. *Baal!* B-A-A-L! He's going to kill everyone."

"I called the police..."

She turned suddenly on the couch and grabbed me by the shirt. Her eyes were rimmed with red, desperate and terrified.

"Not the police! Not the police! They work for the king. Bad energy. Shark energy. They all work together devouring stars. I hid in the trailer. Ijah said they would come and I hid. They couldn't find me."

"Abby, the police …"

"Not the police! *You!* Don't you see? It has to be *you*, Davis. When he comes, you must be here. You must be ready. Will you save me? Will you kill him for me?"

I didn't know what to tell her. I said the only words in my head. I meant them. I wanted them all to be true. Her face was torment. It was real fear.

"Abby, I love you. I won't let anything happen to you. I'll keep you safe."

She threw her arms around me in a hug, sobbing into my neck.

We did not speak for many minutes. Eventually I could feel her muscles starting to relax. I pried her loose and went to the kitchen and brought her back a glass of juice. She drank it with both hands around the glass, like a child.

We talked about small things. The dog up the street that would not stop barking. The tear in her nightgown. The painting of an old three-masted schooner on the wall above the television.

"Simon gave that to me. It's from a shop in London. My father was a sailor."

"Abby, where is Simon?" I asked.

"Gone."

"Gone where? For how long?"

"I never know."

"When did he leave?"

"Four days ago."

"Abby." I waited until she was looking at me. "Are you afraid of Simon?"

Many seconds passed. I could see her thinking about how to answer.

"Sometimes he gets angry."

"Angry at you?"

"Yes."

"Has he ever hurt you?"

"He tries to help me."

"Abby. Has he ever hurt you?"

She closed her eyes.

"Abby, listen. The universe or cosmos or whatever don't hurt people. The universe isn't alive. It doesn't have thoughts. *People* hurt people. *People* kill people. Like those poor people over at Lake Waco. A person did that. Not the universe. Not a shark or a whale or… or a… Baal. A person. The universe is … is just nature, Abby. It's like Lake Waco or an ocean. Sure there's whales and sharks and all kinds of other things in an ocean, but its just nature. It's not personal. Maybe there are energies in space, or whatever, I don't know. I'm not saying you're wrong about that. And maybe you hear things. Maybe you do. But I really don't think there's a conspiracy of energies swimming around space devouring stars and looking for you. If you hear things, it's not personal. Its just nature, doing its thing."

She didn't answer. I could feel her slipping away. I kept at it.

"See, I believe that people are to blame. We people are. *We* kill others. *We* hurt others. *We* kill people we love. *We* hurt ourselves. *We* kill ourselves. I'm worried about you, Abby. Really worried."

She cried and I just sat there trying to comfort her.

"Abby."

"I'm tired. Davis. My head is like… I have to sleep." She wiped her eyes and looked at me pleadingly. "Will you come sleep with me? Will you lie down with me? Will you? Davis?"

She stood and took me by the hand and led me out the back door and across the lot to the shop. I remember seeing the white of that nightgown against the blue trailer door and thinking it was like a cloud against sky. She was that innocent to me. She locked the trailer door and took off her nightgown and lay down on the cot, slipping beneath the sheet. I undressed and wrapped my body tightly around hers, like a shell around some tiny defenseless baby animal.

She felt perfect in my arms. Innocent. I wanted to protect her. So I wanted to believe her. I wanted to believe that it was my job to save her.

It was dark with the curtains drawn. There was muffled birdsong outside. The air was close and still and hot and smelled of incense.

We both slept. We made love half awake, with one foot in each world.

Chapter 37

Sheldon leans on his elbows. Looks down over the side of the little white concrete bridge.

The water slides beneath him, a flat, silvery-gray ribbon. Somewhere in Mexico, or maybe much further south, God sits on a stool pulling it all into a loose pile. Letting it dry in the sun. Then he'll roll the San Antonio up onto an old cracked, wooden spool with all of the other rivers.

He watches the water. Thinks of the little Pecos Bluntnose Shiner causing its trouble up on the New Mexico Border. No bigger than a finger and still likely to cause the mighty Grayson Tate a life-ending aneurism.

No Shiners in this thread of the San Antonio, he thinks. Shouldn't even be a river at all. The city pumps upwards of five million gallons a day into what would otherwise be a bone-dry ditch. First they pumped it out of the Edwards Aquifer.

Five million gallons a day. Every day.

Then someone with grandchildren and half a brain decided that wasn't such a great idea. Since the mid-nineties San Antonio has been filling the ditch with retreated sewage. Sheldon knew the research cold. Everyone selling the Corbin Redevelopment Project knew the research. The San Antonio history was required reading.

Initial plans for the Corbin project had called for tapping the Edwards-Trinity Plateau Aquifer. But then some savvy executive at Quinco International with a corner office in London or Hamburg –some *"Russian"* as Grayson would say – had decided to chart a course around the sustainability shit-storm. Part unflinching political practicality. Part inspired commercial *jiu jitsu*. Quinco had budgeted into the Corbin project a thirty million dollar, state-of-the-art sewage treatment plant.

Corbin. Commerce. Conservation. Part of Sheldon's job had been to help sell the interconnectedness of those concepts.

Greening the desert. Greening the economy. Green was good. Give us green. God bless green. God bless Texas.

Not an unfamiliar task for Sheldon. Not for the songwriter turned ad man.

Texas Pete, he's our guy
He's the name in Rodeo Supply
Shoe that hoof and barrel that clown
Texas Pete is the hoss in town
Break that bull and rope that filly
Come see Pete 'tween Polk and McGilly

Another dining barge slips out from beneath the bridge. A dozen people eating salad. They look up at him warily, two at a time as they emerge. Afraid he might drop something onto their plates. A cigarette. Or spit.

He scans the tables beneath the phalanx of brightly colored umbrellas lining the other side of the channel. All of the same people. Eating. Drinking. Talking. Feeling the jazz through their hair like a breeze.

Table by table. Person by person.

None of them are her.

He looks over one shoulder. Then the other. A man on the other side of the bridge is taking pictures of the water. He reminds Sheldon of Nicholas Voss. The icy blond hair. The frame. Always with a camera. Like a detachable appendage.

He turns back. Remembers Nicholas in his home, sitting at the kitchen table. Christi flitting nervously about behind him, a trapped bird looking for open windows. She had not expected him home so early.

His wife was not a particularly good liar. Not her face. Not off the cuff. Her true intentions tended to freeze into her expression, hoping to blend in with their surroundings.

Sheldon seriously doubted that she was having an affair. Possible he supposed. But he doubted it. Christi got too much satisfaction out of being righteous. Being the example. Shoulders back. Chin up. People were watching. Always watching. Waiting for the stumble. For the slightest bobble. A life of pageantry training had beaten the rectitude into her. Stoop, even once, and the crown falls off your head.

And if she was going to have an affair, Nicholas Voss, for all of his rugged Nordic allure, seemed a particularly unlikely choice.

For starters, he seemed wholly indifferent to other people. To Christi and to everyone else. And if there was one thing Christi needed beyond her father's approval, it was a lot of personal attention. Fawning. Magnanimity of devotion. Sheldon had never even seen Nicholas smile. Not once.

More importantly, Christi would never risk the wrath of her father. Grayson's reaction to an adulterous tryst between his daughter and someone who was even loosely associated with a business client would be volcanic. Ironic, given his own adulterous past, but volcanic just the same.

So, no. He did not think they were having an affair.

But he thought that Christi at least liked to *think* about having an affair. And that was the expression on her face when he had walked into the kitchen five days ago. She had been *thinking* about it. Nicholas was back in town on some business or other and had dropped by the house to pick up the camera lens he had forgotten on the deck railing... and Christi had been *thinking* about it. Poured him a cup of coffee. *Thinking* what it would be like to let Nicholas Voss knock her crown to the floor and bury it with her clothes.

And yet.

And yet, if it was so unlikely, why did he keep dwelling on it? Imagining it. Imagining them. And why did he keep imagining Nicholas Voss everywhere he went?

He looks back over his shoulder. The man with the camera is gone, replaced by an older couple. They're trying to fold a San Antonio River Walk map. She knows how, but he won't let her try.

Sheldon scans the umbrellas again. Nothing.

Looks at his watch. Still a little early. She's probably camped out on some other bridge. Looking for *him*. Looking to see if *he* brought reinforcements. Looking to see if he was talking into his sleeve.

Maybe she was looking at him now. Watching him look for her.

He nudges the leather satchel with the toe of his shoe. There is nothing but old newspaper inside. But to whoever might be watching him, it *could* be full of money. It could be holding a quarter of a million dollars. If this was going to be an ambush, he wanted to get it over with on a bridge full of people. He wanted the whore-thugs to take the bag and run. Just so that he would know what he was dealing with. As long as he stayed out among the public, they —whoever *they* were, if anybody —would not hurt him. They'd just go for the bag with the cash.

He straightens. Takes a couple of steps away from the bag as if to view the passing barge from another angle. Two feet away. Three feet. Four. If she had brought muscle, now would be the time. Just take it and go.

Nothing.

He feels Christi's 9mm in the pocket of his sport coat knock against his hip. He thought it might lessen the anxiety. It doesn't. The gun only makes it worse. Even without bullets.

Across the water a dozen or more servers carry pitchers and glasses and trays of food. Most of them are headless behind the wall of umbrellas. He watches their arms and shoulders come and go. Looks for new arrivals. One of the servers threads the tables and chairs, pausing for a fat man with a Macy's bag, then pushes forward to the red umbrella on the end. Behind the server is a headless woman in a white blouse. Jeans. Boots.

She moves with a limp.

Sheldon knows it is her before she sits. Before her head drops beneath the umbrella scallops. Something in his chest.

Rose, says the chest.

Olivia, corrects the brain. *Whore.*

He makes her wait. Ten minutes. Fifteen. Looking for others. Watches her read the menu. Drink her water. Talk to the headless server.

He picks up his bag. Starts the recorder in his shirt pocket. Heads off across the bridge.

"Sorry I'm late," he says. Ridiculously. Like they are old friends. He pulls out the opposite chair. Sits. Positions the bag on the ground at his feet. He leans back, looking at her for the first time across the white tablecloth and its outcropping of glass candle and ceramic cactus shakers.

The scars cut him like hot, sharp blades. He can feel them on his own face, shaping his expression. He can't help it. He wants to gasp. He wants to cry out.

He can see that she sees. She looks at her watch.

"Did you think that bridge was a café?" She looks back up at him, deeply expressive brown eyes as cold and as hard as they can manage. "You think someone was gonna bring you a table and two chairs and a glass of wine up there?"

He flushes. Feels the blood in his face. He can't look at her.

"I… wanted to make sure you were alone."

"Yeah. Sheldon. Well, I've been alone for the last twenty minutes."

An overcompensation of anger only makes his face redder.

"Well, I'm sorry. *Olivia.* I'm new at this. Okay? Okay? I've never been blackmailed before."

She leans forward, into the table, pushing the scars closer. Opens her mouth to speak.

The server is suddenly upon them. He has a head on his shoulders and carries a pitcher of water. They listen to the specials. Chicken something. Fish something. Sheldon steals glances. Watching her listen. Her head is turned sideways. His eyes are fingers. He traces her scars. Her lips. The line of her jaw. Down the slope of her pure neck.

Capers. Beurre blanc. Truffle sauce.

The last time he had seen her neck it had been covered in blood. Before that, the explosion. Before that, dragging her across the hot pavement, leaving a wet, red snail trail. Before that, yanking her out of the burning car. Before that, thinking she was dead.

He blinks hard. Reaches inward. Gropes blindly for the hate and the rage. Gropes for the maddening worry. But those feelings, having brought him to the table, have now abandoned him to other feelings. Older feelings.

Before that…

Olivia hands up her menu to the server. Salad and a beer. They both look at him. He hasn't been listening. They wait.

"He'll have the crab cakes," she says at last, snapping away his menu and handing it up. "And the house chardonnay."

They are alone again. She crosses her arms, holding something back. Fear. Rage. Something.

"You can call this blackmail if you want to," she says. "You can call it a train robbery if that makes you feel better. But we both know the truth."

"The truth? Ruining my reputation? My marriage? How is that not blackmail?"

She takes this in. Seemingly confused. As if pondering it for the first time.

"Listen. *Sheldon.*" She spits his name out on the table. "You have fucked up my entire life. You get that? Take a good long look."

He does. Then he can't.

"So if you're feelin'... I don't know... *exposed...* 'cause I live in a whorehouse... or 'cause you've been steppin' out on your wife... to buy sex four hundred miles away in quaint little Corbin... then you'll excuse me if I don't give a good rat fuck."

"I didn't run you off that road. You know that."

"Oh really?" She laughs to herself, contemplating her fork. Then looks up. "I didn't come here to debate what I know, Sheldon. I know everything there is to know. Is that what your wife calls you? Sheldon? Shelly? Shel?"

He crosses his arms. Looks off at the water sliding away through its engineered groove. Listens to the word in his head. *Wife.* She wants that word to hurt. To cut him. And it does hurt. *Wife.* He regrets the word. Regrets the emptiness. Regrets its dry riverbed of fact. He hears it as an accusation.

As if from a lover.

He looks back into her young, now imperfect face. His accuser. His lover. Waiting for an explanation. Waiting for lunch and wine beneath a riverside umbrella. He wants a different conversation. A server delivers heaping red plates to the neighboring table.

"I'm not really hungry," Sheldon says. She follows his gaze.

"Then maybe you shouldn't have insisted on meeting at a café."

Their eyes lock. He sees past the scars to deeper wounds. Loathing. Desperation. He cannot find a calculating blackmailer.

"I'm sorry," he says at last. "For the accident. I didn't mean to suggest I wasn't sorry. Putting the question of fault aside... I *am* sorry."

But her river is not so easily diverted.

"Don't want your pity. I want compensation."

"I don't have that kind of money."

She leans back. Soaking that one in. Readjusting her expectations.

"Then why am I here? What's in the bag?"

He glances down at the satchel. "Nothing. There's nothing in the bag." He reaches for it. Pulls it up. Opens it. Shows her the newspapers.

She pulls the napkin up from her lap and drops it on the table in front of her. Uncrosses her legs.

"Enjoy the crab cakes."

"Wait." Sheldon holds up his hands. "Wait. I have money for you. Just not... not what you've demanded. I have a proposal. It's all I can do. Olivia. It's all I can do. Hear me out."

She leans back. Interlaces her fingers. Waits.

Sheldon pats the breast of his sport coat. In the lower pocket, he can feel the weight of the empty 9mm. In his shirt pocket he can feel the recorder.

"I am prepared to give you a hundred thousand dollars. I know you have demanded two fifty. I don't have that kind of money."

He is talking too fast. He swallows. Breathes.

"I know you must think I'm a very wealthy person. You're wrong about that. I have very little money that is truly my own. Everything else has strings attached. Business strings. Family strings. I can't give you anything more than a hundred without... without people knowing. And consenting. And they won't consent. Not ever. I promise you that. They would sooner cut me loose and see my life ruined. So the price that I'm willing to pay you to *avoid* ruination is no more than a hundred. Above that, it's all the same result to me."

He pauses to measure her expression. There is none. Only her words.

"You'll pay whatever a judge orders you to pay. Sheldon. He'll bleed you 'til you're empty."

She's a smart one, he thinks. She's not going to risk words of extortion. She's been coached to talk only of judges and lawsuits. The recorder in his pocket was a wasted precaution. Like the bag full of newspaper. And the gun.

"Maybe," he says. "But not my business. And not my family. A lawsuit isn't going to touch them. As I say, judge or no judge, I can only pay what I can pay. You don't have a solid legal case anyway. Your accident wasn't my fault. I saved you."

"Saved me? *Saved* me?"

"Yes, you're lucky I..."

"You were fuckin' *chasing* me."

"No... I... I was trying to get your attention. My car never touched your car. You swerved. The police dismissed the case. You won't get what you want in court. You won't get what I'm offering you now. You're likely to get nothing. And your lawyer is not going to come cheap."

Another dinner barge floats lazily past. Someone is toasting a bride and groom. He continues.

"Even a hundred thousand is almost impossible. It's going to be tough. Really tough. I can only do what I can do, Olivia. I have to spread this out. Ten thousand a month. Starting today. Starting now."

He pats the hidden envelope. Watches her eyes. Feels her thinking. Continues. "We meet here. Just like this. Once a month. Nine more months. But understand this." He points at her across the table. "One word to my family… or anyone else… about *anything*… and the payments will stop. I will notify the police and they will prosecute you… and Libby Holder… for extortion. And for whatever drugs go into those cookies. And the wine. That *Rio Lobo* crap. If I see any more letters or notes or videos or photos or… *whatever*… I am going to the police. And when these payments are finally done… then it's all over, Olivia. Then I'm done. One demand after that and I'm going to the …"

Their server cuts him off, lowering plates and glasses and asking questions about fresh cracked pepper that go unanswered. They both ignore him, staring at each other across their food. When he is gone, Sheldon slips the envelope from his pocket. Places it on the table.

"Those are my terms. It's all I can do. Do we have a deal?"

She uncrosses her arms. Reaches for her beer. Drinks. Returns the glass. She looks at him for a long, hard minute. Nods. Reaches for the envelope. He intercepts her hand, pancaking it against the envelope.

"One more thing," he says. Her warm skin wriggles beneath his. "I want my stuff back."

"Stuff?"

"Wallet. Ring. Business papers in a green folder. I want it all back."

"I don't have your… *stuff.*"

"Bullshit. If you really think that's true, then I suggest you ask your partner in crime. Unless this is all the money you want."

He does not want to lift his hand. He wants it to lie atop hers for another minute. For another hour. He lets it go.

She slides the envelope discretely into her lap. Opens it. Counts. Sheldon watches, daring to hope that he has found his way. He eats a bite of crab cake. Reacquaints himself with his surroundings. The ribbon of recycled water slides past him through the bright green desert. The air smells of flowers and food. Someone is laughing. Someone is singing.

Behind him, from some unseen courtyard, floats the sound of live music. Bouncy, swishy jazz. A horn carries a clear and hopeful voice. It cajoles an old blues standard out of its porch rocker, browbeating it into being something it isn't. The song about having notions to jump into oceans and about that not being anybody's damn business now, suddenly, a whimsical splash in a fountain.

"So," he says. Takes a drink of wine. "How 'bout this weather."

Chapter 38

Davis spends the morning with Libby Holder. They sit out in the orchard beneath a pecan-laden canopy.

Third meeting and it's still slow going. Cutting through her bullshit. Coaxing out the truth, a bashful sea creature hiding in a hole in the reef.

Every time the story begins to emerge, she shoves it back down into the hole.

He refuses to talk inside the house. She teases him. Insinuates he is less of a man for fearing the police. They laugh about their last adventure. It is a good distraction.

"Las' time was t'afternoon, baby. You safe. Po-po ain't do shit at nine-o'fuck in the mo'nin'. We can go fuck out in the middle of the damn road and ain't see no po-leece. Hey…" she leans forward. Stage whispers. "What say we go fuck out in the middle of the road?"

She plays with herself through her shirt.

But he gives her nothing. Waits. Lets the octopus ink dissipate and float away in currents of warm air.

"Just fuckin wit'chu, baby. You can relax that fuck-all-day face. Pick up yo' lil' pen. We got to get you a sense of humor, baby. *Damn.*"

Then he sets out to find her again.

Question. Evasion. Game.

Question. Evasion. Answer.

Question. Answer. Evasion.

Question. Answer. Answer. Answer.

The real story is not far away. It never is.

She is like all of the others. Once she starts, she cannot stop. The truth swims in quiet circles, just beneath the surface of her life. Waiting. Waiting for her to jump out of the boat. Then, one stroke, one cupped hand to pull her forward, one kick into the depths to propel her out to sea, and it has her by the ankle. No more games now. No sir. No more bullshit. She is in the jaws of her own story. Just like we all are. Only now she can feel the teeth. Now, suddenly, again, she is conscious enough to put a name to the pain that is always there.

It feels good.

No. Not good. It feels the opposite of good in every way imaginable. It feels terrible all over again.

But it feels *real.*

He breaks off after an hour. She is disappointed. Ernest. Wanting more. She tries to seduce him into staying.

"C'mon, baby," Libby says, unbuttoning her shirt. "You need you a good fuckin'. Cain't keep lookin' at that sad, fuck-all-day face and not reach out to help. See how I am? I throw that humanitarian shit in fo' free, baby. Wit' a cookie an' a glass o' Rio Lobo too. Like this a open house or some shit."

He smiles a little. Sad. Apologetic for what he has done. She can see the empathy in his eyes.

'*See how I am?*'

Yes, he can see how she is. He cannot un-see any of it. Not now. And she knows better.

He stands. Puts away his pen and pad.

"Sorry, Libby. Gotta go to Houston." He heads slowly for his bike, leaving her in her chair beneath the pecan tree. "We'll pick it up later."

He rides east into the sun. Tries not to think of what is ahead of him. Tries to hide himself inside Libby Holder's story. Writing it in his head. When that is gone, like a mist, like receding weather, he tries to lose himself in the vibration beneath him. Lets the cracked, bleached-gray ribbon of the road unspool like it has no end.

But it does have an end. This road back in time. He knows this. The road ends where it always seems to begin. In Houston.

In six hours he is sitting in a worn, leather booth, listening to Hank Williams and Charlie Pride. His body is still buzzing from the ride. He glances up at the two urban cowboys in their *suits-n-boots*, laughing on their way out. The bell jingles as the door closes behind them. Davis eats the last of his cheeseburger.

"Sure you don't want some fries?" he asks. "First time I've ever seen you not eat. Kinda weird."

"Wife has me on a diet," booms Buddy. "Afraid my arteries are out to kill me." He slaps his prodigious gut. "So I'm cuttin' back."

"Buddy Lincoln on a diet. Miracles never cease."

"No." Buddy says this too seriously. His voice is solid rock. An island in the ocean. He leans forward a little. "Miracles never cease, Davis. Never."

Davis lets it go. "Does that mean no more beer either?"

The question is intended to distract. A game to avoid the real issue. They have exhausted his update on the interviews for *Voices*. For once, Buddy is not interested in what he is writing or the magazine.

"You gon' be hungry again in two hours?" asks Buddy. "You'll ruin your appetite." Davis swallows. Drinks his Coke.

"In two hours I won't have an appetite anyway," he says.

Buddy wrinkles up his broad forehead, now resembling a furrowed field of rich, dark loam.

"This is your father we're talking about, man. He's reaching out. If you ask me? You need to forget about the past. Help him make this right."

"He's not reaching out, Buddy. He just wants to make his point. *Again*. He wants to remind me. Now that he's sober."

"Well now you're *both* sober. So maybe now's a good time to have this conversation. Maybe it's time to stop hating each other."

"He just wants to feel good about himself. At my expense."

Buddy shakes his head. Picks up the crumpled letter again. Reads.

"*Dear Davis. I hope...*"

"I know what it says, Buddy."

Buddy gives him that look. Davis sighs.

"*Dear Davis. I hope this letter finds you. I only have your old address, but I assume it will forward. If I had your phone number I would have called you. I know this is awkward. It has been a long time since we tried to connect. I would like to try again.*"

Buddy stops. Lowers the crumpled page to reveal his face. Raises his eyebrows at Davis. Continues.

"*I am better now. I hope you are better now. Time has a way of healing wounds. It helped to finally move out of the house. It helped to finally finish the book. I suppose you heard that I sold the bookstore. It took a long time to realize that place was part of the problem. I'm a copy editor now for Saddlehorn Media Group. It feels like a new start and I want to stay on that road. I'm having a book reading as part of the launch. I would like you to be there. It's important for you to be there. Important for me. You know it would be important for her. The flier is enclosed. We can grab a bite to eat and then catch up. I hope to see you, Davis. Love.*"

Buddy folds the letter. Hands it across the table. Davis puts it in his shirt pocket. "It's bullshit, Buddy. It's the same old bullshit."

Buddy Lincoln leans back in the booth, crossing his massive arms. It is the old seat vinyl that groans, but the sound seems to come from the threads holding Buddy's shirtsleeves to their shoulders.

"Awfully long ride for that *same old bullshit*," he says, dubious.

The server swings by and refreshes his coffee, leaving the bill on the table. Davis doesn't answer. There won't be an answer.

"You gonna be okay tonight, Davis?" he asks. "Elvis thinks you're solid, but if Daddy-O is gonna rock your boat tonight..."

"I'm done with that," says Davis. "I'm good, Buddy. I'm okay." He picks up the bill. Buddy snaps it from his fingers before he can read the total. "Buddy, I'm the only one eating. You can't…"

"Oh, shut up, Davis. I can do whatever I goddamned want. It's on me. Magazine expense. Just write this shit off."

Davis sighs. Nods.

"Thanks. For everything. I mean that."

Buddy scoffs. Waves him away. He pulls a twenty out of his wallet and hands it to the server as she passes.

"He's right, you know. Your mother would want this."

Gratitude evaporates. Davis stares. Blinks. Leans back. Pushes his empty plate away.

"You never knew my mother, Buddy. No disrespect, but…"

"I don't have to know your mother, man." He pokes himself in the chest. "Had my *own* mother. My *kids* have a mother. That shit's the same everywhere, Davis. You count on it like you can count on water bein' wet and the ocean bein' deep. Doesn't matter whether she is near or far, here or gone. Good or bad. She would want this."

Buddy waits. Watches Davis look out the window at the street.

"But you already know that."

Davis looks back.

"Oh?" Snotty. Defensive. Childish. He regrets the tone before the sound of it is gone. Buddy smiles like the man-in-the-moon. Nods. Cocks his head.

"You're here, aren't you?"

He doesn't need the flier. He knows the bookstore. *The Crow's Nest*. A dying independent owned by one of his father's colleagues. Albert Espinoza. His father used to hate Albert Espinoza.

"*Let him leave. Stupid, stupid man. Good riddance. He'll never make it on his own. He'll stock the commercial dreck and get plowed under by the box stores. You just wait. Al's got no sense for business.*"

He also remembers *The Crow's Nest* because it's just down the street from *Billy Budd's Saloon*. He remembers, sprawled over the sidewalk outside *Billy Budd's*, looking up at *The Crow's Nest* one night. After last call, of course. After *Billy Budd's* had kicked him out and locked the door. He remembers the pitch and yaw of the dark glass cage of books up the street, the whole building sliding one way then the other, full tilt on the liquid street. Remembers watching for the books to slip off the shelves. Into the deep.

Remembers not remembering. And how good that felt.

The glass cage of *The Crow's Nest* is still now. Fully lit. It glows yellow with enough light left over to paint the sidewalk.

Davis parks the bike. Breathes.

There are maybe thirty, thirty-five people inside. Four broken rows of folding chairs. Some people stand, leaning against bookshelves. Holding paper cups. Listening with coffee. Some stare at the floor.

Author's Anonymous, he thinks.

My name is Conrad Payne and I finally published a fucking book.

Hi, Conrad.

The room holds his father's voice like a scent. Like coffee. Like the smell of ink and leather. Davis stands in the back, between *Classics* and *Poetry*, partly obscured by trailing ivy.

Conrad is behind a blond wooden podium. Sport coat. Clean white shirt. New glasses. They are rounder than the ones he remembers. They splash with light as Conrad moves. No hat. Fully bald now. No more pretending on that score.

But the dungeon pallor is gone. He has been in the sun. He is leaner. Not leaner-emaciated. Leaner-fit.

On the table next to the podium is a bottle of water and a cardboard placard leaning up against a small pyramid of books.

Eyelash Lake, it is called.

The title font is loose and soggy. Like something washed up on a shore. Its blue letters slop over the single image of a bleached wooden prow. The background is a pale, watery green. He closes his eyes to the sound of his father's voice, reading his own book.

… because he could not fathom what she was telling him. The young officer smiled painfully, removing the chunk of blue stone from the evidence bag.

"The investigation is closed," she said. "We don't need this any more. I think she would want you to have it. I mean… obviously."

She placed it in his hand, which then sagged in the air beneath its weight.

For the first time, Spencer saw the thing for what it was. Not a soapstone whale; but a warning. A comeuppance. A promise. A confession. An apology. Forgiveness. All in advance. A message from his wife –from Elizabeth –that she had carefully sculpted before they had ever met and then precisely hidden, years before her death, at the bottom of a lake, knowing –somehow, inexplicably knowing –precisely when and how he would find it.

Did he believe? No. Still, his answer was the same. No. He did not believe. He could not believe. It was too much. Too far.

And yet it was impossible not to believe. The proof was in his hand.

"People warned me that Elizabeth was crazy," he said finally. "My friends. Her friends. The way they talked about her…"

"Crazy is an ugly word," the officer said. "She was… troubled. Mixed up."

Spencer opened his mouth to speak but then fell still. It began to sprinkle.

Drops spattered off the shoulders of the officer's jacket.

He might have invited her in. She was no longer the enemy. There was no reason to fear her. Neither of them moved.

"But you're not implicated," she said. "Not criminally. Not for Jennifer. That's what is important now."

"But Elizabeth knew that I *would be* implicated. That's what she wanted. She knew it would look like... like I..."

The officer smiled sadly. The condescension was too much for her to hide.

"Is that what you believe, Mr. McClure? Really? You believe that, years before she married you, Elizabeth foresaw all of this? That she carved this thing? This whale? That she inscribed it for you? You whom she did not even know at that point? Knowing then that she would meet you. Marry you. That you would treat her like you did. That you would find this thing at the bottom of Eyelash Lake, where she sunk it years before any of this happened? Knowing that of all places, *that* is where you would find it? So that you could use her inscription on the bottom of that thing to exonerate yourself? Really? All after going through the trouble of setting you up for the murder of your own mistress? Is that really what you believe?"

He couldn't answer her. Couldn't look at her. She pressed on.

"Look. Had you not tried..." she hesitated for a beat, trying to be delicate. "Had you not tried to drown yourself, you'd never have found this thing. Right?" Her expression was more intense now, betraying her emotional investment in the case. After that first day she had always seemed so coldly professional. "Mr. McClure?"

The rain was coming harder, hissing into the trees and pocking the lake. The water looked like it was just beginning to boil. Spencer nodded.

"She believed..." he swallowed. Then he continued, speaking slowly, as if speaking to the stone whale in his hand. "Elizabeth believed that the barrier between life and death is... *porous*. That was the word she always used. *Porous*. She believed that linear time is just a conceptual crutch for simple minds. She believed that there is only... the *now*. That the past is now. The future is now. It's all happening now. All at once. In the same moment. And that single moment of happening is all there is and it lasts forever. She believed that the truth of our existence is simply beyond our perception."

He could sense the incredulity in the air between them. He could not tell whether it was hers or his. She shifted her weight, resting her hand on the butt of her holstered gun. The empty evidence bag rattled in the rain. He could tell she wanted to speak. But she held her tongue. Spencer kept pushing out the words.

"She always scoffed at the idea of an exogenous god. She believed in a god that was all-encompassing. All things. All creatures. All places. All times. She believed we are merely molecules of an eyelash on the face of divinity, cursed with self-awareness. There is no god to worship because there is nothing but God in the first place. Boats are made to carry an illusion. We are all made of water." Spencer looked up. "That's why she drown herself in that lake. She believed she could move on. Escape the prison of this plane. This limited vibration."

"Why? So she could frame you?"

"Yes. To punish me. For loving Jennifer. And for not loving her."

Officer Flask shook her head.

"Oh, you did a lot more to Elizabeth than not love her."

Spencer did not answer. He did not have to answer.

"I don't care what Elizabeth believed," she said. "So answer the question. That's what it took for you to find this." She tapped the whale on the head. "Right? It took your own attempted suicide to put you in that lake. The only way you would have ever found this whale. You had to almost drown."

He nodded, sighing this time, as if her words were coming from inside his own head and he was tired of chasing those words on their endless loop of logic. Tired of being chased.

"Right," she said, anger finally in her tone. "So that's not an explanation. That's not possible. We have to deal in the real world, Mr. McClure. Facts. Evidence. Flesh and blood. Elizabeth was flesh and blood. Just like Jennifer. None of this is about spirits or God's eyelashes." She pointed sharply to his hand and the thing it held. "This... *thing* exonerates you. You're not a suspect. And I don't know if it clears your conscience. That's between you and your God and Elizabeth's memory. Maybe you forgive yourself and maybe you don't. But I do know this, Mr. McClure: there is a past, there is a present, and there is a future. The things we do have consequences. We have free will in this life. You have to *choose* to marry your wife. You have to *choose* to cheat on her. You have to *choose* to hit her over and over until her face swells up and the neighbors start talking. You have to *choose* to abandon her for a bottle of booze. You have to *choose* to jump out of a rowboat with weights on your ankles. These are choices that you make in the moment. They are not theoretical or figments of your imagination. You don't get to opt out of linear time. You have to live with the consequences of those choices. Elizabeth chose to kill Jennifer. Then she chose to kill herself. Are those decisions a consequence of how you treated her? I'll let you wrestle with that one on your own time. But what you don't get to do is pretend that Elizabeth drown herself just so she could pop up on the other side of a cosmic wormhole and stick it to you and then save you from prosecution. You don't get to do that. Because that's not real."

Spencer looked up into Karen Flask's eyes, now full of rage and accusing him all over again, like that first terrible night when she had come for him, finding him in the woods covered in Jennifer's blood. Not the blood of murder. The blood of discovery. But it all looks the same to the police.

Spencer looked down at the whale. The tail. The blowhole for a flower. The sly smile. He remembered it from the dresser. From the étagère. From the bookshelf. He remembered it from every home of their marriage. He had felt the inscription, too small for him to find his glasses and read it. He never cared. He remembered Elizabeth saying she was tired of it; that she was going to sell it. Donate it. Years ago. He thought she had.

He extended his hand, raising it, holding the slick blue stone within inches of Karen Flask's face. The rain splatted in soft, wet detonations. He turned the flat of the belly toward her, so that she could reread the inscription: *"Spencer, I forgive you. The knife is in her watering can. Elizabeth Bohn. January 12, 1972."* His eyes asked the question more than his words.

"Then you tell me, Officer Flask. You tell me how I'm supposed to explain this. Are the lab tests wrong? This has been down there in the muck for years. So just how do *you* explain this?"

In a quiet instant, the air around them had become a torrent. The lake was roiling. Spencer saw from her face, losing its tension as the rain slid down her cheeks, that there was no answer to this question. There was no answer except the answer neither of them could accept as possible.

They go to *Murphy's* for a bite. A booth in the back. Dark. Narrow. Too small. Like a rowboat built for one. But it's the only thing available. His father orders a steak. The server is young and timid.

"I'm good," Davis says, handing up the menu. "Iced tea."

"What?" Conrad looks offended.

"Already ate." Davis nods again at the server. She leaves.

"I invited you to dinner."

"You invited me to a reading. I came. You read."

Conrad sighs. Looks at his son. He nods, acknowledging the steepness of the hill in front of him.

"Okay," he says. "Okay."

They talk of small, innocuous, inconsequential things. Weather. The Astros. Like strangers sharing a cab to the airport.

"So," says Conrad. "Little Corbin, Texas. That's a surprise. You liking it okay?"

"It's okay. Small. Probably what I need for awhile."

"Doesn't sound like it's gonna be small forever. That Corbin River Walk thing? Sounds like a fool's errand to me."

"Never know," says Davis. "Could be."

"I've been reading the old *Ocotillo Review* back issues. Good stuff, Davis. Good stuff. Must be in the genes. Can't be enough to live on though."

Davis nods. Drinks his tea. Watches his father chew.

"Your aunt died," Conrad says, watching it register. "Ann Marie sent me a letter with the obit."

"Tallulah? When?"

"Last month. Neighbors found her at the bottom of their pool. Middle of the night. Nothin' on but a sock."

"Oh God."

"Figured you'd want to know."

"I should have been there," says Davis.

"The pool?"

"The funeral."

Conrad jolts with a soft laugh. Cuts his rib eye.

"Was no funeral. Ann Marie said Tallulah had been very clear on the subject of funerals. Would not abide ceremony of any kind. Particularly the religious kind." Conrad chews. Shakes his head. "Poor woman. Crazy as the day is long."

It is the same old attack on Tallulah. That it was probably true did not make it less offensive. That she was dead made it more offensive. But Davis lets it go. Tries.

"Do you need money?"

"No." He waits a beat. Then adds, "Buddy Lincoln is helping me out."

He notes the pause in the chewing. The irrelevant father. Conrad nods. Swallows. Climbs back up on the horse.

"Where you working?"

"Here and there. Restaurant work mostly. Demolition work for Dallas Letti."

"Dallas Letti? *The* Dallas Letti?"

Davis nods.

"I'll be damned," he says. "Thought she was dead."

Davis shakes his head. "Nope."

"Demolition work. You mean like…"

"Couple of old structures on her property. Hauling it off to the dump one truckload at a time. It's some money."

"Your mother loved Letti Blue. Woman could sing. How the hell did that come about?"

Davis gives Dallas Letti a makeover. They have become fast friends in his version. She is generous to a fault. The mother he no longer has. The story eats up another ten minutes but then empties into a chasm of silence that neither of them knows how to fill.

"What'd you think of the reading?" Conrad wipes his mouth with his napkin.

"I think you gave away the ending."

Conrad smiles. "That wasn't the ending. That was from the middle."

"The middle? What the hell happens after that?"

"Maybe you should read your old man's book and find out."

The smile tumbles out onto the table like the bullsnake out of that ceramic pot. Same old Conrad. All about him. Always was, always will be. Fuck the past. This wasn't about the past. This was about Conrad, the new man with no history.

It is almost more than Davis can take. He drinks his tea, an effort to drown the words in his throat. His father sighs.

"What's wrong, Davis?"

"Nothing. Nothing's wrong."

"I want to see you. I want to spend time with you. I want us..."

A bitter laugh escapes. A fetid gas bubbling up from the depths. From the sunken, broken hull. Davis shakes his head. "Little late for that."

"It's never too late."

They look at each other for a long moment. The server starts to make a pass with a silver pitcher. But she is as perceptive as she is timid. She aborts at the last second, picking another table. Davis goes first.

"I wonder what she'd think. After all the shit you gave her. Cuttin' her down for what she believed. For who she was. Year after year. And now it's all out there. Loud and proud. Right there in your... fuckin' novel."

"Davis..."

"*The barrier between life and death is porous?* Really Conrad? *Molecules of an eyelash on the face of divinity, cursed with self-awareness?* You're going to use that *now?* For *yourself?* Like those ideas were ever in *your* head? Like you never tore her apart for believin' in somethin' different than you?"

Conrad leans back, the structure of his expression starting to crumble like a bulwark of dry sand. He glances sideways out into the restaurant. "Son..."

"No. Don't call me son. Like that word has some special power. It doesn't. How dare you try to profit from her. From who she was and what she believed. How dare you write about her. Prostitute her. You didn't even have the decency to change her name."

"We need to forgive each other."

"And a goddamned *whale?* Really? Like the porcelain one that you smashed against our wall the day she died?"

"Davis. This needs to stop. For once. We need to forgive each other."

"No," he says, feeling the rowboat shake beneath them. "No we don't. I will never forgive you for how you treated her. Like dirt. Running her down like she was nobody. How many times did you yell at her? How many times did you shit on everything she believed in? How many times did you make her afraid?"

Conrad shakes his head. Sighs. Nods.

"Too many times." He stares at the bits of gristle on his plate, remnants of the past. "I won't deny that. I can't. Sometimes she was afraid. For no reason. I'd never hit her and I never would have, but she..."

"But she fuckin' knew better, Conrad. She knew you were capable of anything."

Conrad takes a deep breath. Not looking. Waiting to start again.

"She had these… dreams. Nightmares. Christ." He stops. Lets some air out of his nose. His lips tighten in a spasm of memory. "She'd wake up screaming and shaking. I could never calm her down. I just made it worse. It was like she woke up in the middle of a fight."

"A fight. What kind of fight?"

Conrad looks. "Me beating on her. Drunk. Angry."

"Right."

"Look. I'm just trying to tell you that I know how bad I was. I never hit her but I probably had a lot to do with those nightmares. I know she was afraid sometimes. And she was unhappy in the world. I was most of that. I want you to know I acknowledge that."

He looks up at Davis, hope in his eyes.

"What. You want some kinda' fuckin' *credit* now? For admitting…"

"No. I don't want credit for anything, Davis."

"You're pathetic, Conrad. Still. Even off the sauce, you're pathetic."

Conrad shakes his head. Laughs bitterly to himself.

"Tallulah really poisoned you. Like she poisoned Eliz…"

"No. I was there. *I* was. Not Tallulah. *Me*. My own eyes. My own ears. I was always there the morning after. I was there more than enough."

There is a flash of rage in Conrad's eyes. The heat lightning of old memory.

"You were *not* there for all of those times that she… that *your mother*…" He breaks off. Looks away. Fights for control. Comes back. "You were young. Davis. You were too young. Your mother believed… Elizabeth was…"

"If you say the word *crazy*… if I even see that word on your face… so help me God I will come across this fuckin' table."

Conrad closes his eyes. A vein on his scalp throbs, helping him count to ten. "I was going to say…"

"Music." Davis nearly spits the word. "Forget whatever in the hell you were going to say. Forget Aunt Tallulah. Forget the Motherverse. Forget her cosmic loops. Forget her god. Mom believed in music. *Music. Blues music.* Remember when you smashed all of her records? Remember *that* drunken rage?" He pretends to laugh. "There were so many. But do you remember that one?"

Conrad pushes away his plate. As if his uneaten food disgusts him or he is suddenly too exhausted to eat.

"Well *I* do. I helped her pick up the mess. You broke them in half. Shattered them against the wall. Every last one of them. Bessie Smith. Ma Rainey. Dallas Letti. Billie Holiday. All of them. Just because she loved something that wasn't you. If it wasn't about you, then you wouldn't let her be happy."

Conrad is silent. Taking his medicine.

"So, no, you can't just wipe that slate clean, Conrad. You don't get to publish a book and forgive yourself."

Another ugly bubble, wobbling in its distorted spin up from the depths. It sneaks to the surface behind the others. Too quick for him to catch.

"You've sure as shit never forgiven me."

Conrad looks up. "I do forgive you," he says. "I do."

"Bullshit. You always blamed me. *She died for nothin' Davis.* How many times did you tell me that? *She died for nothin'.* Well, she fuckin' died trying to save *me.* I'm the *nothin'* she was tryin' to save."

"Water terrified her. She couldn't swim. She was fully clothed. You were half way across the lake. No way she could have saved you. I was just saying... the park attendant saved you... I wasn't saying..."

But he's not listening.

"*If it hadn't been for you, Davis... If it hadn't been for you...* How many fuckin' times did you tell me that? *Conrad.* How many fuckin' times?"

"I... was deep in the bottle. You know that. I was a lousy drunk. Losing her made everything worse. And look, you had your own problems. You went off the deep end too. I know that whole horrible drama with..."

"Don't."

"... with Abby was because of your mother."

"You fuckin' leave her out of this. She has nothing to do..."

"You were a mess, Davis. And you made some bad, self-destructive decisions. You associated with someone..."

"Enough!" Davis brings his fist down on the table, clattering the plates and upending the steak sauce. They let it bleed in slow brown drips.

Breathing. That's all there is for a long moment. Breathing in and out. One, then the other. Like the ebb and flow of a dirty tide.

"I went broke for you, Davis. Because I love you."

"Right. Public defenders are paid by the taxpayers, Conrad. You went broke on the cost of bourbon."

"Well, you didn't *start out* with a pubic defender. The taxpayers were a last resort when *I* ran out of money." There is a flash of anger in his father's eyes. "And who do you think paid Dr. Bees? He wasn't free for your mother and he wasn't free for you either. Think the fucking taxpayers paid *him?*"

The question is a lead pipe across the skull. He had always assumed that his counseling had been paid with compassion and with loyalty to the dead.

Conrad holds his breath. Counts. Breathes.

Continues.

"I'm just trying to tell you that... that as bad as things were... *Davis... son...* As bad as things got... I still cared. You're right. I was not a good husband. Or a good father. I was not a good man. I was a drunk. Your mother had her own problems. A lot of them. I know that does not excuse my behavior. But… I never stopped loving you. Just like I never stopped loving her. You must know that. You must know…"

"No." His eyes are drowning, shot through with red lightning. "Here is what I know. What I know is that you abused her to the water's edge. And then I pulled her in. I held her down. That's what I fucking know. Neither of us gets forgiven. Not for her. Not for mom."

Conrad wants to speak. Opens his mouth. Davis points.

"And you sure as fuck don't get to write a book in which you cast yourself as a reluctant believer who loved his wife. The distraught widower. Because you never believed. And you never loved."

"I did. I did love her. I never believed. I had a hard time with what she believed. She and Tallulah. My own religion just ran too deep, Davis. My own religion saved me. It saved me every day. I did love Elizabeth. Like I love you. I did treat her poorly. I admit that. *Eyelash Lake* is my confession. If you would read…"

"No, I won't read. Fuck you, Conrad. I won't read. Not a fuckin' word."

He pushes himself out of the booth. Stands. Steps away.

Stops. Turns.

He comes back and leans down.

"Of the two of us, I was the one who loved her. If I have to own her death, then you have to own what you did to her life. So you just keep on writing your stories. Because forgiveness is fiction."

Chapter 39
Mable and Libby

He saved them. No question. Saved both of them.

Ten more minutes. Maybe five. The house would have been near invisible by then. Just the tip of a roofline above the water; a hard wooden seam laid out on top of the muddy froth like a floating plank. Five minutes after he had them, the poorly built ramshackle thing just dissolved into sticks. Floated off like a bird's nest coming apart.

Saving themselves was never an option. Certainly not for Mable Holder. Every last one of her two hundred eighty pounds was afraid of the water. Also wasn't an option for little Libby, who could float like a leaf. Libby was young and lithe and lean, but she'd never learned to swim. Even if she had, she'd never have been able to muscle her way out of a hurricane.

And she'd never have abandoned Mama Mable anyway.

So that should have been it. Nothing but Bayou bubbles.

But then there he was. Antoine Beaudaine Cherish. The *ABC Man*, as Libby would eventually call him, moving like an oil slick over the top of the water. Floating up alongside their second story bedroom window in his little rusty blue skiff. Flicking away the dislocated water moccasins with a boat hook.

To keep from blowing away, the ABC Man had jammed that boat hook into the hole that used to be a bedroom window. Almost did blow away, taking the whole soggy wall with him.

But it held. And then there he was, framed like a picture in the window hole.

Truth is, they'd heard the motor first. A ragged, tinny buzz, like a sun-drunk bee in the wind, just above the low notes of the lashing storm. But it was Antoine's dirty, smiling face in the window hole that they would remember.

That was the sign that they were going to live another day.

They'd lived with Antoine for a month or two after, until Mother Mable's people in Gretna found them a new place to live. Too late by then. Mr. ABC was already in. Already part of the future.

His home sat alone, outside Thibodaux in Lafourche Parish. It was dirty and small and smelled of old grease. But it was dry. Strangely unscathed by the violence in the air.

He gave Mable the bed. Libby got the grimy, blue felt couch. Antoine slept in the back seat of the moss green Impala parked out front beneath an enormous pecan tree, stripped of its leaves, scattering moon shadows like dark bones over the surrounding field.

He was gone when they woke that first morning. But he'd come back in the late afternoon with some clothes and food. Mable cooked for them in the evenings while Antoine sat on the porch and whittled and played his fiddle and taught Libby how to play cards.

Sometimes Mable would call out from the kitchen to ask if Antoine could play some old blues song she missed. Songs that called out to her slow and soggily from the depths, drowned in the storm with her record player. Antoine never knew the songs Mable mourned.

She was happy to cook and clean for this man she did not know. The man who had saved her life and the life of her twelve-year old daughter. The man who had so easily accepted the inconvenience of putting them up.

It was the least she could do. Did a lot of other things for Antoine too.

None it was new to Mable Holder, of course. She'd done it all before. Those *other* things. The men always left satisfied and always came back.

Mr. ABC was no different.

Chapter 40

April March leans into his office. Wrist bangles clatter against the doorframe. Her hair is pulled into a ponytail, like a blonde waterspout gushing from the back of her head. Lacquered nails like ovular drops of blood on the eggshell wall.

"Okay, boss man. I'm off like a prom dress. It's just you now. See you in the mornin'?"

Sheldon looks up from the invoice. Nods.

"I'll be here. Thanks April."

She flings one of the blood drop nails in his direction. Points.

"Don't you work too late, now."

Sheldon clenches his jaw. Smiles as best he can. It's that maternal tone of hers. *Now, Shelly, don't you eat too many of those cookies or you'll have a tummy ache.* He manages a salute. April March laughs and turns. Swishes out of sight down the hall.

He listens. Hears the front doors close behind her. Then the sound of emptiness. The *memory* of sound.

He looks back down at the invoice in his hands. It would seem that Houston Market Research owes the Houston Media Law Group just over eleven thousand dollars.

Services rendered regarding action for libel/Chachalaca Gazette. $11,250.

Eleven thousand dollars might be a lot to pay for a month of legal representation. Sheldon was not entirely sure. He was not enough of a consumer of legal services to make that evaluation.

Whether the fees were an *appropriate* business expense was entirely academic. No one was going to question that the business was paying his legal bills. Grayson Tate had been clear enough.

"Don't care what it costs, Shelly. If you have to sue the sons of bitches, then sue 'em. Run the legal bills through the goddamned business. You just get this mess cleaned up. You don't clean this up, Shelly, then there *is* no business."

Sheldon was free to take that any way he wanted. Either the consequences of not "cleaning up the mess" would be so catastrophic to the Corbin Development Project account that the business would implode or, alternatively, Grayson would be so angry that he would cut off all support and steer clients elsewhere. Either was possible. Hell, *both* were possible. But the latter was likely.

Grayson had not said, 'run the legal bills through *your* business.'

He had said '*the* business.'

Grayson no longer thought of Houston Market Research as Sheldon's business in any but the most technical sense. He thought of it as a business that he had supported and to which he had fed a steady stream of clients comprising the core of the agency's revenue. As Grayson saw things, all of that support meant that Sheldon operated the agency for the benefit of Christi. *Christabelle*, who was Grayson's daughter first, and only incidentally Sheldon's wife. Never mind that Houston Market Research was a going-concern before Sheldon and Christi had ever met.

Of course, if HMR had been a going-concern before Sheldon married into the Tate family, then it had not been going anywhere very fast or in much of a straight line. Were it not for Grayson Tate, the agency would likely be dead, or one-fifth its current size. There was no arguing that point.

Might have made sense for Grayson to own a big chunk of HMR stock. Sheldon had offered it up almost immediately after the wedding. But Grayson preferred a softer kind of control. Softer and far more complete. It would have demeaned Grayson to be allocated a legal vote tied to a certain number of shares of stock. He already had the only vote that mattered. They both knew that.

Grayson wanted to be a silent investor. Or a not-so-silent investor, full of folksy, sage advice and, purely as a courtesy, entrusted with a right to have his accountants take a monthly look at the books. If there was a problem on the horizon, Grayson Tate wanted to see it coming. More importantly, if the shit ever hit the fan over at Houston Market Research, then Grayson Tate was damn well keeping his suit clean.

Grayson generally let Sheldon pretend that he was still in control of HMR. That he had full authority to determine its destiny.

"It's your baby, Shel. Whatever you say goes. I'm just tossin' in my two cents."

And, most times, Sheldon pretended it was *his baby*.

But it was all just an illusion.

No. It was a *lie*, plain and simple.

Just like *The Houston Media Law Group* was a lie. Of sorts. It was an actual law firm. It just was not a law firm representing the interests of Sheldon Davis. Not any more. Not for at least ten years when *The Houston Media Law Group* had put together a basic suite of business contracts for HMR that HMR had adapted and recycled endlessly ever since.

But Sheldon still had an old but well-preserved *Houston Media Law Group* invoice. It had not taken much for him –hunched down into the late-night glow of the printer-copier-scanner –to turn it into a new invoice with a new address, one that corresponded exactly with Sheldon's new post office box, registered to a brand new company called *HMLG, Inc.*

Sheldon looks down at the invoice in his hand.

Services rendered regarding action for libel/Chachalaca Gazette. $11,250.

It was the second of what would be ten invoices. Over a ten-month span, the average monthly charge for legal services rendered by *The Houston Media Law Group* would pencil out to about ten thousand dollars. Almost exactly.

Imagine that.

He pulls a blue pen from the drawer and scribbles a note to his bookkeeper across the face of the invoice.

Alice: Approved. Please Pay. Thx. Shel.

He walks it down to Alice's office, turning off the lights as he goes. He places it upside down on Alice's chair.

On Alice's desk is an old Houston Oilers Football clock. A relic from the days before the Oilers had run off to Tennessee and changed their name. A little football at the end of the second hand moves jerkily across little white yard lines painted on a circular green field.

Shit.

He confirms the bad news with his own watch. *Shit.* He was going to be late. And there would be hell to pay.

The Texas Pageant Association likes to throw parties. Fundraisers. Award Ceremonies. Spirit Galas. Booster Pageants. The TPA is keen on lavish self-appreciation. At least one big pat on the back every other month.

Always black-tie formal, these things. Always in the grand ballroom of some high-rise hotel in one of four venues: Houston, Dallas, San Antonio, or Austin.

There was a stir several years back. Some of the less populous cities circulated a petition among the TPA membership and board. The heart of Texas, the petition declared, is not confined to its four largest cities. Smaller towns were just as fertile a source of that uniquely Texan brand of American talent and beauty and should be acknowledged with the occasional spotlight. Bowing to political pressure, the TPA Board had tried hosting one of these soirees at the Sheraton in Odessa.

That will never happen again.

Christabelle Tate Davis, former Miss Houston, receives a two-month advance notice whenever the TPA decides to throw a shindig in Houston. A common courtesy. All resident "crown-bearers", board members, and program donors get the same letter in advance of the formal gilded invitation. Christi, as a bearer-member-donor, should have received at least three notices to the event. Grayson's notice would make it four. Sheldon's notice as president of Houston Market Research, a Platinum Level donor, would make five notices.

But one notice was more than enough to do the trick.

Christi treated the Houston events on the same level of importance as a royal wedding that, at the personal request of the Queen, she was hosting in her own back yard. Even in the years when she was not, technically, on the Houston TPA organizing committee, Christi was right in the thick of it with all of the others, swinging her perfect fifty year-old elbows.

Even after he arrives, it takes Sheldon thirty minutes to find his wife. From one end of the ballroom to the other, he bobs disconnectedly in the rolling, sparkling sea of Texan glamour. Eyes. Teeth. Naked throats. Storms of hair. Everywhere tuxedos. Plunging necklines. Open backs. Bejeweled pumps.

People that he knows. That Christi knows. Everywhere. The same people every time the event comes to Houston. Fins in the water circling the tables. Looking to show their teeth.

He tries to spot them in advance, adjusting his course. He is mostly successful. But it's like trying to walk between raindrops or dodge the perfume clouds in Houston department stores.

He turns in time to spot Gillian Reed coming for him from behind.

"There he is," says Gillian, former Miss Dallas, Class of '79. "Handsome devil."

She's as thin as her name. Her hair is a friable copper coif that she carries on her head like a perched vase. She moves in slow, smooth strides, always turning from the shoulders or below, never at the neck.

"Gillian," he says. "You're looking radiant. Where's Chet?"

"The usual. Off where I can't see him drooling over the horse flesh."

"Your Chet? I don't believe that for a second. He's only got eyes for you."

"Sweet. Y'all stick up for each other, Shelly. Can't fool me."

"Hey now. You can trust *me*, Gillian."

"Not what I hear, Tiger." She winks. The entire *Chachalaca Gazette* article is in that wink, along with a note of gleeful diversion. She pats him on the chest with the flat of her hand, holding him in place with her eyes. "Your woman's lookin' all over for you, Shel. I told her you were probably off with Chet, eyein' the goodies. She didn't think that was funny. Best not keep her waitin'."

He blinks. Too long. Too slow. Gillian's smile is subtly crafted and something to behold.

"Where is she?" he asks.

She points and glides away, trailing her fingers across his shoulders.

In a far corner, the members of *Tonky Honk Rodeo Swing* whip their way through *Deep in the Heart of Texas.*

Sheldon listens, waiting for Christi to finish her loud, arm-waving laugh-fest with two other former crown-bearers and their hopeful daughters. When they are finished, Christi wipes a tear of laughter from her eye with a knuckle. She turns. Sees him. Looks at her watch. Looks back at him. Scrunches her entire, flawless face down into the shape of a perfect, pink puckered anus.

"Where in the Sam Hill, Shel? You're an hour late. An *hour.*"

"Things went long at the office."

"And where is your *tux*?" She looks at him aghast. Palms open. "You're... You're..."

"I came straight from the office. I don't wear a tuxedo at work, Christi."

"Shelly, it is bad enough that I have to hitch a ride with Daddy to an event I helped to plan..."

"You could have driven yourself," he says.

"In this?" She takes a step back so that he can better appreciate her full-length gown, black as space and glittering with stardust. "You think... I am gon' drive myself... in *this*?"

"Look..."

"Shelly," she looks furtively in several directions. Then back at him. Lowers her voice. "It's bad enough Daddy has to change his plans so he can bring me, but for you to show up an hour late and not dress appropriately is almost inexcusable."

"I'll settle for almost," he says. Christi draws a breath, ready to unload.

A raven-haired woman wrapped up to her arm armpits in a white lace towel breezes by. Slows. Touches Christi lightly on the shoulders.

Christi's expression is a time-lapse film, missing all of the in-between shots, blooming instantly from puckered anus back into the fully lit face of a carnivorous beauty queen.

"Darla!" she peals, wiggling her fingers at the woman's half-turned back. "Don't you just look divine?"

Darla keeps moving. Christi, spring-loaded, returns to center, shoulders squaring again with Sheldon, face collapsing back into its scowling pucker. *Tonky Honk Rodeo Swing* slips into a jittery version of *New San Antonio Rose*, shaking the room like a can of warm soda. Someone is whooping.

"What has gotten into you, lately?"

"Nothing," he says. "I'm here. After a very long day, I'm here. So I don't appreciate being mowed over. That's all."

"Oh, well 'scuse me, Mister. You' think you're the only one who's had a long day? You think all of this," she gestures expansively at the frothing ballroom around her, "happens all by itself?"

He notes that she has gone with metallic cranberry for the nails and the lips. A week of fretting finally put to rest.

"You spent half the day babysitting Nicholas Voss," he says.

"Half the day? We had lunch, Shelly. *Lunch*. A couple hours at *The Cattleman's*. And that's all. Daddy had to cancel a meeting and insisted I take him out. Nicki doesn't know up from down anywhere in this state 'cept for Corbin. You know that."

"Nicki? He's Nicki now?"

Her face grows still, reclining into some new serenity he cannot explain. She smiles. Blinks. He realizes she is waiting for someone to pass out of earshot.

"Hey, Didi," she sings over his shoulder, face like an exploding star. "Lookin' lovely t'night. See you Sunday. I said I'll see you Sunday." The music is in the way. She mouths the word in slow, exaggerated motion. *Sunnnn...daaaay.*

Like she is gnashing at his face.

She laughs. Smiles. Laughs some more. *Gosh darn music!* Waves. Refocuses.

"Nicki is his *name*, Shelly. It's what he prefers." Her luminous blue eyes slash the room quickly in all directions. "And he's here tonight so you just watch your mouth. Stop actin' like a jealous fool. It don't suit you much. And *you* can give *me* a tone like *that* as soon as *I* get caught by a newspaper payin' gigaloads for sex."

"Gigolos."

"Man prostitutes, Shel. You know what I mean."

"They're called gigolos, Christi."

"Well you would know, wouldn't you?"

"None of that is true, Christi. I told you..."

"Yeah. You told me. But did you ever tell the readers of *The Chacha?* Gillian Reed is like the cat that ate the damn canary."

"Saw her. I'm working on it. It's not as easy as all that, Christi."

"Nothin' is easy with you, Shel. But *nothin'*." She reaches out and yanks at his hand, letting it go. "And where's the ring I gave you?"

"At home."

"At..."

"It's not my ring, Christi."

"No. It isn't. You mysteriously *lost* your wedding ring. *Shelly*. It's behind some floozy's nightstand."

"It was stolen out of the car. Do we really have to do this now?"

Christi smiles broadly, teeth like Grecian walls, cheekbones rising, blue eyes shining like sunlit seas. Her lips move in the slight quiver of a ventriloquist.

"I went. To the trouble. Of buyin'. A new damn wedding band. Just. For this. Event. So people would *not* be talkin'."

"It's too small. I can barely put it on."

"Well then keep your hand in your damn pocket. Try not to play with yourself."

New San Antonio Rose comes skidding to a stop. Someone from the band announces that dinner is served, calling for people to make their way to their assigned tables.

"Where are we sitting?" asks Sheldon. "What's the table number?"

Christi turns and walks off. She holds up three fingers as she goes. Including the one with the ring and its taller more rigid neighbor.

"Nicki" Voss can fill out a tuxedo like nobody's business. Baby blond hair curling softly behind his ears, working with the lips and the eyes, like soft water over rock, to feminize the hyper-masculine cut of his jaw.

Sheldon tries not to be too obvious. Difficult, since Nicholas and Christi are sitting directly across from him. Blond. Blond. Blue. Blue. White. White. Like a couple of purebred Samoyeds waiting for bowls of fresh salmon.

Sheldon is on the other side of the circle, flanked by Grayson on his left and Raeleen McKibben on his right.

Raeleen McKibben. Miss Dallas Runner up 1961. The hair is gray now, but it's all still there, all fourteen inches of it, piled on top of her head, stabbed with ornamental chopsticks and sprayed with a kind of gluey glitter to keep it in place. She looks distressingly like a dirty snow cone melting in the sun. Raeleen has buried three husbands and three children. House fire. Suicide. Cancer. Hunting accident. AIDS. Cancer. Still coming to the damned TPA fundraisers.

He makes small talk with Raeleen, but most of his attention is across the table. When he looks up, he tries to do so in a way that perfectly aligns the red plastic table number sign, hoisted on its silver spindle, with the square of Nicki's perfect Slavic face.

He supposes that Christi is making a statement. Sitting next to Nicholas. Well. Three statements.

One statement, clearly intended for her father, is that Grayson can count on her to be of assistance whenever the need arises to keep his high-rolling clients entertained. It is a task that had previously always fallen to her mother, Layla.

Layla Fennimore Tate, in all other respects a proper Christian woman, knew how to flirt and tell a dirty joke. She could down a shot of Jack without ever taking the cigarette out of her mouth. Layla could do those things all night long and then go play eighteen holes in the morning and shoot birds in the afternoon and then go cook dinner if called upon by her husband, the wheeling-dealing Houston real estate tycoon. It was a devotion, often against principle, that Christi admired.

"You take care of the son-of-a-bitch," Layla had admonished Christi before checking out for good. "He's gonna need you."

Not that Layla Tate had had any illusions in the end. Layla, propped up on her deathbed, Parliament stuck to her upper lip, had looked over at her gorgeous, destroyed, bleary-eyed daughter and croaked out the words Christi never forgot.

"Well sure he's a cheating bastard, baby. Your daddy's a *man*, just like the good Lord makes most men, with a head for business, a dipstick to worship, and a blind spot for trouble. But he's *my* cheating bastard. That ain't nothin'. You can only truly love what you truly know. And you'll never truly know a man 'til you've scraped a bit of the tar from the bottom of his miserable soul. So I truly love your daddy, Belle. I truly do. And now that I know what he's been up to all these years, and now that he *knows* that I know, well that just means I've got his soul by the oysters, plain and simple. I'm gonna squeeze and pull those gonads all the way up to the Pearly Gates and when I let go, the snapping sound will be so loud that the Devil himself is gonna wince."

But it was ultimately the *last* thing Layla had said on the subject of Grayson that had endured the longest with Christi. The part about *taking care of the son-of-a-bitch*. And so here she was, doing just that. Taking care of the son-of-a-bitch by taking care of Nicholas Voss, a representative of the biggest client in the biggest deal by any measure that Grayson Tate had ever scored in his entire life.

The second statement inherent in Christi's choice of seating arrangements, Sheldon figures, is intended for Gillian Reed and all other attendees who were aware of *The Chacha* article. Or, if not the article itself, then at least the resulting rumors. And that message is simply that Sheldon is in serious trouble with the Missus. Christabelle Tate Davis was, first and foremost, Christabelle *Tate*, former Miss Houston, daughter of Grayson and Layla Tate, neither of whom had raised a fool nor a person who could grow up to look indifferently on a man stupid enough to land himself in a newspaper in such a fashion and to then allow the story to go uncorrected. Nor was she the kind of person who easily swallowed flimsy stories about a missing wedding band.

So, had the seating arrangement actually been able to talk, it likely would have cleared its throat and said: *Sheldon, the one across the table from his wife, is sleeping on the couch.*

But the third statement to be taken from Christi's choice of seatmates is clearly intended for Sheldon, her husband. Five words: *Don't take me for granted.* Or maybe four words: *You are not indispensible,* which for Christi is more realistically reduced to three words: *Y'aint all that.*

Although Sheldon knew that the entirety of Christi's silent public statement to him could be folded neatly into the four corners of a single two-syllable word: *grovel.*

But, then, why burn two syllables when one will do? *Beg.*

He knew that begging for forgiveness, or even something close to it, for having embarrassed her, for having exposed her to scandal, would probably go a long ways with Christi. She did not like marital disharmony, or the appearance of it, any more than he did. He also knew that Nicholas Voss was just a tool she was using to get his attention. Even if she was inclined to carry on with someone, and he doubted this, Christi would never carry on with a representative of her father's client.

All Sheldon needed to do was concede. Write her a little poem of contrition. Go up on stage, turn on the microphone and recite it to her in front of four hundred some odd exceptionally well-dressed, criminally attractive members of the Texas Pageant Association.

Or one of his little songs. Something that worked in the words *idiot* or *imbecile*. And *Chachalaca*. That would go a long ways with Christi.

There were now two women in his life that felt grievously wronged and entitled to an apology. But there was only one for whom he could find the rhymes.

Table No. 3 is front and center to a makeshift stage. Stairs on each end, running half the width of the room. Dead center is a twelve-foot rectangular protrusion that juts into the field of round, cloth-covered tables like a jetty stretching out into a sea of pale, floating jellyfish. Sheldon's back is to the stage, which means that he cannot see Emmet Culpepper, current Director of the TPA, clutch the microphone and rattle on about the year ahead.

If this backwards orientation was intended as part of the seating arrangement comeuppance, then it has backfired. He has seen Emmet hold court at these events before. Too many times. Deeply tan. Slick silver hair. Bent at the shoulders like a straw. He has a distracting facial tick. Always looks like he's winking. And he likes to point with both of his knobby-knuckled hands; the game show host announcing that you've won a new car. Before Emmet was the Director of the TPA, he was a Baptist Preacher from a large and high profile Dallas ministry. The TPA Board seems to appreciate the evangelical fervor —*energy* is the word they use —that he has brought to the pageant business.

Sheldon does not need to see Emmet Culpepper. He is content to eat salad and look at his watch. Every now and then he steals glances across the table at the Samoyeds, who can see everything.

Tonight Emmet is particularly enthused about the TPA Youth Program, the Pageant College and recent headway in collaborating with the schools in Dallas and Houston. He shouts over the clattered conversation of silver and porcelain and crystal.

"*The earlier the better! Am I right?*" A wash of applause. "*Praise God. Can I get an Amen for extracurricular credit?*"

"Looking lovely tonight, Miss Raeleen," says Grayson leaning sideways over

Sheldon's plate. Sheldon puts his fork down. Leans back to allow the conversation. Raeleen nods. Smiles. Her mouth is too full to answer. Grayson corrects his posture over his own plate.

"How goes the *Chachalaca* business?" The question slips from beneath the end of Grayson's mustache as he decapitates a spear of asparagus.

"Working on it," says Sheldon. "My lawyer says it looks like a fight."

"Lemme guess. First Amendment bullshit."

"You got it. Freedom of the press."

"Not for libel. They don't have freedom to lie. To ruin a man's name."

Grayson starts with the head shaking. Sheldon can feel the irritation.

"That's what we're telling them, Grayson. And forcefully. But it looks like they may want to play a round or two before they even investigate the facts. Could get expensive."

Grayson grabs Sheldon's wrist. Points at him with his fork. Whispers.

"Whatever it takes, Shelly. Hear me?"

Raeleen McKibben, now having swallowed, is suddenly listing her way, hair first, over Sheldon's plate. She beams at Grayson.

"Thank you. Charlie bought me this dress. I haven't worn it in ages."

Grayson sighs. Smiles as best he can. "Well you're a knockout in it, Raeleen. A real knockout. You're puttin' people to shame tonight."

"Oh, Grayson," says Raeleen, clearly pleased. She intends on prolonging the compliment but Emmet Culpepper is suddenly everywhere with fresh force, pulling her attention back up to the stage.

"Ladies and gentlemen we have a treat for you tonight. A treat! How many of you would like to see the future Miss America walk out on this very stage tonight? Amen!"

Grayson squeezes his wrist again. Whispers.

"Fuck the money, Shel. Whatever it goddamned takes. It's a business expense. This is an attack on your integrity and if you don't turn those bastards back, it'll hurt your business. *Our* business. You want me to weigh in?"

"No. Grayson. Your hands are full enough. We're on it."

"Who's your man?"

"Mel Weinstein. He's with HMLG."

"HMLG?"

"Houston Media Law Group."

Grayson nods. Lets go of Sheldon's wrist. Stabs the asparagus head. "Nothin' like a Texas Jew to make 'em wish they left you well enough alone. Let's hope. And the sooner you clean this mess up, the sooner Belle will climb down out of the goddamned rafters. Just like her mama. Hellfire on tap." Grayson pokes him in the side with an elbow. "Weather the storm, boy."

They chew through their salads in a strange sort of solidarity, listening to Emmet Culpepper welcome ten pageant hopefuls from around the state. Ages twelve to seventeen, he says. He invites them up for a presumptive bow.

"Come on out, girls. Young ladies I should say. Come get a taste of what it's like to be up on the big stage. Think of this as a dry run without the TV cameras and the flashbulbs. And y'all out there give these girls a big hand. Show 'em what Houston thinks of the next Miss Texas! The next Miss America! Come on, gang! Show the love! Show some TPA spirit! Amen!"

The room rises in whoops and applause. Sheldon stands. Turns as he claps. Two lines of girls, five at each end of the stage, climb the steps and make their way to Emmet who is waiting for them at the microphone, arms wide, mouth open. Like he intends to eat them.

They are lovely and grotesque. Each of them half naked and two inches taller than nature intended, beaming at the ovation. They each have the gate and the posture and the swishy-wrist pageant wave down pat. More of a salute than a wave. These are soldiers.

Sheldon rotates back to the table. Christi and Nicholas are applauding. Nicholas, expressionless as always, says something, inclining his head slightly sideways, flaxen wisps falling away from his neck. Grazing his collar. Christi laughs, covering her mouth with her fingertips. Sheldon turns to Grayson.

"So how are things shaping up in New Mexico?"

Grayson looks at him. Shakes his head. They lower themselves back into their chairs with the rest of the room. He picks up his fork and impales a leaf. Stuffs it in. Chews angrily like he might not answer the question. Then he shakes his head again. Swallows.

"Like goddamned shit on a shingle is how it's shapin' up. Goddamned federal judge says he's gon' take it under advisement. Meantime, goddamned temporary injunction stays in place. No one can do a goddamned thing 'til he makes up his mind about a goddamned fish the size of my pinky. Wants to decide whether the EPA should be a party. Now every tree-huggin', fish-lovin' environmentalist west of the Mississippi is writin' letters to the goddamned editor of the New Mexico *Let's-All-Fuck-Texas-In-The-Ass* Gazette."

"But we're a long way from doing anything to divert the Pecos, aren't we? It's not like Quinco's got idle contractors and equipment ready to start digging."

Grayson chews. Swallows. Shakes his head.

"You're missin' the point, Shel. This is all 'bout public perception. Public perception drives investor perception. Little wrinkle like this makes people think that maybe it's not such a good idea to invest in the Corbin River Walk. Maybe they'll just wait and see how it all comes out. They'll play wait-and-see even though there's no chance in hell that New Mexico and the… the goddamned Pecos River Commission can tell Texas what it can do with its own goddamned water. People will wait and keep their money on the sidelines. We can't have that, Shel. We can't. This thing gets jammed up in court for ten years… I mean if we really have to litigate the thing? Or if the press gets nasty 'cause the tree-huggers don't have anything better to do than jerk off over a goddamned fish? The Russians will just pull the goddamned plug."

Grayson snaps his arm back off the table like he is pulling an electrical cord from a socket. "I mean right goddamned now. Quinco will put its money to work someplace with enough goddamned common sense to see the golden egg as its pops out of the chicken's ass."

"Goose," says Sheldon reflexively, immediately regretting it.

Grayson looks up. Sharply confused. Ready to be angrier than he already is. Emmet Culpepper comes to the rescue.

"And who is this lovely young thing?"

"Katie Dixon."

"Well, Miss Katie Dixon, tell us how old you are and where you come from."

"I am twelve years old and I live in Sugar Land, Texas."

"Sugar Land. Well that's just fine! You a church-goer, Katie?"

"Yes sir."

"Well I could tell by the gleam in those pretty blue eyes. You're already on the path. Tell us, Katie, what are your plans on this side of the hereafter?"

Katie counts the mileposts off on her little fingers.

"First Miss Pre-teen Texas. Then Miss Junior Teen Texas. Then Miss Teen Texas. Then Miss Texas. Then Miss America. Then Miss Universe. Then a marine biologist. Then feed the poor in Africa and teach them how to speak American. Then..."

"What do the lawyers say?" asks Sheldon.

"The lawyers say that this judge just doesn't want to seem like he's acting without *due consideration*. That's how they put it. Son of a bitch Judge Winifred is up for appointment to the Fifth Circuit Bench so he's not gonna throw anyone outta court without takin' his time about it. But the lawyers say Hell will freeze over before *any* judge grants a permanent injunction on something like this. All on account of the goddamned Pecos Bluntnose Shiner? Give me a goddamned break. Our lawyers aren't worried one little bit on the merits. Ain't no merit here at all. This is all just to get what they want on that Lake Avalon project."

"So we just have to wait?"

"Russians ain't gonna wait for shit, Shelly. They got to keep the property values going up. New investor blood is the key. Waiting on the goddamned judge to get reelected sends everything in the wrong direction. Quinco's sending a team from New York to meet with the New Mexico delegation. Sons-a-bitches."

"To do what?"

"See if they can negotiate something. Quinco wants our people on the Commission to drop their objections to the Lake Avalon diversion project. Trade that for a dismissal of this bullshit lawsuit. We'll see, I guess. Whole thing is giving me a goddamned ulcer."

"My word, Miss Katie, that is a whole pile of ambition for such a little firecracker. You have any talents? Things you like to do?"

"Oh, yes sir. Concert piano. Clogging. Archery."

"Archery?"

"Gymnastics. Dressage ... "

Sheldon does not know what makes him think of the lime green folder. The one he no longer has. The one with his notes from the ill-fated trip to Corbin he never should have made. Maybe it's the last baby green leaf of lettuce that has flopped off of his salad plate and lays bent in half, glistening on the white tablecloth.

Or maybe not. But something makes him think of it. That missing folder.

Whatever the trigger, the question is out there on the table with that slick baby leaf before he can think twice about it.

"So, how many of the Tier-One properties are left to be sold?" he asks.

Grayson leans back in his chair, nudging away his plate. Wipes his mustache with a finger.

"How many? None. They're all gone."

"All of them?"

"Far as I know. Quinco used San Angelo Property for the Tier One sales. They brought Tate Realty in to handle the later tier sales. Tier Two, Three and Four. Tier One was sewn up before we got involved. Thought you knew that."

"I guess I did." Sheldon says, nodding. "Guess I did."

"Didn't take any time at all buyin' up Corbin desert. Quinco paid double. Triple. That's all gone. No one's turnin' down that kinda money for a piece-a-shit house on a square of dry dirt. And as for the undeveloped parcels, Tate Realty reserved... "

"I know. Four percent in the south and six percent in the north. That much I remember. I was just curious about the developed lots."

"Gone. Quinco snapped up every last one of those puppies. And got 'em for a song 'cause it was before anyone knew about the development plans." Grayson twitches his lips into an admiring smile. "You can bet they've already flipped most of those lots for a pretty penny. Those people know what the hell they're doin', Shelly."

"And I can tap dance and sing at the same time."

"Go on now, Katie! You wouldn't pull an old preacher's leg!"

"No sir!"

"Alright then, what's the tune?"

"Big Spender from the musical Sweet Charity."

"Have at it young lady. Give her some room girls."

Sheldon lets the subject go, thinking of Libby Holder *aka* Liberty Cherish. Liberty the whore. Liberty the thief. If there was one person on the planet that he knows he cannot trust, it is Libby Holder. It is possible, he concludes, that his Quinco lot map was wrong. Outdated. It is possible that the acreage belonging to *Libby's Nuts* did not actually sit on the outer rim of the Quinco Tier One properties.

More than possible, he thinks. *Likely.* All of the Quinco real estate data comes to him second hand. He just does the marketing. The realty piece belongs to others.

"... spend a little time with meeeee ... "

He steals a look across the table at his wife. Christi is taking in little Katie Wunderkind. Eyes fixed, mouth slightly ajar. She twitches sympathetically with the slapping and stomping sounds behind him. It's like watching a four-year old at a puppet show.

But it is not just Christi. All of them on her side of the table have the same slackened expression. Or some version of it.

In fact, as he pans the faces around him, everyone in the ballroom, including Emmet Culpepper, is utterly transfixed by this juggernaut of talent from a twelve-year old. Even Grayson has surrendered.

Little Katie Dixon from Sugar Land, Texas, owns the room and absolutely everyone in it.

Everyone except Nicholas Voss.

He sits unmoved. As still and as stoic as an owl on a branch. Listening. Marking movement. Waiting for the sun, glowing like the tip of God's cigarette, to finally snuff itself out into the dirt.

Chapter 41

Celia Morales' voice has an edge this morning. Hard to believe that is even possible. Sitting in her chair on the patio. White Mexican dress. Sandals. Dewy, sweet face sipping her prickly pear lemonade. Like she is sipping the sound of the school children playing across the quiet street. And that keeps her innocent.

But there it is anyway. Anger. Rage. Hate.

He does not take it personally. Celia is not in control any more. The story has taken over, like it always does.

Same with every other interview. He's reached that familiar point when it ceases to be an interview. He needs to ask very little now. Almost nothing.

Used to be, like it always is in the beginning, questions were what got the story moving. Like he was one of those old locomotive engineers with an oil can lubricating the iron wheels. Squirt a question here. Drizzle a question there. Anything to reduce the friction of going back. Remembering. That can be a lot of freight to pull in a story like Celia's. The past sits heavy on those rails.

Train is moving fine now. He just has to listen to the thing roll forward. Or backwards. He makes notes of what he hears.

Celia and Paola.

Paola and Celia.

So it's not about asking questions any more. It's about listening. He's an anthropologist now. A shrink. A priest. A placer miner. He runs the river of her story through a sluice box. Picks out the heavy, shiny bits. Tucks them away.

Not a happy story. Or painless. It has reacquainted her with the jagged blade lodged in her memory. And it's still cutting. It still hurts. Whenever Celia looks up, she does not see him. She sees through him. He is a portal now. A tunnel for the train. A wormhole to another time. Another Celia.

He tries to stay with her. Stay in the moment. Listen. But he can't help thinking about the box.

He tries to shake free of the image. Tries to focus only on Celia. And Paola. And now Lyle.

But the box keeps floating back into view. In his head, it is still sitting propped up against his front door. Three days now and it is still all he can think about. The box.

Not the box itself, really. The letters inside. Two hundred and six letters. *Dear Lula... Dearest Lula... Dear Lula... Dear Sis.* *Love Liz.*

Two hundred and six. He had counted. That first day, count them was all he could do. Count envelopes. Each one slit precisely up the right side, corner to stamp. Tallulah had used a razor to open them.

They were not organized. You'd think letters in a box would be chronological. These were not. Tallulah did not believe in time.

It was not until the second day that he could bring himself to read one of them all the way through. Four pages of his mother's script. It was like seeing her voice. After all of these years. The signature was her enigmatic smile. *Liz.*

Same as always. *Liz.* Mom. After all of these years.

When he had finished, all he could do was sit in his screaming geranium chair and stare out the window at the poplars in the front yard. Only not the poplars in the front yard of the place he lives in today. The ones in the front yard of the place he lived in thirty years ago. It was a kind of paralysis. A kind of timeless coma wrapping itself around the shoulders of his conscious perception. A narcotic.

When he had come back to the present it was with a kind of alarm. An hour had passed imperceptibly. He found he was starving for her. He wanted to gorge himself with her words. With the sense of her. With the sudden newness of her presence. He wanted to forego eating and sleeping just to be with her.

But he saw the danger immediately. Felt it in his chest. The letters were not of this world. Not of this time. They were an escape. An excuse.

My name is Davis Payne and I'm an alcoholic.
Hi Davis.

He wanted to binge. All two hundred and six paper bottles. One after the other. Guzzling her words. He wanted to drown in a lake of cursive ink.

But then the paper bottles would be empty. And she would be gone. Again. Gone. There would be no hope of her being new. Not ever again. He would re-read them. All of them. Coaxing out every last drizzle and drop. Then they would all be empty. Dry.

And then he would put away the box of letters and go buy himself a drink.

He had thrashed about, sitting in his geranium chair. Looking for something to grab. Something that floated. Something to keep him from sinking.

Rules. Dr. Bees liked rules. There had to be rules.

Rule one: No more than one letter a week.

Two: Only one letter out of the box at a time.

Three: At least six months before starting over with a letter he had already read.

He wrote down the rules. Twice. Signed his name to each slip of paper. He put one in his wallet. The other up on the refrigerator beneath the cactus magnet.

But these rules of conduct had nothing on his thoughts, which collectively were like a gas wafting through the bars of his self-restraint.

The box. The box. The box.

Dearest Lula… Love Liz.

It is hardly fair to Celia. Pouring her heart out over her little patio. Recalling for him the day Paola stepped out of her car before it had fully stopped.

Lyle Cross. Alone. Materializing out of the windblown dust on the road up ahead.

Celia has become more than merely emotional. She is afraid. All over again. She is afraid of these memories.

She is quiet now. Stabbing her straw into her glass. Trying to pull herself together.

"You blame yourself," he says. "For not doing something. For not making Paola get back in the car."

Celia nods slowly.

"Yes."

"But… how could you have known, Celia?"

Her mouth opens to let out some explanation. Closes again. Opens.

"That's just it. I think I *did* know. It's like something in me knew from the very beginning. Like…"

"What."

"Like somehow I already knew and that's why I was there. And maybe that's why I was in her life in the first place. That's why we met."

They are silent after that. He watches her remember. Lets his attention slip in and out of the box sitting on his kitchen counter, full of his mother's voice. *Dearest Lula… Love Liz.*

A minute. Two. He stands.

Celia looks up. Wipes her eyes. She doesn't want him to go. There is more to tell, she says. About Paola. So much more.

"I'll be back," he tells her. "Gotta go to work."

He thanks her for the lemonade. Pats her on the shoulder, letting the last one linger. Shows himself out.

The Harley needs a new seat. The puncture had grown up to be a gash. Now the leather wants to split all the way up the middle. Duct tape can only do so much. Too many miles. Too much heat. Too damn dry.

He straddles the seat, kicks the bike to life and roars off past the schoolyard to the corner. The kids watch him go. He can feel their wondering eyes, like little fleshy fingers at his back.

He rides out into the desert furnace beneath a smear of burnt blue brightness veiled with whitening ash. His mother is in the hot breath of the road. Her voice comes in fragments of black cursive loops.

...Tell me again, Lula, the point of this life.

...Another dream. I have them all the time now.

...Like a loud horn, or a voice, but a long ways off and from all directions.

...I played an old Sippie Wallace record yesterday: Mama's Gone, Goodbye.

He can feel the letter. Down there in its little compartment. It burns a hole up through the split in the leather seat beneath him. Three pages. He has read it twice already. *No more today*, he tells himself. *No more.*

But he knows better.

And now, the fragments. Bits and pieces of her, torn loose from the bottom. New flotsam surfacing here. And there. And there. Some new. Others he thought he had drowned a long time ago.

Here's one. *His mother... sprawled out on the living room floor crying and singing along with Memphis Minnie about making a change because she couldn't take any more —trav'lin' on her mind —no idea he was watching.*

Another. *His mother... eyes wild, shouting, "You don't understand! Conrad! None of it is real. It's all a goddamned hoax!"*

Another. *His mother... the last of her green dress disappearing behind the door to the sky-blue building where Dr. Bees worked; his father asking him about school in the rearview mirror, accelerating.*

Another. *His mother... on her knees in the kitchen, steak and beans and a broken plate, eyeliner like gangrenous scars down her pale cheeks, squeezing his hands until he thought they might break —"Davis... Listen to me. You have to listen to me, baby. I... Will... Never... Leave... You. Understand? You will feel alone in this life, but I am always gonna be right there for you."*

These broken bits of her. Living pieces of Elizabeth Payne that have been locked down in the sunken hull.

But now. The letters. The old voice inflating new words. And the memories are now like children barreling up the basement steps and smashing down doors to be with their mother.

Another. *His mother... whispering, hunched over the bedside phone, "Lula... I'm drowning. All I see is stars. I can't breathe anymore."*

His father joins them about halfway to *Broken River Road*. He is a brooding presence. Judging his memories of her. Davis tries to shut him out. Exclude him. It is his head, after all.

But Conrad is going nowhere. Davis sees him sitting across the table at *Murphy's*. Pushing away that rib eye. Words are unnecessary. It's all in the face.

I'm your father.
I loved her too.
We need to forgive each other.
I'm trying.

Pepitas saves him. The sight of it reasserts the here and now. He pulls his bike into the small dirt lot at the back of the building. Parks by the dumpster. Heads inside.

The place is already at half capacity. The kitchen is in full steam. In another hour *Pepitas* will be packed. He will be too busy to notice time passing. Too busy to hear his mother in his head. And then, it will occur to him to look at his watch and it will already be four o'clock and time to head up to see Dallas Letti. To see if he still has a job. He is glad for the distraction. He needs to keep moving.

Eladio Rivera is working the counter. He looks up. Waves. Davis waves back. Heads to the kitchen. Accordions and horns like little fireworks. Hector is on the grill doing his Tejano shuffle.

"*Hola, chavo!*" Hector shouts. Hector had gone a full month without knowing Davis' name. By the time he learned, *dude* had stuck for good.

"*Hola*, Hector."

Hector makes a swivel move with his hips. Points his spatula to the garbage can. Already full. Davis nods. Puts on an apron. Hair in a ponytail. Bags up the trash. He takes it out to the dumpster and returns to wipe down tables and clean the restrooms.

On his second trash run of the day he kicks open the back door with the side of his boot and walks out into the back lot for the dumpster.

The one sitting on his Harley wears a backwards baseball cap.

Fuck U Athletics.

The other —stocky, like an overstuffed sausage casing —wears a black t-shirt with a pirate skull. The boots look new.

The one is working the clutch. The other is looking through the papers that used to be in the little compartment beneath the seat. The article clipped from the *Chacha.* And his mother's letter of the week.

Davis lets the door close. They both look up and around.

"You need to get off of the bike," he says. "And you need to give me those papers. Now."

"Nice hog, man," says the one. "How much you want for it?"

"Not for sale. Get off. The fucking. Bike." Davis drops the bag of trash. Holds out his hand to the other. "Papers. Now."

The one swings his leg off the bike. Turns. Sticks his thumbs in his belt loops. "Okay, bitch. I'm off. Now what?"

"Give me the papers," he says. "No harm, no foul."

The one laughs up to the sky. Thumbs out of the belt loops.

The other throws the papers on the ground. "Let's go, man. Hippie ain't worth…"

"Fuck that," says the one. "Hippie here wants to dance."

Davis turns away. Bends for the letter –his mother's cursive voice –lying in the dirt. He is on his back before he knows what is happening. The one is on top of him, knees pinning his arms to the ground at the biceps, laughing through his rows of perfect pearlescent teeth.

A brownish bird alights from the roofline above. A plain dusted thrasher of some kind. Or a thrush. Gone.

He sees the fist coming. There is nowhere to go.

Again.

Again.

There is a wet, popping feeling in the center of his head. Points of light winking on and off around the grimly satisfied face of the man on top of him. Like the man's teeth were shooting sparks.

"Come on, man," says the other. Urgent. Uncertain.

Again.

Again.

His neck aches, trying to turn his face away, into the earth, pushing against the planet with his left cheek. But the planet will not move.

Again.

Again.

"That's enough. *Travis!* That's enough, man. That's…"

The other does not finish his thought. Or Davis does not hear it. He is looking for the fist, trying to wriggle free from knees that are like iron spikes through his arms. Bracing for the next explosion of pain between his eyes. His mouth is slick with the taste of metal.

But the fist does not come. There is no next explosion. The one –*Travis* –is climbing off.

Davis throws his hands up, ready to ward off a kick to the head. The trouble is in seeing through the sheen of blood. It feels like his heart is trying to come through his nose and eyes and lip.

"Ain't your fight, man," says Travis to the dumpster. "This shit don't concern you."

Davis throws his head back, trying to see behind him.

"No," says the Mexican. A Louisville Slugger rests over his shoulder. At his feet, the still nameless other is curled up into a ball holding his stomach and trying to breathe.

"No. This shit don't concern me. Not one bit. But maybe it should concern you. *Ojete.*"

The Mexican spits. Kicks the other hard in the chest. He cries out, clutching at a rib likely broken.

Davis seizes the moment. Hooks his foot sharply up. Catches Travis hard between the legs with the toe of his boot. Travis falls to his knees, clutching himself. Eyes closed.

But he is no dummy, this Travis. No time for pain. Not with the Mexican and Slugger around. He recovers quickly, staggering in a drunken beeline for the alley that connects with *Broken River Road.*

The Mexican intercepts in four calm steps. Swings hard for the fences. Slugger closes the distance, connecting with the right elbow. There is a terrible snapping. Travis howls. Keeps running. Gone with a keening sound of pain like a dog close at his heels.

That leaves the other. Huddled. Crying.

The Mexican walks back. Four steps. Stands over him.

Then squats.

"*Nombre,*" he says quietly. Nothing. Again. "*Nombre.*"

"Harlan."

"Harlan..."

"Wickett."

"Apologize to *mi amigo,* Harlan Wickett."

Quavering silence. Slugger rolls smoothly in the palm.

"I'm sorry. I'm sorry. Oh God, don't please. I didn't want... Travis was..."

"Travis?"

"Travis."

"Travis..."

"Shumaker. Travis Shumaker."

"From..."

"Houston."

The Mexican smiles. Slugger rolls.

"Lie to me again, Harlan Wickett."

"San Angelo. San Angelo. It's the fucking truth." He is sobbing. "I'm sorry. I'm sorry. Fuck me, I'm sorry. I didn't want this."

"Okay, Harlan Wickett. Go find Travis Shumaker from San Angelo. He has a broken elbow. You have a broken rib. Go to a hospital. Go home to San Angelo. Wait for the Sheriff. Never... *ever*... come back to Corbin."

Harlan looks up at the Mexican. Afraid to move.

"I will count to ten, Harlan Wickett. But after that..." He smiles in a beautiful, sad sort of way. Slugger rolls. "*Uno. Dos.*"

Harlan is up and moving before *cinco.* Fast as a broken chest will allow. He is out of sight around the corner before *nueve.*

The Mexican stands. Walks over to the letter and the folded *Chacha* page and the other things. Picks them up out of the dirt one by one. He brushes them against his pant leg. Hands them down to Davis. Pulls him to his feet. Now they both have bloody hands.

"San Angelo punks," he says. "You okay?"

Davis spits. Once. Twice. Long, red ropey strands swing from his nose. He has to keep his right eye closed.

"No." Spits. "But a lot better than I would be. Never been much of a fighter." He turns his head slowly, like his neck is suddenly gripped with rust. He squints at the Mexican with his one good eye. His nose feels like a split guava.

"Davis." He holds out his hand again. "I owe you big."

Miguel Rivera props the Slugger back on his shoulder. Shakes. "Miguel. You're a mess, Davis. Let's get you cleaned up."

Eladio brings him another damp towel with an ice cube in it. Takes the old one, rolling it up, bloody side in. Davis leans his head back against the booth. Groans.

"Have you ever seen them before?" asks Eladio. The excitement in his voice shaves off some years. Davis presses the towel against the side of his face. He answers with a slow shake.

"I have," says Miguel taking the seat next to him, drying his hands. He leans the bat up against the wall. A tongue of black hair droops over his forehead. "San Angelo white trash. They like to leave their bottles and cans in our desert." He rakes his fingers through his hair. "We're just a litter box."

"What did the Sheriff say?"

"Eladio…" Miguel crosses his arms over his chest.

"What?"

"I didn't call the Sheriff."

"What? Why the hell not, Miguel?" Eladio gestures with both hands to Davis. "Look at him, man."

Davis holds up the rag. Rotates it. Reapplies. Speaks.

"'Cause your brother broke some bones out there, Eladio. Those guys got the worst of it with hospital bills to prove it. They'll make up their own story about it. No need to report this. I'll be fine."

Eladio scoffs.

"You'll be fine? *Fine?* Tough guy. They nearly killed you, man."

Miguel points to the front counter. Ten people shifting weight from one foot to the other. "Customers, Eladio."

"*Papá estaría de acuerdo conmigo, Miguel!*"

"Eladio, *Papá* is not here. *Andale. Chilito. Andale.*"

Eladio looks hard at his brother. Spins. Curses under his breath. Disappears.

"Ah, Eladio," says Miguel to himself. Then to Davis. "Too innocent for this kind of thing. He is very sensitive."

"*Chilito?*" asks Davis.

Miguel laughs. "Little penis," he says. "He hates that."

Davis laughs. Closes his eyes. "Ow. Fuck. No laughing."

"Sorry."

"You always carry a bat around?"

"No. My turn to coach *los chamacos*. Once a month. Four of us take turns."

"Shit. My lucky day."

Miguel shakes his head.

"What?"

Miguel shrugs. "Luck."

"So?"

"My truck wouldn't start. My friend Carlos drives by. He works at the *Coahuiltecan.*" He points up the street, through the kitchen wall, to the Indian trading post. "So I hitch a ride in with Carlos. I tell him I want a *carne asada* burrito before practice and that I'll just walk to Draego Field. Carlos drops me at the corner."

"Okay."

"So Carlos drives a piece of shit Fiesta. Little white, second hand *chingalera*. Bullet holes and shit. Thing almost never starts. I'm always givin' *him* a ride. My truck always starts. But not today. I'd have driven straight to the field."

Miguel shakes his head again. Gives a sideways glance. Raises his dark eyebrows. "And I never eat lunch." He leans back. Elbows Davis gently in the side. "Someone's looking out for you, *mi amigo*."

Davis grunts dismissively.

"Then *someone* was a little fucking late."

"*Si. Posiblemente.* Or maybe just in time."

Davis repositions the towel. Curses the pain. Opens his eyes.

She is the first thing he sees. Standing in line at the threshold of the front door. Half of her is in the shade. The other half, the half away from him, is on fire. He remembers instantly.

'Livia, baby. This here my new writer friend. He want me to confess my sins. Fo' a magazine. How 'bout that shit?

It is her. Olivia. The woman from Libby's Nuts. From before he was wrongly arrested for soliciting a prostitute. From before she almost died. The woman whose life he supposedly saved. Miguel takes note. Turns to see what he is seeing.

She is looking at them now. Straight on. He can see the scars.

"Ah, Olivia," says Miguel. "You know her?"

"What?" He glances at Miguel. He doesn't know, he thinks. "No. No." Davis rotates, just a little. "Why? Do you?"

Miguel smiles. Raises his hand. Waves. Beckons.

The woman, Olivia, turns away. Scans the room like she is looking for someone in particular. Someone not him. Someone not Miguel. Like she has not seen them. She keeps turning, rolling out of line and into the white sun. She burns into flakes of ash and is gone.

Miguel is shaking his head. "Sad. Poor Olivia."

"Why?"

"Bad car accident. Almost died. Some guy from Houston comes by, pulls her out of the car by the fuckin' hair. Then *boom*. Car explodes. She's got scars now. Bad ones." Miguel moves three fingers up and down in the air. "On her face. Some bad shit. Fucked up her leg too. Olivia was antisocial before. But now. Like trying to talk to a ghost, man."

"But she's got family, right? Friends?" He is fishing.

"Olivia?" Miguel shakes his head. "Not really. Some people were meant to be left alone. She's one of 'em. Lives in a whorehouse."

"What?" He feigns surprise, keeping to the shadows. "She's a hooker?"

Miguel huffs out a laugh. "That's the last thing she is."

He looks at his watch. Grabs Slugger from the wall. "I gotta get over to practice. *Niños pequeños* with bats and balls. Nothing but trouble. You gonna be okay?"

He wants to know more. Wants to know everything. Lets it go.

"I'll be fine," he says. "Thanks again."

Miguel stands. "*De nada.* Hey, my family is having a thing up at my parents' place. Tomorrow night. Nothing big. A few friends. Good food." He nods to the kitchen. "Hector will be there. And Eladio. Want to come by?"

Davis hesitates. Eladio thinks he is a hero. He imagines the conversation. Nods anyway.

"Sure."

* * *

They have found each other. The mottling four o'clock wound in the sky and his bloody, swollen, throbbing eye. It is a gruesome fascination.

The sunglasses and the wisp of cloud are pointless. He tries to keep his eyes on the hot strip of concrete slipping beneath his bike. *Look down. Look down.*

Doesn't help. Nothing can keep them apart. Heaven and earth connected through pain. Or is it empathy? Or merely our longing projection up into the veiled mirror and back again?

Doesn't matter. The only thing that matters is the hurt. His entire face is hot and swollen and every heartbeat is a dull needle stabbing into a fat nerve. The vibration beneath him is a kind of sonic sandpaper over raw, newly burned flesh.

He needs the opposite of this. Needs to be perfectly still.

But he is going anyway. He throttles up to cut the time. Tries to keep his eyes down. He makes the turn at the gateless gatepost and rumbles for another mile through the scrub.

He stops the bike at the wall and cuts the engine. Below the neck, his body goes numb in the sudden stillness. Above the neck is another story.

At first he thinks that she is inside. He walks slowly along the stone wall. Passes the opening to the yard. He makes it to the corner.

"Hero think he still got himself a job."

She is not inside. Dallas Letti stands from just on the other side of the wall. Knocks an iron hand spade against the rock and cleans the dirt off with a glove.

Davis stops. Hands on his hips. Head down.

He thinks of telling her off. Turning around and getting back on his bike and sending a fantail of dirt over the wall. Riding back to Corbin.

But that is not what he wants to do. He needs the world to be still.

There is too much vibration.

He looks up. Takes off his glasses.

He and Dallas Letti glare at each other over the wall. Her sharp dark eyes tell him what he already knows: that this is his first appearance in a week. First time since he took a day off to see his father. *You not here tomorrow then don't you come back. Hear me?*

But her eyes also reflect the carnage of his face. They look at him in questions. Surmise that he has paid for something. That it is painful to be here.

That this is penance.

Those eyes make a slow, wandering inspection.

Then Dallas turns away from him. Lowers herself out of sight, back beneath the edge of the wall. Stabs her spade back into the dirt.

Again. Again. Again.

Davis replaces his glasses and rounds the corner, aiming for the dirty, white truck parked around the back of the house. Just where he left it.

* * *

Abandoned.

Condemned by time.

It is all still waiting for him. Every busted plank and rusted nail and shard of porcelain. Desiccated pilings. Corrugated roofing crumped and lying about like discarded tissue. Glass. Stained and broken.

Davis takes it all in from the cab of the truck. The wounded sky seeps its color, the last of the day bleeding out over the wreckage in a flood of wasted light.

It is not in him to work. He is not here to work.

He is here for the stillness. Nothing for miles. In any direction except Dallas' home which is out of view and may as well not exist.

He climbs out of the truck. Slams the door. Walks around the back of the broken building. To the boat. The ark.

He opens the narrow half-door in its faint memory of blue. Steps inside.

The air does not move in this place. The sound of his boots on the wooden, sand-strewn floor is swallowed whole. The light is dim and old.

Davis looks through a small, paneless window. The desert sweeps out to the east. Nothing moves. No sound.

Stillness.

He sits in the dirt beneath the window. Leans his aching head back against the wall. Closes his eyes. Pulls the letter from his pocket.

It's sticky and stained with dirty blood.

Davis opens his eyes. Reads.

... Tell me again, Lula, the point of this life.

Chapter 42

The towels are hot and tangled inside the driers.

The first ones are always reluctant.

Olivia has to yank them sharply to get them out. Like she is separating clinging family members. Then the others follow easily enough.

She drops the towels into the bin. When the driers are empty, she rolls the bin over to the tables next to the boiler. She takes out a small pile. Starts to fold.

Dooley Simms is working the washers. He is tall, with gangly limbs. Big, red-knuckled hands burrow into the dirty towels like rodents tunneling into cottony soil.

Dooley is normally an attentive sort. Always aware of when she enters the room. Always asking her to come to one of his parties. *Shooters*, he called them. *Just me and some friends.*

Dooley knew the odds. He had to. Olivia had never accepted. Ever. She didn't like parties. Or friends. She kept her own company.

No matter. Dooley was always asking anyway.

But not today. Not since she had come back with a limp and a release to work. Now Dooley just looks at her a lot. Across the laundry room. Stolen glances. Guilty. Regretful. He can't get used to the new face. Nobody can.

She doesn't need to be here. She shouldn't be here. The laundry is Dooley's job. She should be out wiping down the free weights. The ellipticals. The stretching mats.

But she can't. Too many people. Too many mirrors.

She folds a small stack. Pushes it to the back of the table to make room. She only has but so much time before Mr. Pete comes looking.

"There you are." From behind her. As if on cue. He's wearing the kelly-green version of the *Longhorn Fitness* t-shirt tucked into a pair of gray dress slacks. And boots, of course. Hands on his hips.

"Ain't your job, Mocha. Not gonna' tell you that again."

"Didn't want to start anything," she says "I've got a session in fifteen minutes. Just thought I'd help Dooley out."

"You don't have a session," says Mr. Pete.

"What?"

"My office."

He turns. Walks out of the room spinning a set of keys on his finger. Olivia looks over at Dooley. He looks away, towel rodents plunging back into the washer.

"'Cause you don't have a license, that's why."

Mr. Pete talks to the plastic longhorn rack screwed to the top of his desk. One of the tips skewers a small foam football. He glances up at her. Looks away.

"I've *never* had a license," she says.

"Yeah, well I can't take the chance. I can't get shut down."

"You're not gon' get shut down. You haven't gotten so much as a warnin'."

"Mocha..."

"Name's Olivia," she says. "Use it."

"Fine. Olivia," like he is so tired of the conversation. "We could get sued."

"By who? All my clients know I'm not licensed. They sign the little... *thing*. Every time. They're not..."

"Can't risk it. You need a license."

"That's like... five hundred hours of course work. That's a lot of time and a lot of money. Meanwhile, I need those tips."

He looks at her in the eyes for the first time. His salt and pepper hair has the coarseness of horsetail. Same with the eyebrows.

"What do you want from me?"

Hopeless. She sees that now. Her mind gropes. It finds the ten thousand in cash, huddled in the bottom of her sock drawer. It grips the wad. Snaps off the rubber band. Fans the bills. Spreads them out in the air.

She can't touch it. She'll need every dollar. She needs to work.

"So you're saying if I go get certified... pay the money, take the time... I can take appointments. You're *promising* that."

Mr. Pete clears his throat. "Can't make any promises, Mocha. Olivia."

"Why not?"

Pause. Swallow.

"*Triple M* is coming in."

"What?"

"*Muscle Menders Massage.* Jackson's got 'em on contract now. They're gonna do all the clubs. They start the first of the month."

"What the..."

"They're licensed. Based in Houston."

"I know who they are, Pete. If I see one more *Muscle Menders* bikini car wash..."

"They're… licensed and bonded."

"They're glorified pole dancers."

"They bring in business."

"I'll bet they do. Look at me, Pete. Look… at… me."

He does. Then he can't.

"Thought so. Fucker."

"No," putting a finger in the air. "Not my decision."

She looks around the tiny, cluttered room. Spreads her arms. "Well there must be a bull in here somewhere, Pete."

He sighs. Exasperated. *Fucking employees.*

"I'm sorry. Okay? I am. Look. You still have a job. Not Dooley's job. Your job." His fingers find a pen. He uses it to point through the little window in the door at the metal forest of machines on the other side. "Out on the floor. Speakin' of which."

She doesn't know what to do with the sudden free time. Dashboard Jesus, arms spread, is befuddled. *What are you doing? Where are we going?*

She steers Jesús Batista's battered brown Falcon randomly around San Angelo. Looks at the people floating above the desert in their little bubbles of shade. House bubbles. Car bubbles. The *Target* bubble. *Albertsons. Wal-Mart.* The university bubble. They are in groups, mostly. Inside these bubbles. Twos and threes. Families. Lovers. Friends. Bonded like molecules of humanity. She can see them, going about their lives. If they can see her they don't let on.

She ends up on Knickerbocker. Drives past the school. Kids are playing baseball in a diamond of brown, burned out grass. She pulls in and parks. Turns off the engine. The desert sky is a blue-green beryl. Like she could drink it. Like she could puncture the upper wall of her bubble with a straw and suck it down.

No one can throw. Or catch. Or hit. The ball has a mind of its own. There is a lot of chasing and waiting and spitting in the dust.

She remembers Sheldon Davis. Remembers, as if she had ever stopped thinking about him. Under that red umbrella. Drinking his wine, the trickling San Antonio River behind him like something leaving. She thinks again of the ten thousand dollars in her dresser drawer. Thinks of the ninety thousand to come. Nine more months. Gestation for a new life. She pretends to wonder if it is enough.

She knows better. But pretending is better than knowing.

Maybe, she thinks. Maybe it is enough. Papi's deal could fall apart.

Swing and a miss. The ball ricochets off the shoulder of the catcher, over the bullpen. Skitters up onto the empty aluminum bleachers.

The runt with the bat is upset. Life is betraying him in sets of three. He throws his hat in the dirt. Spits. Olivia starts the car.

She lights a cigarette as she merges onto the 67. Rolls down the window. The Devil's breath is hot and savage in her hair. She blows smoke in his face just the way he likes.

She thinks of Papi. *Maybe it is enough. Maybe.*

She works the cigarette. Tries to find the melody in her head; tuning it in like a radio signal wandering lost in deep space.

Mother Ocean. Mother Ocean.

Your sorrow so deep.

There is a dark lump by the guardrail. And another.

Three.

Four.

She is not used to *Pepita's* this early. Actual lunchtime. People eating. People waiting to eat. The tables are full. Mostly locals. There is a line stretching almost to the door.

A *Tejano* beat punches out from the kitchen. Lively horns and guitars. The music comes with an aroma of searing chicken and beef. Hot tortillas. Beans and onions and garlic. Cilantro and fresh lime.

Olivia shuffles forward at the end of the line, into the sound and aroma, shifting her weight back and forth to keep her leg from hurting.

A large, pit-stained man in a backwards hat is sitting in her usual seat. He reads a story from the *Chacha* into his cellphone over a half-eaten enchilada. At the front of the line Eladio Rivera is doing his thing. He looks up in time to catch her eye.

"Olivia! *Hola, chica!*"

Too loud. Too sincerely enthusiastic. People turn. Look.

She doesn't want the attention. It burns her face, lighting up the scars. She looks away into the restaurant. Two men sit at a table near the back door. They are looking at her. Looking hard.

One of the men is Miguel Rivera. Fucking small town.

The other she does not know. But she has seen him before. Has seen him here. At *Pepitas.* He works here. Kitchen help.

And she has seen him in the place she lives. *Libby's Nuts.*

He is the writer.

'Livia, baby. This here my new writer friend. How 'bout that shit?

The writer is holding a bloody white rag to the side of his face. To his right eye and to his nose. She sees him straighten. He stares. Says something to Miguel.

Miguel holds up a hand. Waves. Says something to the bleeding writer. Beckons.

Olivia pretends not to see them. Keeps turning in place. Looking elsewhere. She knows she is not convincing. Nothing to be done for it. She needs out. Too much motion. Too much noise. She needs to be still. She turns and leaves, pushing her way through three ranchers coming in through the front door.

She walks up *Broken River Road* to the *Coahuiltecan Trading Post.* Wanders the narrow aisles collecting as she goes. Beef jerky. Bag of nuts. Bottle of water. Lucela Flores is at the register. Reading her romance.

"Lucela."

"*Hola,* Olivia." She smiles. Shy. Hesitant. Takes the five. Doesn't look up. "Glad you're back. Glad you're okay. That was bad. Mom and me prayed for you."

"*Gracias,* Lucela. Thank your mom for me."

She takes the bag up the street to City Hall where she sits on the flat edge of the fountain. Her hip groans in relief.

Pish. Pish. Pish. Pish. Pish.

Recycling water ministers in soft gushes. She lies back on the smooth stone. Looks up at the sky. Dips in her fingers. Closes her eyes.

She imagines that Papi will be here. Like last time. She will hear his voice and open her eyes. She imagines the conversation. Imagines the smile on his saggy kind face. The nod. *Yes,* says Papi. *The deal just came apart. Yes. Must have been meant for you. Yes. Yes. Yes.*

She imagines that it will be enough.

Pish. Pish. Pish. Pish. Pish.

A warm bath of minutes, pooling up around her.

Then a coolness of shadow crosses her face.

Papi, she thinks. *He is here.*

"Wha you doin', O?" says Manny Soto. "You think you at the fuckin' beach?"

She opens her eyes. He is a brown, pock-marked brick in a hat. He is smiling. Or showing his teeth. The gold cross swings over her face on its chain.

"Manny Boy," she says flatly. Closes her eyes.

"You gettin' a beauty sleep?"

"MmmHmm."

"'Cause it a beautiful day today, O."

" … "

"Beauuuuutiful day."

" … "

"Sun shinin'."

" … "

"Birds singin'. Waves crashin' out there in…"

"Manny."

"Yes, O? Are you invitin' me to join you on the beach?" He laughs to himself. "Okay, okay. If you insis'. I will Join you."

He sits on the ledge of the fountain, pressing his leg up against the heels of her boots. She can feel him looking up the length of her body. His eyes scaling her chin. Traversing her cheek. She keeps her eyes closed.

"What do you need, Manny?"

"O. I don' need. I jus' sayin' hello. You workin' toonye?"

"You know I am."

"Ahhhh. Thas rye, thas rye. Toonye you on the schedule to clean up."

Eyes open. He is dripping water on the toe of her boot with a finger.

"What?"

"Got to keep da' place clean, O. You know da'. Bathrooms get nasty."

"I did it last week. Once a month, Manny. It's supposed to be once a month."

"Kelly sick as a mutha *fuck*a. She call me on my cell phone. Ricky still in Baton Rouge. Da' mean you... an' me... an' Gary... an' Kim, O. An' you know Gary ain' cleaning no toilets. An' you know *I* ain' cleaning no toilets. So da' leave you an' Kim."

"Then it's Kim. She never has to do that shit."

"I know. You rye about da', O. You rye. But it you name on da' schedule. So..."

"Fuck." She closes her eyes. Resists connecting the toe of her boot with Manny's chin, knocking him back into the fountain.

"We can' give no special treatment, O. Accident or no accident."

"Ain't askin' for special treatment, Manny. I have never asked for special treatment."

"I know. But Kim get along nice wi' Gary. You know? She show her manager some respec', O. You see da'. You know wha' I sayin'?"

"If you mean that Kim's fucking Gary to get out of cleaning the bathrooms, then yeah, Manny, I see that. Everybody sees that."

"No, no, no. Not fucking, O. I ain' see nothing like da'. I sayin' respec'. See? Jus' a little respec'." He waits. "You know wha' I sayin', O?"

She doesn't respond, marveling at what disfigurement and a limp has done to embolden Manny Soto. Every shift a little more confident. Less combative. Less intimidated. Smiling. Joking. Holding the door. *Mucho gracias for all you har' work toonye, O.*

She is marked for desperation. Abandoned by the herd of women with whom Manny Soto has no chance. She is slower now. Grateful for the company of jackals.

"I tell you wha'." Manny places a hand lightly on the top of her foot. Gives it a squeeze through the boot. "I see wha' I can do about da' schedule. Maybe you don' have to clean for a month. Maybe two. We see wha' we can work out."

A harder squeeze. Pain travels the bones of her foot, skittering up to her hip like electricity through a wire. She clenches her jaw.

"Wha' if we make da' shit permanent, O? You like da'? Wha' you think?"

She opens her eyes. Props herself up on her elbows. Smiles.

"I think we should make it permanent, Manny."

He stops squeezing. "You do?"

"Yes."

Manny smiles. Perfect teeth catch the sun. It is finally safe to look her in the eyes. So he does. She smiles back at him, scars warping.

"Yes. You make sure I am on that cleaning schedule. Permanently, Manny. Permanently. Every shift. Starting tonight."

A beat. Two. He is trying to understand.

"Wha? O, you bein' crazy now. I sayin'..."

"No, Manny. Seriously. I'm just trying to show my respect. Each night? When I scour away all the shit? I'll think of you. Out of respect. So sign me up. Make it permanent."

She leaves Manny in the town square, perched on the fountain. The stone spire rises up behind him from the center of the pool like the spindle of an old Victrola. She looks back. He raises a hand. She imagines the fountain spinning, sending Manny into an orbit of thirty-three and a third revolutions per minute. The needle in her mind is made of sharp, hot iron.

Manny Soto: human scratch.

She walks back up *Broken River*, crossing the street past the *Lone Star Laundry* and the *Lick-n-Tipple* and the *Jewelry Works*, wanting to avoid *Pepita's* and Miguel Rivera and the bleeding writer. When she is safely past she crosses *Broken River* again and heads for the car.

The sun is high and white in the sky. It has stolen her fluid. Her river. Her ocean. It begrudges every trickle. Every drop. Her throat sticks. Each eyelid tight against the ball. The dry air rattles in her lungs like tattered paper.

Her hip hurts. Like the socket needs oil.

She finishes her water. Slips the bottle into a trashcan. It clunks like a tiny bucket into a dry well.

Two Mexican kids are sitting on the hood of the shit-brown Falcon smoking cigarettes and laughing at something on a cell phone. Sixteen, she guesses. Maybe seventeen. Hard weathered feet in leather sandals. No shirts. All muscle and bone. Dusty black hair. Rancher kids. They see her limping their direction and pulling on a piece of jerky. They come to a kind of attention.

"Ain't a park bench, boys."

"This *Jesús'* car," says the one, squinting up into the sun.

"*¿Dónde está Jesús?*" asks the other at the same time.

"Toluca," she says.

"Toluca?" asks the one and the other in unison.

"*¿Cuando se vuelve?*" asks the other.

"He's not," she says. "He ain't ever coming back."

Olivia climbs in. Closes the door. Rolls down the window. Waves the smoke away with her hand.

"Those things'll kill you." She holds out the rest of the jerky and nuts to the one. He takes it. She adjusts the cushion. Sticks the keys in the ignition. "Why aren't you in school?"

"Don't go to school," says the one.

"Then go home to your mothers. *Vete a casa a sus madres.*"

But the other scrunches up his face as if to a foul smell. Like he does not enjoy the idea of having a mother.

"*¿Mi madre?* Bitch don't care what I do. I'm the man of my house." He takes a drag. Blows it out in a tight stream. Smiles.

No doubt it belonged to his father, that smile. Someone may as well put it to use. He leans in the window.

"Got you a man in *your* house, *mami?*"

Olivia shakes her head. As if in a tiny tremor.

As if to herself.

"No?" The other looks over at the one. Then back to her. "*Jesús* gone, yo. You wan'chu a man, *mami?*"

"Why?" she asks. "You know of any?"

The one thinks this is funny. Punches the other in the arm, laughing at her dig on his friend. The other pulls his lips into a comic sneer. Cocks his head for the payback.

"What happen to your face, yo?"

His expression shows a coming menace. He is young. Still working on it. But he is getting there. The one grows quiet.

Olivia starts up the Falcon. Puts it in gear. She reaches out of the window and plucks the cigarette from his lips. Takes a drag and snuffs it out against the car door.

"Last little boy I ate was feisty." She drops the butt in the street. "I like that in a snack. Feisty, rude and dumb."

She leaves them laughing and punching at each other in the street. Pulls the Falcon off *Broken River* and picks up I-67, headed west, dust flaring up behind on both sides as the car unzips the old hide that wraps the world. She doesn't know where she is going or why. She just drives.

Seven. Eight. Nine.

The turn-off to *Libby's Nuts* comes in a ticking of telephone poles and goes by in a blur of signage and scrub. She can feel the money huddled in her sock drawer as she passes. It glows in her head. A distress beacon.

Hope... Hope... Hope.

She thinks of Sheldon Davis. Sees him in her mind. Sees the envelope of money between the table and his baby-soft hand. Sees his face. Hears his voice. She searches for the old hate and comes up with hope instead. Desperate and tiny and blind, but there it is anyway. *Hope.*

Maybe it's enough.

Ten. Eleven.

Twelve.

Number thirteen is a desert hare. A lifeless lump at the end of a dark reddish-brown smear, stretching out like an arrow that points to the sign about Fort Stockton. Another fifty-two miles.

That's when she realizes where she is headed.

She's going back. Going home. Her words are still in her head. *Vete a casa a sus madres.* Time on her hands and a little distraction and then somewhere along the line the automatic pilot in her brain had completely taken over. Her subconscious was trying to take her back. Kicking and screaming if it had to. As if the last two decades had been an afternoon detour of errands. As if dinner was cooling on the table. Waiting.

That, or maybe somehow Jesús Batista's shit-brown Ford Falcon was cursed. Whoever is behind the wheel gets sent back home. Maybe the government shows up with ICE badges, rips you out of the front seat and sends you back to where you came from. Or maybe the engine just lulls you into a trance on the I-67 and you end up driving there yourself. But, one way or the other, you're going back.

Hell she was.

She slams down on the brakes and skids the Falcon almost to a stop. The pressure sends lightning up her leg. Hip. Spine. Skull. She clenches her teeth. Steers over onto the dirt shoulder and cranks the wheel like she is piloting a riverboat. Then she heads back the way she had come.

Dashboard Jesus. Palms out. *What are you doing?*

She doesn't answer.

Thirteen. Twelve. Eleven.

Olivia watches from the bathroom window.

Libby is out back in the orchard, tormenting Lewis and Darnell McKenzie as they shake the trees and make it rain pecans. She is in her mango kimono, fully aflame in the two o'clock sun. Imitation ostrich feather pumps on her feet. She has to shout over the shaker. Her hands move back and forth over her head like she is pantomiming the wind. Whatever she is saying, or maybe the way she is saying it, has their full attention.

Libby laughs. Lewis and Darnell laugh.

The mechanical shaker will do its thing until someone pays enough attention to stop it. It will shake the nearly nutless tree to death if they are not careful.

Olivia flushes the toilet. Goes upstairs, gritting her teeth at the ache in her leg stabbing up into her hip. She limps to the bedroom. Opens the sticking drawer to Cale Hargrove's old Mexican oak dresser. Checks the money. Puts it back.

She pulls off all of her clothes and leaves them on the floor in a pile. Climbs into bed.

It is too hot for this. She doesn't care. It feels good to be lying down.

The ceiling fan sweeps in slow circles, stirring the air. The muffled drone of the tree shaker pushes its way through the walls.

The cactus people are next to her on the nightstand. All still together. Her family of desert moon people. The boy is waving. The dog. Peppercorn nose. Little pink flower ears. They've all been waiting.

The tree shaker changes into a lower gear. A throbbing, thrumming of sound. She closes her eyes.

The cactus people, her little children, are on the piano now. The piano is in Yvonne's living room. Kevin's chair is next to her, empty.

She plays. Fingers hard on the keys. Jellyroll Morton. Professor Longhair. But there is only a dull rumbling sound that comes from inside the big black box.

It is not a piano, this box. Why had she thought it was a piano?

She lifts the lid. Kevin is inside. Sticks of cheese on his little still chest.

She closes the lid. Looks around. She is not at Yvonne's.

She is back in that... place. Fallen asleep at the wheel, thinking of other things, and now she is back. She listens. She can hear them in the other room. Voices. They think she is asleep. The word-sounds push through the walls, mixing inside the wood, travelling along the old floorboards in a kind of rolling, shaking rumble. When the voices emerge from the wood their sound opens into blood orange flame.

Libby is laughing. Somewhere Libby is laughing.

The cactus people are gone. She searches. Frantic. She finds them. They are above her, up on the shelf in the moonlight. Looking down.

They huddle in panic next to Mother Mary.

Mary stands upon a flaming shelf, arms spread, sky-blue paint bubbling black and streaming from her porcelain robe.

Humming a song about the ocean.

Chapter 43
Mable and Libby

"Mama, tell me again."

"Tell you what, baby. Damn this window all to hell!"

"Mama, tell me 'bout how you come for me."

Odd question for a little girl right before she dies.

Outside, the storm howled like a feral beast with claws of wind. It tore at them like they were live, frightened food inside a tiny wooden box. Hours of lunging at closed windows, warping the glass. Then the howling, gnashing thing had dissolved the frames right out of their rotten moldings.

Not like water wasn't already pouring in through the roof. It was knee-deep downstairs. A third moccasin had slithered out of a cabinet and into the failing kitchen light, ropey shadows wriggling out over the top of the water. They were swimming in to get out of the storm. And then they were swimming out again.

Three was the magic number when it came to snakes. That's when Mable had decided it was time to relocate up to the second floor. She had hauled herself up and down that staircase five or ten times, moving her things up to higher ground. Top of the priority list was moving the records. Then moving the stereo and the record player that had been waiting on a new needle for going on three months. Hard work for a woman her size. The adrenaline helped. They shouted at each other over the storm just to avoid feeling alone.

"Mama?"

"Stay where you at, baby! I'm okay! Almost done!"

But when the beast outside had finally opened that little box of food and began clawing around inside, things had really gotten nasty. Mable was shouting, angry, pulling back at the window frame already three-quarters gone. Libby's voice was a tiny thread of sound.

"Mama, tell me 'bout how you come for me."

"Baby, ain't no time for..."

But then Mable had looked back over her shoulder at little Libby, arms wrapped around the bedpost, waiting for the weather beast to reach in and tear her free. Mable stopped herself. Let the window frame go like a sail. It ripped off and was gone leaving a ragged hole in the bedroom wall.

Mable had heaved herself up onto the bed. Pulled Libby from the bedpost into the pillow of her body. Pulled the terrified girl's face close to her mouth so that she could whisper.

"I know you scared, baby. But ain't nothin' gon' happen to you and me 'cause the good lawd lookin' out. Una'stan? Only take *one good thing* to save you for Heaven. Don't matter who you are or what you done or whether you go to church on Sunday. An' you…" Mable had pinched Libby's nose. "You is that *one good thing*, baby. For me, you that one good thing. Ain't nothin' but goodness in you. An' bein' yo' mama might be the only good thing I ever done in my livelong life, but it enough. And 'cause of that, the good Lawd gon' see us through. He gon' send us one of his angels a mercy."

"Talkin' shit, mama."

"Ain't no shit, baby. Not this time. Help on the way. You believe me?"

Silence from little Libby. Silence louder than that bestial storm. She trembled and cried to herself. Mable rocked her back and forth humming. The words weren't necessary. Libby knew her Bessie Smith backwards and forwards. The words bloomed in her head like flowers in a rain-soaked garden. *Hallelujah. Blood of the lamb. Raise those voices. Everybody gone to paradise.*

Brown water streamed down the walls. The roof above them banged and chattered violently in the wind. Whenever the storm took a breath they could hear sloshing beneath the floor.

"Mama, tell me 'bout how you come for me."

"How I come for you? Baby I tol' you 'bout a hundred million billion time already."

"Mama."

"How 'bout you tell it back to me this time."

Libby sniffled. Took a breath.

"A lonely ol' Chinaman name of Mr. Lee had me in the hugest most beautiful garden an' I was just a little bitty China baby and I cry an' cry and Mr. Lee did not know what to do so he invite all the women in Jefferson Parish to come see me and you and your friend Maggy went to see what the fuss was about and Maggy ain't short for Margaret 'cause it short for Magnolia 'cause her mama a crazy ass woman who don't know a pretty white flower from a chubby black baby so you just roll your eyes and call her Maggy and sometimes just *Mags* when you mean business. And when you and Maggy got to Mr. Lee's garden whole bunches of other women were coming out t'other way sayin' I was the cryin'est little baby they ever did see…"

Something hard and heavy had slammed into the back of the little house and everything shook. Little Libby turned rigid in Mother Mable's arms. Mable stroked the girl's long, silky black hair.

"Don't worry none, baby. Now you gon' keep me in suspense? What happen next?"

Libby looked up. Softened. Spoke.

"You an' Maggy come up on me in a little bitty bed surrounded by flowers an' Mr. Lee the Chinaman was there an' he point down to me an' say he found this little bitty China baby in his garden an' no idea how she get there an' he thinks someone put me there and snuck away in the night or maybe I growed up out the ground like a flower but Mr. Lee did not know what to do 'cause even if I was a flower I was the cryin'est flower he ever did see an' he did not know how to make me stop so he figure I needed me a mama."

"I see. MmmHmm. What he do then, baby?"

"Mr. Lee invite all the women of Jefferson Parrish to come see but ain't none of them make me stop cryin' neither so he don't know *what* to do. And then Maggy pick me up an' start coo-cooin' and swingin' me in the air but I kep' yowlin' my little head off and so Maggy start shakin' her head wantin' nothin' more to do with me even though Maggy was always on an' on about wantin' her a baby real bad on account of her man bein' all mean and her needin' someone to love her but no amount of coo-cooin' would satisfy me an' so Maggy start to put me back down in the bed an' that's when you say to Maggy *don't you put that baby down, Mags*', an' you reach over to Maggy an' take me into yo' arms an' just like that I stop cryin'."

Libby had looked up into Mable's face. Holding her breath. Waiting to see if she had gotten it wrong. Fearing her own doubts. Mable had shown soft astonishment.

"Goodness gracious. Just like that?"

Libby smiled for the first time all day. Nodded.

"Just like that I stop cryin' an' I hug you around yo' neck an' you say to Mr. Lee every baby need a mama an' not just any ol' mama but the right mama fo' the right baby an' Mr. Lee, I do believe this here is *my* baby an' I am takin' her home with me, an' then Mr. Lee an' Maggy start cryin' 'cause it was so happy an' beautiful that we found each other."

Mable had pushed back the swelling fear in her heart. Fear of the gnashing beast reaching for them from every direction. Fear of the wet and lonely darkness coming just before death. Fear of being wrong about it only taking one good thing to earn mercy. She had pushed it all back and had beamed down at the girl. Squeezed.

"Tha's it exactly, baby. Yo' mem'ry the same as mine. That how we found each other alright. An' then I take you home an' name you Libby after my own mama 'cause ain't a day go by I don't miss that woman."

Then the world had fallen away.

The entire house had slipped suddenly sideways as the foundation let go, rolling them both off the bed and into the wall. Fear took them both. The torrent of questions Libby always had after the story of Mr. Lee in the garden did not come this time.

So there had been a thin sheen of relief spreading atop Mable's terror. She knew the lie would not hold forever. But it would hold for another day.

If there *was* another day.

Eventually, if there was another day, Libby would know the difference between a garden and a brothel. Know that babies don't grow out of the ground. That yowling babies are bad for business and have to go someplace for business to continue.

She had often imagined, even pretended, that Libby was hers. That Libby had *come from* her. Imagined those nine months. The delivery. A kindly white doctor handing over a tiny life wrapped loosely in pink gauze, cord still attached.

But there is no rewriting the past. She had known Libby's mother. Magnolia. She had hated her. Envied her. They all had. Mr. Lee only slept with the best of them. And coffee-with-crème-colored Magnolia was always the best. Month after month.

There were other privileges too. *Incentives*, Mr. Lee called them. Magnolia had never been gracious about winning. No reason she should have. She saw herself as a delicate brown bird flitting among lumbering black cattle. All the men wanted Magnolia. Her real name was Constance. The women all called her Mags.

Magnolia's fall from grace had been spectacular in its cruelty. Mr. Lee had taken no responsibility for his role in the swelling belly, which angered him to the point of violence. Favoritism and kindness had evaporated like the morning dew. Mags was assigned the worst work. The worst customers. Always last in line.

"You no take shit befo' every other take shit! You no take wash befo' every other take wash! You only take customer no other take!"

Mr. Lee had demanded an abortion, of course. Mags fought back with promises to work for free.

"This our baby, Mr. Lee. Our son. After he born, I be better than ever in this house and ain't no sense in me takin' nothin' fo' my own self. It all for you an' yo' boy. He gon' grow up to be a great man jus' like you. Wha'chu' gon' name him, Mr. Lee?"

It was a healthy mix of pride and greed that had saved Libby's life, all wrapped up in the feminine guile of a desperate mother.

Couldn't just leave. None of them could just leave. They all owed Mr. Lee more than they could ever repay. Housing. Clothes. Food. Jewelry and perfume. Drugs. Mr. Lee had a solid reputation in Jefferson Parrish for both generosity and precise accounting. He also had a reputation in Thailand, allegedly, for criminal savagery. They all needed him. They all feared him.

Mags, for all of her fine-bones and light skin, was no different. Permission to bring her baby to term had turned the screws into her daily existence. She was made to suffer for allowing one of her eggs to accept one of Mr. Lee's sperm. Mable had not been sympathetic. None of them had been sympathetic. Mags had it coming.

But none of them had particularly wanted Magnolia to die. Not even Mr. Lee. Near the end he'd begun talking optimistically of a post-partum return of her profitability. He planted a tiny vegetable garden out behind his house across the street and when any of them came over to report on business, he had mused about all of the things he would teach his son.

The gender had been a surprise. Mags told everyone she was carrying a boy.

"Doctor say he gon' be strong and beautiful. Show me his lil' wee-wee an' eva'thing. He gon' be just like Mr. Lee."

Which meant Magnolia had anticipated Mr. Lee's reaction. Delaying the inevitable as long as possible. She had known there would be a reckoning.

And there was. The gender revelation sparked a resumption of Mr. Lee's briefly abated rage. The threats were constant.

"No crying baby! All the time cry! I hear from across street! Bad business! Bad Business! You get rid or I drown in bathtub!"

Just as surprising was how little affection Magnolia had for the child, who she called simply, "the baby" and "baby girl" and "her." Naming is an act of inspiration. There was none of that.

"Name ain't none of yo' damn business is what the name is. Namin' is for Mr. Lee. It his baby."

They had all accepted the excuse. But the truth was that Mags never attached. Once the cord was cut, the wailing, wriggling bundle was a thing apart. A thing not from her. Not *of* her. And then, suddenly, Mags had seemed to have a hard time attaching to her own life. Like the alienation from her baby was merely part of a greater alienation from herself.

So that *she* was not of herself. So that *she too* was other.

To investigate the sound of crying, which they all did if for no other reason than to keep Mr. Lee from storming across the street, was to find a kicking, red-faced infant in one corner of a room and a stoned, disheveled, red-faced crying Magnolia, former queen of the house, in another corner.

They all tried to help, despite the common disaffection for Mags and her unrelenting abuse. They each bounced and coddled and cooed at the little girl. Carried her around the kitchen and living room and the back yard whenever a customer needed attention. Or when Mr. Lee was over. Or when Mags was off to the store for supplies.

But the crying rarely stopped. None of the women who came and went in that house, a few of them already mothers, had the right touch. The right voice.

None except for Mable.

Whenever Mable approached the screaming child it was like a cumulous cloud scudding in front of a merciless sun. A cool breeze of silence blowing through the house. Every time she picked her up. Every time she touched her. Every time.

"Should be yo' baby, Mable," Mags had said once. "You the motherin' type. That shit's either in yo' blood or it ain't. Like bein' fat and black I guess. Too bad you can't get you a man."

Week four. Mags left the baby with Mable to go to the corner market for formula and diapers. Never came back. Passed the corner market and kept on walking. Took a bus west. Got off and walked some more. Walked until she decided to step out in front of the 3:50 BNSF pulling into Avondale Station.

Took awhile to get the news. No one at the scene knew who she was or had ever seen her before. Magnolia would have hated the name Jane Doe. Mable and the others could believe easily enough that Magnolia had just kept walking. None of them had considered that she had stopped walking forever.

But then it all made sense.

A couple of days. Maybe three. Then Mable had stepped up. Had traded need for need. Fear for fear. Mr. Lee had a problem and she was the answer.

"Don't owe you nothin', Mr. Lee. Nothin' if I do this. We una'standin' each other?"

Mable had shifted the sleeping baby from one arm to the other. Waited.

Mr. Lee had stood up from his garden. Brushed the dirt from his hands. Looked up at the sun. Nodded.

"You take. You go. I no see no mo'."

It was her mother's voice that had come to her in that moment. Mama Libby, calling out all the way from those growing-up days beneath the lengthening shadow of a giant Mississippi pecan.

"Only take one good thing to get you into Heaven, baby. You know it when you see it. But when you see it, you best step up and take it. Good Lawd give you that chance? Don't ask why. Just do what you got to do."

And she had. Left Mr. Lee. Left the house. Left the business. Never looked back. Moved down to Jean Lafitte in Jefferson Parish where she shared a beat-to-hell two-story house with her cousin Janeese. Isolated, but close enough to civilization that a twenty-minute walk and a thirty-minute bus ride got Mable a part time job cleaning hotel rooms at a Radisson.

Janeese had a good part-time job serving food at a hospital cafeteria. Their schedules fit together like the gears of a machine so that one or the other of them was always available to stay home and tend to Libby. By the time Janeese met a man nice enough to move in with, Libby was old enough to be alone, Mable was working a regular shift and making enough to pay the full rent, and they had the house to themselves. It all seemed meant to be.

Janeese even left behind her second-hand Panasonic stereo, turntable, speakers and collection of old records that she had picked up at a garage sale. Janeese's man had his own stereo. His own music. He wouldn't be listening to Bessie Smith. Or Ma or Billie or Victoria or any of the others. And so neither would Janeese.

But Mable and Libby listened to them every night, from the minute Mable fired up the oven to the minute Libby had dried the last plate and usually well after that, night after night, month after month, year after year, until the needle had worn down to a nub and needed replacing.

Mable made mostly right decisions as a mother. Mags had suspected that it would come naturally for her, and it did. But for all of those right decisions, the decision to defend the house against a hurricane was not one of them.

There had been plenty of talk about the storm never making landfall. Best option had seemed to stay put. But nothing changes quite like the weather. By the time the storm threw its left hook into the levees it was too late to leave. The decision had been made. It had become a test of faith.

When the house finally slipped off its foundation, so that the wet gunmetal sky seemed to twist sideways through the ragged hole in the bedroom wall, Mable had grabbed for Libby's wrist and yanked her up off the floor to keep from being crushed by the bed. Libby shrieked. Mable felt the fear that she had been wrong wedge itself into her heart.

She wondered in that terrible moment about her *one good thing*. Wondered if Mags would have been able to keep Libby alive any longer. Wondered if Mr. Lee might have found her a better mother. Wondered if all of the foundations in her life were waterlogged and rotten. Wondered if there was no angel of mercy after all.

The needle in Mable's brain had jolted with the foundation. A new song as she tried to pull Libby upright. Bessie again. But in just a whisper this time. Too easily ignored. On about how the devil is a comin' like you was born to die.

There was a buzzing in the air around them. Like a sun-drunk bee fighting the wind. Louder. Louder.

And then the grizzled face of Antoine Beaudaine Cherish, Mr. ABC, framed by the hole in the wall that used to be a window. He flicked a snake away from the skiff.

Looked at Mable with something like a smile.

Chapter 44

It's her in the boat. Olivia. Alone. The boat is just big enough for one.

Beneath her is sand. In every direction. Only sand. Still and brown.

Every so often it all moves beneath her. The sand. The boat. Enough to make her clutch for the edges. Then stillness. Again.

The shore beyond is a liquid silver. Shimmering. Distant.

No oars.

She scoops handfuls from around her feet. Dumps it over the edge. Again. Again. Scrapes the bottom with her fingernails, down to the bright blue wood. Then the blue is gone again. Buried. She can't tell how the sand is getting in. Her hands are too small. Like tiny wooden spoons, ugly and cut with scars. Riddled with holes.

From the liquid silver shore there are arms. Lots of them. Like little sticks. Moving. Waving. Pushing tiny thin voices up into the air. Threads of smoke.

She listens. Closes her eyes. Reads the sound of the smoke.

Fire, says the smoke. *You're burning.*

Opens her eyes. A coyote is in the boat with her. Lean and soft. A new born pup wedged gently in her jaw. She reaches but the coyote leaps over the edge, into the sand. Swims for shore, pup held high.

She wants out. Tries to move. Tries to dive overboard. Tries to follow. But her leg is caught in the hole, somewhere beneath the sand. The smoke from the shore is everywhere now. *You're burning.*

Her wrist. Someone is pulling. Not hard enough. She wants to scream —*pull harder... pull harder.* But they are only thoughts. Silent wishes. Only the smoke has a voice. *You're burning.*

Olivia DeLuna opens her eyes. The cactus people are looking at her from the nightstand. Her little moon family. The wall behind blazes in late afternoon sun.

"I said... you burning up, baby." Libby gives her wrist another tug. "Fo' hundred degrees outside an' you up in here under the damn covers."

"Libby..." She rolls over. Yanks her wrist out of Libby's hands.

"You sick, baby?"

"No. I'm just…" She doesn't finish. The air is close and hot. Libby puts a hand on her bare shoulder.

"Jus' what?"

Olivia kicks off the covers. The breath of the ceiling fan blows over her damp body, cooling the sweat.

"Tired," she says. "And hot. *Fuck* it's hot." She takes Libby in for the first time. Propped up on one elbow. "Libby… why are you always naked?"

"Why? 'Cause *fuck it's hot.* You jus' said so. An you nekid too, baby."

"I'm in bed."

"Me too."

"I'm in *my* bed, Libby."

"*MmmHmm.* I'm in yo' bed too. See?"

Libby sweeps her arm away from her familiar body to show the obvious. Olivia closes her eyes. The McKenzie brothers are still outside picking up nuts. Darnell says something to Lewis about fertilizer. The words are lost in a panicked conversation between two chachalacas off in the direction of Old Faithful. Something about the end of the world.

"Doesn't matter if it's hot," says Olivia. "You're always naked."

"*MmmHmm.* You right. You right. You want me go get in my pee-jays an' come back? Maybe I go find me a snowsuit. An' a hat. An' some big ass boots." She pretends to roll away. "You wait here an' I come back as a Eskimo girl."

Olivia smiles. Sputters a laugh. Opens her eyes as she grabs at Libby's wrist. Libby rolls back in. Kisses her on the forehead.

"You had you wunna them days, huh?"

Olivia nods.

"You want to tell me all about it?"

She shakes her head. "No."

"You spose' to work tonight?"

Olivia remembers. Sees Manny Soto sitting on the lip of the fountain. Nods.

"Well fuck that, baby. Call in sick."

"No."

"I write you a note. Pretend to be yo' mama. Say you coughin' up blood and got green goop comin' all out…"

"Libby."

"… you nose. Okay. Okay. But I would."

"I know you would." She squeezes Libby's wrist. Stares at the fan, sweeping the dry air. "Thanks. I'm fine."

Libby pulls her fingers through Olivia's hair. Long, slow strokes. The chachalacas are still at it.

"Tell me, baby. You still wish you had yo mama 'round to talk to? Look after you? Even though you a grown up woman?"

Olivia rolls her head over. Looks at Libby. Lies.

"Of course."

"Me too," says Libby.

A minute. Two minutes.

"Sometime I have dreams. Mama Mable right there on the stoop, rockin' in her chair, listenin' to her records, talkin' on an' on like nothin' happen. You do that?"

"No."

"Mmm. Sometime the dream is more real than when I wake up. You know how that shit is? You had you dreams like that?"

She remembers the only dream in her head at the moment. The boat. The silver shore. Waving arms. Smoke and fire.

"Sometimes."

"'Course, my mama pass when I was seventeen. An' we was close, me an' her. Yo' mama pass when you what? Twelve?"

"Fifteen."

"MmmHmm. Still a baby. That some shit. She do that a lot? Drive while she drinkin'?"

"All the time."

"Like puttin' a damn gun to yo' head. I don't do that shit. You two talk much 'fore that happen?"

"She didn't like me much."

"Come on now. 'Course she did. You her baby. She jus' angry at yo' daddy for ditchin' out. Mama an' me talk all the time. Woman-to-woman like. We talk all kinda' shit. 'Bout eva' thing. Men. Sex. Life. Now she dayid an' still wanna talk about shit. So she jus' pull up a chair in my head an' rattle on an' on."

"Do you talk back?"

"Talk back? What'chu..." Libby pulls her head back. Wrinkles her forehead. "Baby, the woman is *dayid*. I ain't no crazy person." Then she laughs to herself.

"What?"

"I tell that shit to my new little no-kinda-priest writer friend with the ponytail an' the fuck-all-day face an' you know what he ask me?"

Olivia looks. Remembers the man with the bleeding face.

"He want to know if mama eva' talk to me when I *awake*. You know, walkin' 'round doin' shit. An' I tell him she do eva now an' then, but baby, there a diff'rence 'tween dreamin' an trippin'. Mama don't show up in my head when I'm trippin'."

"What'd he say?"

Libby shakes her head.

"No-kinda-priest don't say much at all 'bout *anything*. I tol' him that me an him should go out an' fuck in the middle of the road."

Olivia looks. Winces.

"You did what?"

"You know, just to rattle his ass. He jus' look at me like I crazy. Sat there waitin' to write shit down on his lil' notepad."

"You *are* crazy, Libby."

Libby lets out a deep, rolling laugh. "I am too crazy, huh?"

"Yes you are."

From outside, farther away, the chachalacas agree.

"I saw him today," says Olivia.

"Saw who? Ponytail fuck-all-day-no-kinda-priest?"

"Yeah. At *Pepitas.* Looked like he'd been in a fight. His face looked pretty bad."

"Really? My ponytail writer friend?"

Olivia nods.

"Someone fuck up that pretty 'lil face?"

Olivia nods.

"Well ain't that some shit? I wonder what happen."

"Don't know."

"Hope he okay. Hate to think someone mess up that face."

Olivia waits for her to say '*Like what happened to you.*' But she doesn't.

"He was with Miguel," she says. Libby scrunches up.

"What? Miguel? Yo' Miguel?"

Olivia looks. Scowls back.

"He's not *my* Miguel, Libby. He was never *my* Miguel. Looks like he's Yvonne's Miguel now."

"Yvonne? Miguel fuckin' that skank ass thing now? You sure?"

"Yeah. Pretty sure."

"Well mutha fuck. How a man that fine get so desperate? She a old married bitch with a sick little baby."

"Kevin's not a baby. And Yvonne's not old. And she's not a bitch. And since when are you defending the institution of marriage?"

"Look. I'm the biggest fan of bein' married you will eva' see, baby. People bein' married keep my shit in business. Unna'stan'? I'm jus' sayin a man lookin' like Miguel can do himself a whole lot better than Yvonne Laundry."

"Lawry."

"I know the bitch's name."

"She's a good enough catch."

"Oh he gon' *catch* somethin'. He be lucky his dick don't look up one day an' start prayin' *Lawd, take me now, 'cause I ain't nevah goin' back in there a-gain.*"

They both laugh. One high, one low. Chachalacas too.

"Ain't enough shuga' stick cookies in this worl' to solve *that* problem."

Lewis and Darnell are picking up their bags and rakes. Heading for the barn, as they say. Something about beer and it being too hot. Libby resumes raking Olivia's hair.

"Miguel should be beggin' you fo' fo'giveness is what."

"I don't want him back, Libby. Seriously."

"Well. You need to get you a man, baby. Not a man-man. A *good* man. An' Miguel 'bout as good as they come. Fo' a no-account piece a shit anyway."

"I think my man-getting days are officially over," she says, voice breaking. Emotion finds its way to the surface. She wipes her eyes. "Fuck."

"Yo' face hurt, baby? Yo' leg?"

"It all fuckin' hurts, Libby. All of it."

"You still using them ointments? Whad'ya call that shit?"

"Steroidal…"

"Yeah. That mess helpin' any?"

"No." Anger now, like a flame to straw. "*Nothin'* fuckin' helps, Libby. I'm a goddamned freak show. I'm a fuckin' monster."

Libby wraps a dark strand of hair around her finger. Tugs.

"Come on, girl. Stop that mess. Jus' stop it. Don't you be feelin' sorry fo' y'sef. Body like this here? *Sheeit.* Miguel a damn fool is all."

They lie in silence. Minutes pass. Long enough for the wall to change color. Deepening from flame to embers. Olivia sniffles. Speaks.

"Miguel's a good-enough guy. But…"

"You two was good, baby. 'Til he lose all control of his dick."

"No. I don't really blame him for what he did. I'm not… we just didn't… we don't work together. I'm not sure I really work with anyone." She shakes her head hard. Sniffs again. "Anyway. A man is the very last thing I need."

"Then what is the very first thing you *do* need? Tell me. I go out an' get it fo' ya'. 'Cause we got to pull yo' ass outta the blues, baby. You worse than Ma Rainey, singin' 'bout *Yonder Come the Blues.*"

Libby hums. Starts to sing.

"*Went down to the river, each*… Sing with me, baby. Come on."

"I don't know those words," she lies. Libby elbows her in the side.

"Listen to you lie like a dog."

"Well I don't."

"'Bout how Ma Rainey go down to the river every last day? Tryin' to keep from cryin'? Tryin' to keep from ending herself? *Do myself away* is how Ma Rainey says it. *Keep from doin' myself away.* And she walks until her shoes done wore out just so she can keep on livin'? 'Cause sometimes walkin' is the only difference 'tween livin' and dyin'. Puttin' one foot in front of the other. Step, step, step. But then Ma Rainy can't walk no more and she look up and she say, *Yonder come the blues.* Come on, baby. Sing it with me."

Olivia does not sing. Libby sings it herself. Works devolve to humming. Silence. Then she turns her head to Olivia.

"Got to keep on walkin', baby. Even on yo' bad leg. You hear? Got to keep on walkin'. Ma Rainey talkin' to us from the otha' side. Like we her babies. Tellin' us she know how deep the shit can get, but we got to keep walkin'."

Silence. Even the chachalacas are gone. There is only the sound of embers. The sound of hot glowing.

Libby brightens. Laughs. Squeezes Olivia's shoulder.

"I know what you want, baby. You want that damn juke joint. Don'chu? Tha's what you want. Want me go get that shit fo' you?"

Olivia thinks about the ten thousand sitting quietly across the room in Cale Hargrove's old dresser. About the ninety more to come. She can see *Papi's* in her head. Not the checkerboard floor, but the lake of dark wood beneath it. And the velvet wallpaper. Table candles in hurricanes of thick amber glass flickering in the smoke. The old-timey microphone, like the one in the photo of Billie Holiday.

She can feel *Papi's* in her chest. The way it used to be. Before *Papi's* was *Papi's*. She can hear how it all used to sound. Like listening to the memory of an ocean in the boney curl of a conch.

She considers telling Libby everything. The letter she had written to Sheldon. Meeting with him in San Antonio. The money. The plan. The hope. Everything. She wants to tell her everything.

But no.

It's the hope that's the problem. It's bigger now. Big enough to be afraid. Enough hope to be spotted by her own fate. Targeted. Exterminated. The bigger it gets the more it feeds. The more it feeds, the bigger it gets. Now the hope is too big. Too big for the door of her larynx. Too big for the arms of her own words.

So none of the details can make it out either. The letter. Sheldon. The ten and the ninety. It all stays inside. The hope presses its fingers against the windows of her eyes, looking out across the pillow at Libby. The hope, like some abandoned, imprisoned, overfed child.

"'Cause I *will*, too," continues Libby. "I will tear that fucka down, baby. Brick-by-brick. Then I bring all them bricks back here an' rebuild *Papi's* right back there in the orchard. That what you want? 'Cause, baby... I want..." She taps a finger on the sternum between Olivia's naked breasts. "... whateva *you* want."

They stare at each other, Libby's long black hair brushing over Olivia's shoulder. Olivia furrows. Ten seconds. Twenty.

"Why are you so good to me?" she asks.

Libby smiles. Strokes Olivia's face with the back of her hand.

"'Chu mean, baby? You my sexy 'lil live-in massage-massage housecleaner. Got to keep yo' shit happy."

"You didn't pick me up because you were looking for a housecleaner."

"No. I pick yo' ass up because you had yo' *thumb* stuck out, pullin' yo' big-ass bag up the road. Hitchin' in a temp-a-ture of two hundred mutha fucks. Sun beatin' all down. An' you look like road kill walkin'. You was some kinda messed up. All bleedin' an' shit. Ain't gon' leave no beat-up woman to die in the dirt."

Olivia scoffs. "Wasn't gon' die in the dirt."

"Yes you was, too. Maybe not right then. Maybe it take another man to fuck you sideways and then beat you silly. Maybe it take another two. Or three. But it was comin' baby. Sho as shit. So I says to mysef, *Libby, pull over an' see if this almost dead woman with her thumb stuck out and her big-ass bag want to clean house and learn how to stick up fo' her damn self.*"

"You did not."

"Did too. Mama always tell me we got to look out fo' each other. I say, mama… how you know who need the help? And Mama Mable say, *baby, you knows her when you sees her is how.* She also say it only take one good thing to get yo' ass into Heaven. An' you my one good thing, baby."

"Me?"

"*MmmHmm.*"

Olivia snorts. Laughs to herself. Shakes her head.

"Ain't nobody's ticket to Heaven, Libby. Ain't no charity case, either."

"Sush. So there I am drivin' along an' it like Mama Mable right in my head. *They she is, baby! They she is! Pull over.* And I did too. Pulled right over."

"You were trippin'."

"Weren't trippin'. I never drive when I'm trippin'. That was mama alright."

Olivia rolls her eyes. Lets it go. "Okay."

"Look. I don't got no babies of my own to look after. So I figure I jus' look after *you* while you cleanin' up after *me.* See how that shit work?"

"Like it was meant to be."

"*MmmHmm.* Like it meant to be. Yo' *massage*-massage skills just a surprise bonus. Even though you don't get too much of a chance to *massage*-massage anybody in *this* house. Eva' so often I 'spose. Most men get what they come fo." A rueful laugh. "'Cept *massage*-massage-all-the-way-married. Wonder how that dumbass mutha fuck doin' anyway."

"Sheldon? I dunno. He's not so bad, Libby. Do you think?"

Libby pushes herself up on one arm.

"Not so bad? What the… *not so bad?* All-the-way married ran you all the way off the damn road then blowed up your damn car. Nearly killed yo' ass all the way dead. What the hell you mean he not so bad?"

"Nothing. I mean… I don't know. I kinda feel sorry for him."

"Sorry? You… that mutha fu…"

Olivia rubs her face with both hands. Tries to find the words to excuse and defend. Or at least the words to explain.

"I mean. Look. He shows up, scared half to death so he comes upstairs with me, stoned out of his mind…"

Libby laughs. "Sheldon love him some cookies. He stoned and hard as a damn brick."

"We were talking and… I don't know. He seemed like a pretty okay guy. He's big into the blues."

"He was too. He knew Big Mama like *that.*" She snaps her fingers.

"And then the second time…"

"*MmmHmm.* Second time he was comin' for you, 'Livia. Getting' all grabby an' shit. Not in *my* house. Not wit' you anyway. No, no, no."

"That's what it seemed like, but I don't know. I was jumpy that night and the whole room was probably spinning for him. And…" She sees Libby smirk, squeezing her lips together. "It's not funny, Libby. You can't just… drug people up without their knowledge."

"I know, baby. I know."

"You could really hurt someone. Kill someone. What if they have some kind of reaction? Seizure. Heart attack."

"I know. You right. I got to knock that shit off, huh?"

"Yes. You do."

"Yes I do. Yes I do."

"So anyway…" But Olivia is starting to smirk too. She stops talking long enough to let it subside. "He's standing there… trying to hold on to the table… with his… his… *thing* just…" She rams her arm straight up into the air towards the fan. Closes her eyes tight, trying to keep the laughter in. No use. Out it comes in fits and sprays. "Like some kind of… of…"

"Like he done swallowed the damn Number 5 bus to Houston…" Libby is clutching the sheets like she is in danger of laughing herself off the bed. "An' it leavin' without him!"

It is a moment or two before Olivia can stop laughing long enough to speak. "So then… so then… ahh… this is *not* funny, Libby. This is *not*…"

"I know, baby. I know. This shit ain't one 'lil bit funny."

"So then I punched him in the face."

The words, the image, destroy them. They are fetal and rolling, clutching themselves. Gasping and crying.

"He out there… he out there… he out there in the front yard… crawlin' round'… lilly-white ass in the air… holdin' his nose with one hand an'… an' lookin' fo' his draws with t'other."

"Oh, God. Libby. Libby stop. This is so…"

"People be drivin' by thinkin' damn, Libby Holder gots herself one of them shaved… one of them shaved… five-legged dogs."

They coast to the bottom of the hill like a car with only two tires and a broken axle. Panting. Holding hands. Olivia is the first to speak.

"Poor Sheldon."

"Po' Sheldon my ass. *Massage*-massage-all-the-way-married run you off the fuckin' road. A punch in the nose is one thing. Nearly killin' yo' ass is another. If I *eva'* see that mutha fuck again…"

"What did you do with all of his stuff?"

"What stuff?"

"Libby."

"Oh, you mean his damn wallet?"

"Yes."

"An' the fo' hundred fifty-two mutha fucks *inside* the wallet that he decide not to put into his pocket?"

"Yes."

"An' the weddin' ring that his wife put on his damn finger when he swear to her *I do in sickness an' in health an' even if I get a rock-hard dingly-dang 'cause I just happen to drive fo' hundred miles fo' some ho-house cookies?*"

"Yes. Whatever you have, we need to give back."

"Oh *hale* no. I ain't givin' nothin' back to that jackass."

"Libby, I don't want any more trouble. Okay? I don't want to be dragged off in handcuffs for stealing. Neither do you."

"Baby, if they was gonna do it, they'da done it."

"You don't know that."

"*Massage*-massage don't want trouble with me. Besides, he the one who left that shit behind. Ain't my fault if he don't have enough sense to get his own things."

"That's not what he says."

Libby looks sharply. "What? You been *talkin'* to that shithead?"

A beat. Two.

"No. Libby. That's what you told me he was going on about when he came pounding on the door. Before I ended up in the hospital and you were arrested. He's worked up into a lather. All he has to do is decide to file a complaint. They already arrested you once this month. You want to go again?"

"No."

"Me neither. My life is already fucked up enough. I don't need that kind of trouble."

Libby's face clouds into a disgruntled pout. "Mutha fuck try to kill you, baby."

"Libby."

"Fine. I just put it all in a bag full'a rocks and tho it at him next time I see his sorry ass."

"How about you just give it all to me."

"So you can do what?"

"Mail it to him," she lies.

"No, no. Oh, hale no. You done with that mutha fuck. *Fo'eva'*. You hear me?" She taps her chest. "*I* mail his shit back."

"You sure? Because I can…"

"Baby, look at me."

Olivia looks.

"Do I look confused about this shit?"

Not a good development, Olivia thinks. Not good.

"No," she says. "You don't."

"Damn right, no I don't. *Massage*-massage best sleep out by the fuckin' mailbox, wit' his pillow an' his teddy bear an' his glass o' warm milk, 'cause Liberty Cherish gon' have the last word with this mutha fuck."

Chapter 45

Sheldon stands at the upstairs window. Looks out at the deep green hill sweeping out away from the house down to the horsehead gates and the road on the other side. Christi's Beemer rolls slowly into view down on the driveway, like a tube of red lipstick on wheels.

It stops. Idles. The gates grind open along their leisurely arcs. The black ragtop moves sympathetically. Separates from the windshield. Crumples, gathering and disappearing into a discrete cavity between the back seat and the trunk.

The horses wait at attention now. His wife fusses in the rearview mirror.

Hair. Lips. Hair. Eyes. Hair. Glasses. Tongue swiping over teeth. *Big smile!*

It doesn't matter where she is going. He has no idea where she is going. Doesn't matter. The pre-stage beauty-check ritual never changes.

Hair. Lips. Hair. Eyes. Hair. Glasses. Tongue swipe.

Big smile!

No coincidence that he should happen to be at the window to witness the ritual. That is precisely why he is here. Well. Not to watch the ritual, exactly, but to watch Christi drive away. To watch her pass the mailbox on her way to wherever she is going. Because, he figures, *that* moment –which is now *this* moment –is the most dangerous moment of the day.

Not that he could ever recall a time in which Christi had actually intercepted the mail on her way out. He almost always brought the mail in when he returned from work. Mail collection was usually *his* thing. Not by any formal assignment. It just was.

But still. There was a theoretical chance that the mail truck would arrive just as Christi was leaving, and that the postal carrier would hand her whatever contents of that truck bore their address.

It was possible.

Of course, Christi would never actually *open* his mail. But she would likely ask him about it. She would certainly ask him about a package. He rarely received packages. And she would sure ask him about a package with a return address of Corbin, Texas.

Whoreville.

So if there was any chance at all, he needed to be watching. Prepared.

Christi straightens the mirror. Drives off down the rest of the hill and through the gates. She pushes the button on her visor to reunite the misaligned horses, lip to nose.

And... *gone.*

Sheldon leaves his lookout post and returns to his study. He sits on the worn leather couch and listens to the empty house. He looks at the desk, heaped with papers.

It is all for effect, the papers. For the past week he has opted to "work from home" in the mornings. He told Christi that he was having trouble concentrating at the office. Feigned anger at the telephone and his callously interruptive staff. Unfairly maligned April March for not knowing how to do a job herself without needing to consult with him every fifteen minutes.

"I just need a few hours in the morning to focus. The afternoons I can handle. But the mornings..."

Or at least until the mail was delivered.

Not that Christi had asked for an explanation. Not that she cared one way or the other about him working at home. They each had their own corners of the house and it was not like he was underfoot. By the time she was up, bathed, scented, painted, adorned and ready for life outside of her bedroom, he was already in his study with the door closed. For all she could tell, he might as well have been downtown ensconced in his *actual* office at Houston Market Research.

But he had decided some explanation was appropriate anyway. Trouble concentrating.

Christi had received and apparently accepted the explanation with a shrug. As if he had told her that since his right nostril was inexplicably clogged, he had decided to make greater use of the left nostril rather than searching for a tissue.

It was silly, frankly, for him to have thought that she would care about *anything* he had to tell her. Given her general state of dizzy preoccupation, she would have shrugged off, in precisely the same way, an explanation that involved an office infestation of vampire bats. Vampire bats, her shrug would say, simply did not concern her.

What *did* concern Christi, in fact, by all appearances, the *only* thing that presently concerned Christi, was her contribution to the Corbin Redevelopment Project. She had stumbled upon the idea that would allow her to share, at long last, in the business obsession that had so consumed her father and her husband and, not to be forgotten, Nicholas Voss. Hers was an idea so obvious —not in the sense of being *good*, but in the sense of being *predictable* —that Sheldon was amazed he had not seen it coming sooner.

Christi's revelation had made its debut at dinner with Sheldon, Grayson and

Nicholas Voss at *The Branded Calf* in north Houston. Decidedly upscale, *The Branded Calf* was located two levels beneath the lobby of the thirty-five floor Chemstat-Acres Building. A mainstay on Grayson's list of quality restaurants to take important clients. Dimly lit. Dark tablecloths. Tall, padded leather booths. Wine-colored concrete walls, slickly painted and hung with thick, matching drapes to dampen the ambient noise.

Like dining tucked neatly away in a cranny of someone's lower intestine.

Much of the evening had been given to Grayson's grumbling discontent over the environmental politics that he increasingly feared would threaten investor interest in the River Walk project.

But this was not a discontent that Grayson could let off the leash. With Nicholas Voss at the table, Grayson was conscious that a representative of the client was listening to every word. Weighing every tone. In this way, Grayson had been at war with himself all evening: furious and worried on the one hand, dismissive and unconcerned on the other. The need to vent and the need to keep an optimistic outlook locked in mortal combat over his cut of prime rib, extra bloody.

For his part, Nicholas Voss –*Nicki*, as Christi now called him –rarely contributed to the conversation. Nicholas watched. Listened. Took barely perceptible mental note. His face registered its comprehension in minute wrinkles.

A nod.

A small smile.

Then back to cutting his meat as Conrad groused.

"Goddamned court doesn't care. After all of that. Quinco sends its people in…" He had pointed his fork at Nicholas. "Impressive people. I mean these boys know what the hell they're doin'. They get Texas and New Mexico in a room and come out with a deal. *A goddamned deal!* I mean are these guys good or what?"

Grayson had held both hands out across the table, knife in one, fork in the other, as if giving Nicholas some personal credit.

"A goddamned deal. Texas is gonna drop its objections to a diversion of water north of Lake Avalon. New Mexico is gonna drop its support for a lawsuit, on behalf of a goddamned *fish*, to prevent Texas from diverting a trickle of spit from the Pecos to green up Corbin. *A goddamned deal!* Right? *Hallelujah.*"

Grayson had looked at each of them in turn, allotting one forceful chew for every incremental turn of his face.

"Except the goddamned judge is looking to move up to the Fifth Circuit bench. Bastard's got skin in the game. And so he decided he needed to allow every half-baked, hair-brained, roach-kissing environmental organization to intervene in the goddamned case. Now he can't dismiss the damn thing."

Here, Grayson had once again remembered his audience and had looked up at Nicholas.

"Not that it won't get dismissed eventually. No one thinks otherwise. Case is going away –and I mean *a-way* –because there's no goddamned merit to it. It's just a goddamned irritation is all. Same with all of these environmental blowhards that like to write letters to the newspapers and have their bullshit press conferences and twitter and tweet or *whatever'nthehell* on their goddamned phones. They all know the dust is about to settle and they'll all be forgotten like a pile of shit in the dirt."

"Daddy!" Christi had scolded.

"Sorry, darlin'. But they know it. This ain't Oregon. This is *Texas* and these sons-a-bitches know that they are little fishes-outta-water in this state. They damn well know the end is near. So they want to make a nuisance of themselves while they can. Nothin' to worry about. All we need to do is keep the media focused on the positive."

Grayson had chewed with purpose, trying to masticate his irritation into a call to action.

"Shelly, you and your team have got to keep blowin' sunshine up the ass of every newspaper editor in this state. We need to keep them focused on that pretty little jewel, that little drop of blue water, glittering out there in the desert. You get what I'm sayin'? Got to keep everyone focused on the water."

That might have been the trigger for Christi. *Glittering, pretty little jewel.* That, after all, was how she thought of herself.

"Oh… My… God."

Her eyes had grown wide and fixed, apparently focused on some point in space over her father's right shoulder. Grayson had stopped chewing. He looked behind him and then looked back at his daughter. Then everybody had stopped chewing.

"Daddy. I have… *Oh. My. God… Oh. My…*"

"Dammit, Belle, spit it out! I don't have all goddamned night."

Grayson's irritation had melted too slowly into something pretending to be playful. He had smiled at Nicholas and rolled his eyes. Christi, oblivious to his tone, had slowly spread her hands out over the table, as if smoothing out a newspaper headline or brushing her palms against the hot bulbs of a lit marquee.

"The Corbin… River Walk… Queen."

"Belle, darlin', what *are* you talkin' about?"

"Daddy… I am talkin' about… a *beauty* contest. A pageant. At the next Corbin Moon Garden Festival. We get… the TPA… to host a beauty pageant… to coronate the first Corbin River Walk Queen."

"Belle. Sweetheart…"

"Wait, wait. Daddy. Hear me out. Texans love beauty pageants. So… therefore… newspapers and television networks love beauty pageants. You know it's true. It's great publicity for the project 'cause it's right there in the name. See?"

Again with the floating headline. "*Corbin... River Walk... Queen.*"

They had all stared in silence at the imaginary words above the table. Christi continued.

"We've got how many months 'til the next Moon Garden Festival? Six? Seven? Plenty of time to get it off the ground. Shelly can get to work promoting the heck out of it. Let's use the Moon Garden Festival to launch a party for the River Walk project! By the time the Corbin River Walk is actually built, the pageant will be a ten-year tradition. And what better way to focus the attention of the whole state on the festival than a beauty pageant that will put a crown on the head of the Corbin River Walk Queen? And keep everybody's mind off that little bitty fish."

Before Grayson could make another naysaying sound, Christi had looked at Sheldon. Had told him with every inch of her perfect, award-winning face what he needed to understand: *this right here, fella, is your time to cowboy up.*

"Don't you think, Shel?"

Sheldon had swallowed. Taken a drink. Looked up at his wife.

"I... think... that is a... *brilliant* idea," he had said. "Brilliant. Just like Grayson said, we need to focus on the positive. And pageants are a great way to get that kind of focus. And with Christi's TPA connections, it should be an easy sell to get their backing."

Christi had beamed. Grayson had opened his mouth to speak, but Christi had known better than to let that happen. She rotated her head quickly to Nicholas Voss.

"Nicki? Think CDC and Quinco would approve?"

Nicholas had found a way to intensify the blue in his eyes so that they did all the smiling. "I will recommend it," he said, nodding once. Christi had squealed and clapped and jiggled in her seat like a six year old at her own birthday party. Then, suddenly, it was safe to turn to Grayson.

"Daddy?"

Grayson's eyes had made the rounds. They closed for a microsecond longer than a normal blink as he brushed his mustache with a finger.

"Sugar, you are as smart as you are pretty."

The rest of the evening had been devoted to dressing Christi's over-empowered brainchild in little outfits and watching it strut back and forth across the table, posing in the limelight and issuing commands. Christi would work on convincing the Texas Pageant Association to recognize and sponsor the pageant. Nicholas would get the blessing of the Corbin Development Corporation board and, if necessary, the Quinco International leadership to use the project name and contribute enough money to smooth over any resistance the TPA might have to owning yet another pageant. Sheldon would work up the publicity campaign. And Grayson, for his part, would stay the hell out of the way and be supportive.

In the days that followed, the Corbin River Walk Pageant had become a real thing. Real enough to earn its own acronym –*CRP* –letters that Christi flicked into every conversation like drops of holy water. Sheldon had done his best to withhold criticism and to be supportive. The sourness with which Christi had, of late, treated him and their marriage mostly dissipated to make room for her need to speak expansively about this new, day-saving aspect of *their* project.

It had helped immeasurably that Sheldon had accurately read her face at the dinner table and stepped up. Had he expressed any hesitation at the idea, let alone disapproval, Grayson would have seized the moment and snuffed it out before its first real breath: *Belle, last thing this state needs is another goddamned beauty pageant.*

So Christi was grateful. And she had expressed her gratitude by easing up. By letting her withering discontentment with him dissipate. At least enough to allow him to join her in obsessing over her great idea.

All of which had been more than fine with Sheldon. He was happy to feign enthusiasm. Happy, even, to roll up his sleeves and re-engineer the HMR project promotion mission to include a measured rollout of a new beauty pageant. All of that was better than constant recrimination for losing his wedding ring and making the newspaper for soliciting a prostitute.

And, for a while anyway, life had seemed a little kinder.

But then, one evening on his way home from work, his cell phone had cleared its throat at a stoplight. He did not recognize the voice.

"Sheldon. It's me. You've got to watch the mail."

"What? Who is this?"

"Olivia," said the voice.

A horn behind him had jolted him out of his stupor. He had pulled over into a *Rodeo Ribs* parking lot. Turned off the car. Closed his eyes. Listened.

He drank in the sound of her.

It was not until the call was over and she was gone that he had actually comprehended what she had said: Libby, Liberty Cherish, the Corbin whore, was sending a package… to the place where he lived.

"You've got to watch the mail," she had said. By which she had actually meant, *you had better intercept the mail and make sure your wife does not open it because there is no telling exactly what is inside. A nasty letter. A video. A rattlesnake. Could be anything. Because we're talking here about Liberty fucking Cherish.*

That's what she meant.

And *that* had gotten his attention. Sheldon had sped out of the *Rodeo Ribs* parking lot for home, slaloming traffic and using his horn. Things he never did. In his imagination, every car was a slow-moving mailbox and every antenna a little red flag. *You've got mail!*

As it turned out, skidding up alongside his actual mailbox, he did in fact have mail. And so did Christi. Bills and magazines and catalogues just like every other day.

But nothing from Corbin prostitutes.

For the next three days, Sheldon had returned from work earlier than normal. Unable to concentrate for having to imagine his unguarded mailbox, standing at attention on the side of the road, waiting in the hot sun to be opened.

Inconveniently, Nicholas Voss had chosen that week to spend time at the offices of Houston Market Research to sort through the thousands of stock photos that HMR had accumulated over the years, looking for those *quintessentially Texan* scenes that might be useful in materials to be assembled for European investors. Sheldon had offered to put them all on a flash drive so that Nicholas could sort through them at his leisure. But Nicholas Voss had arranged his face in his politely negative expression. Wrinkled his nose. Shaken his head.

No. That's okay.

So Sheldon had given Nicholas an office down the hall from his own. He had tasked April March with showing Nicholas how to access the image file database on the HMR computer system. April, not so discretely admiring the cut of Nicki's suit and the sheen of his hair and the gemstone lapis of his eyes, was all too happy to oblige.

But that meant that Sheldon was stuck at the office until Nicholas decided he had had enough for the day.

Of course, he might have simply left. He might have raced home at noon each day to inspect the contents of his mailbox and then race back. He was the boss at HMR, after all. He did not answer to Nicholas Voss.

Except in some strange and convoluted way he did. He *did* answer to Nicholas Voss. Leaving while Nicholas was working in the next office –Nicholas of the CDC, Nicholas of Quinco –felt inexplicably wrong.

No. Not wrong. *Unwise.*

Besides, Nicholas had questions. Several an hour. *Where was this taken? Are these wild horses? How do we contact his photographer? Where are your Corbin project files?* Every time Sheldon thought that going home to watch for the mailman was a feasible idea, Nicholas Voss was darkening his door with printed photographs in his hands and questions on his lips.

So Sheldon had waited until after three o'clock each day to tell his staff that he needed to run some errands. And then he would race home to open his mailbox. But every day produced the same result. Bills, magazines, catalogues. On one of those days he extracted a plain brown box that had nearly made his heart stop.

Turned out it was from a cosmetics company.

Since then, with Nicholas having completed his research session at HMR, Sheldon had taken to "working at home" in the mornings and making his first appearance at the office around one o'clock in the afternoons. Not a schedule he could keep up much longer without seriously complicating his work life.

But it had lessened his anxiety.

He reclines on his home-office couch, listening for the sounds of postal delivery. Listening and thinking. Drilling down beneath the anxiety about whatever Liberty Cherish may be sending him. Drilling down into a reservoir of far more pleasant feelings.

It had taken him a day or two to realize the feeling was even there, and another day to figure out what it was. But then, suddenly, he had realized what it was. He had been able to put a name to it.

Olivia DeLuna. That was the name.

She had called him.

True, she had called him with a warning. She had called to give him a reason to worry. True, her tone had been all business and as tight as an over-cranked guitar string.

But she had called him.

Why? Why had she called him?

Because in this singular respect, if in no other, they were on the same side. They were working *together*. If Olivia wanted her money, then Sheldon would have to embezzle it from his own company to get it to her. The only reason Sheldon would ever take such a risk was to avoid the *greater* risk of his wife and father-in-law learning that the *Chachalaca* article, mistaken though it was, had not been made up out of whole cloth. If Liberty Cherish ratted him out to Christi, then there would no longer be any reason for him to steal from his own company. And Olivia would get nothing.

So they were now working together. And that felt strangely... *good.*

But best of all had been Olivia's sign-off. It was the question she had asked before disappearing into silence. Just before the traffic outside the *Rodeo Ribs* parking lot had whipped his panic about the mailbox into a consuming froth.

"So we're still on then?" she had asked.

"What?"

"The River Walk? Same time?"

"Oh. Yes. Yeah."

"Good. See you then."

See you then. The words were a salve. The memory of her voice, gliding along an endless loop in his head. *Good. See you then.*

Such a round, soft, beautiful name. *Olivia.* A clear stream of water, folding in on itself. That was the sound of her name in his head. *Olivia.* Water in the desert.

What did he want from her?

He did not know.

What did he hope from her?

He did not know.

What did he need from her?

He did not know.

She lived in a whorehouse. Yes.

She was much too young. Yes.

Much, *much* too young.

Yes, already. Yes.

She was scarred and broken and angry. Yes.

She hated him. Yes.

She was interested only in the money he could steal for her. Yes.

None of that mattered. He didn't care about any of it. He only cared that her name was Olivia, and that in his head and in his heart that name sounded like folding water.

That, and he ached with thirst.

The sound of the rolling property of the United States Postal Service, braking with a long and familiar whine, pulls him off the couch. Sheldon hustles into the bedroom. Slips on a starched, white work shirt. Striped tie. Gray slacks.

He is rolling down the driveway in less than six minutes.

He maneuvers the car. Slides the window down. Opens the box. Plunges his hand inside.

Bills. Magazine. Catalogues.

Irritation and relief once again combine to deliver a wholly different emotional impact. He stuffs it all back inside. Slams the little plastic door. Speeds up the road, glad and yet cursing the U.S. Postal Service for its whorish willingness to do business with absolutely anyone.

When he gets to the office he spends a very long time with April March on a tangle of questions regarding how and when to roll out the Corbin River Walk Beauty Pageant. There is an order to unveiling something like this. A lot of moving parts to consider. The prickly sensibilities of the TPA to navigate. CDC and Quinco approvals to secure. A show of deference to be made to the officials of Corbin Texas and the Corbin Moon Garden Festival Organizing Committee. Myriad questions to ask, all for someone else to answer. Contestant eligibility. Fees. Judging. Awards. Venue. Every time it felt like they were getting on top of what they needed to know and needed to do, something else would occur to them.

By the time Sheldon is through with April March it is almost the end of the workday. He barricades himself in his office to return phone calls and email. A late return call from the people at *Texas Beef.* The same account he had been using as cover to disappear down into the den of Corbin debauchery now *actually* needs his attention on a national campaign. It keeps him occupied and behind his desk until after seven o'clock.

When he finally returns home, the house is almost as quiet as when he had left. Christi's rolling red lipstick parade car is back in the garage, but there is no sign of her downstairs where he expects to find her. No aroma wafting from the kitchen.

He takes off his suit coat. Drops it over the back of the couch. Listens.

There is the sudden, muffled sound of plumbing from the upper floor. He nods. Looks at his watch. They are not eating in. Christi is readying herself to go out to dinner.

For the third time this week.

He sighs. Puts his jacket back on. Heads into the kitchen, hoping only that they will not be dining with Nicholas Voss or Grayson or some muckedy-muck from the Texas Pageant Association.

The kitchen is dark. He turns on the light. It is the large island countertop that commands his attention. A slick green marble, veined with pyrite.

On the left of the counter is a flat, brown box. It prominently features letters that had never before made him feel sick to his stomach: *UPS*.

Next to the box is a neat stack of… *things*. Familiar things.

On the bottom of the stack is a lime-green folder.

On top of the lime-green folder is a brown leather wallet.

On top of the brown leather wallet, is a gold wedding ring.

Next to the stack of things is a square of blue note paper.

Sheldon stands in the doorway. Motionless. Listening to his own circulation. He swallows. Steps into the kitchen, sucked in toward the black hole of that green marble island. Looks at the address on the UPS box.

Mrs. Sheldon Davis (Massage-Massage-All-The-Way-Married.)

He looks slowly past the stack of familiar, long-lost things. Looks at the square blue note. Picks it up. He does not read the words so much as hear Memphis Minnie from beyond the grave, singing about that bumble bee. The little bee that only stings her, or so it would seem. About how he makes the best honey and, oh, how he makes her scream.

Chapter 46

He looks. There is no water. Anywhere.

Desmond Vaughn crumples the empty cup. Flicks it off the desk and into the trash. Pops in the aspirin. Chews.

He looks around the *Chacha* newsroom. From one person to another. Every face carries the same headline: *Owners of Failing Desert Rag, Ready to Sever Another Limb.*

Living Arts is worried.

Statewide is bickering with *Community*. They each claim to be essential. Everett and Billy are at it again.

"This is a regional paper, Everett. That's what we are. You get that? People take the statewide news from other places. Okay? What our readers need is the local scoop. *Local.* The shit that's not gonna be printed anywhere else but the *Chacha.* Do you even comprehend that?"

"Don't talk down to me, Billy. Don't lecture me. Get off your goddamned high horse. Most of our readers rely on us exclusively. *The Chacha* is it, man. You understand that? If we don't provide statewide content, then we may as well be a flier on a bulletin board down at the goddamned library. And not some San Angelo library either. The goddamned Corbin library. We're all gonna be out of a job. How you gonna keep Tammy satisfied on a Dairy Queen assistant manager salary?"

"Now listen, Everett. You listen to me. For the last time, leave Tammy out of it. She made her choice. That's the end of discussion."

"You stole her plain and simple, Billy. And let me tell you something. And listen good: *Mom. Is. Pissed.*"

There isn't enough aspirin in the world. Desmond chews.

The Sampson twins are the least of *The Chachalaca's* problems. The readership is a rapidly shrinking glacier. Huge sheets of subscribers are groaning. Calving off. Falling sideways with a booming, chest-rattling thud to the desert floor. Every month. *Thud. Thud. Thud.*

So the owners are sharpening the blade. Again. Everyone knows it. Morale is drying up along with the money. When people aren't fighting, which is always, they are praying to the god of miracles.

Rational calculation is long gone.

Hope of small, incremental victories, gone.

It's all or nothing now. Fear of bankruptcy held at bay with dreams of a jackpot lottery win. In the newspaper business the only jackpot lottery is *the story*. The blockbuster. The exclusive. That one geyser of ink pumping through a derrick of words that every national outlet wants for its own.

They're all looking for the great white whale. In the desert.

Laurie Weaver has all the enthusiasm of an old sloth. She hangs from his cubicle wall with one bare arm. Drops the notepad on his desk.

"I called the ..." starts Laurie. She turns to the bickering Sampsons three cubicles away. "Seriously, will you two give it a fuckin' rest? Or take it outside? You're not helping." She turns back. "I called the number."

"What number?" Desmond drops the plastic bottle of aspirin back in the drawer and slams it with his knee. "I need water. What good is an empty cooler?"

"*What number?* Dez, you've only been hounding me for a week. The number on the list."

"Oh. That. You get a name?"

"Oh, sure, Dez. The name is," Laurie reaches down and grabs the pad. Flips two pages. "Yeah, right here." She drops it back on the desk. "The name is '*Nomynous*. Although there seems to be an alternate pronunciation of *Uhnomynous*."

"You weren't impressed."

"No."

"Man? Woman?'

"Woman."

"You asked her about the list."

"Yes."

"She's the one who sent it to us?"

"Yes."

"And?"

"And she says she got the list from one Sheldon Davis of Houston. She spelled it for me. Gave me his address too. Says that Sheldon Davis of Houston has some undefined relationship with an outfit in New York. *Quinco*. Says Sheldon Davis of Houston suggested to her that Quinco is pretending to buy properties."

"Pretending to buy properties? That's the list?"

"That's the list. She says that Sheldon Davis from Houston is going around to everyone who will listen, saying that some guy at Quinco, Gregor *somethingorother*, is... oh how did she put that?" Laurie leans in. Pulls her finger down the pad. Desmond follows with his eyes. The nail is ragged and half-

polished. "Oh, that's right. Quote: *he a New York no account dumbass cheatin'*
muthafuck with a teeny-tiny lil' thang."

"That's what the Sheldon guy is supposedly calling the Gregor guy."

"Right."

The *Chachalaca* ventilation system begins its inexplicable daily banging
sequence. Rapid sets of five. Like the ghost of reporters past is haunting the sheet
metal ductwork.

Desmond sighs. Closes his lids. "And why, exactly is this Quento…"

"Quinco."

"Why does she think this Quinco outfit is pretending to buy property?"

"She doesn't. She thinks Sheldon Davis of Houston is out telling lies about
his boss. Thinks Gregor of Quinco is not going to be too happy to read about all
of this in *The ChaCha.*"

He opens his eyes. "You're kidding."

"Does it look like I'm kidding, Dez? Seriously. Take a good look at this
expression."

He looks. Her face is a clothing iron. Temperature, but no expression. She is
pretty. Could be pretty. Has been pretty. She is a bird of a woman with precision
to her shape. Honey-ginger hair. Nice smile. But the smile is rare and too often
sardonic. Weariness dims her watery blue eyes. She lives alone. Drinks too much.
All of that, and twenty years abusing each other at the *Chachalaca Gazette*, gets
in the way of pretty.

"Sorry, Laurie."

"I tried to tell you."

"So she wants us to hurt Sheldon Davis from Houston."

"Yep. Don't ask me why."

"Did you ask *her* why?"

Laurie blinks in extra-slow motion.

"Now why… would I… do that?"

"I don't know, Laurie. Because you work here? Because you're a reporter?
Because this woman is trying to use this paper as a shiv for some private
vendetta?"

"Right, so let's not give her the opportunity."

"I'm just saying we should follow up and…"

"Waste. Of. Time. Spike it and move on, Dez."

Desmond scratches his forehead. Picks up his pen. Underlines. Mutters.

"Sheldon Davis. Sheldon Davis. We did something…"

"Yeah. We did. Months ago in *The Docket.* He was busted for solicitation.
The hooker in question was a woman in Corbin."

"Ah. That's right. I remember. What was her…"

"Libby Holder. Proprietor of *Libby's Nuts.*"

"Have you…"

"Have I run a check on the phone number to find out if it matches up with Libby Holder? Why yes, Desmond, I have. Because I'm a reporter and I fucking work here."

"And?"

"It matches."

"Right. Okay. So the hooker has it in for the john."

"Correct. *The Chachalaca Gazette* has become the weapon of choice for Corbin prostitutes. Can we please just spike…"

"*Libby's Nuts.* Have you checked…"

"Have I checked to see if it's on the list of properties? Yes I have. And yes it is."

"Did you ask Libby Holder if she sold her property?"

"She's still living there, Dez. She's…"

"Did you ask her?"

"I didn't check the list for that property until after I called her. I'm not calling that woman back. It's like talking to a… She really makes my head hurt."

"Have you called the other property owners on the list?"

Laurie sinks below the edge of the partition. Groans.

"Laurie."

"No." Her face reappears. "This is bullshit, Desmond. Seriously. *Ser…i…ous…ly.*"

"You got anything better to do, Laurie?"

She closes her eyes. Presses her forehead onto the silver edging on the top of the cubicle. She pulls against it with both hands. It's going to leave a mark. She doesn't answer.

"Check the properties. If it's bullshit, we'll spike it. If not…"

"Desmond…"

"And if not, then *I'll* put in a call to Quento."

"Quinco. *Fuck.*"

"Right. Quinco."

Chapter 47

Tell me again, Lula, dear sister, the point of this life.

I had another dream. I have them all the time now. Sometimes even when I close my eyes just for a moment when the house is quiet. I don't always see things. Sometimes it's just a sound all around me. Like a loud horn, or a voice, but a long ways off and coming from all directions. Or a vibration I can tune into. Like a radio frequency. Like music.

I played an old Sippie Wallace record yesterday. *'Mama's Gone, Goodbye.'* Mid-1920's. You can barely hear her through all of the scratches and pops. One of my favorites. Conrad was out with Davis. I had the house to myself. I sat in a chair by the open window and closed my eyes. It was like Sippie was singing to me from another world out there in space. Like the sound was coming from someplace almost too far away to imagine. When I opened my eyes, nearly an hour had passed. The needle was back in its holder and the house was quiet again. But the music had been in my head the whole time. I was not sleeping, Lula.

Last night, Mama Mae was in the dream. She's in a lot of them. She was standing next to me like I could touch her. In her gown. The green one with white daisies. The one she always wore when she knit. The one they found by the pool.

And then I was her. I was my own mother. I was above your house, floating, and I could see right through the roof like there was no roof. I could see you in your bed. Buzz sleeping next to you. I asked you if Buzz is the reason you stay. I kept asking. *"Is it because of Buzz?"* You always tell me that we can go home any time we want. Like a drop swallowed up by the sea. I wanted to know why you're still here. You wouldn't wake up.

Instead, I was the one who woke up. I couldn't stop crying. I can't tell you why. I felt apart. Separate. I missed Mama Mae horribly. I wanted to call you, but it was much too late. I had to go in the other room so I would not wake up Conrad. I sat in Davis' room and watched him sleep. His little chest moving. He is precious to me, Lula. Sweet little boy. If there is a reason I am here, then I think that reason is all about little Davis.

It's not about Conrad. He's not like your Buzz. We don't speak to each other any more so much as scream. I don't know what I have come to hate more, his writing or his drinking. Drinking brings out his anger. His hate, or something like it. But at least he is present then. At least he is connecting with me in one way or another. When he writes, he is absent. I do not exist for him in those hours. I would rather he scream at me and throw things.

His religion can be a blessing. It makes him want to do better. The lessons of Jesus encourage him to think that it is possible for him to do better. He tries, he really does, Lula. He is not a bad man to the core. There is goodness inside. He knows how he is and he is usually sorry for it afterwards. But he only seems to try to be a better man between Sunday and Thursday. He writes at his book in the evenings until the bourbon takes over.

Even though I mostly hate it, I try to encourage the writing. He does have a way with words. And maybe things would change if he got published. His writing makes him better sometimes. Makes him someone. And then sometimes it does the opposite. Sometimes his writing makes everything worse.

I play along at church. For his sake and mine. There are good people in our congregation. Most of it is not so bad. Except that it is empty. It is too small for me, Lula. I have come to see things your way. You will laugh after all these years and all of our fighting. But slowly you have brought me around. And I cannot go back to the way I used to think. I cannot live in such a small, airless space. I cannot pretend that I am not pretending.

Dr. Bees says I need to talk about it. He says I need to share my feelings. He says I can't keep locking myself up in my own head.

Dr. Bees. Good lord. He thinks I tell him everything and no one else. The truth is Lula I tell him almost nothing. I don't tell him about the dreams. I don't know where to begin. He asks about hearing voices every now and then. I don't tell him anything. And he is always on and on about depression. I talk about that plenty, just so we can pretend there is a point to what we do. There is no point, except that Conrad wants me to go. So I go. But there is no point. Like there is no point to me going to church.

I have tried to explain some fraction of these feelings to Conrad. I think it scares him. There is safety in numbers when it comes to the big questions. He likes a full church. I like to think that he is afraid for me. Afraid for my health. Afraid for my soul. Maybe he is. But I think he is really just afraid of being left alone with no truth in his pocket. He needs me to believe in the same God. And so I have. For his sake, for my sake, for Davis' sake. I have. I have reminded myself that Mama Mae went to church every Sunday and took you and me and Gus with her. How many hours did we spend on our knees growing up? I try to remind myself that Conrad's God is my God too.

But Conrad's God is too small for me. Mama's God too. Any God is too small for me. I see that now. You are the only one who knows that. You are the one who told me in the first place. I know I gave you hell. I was terrible. I did not believe the things you believed. *The Motherverse.*

But that shattering truth of yours has left me alone in this life. Alone except for you, wondering why I am still here. The other day Bessie Smith was in my head and wouldn't leave. – *'Backwater blues done caused me to pack my things and go. 'Cause my house fell down and I can't live there no more.'* –Over and over and over.

So I choose to believe that I am here for Davis and that you are here for Buzz. I'm trying. I'm really trying to keep walking around in the dust.

But the dreams, Lula. Even when I'm awake. Like bright little fish, flashing in the blackness. Like my head has filled with dark seawater. A secret ocean in the desert of living and I have found it or it has found me. One by one it's blowing out the windows. It's like I am already there.

Like I am already gone.

Chapter 48

There are eleven of them out here. Sitting in the dark in a circle with a flame in the middle. Somehow fire brings everything to life. Even a black and empty ocean. Even the desert.

For awhile they are eight, as Miguel and Eladio disappear to help their father, Ernesto, gather more wood. And then they are six as Hector and his girlfriend, Sandra, pull themselves out of their chairs and go back up to the house for more beer. Davis stares through the flames at two men he does not know, each playing a guitar. One picks, the other strums. Their girlfriends –wives maybe, Davis has no idea –sway in their seats as the men croon out a ballad about fishing.

Madre océano
Abre tus brazos azules.
Abra sus arcas verdes.
Alimenta a tus hijos solitaries.
Madre océano. Madre océano. Madre océano.

Behind them, the cooling desert devours the sound. Hungrily. Like it devours the light and the smoke from the fire.

Marcela Rivera, the mother, is two chairs away in a floral housedress. Slowly swaying and tapping a sandal. Broad shoulders. Full head of coarse black hair. Large, compassionate eyes. Perpetual smile. She leans his direction.

"Can I ask you? Davis? How do you like our *Pepitas*? Eh? Is it a good place for you to work?"

Davis leans in. Smiles. Nods. "I like it very much. Thank you."

Marcela winces in empathy. Her large hand floats out in his direction as if of its own will.

"I am so sorry about… about…"

Instinctively, Davis almost touches his mottled, swollen face. Almost. He has done it too many times. He shakes his head.

"It's not your fault. And if it hadn't been for Miguel..." He doesn't finish.

"Yes. I too am glad for Miguel. I am glad to whoever sent him to you in that moment. But it happened at *Pepitas*. I am sorry."

"Thanks, Mrs. Rivera. It doesn't hurt too bad," he lies. "Looks worse than it feels. Swelling will go down in a couple of days."

Miguel, and then Eladio, pass between them from behind, each with an armload of wood. They stack it in a pile away from the flames. Miguel falls back into his chair with a grunt and reclaims his beer. Eladio scampers back between them in a loping run for the house. Marcela's voice catches him before he has cleared twenty feet.

"Eladio! *Deténgase.* I am sure you mean to ask our friend Davis if you can bring him a beer!"

He can hear Eladio skid to a stop.

"Davis? *Cerveza?*"

"I'm good," he says, holding up his water. "Thanks."

"*¿Dónde está Ernesto?*" asks Marcela, looking past Davis at Miguel. "I thought he was with you."

Miguel swallows. Points with his bottle just as his father, clutching four logs, steps into the circle of orange light.

"You worry too much, Marcela," says Ernesto. He is lean, stooped and weathered with silver hair and eyebrows. He drops to one knee and stacks the logs. "What do you think will happen to me between here and the woodshed? Eh? You think I will die of a heart attack? You think a snake will get me?" Ernesto stands. Winks at Davis and Miguel. "Perhaps I will be deported, eh? They will send me off to be with Jesús Batista?"

"All of those things, Papa. Yes. I have to look out for you. You are always getting into trouble."

Ernesto brushes at his wife with his hand. Takes his seat between her and Davis. Speaks.

"You are afraid that if something happens to me you will have to help our sons gather the wood. I know the truth, Marcela. And why have you not offered Davis a beer?" He begins to stand again. "First he is beaten outside our restaurant and now..."

Davis waves him off.

"No, Mr. Rivera. Please. I'm good with water. Thanks."

Ernesto sits back with a loud sigh and directs his attention through the flames. "Luis! *No canciones más tristes.* Dancing! *Quiero bailar! Bailar!*"

Marcela knocks her husband on the shoulder. "Sad song? Ernesto, that was a beautiful song! I love that song."

Ernesto juts a hand imperiously into the air. Shouts. "*Quiero bailar! Bailar!*"

Everyone laughs, including Julio and Luis who pick up the tempo to a chorus of yips and ululation. Their companions stand. Slip out of their shoes. They dance with each other. The firelight pulls at their naked legs and their long black hair. They are intertwining shadows in the desert, born of flame. Ernesto, possessed by the rhythm, claps his approval. Marcela is leaning forward, waving her arm.

"Miguel! Davis!" She gestures. "What kind of men are you?"

Miguel rolls his eyes. But he knows better than to disobey his mother. He stands. Looks down at Davis. Extends his hand, just as he had outside *Pepitas.*

"Lo siento, mi amigo."

There is no resisting. He grabs the hand. Stands. Follows Miguel around the fire out into the desert.

He dances with women he does not know to songs he has never heard. It is awkward. Clumsy. A cringing contrast to the way these women move. His is an affront to rhythm.

It is terrible.

It is lovely.

He laughs for the first time in a long time. Hector and Sandra return from the house with a full cooler. They join in. Shoulders and elbows collide. And then, suddenly, Eladio is there too, pulling his mother by the hand into the middle, dancing slowly, defiantly, as if to another song entirely. As if to orchestral strings, they sway to an invisible tide.

"None of you know how to dance!" crows Eladio. He turns Marcela slowly.

They all follow suit, laughing, dancing folded in each other's arms in a slow, washing movement, ignoring the frenzied flamenco. Davis holds the woman with no name, the woman with only a laughing smile and dancing eyes and a topography of skin against his body. Her long hair brushes the back of his hand pressing into the small of her back.

It has been so long. This feeling. Being held. The smooth palm on his neck. Arms around him. Envelopment. So long.

He laughs with the others, dancing slower as the music grows faster. He laughs. But he laughs around the knot in his throat. He can feel the shape of his emptiness. She has defined it for him. They all have. He closes his eyes to the fire. Drinks in the moment.

The dancing continues to slow until only hips are moving. Bodies rooted to the cooling earth like tangled ropes of seaweed clinging to a seabed. Ernesto bellows a pretended protest from beyond the sparking tower of flame, laughing and clapping.

The moment dissolves before the song is over. Movement and music forgive each other, coming together again in playful celebration. Young Eladio cuts loose. He is an elegant blur. Arms, hands, fingers, legs, feet, smile, all proving his claim to be the best dancer. Others try, of course. Miguel. Hector. But it is no contest.

They cannot touch him. They are too convinced that gravity is a real thing. That our essence is terrestrial.

They all dance until they are panting, returning to the fire in pairs. Eladio swaps partners with Davis, who walks Marcela Rivera back to her seat.

"*Gracias*, Davis," she says. She groans as the low-slung folding chair resumes custody. "Eladio tells me you are a hero. Saving Olivia. He showed me the newspaper."

He doesn't know what to say. He thought he was prepared for this subject. He had rehearsed it in his head. But he is not prepared after all. He smiles down at her. Shrugs. It looks like modesty.

"Brave thing you did."

"I'm glad she is okay," he says.

"Yes. Me too," says Marcela. "I only hope she is grateful. Olivia does not always appreciate a good man."

"*Madre. Suficiente.*" It is Miguel from behind, his tone gently warning. He places a hand on Davis' shoulder. Nudges him towards his chair. "Time enough for you to leave that alone."

Marcela scoffs softly.

"Eladio tells me you are now with that... *Yvonne*, Miguel. I am hoping Eladio is not telling the truth this time. She is a married white woman, Miguel. With a sick child. You should stay away from..."

"*Madre. Suficiente. Por favor.*"

Marcela purses her lips, pinching closed her opinions. She holds up both hands in surrender and then brings them together forcefully, clapping with the others. Watches Eladio showing off with Julio's girlfriend.

"Don't mind that," says Miguel as they are sitting. He pulls another beer out of the cooler. Opens it. Drinks. "She is a protective mother. That's all."

Davis thinks. Weighing. He asks anyway.

"What happened?"

"Olivia? Oh. Just didn't..." He laughs to himself. Shakes his head. "Didn't really work out. She's a good person, but she's pretty tough. She's just..."

He takes another drink rather than finishing the sentence. Davis waits.

"She's just really fucked up."

"Fucked up how?"

Miguel whoops and whistles at his little brother. Davis waits.

"She can't..." Miguel puts down the beer, holds his hands out, interlacing his fingers and then separates them again. Repeats. "She can't attach. She can't trust. She was made to be alone, that one."

Davis waits.

"We tried. I tried. We were fine when we were just flirting. But then... *mierda*." Miguel shakes his head. Drinks. "Olivia never really came out of her shell. You know? She just stayed locked up in her own little world. She lives in her head."

Davis waits.

"So I gave her what she really wanted. What she needed."

"Which was what?"

Miguel turns. Looks. Smiles a beautiful sadness in a wash of flame. Drinks.

"A really good excuse. The oldest of excuses." He nods to himself more than to Davis. "I gave her a way out. Didn't realize it at the time. But that's what it was."

Miguel snakes a hand deftly into the cooler and pulls out another beer. He reaches in again. Hands Davis a bottle of water.

They drink and watch Eladio gather the nameless beauty in his arms and dance her across an imaginary threshold. She encircles his neck with her arms. Laughs up into the stars.

"Eladio will break a lot of hearts in the world," Marcela calls out proudly.

Miguel leans forward. "If he doesn't put her down soon he is going to break something else."

Marcela scoffs again, but Ernesto roars with approval. "Don't break her Eladio! Julio will beat you with his guitar!"

They all laugh and clap. Eladio pretends to struggle and stumble out of the light. More laughter. Except Miguel.

"So I know you say you saved her, Davis. You can say that all you want. And others may even believe it. You can even believe it. I read the article. But I know otherwise."

Davis turns. Looks at Miguel. Not knowing what to say. He swallows. Waits.

"Olivia can't be saved," he says. "She is scarred. Broken. Lost. Keep moving, *mi amigo.*" He sends his hand, fingers together, slowly cutting through the night air towards the fire. "Keep moving."

An hour later, the fire has simmered to a low magmatic glow, savoring the last of the wood. Luis and Julio take turns with fat, romantic chords and slow, contemplative pizzicato. People around the circle sway in silent intoxication, the desert at their backs. An impenetrable blanket of space beneath a spray of phosphorescent starlight. A mother's cool wet hand on the body of her febrile child.

In the distance, a coyote howls. Another joins. Another.

"Oh. *Spooky,*" says the nameless one. She snickers and leans in to Julio as if for protection. Ernesto laughs, sensing a moment.

"*Ahh.* Perhaps that is *La Llorona,* coming for you Ana." He holds out his hands like claws. Finally she has a name. *Ana.*

"Who?" She asks. Ernesto leans forward, elbows to knees, incredulous.

"You do not know the story of *La Llorona?*"

Marcela looks, swatting him on the shoulder.

Eladio laughs. "Tell the story, Papa."

"Oh. *Well.*" Ernesto leans back. Strokes his mustache. Lets the attention build. "*Llorona. Llorona.* The Crying Woman. Yes, well the story of the crying woman goes back to old Mexico. *La Llorona*, you see, was a beautiful woman who lived long, long ago. She married a man and gave him a family of beautiful children. They were together for many years. But then *La Llorona* fell in love with another man in a nearby village. This other man did not want a woman with children. He rejected *La Llorona*. Again and again, she tried to win his heart and he rejected her. He would not take her, you see? So what do you think she did, *La Llorona?*"

Ernesto looks slowly around the fire. Marcela crosses her arms. No one answers.

"She took each of her children, one by one to the river that flowed near the place they lived. And one by one, *La Llorona* drowned each child. And one by one, she let each child float away down the river to the sea. When, at last she was childless, *La Llorona* walked to the next village and presented herself to the man she loved. She showed him that she no longer had any children. And what do you suppose he did?"

Ernesto looks. Pivots. Looks.

"Does he take her? No, no. He does not take her. He was aghast. He rejected her. He wanted nothing more to do with her.

"So, grief stricken, *La Llorona* went back to her home. Back to her husband. But now he would not have her either. She has betrayed him and murdered their children."

Ernesto takes his time. Looks. Rotates. Looks at each of them.

"So here is *La Llorona.* She has no man and no children to keep her company in her grief. What do you suppose she does?"

Looks. Rotates. Looks.

"Well. *La Llorona* goes down to the same river and she drowns herself. Her body floats down the river to the sea, as if to follow her lost children. But, of course, her children are long gone.

"And ever since that terrible day, *La Llorona's* spirit circles the earth wailing and weeping and howling, searching for her children and not finding them. And when she does not find them and does not find them and does not find them she grows angry and vengeful. She looks to take the children of others, claiming them for herself." Ernesto points at each of them in turn. "Especially children who are foolish enough to disobey their own parents."

The circle laughs into the fire. Julio digs his fingers into Ana's sides and she yelps in surprise. More laughter. Ernesto claps his approval.

"I have never liked that old tale," says Marcela, not laughing. "That is not right, Ernesto."

"Oh, Marcela," complains Ernesto. "It is the story. That is how it goes. There is no changing it. What do you know about it?"

"I am a mother. I know different. *Mi madre oró a La Llorona*. And I have too. I have prayed to *La Llorona*. Because you see once she died, *La Llorona* understood what she had done. What she had lost. Her guilt keeps her close. Her sadness keeps her close. She has not floated out to the great sea. She is here. Among us. She looks out after our children. Protects them. She uses the living. Whispers in our ears. *Marcela, why is Eladio not home? Call his friend Oresto to see if he is safe.*

"Whispers. *Ernesto, open your business to all of the boys who have dropped out of school. Let them harvest your trees. Pay them a good wage. They will soon be into trouble with so much time on their hands.*

"Whispers. *Miguel, go to Pepitas today. Inmediatamente. Davis is alone and needs your help. He is somebody's child. Bring him back to dance with your family.* That is what I was taught about *La Llorona*. She carries a mother's grief for all mothers."

Silence except for the hissing fire. Ernesto pats his wife on the knee. There is another chorus of howling in the black, starlit distance. Laughter.

"*Ooooo*." Ernesto wiggles his fingers in the air. "*La Llorona*."

Miguel cups his hands to his mouth. Stage whispers.

"She is saying '*Eladiooooooo. Go clean up your rooooooom. You are a pig.*'"

Ernesto howls with laughter, drowning out the others. Eladio stands. Balls up his fists. Miguel flicks his fingers. The circle eggs them on. It is Ana's voice when the moment finally passes.

"Mrs. Rivera, you should wear a *La Llorona* costume at the next *Day of the Dead*. Help keep the celebration safe."

Marcela points across the fire back at Ana. Nods. She thinks the idea has promise. The others agree.

"You will not believe this," says Ernesto. "But they have scheduled the Moon Garden Festival for November 1 this year."

There is a collective consternation. A turning of heads. *What? Day of the Dead? Really? No!* Ernesto nods.

"I know. I know. I objected. I said it would take away from the *El Día de los Muertos*. The Moon Garden Festival is to honor life and the living. *El Día de los Muertos* is to honor those who are no longer living. You cannot combine the two. The living and the dead. I tried to tell them. One is full color. The other is black and white."

"You mean one is white and one is brown," says Hector.

Ernesto shakes his head.

"No. Green is the most important color, Hector. That is the color that matters. Money has a louder voice in those meetings than an old Mexican nut farmer. The Corbin Community Council wants to save money by combining. You see? So they have moved the Moon Garden Festival three weeks later." Ernesto raises a fist to the sky. Shouts. "Where was *La Llorona* when I needed her most?"

In the laughter, Miguel leans towards Davis. Shoulders touching.

"Papa has been on the Moon Garden Festival organizing committee for years. He likes to complain about being the token Mexican. But they listen to him. Between the nuts and the restaurant, he's got some influence."

"Not enough, I guess," says Davis.

"It's too bad. He's right. Combining things will really fuck things up. Ever been to the Moon Garden Festival?"

Davis shakes his head.

"Already a cluster fuck, even without mixing it into *Day of the Dead*. People come from all over. They bring in carnival rides. Put on a bullshit rodeo and a little cattle auction so we can pretend for a day that we're like Houston. People come and set up their tents to sell hats and t-shirts and trinkets. Corbin's not big enough for that shit. But the businesses love it. *Pepita's* makes a killing. *Lick-n-Tipple. Coahuiltecan Trading Post.* All of them. People come and leave their money and their beer cans. Day-trippers drive down from San Angelo." He nods at the wreckage of Davis' face. "Like those shitheads at *Pepitas. Culeros.* They trash up our desert. Takes us a week to clean it back up. I tried to stay home last year."

"Tried?"

"Papa makes all of us go. Civic duty. He's big on community. There's no getting out of it. You too, *amigo*."

Davis stops filling up his empty water bottle with dirt. Looks up.

"Me?"

Miguel laughs a little. Nods over at his mother, struggling to push herself up out of her chair.

"You heard her. *La Llorona* has been whispering."

Chapter 49
Abby and Davis

We lay there for nearly three hours. I was awake for much of it and uncomfortable on the saggy cot. But I tried to be still and let her sleep. I hoped that whatever was causing her such distress, real or imagined, would weaken with some rest.

When she woke, her eyes fluttered a moment before focusing on my face. She smiled. She seemed calm. Back to her normal self. Like everything had been a bad dream.

"Davis," she whispered, stroking my face. "My love. My savior. You're here."

She kissed me and I responded. We touched each other. I wanted to forget everything of that morning as though it had never happened.

You are an expert in crazy, Dr. Bees. So you tell me who is crazier? Abby for believing the things she believed? Or me for believing that she did not really believe those things?

We made love, vigorously that time, knocking the cot off its foundation, laughing and then continuing on the floor of the trailer. I felt relief pushing away worry. I felt lust pushing away confusion. I wanted to believe that Abby was, once again, Abby *–my Abby –*and that all of the drama that had brought me flying down the highway to her house after that phone call was all just a bad dream. Had I really thought about it more carefully, I'd have known that wasn't true. But the sex helped me to not think about anything too carefully. Neither of us spoke about it.

When we were dressed, Abby asked me to help her carry boxes of her aromatherapy candles into the house. The boxes were flimsy white cardboard cake boxes arranged in two neat stacks of five on the counter. There were eighteen candles in each box with enough room between the candles to make the load unstable and difficult to carry. We each took a stack and moved slowly to keep from dropping everything on the ground.

"What are you going to do with them?" I asked.

"Sell 'em. Silly goose."

"Sell them to who?"

"Customers, Davis. Who do you think?"

"Can I buy one?"

"No." Abby opened the door to the house with her foot and we went inside, putting the boxes on the kitchen counter.

"Why not?"

"Because I'm going to make you a special candle with a blend of essential oils just for you. Nothing generic for you, love."

In one of the boxes were fifteen or twenty round tins about the size of a silver dollar but maybe a half-inch thick.

"What are these?" I asked, taking one out of the box. She took it from me and opened it with a twist. There was wax inside, or something like it. She pulled her finger across the wax and spread it on my lower lip. It smelled of beeswax and cocoa butter. And maybe lavender.

"Lip wax," she said. "Aromatherapy balm."

"That feels good. I'll buy some of that. How much are one of those?"

"Davis. I'm not selling you anything." She slipped the tin in my pocket, then draped her arms over my shoulders and kissed me for a long time. "I'm going to give it to you as a gift. Because I love you. Because I don't quite know what I would do without you."

We both stood in the kitchen, looking at each other, letting that declaration grow heavy in the air.

"The balm tins are basically throwaways," she said. "Gifts with a purchase. But these candles have already been sold, you see. That's how it works in the dash-bang world of aromatherapy. I take orders, I make candles, I deliver candles and I collect my fee." She tapped me on the nose with her finger. "Today is delivery day."

"Where?"

"All over."

"Do you need help?"

"Nah. I've been enough bother for one day I should think."

It was the first reference from either of us to the craziness earlier that morning. I resisted it. I did not want to go backwards.

"No you haven't. I can't get enough of you, Abby." I kissed her. She kissed back. We were at it for awhile. When we separated I said, "Let's deliver these things together."

"Awfully boring, you know. And the locations are all a bit dodgy. I've a duty to warn you."

"I'll drive. You do your thing. We'll get some lunch."

I could tell she was pleased. She still looked ragged and tired, but the light was back in her eyes and she smiled and laughed a lot. It was easy to see her as the person I had first met at the fair. A little bit of makeup and attention to her hair and she seemed almost as good as new.

We loaded the candles carefully into the back of Fat Jack's stolen truck and headed off to the city. We played the radio loud and sang horribly off key to classic country songs about people down on their luck and out of time to make any difference.

Abby's customers were tiny businesses, mostly. Cult bookstores. Sex shops. Massage joints. Head shops. They were scattered all over Houston along with a few private homes and apartments that we always seemed to have difficulty finding. Abby made the deliveries as I waited in the truck for her to come back and cross off a name on her pad of paper and tell me where to go next.

It took us most of the day, but we were able to cross off everyone on the list except three customers –two of them not home and one we couldn't find. That left us with most of one box of candles. I offered to circle back around and try them again, but Abby was satisfied with the effort and was ready to head back. She fell into an odd silence as I drove. She closed her eyes in the hot air blowing in off the road as her hair lashed around her face. We went for ten or fifteen minutes without a word.

"You need your own store," I said finally. I had to shield my eyes from the setting sun blasting through the windshield. "Get people to come to you so you don't have to spend your time and gas money delivering."

She looked over at me, scrunching up her forehead.

"You want gas money, is that it?" She reached into her purse and pulled a twenty off a stack of bills. I pushed her hand away.

"That's not what I'm sayin'. I'm just sayin' that if you…"

"You asked if you could come. You wanted to drive. I didn't force you."

"I know that. I don't want money. Jeez-Louise, Abby. I'm just makin' conversation."

After a moment, she smiled an apology.

"Sorry, love. You didn't deserve that. I was sitting here… contemplating whether you think I'm raving mad. Bit defensive, me."

I didn't respond. I should have changed the subject.

"Well?" she asked.

"What?"

"Do you think I'm mental?"

"No. Of course not."

"Liar."

"I don't. Really."

"Fine. Fine. I see. So you believe me then, do you? You believe me when I tell you that the universe is full of crackling intelligent energy? Electric energy? That the energy connects into something like… like *kingdoms* in space? That these kingdoms are like sentient beings that are capable of great feeling? Great anger and wrath and sorrow and compassion and jealousy? Like they were Egyptian gods? You believe that, do you? You believe me when I tell you that I understand the language spoken in these kingdoms of energy? That I can decipher the code? That I have heard terrible things I should never have heard? That Ahab is king and that I have been warned by Ijah? That Baal has loosed the whale, terrible white with black eyes, to devour the stars? That the bobbies cannot be trusted? The coppers? You believe that? That they cannot be trusted? That everyone will die if you trust them? That I will die unless you save me? Are you telling me that I am not crazy because you believe all of that?"

It was a storm of words. I didn't answer.

"Well then. What a bloody relief. I feel so much better."

She collapsed back into silence for many minutes. Desert air blew into the cab of the truck. It smelled dead. Empty. It smelled like nothingness.

"I don't believe those things," I said, finally. "I can't. Maybe I'm wrong. But I can't believe what I don't believe. I can't believe what I don't understand. But listen. Abby. *Abby?*" I waited until she looked over at me. "I believe that *you* believe those things. And I'm not saying that makes you crazy. We can believe different things. That's okay. I just... I just want you to be safe. And happy."

She nodded. "Safe and happy. That's dandy. Safe from what then?"

"Anything. Anyone."

"Simon, you mean?"

"Yes."

"Right." She yanked up her sleeve angrily and thrust her bare arm over the dashboard for me to inspect. "Safe from myself, you mean?"

The scars were not quite parallel, like railroad tracks converging on the horizon. I didn't know what to say. I said nothing. She retracted her arm.

"You think I did that because I wanted to?"

"Abby... I don't know... I..."

"I had no choice." She stabbed at her temple with her forefinger. "I *know* things, Davis. Terrible things. Terrible, terrible things. I didn't want the knowledge, but it came to me. I heard it one night and there it was in my head. What was I supposed to do? If I had the information in my head, then that meant the information could be *found* in my head, couldn't it? It could be *taken*. It could be *used*. Baal couldn't risk that. He was going to snuff me out sooner or later. So I didn't have a choice. May as well do it myself. It seemed like the only way to keep him from finding it."

"But you didn't..." I tried to say the word. I couldn't. "I mean..."

"No. I didn't. I failed. I'm here aren't I? You know, Davis, you won't actually go to Hell for just saying the word *suicide*."

"I don't believe in Hell," I said. It was a clumsy attempt to change the subject.

"Well neither do I. Silly. Universal retribution, check. Karma, check. I believe we are made to suffer and pay for the wrong that we do in the world. The wrong that we think and the offense that we give. Check and check. I believe that our thoughts are only another form of energy and that ultimately there are no secrets from those who would punish us or take mercy on us. There will be a consequence to the things we do. The things we plan. The things we think about doing. But *Hell?* The whole pit of fire thing? Utter rubbish."

"Have you … done *things?* I mean… are you afraid of being punished for something?"

"I'm not a good girl, Davis. You know that."

"No. I don't know that."

"I've done bad things. I've had bad thoughts. Very bad indeed."

"Suicide, you mean? Are you afraid that's, like, a sin or…"

"Suicide? A sin? Yeah, suicide's a sin. So is shagging a handsome lad half your age, which all might amount to something important if you believed in sin, or God, which I don't so that's quite enough about sin."

"Then tell me. What have you done that's so bad?"

She shook her head and looked away, thrusting her face back into the wind.

"Yeah. Can't tell you that."

"Why?"

"Because. You don't know how to hide your thoughts. I do. Telling you anything is like sending up a flare. They find you, then they find me. It's too early for that. I'm not ready to die."

"You tried to kill yourself."

"Right. Well. Part of me wanted to be found I think. Nosy neighbors. I should have locked my flat. I'd never killed myself before. I was an amateur. Just as well. Turned out there was another way."

"Which was what?"

She looked at me directly for the first time in many minutes.

"To stop them. To find you. Davis. To find you and stop them. That was the other way. Ijah convinced me."

"Ijah. Ahab. Baal. Abby, I don't… I don't know what to do with any of this."

"Accept it. Do *that.* Just accept it."

"I don't know what you want me to do. I don't know who I'm saving you from. Stop them from doing what?"

"Well, killing me for starters."

"I don't even know…"

"You'll know everything when the time comes, Davis."

"What time? When?"

"I don't know *when.* I suppose we'll both find out together. Won't we?"

"This is crazy."

"Ahh. There's the word."

"Didn't say *you're* crazy. I said *this* is crazy. The situation. Not knowin' anything. I don't live in your universe."

"Well just what's *your* universe all about then? Reads like a bus schedule, does it? So that you know what's going to happen when? Is it all that predictable?"

"No. Yes. More logical, I guess. You're treatin' nature likes it's a person."

"Am I? Fascinating."

"Yeah. I mean if you could figure out the logic, the universe –my universe, let's just call it that –my universe would be predictable. My universe follows, like, certain natural rules. If we don't know what's going to happen next, it's only because we don't understand the rules."

"I see. So what was the logic behind those poor souls up at Lake Waco? Was that logical, Davis? Was that predictable?"

"Humans did that, Abby. People. Not the universe. They were not being punished by Baal or Ijah or Ahab or whoever. They were in the wrong place at the wrong time. Bad things happen to good people. That's a universal rule. Bein' a good person, havin' good intentions, don't mean anything to the universe. Good thoughts and intentions won't protect you. Innocence won't protect you. You could get a bolt of lightning just like the next guy."

I listened to the words tumble out of me like they belonged to someone else. They could have belonged to you, Dr. Bees. Like you were sitting in your office drinking your tea and wiggling your pen like it was some sort of remote control that made me speak your stupid words. I didn't believe a word I was saying.

"Misfortune ain't punishment, Abby."

"Mmm. And if you're bad? If you have evil thoughts? Do evil things?"

"Universe don't care. It don't judge. You can't offend it or anger it. Bad things happen to good people and good things happen to bad people. The rule is that there is no rule."

"Oh that's rich, innit? Now who's crazy? Let me ask you this. If your universe doesn't punish, how does your universe forgive?"

The question hit me sideways. It took me a moment.

"It doesn't," I said. "It can't."

"Your universe sounds rather like a dull and bleak cunt to me."

"Maybe. But yours has too much drama."

Abby looked at me, lips tightening. I thought she was going to cry or scream. I braced myself. The laughter was a relief.

"It does, doesn't it?" she said. "Too much bloody drama."

"Yes."

"You poor dear. I'm a wretched friend aren't I?"

"No you aren't."

"I am and you know it." She pointed at a crossroad leading off into the darkening west. "Pull off, Davis. This one here. This one. This one."

"What? Why?" I didn't know what she wanted. I did as she said anyway. Like always.

Abby smiled, scooted over and licked the rim of my ear.

"Another mile. There's a field." Her hand slipped under my belt. "I want to show you how sorry I am. In my universe, absolution is there for the earning."

* * *

It was completely dark when we rejoined I-45. Abby sat close to me in the truck, head on my chest with my arm around her shoulder. We were mostly silent, maybe both aware that more words would only spoil the mood. Abby sat up when we pulled onto her street.

"Shit," she whispered.

"What?"

"Simon's back."

I saw the green Charger in the unlit driveway and hit the brakes reflexively. I pulled over to the curb and turned off the headlights, not because I was afraid of Simon (though I was), but because I knew that if Simon was home, then my last moments with Abby that day were rapidly running out. I wanted more time. There was never enough time. Abby chuckled.

"What. Are you going to make me walk the rest of the way? Is that any way to treat a girl who did what I just did? I banged my noggin on the steering wheel for you."

"No... I ..."

"He's perfectly harmless, you know."

"Somehow I doubt that. He seems jealous. And I don't even know what he does. He could be some kind of criminal for all I know."

"Simon? A criminal? Are you mental?"

"Well I don't know. So what's he do?"

"Oh he's a right fishmonger, 'im. Works for one anyway."

"I don't... a what?"

"Means he sells fish, love." I must have looked skeptical. "Don't you believe me, Davis?"

"Don't really see a lot of fishin' in Fairfield."

Abby laughed in that way I loved. It was like a song you want to go on forever.

"A bit daft, aren't you? He's not *catchin'* the fish. He's driving them to little groceries and restaurants scattered from Houston to Dallas and back. They got big men on boats see? They pull the fish out of the Gulf. Did you really think I meant he caught them? With a pole and a bit of twine down at the creek?"

"Don't know," I said, shrugging. "I guess."

She had another good laugh at my expense. I was partly playing dumb. I liked it when she teased me. It made me feel close to her. The way she could have been mean but never was. Her last bit of laughter turned into a shudder.

"What was that?"

"Fish," she said. "It's all Simon eats because he gets it for free. I used to eat fish all the time back home. My daddy was a fisherman. Then his boat sank and he drowned and was lost at sea and the fish ate him just to have their revenge. I bloody hate them now. Make me gag."

"The taste?"

"Taste. Smell. Sight. Our freezer's so full of it there's no room for anything else. Can't open it or I'll toss me guts. Do you like them, Davis?"

"Fish? I guess. Not much call to eat it. 'Cept tuna. I eat that enough. I'm more of a steak man though."

Abby wasn't listening. She looked up the street at her own house. Remembering.

"This one Fourth of July, Simon and two of his mates were over. Completely pissed. Sitting out back listening to music and lighting firecrackers and grilling fish. One of 'em slit open a nasty-looking grouper that was too old to eat and they stuffed it with some kind of firecracker. M-80's or whatever. Blew the bloody thing into disgusting chunks. They had so much fun the first time, they kept doing it. Blew up more fish than they ate. Fish-bangers they called them. Hilarious. Few days later, the smell and the flies were so bad around the trailer I couldn't even use it."

She looked at me. I made a face.

"Oh, you don't even know, Davis. I finally got a rake and dragged a big bit of grouper out from under the trailer. So wriggling with maggots I couldn't barely see the fish. I chundered right there."

"Chundered. Wow."

She laughed, pushing me.

"Stop making fun."

"Right. Like you never do that to me."

"I could say *vomit*. Is *vomit* better? Does that please you, Master Linguist?"

"I prefer the term *barfed*." I flicked my fingers without looking. "Proceed."

"Alright then. I *barfed* all over the bloody, wriggling thing. And that was finally it for me and fish. Between daddy and the fish bombs and the maggots, they all look like a kind of death to me. Eating them is unthinkable. They're all rotten and wriggling inside as far as I'm concerned."

She shuddered again, then curled up against me and kissed my neck. I couldn't stop looking at Simon's car. Eventually Abby laughed.

"Are we going to sit here at the bloody corner all night because you're afraid of Simon? Are you going to make me walk?"

"You said… sometimes he gets angry. Has he ever hurt you?"

"Simon? Never. You worry too much, Davis." She sighed, stroking my cheek. "Sweet boy. I wasn't myself earlier. When you came to my rescue. But I suppose it's all just as well if you don't go in. Right? Never know what mood he's in. Just let me out on the drive."

I eased the truck forward toward the house, pulling into the driveway behind the Charger. Abby gave me another small peck on the cheek and opened the door. In front of us, the interior lights of the Charger glowed to life. The door opened and Simon Dore stepped out.

"Where 'ave you been?" he demanded.

"Simon," she said with light surprise. "I thought you'd gone. I've been selling my candles. Davis has driven…"

"Selling candles? Selling fucking candles?"

"Calm down, love. We're just…"

Simon reached out and grabbed her roughly by the elbow, yanking her between the two cars. He began marching her towards the house. Abby looked over her shoulder at me.

It was like a bullet through my chest.

I don't know when, she had said. *I suppose we'll both find out together.*

I opened my door and stepped out onto the drive.

"Hey," I said. My voice did not sound like my own. My head was buzzing.

Simon spun around to look at me across the yard. He pushed Abby inside the door and marched back across the yard to the driveway. I took a step back.

"Got something to say about it, little man?" I could smell the alcohol. His face was flat and hard. His skin was greasy.

"Don't you hurt her," I said.

"Oh, I'm not gonna hurt her. I'm gonna hurt you. You think I don't see the stiffy in your knickers? *Eh? Eh?*"

"Listen, Simon."

He slapped me hard across the face with the back of his hand. Then he did it again the other way. I stood there and took it. I was too stunned. I could see Abby over his shoulder in the doorway. I felt hot blood in my nostril.

"No, you listen. Davis. That your name? *Davis?* You come around here ever again and I will end your short, miserable life. Now, you run on home to mum. And you take your stiffy with you."

He turned and marched back across the yard to the front door. We all looked at each other. Abby and Simon at me and me back at them. Everyone knew the next move was mine. If I had any bit of man in me, any Texan at all, it was time for me to walk across that yard and start punching Simon Dore in the face.

And if I was a chicken shit of a man, then it was time for me to smash a window on his car.

Or, if I was really a chicken shit of a man, then it was time for me to ram his car with the truck and then speed off.

But one way or the other it was time. I had to do something. We all saw that. I swallowed and took a step.

Abby clasped Simon's face in her hands and pulled him close, kissing him deeply. Their bodies separated and she stared a longing apology into Simon's eyes. Then she looked at me. Simon pulled her back into him, mashing his lips into hers. He pushed her inside and followed, slamming the door behind him.

I stood in the driveway for a few long minutes listening to them scream at each other inside. I didn't know what to do. I was not a Texas man. I was not a chicken-shit man. I was not the man who could save Abby Palmer from anything.

I was not a man at all.

I climbed back up into the truck, blood pooling on my upper lip.

I drove home.

Chapter 50

She can feel him. Waiting. Watching her.

Jesus was like that. Nowhere to go. Sandals glued to the hacked-up dashboard. He is all bemused attention and forgiveness.

Olivia blocks out the piercing blue eyes. The open hands.

Olivia, my child, what are you doing?

She looks back up at the mirror. Applies another layer of foundation. Fingertips trace the ridgelines of her disfigurement.

Can still see them, says Jesus.

I know.

Make-up is pointless.

I know.

Now you just look like Jezebel after a car accident.

Shut up.

Dashboard Jesus is right, of course. He was always right. She wonders why Jesús Batista chose not to listen.

Jesús, my child. You realize they're waiting for you at the house? You can't go back to the house.

Right. Whatever.

Sure enough, there they were. Waiting for him.

Jesús is gone now. She's got his car.

She looks down at the rubbery plastic savior and then back up into the rearview mirror. Adds another coat on her cheek. She never wears cosmetics. Hates the stuff.

Although Libby has dolled her up before. Full Kabuki theater after a night of too much *Rio Lobo*.

"Where yo' big-ass red clown shoes at, baby? We done make you a circus ho!"

They had laughed until they cried. She couldn't wash the stuff off fast enough.

She sighs. Leans back into the sagging, crooked seat of Jesús Batista's car. Lights a cigarette.

Lung cancer, my child. Blue eyes. Open hands.

She exhales over the dash. Finds her *Diamondback* t-shit in the back seat and drops it over his head. Takes another drag.

She readjusts the sofa cushion. Looks at her watch. Still forty-five minutes to go. She could head out now. Grab a table. Wait for him.

But she does not want to be early. Not after that first meeting, when he had stood there on the bridge and watched her like a bug under glass.

For their second meeting she had been deliberately late. *She* had watched *him* sitting under the umbrella. Watched *him* as he looked at his watch every minute. Watched *him* track every movement around the table.

The third time she had been accidentally late, having been forced to detour in San Angelo for gas. When she finally showed up, he was there waiting for her. Relief on his face. Irritation in his voice. He had said that he was *this close* to leaving.

Bad liar, Sheldon. He'd have stayed until they pulled the tablecloth off the table and told him to leave. His face had told the truth. *Olivia,* said his face. *Thank God.*

And, strangely, that relief had meant something. Someone was relieved to see her.

This would be meeting number four. She wanted to be… *anticipated.* Wanted every minute that she was not there to feel empty. Empty except for the concern that maybe she might not show up. She did not want to be early.

Vanity is a sin, mumbles Dashboard Jesus beneath the shirt.

Was she really trying to make an impression? Entice him? *Him?* Sheldon Davis? *Massage*-Massage? Almost twice her age?

No. Was she?

She takes another drag. Watches three women rappelling out of a gleaming red pick-up perched upon giant tractor tires. Two are in heels and micros. The third, boots and spray-on jeans. Above the waist all three are loose and airy and ready for whatever. They are young and full of themselves, feeling power and perfection in their veins. They move through time like boneless sylphs, exempt from physical laws. Immune to cause and effect. Invisible to the vicissitudes of good fortune and its ugly, hateful twin.

They are already laughing at *something else*, before any of them turn to look in her direction, seeing her through the cracked windshield of the beaten, scarred, shot at, shit-brown Ford Falcon in the corner of the parking lot.

Something else. She knows that. Nothing to do with her. She knows that.

The women laugh with fresh force and glide off toward the River Walk.

Olivia looks away. Exhales in a long, white stream. Like she is freezing.

The question of Sheldon Davis is still waiting for her. She changes the channel in her head. Thinks of Papi, three nights before, sitting at his table nursing his bourbon as the club slowly filled up behind her.

It is the sadness in his baggy brown eyes that she remembers first. Not sorrow. *Sympathy*. Eyes that see an ugly five-legged spider desperately trying to climb out of an empty wet bathtub.

Papi's mistake was in giving her some hope. He did not know what he was doing, of course. She had asked her usual questions, pretending idle curiosity, and he had surprised her with what he believed was a report of bad news but that to her had been like music. Like birdsong.

"Deal fell through, Olivia. Buyers' jerked me around to the last minute –to the last damned minute. Then they put their pens away sayin' the plumbing trouble had not been fully disclosed. Now *that's* a load a shit. I told them everything. Showed them everything. Plumbing is fine. For now anyway. Truth is they found another place to park their money and they wanted out."

She had tried not to dance in her chair. Had commiserated as convincingly as she could, thinking all the while of the money in her dresser. Thirty thousand now, evenly divided. Three clean, white envelopes. Real money. And more to come. She couldn't help herself.

"Papi… what if I told you that I could hand you, oh, I don't know, let's say thirty thousand up front… and another… oh, seventy by, say, March of next year… and…"

"Olivia…"

"And then make payments out of the profits, and over time…"

"Olivia…"

Papi's sad eyes had watched her struggle up the slick porcelain wall of that proposal. His big hand had enveloped her own. His misshapen lips had then shaped for her the business realities of money and time and need.

She had done her best to show that she had just been trying to help him. That he, not her, had been the hapless, pathetic spider. But Papi had known better. She knew that. It was in his eyes.

She could see herself in those eyes.

Why else would he lecture her about the past?

"You can't go back, Olivia. All of that is done. Understand? You have to go forward. Forget all of that. You're wasting your time. Your life. Your money… if you really have any. If you knew what was good for you, you'd get the hell out of this place tomorrow. Go to California. Better yet, move to Hawaii. Florida. Someplace it's wet. Not Houston-under-Harvey wet. Talkin' about wetness in the air. I'll miss you like my own daughter, but you need to let go of all this shit. Understand? You like to say this all used to be ocean? Well guess what, sweetheart…"

She looks at her watch. Stabs the barely smoked cigarette against the side of the car and drops it in the ashtray. Frees Dashboard Jesus. They look at each other. *Olivia, my child…* He hasn't changed a bit.

She climbs out. Slams the door. She heads out across the lot, toward the shops and cafés that line the banks of the San Antonio River's commercial tributary, trying her best to disguise her limp inside a slow, casual gait. People pass, looking at her cosmetic mask. Irritated. Like they want to know the truth of who is underneath. *What are you hiding?* The scars had given people as much of the truth as they wanted. Used to be they couldn't look away fast enough. Horrified. This is worse.

She is surprised to see him at the table. She was prepared to be disappointed at being early. At not being anticipated. But there he is. She looks at her watch as she slowly closes the distance. She is early, but he is earlier. Anticipating.

He stands, jarring the table. Smiles. Pulls out a chair.

"You're looking lovely."

She does not acknowledge the compliment beyond a perfunctory smile, pretending it does not matter and wondering in secret why it does. Wondering why it hurts to hear the words. She sits.

The clean white envelope is already beneath her napkin. Number four. She drops it into her purse.

"You eating?" he asks, retaking his chair. She looks at him as though it is an open question. He is wearing a dark blazer and a crisp white shirt. She realizes that he is handsome in his own way. Nice eyes. Boyish lips. Still not too far from a younger version of himself. The sandy brown hair is thinning, but holding its own.

"I'm buying," he adds, tone hopeful.

Olivia nods. "Guess I could eat."

Sheldon flags a server. Menus pass from one to the other. She watches the manicured hand. Notes that after three months he is still wearing his recovered wedding ring. The inset diamond gathers the sunlight in its setting of brushed gold. She supposes that for all of the panic, his wife has decided to forgive him. Or at least keep him. Or that he had somehow managed to lie his way around the truth and she had stupidly chosen to believe him.

It wasn't really her business. But still. She can't stop looking. The ring is like a crown that has slipped down over the body, pinning imaginary arms. It gleams in its confidence.

The server is suddenly there again with his pad and his muscled cheeriness. Iced teas. They order cheesy, bacon appetizers. Salads. He scribbles and leaves them alone. They look at the river, grey and silky, slipping soundlessly past.

This part is always awkward. The interlude between purposeful discussion. Same with the second meeting. And the third. A month is too long of an interval. It requires starting all over. They always have to chip away at the ice.

They stare out silently at the water that shouldn't be there. The barges give them an excuse. Soon the barges will be gone too. Then what will their eyes do to pass the time in silence?

People on a barge with bright blue railings float past. They aren't talking either. One of the women raises a glass of gold-colored wine. Sheldon gives a nod and a wave.

"She looks like she wants off," he says.

"You like boats?" It is all she can think of.

"Yes," he nods. Smiles a little. "I like boats a lot. As long as I'm not on them."

"Motion sick?"

"Doesn't take much. You?"

She holds up an index finger.

"Only been on one boat in my whole life. Knew a guy who had friends. They had this sailboat up on Canyon Lake." She gestures vaguely over her left shoulder beyond San Antonio proper. "'While ago."

"And you liked it?"

She feels him looking at her. At the scars that he is not supposed to be able to see. They burn like kerosene ropes beneath her mask.

"Lot better'n I liked him."

"Boyfriend?"

"Somethin' like that. But the *boat* never made me sick. Boat almost made him worth it."

Sheldon laughs. Drinks. He seems nervous, which makes her feel better. From up river comes tinkling blues piano. Someone singing.

"Big Mama Thornton," he says, finger in the air, pointing to invisible sound waves like passing birds.

Olivia nods. Thinks of Libby. Imagines the look on Libby's face as if she could see them now. At this table. Talking about Big Mama. *Baby, what in the... you havin' high tea wit' him? Wit' Massage-Massage-All-the-Way-Married-Run-Yo-Po-Raggedy-Ass-Off-the-Road-an-'Bout-Kill-You-All-the-Way-Day'id? You lost yo' got-damned-evuh-lovin' mind?*

"I'da guessed Bessie Smith," she says. "You're prob'ly right."

"*Born Under a Bad Sign.* Before she went off to tour Europe. Before the Newport Jazz Festival. Before she did *Blues is a Woman.* It's a bizarre arrangement and whoever's singing has a voice for jazz, not blues, but..." He breaks off. Closes his eyes. Listens. Bobs his head. "That's Big Mama. I guess Albert King should get the credit. *Born Under a Bad Sign* is his song. But I always hear it in her voice. Bet they'd both hate this version. I sent her a song once."

"What do you mean? Big Mama Thornton?"

He opens his eyes. Like he's surprised to learn he's been talking out loud.

"Oh." Waves his hand dismissively. "Yeah. I wrote some songs when I was a kid. Sent them around to musicians hoping they'd pick them up. Big Mama was one of those unfortunate artists. Albert King too." He laughs at himself, embarrassed.

"Any luck?"

Preposterousness puckers his face. He shakes his head.

"None to speak of. I think I just liked the idea of hijacking someone else's talent to hear myself on the radio. Her agent wrote me a nice letter. Well. More polite than nice."

"No thank you."

"Right."

The appetizers arrive, salads close behind. They eat and talk, invoking the legends, plowing up the rich blue musical earth from one end of the Gulf Coast to the other, detouring northward on a loop through Chattanooga, Belmont, Chicago, St. Louis and the Arkansas Delta.

She is trying to impress him with her command of the subject. She does not recognize the agenda at first. Denies it firmly to herself. She is only doing what comes naturally.

But then Sheldon tosses out a name. *Juke Boy Bonner* from Bellville. She doesn't even bat an eyelash.

"*Oh, he was always good,*" she says with authority. She has never heard of him. So there is no denying it to herself now. She is trying to impress Sheldon Davis.

"You know your stuff," he says, draining his glass. Olivia shrugs.

"Just know what I like, I guess."

"Why blues?"

"Why not blues?"

She might have just let it go at that non-answer. But he doesn't move on. He is waiting for some elaboration. Waiting to go deeper. Drinking his tea. Waiting for a look inside. She clears her throat. Hesitates.

"There's somethin'... I dunno. Somethin' true. Somethin' terrible. And sad. And real. Unashamed. I think it's brave music. Honest music. Human music."

Sheldon nods a little. Waits.

"Jazz, like, tries too hard. Pop music..." she shakes her head as if it is not worth the effort. "Classical... it's... so... mental. It's all from the head. You know? Too..." her fingers try to shape the word. "Too complicated. But the blues is like... *raw*. It's raw music. Right off the tree. Unwashed. It's the mother of all music. Suffering and triumph, sin, redemption all there in the same notes. At one end of the blues, you've got the field holler and slaves keepin' up with their families. And at the other end you're into gospel. Everyone testifyin' to their maker. The blues is just... like... *this is who I am... where I come from... what I've done... how I feel... this is the best of me... the worst of me... why I hate myself... why I love myself... what I hope for... what I fear... and I'm gonna sing about my miserable life 'cause that's the only way I know I'm alive. It's the only way you'll ever remember I was even here.*"

She could go on. Almost does. There is so much more to say. But she is suddenly uncomfortable. She doesn't share easily.

"Anyway. That's why."

Sheldon does not answer. He stares at her from across the table, not moving, waiting for something neither of them can name. She is unnerved. Vulnerable. She has said too much. Spoken too truly. It makes her feel cheap. Laughter, two tables away. She speaks in a kind of desperation.

"I don't trust anyone who doesn't like blues."

"That mean you trust me?"

Her eyes slice up and away again.

"No."

"I trust *you*," he says.

"Well, you shouldn't."

"But I have to, don't I?" He waits. "Give you all this money and then you and your friend do your damage anyway."

"I'll say it again." Head down, twisting her napkin into a rope. "I ain't a blackmailer. I'm a hit and run victim."

"I didn't hit you and I didn't run. I saved you."

"You ruined me. I'm not having this conversation again, Sheldon."

Too much contempt in the sound of his name. Their eyes catch over the table. She can't leave it at that.

"Think I'm all fixed, do you? All better."

"Look, I…"

"My tibia no longer likes my femur. My femur no longer likes my pelvis. Ain't a good fit any more. The three of 'em fight all night long. It keeps me awake. Good thing walking is painless. *Oh, wait…* it ain't painless. Or pretty. If I ever want to walk like a human again it's gonna take at least two surgeries. Good thing I have a lot of money socked away. *Oh, wait…* And then there's the plastic surgery. That'll probably come cheap. *Oh, wait…* Well maybe I can just have my insurance company pay for it. *Oh, wait…* none of my four employers offer any insurance. Too bad the asshole that ran me off the road and nearly killed me is destitute and don't have any money. *Oh, wait!* He owns his own business! He has a big metal gate outside his house! With horses on it! Probably owns horses too! Maybe he'll be decent enough to foot the bill." Her face is lit up in mockery. Big eyes. Hopeful smile. It all melts. "*Oh. Wait.*"

"Decent? I'm paying you a hundred thou…"

"Chicken feed."

"Chicken… It is *not* chicken feed. That should be more than enough. And you think I can just pull that kind of money out of my ass? I told…"

"I think you're pullin' something out of your ass."

She mumbles this. Looks away. She can feel his eyes.

"Why do you live in a whorehouse, Olivia?" Not anger. Nothing so informed. Reflexive. Defensive.

"Really? Why do you visit whorehouses? What's your wife think about that little pastime? How's the whole marriage thing workin' out for you?"

They avert. Look out at the water. Grey, uncaring, liquid time. Sheldon sighs.

"I'm sorry," he says finally. "It's none of my business. Where you live."

"I'm not a blackmailer *or* a prostitute."

"Okay." Hands up. "I believe you. I'm sorry."

But her blood is up. The apology is not enough. She wants her answer anyway.

"So? Let's hear it. Why?"

He looks away. Like he might not answer.

"I don't visit... I... I mean I *did*. Obviously. That time. Those times. I did. But it's not something..." She can tell that whatever it is inside him wants out. Wants to breathe the hot air and feel the music wafting over the river. But he abandons the effort. Picks a different path. "My marriage is... my wife might be stepping out. Or thinking about it."

"So you're gonna go *pay* for it? Just go out and buy you some flesh? That's a bullshit way to deal with a cheatin' wife. If you ask me it is."

"Yeah. Well. I didn't ask you."

The server wants to pick up the plates. He leaves the bill. Sheldon fishes through his wallet. His words hang in the air; little dark clouds in a breezeless sky.

"Cheatin' with someone you know?" she asks. Sheldon sticks some twenties into the folder. Nods.

"I know him," he says.

"I mean is he like, a friend, or just someone you know?"

"More like a business associate. Keeps turning up in my kitchen."

"Why don't you show him the fuckin' front door? And then tell her to clean her shit up."

"Hard to do. After that note from your... housemate."

"You said you lied your way though."

"I said I *tried* to lie. Christi's not stupid."

"I tried to warn you."

"You said she was mailing something. I didn't think about UPS."

"UPS *is* mail."

"No. *Mail* is mail. UPS is... is... package delivery."

"Right. Mail."

"No."

"Look. You didn't do anything. Right? You paid for a massage. Why can't you just tell her the truth?"

"It's complicated."

"Not if you want to save your marriage."

She waits for him to look up from the table. There is a long moment between them. No words. Just the eyes doing their thing. She can see him thinking. Or wanting. She imagines him younger. It isn't difficult. She cannot decide if he is handsome or if it is something else. Some part of his quietness.

It is Libby's voice she hears, filling the void. *I'm the biggest fan of bein' married you will evah see, baby. People bein' married keep my shit in business. Unna'stan'?*

And suddenly she does understand. Understands with a spark of clarity that scares her. Understands why Sheldon Davis went to a whorehouse. Understands why she lives in one. Understands why it had never worked with Miguel and why he had thrown it away so easily. Why Yvonne had snapped him up. Understands why she is always alone.

And then she understands, again, what she had always understood. That the blues was her confessional. Her twelve-bar salvation. Understands that the blues was still there –always there, like the mother she never had –ready to forgive her whenever she did what she had to do.

No matter what that thing was.

He pay you anything you want, baby.

I don't do that.

Not fo' no relations, dummy. Jus' to see you. Jus' to lay his rich, married eyes on yo pretty lil' face. He let you give him ten massage-massages a day. He sleep outside in his 'lil silver car 'til you ready. And Sheldon worth a lotta money.

"Is it a marriage you want to keep?" she asks.

"It's complicated," he repeats with an apologetic smile.

"What would she do…" she stops. Shakes her head.

"What."

"None of my business."

"Seriously. What."

She looks at him. They listen together at the new song floating over the water, pushing the barges south. Deep and throaty with a hint of Bayou. A black-hearted parody of Ethel Waters, pre-Vaudeville –before Fletcher Henderson and Elia Kazan and the Hollywood happy machine –always singing about the weather. A change is coming, the song predicts. A change in the weather, a change in the sea, a change in me. Nothing will be the same.

"What'd she do if you were… you know…" She twists her napkin like she is wringing the words from the cloth. "If *you* were *actually* stepping out?"

He laughs. Shakes his head, like whatever the answer is isn't really funny.

"She and her father would put my balls in a jar. And that's just the beginning."

"Yeah?" Olivia drains the ice melt from her glass. Coaxes the last reluctant cube into her mouth with her tongue. The scars burn in her mind's eye, sloughing their cosmetic skin like snakes. She swings her eyes his way. Tells herself that she is ready to do what it takes to get what she needs.

"Well then tell me, Sheldon-*massage*-massage. Where are your balls now?"

Chapter 51
Celia and Paola

She shouldn't have been surprised. The last day of school is never worth much. Every kid teetering on that ledge of freedom. Feeling the visceral pull out into the season of hot open sky. Waiting for that bell. And then, one step out and down into summer's hay bale.

Not that skipping the last day was expected. But it wasn't uncommon. And Paola's attendance had always been spotty, even without the suspensions.

When the after-lunch bell rang, Paola's seat was still empty.

Celia had waited. Then she'd started without her, one eye on the door.

Maybe surprise is the wrong word. Profound disappointment can feel like surprise. It's not the event itself that knocks us over, so much as the depth of our own feeling about it. It's how much we care that always gets us. Shakes us.

Frightens us.

Paola's empty desk on that last day became a gaping hole in the room. Like staring down into a well. A well deep enough that light does not reach the bottom. Mortared rock wrapped tightly around a column of emptiness. Cold. Still.

Celia had felt the emptiness in her own chest that day. Had realized as she struggled to represent Tom Sawyer and Huckleberry Finn, that Paola –the thought of her, the sight of her, the hope of her –had come to fully occupy Celia's shape in the world. Mentally. Bodily. For the entire school year. But then suddenly, as of that last day of school, with no hope of a Paola tomorrow, or the next day, or maybe even a forever of next days, all of that had drained away. Celia was hollow again.

Empty. Again.

It had not helped that Celia's expectations were high. Paola's parting words on the road had given her some hope: *"If you want me to talk to you again sometime, if you really want to be my friend forever and ever amen…"*

The words had imparted that those things were okay with Paola. Talking.

Friendship. And the fact remained that Paola had *chosen* to wait for Celia to leave the building. To chase down her windblown papers. To ask her for a ride. To open up about Garvin beating Maria. To weep in the seat next to her. All of that meant, Celia had told herself, that Paola wanted to connect. Wanted *her*. Wanted Celia.

It had felt like a breakthrough. And just in time too. The last day of school, Celia had expected, was to be a new day. A beginning. Another big step forward by Paola. Toward Celia.

And yet, the last day of school had not been a new day. Paola had not even shown up. Instead of Paola, there was just an emptiness where Paola used to be.

And then, the bell. And like they do every year, all the children had left.

Gone home to parents. Home to siblings.

Gone from her.

The dream from the previous night had stayed with her all day, lurking in the background of Celia' s hope.

Magdalena. Young. Singing to herself. Playing in the dirt with a scorpion. She'd pinched the scaly, dark brown body, gently between thumb and forefinger, lifting it up to her face. Singing '*La Linta Manita*' in a high, soft, sweet voice.

Like it was a plastic baby doll.

Like the scorpion was the closest thing Maggie could get to a pretend baby. A living stand-in for a plastic stand-in for a living baby that Maggie did not live long enough to make for herself. As she sang in the dream, the scorpion slowly relaxed its tail. Lulled. Assured.

Yolanda had appeared in the dream. Prettier than she had been in prison. Full hair. Missing tooth back in its socket. Drinking from a bottle, as always. She had picked up Maggie's lullaby in mid-verse.

La linda manita.
Que tiene el bebé.
Qué linda, qué bella.
Qué preciosa es.

Yolanda had tipped the mouth of her bottle to the scorpion, as if to give it a drink of whiskey. But that had not been the point. The point was impossible. Preposterous. Yolanda and Maggie worked at it anyway. It seemed to be all in the angle of the bottle and the angle of the scorpion, using the lullaby and the whiskey as a kind of lubricant.

Suddenly, success. The scorpion was inside the bottle. Yolanda and Maggie had both fallen backwards in the dirt laughing and cheering.

Then Yolanda had stood. Brushed herself off. Walked over to the shade of the *palo verdes* from where Celia had been watching, shoulder-to-shoulder with Father William. Yolanda held out the bottle. Spoke.

"*Aquí está, Celia. Beber.* Here she is, Celia. Drink."

Celia had not known what to do with herself after that final school bell on that final day. She had slowly gathered up her things. Lied about busy summer plans –travel, relatives, nonsense –to half a dozen teachers and staff. Stopped in to thank Principal Deazy for a good first year. Hoped to see him in the fall.

He had smiled. Nodded. Made no promises.

On her way to the parking lot she could not help but look for Paola. Imagined her sitting beneath the *palo verdes.* She had known better, of course. But she had looked anyway. The spot was empty. Detritus circling in the wind, which had not abated. If anything it had grown stronger over night, feeding on itself in the dark.

Wind. She had remembered the day before. Wondered what would happen if she let slip one of the papers in her hands. Wondered whether Paola would appear from thin air to chase it down and bring it back to her.

Worry had not shouldered its way into her emptiness until the sky began to darken. Contrails over the desert glowed deep red. Hot scars cut by the sun, clawing into the sky on its way over the cliff.

That's when she'd first really started to wonder. What if the empty chair in that classroom was not just Paola being Paola? Not just last-day apathy?

What if something was wrong?

Celia had brushed the notion aside several times. It kept returning like a stray cat to the back door. Demanding.

What if something was wrong? Go away.

What if something was wrong?

After dinner she had planned to watch *The Sound of Music* on television. But the wind had knocked the power out just as little Gretl was skipping into the VonTrapp living room. Celia had heard a popping noise and then all light and sound had collapsed in around her, as if she'd sunk to that depth where the pressure is just too much, imploding all artificial bubbles that pretend to sustain us.

Celia sat in the dark. Listened. Even the television had abandoned her. The air conditioner. The refrigerator. Just the wind was left. Whispering that question. Then howling it.

What if something was wrong?

Engine. Headlights. Seatbelt ding.

The car had offered some comforting pretension of life amid the surrounding semblance of deadness. She had driven aimlessly at first. Steering a serpentine route through Corbin proper. Up and down the length of *Broken River Road*. Then to *Corbin Middle School*. Then *Corbin Elementary*. Up past the *Chachalaca Gazette*. Over to the *Evangeline Huerta Library*. Power seemed to be out everywhere.

Others were on the road, but she had steered clear. Aimed for darkness. Aimed for absence.

Just wind, curling and uncurling itself over the desert in restless fits.

She did not imagine she had taken on passengers until she had made the turn onto I-67 and headed west. Magdalena in the front seat. Yolanda stretched out in the back, holding Celia's baby. The baby she'd told Yolanda had just never taken. The baby Celia had named anyway.

They were a quiet group. No one spoke or cried. They just sat there as she rolled the car through the dark wind. Looked out the windows. Watched the headlights sweep the road, pushing the dust and debris in front of them up into the air. But they were all thinking the same thing.

What if something was wrong?

Celia had considered driving all the way down to Iraan. Or further. Keep going. Pick up the I-10. Head over to Fort Stockton. Just keep driving.

But as the car approached the little unmarked dirt road bisecting the highway, Maggie had reached over. Given the wheel a little tug.

Celia had wanted to stop, to turn back, a thousand times as the car rolled along the scratch in the dirt, bending in slow curves until the highway was out of view, passing the spot where, just the day before, Paola had opened her door and Celia had skidded to a stop. *"If you want me to talk to you again sometime, if you really want to be my friend forever and ever amen..."* Celia had wanted to stop again in that same spot. Had wanted to turn back. Again.

But that night Maggie was in control. Maggie was steering.

So the car kept rolling forward.

Eventually, though, Celia had asserted herself. Stopped the car. Just as soon as she had seen the lights.

Two structures —a modest two-story house and a large detached shed —marked the end of the road. The house was ablaze with yellow light, every window a kind of burning hole, the blowing dust in the middle distance like a kind of smoke. She had waited for solid interruptions in the glare. Like astronomers look for signs of planets passing in front of distant suns. A body in motion, blocking the source of light.

But nothing.

She looked for Garvin's red station wagon. Nothing.

Vehicles of any kind. Nothing.

Celia had decided this meant that Garvin must still be away, up in Haskell fighting off Maria's sister, Arlene, and quoting whatever bits scripture would convince Maria that a man and his wife must be together. That reuniting was God's will. That her bruises would heal faster if she just forgave him and came on back home. Think about the kids, Maria. Praise Jesus.

The car had seemed to ease forward on its own, as if Maggie had reached down and pushed on the gas pedal with her little dead fingertips. They rolled slowly up the grade, until the bumper was nosing up against the perimeter of light from the house.

Celia had cut the engine. Climbed out into the wind. Closed the door.

There were two sounds cutting through the gusts. In the background, from somewhere beyond the house, the unmistakable rumbling whine of a gas generator.

In the foreground, music.

Not music.

Noise. Angry, electronic retching. A muffled, convulsive rage of sound, like a frenzied sawing of high-tension power lines. An undisciplined, rapid-fire spray of percussive bullets. The sound of violence, locked inside a box of glass and wood.

Pretending some certainty of purpose, Celia had stepped into the nimbus of yellow spray, alive with flying dust. Walked to the nearest window. Peeked inside.

The window, white gauzy curtains half-pulled, belonged to a small, messy kitchen. Sink full. Counters littered. Crumpled bags of chips. Empty pizza box. A dirty frying pan holding a picked-over chicken carcass in a solid puddle of pale, congealed grease. Oven door wide open.

And bottles. Empty. Half-full. Gin. Whiskey. Beer.

Past the far end of the kitchen, through a narrow doorway, was a larger room. An oak dining table. Three high-backed antique chairs. The fourth was missing.

Jesus was in the center of the table. Fourteen inches. White robe. Arms spread. Standing in a circle of dusty silk foliage.

Celia had waited. Hoped Paola would pass into view. The storm of sound pounded at her from inside the window, like something savage determined to get out, angry at the easily escaping light. Above, an aerial antennae cable slapped against the side of the house in the wind. Again. Again.

Celia had waited. Watched. Nothing.

She had decided she was wrong to involve herself. That it was not her place. That Paola would hate her for intruding. That was too much to risk. So she had turned away from the window, resolved to leave.

Then she had looked down. Stopped.

Movement. Between the tip of her shoe and the foundation of the house. Something traversing the narrow lane of shadow where the light from the window did not fall.

It was a small scorpion. Gone from view, swallowed into blackness, almost immediately. Celia had taken it as a sign. Pushed on.

She had knocked. Waited.
Pounded. Waited. Then tried the door.
So many years later, she does not know what she would have done had the front door been locked. She marvels now at how that might have changed everything. A simple two-inch bolt of metal pushed into its little hole. She would have gone home. Everything would have been different. For better. For worse.
But the front door was not locked. Celia had not gone home.
She had pushed the door open.
The sound from inside had rushed over her like an un-caged animal, pushing her back, raging out into the desert. She stood in the doorway as if it might pass behind her and then be gone, howling and keening out into the night.
But it kept coming. And coming. Eventually less an animal from a cage than a flood of something vile from a ruptured pipe.
She looked forward. Focused through the sound. She could see through the dining room, over the oak table, and in through the narrow kitchen door.
The window over the sink had glinted light.
She remembers, all these years later, that of all the things about that night she has forgotten, repressed, and so many other things that never registered in the first place, she remembers searching for her own face peering back at her in through that kitchen window. As though she had never decided to come around to the front of the house. As though she were still there, waiting for some sign of Paola.
Three cautious steps forward. Another room had come into view.
It had not looked much like a living room except maybe for the dirty tan wall-to-wall carpet and the long, green velveteen couch that occupied much of one wall, hunching beneath a bank of three windows. The couch was sagging in the center, two cushions ripped and beginning to extrude their stuffing. The windows behind were draped with the same hand-made, white gauzy curtains Celia had seen in the kitchen.
She still remembers that the curtains were too long, pillowing up on the back of the couch. It had made her think of snow beginning to cornice on an eave. Something she'd never seen in her entire life except maybe on television or in the Christmas catalogues.
Priority in the room had been given to the folding chairs. Cheap and wooden. Nine or ten of them arranged in a single row, curving gently against the far corner. The chairs faced a wooden lectern draped in a purple velvet cloth.
She remembers all of that now, decades later. She had somehow absorbed all of it without really seeing it. The large wooden cross on the wall. The portrait of

379

the crucifixion. A Crown of thorns hanging like a wreath. She had somehow taken all of it in to remember it later. But at the time, standing in the storm of furious electric sound, the only thing Celia consciously acknowledged in that room was the piano.

A restored antique. Burled, orange-toned wood, chipped and gouged in places, with three thick, muscled legs, tarnished brass pedals, and a set of dingy white keys. Behind the piano was the missing dining room chair.

And yet it was not the piano itself that had caught Celia's attention. It was the pasty white, nearly naked body of Lyle Cross, draped backward on top of the thing. That was what she had seen first.

Black underwear. One black sock. Nothing else. All four limbs spread out over the curving edge of the piano. Arms stiff, legs dangling limp.

His face was turned away from her, as if in some debilitating shame or modesty. Or death.

That was the first thing that had occurred to her. *Here was Lyle Cross, dead.*

The candles on the piano, burning around his head and one of his arms had also made an impression. Three fat white candles burning tall, sooty flames. One large black ceramic oil lamp burning a pure yellow in its glass hurricane.

The candles were not, in that first instant, indications of a power-outage. Sources of light before someone had fired up the generator.

Instead, they suggested ritual. Scripted observance. Signs of passing. Candles lit to mark the fallen and to honor the dead.

All of that –the piano, Lyle, the candles –had consumed one beat. *One.*

Two. On the floor, directly beneath Lyle, was Paola. Face down.

Three. A length of white rope connected her left wrist to a leg of the piano. A length of black electrical cord tied her right wrist to a piano leg on the other side.

Four. The hair on the back of Paola's head had been cut short, down to soft stubble, revealing a circle of scalp. Long, thick drizzles of white wax crisscrossed the circle. It trailed along the length of her bare neck and off the sides, covering the collar of her t-shirt like an old lava flow, down to pale sooty pools on the beige carpet.

Celia does not remember how many seconds passed before she could comprehend. Her eyes were uncaring, insensitive ambassadors from some other world, speaking an alien language. It was, at first, visual gibberish.

She remembers a screaming in her head. Remembers Maggie's voice. Remembers the sound of Maggie shrieking, trying to be heard over the rage of noise around her. She does not remember how long all of that lasted. She remembers only that it did not feel like seconds. It felt like minutes. Minutes of standing and not comprehending.

But, eventually, she had moved. She had acted. Even if she cannot account for why she did what she did. And what she did not do.

She did not cry out. She did not shout Paola's name. Somehow she had known to be quiet.

Celia had slowly lowered herself to the floor. Crawled across the room. Tried to burrow beneath blaring light and sound.

She reached the piano. Placed a hand on Paola's left wrist.

The girl jolted. Yanked hard and repeatedly at the rope. Wrenched her face up and back. Saw Celia looking down at her. Froze.

Paola's expression had been part rage. Part horror. Part plaintive. Then all of it had slowly dissolved into confusion. Her face was red and streaked in tears. Nose clogged. Hair caked in blobs of smoky-white wax.

Celia had placed the tips of her fingers over Paola's mouth. Tried to hold the girl's bloodshot eyes in her own. Tried to *really* look at her. Then she had turned away and went to work on the knot.

Paola had been well tied. Her hand was bluish white and cold to the touch. It took time. Too much time. Each second elongated, making room for itself in the heart of the next. The sound of electric gnashing, screeching, came from everywhere.

When she had finally freed Paola's left hand, Celia had moved herself across Paola's body, first one knee then the other, careful to duck beneath Lyle's dangling bare foot, and had begun working on the electrical cord that tied the right. It was harder than the left hand. It took longer.

Then Lyle's foot had twitched, kicking her in the back of the head.

It was Maggie's voice, suddenly, deep inside her head: *Not dead, not dead, not dead. Still alive.*

Celia had frozen in place. Beneath her, Paola had felt the change. Had felt Celia stop working on the knot. Paola had rotated her face up again. Had watched Celia watching Lyle's swaying foot.

Then they had stared at each other, feeding on terror. Utterly together in that moment. A single pulsing heartbeat. *Celia and Paola. Celia and Paola. Celia and Paola.*

Celia had resumed her work, frantically trying to loosen up the electrical cord. Broke a fingernail. Used her teeth.

The cord loosened. Resisted one last time. Came free.

Paola reclaimed her hand. Rolled over on her back. Sat up clutching her wrist. Opened her mouth to speak.

But it was Lyle's voice coming through the sound.

"What in the *fuuuuuuck*!"

Celia had clutched Paola by the shoulders, squeezing and lifting with her hands at the same time, shouting with her eyes, forming the same single silent syllable with her lips as she had done that day behind the dumpster.

Go!

Paola was up and running for the door before Celia could get up. When Celia tried to stand, her right shoulder rammed up against the underside of the piano forcing her back down to her knees.

She did not get a second chance. She felt one of Lyle's hands grab the side of her face like a football. Felt him ram her head into the side of the piano.

Once. Twice.

She felt herself go limp. Felt the black water pouring in through her ears.

She dreamed of floating. Dreamed of a body of water, dark and calm and shoreless, flecked with bits of light that disappeared when she looked at them. Dreamed of sinking beneath the noise, down into the depths, her body like a falling leaf. Like a feather spiraling from the wing of a passing bird.

Dreamed of stillness.

Then dreamed of movement. Movement.

Around her. Beneath her. Movement. Large and sleek and swimming. Something pushing aside trillions of tons of water to get up to her.

Dreamed of singing. *La linda manita. Que tiene el bebé. Qué linda, qué bella. Qué preciosa es.* Dreamed of her mother's voice in the dark.

Floating. Rising. Rising.

Rising.

She had returned to her senses as Lyle was dragging her backwards by one hand out from beneath the piano, over knobs and streaks of hardened wax and through long, severed strands of Paola's hair.

Lyle let her hand drop. Towered over her, almost naked, like some waxen golem. Dirty-blond hair matted against his blemished face. Socked foot stepping on her left wrist. Bare foot stepping on her right. Ankle pocked with pink, scabbing needle tracks.

In his right hand, Lyle held a large pair of scissors. He'd shouted at her over the sound.

"Oh, teacher want? Teacher want!"

He snipped the blades twice. Reached over the piano with his other hand for one of the candles. Tipped it sideways.

Celia had looked away in time. The stream of wax found her right cheek and trickled into her ear. She writhed violently, kicking up her feet. Lyle put the candle back. He bent down, bringing his upside-down face close to hers, holding the point of the scissors to just above her left eye. Smiled. He had his father's teeth. The breath of a scavenger.

Celia fell still. Lyle ground out the words like metal filings.

"Then why. Is teacher. In my. Fuckin'. House."

She has no recollection of choosing her words. Only having said them,

"I am here. To pick up. Your sister. *Let! Me! Go!*"

Lyle straightened. Stood again, crushing her wrists into the carpet. Screamed at the ceiling as if he were shouting lyrics to whatever song was punching through the walls.

"Ain't. My fuckin'. *Sisterrrrrr!*"

She remembers seeing the bottle fly past his hip. Hearing it glance off the piano with a *thunk* and disappear somewhere in the room beyond. Lyle turned. Celia arched her back, rolled the top of her head against the carpet, to look upside-down through Lyle's legs and behind her.

Paola stood across the room, both hands out, trying to keep the gun from shaking. It was large and black and looked older than the piano.

"Get off of her!"

"No! Paola!" Celia remembers saying the words. But not shouting them. Not screaming them. Weeping them. So they went unheard. Unheeded. "Paola. Please. Put the gun away. You don't need a gun."

Lyle. Screaming. Laughing. Bearing down on her wrists with his feet.

"Little shit! Thing don't fuckin' work! Ain't no fuckin' bullets anyway!"

"Does too! Leave her alone, Lyle! I will shoot!"

Lyle turned, stepping off of Celia's wrists, and moved quickly for Paola. Five steps would do it. Paola had closed her eyes. Squeezed the trigger.

Celia remembers the muzzle flash. A dullish low boom. A sound of shattering glass. Wind, suddenly, had gushed in from behind her, flowing over her body for the open front door. Paola stood stunned. The kick of the old pistol had rotated her arms straight up over her head. Celia still has nightmares about the look in Paola's eyes.

It was all too fast for Lyle to even think about pausing. So he hadn't.

He was on Paola in an instant. Ripped the gun out of her hands. Threw it across the room. Slapped Paola hard across the face.

There was a moment of stillness in the tornado of sound before Paola went at him with every ounce of fear and rage in her little body. Even as she was pulling herself to her feet, Celia had wanted to shout for Paola to run. Not to fight him. To just get the hell out.

But the moment of stillness was too brief for words. Paola was clawing at him. Kicking. Punching. Trying to climb him. Going for his face.

Lyle was too big. His left hand quickly found the girl's throat. Pushed her against the wall. Squeezed. She flailed pointlessly. Began to choke.

Yolanda, then.

Whispering to Celia through time.

Whispering all the way from Gatesville, Texas, over the metal table in the visitor room of the Mountain View Corrections Unit. Whispering so the guard couldn't hear.

"They were trying to take my little girl. *Mi pequeña niña.* My little Amalia. No one does that. You understand me? No one. I burned them to the ground.

Gilipollas. I'd do it again. You will too, Celia. You will too."

Not 'would.' '*Will*.' Yolanda had said she *will* do it.

It was Celia's scream that got Lyle's attention. It made him turn his face away from Paola and back to the piano. But it was the sight of Celia hurling the large kerosene hurricane against the nearest wall that made him drop Paola to the floor.

That old green couch. Those piling, snowy curtains.

The air turned bright orange.

Lyle came for her. Turning. Moving in fury and certain panic. Shouting something she never really heard as she had braced herself for a fight she could never win.

But Paola, even as she was crumpling to the floor, had seized Lyle's ankle.

A single, terrible moment. Broken evenly into four-four time.

One. Lyle fell fast and hard, hands out in front of his body, reaching for the carpet.

Two. The scissors in his hand slipped in through the white flesh of his neck. Found both carotid arteries like two strands of crimson yarn. Broke through the spine on the way out the other side.

Three. Nothing but ragged sound and flame and blood. Her own heartbeat, her own breathing, gone.

Four. The carpet. The adjoining wall. The ceiling. Like the sound itself had turned incendiary, igniting everything in its path. The couch was a flaming green log beneath cushions of dry hay.

Paola was still on the floor. Oblivious of the fire. Transfixed by Lyle's still body seeping a dark lake over the dirty tan carpet. Her hands still clutching his bare, needle-pocked ankle.

Celia has no memory of crossing the room. Only suddenly standing over Paola. Hacking. Gulping in toxic air. Pulling Paola to her feet. Shoving her toward the door. Shouting at her to get out. Shouting at her to go to the car. "Go to the car! Go to the car!" Paola ran.

A twitch on the carpet. Another.

She had tried to force herself not to look at Lyle. It was too awful. She thought that she should make the effort to see if he was alive. To do what was necessary to save a life. A life was a life was a life.

The back of his head, above the scissors, was normal. Gently curling wisps of dirty blond hair. A mother's hand had washed and cradled that head. Smelled it. It had once fit snugly in a mother's palm. Maria Cross' palm. If she did not save him, then a mother would lose a child.

But she couldn't look. To look was to risk paralysis in horror. All she could afford was turning away. Running. Chasing Paola. She stood.

Thoughts in her head. Yolanda. Again. Suddenly. Cutting through the chaos. *El arma, Celia. Get the gun. You need to get the gun.*

The gun. Paola. Fingerprints. She needed the gun.

She'd dropped back to her knees. Crawled beneath the smoke. Away from the inferno. Away from the front door. Into the dining room. She felt the fire move in behind her. Racing for her. Gobbling up the carpet. Blocking the exit.

The antique pistol had landed beneath a chair. Celia clutched the thing in one hand. Felt the heat behind her become a wall. She crawled forward for the kitchen. There was no going back.

She crossed the kitchen floor. Stood at the sink. Raised up the window, giving the gusting wind outside exactly what it wanted: another clear path through the house. The fire exploded into the dining room, flaring into the kitchen. Celia climbed up on the counter. Kicked out the window screen. Threw herself forward, down into the dirt where the scorpion had been. Where she had once stood deciding whether to involve herself.

When she reached the car she had found it still. Dark. Empty.

She had shouted Paola's name into the wind. Listened. Shouted. Listened. Flames stretched out of the eaves of the house to the sounds of popping and cracking like something large and lumbering stepping on bones.

Celia moved away from the car. Away from the house. Toward the darker desert beyond.

Then a light. Quick. Moving. Steady. Moving.

It came from inside the shed. There and gone again.

But then the glowing orange nimbus from the flaming house had corrected Celia's first impression. It was not a shed. Or a garage. It was not a building.

It was a boat. It was an ark.

Celia had pushed open one narrow blue door. Stepped inside.

Paola. There. Kneeling on a mattress, flashlight burning at her side. Bare scalp like a third eye glowing through the hole in her hair.

Above her on the wall was a narrow plank made into a shelf. On the shelf, a porcelain figurine. Mother Mary. White robe. Bright blue cowl that matched the door.

Celia's voice was too loud and frantic for such a small, close place.

"You're praying? No. No, Paola. We have to get out of here. Now!"

Paola's voice. Panting. Afraid. Shaking. But determined.

"Ain't prayin'. Go start the car."

"Well, what…" The gun felt heavy in Celia's hand. She'd forgotten she still had it. Something up in the house behind them exploded. She felt the wax still in her ear.

Paola reached up to the shelf. Next to Mother Mary were other figurines. Smaller. Made of wood.

No. Not wood. Made of lacquered painted cactus. A whole family of them.

Paola plucked each of them off the shelf and laid them in a row on a blue velvet cloth in a small silver box. Closed the lid. Turned. Looked up.

Her face was white in the glow of the flashlight.

"Ain't never comin' back to this place again, Miss Celia. Not ever."

Chapter 52

Olivia DeLuna is in his head.

She lives there now. Drinks his every thought. Eats his unspoken words. Rolls up his attention and smokes it.

She is always there.

Sheldon nods gravely at Grayson, who is going on about the Corbin deal. Investment figures. Land prices. Government approvals. The Russians this and that. *Blah, blah.* The silver mustache dusts the top of the words and sentences as they clear his teeth, just before they drop to the pavement in a pile of instantly forgotten sound.

Olivia is all he can think about. The feel of her hand in his. The smell of her hair. Those eyes.

Time stopped flowing forward last Wednesday. He is in an eddy now. He and Olivia are in a boat, together, in an eddy. The eddy is called *Wednesday afternoon.*

"Don't you think?" asks Grayson.

"Sure." He responds quickly and with certitude. "Sounds about right to me."

The sound of her voice. The way it folds around him like a kind of incense cloud. The way it shapes his name. *Sheldon. Sheldon.*

Her guarded laugh. Like some timid, wild animal.

Her love of music. That secret enthusiasm. The way it fills her to the brim, like water, always sloshing out around her when he jars her with the right question. The way she smiles at him and sputters at his stupid jokes.

"I think we should be making another run at Derrick Pike and his people. Is it Pike or Pick?"

"Huh?" He looks at the question on Grayson's face.

"Derrick Pick? Pike?"

"Pike, I think."

Olivia. Olivia.

Of course, somewhere in all of the smiling and handholding, Sheldon knows he is being worked. He isn't stupid. He is too old for this to actually be what it feels like. She was too angry and desperate for this to be what it feels like. It was about his money. He knows. Wasn't about him. He knows.

But it *feels* like it is about him.

He *wants* it to be about him.

And so it *is* about him.

And if money is the price –if this is about him only because he has access to money –then he will pay the money. He will find a way. He is not above paying to feel this way. Does that make her a prostitute and him a john? No, of course not.

Well. Maybe. He doesn't care.

"So tell me what's doin' with those bastards at the goddamned *Chacha*."

Sheldon's full attention zips down into a sharp focus. *Goddamned Chacha.*

Grayson Tate strokes his mustache. Nudges his hat up with a knuckle. Leans a little more out the window letting his hand brush against the side of the door. His fingers caress the metal flank of the vehicle like he's on a black stallion in need of some assurance.

The people at Mercedes-Benz don't make horses. But SUV's they can do.

The big black thing towers above Sheldon's silver coupe, a relative pony. They are side-by-side at the bottom of Sheldon's driveway. Stallion pointing downhill towards the street. Pony pointing up towards the barn.

"Sure you don't want to come in and have a drink?" Sheldon asks on the thin hope that a tumbler of bourbon will get Grayson side-tracked on other issues.

Grayson shakes his head.

"Hell. Been here for an hour already. I gotta be anywhere but here. Christi won't shut the hell up about that goddamned Corbin pageant. I'm not sayin' it's a bad idea or anything, but I'm sick of her goin' on about it. And Nicki Voss is in there drinking your vodka, calm as can be on the outside but I'm guessin' on the inside he's ready to shoot himself in the head. Or her. God knows what he reports back to Adrian Hewitt at Quinco. I try nudging her off the subject but you know how Christi is. Once somethin' finds its way into that head of hers…"

He leaves the thought hanging. Looks out over the steering wheel, between where the twitching ears of the stallion might be, and down at the metal gate that separates the driveway from the street. He takes off his Stetson with a thumb and two fingers. Drops it in the passenger seat. Rakes his thin, silver-white hair. He looks back down through the window at Sheldon.

"She's pretty to look at and loyal as the day is long, and I'll kill any man that hurts her, but sometimes Christi has the sense God gave a turnip." He looks guiltily in the rearview mirror, like his daughter might be in the back seat. "That's between you and me. I've just had my fill of pageant-talk for the day. So I'm goin' home. What's the word on the sons-a-bitches at the *Chacha?*"

Grayson cuts the engine so he can hear the answer.

Sheldon had hoped, without much reason, that he had heard the last of the questions about the *Chachalaca Gazette*. Grayson had been so embroiled in clearing brush for the Corbin River Walk deal that Sheldon's supposed defamation by the *Chacha* had fallen off into the scrub along the road of Grayson's attention.

Helping matters greatly, Christi's preoccupation with her very own beauty pageant, and her recent unwillingness to confront his supposed perfidy, had meant that there was no one in Grayson's face to fan the flames of indignation. No one to remind him of a family honor in need of rescue.

Sheldon had hoped that state of affairs would continue indefinitely.

But the landscape beneath Grayson's boots had been shifting. Obstacles had moved. Brush cleared. Quinco International had hired a team of lawyers to address the Pecos River Commission and help negotiate a truce between Texas and New Mexico. Texas had removed its objections to New Mexico's Lake Avalon diversion project. In exchange, New Mexico had agreed not to bitch about a diversion of the Pecos River east of the New Mexico border so that Texas could green up the desert around Corbin. As part of the truce, New Mexico withdrew all support from the environmental litigation to enjoin the Pecos River diversion.

In a confluence of fortune, the presiding judge had lost his bid to be appointed to the Fifth Circuit bench. The Administration in Washington, troubled with the consistency of Judge Winifred's rulings on sensitive environmental issues, chose to back another horse for the open circuit position. But that political disappointment, it turned out, had come with a certain judicial liberation. No longer concerned about the controversy of environmental activists picketing the Pecos County Federal District courthouse, Judge Winifred had extended an enthusiastic Bluntnose Shiner-sized middle finger to those who would judge him for his environmental insensitivity and dismissed the lawsuit with the toe of his boot.

So. Pending appeal, the Pecos Bluntnose Shiner was on its own.

But then again, that was environmental politics. Never really know which way that fish was going to flop.

The news had left Grayson feeling vindicated, buoying his spirits and lightening his step. In the wake of the lawsuit dismissal, he had carried on with extra *bravado*, as though somehow he had been responsible for the victory. As though he had done something other than watch from the sidelines and bellyache. "We showed those sons-a-bitches. Those fish-fuckers. Did I tell you, Shelly? Did I? Kicked their asses but good."

For a week or so, a smattering of protesters from a handful of environmental organizations walked in dusty circles outside the Pecos County Federal

Courthouse chanting bad rhymes. The news coverage of the protestors only served to heighten Grayson's pleasure, prompting fits of taunting directed at Sheldon's television.

"You ever seen a more pathetic sight than that? How many are there? Eight? *Nine?* Look at 'em. May as well take your fish and go back to Oregon, you pussies! Don't mess with Texas!"

Not that Judge Winifred's decision had issued without some broader attention. The newspapers in Texas, New Mexico and throughout the southwestern United States had covered the story. The op-ed pages lit up in vituperative argument and the national talk shows briefly swelled with segments devoted to issues like the unseen environmental costs of commercial development. The precariousness of green desert economies. The growing interstate battle over western rivers. More than any expert on the subject, the media was most fond of quoting Mark Twain: "Whiskey's for drinking, water's for fighting about."

In all of the media dust-up, there had been a handful of segments that specifically honed in on the Corbin River Walk project for whose success the Pecos Bluntnose Shiner, and perhaps other desert inhabitants and ecosystems, would be made to suffer. They were not comfortable stories to watch or read.

The consensus of the media snipers had been predictably bleak and cynical. Water allocation, they noted, was always a zero-sum game. Water diversion always came at a cost. Hurricanes aside, the American west was in the grip of decades-long drought with no end in sight. Global warming was rapidly rolling past the tipping point of recovery. Agricultural supply was in increasing peril. Irreversible environmental calamity wrought by over-development and unsustainable population growth was on the horizon. And, not to be left out of the consensus, the developers of the Corbin River Walk would make an absolute financial killing by turning the Texas desert into an unsustainable oasis of golf courses, high-ended shopping and riverside dining. The head-shaking, shoulder-shrugging sign-off to these various stories had been that greed had the only voice in the debate.

Grayson had avoided the criticism entirely, leaving it for Sheldon to evaluate and, as necessary, to defuse with a statewide blitz of well-placed positive stories about greening deserts. Commerce. Jobs. Tourism. Songbirds. Arts and culture. Stories about the San Antonio River Walk. Story after story about the upcoming *Corbin Moon Garden Festival* and the crowning of the first-ever *Corbin River Walk Queen*.

Grayson had been determined to turn the page on all that had been keeping him a raw nerve. He had flown to New York at the invitation of Gregor Buchvarov, *the Russian* himself, to share his perspective on the progress of the Corbin project with Adrian Hewitt and the other Quinco Project Directors. He had returned to Houston with extra swagger.

"Goddamned Russian is somethin' else, Shelly. Man knows how to run a meeting. When it came to my turn I gave them the low down 'bout how we'd been kickin' serious ass down here, right? I talk about the goddamned lawsuit. And how I've been workin' those last few sons-a-bitches in the state house and about my lunch with the Governor. And the Russian looks at me from the other end of that room –lookin' out over Manhattan, I mean what a goddamned *view*, Shelly! What a goddamned *view!* –and you know what he does? He doesn't say a fuckin' thing. He just brings his massive hairy fist down on that table one time – just once –like he just might break it into splinters, and then he stands up, goes to the mini 'fridge, opens a new bottle of Stoli, and pours everyone a drink. He holds his glass above the table and we all do the same –all goddamned fifteen of us –and he says one goddamned word. Know what word he says?"

Sheldon had had no idea.

"'*Texas*.' That was it. Just '*Texas*'. And so we all drank to Texas. Never been prouder to be a Texan in my whole goddamned life than to hear that word comin' outta the mouth of the Russian. Meeting over. Done. We kept drinkin'. The Russian and me and half dozen others went strip clubbin' for the rest of the night. You know I don't normally go in for that sort of thing, but I don't say 'no' to the Russian. No one says no to the Russian. When goddamned Gregor Buchvarov tells you to do something then you goddamned do it. If he tells you to walk naked out into traffic, then you drop those pants and get to walkin' because somehow, someway, you're gonna shit a pile of money if you make it to the other side of the street. And the Russian thinks we're the fuckin' bees knees, Shelly. You and me. Said so himself and near broke my shoulder tellin' me. He likes your roll-out. Best he's seen from anyone. Even the national firms. Son-of-a-bitch knows what he's doin', Shel. He's got big plans for Corbin. The Russian's not fuckin' around."

And so on for most of a bourbon-soaked dinner.

But with the reblooming of Grayson's optimism had come a renewed attention to things that had previously been too small to care about. Libel. Family honor. No-account desert rags masquerading as real newspapers.

"What's the word on the sons-a-bitches at the *Chacha*?"

Sheldon looks out the windshield up his driveway to the house. Why had he left work so early? Two hours ahead of his usual routine. Hell, had he driven home just a little slower, had he caught just one more stoplight, he could have avoided this entire conversation. He looks back up at Grayson. Dives head first into the lie.

"I think we're going to have to sue 'em," he says. "Newspapers won't budge until it hurts."

Grayson nods. "Bastards. Your lawyer think you can win?"

"*Lawyers.* Plural. They've put two of them on the case. They say that there are Constitutional issues that will make it tough, which is why the paper is playin' hardball. They say they're going to have to take some time to get prepared. Get their ducks in a row. It's going to take some money, Grayson. Good lawyers don't come cheap."

Grayson juts his hand out of the window, pointing. Sun splashes off the gold ring. "Nope. Already said my piece on that, Shel. Money is no object. If you think this is important, then don't you worry about the money. Run it through the business. We'll all be rollin' in money like pigs in shit 'fore we're done with Corbin."

A pause. Grayson looks away. Down at the street past the mailbox. Then back.

"Question you got to ask now is whether it's even worth it at this point."

Sheldon takes in half a breath but then doesn't know what to do with it. "Worth it?" he asks. "What are you…"

"I know, I know," says Grayson. The rest of his hand opens up to join his index finger. "But look. All this whorehouse cattin' around bullshit has died down now. It's old news. You go filing a lawsuit, you'll just stir it all up again. *The Chacha*'ll cover the lawsuit and the real newspapers might too. Christi will get all wrapped around the axel…"

He is right, of course. Sheldon knows this. It has been for this very same reason that he has never actually hired an attorney nor made any contact whatsoever with the *Chachalaca Gazette*. And yet.

"Grayson, this is my *name* we are talking about. This is my *name*. My *wife's* name. My *reputation*. It's in the public record now. I can't just let them get away with…"

Sheldon is surprised by the indignation. Surprised by the vehemence in his own voice. Even a tremor of anger. Grayson takes on a mildly irritated expression.

"Calm down. Calm down. Christ. I'd do the same. I'm just sayin' that your lawyers better know what the fuck they're doin', Shel. If they're gonna shoot, then they damn well better aim for the heart and put those fuckers down and put 'em down fast. You can't file suit, stir up all the shit and then settle out of court later for some money. It ain't about money. If you file suit then the only option is to clear your name. Understand?"

"I understand perfectly, Grayson. But I can't just cave in. I can't turn away from this fight. And there's Christi."

"I know."

"This whole thing has hit her hard. She needs this cleared up. Her friends…"

"I know. I know. Bunch'a barracudas in designer shoes."

"And I know it's going to take money. Maybe a lot of money. But…"

The impatience is back on Grayson's face, flirting with anger.

"Spend the goddamned money, Shel. How many times I gotta say it? Your name is always worth the money. Reputation is everything. The business'll take care of the money and if you need more, well then come see me and we'll work something out. It's not about the goddamned fees. I'm just givin' you things to think about is all."

Grayson looks away. Turns the key. Puts the stallion in gear. Looks back down at Sheldon on his little silver pony.

"Give 'em hell, son. Give 'em hell."

Sheldon watches him in the rearview mirror, rolling away down the drive.

Son. The word is alien and uncomfortable. Homeless. It bounces and rolls fitfully along the ceiling of the car like a black, stringless balloon.

* * *

The garage door slowly severs the sunlight. He extracts the keys. Stops. Sits there. All is still and cool and concrete. Before the overhead light times out, he is back to mooning over Olivia. Thoughts like leaves, floating in circles.

Wednesday afternoon.

How different she had been. Different than at all of their other meetings. How engaging. How easily she had reached for his hand as they had strolled the San Antonio River Walk. Music in the air like a blossom-scented breeze. Her hand in his. As though that was the most natural thing in the world. As though it belonged there.

He replays their entire conversation, again, stroking it from beginning to end like he is petting the gleaming hide of a large, magnificent animal standing in the sun. Each recollective stroke is a kind of breath. A tidal surge. A hit of something intoxicating. Soothing and exhilarating at the same time.

They had met earlier than normal. That had helped. Time was not a factor. Neither of them had been in a hurry. They had reclined into the afternoon beneath a brilliant ocean blue sky. An armada of scudding cotton clouds had sailed into battle all afternoon, taking the edge off the sun, dappling their private bend in the river.

The white envelope beneath the napkin. Same as always and yet, somehow different this time. Off the table and in the purse. Never spoken of. Not once. As if the money was not the point. As if *they* were the point. *He* was the point and *she* was the point. It was not about the money.

Maybe, he had thought more than once, *that* should have told him that it was more about the money than ever before.

But that's *not* what it told him. That's not what he chose to understand.

Laughter over lunch. Silly things. Her names for passing strangers. His self-deprecating parade. How strange to see her sadness so clearly, lit in accidental light-heartedness. Like glimpsing a seabed in filtered light. Anger and longing and desperation, there and gone and back again like watery ghosts. A history of shipwrecks down there, guarding her secrets. Entombing her gold coins. They flash for an instant, finding their way up in that enigmatic smile of hers and the hazel glint of her eyes.

Tussling over the lyrics to old blues songs. *I'm a Mighty Tight Woman* and *Ma Rainey's Black Bottom.* Sex, he had claimed, was a subversive instrument of feminine power. Sex, she had argued, was a flag of surrender, no more an instrument of power than a pair of stiletto shoes.

"When that's the only tool you got left? When that's your only weapon? Then you've lost the war, Shel."

"It's not a war."

"Ain't it? Most women got no idea what they're doing."

"Sippie Wallace and Ma Rainey knew exactly what they were doing."

"Yes they did. They were testifyin'. Showin' you what it's all come to. Showin' you what's left. They were singing the blues, Shel."

Dessert. Chocolate and creamy. "Pretty big for one," said the server. "We'll share," Olivia had said without any hesitation. Most delicious was her assumption that she could speak for him.

The server took away the dishes. Took away the bill beneath its blanket of money. Took away their remaining time.

Or so he had feared.

Then her suggestion –*hers!* –that they stroll over to listen to whoever was playing *St. James Infirmary,* the clear, somber trumpet cutting through the early afternoon, haunting them, carrying them above the crowd on its brassy shoulders. And then, when they'd found the trio, set up on a makeshift stage at a bend in the river, her hand slipping into his. Suddenly. Wonderfully. Pulling him to a nearby bench where they had sat and listened to the rest of the set.

The trio had ended with a slow, blue version of *Since I Fell for You.* Olivia had closed her eyes. Swaying against him. Pushing her shoulder against his on every other downbeat.

And he had moved with her. They were like a tiny, self-contained ocean on a park bench, ebbing and flowing. If she had known he was looking at her, she hadn't let on. She was someplace else.

"Didn't take you for a Lenny Welch fan," he had said finally. She had opened her good eye and then closed it again. Shook her head.

"Sheldon, Sheldon, Sheldon. You disappoint me. This song belongs to Ella and Buddy Johnson. This here is a straight-up blues tune. Should be anyway. Lenny just poured a bunch of sap all over it." She had pointed across the walk at the trio. "And these cats know all about Ella and Buddy. You can tell. That sax?" She broke off, listening. "Like a ladle full of hurt. Ain't a romantic dancin' song. It's a cryin' song."

He had watched her listen. Watched the fullness of the sax pour over her. Watched the whisper of a smile on her lips. As if sadness, or the sound of it, gave her the most pleasure.

A couple had walked by sharing a cone. He wasn't thinking.

"Ice cream. You want some ice cream?"

She hadn't opened her eyes.

"This a date? Sheldon? Feels like a date."

He had looked away, blood rising in his cheeks, realizing she was right. He'd felt transparent. The words tumbled out like loose stones.

"If I could pay you more I would. Olivia. I would. I'm already basically stealing the money as it is."

"Right. So if you're already stealing it..."

She hadn't finished. She didn't need to finish.

The song ended. Olivia had stood, leaving him on the bench. Limped across the walkway to the little stage. She pulled a crisp hundred from the envelope in her purse. Folded it up and put it in the fishbowl perched on the empty chair.

"Hell of a tip," he had said when she returned, standing over him.

"Only thing I got," she'd said, extending a hand. She pulled him off the bench. "And it was stolen."

Then that wry smile of hers that was still lodged in his brain like a feathered hook. The smile that said they were in on something together. He just didn't know what that something was. A joke maybe. A thing they knew about each other. A secret. A song. A crime. A swindle. A blues riff. Maybe something else. Something deeper. Something wonderful.

"So the ice cream's on you."

Sheldon climbs out of the car and goes inside. Head still sloshing with her. His heart still thrilling to her strange, sad, beautiful music.

The only flat note in this memory is the money. He is paying her money. Paying her in exchange for something he could not name. Money that is not his to spend.

Voices in his head.

"Right. So if you're already stealing it..."

"Spend the goddamned money, Shel. How many times do I have to say it? It's not about the goddamned money."

Voices like sea spray against the rocks of his brain.

"Right. So if you're already stealing it..."

"Spend the fuckin' money, Shel."

They carry him all the way down the hall to the kitchen before he has any presence of mind. Before he realizes that the voices in his head have substituted for the voices he had been expecting to hear in his house.

Christy. Nicholas.

He listens. Cocks his head in the doorway of the fully lit kitchen.

There are no voices. The house is quiet. He thinks back to the driveway. Sees the black Tahoe rental all over again. Walks to the empty living room. Two drinks on the coffee table. Half a glass of wine. Half a tumbler of vodka.

Listens.

There *is* a sound after all. Water. From upstairs.

Shower water.

He does not think about what he is doing. Thought is not part of the equation. Something else is in control now. His heart beats out in alarm at the stranger in his veins. He moves to the bottom of the stairs. Pauses, one hand lightly on the railing. He takes them quietly. Listening. Peels back the sound of the water. Tries to hear between the drops.

In his mind he has already found them. They can't hear him because of the water. They can't see him because of the steam on the glass. He has no idea what to do next. What to say.

But then Olivia is there, inside his head with the rest of them, giving him that feathered fishhook of a smile. *"Right. So if you're already stealing it…"*

So then he suddenly *does* know what he will do, doesn't he? He *does* know. He will stop worrying about his marriage. He will give Olivia everything she wants. He will defraud his own company. He will loot it into the dust. He will direct ever-larger payments to a law firm that does not really exist. Send the payments to a Post Office Box for which he has the only key. Cash the checks at the S & L where his new company –not *Houston Media Law Group* but its acronym, *HMLG, Inc.* –has an account. Put the cash in an envelope. Drive to San Antonio.

Again. Again. Again. Until it's gone.

He will tell her how he feels. He will summon the courage. He will kiss her beautiful mouth and trace her scars with his fingertips and he will tell her that he loves her.

And then, whatever comes, he will be free.

That is what he will do.

And so what? Was that to be the end of everything? Maybe. They would find out eventually. Christi. Grayson. Yes. Maybe. So what. Whatever comes.

Christi had already stopped almost all genuine engagement in the marriage. Ever since the day UPS had returned his belongings. Not that he hadn't tried.

"Christi, can we just, you know, talk about this?"

"No, hon'. We can't. Not ever. And we're meetin' Daddy in twenty-five minutes so you best change outta that god-awful shirt."

"Christi."

"Go on, now."

He was, at best, a socially significant status. A *spouse*. Not a person. She had decided, apparently, to freeze him to death with the blue eyes that now fully believed in, but never openly acknowledged, a Corbin Texas indiscretion. She had not told her father about the UPS delivery. And she had not ventured any opinion whenever Sheldon had updated Grayson on the status of his fight against the *Chachalaca Gazette*. His charade –for that is what Christi had obviously come to believe it was, a charade –had become a sick kind of spectator sport that she indulged with an implacable detachment.

To what unnerving end Sheldon had never been sure. Maybe she was working towards a one-off, boys-will-be-boys rationalization. Maybe she had remembered Layla, her template for all things matrimonial, on her deathbed. *"Well sure he's a cheating bastard, baby. Your daddy's a man, just like the good Lord makes most men, with a head for business, a dipstick to worship, and a blind spot for trouble. But he's my cheating bastard. And that ain't nothin'."*

Or maybe Christi was unwilling to feed her soiled marriage to the school of pageant piranhas that swam from one TPA function to the next. The fall out from Tig Larson's escape to Venezuela with a Dallas Cowgirl had been horrible enough. But being dumped for a slutty South American cheerleader was like being invited to tea with the Queen compared to being thrown over by husband number two for a south-Texas whore.

Or maybe she was just waiting. Watching fluctuations in the exchange rate between knowledge and power.

Whatever the explanation, Christi had clearly decided that his trip to Corbin had justified, maybe even retroactively justified, an affair with Nicky Voss.

Difference, of course, was that Sheldon's trip to Corbin had resulted in half a massage and an almost broken nose whereas the ice-eyed Samoyed twins had, apparently, been fucking daily in his own shower.

So. Whatever comes. He will shovel as much money out of that business as he can lift. For as long as he can get away with it. Olivia's need was now, suddenly, unapologetically, his mission.

He pauses at the top of the stairs. Listens. Moves to the end of the hall. Closes his eyes. Listens. Breathes. Steps into the bedroom.

Christy's clothes are in a pile on the floor. The bed is rumpled. Not unmade. But rumpled. Bathroom door, cracked open. He walks into the room far enough to see his wife's award-winning shape in the cascading water.

She is… alone.

Sheldon looks around. Eyes reading the bed rumples like fingertips to braille. Backs out of the room into the hallway. He is as silent as he can be.

"You are home." Nicholas Voss closes the door to Sheldon's office at the other end of the hallway. "I am glad."

Sport coat. Crisp white shirt. Open collar, disappearing beneath the ends of his fine blond hair. Dark slacks. Clean black shoes. Nothing out of place.

Nothing.

Nicholas closes the distance. His face, as always, like it is coated in glass or some weather resistant polymer to which expressions cannot bond. Nothing stuck to that face. Even the whisper of a smile on his perfect mouth slips over and off of his square jaw onto the carpet like a cheap costume mustache.

He is holding a sheaf of paper. The top page is a grainy copy of a photo.

"Nicholas. What are you…"

The photo is of a house. Someone's home.

"Fax machine. Your wife showed me where it is. I'm getting errors. *Error 72?* What does that mean? Something is wrong."

The water behind him stops. Christi's voice, a wet tendril of sound, bends out into the hall.

"Nicky? You still up here?"

Then he realizes.

The photo. The house. The home. It is the home of Libby Holder.

Liberty Cherish.

Yes. Something is very, very wrong.

Chapter 53

He is in the boat. The ark. Sitting on the dirty wooden floor beneath a paneless window. Back against the wall. Like the flood is coming and he's the first animal on board. Waiting.

Or like the waters have already receded and he doesn't want to leave. Like he doesn't really believe that God is quite done.

The wall opposite glows blood-orange. He re-crosses his legs. Flips the page over in his hands.

Because whatever the past, whatever the misunderstandings, whatever the blame —I will take the blame, Davis, I will own all of the blame if that makes a difference to you —this is not how it should be…

There are only four small rooms. Two below and two above, connected by a tiny, splintered staircase and arched doorways. It was never intended as an actual boat. Or something made for sleep or shelter. It was nothing more than a symbol. A large yard ornament for a church. Something for the children to play in while the adults were up in the main building —the house made into a church —reciting the gospel. Foretelling the rapture.

This is not how it should be between fathers and sons. You can hate me if you want. I can't stop that. But I am and will always be your father. And you are my son. My only…

He used to like sitting in the ark after two hours of breaking the house-church into pieces small enough to fit in the bed of Dallas Letti's truck. It was a place to catch his breath. Watch the sun snuff itself out into the dirt.

My only family. That means something to me, Davis. I'm not asking to be best friends. You don't have to like my book. But you know your mother would not want things like this. All I'm asking…

More recently he had taken to sitting in the ark for a few minutes just after he gets here. Before he starts tearing things up and hauling them away. While the sun was still high enough in the sky to blast its dying light through the window in the upper room. It is a respite between the chores of his life, to be sure.

But it is also a kind of sustenance. It fills him with an emotional protein to burn off as he swings a sledgehammer and rips into old sheetrock.

All I'm asking is this:…

Davis folds up the letter. He has read it too many times already. Once was enough. His father's voice is now too prominent in his head. He slips the letter into his back pocket. Trades it for the other one, this week's bittersweet antidote. He starts in the middle of the third page.

It was terrible, Lula. Terrible. I didn't recognize myself. Like I was looking down from the ceiling watching some other woman shriek. Snot and tears. Calling him names. And Dr. Bees was so calm. Legs crossed. Hands clasped. Waiting for me to wear myself out. And I finally did. And then when I was quiet he asked me one question. "What is the thing you love most about this world, Elizabeth?" I didn't have to think about it for half a second, but I was quiet a long time before I answered. He waited. I think we both appreciated the stillness for a change. And then I spoke the truth: "Davis is the thing I love most in the world. I love my little boy."

He rereads those words. Swallows. Reads. Again. Again. Like he is tracing a scar with his finger. A faint sound from out in the desert slips up the side of the ark. Drops in the through the window above his head. He blocks it out. Reads.

And then I said the thing I never should have said. It just slipped out. But it was the truth that slipped out, Lula. I told him that Davis is the only reason I'm still here. The only reason I'm still living. The truth. Well you can…

The sound again. Tiny and light. He listens with his eyes. Pans the shafts of suspended sunlit dust. Imagines a jackrabbit. Reads.

Well you can imagine where it went from there. He wants to see me twice a month now. I almost told him everything. I wanted to. It would have been a kind of relief. He would have locked me up as a certifiable loon, but it still would have been a relief. I told him nothing. I lied to him about the medication. We talked more about depression. We talked...

"Hero! Wake up! Ain't payin' yo lazy ass to sleep."

Dallas Letti's voice is like an arrow. It quivers for a beat in the trapezoid of drying light on the opposite wall. Davis stands quickly. Folds the letter. Stuffs it in his back pocket with the other. Looks out the window.

Dallas is directly below looking up. Floppy green gardening hat. Knobby hands on her hips. Face like a slab of black schist. No sign that she has walked all the way from her house up through the desert scrub.

"I was just looking around," he calls down.

"Don't you lie to me. You either sleepin' or spankin' yourself."

"No, seriously..."

"Shut up, boy. I don't care which it is. Either way y'ain't workin'. Now put the po'nography away an' get yourself on outta there."

He does as he is told. When he emerges out into the sun, she is already halfway up the short slope to the broken church. He follows.

She stops inside the threshold. Looks from one pile of rubble to the next. Kicks at a two-legged chair. He stands quietly behind, hands in his pockets.

"Ain't done a goddamned thing."

"That's not true."

"Damn, boy. Payin' you for *nothin'*."

"You pay me by the truckload, Ms. Letti. I told you, if you want this done faster then you need to hire a crew with a bulldozer and..."

"Don't start in on all that shit again. Not gon' hire no crew to charge me a fortune. So they can come look at me through my windows. Bulldoze everything in sight. I like my peace."

Dallas turns. Takes a step closer. Looks up into his face.

Her breath is flammable.

"But I don't let you up here so you can spank yourself in the goddamned boat. Unna'stand me, Hero?"

"I wasn't..."

"Do. You. Un. Der. Stand. Me. Hero."

He sighs. Closes his eyes. Spreads his arms. Nods.

"Yes ma'am. I understand. No spanking in the boat."

"Good." She turns back around to face the interior wreckage, steeping in its sticky syrup of burnt orange light. Her hard black eyes sweep back and forth too many times. "You find anything of value?"

"Ms. Letti, how many times do you have to ask? Don't you think I'd tell you?"

"I think maybe you'd keep it all for yourself. Poor boy like you."

"Oh, please."

"No, no. Don't you take a tone with me, Hero. I'll fire you in a quick second." She does not look at him this time. He understands suddenly that they are just words. It's just how she is. If she hadn't fired him by now…

"That's why you don't want any bulldozers, isn't it? You want someone to pick through everything. Piece by piece. Lookin' for salvage."

Dallas turns. Pushes past him without looking up. The brim of her hat hides her face. He imagines her expression as she walks away, out into the front clearing ringed by debris. He imagines the thoughts on the inside of that expression.

He watches her leaving.

She cannot talk about it, he realizes. She would rather walk away than talk about it. Why?

Why? It is the writer's question he hears over and over in his head. *Why?*

Suddenly the feeling is everywhere inside, like a Geiger counter passing over a vein of uranium. A sonar ping echoing away through a deep ocean, rebounding off an invisible shape in the dark. He always knows it when he hears it. Always. This was the thread to pull. *This,* whatever it meant, was the story.

She is outside the ring of debris now, moving towards the slope that connects to the swath of desert that leads to home. He wants her to stop. He reaches out with his voice, feeling no shame. Feeling only a shape in the dark. Feeling only hope.

"I hear you're planning on singing at the Moon Garden Festival."

She stops in her tracks. Turns. Marches back in his direction.

They meet in the middle.

"What did you say, Hero?" she asks. "Who told you that? *Who?*"

"Guy I know," he lies. "He heard it from someone who heard it from someone. People are talking. Hey, me? I think it's great."

"It's a goddamned *lie*. I'm done with that. You hear me?"

"Well don't get mad at *me*, Ms. Letti. I'm just telling you what I heard."

"I'm done with that."

"Okay. Okay. I'm just… *Jeez*. Did you tell someone you were going to the festival? Maybe that's how the rumor started."

"Not goin' to the goddamned festival."

"Not even to just, you know, eat cotton candy and listen to some good…"

She wheels on him.

"Not. Goin'. To. The. God. Damned…"

"Okay. Okay. I get it."

He looks down at the dirt. Her body casts a long shadow over a pile of pulverized drywall. He figures he has another second. Maybe two. He looks up.

"You know they're puttin' on a beauty pageant? Gonna name the first ever Corbin River Walk Queen. I think you'd make a good one. You should be the first. You're the most famous person this town's ever had. They should start with you, don'tcha' think?"

She blinks. There is an empty beat between them. Derailment by absurdity.

Then the beginnings of a smile. She tilts her head back, face to the only cloud in the sky, almost the color of strawberry. Sunlight splashes off the brim of her hat. She laughs.

Dallas Letti laughs.

"Hero, that'll be the day Hell has frozen over and the Devil takes up ice skatin' and makes himself a goddamned snow cone." Another laugh. Like she is exhaling an old breath. "That about the *dumbest* thing I ever heard in all of my years. Damn Moon Garden Festival bad enough all by itself. I am *not* puttin' my name on that mess. River Walk Queen? *River Walk Queen?* That's some shit, boy."

"Well, then how about we skip the stupid festival together? You and me. I'll come over after work and we can hang out and talk about whatever comes to mind."

"Talk?" Still in her frozen mirth. "What you and me got to talk about, Hero?"

"I dunno. Music maybe. Or what's wrong with the world today." He gestures at the dilapidation behind him. "Or this place."

Her expression slowly melts. The muscles in her face letting go of the strawberry cloud like it was a helium balloon.

"Y'ain't writin' a damn thing about me in your damn newspaper. Get that through your lil' head."

"I wasn't talking about writing anything. I was just talking about... about *talking*."

But she has already turned, walking, pulling her lengthening shadow away from him. It scrapes the top of a broken windowpane.

"Work to do, Hero. Best get to it."

* * *

"My name is Sarah and I am an alcoholic."

"Hi Sarah."

She's a talker, this one. Every meeting something new to say. Some looming new threat to a six-month sobriety. Before that she'd managed to put eight months behind her. Before that, seven. She's coming due. She's afraid to stop talking.

Elvis Broussard shifts in his chair. Sets his empty cup on the floor and crosses his arms. Elbows Davis in the shoulder.

Davis looks. Elvis tosses up an eyebrow. His way of asking if Davis plans on saying anything. Davis shakes his head. He is here to be counted, not heard. Not tonight.

He likes the weekend meetings better than weeknights, but Elvis had insisted. So he is here, shellacked in dried sweat and flecks of plaster and dirt. His muscles ache and his hands are raw from loading up Dallas Letti's truck. Heavier things this time. Chunks of wall and flooring. A bathtub. Hauling it all out to the landfill, and then unloading everything.

The ride to the dump had somehow made everything heavier. By the time he had returned Dallas' truck, collected his pay and reclaimed the Harley, it was past eight. No time to change clothes. He'd come straight to the meeting. Ten minutes late. Not that anyone cares.

Except Elvis, who had looked at his watch and pointedly not said anything. So, no. He is not interested in speaking. He is too tired to stand. His attention is elsewhere. It's in his back pocket with Conrad and Elizabeth. Out in the scrub with Dallas.

What was there to say anyway? He had been savagely beaten. He had been befriended. He had danced in the desert. He keeps busy during the day. He writes at night. He is still sober.

Was he tempted? No. Nothing to be tempted by. He thinks of booze like it's a poison gas. Sarin. Hydrogen cyanide. Like it might waft out of the *Lick-n-Tipple* as he passes by and slip into his lungs. So he just stays away from it. The Rivera party was tough. All night, Miguel diving into that cooler full of beer. But he had survived.

Sarah tortures a lock of brown hair with her fingers. Talks about her kids. She is worried for them. She's always had a man around to help put her back together. Now she's a single mom. What if something happens? What if she slips up? The *what ifs* keep her awake at night.

"I've decided I have to leave for the festival. I hate to do it. The kids will hate me for it. Everyone in their school is buzzing about it. And my friends all want to get together too. They're supportive, but they're all going to be drinking. I mean, Moon Garden *and* Day of the Dead? On the same damn weekend? What genius thought that one up? This place is going to be crazy and I just…"

She chokes up. Breaks off. Her hand worries around her nose and mouth. They all wait. Elvis crosses his legs.

"I just don't feel safe. I have to leave. I'm just going to put everyone in the car and drive. Just…" Her hand slices a path away from her rail-thin torso out over the rows of gray folding chairs. "Just drive."

It is a longer meeting. People want to talk. The coming festival is starting to change the barometric pressure inside their addictions. They can feel the clouds gathering. Uncertainty reigns.

The steps outside the church are dark. Only one of the lights beneath the eave is working. Davis leans against an iron rail watching the addicts shuffle past two-by-two, making their way to their cars. Some nod as they pass. Davis nods back. He waits for Elvis who is still inside. Holding his empty cup. Giving Sarah the advice she doesn't want to hear.

"You can't run away from it. You can't just get in a car and leave it behind. It loves a good chase. It's a beast, Sarah. It has a nose for blood and fear. And it damn well knows your name. You gotta sit still and look that fucker in the eye."

Eventually they emerge together, Sarah wiping her eyes. Elvis pats her shoulder. She waves goodnight. Davis raises a hand. Nods. They watch her leave.

"She's a mess," says Elvis, lighting a cigarette. He lets it out in a long white stream up into the light, scattering the bugs. "Storm is comin' in her life. You can feel it. She's goin' in again."

"Been there," says Davis. Elvis nods.

"*Mmm Hmm.* And you goin' again too."

"Me?"

Elvis nods. "You."

Davis shakes his head. "You're wrong. I'm done with that."

"Well." Elvis takes another drag. Lets it go. Bugs scatter.

"Well what?"

"You'll be done with it, Davis…" He turns. Points at him with his cigarette hand. "You'll be done with it when you realize that you're *never* done with it. Long as you think there is such a place as bein' done, bein' free, a place where you no longer have to be *you*, then you're goin' in again. Sure as shit. Sarah wants to get in a car and outrun herself and you want to pretend that you're not who you really are. Like the *Corbin*-Davis a different damn person than the *Houston*-Davis. Like you put on a little mask and pretend that the person in the mirror has his shit together. *Look at that handsome fuck in the mirror with his little mask. He ain't no alcoholic.* All of that leads to more misery, man."

"Nope."

"Yep. But, hey, you're right on schedule. That's the road to recovery. Be nice if we could avoid those potholes. Some do I guess. Most don't. I didn't. Thinkin' that way fucked me up for years."

"Elvis…"

Hand up. Head shaking.

"Don't Elvis me, boy. Take it or leave it. You think playing hide and seek with the bottle has fixed what's broken?" Elvis makes a face to answer his own question. "Listen. I'll be here to pick you up and dry you out and hear you tell me how right I am. Meantime, know this: You weren't born an alcoholic, but you sure as hell one now. Whatever happened between then and now, whatever fucked you up inside, is a part of who you are. You can't un-happen that shit. It's here to stay. Feel me? Best you can do is understand it. Make your peace with it. Forgive yourself. And then move on. Do the steps. Or don't do the steps. Whatever the fuck, man. But you can't ever stop bein' you. You gonna always stick to y'own self like skin. And when the shit gets bad, when that rain comes, and it *will* come, guess what you're gonna want to do? Only thing that can save you then is knowing who you really are and what your life is really all about."

Elvis leaves him on the steps of the church, shuffling across the dark parking lot to his truck. Davis watches him chug away, disappearing behind the mesquite on the corner. He pushes off from the railing. The letters in his back pocket crinkle. Words, typed and cursive, pass through each other in his head like smoke rings, linking and unlinking.

No. Not words. Voices.

He makes his way to the Harley, floating alone beneath the moon of a streetlamp above a dark gray sea of pavement.

* * *

The I-67 is full of trucks this time of night. Too many trucks. Like his old Harley is the coupling that connects boxcars in the middle of a Santa Fe freight train. Nothing to do about it. It's the fastest way home. He just wants to be in bed.

So he sticks it out.

He revs up. Passes a semi. Tucks back in line to get out of the way. Elvis is still in his head. *Whatever fucked you up inside is a part of who you are. You can't un-happen that shit.*

But not just Elvis. His mother is in there too. Like the letter in his back pocket has its own frequency, cutting in and out. *Davis is the only reason I'm still here. The only reason I'm still living. What is the thing you love most about this world, Elizabeth? Davis. My boy Davis. Davis. Davis. Davis. The spur. Up ahead. Here. Turn. Turn. Turn. Turn. Turn.*

He turns. He does not know why. He just does. He sees the sign and takes the exit. He reaches for the reason. *Why?* He just wants to stop. Too many trucks. They run in packs. He will let them pass. Why was he in such a hurry? He's in no hurry.

Out here it is still. Dark. No traffic. Only his small headlamp washing over the low scrub, like he is in a submersible exploring a trench, revealing an ocean floor a few feet at a time. The highway whine recedes beneath his singular rumble. Desert stars spill out ahead. Blue phosphorescent algae washed up on a black sand beach.

It's everywhere. *Everywhere.*

He wants to stop. Wants silence. Stillness. He keeps riding. He doesn't know why. He just does. There is an ever-greater stillness ahead. It pulls him forward. He is not pushing. He is being pulled. He is falling.

Davis is the thing I love most in the world.

There is a shape in the dark. Solid. Large. A faint glint of metal or glass. He slows, not knowing. His headlamp peels back the night tarpaulin as he passes. He keeps riding, examining the image in his head as it resolves.

A shape.

A car on the shoulder.

Something on the hood.

A body.

He keeps riding. Passes it. Replays the image.

A shape in the dark. A shape on a shape. *A body.*

He stops the Harley. Thinks. Turns around. Stares back into the starry void. The dark lies heavy over the road.

Then forward. Slowly. Slowly.

The body is rising as he approaches, propping itself up against the windshield. He pulls up alongside and stops. Plants both of his boots on the pavement.

"Everything okay?" he asks.

"Yeah," says Olivia DeLuna. "I'm good."

He is stunned to know the name of this shape on the road. Stunned to know her face. The scars, like a kind of relief map. He can see her in the doorway of *Pepita's*, light exploding around her. He can see her in the doorway at *Libby's Nuts*, the day of the accident. An hour before the wreckage he had never actually seen. Shortly before he was arrested for solicitation.

"Oh she real nice. An' she off the damn menu. Ain't tellin' you shit 'bout Olivia. She private as can be."

Her expression is now tense with the uncertainty of this moment. Uncertainty about *him*. She is ready to roll off the hood and dive into the car. She is ready to flee out into the desert. She is ready to use whatever weapon is within reach.

"You sure you don't need any help?"

"Just want to be alone."

She reclines against the glass, pulling her face out of the wash of light. She returns her gaze skyward in a show of unconcern.

But her fist is still in a ball against the hood. She is waiting.

It occurs to him, suddenly, like a kick in the head, that *this* is the road. *This* is the spot. The blood has faded to invisibility, but her DNA is smeared across the surface of this strip of pavement.

He wants to make the connection for her. Tell her his name. *Davis Payne.* Wants her to believe the *Chacha's* mistake. Wants all of that to be real.

Elvis, suddenly: *Look at that handsome fuck in the mirror with his little mask.*

"I... I know your friend," he says. "Libby." He can see her body take the sound of that name. "Libby Holder?"

Olivia turns her head, looking with new eyes. She sits upright. Studies him.

"You're... the writer?"

"Yeah. I'm Davis. I'm interviewing her. You're Olivia, right?"

"Yeah. Man... what a..." She doesn't finish.

"Right?" He laughs a little. "What are the odds? Small world I guess."

"Yeah, I guess so."

Neither of them speaks. The moment elongates. Floats inside the bubble of light. Rises for the surface.

"Well, look, I don't mean to intrude. Just wanted to make sure everything was okay here."

"No, no, it's fine. Yeah, everything's good."

"You feel safe out here?"

She nods. "Do it all the time."

"Peaceful."

"Yeah."

The awkwardness grows heavy, like a sudden humidity. For it is surely less peaceful out here with an idling Harley.

There is movement ahead of him, toward the freeway. They both look. Headlights. He has maybe a minute before he will have to move. Or move on. He does not choose his words. It's like they are chosen for him.

"Not gonna to be so peaceful come the festival," he says. Then he corrects. "*Festivals*, I should say."

There is something like a laugh from the hood.

"Got that right."

"You goin'?" He has no idea what he is saying. She rolls her face his direction.

"Not even if my life depended on it," she says.

"Me neither."

"Already can't wait 'til it's over and done."

"Me too."

They both laugh a little. And look. Headlights. Like eyes in the dark.

"Alright then. Olivia. I look forward to *not* seein' you at the festivals."

He throttles up. Moves forward. Inches. Then feet. The coming headlights, like a white leviathan swallowing everything. If she speaks, the sound of her is lost.

So he is left to imagine.

Davis is the thing I love most in the world.

Chapter 54
Dallas and Etta

Dear Pablo:

If you are reading these words, well then that means you opened the envelope without tearing it into pieces. It means I sent it to you without tearing it up my own self. I may regret sending it and you may yet regret reading on. I don't know. I hope not. But Lord knows I am not a writer of letters. If you made it this far, then I'm grateful. It's still morning so maybe this'll read like it's a sane person who wrote it. I'll be drunk as a skunk long before the sun goes down. I'm most likely to rip it up and go on to bed. Guess we'll see.

Been a lot of years, Pablo. Long time since we spoke. That last time was more yelling then speaking. We said some words, didn't we? I know you don't think of me as a friend. Probably hate me for what I did. Or maybe you don't care enough any more. Hating takes energy. Does for me anyway. People think I'm full of hate. But I don't hate other people. I can't think of a single person I hate. I save it all for myself. I don't spread the hate around. I don't share that shit. I hold the hate close. Maybe that makes me greedy. Maybe the hate for me ain't worth your energy. Don't know. But let me just say, Pablo, that I consider you my oldest friend. Not because we like each other. I guess we don't. But it's because you are the oldest best memory I still have in my head. The memory is more about me than about you. Like any memory, I guess. But you're the one I see inside that memory when I close my eyes.

This is the memory. *Mother Blues* at about nine o'clock. I'm up on that little wooden stage. Blue lights in my eyes. Place is packed. Like always. Smells like tobacco and weed and sweat and liquor. Barbeque tang coming in from out back. Candles on those six tables up front. Pool balls clicking off in the corner under the glow of that big ass Michelob lamp. Headlights passing to and fro in the dark out the window. Men leaning back against the brass rail of that raggedy bar, drinking and talking sideways at each other as they look at me on that stage. No doubt sayin things that would shock their wives and mothers.

Place really held on to the sound, Pablo. Held the sound in its arms like it was a baby. Cradled it. Oh, I could rattle that room. Not saying I couldn't. I could shake it like a can of hot beer. I could blow the windows out into the street. You know I could. And I did too. But it's the slow, deep tunes I remember most at *Mother's*. Like dropping into a lake from the top of July. Make everybody heartsick. See all them heads shaking. People cryin. Make them all remember what they've lost. What they want from the world that the world won't give up. I'm not telling you anything you don't know.

Anyway. The memory. There I am. I look out over all of those faces and your handsome mug is right there in the middle. You always liked to be right in the thick of it. Like you were just one of the regular customers. You said you needed to check the sound balance. Which was always horseshit, Pablo. You just like being in the middle. You like surrounding yourself with other people. You like being up in their business like the whole world is your family and you have an equal say. Balancing the sound, my black ass.

But looking at you was how I checked *my* sound, Pablo. I could always see my voice on your face. Or imagine it. Little Etta sittin right next to you drinkin her soda. Like you were her daddy. Made me feel beautiful when I looked out at you, Pablo, lookin back up at me. Felt like something special. I was so young. No idea what was coming. No idea I would be packing auditoriums and cuttin albums. As far as I knew it would never get any better than singing in your little blues joint. In a lot of ways it never did get any better than that. More than a few things got a whole lot worse.

So why in the hell am I writing to you? That's what you're askin. Good question. I'll try to answer best I can. If you've made it this far, you may as well go the distance. Don't rip me up yet. If I didn't then you shouldn't either. Let's just see.

I got this young guy coming up to the house a few times a week. Wears a damn ponytail. Rides a motorcycle. But he's nice enough. Good lookin thing. You've never been up to my place since I got back to Texas. I never invited and you'd never have come anyway. I bought a house that's about half way between Corbin and Fort Stockton. Middle of nowhere. Also bought me some land about a mile north. A few acres of nothing with a house on it. A fire destroyed the house years before I came back. It's just sitting up there in the desert a black, broken shambles. Just like me.

Anyway, I hired this kid to tear it all down and haul it away. We were up there the other day looking at the wreckage and this kid says he wants to write my story. Ain't the first time either. He's been at me for awhile. He writes for some magazine in Houston. You can imagine what I told him. Or maybe you can't imagine. Maybe you think I'm still a whore for the publicity. Well I'm not. Been a whore for too long. Publicity. Drugs. Love. Done a lot of whoring in my life, Pablo. Don't need to tell you. But all I want now is to be left alone. So I told the kid where he could stick his questions. Then he tells me that people are talking about me singing at the Moon Garden Festival, which is a load of shit. Can you imagine? At my age and stage? Then he tells me that I should enter the pageant and be the first *Moon Garden Queen*! Can you even believe? They'd all be screaming for the exits. Can you see me in me in a damned swimsuit?

Not much funny in this letter, Pablo, so I hope the vision of me wearin a beauty queen sash over my mostly naked, shriveled up body trippin over my four inch heels put a smile on your saggy old puss. Laugh while you can. Anyway, the boy is pretty enough to look at but he's as dumb as a rake if he thinks I can't see him tryin to flatter me into telling him my story.

But it got me to thinking. Maybe I need to tell somebody. Maybe it would be a good thing. Unburden myself. Not to a stranger. Some ponytailed writer I don't know? Chicken shit way out if there ever was one. You're the one I need to tell my story to, Pablo. Not the whole story. Wouldn't want you to kill yourself having to read the whole thing. But there's one small part of it that would be good to tell you. Because you're my oldest friend. And because you already know most of it anyway.

And because Etta thinks of you like a father. Least she did. Maybe you two had a falling out. Maybe she hasn't spoken to you in donkey's years either. Maybe she's cut us both loose forever. If so, then I'm sorry. That means maybe you have the same kind of broken heart that I do.

But she used to, Pablo. She used to think of you like her daddy. On the ride home from the club every hot night of those few months she'd squeeze up next to me in the front seat, then she'd scooch down and put her head in my lap, and we'd sing together —she liked all the old timey music, Bessie and Ma and Mamie and Blind Willie and all the old gospels too —and I'd stroke her little head as I drove that piece of shit car all the way back to Corbin. Open up the window and have me a smoke every few miles just to stay awake and on my side of the road. And every trip she'd lift her head and look up at me and ask why couldn't you be her daddy. Every trip. Probably asked you the same thing herself once or twice.

I'd tell her it was because you only have one mamma and one daddy as God intended and everybody else has to be somebody else. Just the way it is. She'd lay her head back down on my leg and we'd start another song. But I could feel her thinking.

So if I'm going to tell any part of my story, even just this one little bit, it has to be to you. Because most of what I have to say is about Etta. And because forgiveness is cheap and easy from strangers. I need to tell someone who knows enough about all the shit of my life to withhold forgiveness. I don't want forgiveness Pablo. I'm counting on you to read this pitiful mess, if I ever send it to you, and to know better than to think something soft and stupid like I was just trying to do my best. Or I got confused because of the drugs. Or the fame. Or I'm really a good person deep down. None of that is true. I'm counting on you to read it and *not* let me escape. To hold my face down in the shitty stink of what I've done and who I am. And I'm counting on you to share it with Etta. God help me, Pablo, but that is what I want. I almost change my mind as I write those words.

But it's the coward's way to hide in shame. Better to stand out in the cold light and take it. So that's why I'm writing you a letter that I may or may not have the courage to send. I don't want to die a coward.

Oops. There it is. In ink too. Can't erase it. Guess that's why people do their computer mail. I don't hate people but I do hate computers. Wouldn't own one of those contraptions for a million dollars. But if I wasn't writing this long hand, I bet I'd have erased that last part. Deleted I mean. In case you haven't figured it out, the drinking part of this letter has already started. Can tell already this is going to take more than one session.

Anyway, it's true I am a dead woman walking, Pablo. Dead woman writing. Going to be riding that black coach of sorrow that Billie Holiday sings about in *Gloomy Sunday*. Don't know when exactly. But the black coach is coming. I can hear it. I can feel it rolling my way, rocks breaking beneath them iron wheels. I guess Billie would know too, wouldn't she? I was having these terrible headaches. For the longest time I just blamed it on the booze. Then I started passing out even when I wasn't drinking. Then the hallucinations. Seein things. Hearin things. And I thought, Dallas, you have so completely pickled your brain over the years that you have crossed a line into some kind of constant *shitfacedness* if that's a word.

But no. Doctors in San Angelo tell me ain't nothin to do with the hooch. Got a tumor in my brain, Pablo. Big old long name I can't spell. Not a thing I can do either. They got all kinds of things they want to try. Doctors. They just want to play with me like a rat in a cage while I'm still living. And not a one of them looks old enough to buy a beer. Well, point is they can't get the thing out. That's the bottom line. It's growing and they can't get it out. I can see in their faces that everything else is just something to pass the time. Just a way to play doctor, and not the good kind of playin doctor either.

So if I'm going to get anything off my mind, the time is now. Guess I'm still a coward for not just tracking you down and callin you up on the phone. Probably wouldn't talk to me anyway. Same if I tracked down Etta. She'd run me down in the street before she heard a single word from my lips. So then maybe this is the only way to go. Write you a damned letter. In pen so I can't take anything back. Guess we'll see.

Chapter 55

She needs to buy a good pillow. Maybe two.

The old sofa cushion is like a fuzzy sheet of cardboard. A poor substitute for an actual seat. She hurts enough as it is.

Olivia opens the door. It groans and pops loudly on its hinge. Once. Twice. Always twice. Always upon opening. Never closing. She steps out onto the parking lot. Looks at her phone. Ten-thirty. She slams the door. The window inside rattles.

A petite, brittle blonde in yellow silk and gold bangles approaches a nearby Range Rover. Shopping bags in one hand. *Macy's. Victoria's Secret.* Seven-year old Mini-Me in the other hand.

Mini-Me wants ice cream. Doesn't really care about spoiling her lunch. Wants to ride on one of the river barges. Wants to eat ice cream on a barge. She and Daddy *always* eat ice cream on a barge.

Because *Daddy* loves her.

Olivia turns and stretches against Jesús Batista's shit-brown Falcon, pressing against the door with her abdomen and pushing her hands up over the car into the robin's egg sky. The top of the car is too hot to touch. She wants to curl up in the shade of the backseat and go to sleep.

She reaches inside the window for a cigarette and lighter. Turns. Leans back against the door and watches Mini-Me play the guilt riff like a bottleneck slide on a steel guitar.

"How come you don't love me as much as Daddy does?"

"I love you just as much, Honey. I'm the one that stayed, remember? I'm your mother. It's all on me. *Me.* Get it? So stop your whining and get in the damn car."

"I'm telling Daddy you cussed."

"Get in the car."

"And he's gonna tell Pastor Blake."

"Get in the damn car. Now."

There is a harsh exchange inside the Range Rover that Olivia cannot hear. The thing roars to life. Lurches forward with a screech.

She watches it go. Puts the cigarette to her lips. Almost lights it. Sighs. Tosses the lighter back through the window onto the sofa cushion pretending to be a seat.

She doesn't want smoke on her breath. Not today.

Sheldon tolerates it, but she's pretty sure he hates it.

She plucks out the cigarette. Examines the lipstick. Tosses it in the front seat with the lighter. Looks at her phone. Ten thirty-two.

He had not explained the change of routine. *I'm paying the money, so I'm calling the tune. No more questions. Be there at 10:30.*

Just as well. Or should have been. She'd worked at *Papi's* last night. So that had put her in Austin, a damn-sight closer than Corbin. Only ninety minutes. May as well start early.

But then she had not expected having to work at *Papi's* until two-thirty in the morning. And she had not expected *Drifter Jack's* to be so full of lodgers. Or the sounds of snoring, fucking and muffled sobbing assaulting her in the dark all night long from different directions. Three hours of sleep was a generous estimate. Getting herself ready and on the road by nine had been a challenge.

Getting ready. One part showering, one part dressing, ninety-eight parts putting on makeup at a dirty bathroom sink as a girl named Silvia vomited repeatedly in one of the stalls behind her.

"Fuckin' Brian." A gasping whisper after each heave. *"Fuckin' Brian."*

"You okay?"

No answer from the stall. Another wretch.

"He's just fuckin' lucky I'm not fuckin' pregnant. That's all I can s…"

"You okay?"

"Don't even know what my mom fuckin' sees in him. I mean what the fuck? He manages a fuckin' Burger King. They fuckin' deserve each other. And you can't kick me out if I've already fuckin' left. Like a fuckin' month ago."

Olivia hadn't worn makeup for a month. Not since the last time she'd met Sheldon. She hated the feel of it every bit as much as she had last month. But she hated even more the idea of seeing him without it.

Which was curious. She should want those scars, those claw marks of fate, to be in his face as much as possible. She should want him to be uncomfortable. *Look at what you have done. Shame on you.*

Except that wasn't the game now was it? The game now was different. The oldest game there was.

It just didn't feel like a game.

Sylvia had staggered backwards out of the stall to stick her face under a faucet. A barely-legal dirty blonde with a purple streak, wearing only panties and a bra.

Probably her father's eyes and her mother's name. Drunk as a skunk.

"Fuckin' Brian. Fuckin'…" Sylvia had looked up. They'd connected in the mirror. *"Damn, girl. What the fuck happened to you?"*

Olivia looks at her phone. Ten thirty-five. She rethinks the cigarette. Turns to reach inside the window. Stops. Sheldon's car is making its way across the lot like a little silver bullet. To her that car will always be the last thing she had seen, right before the world spun out from beneath her. It is the gleaming image in her consciousness that abuts chaos and pain. The last thing she had seen in that split-second before everything changed.

Well. The second-to-last thing she had seen.

But she doesn't like to think about that.

Sheldon rolls to a stop. Looks up at her. Pulls his sunglasses down with a finger. Smiles.

"Wow. You look… amazing."

"Thanks."

"Hop in."

Her face is distrusting.

"Where we goin'?"

"Surprise. Hop in."

He reaches into his sport coat. Drops a fat white envelope onto the passenger seat. She climbs in and closes the door. Puts the envelope in her purse.

It's fatter. Heavier than the others. She doesn't need to fan the bills like they do in the movies. She can tell.

They head north. Up the 281. The little car cuts through the hot air. Doesn't smell as much like desert breath. Never does north of San Antonio. Not like Corbin. Big, sprawling mesquites slip past on either side, rising up between the houses. All of the branches seem to like each other up here. They stick together like families should, unlike their rangy southern cousins.

And they keep coming, one after the other, like they aspire to make a big green leafy fence.

The air bends around the convertible. Her hair barely moves. She unfolds her right arm. Opens her hand. Like she is brushing her fingertips across the face of a waterfall.

"Want me to put the top up?"

"What?"

"Put on the air?"

"No."

They ride in silence, mostly. Not awkwardness. They are past that. Past the nervous prattle. They are in something together now. Whatever that is. They are both inside of it and moving. It is the intimacy of 'not talking' that she feels. He does too, she guesses. Not an intimacy that has been earned. Not yet. They are ahead of themselves. She has not kissed him. He has not touched her in that way. Not yet.

But here they are anyway. Together. Not talking.

Like old lovers.

Sheldon passes a semi. Pokes at the dashboard. An old Victoria Spivey tune sticks a steel blade into the tunnel of wind, carving lyrics like a kind of sonic graffiti. Victoria don't trust nobody. Not even her own mother. Just the good Lord, above, she sings. *People just love you 'til you spend all yo' dough. Once they get what they want, they just don't love you no mo'.*

Sheldon shakes his head to that pitiful state of affairs.

Olivia looks at him. Watching. He can only hold it but so long. Then he breaks, smiling. Playful. Mischievous. Looking innocently off into the distance. She laughs in spite of herself.

"You can be a real shit, you know that, Shel?"

He feigns protest. Eyes wide, mouth open. Looks at her aghast.

"Oh, right," she says. Laughing. Pulling her fingers through her hair. "Fuck you."

"Not a Victoria Spivey fan, eh? Good ol' Houston gal like her?" He shakes his head. "I'm disappointed, Olivia. I truly am."

Victoria sings on about leaving the country. Crossing that deep, blue sea. Sheldon sings along, blowing the lyrics out into the wind. *Friendship will never travel that long, long trail. Because you fool with Mama's money and off you go to jail.*

"You're an ass," Olivia laughs. "But you do know your blues divas. I'll give you that." She nods, as much to herself as to him. "I respect that in any man."

It is not until they cross the Guadalupe and head east on the 306 that she realizes where he is taking her.

"Really?"

"What."

"Canyon Lake?"

He smiles. Shrugs like it is all a mystery to him too.

Another fifteen minutes and they are pulling into a dusty lot in front of a two-story building. Yellow painted brick on the bottom. Dark wood siding with aqua trim and shutters on top. All beneath a roof of corrugated metal. A low brick wall separates the parking lot from a small green lawn. A palm-lined walkway leads off to a chalk sandwich board trimmed in turquoise.

Sheldon parks beneath the sign. *Baja BBQ Shack. Canyon Lake, Texas.*

In the background, off behind the building, filling in all of the empty spaces between piling and palm, lawn and roofline, sign and sandwich board, is an expanse of shimmering liquid blue. Sheldon climbs out. Stretches.

"Hope you're hungry."

The server seats them on a large wooden patio, beneath a miniature version of the same metal roof. The table is in the corner near the railing overlooking the Canyon Lake Marina. Long grey piers stripe the near shore of the lake. Sailboats sunning in their slips. The water is soaked with sky.

They are alone in their cozy corner neighborhood. There are others here, dining in threes and fours, but not nearby. Off to their right is a flange jutting out from the rest of the patio. Three microphone stands. Stools. Speakers. Garlands of glass beads along the roofline fracture the sunlight into arrows of color that dart through sprays of palm.

A woman perches on one of the stools hunched over a battered Gibson. Sixties. Weathered. She has dirty gray hair that spills out from beneath a black baseball cap. She shakes her head in pitiful commiseration with someone. Probably BB King. Nobody loves her, she sings. Just her mother. And there's no tellin' about her either.

They order salads and barbeque plates. Olivia a beer. Sheldon a Texarita. They sit and listen and applaud. The woman nods. Tips her hat.

"Anyone out there like Bonnie Raitt? Linda Ronstadt? Alright then."

She starts in on the song about a woman named Louise.

The drinks arrive. Sheldon holds out his frozen green glass. Olivia lifts her bottle.

"To what?"

He smiles.

"I don't know. To us. To *this*. To somethin' different."

He drinks. She watches him. Glances out at the boats. Then she drinks too. He licks the salt off his lips. Holds out the glass again.

"Mmm. Here. Try this."

She smiles a little. Shakes her head.

"Me and tequila…" She doesn't finish.

"Trouble keeping it down?"

"Trouble stopping."

He nods at her bottle. "But beer…"

"We have an understanding, me and the beer."

"Oh?"

"We like each other enough to be *amigos*. Nothing more. We know when to leave it alone. But tequila's got only one thing on its mind. Tequila don't play by the rules."

"Ahh. So there are rules."

She smiles. Drinks deeply this time. This is not what she wants. Games aside. Calculated pretense aside. Unusually fat envelopes of money aside. *Papi's* aside. This is not what she wants.

But the flirtatious patter is irresistible.

"Oh, there's always rules, Shel." Closes her lips over the bottle. Drinks. "There's always rules."

It's not made up of words, this thing happening between them. She knows.

It's a beat. A very slow rhythm. A tree branch in the wind, knocking up against the house. Gnarled knuckles against the face of a beat-up six-string. Weathered shoe leather keeping time against a dirty floor. It's a groove on a record, pulling the needle of conversation ever inward. Ever down into that old feeling. Into the dark lust of the raw, uncontrolled moment. Somewhere down there, beneath her, just follow the beat, all is molten and she is nobody.

Down there she is less than nobody. She is food for a beast. She knows.

"I see," he says. The smile. The sideways glance. Eyes back to her. "And just what are your rules, Olivia?"

Were she to tell him the truth, she would say that there are only two rules. One for him. One for her. The rule for him is the one that applies to just about everyone else on the planet: *leave me the fuck alone.*

The rule for her: *trust no one.*

But she does not tell him the truth. All she has for him is the next downbeat in the dark rhythm that will not quit.

"My rule is simple." She drinks. Leans in. Tucks her long dark hair behind her ear with two fingers. The leather bracelets on her wrist slip a little down towards her elbow. She can see his eyes move. Linger. He sees the scars. Not the new ones. The old ones. The tiny ones. She lowers her arm to the table, wrist down.

"And what rule is that?"

She slips him a sideways smile.

"Don't disappoint me."

She can see that he wants to say something. Do something. Take the next step. His eyes are quiet but restless. There is a familiar vibration in her stomach. A buzzing, as if from some cockpit instrument that registers sudden changes in topography. A vibration that defines the edge of a cliff. The talent on the stool channels Bonnie Raitt. Sings about Louise coming home on the mail train. Ugly end for Louise. How it goes for girls like her. Too bad.

She is rescued by the server with plates of barbequed beef. The act of eating and reordering dilutes the moment enough to escape its grip. She reaches for the only thing she can think of, a branch of words shaped like a question, trying to pull herself up out of the groove onto dry land.

"So how's the wife?"

It registers on his face. Too abrupt. Too fraught with meaning. Not what he wants to talk about. So she feels better.

The woman in the cap takes a sudden liking to Willie Nelson. Mamas and cowboys. Sheldon chews as he thinks.

"She's definitely sleeping with this guy," he says to his plate. "Nearly caught them in the act about ten days ago. I came home early. They were both upstairs. She was in the shower."

"Did you call her on it?"

"No."

"Why the hell not? Wait. Let me guess. *It's complicated.*"

Sheldon gives an apologetic smile. Nods. A motor surges down on the lake. He looks up. Then back. Nods again.

"So, what, you're just going to let it go? You're not going to do *anything*?"

"Didn't say that. I will. I am."

"Good. What are you doing?"

But then she knows what he is doing. She thinks of that envelope nestled too heavily in her purse. And suddenly she knows.

He's going to bleed the business. For her. Before everything in his life goes to shit. Libby was right. He'll do anything.

Great forces collide inside of her, struggling to plant a flag in her heart. Her hope and her shame are evenly matched. She focuses on her food. Swallows. Drinks. Such invisible drama.

"I'd rather talk about you," he says. She shakes her head.

"My least favorite subject. If Christi was in the shower, what was he doing? What's his name again?"

"Nicholas. He was down the hall in my study pretending to use my fax machine." There is a flicker in his eyes. Something new. An escape from the subject of his wife. He puts down his Texarita. "Can I ask you something?"

She shrugs.

"Has Libby ever talked to you about selling her property?"

She shakes her head. "You lookin' to buy a whore house on a nut farm?"

"No. Is that the kind of thing she'd normally talk to you about? I mean is that somethin' you'd know? If she'd sold it to someone?"

"Not many secrets between me and Libby. Why are you asking me these questions, Sheldon?"

His glass is empty. He drinks anyway. Looks around for the server. Waves his glass in the air.

"The Corbin Redevelopment Project. Sometimes I get... I'm not directly involved in any of the real estate sales... that's all handled through Quinco..." he flicks his fingers. *Out there. Far away places.* "But sometimes I get information. I saw something once..." He stops, stuck in the mud of his own story. Sighs. "This is so inappropriate."

"Sheldon." Sideways smile. "Ain't a thing about us that's appropriate."

She thinks it is the word '*us*' that gets him unstuck. He sighs.

"I saw something once. A list of properties. It showed that Libby had sold her property to one of the CDC subsidiaries. House. Orchard. All of it. And when I went out there... that first time... before anything else, you know... *happened...* I asked Libby about it and she denied that she'd sold anything to anyone."

"Well we're still living there, aren't we?"

"Yeah. You sure are."

"So then your information is wrong."

"Right. The list is wrong. Or, well, the list was probably right but it was probably just an old list of target properties and not a list of acquired properties."

"So then what's the problem? I'm not..."

"Problem is that Libby told me she'd never even been *approached* about selling. If her property had been targeted, she'd have been approached. They'd have made her an offer. Seems to me."

The server drops off another round. Olivia waits for her to leave.

"She probably didn't like the idea of givin' you information about who she's been talkin' to about what. Libby's like that. Prob'ly ended up... *entertainin'* the person who was doin' the asking."

He nods too readily at the euphemism. *Liberty Cherish. The 'entertainer'.*

"Just like she entertained you," she adds. Watches him blush. "Libby don't talk about her business."

"That's what I thought. That's what I assumed. Prob'ly what it is. They tried, she declined. The property maps are just wrong."

He is quiet. Thinking.

"But?"

"Nothin'," he says.

"Clearly something."

"No... I saw Nicholas holding a photograph of Libby's house. Your house."

"*Nicholas*-Nicholas? *That* Nicholas?"

Sheldon pushes back his plate. Drinks. Nods. "*That* Nicholas."

"Why would he have a..."

"I don't know," he says. "Maybe... I don't know."

"What."

"Maybe that article in the *Chacha* –the one about me –has finally made its way to the Quinco home office. I know that sounds paranoid."

"And so what? They're... *investigating?* What do they care?"

"My father-in-law insists that these people will cut loose anyone associated with scandal. Image is everything. Squeaky-clean. They severed ties with another Houston real estate firm when a vice president was arrested on charges of domestic assault. And he wasn't even working on the account. 'Course, he put the poor woman into a coma. And the coverage was pretty colorful. But still."

"When did that happen?"

"Three years ago maybe."

"This project's that old?"

He nods. "The publicity phase you're seeing is just the tip of the iceberg. They've been at this for years."

"So you think... The article comes out and..."

"Look. I'm not tryin' to be all self-important or anything. But I'm the owner of the ad agency in charge of spreadin' the gospel about the largest development project ever to hit south Texas."

He opens his hands at something self-evident.

She finishes her beer.

"Or maybe I'm just a paranoid fool."

From the dock, the sun on the lake is so bright she cannot even look at the water. But she can sense it. Smell it. Wet sunlight has a smell. She is porous. It finds its way in, filling her.

Sheldon walks back from the rental office. Behind him a man in a red shirt and a beard points to the end of the second pier. Sheldon looks back. Nods. Waves.

"Which one?" she asks when he reaches her.

He points. It's blue and three times larger than they need. It reminds her of the River Walk barges. She guesses that is the point.

"Pontoon boat," he says, taking her hand. They walk the rest of the way together.

The starboard cushion is hers. She is fully reclined in the sun. Shoes off. Eyes closed. Sheldon cuts the engine somewhere near dead center. The boat slides into quiet, slipping beneath the faint, distant drones of other boats.

Sheldon rattles on about the Corbin makeover plan. She has come to like the sound of his voice. Not the words. She discards the words like peanut shells. Just the sound, carrying a scent of the shore misting over the water.

She imagines the hidden topography. The canyon beneath her. Imagines her suspension above the deepest point. Imagines the distance a stone would have to fall to find the bottom. In her mind, it never does find the bottom. It just keeps falling, punching through watery ribbons of light. The farther it falls, the greater her sense of suspension.

Floating.

Weightless in the world.

Happy.

Not happy. Wrong word.

Relieved. Sheltered. Like she has found a patch of shade in the desert. There is water in the shade. Just enough water. For this moment, just enough.

And the reception out here is good. She can find the melody without any effort. More like it finds her. Like a breeze. The words are scudding clouds.

Mother Ocean. Mother Ocean. Your sorrow so deep.
Your children have floated astray.
Down in green coffers
Such mem'ries you keep
Are you sorry you sent them away?

Sheldon is above her. She opens her eyes.
"You were sleeping."
"What? No…"
"A good ten minutes."
"You were talking. About the pageant."
"Not for awhile now." He smiles. "You looked peaceful. Beautiful."
He sits at the end of the cushioned bench, pressing his leg against the soles of her bare feet. Lays his hand against the angry welt disappearing up into her pant leg. Brushes it with his thumb. She could respond in any number of ways. She does nothing. He speaks, as if to the scar.
"I'm sorry. Olivia. It was a reckless way to get your attention. You didn't deserve this. I was angry. Afraid. Possessed. I think you're a good person."
She cannot say what she wants to say. Not now. Too much has happened now to untangle the accident. So she doesn't. Instead:
"Then you don't really know me. I'm not who you think I am."
He moves his hand to rest on the top of her foot. His palm is smooth. Soft.
"I know you're smart. That you've got music in your soul. That you're stunning."
Libby is suddenly in her head. *What I tell you, baby? Massage-massage-all-the-way-married in love all the way up to his pretty 'lil nose. He 'bout to start speakin' in tongues or some shit. He do anything fo' you now. He set his lily white ass on fire an' run 'round singin' Dixie if that what it take. You gots 'im by the pecans, baby.*
She hates herself.
"You're one for three, Sheldon."
"I'm three for three and you know it. Scars and all."
She reacts to that, muscles everywhere clenching a little. He sees it.
"I'm sorry. I didn't mean… Point is I don't care about any of that. You're an amazing person. You should be the first Corbin River Walk Queen."
She lifts her head to look at him with an expression of horror. Lays it back down on the cushion, still feeling his hand.
"What. I'd vote for you."
The laughter –hers, then his –takes flight. Combines in the air. Sails out over

the water. To others it is the cry of some exotic bird, coming from everywhere and nowhere. Or it is the sound of cold dark water stirring in this cup of granite, the song of this tiny inland sea.

It is nearly three when they bring in the boat. Sheldon is preoccupied with the story he will need to cook up for his wife. He says Christi is expecting him for some benefit dinner that he will now not be able to attend. He ties up the boat and extends a hand. Helps her up onto the pier. She wants to groan at the pain in her leg.

"I'll just tell her the meeting ran long," he says. "She knows I'm in San Antonio, so…"

"This feels like an affair," she says, eyes impatient, letting go of his hand. "Is that what this is? Lyin' to her to be with me? That what this is for you?"

He puts his hands on his hips. Stares for a second down at the pier. Looks up. "Is that what you want it to be?" he asks. "An affair?"

"That ain't me, Shel. I don't like affairs. Lovers. All of *that*. I'm not an affair person. Hell, I'm not even a *people* person. Can't trust a one of 'em. Give me a good dog any day of the week. As fucked up as affairs are, I'm too fucked up for an affair. And I don't want to hate myself more'n I already do."

Sheldon shakes his head. Laughs a little. Like that might cover up his disappointment.

"What then? It's about more than the money, Olivia. Isn't it? I mean…" He spreads his arms a little, Canyon Lake swallowing up the background.

"I don't know," she says.

"This has to be about more than money. What are we sharing here?"

The invisible chasm beneath them waits. Silent. Expectant. Dark water stirring unseen.

"Music," she says quietly. She turns and heads for the shore. "Let's make this about the blues. Let's share that."

She limps past an attendant in a *Canyon Lake Marina* baseball hat. She can hear him asking Sheldon about the boat. She keeps walking. At the top of the pier, leaning up against the corner of the rental office is the man in the red shirt and the beard that had first pointed the way to the boat.

"How was it?" he asks, painting her with his eyes. Taking her in.

"Like Heaven." She smiles a little. Keeps walking. Red shirt says something *sotto voce* with a breathy laugh.

There are two of them, she realizes, as she clears the corner of the office. Another man is there, back turned to her. He is bent in half, tying his shoe. Fine blond hair obscuring his face.

Chapter 56
Mable and Libby

"'Cause I'm the ABC man, is why. I'm all the schoolin' she'll ever need, baby."

"Don'chu you *baby* me."

"I never went to no school. Don't need it."

"Antoine, now you listen to me. I'm her mama. I say if she go to school. *Me.* Not you. You can't just pick her up an' take her away. School call my work in the middle of the day an' say *what the fuck, Mable?* Only I don't got no phone at work so that mean they callin' my boss an' he got to come up an' find me and pull me out one of the rooms so I can come downstairs and call the school back so they can ask me what-the-fuck *di-*rectly."

Antoine had let slip a small laugh. Shook his head. *All that commotion over little ol' me.* Didn't say that, exactly. But that's what was on his face just before he stuck a bottle in it and sucked down the last of his beer as Mable watched. Not his beer. *Her* beer. Out of *her* fridge.

He had a triangular head. Wide set eyes, like green olives floating in pools of dirty milk. Narrow, dimpled chin. His hair was a soiled mop of sandy corkscrew curls that he wore too long and never washed. He also never smiled much, which was a good thing. His teeth were all there but they were dingy and crooked. There was a lot to get past to find the charming center of Antoine Beaudaine Cherish, but it was in there someplace. And he knew how to dip into it if ever he needed. Confidence was part of it. People are always drawn to confidence.

Antoine had put the bottle on the table with a *thunk*. Leaned back in his chair. Crossed his arms.

"Go on Mable. Say what you got to say."

Mable had turned back to the sink and resumed scrubbing his plate, deciding that the conversation was pointless. Knowing the look on his face and deciding that she did not have the energy. Then changed her mind.

"I'm sayin' she need to be in school. She fifteen an' she need her some friends."

425

"I'm her friend. I'm her best friend."

"No. Antoine. You ain't. And she got to learn."

"I teach her what she need."

"Like what, exactly? How to drive round emptyin' one shitty seppic tank afta' anotha'?"

"Sep-tic. *Septic*. How many times I got to say it, Mable? Goddamn, but you the one need some schoolin'. Look. If Libby don't want to be there, then she ain't gon' learn nothin' anyway. Might as well enjoy herself. She keeps me comp'ny and I teach her about the world."

"Hell you do."

"Teach her how to fish. How to shuck oysters. How to throttle that motor just right to make it purr on up river."

"Oh, you must mean you teachin' her how to steal *otha people's* crab an' crawfish an' turtles. Buzzin' 'round in yo' li'l boat. You teachin' her to find them jug lines an' hoop nets an' crab traps."

"I work for a livin', Mable."

"MmmHmm. So then you teachin' her all about shit. Antoine. Sep… tic… shit. That ain't enough."

"Enough to pay the rent for this place you can't afford. I'm the one keepin' you in this fine three bedroom, Mable. That's me doin' that."

"I can't raise my baby in no itty-bitty studio. Sleep on no couch. She need her some space so we not in each other's business ev'ry time we turn around. Hurricane took my damn house."

"Right. Three years ago. I was there. You'd be dead. And her too."

"I think I show my gratitude on a regular basis. An' I'm lookin' for a cheaper place all the time. An' I don't *always* need yo' help. Not all the time."

"Hell you don't. Your toilet-cleanin' ass come up short every month. I ain't the only one in the shit business, Mable."

"I clean the whole damn room, Antoine. Each an' ev'ry last one. And the lobby. And the laundry. An' the hallways. Not just the toilets. And we both know I pay you for that rent. I cook for you whenevah the hell you show up. Like tonight." Mable had raised the frying pan still wet from the sink. Exhibit A for the jury. "An' we both know you ain't evah gettin' any of that *otha* thing I do for you without payin' for it. See, I'm the one that keep you from gettin' sweet wit' the possums an' the goats. That's me doin' that, Antoine. That's me."

"Maybe I don't need your fat darkie love so much as you think."

A smirk. A wink. *Just foolin'. So cute when you're mad. Lighten up.*

"Hell you don't. Sure keep comin' back for it. I should be getting' enough rent for a five-bedroom lake-front condo for this here *fat darkie love* as you call it."

"Okay, okay. I didn't mean nothin'. Damn, Mable."

But the words had never reached her. Mable pointed to herself with her free soapy hand, water drizzling down to the vaguely continental stain on the linoleum.

"You ever want any of this again? You gon' do what I say when it come to Libby. She *my baby*. An' it my job in this world... to do right by my baby... or die tryin'."

"Oh you die for her would ya'?" Antoine had restrained a mocking smile.

"In the time it take you to step on a damn rake."

"You sure? 'Cause, I don't know if you've ever took a real close look at her, Mable," Antoine had paused, looked both ways, then whispered, "but she ain't your baby."

The frying pan had taken on new meaning. Different exhibit. Different jury.

"Maybe time you get on up out this house, Antoine. 'Fo' I say somethin' I regret."

Looking back, ever since they had moved out of his place in Thibodaux over to Gretna, the skirmishes with Antoine had been regular. Predictable. Starting from a dozen tripwire issues and ending more or less on cue. He knew how to pick the fight. She knew how to stand up for herself and hers. He seemed to know when enough was enough and to move on to other forms of entertainment. She seemed to know just how long to hold a grudge.

But Mable's skirmishes with Libby had been another matter. Unpredictable. Ferocious. Arising without warning and without any rules or promises about how they would end. Libby was desperately close to Mable. Too close.

Somewhere down at the heart of it was fear. Fear that the love would just evaporate. That Mable would suddenly see her for the worthless Black Asian whore baby that she was and abandon her to fates unknown. Fear that the abandonment was inevitable. It lurked in too many of their moments, coiled and quiet and waiting like a snake beneath the seemingly innocuous ground cover of normal words and expressions.

No surprise then that Libby often led with her anger, looking to flush out the inevitable. To provoke the unseen threat and pull it by the tail out into the open. Mable did what she could. It had made for challenging childrearing by anyone's measure.

School almost instantly became the precursor to the abandonment Libby feared. School was the place away. The place apart. The place Mable was not. The place Mable did not want to be. If Libby ever had any inclination to trust that she was not alone in the world, it did not survive junior high school.

High school was even worse. In that world, she was very much alone. She may have sounded the same, talked the same, but she sure *looked* different. The skin. The hair. The eyes. Not like the others. It had kept a bull's eye on her back. The outsider trying, ridiculously, to pass. She was reminded daily, and cruelly, that how she talked –how she sounded –counted for nothing. That *looks* mattered most. That, except for Mable, she really was alone.

A boyfriend would have helped. Someone to stick up for her. Vouch for her. Someone others respected. But there was none who would have her. Not delicate little *Libby Ching-Chang-Chop-Suey*. Not openly anyway.

There were more than a few boys who were willing to secretly trade on her desperation. But of course there are no secrets. Not there. Not at that age. Word spread that Libby Ching-Chang-Chop was good at some things. Really good.

Irony was, Libby had never like boys in the first place. Her crushes always went the other direction. But the girls of Jefferson Parrish, a territorial and warring species, all lived on another planet. They refused to recognize her as one of their own.

Not that she hadn't tried to attract the girls. To lure them around. Having gushed over the photo of a Hawaiian woman in a magazine Libby tried wearing a different flower in her hair every day. Just to be as girlish as she could possibly be. The girliest of the girls. She snuck bits and pieces of Mable's jewelry out of the house. Make-up. Perfume. Grown woman stuff. Stuff that Mable forbade. She'd taken some feminine pride in the fact that despite her slight, waifish build, she developed breasts earlier and more prominently than her contemporaries. She had felt like it was something to highlight. She thought it would help.

But the *girliest of girls* strategy had the opposite of the intended effect. Ridicule. Contempt. Serrated whispers. By trying too hard, Libby had shown the pack the soft underbelly of her need.

No coming back from that.

At least she had something the boys wanted. They may not have held any intrinsic hormonal interest for her, but at least the boys were nice to her, thirty minutes at a time. Sometimes they even gave her things. Sometimes they confessed that they did not really like their girlfriends and swore her to secrecy. Secrets like those substituted for any sort of deeper bond. They conferred a sense of value. That, anyway, is how it translated. *Value.* She had a value.

The boys, it turned out, shared a general understanding of value and how the world worked. You had to give a little to get a little. Give a little more, get a little more. And that was true even if the person you wanted to get a little from was little Libby Ching-Chang-Chop.

Antoine wasn't entirely wrong. Mable knew that. Knew Libby hated school. Knew that the kids picked on her. Knew that in addition to saving her life Antoine was providing a different kind of rescue. That even if he was wrong to encourage her truancy, he was making Libby happy. Or at least happier than she would have been otherwise. That was something.

But it was not enough. Happy *in the moment* was not enough. *Stupid and poor* ate away at the *happy* like termites in the walls and rats in the rafters. Happy moments here and there, pretending that you can't hear the chewing, was not enough for her baby. Mable wanted more for Libby. Wanted her to have the strength and smarts and courage to make her own way in the world. To be able to live in relative comfort and security and to look back and remember Mable and think to herself, *thank God for my mama.*

Thank God not just for working so hard to keep her from going hungry. Or to keep her warm and dry and safe. But also for keeping her in school. For teaching her to look out after herself. For teaching her to cook and sew. For singing every blues song ever written as she walked around the house doing laundry and cooking food and sweeping floors, so that the words would fill Libby's head, preserving her mother's voice long after she was gone. That swaying, empathetic lullaby. Singing those bleeding hearted blues. *Mama know, baby. Mama know. Jus' like Bessie know.*

Thank God for my mama. For pressing into the wet mud of Libby's soul that indomitable blues rhythm that would become a like second heartbeat.

Too many troubles at the door and friends that can't be found.
Plead all you want to
But ain't no other soul around.

And she'd need it, too. That second heartbeat. The pulse pounding out that twelve-bar solace. *You are not alone. You are not alone. You are never alone.* Keeping Libby's head up above the floodwaters when they came. Because they would come. Again and again.

Mable did her best. Not that life ever cooperated. Libby's vigilance for signs of abandonment —always testing those waters, always looking to unmask her mother's secret, inchoate perfidy —had kept the bond under constant internal pressure.

And then there was the money. Never enough. Never certain. Mable changed jobs four times in six years. Each change marked a financial and emotional precipice. Prospects of food and clothing and shelter and medicine, all teetering.

All of it had seemed to swing terrifyingly from the rusty hinge of capricious middle managers. The Gretna hospitality industry was never particularly healthy even in the best of times and the labor market at Mable's level was busting at the seams. There was always someone else to wear the uniform, so second chances were rare. Meanwhile, the river of time was not much of a river. Some of that old Jim Crow water was still around, swampy and fetid. You lived with the smell of it. Got used to it. You measured each day against its immediate predecessor. Happiness was all about the framing of perspective.

But that dankness was always there in the background.

The iconic example was Harry "Hal" Meeks, day manager of the Gretna Sunrise Suites. Hal was a wiry, good 'ol boy who belonged in a greasy uniform bent under the hood of a car cleaning dipsticks. He did not belong riding herd over hotel staff in a dingy black tie and a wrinkled ochre shirt. The mustache made him a man. The wire-rim glasses made him smart. His race made him right.

Mable worked the L-shaped, three-story shoebox of the Gretna Sunrise Suites for eighteen months. She was late for work four times in the first six months, which put her on Hal Meek's *you just give me a reason'* list permanently.

Mable lasted as long as she did mostly because she was thorough and efficient in her work and because just about everybody except Hal Meeks liked her immensely. She always had good stories to tell in the lunchroom and she covered other shifts whenever it was possible. She sang softly to herself as she worked. People liked that. They found it strangely comforting.

Mable's eighteen months came to an abrupt end the day one of the guests –a bluish-haired Nebraskan in town to see her grandson get married –accused her of stealing a broach. Costume jewelry. Worth less than the collar of the thirty-dollar tangerine jacket to which it had been pinned.

But the thing came up missing. And Bev Dickson was upset.

Bev had hunted down Mable vacuuming another room and accused her directly, rummaging through her service cart. Digging through the trash bags. Flinging towels and pointing fingers at Mable's smock pockets. Mable took as much as she could. But there were limits.

"Ma'am? Let me tell you this. I gots a job to do. I didn't take no jewl'ry. You need to leave my cart alone, an' leave me alone, an' go on back to wherever you come from, or you an' me gon' have us a big problem."

The cheap broach and its broken clasp eventually turned up on the closet floor behind the luggage where it had fallen from the jacket lapel. Made no difference to Hal Meeks. The issue wasn't the broach. It was never the broach. It was the insulting and threatening manner with which Mable had accosted a paying guest. *That* was the complaint. Not the broach.

And, anyway, maybe if Mable had cleaned the closet with better care –maybe if she had cleaned under and around the luggage –she'd have found the broach and put it someplace in plain sight so that there might have been no concern in the first place.

Blue Hair Bev from Nebraska thought maybe Mable had intentionally hidden the broach on the closet floor so she could go back for it later. Hal didn't believe that. Of course not. But Mable's *manner* was inexcusable. *That* was the issue.

Mable had given Hal Meeks what for. Turned in her keys and uniform. Stormed out of the Gretna Sunrise Suites at 11:30 in the morning, fuming all the way to the bus stop. The anger was like a high-pressure system in her head, holding at bay the rest of it.

Anger is good that way. Black thunderheads towered on the horizon. Waiting. The Number 64 Bus showed up about the time the anger burned off and receded. Mable boarded the bus and took her seat as the storm clouds of despair and worry advanced and then fully occupied her head.

The tears had come in quiet torrents all the way to her stop. When she disembarked she felt like she was drowning. Again. Always on the verge of drowning.

Antoine's moss green Impala –the car in which, having given Mable and Libby his house, he had made his bed after the hurricane –was sitting out front.

Mable had taken it as a sign that whenever she seemed about to go under, when the foundation was slipping out from beneath her and even the snakes were swimming for their lives, Antoine Beaudaine Cherish showed up in his little blue skiff, tossing a rope out over the water.

She had taken a deep, rattling breath. Ready to say nothing about him coming by to steal her food and beer in the middle of the day. Ready to keep giving him anything he wanted from her. Pleasing him when and where and how. All of it. Ready to ask for help. Again.

But Antoine was not in the kitchen with his feet propped up on the table.

Was not sucking on a beer and eating pretzels.

Singing. Singing about the knock on the door, so early in the morning.

Ooooo, I know, I know, I do surely know.

Antoine was in the shower. With Libby. He was singing.

Hello Satan, he sang. *Must be time to go.*

Libby was laughing. Laughing too hard. The sound was high-pitched but desolate. Wind blowing over something small and empty and discarded.

Their naked backs were to the bathroom door.

So neither of them had seen her.

Chapter 57

One of these things is not like the others.

That has always been the feeling of this room. Not belonging.

It's one of the animals that sees him first. The longhorn. Or the water buffalo. The buck.

Not the shark. Glossy black eyes probing sideways, away from him. Away in a quiet, preoccupied disinterest. But that's always the thing with a shark. It doesn't need to see him. It knew he was coming. Of all of them in this room, the shark knew.

And with greater interest than all of the others.

"Shelly!" Grayson points at him with a pair of silver ice tongs. The four human heads between them swivel, eyes following Grayson's words across the spacious leather study to the doorway. Sheldon gives a polite nod. "Great timing, boy. We just got here. Thought you were in Dallas."

"Cancelled," he says, shrugging. "Fine by me though. Got a lot of work done."

"Well good. Good. Come on get yourself a snort and sit down."

The room dimensions are too spacious for a den. Too far across from one wall to another. And yet, somehow, it still leaves him feeling a little claustrophobic.

The appointments are compensatory. They make the space smaller. Darker. Oversized Mexican furniture. Slabs of weathered, lacquered pine wrapped in hides and draped in designer saddle blankets. Twisted, wrought iron lamps spray yellow, low-wattage light. A bleached elk-rack chandelier, eight separate racks, as if to commemorate the tragic head-on collision of an entire herd, hangs from braided ropes above a low, fossilized redwood table on a large cowhide rug. The corner desk at one end of the room, and the corner wet-bar at the other, are roughly hewn bookends, carved from large arboreal siblings.

The high ceiling threatens to lighten the mood.

But the animal heads have fixed that problem.

"Shel, you know Danny Broderick?" Grayson's back is now turned as he plunges the tongs into a leather-wrapped bucket.

Christi. Adrian Hewitt. Nicholas Voss. There is only one pair of eyes in the room Sheldon has never seen. They are large and round behind silver-rimmed glasses. Broderick is short and thick and doughy, uncomfortable in his suit. He raises a hand from his chair. Sheldon detours on his way to the bar to shake hands.

"Daniel," he says. The man reaches out. Firm grip. Single pump.

"Danny's VP of Project Accounting for Quinco," says Grayson. "Dan, Shelly here is the man behind Houston Market Research, HMR we call it, which is doin' a bang-up job rollin' out this little project of yours to the great unwashed."

"Nice to put a face to the name," says Sheldon, moving on. "I'm pretty sure I see your signature in my sleep."

Broderick deflects with a sip of scotch. Arranges his expression. Blinks. "Mr. Davis." The British accent is arresting. "The project team is quite impressed with the work your firm has done on the Corbin project. Top drawer. Top drawer."

"Thanks," he says. "I 'preciate that. I do. We're all workin' real hard on this Corbin project. Real hard."

He takes the tongs from Grayson who leaves him at the bar and assumes his place on the leather throne that the others have left for him. He props his boots up on the table. The dress boots. Slick black snakeskin to go with his suit. He crosses his ankles. Rattles the ice cubes in their little sea of amber. Sips.

"Shelly also happens to be my son-in-law, but I don't hold that against him."

"Daddy," scolds Christi. She lolls her head sideways in a half-turn towards the bar, yellow hair slipping from her shoulder. "Don't you listen to that mess, darlin'. He just needs his drink and he'll be fine."

Sheldon drops some ice in a tumbler. Adds a splash of bourbon. He closes his eyes before he turns. A long blink. In that fleeting darkness he is not in this room. He's on a floating dock.

Sun washing over his back.

Sun splashing onto her face.

This feels like an affair. Is that what this is for you?

"I must say that you have a rather impressive array." Broderick holds his glass up, pointing to a wall. "I think I should not like to make you angry, Grayson."

Grayson twists in his chair. Looks up at the trophies. Uncoils again.

"Used to do a lot of huntin' when I was younger. Not so much any more. Prob'ly have one or two left in me I guess. Just need to make the time." He points backwards over his shoulder without needing to look. "Water buffalo came from Kenya. Siberian brown bear from Kamchatka Peninsula. Som'bitch damn near killed me hauling his fat ass outta the woods. And the Ruskie guides were damn near as big as he is. Let's see."

He turns. Points.

"Dahl sheep come from Alaska." Points. "Moose come from up in Montana."

Points. "Longhorn Larry there comes from Mexico." Points. "Bagged that ten-point buck down in Crockett County, not but maybe couple hours from where we were today."

"And what about this beauty?" asks Broderick. He is looking up at the one that is not like the others. Then they are all looking. Everyone except Nicholas Voss, who is seated directly beneath the thing.

"Ahh. Great white," says Grayson. The shark is mounted on a rod that protrudes from the wall so that it appears to be swimming down from the ceiling and out into the room.

"Shark." Broderick jerks his thumb in the general direction. "It's a bloody white whale, that."

"Key West. Son-of-a-bitch fought me for four goddamned hours. Thought my arms'd fall off. We were out lookin' for Marlin. But this is better." Grayson laughs with a raw, unapologetic gusto. "Much better."

Then they all laugh.

All except Nicholas. He sits quietly beneath the fish that is much better than a Marlin. Sipping his vodka. Looking across the room at Sheldon Davis.

"You're terrible, Daddy," chides Christi. "All these majestic creatures just mindin' their own. God didn't put 'em on this earth just so they could hang on your gosh-dern wall."

Grayson pulls his boots off the table and sets his drink on the arm of his chair. He leans forward, elbows to knees. Holds out a finger.

"Baby... okay, one, these *majestic creatures* as you call 'em all had plenty of time on God's earth before I took 'em and, two, except for sharky up there, I always donated the meat, and three, you sure sang a different tune wearin' that fur around Switzerland a few years back."

"That's diff'rent."

"Hell it is. And you know what else? Your mama could plug a buck at a full run from fifty yards so you prob'ly got it in your DNA, babydoll, if you should ever decide to shoot a gun rather than shootin' off your mouth."

"Hey, now!" Playful. All in good fun. "I shoot my guns on a regular basis I'll have you know."

"Target practice with the gun club as you gossip with Delores and Betty Ann about the latest pageant scandal is not, is not, is *not*... darlin'... the same thing."

Daniel Broderick laughs, amused at this bit of Texan family theater. It is a high, strangely lilting sound from such a low, dense body. He adjusts his glasses with a pasty hand.

"And what about you then, Sheldon?" he says. "Fancy a hunt every so often?"

Grayson is shaking his head before Sheldon can speak. "Nah. Neither one of 'em hunt. What kinda' damn family is this anyway? I'll bet Nicki over there hunts, don'cha Nick?"

Nicholas gives a slow-motion blink, eyes releasing Sheldon, sliding sideways to find Grayson. He nods. "Yes. Many times."

"Thought so. Adrian?"

"I'm afraid I'm with Christi one this one," says Adrian Hewitt, loosening his tie. Navy with yellow paisleys. "Never really had the stomach for it."

Grayson resumes his reclined posture, boots up, drink in hand. He waves the other hand, dismissing any concern.

"Ahh. To each his own, Adrian. T'each his own. You boys were out huntin' for money this week. Huntin' bucks. *Real* bucks. And I dare say you found you some."

Adrian smiles broadly, a bleached-white butterfly opening to daylight. The salesman's smile. He looks at Daniel. Nicholas. Then back again.

"I think it has been a successful few days. Yes. Daniel? Wouldn't you say?"

"Oh quite, quite," says Broderick. "I'm rather satisfied with the progress."

There is a feeling. A pressure. Sheldon glances up over his drink at Nicholas Voss. But it is not Nicholas he feels this time.

It is his wife. It is Christi. He looks. Her face is placid, smiling. It does not betray what disgusting tawdriness she believes to be true about him. Does not betray the state of things between them. She is working now. On the clock for daddy.

And she does not blink. Not once.

Which means she is irritated. Christi does not like his penchant for aloofness in social situations. It is less about bending him to her will than avoiding a genuine humiliation. His diffidence, his preference to lean back against the bar, somehow, reflects poorly on her. She pats the leather cushion next to her on the loveseat.

He doesn't want to play this game. The *marriage* game. The *couple* game. The *love* game. Doesn't want to pretend. Not for the clients. Not for Grayson. Not for Christi. Doesn't want to be the water buffalo, feigning polite interest. He wants to feign illness. Or pressing business. He wants to excuse himself to be alone someplace quiet.

He wants to be with Olivia, if only in his thoughts.

This feels like an affair. Is that what this is for you?

These are not simple thoughts. They are complicated. Riven with colorful contradiction. Shot through with guilt and longing and uncertainty. Regret. He looks at his wife –Christi, the woman he married –and he sees a beautiful, nearly flawless husk of an ideal that he can no longer explain. She is bedding that perfect, glacier-eyed specimen sitting so calmly beneath the shark. He is sure of it. Disparate clues have started to join hands. His bed is their bed. He merely borrows it in the evenings. They loan it to him for the sake of appearances.

His imagination has been meticulous and unrelenting.

The mental images should fill him with rage and indignation. They should. He often pretends to himself that they do. How dare she rake him over the coals for something that never actually happened in Corbin while she was gettin' it good from Nicki Voss? Maybe, he thinks, this is why she no longer confronts him about Corbin. She knows he knows. Or suspects he knows. Or knows that he suspects. This is the marital version of the US-Soviet geopolitical game of mutually assured destruction. They each had their missiles locked and loaded and maybe that was the thing keeping the peace. Maybe.

In the meantime, his head is full of blue-eyed Samoyed carnality in the room where he sleeps. The images should bother him. But they don't. They fill him with a sick sort of relief. There is an odd happiness buried in that pornographic rumination. An odd kind of freedom. An odd kind of music. Old music. Like a sticky-sweet serum slipping into a vein. Bringing him back to her. Olivia. Over and over.

Music. Let's make this about the blues. Let's share that.

It's complicated. How many times has he said that to her? *It's complicated.*

Because it *is* complicated. Nothing about these feelings is simple. It's not like he has forgotten the poverty of canned beans for dinner every single night. Not like he has forgotten shaving in the men's room at the bus station, his six-string propped against the sink. Not like he has forgotten seeing Christi for the first time, full of his newly minted ad-man swagger, selling her a bill of goods.

The businessman going places.

The up and comer.

The up-from-the-bootstraps, good-looking songwriter with an eye for the finer things and yet with the bonafide anti-establishment hippy roots perfect for pissing off daddy.

He thinks of the clothing on his body. The silky swing of his tie. The comfort of his shoes. The sanctum of his automobile gliding over the earth. He thinks of the business that makes it all possible. Thinks of Grayson, who had seen through all of the ad man bullshit. Grayson swallowing hard. Grayson pouring buckets of money into Sheldon's pockets, propping up Sheldon's mediocre business instincts, all for the sake of his daughter and the Tate reputation. Grayson, throwing down for family and to honor the dead.

So it is a betrayal.

No doubt about it. It is looting pure and simple. The money does not belong to him. Not really. And so it also does not belong to Olivia.

But he will loot it anyway. He will surreptitiously bleed his business ten thousand dollars at a time. More if necessary. For as long she needs him to, or until HMR starves and desiccates and blows away in the hot breeze.

Why? Why has he done this? Why will he continue to do this? He does not know why exactly. Because he has hurt her?

Yes.

Because she needs it?

Yes.

Because she needs him in order to get it?

Yes.

All true. And, at the same time, all horseshit. For the life of him he does not know his own motivation. He only knows that he is chasing a truth he cannot fully comprehend. Every morning now he wakes up.

Wakes up.

Wakes up.

Every morning he wakes up in his wife's bed and cares nothing about his marriage. Or his business. Or the Tate family honor. The only thing he cares about now is Olivia.

Every morning now he wakes up.

It is unclear what Olivia means to him. He pretends, convincingly, that this is love. Pretends she is a woman. Pretends she is a person. It is easy to do. For all of that is true. And yet that is all wrong.

She is not a woman.

She is not a person.

She is a memory. She is a pulse. A melody. A song. An old frequency traveling by night, crackling over the desert in his dreams. He wakes up in his wife's bed, every morning, imagining what must have happened on those same sheets eighteen hours earlier, and then, inexplicably, wanting to write music again.

Music. Let's make this about the blues. Let's share that.

So. It's complicated.

Christi arches an eyebrow. A silent shout. She pats the seat cushion with a force that is almost a slap. Sheldon pushes off from the bar with his hip and heads for the loveseat.

The love seat.

"So it sounds like everything went as planned," he says, overcompensating. He sits. Christi pats him on the knee. Good dog. "What can you tell me?"

"These boys are pros, Shelly," says Grayson. "I mean they know what in the hell they're doin', I tell you right now. I mean they had those sons-a-bitches eating out of their hands. Tell 'im, Danny."

Daniel Broderick smiles, a complicated expression torn between the flattery and his apparent distaste for the name *Danny*. He clears his throat.

"Indeed, it has been a successful few days. We have been negotiating for months with Corcon. Yesterday we had our meeting with everyone 'round the same table and we got a deal. A *good* deal. A *bang-up* deal."

"What is Corcon?" Sheldon asks. He knows what Corcon is. He asks anyway.

"Right. Sorry. Stands for Corbin Construction. It's a joint venture consisting of eight construction companies that have now agreed to do roughly ninety percent of the construction work for the CDC on this project. It's a crucial element to the entire project because the construction costs will be enormous. I mean, really bloody astronomical. If we can't get the construction costs in line then the whole thing collapses, see?"

Broderick interlaces and then pulls apart his pudgy white fingers to show something coming violently undone, more an explosion than a collapse.

"You found eight construction companies in Corbin, Texas?"

"No, no. None from Corbin. They're from all over."

Grayson clears his throat. Moves his hand through the air, fingers spread wide, in a slow sweeping motion.

"Shelly, these boys, see, know what the hell they're doin'. Okay? They took bids from all over the damn place. California. Texas. Louisiana. This is gonna be one helluva big job. And they made sure two of the companies are owned by Mexicans just to help with the lending bit of it."

"Well," says Broderick correctively, "the lending, yes, but mainly so that we can bring in the federal highway funds. We'll be messing about with Interstate 10 and your State of Texas made it quit clear it was rather disinclined to go it alone. So we need some ethnic tokens in the mix, don't we?"

"Those Mexican boys'll do you fine, Danny. They're hard workers, long as you've got good oversight. Long as they know where to put the shovel." Grayson points at Broderick. "Watch the money, though. Watch the money. They'll work hard but they'll rob you blind if you let 'em."

"We're not worried a bit about the oversight. We know what we're doing, as you say. The Corcon joint venture will be impeccably managed and accountable to the CDC and Quinco at every step. And that relationship is crucial. As I say, if we can't get the construction costs in line then the whole thing collapses. First thing serious investors want to look at are the projected construction costs. They have to pencil out favorably against the returns, and by a wide margin, mind you," finger in the air, "or everybody gets cold feet. The banks too. And the public utilities. No one wants to really commit to this beast until we have a deal on the construction costs. See?"

Sheldon nods, nursing his bourbon.

"And yesterday we managed to cut the projected costs by a full thirty-eight percent. Twice as much as we were hoping. We would have felt good about shaving seventeen percent. Hell, fifteen."

Broderick looks at Adrian Hewitt. Adrian nods with enthusiasm.

"Let's be honest here, Daniel" says Adrian. "I'd have been smiling at ten percent and writing home to mother at fifteen."

Broderick laughs in his girlish falsetto, slapping his knee.

"Right, right. Ten would have done. But thirty-eight? Bugger and blast, man! *Thirty-eight?*"

"Wow," says Sheldon. "How… can I ask how you did that? I mean is that confidential or …"

"Well, of course it's *confidential*. Lawyers outnumbered the hardhats two to one at this meeting." He glances sideways at Adrian. Then back. "But I can tell you this much: all of these people know what the property around Corbin Texas is about to be worth. They can all see it."

There is a pause. Even the dead animals are thinking about that one.

"You're paying them in property," says Sheldon. "The construction companies traded dollars for a piece of the action."

Daniel Broderick smiles. Hands in the air like he is disclaiming or surrendering. He leans back in his chair. Reclaims his drink.

"Did I say that? I'm quite sure I said nothing of the kind."

Laughter around the table. It looks like Broderick might leave it there. He doesn't.

"But I will say this much, eh? I will say this much. If the joint venture *were* of a mind to do such a thing, trade dollars for real estate, it would make a bloody fortune as that desert greens up and blooms with commerce. A bloody killing. They should do the work for free."

Grayson rattles his cube for attention.

"So then, Shel, *then*, these boys go sit down with the utilities. Those mean-spirited, sanctimonious bureaucratic mutherfuckers…"

"Daddy…"

"Well pardon my French, baby, but it's the goddamned truth. Those bastards live to tell people what they can't do and how much more they have to pay for less service. But Danny and Adrian and those fellas from the banks sat down with these peckers and… well you tell it Danny, you were there."

Danny does not tell it. Not that he wouldn't. His mouth opens. But Adrian is first out of the gate.

"It was beautiful. They gave us exactly what we needed."

"Which is what?" asks Sheldon.

"A long, slow ramp up on the rates until year five post-completion. Year *five*." Hand out, fingers spread. "The pre-completion rates are almost nothing."

"And they did this because…"

Grayson steps in. "'Cause the sons-a-bitches know a green title wave when they see one. Every last one of 'em can smell a budget surplus. They want this project done yesterday, Shelly. I tell you *what*. They'll all take a bath on the rates in the short term if it will speed things along."

"Right," says Broderick, spitting an ice cube back into his glass. "And the bankers and the insurance underwriters had a front row seat for all of this. That's the thing, see? Not at our invitation, mind you. To tell you the truth it makes me a bit nervous. I'd rather get all of my little ducklings in a nice neat row, thank you, but they insisted see? They wanted to ask their questions. And they did too. We had, what, about ten of us altogether, three days ago, walking around the desert in our starched shirts, one million bloody degrees, pointing this way and that and I thought to myself that these buggers have no bloody idea what we're about. Adrian too. Didn't we?"

Adrian nods.

"I've never seen such a lot of skeptical wankers in my whole life. And I've seen a lot, let me assure you. But then these past two days, meeting with the Corcon people and the utilities... I think they could feel the enthusiasm in the room. I mean it was palpable. You could spread it on toast like jam."

"So they're satisfied?" asks Sheldon.

"Well, they're stoic to the end, these bastards. I think bankers all go to university for that sort of thing; just so they can look grim even when they're excited. But I have no doubt that they are going back to their boards of directors and they will recommend approval for most of what we are asking. We're going to have more than enough to cover whatever the private investors will not."

"I thought the private investors were really coming through," Sheldon asks.

"Oh, private investment is smashing. Beyond our expectations. But in our experience only a certain percentage of that will actually materialize. Hopefully a very large percentage. But the reality is that it is easy to *promise* the money and then life, you see, intervenes. A hurricane destroys your hotel in the Caymans or the futures market for orange juice takes a blow or the missus decides she wants to invest in a new pair of *Manolo Blahnik* shoes."

"Hey now!"

Christi pretends to take offense. She extends a shapely leg over the table, rotating her foot one direction, then the other, showing off her own pair of black *Blahniks*.

Daniel Broderick and Adrian Hewitt readily take up the invitation to admire the slope of his wife's award-winning calf. Sheldon looks away, wanting to avoid whatever feelings he should have as Christi's husband. He glances over at Nicholas Voss. They lock eyes. Sheldon smiles. Nicholas does not.

"Just what're you implyin' there, Danny Boy?" says Christi.

She retracts her leg and scrunches up her face to show she is not serious. She leans forward like she is preparing to pinch Broderick on his pudgy white cheek, which rapidly takes on color.

"I can assure you that was meant as no slight to you, Mrs. Davis. No indeed. In my experience, women tend to be the better investors. When you get right down to it, right down to the nitty-gritty, men tend to invest because they want to *prove* something. Whereas women invest because they want to *get* something. All I was saying is that as a general group, without accounting for gender, private investors are a fickle lot. So we at Quinco have to prepare for the worst on this project. And after this week..." Broderick shrugs. Leans back in his chair. Sips. "I think we have."

"Still a lot of activity out there on the environmental issues," says Sheldon. "Lawsuit went away but, you know, that hasn't stopped the ..."

"Ahh, now don't go steppin' into that horseshit again, Shelly." Grayson's voice is tight, pinching down on the anger rising to the surface. "Those boys got their asses handed to them. Goddamned New Mexico. Held Texas over a barrel for their goddamned Lake Avalon project. That's extortion plain and simple. They ought to be kicked out of the union for that. And the environmentalists have no goddamned idea they were just used as a tool. They got nothin'."

"I know. I know. Just... there's a lot of talk about demonstrations at the Moon Garden Festival and..."

"Well why do I give shit about that? Let 'em come. They can all ride in with the homosexuals and the cross-dressers who think it's funny show up at a wholesome gathering of God-fearing Christians and rub their business in everyone's face. All I care about is that the court fight over that stupid goddamned fish is done and over. Should'a cut the head off of one those slippery little fuckers, one of those bluntnose shiners, and put it up there on my wall."

"Right, but..."

Christi squeezes his knee. She has an instinct for the limits of her father's self control. For knowing when enough is enough. She body-checks the conversation in another direction.

"Which'a y'all are comin' to the pageant?"

"What pageant?" asks Broderick.

"What pageant?" Mouth agape. Eyes like baby blue dinner plates. "Darlin', there is only one beauty pageant worth talkin' about right now."

Grayson sighs into his glass. "Belle, honey, don't go gettin'..."

"I'm *talkin*'," her eyes pivot over to her father and then back to Broderick, "about the First Annual Corbin River Walk Queen Beauty Pageant. Surely daddy has been keepin' you apprised."

Daniel Broderick knows little and cares less. But he is not a fool.

"Oh yes. Right, right, right. I am fully apprised of the pageant. Looking forward to seeing that take shape. Top idea. Brilliant."

"Less than six weeks to go now," says Christi beaming, bouncing her legs. She squeezes Sheldon's knee. "It's all comin' together. Hundred seventeen girls applied. One *hundred* and seven...*teen*."

She looks from one face to another, waiting for reaction. There is none.

"Come on y'all! One hundred seventeen? For a first time pageant all the way out in li'l ol' Corbin? That's pretty dang good. We're gon' have to have two elimination rounds just to limit the field to fifteen for the day of the Moon Garden Festival. And these girls are knockouts, I'm tellin' you what. *Knockouts*.

And this little pageant has lit a *fire* down in Corbin and San Angelo. The TPA has had no problem gettin' sponsors. Every business out there wants its name on this thing. And the publicity? *River Walk this* and *River Walk that* all day long. *When's it gonna be done?* and *What stores are comin*? Everybody's talkin' 'bout y'alls River Walk Project. I think it has really helped to get the word out, don't you?"

"Oh, absolutely," says Adrian nodding, twisting his ring. "Absolutely." He looks over at Broderick, who is also nodding.

"Top idea. Top."

"And next year it'll be even better. By the time y'all are done bringing the water and puttin' up buildings, this pageant is gon' have a real set of legs on her."

Laughter. Something in the visual appeals to them.

"So…" she moves her finger in a line, from one to the next, "are y'all… gonna be there… to see the crowning… of the very first Corbin River Walk Queen?"

"I'm afraid I will be missing the pageant," says Broderick. "And the festival too. *Festivals* I should say. Curious development there. Combining it with the *Day of the Dead*."

"Oh, I think that's just despicable," spits Christi. "Why can't they have their own damn day? I'm tryin' to put on a wholesome beauty pageant here. Somethin' worthy of Texas. Somethin', you know, all-American. This zombie holiday of theirs is downright gruesome. It's anti-Christian if you ask me. They should go across the border and celebrate. God knows they'll all get back in."

"Local politics," says Grayson. "No way around that. Hell, it's better combined anyway."

"Daddy, you can't mean that."

"I do mean it, Sugar. More people, more coverage, more attention. Ain't that right, Shelly?"

Sheldon nods. "Yeah, probably works better for us. If people behave. It's a bigger splash."

"Well, anyway," says Broderick, "much as I would love to be there. I am needed in London that week. Can't be helped I'm afraid."

Christi, her face a beautiful pastiche of scolding and disappointment, looks to Adrian.

"We'll just have to see," he says. "Too soon to tell. I always have a crowded calendar in the last quarter. All of my boards trying to get things done before the clock strikes midnight."

She is looking away, moving on, before he has finished shaping his excuse.

"Oh come on, y'all. Nicki? Surely you're plannin' to come. You've got to take your pictures."

Nicholas Voss looks up slowly from his drink. Like his head is moving through water or clear oil beneath the dead thing in the room that is unlike all of the other dead things. Eyes like lost coins glinting in blue moonlight.

The barely perceptible smile is for Sheldon.

"Wouldn't miss it."

Chapter 58

Kevin does not like the wind. His senses are tiny vessels.

Too much stimulation all at once.

The invisible torrents mean too many follicles are shouting to his brain at the same time. The overload will have consequences for the rest of the day. Spasms like aftershocks.

Olivia shudders. Rubs his arms and shoulders with her hands. Closes the door to the deck. They watch the flailing trees.

Yvonne had not understood.

"Breezy today! You like a good breeze, don't you, Kev? Maybe if you're lucky Olivia here'll bundle you up and roll you out on the deck for awhile. Would you like that, baby? Would you like that? 'Course you would. Feel that cool air? And no cheese, Olivia. I mean that, now. Okay? And make sure he's bundled up. Don't keep him out there too long. He doesn't like the cold."

But she was wrong about that. It isn't the temperature.

It's the wind. Too light. Too dry. It carries the full weight and promise of nothingness. Of absence. The blowing is an act of leaving. An atmospheric escape before the sealing of a vacuum. Waterless drowning.

All suffocation is the same. It's the breath of death, this wind, holding the past in its arms like a corpse. The ghost of a river. The ghost of an ocean.

That's what he doesn't like.

His mother has the same misguided inclination every fall as the heat relaxes, pulling its talons out of the earth. It's not the temperature.

So they have come in. They spend some time up against the windows. Eat thin strips of American cheese and watch the invisible torrents yank cruelly at the limbs of the living.

Olivia removes the blanket from around Kevin's shoulders. Folds it. Drops it over the back of a chair. She sits and watches him moving in his wild rhythms. Jerking in solidarity with the trees.

Yvonne has stopped making any pretense about what she is doing. Out fucking Miguel Rivera in the shadow of some sign without enough letters on it to spell the word "Best" or "Suites" or "Comfort". At least three days a week now, whenever Brent is out of town making his money. Climbing his ladder.

They have agreed to simply not discuss it. Have agreed that it is none of Olivia's goddamned business. That since Olivia lives in a goddamned whorehouse she is in no position to judge. That if she wants to spend her time judging, then she knows where to find the front door.

And she might have done that. Found the front door. She might have.

But she didn't.

Yvonne surely concluded it was all about the money. Not a bad guess.

Wrong, but not ridiculous.

Sure, she was saving. Every little bit helped. She was determined not to touch the soft bricks of cash piling up in the old Mexican pine bureau. Determined.

She had even limped back into *Longhorn Fitness* like nothing had happened. Had ignored Mr. Pete's lopsided smile and had started wiping down the machines, choking on the sight of the short-shorted *Muscle Menders* minx in and out of that massage room. *Ginger.* Swinging a towel. Working the floor for clients.

But it was not like she needed Yvonne's money all *that* badly. An extra shift at *The Diamondback* would have made it up.

Wasn't about the money.

She palms the back of Kevin's head, moving atop his writhing body, twisting and curling around his spine. She imagines not doing this. Imagines Yvonne trying to find someone else. Imagines Yvonne and Miguel in the guest bedroom down the hall, door cracked just enough for Yvonne to keep an ear on the living room. *You okay out there, Kev? I'll be right out to fix you a snack, honey.*

Wasn't about the money.

But it also wasn't entirely about Kevin.

"Want to play some music?" she asks. Kevin jolts forward and sideways. It's not an answer. But she pretends it is.

She rotates his chair. Rolls him over to the Baby Grand. Shoves the bench over with her foot enough so that they can share the keyboard space. Locks his wheels. Sits.

She tries to extend his hand enough to reach the keys, but it does not extend today. It stays clutched tightly up against his chest, fingers curled, as if holding him back in his chair. His head jerks sideways, pulling at his neck in that secret wind.

She plays.

Slow. Easy. Sad. She lets the notes fall, almost disconnected. Rain on a tin roof. Drips in the garden wheelbarrow.

Texas Flood. And *God Moves on the Water.* And *My Mama Don't Allow.*

It helps a little. But not much. The wind in Kevin's head dies some, but the gusts still pack a punch. His body is a flag.

So she plays the other song. The one that never really lets go. The one that is never finished. Closes her eyes. Sings.

Mother Ocean
Mother Ocean
Your sorrow so deep
Your children have floated away

The calmness next to her is sudden and shocking. She forces herself to keep playing. She repeats the words. The only words there are.

Down in green coffers
Such mem'ries you keep

Again.
Again.
The still eye of Kevin's private tornado holds its position.
She remembers the doe.
In April. Kevin in his chair out in the yard. She had run up for more apple slices. When she had returned, the doe, nimble and suede brown, was slowly approaching. Unsure, perhaps. But unafraid.

Kevin, through some force of will that she could not fathom and that should not have been possible, had been as still as granite.

The doe had stopped within inches. Sniffed. Feinted. Sniffed. They had looked at each other. And then she had brushed past and away. Gone.

That ninety seconds of control had left him without any control for the rest of his day. Exhaustion had left him helpless, a leaf in violent air. But she knew it had been worth it. Connection. Understanding. Grace. Ninety seconds of grace.

And now here he is again. Perfectly still. Listening to her voice. Every muscle holding its breath.

Holding.

Down in green coffers
Such mem'ries you keep
Are you sorry you sent them away?

Holding.

Hanging on. Soaking it in. She tells herself that it is the song. The melody she uses as a homing signal. Each note connected to the next by the smell of the sea. Something about it has opened a narrow channel through the lightning storm around his brain.

Connection. Understanding. Grace.

She has no choice but to believe it is the song. The music.

Because to understand that the music is just a medium, a sonic ocean through which we can move, suspending the heaviest parts of ourselves as if weightless; to understand that it is not so much the music itself that has arrested Kevin, but his feelings for her, floating within the music, and the possibility that Kevin actually loves her –to really understand that, that he actually loves her –would be more than she can bear.

Ninety seconds. Ninety-one. A new record.

* * *

The Diamondback is jammed with Friday night regulars. Ranchers. Nut farmers. The oil boys. All here. Hands streaked or dusted with the residue of whatever they choose to turn into the money that they trade for alcohol. Mostly they're Corbinites. But also some up from Iraan. Some over from Fort Stockton. Folks looking to do something different as Saturday rolls into view. Not *different-*different, of course. The *same-*different. *Routine-*different. Friday night different.

Olivia does not like the press and frenzy of Friday nights. But it is better in some ways than when the place is only half-full. People come in groups. They have things to say to each other. Shout to each other. Jokes to tell. Songs to sing. They have brought their own entertainment.

So sometimes she is able to slip behind the chaos, squeezing between the country rock standards blasting out of the jukebox and all but disappear, delivering and collecting and setting up tables like some faceless machine.

Helps, too, that the owners bring in Dina to work on Fridays. If there is unwanted attention to be had, Dina draws most of it. All legs and hair and boobs. No scars. No limp. Dina eats it up and spits it back out in a way the men love.

Manny Soto is too busy to bother her. Another blessing.

But he *wants* to bother her. She can tell. Manny's a watcher.

He looks at her as he shouts to others over *Lyin' Eyes* and *Sweet Home Alabama* and *Friends in Low Places*. He says something to her every so often when she passes with an over-burdened tray. She scrunches up her face in mock confusion. *Huh?* Shakes her head. *Too loud.* Keeps moving.

She thinks of him sitting on the fountain in the town square. Hand on the top of her boot. *"I see wha' I can do about da schedule. We see wha' we can work out."*

She will not be lucky for long. She knows better. Manny Soto does not give up. It would be easy to mistake his single-mindedness for plucky determination.

It's not plucky determination. It's a tragic failure of perception. He never sees the brick wall until he hits it. And even then.

He finds her after closing, cleaning the women's restroom. Lynyrd Skynyrd floods in with him.

"O. Here you be. Wha you doin', O?"

She turns. Looks at his pocked brown moon face in the doorway. Smile spreading like an oil slick. She dangles the toilet brush. Turns back. Resumes.

"Ice skatin', Manny. What's it look like I'm doing?"

She is bent at an odd angle to avoid any part of her coming into contact with the stall. Her leg hurts from the evening. This is not helping. She imagines the titanium screws and pins anchored into her bones. In her mind they are black spots on an x-ray, emitting little red radioactive waves of pain every time she moves.

"Look lye you cleanin' da' toilet, O. Da what it look lye to me. Cleanin' da' crapper. *Again*. Damn, O. You mus' lye cleanin' shit. You do this every damn shif'. You lye da, O?"

"It's my very favorite thing, Manny."

"No it ain', O. You want I give Dina a turn on dis shit?"

"Right. No chance in hell you boys would ever give Dina this job. Told you I'd do it. So I'm doing it."

Manny steps in. The restroom door closes behind him, muffling the lead in to *Cat Scratch Fever*. He leans against the opening to the stall, one arm out, clutching the opposite side. Blocks her in.

"I go get Dina. Rye now. You want me to? She do dis shit if I ask her. You don' haf to, O. *See?* Jus' give me da word, *mamacita*. But you haf a do for me, O. Unnastan? You haf a do for me."

He says this in his shoulder-shrugging *rules-are-rules* tone. She keeps her back turned.

"Nope. I'm good, Manny."

"I know you good, O. I know da fo' shu. Livin' in da ho' house lye you do. I know da *fo' shu*."

He uses both hands. One for each cheek. Each of his ten stubby sausages want to go their own way on a Friday night, pulling at the black nylon skirt that *The Diamondback* makes her wear. Each finger carries a thousand volts.

So she starts. The old, hot panic is right where she left it.

She wheels in place, hot lightning spitting up her leg on its way to the pain receptors in her brain. She swings the plastic toilet brush like a club. Once. Twice. Three times. It connects wet and hard across the front of his face, slapping against the side of the stall in a spray flecked with brown and black drizzles.

Manny Soto falls backwards out of the stall. Sputtering. Wiping furiously with his white sleeves. Again. Again.

"O! O! You fucking bitch, O! Why you do da? I jus' playin' wichu, O! Damn! *Damn!*"

She steps forward. Points Excalibur. Manny crabs his way backwards out of the stall against the wall, still sputtering, face trying to leave the scene without waiting for the rest of him.

"If you are not out in three seconds, Manny, I will start scrubbing your fucking tongue. And if you ever touch me again…" She does not finish.

"O, you a fucking…"

"*Uno.*" Another half-step forward and he is sliding himself up the painted brick wall.

"You a ho house cunt, O! I fire you filthy ass. Fucking scarface, limpin' ass bitch."

"Let's go talk to Gary and Lou together," she says. "But you might want to get cleaned up first. 'Cause you stink, Manny Boy."

"O, you…"

"*Dos.*"

* * *

She should have kept it to herself. She knows that now. It takes Libby a good twenty minutes to come down off the ceiling. Olivia can't say that she'll handle it one more time. But she does anyway.

"Libby. I said I'll handle it. Will you just…"

"Naw, baby. You keep sayin' you handle it. *I* gon' handle this shit. Hear me? That no good muthu fuck gon' wished he was dayid."

"Will you just come away from the window? Or put some damn clothes on. Aren't you cold? You want Lewis and Darnell to stand out there gawkin'?"

Libby stops. Turns her back to the bedroom window, morning sun breaking over her bare shoulders like sea spray. Olivia re-props the pillow. They look at each other.

"You think I care one li'l bit 'bout the McKenzie boys? They want my pecans then they jus' gon' have to put up wit' my peaches in this here winda'. Men know how to turn away from ugly, baby."

"I never said ugly. But you could put on some clothes once in awhile, Libby."

"Don'chu *Libby* me. This *my* house, baby. If I want to wash my windows wit' my tongue and mow my grass without a stitch, then guess what I'm gon' do?"

Olivia sighs. Rubs her eyes. Pats the bed.

"Then get away from the window. Please."

It takes a few seconds. But Libby does as she is told. Stretches out on top of the sheets. Breathes.

"I tol' you to quit that place, baby."

"I know you did. I need the money. There are no other jobs in Corbin. And back and forth to San Angelo is killin' me."

"I know, baby. But ain' no money worth that shit."

"Could move. San Angelo. Houston."

Libby's face is half shock. Half pain.

"Move? You lost yo' mind?"

"To find a job."

"MmmHmm. And you find you some rent, too. So you can take yo' paycheck an' hand it right over to some lan'lawd. Then where you be, baby?"

"I know." Olivia rolls her head sideways. Looks at Libby. "Can't very well quit now anyway, can I?"

"An' let the no good mutha fuck Manny Soto win? Aw, *hale* no. This shit's war now." She is silent for a beat. Two. Three. She looks up at Olivia. "You really hit him 'cross the face wit' a shit brush?"

It's a little smile. That's all it takes for Libby to cut loose. She roars at the thought of it, kicking her legs on the bed.

"Li'l bits a mess all eva'where, huh?"

Olivia nods. "So disgusting. Then I had to clean it all up."

"Don' matter. He had that shit comin'. But now he one angry li'l mutha fuck, huh? He afraid an' angry all at the same time."

Olivia nods. "I've never seen him so mad."

"MmmHmm. What'chu' gon' do about it, baby? Tell me."

"Guess I'll talk with Gary. Or go to San Angelo and sit down with Lou Diamond. Get him fired."

"You think they back you up on this?"

"One way to find out."

"MmmHmm. An' if they don't?"

Olivia sighs. Lolls her head sideways. Looks at Libby with arched brows.

"I'll handle it, Libby."

"Oh, you handle it, huh? Like you handle *Massage*-massage-all-the-way-married?"

Olivia examines the cuticle on her thumb.

"Sheldon? There was nothing to handle."

"Mmm-Hmm. See what I mean? Fool try to kill you wit' his li'l bullet car an' you just wanna let that shit go? I had to handle that mutha fuck too."

Another beat. Two. Three.

Four.

"What... Libby what'd you mean that you had to handle that too?"

"I mean I got yo' back like any good mama would, rhas all."

Up on an elbow now. Brow arches collapse into deep furrows.

"You ain't my mama, Libby."

"You right. You right. But I'm the closest thing you got to one, ain't I?"

She doesn't know what to do with that. Terribly wrong and yet, when she really looked at it, absolutely correct. She lets it go.

"What did you do, Libby? Tell me. I have a right to know."

There is a long moment. Olivia glances down at Libby who looks up at the ceiling. Some gas-powered yard thing fires up in the distance, blowing away the birdsong. She can see Libby sorting through the facts, choosing which ones to let out and which ones to keep stuffed away. Olivia has no illusions she is going to get it all. She waits.

"Well... I send the fool all his shit like you tell me to. Address the box to *Mrs. Massage-Massage-All-The-Way-Married.* An' I put a little song in there fo' his wife. You know that *Bumble Bee* song? Memphis Minnie?"

"Oh, Libby."

She feigns shock. Disappointment. Does not want Libby to know that Sheldon has kept her informed. She does not want Libby to know anything of her meetings with Sheldon.

She just doesn't know exactly why. Libby would love the idea of her wringing money out of Sheldon. So why not tell her? She tells herself it is to protect Libby, just in case it all goes south and the law gets involved. The less Libby knows the better.

Except that wasn't it. Not really. It's something else.

"Oh Libby..." she says again.

Libby enlists her face and her hands and her naked body to help her sing.

"*I gots me a bumble bee, don't sting nobody but me. And I tell the world, he got all the stinger I need.*"

"Oh Libby..."

Liberty laughs a little under her breath. "Liked to seen his face when his woman show him that note. Bet they done now fo' sho'. Either that or he sleepin' in his pretty lil' bullet car wit' a bag a ice on his dick where she kicked him wit' her little pointy rich-bitch shoes."

"Okay, okay. That it? That how you... *handled* things?"

"Oh, baby. Who you think you talkin' to? I mean really. That shit was me jus' gettin' started."

"Just great. What else. Tell me."

"When *Massage*-massage first show up at this house, he askin' me all kinda questions 'bout if I sold this property. Tells me it part of his job to know. I tell him I ain't sold nothin' to nobody. An' he open up this green folder and show me a list of names. And there I be. Libby Holder. An' he want to know if there were any other owners and I tell him I used to be wit' Antoine Cherish but he nevah own this place. An' I lef' out the *mutha fuck* part of Antoine's name, too. Should'a said Antoine *Mutha Fuck* Cherish. But I didn't."

"Libby…"

"Alright, alright. Anyway, I reco'nize buncha other names on that list too but I don't say nothin' 'cause I don't really know what the hell he talkin' 'bout and I don't care neither. Hell," Liberty points across the room and out the window, "*Darnell's* name on that list. Anyway, I don't say nothin'. All I say is that I ain't sold nothin' to nobody and wasn't goin' to neither. An' he say he must have a bad list, or a old list, or some such. And I let that shit go."

"Okay. So?"

"So then, 'ventually, dumb ass mutha fuck *Massage*-massage-all-the-way-married get all grabby in my home wit' you and then try to kill you with his car and put yo' ass in the hospital and…"

"Libby. I know that part. What the hell'd you do?"

"I found that green folder in his car…"

"You mean you broke into his car and you stole it before any of that other stuff had even happened."

"I mean I wake up one day and that folder in my hand and I don't know how it get there but I had it. You gon' let me tell you what I done or you gon' cross-examine me like some bitch-ass legal beagle?"

"Sorry. Go on. Let's hear it."

Libby waits. Her face placidly uncaring in its control.

"Libby. Okay. I said I'm sorry. Just…"

A sigh. A gathering of sufficient interest to slowly continue.

"So I print me out a li'l picture from my camera. The one I gots behind a mask in the boom-boom room downstairs. *Massage-massage* in his lil' draws like a damned circus tent, 'cause he on cookie number three at that point. Eyes all big. Tongue hangin' out. Got my purple feathers round his neck. An' there I am too, in the background, nekid as a baby. An' so I send this li'l 'ol picture to the address that was on a letter in that green folder with that list of names. I don't put in no note or nothing. Jus' the picture. 'Cause that shit speak a thousand words all by its damn self. That should be enough to get his dumb ass fired."

"Libby… shit. You mailed it?"

"I did, baby. I did. Laughin' all th' way to the mailbox too."

"Who'd you mail it to?"

"Who? I don't remember who? This was like… fo'eva ago. Some long-ass name with too may letters. Figured it was *Massage-massage's* boss. Work at a place called *Quento* or *Quinky* or *Quinnycunt*. Some shit like that. New York City, baby. *MmmHmm.*"

Olivia rolls flat against the bed. Back of her arm over her eyes. Listens to the distant droning. Imagines Sheldon's face as she tells him. Imagines his expression like a slide show. Confusion. Alarm. Anger. Hatred. Imagines him snatching back a fat envelope. Slapping it across her face. Imagines his words: *We are done.*

"You mad at me, huh," Libby asks.

"Shouldn't have done that, Libby."

"I only done what yo' mama would'a done if she were here to do it, baby. An you know that shit's the truth."

Olivia finds Libby's hand on the sheets without looking. Squeezes it. Libby laughs her low, slow little chuckle.

"You fo'give me, huh baby?"

"Yeah, Lib. I forgive you."

And she does. Because, in the end, she knows *that shit,* as Libby put it, is *not* the truth. She knows, for a cold certainty, that her mama, were she here, would never have done something like that. Would never have cared to do something like that.

"Just…" Olivia rolls back onto her elbow. Looks hard. "Tell me that's it, Libby. Tell me you haven't done anything else. No more."

The pause is just long enough to be uncomfortable.

"Thas' it, baby. Ain' no mo' shit to tell."

A lone chachalaca is in the orchard behind the house. Racing from tree to tree. Shrieking its alarm.

Spreading the news.

Calling the lie for what it is.

Chapter 59
Dallas and Etta

Another day, Pablo. Another day and another go at this letter. I was thinking as I was lying in bed trying to wake up that I probably won't even send it. Going to be a short day too. Didn't wake up until close to noon and my head hurt so bad all I could do was lie still. Listen to the fridge turn itself on and off. Medicine they give ain't worth a boat in the desert. Here's some advice, Pablo. Try not to get a damned tumor in your brain. Aim for the elbow. Get a thumb tumor.

I don't really know where to start so I'll start where everything else always seems to start and that's with Mama. I gave an interview to Billboard Magazine back when '*Mama's Girl*' was hittin big. No, that's not right. '*Mama's Girl*' had already hit and '*My Man for a Dime*' was comin on strong. Billboard asked me about my family when I was comin up. I told them something I thought would sell me better than the truth. Funny how we always think people will like the lie better than the truth. I had a better blues story than I could ever make up and I made up a story anyway. I was worried about being too blue. I told them I had five siblings. Three brothers and two sisters like I come from some dirt poor black Texan Brady Bunch. Said we all went to church together with my mother who sewed clothes for a living and my father who was in the army. Even referred to them as 'mother' and 'father'. Like buried beneath all them blues was a real wholesome family girl who said things like 'yes, mother' and 'thank-you, father'.

Well, as you might imagine, that led to questions about growin up in such a big, close family. All the love, all the love in that big family of mine. Lord, have mercy. One lie just led to another and another. I had to make up names and had to try to keep them all straight. Interview about killed me, Pablo. I slept for two days just to get my strength back up from so much lying. Then Billboard published the story. People I knew come up to me on the street: '*Dallas, I read that interview. I didn't know you had such a big family! Come sit down and tell me what each and every one of your brothers and sisters is doing today! And let's see us some photographs too!* The lesson should have been don't lie. Lesson turned out to be don't do interviews. I kept on with the lying. My whole life. Until now anyway.

Truth is I'm an only child. Mama was an assistant to a fat man named Louie Perl who served as the county assessor. My daddy is either Fat Louie or Earl Letti, the thin mean man she married and that beat her with his ring hand three days a week. Can't tell you for sure. Every person who might know is dead and I don't care much anyway. I favor Louie, but I got Earl's last name and Mama swore up and down he was the one. Course, I come by my lying honest. If my Mama told you the sun was out you best go to the window and see for yourself because it's just as likely to be snowing.

Anyway, whoever my daddy was, Mama squeezed me out and then gave up the baby-makin business for good. She had two miscarriages after me and I know its because she willed them babies to call it quits before they ever saw daylight. She regretted me and did not want another one. Earl didn't either. That's my guess anyway. Can't imagine why he would. That didn't stop him from doing the deed whenever he wanted. And then one thing lead to another. Twice. So Mama did not have much choice but to use her own stubbornness and force of will to snuff out my siblings in the womb. Plus Earl tended to let up on the beatings when she was showing so I suppose the longer she took to get the job done the better off she was.

But she sure didn't want babies. I figure I was lucky to make it out alive. Before she knew it I was crawling around her kitchen floor messin up my diapers like I messed up her sex-on-the-side with Fat Louie. She started swellin up with me and Fat Louie suddenly loves his wife and his own kids after all. Fired Mama and hired a secretary who didn't have a bun in the oven. And before she knew it there I was, on the floor in my shitty diaper. Too old to snuff out.

Guess I shouldn't speak ill of the dead. She gave it a go. I think she tried. She did her best to settle into mothering. But she wasn't much good at it and she didn't ever seem to like it. Or me. I know that's a sorry ass sad-sack thing to write down in a letter. But it's true, Pablo. I'm trying to tell the truth for a change.

In all my years on the road, there was plenty a time when someone in the band would ask if his wife or girlfriend could ride with us on the bus from one city to the next. And I'd always say yes cause I'm really not the bitch everyone thinks I am. And then, sure enough, a woman would come on board with a baby in her arms. One gal come on the bus draggin a three-year old. I fell for it every time.

Cause what am I gonna do? Say no? Say 'you and your yowlin baby got to *walk* from Louisville to Chicago'? Guess I could have. It was my name scrawled across the side of that bus. *'The Letti Blue Rollers'* in big loopy letters. My bus, so I could have throwed off anyone I please. But, like I say, I always let them come on.

Anyway, sometimes I'd wake up in the middle of one of those long stretches of road and look over at the woman with the baby in her arms, or look over at the woman with the toddler asleep in her lap. Everybody but the driver sacked out and sleeping and there I am, Letti Blue, awake and looking. And as hard as I looked, Pablo, I never saw me and Mama. I never had that with Mama. Not as I remember.

And how do I *not* take that shit personally, Pablo? Damn right I took it personally. It was *me* Mama did not want. *Me* she did not like. *ME.* But I don't think it was actually personal. I think she'd have treated any child of hers that same way. Any child would have been a burden. Any child would have kept Mama from being who she wanted to be. Which, you ask, was *what?* Free, I think. She wanted to be free. Mama didn't want to be a mama. She wanted to be Maybelline Louisa Nogales, a half-black, half-Mexican sex maniac from Las Cruces who wanted to dance up on a stage and fuck around back stage. She married Earl cause he played alto sax in a little Jump Blues band that toured around New Mexico for about ten minutes. Fool thought himself the next Louis Jordan. Mama and another girl got to shimmy and shake their goodies, do a little sexed-up swing dancing and fox trotting out front just to get people in the mood.

Not so fun when they moved to Texas though. Earl got himself into rough necking. Sold his horn and started following the tool pushers up and down the state line from one pumpjack to another. Mama said he called it *humping dinosaurs.* Come home all covered in oil and grime and upset because Mama didn't have his chicken and beer ready for him. She told me she was always late with supper because she was off assisting –and by 'assisting' I mean 'bending her ass over for' –the County Assessor who worked a slow bus ride away from where they lived. That was Fat Louie.

People say the funny part was that Earl was happiest when Mama was home early to get him supper. Funny because she was only home early when Fat Louis gave her a ride home, which he did so they could pull over out near the quarry and fuck in the back seat of Louie's Ford Deluxe station wagon with whitewalls and hickory panels along the sides. Only car like it in South Texas and the only reason Louie had it was because he had a well-to-do uncle in Chicago who died and left it to Louie's daddy who then died of a stroke before the damn thing was even delivered. So Fat Louie Perl, not much better off than anyone else in South Texas, got the car. A fine ride to hear Mama tell it. Called them cars 'Woodies' back then. If you can believe that shit.

Mama went to work shuffling papers for Fat Louie because, well, one, they needed the money and, two, because she thought being an assistant to a government official made her special somehow, and three because Fat Louie played a mean piano in the Baptist church they attended, and four because Fat Louie had seen her dance and told her that she should be up on a stage somewhere. Fat Louie was full of talk about quitting his job and going to Europe. He had some friends in London. Said all they did was play music and drink beer and fuck. That kind of talk was like Spanish Fly for Mama. She'd bend herself over Fat Louie's back seat nine days a week just to hear him go on about leaving his wife to go live across the damn pond. Which was all shit, of course. Only place Fat Louie ever took Mama was to and from that damn quarry. Europe my ass.

Earl Letti was the one who went to Europe. Got himself drafted just after we entered the war. Shipped off to France. Come limping back ten months later with a bad case of the Clap and a cane and a hole in his foot from his own damn bullet. He hobbled in the front door, dropped his duffle, and there I was waiting for him. On a blanket on the floor. Poopy diapers. Screaming my head off. I could sing even then, Pablo. I could really shake up a room.

Mama had a real tough go of it starting then. She'd fucked herself right out of a job cause Fat Louie was not interested in giving a pregnant woman Woodie-rides to the quarry. He fired Mama and hired some eighteen-year old thing from the church to shuffle his papers. Not that Mama had any choice once I was born anyway. Once I showed up, she was chained to that tiny house. Earl tried to go back to roughnecking, but that didn't last but a month. They didn't want a cripple around the iron dinosaurs. So he got himself a job at the slaughterhouse. Stopped seeing his oil crew friends. Started drinking everyday after work. Come home drunk and angry and take it out on Mama. She said she would have left him a thousand times, but then there I was, looking with my big baby eyes, crying, needing, complicating everything. So she stuck it out. Made sure his chicken and beer was on the table when he got home. Took her beatings. Got herself knocked up twice more, but like I say, neither of them took. Just me. I was the only one.

Five years after he got home from the war against his own foot, Earl got himself killed in a bar fight. A knife to the gut over a two-dollar bill. Not wasting any ink on details you don't need to know. This letter is not about that miserable excuse for a person, Earl Letti. Point is that the knife to Earl's gut left Mama alone with a six year old that she never liked in the first place. Just me and her. No survivor's pension from the Army because Earl already been discharged too long at that point. So there was wasn't even enough money just for Mama, not to mention me.

We were a charity case for a long spell. Mama did what she could. Cleaned a few houses for a while, drag my little ass up and down the stairs, sit me in the corner and clean around me as I cry and carry on. Must have drove them white people out their ever-living minds. But they kept her on. Didn't have much of a choice, really. Like the very idea of me tellin a mama and her baby they can't ride on the Letti Blue bus. Hard to look us in the eyes and say don't come back. Go on and starve.

Eventually, someone at the church gave her a sewing machine. Big black monstrosity. Looked for all the world like one of those iron dinosaur pumpjacks scattered around the desert. She worked that thing day and night. Patching holes. Making clothes. Made hats. Shirts. In three years time, half the county was walking around in something that Mama pulled out of that black iron sewing machine. Really wasn't another seamstress competing with her, so that helped. It was enough to put food on the table, but not much more. She made all of my clothes too.

My earliest memories are sitting on the floor of our little bitty house listening to the radio as Mama sewed. She said I always stopped my wailing when the music was on. So that meant it was on almost constantly. That's where I first heard the blues. Bessie Smith on the radio, fighting with the angry growl of that big black sewing machine. And Big Joe Turner and Big Mama Thornton. Billie. Ella. Odetta. Mississippi John. Blind Willie. Lightnin Hopkins. Alberta Hunter. Victoria Spivey. All of the good ones, Pablo. They just came pouring out of that radio. Entertained me. Rocked me to sleep. Paid attention to me.

Mama fed me; I'll give her that. She worked hard to feed me and keep me dry. But the blues mothered me, Pablo. Cared about me. Understood me. My real mama was the blues itself. Sounds silly. Sounds like I'm back doing that Billboard interview. But it's truer than anything I know.

By time I turned twelve, Mama got the itch. With enough food in the fridge to eat, she got back to thinking about men again. I was the wrong kind of company. There was a man or two during that time that took to having their inseams measured every Sunday. Those boys just never seemed to run out of pants! Both of them as married as married could be. Mama took me to morning service at the church and left me with Mr. Roop, the choir director, most of the afternoon. Cornelius Roop. People called him 'Corny' behind his back because he thought himself so proper and refined. Always in the same shabby black suit and tie. Cologne so sweet he walked around in a cloud of bees. Corrected everybody's grammar. Got angry at people when they swore, protecting God's name every which way. But he could sing. Corny had a voice. In all my years with Corny Roop, while Mama was out measuring inseams, I was at the church learning just what kind of voice I had in me.

He discovered me. Corny Roop found my voice and he taught me how to use it. Also taught me how not to use it. Taught me to sing. And he taught me how to keep a secret. We sang a lot of gospel and blues every Sunday afternoon. And we kept a lot of secrets, Pablo.

Never told anyone about that. Not even Mama. You the only one. Since Corny Roop is pushing daisies going on forty years now, that means it's just you and me that know. Pretty soon it'll just be you. You do with it want you want, Pablo. I just needed to get it out. I won't say I didn't know any better. Wrong is wrong and it felt all wrong every time and I felt bad about it. I did. But Corny Roop was nice to me. Paid me attention. Thought I was something special. Told me I would be great one day. So I paid him attention back.

Mama died of the crazy when I was nineteen. Threw herself into the same quarry where Fat Louie used to take her in his Woodie. Swallowed up by the earth.

I'd been gone for a whole year by then. I'd moved down to Corbin and set up with my very first group, "*Otis D's Hot Fivers*", doing our little gigs. Sometimes, when Otis was feeling generous, we'd be "*Otis D's Hot Fivers featuring Rosetta Letti.*" That always felt good. Sometimes we'd be playing in some beat-up club, or out back behind some pig roast pit on the Fourth of July, or playing the Moon Garden Festival, and I'd imagine Mama looking at the words on that sign, "*featuring Rosetta Letti*" and I'd imagine what would be going through her head. Always hoped she'd be proud. Proud that I had a gift. I imagined that she'd suddenly love me for my voice and want to brag on me to others. Hell, last time I played Chicago I imagined Mama somewhere in the crowd. Clapping and cheering. Guess that makes me just a little bit crazy too.

Long before I left home, Mama could see me becoming a woman. I developed early. And, as you well know, I knew how to flirt like nobody's business. Didn't matter the age. It was a game to get the men to look and smile back. And they did. I think my flirting scared Mama to death. Not so much for what being a mother would have done to my life but because she saw herself having to raise a sixteen-year old and another yowling baby. So she came down on me hard. I got punished every time I so much as looked sideways at a man. Except for Corny Roop, of course. Corny made the cut because he was a deacon and I'd known him since I was just a girl. And Corny was the one that made it possible for Mama to go out and do her thing. Measuring inseams. And, anyway, Mama trusted Corny. But every other man was suspect. If she caught me looking sideways at a man she'd lock me in my room for the rest of the day. No supper. No money for candy. No radio. But I kept looking sideways at men anyhow. And they always looked back.

Mama was always dead-set against me having a baby, and I mean *ever* having a baby. Our mother-daughter-birds-and-the-bees talk was one for the ages. She basically told me that I'd be a terrible mother. That it would be a crime for me to ever have a child and because of that I should stay away from all men forever and ever. That's when she told me point blank what I already knew; that she should never have had me in the first place. I think it was her way of owning up to what a shitty mother she had been for me. *"You be 'bout as good at it as I was. You be about as good for a baby as I have been for you."* It was as close as I ever got to an apology. *"Don't you bring into the world a baby you ain't prepared to throw your entire life away for. You got one life and you can either keep it for yourself or you can give it all away to the baby. You want you a man? You want you a good time before you get old, wrinkle up and die? You want you to sing for the people like Bessie Smith? Like Corny Roop say you can sing? Then you best keep your life for yourself. Don't go throwin' it away for some tit-suckin little maggot. You keep it for yourself."*

The crazy came gradual at first. Just a little extra angry or a little extra drunk or a little extra lonely. *Acting* crazy is different than *being* crazy. But then Mama started *being* crazy. She'd stay up all night sometimes, walking the house, talking to herself. I'd go to sleep to it and wake up in the middle of the night to it. I woke up one Sunday morning and she had glued big sheets of blue poplin to every door in the house. I asked her why. She laughed and shook her head. *"Doors? Can't you see them's windows?"* And I said, *"Mama, those are doors and you know it."* And she said *"Well, they's windows now."* And I said, *"Mama why on earth?"* And she said *"Well how else am I gonna see out and how is she gonna see in?"* And I said, *"Who are you talkin about, Mama?"* And she said, *"The woman who says things to me, that's who."* And I said *"What woman?"* And she said *"The one with the voice. Oh we have us some good conversations, too. All night long."*

That's when I knew I was dealing with *being* crazy, not *acting* crazy. Mama's crazy made an impression on me. I know part of me believed Mama when she told me I would never be a good mother. That it would be a crime. That I would cause misery and pain if I even tried. She wanted me to promise. Begged me to promise. I didn't promise anything. I just left home for good. Didn't look back and never saw her again. I had no idea in this world what I wanted. But I knew whatever it was I wanted, I wasn't going to get it in that house. Like Billie Holiday wishing on that moon for sweeter roses and softer skies and all the other things she had never known. April days taking their time.

More than anything, I think I was determined to believe that I was nothing like my mother in any way. Turns out I was wrong, Pablo.

Truth is, I turned out exactly like my mother.

Chapter 60

She is a different person, Laurie Weaver. No longer a *Chacha* newsroom sloth. She is over-caffeinated. Nails freshly bitten. A band of irritation across her forehead. She is now two cigarettes behind for not having had time for a smoke break. Withdrawal is tightening the vice from the inside.

She leans into the table, impatient at the pace of seconds, marching single-file. Always single-file. She raps her pen against her notepad fast enough to qualify as a vibration. Trying to make the seconds march faster.

She is evening up her thumbnail when the door pushes into the room. She spits out the invisible fragment. Opens her mouth to speak.

Desmond Vaughn raises a finger. Says something over his shoulder to Everett Sampson. Everett calls out to his brother Billy and moves on as Desmond closes the door behind him. He pulls out a chair. Sits.

"Dez…"

"Laurie. Just wait. You want money. I get it. I don't have money."

Irritation. Impatience.

"Have you asked?"

"I don't need to ask. There is no budget for anything investigative. You already know that."

"Damnit, Dez."

"Laurie, our goddamned water cooler is empty because I can't get anyone to renew the contract with the supplier. Understand? We can't spend even on *water*. How can this possibly come as a surprise?"

Laurie sits back hard in her chair. Crosses her arms. Looks out the dirty window of the shabby conference room out into the bullpen. A quarter of the desks are empty. Half of the remainder may as well be empty. It's a pathetic tableau. *Still Life of a News Room.*

The gremlins inside the radiator start in with their little hammers. This season is always an irritant. Cold in the morning. Warm in the afternoon. So they bang out their discontent in the usual code. Three fast. Two slow. One alone.

Laurie waits for the last little hammer.

"Desmond. You were the one that asked me to look into it. And now you want to just let it die?"

It is Desmond's turn to be irritated. His face pinches inward.

"Now wait a second. I…"

"You can't expect me to…"

His right hand is up, stopping traffic.

"Wait… a fucking… second. Just stop. Just. Stop." He drops the hand. Sighs. "I'm not asking you to let anything die. *Laurie.* But I can't just pull an investigation budget out of my ass. If there's really a story here…"

"If there's really a *story*? Desmond," she jabs the point of her pen onto the face of her notepad. "This shit is not adding up. Something is wrong here."

"Well, something is certainly *weird*. It may or may not be *wrong*. It's all still preliminary. If you start jumping to conclusions and we run a half-baked story…"

He lets his eyebrows finish the sentence, adding a little gravitas to the thing unspoken. Laurie is not impressed.

"No half-baked stories. Got it. Good to know. Gee, Dez, sounds like some investigative journalism might just be a great fuckin' idea."

Desmond sighs and leans back. Absorbs the sarcasm. Laurie is the only *Chacha* reporter in motion on anything. Usually he is lucky if she shows up on time and not hung over. Suddenly she's a force of nature. He rubs his face with both hands.

"Right. Fuck. Okay. Tell me again. Where are we?"

She opens her note pad. Flips through the pages. Stops. Counts to herself.

"I've talked to six of them so far."

"Including Lib…"

"Including Libby Holder. And her next door neighbor, a guy named Darrell Lewis, who harvests Libby Holder's pecan crop. So six property owners who say they have not sold anything. To *any*-fuckin'-body."

"Six. I thought the list from Libby Holder had seventeen."

"Nineteen."

"And?"

"Jesus, Dez. I'm doing what I can. I got through to six of them. I'm working on the others but they have to decide to call me back first."

Desmond closes his eyes. Takes a breath. Lets it go. Continues.

"So as to the six… the county property records show…"

"Yes. Yes." She is already flipping back the pages. "And the county property records show that each of those properties has been sold in the last… wait… in the last eighteen months."

"Sold to whom?"

"Six different buyers. Two individuals. Four companies. All out of state."

"Have you…"

"Goddamned right I have. And no luck connecting with any of them. *But.*" She points. *Flips. Flips.* "But." Finger in the air. "*But.* All six properties have flipped at least once. Two of them have flipped twice. One of them three times. Price has doubled. More than doubled."

"On all six?"

"Yes. And get this. All six properties at some point in time have been owned and sold by one of three companies operating as a subsidiary of the Corbin Development Corporation."

"The River Walk people."

"The fuckin' River Walk people."

"Okay."

"And the Corbin Development Corporation is a wholly owned sub of Quinco International. New York, London and …" *Flip. Flip.* "Hamburg."

"Okay. Any comment yet from them?"

"Nothing worth a shit. Quinco gave me three different referrals in two different countries each of which referred me to a media relations office in London that still will not return my calls. The time difference is killing me. After a billion or so messages to Corbin Development I finally got a call back from a guy named Adrian Hewitt, Vice President of Projects. He called to tell me that there is nothing he can tell me because…" *Flip. Flip.* "Because, quote, the CDC is prohibited from discussing its commercial transactions without approval from its parent."

"Which is Quinco."

"Right. So Adrian Hewitt referred me to the same media relations office."

"So Corbin Development owns all six properties?"

"No. Corbin Development currently owns two of the six. It flipped the others."

"To who?"

"Whom."

"Fuck you."

"To four different construction companies."

"Okay, wait. All four of those buyers are construction companies?"

"Yes. All four."

"Have you talked to them?"

He can see her biting her tongue. She wants desperately to make a point about his expectation that she conduct herself like an investigative journalist while at the same time lecturing her on the impossibility of investigative journalism at a publication one breath from extinction.

"Laurie, just…"

"Yes. Dez. I have tried talking to them. There is no way, no *fuckin'* way, to get this information over the telephone. Doesn't work that way. Only one of them has called me back. A minority-owned outfit out of San Angelo. *Sanchez Construction.* So I push a bunch of work off on to Billy and I make the drive and do some digging."

"Okay. So?"

"So this is a small operation, Dez. Only a handful of modest projects in a year. All residential. All in San Angelo. All Hispanic labor."

"Okay."

"I paid them a visit. Spoke to a Jaime Sanchez, son of the owner. He acknowledged the purchase from Corbin Development as investment property. No big deal, right? So I go back to the county records. Sanchez Construction – little teeny, tiny Sanchez Construction –has acquired seven lots in and around Corbin over the past two years. *Seven.* It still owns two of those, plus the one I went to ask them about. The other five properties it sold off to those same three CDC subsidiaries."

He scratches his head. Leans in. "So…"

"Wait. So when you add up the acquisition price of those seven properties… the total cost to Sanchez Construction…" *Flip. Flip. Flip.* "It comes to almost three million bucks. If I was a *real* investigative reporter with an *actual* budget for investigative journalism I'd be here telling you that Sanchez Construction is lucky to net one million in a good year."

"So…"

"Wait. So when I add up the book value of those seven properties today… the three that Sanchez Construction still owns, plus the four it sold off to the Corbin Development subsidiaries, which promptly flipped them over to other buyers… guess how much."

"All seven?"

"All seven."

"More. I don't…"

"Five point two million." Laurie stabs the pad with the point of her pen for emphasis. "*Five. Point. Two.* That's a seventy percent increase in less than a year, Dez."

She falls quiet. It is his turn to speak. He doesn't.

His eyes trace the grain in the table between them. The same coffee-stained, gouged, ink-streaked table that had once regularly supported four, five, sets of elbows at once in heated meetings about journalistic priorities and standards. Who to endorse for the Crockett County School Board. For Governor. For President. Whether an entire National News section, as opposed to a single page, was worth the extra ink. The epic, friendship-ending fights over whether Molly Ivins and Mike Doonesbury were purveyors of subversive propaganda harmful to Texan and

American values or a worthwhile counterbalance to the undeniable journalistic tilt. For such a provincial rag, *The Chacha* had always seemed to fold irregularly over shifting political fault lines. Allegiances –between staff and editor, editor and owner, owner and the rest of the political and publishing world –had always been critical and unreliable. Flimsy rope and wood-slat bridges swaying above deep rock chasms that split the world between where one stood and where one needed to be.

And here he was again. Wondering if the bridge would hold.

The radiator gremlins start swinging their hammers. The door opens behind him. He glances up at Laurie's face like it's a rearview mirror. Billy Sampson's voice falls over his shoulders.

"Everett says you want *me* to pick up the slack on *The Docket*. You want *me* to do that. *Me*."

Desmond closes his eyes. Does not turn around.

"I'm in a meeting, Billy. We all have to pitch in. You guys will just have to work it out. Someone's got to fill the column. It's half-done already."

"I'll do it, Dez," says Billy. "I'll do it. *Again*. But just so you know? This is bullshit."

He closes the door too hard. Desmond opens his eyes. They find Laurie Weaver where they had left her.

"Anyway," he sighs. "So the River Walk people are inflating the market. That's what you're saying."

"It's not rocket science, Dez. The guy I went to see at Sanchez Construction? He had a CDC development plan brochure right there on the fuckin' desk."

Desmond lets a soft laugh escape.

"So? Who hasn't gotten one of those? They're everywhere. I got one too."

"Really?" She is mocking. "Where is it? Do you still have it?"

"I don't know. No."

"Right. They came out a year ago. You'd need an archeologist to find the shit I received a year ago. This thing was right there on top of the man's desk."

"But that really doesn't prove… anything, does it?"

Laurie Weaver's forefinger and thumb hover above the table, pinching the air between them until they are almost touching.

"It proves that Corbin Development is on the teeny-tiny-itty-bitty radar of Sanchez Construction."

"So what, Laurie?" Desmond's arms widen, palms up, embracing the obvious. "If you were Sanchez Construction, why wouldn't you have the CDC on your radar? You'd do anything to get a piece of the biggest construction project South Texas has seen in a century."

Laurie's face lifts at every corner. "Exactly."

Desmond lowers his arms. His eyes, as if struggling against gravity, go back to looking at the grain in the table.

"Something stinks here, Dez," she says. "There's a story here. Maybe a big one. Maybe the one this paper needs."

There is a moment. Two. Three. He looks up. Speaks.

"You know how many jobs the Corbin River Walk will bring to this part of Texas? You have any idea of the investment money that is hangin' above Crockett County like some sort of... some sort of fucking cornice just waiting to drop? You realize the political muscle lined up behind this thing?"

"Who said anything about taking down the River Walk project? Jesus, Dez. Back up a second. This isn't about the River Walk. I'm just sayin' that some of these property transfers are... hinky. *Could be* hinky. Could be."

"Stop working me, Laurie. I'm trying to tell you that what you're askin' is not going to sit well with the owners. They're not gonna like getting' those kinds of phone calls."

"I'm not askin' the owners. I'm not askin' Cal Aronson. I'm askin' you. If this story finds a spotlight, I mean *really* hits a nerve, the owners won't care who's ringin' the phone. The phones'll be ringin' all the way back to the good ol' days. Cal Aronson'll break out the good hooch."

He sighs. Rubs his eyes. Keeps them closed. They resemble half-deflated, post-accident airbags.

"What do you want?"

"All roads lead to the Corbin Development Corporation, which is an instrument of Quinco International."

"Right. So you want to knock on doors in New York. London."

"Damn straight."

"I can't do that, Laurie. I can't pull a travel budget out of my..."

"Please stop talking about pullin' things our of your ass. I know you can't. Which is why I want to reach out to Rick."

Eyes open.

"Rick? Rick Stoddard? Fucker left us for dead."

"Yeah. He did. Naked, barrel-chested ambition personified. But look. If you could choose between this dump and CBS, what would you do?" She doesn't wait for an answer. "Rick has always been in it for himself." A pause. "But Rick owes me big time."

"Why?"

"Never mind why."

"*Really?* Really Laurie? Never mind? Do you want my fuckin' approval on this or not?"

Laurie looks away. Considers her thumbnail. Starts to chew. Looks back.

"It's personal."

"So?"

"We had a... *thing*. Okay?"

He absorbs the truth in the cavity of his chest. Does his best not to react. He sees in her eyes that he has failed at not reacting. Speaks.

"A *thing*. Nice. Before or after he married Angie?"

She crosses her arms. Watches him putting that moving image together in his head. Says nothing.

"Jesus," says Desmond.

"Oh, don't look so fuckin' surprised. Boy Scout. I don't see any merit badges on your chest. You of all fuckin' people."

"So, you mean Rick owes you big time in a *blackmaily* kind of way. They've got a three year old girl."

"Yeah. I'm aware, Dez. Look. Not that it's any of your business, but he was cheatin' on *me*. With *her*. Kind of. Angie is just another rung in the ladder for him. Part of his résumé. Not sayin' blackmail. I'm just sayin' that there's likely something still there."

"Oh, so… what… you're just going to promise him some good phone sex?"

"The point is… *Fuck*." She uncoils from her defensive crouch. Leans back in. "The point *is*, Dez, that if I can get Rick interested in this thing, maybe we can ride on the coattails of *CBS*'s budget. CBS can knock on doors in a way that the piss-ant *Chachalaca Gazette* cannot."

"And… well *Hell's bells*, Laurie, what good does that do *us*?"

"If there's a story here, the *Chacha* gets the print headline. We become the source for CBS. We get the local coverage and they identify this paper in their reporting, which broadens our exposure. If there is a story in New York or London or Hamburg or the fuckin' moon, then CBS gets that for itself and we can use whatever they find to fill out our local coverage. We promise not to share with the AP or UPI. We promise them everything we've got."

"Which is almost nothing."

"We've got more than nothing. We've got six property owners on the record and more to come if you give me the time to really dig in locally. And we've got a list from the files of the CDC and Quinco. We've got Libby Holder and Sheldon Davis…"

"The vindictive hooker and her erstwhile john. Great."

"We've got Sanchez Construction. We've got the list."

"Okay, yeah, we've got the list. You already said that. It doesn't count twice. CBS can get almost all of the rest themselves."

"Only if they know where to start diggin'. Besides, how is it our fault if Rick Stoddard's ambition causes him to jump to unfounded conclusions about how much we have?"

Desmond opens his mouth. Laurie points.

"No. Don't give me the Boy Scout ethics lecture. We need a good story. And this one's got legs. I can feel it. So don't for one fuckin' second get hung up on doing right by Rick Stoddard. This gives him something fresh to take to his editors. He's looking to make a name for himself. Everybody wins."

"If there's a story," he says. "But if there's no story?"

"Then there's no story. We will have wasted our time, and some of CBS's time and budget, but we'll all just go about our business."

"*Fuck*," says Desmond quietly shaking his head. The rope bridge starts to sway beneath him. "Okay. Fuck."

"I'll need to get someone to take some of my load."

"Oh come on. Like who?" He jerks his thumb over his shoulder toward the bullpen on the other side of the window. "Billy? You want me to ask Billy to do your work?"

"I don't care, Dez. Someone. This is going to take some serious time. I can't be worried about fender benders and coyotes in the chicken coop."

"Fine. Shit, Laurie. You're going to lose some friends around here."

"I don't have any friends." She beams with insincerity. "'Cept you."

It's the closest he will get to a thank you.

The door opens. A disembodied head appears through the crack like a dour-faced helium balloon sporting a dirty-blonde wig.

Sylvia Bloom is responsible for *Living Arts*. And the obituaries. Between art and death she also answers the phone.

"Sorry to interrupt," says Sylvia. "Laurie, Rick Stoddard called. Told me to tell you that all lights are green on his end. Said you'd know what that means, which is good because I certainly don't. Wants you to call him ASAP. Dez, the fucking copier is down again. What's the word about getting a new one to replace that piece of shit?"

Desmond does not answer. He watches Laurie stand and make her way furtively around the table. She is smart enough to know that she needs to get out now, before he retracts his consent in the shadow of its apparent irrelevance.

But she cannot get to the door without coming within inches of his left side. He pinches her notepad between his fingers. She stops. Looks down at him. Waits.

"Take me off of your fucking friends list."

Chapter 61
Abby and Davis

The month that followed Simon Dore's hand across my face was like the column of air in a black well. It was like that slap had knocked me backwards over the edge and I was falling. Totally disoriented. The dark, open space below devoured me whole. I kept expecting to land on some realization or some truth or some relationship –my father, my friends, my teachers –that would break my fall. But I just kept falling.

I skipped as much school as I could get away with. I kept to myself. I held everyone at a distance. The only voice in my head was Abby's telling me in her kitchen that she loved me and that she did not know what she would ever do without me. And the only vision in my head was Abby kissing Simon in her doorway. Kissing him the same way she had kissed me. Kissing him with that same look in her eyes. The look that belonged to me. Or that should have.

I told myself that she had kissed Simon to protect me. That she was only convincing Simon I was not a threat and not worth the trouble of hurting. I even believed it. I still do. Despite everything, I still believe that.

But I also believed the opposite. That she loved Simon more. That she had never loved me. That I meant nothing to her. It was a kind of relief whenever I could convince myself that she had been trying to save me. It meant that at least she cared. But even that thought was poisonous. Because Abby was not supposed to save me. I was supposed to save *her*. To think she had sacrificed herself to Simon to save me left me feeling pathetic and weak. Every so often I felt angry at her for even thinking that I had needed her protection.

But there was nothing I could do with all of that anger except to let it grow heavy in my chest and let it pull me deeper and deeper into the well. Because it was true. I *had* needed saving. Simon would have hurt me. I proved that I could not actually defend myself or Abby. I'd just stood there on the driveway and bled.

Everyone in my life knew something was wrong. When I wasn't locked off someplace alone, I was taking my anger out on someone who didn't deserve it.

My dad started to show a lot my interest in my life. Suddenly he wanted to do things together. Football games. Movies. I always turned him down. He kept coming back. We went out to dinner a few times and he always asked me to drive. Like it was a big deal for me to drive a car. I wanted to tell him that I drove all the time. That I didn't need his permission or his charity. That I was a man with a broken heart. That I had logged more miles on the road in the past six weeks than he had all year.

I didn't tell him any of that. But I refused to drive every time he asked, letting him think that I was afraid to drive. What was one more person who thought of me as a helpless chicken-shit? What did I care?

At one point, after I had bitten his head off for something stupid, Dad asked if I wanted to come see you. He had decided that whatever I was going through had something to do with Mom. He said maybe it would help to talk about it with someone who knew mom. A professional.

That's how he referred to you. "*A professional.*" As if that meant something. It meant nothing to me. It still means nothing. The certificate on your wall doesn't mean that you know anything. Sorry, Dr. Bees, but that's true.

I wanted to slap him. I wanted to hit my dad across the face like Simon Dory had hit me, over and over again until his face was red and his nose was bleeding. I wanted to scream at him that nothing I was feeling had anything to do with Mom. That he didn't understand anything. He eventually left me alone, but I could tell he was worried. That might have been the only thing good in my life.

Fat Jack and Skinny Kenny also knew something was wrong. I told them that I was having problems with my dad and that I didn't want to talk about it. I don't know if they bought that or not, but they mostly let it go. I tried to see them as little as possible. I couldn't go back to that world. As much as I wanted to go back, as much as I wanted to escape the hurt and confusion in my world, I knew I would never fit myself back into the life of a teenager. I couldn't imagine caring about grades or girls or dances or high school football. All I cared about, all I could think about, was Abby. How much I loved her. How sickeningly awful it felt to not be able to just jump in the truck and drive out to see her. The fantasies in my head were constant. Brutalizing Simon with my fists. Carrying Abby away. Making love anywhere. Everywhere.

But I knew none of that was possible.

I called her once. It was the beginning of the second week after Simon's slap. I didn't think about it and I had no idea what I was going to say to whoever answered the phone. It was ten o'clock at night and I was lying awake in my bed in the dark and without any plan whatsoever I reached over, picked up the phone and dialed her number. She picked up on the second ring.

"Abby."

"Davis. Don't call me. I mean it."

Her tone was soft. Pleading. But the words were hard.

"Abby... I..."

"I mean it. We're very busy. Goodbye, Davis."

The line went dead. All I could do was stare at the phone as my chest crumbled into dust.

We're very busy.

We.

She was trying to tell me that Simon was still nearby. Still dangerous. Maybe that was her way of explaining herself. It's not Abby, it's Simon. Abby still loves you but Simon will still kill you.

Maybe.

But all I heard was that it was Abby *and* Simon. Together. Busy.

At one point the torture of seeing Jack's truck down the street in the cul-de-sac was more than I could take. The temptation to do the thing I could not do was slowly killing me. I needed to forget her. I needed to make her impossible.

I cornered Fat Jack after Biology and held out the keys to the truck. I told him he needed to take it someplace else because Dad had started noticing it every time he drove into the driveway and wondering out loud about who owned it. That was true enough. Dad had started taking notice. But I really did not care anything about whatever Dad thought about the truck. I just needed to make Abby impossible.

Jack assured me that he could take the truck back soon, but that he was not ready yet. I pressed him for details, but he refused. He kept asking for me to trust him and to be a good friend. "Just a little longer," he kept saying. "Just a little longer." I didn't have the energy to argue.

I felt things begin to change a little in the fourth week. I woke up that Saturday feeling a little lighter. Still falling down the dark well, but maybe not falling quiet so fast. Or maybe the difference was that for the first time I really wanted to stop falling. Stop hurting. Stop wallowing in it. Like maybe I was ready to be done with being overwhelmed with it all.

By the next Monday I was actually joking around at school and acting mostly normal. Kenny told me that someone had told him a senior named Deena Baker wanted me to ask her out. I had no interest in Deena Baker. Less than no interest. But the idea of it felt kind of good anyway. Jack and Kenny razzed me about the very possibility of dating an older girl.

Had they only known.

That Wednesday, the fifteenth, I invited Jack and Kenny over to play video games and, we told ourselves, to study for our looming chemistry test. I knew Dad would be out at the bookstore and that we would have the place to ourselves until maybe seven or eight. After school Jack and Kenny took my bus and we all walked together from the bus stop to my house.

It felt pleasantly familiar, the three of us walking together. Ragging on each other. Talking trash. Punching each other in the arms. It felt normal. I caught Jack's truck out of the corner of my eye as we walked up the driveway. I pushed everything that truck represented out of my mind.

I had stopped falling. It was the first step up on my way out of that well.

We ate crap and played video games all afternoon. No one opened a chemistry book, of course. Kenny pulled the bad porno tape out of his backpack that he'd been carrying around all week. We watched it for a few minutes on the VCR, laughing at the facial expressions until we nearly cried. I felt almost normal.

That was when the phone rang.

I answered it in my bedroom in case it was Dad. I didn't want him to hear what was coming out of the television.

"Davis?"

Her voice was ragged and hoarse, like the last time she had called, but not hysterical. She spoke slowly.

"They've found me," she said.

"Who's found you?"

"You know who."

"No. I don't."

She kind of laughed.

"This bit again. Doesn't matter, love. It will be over soon. This is it, I'm afraid."

"What do you mean, this is it? What's... Is Simon there?"

"Simon? No. Simon's not back yet. Listen, Davis. I don't have much time. I want to tell you something." She paused. "I want to tell you how sorry I am. I have never deserved you. You're a brilliant boy and I have never deserved you."

She was crying then. I tried to understand but she wasn't making any sense. I could hear Fat Jack braying like a donkey out in the living room.

"Abby..."

"Tell me you love me, Davis. I love you. Tell me. I need to hear that."

The words came on their own. I couldn't stop them. I never considered them.

"Abby... I do. I do love you. I love you so much it's killing me inside. Abby? Abby, tell me what's wrong. What's happening?"

There were waves of sobbing. All I could do was wait.

"I thought you could save me."

"I can. I will."

"No. I see that now. It was wrong of me to ask. I was afraid. I'm still afraid. But you're a brilliant boy. Like a star." Then more sobbing.

"Abby..."

"The white whale. Black eyes like a shark. Devouring stars, Davis. You need to be careful. Don't trust the bobbies. They will know about the wax. Don't tell them about the wax."

"Abby. Enough of this. Listen. Everything is going to be okay."

"No. Davis. My love. My lover. My brilliant boy. Everything is not going to be okay. Not ever again. Because there is something in the wax."

"I don't know what you are talking about. What's in the wax? Chamomile. Essential…"

"Bad energy. Death is in the wax. God is in the wax."

"You don't believe in God."

"Ija is never wrong. They know I know. They are coming for me. Simon locked me in the trailer. There is a hole in the floor. Under the table. I crawled out. I had to call you. I have to go back in now. Simon will be angry with me. I have to go back. I love you Davis. It's not your fault, Davis. It's not your fault. Ija is never wrong."

"Abby…" I paused. Moaning, pain and pleasure, crawled under the door from the living room. Then there was a sharp intake of breath over the phone. Abby's next words were barely audible. A ghost, trying to move the air.

"He's back. Goodbye, love."

The connection clicked off before I could say anything. I hung up the phone. I wanted to call her back, but I didn't dare. I knew it would be Simon who answered.

I stood up and looked around, as if the answers could be found in the chaos of my bedroom. All I saw were the keys to Jack's truck.

I walked quickly through the house, hoping to avoid the living room and make it outside without anyone noticing. I heard Jack's voice at the front door before I had made it off the driveway. I broke into a run for the cul-de-sac.

They were running towards me across the lawn, Fat Jack in the lead, waving his arms, as I started the truck. I hit the gas and swerved wide to avoid them. Jack slapped the side of the truck with his hand. I didn't slow down. I didn't look back.

I hit I-45 like I'd been shot out of a canon, hunched over the wheel, taking everything that damn truck would give me. The name "FRED" on that steering wheel was like a roller coaster car at the Texas State Fair.

Simon's face was on the windshield the whole way, pulling me forward. All of the anger and humiliation from that night was still inside. I imagined myself back in Abby's driveway, Simon's rotten breath mixing with the smell of blood in my nose. I had no idea what was happening. I had no idea what I would have to do when I got there. I only knew that I was going to save Abby Palmer, just as I had promised, and that I was willing to kill Simon Dore to do it.

I was easily going twenty miles an hour over the speed limit when I blew past the Trooper just on the far side of Huntsville. He hit his lights and siren and chased me down. I was so wound up I actually considered trying to outrun him for the rest of the way to Fairfield. After a minute or so, I realized I'd never make it.

I pulled over at a gas station and sat there fuming, watching the Trooper in my rearview mirror taking his time calling in the plates. I used the time imagining Simon surprised to find Abby outside of her locked trailer prison. I imagined him beating her.

I imagined her screaming my name.

"License and registration." He was beefy with short, black hair. He wore his hat so low I could barely see his eyes. Dark sunglasses hung from the shirt pocket of his uniform. His name was Trooper Clapp.

"Don't have any," I said.

"What's your name?"

"Davis Payne. Look, officer, there's an emergency... I've..."

"How old are you, Davis Payne?"

"Seventeen. Sixteen. Sixteen. I've got to go. There's..."

"This your truck, Davis Payne?"

"No. It belongs to a friend of mine. Please, please, listen. I've got..."

"You aware this truck has been reported stolen?"

"What?"

"You aware this truck was involved in a hit-and-run?"

"No. I ... I just ..."

"Get out of the truck. Leave the keys in the ignition."

"But..."

Trooper Clapp opened the door.

"Out."

I turned off the engine and stepped down. He turned me around and frisked me. He walked me back to his cruiser and opened the back door.

"Officer," I said. "Please. You have to let me go. I have to stop something really bad from happening. I don't know anything about the truck. I'm just borrowing it. I was speeding, I know. I'll pay the ticket or whatever but I have to go."

He put his hand on the top of my head and scrunched me down into the back seat and closed the door. Then he sat down in the front seat, door open, one boot on the ground, and radioed in. He made arrangements to get someone out to examine the truck and drive it back to the impound lot. He and whoever he was talking with went back and forth about what to do. Trooper Clapp would wait until Jack's truck was secure, then he would bring me in for questioning.

"We'll need to get up with his parents first," he said. He didn't know I didn't have parents. I only had a parent. Just one. I started thinking for the first time what I would tell my dad.

The accident happened in a split second. Trooper Clapp was asking me a list of questions about where I lived and the name of the owner of the truck. I could see the car on the road out my side window. It was a little white thing, just turning across I-45 for the gas station. I don't know whether it stalled or was just moving too slow, but the semi coming from behind clipped the rear bumper and sent that thing spinning up into the air like some kind of carnival ride.

It landed upside down on the other side of the road. The semi overcorrected and plowed off the road onto its side. It was all over in about six seconds and after the shock of so much noise, Trooper Clapp and I spent a few more seconds together in complete silence.

Trooper Clapp shouted into his radio for an ambulance and ran off, closing his door behind him. I watched him run across the gas station lot and across the road to the smashed white can that used to be a car. Men in blue mechanics uniforms were coming out of the gas station, moving carefully toward the wreckage.

It probably makes me a bad person for not being more concerned. For not caring. But there was nothing I could do to help those people. The only sound in my head was of Abby Palmer screaming for me.

I tried the back door but it was locked. I crawled over into the front seat and climbed out of the passenger side. I thought for a second about taking the cruiser. The keys were still in the ignition. But that idea scared me. Then I thought about just taking the keys so he couldn't follow. But I didn't want to strand him if he needed to race someone to the hospital. I decided to take my chances that Trooper Clapp had his hands full. He knew where I lived. I would turn myself in.

I climbed back into the truck, started the engine and drove off. Trooper Clapp looked up as I passed him on the road. His big white face followed me as I picked up speed. Our eyes met and I could see that he was having trouble understanding or believing what I was doing. I looked away. I heard him shout something. In the rearview mirror I saw him pull his radio from his belt.

I drove as fast as I could, frantically looking for the police cruisers that would be searching for a white pick-up with an underage fugitive hit-and-run car thief behind the wheel. I figured that if they came for me from behind, I could still make it to Abby's place, although I knew that the *last* thing she would want was to see me leading a parade of six police cars to her house.

That thought made me take my foot off the gas for a second. She would hate me. She would never trust me again.

But the hesitation did not last but a second or two. A much larger part of me did not care about Abby's irrational fear of the police or even if it was a long time before she forgave me. If Simon really was beating her up, none of that would matter. As terrified as I was, and as much as I did not want any further complications with the police, I craved the look on Simon's face when the Calvary arrived, lights flashing.

But I encountered only two police cruisers and they were both speeding the other way, no doubt in response to the accident. When I screeched into Abby's neighborhood, my rearview mirror was clear.

Had I arrived two minutes later, I would have been able to see the smoke from a mile away. But when I skidded to a stop across the street, the black oily billows were rising up over the roof of Abby's house, just barely taller than the largest pecan tree on the neighboring lot.

I am ashamed to say that I barely noticed the smoke. I was too concerned with the sight of Simon's car in the driveway. My blood turned to ice water. Now that I was there, I started to panic about the reality of confronting him. I opened the car door and stared across the street, not really knowing if I could do whatever needed to be done.

It was the smell that brought me to my senses. Sickeningly sweet. It smelled like Abby's oils. It smelled like incense.

I shot out of the truck for the house. Visions played through my head like I was seeing the future. I saw myself searching the house through the smoke for Abby. She is locked in a room. She is tied up in a closet. She is wounded on the couch. He is beating her in the kitchen. I had to find her. Pull her out. I was cutting the ropes with a knife. I was holding the fabric of my shirt over her mouth to keep the smoke out. I was punching Simon in the face. I was wrenching the gun from his hand. We were wrestling on the floor as Abby coughed and hacked and bled nearby. She is choking in smoke. She is saying my name. She is reaching for me. *Davis, save me!*

I pounded twice on the front door and then opened it. The house was quiet. I stood in the living room and shouted her name. I listened intently.

Nothing came back to me. I was ready for a strangled whisper or a muffled scream or a foot stomping on a wall. All I heard was the sound of burning. Wet pops and hisses. The smell was overpowering. I was breathing hard. Ready for anything. A hammer was sitting on the back of the sofa. I picked it up. It was my only weapon. I called out again.

I realized then that even in the universe in which I was ready for anything and everything, something was wrong. Something I had not expected. I sharpened all of my senses.

The house was not on fire.

The house was as it had always been. Calm. Quiet. Like Abby might come walking out of the kitchen with two beers in her hands and wearing the *Longhorns* nightshirt that barely covered her privates.

I walked into the kitchen.

I stood, looking out the windows across the back lot.

It was Abby's shop that was on fire.

Jets of thick, black smoke were boiling out of the tiny windows. Blades of bright orange flame stabbed out of the smoke like lightening.

I screamed Abby's name. I dropped the hammer and nearly ripped the kitchen door off its hinges trying to get outside. I ran several steps before feeling the slap of heat in my face. My eyes started to water. I kept moving. I kept screaming Abby's name. I aimed for the rectangle of blue metal that was the door of the trailer. Flames and smoke were belching out of the windows on either side, but that door was the same blue rectangle it had always been. It was the same shape and space I had entered before my life had changed.

I did not see Simon until I was halfway across the back lot. He came from around the back of the trailer. He was in jeans and those same black boots and a white t-shirt covered in grime. His face was bright red with rage and smeared with black soot, like the fire had taken human form.

He came at me in a dead run, arms wide, fists clenched, screaming. I was so freaked out, I threw the first punch early, completely missing his face. As though in all of my excitement I calculated that he was moving faster than he really was.

He ducked the punch and hit me head-on with his entire body, each of his arms ramming under my armpits like metal prongs on a forklift. He had so much momentum, the collision carried me backwards a good ten feet before we hit the ground. He fell directly on top of me and knocked all of the wind out of my lungs. I felt like I couldn't breathe. I fell into a blind panic, gasping for air. Simon sat up and I started throwing wild punches at his face. He avoided them all and punched me hard in the cheek, screaming at me words I did not understand.

The trailer behind him exploded. It was a sound I do not know how to describe. It wasn't a sound. It was a feeling. Like the bursting of internal organs. The ripping open of a human heart. The day turned bright orange like the sun was swallowing the earth. Simon fell on top of me, his chest mashing against my face. I heard bits of metal siding and cinder block smash against the back wall of the house behind me. A window broke. My lungs felt like they were bleeding.

Simon pushed himself up again, still sitting on top of me, and screamed up into the sky. Behind him, over his shoulder, was a knobby, bubbling tower of coal black smoke, shot with flame and framed in perfect blue.

I was not thinking. I was surviving. I swung as hard as I could. I felt his nose break. The blood was like rain from a cloud in the shape of an angry face. Simon looked down, shock in his eyes, and let me have it. He snapped the bridge of my nose with one punch, split my lip open with the next and hit me twice in the temple so hard I felt myself go numb. I just lay there, waiting for him to finish me.

I'm not a fighter. I guess you already know that.

He pinned my arms beneath his knees and screamed at me, blood spraying from his lips.

"You stupid bloody fuck! You just gonna reach into the fire pull her out? You think you're a hero? Is that it?"

"I love her!" I screamed. Blood drizzled over my face in long, sticky ropes from his nose. He slapped me hard across the face. I shut my eyes, waiting for the next punch.

"Oh yeah? Hero? Well, I love 'er more than you ever could! I told you to fucking stay away from her! She thinks she's saving *you!* She was saving *you!* She…"

He stopped. I opened my eyes, watching him. He looked like he was seeing something in the air behind me. Some kind of ghost. But then I realized he was listening intently to something.

He heard the first siren before I did. I didn't hear them until he was off of me and gone, disappearing around the corner of the house. I lay on the ground, not feeling my own pain, staring up at the smoke like the coming of night as it covered over the Texas blue sky and drifted past the roofline behind me.

It is not possible that I could have smelled anything through the blood in my nose. But I remember smelling lavender. And thyme. And jasmine.

In my mind, Simon's smoky, bloody, angry face was still hovering above me, almost like he was still there. I studied the memory of it. *'She thinks she's saving you.'*

He had gotten that backwards. I was supposed to save her.

But it occurred to me then that maybe I had been wrong about the anger.

Turned out I had been wrong about almost everything.

Chapter 62

But I was not broken beyond repair. We are never broken beyond repair. You, Davis, are not broken beyond repair. I have worked hard to put myself back together. It has been a long, steep...

Davis folds the letter, shaking his head. Halves. Quarters. Slips it in his back pocket. He rubs his hands together in the morning air, still a good twenty degrees from comfortable. Zips up his jacket a little more.

The sun has only been up for thirty minutes. It's nothing he can actually feel. A smear of paint on the canvas. Still just an idea. The artist is undecided.

He pushes off from *Pepita's* locked door. Steps out onto *Broken River Road*. Looks both ways.

Still no sign of them.

He steps backwards. Leans back against the door and wedges the heel of his boot back under his haunch. The letter in his pocket crinkles. He pulls it out. Unfolds it. Shakes his head at Conrad's latest self-serving effort. It took him two weeks to open it. Threw it in the trash once. Fished it back out.

He can't help it. He hates himself for that weakness.

His father is a bottle of a different kind.

He flips through the pages. He wants to rip it up without finishing. Without dignifying. Halves. *Rip.* Quarters. *Rip.* Eighths. *Rip.* Sixteenths. *Rip.*

But the words burn brighter than the nimbus of light slowly engulfing the *Lick-n-Tipple* across the street.

The anger helps keep him warm.

But you don't need to do this for me. In fact, don't do it for me. Do it for you. You have to let all of it go, Davis. You need to cut us all loose. Me. Your mother. Abby Palmer, too. All of us. You have to save yourself. You have to let it all go.

I have something I want to share with you. I almost…

"Davis!" Ernesto Rivera is waving an arm out the window of the pickup, angling across the empty lane for the sidewalk. *"Buenos dias, amigo!"*

Davis folds the letter. Stuffs it back into his pocket. Pushes off. Crosses the sidewalk to the curb. Marcela leans over from the passenger seat. She smiles at him from beneath the brim of Ernesto's hat. They are in matching black fleece.

"Buenos dias, Davis."

"Mornin'," he says. He tries to shake off the letter with insincere enthusiasm. "Beautiful day!"

"Sí, pero frío!" says Ernesto.

"A little. Yeah."

Ernesto takes a plaid thermos from Marcela. Holds it out the window. "I have hot coffee for you. Miguel has his own."

He takes the thermos. Marcela smacks the back of the cab with her hand. *"Levántate,* Miguel! We're here. *Miguel!"*

"I'm awake." The words come reluctantly from the bed of the pick up. "I'm up. I'm up." A hand slips up into view, clutching an identical thermos. "Mornin' Davis."

Marcela laughs at her son. "Miguel. Sleeping the whole way here. You should not drink so much at night." She pats the seat next to her. "Davis, we can make room for you in here with us, where it is warm."

Miguel, *sotto voce*: *"Sí, sí.* Sit up front. Pussy."

He rattles backward into the rising sun. The world spins away out from beneath him, a cracked, round clod of dirt. The scrublands vector inward from either side of the truck, a triangle split up the middle by the strip of gray pavement that disappears at a single point on the horizon. Miguel sleeps on a sheepskin pad, face beneath his hat, boots pushing up against a row of six cardboard boxes marked *D.A.F.* in a fat, black script. He is too hung-over to be convincingly sociable.

Fine by Davis.

He leans up against the back of the cab. Crosses his arms. Watches the blush of morning push the world away. The words in his back pocket are restless. They pick the locks. Open the valves. Anger seeps back into his bloodstream.

Your mother was my wife. You seem to forget that… I am a better man now.

"Gracias." A mumble from deep inside Miguel's hat.

"For what?"

A loaded horse trailer shoots into view, tails twitching. He repeats.

"For what?"

"Huh?"

"Go back to sleep."

And he does.

The fairgrounds emerge and recede on either side of him in a succession of *whooshes.* Unhitched semi-trailers arrayed like dominos on the side of the road. What a few days ago was bare desert is now a burgeoning erector-set city. A Ferris wheel lays in broken pieces on its side, a dismembered carcass beneath the great metal necks of other rides arcing up into the sunlight like dinosaurs slowly bringing the distant past to life.

Whoosh.

Whoosh.

Whoosh.

The *Octopus.* The *Slingshot.* The *Banzai.* The *Fireball.* The *Scrambler.* They recede behind him, one by one.

Whoosh.

A roller coaster snake uncoils across the warming desert.

Whoosh.

A nascent tent city, skeleton rows of naked metal frames extending off to the south, comes and goes, teeming with sensate ghosts. He imagines he can smell sugar in the air. Hotdogs. Incense. Cow manure. And old feelings, still there, attached to him in the funhouse mirror like phantom limbs.

You will see this as a selfish effort… You need to cut us all loose. Me. Your mother. Abby Palmer, too. All of us.

Whoosh.

Then the stock yards. The rodeo grounds. A small Porta-Potty township in the making. Gnome condos, aqua with quaint white roofs, clustered and bound by the dozen on flatbed trailers.

Whoosh.

A new sign. Familiar lips around that plump red tongue. *The Lick-n-Tipple: Proud Sponsor of the Corbin Moon Garden Festival. Right on Broken River Road. Three Miles.*

Whoosh.

A new sign. A smiling skull in a black sombrero. No lips. No tongue. Just teeth. *The Lick-n-Tipple Celebrates Día de Muertos! Right on Broken River Road. Three Miles.*

The truck turns off the highway and the sun hits him sideways. Miguel sits up. Stretches. Yawns. Puts on his hat. He pushes the boxes with his boot. Scoots back up against the cab.

"*Mierda.*" More of a breathy sound than a word.

"You okay?"

Miguel winces. Forefinger to lips.

In a few minutes they pull into a parking lot, squeaking to a stop in front of a small white church. There is a hand-painted sign in a patch of yellowing grass near the steps. *The Holy Mission of St. Rachel the Matriarch.* Marcela slaps the flat of her hand against the window at his head.

"*Vamos, muchachos.*"

Ernesto cuts the engine. Climbs out. Opens the tailgate. He slits open the boxes one-by-one with a pocketknife. Marcela joins him. They dig through each box, extracting contents. Bright yellow t-shirts. Rubber wristbands. Baseball hats. Stacks of folded brochures. Miguel stands. Stretches. Steps up onto the side of the pickup bed like it's a ledge. Jumps.

"Give Davis a t-shirt, Papa," he says. "Or a hat. He should get something for his trouble."

Ernesto smiles from beneath the brim of his hat. Flicks a t-shirt out of the box. Davis catches it.

"Yellow this year," says Marcela proudly.

The logo is an ark beneath a rainbow of words. *Desert Ark Foundation.*

Miguel is already walking away. His mother calls out.

"You know where to find it, Miguel?"

"*Sí, Mami.* Let's go, Davis."

Davis leaves the shirt. Spills himself out of the truck. Follows.

They walk around the side of the building to a courtyard bordered on three sides by flowering olive trees. Saint Rachel the Matriarch is full-sized, cast in smooth white stone, standing in a semi-circle of stone benches. Her head, sheltered in its cowl, is lowered and turned away in the supplicating way of saints. Water spills across her open palms, burbling down into a marble basin.

Miguel threads the benches, walking over to the far corner of the courtyard. He stops at what could have been St. Rachel's black stone umbrella, now upside down on the grass. The basin is littered with small rocks and twigs. Miguel finds the power cord and coils it up in his hand. "Okay, cowboy," he says.

Together they tip the fountain sideways, up on its rim. Miguel brushes out the detritus. Bits of colored glass are imbedded in the black concrete basin. It reminds Davis of Celia Morales and the fountain that sits in the foreground of her line of sight to the school playground across the street.

They let the fountain fall heavily back to the grass with a resonant thud.

"Well they sure traded up," says Davis, brushing off his hands and glancing back at Saint Rachel. He moves around to the other side of the basin, across from Miguel. Kicks it gently with the toe of his boot. "And the DAF gets the hand-me-down."

Miguel nods. "The DAF is all about the hand-me-downs."

It is a cumbersome, difficult lift for two people. They could have used a third. Eladio or Hector, if they hadn't had to open *Pepita's.* But they manage, stopping every forty, fifty feet, shuffling slowly sideways around the church to the parking lot like two crabs fighting over a large shell.

They have the fountain in the bed of the truck by the time Ernesto and Marcela emerge from the church, arms now empty. Ernesto reaches over the side. Slaps the fountain dismissively.

"Eh? Like a feather. You see? Like a leaf." He laughs, squeezing Davis hard on the shoulder.

They spend an hour crisscrossing Corbin, stopping at a dozen or more places. Churches and businesses mostly. A couple of homes. Each time, Ernesto and Marcela load up on charity swag and make their deliveries. Davis and Miguel stay in the truck, stuffed into the open corners of the pick-up that the curvature of the concrete fountain cannot reach.

"You taking someone to the festival?" Miguel asks, watching Ernesto, silver hair flashing in the sun, disappear behind a closing door.

"Me?" He thinks of her, then. Olivia. Propped up against her windshield under the stars. "No. Probably not even going."

"What? *Loco*? You have to go."

"I do?"

"Yeah, man. You do."

"Why?"

"Because you just do. It's the *Moon Garden Festival…*" Miguel slaps his right hand down over the back of his left hand, "stacked on top of *El Día de los Muertos*. It's like a double-decker festival sandwich, man. Can't pass that shit up. There's even gonna be a beauty pageant this year. Can you believe that? Someone's tryin' to put Corbin on the map."

"Thought you were down on all of that. The whole River Walk thing."

"You know it, man. The day that shit really happens *–if* it really happens *–is* the day I move. And in the meantime, the festival is a pain in my ass too. My family will spend two weeks picking up bottles and condoms after all of the *pendejos* have gone back home. Seriously. Two weeks. Maybe three just to put the desert back to what it was."

"Right. So why are you…"

"Hey, I may as well get some rides outta the deal." He laughs. Teeth gleaming. A child, suddenly, in a man's body. "Get me some *Scrambler* action, man. And some *Octopus!*" He backhands Davis on the shoulder. "Am I right? And this year a stage full of long-legged *senoritas* singing and dancing and playing guitar? In bikinis? Shaking their maracas? Come on, man. Who sits that shit out? You think I'm gonna pick up trash after the party and not *go* to the party?"

"Can't argue with that," says Davis. "You taking someone?"

He nods. Hesitates.

"I'll be at it all day. I'll have to help my parents set up the *DAF* booth in the morning. Then I'm picking up Yvonne and her kid Kevin in the afternoon. That'll be the day right there."

Davis thinks about it. Says it anyway.

"Thought she was married."

Miguel looks. The smile is small. Complicated. He nods. Looks away.

"So then what are you doin', man?" The *doin'* is a small knife with a dull blade, but the point breaks the skin.

Miguel winces. Then shrugs.

"She wants her kid to go to the festival. He's got MS. Like, you know, seriously. He's got a special chair that weighs more than this fuckin' thing." He kicks the side of the fountain. "In and outta her van. All of the people at the festival. It's gonna take two."

"Okay. Great. So why doesn't her husband…"

"He's off in Bahrain or some shit."

"Military?"

"Nah." Miguel shakes his head. "Big oil. Big shit. Never home."

"Isn't she concerned people will, you now, start talking?"

Miguel looks up. Face hard. He is once again the nameless Mexican out behind Pepita's, Louisville Slugger rolling in his palm.

"*Suenas como mi madre, hombre.*" A beat. Two. Three. "I'm just helpin' her take her kid to the festival. You think I'm going to fuck her in the line for tamales?"

Davis holds up both hands. Looks away.

Ernesto and Marcela reemerge, crossing the yard to the street with purpose. Ernesto smacks the side of the bed twice with his hand.

"*Está bien, muchachos.* Now is time for the fountain."

They ride backwards in silence until they are most of the way to the fairgrounds, each surveying his own side of the desert, an old hide splitting up the middle, sliced open by the blade of Ernesto's tailpipe. It is not a bloodless wound. Just looks that way. It is easy to dismiss the dust billowing out from beneath their rolling knife, golden yellow in the late morning sun.

And yet, Abby is in that cloud. So is his mother. Even if he cannot recognize them, they are there. Something powerful swims beneath him. All he feels is movement. Displacement within the unseen, unknowable medium.

His father's voice. A vibration in his head. *Your mother was my wife… You have to save yourself… You have to let it all go.*

He clenches his brain. Wants desperately to change the channel. Anything. Anything else will do. Just not this.

Olivia DeLuna is the first *anything*.

And then she is the only thing.

You going?

Not even if my life depended on it.

Me neither.

They turn off the highway and Ernesto navigates the truck to an access road. It leads past a phalanx of semi-trailers and then out into the skeletal subdivision of tent city. They trundle bumpily past square frame after square frame of bare silver piping, each with a roll of brightly colored tarp somewhere nearby. None of the skin is on yet. Just the bones. Plastic signs tied to the frames give each assemblage a name. Ernesto squeaks to a stop at the one that reads "*D.A.F.*"

Miguel sighs. Adjusts his hat up and back. Up and back. Looks over at Davis. "Forget it, *amigo*," he says. "All that shit back there? That's on me. Not you."

"Don't worry about it," says Davis. "None of my business anyway."

"You're just walkin' through the scrub and don't know where the fuckin' rattlesnakes are."

Davis smiles. "I do now."

"*Hermano*," Miguel laughs. Shakes his head. "You have no fuckin' idea."

* * *

He works his shift at *Pepitas* in his new yellow *D.A.F.* shirt. It earns major points with Marcela and Ernesto and a good laugh from Eladio and Hector, who make no effort to contain their amusement.

"*El hombre en amarillo!* Oh, shit, D! You must like spendin' time wit' yo' own self! You ain't evah, evah, *EVAH* gon' get you some in that shirt, brah!"

"Funny. I know they do this every year, Eladio. And I know that at least once your mother did not let you out of the house without you wearing this shirt."

"No, no, no. I wear the one from five years ago, D. It's a stylin', fire-engine red. *Chicas* see me bustin' my moves in that shirt…" Eladio freezes in mid-Flaminco for cameras that are not present. Eyes closed. Lips parted. Right arm up. Left arm out. Reaching for the hand of the woman who is not there. "And the shit is on. Know what I'm sayin?"

Davis puts on his apron. Ties it in the back. Picks up a bag of trash.

"Yeah. I think you're saying that the catsup-colored shirt you wore when you were twelve or thirteen still fits you so, yeah, good luck with the ladies there Eladio."

Hector loses it in the kitchen, slapping the counter and stomping his foot with approval. "Oh, damn! D smoked you a good one, Eladio. *¡Mi hombre!*" Hector holds out a beefy fist. Davis obliges the bump as he kicks open the back door for the dumpster. He looks back at Eladio as he goes. Points, as if to say, *let that be a lesson.*

Eladio laughs in spite of himself, adorably acknowledging defeat in a blush of innocence. He pivots seamlessly to take the order of two twenty-somethings at the counter, clearly on a joyride escape from San Angelo. As the back door closes behind him, Davis feels the truth hit him in the back of the head. Eladio's entire display, even the defeat, *especially* the defeat, had been for the benefit of those two women. Eladio was always dancing. Even when he wasn't.

After his shift, Davis straddles the Harley in the back lot. He strips off the yellow tee for the chambray button-down with which he had started the day. He cannot picture working for Dallas Letti, splintering her abandoned structures, taking her soggy abuse, in something so unapologetically sunny. He folds the tee shirt. Halves. Quarters. Tucks it inside the duct-taped, split leather seat. Closes it. Sits. He feels the letter from his father.

I have tried, Davis. Tried to connect. Tried to apologize. Tried to put the past behind us. Tried to start again. Your mother was my....

He blocks it out. Puts on his jacket. It's too warm now for the jacket. He zips it up anyway. Kicks the Harley to life.

There is a haze over the sun. The fingertip of weather gathering out in the Gulf. It glows like a burnt-orange scarf over a lamp, frayed and tattered at the edges.

He tries to throttle past his father's voice. No good. The voice has commandeered the Harley as a larynx. Riding faster only increases the volume. The essence of his father fills the spaces in the vibration beneath him. There was no separating them. The voice is an arm draped heavily over his shoulders. The voice wants to buy him a drink.

So he tries to leave the vibration altogether. Tries to get out of his body, watching himself from above, high enough that he is just a silent dot in a line of silent dots, slowly tracing the necrotic scar that cuts across the desiccated hide of South Texas. He absconds into abstraction. Into Eladio's beatific perfection. Into Hector's approval. He thinks of big, loyal Buddy Lincoln. Thinks of Celia Morales. And little Paola. Tries to choose the words with which he will tell her story. Thinks of Libby Holder. Another story. Other words.

Elizabeth.

Olivia.

From out of nowhere. Two independent abstractions. Together.

Elizabeth. Olivia.

Elizabeth-Olivia.

They are intertwined, these two thoughts. Clinging to each other. Like vines on a fencepost. Like children at the foot of an immense and looming wave.

He is no longer above himself. No longer a dot among dots. Without warning he drops like a stone back into an ocean of sound, the Harley pouring back into his ears. The crossroad is only two hundred feet ahead.

Closer.

Closer.

There is no thought, only impulse. He signals. Turns.

Conscious thought returns to him, disheveled and half-dressed, before he arrives. Preparation begins in earnest.

I was in the neighborhood.

I thought I would drop by to see if you were home.

I thought maybe we could not go to the festival together. Someplace. Anyplace.
Pizza. Movie.

He parks where he always does, in front, beneath the stately pecan. He sits for a moment, sudden stillness beneath him, all vibration seeping back into the earth. How is he here? He marvels at his own unaccountability. A chachalaca screeches, racing across the small lawn for cover.

He dismounts. Walks to the door. Runs his fingers through his hair. Knocks. It opens almost immediately.

"*Ooooo-Weee!* Will you look what the sex fairy don' lef' on my stoop?"

The robe is a deep, nearly transparent fuchsia, trimmed in velvet. Libby's bare knee opens the robe, pushing the flap aside to see who's at the door.

"Lawd, I mus' be dreamin'. My sexy li'l writer wit' the ponytail an' the fuck-all-day face? Knockin' on my do' fo' I don't know why."

"I…"

But there is no starting anything before Libby is finished. She looks backwards inside the house. Looks back at him. Leans in, shoulder against the doorframe. Whispers.

"You lookin' for a li'l *sumpin'-sumpin'* baby? Go get you some food and come back in one hour." She looks over her shoulder again. "No. Come back in two hour. Imma' need to rest up, if you take my meanin'. *Damn.* When it rain it pours, baby. Fine lookin' men beatin' on my do' today. I'm startin' to worry God's about to call me home. But I sho' die a happy woman."

Her face suddenly pinches into concern.

"Baby, I cain't jab wit' you now. I got comp'ny. Come back in two hours. Go get yo'sef ready. Go do some push-ups or wash yo' li'l ponytail."

She has almost closed the door in his face. He stops it with the toe of his boot.

"Lookin' for Olivia."

The door opens. Libby's face reappears.

"Say what?"

"Olivia."

"Ain't here, baby. What you want with Olivia?"

There is no need for him to speak. So he doesn't. She steps closer, almost on top of him. Her mostly open robe grazes the back of his hand.

"'Livia is my *baby*, baby. Unastan? Last thing she need now is a man on a motorcycle wit' a ponytail and a face that say he only good fo' one thing an' that one thing is fuckin' all day long."

"I'm good for more than that."

"You lyin' through yo' dick. You a muthafuck out pickin' up low-hangin' fruit."

"No."

She stares at him. Stares *into* him. He stands there. Takes it. She leans in.

"I tol' you my story."

"You have. I took good notes."

"You believe me?"

"Yes."

"Every word of that shit?"

"Yes."

Libby's face sheds every soft, feminine charm it has ever known, hardening to iron. It is the most naked she has ever been in his presence. She whispers razorblades.

"So then you know... jus' how *dayid...* I can make you."

Movement. Behind her. A man –*a customer* –pretending not to listen. He finds Davis' eyes, just for a moment. Looks away. Walks slowly out of view.

But the man leaves a residue. An image. A memory. A ghost.

Simon.

Where the man used to be, that is the person Davis sees. That is who he feels in the churn of acid releasing into his gut.

Simon.

Silly. Stupid. Because they look nothing alike. The man inside is much taller than Simon. Better built. Cleaner. More polished.

Clear blue eyes. And fine blond hair grazing the tops of his shoulders.

Chapter 63

"They don't want catchy."

She is taller today, April March. She has wedged herself into a new pair of designer boots. They push her two inches higher up into the air. Pants might also be new. Like black, tubular seaweed. Covering and uncovering the tops of the new footwear.

"They said, *light-hearted*," says Sheldon. He leans forward in his chair, arms on his desk. "They said *humorous*."

"Yeah, well, they don't want that now, boss man. Doris called last night. Says Bruce and Chip and the others just plum hate it. I reminded her about light-hearted and humorous. That's not how they remember it. She says they never wanted a jingle. They want a cowboy song. Simple. Just a guitar. They don't want a jingle."

"That's *exactly* what they said they wanted. They used that very word. *Jingle*. Bruce wanted *catchy*. Chip wanted *country-catchy*. I suggested a tapestry to accompany a montage, but they wanted to lighten things up and go with a jingle. So I asked TMM for a jingle and TMM sent them a…"

"Maybe you just misunderstood." But April can see she has gone too far. She self-corrects before he can speak. "Look. I don't know what all y'all said t'each other. I wasn't there. All I know is they wanna go a different direction."

Sheldon leans back again. The chair groans. April spreads her arms; models a concession to a reality that must be accepted. "*Is-what-it-is*, Shel."

The blouse is familiar. Paper white. Billowy at the sleeves. Trim at the waist. It's a regular in the rotation. Her straight blonde hair is out of its ponytail today, fanned and flattened into the grip of a black velvet barrette.

She is strategically colorized. Like a Texas belle who has wandered into a Frank Miller film. Head-to-toe hard-boiled black-and-white, but shockingly over-saturated here and there. Lips. Nails. Irises.

"Well what other direction do they want?" Sheldon asks. "Anything specific?"

"I'll send you Doris' email. They want to go more classic. Western retro. Bruce keeps bringing up *Rio Lobo*."

"*Rio Lobo?*"

He knows what she means. She means the movie. But that's not what he hears. He hears Liberty Cherish in his head. "*You want you a Rio Lobo? That a Char-do-nay, baby.*"

"Yeah, you know, full-on cowboy. Out-with-the herd... bedrolls under the stars... campfire... whiskey... strummin' and singin'. That kinda' thing."

"You mean *Rio Bravo.*"

"John Wayne."

"He's in both of them, April. They're looking for Dean Martin and Ricky Nelson."

"*Wellllll...*" April cocks her head to the side and squints. Like he is a child thinking about picking his nose. "Dunno 'bout that, boss. I think it's about John Wayne. They want to play up the *Texas* in *Texas Beef.* I think they want a kinda... romantic... classic.... sorta, oh what am I tryin' to say..."

He stares up at his leather-stilted assistant. Marvels at her empty, southern belle perfection as she tries to translate the thoughts in her head. Her effort only intensifies her cringing, dubious *are-you-really-that-dim-don't-make-another-big-mistake* expression.

He sees his wife in that expression. Sees Christi. The wryly-twisted lips. The narrowing shocks of blue. Hears the words she has never actually said.

Why should I ever trust that you know what in the hell you are doing, Shelly? If it weren't for daddy...

"Mr. Tate says sellin' beef has got to be about takin' care of your family," April is saying. Like she is reading his mind. "Livin' by a code of honor. He doesn't think..."

"Grayson?" Uncensored. Too sharp. He can see the tone register on April's face. He over-corrects into something much too casual. "So when did you talk to *him?*"

She does not smile, exactly, but he can see that she wants to.

"Last night. After you left. He was in to have a look at the River Walk files. Then he wanted something in accounting that I didn't ask about. I'd just hung up from Donna, so," she shrugs, "we got to talkin'. He doesn't think your *Texas Beef* campaign is masculine enough."

The reaction seems to start somewhere close to the sternum. It splits immediately in two directions. Rage boiling up toward the heart. And then a kind of panic-laced sickness, threaded with self-loathing, sinking down into the pit of his gut. There is no place for his brain in this reaction. So it is not a *thought* that pops to the surface. It's a *feeling*. And the feeling is that he wants to be done. All of it.

He wants to be free of this place. This life.

His face has to hold everything together. He does his best to smile.

"Okay," he says. "Send me the email. I'll figure it out. I'll talk to Dill and Marty at TMM this afternoon. See if I can get them working on something new."

"Want me to meet with them?" April offers, her ambition showing some leg. There is nothing she would love more than to save *Texas Beef* from his incompetence and then go running to Grayson.

"Nope. I got it. I'll handle it. I need to get on the same page with the client. Just pull together the project sub-file for TMM. I'll take it with me."

April turns and disappears through the hole in the wall. Closes the door behind her in a waft of cosmetics. The aroma settles in his head like a cloud of dust. When the dust settles, he can see himself, out there on the horizon. Just his silhouette. Sauntering away. Getting smaller. Smaller. In the back of his mind he can hear Dean Martin crooning as he clops through Rio Bravo. Dean's giving up roping cows and counting strays. There's a woman waitin' 'round the bend. All she cares about is his rifle, his pony and him. Were it only true.

The door opens again. April.

"Forgot to tell you. Pepper Clark-Bean? She sent me an email."

"Great. What now?"

"Well. Pepper's startin' up an investigation-security business."

"Pepper just *bankrupted* her investigation-security business."

"Right, but this is a new one. This one is using drones."

"Drones?"

"Drones." April's hands flatten out and sail off in different directions. "You know. Drones. No employees. Part of the bankruptcy reorg."

"Well who's operating the drones?"

"Shel," April's drones come in for a hard landing, one on each hip. "You really want me to try and make sense of Pepper? Woman's about two sandwiches shy of a full picnic."

"You got that right."

"She wants us to start thinkin' about a campaign. What do you want me to tell her?"

"Tell her she still owes us ten thousand dollars."

"Twelve thousand. Got it."

April is out and gone.

Sheldon closes his eyes. Sees Grayson's face. Imagines Grayson hunched over the accounting desk, leafing through files. Following the money. Following the green river that flows to a post office box supposedly belonging to the Houston Media Law Group. Initially nine to eleven thousand a month. More recently fifteen to twenty. Sees him looking up from the invoices. Leaning back. Scratching that mustache. *Thinking. Thinking.* Slicking it down again with his lower lip. *Thinking.*

Not good.

The door opens. April.

"Sorry. Forgot to tell you. Megan told me to tell you that Laurie Weaver woman called you again. *Chachalaca Gazette?* Wants you to call her back ASAP. That's like the fourth or fifth time this week. What in the Sam Hill, Shel?"

He suppresses the adrenal surge. Smiles again. Shakes his head in a kind of mirthful admiration.

"Gotta hand it to them," he says. "That's a scrappy little rag. She's trying to squeeze me for information on the Corbin River Walk. Doesn't want to take no for an answer I guess."

"Well, okay then." She furrows. "Don't we want the publicity?"

"CDC is very tight on the rollout. Strategic pacing. Information control. They have a very strict disclosure campaign. It's not for me to give interviews anyway."

"Want me to call her?"

"Nah. I'll deal with Laurie Weaver."

April nods. "Okay." She recloses the door. He recloses his eyes.

Laurie Weaver.

He tries to pretend to himself that he has no idea why the *Chachalaca Gazette* is really calling. Tries to tell himself that for all he knows she really *is* trying to squeeze him for information about the Corbin River Walk. Tries to tell himself that the lie he just told April was actually the truth.

But he knows better. He knows exactly why Laurie Weaver is calling. Which, he suspects, is the reason he has not been answering.

He slowly rotates his chair around to face his computer. Looks up the number for Texas Media Music. Reaches for the phone.

"Dill? Sheldon. Good. You? Doin' fine, doin' fine. Look, I need to pop over to talk about Texas Beef. Well, they're still unsettled. Wrong tone. Yeah. We need to rework it. No, all of it. Yeah, the whole thing. Yep. Everything. Sorry. How it goes sometimes, I guess. Can you spare an hour? What time? Good. Yep. Good. Okay. See you then."

He hangs up.

Laurie Weaver. The sound of her name is still in his head waiting for him. Waiting to talk to him. *About what?* About a solicitation of prostitution story and why there is suddenly so much interest.

What he had feared was now, he imagines, actually taking shape. Grayson Tate had stirred the pot. He had gotten his own lawyers involved to shake up the *Chachalaca Gazette* about a retraction. Grayson had started to apply the pressure that Sheldon had been steadfastly assuring he was already applying. Now *The Chacha* was interested in him all over again. *That* was what was going on. Must be. Just as he had feared.

Sheldon suspected, though, that he had not been entirely on the mark. He had initially expected Grayson would act from impatience. Too many months without seeing any results. Grayson wanted either a retraction or legal action and there had been neither of those things. For months now. Nothing. Eventually, Grayson's resolve to let Sheldon fix the problem would simply wear out. Then, he had predicted, Grayson would pick up the phone and instruct his own lawyers to get tough and do whatever it took to clear the family name. Or maybe Grayson would bypass the lawyers and do it himself.

But now that it was actually happening, Sheldon guessed that Grayson was acting less from impatience than from outright suspicion. It was possible, even probable, that Grayson was starting to suspect that his son-in-law was stringing everyone along; that he had never had any intention of getting tough with *The Chacha.*

Because maybe, just maybe, Grayson was likely surmising, *The Chacha* had been right all along.

Of course, it would have been easy enough for Grayson to do a little research and see that the name *Sheldon Davis* does not appear on any list of people charged with a crime in the state of Texas. It would be easy enough for Grayson to conclude that *The Chacha* had been wrong about at least that much.

But that alone would never satisfy Grayson. *The Chacha* story had come from *somewhere.* The paper didn't just make up the name Sheldon Davis and plug it into a story about prostitution in Corbin. Rather than confronting Sheldon about it for a new round of lies and deflection, Grayson had likely asked someone to get to the bottom of things. And while they were getting to the bottom of things, they may as well go ahead and bully a retraction out of a newspaper that was rasping out its dying breaths. A newspaper that may have actually printed a lie but that had somehow managed to accidentally get the story right anyway.

And now, here was Laurie Weaver, responding on behalf of a paper suddenly under attack from Houston.

Mr. Davis? Laurie Weaver here. Chachalaca Gazette. What the fuck, man?

That, anyway, was what Sheldon imagined. Grayson taking action. Laurie Weaver responding.

So he had never called her back. And he would not return the most recent call either. Nothing good could come from that discussion. Outright evasion seemed to be the most prudent, and easiest, course of action for avoiding catastrophe.

But, at the same time, he did not want anything to do with avoiding catastrophe. He was tired of avoidance. Tired of worrying. Of lying. Maneuvering. Protecting things about which he no longer cared. He wanted to let it all go. The Tate family name. The business. The money. The security. The marriage. He wanted, increasingly, to just walk away and never look back. Enough with ropin' cows and countin' strays. There's a woman 'round the bend. She'll be waiting.

It was impossible to have these thoughts without also thinking of *who*, exactly, might be *waitin'*. Imperceptibly Olivia had become a destination. An answer. An alternative. A vibration truer than any other vibration in his life. She was the only string in his guitar that was in tune.

And that –the one true vibration –always brings him back to reality. He can't walk away from the money. He needs the money. He needs it for her. Not because she could ruin his life with a well-placed disclosure. She could not ruin a life he no longer cared about. Blackmail was a hollow threat at this point. No, he needs the money because he is not stupid. He is not so vain as to think he is enough for her. Not yet. She cares about the money. The last phone call was proof enough of that.

"*Are you going?*"

"*Where? The festival? Lemme tell you, Shel. Not if my life depended on it.*"

"*I'll be there. Saturday.*"

"*Why? Oh, right. The pageant.*"

"*The pageant.*"

"*Well you just have yourself all kinds of fun, Shel.*"

"*Let's meet. I can slip away for a Ferris wheel ride or something. Christi will be occupied.*"

"*Not a chance. Too many people. I don't like people. We can go get a burger or somethin'. Whatever you do, just stay away from my place. Libby'll put a bullet in your head.*"

"*My leash won't be that long, Olivia. It'll stretch as far as the Ferris wheel.*"

Sorry. I'll just see you in Austin. I'm not goin' to the Corbin Moon Garden Day of the Dead clusterfuck."

"*I'll have somethin' for you. Heavier than normal.*"

"*...*"

"*Still there? Olivia?*"

She needs him. Not that she couldn't eventually be persuaded as to his merits as a person. As someone to *want* to be around. To be *with*. But, for now anyway, she needs him for the money. Maybe that's what keeps her waitin' 'round the bend. Maybe that's the only thing.

So he can't afford to let anything go. Not one thing. Not yet. He can't walk away from the business. Or the marriage. Or the Tate family name. He needs to continue protecting the things about which he no longer cares. He needs to worry. To lie. To maneuver.

He needs to embezzle from his own business. He needs to continue diverting a stream from the river of revenue, largely fed by the Grayson Tate and the CDC River Walk reservoirs. He needs to send the stream out across the desert to make a paradise where currently there is only a kind of desolation –a wreckage of bone and tissue and spirit –that he had helped to bring about. That was what Olivia wanted from him. That was what she needed. And so that was his importance to her.

And he will do whatever it takes. He is not entirely sure why. What she means to him. But he will do whatever it takes.

He busies about. Shuffles from one paper distraction to another. Tries to keep his mind away from the edge of reason. Thoughts of Grayson and Laurie Weaver are like a pick-axes working through the thin, membranous walls into a place of conscious attention. He reschedules two meetings that now must go to TMM and Dill Mathers and the recalibration of the *Texas Beef* campaign.

April March brings him the Texas Media Music sub-file as requested. He rereads the notes of his meeting with Bruce and Chip. *Country-catchy jingle.* Right there in black and white.

The phone rings three different times. Each time he is prepared for Megan at the front desk to put through a call from Laurie Weaver. Each time he tells himself that he will take the goddamned call and brace himself for Laurie Weaver's explanation about how they have gone back and re-interviewed Libby Holder who has confirmed both solicitation and assault and the paper would now like to know if he would care to comment before they print a "correction." Each time he is prepared to feign apoplexy. Demand a proper retraction. Threaten repercussions. Defend his wife's honor and the family name.

But each time it is not Laurie Weaver. Each time he is relieved.

He only lasts an hour and fifteen minutes in the office. He cannot concentrate on work. He has to get out. He wants to drive. Doesn't matter where. Just drive. He needs to outrun his own thoughts. The faster the better. He gathers up his things.

"You're leaving?" asks April from halfway down the hall, one hand, fingertips wide, pushing against the door to the ladies room.

"Meeting with Dill and Marty at TMM." He keeps walking. Pushes open the main door. "See you tomorrow."

He buckles himself in. Turns the key. Pushes the button. The roof folds away to reveal a sky of darkening slate, rippled in long cottony waves washing in from the Gulf. They've been talking about it all week. And now here it is.

He had secretly wanted a hurricane. Harvey. Irma. Not really. But violent weather might have been oddly therapeutic. He would snap trees himself if he could. Demolish buildings. Toss trawlers.

But meteorological catharsis is not to be his. After a lot of hype, the most the weather gods can offer him now is a tropical depression. Lowering the ceiling. Darkening the horizon. Squeezing him into a narrowing channel of existence closer to earth. More pressure without release. Exactly the opposite of what he needs.

He navigates the lot. Heads north.

He thinks again of Grayson. Personally reviewing the agency accounting. And at a time when he knew Sheldon would not be around.

Not good. The queasiness deepens.

He needs to shake free of these feelings. His best bet is the I-10. It takes him another fifteen minutes to reach the on-ramp. He picks a lane. Accelerates. Feels the rush of cool air. Tries to think of Olivia. Tries to be free.

* * *

He is better by the end of the day. Considerably better. The garage door closes behind him and he is glad to be home. Christi's car fills the space next to his. Grayson's truck is out in the driveway. He doesn't care.

He should care, but he doesn't. He is finally in a place that can provide him with a hot shower and a stiff drink. That's all he really cares about at the moment.

The afternoon's anxiety about Grayson and Laurie Weaver has seeped into the soil of his mood, which is still spongy, but at least no longer sopping wet with dread. It all has the feel of over-reaction now. A regrettable, but temporary loss of perspective. Self-justification has reacquired its grip.

It is *his* business, after all. *His* money.

He owes the mood improvement entirely to the two-hours he spent with Dill Mathers in the TMM recording studio, insulated on all sides by spongy orange soundproofing installed before April March was even born.

He and Dill went back a ways. Before TMM. Before HMR. Before life had cooked his creative essence down into an acronym. Dill had always been a man of few, well-chosen words. He spoke like a songwriter.

Sheldon had laid out the problem with Texas Beef and Dill had run his fingers through his shaggy, sandy brown hair and leaned back against the soundboard.

"*Rio Bravo*, huh?"

Sheldon had shrugged and Dill had stretched backwards, reaching for the Gibson. He picked out a few notes in a vaguely horse-trotting cadence. Took his voice up two octaves and gave his best Ricky Nelson impression.

Oh that movie Rio Bravo
Was not about... cattle
That's just Texas Beef
Tryin' to sell you... a saddle.

Sheldon had laughed for the first time all day. Maybe all week. Dill had nodded at the Martin in the corner. Sheldon had climbed off the stool and pulled the strap over his neck. Strummed. Closed his eyes. Strummed. Strummed. It was like a hand on his back. His father's hand. His mother's hand. *Strum. Strum. Strum.*

One thought: *God how he missed this.*

Dill had slipped back into plucking out a horse trot. Lifted his face. Sang. Sang the boiling-red sun down beneath the western horizon. Sang the cattle down to the creek. Sang the redwings to roost. Sang a purple light like a satin sheet over a dreaming cowboy. *My Rifle, My Pony and Me.* Of all the songs, only Dill would know to start in on that one. Sheldon had laughed. Dill had laughed.

"Come on partner," Dill said. "You and me."

Then he had nodded at Sheldon, who had adjusted the Martin on his knee and pulled his own six-string horse up alongside. They sang it together like a couple of lonesome and worriless cowpokes. And when they had finished that one, they had moved on to *Restless Kid* and then, inevitably, to a rousing *Cindy Cindy.*

"That was truly, truly terrible," Dill had laughed, raking back his hair with his strumming hand. And he was right. It was terrible. Both of them had forgotten the words and Sheldon could not keep up with Dill on the guitar. It was terrible. A rhythmic train wreck littered with broken, made-up phrases.

Except that it wasn't terrible. It was wonderful. Just being there. In the studio. Back inside the womb of *Mother Music*, where all things were still possible.

There had been a wave of nostalgia. Like a warm bath.

He had once *created.* Now he *sold.* Now he *marketed.* But once upon a time he had created music for its own sake. Hoping to sell. Hoping to eat.

But sell or not, eat or not, the music had come into the world anyway. Dozens upon dozens of songs. Dozens upon dozens of little lovely rhyming children.

"You okay?"

"Hmm? Yeah. Yeah."

"When's the last time you wrote one of your own?"

"Long time, Dill. A lifetime ago."

"You wrote some humdingers, brother. You surely did. I learned a lot about writin' music from you."

"You flatter me."

"I do no such thing. You were the one that told me to figure out the center of the song first and then write outward in circles from there. Like a rock dropping into a lake. That's what starts the music. Gotta start in the center of the thing to know what it's all about. The heart of it. You called it the mother verse. Never forgot that."

"The mother verse. Damn. That's a whole other life, Dill."

Dill had smiled with just a little sadness.

"It's all the same life, Shel. It's all one thing."

Sheldon had nodded, conceding the point. Dill had picked out a slow blues progression. Closed his eyes. Repeated. Shook his head. Sang.

Just got outta prison, baby,
Been dreamin' 'bout you all year long.
I said I just got outta prison, baby,
Been dreamin' 'bout you aaaaaall year long.'
But your heart is locked away now, baby
And the only thing free is this song.

Sheldon had closed his eyes. Listened. Remembered.

You say you had to go on livin', baby,
'Cause life is here and then it's done.
You just had to go on livin', baby,
'Cause your love is here and then it's done.
But I weren't made for givin' up now baby,
'Cause I know that I'm the one.

Dill had riffed and embellished his way around every last note and had sung every verse. Sheldon had received it like an unexpected visit from an old friend. Every sharpened feeling that had lashed at him on the way over to the TMM studio had fallen away, cowering in the shadows like something savage staying out of the firelight.

When the studio was quiet again, Dill had folded his arms over the top of the Gibson. Had looked over at Sheldon, clearly touched, without a smile.

"That's one of many of yours, Shel. I know most of 'em. It's in your blood. You wrote some truly good music in your day. And you know what else, brother?"

Dill had raised his eyebrows. Waited. Sheldon had not spoken.

"It's still your day. It's all one thing. One song. Maybe you just need to rewrite a lyric or two is all."

* * *

Sheldon climbs out of the car. Heads inside. The voices of his wife and father-in-law tumble down the hall from the kitchen. He pauses, one foot in, one foot out. Listens. Christi gushes about the impending pageant. Grayson rattles his ice cubes, trying to get a word in edgewise.

"Well that's good, Belle. That's good."

"I mean who knew Waco could produce such a good-lookin' thing? Galveston too. Daddy, we got ourselves a real contest. Wait 'til you see. These girls'll knock your socks off, I'm tellin' you. And we got hard confirms from seven television stations. Seven! Two're comin' all the way from Dallas."

"Texans do love their beauty pageants, sugar."

"Now all we need..."

"Gimme another splash there."

"Now all we need is for the gosh-darn weather to cooperate. I mean *honestly*. Three hundred sixty odd days in a year and this mess out in the gulf chooses this weekend?"

"Gon' be fine, Christi. It's dwindlin' almost down to nothin' already. It'll fizzle. Go on warm up the oven. He'll be here soon enough. And where the hell is Nicki? Haven't seen that boy in a week."

"Nicki? He's already out there doin' his thing, daddy. He's gon' pick us up at the airport and takes us into Corbin."

"Okay. So then Saturday mornin' it's just you and me and Shelly in the plane."

"None of the others comin' down? Adrian or whatshisname? Dan Broderick?"

"Not coming. Other things going on. These are busy people, darlin'. Got bigger fish to fry than your pageant and the Corbin Moon Garden Festival. Plane only seats six anyways. Will you fire up the goddamned oven or do I need to get up..."

Sheldon wants to detour through the living room. Just head upstairs for the shower. Twenty minutes. Thirty.

The hallway door to the garage closes behind him with its telltale click. He winces. Slumps.

"Shelly?"

Oven-baked brisket. Green beans. Cornbread. Grayson reaches here and there, helping himself to some of each of it as he speaks.

"Bless-us-O-Lord-and-these-your-gifts-which-we-are-finally-finally-finally-about-to-receive-from-your-bounty-through-Christ-our-Lord-Amen-pass-the-damn-barbeque-sauce."

"Daddy..."

"Well, I'm sorry, Belle. Good Lord understands hunger at the unholy hour of ten o'clock."

"It's not even eight o'clock."

"Feels like ten. God*damn* this is good brisket. You cook like your mother."

Christi does not pick up where she had left off about the coming pageant.

She starts back from the beginning.

She does this for his benefit, not caring that Grayson will have to endure every organizational detail, every snippet of gossip, every niggling worry, all over again. He does not often pity his father-in-law, but tonight the suffering is palpable. The first opportunity to nudge the conversation onto another track does not come until the brisket is gone.

"So what's the plan for Saturday?" he asks. He looks with interest from one to the other, seeing neither. Seeing only Olivia. Waiting for him at the Ferris wheel.

"Daddy's taking us in the plane first thing Saturday morning," Christi says, standing and gathering up the plates. "Nicki's pickin' us up at the airport and we'll drive over from Odessa. Just the four of us though. 'Cause Danny Broderick and Adrian got *more important things to do.*"

She bugs her blue eyes at Grayson who sours his expression as he tongs another cube of ice into his tumbler. Christi continues.

"Janey and Bill and the rest of the team will be there on Thursday to start sweatin' the details. Nicki's already out there workin'. Photos and whatnot. Says he's got a whole long list."

Grayson intones. "Speakin' of Nicholas."

He leans back in his chair. Rests his glass on his leg. Looks up at Sheldon.

"Belle tells me... that Nicki told her..."

"Daddy..."

"That he ran into you a couple weeks ago over at Canyon Lake."

From the sink, Christi rotates sharply at the waist to look at her father.

"*Saw*, daddy. Not ran into. *Saw.* Don't even know why you're bringin' that up."

"Well, fine then. *Saw.*" Grayson strokes the bottom of his mustache with his lower lip. Then he takes a small drink. "Just curious what's goin' on at Canyon Lake."

Sheldon knows better. Grayson Tate is never *just curious* about anything. He either has a keenly self-interested reason for wanting to know something or he has no interest at all. Not a man to indulge irrelevance, let alone go looking for it. Last time Grayson had been *just curious* about something had been at the wedding, when he had asked whether Sheldon had any crazies or criminals in his family.

Daddy!

Just curious, baby. Just curious.

Christi turns back to the sink, pretending to clean a saucepan. But she has turned off the water. He feels them waiting. Denial is tempting. But a trap.

The only way through is right up the middle.

"Yeah, I met Pepper Clark-Bean out at the *Baja BBQ Shack* to talk about a new business she wants to start. Wants to build an investigation-security business around a fleet of drones, if you can believe that. Thought I'd have an idea or two about a campaign. 'Course Pepper's got more crazy than you can shake a stick at. You know her?"

Grayson shakes his head. Drinks.

Christi reaches. Water hisses into the sink.

"Pepper's daddy, Conwell Clark, was behind Lubbock Oil & Gas before Exxon ate LO&G for a snack."

But the Clark family saga lays lifeless on the table. No takers.

"Drones, huh?" says Grayson. "Y'all out there talkin' 'bout flyin' robots."

Sheldon nods. "So what was Nicki doin' out there? I sure didn't see him."

No one answers for a moment. Two. Three. Then Christi.

"Oh, you know Nicki. Out and around, takin' his li'l pictures."

"Well I wish he'd pulled up a chair. I'd've bought him a drink, excused myself to the men's room and just kept on walkin'. Could've skipped out on that ridiculous boat ride."

Grayson. Not looking. "Went on a boat ride, did you?"

"Paid a ransom for it too. Bunch'a pirates out there if you ask me."

Grayson nods. Stirs the ice with a finger. Speaks down into the glass.

"Gotta watch out for the damned pirates, Shel. Pirates'll take your woman, rob you blind and leave you for dead." Glances up. No smile. "It's what they do."

"Well." Sheldon laughs, as if at the hyperbole. "Or just take you for an expensive boat ride."

Grayson gives a big, breaking smile. Eyes, milky and irritated from drinking, widening with counterfeit mirth. He laughs. Christi tenses at the sound, fumbling a fork into the sink.

"Right, right. Or just take you for a very expensive fuckin' ride."

Chapter 64

Dear Davis:

It was with enormous shame and disappointment that I read your letter. I have tried my best. Tried to connect. Tried to apologize. Tried to put the past behind us. Your mother was my wife. You seem to forget that. Yours is not the only loss. She has been gone a long time now You seem determined to keep knifing open this wound.

Yes. I blamed you. I do not know how many times I must admit that to you so that it sinks in. You are *correct*. I blamed you. And I know what that did to you. I have carried that shame a long time. I still do. I have tried to take responsibility for who I was in those terrible years. I have tried to own up. I know I was horrible. I felt like a failure. I wanted so much more out of my life. I was full of anger. It's not an excuse. It's just the truth. There was not enough booze in the world to numb that pain. I was broken.

But I was not broken beyond repair. We are never broken beyond repair. You, Davis, are not broken beyond repair. I have worked hard to put myself back together. It has been a long, steep hill with many setbacks. But I have done the work. I have a healthier perspective. I have triumphed over my addiction. I am a better man now.

But you are the piece in all of this —the piece in me —that is missing. I need you to set down the past. I'm not asking you to pretend that none of it happened. I am not avoiding my share of blame. I am to blame. I am asking for a chance to earn back your love. Your letter, like your attitude at dinner, threw that effort back in my face. It hurts more than you know.

Maybe it is not fair of me to ask that you let go of your anger. You will see this as a selfish effort. Well, son, it *is* a selfish effort. I am trying to cut myself free of the past and live a good life, but I cannot do that unless you allow me to be a new better man. So it is a selfish effort. But you don't need to do this for me. In fact, don't do it for me. Do it for you. You have to let all of it go, Davis. Cut us all loose. Me. Your mother. Abby Palmer, too. All of us. You have to save yourself. You have to let it all go.

I have something I want to share. I almost mentioned it at our dinner, but that night went another direction. There is no one else I can share this with. So if you are still reading this letter, I hope you will keep reading.

Years ago, the winter before Elizabeth died, she told me that my God was just a mask. A disguise. She was angry. I was drunk. She was trying to hurt me. She succeeded. She said things like *'your God'* to make it clear that *'my God'* was not *'her God'*; to make it clear that we were so fundamentally different from each other that we even answered to different gods. I took her to be calling me a phony who used religion to make myself look better than others. Better than her. But three years ago I realized that, for all of this time, I might have misunderstood her meaning.

I was rereading about Ahab (Melville's doomed sea captain, not the idolatrous Old Testament king). My editor seemed to think it would do me some good to reground myself in the classics. So I picked a chapter at random. Ishmeal is trying to learn the moral essence of the sperm whale by studying its face. *"I try all things,"* he says. *"I achieve what I can."* He goes on about how ancient cultures would have made the thing a god because it doesn't have a nose or a tongue. A god! The poor guy ultimately gives up trying to understand.

I can't tell you why, but as I read that chapter, I kept hearing your mother. *'Your God is just a mask.'* It occurred to me for the first time that it wasn't an insult; that she might have been telling me that my God was not who or what I thought he was; that my God was *disguised from me*. The idea would not leave me alone. When I closed my eyes it was like she was still here. Still looking at me. Still shouting at me so that I would understand.

I picked another chapter. Actually, I let the book itself pick the chapter. I set it on its spine and let it fall open. Chapter thirty-six. Elizabeth's age when she died. The sentence at the top of the page was Ahab lecturing Starbuck. His words, the first words I read, were like a slap in the face: *"All visible objects, man, are but as pasteboard masks."* Davis, I actually gasped. Edited a bit for length, here is what he says:

All visible objects, man, are but as pasteboard masks... If man will strike, strike through the mask! How can the prisoner reach outside except by thrusting through the wall? To me, the white whale is that wall, shoved near to me... That inscrutable thing is chiefly what I hate; and be the white whale agent, or be the white whale principal, I will wreak that hate upon him. Talk not to me of blasphemy, man; I'd strike the sun if it insulted me. ... Who's over me? Truth hath no confines.

After decades of hearing her words as an insult, I have now convinced myself that your mother was pleading for me to punch through the mask of *my God*, pleading with me to learn what was on the other side. As though she already knew. As though she and Tallulah already knew.

So many years later it was like she was still trying to make me understand. I dreamed of her. I woke with her voice ringing in my ears. No words. Only sound. Just the sound of her, like from the other side of a thick iron door. Or deep beneath the surface of the ocean. I spent a day spot-reading *Moby Dick*. I went to church. I prayed. None of it helped. I could not write. I drank to block her out. It did not help. I dried out and went to church and prayed for clarity. It did not help. My own faith, increasingly, was meaningless.

I forced myself to confront Tallulah's nonsense. It was the only way I could think of to understand your mother who could not talk about these things with me. I think that's why her music was so important to her. All of that blues. Those songs. Over and over. It was a kind of sonar that she sent out into the deep. Tallulah was the only one who ever answered.

I will spare you my thoughts about Tallulah. You already know that I believe she was just this side of bat-shit crazy. But your mother loved her. Tallulah took pleasure in provoking me into defending my religion. She liked quoting the Bible just to mock it. I always took the bait and I always regretted it.

One summer the three of us went to the state fair. You were five. Maybe six. I doubt that you remember. You and Elizabeth were off at the ring toss winning a stuffed bull. Your aunt and I sat on a bench and waited. It was hotter than hell and I wanted to go home. Tallulah suggested that maybe Jesus could pay closer attention and speed things along for me. That started things off. Eventually, I was shouting at Tallulah and she was laughing at me. We fought all the way home. Your mother kept swatting her in the leg to get her to shut up, but Tallulah never stopped. Most of the details are gone. But I do remember her leaning forward so that her face was right behind the driver's seat. Then she whispered.

"Makes sense that you worship a vengeful God, Conrad. You are a vengeful person. You're just a splinter of light stuck in your own eye. God is a mean drunk with a chip on his shoulder. You *are God, Conrad.* You.*"*

It was gibberish to me at the time. It was enough to make me even angrier, but I had no idea what she was saying. *'You are God.'*

Since then, I have found a new sympathy for poor Ishmeal, trying to read that inscrutable face. But I'm beginning to think it's only a mirror, Davis. When you punch through the mask? If you tear it away? *You are God*, Tallulah had said.

I have not come to terms with your mother's death. I never will. It was all too easy to blame you. I shouldn't have. It was not your fault. But blaming you kept me from blaming myself. Better that she died trying to save you than that she died to get away from me. The truth is even worse than that. There are lots of ways to get away from someone. Elizabeth was not just getting away from me, she was getting away from life. She was done with all of it. I am partly to blame for that. I abused her all the way to the water's edge, as you so cruelly but accurately put it.

But I was not the only problem. She was also part of the problem. The thing that you don't like to acknowledge is that your mother had mental issues. Your grandma Mae had similar problems. Tallulah too. So Elizabeth got it honest. And I made it worse. Dr. Bees told me over and over how my anger was only driving her deeper into her own head. But I didn't listen. I kept at it. I kept drinking in the anger and I kept taking it out on her. And just as Fredrick predicted, she kept sinking like a stone.

I regret telling you about the dreams. I don't know what they meant to her. I know they terrified her. I know they lingered and returned. She carried them around like memories. Those dreams came from an illness, Davis, one that smudges the line between the real and the imagined. She pretended to take her medication. Then she outright refused, saying it made her depressed. But that was just an excuse. Tallulah hated doctors like she hated ministers. She convinced your mother that life is just a conspiracy among the living. A kind illusion. Just so we can believe that we understand.

So why, then, did she die? To save you? To leave me? I don't know what she saw in that moment. I spent years pretending to know, conveniently blaming everyone but myself. It was always so clear.

More recently, I find myself less and less certain about everything. I no longer know where to find the water's edge. I sense that Elizabeth has been guiding me. I feel her on the other side of the wall. The other side of the mask. I hear sounds in my head that I know belong to her. Sometimes I can see the lake through *her* eyes. I can feel the cold water against *her* skin. I can sense the choice in *her* heart. I know all of this sounds like I have gone crazy. Maybe I have. How can any of that be possible? And yet…

Three years ago, when drinking could not banish your mother's voice, I quit the bottle for good. I also spent some time with Fredrick Bees, if you can believe it. He put little stock in the value of God's forgiveness. He encouraged me to look for answers much closer to home. The sobriety stuck. Life improved. I threw myself into *Eyelash Lake*. And with all of that eventually came a relative peace.

But there is also something else. I no longer know what to believe, Davis. My old faith feels like an empty and useless vessel. If there are answers, then they are much deeper, beneath my religion, where I have great difficulty reaching. I still dream of her. Almost every night. She is always a shadow in deep water. She is always swimming.

I understand that you hate *Eyelash Lake*. You think I'm looting her beliefs for my own material gain. But it was never that. I was trying to dive deeper than my religion allows. I was trying to understand her. I still am.

I am trying, Davis. I promise to you that I am. Maybe that promise means nothing to you and, if so, then that is my fault. But I cannot move on unless you can forgive me and allow me to be a different person. Otherwise, part of me will always stay lashed to the body of the old hate and anger. I cannot move on until you have moved on. And you cannot move on until you allow yourself to let go of all of those old feelings. It's not enough to stop drinking. It's not enough to isolate yourself in the Godforsaken scrublands of south Texas. You have to make your peace. You have to let go of all of it.

Your letter expressed some anger at Buddy Lincoln for giving me your address. But Buddy has not failed you. I have failed you. It no longer works for me to ask God's forgiveness. I need your forgiveness. And I do not think that can happen until you forgive yourself. So, once again, I will tell you what you refuse to believe, deep down in the dark bottom of your ocean where all words are merely sound: *It was not your fault.*

You are right, Davis. This is a selfish letter. But there it is anyway. I try all things. I achieve what I can.

Chapter 65

Eleven penises.

An amateur will try twelve. Thirteen.

Twelve is too many. Because they expand.

But she's a pro. She's got it down to a science of numbers. Properly arranged on a 17 x 11 inch cookie sheet, eleven slow pours into half-inch molds. Three hundred seventy-five degrees. Eleven minutes.

She has made the mistake of twelve. The mistake of thirteen.

She had also made the mistake of six. Much too big. The long bit always out of proportion with the round, bulbous bit. Usually burned. Easily broken.

Doesn't matter what you are wearing or not wearing. Can't hand a man a broken penis and expect him to eat it.

So. Eleven.

She sings.

"Mmmmm. I'm gonna bake my biscuits, bake my biscuits."

Libby pours the last of the batter into the eleventh tin-foil mold.
Puts the sheet into the oven. Closes the door with her hip.

"I'm gonna bake them biscuits, bake them biscuits."

She turns to the sink but is pulled up short. Opens the oven door again. Yanks out the sash to her lavender, above-the-knee kimono. Closes the door with her hip. Shakes her head in a slow roll. Keeps channeling Memphis Minnie.

"Gonna want my biscuits. Gonna taste my biscuits."

"Thought you were gon' stop making those cookies." Olivia leans a shoulder against the doorway. Watches Libby, framed perfectly by the window over the sink. Outside is nothing but dark, slate gray air and bending trees. Water slips down the glass in ropey rivulets. She crosses her arms.

Libby looks. Turns back to the sink. Rinses.

"Cookies? Ain' no *cookies*, baby. These here is shuga sticks. An' you didn't believe that shit anyways. *Gonna shake my biscuits. Shake my biscuits.*"

"You're gonna get yourself in serious trouble is what you're gon' do. All that junk you put in the batter."

Libby slaps off the water. Talks to Olivia's airy reflection in the wet window.

"Junk? Pixie dust is what makes 'em special, baby. Don't go callin' my shuga sticks junk." Liberty turns suddenly, face lit in a smile. Laughs. "Wait, wait, wait. They is too *junk*, huh? They *dick* cookies! *Junk!* This like the *ultimate* junk food."

"Libby…"

"Next time my serious blond sex-machine come by I'm gon' hold out a shuga stick and look into them freaky blue eyes and say: *here, baby, you go on and eat you some junk food.* That make him smile. I tell that man one joke after t'other and the muthafuck don't even crack a grin. *Whooo-Wee.* That man fuck you with his eyes. Don't even need a dick." Libby lowers her chin and her voice. "But he got himself one of them too. Lawd have mercy, he gots one a them."

"Who?"

"My serious blond sex machine. Yestaday he come by wearin' a suit! An' he…"

Olivia holds up a hand. "Never mind. I don't want to know." She pushes off from the door. Limps for the refrigerator.

"*Mmmmm.*" Libby points. "Leg hurt today, don't it?"

"I'm good."

"Oh, you good huh? Limpin' like a peg-leg pirate?"

"Okay. Thanks for that."

"I don't mean nothin', baby. Don't like to see you hurtin', is all."

"They said I could expect this. It's the weather. This rain. Makes the mornings colder. That hurricane just sitting out there in the gulf. Not moving. It's the pressure."

"Ain't no hurricane, baby. It a *system.*"

"System. Whatever. Nice weather for a festival."

Libby packs a laugh into one syllable.

"Oh, this shit pass befo' then. Whatchu' care anyhow? Thought you wasn't goin' to the festival this year."

"I wasn't, but now I …" It is too late to put the words back into her mouth. "I gotta meet someone tomorrow."

Libby beams. Lowers her head, looking up at her from below. Points with the spoon. "Oooo. 'Livia gon' get her some on the fuckus wheel."

"Ferris wheel. And no. Nothing like that."

"Who you meetin', baby? Don't tell me you meeting that Yvonne bitch."

There will never be a better chance to derail the train before it runs smack into the truth about her and Sheldon. Olivia points back. "You know, I really don't know why you hate her so much. Y'all are more alike than different."

"You lost yo' mind?"

"No, thank you very much. You're both women with a shitty track record tryin' to find a good man. You should sympathize."

"Hell, baby, we *all* in *that* leaky boat. We all women. An' men always be what they be. But I'm a *cat* woman. An' Yvonne a *dog* woman. That make me all pussy and Yvonne all bitch. Jus' like I say. So we ain't the same."

"Fine. Not arguing with you about Yvonne. I'm just sayin' the weather sucks for a festival. That okay with you?"

Libby makes a half turn. Looks out the window. Turns back.

"Might be gray as fuck but ain't gon' keep rainin'. Ain't never rained on the Moon Garden Festival. Evangelina Huerta up there on her li'l cloud lookin' down on her li'l moon flowers. Protectin' her lil' babies. Hell, the sun probably gon' come out. People worried about the rain gon' be usin' they umbrellas to keep the sun off. People in raincoats slumped on the side of the damn road, dyin' a heatstroke. They all be *prayin'* fo' anotha hurricane 'for its over."

"Don't think so, Libby. Not this year."

Libby laughs. Shakes her head. "Mama an' me rode out a hurricane once."

"Yeah? Which one?"

"Which one? I don't know the bitch's name. *Hurricane Bitch.* And she *was*, too. Weren't no Harvey or Katrina but she big enough an' mean enough to kill my ass. Eva'one else got the fuck outta Dodge. Not mama. No, no, no. She say whatever the good Lawd send yo' way, you supposed to receive that shit. If it kill you, then thas' because it yo' time to go. If it don't kill you then it make you stronger. Makes you better. Brings you closer to God. But if you run away? If you turn yo' back on what God sends to you? You gon' die fo' sho'. Even if you live, you be dead inside 'cause God gon' say *fuck it I ain't wastin' my time on you.* So we hunker all down, jus' me an mama in our little piece-a-shit box we call a house an' cover eva'thing in plastic and blankets and pray to Jesus."

"What happened?"

Another punch of a laugh. Outside, the trees react to the stupid question.

"Lost *eva'*fuckin'thing is what happen. Like God rip off the roof and pour in the fuckin' Pontchartrain. We like a couple'a damn fish in a leaky wooden bowl. Water moccasins swimmin' all every which way, in one window an' out t'other," she points the spoon in the direction of the front yard, "tryin' to get the fuck … *out. Mmm-mmm.* Thought we was gon' die fo' sho'."

"But you didn't."

"No. We did *not* die. We did *not.*" Libby holds the spoon like a sword. Lets it drip. "An' you know why?"

"Why?"

"'Cause one of them snakes swimmin' in through the windows was the ABC Man in his li'l beat up motorboat. He won't tryin' to get the fuck *out*. He was tryin' to get the fuck *in*. Thas' what the Lawd sent Mama an' me. Antoine Beaudaine Cherish. Mama say God sent Antoine to save us. So she grab snake Antoine right around his middle and held on fo' dear life. We both did. Like he was some kinda fucking rope."

Olivia opens the refrigerator. Leans in.

"Well, I guess *that* explains your relationship with the man upstairs." She winces. Kicks herself for letting the remark slip past her better judgment.

"Man upstairs? Ain't no man upstairs, baby. No, no, no. The *Man*… live *downstairs* here with us. He the one wit' those three little fuckin' horns. Two up top an' one down below. Una'stan' what I'm sayin'? Only Mama upstairs. Yo' mama… an' my mama… an' eva'body else's mama. I believe in Mama to shine that light. Show us the way in the world. Protect our sorry selves. Man upstairs my ass. Jesus may be a man, but he a mama's boy. He out doin' her work jus' like she say."

Olivia inserts her head further into the open refrigerator. Rummages. The conversation teeters on a familiar precipice. One more word on the subject and the whole thing will tip downhill.

"Man upstairs my ass."

Religion is constitutionally offensive to her. All of it. When people speak of religion, any religion, the words have an odor. Like a gas. Or smoke. They carry a stench that triggers in her a kind of psychic gag-reflex. It's a kind of sickness. A hidden emotional rockslide of inexplicable rage thundering down into emptiness.

"Man in the damned *basement* what you mean to say, baby. Ain't upstairs."

She has tamed the reaction. Has learned how to beat it back. Has learned to smile and nod. It is the quickest way to dissipate the fumes and make the stench go away. Libby's religious kink *–mamas in Heaven lookin' afta' they babies –*is somehow more noxious than the others. More deadly. And once Libby starts, she doesn't stop.

"'Cause I *know* the Devil. An' *that* muthafuck a man fo' sho'."

Not another word of religion. She needs to protect the delicate feeling in her chest. Today just might be a good day. A genuinely good day. The first in an unbroken series of good days. It might be. It could be.

It is just an inkling of a feeling. A newborn baby bird of a feeling. It does not yet dare step into the harsh light of conscious thought for more than a second at a time before tumbling back into shadow. It will not survive a discussion of religion. Or mamas. Not today. Not now.

So she waits, head in the cold air between the orange juice and the *Rio Lobo*. She rummages until she hears the water running again in the sink. Then she pulls halfway out.

"No eggs?" she asks.

"I just used 'em up."

"Right. The sugar sticks. How silly of me."

"Baby, you an' yo' attitude up *early* today."

Olivia briefly glances up over the door of the open refrigerator.

"Lots to do. Got a mornin' shift at the club. Then I'm meetin' with Lou Dimond about Manny Soto. Then I got a shift at *The Diamondback*, which is gon' to be awkward as all hell 'cause Manny's workin' tonight. Unless Lou fires him on the spot. I'm gon' insist on different shifts at the very least. If we have to work together Manny's getting' another shit-brush in the face."

"That mutherfuck so much as look at you the wrong way…"

"I'll be fine, Libby."

"*MmmHmm.* I make it so no one can call him Manny no more. He ain't gon' be a man after I get done."

"Libby."

"Alright. You handle it. You still ain't said why you up so damn early. 'Cause I happen to know you ain't due at *fuck-all-fitness* 'til eleven."

"Longhorn Fitness."

"Thas' what I say: *Fuck-all-fitness.* May as well come clean, baby. You usually like wakin' up a dead person this early."

Olivia sighs.

"It's nothing. I'm meetin' someone."

Liberty shuts off the water again. Turns, arms crossed. Waits.

The silence brings Olivia back up over the edge of the door. She looks.

"What."

"I can wait all day, baby."

"Libby…"

"Uh-uh. Don't you Libby me. Ain't gon' slip out this house to meet up with some no good man at fuck o'clock in the mornin' without me knowin' who."

"You're not my mother, Libby."

"No I ain't. But yo' mama up there in Heaven jus' waitin' to fuck me up if I don't look after her baby. An' if she don't do it, *my* mama sho' nuf will. 'Cause you my one good thing."

"I don't think it works that way."

"*MmmHmm.* You hookin' up with my li'l writer friend, ain't you? That who you meetin' t'morrow too, huh? Y'ain't meetin' up with no Yvonne. You meetin' up wit' my li'l writer-ponytail-no-kinda-priest with the fuck-all-day face. You tryin' to make me believe…"

"Libby, I really don't think any of this is your business."

"Baby, my business is keepin' you from doin' somethin' stupid. That boy want you in a bad way. It's all up in his eyes n'shit. He been after you in his dreams. He could give a shit 'bout me. I pull out my titty three time and the man jus' keep writin' in his li'l notepad like I showed him a li'l green tree frog that live inside my shirt. But *you?* Baby, it like he gon' mess his draw's sayin' yo' name on my front stoop."

Olivia suddenly sees him in her head. Davis. Sees him in Libby's parlor. Sitting on the purple settee.

Sees him at *Pepita's* with Miguel. Sitting at a table. Blood on his face.

Sees him on the dark road under a torrent of cold stars. Sitting on the idling Harley. Hears his voice. *Alright then. Olivia. I look forward to not seeing you at the festivals.*

She had hoped that would be the last of him. She doesn't want any of that. Not anymore. Not now. Not ever again. She is done.

But he has come looking. Davis. Knocking on her front door. Wanting to *not* go to the festival together. Festivals. And he will be back. In broad daylight he will be back and up close and he will ask his question because those are the words in his head, formed and arranged before he could get a good look at her. She will see herself in his recoiling face. Like a funhouse mirror.

But it will be too late for him. For Davis. He will stand by his reckless, ill-considered words and it will be up to her to correct his mistake. And she will. Coldly. Heartlessly. Because she is done with all of that. Done being in the world that way.

Done.

Sheldon, *massage-massage-all-the-way-married*, is suddenly in her head, standing at the door with Davis, leaning in, his face a tortured question, envelope in his hand. The answer she gives to the question on his face is quick and practiced: *blackmail.* Fear of exposure. That is the only explanation for Sheldon. An old man looking for peace of mind. Protecting his shitty marriage.

She snatches the imagined envelope. Slams the door in her head. She does not want the darkness. Not now. Not today. There is only one thing she wants. Just one. The tiny bird in her chest flutters. She looks at Libby.

"So you're jealous? This is what you're saying?"

"*Jealous?* I am protectin' yo' ass is what I am. I got to remind you that you seen my *No-Kinda-Priest-Fuck-All-Day* at *Pepitas* wit' his pretty li'l face all beat to hell?"

"So?"

"So? So that mean up inside his cute li'l writer head is a fighter. He a violent man." Libby balls up a hand, tightening her lips. "He like to beat on people. And you's people."

"Will you stop?" She grabs the orange juice. Closes the refrigerator. Swigs from the plastic jug. "Not every man is Antoine Cherish. Anyway, I'm not meeting... *him.* Whatever his name is. *Davis.* Not tomorrow and not this morning."

"You lie like a…"

"Libby."

"Who then? Oh you roll them pretty eyes. Y'ain't leavin' 'til I know."

Olivia closes her eyes. She feels it, the smile, suddenly, slipping over her mouth like a tongue of honey. She can't help it. She can only hope the plastic jug can keep it hidden. She drinks. Can feel Libby waiting. Closes her lips, pretending now, prolonging the posture. Waiting for the smile to recede. She does not want to talk about it. She does not want to jinx the promise of what might come. She should not have come into the kitchen in the first place.

But there is no changing it now. Libby will never let it go.

She lowers the jug to the counter. Wipes her mouth with the back of her hand. Composed. Looks across the kitchen, out the window. There is a moment of stillness outside.

"Papi," she says. The tiny bird in her chest stirs again. Ruffles its little feathers.

"*Papi?* You mean *Papi*-Papi? Baby, he *waaayyyy* too old to fuck. His sad li'l heart just say *fuck it* and give up 'fore you unbuckle his damn belt. 'Specially in the mornin'. See, this why I got to be involved. Don't you go killin' that man."

"Oh, come on! You can't be serious. Ain't hooking up with…" But then she can see Libby crack.

"*Oooo Wee!* You easy pickins today. I'm jus' playin', baby. Cain't help myself. Why you meetin' up with Papi?"

It is not a question she wants to answer. The hope is still too delicate. It will shrivel and die in direct light. She doesn't want to let it out. Not yet. So she gives only a scolding expression.

"*MmmHmm.* You still talkin' 'bout that juke joint ain'tcha? You still workin' that poor man."

"Can't hurt to keep talking," she says, taking a last swig. She returns the jug to the fridge. Closes the door.

"That old man jus' gon' keep breakin' yo' heart, baby."

"I know, Libby. I know."

But she doesn't know. Not any more. Not this morning.

She limps through the ghost gray light, rainwater streaking her face. Aims for Old Faithful, usually so stoic but now with branches like a carnival ride. Beneath it is the battered, shit-brown Ford Falcon that Jesús Batista has been forced to abandon for a new-old life in Toluca. It waits for her, not for Jesús anymore, but for *her* now, in the wet, restless gloom.

She climbs in. Slams the door. Adjusts the sofa cushion. Slicks the water off of her face. The weather has sealed in an odor she cannot identify.

Dashboard Jesus is touched to see her again. He doesn't mind the stink.

She starts the car. Backs out. Libby is at the window watching. Waving. A pan of penises in her mitted hand. She jolts forward.

He had called *her. Papi* had called *her.*

That made all of the difference.

Usually she was the one pushing the issue. But this time, he had called her and left a message that now ran on a loop in her head.

"Olivia. Papi ringin' your phone. I'm coming to Corbin. Willa and the kids dragging me to that damned festival. In the rain it's lookin' like. Anyway, come by the church Friday morning. Say eight, eight-thirty. Want to talk to you about this club. May as well be in person and you're not on the schedule for a couple of weeks yet. Hope to see you. If not, we'll just talk whenever. Bye now."

She had returned the call. Twice. Hungry for more information. But Papi was notoriously hard to reach. He had a cell phone "for emergencies." Turned it on to make a call and turned off when he was done. Best chance to reach Papi was always to call him at the club. Whoever was tending bar would take a message and, if you were lucky, Papi'd call you back.

Well, she wasn't and he hadn't.

Which left only the loop of memory in her head. *Want to talk to you about this club. Want to talk to you about this club. Want to talk to you about this club.*

That could only mean one thing.

She hits the highway. Heads for town. Thinks about the money stacked neatly in the back of the old Mexican dresser. Stacks of soft green paper inside of a soft paper bag, inside of a brown cardboard box, inside of an old pine dresser, inside of a sparsely appointed room, inside of a whorehouse that smelled like freshly baked penis cookies. The money makes her think of Sheldon again. Sheldon was already working his own little memory loop.

"I'll be there. Saturday. I'll have something for you. Ahead of schedule. Heavier than normal."

Heavier than normal. Heavier than normal.

And now. Papi. *Want to talk to you about this club.*

It could all only mean one thing. Not mamas in Heaven. Or the white-bearded man on a throne. Or the brown-bearded man in sandals hanging ten on the dashboard. But only the power of her own earthy desire to secretly shape events. To delay them. Accelerate them. Steer them. To bring them into perfect collision. *She* had done this. *She* had brought all of this about.

Somehow, suddenly, she knows this.

She, Olivia, had been orchestrating things from the very beginning.

The careful seduction of Sheldon Davis. Businessman. Houston, Texas.

His violent ejection onto the lawn of Libby's Nuts. Make him mad. Make him lovesick. Make him crazy. Somehow she had known to do that.

Somehow she had known to do *exactly… that.*

The collision that had been no accident. Not really. Not in any way that really mattered. Something in her had known. Something in her had steered that little blue Civic in just the right way. Hooked those cheap, balding tires on the edge of the road. Pulled the wheel. Yanked it hard at just the right second. It had had nothing to do with the coyote, pup wedged into her maw. Not really. Somehow she had just known to take her timing cue from the natural world. *Yank the wheel! Now! Pull!*

That was not God. That was *her*. It was the gravitational pull of her desperate need for the one thing that would allow her life to make any sense –the one thing that would fit the jagged empty shape in the puzzle of her existence. The vibration. The note. The melody. The rhythm. The missing sound that would fill a very particular silence in her soul.

She had been writing this song from the very beginning. And that meant that she was in control of the time signature. Four beats in every bar.

One-two-three-four.

A quarter note for every fifty-foot stretch of cracked, sun-bleached road.

One-two-three-four.

She had known the precise moment, as Sheldon Davis sped along next to her, red-faced and yelling at her through glass.

One, two, three … Yank.

That quarter-note moment had connected to the next quarter-note moment. *One, two, three, four.* And the next. *One, two, three, four.* And the next. Until the neat little paper stacks had started accumulating; piling up inside the bag inside of the box inside of the dresser inside of the whorehouse. *One, two, three, four.*

And now, *now*, just when Sheldon Davis, businessman of Houston, prepares to bring something for her that was *heavier than normal*, here comes *Papi*, Austin juke joint owner. Calling her on the phone.

He has called *her*.

Wanting to *talk about this club*.

She feels sick with hope.

She finds him in the Activities Center sitting at a long, empty table that belongs in a school cafeteria. The window behind him looks out across a small, nearly submerged pathway that serpentines frivolously to the side of the Corbin First Methodist Church. Willa is across from him folding green fliers and slipping them into envelopes.

Papi sees her across the room in the doorway. Points a crooked black finger to a large stainless steel coffee pot on a table in the corner.

She looks. Shakes her head. Keeps walking.

"Morning," she says.

Willa looks up. Smiles. She has a sweet, doughy face. Scattered freckles. Her father's eyes, for better and worse. She leaves a flier half folded.

"Hey, Olivia," says Willa. "How you been? Haven't seen you in awhile. You healin' up okay?"

"Slow. It all still hurts," says Olivia. Inside she cringes. Not that. Anything but that. She pivots. "I catch glimpses of you here and there. Out-n-about. Usually with your arms full."

"Staying busy," says Willa. Rolls her eyes. "Those kids."

"And still working for the city too, right?"

Willa nods. "Tryin' to pull off another festival. In the rain this time. Good Lord, give me strength. And the church." She drops her hand onto the fliers. "Trying to raise just a little bit of money to do just a little bit of good."

"Don't know how you do it all, Willa."

"I don't either. I called for reinforcements."

They both look at Papi, inviting interruption. He does.

"No coffee?" he asks.

"Nah." Olivia shakes her head and makes a face. "Can't drink coffee without some food in my stomach."

Papi looks at her with a deadly seriousness she knows cannot be real. He points the crooked black finger again, this time at her.

"You think... I was pointing at the coffee pot... for *you*?"

Willa laughs. Hits him with the nearest envelope.

"You be nice."

"Well... what's a man got to do to get himself a cup of coffee?"

"You just said it, Daddy. A man can *get himself* a cup of coffee."

"But, but, but..." Papi feigns incomprehension, looking around the room, spreading his arms for help. Willa stands.

"I will bring you your coffee. Stubborn old man. Then I have *got* to find those kids. Probably knee-deep into something they shouldn't be. Sit Olivia. Keep an eye on him. He's worse than my girls."

Olivia sits. Finishes folding the flier. Sticks it in the envelope. Picks up the next one. Reads out loud.

"*Church auction. Free cookies. Treasure hunt.* You gon' be down in Corbin hunting for treasure, Papi?"

He closes his baggy eyes. Nods.

"If Willa has any say..." he breaks off and smiles as his daughter bustles back by the table, slowing enough to hand him a Styrofoam cup.

"Black as night, no sugar, no cream," says Willa.

"Thanks honey-bun." He sips. Watches her go. Nods. "If Willa has any say I'd move down here permanently." He laughs to himself. Shakes his head. "Sure as hell not doing that. Austin suits me better. Best thing about Corbin is Willa and those kids. Weren't for them I'd never be down here. And I mean *ever*."

She folds the flier. Stuffs an envelope. Picks up the next. Folds. Papi watches.

"Still don't know what keeps you here in this dust pit, Olivia. You should move up my way."

She forces herself to keep folding. The words come with an electric charge. They riot through the streets of her central nervous system. Of course he would suggest that she move up his way. She would *have* to move. She pretends to ignore the significance of the remark. Folds. Stuffs.

"Dust pit?" She nods in the direction of the rain-streaked window behind him. "You see any dust out there, Papi?"

He doesn't turn. "A Moon Garden Festival for the record books, that's for damn sure. *And* Day of the Dead. Mercy. You goin' to that mess too?"

"Not for long. But I've got a friend I have to meet, so..."

Papi smiles broadly enough to stretch taut his saggy lower lip. "Oh. Well now. Well... now. Meetin' a friend are we?"

She feels the blood in her face go hot. Feels the scars glow white. Feels exposed. Transparent. Like Papi can see her working poor Sheldon Davis, businessman from Houston. Like he can see everything that has led up to this point. Like he can see Sheldon's feelings for her. Can see him handing her an envelope, *heavier than normal*.

"Trust me," she says. "It ain't what you're thinkin'."

"All I'm thinkin' is that what you need..." His hands search for the words in the airspace around the coffee cup. "It'd be nice to see you in some kind of... of..."

She shuts him down with a sharp shake of her head.

"No. Nope. Don't do that, Papi. You're not qualified to be givin' me relationship advice."

"Well ain't that the God's honest truth. But I'm not giving any advice. I'm just sayin' that if you got somethin' goin' then I hope you *keep* it goin'. I'm sayin' I care about what happens to you."

"I know, Papi. I..."

"I see all kinds of girls... *young women* I guess I should say. Willa's all over me about my words. I see all kinds of *young women* movin' through that club. I hire them and they stay for a while and they move on and I hire someone else. I get to see all of their little quirks. Their problems. And I'm here to say I've seen it all. Good and bad. Some of it really bad. Half of the trouble comes from the music end of it. Those guitar players. The drummers. Most of 'em high on something with no damn sense. I've lost more help to musicians than I can count. I don't have to tell you that."

She makes a sound that could be a laugh of agreement.

"Could have probably avoided a lot of problems by pullin' the plug on the live music. Just have a bar with good food. Bring in a juke box."

"Not an option, Papi. Not there. You want *Papi's* to be just another *Diamondback*?"

"No. I know. I'm just sayin'. The musicians always bring the trouble it seems. Anyway, after a while they all sorta start to look alike, these young women. Except you. You've always been… I don't know… *different*. From a different kind of place. On your own little island. Even before the accident. And, far as I can tell, you don't let another living soul set foot on your little piece of dry land. Not the people you work with. Not me. Maybe you got some friends down here that you let come ashore. Maybe they provide you with whatever it is you need. But that would surprise me. It truly would. You're the most alone person I know."

She is silent. Folding. Stuffing. Listening.

"So I'm just sayin'… I don't know, Olivia. I'm just sayin' that I care what happens. That's why you're here this mornin'. I didn't want to wait 'til you came to me. And I didn't want to talk on the phone. I hate the damn phone."

She stops. They look at each other over the table. Weather lashes at the window at his back, trying mightily to reach them. She sets down the flier. Swallows.

"Tell me what you want to say, Papi."

"I sold the club, honey. The ink is dry."

She does not answer. Does not move. Feels the baby bird in her chest seize, struggling for air.

"She's gone. And I'm sorry, Olivia. I really, truly am."

Olivia nods. Once. Twice. Folds. Stuffs.

Again. Again. Just the sound of skin on paper.

"Who?" she asks finally.

"DCPM."

"I don't… DC…"

"Dallas Commercial Properties Management, LLC. Cash offer. My lawyer said I wasn't going to get a better deal. So I took it."

"How much?"

He smiles sadly.

"Ah. Can't tell me, can you?"

"No. Doesn't matter, honey. It was for more than you could have scraped together. I know you wanted it. And I know *why* you wanted it."

She looks. Looks away. Folds. Stuffs. Folds. Stuffs. Folds.

He lays his big hand on both of hers. She tries to keep going. He presses down. Stillness. She looks up. Something wet and plastic sticks to the window and is torn away in the wind.

"If I could have saved it for you, I would have. I couldn't wait. I had to take it."

"I know, Papi. I… It's okay."

She pulls her hands from beneath his. Stuffs an envelope. Folds. Slower now. He watches.

"What are they going to do with it? Probably can't tell me that either."

Papi sighs. "I don't know what they're going to do. Nothing good, I'm afraid."

"Why?"

"They didn't care enough to even inspect the place. Which means they're going to bulldoze the whole thing. Or gut it and move in a fried chicken franchise or sell footballs or some shit. I don't know. Or just jack up the price and flip it to some other buyer. It's just money to them. This is what they do. Buy and sell. I feel like a soulless traitor, Olivia. And I don't know how to tell you how sorry I am about this. I don't have any goddamned choice. But I am so sorry."

They sit in silence. Listen to the world outside, lashing at their bubble of glass. Listen to the rhythm of dry paper. Creasing. Sliding. Stacking. All of that water outside and she feels like she will crumble into dust. Death by desiccation.

She sees the stupidity of it now. All of it. Sees her own hope, framed in the windows of her eyes. Laughing at her. Pointing. It had all been so ridiculous.

Willa is in the doorway, finishing a conversation with someone out of view. Walking and talking. Heading their direction.

"I know, Papi," Olivia whispers. Not because she wants to whisper. There is not enough breath in her lungs for anything more. "I know you are."

Chapter 66
Mable and Libby

The ABC Man had been at a serious disadvantage.

Naked, for one thing. And the tub was slick.

Mable, newly fired over a missing broach she had never seen but accused of having stolen, was already soaking in rage. Antoine, his back to the door, was otherwise engaged with young Libby. And singing.

He never saw it coming.

Antoine's throat fit neatly in the crook of Mable's elbow. She'd yanked him out of the tub so hard he fell backwards, head like a hollow melon against the floor. Before he could make sense of things, Mable had ripped the towel bar out of the drywall and was swinging it like a club. It connected once with Antoine's cheek, opening the flesh. Second swing caught his shoulder as he was crabbing backwards for the door, screaming about how she'd gone crazy and something about it being Libby's idea.

The third swing went for the groin. Adrenaline and instinct served him well. He'd rolled away from the swing and she missed, shattering the full-length mirror on the wall. Antoine scrambled out of the bathroom in the reflection of a hundred falling glass daggers.

She'd let him run. Turned to face Libby, cowering naked and terrified under the streaming water. Looking down at that towel bar like she might be next.

Mable had not moved for a long time. Breathing hard. Listening to Antoine in the apartment behind her. Dressing and shouting. *"Whore! Worthless whore!"* Stumbling. Bleeding.

Leaving.

A minute after the door slammed. Two minutes.

Three.

Four.

Mable had dropped the towel rod. Dropped herself to the floor, sobbing.

It was a profound moment for Libby. The sound of Mable's weight hitting

521

the glass-strewn floor. Returning her to human. Libby had blinked again for the first time in that revelation. Her mother would do anything. Risk everything. Kill anybody. Die trying. Her mother would never leave her. The very idea that Mable would choose to abandon her to the world was suddenly as unlikely as the story of a kindly Mr. Lee finding a beautiful baby girl in his garden. Suddenly she had understood the world. She was loved. Desperately loved. And she would never, ever be alone.

Because her mother would never let that happen.

They had moved after all of that. Took Mable three weeks to find another job that paid almost as much as the Sunrise Suites. Their old three-bedroom apartment was suddenly a fondly remembered *Taj Mahal*. The new place turned up only a mile away at just the right time; meaning just before they were sleeping out in the tall grass under a moon dripping with the humidity of a Louisiana July.

The place was small and hot and looked out over a pile of uncleared bramble that seemed to writhe and twitch in the lengthening shadows of afternoon. The wretched couple living on the first floor were randomly indifferent and resentful at sharing the building. It seemed to depend on the day. Or the temperature. Usually it was the wife who was resentful and the husband who was indifferent, but they mixed it up just enough to keep things interesting when Mable came home from work.

"Afta'noon Mr. Greavy. How you today?"

Always out in the yard, bent under the hood of his black Pontiac. Mostly black. Driver's door was a dingy yellow. Trunk was white. Whitish. Sometimes he'd answer. Mostly he'd just look up at her warily and nod. Then he'd get back to work, Lynyrd Skynyrd on a loop blasting out of one speaker.

Every so often his wife would be standing in the screened doorway. *Vye* or *Vyra*, he called her. Thin and rigid. Red nails and dirty-blonde hair falling below her razor shoulders. Just to remind everyone what she was made of. To remind Clayton whenever he happened to look up from under the hood or came in for another beer.

The Greavys shouted at each other in the evenings and played the stereo and the television too loud, which should have made the building intolerable. But Mable could afford it without any help from Antoine or anyone else. That was the selling point. It would do. It was temporary.

As predicted, less living space had meant Libby and Mable were always *up in each other's business*. Libby bristled, just as any teenager. They fought over little things. Libby invented friends she didn't really have, just to get out and to be away. When the season came, she went back to school in the mornings. Most of the time she actually made it through the front doors. But she rarely stayed in the building through the end of the day. The administration stopped caring. Stopped calling. It was just easier.

Mable waited for Antoine. No question that he would be back. They were easy enough to find. He would be back and he would try again and she would put him in the hospital. Police would be no help. She'd have to do it herself.

So then she would.

She slept lighter. Listened through the crickets. Switched up her work shifts at random. Kept an eye out for that moss-green Impala.

Months passed. A tropical depression shouldered itself into the Gulf and brooded its way into a storm. The air turned liquid and the wind took out the power for six hours. Mable and Libby sat in the dark eating stale potato chips and listening to the weather against the walls. Feeling the building shake in the wind. They were both thinking about that one hurricane. Impossible not to think about it.

"Think Antoine out in his skiff tonight?" Libby had asked. His name was always good for a long pause.

"Most likely. Takin' what ain't his while folks is huddled up inside."

"Getting' bad out there, mama. What if Antoine in trouble? He ain't got no people. Not that I know of. What if he need help?"

Mable had tightened up her face so hard that Libby could feel it on the other side of the dark room.

"Baby. Now you listen to me. Antoine… don't need no help… from nobody. Antoine helps himself. You evah see Antoine Beaudaine Cherish again? You turn and walk away. Unastan' me?"

"But eva'body need help sometime. You said so."

"Not Antoine."

"You said that one day I will see a man on the road in need of my help and that it ain't right to judge nobody needin' help 'cause it could be anybody on that road an' that I would know that it was my turn to be a mama to that man jus' like he was my own baby."

Quiet in the dark for a moment. Just the wind and the rain. Beneath them Vye and Clayton Greave yelled at each other. Mable sighed.

"You right, baby. I did say that. 'Cept I did *not* say you would see a man on the road. I said you'd see a soul on the road. Could be a man. Could be a woman. Could be old or young or in between. So I said soul to mean all them kinda people. Could be some kinda hurt animal too. But when the time come, you gon' know it your turn to be a mama to that poor soul. Maybe you have y'own kids when it happen. Maybe not. Don't matter 'cause a soul is a soul is a soul, baby. My own mama tell me that many a time. Sitting under that big ol' pecan. Watchin' the fireflies wink on an' off. Many a time."

Another long pause. An exploding transformer flashed in the distance. Exclamation from below. Mable cleared her throat.

"But Antoine Beaudaine Cherish ain't got no soul, baby. He ain't the one on that road needin' no help. Not from you. Not from me. I see his ass on the road, I'm gon' run it over."

Silence after that. Just the wind and the rain. The airborne ocean and all of its memory trying to get in.

The storm passed. Months passed. Then nearly two years. The ABC Man never showed. The muscles of vigilance ached from strain. Always watching. Always listening in the dark. Then, eventually, they slowly relaxed.

The call came one morning from a new Jefferson Parish Public School District employee. Rules and policy still meant something, it seemed. Libby's truancy problem had reached levels that precluded graduation.

"Ma'am, she can't just leave whenever she wants to leave."

Mable had resisted. There must be some mistake.

"Nope. No mistake, Ma'am. Just this morning, not two hours ago, Libby left the building, got into some car with some man. No... I... I... Listen. I don't know what kind of car, Ma'am. It was green. Okay? Ma'am? Ma'am? I'm not concerned about the kind of car, I'm concerned..."

Mable had called the house. No answer.

She had then searched out her Day Manager. Feigned illness. Headed straight for home. The bus was late for not being early. The ride was excruciating for being normal. Pushing through nearly unbearable heat, she'd walked the last half mile as fast as she could move her large body, sordid vignettes playing in her head –the shower, the bed, the couch, the kitchen counter –expecting to find that history had uncoiled itself and slithered over the threshold up into the present. Expecting to see that moss green Impala out front.

But it was not out front.

Clayton Greavy was out front. Bent under the hood of his own car, half-devoured by a mostly black metal lawn beast. Engine running. *Sweet Home Alabama* blaring. Mable huffed past him without a word and thundered inside and up the stairs. Ready for anything.

But the apartment was empty. She looked for signs. Felt the shower walls. The beds. Inventoried the beer in the refrigerator. Nothing suspicious. They hadn't been there. He'd taken her someplace else. Because Antoine was evil, but not stupid.

She paced. Waited. Looked out the window down at Clayton. Thundered downstairs and back out into the sadistic sun. She had to shout over the music and the engine.

"'Scuse me, Mr. Greavy, how you doin' today? Oh... I said how you doin' today? I am so sorry to bother you, sir, but have you seen Libby this mornin'?"

He'd stepped back. Stood up. Hands on hips looking at her in her dingy blue uniform so thoroughly drenched in sweat you'd think she'd been swimming.

"Libby?"

"Uh, yes sir. Libby. My daughter."

"Your daughter? China doll?"

A beat. Two. "Yes sir. You seen her today?"

"Naw. Not today. Slipped her leash, did she?"

Clayton had laughed a little. Then he turned from her, ready to burrow back under the open hood. Vye was suddenly in the doorway, chewing on a nail. Then she shouted.

"She was here this mornin.' I saw her. Came and went in about five whole minutes. Man waitin' for her in a car up the street."

"What man? What kinda car?" The question had been too direct. Too forceful. Almost accusatory.

"How the fuck do I know? Ain't my job to keep track and take notes. She ain't my wild child, honey. I seen half of the man's left arm hangin' out the window. Car had four tires and a steering wheel. Green I think. You ask me? They were off to his place where they don't have to worry 'bout you coming home early askin' a lot of questions. Way she was dressed I'm thinkin' she knows what the hell she's doin'. Clayton, turn that shit down and come in here and help me move this goddamned dresser. Ain't gon' say it again."

Vye had disappeared into shadow. Clayton had not turned any shit down, but he had spit and thrown a wrench down into the dirt with some disgust and stomped off inside after his wife. The shouting had started before the screen door had slapped closed.

Mable had stayed rooted in the yard, staring at the spot Clayton used to occupy. Bludgeoned by the chorus to *Sweet Home, Alabama*. Taunted by Vye's ugly surmise.

Of course that's where they were. Of course it was. All this time. All this time they had been going to his place. How long now? A year? Two?

The rest had come without any thought. Something automatic had taken control. Something bigger. Deeper. Something other. The hood had slammed closed on its own as she accelerated backwards out into the street. She stopped hearing Lynrd Skynrd altogether. In her head, rage and fear shook the foundation like a category five storm.

The drive to Thibodaux had taken just over an hour. Long enough so that by the time she had turned off East Bayou for Laurel Valley, where the canopy of large Southern Oak grew dense and the blue Louisiana sky became like the eddy in a river, choked with dark debris, the full boil of her emotion had slipped back into a queasy simmer. Distractions floated on the surface of her anger like little battered skiffs, moving closer. Worries that had once seemed so inconsequential took on greater proportion.

She had stolen a car.

The car did not have enough gas in it to get home.

She had no money. No credit. No identification.

She was heading for Antoine's turf. Without a towel rod.

The small house was right where she'd left it. Out in the middle of nowhere, beneath a brooding horizon of dark foliage. Curtains of Spanish moss hung from the branches like a sloughing skin.

The towering Pecan was still there. Like an iron stanchion holding up the last of the daylight. It knew everything, that tree.

She sat in the idling car for a long time. Burning gas. Watching. Nothing moved. No moss-green Impala. No lights in the windows. There was only the structure itself and her memories of it. Keeping it clean. Cooking food in the tiny kitchen. Looking out of the dirty window that first night at Antoine making his car into a bed. Antoine driving up the next day, stepping out of his car with an armload of borrowed clothing. Antoine on the porch playing his fiddle. Teaching Libby to play cards. Hearts. Spades. Pedro. Tonk. Antoine had his own rules and he enforced them.

Mable took a breath and pulled in. Cut the engine. Stepped out and headed for the door. Ready for anything.

She did not bother knocking. If anyone was inside, they already knew she was there. Antoine never locked his door. No need way out there. She pushed it open. Stepped inside.

It was empty of life. A dirty, dimly lit wooden box full of Antoine's things. Antoine's smell.

She walked. Slowly. Quietly. Stepping around. Stepping over. Looked for signs of Libby. But she found nothing. The anger, the fear, the worry, the hope all began to deflate. Exhaustion flooded in to fill the empty space, pushing everything else out. She had wanted to cry. Wanted to lie down on the floor of Antoine Beaudaine Cherish's filthy little house and wail.

The sound of tires out front had changed all of that. Everything had reversed itself. Hope, worry, anger, fear. Everything had reinflated in an instant. She flung open the door. Stepped out on to the front porch.

"Who the hell are you?" He was bald with a muddy, indecipherable neck tattoo. A soggy spider web that had captured some cursive red letters. The barrel of a shotgun angled out of the window of the rusted white pick up. He, too, was ready for anything.

"Lookin' for Antoine," Mable had said.

The man narrowed his eyes like he was talking into a sandstorm. "You a friend of Antoine's then?"

"Yes sir," she lied. "Just need to talk to him about some things is all."

"He give you permission to be in his house?"

"No sir. I'm just tryin' to find him. Ain't stealin' nothin'." She held up her hands to show she wasn't holding anything. "Just tryin' to find him. Know where he at?"

The man closed a fist around the tip of the barrel. Pushed the gun back down into the cab. He spit a rope of chew out into the dirt.

"What's your name then, honey?"

She didn't want to give up her name. Wasn't sure whether it was in her interest. Wasn't sure she wanted Antoine to know she had come looking. But she did anyway.

"Mable."

"Mable, huh. Mable who?"

"Mable Holder. Antoine an' me known each other a long time. You know where I can find him?"

The man put the truck in reverse. Backed up a little.

"Why don't you come on outta there, Mable Holder. Antoine's up at the lake fishin' with a friend. Don't think he's gon' want to be disturbed. Not for awhile anyway."

"What friend?"

The man had laughed. Scratched at the muddy symbols on his neck. Looked away. Looked back.

"Oh, Antoine got him all kinda friends. Young and old. Pretty ones and ugly ones. Skinny and fat. Sweet and mean. You got to be young, skinny, pretty and sweet to get invited to the lake. Guess that leaves us out. Don't it?"

He let the insult hang in the air like an odor. Smiled a little, if you can call it that. Turned the wheel.

"Run along on home, Mable Holder. Don't want to find you here when I come back this way. Bye now."

And off he went.

Mable watched him disappear up the road as she walked back out to the car. She climbed back in and closed the door, feeling lots of things all at once. All of them bad. Started the engine. Drove back out to the fork.

Right would take her back the way she had come. Until she ran out of gas.

Left would take her along the back roads to *Lac des Allemands*, the twelve thousand acre lake that fed the *Baie des Deux Chenes* and on which Antoine kept a cabin on a marshy parcel that had been in his family for three generations. It featured an oily boathouse and a long dock with rotten, stained boards and a sag in the middle that dipped the left end of four planks into the lake. Mable and Libby had been to the cabin twice while they had been at the mercy of Antoine's hospitality. Both times Antoine had gone out fishing for dinner while they stayed back and picked up the place to make it more habitable. To make it bearable.

Mable sat there. Idling. Thinking. Feeling.

Libby's voice was suddenly in her head. Not her daughter, Libby. Her mother, Libby.

This ain't somethin' you want to do, baby. Go on home, now. Right. Right. Right. Turn right.

But Mable's imagination was already drifting to the left. She could see her daughter in that tiny, filthy place. Could see her face. Could see the expression in those beautiful Asian eyes that acknowledged she had made a mistake. That she had trusted Antoine again. That she needed help. That she needed her mother. Mable could see the screaming infant that the bird-boned, coffee-with-crème-colored Magnolia –*Mags* –had chosen to abandon. The screaming infant that Mr. Lee wanted out of his sight. The screaming infant that had always stopped screaming in Mable's arms and that Mable had stepped up to save all of those years ago.

She pulled the wheel to the left. Accelerated.

The stolen car rolled beneath the towering oaks and the swaying vines of moss even as night came forward out of the trees to meet her. It came not like darkness descending. More like the light itself was steadily draining away from the hearts of living things.

Disappearing down into the cooling soil. Leaving only the dark.

The bald man in the white pick-up with the gun and the soggy spider web on his neck would remember her as a nice enough gal. Never found out her name but remembers the car. Black with a different driver's door. Different trunk. She'd flagged him down on Laurel Valley and Choctaw. Wanted to know how to get to the lake. Didn't say why and didn't seem to know the difference between *Lac des Allemands* and *Lake Boeuf*. Didn't seem to be up to any mischief though. He'd given her directions to both lakes. Had no idea the car was stolen. No idea whatsoever.

No idea on this earth that he may have been the last person to see that poor gal alive.

Chapter 67

The sound fills the widening crack. Like water into rock.

Laughing. Squealing. Singing.

He can hear them. Louder. Louder. The door pulls slowly ajar.

Louder. Like they are all inside of her house.

But Davis knows better. There is no one inside this house. No one but her.

It's like listening to ghosts. He waits.

The door swings fully open. He can see her muscles tense, hand on the knob. She is not prepared for him.

"Oh." It is all Celia can say. Expression slack and unformed. Dark eyebrows like a sagging bridge, barely holding up the weight of her forehead. Eyes shot through with blood lightening. She is wrapped in a dingy white serape.

He knows a hangover when he sees it.

"I should have called," says Davis. "Sorry."

Celia's countenance assembles itself. The old ebullience shakes out its skirt. Blood, almost like a sanguineous gas, inflates her face. Tightens up the bridge. Lifts the brow. A secret wind blows in a big smile. *Show time.*

"No, no! No problem. I was just having my breakfast. Come in, Davis. Come in. Get out of this rain!"

He can see that it hurts her. This sudden spike in energy. This pretention of civility. He wants to tell her that he knows exactly how she feels. How many times he has been on the other side of that door.

But he doesn't. It's her façade. He lets her keep it.

She pushes open the screen door. Holds it and steps aside, allowing room to pass. He does his best to shake himself off. Takes off his dripping hat. Slaps it against his leg. Steps in.

"You really riding that thing in the rain?" she asks, laughing for no reason. She points to the bike in the drive as the screen door closes itself. Davis looks back. Shrugs.

"Not much choice."

He slips out of his coat, passing the gallon plastic bag from one hand to the other. Drops the coat on the floor by the door. Then the hat. He starts with the boots."

Celia waves her hands.

"No, no, no. You can just leave those on. My goodness. It's just water."

She is laughing again. Overselling. Trying to convince the both of them. She walks away, through the living room, leading him toward the back. The sliding glass door is already open.

"You're lucky I'm here. I should be at the school. I'm feeling a little under the weather today so I called in."

He joins her on the patio. She is lowering herself into her usual chair. On the small side table is a messy plate. A carnage of uneaten beans and eggs next to a blue ceramic mug.

Davis looks down at her. "Sorry you're sick."

"Feels good out here," she says. As if to explain why she is not curled up in bed with a thermometer in her mouth. "Helps clear my head. I'd offer you some coffee…"

Davis shakes his head, cutting off the apology. He knows Celia Morales only makes coffee for one.

"Can't stay. Just wanted to come by and give you this to review. Didn't want it to get wet."

He puts the sealed plastic bag on the table next to the plate. Sits in the only other chair under the roof. Painted wicker with a green and pink hummingbird cushion. The chair creaks under his weight.

The rain has abated for the time being. As if the gods are no longer interested now that he is off of his bike and sheltered. He leans back. Takes out his ponytail. Rakes his fingers through his wet hair. Puts it back the way it was.

Celia opens the bag. Pulls out the sheaf of paper. Eyes wide. Sharp breath.

"This is the article? For the magazine? For *Voices?*"

He watches her read his handwritten cover note. Lips and brow working to untangle the scrawl.

Just a draft.

Will be changing the names.

"No." He leans forward. Elbows to knees. Looks at her. "No. This is just the narrative I wrote up from your interviews. The way it works is that I take this narrative and cut it way down. Like to about a quarter of this size. And then I combine it with two other interviews and work it all into a single piece. Like a short story with three characters connected by a common theme. I just wanted you to read your part of it. Make sure you're comfortable. Like I promised."

Celia does not respond. She is already lost. He watches her eyes. Gulping in the words. Examining herself in their patterns. Gorging on her own story. On

Paola's story. There is too much here for one sitting. Her bottomless brown eyes dart erratically, sampling. Page one. Five. Three. Seven.

He watches in silence. Looks away. Gives her time.

Dripping comes from all directions. The fountain in the yard is full. The glass-cubed basin glitters from beneath a clear, rippled skin. The saguaro is now variegated beneath streaks of rain. All of its wren holes are empty. Lifeless. Babies long gone.

It makes him think of the baby that never was. The wren that never emerged from the nest. Remembers Celia's practiced nonchalance that first day. *Long time ago. I've got lots of children in my life. Always have.*

The things we tell ourselves.

Across the street, over the chain link, through the mist, there are children. Slick smudges of color. Like blurry traffic lights on a wet windshield. Swinging. Sliding. Seesawing. Their sound is in the air. A kind of watery birdsong. It drifts over the fence. Across the street. Past the fountain and the empty saguaro. Through the home of Celia Morales. Condensing. Accumulating. Pressing out against the walls. Barricading the front door from the inside.

"They get to play in the rain?" More to himself than to her. "Never let *us* play in the rain."

But Celia is elsewhere.

"Who are the others?" she asks, not looking up. "The other two characters. People, I mean. People you interviewed."

Davis smiles apologetically. He doesn't need to answer. He stands.

"Take your time reading it," he says. "I'll come over another time and we can talk about whatever I might have gotten wrong. I want you to feel comfortable that it's accurate."

She keeps reading. Nods. Does not look up. He tries to discern an opinion from the face he almost cannot see. Approval. Disapproval. Satisfaction. Horror. His writer's insecurity always so close at hand. He wants her to approve. Wants to assure her.

"No one will know its you, Celia," he says.

"It's got our names in it."

"Well I'm changing the names. This is just... I'm just capturing facts here. The names will be totally different. And it could have happened anywhere. Houston. Dallas. Lubbock. Know one will know. When I work this into the finished article, I'll substitute a fictitious name for you and Paola. Something Anglo. Maybe Ann and Lucy. Or something you like better. Whatever you want."

She is quiet. Looks at him. Blinks slowly. "Buddy will know."

"Buddy will *not* know," he says.

"You got my name from Buddy. Buddy's your boss. Of course he'll know."

"No. Celia. Look."

He lowers himself again. Sits on the edge of the hummingbird cushion. Elbows, knees.

"Look. Buddy gave me your name as someone I might want to meet. I was new to Corbin. Buddy grew up here and he knew it would be important for me to meet people he trusted were good people. He has no idea I'm writing you. Writing *about* you." He waits. Points at the papers. "Have you ever told Buddy anything in that story?"

She looks down at the sheaf. Hesitates. Looks up again.

"No."

"Okay then. So there's no way he can know."

Unless you tell him. It's the response she doesn't offer. She doesn't have to.

"And I never reveal my sources to anyone, Celia. Not even to Buddy Lincoln. And he knows better than to ask."

Celia resumes reading. Slowly nods her head. "Okay," she says. "But you're changing the names."

"Anything you want. You just let me know. Think about *Ann* and *Lucy*. I kind of like that."

Celia smiles broadly. Laughs. Waves her hand dismissively.

"Not that it matters. I put all of this behind me years ago. I just moved on."

But he sees her clearly now. There is not a lie her body could tell that he would believe. Celia Morales has not moved on. She will never move on.

Davis nods. Slaps his knees. Stands again. Holds out his hands as if stopping traffic. "Don't move a muscle. I have to go. I just wanted to give that to you. I'll show myself out. Feel better soon?"

She nods. Smiles wanly.

"Good. We'll talk again in a few days."

He leaves her on the patio, flipping back to page one. Makes his way back through the living room to the front door. Puts on his sopping coat. Picks up his hat.

He takes in the space around him as he reaches for the knob. Dark, brooding furniture draped in shocks of color. The poppy cotton throw, arranged across the corner of the couch like some accumulation of petals blown in through the window. The sun-colored pillows perched in each chair. Like that patina of cheer will change the geology of time. Eons. Millennia. Centuries. Decades. Years. Months. Weeks. Days. Seconds. Layers of temporal sediment. The desert is always there. At the bottom. Waiting beneath the ocean.

He considers Celia's windblown smile at the door. The poppy cotton throw. The sun-colored resolve to leave the past behind. All an extravagant lie to herself. A flapping flag on the eighteenth hole of a lushly green golf course carved into a desert made of powdered mollusks. She hasn't put the past behind her.

Because the past is not behind. It's *beneath*. It's a condensed mass of seconds. Moments. Triumph. Regret. We walk around on it. Build on top of it. It creates its own gravity. There are ashes in the dust. There is no escaping.

Musical taunts waft in over the patio and through the open door, disintegrating into an atomized laughter. In the back of the room is a heavy wooden étagère. Artifacts of faith and regional kickshaw. Jesus in an oval frame. A cactus clock beneath a gilded flicker. A dark lacquered cross.

On the top shelf is a small pink pillow with tassels. To one of the tassels is tied a pair of small, pink booties with decorative yellow laces. A name is embroidered in turquoise across the front of the pillow. The yarn seems phosphorescent.

Paola. Like it carries its own blue light.

* * *

"You want to tell me again why we're open?" Hector sits heavily in a booth nearest the kitchen. Eladio drapes himself over the front counter. Responds to the floor.

"Just because it's rainin' don't mean people stop eating. People still need to eat, yo."

"You see any people in here, Eladio?" Hector spreads his arms to reveal an empty restaurant. Eladio snorts.

"I seen you put away two chimichangas in the past hour," says Eladio. "Does that count? I see Davis over there eatin' himself a burrito."

Hector scoffs.

"Didn't need to come all the way into town to make myself breakfast, dumbass. I could do that shit at home, man. In my damn pee-jays. Then go back to bed. Sleep 'til noon? Listen to the rain? Sweet."

Eladio rolls over on his back. Looks upside down across the room at Hector. Screws up his face in mock confusion.

"Say *wha*? You still sleepin' in pee-jays? How old are you again, man?"

"Right," says Hector. "Like you don't. Probably have little feet on your pee-jays. Little moons and stars and shit all over."

"Nah. No jammies for me. I sleep in the raw, yo. *Al igual que una máquina del sexo.*"

Hector laughs fully, filling the empty room. "Eladio, the *last* thing you are is a sex machine."

Eladio sits upright on the counter, legs dangling.

"Laugh if you want to, man. But when the ladies come tappin' at *my* window? In the middle of the night? And I get outta bed to see who it is? Pull back that curtain? There I am. Boom. Ready. Wearin' nothin' but a smile."

"And that's when Marcela shouts through the window '*Eladio! Get your jammies on before I come in there and beat your bare ass!*'

All of them lose it over that one. Even Eladio, who is forced to abandon the campy machismo. Even Davis, mouth full of burrito, mostly still thinking about Celia Morales and not particularly interested in the banter.

Hector slaps the table with his massive hand, over and over like he is trying to break it. He keeps repeating Eladio's name in Marcela's voice. *"Eladio! Eladio! ¡Oh Dios mío! Eladio!"* It only makes it worse.

"Hey, Davis." Eladio has recovered. Looking for more. "You sleep in jammies? You do, don't you? I know you do, man."

Davis wipes his mouth. Swallows. Drinks. Steps up to the challenge. "No," he says dryly. *"Sólo mi verga."*

Hector and Eladio disintegrate all over again, howling into their hands. Davis feigns mild offense.

"Seriously. Just like, you know, a tube sock with moons and stars. Stuffed into one big ol' boot."

Eladio is the first to pull it together. "Jammies for your thang? Why in the hell, man…"

"Dumb ass. In case it has to get out of bed to see who's at the damn window."

Eladio is vindicated in the end. People still want to eat. Even in the rain and chill. They still get hungry. *Pepita's* hits only a fraction of its usual lunchtime traffic, but it is enough to keep them all reasonably busy.

At two, Davis takes his break. Walks up *Broken River Road* toward the *Coahuiltecan Trading Post* for some gum and a stamp. The road glistens in a cottony light from a sun no one can see, slick with rain that is no longer falling. The sky is a wet gray sweater.

He feels better today. Better than in a long time.

Not happy. But better.

There is no accounting for it. Probably nothing in particular. Probably everything together. This dusty little town. The simplicity of it. Its remove from the world. As usual, Buddy Lincoln had been right. Corbin was exactly what he needed.

He thinks of Houston. Remembers floating, literally at times, from shelter to shelter with the countless others that *thousand-year Harvey* had dispossessed of everything. Remembers killing time by wandering the gymnasium neighborhoods and stadium suburbs of dingy cots and mattresses beneath tiny dank piles of possessions, looking for people who might share a dollar or a joint or a bottle. Pretending to interview people about what they had lost and the lives they used to have. Telling people he was a writer. That he was collecting stories. That it would all mean something with the right words. All of those voices.

Remembers having nightmares about what the world would look like when Harvey finally left. About what was under all of that brown, oily water.

No. Not *what* was underneath. *Who*.

And then Harvey had left. And the land had dried out.

But he had not dried out. He had been wetter than ever.

He imagines where he'd be right now if Buddy Lincoln had not intervened. Had Buddy not let him stay in one of his rentals. Given him a beat up Harley. Given him a job writing for the magazine. Given him advice and rules that his addiction would not abide. Had Buddy not bailed him out of jail and made him abandon Houston altogether. He imagines the cell. Imagines the hospital. Imagines the flea-infested couch of some stranger. The back seat of some junked car. Imagines the stainless steel drawer with his last name on the front, opened quietly for his father.

But now. He thinks of Eladio and Hector. The slow-blooming friendship with Miguel. The kindness of Ernesto and Marcela.

Thinks of the possibility, just the possibility, of something, *anything*, with Olivia DeLuna. The woman who might have died but who, according to the local paper, did not die because of him. *Davis Payne.* Right there in black and white.

Crazy, he knows.

But no crazier than any other omen. No crazier than a burning bush. Or a rainbow. No crazier than the voice of the dead telling you when to steer your Harley down an empty desert road.

It meant something. It had to.

Thinks of Elvis, wise man of the AA confessional: *Shit does not just happen. You happen. What you choose to believe about the world is the only thing that ever matters. That's what's going to kill you, man. That's what's going to save you.*

Thinks of the therapy of writing. Finishing the draft for Celia Morales. Almost done with the draft for Libby Holder. He is good at something. He had allowed himself a small measure of pride at being good at something other than being a fucked up drunk ahead of his time. Good at something other than letting people die. Good at something other than inspiring people to kill themselves. That had not happened in awhile.

Which was also good. Death had left him alone. The Reaper was not interested in coming all the way out to Corbin just to sport with his self-concept.

Thinks of the steady stream of new-old words from his mother, pressed like flowers into dusty letters, perfectly preserving her essence. Like she is not dead. Like she has never been dead. Like this is how he was always supposed to know her.

Or maybe it was just today. The weather. The miracle of water in the desert. The merciful intervention of cumulus. He had no idea why.

But he felt measurably better.

Three men in a white utility truck roll slowly up the opposite side of the street. Matching yellow slickers. Black baseball hats emblazoned with the ghostly blue *Moon Garden Festival* logo that all Corbinites have come to see in their sleep. They stop the truck every twenty feet to fasten garlands of lights and flowers to phony green street lamps that someone has bolted into steel plates embedded in the sidewalk. They have done this before.

A boisterous foursome foams out of the *Lick-n-Tipple*. Matching baseball hats. Swinging sunglasses. Knee-length basketball shorts. Big, day-glo neon shoes. Somewhere within walking distance is a motorhome with three or four girls inside, equally oblivious to the wet, chilly weather. Frayed cutoffs and bare midriffs. Maybe two motorhomes. Two couples each. Or maybe the girls are coming later. Maybe they're still on the road on the way from whatever college sells the hats and shorts. This is destined to be one of those *'remember that time'* weekends. Ten years from now. When shot gunning beers on the *Scrambler*, and then getting sick, spewing vomit six ways from Sunday, will have become the stuff of legend.

Or *twenty* years. When the girls are gone and only two of the four men are still in contact. And those two men will meet up at a bar every so often. Toast. Drink. Lie about their kids and careers until the conversation starves. One of them will shake his head.

Oh, man.

What's so funny?

Remember that time... In Corbin...

The double glass doors to the *Lick-n-Tipple* close behind them. It's all *tipple* for these guys. Not a single twisted spire of soft, frozen, sugared dairy between them. Each has a case of beer under one arm and a full bag of different glass bottles under the other. They exchange head-nods and a *buenas tardes* or two with the workers, one of which points and says something about stocking up on provisions for the festival. They all laugh knowingly. Like the sound is a secret handshake.

But it's not so secret.

Davis stuffs his hands deeper into his pockets. Congratulates himself on being on the right side of *Broken River Road*. Congratulates himself on the purity of a mission to buy a stamp and some chewing gum. Keeps moving.

The stamp is for the envelope sitting on his tiny kitchen table. He has sealed it so he will stop second-guessing his own words.

Conrad:

Got the letter. It took me awhile to get through it. It took me even longer to figure out what to think about it. I still don't know.

536

If you want me to solve your crisis of faith, I can't do that. If you want me to decipher Herman Melville, I can't do that either.

You ask me to let go of the past, and to start over, apparently for your sake. Forgive you. Forgive myself. Let Mom go. Let Abby go. I seriously doubt I can do any of that either. But I can try. I know I should try. I know Mom would want that. I don't take back anything I said to you at dinner. But I do regret how I said it. I regret being out of control. I had so much more to tell you, none of it good. All of it real. All of it needed to be said.

I have ordered a copy of Eyelash Lake. *I will read it. I will meet you someplace that neither of us like and I will tell you what I think of it. I can't promise a pleasant conversation, but I promise to be civil. Then maybe we can take things from there and just see where it leads. I'm willing to try that if you are.*

The *Coahuiltecan* is empty. Brighter than normal. They have clamped colored spotlights to the end of each row of wooden shelving, painting the white plaster ceiling with oval smears of pink and red light. The walls are covered in bright paper flowers. Columbine. Globe mallow. Monkey Flower. Mojave Aster. Garlands of marigolds line the front counter and the window behind. Fresh cut marigolds in white plastic buckets line the wall.

Skulls, too. Everywhere. Some made of porcelain, others of painted white sugar. Skulls wearing black sombreros, brims laden with bright orange marigolds. Skulls chewing on cigarillos. Skulls adorning key chains and shot glasses and refrigerator magnets. *Calaca* dolls and masks. Plastic tubes of black and white face paint. Three sizes of black tee shirts, wearable x-rays showing bleach-bone ribcages.

A life-size cardboard cut-out of a tuxedoed skeleton, rose clamped in his enormous teeth, plays a *guitarron* between the door and the front counter. He stands on letters of white smoke: *Dance with the Dead.*

A far-back corner of the store has been made into a kind of altar for altars. Candles and incense. Sugar skulls and bowls of hard candy. Small porcelain and black metal picture frames. Along the base of the altar, orange sugar has been stenciled into cursive lettering: *El Dia de Los Angelitos.*

Davis walks the aisles, looking, heels of his boots knocking on the wood floor. He finds the gum. Heads up to the counter. Lucela Flores smiles, dimples in the dough of her cheeks.

"*Hola*, Davis," she says. "Spending it all in one place?"

She wants to flirt. Wants to pick up the relaxed, overly familiar patter where they had left it the last time he was in. An easy rapport over commerce and weather had gradually relaxed into something less transactional. It would accommodate a tease just now. A knowing wink.

But Lucela is much too shy to really flirt. And he's not in the mood anyway. Not today. He smiles back. Asks for the stamps. Thinks of the letter on his kitchen table.

"Going to the festivals?" she asks.

He shrugs. Shakes his head. "In the rain?"

She frowns, wounded by disappointment.

"Rain stopped. And anyway, it's a blessing. Need to green things up a little for when the spirits come home to visit." She smiles, lifting the singular freckle above her lip. Sighs. Pats the top of her chest with her hand. "*Mi abuela.* She loved the rain. I'm so happy it has rained for her this year."

"And don't forget about all of those moon gardeners," he says with a wink. Teasing. Flirting in spite of himself. Just to see her light up. "They've got to love the rain."

Lucela gasps. Like the sound comes from her eyes.

"*¡Sí! Los jardineros de la luna!* Have you seen the fountain this morning?" He shakes his head. "Oh! So beautiful this year! They have been working for three days and the flowers are everywhere, Davis!" Her hands are in the air now. Painting for him. "In the fountain, and on all of the benches, and in great big baskets from all of the churches and the schools and someone has placed pink and yellow monkey flowers one-by-one," she pinches thumb to forefinger with each hand, pretending to insert something small and delicate into an invisible opening, "*inside* the vines of the bougainvillea around the top of the fountain. Like flowers woven into the hair of a goddess."

"A moon goddess, I'm guessing," he says narrowing his eyes. Lucela laughs.

"*Sí. Madre luna.* Watching over her children. I have never seen the fountain so beautiful and I have lived here my whole life. It will make for such a special *Día de los Muertos.*"

Lucela's wide brown eyes glisten wet, lit from within. Her innocence is arresting. *She knows nothing,* he thinks. *Feels everything. Is nourished by everything. Regrets nothing. There is nothing in her to numb. Nothing to drown. The rain is a blessing and the dead all come home to visit.*

In an instant she sees herself. Blushes at her own girlish enthusiasm. Lowers her hands to the booklet of stamps she had abandoned by the register. Slides them across the counter beneath two fingers until they come to a stop, wedged snugly beneath his own.

He walks the rest of the way up *Broken River Road* to the *Fuente de la Luna.*

Lucela is right about the spectacle. The fountain itself has been turned off so that four men can cover every last square inch of marble with flowers and lights.

Extravagant woven baskets and large hand-painted pots ring the basin, exploding color. Each has a bluish bone-colored plastic flag in the shape of a moon rising up out of the center. Each moon has a name.

Corbin Elementary
Matilde of the Sacred Heart.
McGuinley Ranch

But it's more than just the fountain. The two-story shoebox town hall is festooned with long pink and red garlands. Thick floral vines scooping color from corner to corner, window to window, door to door. From the center of the roofline four braided cables radiate out over the fountain to tall poles at the four corners of the town square. Each cable is wrapped in flowers and fixed with large blue-colored bulbs.

He makes a slow tour of the fountain. Reads each of the moons above each of the baskets.

St. Matthews Episcopal
Desert Ark Foundation

To the east of the town hall is the beginning of a wooden stage tucked beneath a sloping white tarp. A small brown man in a dirty blue shirt is up on the platform, hunched over a tangled nest of black wires. He slaps them against the stage like he is whipping snakes into submission.

Davis looks at his watch. Turns back up *Broken River Road.*

That's when his phone rings. Eladio, he thinks. Answers.

Buddy Lincoln is not without compassion. But the truth always comes first with Buddy, who aims that double-barrel baritone and gives it to him straight.

The words register in the center of Davis' chest. After he's done, Buddy is silent. Waits. Then adds: "I saw it on the news. This morning. I waited until I could confirm. Didn't want you to find out on your own."

Davis lowers himself onto a wet bench, next to a basket of flowers. Watches the snake-whipping man. Buddy is talking.

His head empties.

Silence. Silence. Buddy is talking.

But there is only silence in his head.

As if he has dropped a stone into the center of a still, inland sea and he is waiting to hear it, or feel it, come to rest at the bottom.

But there is no bottom. Only falling.

"You okay? Davis? Are you..."

Falling.

"Davis?"

"I'm fine. Buddy. Yeah. I'm... I'm..."

"Where's Elvis?"

"I'm fine."

"Nope. It's a new question, Davis. Where's Elvis?"

"How should I know? He's…"

"You need to call him. Will you do that? Davis?"

"Yes. *Fuck.* I'll call him."

Falling. He has to ask.

"Was it… Was it…"

"It was bad, son. Lucky he didn't take out anyone else. Doin' a hundred. Maybe more. Missed the off-ramp by a couple hundred yards. Must have been lit but good, Davis. He must'a been seein' triple. Thought he was through with all that."

Falling.

"Davis?"

"I gotta go, Buddy. I …"

"Davis? Listen to me. Call…"

He sits for a long time watching the man with the snakes. Slapping them against the stage. Extracting them from their tangled nest. They keep coiling around his boots.

He's only waking them up, Davis thinks. Making them mad.

He stands. Walks up the road, back toward *Pepitas,* scuffing his heels against the pavement. He slips the phone in his pocket. Feels the pack of gum. Feels the book of stamps.

Conrad: I got the letter. It took me awhile to get through it.

Laughter. Someone sings a playground taunt in Spanish.

Universal languages. Laughter. Singing. Taunting.

He looks up. Over. The workers stringing lights and flowers from the back of the truck inch forward. Laughing. Singing. Taunting. Just past the *Lick-n-Tipple.*

Another veil of mist descends.

The street between them glistens.

Chapter 68
Celia and Paola

Sheriff's investigators worked in circles. Re-examining. Re-interviewing. Like looking for a lost set of keys in all of the same places. Over and over. They were less than fully satisfied.

But the story held up just enough.

Celia credits herself for thinking things through. Sitting in the car, Paola shaking at her side, watching the fire scorch the dark desert sky. Watching the wind whip the smoke one direction, then another. Like the murmuration of starlings at twilight or a plague of locusts, packed by the millions into the rafters, escaping the flames.

She watched in silence. Trying to think of what to do. Forcing herself to contemplate Lyle Cross, dead and boiling face down in a bloody carpet swamp. Forcing herself to plan for the future. Pulling Paola tight into her body with one arm. Absorbing her tremors. *'Don't you worry, now,'* she'd said. *'I'm here, baby. Mama's here.'*

Backing up. Turning around. Driving. Watching the fire shrink in the mirror. Thinking. Thinking. She gets credit for those early steps.

For driving a half-hour east, then back up into the desert, off an old ranch access road to bury the antique gun. For then turning around and driving Paola west all the way to Fort Stockton. For making her get out at a truck stop diner to ask for change so she could make a phone call. For making her sit there in a window booth alone for over an hour. Picking at the wax in her hair.

They showed up at the Sheriff's office after one o'clock in the morning to explain a plausible version of the truth. Maria Cross had left after a beating. Garvin Cross had left to bring her back home. Which had left Paola home alone with Lyle. Lyle Cross, out of his mind on three types of liquor and whatever he was shooting into his veins, angry for reasons only Lyle could know, had spent the evening tormenting Paola. At first, tormenting her in all of the same ways. Petty, demented-sibling ways. And then, when the winds had taken the lights out, in *different* ways. He had choked her. Tied her up. Cut her hair. Drizzled her with hot wax. It was horrible. Paola feared for her life. Feared that he would eventually get around to doing again the thing he had managed only once before.

All true. Every bit of it.

But then the story had taken a detour. A diversion. Like water siphoned away from a river on its way to the sea, out into the dry desert where it might have been needed but did not really belong.

Lyle Cross had passed out on top of the piano, surrounded by burning candles. Scissors still in his hand. Paola had escaped her bondage. She had bolted. Never looked back. She had walked in the dark all the way to the highway. Then she had walked west, thumb in the air, until a trucker picked her up.

"Trucker. What trucker? What was his name? Can you describe him?"

Big guy. Greasy black hair. Unshaven. Smelled bad. One-syllable name. *Bob* or *Sam* or *Fred*. Didn't exchange more than twenty words the whole trip. Country music blaring from the radio. She explained that she had pretended to sleep because she did not want to talk. Not to him. Not to anybody.

"What kind of truck?"

Big, long truck. Eighteen wheeler kind. Seems like there was writing on the side. Maybe. She wasn't paying attention to the truck. It was dark. *Bob* or *Sam* or *Fred* or *Mack* or *Bill* had dropped her off at a truck stop in Fort Stockton.

"Truck stop. What truck stop?"

Rig something. *Rig Rest*. She had asked the lady behind the counter for some change to make a phone call. Her nametag said '*Edith*.' Edith was concerned and kept asking questions. But Paola had not wanted to tell her story to a stranger. She had told Edith that she was fine. Slumber party pranks gone a bit too far. That she was calling her mom to come pick her up.

"So did you try to call your mom?"

No. Could have called Maria's sister. Could have asked Directory Assistance for the number. But she didn't know the woman's last name. All she knew was the first name. Arlene. Arlene in Haskell. And even if she had known, she did not want to talk to Arlene or Maria or Garvin. The only person Paola could think of to call, she had told them, the only person she really *wanted* to call, was her teacher. Her friend. Celia Morales. *Miss Celia*.

And then Celia had come running. Had made the trip to Fort Stockton in record time. Had picked Paola up and brought her straight to the Sheriff's office. That was the first time either of them had learned anything… about *anything*.

"A fire? What? How? Where's Lyle? What happened to Lyle? Is Lyle okay? Did he get out okay? Did you find Lyle?"

There had been just enough corroboration, and an absence of contradiction, to hold the story together. Ligature marks on the wrists. The circle of missing hair. The wax. The bruising around her neck. Edith at *Rig Rest*, who had been credible and emphatic. One of the diner regulars had leant some assistance. Kid sat in a window booth for over an hour. Pickin' wax outta her hair. Left a little pile of it on the table. Then a woman had come by and picked her up. *Yessir, that's the car.*

And over multiple interviews, Celia and Paola had lined up with each other exactly, even when the diverted tributary had been forced to accommodate unanticipated topography. Diversions from the diversion. Tributaries from the tributary. Like explaining Celia's tire tracks around the house. And her footprints to and from the ark. Everything only partial after that wind. They had each explained that Celia had been up to the house the previous day. That Paola had given her the tour.

Celia's phone records had shown the call coming in from the diner. That too had helped. But it was the only record of any call Celia had ever received from any phone number associated with young Paola. *Odd.*

"So you remembered Miss Celia's number at the diner, but you can't remember it now?"

Paola couldn't tell them, of course, that she had written the number on her hand sitting in Celia's car in the diner parking lot before going in, and then washed it off with spit on the road to the Sheriff's office over an hour later.

"What are you saying? You don't believe me? You don't believe me?"

If Celia gets some credit for thinking things through, Paola gets credit for acting; for tapping a river of genuine trauma and diverting it for an artificial purpose. Tears. Wailing. Distraught incomprehension that these two uniformed men –Salvadore and Martinez –might not believe her. Turns out they both had daughters of their own. They wanted to believe. Wanted her to be okay.

Another problem. Celia's face. The piano side of Celia's face was swelling, reddening. All night. Blooming signs of trauma. So they asked, point blank. Investigator Salvadore had rotated her chin with the tip of his pen.

"What's going on here?"

She had answered easily, not knowing where she found the words. The power was out, so it was pitch black when she headed out to the car in a hurry to pick up Paola. She had tripped on the step outside her front door. Landed on her face. Yes it hurt. Aspirin would help. Did they have any aspirin?

Different day, different problem. Having combed the charred house, the forensics people eventually found a partial print on a shard of the shattered oil lamp. The partial print was a partial match for Celia's forefinger. Another partial match came from a pane of scorched kitchen window glass. But the shards were too small to make the partial prints conclusive.

Might be Celia's, might not be. Lot of head scratching.

So they had taken a deep dive into the life of Celia Morales. Turned over every rock they found. Lots of questions about Mama Yolanda's crime; murder by arson of all things. And lots of questions about that restraining order to protect little Amalia and her new family.

But the road eventually brought them to the newly installed Auxiliary Bishop of Austin. And Father William had stood up. Had vouched for Celia's character with great conviction. Had exorcised his own secret guilt over that new soul that never was. Salvadore and Martinez had both thanked him profusely, genuflecting like the good Catholics they were. Taking his blessing with gratitude on their way out.

"Thank you, Father. Thank you, Father."

So there had been some concern about the story. *Niggling. Nagging.* They could each see it in Salvadore's wrinkled brow. In the squint of Martinez' green eyes. In the long silences between questions.

But the niggling concerns were not enough. In the end, the artificial tributary had rejoined the river of truth miles downstream as if it was always meant to be so and precisely as nature intended. The story held.

It had actually occurred to Celia to simply tell the truth. Self-defense was the truth. Defense of a young girl was the truth. Accidental death by scissors was the truth.

Except that mere exoneration was not the goal. Mere truth was not the goal.

Not as she sat in her car watching the house burn and feeling Paola's shaking body next to her. Not as, minutes before, she had shouted Paola's name frantically into the night, searching for her. Not as, minutes before that, she had heaved the oil lamp against the wall with every intention of not only saving Paola's life but of destroying the prison of her home and family.

The goal was not merely exoneration. Or truth. The goal, the *real* goal, if she was to be honest with herself, was adoption. The real goal was to be a mother.

Intuition had been her guide. Whispering between the beats of her terrified heart. Whispering in a voice she recognized. *'She belongs with you, Celia. She needs you to protect her. Don't let them take her like they took Amalia.'*

Adoption. That was the goal.

So better that Celia was never at the scene. Better that she not be the person who, for whatever reason, had burned down the home, incinerated all of the evidence, and walked away with the girl as Lyle bled out on the carpet. Better that her only connection with the carnage was that she was the one person to whom Paola had reached out when she most needed help. Better that Paola make no effort to contact Maria at her sister's house in Haskell. That she reach out to Celia.

Only to Celia.

Paola needed no convincing. She wanted as far away from her life as possible and she knew Celia was the answer. When the questions came about Garvin and Maria Cross, she had not pulled any punches.

By the time Garvin returned home with Maria, eyes black as a raccoon's, the Sheriff's office and state investigators were already digging. Maria's sister Arlene up in Haskell had a lot to say about Maria's marriage. Eventually, before her swelling had subsided, Maria did her own talking. Blamed Garvin for everything. Lyle's death was like water freezing and expanding in the fissures of a rock. There was no holding it together. After Lyle's funeral, Maria moved in with Arlene. Found a lawyer and filed for divorce. Pressed charges for assault.

Just as Paola had said, Garvin and Maria Cross were not her parents. She had never been adopted. She had been abandoned, passed from mother to friend and then claimed by Garvin in his capacity as a self-proclaimed minister of God's will. Paola was, he believed, a divine gift entrusted to his care.

Not that the State of Texas would have ever agreed with that assessment. Garvin had known that much. A previous record for domestic battery made him a bad bet as an adoptive parent. Maria, his second wife, had agreed. Formal adoption was clearly *not* God's will.

So it had taken some time. It had taken a full year before Maria had stopped blanching at the word '*daughter*' to describe Paola's place in the family. They had kept her out of the school system entirely, explaining to anyone who asked that Paola had personality issues better suited to home schooling. Her birth mother, they said, had had a drug problem. There were some emotional issues. Anger issues. Lashing out.

All true. And yet, completely wrong.

They had done their best at home schooling, an uneven mix of religious and secular instruction. Writing out each of the Commandments in cursive. Adding and subtracting and multiplying the Disciples. Six thousand years of history, before and after the great flood. Most of the instruction fell to Garvin, who rewarded Paola's efforts with time at the piano and who disciplined her, however rarely, by forbidding the piano. Garvin had marveled openly at Paola's musical aptitude. She had been entrusted to him by God for a purpose. A purpose revealed more and more with each passing day. A purpose that just might be music itself.

"He's in her fingertips," Garvin sometimes whispered to himself, clutching the neck of a bottle. "He's in her voice. He has a purpose for her."

Maria had resented Garvin's near obsessive devotion to Paola, which she knew came at her expense. Garvin swooned over Paola's perfection. Her physical beauty. Her perfectly proportioned face. Exceptional eyes, teeth, lips, skin. Fingers. Hair. She was perfect. She was a gift.

Maria Cross, sallow, pudgy with small pinkish eyes, having given Garvin a pale, unappealing son, had taken Paola as a damning contrast. So Maria had provided, at best, a perfunctory mothering. Critical and disciplinary. Over-compensating for Garvin's tendency to spoil. On Garvin's teaching days, when he and Lyle were at school and it was just the two of them, Maria had forbidden Paola any contact with the piano. Chores and lessons provided opportunity for Maria to say everything she could not say when Garvin was home. There were consequences for complaining.

Lyle was no better. Already well on the path of self-destructive attention. He abused his classmates, lashing out for reasons he only partly understood. Then, when the trouble he caused at school did not make him feel any better, he abused Paola.

Little things at first. Words. Taunts. Sibling cruelty. But it grew much worse. It became physical. Pinches. Punches. Slaps. Pinning her to the ground with his weight and not letting her up. Tearing her clothes. Twisting welts into the flesh of her arms. Taking her clothes. Her towel. Making her cower naked. Poking at her.

And then there was the one time. Just the beginning of something horrible. It had scared Lyle too. But in a good way.

Lyle liked to trap desert hares. Kill them. Skin them. Cook them. He liked the noises they made at the end. They were easier to catch than coyotes.

Paola was easier still.

Garvin punished him, which only made it worse. Lyle seemed to take the pain from Garvin's wide leather belt. Soak in it. Let himself steep in humiliation for a week or two and then channel it back into Paola. Later, around the time Lyle discovered a heroin supplier in the man who delivered fresh eggs every week, he seemed to actually *want* the belt. As if the pain was an opportunity. An answer. Palliative.

The most effective punishment for Lyle was never the belt anyway. It was the hall closet. Lyle could take the belt. But not the spare closet. Small and dark, smelling of rodent. It locked from the outside.

An hour was usually all it took. Then the tears. The apologies. The promises. He'd come back out into the light, docile and blinking. The closet corrections had always lasted a lot longer than the belt corrections. Weeks, not days.

No one had a good feel for how the claustrophobia originated. Maria blamed a difficult birth, mostly as a way of countering Garvin's reminder about her crazy brother Llewellyn who walked in his sleep and thought foreign leaders took turns controlling his mind. No one really claimed to know for sure, but they all seemed to accept claustrophobia as the go-to solution when Lyle's hostility slipped into high gear.

Just put him in the closet.

The condition had been a blessing to Paola. Not just because it allowed for effective punishment. The real blessing was that Lyle had never liked the ark. If she could make it to the ark, he'd leave her alone. He'd go off and trap rabbits. He'd wait for later.

The year that Garvin and Maria purchased a new mattress, Paola had asked if the old mattress could go in the ark. Not to sleep. Just to make it more comfortable. Maria was dead set against it. Snakes. Scorpions.

But Garvin had agreed. Because Garvin understood.

The ark was never her actual bedroom. She always had to sleep inside the house. But it was a place she could go. A place that was hers. The ark had been a selling point for the property. Garvin had seen it as a sign. A promise from God to encourage his passion for a home-ministry that would lead to a church with an *actual* congregation. And then to a true following, maybe throughout the state, in the name of the Almighty. It appealed to him that the home had previously doubled as a church for the South Texas Fellowship of Charismatic Nazarenes.

Not that *he* was a Nazarene. But still. It came with an ark. It was a sign.

And not that Garvin had ever used the ark for much of anything. Mostly just a prop outside his living room windows. Something that he could point at and work conveniently into his weekly sermons.

If Garvin had been sensitive to Lyle's abuse of Paola, Maria had mostly turned her back on it. Let it happen. Minimized it when she could. When she couldn't minimize it, she defended her own flesh and blood. Made it all less about Lyle acting out and more about Garvin's *'perfect gift from God'* just asking to be taken down a peg.

By the time Paola turned eleven, the pressure mounted to enroll her in Corbin Elementary for the sixth grade. As a part-time teacher, Garvin knew too many people with an educational mission. They pressed. Garvin firmly resisted. Home schooling was God's plan. Paola was their responsibility, their daughter, and they knew what was best. They had prayed on it many times. Many times.

As that year came to a close, the pressure resumed for them to enroll Paola in Corbin Middle, the school where Garvin taught music and Lyle confounded his teachers. The colleagues pressed. Garvin resisted. Home schooling was the still the answer. Still God's plan.

But then Maria had switched sides. Forcefully. Wanting Paola out of the house. Wanting her away. Wanting to disrupt Garvin's fixation. All in the guise of a quality education and proper social interaction.

"One night they, like, really fought over it. A yellin' fight. He didn't hit Maria that time. Prob'ly wanted to. But Maria stood tough. That's how much she wanted me gone. Enough to risk another beatin'. I didn't have any kinda say in it."

Eventually Garvin relented, giving way like the outer bank of desert soil accommodating a new, deepening bend of water. He knew it was pointless. Sometimes you just know when you're on the wrong side of history. Garvin knew. But by God he would drive her to and from school every day. He insisted on that much. She still belonged to him.

So Paola had gone to school. Smoked Garvin's pilfered cigarettes in the rain. Kept to herself. Took solace in solitude. Resorted to violence, beating Mandy Klutch senseless. Met Celia Morales. One bend in the new river leading inexorably to the next. All connected. All one thing. Through wind and blood and fire. Never stopping.

Temporary custody had been easy enough, even as the investigation was pending. Maria Cross, convinced Paola was somehow to blame for Lyle, wanted nothing more to do with her. Garvin wanted everything to do with her, of course. *His perfect gift. His sign from God.* But Maria's claims of abuse against him precluded custody. Turned out that neither of them had any legal claim to her anyway.

Possession was nine-tenths. She stayed with Celia.

Paola took Celia's room. Celia took the couch. They took turns in the bathroom. Just the two of them. Celia and Paola. Not mother and daughter. Not teacher and student. Not close friends. None of those things. All of those things. Crockett County Social Services approved the arrangement on a provisional basis until something more suitable could be put into place. The wheels of the *in loco parentis* bureaucracy turned slowly.

Cruelly. Because time brought hope.

They settled in. Uncertainty solidified into expectation. Mother and daughter. Celia and Paola. Confiding. Bonding.

June.

July.

Hotter. Drier. The earth split and crumbled. Flora shrank. The primrose. The lantana. Shriveled. Desiccated. And yet, slowly, haltingly, Paola began to blossom. Began to trust. Smile. Laugh. Began to open like a flower with one root tapping a secret pocket of damp relief.

August.

They waited for resolution. Watched movies. Took turns cooking. Drove places. San Antonio. Austin. Pizza. Shopping malls. Paola picked out a thousand-piece puzzle. A blue whale behind a school of dolphins. Vines of kelp. Glittering starfish. All beneath an unsuspecting boy asleep in a rowboat. They spread it out on the dining table and started eating meals in the living room. It took ten days to put it together. They celebrated. Paola broke it up and started over.

September.

Something about the school season prompted Social Services to make a decision. They were all very sorry. Celia did not have the resources. Did not have the space. The investigation into Lyle's death was still open. The agency just did not feel comfortable. They needed to be comfortable.

Comfortable. Like the agency was buying a sofa.

The foster family lived in San Angelo. It felt to Celia like losing a limb. It felt like Amalia all over again. It all came rushing back. She raised hell about the school.

"You do not understand. Her place is in Corbin!"

"Ma'am…"

"She goes to school in Corbin!"

"Ms. Morales. She's already been transferred. I'm sorry. She's…"

"I will pick her up myself! I will drive her every morning! That is what she wants! That is what I want and she is going to be my daughter! I have petitioned…"

"I understand that, Ms. Morales. But while the petition is pending we have a responsibility to make sure…"

A losing battle. Paola attended Davey Crockett Middle School in San Angelo. Celia resumed teaching at Corbin Middle. Had there been an opening for teachers, she would have transferred. Would have moved to San Angelo. Would have slept in her car.

But there were no openings. So they waited. She did not press her luck. She had learned her lesson with Amalia. They spoke on the phone. They waited.

October. November.

The denial of the petition for adoption fit on a single piece of paper, folded in thirds, tucked into a thin white envelope. It waited alone in the mailbox, orphaned. Celia opened it. Read. Held it in her hand, standing over the half-completed puzzle she had started all over again as a kind of prayer.

It weighed nothing, that sheet. Those squiggles of ink. That serrated signature.

It weighed nothing.

And yet it crushed her.

'Insufficient means of support.' That was the reason. But she suspected that there were reasons behind the reason. Yolanda and murder-arson. Maggy and heroin. Suspicions of genetic criminality. Her restraining order. Her violation of the restraining order. Her attempt to abduct Amalia. Strong words from a Dallas County judge not long enough ago. Father William, it seemed, did not have any stroke with the Texas Department of Family and Protective Services, full of Protestants.

Celia had wrapped herself in telephone cord. The phone became the only thing in her life that floated. For a while it was every night. Clandestine. Whispers in the dark.

"I hate it here, Celia."

"I know, baby."

"I want to be with you."

"I know. I know. I want to be with you too."

"No one understands me. I want to be left alone. I hate them. I hate the school. I hate my teachers. Why can't I be with you?"

They burned up the phone lines until Alice Kendricks caught wise. Decided it was unhealthy. Dangerous. Flexed her foster mother muscle. The TDFPS scolded Paola. The calls began to dry up. Every couple of days. Once a week. Then less.

Alcohol picked up the slack. Kept Celia company. Gave her something to do. Working the puzzle. Waiting on that phone to ring.

Desperate, she pressed her luck. Called in sick. Drove out to San Angelo. Found the school. Waited across the street. Watched. Scrutinized the areas where the other kids were not. Looked for loners. Looked for places most hospitable to castaways.

There was a large *palo verde* near the corner of the building. Sure enough.

She took Paola out to lunch. Drove her in circles. Parked. Talked. Cried.

Twice more. Same thing. Just a flash of headlights from across the street did the trick.

But each time, she found Paola had drifted farther away, unmoored from anything or anyone connected with dry land. Increasingly self-contained. Less able to trust anyone. Less able to trust even Celia, who had not done what she promised. Celia, who could not be counted on.

"They signed me up for this music camp thing," Paola said from the bottom of a milkshake. "This summer."

"Well… that's good, isn't it?"

"I guess." She shrugged. Slurped. "Alice is prob'ly just lyin' about it to make me talk to them. I hate talkin' to them."

"Maybe… maybe you should give them a chance. I mean… maybe they're trying."

"Yeah, right. Next time she touches me I'm gon' punch her in the face."

"Touches you how?"

"Not like that."

"Then like how?"

"Like she gives a rat fuck. Larry too. Next time he *acc-i-den-tal-ly* walks in while I'm getting' out of the shower I'm just gon' drop the towel. Walk around the house naked. Let him watch. Let him get a good long look. See what Alice thinks about that."

"Paola. Don't even joke about that. Are you serious?"

"As a heart attack, Celia. Man's a perv and Alice don't got a clue."

Celia had called TDFPS. She had no credibility. They told her that she needed to accept the decision and move on with her own life. So nothing came of it. They paid a visit or two. Just to check in. Talked to Larry and Alice. Talked to Paola. But Paola trusted the State of Texas even less than she trusted Larry Kendricks.

"You didn't tell them?"

"Who you think they're gon' believe, Celia? *Me?* Where you been? He hasn't touched me. He's just a looker. Least he 'preciates me for somethin'. Unlike Alice."

Time. Lots of it. A full year. Two. Larry and Alice Kendrick proved no match for Paola, determined not to trust or be trusted. Not to love or be loved. Not to be controlled by curfews or house rules. She eventually made good on her threat about the towel. It was Larry who asked for the change.

Another couple stepped into the breach. The Mills. Good Mormons with two kids of their own. Paola changed schools again, this one twice as big as the last. She fell in with a handful of losers. Smoking weed between classes. Drinking. Other backseat conduct unbecoming a good Mormon. But then, that was the whole point.

"Maybe they need to stop tryin' to make me into one of them. Ever think of that, Celia? Ever think that maybe *they're* the problem? I'm just bein' who I am. They already got their two perfect straight-A kids and so maybe they just need to let well enough alone."

Celia had wanted to feel good that Paola was still confiding in her. Still trusting her enough to share her life. Trusting her not to lecture. But even this was cold comfort. Each time they spoke it seemed to Celia that Paola, alone in her little boat, had drifted further away from shore. Each time she seemed smaller. Her voice more distant.

In October the Mills family came to Corbin for the Moon Garden Festival. Paola called ahead of time. They agreed to meet at the Ferris wheel. Five o'clock.

But the logistics were not Paola's to control.

They left late. Then the traffic. They parked in Corbin and had to walk past the *Lick-n-Tipple*. The kids —her perfect foster sibs —wanted ice cream, just like everybody else. By the time they reached the fairgrounds it was after six. By the time Paola made it to the Ferris wheel it was six-thirty.

Celia had been there since four. Had wanted to take the edge off of the anxiety by being early. That didn't help as much as the flask of whiskey in her purse. Five o'clock came and went. Five-thirty. Six. Celia assumed the worst. Anxiety got up and left. Depression took a seat next to her on the bench; watched the big wheel with her. Turning. Turning. Going nowhere.

Paola found her just as she was up and walking off toward the parking lot.

"Celia. *Hey. Celia.*"

Hands in her pockets. Distant. Different. Taller. Older. Not a girl.

The hug felt perfunctory to Celia. So she hadn't let go. Had tried to melt the ice with the warmth of her body. Cried. Paola had wrenched herself free. Looked around uncomfortably.

"My God, Paola. You're so… You're such a young woman now. You're so… you're beautiful."

"I'm a lot of things. Beautiful ain't one of 'em, Celia. I'm late. And I'm sorry. And you're drunk. Let's sit you back down before you fall down."

Thirty minutes on a bench. Like a single drop of rain in the middle of a hot empty desert. Gone, evaporated, before it even hit the ground.

Paola did the talking. Reporting. Accounting. Boyfriends, zero. Friends, zero. Suspensions, two, both for fighting. Arrests, two, both for shoplifting. Adoption prospects, zero. Not that she wanted any. She wasn't a kid anymore. She just wanted out. Anywhere but here. California. Florida. Didn't matter. She just wanted out.

The sleeves of Paola's jacket were not quite long enough. Celia had seized one of her wrists. Flattened it to the full moon.

"Paola..."

She brushed the ridges with her thumb. Her eyes filled.

"Paola..."

But the girl, no longer a girl, yanked herself free. Stood.

"Gotta get back. I have to go."

"No. Paola. You have to tell me. You have to talk to me. Come home with me. Let's just leave. Let's just go home. Come home."

She did not know what she was saying. Did not know she was crying. Clutching.

"Y'ain't my mama, Celia. I have to go now. Take care of yourself. Please don't drive. I'll call you later."

A hug. Paola sat her back down on the bench. And then she was gone.

Paola did call. The next day. Wanted to make sure she got home okay. But that was it. For weeks. Then months. Another school year. Another final bell. All the children left. They always leave.

So Celia prefers the memories to anything new. The look on Paola's face when Celia had plucked that cigarette out of her mouth out by the dumpster behind the school. Paola beneath the *palo verde*. Paola chasing down papers in the wind. Paola on the road in the desert, one hand on the car door: *"I like you Ms. Celia. Don't exactly know why, but I do."*

And there is another one. One more favorite. *The* favorite.

They had just finished the puzzle for the second time. Possession was still nine-tenths. Anyone could see that adoption was certain. Of course it was. They reclined at opposite ends of the couch. Bare feet intertwined. Dorothy was on the television with Toto, no longer in Kansas.

"When the adoption is final, will my name be Morales? Like yours?"

Celia had smiled. Nodded. "Is that okay?"

"Fine by me. Heck, I wanna change my first name too."

"What? Such a beautiful name. So round and soft. Like water. Round like the moon."

"Right. A name from a woman who may as well be *on* the moon. And who ain't my mother. She won't be soon enough anyway. Soon as you're official. She can have back her stupid ol' name. Give it to some other girl. Probably got a dozen kids by now. Can give it to one of them."

Dorothy and Toto had followed the bricks. There was a scarecrow in the field.

"What name would you want?" Celia had asked. "What would you want me to call you?"

The girl on the couch, for she was still just a girl then, had pointed over Celia's head. Pointed to the top shelf of the heavy wooden étagère behind her. To the small pink rectangular pillow with the tassels and the little booties.

To the name embroidered in blue yarn across the front.

That, of all names, was the name Olivia had wanted Celia to call her.

Paola.

Chapter 69

Nineteen. Twenty. Twenty-one.

The I-67 glints in the weak morning light like a slick, dirty blade. Like a scythe left behind at the scene.

Twenty-two. Twenty-three.

The dark lumps keep appearing on the horizon of the wet gray road. Popping up left, right and center on a macabre ribbon of braille. It wraps the world, this steel ribbon. Wraps the cylinder of God's music box.

It's a song.

She stubs out the last of a cigarette and tosses it on the floor of Jesús Batista's shit-brown Ford Falcon. Lights another.

Music cannot save her. That much at least is now clear.

Music cannot save her. Not the music she had thought she heard all of these years. Not the music she had hoped for. Prayed for. Mother music. Mother blues.

All horse shit.

Music was not her mother. Music was a preacher, calling her in the night.

Calling her out to the road.

Twenty-four. Twenty-five.

Dashboard Jesus is brimming with compassion and understanding this morning. Head slightly atilt. Palms open. *Now, now my child.*

Olivia puts the cigarette in her mouth. Opens the window. Rips Jesus from the dash. It takes some effort. There is some bend in the legs. But she manages. A small, leather-crusted, pyramidal wedge of foam dashboard goes out with him.

Like he had been digging in with the toes of his sandals.

The place where he used to be is now a perfect notch for her lighter.

The metal in her leg howls, like something chained in the dark, separated from its mother.

She leaves the window down. Lets the road spray soak her left arm. Blows smoke out into the rain. Accelerates into the hissing gray sky.

554

By the time she rolls up on the outskirts of San Angelo, the pointlessness of her existence has come into sharp relief. She has awoken, violently, from the pipe dream of *Papi's*.

She needs to leave. Needs to cut every tie. Dissolve every bond. Set fire to everything. Disappear.

She limps in through the front doors of *Longhorn Fitness*, knowing there is no point in putting on the uniform wadded up in her hands. She uses it to blot the rain from her face. Wraps it around her hand like a tourniquet.

She moves unevenly, compensating for the pain. Weaves her way through the equipment —navigating weight machines, ellipticals, bikes, and treadmills — directly for Mr. Pete's office.

Trish Dale, Assistant Manager in charge of snacks and tanning and lost-and-found and petty, bullshit interference, plots an intercept course. Arms swinging. Trish was born with a coffee cup emerging from one wrist and a cell phone from the other.

"He stepped out," says Trish. Beneath the spongy perm, she is an oiled, sweet potato orange.

Olivia keeps moving. Reaches the door of Mr. Pete's office. Takes a seat.

"I'll wait."

"Can I help you with somethin', Olivia? Can I ask what this is concernin'?"

"No. You can't. I'll just wait for Mr. Pete."

"Well, maybe," Trish gestures vaguely, the twenty-ounce caffeinated appendage and the wi-fi appendage moving in opposite parabolas, "you should just go on and get dressed and start your shift and when he gets back you can pop your head in. How does that sound?"

"Sounds like you weren't listenin'."

Trish makes a noise somewhere in the middle of her nasal sinus. Then she is gone from the doorway. Olivia stares fixedly at the rack of plastic horns screwed to the desk in front of her. Each horn skewers a miniature *Longhorn Fitness* basketball.

She twists the damp uniform in her hands, wringing it of something invisible.

Someone lifting weights out on the floor is making a loud production of it. Banging and groaning. Like he is pounding hot iron into a sword.

Someone on a treadmill is flat footed, stomping on rats.

Someone on an elliptical is shoveling mud. Digging a grave.

"He's gonna be awhile," says Dooley Simms. His gangly frame is leaning against the doorway. Olivia looks up. Nods.

"I can wait."

A moment. Two. Three.

"My friends and I are having a shooter tonight. You can come over if you want. Buddy of mine got a bunch of new fireworks. He was gonna take 'em down to Corbin for that festival but he decided not to go 'cause of the rain. So. I mean. There's a shitload. Plenty of beer. It's no big deal or anything but…"

Olivia looks up. Dooley is looking away, out into the stubby black forest of machinery, worrying his spindly, chapped hands. He pops his knuckles in sequence. He already knows the answer. They both do. She tries to smile.

"Thanks, Dooley. I've… I'm… tonight ain't a good time."

He is nodding before she is done talking.

"Pete's gonna be awhile," he says. "They just started about twenty minutes ago. Yesterday it was like a full hour. So."

"What?"

Dooley nods in the general direction of the yoga, aerobics, warm-up, massage part of the club.

"Massage."

He looks down at her directly for the first time. His long, red fingers rise to scratch quotation marks in the air. He pushes off with his shoulder and is gone.

She stares for a moment at where Dooley used to be. Stands. Leaves Mr. Pete's office, cutting a diagonal across the floor of the factory of sound and stench. The workers, the inmates, watch her hobble past, heads rotating on sweaty necks. They've got the country station on again. She hates country.

The sign is on the door. She tries the knob. Locked. The key is still on her ring. *Insert. Twist. Push.*

Mr. Pete is in up to the hilt. His face beneath the bill of his green *Longhorn Fitness* cap is pinched and red and bobbing and streaked with sweat. The girl beneath him, slick with oil, clutches the table like it's a surfboard in rough water, blonde hair fanned out over her glistening back.

She's eighteen. Maybe.

They both look up in unison, eyelids flying open, as if at the gathering curl of a large wave.

Mr. Pete's expression cycles through half-a-dozen emotions in a single syllable. "Hey!"

He looks around wildly. Wants to pull out. Wants to cover and assert himself with authority. The girl beneath him has a similar instinct. She flinches sideways on the table.

But extraction will only make it worse. All of his authority is heaped in the chair beneath the girl's *Muscle Menders* uniform. So he pushes in further, as if to hide as much of himself as possible, keeping the girl between them as a shield. Hisses.

"What in the *fuck* do you think you… You get the *fuck* out of this… If you are not out of this fuckin' room in…"

The girl squirms beneath the broken and abandoned sentences. Mr. Pete pulls her body against him for protection.

Olivia steps in. Drags the chair forward. Pins the open door against the wall. Garth Brookes, out in the factory of sounds and smells, shoulders his way into the tiny room with some scouring fluorescent light, singing about his lowly friends.

"Sure glad she's licensed and bonded, Pete," says Olivia.

"Olivia, so help me God…"

"No. I really wouldn't count on God givin' you much help. Way to keep the faith though. Prob'ly get some points for that."

She drops her wadded uniform onto the pile of clothes. Bends. Gathers everything into her arms.

"Olivia, goddamnit…"

Sets the pile on top of the stack of neatly folded white towels. Picks up everything.

"Olivia… *Olivia!*"

She leaves. Hobbles up the hallway past the locker rooms to the laundry. Dooley Simms is pulling hot towels out of a dryer, dumping them into a rolling hamper. He straightens as she enters. Hands on hips. Watches.

"These are filthy," she says. She opens up a washer with an elbow. Stuffs in the load. Mr. Pete's pockets are full. Wallet. Keys. Phone. She slams the door. Hits the button. Watches the water through the glass. Remembers the water gushing up against the church window over Papi's shoulder.

I sold the club, honey. The ink is dry.

She turns to Dooley. Smiles. Feels the scars shift to accommodate the expression. "Maybe wash these twice."

Dooley nods. Swallows. "Okay."

A moment. Two. Three. He has to look away.

"It ain't you, Dooley," she says. "It was never you. Take care of yourself."

The hours that belonged to *Longhorn Fitness* are released into the wildness of time. They scatter like caged birds through an open door.

She eats an early lunch in a wet drive-through parking lot, watching San Angelo traffic. Imagines that this is what *Papi's* will be a year from now. A fast food drive-through. Paper hats. Fries. Soft-serve cones.

In her head, where the music used to be, she is stuffing Sheldon's money into a bag. Bundle by bundle, until the dresser is empty. *What else?* Some clothes. *What else?* Family. She gathers up the cactus people. Parents. Siblings. The little dog with the cactus flower ears. Arranges them side-by-side in the little box. Wraps it in a clean t-shirt. Sets it on top of the clothes. She cinches the bag and tosses it over her shoulder. *Now what?* She tries to imagine where. *New Orleans? St. Louis? Nashville?* No. North. *Fargo. Cheyenne.* Anywhere but south Texas. Away. Away.

She chews her burger. Stares into the middle distance. In the airspace above the road. Kevin is in his wheelchair, bent nearly in half, twisting sideways. Yvonne rolls him into the doorway of the bedroom. Then it's not Yvonne. It's Libby. Libby, with not a stitch on, leaning against Kevin's chair.

Oh I sees how it is, baby. MmmHmm. Yo' li'l feelin's get hurt so you gon' take that money an' go, huh? You gon' disappear yo' sorry half-black ass. MmmHmm. I ever tell you my hurricane story? Me an mama? You pussy out an' turn yo' back on what God sends to you? You gon' die fo' sho'. Even if you live, you be dead inside because God gon' say fuck it I ain't wastin' my time on you. An' it be jus' like yo' mama sayin' it. You on yo' own baby. Ain't that right Kev?

Kevin convulses his answer.

MmmHmm. Even Kev here know that shit, baby. But you jus' go on wishin' for what ain't no one eva' gon' give. Like Bessie sing about how she wished she had her own heaven so she could give all them poor girls a long lost happy home.

A blue pick-up is slow off the mark at the corner light. The flatbed behind hits the horn. Olivia sucks down the last of her soda. Stuffs the cup in the bag. Drives.

She has hours to kill before she meets with Lou Dimond. She moves in aimless circles through San Angelo. Seeing but not seeing. Tracing the disappearing loops in her head. The *Papi's* loop. The Sheldon loop. The Libby loop. The Miguel loop. Even the wisp of a Davis loop. They overlap, snarling like tangled fishing line in a drawer. Then, within a couple of hours, they are all atomizing. Disintegrating like dirt roads in a flood. They lead everywhere and nowhere. As loops, they never had any real direction in the first place. But they had that illusion. Always on the road back to the place we never left. The reassurance of the familiar. *Still on track. Still on track.* That was something at least.

But now. When the water in her head recedes, as the brine pops and fizzles in the sun, the loops will all have been wiped clean. She will be back to empty desert, abandoned by the sea. Back to the only loop that ever really matters.

Back to the mother loop.

She stops to pee at *Lone Star Reads*. Loiters. Picks up books. This one and that one. Turns them over in her hands. Puts them back.

She is not a reader. It's the covers that clamor for her attention. Here, a horse with a mane of white flame. There, entangled silhouettes, each with gun. Here, the bleached wooden prow of a boat, rain-pocked lake in the background, draped with the soggy tendrils of a watery blue title. *Eyelash Lake.* She picks it up. Flips. Reads. Flips. Reads.

She always scoffed at the idea of an exogenous God. She believed in a divinity that was all-encompassing. All things. All creatures. All places. All times. She believed we are merely molecules of an eyelash on the face of divinity, cursed with self-awareness. There is no God to worship because there is nothing but God in the first place. Boats are made to carry an illusion. We are all made of water.

She moves on, ahead of schedule. Ready to be done with it. Lou Diamond walks through the bar to the back staircase, pushing through heavy curtains of country rock noise.

"Bit early, aren't you?" he asks.

Diamond Lou's in San Angelo is no different than *The Diamondback* in Corbin. Just bigger. Louder. It also has a sawdust dance floor, dead-center, surrounded by small, low, two-tops and beat up chairs. In the middle of the dance floor is a battered mechanical bull, saddled up and glaring at itself in the mirror over the bar. A rubbery diamondback rattlesnake is spooled round the horns. Head up and fully flared.

She's heard about the bull. It hasn't twitched its tail since the lawsuit. Now it's just a fixture. A prop for a drunken selfie.

People look as they pass. The big boss man leading the girl with a limp and a fucked-up face. It looks like she's in trouble. Like some kind of justice is imminent. They all have the same expression, hiding behind the mugs and bottles: *wonder what this is all about?*

They pound their way up the narrow stairs to the office. Lou is a big man. Not fat. *Big.* But the fat is coming soon enough. The bad knee joints are already making the top of the staircase interesting. They have that in common.

"My afternoon opened up," she says to the small of his back. "Thought I'd come by early and see if you were here."

"Well where the hell else would I be?" He doesn't want an answer. He crosses the landing and opens the door to his office with a push. Points to a long leather couch against the wall. "Sit. You want something? Beer?"

"No. Thanks."

She sits heavily, devoured by wheezing cushions, slowly sinking beneath framed photos of Lou striking poses in a Dallas Cowboys uniform. She watches him thunder off to the corner refrigerator. He pulls out a beer. Twists off the top and tosses it into the trash. Leans back against the wall. Drinks. He clinks a big metal ring against the bottle, keeping time with the thudding that beats up through the floor.

It's not a Super Bowl ring. Everyone knows that. Except the people who don't.

He doesn't look like the pictures. Not really. His face is fleshier. Eyes smaller. Losing his hair. He tries to hide it by letting it grow long. It slips out from beneath the black Stetson like brown moss off a white stump.

"So," he says eventually, knocking the heel of his boot against the floor.

"Manny Soto. Sounds like you two are having a time of it out there in little ol' Corbin."

"Guess that's one way to put it," she says, crossing her arms. "Another way to put it is that Manny's a dangerous pig who shouldn't be workin' for you."

Lou laughs a little. Drinks. The bottle leaves a smirk.

"Dangerous pig, huh? That's why you called this meeting? You want me to fire Manny Soto 'cause he's a dangerous pig."

"He's gon' hurt someone before it's done, Lou. Or get hurt."

"Little ol' Manny?"

"Little ol' Manny. I want you to know what kind of person you got on the payroll. Figure the rest is up to you."

He nods. Drinks. Sizes her up.

"Manny tells me *you* assaulted *him*. With a toilet brush. Got shit all up in his sinus passages. In his eye. Says *you're* the dangerous one. He's givin' me doctor's bills and threat'nin' to sue me unless I fire *you*. What do you say to that?"

There is a hot lick of lightning up the metal in her leg. Her eyelids close until it passes. They open again. Lou and his question are still there.

"I'd say it don't take a rocket scientist to figure that I didn't hit Manny with a shitty brush just for the hell of it, Lou. That I must have been reactin' to something he did to me first."

Another swig. He crosses his big arms. Smiles. They look at each other.

"You think I don't have Manny's number? You think I can't see that dumb fuck comin' a mile off?"

Olivia shrugs. "Don't know. Can you?"

"Like he's wearin' a goddamned neon sign. Everybody can. So I get it, okay? He made a grab and you let him have it. And I say good for you." He uncrosses his arms just long enough to point at her with a beefy finger and the tip of his bottle. "Good for you, Olivia. I say Manny got what he had comin' and that's the way it should be. Action, reaction. Behavior, consequence."

"Okay. So?"

"So I say he's not likely to pull that shit again. Not with you, anyway. And if he does, you're gonna' let him have it but good. And Manny'll come cryin' to me askin' for your head on a platter and I'm gonna tell Manny what I told him not thirty minutes ago in this very office in the very spot you're sittin' now."

She is not expecting this. Stiffens.

"Manny was here?"

"Oh, relax. I sent him on his way. You think a fair man listens to only one side of the story? 'Course he was here. I'm just glad you weren't any earlier 'cause that would *not* have turned out particularly well. He is not a happy man right now. Point is, Olivia, I told him that he got what he had comin' and that he needs to steer clear. I spanked that *chico petito* but good."

The throbbing in the floor stops. Starts again.

Lou drinks. Clears his throat.

"I'll be honest, Olivia, it don't help matters you livin' in a whorehouse. That's pushin' a lot of Manny's buttons. Get's him worked up. You know? Encourages him a little?" He waits a beat. Then holds his hands out her direction. "But that's your business. What you do off the job is between you and your God. Not for me to judge." He points again. "And not for Manny to exploit. You hear what I'm sayin'? Your job with me is safe. Gary always has good things to say about the work you do. You're on the team and I got your back, girl. I do. I got no intention of firin' you."

"Or him." She smiles. Or someone could call it a smile. Lou points again.

"Don't go gettin' greedy on me, now. Manny's gettin' the shitty end of this stick in more ways than one. Like I said, he is pissed but good. I got his number and he knows it. You just keep doin' a good job. You're comin' up for a raise soon and if you play your cards right I'll put you in for the next opening that we have here at *Diamond Lou's.*" He spreads his arms to encompass the entire building beneath them. "This here's the flagship. Or I can look at what we got in the *Diamondback* in Houston if you want. How's that suit you?"

There is no immediate response. Lou fills the void.

"You should come up more often, Olivia. I'll make time. You can fill in here and there. We could get to know each other a little better. Manny'll like that 'bout as much as that toilet brush in his face."

She wrestles herself free of the couch, leg howling. Stands.

"I came here to quit, Lou. Turns out that was the right decision."

"Oh come on now. Olivia. *Olivia.* Wait now, Olivia. Let's talk about this." He takes off his hat. Puts it back on. "Aw hell."

He follows her out of the office to the top of the stairs. Leans against the jamb.

"Game don't go exactly the way you want so you're just gon' to take your ball on home? Is that it? Do I have that about right? You gon' pussy out on me?"

Her shoes make an uneven clopping sound as she descends, the echoes tumbling down to the door that will open back into the bar.

"No Lou. I'm taking *your* balls and goin' home. Seein' as how you don't have any use for 'em."

She drives through intermittent rain. Each jerk of the wheel an impulsive twitch. She follows a blinker. Follows an arrow painted on a brick building. Follows a gust of wind in the other direction. She should just go home. To *the whorehouse.* Stuff everything she owns into a bag and leave before morning. Leave where? Anywhere. North.

Quicksilver. A bar. The letters look like liquid in the failing light. The wheel yanks.

It's barely open. Dark. Quiet. Perfect. A mounted television shows a map of the Gulf. The word '*Mute*' floats just offshore on swirling animated clouds.

She orders a beer without stopping. Collapses into a back booth where she can stretch out her aching leg on the opposite seat. The shaggy kid behind the bar follows her with a bottle and an empty glass and a cracked wooden bowl of nuts and pretzels. She hands him back the glass.

"I'll be in the back. Holler if you want another." He shuffles away.

"Hey," she says. He shuffles back. Waits. She looks up. "Don't turn on any music."

He nods and slips away. She closes her eyes. Surveys the abandoned, dusty barrenness in her head. Back where she started. Same as it ever was. And not a sound. Not a single broken melody. Not a note. Just the wind.

She drinks. Breathes.

The *Quicksilver* door needs some oil. She should have faced the other direction. She should have kept driving. She wasn't thinking. She feels him behind her.

"No, no, no. Why you drinkin' all alone, O? Good lookin' piece of tail lye chu? Shit ain't rye, O."

He slides in across from her. The table wobbles. She keeps her eyes closed.

"Fuck off, Manny."

There is a shuffling sound in the back. Manny calls out.

"Shot an' a beer, yo? An' bring her another."

"What part of fuck off did you not get?" She opens her eyes. Looks at Manny. He's already lit. A swarthy fireplug in denim and a black *Diamondback* baseball hat. His shoulders are wet with rain. His right eye is swollen and bloodshot. "And why are you following me?"

Manny shrugs. "Lou give me da fuckin' boot, O. I meetin' wit' him and he say he meetin' wit' chu an' I can't be aroun'. Wha da fuck? So I jus' wait, O. 'Cause I think he jus' fuckin' wif me, see? 'Cause da man ain't got no balls and don't want to hear wha I got to say. Unnastan? So I wait. But den here chu come. Jus' lye Lou say."

The shuffling kid shows up with the drinks and another bowl of nuts. Manny looks up at him from beneath the bill of his hat.

"Hey man. Chu know why it so dead in dis place? 'Cause chu don't play no music, see?" Manny taps the *Diamondback* logo above the bill. "Da why we kick chu ass eight day a week. Why don't chu put on some music, man? Somethin' good too."

The kid looks down at Olivia. He wants permission. She closes her eyes in an extra slow blink. Shakes her head. He shrugs his shoulders and saunters off.

Manny has already lost interest. He fills his face, eating out of his own palm like he is feeding a pygmy horse. He chews. Throws back the shot. Contemplates the beer. Drinks.

"So here wha' I wanna know, O. Okay? I wan' know what kinda shit chu say to Lou to get him wrap around chu fuckin' finger. Okay? I wan' know wha' lies chu tellin' him. Or maybe chu makin' promises to suck his Dallas Cowboy dick. Da why chu meetin' Lou today, O? Ride 'em cowboy?"

Another mouthful of nuts. Chews. Drinks.

"'Cause I tell chu wha: Lou get me this job. Unnastan? Me an Lou was lye dis, O." He holds out two stubby fingers like they are sewn together. "Not no more. No, no. Not since chu start makin' 'pointments to limp' da *culo repugnante* up those stairs to Lou's office."

The door squeaks again. Two men. Knocking their hats against their legs in a spray. They sit at the bar and stare up at the television.

Olivia pulls her legs off the bench. Faces Manny. Looks him in his dark little ball bearings. Takes a long drink.

"I'm confused, Manny. You sayin' I got a *culo repugnante* that should not be limpin' up the boss' stairs? Or are you sayin' I got a good looking piece of tail that should not be drinking alone? Which is it?"

Whatever he expected, it is not this. He tries to look under the table but aborts the effort. He is confused. Then angry. His face hardens, like he is trying to push something thick out through his eyes.

"Chu fuckin' wif me, O? Think I playin' games over here? Think I won't ... *do* things? Unnastan me, O?"

She leans back. Smiles a little. Nods. "I know you ain't playin' games, Manny. I know I've got exactly two choices. I can either quit my job... or I can start showing you..." Stops. Drinks again. Looks away and back. Rubs. "A little *extra* appreciation. I got that about right?"

Manny's face relaxes a little. A dry sponge taking in a tablespoon of water.

"It about some fuckin' respec', O. I do for chu. Chu do for me. Chu wan' do for Lou too, well he the boss. I ain' got no say. But in Corbin? I'm the boss, O. Unnastan? Me."

"What about Gary? Am I supposed to fuck him too?"

He leans in. Sincere. Earnest. Like she doesn't understand *anything*.

"No, no, no. I tol' you already, O. Gary is wif *Kelly*. She a tall drink. Gary ain' givin' that booty up for nobody, O. I tell chu wha': Gary try somethin' wif *chu*? Come to me an' I will put that snaggletooth muthafuck in his place. Unnastan?"

"So you'll protect me, is what you're sayin'. From Gary."

He flips his hands, palms up, on top of the table. Looks at her like she has finally arrived. The two at the bar think something is funny on the television.

"*Sí. Sí.* Da wha' I tellin' ..."

He stops. Eyes narrowing. He pushes himself back into the booth. It's the gold chain traversing the opening in his shirt that catches her attention. The one that threads the crucifix she cannot see. But she can feel it.

"You fuckin' wif me, O?"

She gives him a smile.

"You like the blues, Manny?"

"Wha' chu… Lye you mean *music*?"

"Yeah. You know. The blues."

Manny shrugs. Bewildered.

She finishes her beer. Turns the bottle over and over in her hands.

"I had this song in my head for a long time. It's kinda gone now. I lost it. I can't feel it any more. You know? It's just, like, *gone*. And now it's like there's nothing inside me any more. I'm empty. Abandoned. Fuckin' deserted. I can't feel much of anything now." She stops turning the bottle and starts picking at the label. Manny waits. "And so… feelin' empty like that… there bein' nothin' inside… makes me think I may as well fill myself with somethin'. Or *someone*. You know? Maybe I should fill myself with Manny Soto. Maybe I should just let Manny Soto inside. Because, you know, he wants to be there and what the fuck, right?"

Manny nods slowly.

"Rye, O. I feel chu, baby. Dis a cold fuckin' world, yo? Eva'body need them someone."

"Your parents still alive?"

"*¿Mis padres?*" He scrunches up his pocked face, offended. "Wha' da fuck, O? Why chu care about my parents?"

"I don't. Just askin'." She looks up briefly. Then back to the label she is slowly destroying. "There's this old blues song. *Nobody's Fault but Mine*. It's an old Blind Willie Johnson song, 1920-something, that everybody seemed to pick up and cover. Rosetta Tharp. Staple Singers. Nina Simone. Hell, even Led Zepplin. Everybody. They all change around the lyrics a little, but it's the same song."

She focuses harder on the label. Keeps picking at it. Manny sighs and waits.

"And in this song the singer is sayin' she's got a Bible that she never reads. And she's got a father who knows how to preach. And she's got a mother who knows how to pray. And she's got a sister who knows how to sing. And so she figures that if she dies, and if her soul goes to hell, then she's got no one but to blame for that but herself. See? She had her chance. She always had people around to show her the way. To inspire her. Protect her from herself. Protect her from those who want to do her wrong. Keep her on the righteous path. You know? And she blew it."

Most of the label is in a small pile of tatters on the table. She keeps picking. Manny laughs.

"Wha da fuck you tryin' to say to me, O?"

"I don't have a mother, Manny. Never have. Don't have a father. Don't have a sister who can sing. And it's been a long fuckin' time since I been in the same room with a Bible. So I figure, if I die, and if my soul is lost, then maybe that's not on me. Maybe that ain't my fault. Maybe if I fuck Manny Soto six days a week and twice on Sunday 'til he's blue in the face, that shit's on God, not me."

"Rye, rye. I unnastan, baby. Look, O. You lonely, see? Da acciden' fuck chu up an' you feel lye no one give a fuck…"

But she isn't listening. *Pick. Pick. Pick.*

"And by that same logic, I think to myself that maybe if I put Manny Soto into an early grave because he touched me with a single fuckin' atom of his disgusting self…" *Pick. Pick. Pick.* "And if I die…" *Pick. Pick.* "And if my soul is lost…" *Pick.* "Well then maybe that shit's on God too."

She stops. Blows the pile of scraps across the table. Bores into him. Stands. Manny looks up at her, covered in dark paper flecks.

"Should prob'ly have someone take a look at that eye, Manny. Looks like shit."

The two at the bar turn, bottles in hand, and watch her limp for the door. She nods to the kid cleaning a glass.

"Y'all can turn on the music now."

It's raining again. Buckets. The sky is low and dark with clouds made of wet soot. Night falls early. Sheet lightning flashes in the distance. Thunder, as if from a far away war.

Olivia loiters a minute or two. Just to make sure Manny doesn't get any ideas. She ventures a look back in the window. He's still in the booth, nursing his humiliation and the beer he'd bought for her. He is plotting his revenge for the next shift. He is thinking about how he will put her back in her place. She wonders what he will think when he learns that she already quit. That she had the last word at the stupid *Quicksilver* bar in San Angelo. Wonders what the realization will look like on his face.

Then she doesn't care.

She slogs around the building and up the alley to the back parking lot. The water is a torrent. It's like paddling up a river to a dark, square lake. At the far end of that lake, like a rotting log, is Jesús Batista's shit-brown Ford Falcon. Floating next to it is the newer, bigger black log of Manny Soto's pick-up.

She considers its dark, quiet shape, unmoved by the wind and the rain. Vandalism occurs to her. Four flat tires just to salt the wound. But where is a good knife when you need one?

She lets it go. Searches her pocket for the key. It's beneath her phone. She pulls out the phone. Goes back in for the key.

Like any sharp gust of wind, she feels it first in her hair, moving the wet tendrils at her shoulders, then traveling almost instantly up every strand to the nerve endings in her scalp.

Except that it is not a gust of wind. It's a hand.

Her head propels sideways, face smashing against the passenger window of Manny's truck. She experiences the concussion as a sound in the center of the skull. The detonation of a wave against rock. She is too stunned to cry out. Her ears ring and pain spits down her spine into her leg.

"Chu one cold bitch, O," says Manny, his face, dripping with rage, suddenly filling her vision.

She opens her mouth. To speak. To protest. Something. Anything. She is conscious of her phone no longer in her hand. Somewhere beneath her. She wants to bend down. Find it. Roll under the truck. Call for help.

But Manny hits her hard in the face before she can bend or speak, bursting her lower lip. She shouts at him. It is not a word. It is raw sound. A singular note of pain. She lashes out blindly with both hands but Manny connects with a shot to the gut that takes her breath and doubles her over.

She tries to struggle. As he pins her by the neck to the side of the truck. As he opens the door. As he shoves her into the opening. Pushes her. Punches her. Pushes her again until she is inside the cab, sliding along the smooth vinyl of what was once the back seat of some other rig. She tries. Struggles against him.

But her priority is oxygen. Manny's fist to her stomach seems to have taken it all away like a pin into the side of a balloon. She gasps wildly for breath, scrabbling backwards across the front seat towards the driver's door as he comes in after her, pinning her feet with his hands.

Time boils off its excess. Slows. Reduces. Thickens into a temporal syrup. She can see individual raindrops over his shoulder. Like they are floating, just barely heavier than air. She hears him breathe. Smells the alcohol.

But nothing about Manny Soto has slowed. He is the image in an old movie with missing frames. He is *there*, and *there*, and *there*, and then he is suddenly *here*, all in a single blink. He is too fast. He is in. Door closed. One hand wrapped around each of her wrists. One knee on her feet so that the metal in her leg screams up into her bones.

Her neck jams awkwardly up against the driver's side armrest, folding her head sideways toward the seat. She thrashes. Spits blood. Finds her voice. Screams. He punches her again in the face. Her left orbital is a tuning fork. The pain returns her to a stunned, syrupy oblivion. The agony in her head coalesces into a single blood-red strand of vibration. A sound. A melody.

Oh, I once had me a mother.

Manny rams his knee between her legs. Collects her wrists in one hand. Uses the other to go to work on her pants.

And good lord above, my mother could pray.

She feels a sharp yank. Two yanks.
"These fucking pants! Fuck! Jus' relax, O!"
Three.
It is easier, she thinks, to just let it happen. *Relax*, as he says. Who is she to escape time? Who is she to swim against the current of her own life?
Current? There is no current. No ocean even. Never has been. Not in her life.
She has not stopped screaming. There is no one to hear. The rain on the roof is like a rockslide. The windows are now opaque with steam. Manny looms over her, face twisted in hate and flashing amber with the anti-theft light of the stereo.
Four.
The crucifix on its gold chain swings clear of his open shirt. Back and forth. Back and forth. The metronome of memory. Her mind's eye finds Mother Mary. Up on the shelf. Same as always.
She searches for the Cactus People. They are assembled. Bearing witness. They will be there when it is over. Her family. Her family. The mom and the dad and the girl and the boy and the little dog with the pink flower ears.
"Shut da fuck up, O!"
Five.
The waistband of her jeans clears her hips.

And so if I die...

Manny, panting, cursing, tends to himself. The buckle. Button. Zipper.

And if my soul loses its way to heaven...
Ain't no one to blame... but me.

He must wriggle to free himself. It is all more than the sloshing in his brain will allow. His weight shifts. His grip on her wrists adjusts. Her left hand breaks free, sailing outward. She finds the steering wheel. Pushes against the horn because there is nothing else to do.
And because in that instant of liberty she has forgotten.
A wide, deep shaft of sound.
Loud and clear and bolting out into the dark like something set free.
Then she remembers. Manny does not have to remember. It's his truck.
For a microsecond everything in her stops. She can feel everything in Manny stop too. Their eyes, wild and crazed, meet in a kind of stunned wonder.
And then that moment is almost instantly gone.
She pumps the horn frantically, pulling strength from the clarion sound

cutting through the wind and the rain.

Again. Again. She keeps pushing the steering wheel, blaring the horn across south Texas. It is a voice in the dark. It is a kind of music. It is outside of her, this voice. And, at the same time, it is inside of her. A mother's voice.

Six.

The voice of all mothers.

The voice of *her* mother.

Seven.

Oh, I gots me a daughter…

Manny is able to pull her hand off the wheel momentarily, restoring the relative quiet, but the sound is back and blaring away in a second. He swings at her face with his fist. It glances off her cheek and hits the door. His balance betrays him, sending him tilting in towards the dashboard.

It is just enough. Like gravity is taking a breath.

Eight.

I gots a daughter and she can … siiing!

Her right leg frees itself, moving up along the seatback, and then sideways, hard and fast, testing the limits of metal pins holding together shattered bone. The heel of her boot breaks Manny's nose in a single thrust, the cartilage giving way in a wet popping sound like small twigs under foot on a damp forest floor. Ropes of blood spray the dashboard and streak through the steam on the windows.

Again. Again.

Manny howls, recoiling back against the window, pants half down, trying to fend off her boot with one hand and fumble for the glove box with the other.

Again. Again. Ripping open his cheek and fracturing the bone inside.

Manny opens the glove box. Light spills from the cavity revealing a cab smeared with red. He tries to look. Tries to reach. But he is forced to use both hands to protect his face. Eyes closed to the blood, he captures the flailing boot and wrenches it sideways.

It makes her scream.

But she can see it now. The thing he wants. Glinting in the tiny light. Sitting on top of orange rags and a half-empty bottle of whiskey.

Manny Soto is a lover of apples. Every shift he lectures the employees out behind the *Diamondback*, using their fifteen minutes to blow smoke up into the air. *Chu gon' die of the cancer. Wha' wrong witchu people. Apple a day! Apple a day! But chu see da skin? Got to peel da shit off, yo. All chemicals an' pesticides an' shit.*

And here it is. Glinting like the wink of fate. She knows suddenly that the universe, in all of it's supposed infinite complexity, has just boiled down to only a couple of possible outcomes.

She pulls hard against the steering wheel. Pulls her torso upright. Yanks her foot out of the boot in his hands. Launches herself across the seat. The sudden lack of resistance sends Manny back against the window, still clutching bloody leather boot. Olivia dives for the rectangular hole in the dashboard.

He recovers quickly, regaining his purchase and blindly flinging his right hand sideways into the glove box.

But the knife is no longer there. Olivia brings it down hard into his leg, burying the six-inch blade into the soft flesh above his kneecap. She twists. Once. Twice. Feels the kneecap loosen and then pop. Manny roars in pain, his sticky hands clutching at his leg and searching for the knife that is already gone again.

Olivia hurls herself at him, shoulder connecting with the center of his chest and flattening him against the door. The blade misses the eye, but cuts a clean line from the bridge of his pulpy nose down to his chin, crossing the flesh of each lip.

Neither of them are thinking about the scar. Or the limp. Not yet.

But they will.

She wants to take his pants. Cut them free of his legs if she has to. The apple knife is not nearly sharp enough. She settles for a hard knee to his naked groin. Manny bellows. Vomits onto the floor.

She reaches for the keys in his front pocket. He is afraid of dismemberment. His body recoils, curling up in a ball against the door. He wants to kick at her. His legs are pinned beneath his own weight.

She grabs her empty boot, opens the driver's side door and falls backwards out of the truck into the deluge. She rolls over into water. Tries to push herself up. Collapses.

She wants to stay submerged in this rectangular lake. The water is cool on her bruised and bloody face. She wants the rain to never stop. She wants to float, at last, on the shoulders of a rising tide, all the way to the sea. Bessie sings to the pain in her head.

If I should take a notion
To jump into the ocean

Notions in the oceans. Each breath takes in water. She coughs it out violently into the puddle. Nina Simone wafts up through the asphalt. More notions. More oceans. More about that daily struggle to stay alive, keeping your head above water just to be heard, just to communicate the truth about living in the world. The truth about dying in the world.

It is the notion that Manny Soto is not done that gets her to her feet. Concern that he will come out of the passenger door, pull up his pants, wipe away the blood. Jump into the ocean with her. Try again.

She hobbles, one boot on, one boot off, to the Falcon. She falls. Uses the bumper to pull herself back up. She climbs in the passenger side to keep the driver's side locked and between them. Slams the door. Starts the engine. Jams the knife into the hole where Dashboard Jesus used to be. She pulls the gearshift into reverse, crosses the dark flooded parking lot and threads the alley backwards until she emerges, bouncing and screeching, into the empty street.

She does not look back. She yanks the gearshift. Jams her throbbing leg down onto the gas pedal so hard the pain lights up her spine. Drives.

She is no more composed in an hour. She is *less* composed. She shakes so violently with emotion that she is forced to pull off the freeway on the way back to Corbin. Sheets of lightning turn the desert into an x-ray. She trundles forward until she finds a quiet road out into the scrub where she can, for the second time that night, scream and not be heard by another living soul.

She pulls onto the shoulder. Cuts the engine and the lights. Sits. Breathes. Hurts. She pulls the knife out of the dash. Climbs out of the car and up onto the hood. Leans back against the windshield. Spits blood for the thousandth time. Feels Manny's fingerprints on her neck. Her face feels hot and swollen enough to burst open like a seed of pomegranate.

She lies there. Breathes.

The torrents of rain are threads in the air, little filaments, woven into the starless black that covers her like a blanket. A breeze is up. Clouds scud and undulate above her as shadows. Every so often a bluish glow reveals itself in the east.

It makes her think of tomorrow's Moon Garden Festival. And of Sheldon who will be waiting at the Ferris wheel with a package *heavier than normal.* She thinks of *Papi's.* Thinks of Dashboard Jesus now somewhere on the side of the I-67. Thinks of the life that existed before tonight.

She thinks of all of it. Libby and Yvonne and Kevin and Sheldon *massage-massage* and a dresser full of money and a guy named Davis with the *fuck-all-day face* who came knocking at the front door and now none of that seems real.

Thinks of the blown-up blue Civic.

Thinks of Jesús Batista somewhere in Mexico without a car of his own.

She can't connect with any of it. Not even Libby. She can't go home. Can't deal with what will certainly be Libby's homicidal rage. Libby in prison will not help anything. When next she returns to Corbin's notorious house of ill repute, it will be to stuff everything she owns into a collection of bags and disappear.

Middle of the night. No conversation. Gone. She'll call Libby from the road.

Give her a story. Met a great guy. Off to Vegas. Something.

She thinks of her phone, somewhere in a puddle beneath Manny's truck. *Fuck*. How will she call? She'll think of something.

Sheldon is suddenly in her head. *Heavier than normal.* What about Sheldon? She can't just leave him hanging.

Then she knows. *Fuck it.* She knows.

Soon enough she is shaking as much from drenching cold as emotion.

She sits up. Wipes off the knife. Throws it as far out into the soggy scrub as she can. Then, in the other direction, Manny's keys.

She collapses back against the windshield. She thinks about screaming and screaming and screaming and not being heard by any living soul except Manny Soto. As if her voice had been made for only him. Tuned to a frequency only he and his kind can hear.

And the horn. She thinks of that too.

A truck without a voice.

Who need a fuckin' horn, O? Who need a fuckin' horn? It got shit for a stereo and it got shit for brakes an' ain' got no fucking horn.

She can still hear the voice of that horn in her head. The white vibration. A harmony unto itself. And then, the voices nestled *inside* of that voice, like filaments of starlight woven into the cold blanket of space.

Sobbing against the windshield, Olivia wonders who, or what, beyond the Ford Motor Company, had made the sound that saved her.

A breeze. A current. Something swimming. A graceful shape in the shadows. Displacement from something so large, so far away, so close by, it is unfathomable as anything more than a breathy, whispered lullaby in the dark.

Oh, I gots me a daughter. I gots me a daughter, and she can sing.

Chapter 70
Dallas and Etta

Had a dream last night, Pablo. It came from this thing, this little ball of evil I got growing up in my brain. Good dream, but a cruel dream.

It was you and me and Etta at the club. Sitting in one of those back booths. The ones you had in there before you had the fucked-up idea to rip them all out and cover that beautiful wood floor with that ice cream parlor checkerboard shit. Anyway, we were the only ones in the place except for Billie Holiday up on the stage in a midnight blue sparkly floor-length. And then Billie turned into Bessie who turned into Ma Rainey who turned into Big Mama and then Memphis Minnie and I don't know who all because it was a dream where everything was all swimmy, like you're looking at things under water. Every time I looked up at the stage it was someone else in the same dress holding that old-timey microphone.

And it was like we didn't care who it was up there singing. Can you even imagine not caring that any one of them gals was up in your joint, Pablo? You'd have had you a stroke! But in the dream we didn't give two hoots. We just kept drinking our drinks, paying no mind. Laughing at something I don't know. And little Etta was sitting on your lap in her little dress and her little shoes like some perfect little doll drinking her usual Shirley Temple except that it was a blue Shirley Temple and Etta was going on about there being a fish inside her glass pecking at the cherry.

And you know what else, Pablo? I was happy. For the first time in I don't know how long, I was happy. My four gold records did not make me that happy. Sold-out concert tours and the Tonight Show and the BMA Nomination all put together did not make me feel happy like I felt in that dream. Not *happy* happy. *Relaxed*-happy. At peace-happy. Fulfilled-happy. And when I woke up this morning I was so disappointed to be awake I cried for near an hour. Brain tumor gives me a dream just to take it away before it kills me. I'd like to pretend that I don't know what I've done to deserve such cruelty. But I can't pretend, Pablo. Well I can. But I won't. Not with you.

Anyway, it's damn near a miracle I'm sitting here at my table looking out at my sad little desert garden putting down these words. I'm drinking early today. No promises on how much of this will make any damn sense. But I've come this far. If you're still reading, then I'll keep writing.

You know Otis. Better than you wish you did, I suspect. Don't need to waste time on the shit you already know. Drugs aside, Otis was a good bass player for a white Mexican. Good band leader too. But also mean as a snake when he didn't get his way. He'd trade your ass out in the middle of a gig if you didn't have your shit together. We played this one club in Houston, *Kickaroo* or *Kickadoo*, something like that. Sammy Briggs started mixing up the rhythm on the drums in the middle of *Stagger Lee*. We blues'd the hell out of that song too. Lloyd Price must have stopped whatever he was doing in the world at that moment and looked around and thought to himself *'well what in the hell are they doing to my song?'* Anyway, Sammy fucked it all up (too much coke –he was playing *Stagger Lee* on a sprint to the finish while the rest of us were taking our own blue time) and Otis stopped in the middle of the song, took Sammy's sticks away, gave them to Charlie Gris who was our sound man and who also knew his way around the drums, kicked Sammy off the stage and then picked it up again from the beginning. That was the last time any of us shared a beat or a line of coke with Sammy Briggs.

Otis was a beater too. Never used his fist. Always with an open hand. He called it a slap as a way of making it sound better when he was ready to make up and he wanted you to get over it. *'Just a slap baby. No big thing. Come on now, I apologize.'* And maybe it was a slap but it was like being slapped with a frying pan. Funny thing was the drugs always mellowed Otis out. He was sweet and generous whenever he got high. He was fun to be with whenever he was whacked. It was when he tried to sober up and get serious about life that he got jealous and mean. So every one of us encouraged Ms. Mary Jane and Mr. Flake to join the band whenever they wanted to sit in. High as a kite, Otis became a good guy and never missed a beat. Can't say the same for Sammy.

So, Pablo, if you are still reading these words that I still may or may not send to you, I suspect you are asking yourself why I chose to marry a coked-up bass-player with frying pan hands. You always did ask good questions. I guess there are three reasons. One reason was scrawled on the big sandwich board we hauled around Texas in the back of Otis' car: *"Otis D's Hot Fivers featuring Rosetta Letti."* I saw Otis as my ticket up and out. When I was a girl, every Sunday afternoon down in that church basement Corny Roop told me I could sing. He said that one day I would be big. I saw Otis as the person to make that happen. And I was right too. Eventually, people started reading that sandwich board backwards: *"Rosetta Letti, featuring Otis D's Hot Fivers."* No need to get into all of that. I'm not writing a biography. Point is that I stayed with Otis because I knew he could do for me what I wanted.

That was the first reason. The second reason was the drugs. There was no separating the two. To need the one was to accept the other. Humiliating but true. There were other sources for the nose candy but like I say, Otis was generous when he was high. Everything seemed to work better when I was on something. Even just a little something. Everything was possible when I was high. And I was a better person too, just like Otis. Course I know now that being high just helps you forget who you really are for awhile. But the real world is one patient son of a bitch. It just waits until you come back from your Fantasy Land vacation. Then it beats you silly.

The third reason I married Otis, the main reason, is that, like it or not, I have always been my mother's daughter. Mama named me after Rosetta Tharp because Rosetta was singing *'Nobody's Fault But Mine'* on the radio when Mama's water broke in the kitchen. But she may as well have named me *'Maybelline Louisa Nogales II'* because I turned out to be a carbon copy of her on just about everything but especially the four M's: Men, Music, Monkeyin' Around, and Mothering. We both seemed to know how to pick men that would beat us and mistreat us. She picked Fat Louie and Earl Letti. And I picked Otis and a half-dozen others before I came to my senses and just said no to every man for anything more than a night or two. Mama liked to fuck every man that she could tempt and I did the same. Like I wrote a few pages back, I was looking sideways at men ever since Corny Roop opened my eyes.

At the time I was with Otis, I was also making it with most of the others in the group, including poor Sammy Briggs. Plenty of other men hung around the *Hot Fivers* too. Some because they owned the clubs (like you) or worked at the clubs and some because they liked the sound we made and some because they specifically liked the sound that I made (the sound I made singing; get your mind out of the gutter, Pablo). I sized them all up, one-by-one, and eventually I'd get that little buzzing inside. Like a little bee down in my pocket. Whenever Otis had his head turned, off we'd go to some dark, smoky corner of the world.

Course, Otis was no dummy. He'd save it up and then, sure enough, every so often out came those frying pan hands. Made it hard for me to complain when it came time for making up. I knew what I was doing. I was guilty as all hell.

If the universe made any damn sense, Pablo, I'd have had six-dozen children. All the monkeying I did in those years? If there is a God, he is surely shaking his head. Maybe Mama and Grandma Winnie were reaching out from the great beyond pinching and swatting away those little sperms. I spose it's a miracle that only one of them tadpoles got through. I knew it was not Otis' baby growing inside of me from the beginning. Can't tell you how I knew, exactly, because it wasn't like Otis ever went unsatisfied either. I just knew. Soon as I began to show, I'm sure everyone else wondered too, including Otis.

But the official assumption was that Otis and Rosetta were going to have a baby. When I *really* began to show, they changed my name from "featuring Rosetta Letti" to "featuring Big Rosetta" as a kind of joke but I think everyone sort of thought that would become my stage name forever. *Big Rosetta*. Like I was the next Big Mama Thornton. Only I was about half of Big Mama's size. I was a little bitty thing with a great big voice.

She was a beautiful baby, Pablo. Too beautiful to come from Otis. People believe what they want to believe though. They work hard at it. Etta was such a beautiful child that Otis spent the early years of her life believing that he made her. Convinced himself. *"She's got my eyes, don't you think, Rosetta? Like my mother's up there in Heaven looking at us through those big beautiful eyes."*

It is true that Etta did have exactly the same number of eyes as Otis and his mama. But any actual resemblance ended there. Not that there was any reason for me to correct Otis. I played along and so did everyone else. The only person I saw looking out of those eyes was my own Mama, telling me just how bad I had fucked up and just how much this beautiful child was going to suffer in the world.

The band never missed a beat. Etta showed up on a Monday and we were up on stage in Dallas that Saturday. Never had any problem with people wanting to look after that child. Don't know what I would have done had she come out ugly. Had she come out looking like Otis I'd have had to sing with her on my hip or just stop performing altogether until she was old enough to look out after herself.

But she didn't come out ugly, did she? People nearly lined up to play pretend mama in some back room of some beat up Texas club for a couple hours at a time. Don't need to tell you that I guess. You took more than a few turns playing mama.

I was in love with *Mother Blues* from the first note, Pablo. That was about a year before Etta was born. You booked us for two or three gigs and I was hooked. For me it was like singing inside the womb. That sound just wrapped me up like a blanket on a cold night. And Otis hated it just about as much as I loved it. He always liked more bounce in the sound. He liked to feel it come back to him like a slap in the face, which now that I write that down and look at it makes a certain kind of sense. His favorite club was *Blue Bar Billy's* in Houston, which had a concrete floor and hard paneled walls that bounced the music every which way like the room was rejecting every sound we made. But the walls in *Mother Blues* just soaked it all in. Like dry earth taking the rain.

You and me getting on so good did not help Otis like *Mother Blues* any better. I think he knew, Pablo. When he came back to the club that one night. I wouldn't have believed us either. Otis could be mean but he was not a dumb man. He had eyes. He knew it was time to go. Not that *The Hot Fivers* had much choice in the end. You were right to send us all packing. You laid down the law about drugs in the club from the very first night. Otis always did whatever he wanted to do anyway. He was asking for his own kind of trouble just like I was. He never intended to get crosswise with the law, but I also know that when the cops came beating on your door, Otis didn't much care. I always figured he was happy to see some payback come your way. Some pain. Otis thought like that. You were right to kick us all out but Otis was just as glad to go and never come back to *Mother Blues*.

Not me, though. That's when I first remember hating Otis and wondering what the hell I was doing with him.

But it took another six years with that man before I had my fill. We were living in Baton Rouge. He beat me silly one night and I lay in bed with my face swelling all up like a balloon and I looked over at him passed out next to me and I just knew that it was the last time I would ever see him. I pretended to think seriously about sticking a knife in his throat as he slept. But I'm not made of that kind of thing. I picked up Etta and as many clothes as I could and all of the money and drugs Otis had laying around and threw everything in Otis' car and left in the middle of the night. And I was right. Last time I ever saw him.

I drove to the last place he would ever look for me: Corbin, Texas. We all said we hated that place when we left because it was the last place professional musicians would want to live. Which was true. Nothing was ever happening in Corbin. So that's where I went. Sold Otis' car and got one of my own. Little beat up piece of shit with one headlight and springs popping up out of the back seat.

But it worked. I sold some of the drugs and used up the rest until they were gone. Got this little apartment about a mile south of *Broken River Road*. I ran out of Otis' money in a hurry. No more happy, floaty, you-can-do-anything feelings for me. I joined *Corbin First Baptist*, which led to odd jobs cleaning and babysitting for two or three women who knew deep down in their souls that they were better than me and that their ugly ass children were better than my beautiful child. I hated them all from the very first second. But their money was green and I was desperate.

A couple of months of that nonsense and I knew what I needed to do. I put Etta in my ratty Popeye car and we drove up to Austin to see you. To see *Mother Blues*. To get back up on that stage of yours. To crawl back into that womb. Hear that heartbeat close in my ears.

I had no reason to expect that you would take me back. And, if you recall, you didn't at first. But then you did. You've always been too soft for your own good, Pablo. I know it was more pity than anything. But your soft side has always been to my benefit so I'm grateful. And I'm glad we did not start back up. Not that I didn't want to. I surely did. But I'm glad you didn't want to, Pablo. I'm glad that when I came back it was always about the music. I wanted a man, but I sure didn't need one. Not even a man like you. I needed to sing. I needed to find myself without Otis and *The Hot Fivers* and the drugs. I needed to dig until I found water.

You gave me that opportunity, Pablo. I owe just about everything I am to what you did for me that summer. People that read *Billboard Magazine* think I owe it all to Hammy Lewis. Hammy knew how to squeeze ten dollars out of a penny and he knew just about every person that owned a soundboard and he knew how to pack any venue on both sides of the Atlantic. But all that shit is just business, Pablo. The person inside of Rosetta Letti, the person that the world knows as *Dallas Letti Blue*, was born in your club, Pablo. She was born in *Mother Blues*. There are no words in this pen or in the bottom of this bottle of hooch in front of me to thank you enough. I just don't know how to do that.

That summer is still like a kind of magic to me. Like a little dream. Like a smell from a kitchen when you're hungry. Driving back to Corbin every night, Etta's head on my leg, after pumping three sets of pure blues through that club. Richie on the upright. Jay on the Stratocaster. Little Stu on the drums. Boys could play. I've certainly worked with better musicians in my day, but none with so much heart. I'd drive through the dark, dead tired, warm air blowing through the window carrying away the sweat, and I'd replay the whole night, song for song, in my head. Note for note. Etta and I would sing together just to keep me awake. And just about every night she'd look up at me and ask why couldn't Papi be her daddy. Like the answer might change one night to the next.

All these years and all the young people still calling you Papi. I think because you're a good man and they all want you to be their daddy. So they named you that. *Papi.* And Etta was the first to do that. Even before your own children. I spose that's only fair though.

After all, Pablo, you were the one who started calling her *Etta*.

Chapter 71

Desmond P. Vaughn. Managing Editor of the once mediocre and now nearly comatose *Chachalaca Gazette*. Divorced. Two kids sporting college acronyms; one fresh into Texas A&M, the other a sophomore at SMU. Thinning, dirty white hair. Bad sciatica. Failing eyes. Waiting for the rattle in his chest to ripen into a diagnosis. Responsible for solving a thousand unsolvable problems.

Day after impossible day.

And he can do that. Somehow, every day, he manages to make the impossible possible. Not with a smile on his face. Not without a residual desolation setting in earlier and earlier each day of the week that only partly resets itself over the weekend.

But he does it. Desmond holds everything together.

So it should not be so much to ask. All he wants is a drink of water.

Might have predicted it would not be so easy. Even the easiest of things are never as easy as they should be. There is always something –or *someone* –to complicate what should have been very simple.

"You look like shit, Boss," says Sylvia Bloom. She pulls the telephone headset down around her neck with a finger. "You really do."

She has started calling him *boss*. Out of the blue. *Boss*, this. *Boss*, that. Sure thing, *Boss*. Sometimes *Bossman*. Sometimes even *Hoss*. But mostly, *Boss*. He guesses she heard someone on television say it. Some beautiful, hip shithead with great hair. Someone calculatedly free of the responsibilities of leadership and with enough time her hands to mock the pecking order with insincere deference.

So now Sylvia calls him *Boss*. She calls everyone *Boss*. But in Desmond's case it just happens to be true.

"That's because I *feel* like shit, Sylvia."

"You sick or something?"

"No, I'm hung over or something." He points to her neck, meaning the headset, meaning the phone, meaning the phone call, meaning the message. "Can't this wait?"

"Sorry. Cal said he's only going to be there another ten minutes."

"Well, shit. Okay. Hey, do you have any water?"

"Water? Like, *water*-water?" Sylvia looks at him like he has asked if she can tap a vein for a glass of maple syrup. "I've got an energy drink back at my desk. Want an energy drink, Boss?"

"No I don't want an energy drink," says Desmond. "Let's get this over with. Is he at his office?"

"No, he's at that poker tournament thing he does in Vegas. Here's the number." She hands him a ripped square of paper. He takes it. Heads for the conference room. Grumbles.

"Gambling away the rest of our fuckin' money." He stops. Turns and looks back at Sylvia. "I didn't say that."

She smiles. "Say what, Boss?"

He closes the door. Sits heavily at the conference table. Pulls the phone closer. Dials.

His head is a munitions dump. The scotch last night had seemed like such a good idea at the time. It *was* a good idea at the time. Just him, Johnnie Walker, the Marlboro Man, and a stack of old jazz vinyl. *Dizzy. Bird. Miles.* Best mood in a long time.

But the fucking headache. He was not a *hair-of-the-dog* guy. Coffee never did the trick either. Aspirin was good if he had any, which he never did. Mostly he just needed water. Lots of it.

He had overslept, of course. Nearly missed his nine o'clock with the people from Coleman Seed & Mill about a deal to persuade them not to pull their advertising. By the time they left, CS&M had cut their advertising budget in half and Desmond's tongue was sticking to the insides of his mouth like a dead sea cucumber washed up on a beach. He felt like he was swallowing sand.

Water. He needed water.

Bolting from the house, he had been sure that he still had a bottle or two in the bottom drawer of his desk. He was wrong.

Then he was hopeful that there might be a bottle or two in the office fridge that nobody would miss. Wrong.

No way he was drinking from the tap. It smelled of sulfur, tasted of metal and had a slight beige color.

The two coolers in the office had been bone dry for months. One of a thousand ways that the *Chacha* had cut costs to keep buying ink and paper.

The phone rings in his ear. He wonders if drinking newspaper ink would cure a hangover.

"It's about goddamned time."

"Sorry Cal. Things are crazy here today."

"Well, I'm callin' about the crazy, Dez, so maybe this is good timing. I've got about twenty minutes before they deal the first hand of the day and it'll take me five to get down to the floor. So I'm gonna talk and you're gonna listen."

"Okay."

"Got a call from Austin this morning. Governor's office has been gettin' calls from London. Company by the name of Quinto or Quicko or some such is the parent company of the folks that are workin' the Corbin River Walk deal. Anyway, the Quincko people, or whatever in the hell they're called, are all worked up about calls they been gettin' from our people. Somethin' about land purchases in Corbin and who owns what and who's gettin' paid for what and who's dead and who's not dead. With all due respect for the First Amendment, the Governor's office wanted to politely remind us of just how much construction money the Corbin River Walk project is going to pump up the ass of the South Texas economy over the next decade. Then I had to listen to a goddamned lecture on retail, dining and tourism. They suggested that a hatchet job on the River Walk project would not be a good thing for South Texas or for our little newspaper. Get on board or get left behind was basically the message."

"A hatchet... Cal..."

"Then I... just wait a goddamned minute. Then I got a call from Jaime Sanchez over at Sanchez Construction. Jaime's daddy and I go way back to when Carlos was paintin' houses for a livin'. And Jaime wants to know why Laurie Weaver is out beatin' his door down to ask questions about his company's property holdings. Wants to know whether he needs to lawyer up and prepare for whatever negative publicity the paper's got in store for his business."

"Cal, look..."

"Wait, Dez. Then I got a call from some aide workin' for our delegation in Washington. And that little piss-ant wanted to know why CBS News is submitting FOIA requests to the Army Corps of Engineers and the Federal Highway Administration, *in the name of the Chachalaca Gazette,* lookin' for property transfer records, lookin' for right of way agreements, lookin' for correspondence with the Governor's office and God knows what else. Apparently CBS News doesn't think it needs to answer to a congressman from the great state of Texas and so the good congressman figures he'll have better luck shaking down a shitty little rag like ours, 'specially seein' as how every so often we need him for information or a goddamned quote."

"What'd you tell him?"

"I told him that he must have his facts wrong because the *Chacha* does *not* submit FOIA requests, because the *Chacha* is *not,* I repeat, is *not,* engaging in any sort of investigative journalism. See, the *Chacha* walks around and picks up news layin' around in plain sight and we write about it. Maybe take a picture of it before we toss it back into the dirt. *Chacha* don't dig. *Chacha* don't own so much as a shovel or a goddamned spade. I told him that we would be in immediate contact with CBS News and advise them that somehow the autocorrect on their fancy east coast computers is erroneously inserting the words *Chachalaca Gazette* into their FOIA requests. I told him I don't know anything about CBS and that if the *Chacha* was involved in any way, then the *Chacha* would be goddamned *uninvolved* right quick."

"Cal? Can I just say something?"

"No. You may not. I just got the signal from the floor and I'm hanging up, but let me leave you with this, Dez. I know we got a deal, you and me. I'm not to stick my nose into content. You play the content side of the field and I play the money side. But make no fuckin' mistake, Desmond: this is all about the money. I am not payin' for investigative journalism. And I am not payin' for any kind of reporting that will piss off every South Texas advertiser that has ever given us a dollar or that gets our asses kicked from Austin to Washington D.C. and back again. The suits and ties want this river walk thing to succeed. *Badly.* But so do all of those nut farmers and herders and people with South Texas dirt under their fingernails. Hell, *I* want it to succeed. We all do. The only people who don't want this project to go through are those environmentalists trying to protect their precious fish, that… that…"

"Pecos Bluntnose Shiner."

"What? What's that fuckin' thing called? Little…"

"Pecos Bluntnose Shiner."

"Little tiny fucker. What's it called?"

"Pecos. Blunt. Nose. Shiner."

"Yeah, that's the one. My newspaper is not gonna' be on the side of those hippie fuckers. And you can take that to the bank because I *am* the bank, Dez. I'm the goddamned bank. I don't pay you people to investigate. I pay you to keep your dick in your pants and report the news. So, I don't know what your people have cookin' over there, but I want you to turn off the fuckin' stove and uninvite CBS for dinner. Hear me?"

"I hear you."

"Good. And you tell Laurie Weaver that I personally want her to cover the beauty pageant at the Moon Garden Festival tomorrow. I want half a page and I want a full color shot of the winner. And don't give me your speech about content. This is still Texas and the *Chacha* is still a Texas rag and nothin' sells newspapers in Texas like a beauty contest. So this is a money decision, not a content decision. Laurie's gonna hate it like poison, but make her do it anyway. It'll be good for her."

"…"

"Dez? You there?"

"Yeah. Got it, Boss."

It is another ten minutes before he leaves the conference room. He pretends to be on the phone. Silent receiver to his ear. Just so people passing by the conference room window will leave him alone.

It's the need for water that gets him up and out into the hallway. Desmond stands, hands in his pockets, looking across the bullpen. He fixes on Laurie Weaver talking on the phone. Waits for her to look up. Finally she does. He jerks his head toward the front door. Walks.

It's raining sideways. He's drenched before he is halfway across the parking lot. His head hurts too much to run. He keeps a normal pace. Opens his mouth. Swallows. Opens his mouth. Swallows. Drinks in as much irony as he can catch.

It's another five minutes before Laurie steps outside looking for him, hands to the heavens. He flashes his lights. She comes running.

"Jesus, Dez." She slams the car door, panting, slicking water from her face. She smells of perfume and cigarettes. "What in the fuck, mister?"

"I'm thirsty," he says. "I need some water."

"You know that it comes in bottles, right? I mean you don't have to wait 'til it rains."

"Funny." He starts the car. Drives.

"Why am I here, Dez?"

He sends the wipers into a slow, rhythmic sweep.

"Just got off the phone with Cal."

He looks at her sideways. Turns onto Prospector Road. It takes her a second.

"Oh, goddamnit, Dez." She slaps his dashboard. "Don't fucking do this to me."

"He's hot, Laurie. Really hot. You have to shut it down."

"When?"

"Yesterday."

"Why?"

"Pressure."

"Pressure from where?"

"Everywhere. Governor's office. Washington. Contractors."

He lets it sit. The sound of the rain and the wipers fill the small space within their tiny bubble. Laurie finally speaks, as if to herself.

"Goddamnit Dez."

"I know. You already made that really excellent point. But that's the deal."

She crosses her arms like a child. Glowers through the steam thickening over her window.

"But… But we're right on the *verge*. This thing is just starting to break open."

"No, it's just starting to break *up*. There's a very big difference."

"We've got some serious leads, Dez. Don't you want to know what's happening?"

He turns on to I-67. Accelerates.

"No. No I don't. I want to drive to *Piggy's Market*. Buy six gallons of water. Drink every last drop. And then I want to go back and finish my fight with Billy and Everett over the school board election scandal, and…"

She turns on him, almost spitting.

"*Scandal?* You call that a scandal? A few ounces of pot? So maybe it takes a joint or two to put up with those little snot-nosed shits. If Willie Nelson ran for school board you think half the people in this county wouldn't vote for him?"

"Laurie."

"If you want a scandal, I've got the biggest fuckin' scandal you've…"

"Laurie. Damn it. Don't make this a thing. I don't have the energy. Let it go."

He pulls off the I-67 into the parking lot of *Piggy's Market*. Cuts the engine, stopping the wipers at forty-five degrees. He looks at her, pulling rank.

"You're gonna call Rick Stoddard when we get back and tell him we're out. Give him all of your notes. I don't care about that. But the *Chacha* is out of this."

Laurie beats the dash with her fist.

"Fuck! Fuck, fuck, fuck."

"Please don't take it out on my car." He points at the squat brick edifice in front of them. "You want anything? Cigarettes?"

"How about a *real* fucking newspaper? I'll take one of those."

"Suit yourself." He reaches for the handle. Laurie grabs his shoulder.

"What I want, *Desmond*, is to tell you where Rick and I are on this thing. That's all I'm asking. If you're going to kill it, at least know what you're killing. Give it a proper fuckin' burial."

They are silent for awhile. Desmond lets go of the handle. Watches the rain. Laurie watches him. Waits.

"Two minutes. And then I'm gonna get out of this car, swim over to that building, buy some water and come back. And when I come back, Laurie, so help me God, I am not talkin' about it again. This is a business. Yeah, it's a newspaper, but it's a goddamned business. Money comes in, newsprint goes out. Understand?"

Laurie closes her eyes. Nods.

"Okay then. Let's give this thing a proper burial."

It is Laurie's turn to look out at the rain. She squares herself to him. Speaks.

"Got a call. Two days ago. Guy named Chris Dawson. Says he used to work for the Corbin Development Corporation. They fired him three days ago. Want to know why?"

"You wanna use up your two minutes with a guessing game?"

"Because he started asking questions about property transfers. Dawson's job had something to do with right-of-way and easement acquisition. He said things were not adding up. The paperwork he got from Quinco was not matching the county records and so he raised the question. Next day he was fired. They told him it was an economic layoff but he doesn't believe it. He's serving out his two-week notice."

"Okay."

"Dawson says that everyone in his office knows I've been calling. They joke about putting me off; forwarding me to London and back again. *Ha, ha, ha.* So when they canned Chris Dawson, I was the first person he thought to call. Says he had no idea why I was calling only that if his boss did not want to give me an interview, maybe he did. He's in town now. Over at the Super 8. We're meeting in a couple of hours."

"Hell you are, Laurie."

"Dez…"

"No, Laurie."

"Will you just let me finish?"

Desmond rubs his eyes. Lays his head back. Smiles.

"You go right on ahead and finish, darlin'."

"Dawson smuggled out some property records. He wants to compare them with what I've got."

"So you told him what we have?"

"Well, yeah, a little. Just enough to get something out of him. Gotta give somethin' to get somethin'. Guess it's been awhile since you've been on a date, huh?"

"Funny."

"Point is, he's offering us inside information. Only he's real skittish because he's travelin' with other people from the CDC. They all came in on the company dime to support the festival. So I'm supposed to swing by like an old friend, pickin' him up for dinner so we can go someplace else."

She waits. Looks for some change in his expression. Desmond responds to the silence.

"So. That about it?"

"No." Laurie tucks her hair behind her ears. "So Rick calls me last night at home. He's been looking into Quinco. No one at Quinco or CDC returns his calls either. Big fuckin' surprise. So he just gets in a taxi. Finds the building. Rides up the elevator thirty floors and there it is: *Quinco International.* Corner suite."

"And?"

"No one home. Locked up. Lights off. Not even a receptionist. No papers. No blinking phone lights. No signs of business."

"So?"

"One magazine in the waiting room. *The Economist.* Drawing of the Eiffel Tower with a cheeseburger on top."

"So?"

"So it's over a year old."

"What, the magazine?"

"Yeah."

"So?"

"You don't find that odd?"

"I find it odd that you could think for one second that Rick Stoddard reads *The Economist.*"

"He doesn't. He had a hunch and like a real fuckin' journalist he spent two minutes looking it up. Stop being an ass. Don't you find it odd that no one is home at Quinco International?

"They're all on a retreat to the London office. Or Hamburg." He points. "Or they're all just up the road here over at the Super 8 for the Moon Garden Festival."

"Oh come on, Dez. Be serious."

"Okay, so they're not all in Corbin, but … but… *so what* Laurie? Why should I care if Quinco employees come to work?"

"Rick called the CBS bureau in London. Asked a favor. They went over and checked out the London office. Same story. The office is there. But empty."

Desmond is silent. Bites his lip. Tries to swallow. Laurie keeps at it.

"I'm just saying it's weird for such a big international corporation –projects all over the world –offices in three countries –to be closed up tight as a drum on a Wednesday afternoon."

She waits a beat. Two. Keeps pushing.

"And that brochure? About the Corbin River Walk? I found my old copy beneath six tons of shit on my desk. It lists all of Quinco's major projects so I started looking 'em up."

"And?"

"I can't confirm Quinco's name."

"What do you mean?"

"I mean I can't find the word *Quinco.*"

"On any of them?"

"Well, I just started, Dez. I've only looked into two of 'em. Yeah, okay, roll your eyes, but still. Supposedly Quinco was the company behind the big canal dig in Brazil? Huge project? Right? I can't find Quinco's fingerprints anywhere."

"It works through national subsidiaries," says Desmond. "You've got to know the names of the subs."

"Right. And yet the name of *Quinco International* is sure as hell all over the Corbin, Texas brochures."

"Eh. You're reaching."

"And you know who *was* involved in the Brazil canal project?"

"I have no..."

"Quince International. *Quince*. Q.U.I.N.C.E. Only in a cursive logo, with a great big *International* comin' up from behind? I gotta tell ya' Dez, *Quince* and *Quinco* look a lot alike for someone not lookin' very closely. Or seein' what they want to see."

"What was the other project you looked at?"

"Andalusia Spain. Some bridge work across the Nagratín Reservoir. Same thing. I can't find Quinco, but I can sure find Quince."

"Hmm."

"Right?"

"Okay. Let's say I give you a little bit of rope there. So you think they're paying some seriously expensive rent to be empty? Why would they do that?"

Laurie hesitates. Looks away and back.

She's getting to it. Steps closer to the edge.

Jumps.

"What if it's a front?" she asks.

"A front. A front for what?"

"The Quinco International New York offices are leased to a subsidiary called BLV Enterprises, Inc. BLV Enterprises is a Delaware corporation. The registered agent for BLV Enterprises is a Connecticut law firm named *Jones & Block*. Small, ten-attorney outfit that does mostly personal injury and criminal defense."

"Rick dug all of this up, I s'pose?"

"See what a real budget gets you?"

"Not much so far." He says the words, doing his best to hold the line. But he can tell Laurie doesn't believe him. He doesn't believe him either.

"So Rick has a few conversations with the Connecticut Bar Association which points him to some disciplinary rulings. Turns out that the *Block* in *Jones & Block* is actually a palatably Americanized name for Sergei R. Blokovich. Second generation. Parents from Belarus. About ten years ago, Mr. Blokovich got himself slapped with a one-year suspended license for withholding subpoenaed evidence. The case that bought him the suspension was the *State of Connecticut vs. Dudnik*. Blokovich was defending a guy named Vasily Dudnik, a Russian businessman with a long resume. Assaults. B & E. Fraud. He's a thug. Guy's a fuckin' gangster."

"Okay, so..."

"Blokovich withholding evidence was enough to fuck up the state charge, but the feds then stepped in and prosecuted Dudnik for racketeering. Now he's stuck doing twelve years in a cell in Terra Haute."

"So you're trying to tell me... that Quinco International, with offices in New

York, London and Hamberg, is a actually a front for the Russian mob."

Laurie laughs.

"It sounds so ridiculous the way you say it."

"That's because it *is* ridiculous."

"Not if those are basically pretend offices. Not if they are just there for show and to staff up every so often to take meetings for starry-eyed investors. Rick doesn't think it's ridiculous. He thinks…"

"Fuck Rick Stoddard, Laurie. Oh, I forgot, you already have. So then tell him to stop submitting FOIA requests to government agencies in our name."

Laurie looks out at a couple of ranchers slogging through the water to the front door of *Piggy's*.

"Shit," she says. "I told him not to do that. He wanted to get some information before going back to CBS News with a pitch. You have to make a case to get the green light and some spending money. Rick was trying to stay under their radar until he was ready I guess."

"Great. Well the *Chachalaca Gazette* isn't under the radar. We've got lights and sirens, Laurie. You can see us from fuckin' space on this thing. Cal is so fuckin' mad…"

"Okay, okay. That was a fuck up. I'll own that. I should'a been more emphatic with Rick. But it's only 'cause he's so into this story. He really thinks we're onto something here. I mean, why would a multi-national development corporation, with enough money for primo office space in downtown Manhattan, and London, and presumably Hamberg too, why would they be in business with a shitty, teeny-tiny criminal defense firm in Connecticut?"

Silence. Her eyes push at him. She keeps at it.

"Look, I'm not saying that any of this answers any questions or that it proves one single fuckin' thing. It absolutely doesn't. But doesn't it make you want to ask some more questions? Maybe a *lot* more? Isn't that what we're supposed to be doing, Dez?"

Silence. Push. Push.

"And don't say the word *budget* or *money* or *business*. I don't want to hear any of that shit from you, Dez. Or fuckin' Cal Aronson. He's an owner, but you're the fuckin' editor, Dez. I mean *really*. What the fuck are we doin' here?"

Desmond is quiet. The wind comes in sopping-wet gusts that broadside the car, strong enough to shake it. Like they are parked on a beach at high tide.

"It's a big stretch, Laurie."

"Maybe. Yeah. Maybe it's a big stretch."

They are both quiet as the airborne ocean steadily returns to earth. She has one more push left.

"You want to know what that Connecticut state charge was all about? The one that was the first nail in the coffin for Vasily Dudnik? The one that got

Blokovich, Esquire suspended for a year?"

Desmond lolls his head sideways on the seat. Looks at Laurie. She clears her throat. Answers her own question.

"Using a real estate agency and two construction companies to falsify deeds to undeveloped Middlebury and Colchester lakefront properties." Pause. "Then *sellin'* those properties over and over and over again. Properties Blokovich and his companies never owned in the first place."

Air wheezes out of him slowly as if from a slit tire.

"Goddamnit Laurie."

"I know Dez. I know."

"I'm gonna be out of job. You know that, right?"

"We both will. But look. The way I figure it? The *Chacha's* days are numbered. We're about to be out of a job anyway. If I'm wrong about all of this? We're looking for work six months early. Maybe a year. And if I'm right –if *we're* right, Dez –about all of this? Well then this is fuckin' huge. This is national. This is international. This is award-winning investigative journalism. And the *Chacha's* gonna be front and center. *You and I* will be front and center. No way Cal cuts us loose then, but who the fuck cares? You'll be able to get a job anywhere you want."

"A little ahead of yourself, don'tcha think?"

"Yeah. But it's all gotta start somewhere, Dez. And I say it starts here. So let's go out swingin' for the fuckin' fences."

He takes her in. All of her. Wet auburn hair. Plain face. Smoker's mouth. Chipped nails. Protrudent wrist bones. Same old, no-nonsense, last-call loner Laurie.

Except her eyes. They are blue like the sea, wet and wild and deep. Ferocious. Real. He has never seen them before. Not ever.

"What do you want, Laurie?"

"I want to meet with this Chris Dawson guy. Like," she looks at her watch, "in two hours. I want to compare the property information we have with the property information he has. I want to look at all of the projects Quinco International has supposedly been involved with. I want to call Rick Stoddard as soon as we get back to the office. I'll tell him to take the *Chacha's* name off of all the future FOIA requests. I'll tell him to use my name. But I want to give Rick everything we have, right now, so that getting shit-canned by Cal or shut down by the state of Texas doesn't mean the end of the story. Something happens on our end, he and CBS can still run with it. And…"

She waits until he is looking.

"And?"

"And if I get fired? And if CBS reaches out to me so that I can keep working this story? I'm gone in a heartbeat. I'll fuckin' freelance. Just want you to know that, Dez. Nothing personal, but I'll jump."

Desmond sighs. Nods. "What else?"

"I want to take enough time off of work to drive to Terra Haute, Indiana and interview Vasily Dudnik in prison. See if I can connect him with anyone associated with Quinco or the CDC."

"What else?"

"I want to have a stiff drink and then sit down with the crazy pecan prostitute who started this whole thing –Libby Holder –and find out everything she knows. I want to go out to Houston and sit out on Sheldon Davis' front lawn until he agrees to tell me what he knows. Been callin' that fucker all afternoon and I'm gonna keep callin'. You ask me what I want? I want to dig, Dez. It's gonna take money that Cal does not have to give you. But I'm a goddamned reporter and I want to dig."

A fresh squall consumes the car, rocking it like a rowboat. Desmond closes his eyes. Breathes.

"Talk to Chris Dawson. Take him someplace you won't be seen. The longer we can keep the shit from hitting the fan, the better off we'll be. Last thing we want is Quinco suing for an injunction to keep us from using stolen documents. Try to keep Rick on a short leash. I don't want him doing anything we don't know about in advance. Keep all of this out of the newsroom. I don't want any gossip. People ask? Your aunt is sick; she lives in Terra Haute. Report everything back to me. I mean fuckin' everything, Laurie. If you want to dig, then I want to look at every shovelful."

"Got it."

"And we write this together, Laurie. If anything comes of it, then it's a series and we write the whole thing together. If CBS is going to send out a life raft, then there's room for two."

"Absolutely. So what are you gonna do about Cal?"

It is a question deserving a long, soggy silence.

"Well, I guess what I'm gonna do is go out to the festival tomorrow. Take in the beauty pageant. In the goddamned rain. Take a few pictures of the first ever Corbin River Walk Queen. Write it up for Sunday. And I'm gonna put your name on the story."

"What?"

Desmond opens the door. Climbs out into the deluge. Leans back in, rain streaming from his head.

"But first, I'm gonna get a goddamned drink of water."

Chapter 72

Elvis is calling. Again.

The phone still sits where he'd thrown it. Across the ark, half-buried in a swale of dust. The ricochet had not been fatal. It bleats out through the dark like something lost and abandoned in the night.

Between each trill comes the sound of dripping. Up on the deck, accumulated pools have found a thousand different ways to drain in through the old wood. The rain had stopped an hour or more ago. But the water is still coming in.

Water works that way.

It *all* works that way. Everything. Water. Light. Darkness. Time. It all finds its way in to the same place.

Memory is a fiction. A narrative trick to keep the past and the future from becoming a single thing we cannot comprehend. We complicate existence. Break everything into tiny pieces. Everything. Even time. Past. Present. Future. It makes us feel better, pretending to understand. But all of those artificial bits are nothing but poorly made rafts –gnarled logs of convenient reason bound by fear and ruddered by superstition –tossed in a storm of stars. They all come apart in the end.

We are porous, temporary vessels. There is no roof. No hull. Nothing is untouched. Nothing protected. Not for long. It's all coming in. It's supposed to. We are made to be dissolved. Cubes of sugar sweetening the cosmic brew.

So now it's slowly raining on the inside. Because there's no difference.

The trilling sound stops. Just the dripping now. And the sound of the wind blowing through the dark.

Davis finishes the bottle. Hurls it through the black air so he can hear it smash against the inside of the hull. But there is no smash. Only a dull *thudding* sound returns. He opens another. Drinks.

His hands are raw. He knows they hurt, but it is not a pain he can feel. He will feel it tomorrow. For now they just feel sticky and itch.

And they smell like blood.

He had actually called Elvis. Not because he wanted to but because Buddy Lincoln had made him promise he would. So he did, as he walked through the *Lick-n-Tipple* grabbing a tall amber bottle at random and a six-pack, pressing his phone to his ear. The fourth ring was followed by Elvis' voice.

"Yeah, this is Elvis Broussard. If you're sellin' something, I don't want any. If you want money, I don't have any. If you want me to vote for your guy, that just makes me want to vote for the other guy. And if you want me to worship your god, then mind your own business. Otherwise, I'll call you back."

He had put the booze on the counter next to the ice cream machine and the stack of papery yellow cones. The bald, mustachioed man behind the counter had looked over his glasses and pointed to the sign: *Be courteous. Please terminate all cell phone calls before transaction. Thank you.*

So he had hung up. And that was that.

He had not known where else to go. Not back to *Pepita's*, where he would have had to contend with Eladio and Hector. Not home, where he would have had to contend with an unsent letter to his father on the kitchen counter. Not to the church to wait in the basement for a meeting that would do no good.

So he rode around in the rain for awhile, bottles clanking in the seat beneath him. Told himself that as long as he was riding, he wasn't drinking.

He had been there before, of course. Too many times. Holding back that ocean with two hands. He'd known how it would end. Only a matter of time.

But still. He had tried to stay on the bike as long as possible. Translating the roar beneath him as a scream to keep everything at bay.

Not just the voice of his father. Everything. Because every single thing was connected to every single other thing. Each drop was part of the same ocean. It's all connected. It's all one fucking thing.

So that had been his fight on the back of the Harley: keep out absolutely everything. Loud. Fast. No thought to direction. He rode anywhere and everywhere, seemingly to no place in particular.

Until the roaring under him became a roaring around him, shaping itself into a roaring inside of him. A voice. A command.

Here.

Now.

Turn.

He had obeyed. Turned. And the Harley had delivered him to the one place he particularly needed to be.

He had not parked the bike at the end of Dallas Letti's stone fence. Not this time. Not as usual. He had throttled up and past the garden and kept riding up into the desert, through the rain and the failing light, until he had stopped at the corner of the foundation that defined the broken church.

He had dismounted. Grabbed Mr. Jim Beam by the throat and kicked his way through the rubble of wood and glass and metal into what had once been a living room made into a place of worship. A place where metal chairs had once been unfolded in front of a makeshift pulpit. A place where people sang and nodded their heads and pretended to know things they didn't know and felt better for pretending. Paddling their little rafts across the sea.

Consumption was single-minded. A kind of flailing to keep his head above the waves. But every swallow seemed to tune in the voices with increasing clarity. At first they came at him as brilliant bits of static. Assemblages of imagined sound.

What is the thing you love most about this world, Elizabeth?

You can hate me if you want. I can't stop that.

By the time the bottle was half gone, they were echoes from someplace far beneath him. Shifting. Warping. Like fat blades of seaweed.

This is your father we're talking about, man. He's reaching out. If you ask me? You need to forget about the past. Help him make this right.

I am trying to cut myself free... live a good life... I cannot do that unless you allow me to be a better man.

Eventually the sun had fully bled out, absorbed into the dirty cotton gauze wadded up over El Paso, the rest dripping into memory. By then, the bottle was no longer a bottle, shattered to pieces against a sideways oven. The voices in his head were bubbles up from the deep, bursting into soggy consciousness.

You have to let all of it go, Davis. You need to cut us all loose. Me. Your mother. Abby Palmer, too. All of us. You have to save yourself. You have to let it all go.

Davis is the thing I love most in the world. I love my little boy.

He had righted himself. He stood by clawing up what was left of the old kitchen wall. Waited. Swayed in the dark until he had some semblance of balance.

And then Davis Payne, abandoned son of Elizabeth and Conrad, had torn into the temple ruins with his bare hands. Like it was an enemy, sleeping and unawares. Like this was homicide.

Roaring. Wailing. The darkening sky had ruptured, breaking open to release an airborne sea as he lashed at the remnant walls. Smashed blocks of cinder into broken fragments. Grabbed wildly at piles of debris, hurtling bits and pieces of human shelter into empty space, only to hear them reassemble noisily into other piles.

Every puncture and laceration of his skin had introduced itself as a snakebite from a nest of serpents he imagined undulating beneath every plank. He had not cared. He had plunged his hands endlessly into the rubble. Screaming, Hurling. Welcoming the pain. Each bite a kind of perverse consolation.

Long after he had finished the bottle, the bourbon was still somehow finding its way inside. Filling him up in a slow drip. Eventually, the pain in his hands had ebbed away into a dull ache, the way sound slows and fattens and blurs when submerged.

He had started attacking another pile. Hurling planks. Metal. Bits of glass. He had lifted a large sheet of wood. Dark. Smooth, round corners. Pushed it up. Tipped it over into a crash of noise.

There were broken teeth beneath it. Like he'd found the mouth of the thing. A lot of teeth. Slim white wooden rectangles buried in a nest of silver snakes. Then the snakes had resolved as a tangle of metal wire.

A piano. A fucking piano.

The realization had made him laugh. A raw and inexplicable sound. He had squatted, elbows to knees, panting. Wiped the sweat from his face. That's when he had smelled his own blood.

Davis finishes the beer. Throws the bottle. It hits something over there. Maybe the phone that keeps dry the worried voices of Elvis Broussard and Buddy Lincoln.

Voices. Fucking voices.

He hears his mother's voice. It comes from the letter in his back pocket. The latest that he has been carrying around for days. He wants to pull it out. Read it yet again. Feel her close. But he is too drunk to coordinate the effort.

No need. He has read it enough to make the paper irrelevant.

I barely sleep anymore, Lula. Sleep terrifies me. I have so much anxiety I stay awake most of the night. I sleep here and there during the day. I sleep sitting at the kitchen table while Davis is at school and Conrad is at the bookstore. It's about the only way I can sleep without the dreams. Dr. Bees says suffocation dreams can mean feeling emotionally overwhelmed. Or feeling stifled by someone close to you.

I figure he's trying to tell me that Conrad is smothering me. His anger. His religion. His writing. His drinking. Like he's holding my head under the water. Could be. He thinks they mean Conrad beats me. That I'm protecting him. But he doesn't and I'm not.

He never wants to talk about the water dream. It's the one with me and Davis on the Ferris wheel that's half under water —like the wheel on a giant, old-fashioned paddlewheel boat —and it has little gondolas shaped to look like rowboats. The wheel stops turning just as we are touching the surface, calm and sky blue and peaceful. We are so happy, Lula. I know I have to make sure Davis can't fall out and so I close a magnetic cuff around his ankle. I have no idea how it works I just know that is what I'm supposed to do to keep him safe. And then the big wheel starts turning again and under we go. I should be terrified. You know how I am. But I'm perfectly happy and peaceful. We keep going deeper and deeper and we don't seem to care, like everything is normal. Like we don't know we are under water.

Until the beast swims by. Then we know. I don't ever know what to call it. A fish. A whale. It's neither of those things. Huge. Terrible. Wonderful. Mouth open and stars inside. Stars, Lula. Like the mouth is an open window. And then we realize that we are under water and neither of us can breathe. Suddenly I am out of the gondola and swimming down after that thing in the dark. Davis wants to follow but can't. He is yanking at his cuff and I am racing to get to the waiting thing, like a shadow in the deep, before he can get free. All I know is that I have to get there first. And I do. The great mouth closes over me and then I am inside, surrounded by stars and looking out through its enormous eye. Watching Davis drown.

Next thing I know I am sitting up in bed, drenched in sweat. Waking up the whole house. Conrad shaking me like a ragdoll.

So I don't sleep any more, Lula. Dr. Bees has prescribed some more pills. They don't help any. I just end up sleeping while I'm awake, living my little life. I feel like I'm in two worlds at the same time, and still not really in either of them. Like I'm a zombie. The walking dead. Like I'm a fish in the desert. Except that I'm alive. And I can see everything through that eye.

He listens. Dripping. Ever dripping.

He does not remember making his way back to the bike for the beer.

Does not remember leaving the wrecked home and making his way down to the ark. Only seeing its hulking shape through the gloom after getting sick. He remembers waking up in the dark. Slowly realizing where he is. Close quarters. Shelter.

Except there is no such thing. The water gets in anyway. It all seeps in. Everything. You can't keep any of it out. Not really.

He falls off again into shards of dream. Cuts himself on jagged image after jagged image.

Bubbles on the surface of a lake turning a boiling red froth.

A long metal box, glinting, blackening beneath leaves of orange flame.

A small brown bird, alighting from a blue door on a hot desert road.

And voices. Just like before. Goddamned voices.

... It's always Davis. Just Davis.

...You can hate me if you want. I can't stop that.

...Davis. My love. My Savior. Baal has loosed the whale, terrible white with black eyes, to devour the stars.

...Simon locked me in the trailer.

"Hero?"

Opens his eyes. Stirs. Pushes his bloody hands against the floor. Sits up against the wall. Stares into close blackness. Tries to focus.

"*Hero!* You up there, boy?"

He falls away. Plunges back into the dark ocean. Dreams. Comes back up.

She is standing before him now. A shape towering in the dark on the other side of a beam of light. He shields himself with his hands like the light is a club.

"Dallas?"

"Well, who else, fool? You expectin' Jesus? Santa Clause? What the fuck you do to yourself, boy? You kill somebody?"

He drops his hands into his lap. Closes his eyes. Lets his head fall back against the wall. Wasted as he is, he can tell that Dallas is already three sheets to the wind herself.

"Yeah," he says. "Yeah. Dallas. I killed somebody. I'm gettin' really fuckin' good at that."

Dallas plays the light this way and that way. Takes everything in. Then back to the human wreckage. The unopened bottles.

"You gonna share any of that shit or keep it all to yourself?"

He opens one eye a little. Looks down at the remaining beers. Closes it again.

"Only."

"*Mmmhmm.* You know y'ain't makin' any damn sense?"

"Only if you promise to turn off that... fuckin' flashlight."

A gust from outside pushes the half door back against its hinges. Dallas turns. Walks over to the starboard wall. Slams the door closed. Her light washes over the wood, mostly protected from the desert sun all of these years.

Still blue.

She comes back. Finds a spot. She sits in a tumbling of inelegant grunts. Holds out a spindly hand.

"Okay, boy. Let's have one."

"Light," says Davis. She fumbles for the switch.

When they have both been swallowed into darkness, he rolls a bottle her way. Listens to her open it and drink.

"Damn, boy" says Dallas. "Shit tastes like warm coyote piss."

"They were out of cold coyote piss." They drink in silence. Listen to the wind and the rain. "Why are you up here, Dallas? Coyote piss aside."

He feels her eyes in the dark. They are worse than the light.

"Well. I tell you why. My phone ring 'round 'bout midnight. Man by the name of Elvis Broussard callin'.' Says to me he the same Elvis Broussard that brings me my fertilizer every year. Like there might be more than one person named Elvis Broussard. I hung up on his ass 'cause I'll be goddamned if I'm gon' have any kind of conversation with my fertilizer man after midnight. If the goddamned sun ain't up, then I ain't talkin' business on the phone."

He can hear her tip the bottle. Swallow.

"Damn phone ring again. Elvis again. Fool don't waste no time on introductions. Says he lookin' for *Davis Payne*. Thinks you might be at my place. Says he been callin' everywhere so he want to try me too. So I ask the fertilizer man why he think you'd be with me. I ask him if he think you been comin' over all this time to fuck a celebrity. Fertilizer man suddenly can't find no words so I say that if he *did* think you were in my bed fuckin' a celebrity, what kinda *friend*... would *call*... after goddamned *midnight*... to interrupt *that* shit? Then I hung up on his ass again."

Tip. Swallow.

"Goddamn phone ring a-*gain*. One o'clock in the goddamn mornin'. I lay into fertilizer man good this time. I mean, I lay into the man's mamma 'for he can get a word out. But it weren't Elvis this time. Big deep black voice by the name of Buddy Lincoln." Dallas laughs a little. "Now I could listen to *that* voice all night long. So I calm right the fuck down and make my apologies best I can and ask the voice how I can help. Told him I thought jus' maybe I heard your noisy-ass bike go by wakin' me up out of a dream. Said I'd walk up and check. Here I be. And goddamned if here you be too. Holed up in the boat."

"You *walked* up?"

"Now do I look like a drinkin'-drivin' fool who's gon' take her truck... out into the desert... in *this* weather... just to get her tired ass stuck in the mud?"

"No."

"Or turned over?"

"No."

"Damned right, *no*. I walk up here all the time, boy. Ain't nothing."

"Fuck. Sorry. Didn't mean to insult your... whatever. Your ability to walk."

They are quiet. He listens to the beer leaving the bottle. He wants to sleep.

"What'd Buddy tell you?"

She swallows. He thinks she won't answer.

"Buddy tell me your whole damn story. Little bit. Then a little bit more. I kep' pullin' just to hear the man make that sound of his. I kep' pullin' and he kep' talkin' and I kep' listenin'." Tip. Swallow. Silence. "*My-oh-my* but you been through some shit, Hero."

Rage again. Suddenly. From nowhere. From everywhere.

"Don't fuckin' call me that. And I mean... *ever!*"

A long silence after that. Just dripping. Waves of wind against the ark.

"Your daddy made his own damn decisions, you know," she says. "You didn't put him in that car. Ain't no one in this world your puppet, boy."

"I'm not talkin' about this, Dallas. I appreciate you coming up... I'll be gone in the morning. And I won't be back. So just..."

"And your mama. That shit is just... *instinct*. No way you could have kept her from goin' in after you. That's why she was on this earth in the first place. You had nothin' to do with that."

His head is mush. He wants to ignore her. Wants to fall over and sleep. But now when he closes his eyes the world around him begins to spin and he feels sick.

So he keeps his eyes open. Stares up into the dark. Tries to find the edges of the beam above him. Anything with definition.

"You don't even know what you're... what you're fuckin' sayin'. I had everything to do with that. *Everything.*"

"No."

"*Yes.* What the fuck do you know about it? Dallas *fuckin'* Letti. Nothin'."

Silence. She lets it sit. The dark world spins around him.

"Look. If she didn't want to go to..."

He is not in control of anything. It comes up again like bile.

"No! Dallas! It was a fucking birthday party!" He does his best to beat it back. Grits his teeth. It keeps coming. "All of my... All of my friends were there. We were late. My parents had been... goin' at it... fightin'. All night long. My dad was gone, God knows where. Wherever. And my mom was a wreck. But I had to go to the... the... *fuckin'* party. Because it was the only thing I *fuckin'* cared about."

He can hear Dallas lean back against the wall. Waiting.

"And we were late. All of them were already out there. My friends. Way out across the lake. They were going to have a picnic on the other side. They just figured I wasn't coming. So they all took off."

Silence. Darkness. Dripping.

"Mom's still trying to pull herself together. Like everything is fine. We're standin' there on the shore. I'm trying to call them. Wavin' my arms. But they can't hear me. So I throw a shit-fit. I blame her for being late. Blame her for picking a fight with dad, which I knew wasn't true. But I said it anyway. Told her I wished she had been the one to leave in the middle of the night and not come back. That I wished dad had brought me because he didn't have to put on any make-up. That he'd have been on time."

He breathes. He can smell the lake water. Can feel the frustration in his tiny beating heart.

"She walked up the hill… said she wanted to see if she could find someone. Someone who could take me out. It was just to make a show of effort. We both knew no one was around. There was a bathroom. I heard the door close."

Dallas Letti is silent. Like she has gone away. Like he is talking to himself.

"There was one little… there was a blue row boat tied to the dock. The fucking *Pequod*. What…" He laughs angrily. "What campground names a fucking boat after the *Pequod*? Why not the fuckin' *Titanic*? The *Lusitania*."

"I seriously hope y'ain't askin' me, 'cause…"

"I just… there it was. I just… I just bolted. I knew she was never gonna get in that thing. She was afraid of water. Nightmares about drowning. Lots of them. She'd wake up cryin'. She thought they were real. Dad liked to tease her about it. *You're not likely to drown in Houston, Elizabeth*. And so I looked at that little boat and I knew it was my only chance. I just… I just…"

He can't finish. She lets it sit.

Silence. Dripping.

A minute. Two.

"I heard her calling. I was already way the fuck out there. She had this tone. God… it was… it was so… I can still hear it in my head. Half rage. And half… terror. I tried to call back to her. To explain. I was scared because I knew I'd really pissed her off and that I was in the shit. But I was pointed the wrong direction. I was pointed across the lake. I tried to yell back at her. She couldn't… Goddamnit. She couldn't hear me. So I stood up and turned around. I tried to anyway. The whole boat just…"

Silence. Dripping. Wind.

"I don't remember anything. They said I was dead for over four or five minutes. I came to on the deck of a motorboat. One of the counselors had heard all of the shouting. He saw what happened. Flew back across the lake and fished me out."

Silence.

"But it was just him. One guy. And he couldn't do both. Couldn't work on me and try to deal with mom. She couldn't swim."

Silence. A broken sob. Sniffs.

"But she sure as hell tried. She made it over a hundred yards out there. Fully dressed. The counselor testified that he saw her go down for the last time just as he was pullin' me out of the water. Said he saw her face way out there as he hauled me up into the boat."

Wind. Dripping.

"He said they saw each other. And then she just disappeared. He said he kept looking for her as he was giving me CPR. You know. In between breaths. She was gone. Just…"

Silence. Wind.

He gets sick. A long scraping wretch of whiskey and bile followed by a squall of sobbing and a release of raw emotion so old that he believes he is twelve all over again.

Silence. Dripping. Wind.

He rights himself. Pulls himself together. Wipes his mouth. The weather in his head clears a little. He blinks. Finds the shape of that beam in the dark, holding the upper deck in place.

"I feel… bad for that guy. The park attendant. Stewart Ames. I always felt terrible for him. I see her for the last time… through *his* eyes. I see her face. Thinkin' I'm dead. I *was* dead. Seeing my limp body in his arms. And then… just… letting go of the fight. Sinking out of sight. Gone. That must have been… *fuck*. How does that not change you forever? Stewart fuckin' Ames. Poor bastard.

"Dad wanted money. Unattended boat. No life preserver. He knew this lawyer. I was always glad he lost. It was my fault. Not the campground's. Not Stewart's. Not mom's. That was all on me."

Dallas tosses her bottle. It finds its brother. They both shatter.

"You gon' drink those other two?" she asks. "'Cause I surely hope not."

He rolls her one. Then the other. Dallas opens one. Drinks.

"First thing I saw when I came to was Stewart's face. Lookin' down at me. Terrified. Crying. Then relieved. Well. That was the first thing I *saw*. Not the first thing I heard, though. First thing I *heard*, as I was coming to, before I opened my eyes, was mom's voice. Screaming my name. I know I was remembering her from the dock. But that's not how it felt. It felt like her voice was inside of me. Beneath my consciousness. Pushin' it up to the surface. Like her voice alone could do that. Like she had died. Like we both had died. And she was pushin' me back up into the world. With her voice."

Silence. Dripping. Breathing.

"It took years. Getting' her voice out of my head. Fucked me up but good. First just mom. But then there were others. My grandmother. Other voices. Different but all kinda' the same. Every night. Fucked… me… up. Then Doctor Bees. All of his little tricks. Little things to say to those voices. Little things to think about. Eventually it worked. Well. Kind of worked. Until Abby, I guess." He looks. Tries to see her. "Buddy tell you about Abby too?"

Dallas tips the bottle. Swallows.

"Yeah. Tol' me all 'bout Abby."

"Fucker." Anger again. Stabbing. Bursting inside of him.

"Stop it, fool. Don't go blamin' Buddy. He's just tellin' me what he thinks I need to know. Privacy ain't no good to a dead man."

"I sound dead to you?"

"Close to it. Close enough. Far as Buddy's concerned? He may as well think of me as your last fuckin' hope, boy. Maybe you up in my boat with a bottle of hooch and a fuckin' gun. Or a razor blade. Leave me to throw your dead ass out with the rest of the trash. B'sides, I know how to get people to open up when I want to. I'm good at that shit. People think me a mean ol' bitch livin' in a bottle tossed off in the desert. And I am too. I am. But listen here. I put on my bedroom voice? Sing my little song? Out it come, like honey from a hive."

He realizes then that she is right. That she had opened him up easier than she had opened two bottles of beer.

"Didn't kill your daddy," she says. Another swig. "Didn't kill your mama. Didn't kill Abby Palmer. But you workin' mighty goddamned hard to kill yourself, boy. Even if you don't know that yet. But that's what you doin'. Ain't it?"

He doesn't answer. He can only cry. The rain comes again in a short, hard squall. A dark cloud of sound. They listen to it pass over and away. Then the dripping inside picks up.

"And, hey, I could give a fuck, boy. Lot more dead people than there are livin' people. You goin' there sooner or later. Me too. Problem is… if you go before I do… who do I get to clean all this shit off my land?"

He makes a sound. Something like a laugh, but a long ways away from anything like humor.

"You just want to find your… whatever you're lookin' for," he says. "Your secret little treasure."

"That too."

"It ain't up here, Dallas. It just…"

"Oh you don't know shit, boy. Maybe I jus' kill you my *own* self."

"What is it anyway? What the hell are you hopin' to find?"

"Look at you. Drunk as a skunk and still tryin' to get my story. What I tell you about that?"

"Hey, fuck you. I just spilled my fuckin' guts over here."

"Yes you did spill yo' guts. You gon' clean it all up too."

He doesn't care. He wants to lay down. Sleep. He closes his eyes to the dark. The world spins. His stomach wants to follow.

Then she sings. Only just a whisper. But Dallas Letti sings. She conjures that flood.

Mmmmm. When it rain five days…
Ohhhh, I said when it rain five days…

Five days of rain and the water keeps on rising. Five days of rain and the lowlands keep on sinking. Five days of rain and now she can't even get out the door. Five days of rain and nothin' to do for a poor girl. Nothin' but wonder where to go.

"Bessie," he says, more to himself than to her. "*Backwater Blues.*"

"Well, well. You know your shit, boy. Give you a dollar you tell me what that song is about."

"Fuck if I know. The weather."

"No dollar for you. It about the Cumberland River flood. Hit Nashville Christmas mornin' nineteen hundred and twenty six. Bessie saw all that misery. People dead. People homeless. Lives destroyed. Thousands an' thousands an' thousands an' thousands. Mercy. And she wrote that song. *Backwater Blues.* But the Cumberland River flood was just the start. By the time Bessie recorded the song in nineteen hundred and twenty seven, half a dozen states were drowned. Thirty feet of water in some places. Mighty Mississippi just kept overflowin' and overflowin and overflowin' and it kept rainin' 'til everything under water. *Backwater Blues* became like some kinda'… some kinda' anthem. Like a 12-bar life raft people reached out for as it floated on by. 'Cause it sounded true. It sounded real."

Dallas dives back in.

Mmmmmm… Come the thunder and the lightnin' and the wind it start to seethe.
Say come the thunder and the lightnin' and the wind it start to seethe.
Look at all them drownin' peoples, ain't got no place left to breathe.

"Delta Blues come right outta that flood. Muddy Waters. Howlin' Wolf. Bessie. Whole lotta' poor people floatin' face down in the water and the whole Delta Blues era come outta that damned flood. 'Course, white folk had a much better chance of survivin'. They got the *real* life rafts. Black folk got the Delta Blues to hang on to. Best they could get was the voice of Bessie Smith floatin' by in the dark. *Hmmm… Rain five days and I can't even get out my do'…* Black folk got herded up into camps. Which were 'bout as bad as the flood itself. Nowhere to go. No way out but *down*. Killin's. Lynchin's. Bad, bad shit."

"Hard to imagine."

"Imagine? Imagine my ass. I *know* you around for Harvey. People talk about how a flood is always colorblind. May be true that eva'body get wet an' lawd knows eva'body can drown. But the rich folk dry out a whole lot faster than the poor folk. Rich folk come out t'other side and move on. Get a loan. Rebuild.

Move away to higher ground. Poor folk walk aroun' waterlogged the rest of their days. Carry that flood inside them forever like little brown jugs with legs. And what the hell you doin' when Katrina come ashore? You all up inside a bottle back then too? You think that response time might'a been just a little teeny, tiny bit faster if that shit happen to New Jersey? *Rhode Island?* Don't get me goin' on that shit, boy. Don't get me started on Puerto Rico after Maria, neither. Those poor people."

"Whatever, Dallas. I was just…"

"*Backwater Blues. Mmmmmm… Backwater blues done make me want to pack my things and leave… Look at all them drownin' peoples, ain't got no place left for me to breathe..* Song ain't about a flood, boy."

"I thought…"

"Not *only* about a flood. It's about livin' in the world. It about the pain. About the regrets. Just keeps getting' deeper and deeper. 'Til that's all you see from one horizon t'other. *Pain* to the east. *Regret* to the west. *Should'a* to the north. *Could'a* to the south."

Dallas sings. Again. In that old great voice. Not just a breath. Not a whisper. Volume this time. Filling the old wooden space.

Woke up this mornin' and the rain done fill my eyes.
Say I woke up this mornin' and the rain done fill my eyes.
All them drownin' peoples, baby, ain't no one hears my cries.

"Poor Bessie so depressed with the world she can't even get out her own front door. *Backwater Blues* calls to her to pack up her shit and move, 'cause the water comin'. And she can see it comin' too. But she can't move no mo'. Ain't no place to go and nothing to be done. And it just keep rainin' 'til whether you live or drown depend on the song you got in your heart. See? That's the song that will either put a little air in your lungs or it'll hold you under. The Bessie Smith in that song sunk like a fuckin' stone, boy. You can believe it. Ain't no hope in that song. She just let it come."

He clenches the muscles in his jaw.

"You got something to say, just say it."

"My opinion? You workin' on y'own *Backwater Blues*, Hero. Got it half-written already. You ahead of schedule. Got to change the song in your heart, boy. This shit you're cryin' over ain't your fault any more than that old flood"

"Like you'd know anything about it. *Celebrity.*"

"Ha. I know *everything* about it. My shit put yours to shame. You a boy scout, helpin' lil' old ladies cross the street. I weren't so drunk I'd crawl over there and beat the shit outta you with this bottle for sayin' something like that to me. You don't know shit about me, boy. *Damn.* I cannot even be-*lieve* I am sittin' in the dark tryin' to convince a white boy he ain't got nothin' to feel guilty about."

They are silent for awhile. Dallas hums to herself as she drinks. He listens. Floats on the sound. Remembers.

"My mom loved her," he says eventually. "All of them. Bessie. Ma Rainey. Billie Holiday. Big Mama Thornton. Etta James. Loved Etta. *Man.* And you. She loved to listen to Dallas Letti. Played *Mama's Girl* until the record 'bout fell apart. And *Supper in the Mornin'.* And *My Man for a Dime.* You had a good stretch there."

"*Stretch* is about right. Shit was longer than it should'a been. I just kept pullin' and pushin' and stretchin' 'til one day it all snap back into proper shape. Unnastan'?"

"Not everyone is born a Dallas Letti. You were... I mean, like, really good, Dallas."

"Fool. *I* wasn't even born Dallas Letti. Shit." She drinks. "That name's just sellin' records. My mama lift up her skirt to Earl Letti and nine months later, while Earl busy shootin' his foot off in the war, out I come, *whoop*, a wet mess skiddin' right across the livin' room floor. Sister Rosetta on the radio singin' *Nobody's Fault But Mine* and *Down by the Riverside.*"

She plucks a song out of the air. Sings her way down to the river where she lays down that load so heavy and washes away her sins.

"*Mmm-Mmm.* Mama love her Rosetta Tharp. *Layin' down my load so heavy. Down by the riverside. Lay down that heavy load...* that was me."

"What was you?"

"The heavy load. Lil' Miss Rosetta Letti. My mama want to lay that load down just about every damn day. Long about twelve years old my mama lay her heavy load all the way the fuck down. Hand me off to Corny Roop at the church every damn week. Off she'd go measurin' inseams. Or ridin' around God knows where with George Peacock. *Rooster*, they called him. Rooster had him a pea-green 1939 Chevy KC Master pick-up. What they call back then a *Cab-n-Box.* All beat to hell. Mama didn't care none. Havin' laid down her heavy load and all. Rooster's *Cab-n-Box* may as well been a magic carpet. Off they went. Sometimes I stayed at that church singin' in the basement with Corny Roop most of the damn day. Mama don't care none. Only thing she cared about is me not ever havin' a heavy load of my own.

It is his turn to wait. To listen. To let it come.

Dallas hums to the song in her head. *Down by the riverside. Down by the riverside.* Tips the bottle. Swallows. Again. Throws the empty. Opens the next. Drinks. He waits.

And then it comes. First a slow drip. Then a trickle. It's that way with everything. There is no *inside* and *outside.* Not really. Nothing stays dry for long.

She talks until she is done talking. Until her own story is out there and up to their chins. Until he knows everything. Until he can't believe his own ears and his head is spinning from something other than the booze.

Then she is done. Suddenly. Done. She is fully spent. The rain has completely stopped. Daylight maybe two hours away. There is too much to say. Too many questions. So he says nothing. He listens to her breathe. Until the rhythm of it, the in and the out of it, is like a kind of tide. He floats in the dark. They both do.

He dreams in music. Waves of cresting sound flinging words out into the dark air like flecks of white foam. The wind is singing in its ghostly whisper. The words belong to Bessie Smith. *Mama gon' leave, yes she is, and ain't gon' say no goodbye.*

The words, but not the voice. The voice, that sound in the wind rocking him in his sleep, belongs to his mother.

Say Mama's gon' leave her little baby boy
And here's the reason why

It is water that wakes him up. Lots and lots of water. A thick, wet violence that broadsides the make-believe boat and shakes it like a toy. It rips the ark off of its foundation and pushes it over onto its side, plowing the once blue door into the desert floor. There is a sharp crack from above. Something large and heavy falls in a swinging arc, crashing nearby.

The water comes not just from the far windows, which are now, suddenly, above him, like three open skylights in a home built on the floor of an ocean. It comes from everywhere. From between every board and seam.

He is human debris, tossed head first into the wall. He goes under holding the new, sharp pain in his head. Comes up coughing and hacking. Struggles to stay upright, flailing for her, searching wildly in blind panic, swinging his arms in and out of the water just so his hands might make even accidental contact with her body.

But there is nothing. He wheels one direction. Then the other. Screams.

"Dallas! Dallas!"

Nothing but the sound of water. Everywhere water. Like they're in a barrel going over the lip of something bottomless. There is a finger or an arm or a wrist moving across the skin of his neck. He grabs for it, lashing at the water. He comes up empty. No fingers or hands or body. He thinks of the snakes that may have been caught in the sudden churning water.

"Dallas! Dal…"

A series of booming detonations thunder next to him. Explosions of sound as the bits and chunks of broken church become floating battering rams, slamming into what used to be the bottom of the ark.

"Dallas! Goddamnit, Rosetta!"

There is a sound. A movement. Unnatural. Unlike all other sound and motion in a roiling dark world of sound and motion.

But very small. Smaller than he should ever be able to detect.

Again.

Off to the left and behind. Twenty feet. Twenty-five. He knows. He doesn't know *how* he knows. He just does.

He dives, plunging under, groping in every direction until his fingers find cloth. He pulls.

A wrist. An elbow. He grabs her under the arms and stands her up against the upright floor of the ark. Clutches her from behind. Pulls hard. Once. Twice. Three times. Dallas Letti's head droops forward. He spins her. Pushes her forehead up. There is warm liquid mixing with cold. He finds her mouth with his fingers. Breathes, emptying his lungs into hers.

"Dallas!"

Again. Again.

"Dallas! *Rosetta!*"

She coughs up water. Gasps. Gulps in air.

Something large and heavy makes impact nearby. The whole structure spins like a bad carnival ride. The top of the ark now points directly upstream, dark dirty water plowing under the starboard side in powerful gushes, working like a lever. The boat shudders like it is about to come apart. Another loud ramming and the water pushes harder, standing the vessel upright. Sending them backwards, down in over their heads.

But Davis does not let go. He holds her to him and they spin together beneath the surface. Water churns cold in his ears. He kicks his legs but cannot stand. There is no floor beneath him. Only water.

There is music in his head. Amid the chaos and terror, there is suddenly music. The sprinkle of words, pocking the surface of his consciousness, comes unbidden. Comes like rain. Bessie again. She had a dream that she was dead.

Bessie's words. But not the voice.

The voice. Like a scented breeze. Laden with memory. Carrying all of its old magic and terror. The voice belongs to Abby Palmer.

He finds the floor. Pushes himself up above the water, pulling Dallas Letti up with him, hacking and coughing. He holds her to him, pulling her limp and ragged frame into his chest.

Over her shoulder he sees a rectangular hole in the darkness. A shape once filled by a blue door no longer on its rusty hinges. Through that black rectangular hole there are pinpricks of light scattered in a sea of desert sky. The stars wink on and off through the gaps in scudding clouds, like whales devouring them whole. Abby's voice. Singing how she had a dream that she was dead.

I say I dreamt evil everywhere, baby. Evil with me in my bed.

Chapter 73
Dallas and Etta

Morning, Mr. Brown. My long lost friend. Here I am again. I'd be lying if I said I did not sorta like this one-way conversation. No one to tell me to stop rambling on or give me that go-away look.

No way in hell I'm sending this letter to you, Pablo. Just the same, it feels good to get some of this stuff out of my head and on to paper where I can look at it. Where I can hate it out in the open.

The writer kid who is working on my property –the one who wants me to spill my beans for his magazine –he says we all like to talk about ourselves. Says we all have something bottled up that wants to come out. Says we all need a confessor. I figured he just working me. So he can score one with his publisher. *'Lookie who I got to talk to me!'* Probably the truth too.

But you know what, Pablo? It does kind of feel good to write this shit down. Like the morning after a week-long bender when you find the energy to finally pick up all the trash in the house and stuff it all into bags and take it out to the curb and then come back in and open up all of the windows. Feel God's breath blowing through the house again. What about you, Pablo? You got a story to tell? Any trash you need to haul out to the curb? I just bet there is.

Not that I'm opening any windows. Cold as fuck out there. Like it might start to rain soon. This thing in my head is like a little hot coal this morning. Like a little second heart that beats out this rhythm of hurt. It's got some extra punch today. My doctors would probably laugh and shake their little boy heads about my headaches but I think it's got something to do with that low-pressure mess sitting out in the gulf. Folks say their bones ache when the pressure drops. It's doing the same thing to this tumor. Like the ocean's got this long arm with a hand made of cloud that reaches all the way out here into the desert and squeezes that little ball of pain. I've got medicine but none of it touches the hurt. Dr. Johnnie Walker is the only one who seems to help. So I started with his medicine early today.

I woke up with Dorothy Moore in my head singing '*Misty Blue.*' Just that last verse over and over. '*Oh, it's been such a long, long time / Looks like I get you off my mind / Oh, but I can't / Just the thought of you / Turns my whole world /A misty blue.*' Since you are never going to read these words I can be honest and tell you I think it's because this letter has put your baggy face back in my head, Pablo. Or maybe a better way to say it is that all these words have picked a lock, letting you out of the place I've been keeping you imprisoned all these years.

Ten-thirty in the morning. Already a quarter bottle gone. I guess that makes me drunk enough to say that my career cost me the two people I loved the most. Maybe you had no idea, Pablo, but you were one of those people. You and Etta. I think you and me and Etta would all be together under different circumstances. Had I made different choices. I know you have made yourself a wonderful family and you wouldn't wish any different. And I know Etta would not wish any different even though she has not made any kind of family. Not to my knowledge anyway. So I'm not trying to say that you and Etta would wish different lives. But this letter ain't about your feelings. Y'all can go write your own damn letters.

And I don't think it's any coincidence that it was '*Misty Blue*' in my head. Dorothy Moore maybe made it famous, but Etta James covered the hell out of that tune. And last night I went to bed with the memory of you giving little Etta her name. Her coming up to you with her hands on her little hips singing '*tell mama what you want*' and '*tell mama what you need*' having no idea in this world what she's saying except that she's singing after me. I thought you might die laughing but you kept your shit together, Pablo. You pulled her up on your knee and said that from then on you were going to call her Etta like she was Etta James. Like you had any kind of choice. Because from then on she wouldn't let you call her anything else. "*Now, Papi! My name is Etta! You said so!*" And then that rule applied to me too. "*Papi calls me Etta and you do too!*"

And I never really stopped calling her Etta. Truth is, I liked it better than her real name. I pretended that it wasn't Etta James' name she was taking, but the back half of my own name, *Rosetta*. I only used her Christian name when she was in trouble or when I was fighting with her. Which, I guess, turned out to be almost always. The name Etta became an endearment. Like *Papi*.

We ended badly Pablo. You and me. We both know every bit of it was my fault. *Mother Blues* was like that calm in the eye of the storm. Otis on the one side and Casey Zoot and Hammy Lewis on the other side. And in the calm middle is *Mother Blues* with you and me and little Etta tucked away safe and sound and happy in the music that was like the sound of my own breath. Who knows how long that would have lasted. Maybe forever. Maybe not. But I like to think it would have lasted a long while.

I was the one who threw it away, Pablo. If you get nothing else from all of these words, get that one thing: I know it was my fault. Jay took his Stratocaster and chased his girl off to Florida and so I convinced you to hire dumbass Casey Zoot. I say I convinced you. I insisted and you said okay is how it went. Because you were always too nice for your own good, Pablo. (How many people have told you that? You're too goddamned nice!) I never told you that Zoot was part of Otis' old crew. He hated Otis as much as I did so I felt safe that he would not rat me out to Otis who no doubt was still looking for me. But it was Zoot that brought the drugs back into my life.

Didn't take long, did it? Soon enough I thought I could do anything and fuck anybody without a care. I started to think that *Mother Blues* –the place I loved with all my heart –was too small for me. I told myself I was wasting my time and my talent. That I was growing old on the vine without anyone of a mind to pluck me. I began to think that if *you* didn't want me in that way then it may as well be Casey Dumbass Zoot. So I rubbed up against Zoot and then I rubbed that in your face. To this day, even as I move this pen, that last fight makes me want to be sick, Pablo. You were right to send me packing a second time. I said terrible things. Hateful things. To say that it was Mr. Flake doing the talking sounds like an excuse. I'm not trying to make excuses. I'm not asking to be forgiven. But I want you to understand that I loved you even then, in between each of those ugly words I loved you like a favorite song.

So Zoot and I put the sex and drugs and music in a blender and drank until we were sick. And sick was what I wanted because I was sick for leaving you. I never loved Zoot. It was never about love. It was a lot more about hating myself. Probably looked like I was having the time of my life on the outside. We did get around and worked all over the place, but that was a dark time. I was all set to get a lawyer and divorce Otis but then Otis up and died of an overdose in the back of some beat-up Chevy belonging to God-knows-who. Some woman worse than me I'm betting. Zoot wanted to go to the funeral. He thought Etta would one day appreciate the closure. Personally, I think Zoot just wanted to silently gloat as they lowered Otis into the ground. But I was having nothing to do with that so we stayed away. Didn't seem to make any difference to Etta. She never did think of Otis as her daddy. She thought of you as her daddy.

It was a lonely time for Etta. I guess I should say that it was the *beginning* of a lonely time for Etta, because she was just getting started. A whole lot of driving around with me and Zoot and Mr. Flake and Ms. Mary Jane and Dr. Johnnie Walker and all of their friends. Whole lot of waiting around in the back room of some shitty blues bar with some cigarette-smoking stranger pretending to be responsible while I was on stage. Etta always had plenty of people around her, but she didn't have a friend of her own. She didn't even have a mama. Etta was all by herself. I felt horrible on the inside. I saw how things were and I hated myself. Still do. I tried to make it up to her. Play dates and such. Bought her things. Clothes and little trinkets when we pulled into a new town. Told her she was special.

But kids are smarter than that. Etta sure was. Could not give a shit about what you told her. She could smell the lie a mile away. Soon enough she wanted less and less to do with me. Insisted on riding in the back seat. Wanted me to sit up front alone with Zoot. I could see it happen, Pablo. I could see her detach and pull into herself. If I was going to leave her, then she was going to leave me first. She was protecting herself from her own mama. And fuck if I didn't let it happen. Fuck if I didn't *make* it happen. Just like my mama told me I would.

After all these years, I 'm not really sure who showed up first, my dead mama or Hammy Lewis. I think of them together. I know that she started showing up in my dreams about the time that Hammy showed up in Shreveport. It was our last night at the *Bayou Grinder* and I'm out back doing a line of flake off a dashboard and Hammy walks up and knocks on the car window scaring the bejesus out of me. Tells me that I can either die of the junk or he can make me a star and that it was up to me. Slipped his business card through the crack in the window and then he walked back into the *Grinder*.

Anti-Semites come up to me all the time in the early days and ask why I was following a Jew Devil around. Ask why I didn't get me a black agent —someone who knew the blues. Hammy was chalky white and maybe he couldn't sing the blues, but that man knew the business of the blues better than any man walking around on the earth. I think it was those thick black eyebrows that put people off of Hammy. And always in a nice dark suit even when it was 100 degrees. Nice shoes. And the way he seemed to be looking right at you even when he wasn't. I always defended the man and I still do. But looking back, if I am to be absolutely honest as I am trying to be in this letter, there *was* something of the devil in Hammy Lewis.

Anyway, I used Hammy's business card that night to sharpen up my line of flake and then threw it away. Zoot and I finished up the last set, put Etta and the equipment in the car and headed on back to the hotel. Next morning we made the trip back to Texas and I did not think twice about Hammy Lewis. Which I guess makes it good that he followed us home.

Good might not be the right word.

I can tell I'm slipping back into a *Billboard Magazine* interview, Pablo. You don't need all of that shit. You know all about Hammy Lewis. The man made me a star just like he promised. Got me away from Zoot. Got me off the drugs. Got me out of the piss-ant back-road happy-hour dive-bar house-band circuit we had been playing and plugged me into the big blues business on both sides of the Atlantic. Stayed with me near forty years. Hammy hooked me up with that tour bus. He did everything. Because Hammy Lewis knew what was best for the great *Dallas Letti Blue*. And he could not have given two shits for *Rosetta Letti*.

And as for poor Etta, she was just in the way. Hammy never said that exactly. But I know that's the truth. The man never saw a child he liked and that particular child –*my* child –was in the way of my success and Hammy's money. Etta never liked Hammy either so I guess it was mutual. Hell, she liked Zoot better than she did Hammy and most of the time she flat hated Zoot. Truth is, Pablo, Etta seemed to flat hate me too. I know kids act out for attention. Growing pains and all that. But my girl gave up on me early on. Can't say I blame her. I don't blame her.

The only adult Etta seemed to tolerate was Rhonda Brill who was this gal I knew in Corbin after I ran away from Otis. Zoot had him a source for all kinds of drugs out at the *Santiago Chicken Ranch*, which was a real chicken ranch not a whorehouse chicken ranch. We'd drive out there and I'd stay in the car with Etta while Zoot would wander off out behind the coops like he was looking for someone to sell him some eggs. Two minutes of sitting and then here come Rhonda Brill, chit-chatting up a storm about nothing in particular. We'd talk until Zoot come back with an egg carton full of drugs.

Everyone called her Ronni. Odd looking woman. Itty bitty little thing half my size in every direction and thin like a rail but boobs like you never seen. Always talking up the Lord and thinking Jesus was going to find her an open washer at the *Lone Star Laundry*. But Ronni had a pretty face and she liked to laugh. She and Etta hit it off right from the start. Wasn't long before we were getting out of the car and going off with Ronni. We'd come back and Zoot would be in the car already high as a kite waiting for us. Etta started nagging us to go see Ronni and the chickens even when we had more drugs than we needed.

Ronni was about the only one who knew how to make Etta laugh in those years, even though I think some of that laughing was just to show me that Ronni was a better mother than I was. Hell, I already new that. Didn't take much to be a better mother than me. And Ronni loved Etta to death, too. Always saying things like *"There's my precious girl!"* and *"Come sit by Mama Ronni"* and *"You get any prettier and I'm just gonna have to steal you away as one of my own."* Sometimes life spells everything out for you ahead of time and you're just too stupid to read the words.

Ronni had her a girl three years younger than Etta. Called her Dixie. Ronni said that Etta liked to pretend she was helping her be a mama to little Dixie. Made her feel important, pulling that girl around by the hand, teaching her things. Neither of them was in school. Ronni was convinced the public school taught the Devil's work. I wasn't worried so much about the Devil. I just didn't want some teacher telling me that I can't go out on the road to some gig in East Bejesus because Etta was supposed to be in the classroom. Anyway, both Dixie and Etta had home-schooling in common, which means they didn't learn shit from books and they didn't have no other friends.

Ronni and I had some shit in common too. Mostly that we both grabbed our child in the middle of the night and left our man passed out in the bed after a beating. Ronni's man lived up in Little Rock so I guess Corbin felt like a safe distance to her. Still, Ronni was always looking over her shoulder, just waiting for him to show up and drag her and Dixie back to Little Rock by the hair. *Kelsey Brattle.* All of these years and the man's name is still stuck to my brain like some shit stain stuck on the bottom of my shoe.

Even toward the end of Zoot's time, Etta always wanted to stay with Ronni and Dixie. She made me carry her kicking and screaming to the car just so we could haul her off to another gig in Bumfuck, Texas like a piece of equipment. The few times that we left her behind with Ronni for a night or two, everyone was happier. It made my guilt a whole lot worse, but Mr. Flake took care of that shit like a pro. *One line, feeling fine.*

Eventually, Hammy took over. When I finally kicked Zoot and Mr. Flake to the curb, Hammy had me traveling more than ever. Up and down the Gulf Coast. Biloxi. Pensacola. Then north. Played Chicago. St. Louis. Then I started getting some real attention and Hammy started booking me out east. Savannah.

Richmond. New York. Ronni went from being a help to being essential because I was almost never home. I made a fuss about taking Etta along but Hammy was a silver-tongued devil in a suit smoking his Monte Carlos and he knew all the right words. *'The road is no place for a little girl, Rosetta. Bad environment. Out all night. Be a good mother and let her stay. Look how happy she is with the chickens and little Dixie."*

He was right, too. Etta wanted nothing to do with me out on the road. She begged and pleaded and threw a fit or two and then here came Ronni telling me it was for the best and that she liked having Etta around for Dixie. So what was I supposed to do, Pablo? I couldn't just stay home and tell Hammy Lewis to go find another star. Hammy was signing talent like he was out picking cotton and the man's bag was full up. In later years Hammy needed me and I kept him well-dressed and his pocket full of Monte Carlos. But in the beginning I was the one who needed Hammy Lewis. He say jump and I say *'Well tell me how high you want me to be jumpin' Mr. Lewis and let me light your cigarette while you thinkin' about it.'*

I couldn't very well drag Etta along kicking and screaming anyway. So I gave it a try. I left for two weeks on that first trip to New York and Boston and Etta stayed back with Ronni. I called every night. Most nights I talked to Ronni because Etta was out playing with Dixie or feeding the goats or tending the chickens and didn't want to come to the phone.

When I got back to Corbin, damn if Etta didn't seem disappointed. Practically had to drag her to the car from Ronni's place. Then when she got to her own home she always wanted to go spend the night with Ronni and Dixie. Wanted to go to church with Ronni and Dixie. Wanted to go on a walk with Ronnie and Dixie. Wanted to go tend to the chickens with Ronni and Dixie. Ronni tried to make it all about the animals. Some baby goats and two dogs and about a hundred chickens was what they had out there. Ronni and Dixie lived right there on the property and Ronni worked mostly for room and board. She did everything they needed her to do, including deliver fresh eggs to half the county in a beat up station wagon. She said Etta was a big help. Said she didn't know what she would do without Etta. I tried to give her money. I insisted. But Ronni wouldn't take it. I had to start giving a few dollars to Etta to give to Ronni. Then Etta started giving it back. And with attitude too: *"Me and Ronni don't want your money, mama."*

And then, Lord have mercy, here come Casey Zoot again. It would be the last time I saw Zoot, but it was a doozy. My last memory of him is of a Sheriff's

Deputy bending him into the back of a squad car holding a bloody rag to his nose. They'd already bent me into the back of a different car and I remember sitting there looking out the window at Zoot and laughing because I was too high to appreciate just what kind of shit we were in. I was supposed to be done with Zoot and all his nonsense. And I was too. I promised Hammy I was done.

But then here he came. Zoot showed up one night needing a place to stay. Before I knew it I saw that he had brought Mr. Flake along with him and we were right back at it like he'd never left. And then before I know it someone was pounding on the door and then I was sitting in the back of a police car laughing at Zoot and his bloody nose.

The laughing stopped soon enough. Right behind Zoot they brought out Etta. I figured she was still up in her bed. Zoot didn't come over until after she was asleep. But then as I am sitting in the back seat of that black and white, there she was, coming down the steps three feet in the air holding onto the neck of this big deputy. I think they wanted her to be crying and upset and all traumatized but she was as calm as can be. And you know how Etta is —the calmer she is, the angrier she is. She looked at me sitting in that police car and then looked away like I was nothing. Like I was *nothing* to her. I called out to her through the glass. Told her I was sorry. Told her I would come for her. Told her not to be afraid. She never flinched. They put her in an unmarked car and whisked her off to I didn't know where. Turned out to be Child Protective Services who had umpteen questions for her and another umpteen for me along with a few threats that they'd take her away and give her to someone who knew the first thing about being a good mother unless I cleaned my shit up in a hurry.

I did nine months for possession with intent on account of the amount of the shit Zoot had brought into my home and stuffed under my couch when I got up to stop the pounding on my door. Zoot did thirty-eight months for taking a swing at the lawman with the handcuffs and for robbing *The Dirty Dove* in San Angelo after one of his solo gigs. That's how he could afford all of the flake he brought with him that night. Jackass went straight from robbing *The Dirty Dove* to the *Santiago Chicken Ranch* and loaded up. Then he came to see me with the law hot on his ass. Some people belong in jail because they're criminals. Zoot belonged in jail because he was just too stupid to be out walking around.

Like I said, Mama started showing up about the time Hammy Lewis gave me his card that night outside the *Bayou Grinder* in Shreveport. She started showing up in my dreams right about then. Usually nothing too bad, but weird. But when I got tossed in jail Mama came on like a damned hurricane. Hammy Lewis never visited me once in jail but Mama came most every night. I'd like to say it was the drugs that brought her on. Getting drugs in prison was easier than falling out of bed, that's true. But it wasn't Mr. Flake that brought Mama back. I think it was the guilt. I think Maybelline Louisa Nogales could smell her daughter's guilt from the *Other Side* (I won't say from Heaven). I think she could smell my guilt like Sunday morning bacon grease sizzling in the pan. And she came hungry.

I started having these new kind of dreams, Pablo. Bad ones. Wake up screaming in my cell, all the other women jailbirds yelling at me to shut the hell up. Night after night. They all hated me. Called me '*Nightmare.*' That was my name for about the last seven months. '*Nightmare.*' I was afraid to go to sleep at night. I was afraid anyway because I'd never been locked up before and there were some women in that place that would just as soon cut your throat as look at you and there I was screaming those crazy white Texas bitches awake every night. They all knew that there was one way to shut me up for good. And I knew it too. So I was always scared.

There was this one dream I remember the most. Mama dragged me into a solid room. No bars, just four black walls and a bright blue door. But then the door disappeared and Mama let go of my hair and then she disappeared too and the lights went out and there was just Mama's voice in the air singing *Nobody's Fault But Mine.* And I knew that was her way of telling me that she'd told me all along not to have any babies. That I was no kind of mother just like she was no kind of mother. That I'd fucked up and had a girl that I would ruin just as sure as she ruined me, only worse because Etta was going to suffer. My punishment would be to see my own baby suffer.

And then the singing turned into sound, like all possible sounds packed tightly into one sound if that makes any damn sense. So loud I could feel blood coming out of my ears and running down my neck. And then the sound turned into kind of like a feeling. Like my ears couldn't hear anymore but I was listening with my whole body and so the sound was suddenly a feeling and the feeling was cold water covering my feet and rising up over my ankles and then my knees and it kept filling the room rising up my body until it reached my mouth and I could taste salt. That's when I woke up screaming and everyone yelling back at me to shut the hell up and about how they wanted to kill me. I never forgot that dream, Pablo.

Like I said, Hammy never once came out to see me. I never had any visitors. Ronni drove out with Etta to visit me a few times. Etta always refused to come in. She stayed in the car with Dixie. Ronni made it sound like she was just too sad to see me in jail but I knew better. Etta was disgusted with me and I couldn't blame her. Ronni said she'd given Etta regular chores out at the ranch to keep her busy and out of trouble. Said Etta had taken to gathering eggs and feeding the goats and that she was a big help. She minded her manners. She was polite. Seemed happy. She went to Ronni's little church where they all just adored her and she adored them back. I know Ronni was just trying to put me at ease so I wouldn't worry about her. But it was like each word was lead pipe to my skull. I wanted Etta to be miserable without me.

Think about that Pablo: I would have felt better... about myself... if Etta had been miserable. What kind of mama thinks such a thing about her own? Back in my cell it hit me that Ronni was more Etta's mama than I was. That was when I started to realize that she'd most likely be better off without me. Had I been a more courageous person I'd have picked a fight with five or six of them bitches that hated me in that place and let them kill me. They would have too.

Nine months felt like ninety years. Hammy Lewis picked me up when they let me out. I called Ronni and told her not to come. The girls in the cage got together and beat me near to death two weeks before I got out. Kind of a get-the-fuck-out going away present. So I still looked pretty bad and I didn't want Etta to see me that way. I wanted to just get out and go home and heal up before anyone saw me. Ronni told me Hammy had come by the ranch and said he needed to talk with me once I got out. She offered to deliver a message but he said he needed to talk in person. So I knew ahead of time I was about to get dropped. I said to call him and tell him the date and time.

So it was Hammy who picked me up that day. Black suit, red tie, like the Devil himself. So hot outside it was like walking around in a barbeque grill.

He took me for a cheeseburger and a shake. Best thing I'd eaten in nine months and I was so grateful to be out. I apologized for ruining everything and that I understood if he needed to drop me now that I had a record –and not the kind of record we had been looking for. Hammy smiled and smoked and watched me finish my burger. Then he said I hadn't ruined anything. He said I was going to be a big star. He said he'd been hard at work playing all my demo tapes so much that they were all about wore out. Then he told me that he had put together six months of tour dates. Said he'd put together a top-notch band of starving blues musicians and that he also knew some important people in the business who were anxious to get acquainted.

Well you could have knocked my swollen, beat-up jailbird ass over with a feather. I looked at Hammy over my vanilla shake like he was out of his mind. But then

Hammy's smile kind of melted off of his face and he said *"But Rosetta, this is serious business. You're going to have to make some changes."* And I said to him for the umpteenth time that I was done with the drugs and he said he was not talking just about drugs and so then I asked what he hell was he talking about. And I will never forget his words. *"You need to turn your back and walk away from all of this. You need to start over. You need to leave everything behind and start over."*

I opened my mouth at that but Hammy shushed me with one of those harry-knuckled fingers. He lit up another Monte Carlo. Then he started in. *"Rosetta Letti of Corbin Texas, is a junkie with shitty taste in men. She just got out of prison for possession of unlawful narcotics with intent to distribute."* I started to protest but Hammy wasn't having any of it and kept his finger in my face. *"And from the looks of her, she barely escaped with her life. Rosetta Letti is going nowhere except back to prison. Only a matter of time. Prison and another bad man or two. Or three. And then an early grave. Because Rosetta Letti's got a taste for misery in her blood. I've got plenty of talented, locked up clients. Plenty of talented dead clients. So I know it when I see it. And I see it in you. I'm guessing it runs it the family. Like mother like daughter. It just passes on along. But what you've got in front of you right now, what I'm offering you, is a chance. It's the last best chance you're going to get because I'm not wasting my time. You're of no use to me in prison, strung out or dead. You can sing, Rosetta. No doubt you've got the gift. But I need you to be free and alive to sing songs about being locked up and miserable and heart broken and abandoned and all the rest of it. You can either let that hunger for misery devour you, or you can put it to work for you. And for me."*

So I asked him what I needed to do, thinking he was going to tell me I needed to move to San Angelo or some such thing, and he said *"You need to leave Rosetta behind. You need to start thinking about being a different person. With a new name. Something that can sell a blues record. You need to start fresh. You need to get out of the country for awhile."*

Out of the damned country. I about came out of my seat at that. But Hammy calmed me down. Took the straw out of my mouth and handed it to me, then stuck a new Monte Carlo in its place. He gave me a light and waited until I was ready to listen again. He said that all those tour dates he'd lined up were in Europe. England. Germany. France. Denmark. Sweden. He told me about all of these blues musicians who were making it big across the pond. Said the Europeans were crazy for original American blues. Blues clubs all over the damned place. He said he'd got me a spot on the *American Folk Blues Festival* tour as a hot up-and-comer fresh out of prison with blues in her bones. Said I'd be sharing venues with the likes of T-Bone Walker and Sonny McGhee and John

Lee Hooker and Helen Humes. Then he told me that those important people he mentioned, the ones who wanted to meet me, worked with the *Backwater Blues* label in London.

Well. Fuck. A. Duck. Hammy leaned back in his chair in the burger joint and smoked his Monte Carlo and watched me take it all in. And by that I mean he watched me sit and stare at him with a goopy straw in my hand and one of his cigarettes hanging from my lip. I didn't even know what to say, Pablo. Three hours earlier my ass was in prison.

Hammy spoke again before I could say anything. *"If you want this, Rosetta, and if you want me to make it come together for you, then you've got to leave it all behind. And I don't mean starting tomorrow. Understand? Now, if you want to stay in Corbin sending demos off to Sun Records and getting high and fucking men who are going to get you sent to prison, well I've got bigger fish to fry, honey. It's up to you."*

I almost asked him about Etta. About how she fit into his *leave-everything-behind* plan. But I didn't. Didn't have to. Truth is, Pablo, if I'm really going to be honest in this letter that I'm never going to send to you –and I promise you that I am too drunk now to hold anything back –the truth is I didn't want to ask. Truth is I came out of prison without a child to my name. Truth is I came out of prison with my Mama still in my head, right where this tumor is now, singing Bessie Smith like she was meant to be sung.

'I'm a young woman and I ain't done runnin' 'round.'

Chapter 74

Desmond rinses the plate. Slips it into the broken dishwasher to dry. He rattles two more cubes into the glass and splashes in another shot and a half. Shambles into the living room.

He sets the drink on the stereo and flips through the vinyl. *Dizzy. Coltrane. Miles.* Considers Chet Baker. Puts him back. Keeps flipping. He stops at a worn black sleeve with water rings from other tumblers. Rolls the record out into his hand. Blows. No lint, but he blows anyway. Reads the purple circle in the center. *The Billie Holiday Story.* Carol had always hated Billie Holiday.

"Maybe if she had a better voice she wouldn't be so damned depressed."

"Well... just maybe, Carol, just maybe, if *you* had been mostly abandoned by your mother, spent your childhood turning tricks in a brothel, sent to prison before you were fifteen, cooked all that shit down with a lifetime of booze and pills that ravaged your vocal chords and fucked up your liver, then you'd see that it was the depression that gave her the voice not the other way around."

"Lighten up, Dez. You're so goddamned touchy. You'd think I'd insulted your mother."

That was true enough he supposed. He *was* touchy. Defensive over little things. Punctuation. Syntax. Multiple sourcing.

And music. Defensive of those who pushed up against the weight of a world that had rolled over them. Pushed with a cracked, reedy voice. Pushed with a tube of brass bent into a horn. Or a harmonica. Or a beat-up six string. Pushing up against that weight. Pushing like a bluebell shouldering its way up through the heap of broken granite. Up around the chipped edge of the fallen tombstone. Up through the avalanche. Pushing with a sound, a syncopated heartbeat, an ironically jagged lyric. Just to keep from being crushed by it all.

So he was defensive. True enough.

It was the little things they had fought about the most. Carol had let him have all of the jazz and blues. She took the standards. The pop. The disco. Classic rock. Fine by him.

The house. Kids.

The wind slaps the side of the house with another curtain of rain. He slips Billie over the spindle. The living room pops and hisses. He grabs his drink and falls back to the recliner. Her lament is achingly familiar. Her slumberless hours amid numberless shadows. She moves is smokey circles, unwilling to land.

The telephone, suddenly, like a chainsaw chewing through the quiet.

Goddamnit, Laurie, he thinks. *Either call me or don't, but stop playing games.*

He leaves the drink. Stands. Giant steps to the turntable and hits the button to return the needle. Seizes the phone on the coffee table.

"Dez?" It is not Laurie Weaver.

"Oh. Rick. Hey." He does not pretend to be pleased.

"Bad time?"

"It's eleven o'clock, Rick. Big gamble that I'm still awake. But, hey, CBS calls, I pick up the phone."

"Awake. Right, Dez. I know for a fact you're not done with that drink yet. And Miles Davis is still working his horn. Not such a gamble really."

He gives it a breath. Doesn't want the pretense of pattering with Rick Stoddard.

"What can I do for you, Rick?"

"Looking for Laurie."

"And you think she's with me? I don't sleep with my reporters, Rick."

"Okay, Dez. One, that's not my understanding. Two, I'm going to assume that's the liquor talking and just let it go. I need to talk to her about this story. I left her a message but she hasn't gotten back to me. I was just wondering if maybe…"

"You know Laurie. Unless you're a source, you have to leave at least six messages before she'll call you back. If you're lucky."

"Yeah, I know."

"Or she hit the sauce until she hit the pillow."

"Yeah. Yeah, I know. Shit."

"So what's the problem?"

"Nothing."

"Really. Nothing at all, just calling around…"

"I need to talk to her about … do you know about the meeting?"

"Meeting? With whatshisname? The… the guy who got fired…"

"Chris Dawson. Corbin Development."

"Right. So?" It hits him then. He laughs. "Oh. I get it. You're worried they're fucking."

"No, Dez. Jesus."

"Look Rick. I don't pretend to understand what the two of you have going on off the books, but I can assure you that Laurie would never fuck a source. So you can relax. You sure as hell don't need to be calling me at elev…"

"Cut the shit, Desmond. I'm not worried about that. She told me she was meeting him. I called the Corbin Development Corporation office and asked to speak with Chris Dawson. Receptionist told me there is no fuckin' Chris Dawson."

"Yeah. Because they fired him."

"No. That's not the message I got. Like there never *was* a Chris Dawson. Like she had no idea who I was talkin' about."

"They just don't want to talk to reporters, Rick. You and CBS are radioactive."

"You think I identified myself? What the fuck, Desmond?"

"You're over-reacting, Rick. You've spooked yourself." He looks longingly at the drink. "Texas boy suddenly in the big city."

"Well, golly gee-willikers. You think so, Dez?"

"Maybe."

"Laurie tell you about Sergei Blokovich and Vasily Dudnik?"

"Yeah. She told me."

"And you don't think…"

"I think it's curious, Rick. Not dangerous."

"I'm not saying it's dangerous. I know she can take care of herself. I'm just sayin' it'd be good if she knew this going in. That's all. Okay?"

"She doesn't have to account to you. And I'm not sold yet on the cloak and dagger shit, Rick. Pretty thin."

"Okay. Well… time to get the fuck on board, Dez. That train's leaving the station."

"Oh yeah?"

"I've been looking through Vasily Dudnik's trial transcript. I won't go into it. I'll wait for Laurie. Let's just say…"

"Really? Why won't you go into it? I'm the goddamned editor, Rick."

"Right. And I don't answer to you any more. The *Chacha* gave me a start and then it nearly fuckin' killed me. You and your play-it-safe, penny-pinching, dare-to-be-dull vision of newspapering nearly killed me. Okay? And now I don't have to care any more. So I'll wait for Laurie."

"You don't know the first fuckin' thing about what it takes to keep that paper in business, Rick. None of you do."

"I'm sure that's true. I'll leave the newspaper business to you and Cal Aronson and you leave the reporting to me and to Laurie."

"I trust Laurie to do the job. We have that in common at least."

"We do. And I'll leave you with this little tidbit to stir into that drink of yours."

"What."

"There were three UC's in connection with the feder…"

"You sees?"

"Capital U. Capital C. Unindicted co-conspirators."

"Oh."

"There were three unindicted co-conspirators in connection with the federal racketeering case against Vasily Dudnik. All Russian. Two of those three UC's – Leo Volodin and Gregor Yemelin –worked construction fifteen years ago on a huge bridge project outside of Kiev."

"Okay. So?"

"So they lost their subcontracts for padding their time and materials and were then prosecuted for stealing equipment belonging to the contractor. Couple of trucks and a front-end loader. Bullshit stuff."

"Okay, so they're bad people. They hang out with other bad people. Rick, this is just…"

"The contractor working the job in Kiev was Quince International. Not Quinco. *Quince.*"

Silence. Another squall hits the side of the house. A cube of ice cracks open in its amber bath.

"Dez?"

"Yeah. I'm here."

"That's not a coincidence, man. I mean what are the fuckin' odds? You think on that. I thought Laurie might have called you to check in after the meeting. When she does, have her call me."

Rick Stoddard is gone. Desmond stands for a moment. Phone to his ear. Thinking.

Thinking about Vasily Dudnik rotting in a cell in Terra Haute.

Thinking about an international development company with empty offices in three countries and a two-bit Connecticut law firm as a registered agent.

Thinking about bridges in Kiev.

But mostly Desmond is thinking about Laurie Weaver. The call an hour ago had been from her. No connection. No message. But it was her number.

He had called back, of course. No answer. He had blamed the weather. The wind and the lightening.

Maybe. But now who was spooked?

He puts down the phone. Picks up the drink. Goes back to the turntable, hoping Billie can make things right. Pushing up against the weight of things.

He sets the needle. Pops and hisses like electronic rain and wind. Billie sings from among her numberless shadows, riding that slow, sorrowful, black coach to where the little white flowers will let you sleep forever.

Chapter 75

It does not feel like it should. Not like it always has before.

Lifting into open prairie sky.

Bevelling up above the rooftops of Houston suburbia. Houses. Schools. Churches. Brick and mortar sandbags arrayed against the storm of blinding yellow light that sprays over the eastern horizon. Banking one hundred eighty degrees, due west. Texas spreading out beneath him like an inflating relief map, enlarging, washing outwards in all directions, as everything within it simultaneously miniaturizes down to the scale of a tabletop train-set.

Sheldon has flown with Grayson several times. Felt the Cessna 206 –white with a crimson curl along the fuselage, like a wave from the Red Sea, nosing into the morning air –pulling him up into the path of the sun, the light pouring in through the windshield, pressing him down into his seat like a yellow gravity.

None of it feels like it should.

Not this time.

This time it feels like they are still, motionless in a bubble of noise as the world simply drops out from beneath them. Falling away, collapsing, in a deafening drone.

He tells himself that he would feel differently if he had his cell phone. Which is probably true. He feels naked without it. Strangely vulnerable. He had looked frantically, Grayson laying on the horn in their driveway, Christi bleating like a wounded sheep from the doorway, until he had to call off the search. *"Anything?"* Grayson had asked. Sheldon had shrugged. Shaken his head. Tossed his bag in the back. Climbed up into the truck. Off they went.

Odd that such a little device can have such an impact. Like it was some kind of vital organ that he, suddenly, could not live without. The amoebic path of human evolution was swallowing personal technology. The cell phone is the first *ex*ternal organ.

What it feels like, anyway.

Mostly because he now has no way to contact her if he cannot find her. The fly in the ointment is to be there, at the festival, without a cell phone. He doesn't like that. It makes him uneasy. Nothing feels as it should.

"Y'all hear 'bout the mother and her boy flyin' Southwest Airlines?" Grayson shouts at them –Sheldon in the co-pilot seat next to him, Christi in back –as he noses the plane up into a sky of gunmetal, banking west. Leaving Houston behind.

Christi pulls out her left, hot pink earplug. Leans forward. Shouts. "What?"

"See, a woman and her boy are on Southwest Airlines flyin' outta Houston for Chicago. Boy turns to her and says, *Mama, if dogs have baby dogs, and if cats have baby cats, how come planes don't have baby planes?*"

"Daddy…"

"Well, she ain't about to have a talk with her boy 'bout the birds and the bees so the woman tells him that he should ask the stewardess. Stewardess 'ventually comes up the aisle and the kid stops her and asks the question. '*If dogs have baby dogs, and if cats have baby cats, how come planes don't have baby planes?*' All the passengers around them hear the kid ask the question and they're all snickerin'. Stewardess looks over at the mom, who is sittin' there wearin' her earphones and smirking. Stewardess leans in and whispers in the boy's ear and then keeps on moving up the aisle. Mama pulls off her headphones as soon as she's gone and asks what she said. Boy says: '*Ain't no baby planes 'cause Southwest always pulls out on time. She said I should ask you to explain what that means.*'"

Grayson laughs like he is the listener, not the teller. Swats Sheldon in the chest. Pulls back on the stick. The 206 lurches up another hundred feet.

"Heard that one from Coop Simms out at the rifle range on Tuesday. You know Coop? Stock broker with Pickering, Platt, Stevens?"

Sheldon shakes his head.

"Daddy, I can't hear a word you're sayin'! Y'all got headsets and microphones! But the piss-ant in the back of the plane got to use chewin' gum in her ears!"

"Come on now, Sugarplum! You always fly up front. Got to give your man here a turn. You're just bent outta shape 'cause of the weather! It's gon' clear up! I keep tellin' you!"

"You said that yesterday! It's the ugliest day ever, Daddy! No one's comin' to see a pageant in this mess!"

"Forecast says it'll clear!"

"What? I can't hear a thing you…"

"Just you wait and see, Belle!"

"What?"

"Wait and see!"

Christi reinserts the neon plug. Falls back against her seat, rummaging through the purse in her lap. Freshens up her lipstick as she looks out the window.

Grayson confirms coordinates with the airfield tower, speaking in a low, emotionless tone that Sheldon can hear in his headphones as clearly as the thoughts in his own head. Grayson looks at him sideways. Chuckles. Jerks his thumb back at his daughter. Speaks.

"Prob'ly not Belle's kinda joke anyway, I guess," he says. "Her mother'd have busted a gut though. She was somethin', that woman. Layla could talk a blue streak after Sunday church like she was singin' a lullaby so you almost didn't know why you were blushin'. She could plug a prairie dog at fifty yards like she was fallin' outta bed. Cooked like she'd sold her soul to the devil and she could hold her liquor better'n any man in Texas." Grayson shakes his head. "Good woman."

The only thing Sheldon wants to say concerns the six years of Grayson's infidelity preceding the day cancer stopped Layla's heart. Apparently Layla was a better woman after her heart stopped than before.

But he says nothing. Nods with enough enthusiasm to qualify as a response. He looks out the window at the city of Houston slipping away beneath them. Thinks of Olivia. Thinks of the money in the canvas *Cavaliers* backpack stuffed into the back of the plane.

The money and the music.

He watches a familiar liquid shape come into view, revealing itself an inch at a time. *Sheldon Lake* glints a dull, gray reflection of sky from below.

He remembers it like an old slide show of black and whites. Remembers his parents, one and then the other. Cigarettes between lips. Cigarettes between fingers. His mother's horn rims. His father's boots. His big hands. Grabbing fishing tackle. The tent. The food. Piling into the blue Bonneville station wagon with the neighbor kids. Clarke and Dustin. Making the hot summer drive to *Sheldon Lake*. The smell of that car. Food and sweat and camping gear cooked under glass in the heat of a Texan summer and blown out the windows in clouds of white nicotine.

He remembers unpacking. Hauling everything up a trail to the same clearing by the water. The picnic table. The campground. The same campground as it had been ten years earlier than his oldest memory.

Everything had started for him, as a human, in the back of the same blue Bonneville. Right there. *Sheldon Lake.*

Grayson's stewardess is suddenly in his head, leaning in. *Ask your mama to explain that, kiddo.*

Places and names. A person named after a lake named after a person. Like planting a flag in the earth so your kid can measure how far he travels in his life. *You started right here, boy. See your name?*

He tries not to consider how far he has travelled. He focuses instead on the shape of the dull gray lake below, now revealed in full. Then he remembers the opposite. *Canyon Lake.* A shimmering a nimbus of brilliance behind Olivia's head.

"This has to be about more than money," she had told him. *"What are we sharing here?"* It was the question they both had been asking themselves and that she had pulled out into the daylight, glinting. And then she had answered that question.

"Music," she had said. *"Let's make this about the blues. Let's share that."*

And that was his way in. *Music. The blues.*

She had given him a map to understanding her. A map to finding her. In all of her sparsity. In all of her wounded remoteness. A map of musical scar tissue that he can trace with his inner ear. That innate rhythm. That old twelve-bar heartbeat of humanity.

Let's make this about the blues. Let's share that.

It took some courage, some determination, unearthing the evidence of the man he used to be. So much more comfortable to keep it all packed away in the dark. That *other* him. The abandoned self.

But he'd found them. All one hundred and forty-three of them, stuffed into a box beneath other boxes in the basement. Not ditties. Not musical slogans.

Songs.

He had taken them upstairs to his office and closed the door behind him. Stood still. Listened to the quiet house on the other side, fingertips on the door. Then he'd set to organizing the yellowed papers in piles on the floor. Extracted the shit-kicking country tunes. Extracted his misadventures into sappy pop ballads. Extracted the maudlin anti-nuke anthem and turned it over so he could not read the lyrics.

That left one hundred and thirteen. Pure blues. Pure shit-for-luck, misery, heartache and pain all in four-four time. Guitar. Piano. Harmonica. Acoustic. Electric. Delta. Chicago. Memphis. New Orleans. One hundred and thirteen altogether, including the ones he had sent unagented, against his better judgment, to the likes of B.B. King. Etta James. Lightnin' Hopkins. Ruth Brown.

They'd never written him back, of course. But they'd never ripped him off either, at least as far as he knew. It had been worth the shot to send them something. Worth the fitful dreams, hearing those songs in his head. *His* songs. *His* notes, flying off of the strings of B.B.'s *Lucille. His* words, sailing out of Ruth's mouth. He'd lain in the dark every night, hearing all of that in his head.

Just maybe. Just maybe. Just maybe.

He'd had some decent success with a dozen or more artists in the regional market. He'd had the most luck with the vocalists. Carny Heart. Bobby Slim. Dixie Mae Werner. He'd had the thrill of hearing *T.J. Black* rip into *Say it Ain't So, Baby* at the Texas State Fair in 1985. The song had brought the band back out for a second ovation in which they'd played a torched-up *Break it to Me Slowly* and *Just a Half-Pint More* on a bottle slide guitar, all to raucous applause. He'd silently taken the credit and an imaginary bow from the cheap seats in the makeshift amphitheater.

And he'd watched thirteen of his songs, followed by the tiny scripted credit to *S. Davis,* find their way onto twenty-four different records. Just enough success to convince himself, and a handful of others, that he had talent but not nearly enough to pay three months rent.

And so he had set about paying the rent. Gradually at first. In a way that did not feel like much of a course correction. He kept writing songs. It was just that some of those songs were little, short itty-bitty tunes about mattresses and ranching supplies. Then that was mostly all he wrote, taking time here and there to work on an *American Pie* inspired anthem against nuclear war that turned on unfortunate phonetic pairings. *Iran* and *Japan. Fusion* and *delusion. Millions of dullahs* and *killin' the Mullas.* He'd tinkered with it off and on, tuning up his trusted Martin and plucking out a verse or two after dinner in front of the television news. Just enough to tell himself that he was still at it. Still creating.

Which he wasn't. Not really. Not for a long time.

And then he'd made a sharp turn into the *business* end of advertising. Stopped writing even those little, short, itty-bitty tunes, leaving that sort of thing to others: struggling Houston songwriters looking to pay the rent.

Houston Market Research became the only tune in his life that he tried to sell. He sang it to anyone who would listen, hobnobbing relentlessly between Houston, Austin and Dallas in his one good pinstripe until a few executives began singing the HMR tune to themselves in the shower like a bad country-pop hook.

And then the phone began to ring.

And *that*, as they say, was that.

And now here was Olivia. *Let's make this about the blues. Let's share that.*

If Olivia wanted them to be about the blues, well then he could oblige. Odd that after all of those years sharing his songs to anyone who would listen, he felt so exposed and vulnerable to share them with her. Sharing them on paper. Sharing them with someone who knew her music but who was not a musician.

At first, as he arranged the stacks of sheet music across the floor of his study, he had no clue what she was supposed to do with them. *Nothing*, he guessed. Read the lyrics. Appreciate the words themselves.

But then he understood.

What he wanted was to provoke interest. What he wanted was for her to read the songs in the privacy of her own life, in the middle of her scarred and wounded remoteness, and then reach out to him. Suddenly not about the money, but about music. *His* music. A phone call. An opinion, reserved but favorable. *Can you play? Let's get together. Let's meet someplace. Bring your guitar, Sheldon. I want to hear 'Break it to Me Slowly'. And 'The Last Drop in the Bottle'. And 'Still Waiting Across Town'. And 'Delta Dial Tone Blues'.*

That's what he wanted. That's what this was all about.

Just maybe. Just maybe. Just maybe.

So he'd stuffed all one hundred and thirteen songs into the *Houston Cavaliers* backpack that he had never used before in his life. He would just hand it to her. Or set it down between them on a bench as festival goers streamed around them. She'd venture a clandestine peak. *What's this?* She'd ask. *The start of something, I hope*, he'd reply. *Something we can share. Save it for later.* And when he stood and disappeared back into the crowd, he'd leave all of those years, all of him, with her. The next time he saw the backpack, it would be coming toward him, swinging over *her* shoulder as he waited at some picnic table or a park bench, one arm draped over a guitar case.

Just maybe. Just maybe. Just maybe.

On top of the sheet music he had tossed in three fat envelopes of cash. On top of that, an old towel. A plastic bottle of water. Cinched the opening. Closed the flap. Then he had stuffed the entire backpack into a black, soft leather travel bag beneath two small umbrellas, a jacket, a baseball hat, and small camera bag. *Zip.* Done.

He'd caught shit from Grayson about the luggage.

"Goddamn, Shelly. You're worse than Christi. How many costume changes you bringin' anyway? You gon' haul that thing around with you? Y'ain't a beauty contestant are you?"

But then catching shit from Grayson and Christi had been the whole point.

"Funny. I'm packin' for two, Grayson. As her father, you should know that. Umbrellas. Jackets. Hats. Who knows what the hell the weather's gonna do today. There's a backpack in here for the essentials. And you know Christi's gonna load up on mementos. I'm only making one trip back to the car and that's when we're leavin' to come back home."

"Well. Guess you get points for thinkin' ahead."

He could have waited on the sheet music. Given it to her another time. He could have. It's not like she was expecting it. He'd said nothing about it on the phone. He'd simply encouraged her to meet him.

"I've got to be in Corbin for this damned beauty pageant. Thought maybe… since I'm there anyway… I could slip away for a few minutes and…"

She had resisted him mightily. "Ain't going within ten miles of the Moon Garden Festival this year, Shel. I'll see you when I'm supposed to see you."

So he had baited the hook with the only thing he knew would work. The thing she needed. "I'll have something for you. Ahead of schedule. Heavier than normal."

And, sure enough, that had done it. She would be there, waiting for him at the Ferris wheel.

So he could have waited. Could have. But then, once he'd decided, once he had opened that box, laid out all of the old music; that was it. There was no waiting. No choice. Not really.

The Cessna makes a slow arc around Austin's southern bank, bumping over boulders of hard air. The *Ann Richards' Bridge* stretches over the part of the Colorado River called *Lady Bird Lake*. On the other side of the water, the city is a petrified forest of slate gray pilings with rectangles of glass reflecting the silty sky.

Grayson inclines his chin. Shouts.

"You doin' okay back there, Sugarplum?"

He does not look back at Christi and she does not show any sign of hearing, locked away in her jostling world of jagged sound. Grayson speaks as calmly as if they were sitting next to each other in a parked car.

"Mighty quiet there, Shelly."

"No. Just, you know, takin' in the view." He shrugs. Smiles.

"See I figure you're over there thinkin' 'bout your girlfriend. 'Bout how you're 'gon pull off slippin' away in the crowd today to meet her."

Sheldon feels his head whip sideways like some spring-loaded sprinkler.

"What are you talking about?"

"Save it Shel. When you're in a hole, put down the shovel and stop diggin'. And you're half-way to fuckin' China already, boy."

"I don't... I don't..."

Grayson is calm, looking away from him out his own window. He points at something below. A show entirely for Christi's benefit in case she is watching.

"The hell you don't Shelly. The hell you don't. You can lie if you want to. Go on ahead and lie. Won't do you any good. I've seen the photos. *Canyon Lake*, clear as fuckin' day. You want to try tellin' me again that you were meeting with Pepper Clark-Bean? Ain't a person in Texas real estate who don't know who Pepper Clark-Bean is, boy. You should'a picked a different name. Might've believed that. But *Pepper Clark-Bean*? Richest, craziest bitch this side of the Rio Grande? You must think I'm stupid, Shel. Do you? Do you think I'm stupid?"

Sheldon looks away. Swallows. Sees the Colorado River serpentine north, away from Austin and *Lady Bird Lake*. It's not a lake, he thinks. It's not a fucking lake. It's a cheat. It's an obstructed river. Dam to the west. Dam to the east. It's a deliberately clogged drain. Why do they call it a lake? Why do Texans play these lying games with water?

"'Course, had I believed the lie about Pepper Clark-Bean, I'd still thought you were a fuckin' thief. Skimmin' money outta that agency like nobody's business."

He wants to snap his head back to Grayson's side of the plane. He resists the urge. Then he replaces it with an urge to speak words into the microphone of his headset. To say that it *is* nobody else's business. That *HMR* is *his* business and he can do whatever in the hell he wants to with it.

But he resists that urge too. He knows better. Knows that Grayson will be waiting for that argument with a lecture about silent partners. A lecture about who made Houston Market Research the business it is today.

All he can do is sit there. Trace the lower, obstructed intestines of the Colorado River and feel nauseous. Want off the plane almost enough to jump. Listen.

"Had me a good long look at the books the other night. Found out you been payin' a whole lot of money to lawyers. Not such a big surprise 'cause I know those suited bloodsuckers cost money. But seein' that kinda' money goin' out the window made me wonder what in the *hell* you were gettin' in return. 'Cause that's not *angry letter-writin'* money. Or *phone-call* money. Or *negotiation* money. That's not *print-a-retraction-or-else* money. That's honest-to-God *scorched earth litigation* money. And I figured I'da heard about scorched earth litigation against a newspaper. So fuck me, but I was perplexed, Shelly. I was perplexed."

The Cessna hits another hard pothole of air. Grayson noses down a few feet. Looks back at Christi.

"Doin' okay, baby?" he shouts.

"Can't hear you, Daddy!"

He waves backhandedly in acknowledgment. Smiles a little at Sheldon. Shakes his head as if they are sharing a private joke about Christi not being able to hear. Looks back out over the nose of the plane.

"So I did a little research. The law firm is real enough. Good reputation. You got you some kick-ass counsel. Problem is... the checks aren't made out to Houston Media Law Group. They're made out to HMLG, Inc. And they're bein' sent to a P.O. Box that don't belong to the Houston Media Law Group. Don't you just wonder who has the key to that P.O. Box?"

He doesn't have any idea what he is going to say. Maybe that Christi is having an affair under his nose with Nicholas Voss. Maybe that his sham of a marriage is none of Grayson's business. But those are just guesses. All he knows is that words seem to be assembling in his upper esophagus.

"Grayson, listen..."

"No, no, no. This is *your* turn to shut the fuck up and listen, Shel." Grayson, voice calm and cold, points out of the pilot-side window at nothing. "You understand me? You're gonna sit there and you're gonna shut the fuck up and you're gonna listen."

Sheldon does as he is told.

"So you'll never guess what happens after that. I'm sittin' there in accounting, scratching my head over this shit and April March sticks in her pretty little head goin' on and on about how some reporter from the *Chachalaca Gazette* is callin' you a thousand times a day and how you won't call her back and how she –April March, I mean –can't figure out why we don't want a little free publicity on this Corbin River Walk deal. Well, you can bet *that* got my fuckin' attention like a fart in church. So I ask April for the name and number for this reporter gal and I call her up. Laurie Weaver. Leave her a message sayin' I was your executive assistant and that you'd asked me to find out what in the hell she wanted. Guess why she was callin, Shelly."

"You really think she's going believe that you..."

"You really think I gave her my real name? Dumbass. Guess why she was callin'."

Grayson goes silent for a few seconds, baiting the trap, pretending that he actually wants him to guess. But even if Sheldon were stupid enough to guess, he actually has no idea now why Laurie Weaver was calling. It was obviously not, as he had assumed, to find out why Grayson Tate or his lawyers were asking questions and making demands about the solicitation story. No one, it turns out, had been calling the *Chacha* asking questions and making demands. Not him. Not Grayson. Not any lawyers. So why in the hell had Laurie Weaver been hounding him? He waits.

"Woman calls back. Tells me they're workin' on a story about land transactions involving the Corbin Development Corporation. Tells me that she has a source that says you –Sheldon fuckin' Davis –have information that the CDC, our fuckin' client, has been buyin' and sellin' land that it doesn't even fuckin' own."

The sprinkler head snaps.

"What?"

"Oh, you're all surprised, huh? Shocked, I'm sure."

"Grayson, I have no idea, what..."

Grayson pulls back on the stick abruptly, tilting the plane up into space. It is intended to shut him up. It works. Christi makes a sharp squeaking-shrieking sound. Grayson levels off again. Waves his right hand toward the rear of the plane to signal an apology. Speaks.

"So this Laurie Weaver woman wants a comment. And, believe me, I want to give her a comment that she cannot repeat in polite society. But I hold my tongue and tell her the truth, which is that HMR has no information regarding CDC land transactions and even if it did, HMR sure as hell has no authority to comment. Told her she needs to address any such questions directly to the CDC. She said her source gave her a list of property acquisitions. I told her property transfers are public record and maybe she should just do some research rather than bothering you about it. She says you gave her source a memo from Gregor Buchvarov, and did I know who he was and did I know why you would do such a thing, to which I told her of course I knew who Gregor Buchvarov was, just like everybody else does, and that I did not have time to play guessing games with desert rag reporters, which I think just pissed her off 'cause she asked me if you were the same Sheldon T. Davis arrested for solicitation in Corbin, to which I replied that she had the wrong person and hung up on her."

The Cessna buzzes up over San Angelo. Sheldon watches the city of a hundred thousand people disappear into the propeller. Imagines it dispersing in shreds behind them, now confetti in the wind. If he had ever wanted to defend himself, that impulse is now gone. He sits, waiting for the rest.

"So I'm sittin' there thinkin' well *shit-oh-dear*, what in the hell am I gonna do about *this*? So I pick up the phone again and call Nicki. We meet up at his hotel and I buy the man a drink and come clean with everything I know. Well, most everything. I leave out the part about *you*. Leave out the part about you dippin' your wick into Corbin whores. Leave out the part about you givin' out CDC information. Prob'ly to the same whore. Am I right? Some whore and her pimp got you by the balls and now you're payin' 'em off with my goddamned money to keep 'em quiet? That about right Shelly? Well, just so you know, you've been wastin' my money 'cause the whore, if that's who's behind it, ain't keepin' quiet. The whore is now talkin' to the newspapers. Does your new girlfriend know the shit you're into? Oh, hang on a minute. Hang on. She *is* the shit you're into, isn't she? You went and fell in love with a whore, didn't you? Not just someone who *turned out* to be a whore, but your *own* whore. You knew what she is and you still..." Grayson breaks off. Shakes his head. "Goddamned but you disgust me, Shelly. I'd like to throw your ass off this fuckin' plane."

Grayson keeps shaking his head to himself, jaw muscles working. Lower lip pulling down against the edge of his silver mustache. He takes a deep breath. Exhales. As if to let it all go. Continues.

"Anyway. Shit, Shelly. So I tell Nicki about the reporter lookin' for a story about property transfers. Tell him about the Russian's memo too. I'm thinkin' he's gonna want to call up the Russian right there at the fuckin' bar, get his ass outta bed, put me on the phone and tell me to repeat everything. But goddamned if Nicki didn't give me one of those non-smiles of his. Said not to worry about it. Said this has happened before. Someone starts lookin' at old documents for properties that have already flipped again maybe two or three times. New paperwork somehow gets out there before the old paperwork and the paper trail gets all confused to people who don't know what they're lookin' at. And he said the Russian's memo was broadly released. Could have come from anywhere. And believe me... I wanted to tell him that I knew *exactly* where it came from. I mean fuckin' *exactly*. Same goddamned place the property transfer paperwork came from. *You*. But I didn't. I kept my mouth shut, Shelly. 'Cause I'll be goddamned if I'm gonna let you ruin the best gig I have ever had in my entire fuckin' career, you understand me?"

Ten minutes slip beneath the plane, each a continent unto itself, without another word. He begins to think Grayson is done, at least for now. Begins to think they will make it all the way to Bates Field in Odessa and that the next words he hears will be Grayson asking for clearance to land. He is wrong.

"Here's how this is gonna go. Sheldon T. Davis. This is how it happens. I want you out of my life and I want you out of my daughter's life. I want…"

"She's having an affair with Nicki Voss, Grayson. Do you know that? Do you?"

"You're pathetic, Shelly."

"It's true."

"I don't believe that for one fuckin' second. You're tryin' to justify your own affair is what you're doin'."

"I'm not having an affair. Grayson. I'm not. And I haven't given any list of prop…"

"This is how it's gonna be, Shelly. You're gon' divorce my daughter. Tell her whatever bullshit story you want to, but put an end to it. If you don't tell her, then I'm gon' tell her. Then…"

"Grayson…"

"Then I am going to buy HMR out from under you, and…"

"What? Like Hell."

"Yep. Even if Hell is what it takes. And I'm gon' do it for fifty cents on the dollar, less what you have already skimmed off the top. I know you don't like that. Think I'm cheatin' you out of your business. But you listen up real good, Shelly. I'm gonna have my *real* lawyers draw up the papers and you can sign them or not. But if not, then my *real* lawyers, who get their mail at a *real* address, are gon' come after you for a return of my investment in that business. Believe it. I have the legal right to cash in my chips any time I please. And that right there will put HMR into bankruptcy and you know it. While I'm at it, I'll make sure my *real* lawyers represent Christi to sue your ass for support. Don't you forget that HMR is a marital asset. And then I'm comin' after your whore girlfriend. When HMR can't pay me back my money, I'm gonna go lookin' for it up your whore girlfriend's cooch. Olivia."

Sheldon looks.

"Yeah. I got her name. Got her phone number. You're phone is down in the couch cushions in your study, by the way. Guess you didn't look there, did ya? I even know what she looks like. Why you want to throw your whole life away over the Bride of Frankenstein I will never know. T'each his own, I guess. She must be one helluva fuck."

"Fuck you."

"Yeah, okay cowboy. That's right. Fuck me. Looks like you been fuckin' me all the way to the bank. So now it's my turn. Talk your talk. But when you're done spoutin' off you just sit there and do the math. You're gonna let go of the business and you're gonna let go of my daughter. Hear me? You'll either take away somethin' close to fifty percent to spend on your whore girlfriend or you won't have a penny to your fuckin' name. You decide. That's just gonna be whatever it's gonna be. But here comes the important part, so listen good."

Sheldon looks out the window. Listening is the last thing he wants to do. But he does.

"First, you have no more involvement in the Corbin Development project. And I mean none. *Zero*. April March is about to get a great big fuckin' promotion. You're not gettin' anywhere near that deal ever again. If I have to, I will tell the Russian that they need to swap in another ad agency. He'll thank me for putting the interests of the project ahead of my own goddamned family. Second…"

"You think…"

"Sec…. Shut your mouth, boy. Second. We are gonna let Christi have her day in the sun. You hear me? This weekend is important to her. We can let all the shit hit the fan come Monday. But *this* weekend? For the duration of this ridiculous fuckin' two-headed festival? You and I are gon' get Academy Awards for actin' like nothin' in the world is outta place. You're about to rip Christi's life open. So I want her to have a successful pageant that she can carry around like a tiara. When her barracuda friends get hold of the news that you turned out to be a pathetic shit, just like Tig Larson all over again, she's gonna need something to keep her head up and this pageant is that thing. Understand what I'm tellin' you?"

They look at each other. Sheldon says nothing.

"So we… I'm in this too, now. I'm in this too. You and me. *We…* are not gon' do anything… *anything…* to rain on her parade. Understand Shelly? Not a single fuckin' drop of rain. Nicki's gon' pick us up at the airport and you're not gon' say a goddamned thing and I'm not gon' say a goddamned thing and he's not gon' say a goddamned thing except what a beautiful goddamned day it is. Think you can try *not* bein' a pathetic shit long enough to do that? You're so good at lyin', you think maybe you can keep it up for another couple'a days?"

Sheldon takes the headphones off. The chainsaw air almost hurts. The sonic violence of it feels good. It shreds everything. Like the propeller has somehow inverted into the cabin. He keeps looking out the tiny window. Leans his forehead against the glass. Odessa is in view. A collection of low, whitish smudges against the light brown earth. Roads like old scars angling this way and that. Everything gets bigger. Closer.

Grayson rotates in his seat. Taps Christi on the knee. Points out over the nose of the Cessna.

"Enough blue sky on that horizon to make a dress, Sugar! Get yourself ready for a good day! You wait and see! 'Cause hell or high water your daddy is gonna make it happen! Ain't that right Shelly?" Grayson slaps him on the shoulder. "Ain't nothin' I can't make happen! Even the goddamned weather! Y'all just remember that next time you doubt me!"

Chapter 76

It's not the hangover. This feeling in his head.

Desmond climbs into the car. Puts the coffee in the holder. Tosses in the briefcase. Closes the door.

Closes his eyes. Breathes.

It *is* the hangover, of course. The fog is so thick in his head he almost cannot see through his own eyes. To think is, at most, merely to grope for the edges of routine. Five steps, shower. Ten steps, coffee. Thirty steps, car.

But that's not everything. He knows what a hangover feels like. This morning there is something else in there with it. Something hard and dense is in the fog, banging around. Like the steel ball they put inside spray cans to mix up the paint.

Somewhere deeper, beneath the wincing, he knows what it is. That other thing. It's that little ball of worry.

Laurie Weaver is in there. Banging around.

She never called. Rick Stoddard was right. Not like Laurie to drop off the radar. Not so completely. She was always reachable eventually. So the ball bearing in his head keeps ripping through the fog until it collides with bone and changes direction.

Something is wrong… bang!

Something is wrong… bang!

Something is wrong… bang!

He starts the car. The radio comes to life, splitting the close, heavy air like machine gun fire. "… *due to flash flooding reported in the…*"

He winces. Fumbles at the dash. Snaps it off. Drives.

The roads are mostly dry. The eastern horizon occludes the sun but there is promise of clearing to the west. The utility crews are out in force, white pickups wearing flashing yellow hats, parked beneath crooked utility poles.

Even this early the traffic is horrible by Corbin standards. All from the east, headed for the fairgrounds. But at least it's moving. In another couple of hours it will be faster to just get out and walk the last five miles.

He has to wait to cross *Broken River Road* to allow for traffic exiting I-67.

Before ten-thirty the entire street will be lined on both sides with parked cars.

A man in black walks past. A pair of stilts under one arm. A large skeleton head under the other. The man darts across *Broken River*, navigating around a clutch of co-eds, everywhere hair and hats and profligate enthusiasm, leaning into the bed of a parked green pick-up. They pull out square placards and silver cardboard fish at the end of long wooden poles. Dozens of them. They lean the signs, one by one, up against the bed of the truck. The signs keep sliding off the truck to the street. He has to tilt his head to read them.

Protect The Bluntnose Shiner!
Leave The Pecos River Alone!
Saks, Stay on Fifth Avenue!
One Planet! One Future!
No Cartier in Corbin!
Corbin River Walk = Pathway to Destruction
Greed? Again? Really?
Gucci Go Home!
Victoria, Keep Your Secret!
Mother Nature is Most Displeased!

A break in the traffic. He pushes across.

He does not like making the drive into work on a Saturday. It makes the next week feel so much longer. Monday will feel like it should be Wednesday. Wednesday he will expect it to be Saturday.

It had not been the plan to come in. The plan had been to sleep off the Friday night overindulgence, have a late breakfast, and then make it in to the festival about one. Take photos of the pageant. Interview a few mostly naked women. Go home. Write up the story to which he would affix Laurie Weaver's name so that Cal Aronson could have the satisfaction of having reminded Laurie of her place in the food chain.

That had been the plan.

But it had been a long time since Desmond had taken a publishable photograph of anything or anyone. He was a vinyl music guy. He was a word guy. A pen and pad guy. He was not a camera guy, meaning he didn't have a camera except the one that came with his not-so-smart cell phone.

So he needed the camera from the paper. He had had the presence of mind to borrow one from Billy Sampson. Billy was all too happy to oblige upon learning that Desmond was not assigning *him* to battle the festival throngs.

"Battery's dead though," Billy had said. "Takes a couple of hours."

Easy enough. If he had actually remembered to bring the camera home. Which he hadn't.

So. Here he was, driving to work. Hung over on a Saturday morning.

The thing in his head starts up again, just as he approaches the final turn that leads to the place he works.

Something is wrong... bang!

Something is wrong... bang!

The street here is wet. Not just damp. *Wet.*

Streams of water. Lots and lots of water.

The Corbin VFD has three, neon yellow engines at its disposal. Two of them are in the parking lot of the *Chachalaca Gazette*, idling, lights flashing. Two cruisers are parked nose-to-nose in the middle of the deepening lake, enforcing a perimeter.

The administration building, the place Desmond has reported for work day after day after day for decades, is a scorched, smoldering brick husk. Next door, the two-story press plant looks almost as it always has: a stalwart relic from the archives of newspapering architecture.

Almost. There is a bright orange glow coming through the shattered first floor windows. The fire inside is dancing. Laughing at the stream of water.

All of that paper stock. All of that quick-dry paraffin. A building full of wax. A two-story brick-rimmed candle.

He inches the car in slowly, steering to an island of familiar vehicles in the far corner of the lot. Everett Sampson. Sylvia Bloom. Others. Mostly production staff. He parks. Cuts the engine. Gets out. Sylvia is crying. Everett is talking to no one in particular.

"One building? Maybe lightning. Maybe electrical. But *both* buildings? That's fuckin' arson, man. We've been torched."

Desmond stands next to him. Hands on his hips. Watching.

"This is it," says Everett. "Ain't it, Dez? We're done. *Chacha's* dead."

He waits a beat or two. Looks back at the plumes of oily black smoke curling up into the morning sky. Nods.

Sylvia Bloom takes it up a notch, a wailing that unmoors from its human source and becomes just another note in the soundscape of hissing and gushing and popping and crackling and bursts of radio static. It is a wailing like a kind of sonic thread. She is a wind instrument, a horn, lungs emptying into a ragged tremolo, an unsustainable high-C, binding everything together.

Desmond watches the water blasting in through the windows of the press plant until his eyes lose focus and he is no longer watching the fire. He speaks. To everyone. To no one.

"Anybody seen Laurie Weaver?"

Chapter 77
Mable and Libby

We know things before we know them. The weight of knowing accumulates, registers, in places we can feel but cannot consciously reach. There is water in the basement. We know this. Even before we open the cellar door.

By the time someone found Mable Holder, half submerged and partially eaten, tangled in mangroves on the eastern bank of the *Lac des Allemands*, right where the *Baie des Deux Chenes* takes custody of the water, Libby had already known that she would never see her mother again.

Knowing what she already knew had taken four weeks.

Instinctive fear had led the parade. That old worry of maternal abandonment. Mable had simply had enough of her, she decided. Had walked out. Had somehow learned that Libby was not in school; that she had left school with the older brother of a classmate. Mable, she believed, had been filled with such anger and disgust that she wanted nothing more to do with Libby and had left. Libby had vacillated between imagining that Mable intended on teaching her a lesson for a few frightening days, and imagining that Mable had abandoned her permanently.

But then the police had shown up. A long, muffled discussion had pushed its way up through the kitchen floorboards. Low, fat sonorous tones slit by thin bursts of radio static. Libby had pressed her ear against the floor. Vye Greavy's voice was a ragged, metal blade.

"Bitch best bring it back. Best do it right now or never show her face again is all I can say. That ain't her car to just joyride as she pleases."

The police came upstairs and knocked. Two of them. Fat white man. Skinny white woman. Guns and hats. They took a tour. Closets. Under the beds. Libby sat at the kitchen table and waited. When they were done they asked a lot of questions. Mable's whereabouts. The Greavy's car. Wanted to know who the man was that Vye Greavy had seen waiting for Libby up the street in a car. She had denied it was "a man" and lied that he was "a classmate." Just skipping school together, she'd told them. But Skinny wasn't buying it.

"Lyin' ain't a good play here, Libby."

"Ain't lyin'."

"Your friend got a name?"

Libby had shrugged and given up the name. The fat one dropped a card on the table. Told her to call as soon as Mable returned.

Mable did not return.

Libby waited. Propped herself up against the wall in her bedroom listening for sounds of arrival. Looking at the empty chair across the room.

She had gotten up and called the classmate's brother.

"I done the best I can. Bein' as you like a billion years older than me I suggest you get wit' Damien an' be ready fo' that knock. Told you not to park so close to my house but you done that shit anyhow, huh? So this yo' problem now, baby. I got my own problems when my mama get back."

But Mable did not come back. The days found a rhythm.

Two. Three. Four.

The police checked back. Closets. Beds. They opened the cupboards and refrigerator and looked at the dishes in the sink. Fugitives have to eat. But the only one eating in that apartment was Libby, and not much at that. The fat one scratched his gut and wiped his forehead with the back of his wrist and gave her a worrisome look as he stood cooling himself in the light of the open fridge.

"Ain't much here to eat kid. You got family you can call? Need us to call social services?"

She went to live with a friend. Well. A boy she knew from school. A boy who was too timid to do anything but pine for the sexual opportunity her presence implied was possible. It was about as close as Libby ever got to a platonic friendship. But he served his purpose and was rewarded for it in the end. She ate well and did not have to worry about Social Services hauling her off to places unknown and far away from the only place in the world that mattered to her.

She had the living room all to herself, at least until two or three in the morning every few nights when the boy's father would come out and sit politely on the edge of the couch. Like his son, he was too timid to ask. The dark room was too quiet, too still, for spoken language. Just the steady, rhythmic breathing in the rooms around them.

But she understood. Libby was fluent in the unspoken languages.

She had left a note for Mable on the kitchen counter. Phone number. Big heart at the bottom. She came back every day to check for signs, hoping the note would be gone. But it was always right where she'd left it. So she sat down for hours to wait. Worry. To hate herself. To hate herself for being the kind of daughter that would disgust her mother into abandonment.

Except that somewhere, deep down, she knew better.

Somewhere, deep down, Libby already knew everything.

One. Two. Three.

Four.

On the eighth day, she came home to find Clayton Greavy and another man out front trading fishing stories. They stopped talking as she approached.

Antoine had turned. Stretched his mouth into a worried smile. His eyes had grabbed for her, closing the distance instantly. The words took their time.

"Well, here she is. Wonderin' if you'd be by. Clayton here been catchin' me up on what's what. Still no word from Mable? What-in-the-hell, Libby? What in the hell is goin' on over here, darlin'?"

The truth travels in a fraction of a blink. It hitches a ride on the color of a man's eyes. The reasons we know what we know —the logic and the explanations and the connected dots —all take their time crossing the road. Some part of Libby had known from that very instant, if not long before.

The ABC Man was a daily presence. He stocked the refrigerator with food and beer and brought fresh concern and outrage that he whispered so the Greavys could not hear.

"Police ain't gon' do a goddamned thing to find her, I can tell you that. Racist sons-a-bitches. An' if they do find Mable they gon' try to pin on her somethin' she ain't ever done. I don't believe for one second that your mama stole a thing in her life. Much less a damn car. We had our differences, me an' your mama, but I know Mable ain't no thief. Somethin' ain't right Libby. An' I'm gon' figure it out. We gon' figure it out. You an' me."

He searched for Mable during the day, playing private eye with a notepad and a pen he tucked behind his ear. Whenever he saw Libby he made dutiful reports of who he had talked with and what they had said. Neighbors. Co-employees. People on the bus she usually rode to work. Most nights of the week Antoine slept over, holding vigil. He was clear that it did not matter what Libby did with herself. It was just something he needed to do.

"You can keep livin' over at your friend's or you can come on back home. Up to you. But someone got to be here when Mable comes back. If that phone rings in the middle of the night, someone got to be here to pick it up. I owe your mama that much. So you go on an' do whatever you're of a mind to."

Libby did come back home. She was tired of sleeping on a couch. Tired of being away. She had crumpled up her note on the counter. Laid in her own bed with the door closed. Waited. Listened to the darkness outside her window. Antoine brought her food she picked at and sent away. A week passed. Then two.

Three.

Four.

The news had come from the Louisiana State Police. Two uniforms at the front door filled to capacity with large white men. Faces of stone. Locked inside the white stone were the answers. They released it in little pieces, a few at a time, like chips of ice from a machine. Antoine put an arm around her shoulder. He asked the officers all the questions as she cried and convulsed.

Death by drowning, they suspected. Maybe an accident. Maybe not. Hard to tell given the state of the body. Forensics would run their tests. Meantime, they'd found the Greavy's car. A hundred miles away in Vidalia. A scorched metal husk upside down and mostly submerged in a swamp. They had not found any evidence in the wreckage to show that Mable had ever been in the car. Antoine had sounded a note of vindication.

"'Course not 'cause Mable wasn't no goddamned car thief. She was honest as the day is long."

They were curious about Antoine, of course. Who was he? What was his relationship to Mable? Where did he live? When he told them that he lived up in Thibodaux, and especially when he volunteered that he had a place up at *Lac des Allemands*, Libby could feel the room change.

More questions. Short, sharp pen strokes on palm-sized notepads.

Antoine had shown no resistance. He invited them out to Thibodaux before they could ask. Invited them out to the lake.

"Whatever I can do to help you find out who the hell done this to Mable. I know every goddamned person on that lake too. I'll tell you whatever you need to know. When do you want to go? Tomorrow? Now?"

The uniformed ice machines had waited as Libby had called Mable's cousin. Janeese was rightly horrified, even before identifying her bloated, decomposing kin. Janeese had swooped down from Lafayette like some sort of bird of prey. Snatched Libby out of that apartment and taken her away. Smothered her with her own hysterical grief. Evicted her own resentful thirteen-year old daughter, forcing her to bunk with her little brother just so that Libby could have a bedroom she hated. Too perfect. Too tidy. A suffocation in pink cotton with stuffed unicorns to enforce the laws of innocence. No death. No grief. Mothers are immortal.

Libby had longed for the living room couch in a quiet house where words were unnecessary and where needs were easily satisfied. It felt like a prison. Not just the pink bedroom. The whole house. All of Lafayette. It felt like she had been separated from her own heart, still beating alone on the kitchen table, one hundred and forty miles away in the apartment where Mable had channeled all the old great blues divas as she cooked supper and cleaned the dishes. For all of her good intentions, aunt Janeese had made everything worse.

Libby, for her part, had done her best to punish the whole family.

"Don't you touch me, Janeese! Don't you hug on me! Don't you tell me what to do! You ain't my mama! You ain't my mama! You ain't my mama! *You ain't my mama!*"

They all eventually hated each other.

But Libby had resisted the urge to walk out and disappear. She'd stuck it out. Six months. Eight. Twelve. She knew Mable would have wanted it. Knew Mable loved Janeese. Besides, she had no place else to go.

Grief was a kind of scoop. A sharpened, serrated tool that hollowed her out like a pumpkin before Halloween. For all of the times she had imagined herself alone in the world, Libby had never known the depth of aloneness. Not with Mable around. True solitude had been no more possible than true darkness is possible with a single burning candle in the room.

But then, suddenly, there it was. Aloneness. True darkness. Her young life, suddenly, an empty cavern where time was meaningless and the days fell like sedimentary drips that echoed from all directions. Nothing made sense. Nothing felt appropriate and true, except emptiness itself.

Nature abhors a vacuum. Time is an alchemist. Grief, guilt, fear, resentment all steeped under the pressure of tyrannical pink innocence, congealed down into a bubbling black tar of rage. Mable became a crater in the earth where something precious and holy used to stand. The more Libby contemplated the crater, the more she realized what she had known from the beginning. And the angrier she became.

Her mother did not like the water. Her mother would never have climbed into a boat. Not unless her life depended on it. Last time Mable had climbed into a boat of any kind, Antoine was at the tiller trying to keep it steady in a hurricane.

Worst of all, there was only one reason Libby could imagine that Mable would have been up in Thibodaux, Antoine's swampy neck of the woods: she had been looking for Libby. She had stolen a car to go find and save her daughter. Mable had known *nothing* about the horny much older brother of a classmate. She had only known Antoine Beaudaine Cherish.

She had only known *the ABC Man*. And she'd gone off to find him.

Libby realized that she had known it all from the beginning. From that moment Antoine had turned and watched her approaching the house. *"Well, here she is. Wonderin' if you'd be by. Clayton here been catchin' me up on what's what."*

Truth is, she'd known even before that. She'd known the first night Mable did not come home. No telling how she'd known. She just had, even if it took her a year to realize it.

Meant nothing to the police investigation, of course. The *ABC Man* was clean as a whistle. They'd scoured the house and the cabin and the boat and the boathouse. Talked to the neighbors. Nothing. The case itself became an inconvenient corpse lying in a long open drawer. The state of Louisiana had closed the drawer with a hip. Moved on.

So it was Libby who reached out. Called him from Janeese's kitchen phone when nobody was home. Antoine's tone was wary, suspicious beneath the relaxed charm of his words, like a thin mattress on a very hard floor. Antoine inquired and Libby had caught him up, complaining about her circumstances. Janeese. The family. How no one understood her. How no one really cared. How no one could fill the void left by Mable.

But Antoine understood. Antoine knew what Mable meant to Libby. Knew the kind of bond they had shared. They reminisced. Laughed about the good times. Painted over the bad times. Misunderstandings. Antoine owned all of the past turmoil. Mable was only being a good mom. He understood. He had always understood.

"Bless her soul."

Another phone call.

Three. Four.

Libby gave him directions. He made the drive to Lafayette and they had spent the day driving in circles. Talking in circles. Remembering in circles. Pretending they did not know where it was all headed. She'd made a good show of it, burying the thing she knew he wanted beneath layers of grief and emotional need. She had forced his restraint and respect. She had made him work. Made him invest in the future.

And he did. Minded his manners. Invested.

"I want you to know that I will do for you Libby. You understand? I will do for you. You need me, an' I will come runnin'. I owe that to your mama."

He did owe that. He owed everything. And Libby knew it. Turns out she had always known it, deep down where we know everything.

So she met him a second time.

Three times.

Four.

August. Antoine had put the car in park. Cut the engine. His right eye was swollen and purple. Nostrils crusted with dried blood. He spoke without looking at her. His voice was thinner. Tighter.

"Dumbass Spider got himself nipped. Lootin' crab pots and fish traps. An' fuckin'... fuckin' burglary? In broad fuckin' daylight? What kinda..."

"Who?"

"Guy I know. Call him Spider on account of his neck tat. They're on to him now, boy. They're lookin' hard. An' the dumbass come runnin' straight to me. Like some chicken shit little girl lookin' for her mama. I told him a thing or two he didn't want to hear. So I had to make him hear it. Shithead's on his own."

Antoine had picked at the dried blood. Examined it. Flicked it from his dirty finger. Continued.

"Thing is... they catch him? Spider gon' try to bite me on the ass. He gon' make up shit six ways from Sunday an' I don't want nothin' to do with it. I don't want nothin' to do with any of this shit no more. He's a goddamned liar, Lib. Don't you ever believe anything come outta Spider's mouth. He gon' try to trade his way out. He gon' say I... I... Wouldn't surprise me one little bit if Spider was the one who done Mable in."

"What?"

"Don't know it for a fact. Just sayin' he's that kinda man is all."

He'd stared out the windshield, flexing his jaw. Breathing. Then he had turned and looked at her.

"Long an' short of it, Libby? I'm movin' out. Leavin' this shitbird state once an' for all. Sellin' the house an' sellin' my place on the lake even though that land has been in my family for three generations. Ain't got no one to pass it on to so I'm sellin' it all an' startin' fresh. I am done with this shit. Not just Spider an' the shit we get up to an' all the shit he thinks he knows, but all the rest of it too." A pause. A heavy breath. "An' I want you to come with me."

Quiet. Stillness. Just her heart in a steady downbeat.

Two. Three. Four.

The answer was yes, of course. She had made him work for it, but there was never any doubt in her mind. Letting the ABC Man go was never an option. But for all appearances, Libby needed convincing. She'd let the silence accumulate. Deepen. He'd jumped in to fill it.

"Thing is, Lib'... Thing is I love you. I don't want to leave you behind. You need a new life an' I can give you one. You're close enough to marryin' age an' ain't no one gon' care 'bout that. I will give you my name or you can keep your own name if you want. I'll buy you some nice little house somewhere that you can doll up whatever which way."

"What about Janeese?"

"What about her? Bitch ain't your mama. I say do as you damn well please."

"Don't know, Antoine."

"You need help, Libby. Someone to look after you. I'm here to help. Have before and I can now. I saved your life an' I can do it again."

They had looked at each other in silence across the front seat for a long minute, the moss green Impala wrapped around them like a kind of rotting pea pod.

Time collapsed. She saw him suddenly not on the other side of the front seat, but on the other side of a ragged hole in her mother's bedroom wall where the window used to be. She saw him sitting in his rusty skiff. One hand outstretched. The other hand clutching the boat hook that he had buried into the wall. She had seen, again, the odd smile behind his face.

Not *on* his face. Behind it.

Chapter 78

"Don't hear so good, do you, boy?"

She is calmer now. That worries him. She cups her mouth with her hands.

"I. Said. I. Don't. Have. A. God. Damned. Cell. Phone."

Dallas Letti reclines on her couch in a bathrobe. Holds a deep-pink hand towel against her head. It used to be white.

Davis sits on the edge of the coffee table, an arm's length away. Soaked to the bone. He hands her a slightly less pink, freshly wrung replacement. She peels the old one off her head. Hands it to him. He sets it down on the edge of the table. Tries again.

"The reason…"

"Don't you set that mess on my table. Don't got one lick of sense, do you?"

He welcomes the abuse. She has given him the key to understanding, and now he does understand. Abuse is her way of fighting back against all forces of oppression. The guilt that will otherwise smother and crush her. The fear that now taunts her into wanting the thing she cannot bear. Compassion. Connection. He understands that now. The abuse is a kind of heartbeat. Proof of life. It's how she defends herself. From herself.

Davis picks the cloth up off the table. Puts it on his own sopping pant leg. Dallas closes her eyes. Exhales deeply. He pats her gently on the cheek.

"Nope. Nope. I need you to stay awake, Dallas."

"Motherfuck… Don't you slap me, boy!"

"That wasn't a slap. Who in this world doesn't have a cell phone?"

"*I* don't have a cell phone, that's who. Got one but I don't ever use the damn thing. 'Cept to throw at dumbass mother-fuckers lookin' to get they' business up into Letti Blue's baffrobe. That what you all about, Hero? Celebrity coochie?"

That's it, he thinks. *More of that. Keep fighting.*

He leans in. Brings his face closer to hers. Searches. Her expression recoils.

"You gon' kiss me, Hero?"

He straightens again.

"Here's the thing, Rosetta."

"Don't you call me that, boy."

"You keep calling me Hero, then I'm going to fuckin' call you Rosetta. So listen up. I don't like the way you look. Your eyes. I can't tell if you're just drunk off your ass or if you have a concussion. My phone is half a mile up in the desert beneath five feet of water. You're phone line is down. So there's no way I can call for an ambulance unless you have a cell phone around here. Even then, no guarantee I can connect."

"Ain't goin' in no goddamned ambulance. Fool. I just need to sleep it off is all."

"Not gonna happen." He does not tell her that curling up and sleeping it off is exactly what *he* wants to do. Right here. Right Now. "You have a head injury. And you took a lot of water into your lungs. You need medical attention. So we're gonna get in your truck and go to the clinic. I can either…"

"The hell you say."

Her entire face hardens for the fight, soft black skin wrinkling up beneath her nose and around her lips.

He can see her for a moment. Back in her day. Remembers an album cover. *Letti Blue Live.* That face. That deep gaze. She had been beautiful in a regal way. Queen like.

He widens his eyes. Points off behind him, through the wall.

"I can either carry your black ass out to the truck… in your *bathrobe*, or…" She wants to object. Wants to tell him off. He holds up a finger. "*Or!* Or… you can go get changed and come out with your head held high and cussin' a blue streak. But understand this, Dallas. While you're makin' up your stubborn mind, I will not leave your side and I will not stop pattin' your face. Understand? So what's it gonna be?"

Takes awhile, but he finally gets her up and moving. They go another round or two over whether he should be allowed to accompany her to her bedroom, behind a locking door, to change her clothes. She doesn't trust him not to look. He doesn't trust her not to lock the door and go to bed. The compromise is that she can close the door but he gets to keep the knob turned. It takes her a full ten minutes. He only peeks once.

She needs him in order to walk. He is one-half step ahead of her, moving slowly. She clings to his shoulder with one hand and to the crook of his arm with the other. She is quiet. Like she is too exhausted to keep swinging. Too tired to keep up the fight.

And that worries him.

It is not until he is steering Dallas' truck from around the back of her house that he appreciates just how drunk he still is. Adrenaline has sharpened the world around him. Fear of drowning, fear of Dallas drowning, had saved his life. And hers. It had beaten back the alcoholic fog. Gotten them out of the disintegrating deathtrap. It had given him the strength to carry her in his arms away from the raging floodwaters, away from the scuttled ark, away from the broken church, away from his submerged Harley, three-quarters of a mile through the desert to her home. It had given him clarity of purpose.

It had also pushed away all of the dead. It had pushed all of the voices off into the shadows. Everyone had shut up so he could save himself. And her.

But now.

The truck rattles beneath them. They sway and rock together as if to some silent melody. He feels the adrenaline receding. Seeping away into the soil. It leaves a landscape sopping with woozy, inebriated exhaustion.

Dallas' head lolls. He reaches over. Pats her on the cheek.

"Got to stay awake, Dallas. Rosetta? Got to stay awake."

"I *am* awake you white pervert motherfucker."

"Atta girl."

He makes it halfway to the road before it hits him in a wave he cannot contain. Like he has internalized the flood. Like he carries it around inside of him.

He stops the truck. Gets out. Wretches water and bile out into the dirt. Spits. Again. Again. Wipes his mouth. Straightens. Looks around, catching his breath, just long enough to appreciate the world rolling out into the gray of a new morning. Somewhere in the distance he can hear rushing water. He climbs back in. Slams the door. Puts the truck in gear.

"You okay, Hero?" She is only half taunting.

He stops at the bottom of the access road, front tires on the edge of I-67. The closest hospital or clinic is likely to be in Fort Stockton. West and south. Or Odessa. West and north. But in that direction, west, rush the floodwaters that had almost killed them. He suspects they have taken out the road. Not worth the risk.

That's what he tells himself.

The truth is different. Truth is he wants to go east. Towards Corbin. He just doesn't know why he wants to go east.

There is a buzz in his head. A bee on the far side of a curtained window. Vibrating from a world beyond. Hurling itself against the bubble. Again. Again.

East… East… East.

So he does. Cranks the wheel. Hits the gas. Peels out directly into the early sun, stuffed down into its soft grey pocket of cloud. Struggling to rise.

"Where in the hell…"

"Corbin Medical Clinic. Road's probably under water the other way." Dallas adjusts her seatbelt. Leans up against the door. He pulls her wrist so she is upright again. "Nope. Dallas? You need to stay awake. Sing me a song."

"Ain't singin' you no song. *He*-ro."

"Okay, then. *Ro*-setta. I'll give you the first line of a song. If you can tell me the name of the song, then you win and it's my turn to guess. If you can't, then you have to concede defeat to a white pervert motherfucker and I get to give you another one."

"Ain't playin' no stupid…"

"I don't want you."

"Well I don't want your sorry ass neither, no good piece-a-shit…"

He laughs. Incredibly, he laughs.

"No, no. That's the first line of the song. *I don't want you.*"

She is quiet for two hundred yards of mostly empty highway. He keeps checking to see that she is awake. She is.

"Stumped you, didn't I? Hell, Rosetta. Y'ain't so damn tough. Let's try…"

She cuts him off, singing.

"But I hate to lose you…"

An echo of the great Letti Blue fills the cab, measuring that space between the devil and the deep blue sea. It is not a slow song. Not as he remembers it. But Dallas makes it her own. Each phrase is heavy and wet and slow to finally drop. She doesn't want him, but she hates to lose him. She forgives because she cannot forget. Like some overburdened ball of rain from the corner of an old window eave, Dallas Letti holds the sound in trembling suspension before letting it fall.

When she is done, he tosses out another.

"Up in the mornin'," he croons.

There is no delay this time. Dallas dives in, singing about that lucky old sun up in heaven, rolling around without a care for the ache and toil below.

There are two ways to go with that song. Ray Charles is one way: *I fuss with my woman.* Or there was Aretha Franklin's way. He knows which way his mother sang it. He can hear her voice in his head. Elizabeth Payne and Dallas Letti merge into a single sound that is simultaneously inside of him and outside. *Sweating for my family. Toiling for my kids. Wrinkling and turning gray. All while that lucky old sun rolls the heavens above.*

They roll forward, the two of them, bearing down on the lucky old sun throbbing like a bandaged wound on the horizon. A glow behind the gauze. A swollen protuberance of light. Dallas sings. Drifting from one song to the next without needing a prompt. Never from beginning to end. A verse here, a verse there. Like she is dropping in on old friends.

She drops in on Ruth Brown.

"Raaaaiiin … is a bring down…"

He is suddenly in his mother's kitchen, sitting at the table watching her cook pancakes on Saturday morning. Conrad is wherever he is. Sleeping it off. So it is just the two of them. Davis and Elizabeth. She flips the pancake. Turns. Smiles. Winks. Turns away again, flowered cotton blouse pulling against her shoulder blade. Sings in that dreamy way of hers.

Rain is a bring down, she says, just like her man. Dallas draws out all of the vowels, elongating every note. *Raaaaaaiiiin is a bringdoooowwwnn.* Now *he* is the one who has to fight the urge to lean up against the window. Close his eyes. Curl up. Sleep.

He shakes his head. Focuses on the road. They pass a crew trying to pull up a telephone pole, knocked over in the storm. Watches them in the mirror. Focuses on whatever he can. The dashboard indicators. *Speed. Engine temperature. Oil.* The horn in front of him sports the familiar array of raised, block silver letters: **F O R D.**

He stops blinking.

Stares at those letters.

He sees them differently, imagines them differently, for the first time.

F R E D.

For all of the times he has been in this truck, loading it up with bits and pieces of metal and glass and wood, it had never occurred to him. Not once. Not consciously. He looks around the cab with new eyes.

It was the same truck. The truck that Fat Jack had asked him to hide from his uncle Zeke. The truck Zeke had likely stolen from some poor Houston hick named *Fred.* The truck that had given him clandestine, unlawful mobility, precisely when he needed it most. Precisely when his young, love-stricken heart had threatened to explode if he could not find a way from Houston to Fairfield, Texas.

He can see the pink of Abby Palmer's fingertips. Pushing open that screen door. Her flying eyes. *Davis! Come in, love. Come in.*

Not the actual truck, of course. And Dallas' truck is white, not black. But it's the same year, make and model. A 1972 Ford F-100. He brushes his thumb over the center of the steering wheel. F-O-R-D.

F-R-E-D.

His stomach stirs. Like the past and the present are mixing in the wrong proportions. Too much grain alcohol in the punch.

She is everywhere in his head. Her voice. Her face. Her scent.

Abby.

Up ahead, a column of mushrooming black smoke climbs up out of the trees. Narrow at the bottom, widening out as it rises, like a dark funnel. Dallas is looking down at the broken stripes on the road. Singing about how she'd rather go blind than see her man walk away.

As they close the distance he begins to feel sick again. He catches his bloodshot eyes in the rearview mirror. Blinks. He doesn't see his eyes. Blinks. He sees the eyes of the palmist to whom he had paid five dollars the year after Abby died, just before those eyes rolled back into her head and she began convulsing. Foaming. As if she'd been poisoned.

As if she'd taken too much of something all at once.

He wants to pull over. Wants to stop. Then he wants to turn around. Go the other way. As fast as the truck will carry him.

But he can't do any of those things. Because he sees smoke.

He is no longer in a white 1972 Ford F-100 headed east on I-67. He is lost in his own head. Time curls above him like a gathering wave. Collapses. He is in a different 1972 Ford F-100, this one black, barreling north on I-45, hoping to make it to Fairfield before the state troopers catch up and arrest him all over again. In the foreground, through a dirty, bug-spattered windshield, a column of pitch-black smoke boils up into the sky.

Abby.

It is not a name. Or a sound. Or a thought.

It is raw feeling. It is brain lightning.

Here Davis. Here, love.

Turn here, love. Here. Here, love.

Davis!

He yanks the wheel. They are moving much too fast to exit, but he manages to keep the truck on the road and cuts his speed. Dallas is nearly in his lap.

"Boy, you gon' kill us both! What's got into you! Ain't no clinic this way! What in the hell…"

"There's a fire," he says. Eyes wide. Heart pounding. Sickness receding. Fog clearing. Adrenaline once again working its magic. "There's a fire."

"A fire? What fire?"

He points. She bends forward. Looks.

"Well… what… you gon' go *pee* on it? Ain't no fireman, jackass!"

He doesn't answer. Hits the last corner going too fast and overshoots the turn. Slams on the breaks. Dallas spews expletives, pushing off against the dashboard.

"Dammit, boy…"

Reverses. Cranks the wheel. Shoots forward. The lightning in his head keeps lashing.

Faster, love.

Come on, baby.

Save me, Davis.

They skid to a stop in the middle of the road. Dallas lurches forward again but spares him the cursing this time. All she can do is gawk.

The upper floor is a forest of orange flame disappearing into black billows. The air is thick with the smell of soot. Profusions of black smoke speak in pops and snaps. Soft and low. High and sharp. Laughing in long hisses.

Old Faithful, fifty yards away, is untouched, towering over a black Mountaineer.

But *Libby's Nuts* is a goner.

Davis is out and sprinting across the yard before the feeling of Dallas' grip on his wrist, trying to keep him in the truck, can register in his head. He can barely hear her miraculous voice.

"Boy! Davis!"

The front door to the house is unlocked. It opens to a vomiting of hot, acrid smoke that sends him sprawling backwards onto the still damp lawn. He gets up. Hacking. Coughing. Wipes his eyes.

Save me, love.

Takes a breath. Charges in through the door, yelling her name. The sound comes before he can think about it.

"Abby!"

It is the only sound he can make before the smoke attacks his lungs. He drops to his knees. Sucks for cowering oxygen.

"Olivia! Libby! Anyone!"

The smoke answers in pops and snaps that now seem deafening. Glass shatters upstairs as the window frames fall out of the walls. He crawls forward. A tilting staircase ascends steeply into smoke. The top third is fully engulfed. He tries to send his voice up through the roiling hot storm.

"Olivia!"

Again. Again. Nothing.

Something heavy falls through the ceiling of the living room. It's like a bomb. Heat and sound. Flame and smoke and bits of building flying out in all directions. Ricocheting back in from first floor walls not yet weakened by fire. It blows him over onto his back. His head smashes back against the hard floor.

A flaming bed is now on top of the couch. Another corner of ceiling gives way. A burning dresser drops down, shattering the large, scorched mirror that comes with it. Wrapped in its pillow of soot, the glass blade slices through the distance between the ruined dresser mirror and his face. Then buries itself in flesh.

For a moment, before all of the debris has settled, he thinks he is dead. He sees the dead, as only the dead can.

His father. Abby. Tallulah. His mother. Separate beings, and yet all the same. A vision that is also a voice that is also a feeling. A presence. Shifting. Glimmering. Like the image of a coin –one becoming many becoming one again –catching the sun through a crack in a shattered hull resting in deep water.

His mother. Elizabeth. He can see her face. That last expression, before she goes down for good. The look that the poor park attendant testified about as he disintegrated into sobs on the witness stand. Stewart Ames, the man who could not be in two places at the same time. It is through Stewart's eyes that he sees the details of his mother's last expression, registering the sight of a young boy's limp body as it is hauled out of a lake and up into a boat. The expression that registers the death of her only son.

"Davis is the thing I love most in the world."

He opens his eyes. The ceiling paint is blistering. Bubbles grow and ripple outwards from the center, toward the walls. Like they are floating on the surface currents of a square white pond.

But he doesn't see them. The paint bubbles. Not really. Like he doesn't feel the shard of glass mirror in his cheek or the warm trickle down his neck.

Because he is still looking out across the water through poor Stewart's eyes. He can still see the top two-thirds of her face. The only part of her above the water line. Those eyes looking back. They have a voice, those eyes. Tallulah's voice.

"It was her time. When it's your time, Hon, you just go. 'Cause you know it's what you have to do. There is no God. She's a part of the Motherverse now."

The eyes submerge. Just the top of her head left now. Worry lines in her forehead relaxing. Still, Tallulah's voice, at the funeral home, spreading out across the water.

"The Motherverse is love and sadness. It protects us. Looks out for us. It feels what we feel. It knows everything. Sees everything. Everything that happened and everything that will happen. May not happen for fifty years. A hundred years. A thousand. The Motherverse already knows it. Has already seen it. We are each born from her and when we die we each go back to her. Like Einstein said E equals MC or whatnot, only the E stands for energy and the M stands for mother and the C stands for children. We are all children of the Motherverse. You understand, Hon?"

No. He didn't. He still didn't.

Maybe he has been wrong. All of these years. Maybe he has been wrong. Wrong, because he had never thought to question the meaning that Stewart Ames had put to his mother's last expression. He has always taken it as gospel. He has taken it on faith that his mother had simply let go of the world, because she believed him to be dead. *His* death, or the belief in it, had precipitated *her* death.

Except maybe that wasn't it at all. Maybe she hadn't let go because he was dead. Maybe she had let go because she knew he was alive. Or needed him to be. Because she knew what came next. Because she knew *everything*.

What if...

His father's voice. Suddenly. Reading aloud to people seated in a bookstore.

She always scoffed at the idea of an exogenous God. She believed in a divinity that was all-encompassing. All things. All creatures. All places. All times. She believed we are merely molecules of an eyelash upon the face of divinity, cursed with self-awareness. There is no God to worship because there is nothing but God in the first place. Boats are made to carry an illusion. We are all made of water.

What if she had known... everything? Seen... everything. What if *she* was the soapstone whale at the bottom of *Eyelash Lake*? Waiting, all of these years, to be found.

He is a boy, crying in the kitchen, handing her bits of shattered blue porcelain. His tiny hands in hers. She speaks, her voice slicing through time, an arrow of sound and excruciating pain lodged in the side of his face. "*Whatever happens today, I will be there for you. I'm not going anywhere.*"

Abby. Suddenly.

Davis, love? Davis!

He coughs violently. Reaches reflexively for his cheek, cutting his finger.

"Fuck!"

The air is hot and thin. He can hear voices outside. A lone siren in the distance. He feels carefully for the shard. Pulls out what he can.

The living room is an inferno, flames raging up into a gaping hole in the ceiling. He looks in time to see a burning body fall from out of the upper blackness and break itself over the jagged remains of the dresser mirror. The head rolls back and over, pulling the rest of the body down to the floor.

Adrenaline, his old friend. He screams.

"Olivia!"

But it is not her. Not even close. The body belongs —belonged —to a man. A large man. Doesn't matter. It's the only name in his head.

"*Olivia!*"

There is a sound. A human sound. An answer. It comes from the other direction. Away from the living room. It comes from the right. From the parlor. He rolls over, the stream of blood down his face redirects, clinging to gravity. He crawls. Away from the flaming staircase. Through the parlor door. Stops. Listens.

"Olivia!"

Smoke squeezes his lungs. He coughs violently. Listens.

A coughing reply. Davis crawls.

When he clears the settee, he can see bare feet. Ankles. Legs disappearing beneath a mango colored kimono. Libby.

The stairway collapses on the other side of the wall. It pulls free of the lower studs, but rips out the uppers on the way down, pulling open a gaping, flaming hole into the parlor.

Davis scrabbles forward. Grabs a shoulder. Rolls her over. Face, arms, chest, hands. She is covered in blood.

"Libby!" He shakes her. "Libby!"

She coughs. Blinks. Blinks again. Sees.

He shuffles backwards over her body, keeping low. Grabs her ankles. His hands are sticky now, staining her skin. He pulls her back towards the door in short, sharp lurches.

But Libby has her own adrenaline now. She kicks at him. Fights her way free.

Claws forward. He clutches at ankles no longer there. She makes it all the way back to where he had found her. Beneath the record player. Her right arm lands over a short stack of albums. Bessie Smith is on top. *Me and My Gin*. Smiling face. Sequined hat. White feathers spilling over a white dress. Smeared with Libby's blood.

"Are you fucking kidding me?" he shouts. "Are you fucking…"

There is no air to finish.

He lunges forward. Grabs her ankles. Pulls. Something big and loud and awful happens in the kitchen. The wall behind the king-sized bed on the other side of the parlor suddenly blackens. The feathered masks, a dozen of them, dark hollow eyes all watching in horror, light up.

Libby clutches the small stack of records. Uses them to dig in against the force pulling her backwards. Stretches out and forward with her left hand, fingers desperate for the thing he had not seen near the wooden trunk.

A bloodstained pillowcase.

She clutches it. Lets go of Bessie Smith. Lays down her head.

Fresh air. Cool. Clean. Infinite.

It is like falling backwards into water.

They are both coughing violently, face down in damp grass. Large hands are suddenly on his shoulders, pulling him up and away. Deep, panicked voices are calling her name. *Libby! Libby!* Instinctively he tightens his grip on Libby's ankles. But she is suddenly torn away, airborne and gone from him.

He is coughing. Coughing. Floating on his back. Carried by men he does not know. Their faces, beading sweat: *down, up, away. Down, up, away.* Behind their heads, a soft, pale ocean of morning sky.

They lay him down on the road. He cannot stop coughing. His eyes burn too much to keep them open. Something small and savage is clawing into his face. Something vicious is inside his lungs, clawing to get out. Minions of pain trying to meet each other and join forces. In the soundscape around him the fire savages its victim, burying its face into the silken viscera of a broken, wooden corpse. In the distance, seemingly behind all of that, he hears his own name. Pleading.

"Davis? Come on back, Hero. Come on back now, Davis."

By the time the Corbin VFD shows up the only thing they can really do is to keep the beast in one place. Protect Old Faithful. Dowse everything growing between *Libby's Nuts* and Darnell Lewis' place up the street. They even shoot a stream over the flaming structure to douse the orchard behind. He is up and walking around by then. There are still bits of glass in his face, just below his left cheekbone, now beneath a square of white gauze. But the fire in his lungs is finally out. He can breathe and talk without coughing as much.

Libby Holder is propped up against the rear tire of Dallas Letti's truck, watching her home atomize into the atmosphere. They have washed off much of the blood. Wrapped her nearly naked body in a blanket. There is a bruising laceration on the top of her head against which she holds a pad of gauze. Nothing else of her is cut, or punctured or broken. Her right hand is still clutching the bloodstained pillowcase.

Davis looks down at her. At the matted hair. The hands. The pillowcase. Thinks of the soaked kimono beneath the blanket. His bloody handprints are still on her ankles.

Awful lot of blood, he thinks. He can hear the ambulance in the distance.

An arms length away, Dallas is sitting in the passenger seat of her truck, door open, as a fireman bends in, dressing her head wound.

"How you feeling?" Davis asks Dallas. She looks. Doesn't answer. Closes her eyes.

"No, ma'am," says the fireman. "Ma'am? Ms. Letti? I need you to keep your eyes open for me, okay? Can you do that?"

Davis steps around the open door. Squats down next to Libby.

"And how are *you* doing?" he asks. "How's your head?"

She does not look away from the flaming house. Like she is afraid of missing something. But she speaks.

"Saved my no account life."

"Yeah, well you didn't make it easy," he says. "But I did."

She rolls her head. Looks up at him. Laughs with a cough.

"Yeah, you did too, huh? Fuck-all-day-no-kinda-priest show up outta the fuckin' blue and pull my ass out the lake of hell." She looks back to the house. Nods. "You did too. You did. Save my sorry-ass life. But I won't talkin' 'bout you, baby."

"Oh? Then…"

"You saved my ass the *second* time. Mama save it the first time. From the other fuckin' side of the river too."

"I don't understand," he says. Then he looks around. Whispers. "I saw… a man. Inside."

Libby nods. Blinks. Points to the black Mountaineer parked beneath Old Faithful.

"*MmmHmm.* I was lookin' 'round his truck while he inside sleepin' off one too many cookies. I look up an' I see fire in the bedroom window. So I come back in the house, runnin' full out, headin' for them stairs. Like a crazy person headin' fo' them stairs, not an idea in my fuckin' head 'bout what I'm s'posed to do about a fire but I come runnin' in anyway and then there's mama in my head. *Bam.* Hits me like a fryin' pan. An' I stop an' I say in my head, *Mama?* An' mama Mable say *kitchen, baby. Don't you go up them stairs. Kitchen.* So I run my ass into the kitchen. Grab a pot. Throw it in the sink, start fillin' it with water. But mama Mable in my head again. *No, baby,* she say. An' that… when I see… the knife. Right there by the sink. *That's a baby. That's my girl.* Talkin' like she right there at the kitchen table, rollin' out the biscuit dough."

She is silent for a moment, watching the flames.

"Davis?"

"Yeah, Libby."

"I took a knife wit' me to put out a fire. You believe that shit?"

"I…"

"If I'da gone up them stairs with a pot of water, he'd a kill me for sho'."

"Who, Libby? Who was it? Why was he here?"

She shakes her head. Like there is nothing she can say. But then she speaks.

"He a monsta is who. A monsta. An' he come for Olivia. My baby. He come for *my… baby.*"

Tears stream from her face. He waits. Grips her shoulder gently.

"She ain't come home last night. Monsta wait all night, doin' with me as he please, eatin' them cookies, but 'Livia never come home. So he go to sleep, wake back up, go upstairs, an' set my shit on fire. An' then here I come, 'bout to bring him up a pot of fuckin' water like the motherfuck is thirsty. Like he gon' boil himself some eggs or some shit." Shakes her head. Picks at the dried blood on her finger. "But Mama Mable still lookin' out."

She shakes her head. "Still lookin' out from across that river." Cries.

"I surprise' his ass too. Right b'tween the shoulders. Motherfuck come at me again and again, but I kep' at it. Fire all over eva'thing. I kep' at it so long I figure we both just burn up an' turn into smoke. Knife. Knife. Knife. I jus' kep' at it."

She falls silent. Breathing. Watching the fire. Reliving what's inside. She doesn't blink. Davis waits.

"But he finally stop comin'. I got my shit together and got the fuck out. Fell down the fuckin' stairs; land on my head. Wake up in hell."

The fireman has finished with Dallas. He turns to Davis and Libby. Speaks.

"Okay. Ambulance is here. Y'all stay put. Understand? Make sure they both stay awake. I'll be right back." Davis nods and he is gone.

Dallas steps out of the truck. Unsteady. Walks around Davis. Sits carefully down next to Libby. Matching head wounds. Libby looks at her, shaking her head. Still disbelieving.

"Been wantin' to meet Letti Blue my whole life and goddamn if she don't just show up in person to watch my house burn down. *Fuck-all-day-no-kinda'-priest* a writer an' I bet he can't make this shit up if someone put a gun to his pretty 'lil head. *Damn.*"

"Libby?" he asks.

"What is it, baby?"

657

"What's in the fuckin' pillowcase?"

She looks down at her hand. Like she has forgotten it's attached to her wrist.

"Only thing I had time to save. Went back into that burnin' bedroom 'fore I throw my ass down the stairs. Only thing 'Livia owns that she'd care to save."

She hands up the bloody pillowcase. Davis opens it. Looks inside.

"What…"

"Her 'lil cactus friends. They from her mama. God rest her soul. I done my best to look after her baby, but she in the wind now." She half-points at the fire. "An' my ass prob'ly goin' to jail on account of that crispy-fried motherfuck, so…"

She breaks off. Sighs. Shakes her head again. Wipes her eyes with the back of a hand. Dallas is crying now too. Harder than Libby. He kneels so their faces are even.

"Dallas? You okay? What's wrong? Rosetta?"

She doesn't answer. Pulls herself together. She throws an arm over Libby's shoulder. Libby lays her head into the soft pillow of Rosetta's chest. Almost whispers.

"People lookin' for my baby, Davis. Bad, bad people."

Chapter 79
Dallas and Etta

Four in the afternoon, Pablo. Woke up in time to see the sun go down. Except there is no sun. Nothing but heavy clouds out my window. Desert is dreary and cold and wet. First time I've lifted this pen in three days. Feels heavier today. Like someone snuck in my house and put a little bit of lead in the ink. But here I am. Back again. Turns out I miss spilling out my insides. Maybe this does make you my confessor. Should start calling you Father. *Padre Pablo.* It suits you.

Instead of writing this damn letter, I've been putting more time into working my garden. Even in this shitty weather. Been waiting for the sky to clear but there was no sign of that so out I went. My basil and my okra and my peppers have needed tending. Eggplant like little purple watermelon this year. Kale, chard, onion, and broccoli all needed some love. That's all on the west side of the house. On the east side I got my flowers, which don't need so much attention this time of year. Mostly just some paintbrush and cactus. A fire stick plant or two. But I fuss with them anyway. Don't want them to feel forgotten. In the summer it's a different scene. Bright orange penstemons and the red yucca make it look like my garden wall is on fire when the sun is going down. Sunflowers along the house. Hyssop and yellow columbine. Thick carpet of purple wine cups just about everywhere.

I like digging in the dirt. Making a home for my little green babies. Takes my mind off things. I can numb the pain in my head with the good Dr. Johnny Walker and it don't matter one bit in the garden. My plants are used to me being off my ass. I talk to them and sing my songs. I'm out there covered in dirt singing '*Royal Garden Blues*' like Empress Bessie. *That weepin' melancholy strain/ Say, but it's soothing to the brain/ Just wanna get right up and dance/ Don't care I'll take most any chance/ No other blues I'd care to choose/ But Royal Garden Blues.*

Which to me was Bessie's way of saying that the blues start to sound a whole lot like jazz when you're up on stage with Louis Armstrong rolling around in money. I've got plenty of money but my gardening blues don't get anywhere close to jazz and Louie Armstrong ain't called my sorry ass lately. So I prefer to stick to the *T'ain't Nobody's Business'* Bessie when I garden because all my plant babies love the true blues.

In the summer months my favorite time to garden is round about midnight when the moon is out and the air is cool and the coyotes are out on the prowl singing with me as I dig in the dirt. And then just a little breath of a breeze and the air will start to move over the desert like a hand over the soft underbelly of something wild.

Sometimes I just sit on the ground and lean up against my house under that low-slung spotlight moon and drink and feel the world turning on the other side of the garden wall. And sometimes I can believe I'm back up on stage at *Mother's* and that the bottle in my hand is a microphone and that the sunflowers up against that wall are men smelling of sweat and dirt and cigarettes and holding their drinks and pool cues and that I'm singing something sad but true with that blue light in my eyes so that I can't see the faces. I can't see you and Etta sitting out there in the smoke listening. But I can *feel* you listening. You with your bourbon and Etta in your lap with her Shirley Temple and I can feel you out there soaking me in, pulling me toward you like this desert pulling water hundreds of miles in from the gulf. I can feel you coaxing the sound out of me like I coax those little green shoots out of the ground and up into the moonlight. Because we all got a story to tell, Pablo, and we all want to tell it, or sing it, and have someone hear it. But the story never comes unless we can make ourselves believe that there is someone out there in the smoky dark listening.

Which is probably why I am writing this letter even if I don't send it. Because I want to feel you out there listening, Pablo. The only ones listening now are my precious little garden babies.

Whoo-wee, but that is some sad, pitiful shit to be putting in a letter. My apologies, Pablo. My only point is that after three full days on my hands and knees in the dirt my bones hurt now almost more than my head. Good to focus on a different kind of pain I suppose, but I am not a young woman anymore. Just in case you were wondering about that.

You got a hobby, Pablo? If not, you need one. What the hell are you going to do with yourself after you sell *Papi's*? Yes, I know all about that, even living all the way out here in the middle of nowhere. I still got people out there in the world who tell me things. News finds me. Like when you did your little remodel and changed the name to *Papi's*. Made me cry when I heard that. A part of me died that day. Anyway, I don't know if you're good at anything but running that club. What are you going to do when it's not yours? Maybe you should start digging in the dirt too.

I never would have guessed that I could grow anything until Hammy Lewis gave me a little potted olive plant one night in Stuttgart. I figured it'd be dead in a week. But it just kept growing. I took it with me from one city to the next and one hotel to the next. I named my little olive tree *Olivia* and sang to her at night. Had to repot the thing twice. People wondering why Letti Blue is hauling this olive tree around Europe. But that's when I realized well I'll be damned if my black thumb wasn't green! Ever since then I've been growing things. I was in Europe over three years and by the time I decided to come back to the states my little potted baby was a damned *tree* and I had to give it away. Can you believe I cried over giving away that tree? Well I did. No one knows that but you, Pablo. Cried like a damned baby.

We were only supposed to stay in Europe for six months. Those were the tour dates Hammy set up while I was busy getting my black behind kicked but good in prison. But then I suppose you know how Europe treated me. Better than Texas. Falling ass-backward into a pile of clover is what it was. Europe just couldn't get enough of me and my sound. They were hungry for it and Hammy was pleased with himself because he knew they would be. His plan all along was to prime the pump with a six-month tour and then see if I could make me a name before coming back home. I never believed it myself but then the offers and the invitations just never stopped.

I didn't speak a lick of German or French or Norwegian or Italian but they loved me anyway. Probably didn't matter because the blues is the *mother tongue*, Pablo. Don't need to tell you that. It's a universal language. Like laughing or crying. Ain't about talking and understanding words. It's about feeling understood down in your bones. Down in the soles of your feet. It's about knowing the hot trouble between your legs and the worry in your head and the ache in your broken heart beating out that ragged four-four time.

'Course I was just dumb enough to let all the attention go to my head. I was dizzy with it for years. I've used a lot of drugs in my day and none of them compare to the high of feeling like you're something special to thousands of people you don't even know. Letters and cards and flowers by the hundreds. Signing autographs. Holding other people's babies. Can you even imagine? *Other people's* babies. Happened near every time I come down off of some stage. There are so many pictures of me out there holding babies people most likely think I went to Europe to work as a nanny.

Good thing they had no idea about my own baby. At first I called Etta two or three times a week. Tried to anyway. Sometimes she'd come to the phone. Just as often she'd be out with the chickens and goats or spending time with Ronni's preacher. When I heard that, first thing I thought about was Corny Roop down in the basement of my Mama's church giving me singing lessons and I saw history just looping over on itself like a long rattlesnake under the porch. But Ronni swore up and down he was a good man who she would trust with her own little Dixie and that Etta needed to be closer to God and that being as how I was across

661

the damned Atlantic Ocean there wasn't much I could do about it anyhow.

I could see by then that Ronni was already thinking of herself as Etta's mama. When she'd take that tone I'd say something to remind her who-was-who and she'd pretend I'd just misunderstood her meaning. But I know bullshit when I smell it. And the longer I stayed away, the worse it got. I know as soon as I hung up that phone Ronni would fill Etta with stories about how I just didn't love her enough to stay home and wondering out loud so she could hear about me finding some rich Frenchman to marry and have babies with and wondering about how I would love my little French babies more than I loved her.

And I wasn't just being paranoid either, which is what Hammy liked to tell me – 'come on now, Rosetta, let's not get all paranoid' –because last thing Hammy wanted was for my maternal instincts to derail the gravy train.

Maternal instincts. I laugh out loud when I write those words and you can too, Pablo. Wasn't no maternal instincts that was the problem. It was selfish pride, plain and simple. Ronni had something that belonged to me. Didn't matter that she was a better mother. I just wanted Ronni to know her place. And she was just as determined to take my place. No one looking at my life and being honest about it can say I ever had any maternal instincts worth a shit and a shine.

My calls with Etta got fewer and fewer and every time we did talk she'd act like it was killing her to speak more than one syllable at a go. And what she said came out all bratty like she was trying her best not to tell me what was really on her mind. I'd tell her my Europe stories like I'm talking to myself and when I asked her about whatever was going on in her world she'd try to tell me in as few words as possible. Any time I try to tell her how much I love her and how much I was looking forward to coming home to see her and spend some alone time just the two of us she suddenly develop some emergency to take her off the phone. Always the goddamned chickens. And I could hear Ronni in the background so I know they were in on that shit together.

During those three years, I came home three times for about a month each. And every time was a disaster. The comparison with my life in Europe was too depressing to stomach, even for a blues singer. Nobody knew me in Texas and nobody cared either. In Europe I'm smoking and drinking and singing and laughing and living it up with the likes of Buddy and Sonny and T-Bone and John Lee and B.B. and Koko. I felt like I was home. In any of those countries I was home. But Texas? The place that was supposed to be home was more like a foreign country. I hated the house I lived in which seemed like a ratty old shoebox compared to hotel living or the cottage I used in France or even the upper floor flats in London and Norway and Sweden. I had me a five-room summer home in Stuttgart with the most beautiful flower garden you can even imagine. Hammy says to me one day oh I know a guy who knows a guy who's vacationing in wherever the fuck and we can use his house for a few weeks. Place was like out of some storybook. That's what Europe was like: *a storybook*. But trying to get comfortable again in the desert, in Corbin, even for a few weeks, was impossible. I was always itching to get out. People could tell too. They were all counting the days until I left again.

But the real hard part about those visits was Etta and Ronni. Etta was growing like a little weed and was even prettier if that is possible. Coming back that first time, when I first laid eyes on her, she was at the top of the little dirt road leading up to the chicken ranch. Hammy was in the car with me that first time back. (He was afraid to let me come back alone so he made up some excuse. I was like a dog on a leash.) And we get to the top of that road and Hammy pulls down his sunglasses and looks through the dirty windshield and says *who is that?* And I said *Hammy, that's my baby*, and I couldn't believe it myself how much a young girl changes in a few months when you aren't looking.

It was like she was someone else's little girl. And since Ronni was standing right behind her with a hand on her shoulder, that someone else had to be Ronni Brill. Big smile like only Ronni could do. Big ol' soft motherly bosom out to here. But eyes of blue stone. I tried bringing Etta home to my house but that shit didn't last but two nights and she wanted to go back to the chicken ranch where all her things were. I was all about keeping her happy, trying to anyway, so I'd go visit my own child every day at Ronni's place. The whole thing was awkward even though we both pretended it wasn't. Which only made it more awkward.

Ronni and me started butting heads on my second trip back. Stupid things. Testing each other on who had the most influence over Etta. Ronni won just about every one of those tussles, which only made me mad. But there wasn't nothing I could do because I needed Ronni and she knew it. She held all the cards and she knew how to play. Her cards were chickens and goats and dogs and little Dixie and I had no cards at all except a mother's God-given power to punish her own child and a date that I was supposed to be on a plane back to London. Hammy had Ronni's phone number so he always knew where I was and how to find me and he did not think twice about calling to interrupt mother-daughter time which was pitiful anyway. Ronni just loved grabbing hold of Etta's hand and telling her *'Come on, sugar, Letti Blue got to go call Hammy about more important things. Let's go find where Dixie at and go get us a ice cream at the L&T.'* I think that's why Ronni's boobs were so big, for such a little thing –titties full of ice cream. Babies follow her wherever she go. Ain't no competing with that.

On the third visit Ronni and me had us an out-and-out fight. Nothing physical because I think I could have killed Ronni Brill dead. Prison taught me nothing else but how to fight and I could have taken out every last one of them smiling teeth of hers. But it was a whole lot of ugly yelling the day before I left. All while Etta and Dixie were in the next room too. I wanted to take Etta as far as San Angelo where I was meeting Hammy but there was no way to get her back to Corbin unless Ronni drove out too. Ronni wasn't having none of that and made up some bullshit excuse and I called her on it and then she started saying things like if an extra hour with Etta was going to make such a difference then maybe I shouldn't have decided to abandon her to go play around across the ocean. It went from there. Nasty, hurtful business. I was so mad when I left that I barely said goodbye to my own daughter.

Not like Etta even wanted to go with me to San Angelo anyway. She was just as happy to see me out of there after that last visit, like the rest of them. Even my own dead mama. I did not have a single mama dream while I was in Europe. Not one. But she showed up near every night whenever I came back to Texas. Not near as bad as the dreams that woke everybody up in prison, but still, there she was, usually sitting naked behind that big black sewing machine. Trickle of bright blue thread running from spool and bobbin like she was sewing with water. And then I could feel that cold tide again rising up over my bare feet like I could in those prison dreams. Every now and then she'd look up at me across the dream and shake her head like she was disgusted. Like I was taking her away from something she'd rather be doing but if I was going to insist on being around Etta, then she and Hammy were going to chaperone and she was taking the night shift –the *dream shift*. And then she'd look away again and go back to sewing water into that cold rising-up sea and it would go on like that until I could feel the water rising-up over my head. Near every night. But then as soon as I was back in Europe, *poof*, Mama was gone. Reason enough for me to stay away.

But, eventually, Hammy decided that the time was right to make a play for *Uncle Sam* and *Lady Liberty*. In Europe my shit was selling like Sunday morning pancakes and he was ready to bring me home. My label had been itching for near a year and a half to commit me to an American tour, but Hammy kept putting them off saying it was still too soon. But when he was ready, Hammy held nothing back. Fifteen cities, coast to coast, small to medium venues but with a lot of big names just to show people the company I was keeping. I spent one night in Houston on that tour. Angela Strehli and Marcia Ball sat in on that one. I had no idea until Hammy come back stage and says *"Hey, Angie and Marcia are out there and I asked if they'd like to sit in on 'Leave Me By the River' and they said yes."* Then he just walked off like it was nothing. That was Hammy.

Houston turned into one of the best shows of the tour. I had invited Ronni to bring Etta but she said it was too much of a drive. We were rolling off to Phoenix in the morning. Putting the miles on my new bus. The *Letti Blue Rollers* just kept on rolling. We bounced off California and ended the tour back in Chicago with Buddy Guy.

I first got to know Buddy Guy in Germany. We were touring together and we were at the same hotel. Get your mind out of the gutter, Pablo, we were just drinking and smoking friends. Buddy liked to talk up his town and I fell in love with Chicago through his eyes. He told me I needed to get the hell out of Texas and that he would show me around his city whenever I decided to come back. And he did too. We went driving all around after the tour and he stopped his car right outside this white two story house with big brick chimney and a fenced front yard, and a great big cherry tree in the back, and Buddy said, *'Dallas, best friend of my cousin lived here twenty years and he died last month and you need to buy this house before they put the sign in the yard.'*

And I did too. By the next day I was the owner of a house in Frankfort, Illinois, which was comical because Buddy and I first met in Frankfurt, Germany. I was an hour drive from Chicago and I could feel that big-ass lake thirty miles away like it was outside my bedroom window. And it kept pulling me closer. I moved three more times before I bought my place in *Highland Park* right there on Lake Illinois. Like each of those houses was just a bigger and bigger boat floating me to deeper water.

When I bought that first house in Frankfort I called Etta to tell her we were moving. It was the first time in a long while that I had actually wanted to talk to Ronni Brill. I wanted to hear the tone in that sing-songy smiley voice when she learned that I was playing my trump card and reclaiming my daughter and moving her the hell away from the *Santiago Chicken Ranch.* I know that makes me a small person. I knew I owed Ronni for looking after Etta while I was off tending to myself. I knew I was taking pleasure in rubbing my new money and my new fame in Ronni's cute little laughing white face. I know she was the better mother, Pablo. Ice cream titties and all. And I knew it then, too. But even knowing those things, and even knowing that Ronni would be better for Etta me, there was still more malice in my heart for Ronni than gratitude. So I was looking forward to her answering that phone.

Except she didn't answer the phone. Took me two days to talk to anyone. Eventually, the wife of the owner of the *Santiago Chicken Ranch* answered Ronni's phone and told me that Ronni no longer worked there. I told her who I was and she said she knew who I was and she said it in a way that told me she'd heard an earful about me from Ronni. She told me that Ronni's man had showed up the week before and that they had packed everything up and rode off. She was none too happy with Ronni for leaving them in the lurch. I asked about Etta and she said both Etta and Dixie were with them when they drove off. She had no idea where. No forwarding address. Just a couple of tire tracks and a cloud of dust.

I was back in Texas two days after that call, looking for Etta. I talked to anyone who I could find. I talked to everyone at the chicken ranch until they near kicked me out for fear I'd start trying to shake the truth out of the chickens and goats. I tracked down a member of Ronni's little church and she told me I could find the preacher at the school where he taught music and so I tracked his ass down too.

He told me that he always thought Etta was Ronni's adopted child (which I knew was because that was the lie Ronni had been spreading from the beginning). He said Ronni and her boyfriend had reunited and had taken Etta and Dixie to wherever it was her man called home. But the preacher had no idea just where that might be.

I went to the Sheriff's office and told them what little I knew. Only thing I knew about Ronni's man was that his first name was Kelsey and that he was a violent man who lived someplace else. Not much to go on. They put in a half-assed effort to follow up but didn't come up with any more than I did. I could tell they had better things to do than help some uppity black woman who left the country for three years and lost her own baby. Assuming it *was* my own baby. They had their doubts and I could see that in their eyes too. Anyway, the only thing I knew for sure was that there was one place in the world Etta was *not*, and that place was Corbin, Texas.

After a month I sold my dumpy little house and I went back to Chicago to my big new empty house. I was more depressed than I have ever been in my entire life. Never got back into the drugs, thank God, but I was sure one with the bottle for awhile. Me and Dr. Walker were like best friends. Still are, I suppose. (If Dr. Johnny could read, I'd probably be writing this letter to him, Pablo.) Anyway, Hammy was all over me, afraid that I was done as a performer. He had big plans to follow up that tour with another record and it looked to him that Etta being gone was going to fuck all of that up. So he did his best to find her. He called every contact he had in all of the states we thought they might be. He even brought in the FBI to investigate interstate child abduction. Feds took it more seriously than the county Sheriff, but I was still the wrong color and they still come up empty.

Inside, I knew the truth. I knew Etta wasn't abducted. I knew she begged and pleaded to go with them. To not be left behind. Last thing she wanted was to be left alone with me. And fair was fair, too. I had left her and so she was going to leave me. How was I going to complain about that, Pablo? So part of me was relieved when the FBI said they were at a dead end. I knew that if they ever found her the truth would come out that never mind the law and never mind blood relation, Etta did not want me as her mama. Not that I blamed her, but that's a hard truth for even the worst mama to take. So I did my best to stick with the unsolved abduction story. But I knew the truth. Least I thought I did.

I went back to doing the only thing I knew how to do, which was to sing the blues. Riding around in my bus and taking care of my people. Fans and critics held me up as being all about the true blues because money and fame never seemed to change the feeling of my sound. Ain't no *'Royal Garden Blues'* in my repertoire, no disrespect to Empress Bessie. And I will tell you what nobody else knows, Pablo. All of those songs I wrote about having been left and abandoned and beat on by the man I loved – *'My Man for a Dime'*, and *'Hurt Me Blue'* and *'Leave Me by the River'* –all of them were mostly about Etta. Even if I didn't know it at the time, I know it now. Don't need a shrink to figure that one out. Just one more way that I owe my career to my daughter.

As you know, my career was a flame that burned hot and bright but then burned the fuck out sooner than anyone imagined. I should still be at it. Should still be making the rounds in my *Letti Blue Rollers* bus. Packing venues and signing autographs and holding other people's babies. The polyps on my vocal chords put an end to all that shit. Two surgeries only made it worse. Probably why I hate doctors. Sing for ten goddamn minutes and I sound like I'm ninety-six years old. Twelve minutes and my throat starts to hurt like I've been drinking gasoline. Fifteen minutes and you may as well turn off the mic and kick me off the stage. I suppose it serves me right. When I dream of Mama these days she is younger than I am, sexy as all hell, strutting around in her little blue negligee, shaking her head and laughing at her pathetic daughter. Serves my ass right.

Near five years ago a woman come up to me in the *Windy City Liquors* and says she wants my autograph. Cute little blonde thing too. Big blue eyes. I sign her little piece of paper. She walks off but then comes back to me in the parking lot after I got Dr. Johnny Walker in the bag and headed for my car. Tells me her name is Dixianne Draper. Took her three times telling me before I could get it through my thick head that she was *Dixie*. Ronni's little Dixie. It was like some little girl looking out of a grown woman's face. Married with two girls living in Chicago! Working at a damned bank! Could have knocked me over with a feather right there outside the liquor store. Little Dixie Brill.

So I invited her over to my big empty house on the lake and fed her a pizza and we shared my Johnny Walker and we pretended that I cared about her life. And then I started asking my questions. And little Dixie told me everything I didn't know.

Chapter 80

Silver fish, wriggling in afternoon light. Maybe a dozen of them. On both sides of the road. Waving their signs. Shouting at passing motorists.

One of the fish has his head off, tucked under a fin. So he can smoke a cigarette. Grayson rolls down the window.

"Go on back where you came from! Sons-a-bitches!"

Christi stretches forward from the back seat and jabs him in the shoulder with her fingers.

"Daddy, just… Stop. Roll up the window. Don't go gettin' worked up. They're just a bunch of mixed-up jackasses with too much time on their hands. Nothin' they can do but make noise so you may as well let 'em be."

"Let 'em be?" Grayson looks back at his daughter. Points behind her where the school of protesting fish are shrinking with distance. "These sons-a-bitches are *dangerous*, Belle. You know why? I'll tell you why. Because they're ignorant. Because they act in a mob… out of ignorance… and that makes 'em dangerous."

"Daddy."

Grayson turns back around. Rolls up the window. He looks over at Nicholas Voss. "Am I right, Nicki?"

Nicholas shrugs. Adjusts his hand on the steering wheel. Then nods.

"Yes," he says. "They are dangerous. Fanatics will do anything."

"There," says Grayson. "Ya' see?"

"Fanatics? Daddy, they're a bunch of college kids lookin' to be on the news."

"'Parently you don't *take* the news, honey. Nothin' on the news these days but concern that environmental radicals –like those sons-a-bitches back there – gon' take over this whole damn festival just to make a point. News is all about things getting' ugly. CDC's havin' to go into it's own damn pocket for a pretty penny to spend on security. Which is smart as hell 'cause you know if there's any trouble the press will put it all on the project. The press'll side with the damn terrorists."

"Terrorists. Honestly, Daddy."

"Environmental terrorism, Belle. Read the newspapers. It's all over."

"I just… I don't know. Seems extreme is all."

"'Cause it is extreme. Don't underestimate the bastards. Ain't that right, Nicki?"

Nicholas shrugs. Then nods a little.

"Better safe than sorry. Yes."

"What you think, Shelly?" Grayson tips his head back, speaking up to the top of the car so his words will ricochet down behind him into the back seat. "You think these… these… protestors could be dangerous fanatics if they put their collective mind to it? Or are they just a bunch a punks lookin' for attention?"

He doesn't want to answer. Doesn't want to converse. He has managed to stay cocooned in silence for most of the last hour. Ever since Midland. The smell of nail polish has given him a headache.

"You awake back there, Shel?" Grayson's voice betrays nothing of the threats on the flight over. He sounds earnestly in search of support.

"Just a bunch of kids," Sheldon says. "They're harmless. Just makin' a point."

"You're naïve, Shelly. The both of you. Those sons-a-bitches'll do anything."

Sheldon keeps his focus out of the car. For most of the drive the view has been unrelentingly empty. A pale white sky sitting atop an open desert plain, stubbled with light brown scrub. Like they were a foursome of mites traversing a dirty, unshaven face.

Unhappy mites. No one is having a good time. Except, maybe, for Nicholas Voss. He's the same stoic mystery as always.

From Bates Field in Odessa they had unloaded the plane into the rental Nicholas had waiting for them and headed south on the 385. The plan had been to pick up the 67, east to Corbin. They had invested an hour in that plan. But then came the temporary road signs explaining that the 67 east of McCamey was under water from flash flooding. That had left them only two options: west to pick up the I-10 at Fort Stockton, or back to Odessa.

Grayson and Christi had cursed their rotten luck as Nicki turned the car around. Christi had emoted into her cell phone from the back seat, immune to irony.

"The gosh darn road is under water! In the gosh darn desert! I know! It just don't seem right. Can you even believe? Today of all days? I told Daddy it's like the weather gods just don't want this to happen! Wasn't even a real storm. Harvey's one thing but this one didn't even have a name! I know! I… *I know!* Well, y'all just carry on. We'll get there soon as we can."

Back in Odessa, they had dog-legged east on the I-20, stopping at a Midland truck stop for what Grayson promised would be a short but necessary bite to eat. It was not short.

"Daddy. Listen to me. We. Are. Gon'. Be. Late. For. Our. Own. Gosh. Darn.

Pageant. Miss? *Miss!* Just how long does it take you people to make a waffle?"

From Midland it was south again, this time on the 349 to, fingers crossed, pick up the 67.

"Should'a just gone that way in the first place, Daddy. Someone should'a thought to call ahead. All that rain."

Now, as they approached the fairgrounds, the view from the car had changed. Traffic had thickened, slowing them to a crawl as westbound fair-goers cut across the road in search of parking places. The roadway is flanked on each side with vehicles, either already abandoned or in mid-evacuation. People wait for an opening, threading traffic with their coolers and their children, crossing over to a colorful tent city in the foreground of a towering, kinetic, erector-set metropolis of spinning wheels and flinging metal arms.

A lanky skeleton holds out a boney hand. Nicholas stops. Waves him across.

"You're too dang nice, Nicki," scolds Christi. She looks at her watch.

"Should just run his ass over," says Grayson. "Then it really would be the *Day of the Dead* and it'd serve him right."

"Well, why these ignoramuses don't just park in the parking lot like they're s'posed to is beyond me. Too dang lazy to make the walk, is why. They should tow every one of these cars."

Nicholas does not respond to either of them. Does not react in any way. He accelerates smoothly once the skeleton has passed the centerline. Tucks his blonde hair behind his ear.

The scratch along his cheekbone, just below a deepening purple bruise, is a new and disconcerting landmark on his otherwise perfect face. Sheldon can imagine a slippery bathroom floor. With greater effort, he can imagine a pointed corner on hotel bathroom vanity. He has spent much of the drive imagining the point of contact, flesh to cheap laminate. The contorted face. A shriek. Something high and undignified.

But it takes some effort. It is not easy imagining Nicholas Voss, whose every movement seems guided by an innate muscular economy, losing all control of himself as he steps out of the shower. That was something other people might do any day of the week. Something *he* might do.

But Nicholas is not other people.

By the time they make it past the fairgrounds to Corbin proper, it is almost twelve-thirty. *Broken River Road* is clogged with people and cars. The parking place closest to the fountain at City Hall is at the ball field, half a mile away. Christi is in mid-commentary about the number of fat people trolling the sidewalks with cones of soft ice cream. Then she realizes where they are headed. She pushes her voice into the front seat.

"You expect me? To walk? In *these* heels? All the way from east Jerusalem to the *fountain!* That what y'all are thinkin'?"

Nicholas turns the car around. It takes two blocks and five minutes. Then another five to get all the way up *Broken River Road* to within six blocks of the town square. Christi reads the sign aloud.

"*No vehicles beyond this point. Pedestrians only.* Well ain't that just... what kinda' fucked-up town, pardon my French, are we dealin' with?" She shoves open her door. Grabs her purse. Steps out. "Let's go boys. Looks like we're gonna hafta' hoof it from here. Nicki, park the car and come find us."

Slams the door.

The three of them sit for a slowly elongating second in the quiet car, a glass bubble in a froth of humanity. Sharing something unknown. Someone exhales. Two seconds. Three. Then the sound of Christi rapping her knuckles twice on the hood. Grayson opens his door. Grabs his hat.

"Pop the trunk," says Sheldon. Nicholas nods.

Sheldon climbs out and opens the trunk. He unzips his bag. Extracts the *Cavaliers* backpack. Slings it casually over his shoulder like something that does not contain tens of thousands of dollars in cash and every song he has ever written. Grayson is watching. Sheldon holds out the pack.

"Want some water?"

Grayson turns and walks off.

Christi stays five steps in the lead, threading people. Clearing a path. She makes full use of the street and both sidewalks. The whole world is moving too slowly for her.

"'Scuse me. 'Scuse me. Thank y'all. Thank you."

Grayson speaks. "So, we on the same page here, buckaroo?"

He doesn't answer. Keeps walking. Follows the sound of his wife's voice and the cadence of her heels.

It is the sound he follows. Not the showgirl legs. Not the knee-length red skirt. Not the blonde trusses. His eyes are everywhere else. He can't help but look for her. Can't help but touch every female face with his eyes.

Olivia? No. Olivia? No. Olivia? No.

Their arrangement had been to meet at the fairgrounds, not here. Not on *Broken River Road.* Not at the fountain.

But what if she *was* here? Killing time before going over to the fairgrounds to meet him. Having lunch, there, at *Pepita's.* Buying ice cream, there at the *L&T.* It was possible. He has no idea what he will do if he spots her. Grayson is watching. Knows he is looking for her. But he can't help himself.

Olivia? No. Olivia? No. Olivia? No.

They have outdone themselves. The denizens of Corbin. The volunteers. The gardeners. In the heart of the town square, *La Fuente de la Luna* is a geyser of brilliant color. A floral eruption with a clear liquid core. Baskets of flowers ring every level of the fountain, two rows deep at the base, so that the entire structure is itself a kind of kaleidoscopic flower with a storm of petals surrounding a straight pistil made of burbling water.

At the far end of the square, the town hall presides in garlanded glory, streaming bougainvillea. Overhead, stretching from one end of the square to the other is a lattice of artificial vine, a net of green-wrapped cables. Each intersection of cable is fastened together with soup bowl-sized plastic flowers, as if growing down from the sky, opening to the earth. In between the flowers are large, blue bulbs. They glow in the daylight like drops of moon, waiting to be lit.

To the east end of the square is something else entirely. A stage. Large and square, with a pitched roof and a protruding, semi-circular lip off the front that juts out in the direction of the fountain. There is a long, elevated platform in the back, a stage upon a stage, wedged between an American flag on the left and a Texas flag on the right. Stairs slope off of each end of the platform down to the stage floor. More stairs slope off each end of the stage down to the pavement. Red, white and blue bunting hangs from every inch of infrastructure.

In front of the stage, arching out across the square like silent shock waves, are ten rows of folding chairs. Fifty chairs in each row, split up the middle to make a center aisle. Affixed to the front of the protruding lip of the stage, like a kind of blemish, is the great red circular seal of the Texas Pageant Association. A white, blue-lettered banner hanging from the roofline ensures that people know where they are: *Home of the Corbin River Walk Beauty Queen!!*

Christi clops up the wooden stairs to the stage. A knot of people at a microphoned podium opens. Swallows her whole.

Grayson sits down in one of the folding metal chairs in the back. Takes off his hat. Puts it back on.

"May as well wait for our orders," Grayson says in casual resignation. He nods to the chair next to him. "Take a load off, Shel."

Sheldon glances down. Grayson's eyes have brought along some of the menace from the flight over. *Goddamned but you disgust me, Shelly. I'd like to throw your ass off this fuckin' plane.*

Sheldon walks away, toward the stage.

Each of the chairs in the front row has a placard on the seat. Four of the chairs, just north of dead center, bear the name *Christabelle Davis*. He removes one of the placards. Sits. Unshoulders the backpack and sets it on the pavement between his feet. He pretends to watch Christi take control of every last person up on the stage. Pointing. Speaking in that too loud, too encouraging, sugar-shellacked drawl that he knows from experience seeks only one response: *yes ma'am.*

But he sees nothing. Hears nothing. All he can do is think about what comes next. Getting away. Somehow excusing himself, Grayson watching, to the fairgrounds. He looks at his watch. Shakes his head. Looks around. People are in motion on all sides.

Olivia? No. Olivia? No. Olivia? No.

If he cannot escape, he needs to find a way to contact her. No phone. He'd have to borrow one. A stranger's phone. He closes his eyes. Tries to conjure her number in his head. Numbers assemble, cuing up uncertainly, then scatter.

He opens his eyes. Wonders if Olivia, having been stood up, will make her way to the town square. To the pageant. To find him. That was possible. She might just come looking for him. And the money.

And then what? After today, meeting or no meeting, then what? All manner of unpleasantness, was what. From horizon to horizon. The fight with Christi. Removal from his home. Divorce. The fight with Grayson. The business. *His* business. *His* employees. *His* accounts. *His* clients. What was next?

It is all too ugly to even imagine.

"Shel? Shelly? *Sheldon!*"

He looks. Christi is up on the edge of the stage, glowering through her make-up. She tosses a roll of silver duct tape. It hits the edge of a chair five feet away and wobbles under the row.

"Those placards are s'posed to be on the back rest, not the seat." She points a finger that sweeps the length of the entire first row. "You wanna just tape 'em up where they belong? We want this thing done right we're just gonna have to do it ourselves." She points again, this time over his head. "And tell Daddy to get off his duff and help."

He stands. Retrieves the tape. Starts at the far end, stage left, and works his way chair-by-chair. Placard-by-placard. Many of the names he recognizes as TPA members. The regular donors. He wonders how many of them have reconsidered their RSVP, now a month old. Money is one thing. A personal appearance all the way out to Corbin is something else.

He scans the town square as he tears off a strip of tape. People everywhere. Candy-colored tourists. Three men with silver fish impaled on long wooden dowels talking like hay farmers leaning on pitchforks. Kids with ice cream. Couples sitting on benches and chairs eating hot dogs and funnel cake out of their laps.

Olivia? No. Olivia? No. Olivia? No.

Grayson, no longer on his duff, is sauntering his way up the aisle. He stops where Sheldon had been sitting.

"Put you to work, did she?"

Sheldon looks up. Moves on to the next chair. He can see Grayson looking at the Cavaliers backpack at his feet. Grayson kicks it with the toe of his boot.

"Didn't know you were a Cav's fan. Didn't know you even knew what a basket…"

The interruption comes from over Grayson's left shoulder. Gillian Reed, Miss Dallas, Class of '79, tugs on the brim of Grayson's hat. Her sunglasses make her look like an electric purple fly.

"Hey, bull rider. Rodeo's t'other direction. I think maybe you're lookin' for a different kinda horse flesh."

Grayson turns just as Chet Reed is shuffling up behind his wife. Everyone laughs too loud and too long. Christi's voice cuts through from above like a scythe.

"Hey Jilly! Hey Chet! Glad y'all came." She's wiggling four of her fingers and scrunching up her face in a mock, secret excitement. "Shelly, hon, can I speak with you?"

Sheldon leaves the group for the edge of the stage. Christi bends. Her face is now hard. Serious. She whispers.

"I forgot my dang speech. It's in my bag. In the car. In the trunk. In a blue leather folio-thingy. When you see Nicki, send him back for it. Or you go get it." She stands, done with him. Turns. Turns back. "Oh, and a bottle of water!"

There is a second, for which he considers her words as just another request. Maybe two seconds. But not three.

He walks back to Grayson and the others. Hands over the duct tape. Stoops. Picks up the backpack. Grayson watches, eyes sharp and searching, as Gillian gets to the heart of a story about a "'lil ol' midget skeleton outside the L&T tryin' to eat ice cream through his mask."

He unzips the backpack. Stuffs in his hand and extracts a bottle of water. Hands it to Grayson.

"This is for Belle," he says.

He swings the pack over his shoulder and walks away, Grayson's eyes at his back, scanning the crowd both for Olivia and now for Nicholas Voss. He tours the town square, circling the fountain, then heads up the middle of *Broken River Road*. Navigating streams of people. Looking. Looking.

A skeleton Mariachi band is playing *Me Nace del Corazon*. People dance in the intersection near the barricades. He stops near a vendor selling marigolds. Turns in a slow circle.

Nicholas Voss is outside the *Coahuiltecan Trading Post*. An intimidating camera over one shoulder. Grey backpack. Talking to two men. Black t-shirts and hats. The logo is a golden silhouette of a bull standing over stenciled letters. '*EBSecurity.*' Their eyes meet. Nicholas beckons with one hand. The men turn to look.

"Okay. This is Sheldon Davis. He can tell you what I am telling you. His wife is organizing the pageant. I work for the Corbin Development Corporation. Here. Here's my ID." Nicholas fishes a wallet out of his back pocket. Hands over his license. The bigger guy, sweaty reddish hair beneath his black cap, takes the card. Reads both sides as Nicholas holds up his camera.

"We need good pictures." He points up the street towards the fountain. "All I need is maybe thirty minutes on the roof of the town hall. When they are crowning the winner. Perfect angle down onto the stage."

The two men look at each other. The heavy-set one with the black goatee is shaking his head.

"Need a permit for that, sir. Town hall building is closed up for the weekend." Red hands him back his license. Glances over at Sheldon.

"Pretty sure one of the television stations will have a media truck here tonight. Got one of them camera crane things. Maybe you could use that. You're not authorized to be on the roof."

"Okay. You still do not understand, I think," Nicholas says. "My company... hired *your* company. I know Eli Ball. I spoke to him two weeks ago."

"No sir," says Red. "We work for the City of Corbin."

"Right, but the CDC is the entity that hired *EB Security* for that purpose." Nicholas is pushing the limits of condescension. Sheldon surmises that this is where cool-as-a-cucumber Nicholas Voss goes when he gets frustrated. "You see? The CDC is paying the bill? Paying your salaries?"

"No sir. Sorry. No one on the roof. You boys have a good day now."

They turn and step away into the flow of people.

Nicholas returns his wallet to his pocket. Shakes his head to himself. Then whatever feeling he is experiences passes. He shrugs. "I'll call their boss. Eli is sensible. I will see if *EB Security* wants the contract next year. Maybe he does not care about money."

He looks at Sheldon. The mottled red wound on his face seems larger now. Longer than it had in the car. It seems to be pulling slightly at the pale flesh around his right eyelid. Like an insect on fire, clawing its way up to the cold blue water of that eye.

Sheldon shrugs in return. He has never heard this man string so many words together at once. But he no longer cares to figure him out, this beautiful specimen. Nicholas Voss. His wife's reflecting pool. Not now. Not ever again. Christi can have him. Christi and Grayson can have him. They all deserved each other.

"I need the car keys." He holds out his hand. "Christi forgot her speech."

"I'll go back," Nicholas says. Sheldon shakes his head.

"She's got other plans for you. I know what I'm looking for."

Voss gives a single, slow nod. Pulls an errant flaxen strand behind his ear. Holds the camera strap on his shoulder with one hand as he slips the other down into his pocket.

It reemerges with a key ring around an elegant forefinger. The fingernail is manicured and buffed. The skin beneath the curving edge, stained pink.

He does not run. But the restraint takes effort. By the time he makes it to the ballpark parking he is damp and sticky with sweat. The cloud cover is now a high, thin gauze, brightening by the minute. He finds the rental. Climbs in and dumps the backpack in the passenger seat. Blasts the air conditioning. Drives.

It is another trek from the designated festival parking to the fair itself. The road congestion on the short drive has eaten twice the time reasonably needed for Christi's errand. The fast walk becomes a jog. Looking. Always looking.

Olivia? No. Olivia? No. Olivia? No.

He is moving faster than the others. More deliberately. And he is the only person by himself. So it seems, anyway. He navigates clots and clumps of humanity drifting aimlessly, chaotically, in dozens of crosscurrents. He looks for signs of singularity, for she will be alone. He looks for signs of stillness and quiet. For she will be waiting. Looking for him.

But no one is alone. No one is still. No one is looking.

"Tent City" consists of two wide, makeshift avenues. There are even street signs. *Moon Gardener Way* is nearest the entrance. Just beyond that, *Día de los Muertos Avenida.* Quarter of a mile south, both avenues empty out onto the same concrete plain, poured over the scrublands years ago to support a temporary metropolis of whirring, swinging, looping steel.

Sheldon pauses abruptly at the foot of *Moon Gardener Way.* Scans the southern horizon. The Ferris wheel is easy to spot, like a silver metal moon rising up over the city. He looks at his watch. Half an hour late. He moves quickly, checking faces as he weaves his way forward.

Olivia? No. Olivia? No.

A man and a woman wearing black Stetsons play guitars and twang country standards into microphones in the middle of the make-believe thoroughfare. They tap the toes of their boots next to open, felt-lined cases littered with cash. Clusters of people stop to listen. Eating ice cream. Eating hotdogs. Eating pink mountains of spun sugar. He plots a wide berth. Keeps moving.

On either side of *Moon Gardener Way* are booths arranged in loose neighborhoods of interest. Local artisans. Mexican jewelers, painters, metal works. T-shirts and hats. Texan tourist trinkets. Shot glasses.

Then the local charities and the special interest proselytizers.

Then slightly larger jewel-colored tents: face-painters, arts and crafts, vendors willing to pay extra to hedge their bets on the weather.

Then the food, at the gateway to the land of screaming motion. People form lines so long they threaten to merge at their ends, out in the middle of *Moon Gardener Way*, like disparate ropes all knotted together. He slows as he approaches.

What if she has given up? Left the Ferris wheel. Is in line to get something to eat before leaving. What if? He tries to look at every face.

Olivia? No. Olivia? No.

He pushes forward. Faster now. The Ferris wheel looms two hundred yards in the distance. Christi, back at the town square, waiting, looking at her watch, standing on the stage searching the length of *Broken River Road*, somehow breaks through the chaos that insulates his single-minded focus. As if his wife's mounting anxiety was a guided missile that could hone in on his brain waves. Destroy him with anger.

He looks at his watch, considering, now, not how long ago he was supposed to meet Olivia at the Ferris wheel, but how much time was left before Christi, without her written speech, would be expected to address those assembled for the opening of the first annual Corbin River Walk Beauty Pageant.

Grayson's anger has its own guided missile. *We are not gon' do anything... anything... to rain on her parade. Understand Shelly? Not a single fuckin' drop of rain.*

He blocks both of them out. Keeps moving. Keeps looking. Tries to condense his feelings into discrete drops of meaning. Drops of sound. Words. He needed the right words. He imagines telling her that everything is about to change.

Imagines giving her his music.

Imagines giving his strange, inexplicable desperation a voice.

You want this to be about the blues? Well then let's do that. Let's make this about the blues. You want blues? Well then here's a whole bag of blues, just for you. I'll write you another full bag, too. And another. And another. From the first second that I laid eyes on you from the bottom of that whorehouse staircase. Barefoot and stoned out of my mind, I know, but it was like you were floating up in the air. Looking down on me with your quiet, knowing expression that I have come to love, like you knew me. Like we knew each other in some previous life. I have tried to hate you. Judge you. Demean you by association. I have tried to be indifferent. I have tried to reduce you to a financial consequence. A threat to be negotiated. But the truth is that I have not stopped thinking about you since that first night. You inspire me to be someone I have not been in a very long time. I can't explain it. Trying to explain it is driving me crazy. So I've stopped trying. I don't care about why. I don't need to understand why. All I know is how I feel. You want blues? Well then let's start over with nothing. Let's start over together. You're too young. I'm too old. I get that. And I don't care. I know nothing about you and yet I know everything about you. From that first second. You're like an old song I have written but never sung. I want to sing your song, Olivia. I'll do anything for you. Anything you ask.

The words, now fully imagined, have given shape to the feeling behind them. He loved her. There it was. Why? He didn't know why. He just did. It was a real feeling, needing only to be expressed. Sung. The emotion seems to lift him. Carry him. He floats forward on the current of his own feelings, now suddenly new, suddenly clear for having language —words, lyrics —to make those feelings buoyant, lifting them out of the muck of fear and denial. Words, lyrics, like little boats in the great flood of inexplicable longing.

The Ferris wheel towers above him, framed against a beryl blue sky behind a pale, whisper-thin curtain of voile. There are two wheels in perpetual motion. A vertical wheel of steel and gears and brightly-colored gondolas. Beneath that wheel, encircling it, is the only wheel that interests him. A wheel of flesh and bone, moving like a moat of humanity, drifting in loud, lazy circles. A wheel of faces.

He circumnavigates the moat. Once. Twice. Looking. Stopping at each of the five equidistant benches. He comes to a stop where he started. Turns in his own tight, tiny circle. Looking.

No luck. He sits on the edge of a bench next to a woman cooing down into a stroller. He swings the backpack off of his shoulder. Leans back. Watches the big wheel turn inside its fleshy moat, scooping up humans four at a time. He wonders how many times she has tried to call him. How many times his phone has bleated a muffled ring from between the sofa cushions in his study.

Big wheel keeps on turning.

Sheldon considers the ride in a new light. From eighty feet in the air he could scour the fairgrounds. Would he recognize the top of her head? He thinks so. If she is here and moving he will, if nothing else, recognize the limp.

He stands again. Slings the pack back over his shoulder as he walks. Gets in line behind a skeleton.

The dead woman is wearing black pants. A floral bodice beneath a woven black shawl. A headband of scarlet roses over curly, shoulder-length black hair. Her hands, face and neck are painted the color of gleaming bone. Her nose, as if it is no longer there, is painted black. Her lips are full and red with a black rose stenciled on each cheek as if growing from each corner of her mouth. The hollows of her eyes are shocks of turquoise, studded with tiny glass jewels and dusted with glitter.

The dead woman has children. One in each hand. The girl is maybe ten. Eleven. Jeans. Black, long-sleeve t-shirt. A plastic skeleton mask pushed up on the top of her head, empty eye sockets to the sky, elastic band under her chin. Hands of white bone like her mother.

But the boy. He is like a yearling from the forest –silken black hair, large velvet eyes, soft brown skin. He cannot be more than six. He is not dead, this kid. Nor almost-kind-of-dead, like his sister. He is clad in soft blue cotton and fully alive.

But he is quiet. And he is afraid. He is unsure about the big wheel, gobbling people up. The dead woman lets go of his little hand. Strokes and cups the back of his head with her boney white fingers. She turns a little. Looks at Sheldon. Smiles. Sweetly, almost apologetically. For being dead and for having a son who is afraid. Sheldon nods.

The big wheel scoops them up. All four of them. Sheldon and the girl sit on one side of the gondola. The dead woman and the apprehensive boy sit across from them. The attendant locks the aluminum bars over their laps. Closes the gate.

They rise. Stop. The gondola swings.

Again. *Rise. Stop. Swing.*

Sheldon scans the widening view. Examines the top of every head. Every set of shoulders. Looks for limping. *Olivia? No. Olivia? No. Olivia? No.*

"*¿Por qué seguimos deteniendo?*" The almost-dead girl asks.

"Because they have to let the other people on." Says her dead mother. "Then it will start."

Rise. Stop. Swing. The boy across from him grips the bar across his lap. Knuckles now as white as his mother's hands. The finger bones stroke his hair. She smiles down at him. Sings in a whisper.

Luna lunera, cascabelera,
ve y dile a mi amorcito
por Dios que me quiera;
dile que me muero,
que tenga compasión,
dile que se apiade de mi corazón.

He knows the song. *Luna Lunera. Whimsical Moon.* And he can pick out most of the lyrics. *Whimsical moon. Say to him that I do not live of so much suffering. Say to him that he must return to me.*

But the lyrics are not important. It's the way she sings. The breathiness of it. The swaying, unearthly cadence. Drifting, back and forth, up in the breeze. Not words, but clouds of sound. Cumuli of feeling.

Ay lunita redondita,
que la espuma de tu luz
bañen mis noches

Oh, little round moon, let the foam of your light bathe my nights. It's as if she is singing to *him*. To *Sheldon*. To a man she does not know. Thoughts of Christi and Grayson, looking for him, angry, time running out, try to cut in. They can't.

Ay lunita redondita,
dile que me has visto tú
llorar de amor

Oh, little round moon, say to him that you have seen me crying of love. But then he realizes he is wrong. It's not as if the boy's mother is singing to him. No. Not that. It's as if his *own mother* is singing to him. Singing from far beyond this place. From a place without time.

How long has it been since he has remembered his mother? Frances. So many reasons not to remember. So much anger, so little forgiveness, in that struggle to be free. In that struggle to break the umbilical bond. Those wars of attrition.

And then the quiet years, as her mind slowly turned to sand and washed away between increasingly infrequent, perfunctory visits. And then, one summer day, the home had called and, suddenly, Frances was gone. Not just physically removed from him. Not just irrelevant as a practical consequence of her dementia. But actually gone. She no longer existed. The umbilical bond had snapped. Death ties off that knot for good.

The cord is not long enough. It will not stretch across the river.

Or will it? Because now he cannot help but remember her. Cannot help but feel her. *In* him. *Around* him. As if some portal has opened. As if the big wheel were a cosmic satellite dish tuning in a signal that delivers her very essence. Like she is sitting in a bright yellow gondola, directly across from him. Here. Now. Frances Harlow Davis. *Mom.*

dile que me muero,
que tenga compasión,
dile que se apiade de mi corazón.

Say to him that I die, that he has compassion. Tell him to have mercy on my heart. But he is wrong. Again, he is wrong.

It is *not* as if she, this woman, is *his* mother. Frances. Singing to *him.* Singing to Sheldon Davis. No. Not that.

It is as if she is channeling *every* mother. Singing to *every* child. Worrying for *every* child. Aching for *every* child. Because for all of our differences, we are all the same. We are all notes from the same lullaby. Sweet and sad and reassuring. We know it innately as a vibration in our bones. We are beings of musical distillation. We are condensed from an eternal harmony. In the end, we are reabsorbed, back into the cosmic song. In between the beginning and the end we have a heartbeat, measuring out our lives in four-four time. We prop ourselves up against that backbeat. Shoe leather stomping against the dusty floorboards of the world. The dirty palm beating against the thigh. Head swinging, side-to-side.

Counting. Always counting. *One-two-three-four.*

Let's make this about the blues, Olivia had said.

He stops looking. Closes his eyes. Worries now that he was wrong. That he has missed his chance. Not just that Olivia is no longer here. But that she never was.

Chapter 81

Small. Made of stone.

Not the whole house. Some previous owner had put up a granite façade. Irregular chunks of rock held in place by wide seams of grout. Big stone chimney. Stone columns on either side of the front door holding up a pitched portico. A large iron bell sitting at the top of three slabs of granite steps down into a tiny, brown front yard, bordered on each side by silver chain link.

To the right of the house, on the other side of the fence and beyond a broken aluminum swing set, is a house just like it. All wood.

Desmond Vaughn walks across the yard, still squishy with rain. Mounts the stone steps. Knocks.

Waits.

Knocks. Tries the knob. Locked. He calls out.

"Laurie?"

Waits. Knocks. Nothing.

He looks down behind him at the iron bell. The first time he'd stood on these steps he had asked her. *A bell?* A cactus wren flutters off the roof.

So he knew the family history.

John Calhoun Weaver, civilian captain of the riverboat called *The Redemption*. Three boilers. A hauling capacity of three thousand bales of cotton, which it transported regularly between Baton Rouge and Jackson, Missouri. Captain Weaver, a whore-mongering lush by reputation, had found sudden purpose in joining the Union assault on Confederate forces in the First Battle of Memphis. He'd done what he could with what he had, using heavy timber and stolen scrap from the Jackson Railroad Company to convert his steamboat into a floating battering ram tipped with an iron harpoon. *The Redemption* scuttled two Confederate gunboats before bursting into flame and sinking. Years after the war, Captain Weaver's brother had salvaged the bell.

Desmond kneels. Tips the thing back on its rim. Reaches in. The magnetic tin is where it always had been.

He knocks again as he is turning the key. Calls out. Pushes.

All quiet. Still. Dark. Like the façade is not a façade. Like he really has stepped inside stone. Everything that moves, beats, circulates, draws is entirely his. He is alien.

"Laurie?"

He closes the door. Flicks a switch. A frosted glass sun hangs beneath a white, orange peel sky. Illumination sprays outward like a yellowing fog.

He takes it all in. Nothing has changed. Not really.

There is one combined room for almost everything. Cooking. Dining. Living. A scarred oak floor stretches beneath small islands of furniture, between a front wall and a back wall, each with curtained windows. The drapes are a pale green, like they are exhausted from years of encouraging the lawn. They have been pulled closed over the windows. The ridges are dirty and discolored. The troughs are cleaner and brighter. Greener.

The lower half of the far wall is almost all bookshelf. A protruding rectangle full of smaller rectangles, each of them packed. The unit is not deep enough for two rows. Books jut out into the room, only half supported by shelving.

The big rectangle in the center is where the television belongs, facing the sectional couch, next to a silver DVD player and a collection of remote controls.

But there is no television. No DVD player. No remotes.

Only more books, leaning like toppled dominos against a black turntable on top of a stereo receiver and two cinderblock-sized speakers. Another rectangle holds the records. The old stuff. The good stuff. *Lightnin'. Buddy. Howlin'. Otis. Big Joe. Bessie. Etta.* Some of them were his. He'd never asked for them back.

It's all the same as it ever was.

They had only lasted three months, he and Laurie, plus a short-lived, mostly drunken rekindling half a year later, just as his marriage was going down for the last time. They had both lost interest after that. Then they had hated each other for most of a year. But they'd kept feeding from the same teat. Children of the *Chacha*.

Above the shelving, scattered across the wall, hang the same half-dozen canvases with handmade frames. She renders the desert absurdly, in unnatural colors. Chartreuse cacti. Teal tumbleweed. An octopus, Stetson pulled low, drives a stagecoach, pulled by a team of sea horses. An old Spanish mission in a grove of rubbery pink kelp.

"Laurie?"

The coffee table has been cleared. There are magazines, newspapers, on the couch. An ashtray. He moves for the hall.

The bedroom on the left. Door closed. He knocks. "Laurie?" Opens it slowly.

Daylight leaks in, disconcertingly, like a syrup, from behind the same drawstring blinds. Over the sill. Down the wall. He has never seen daylight through those blinds. All of his memories here are nocturnal. The same white duvet is pulled incompletely over a lump of clothes. He backs out.

The makeshift office on the right. Door closed. He knocks. "Laurie?"

Overburdened bookshelves. A desk with a computer monitor and an overturned chair. Dangling cords. No computer. He backs out.

The hall ends at the same bathroom. Yellow light whispers from beneath the closed door. The yellowness slickens the hall floor, reaching him, filling him with a rising tide of emotion too subtle and quiet to name and easy enough to deny.

But the feeling does have a name. Dread.

Desmond hesitates. Gathers the breath he may need. He does not bother knocking or calling her name. He grips the knob. It wobbles loosely in his hand. Pushes.

It is everything he remembers of Laurie Weaver's bathroom. Cluttered vanity. Dirty mirror. Two out of five bulbs burned out. The shower curtain, pulled to obscure the tub, is dingy with age and needs replacing. The end hangs loose, ripped free of the last ring.

For as much as he wants to find her, he does not want to find her here.

He extends his arm, hooks the curtain with his finger. Pulls.

He is relieved. The porcelain is chipped near the drain. It needs a good cleaning.

He turns to go. Blinks. Then sees everything he missed.

A hairdryer hangs by its cord almost to the floor. One end of a towel rack has been pulled out of the dry wall. An aqua bathmat is mashed up into a corner. Cosmetics scattered on the floor behind the toilet.

The doorframe is splintered at the lock.

He steps forward. Pushes the door closed.

An aqua towel hangs from a hook on the back of the door. Smears and streaks of red, like an enormous red spider has been smashed beneath the towel, stain the wood. He pulls the towel aside.

The color of Laurie Weaver's lips. A list.

"Chris Dawson" = V.D.
6 ft. Blue eyes
Shlder length blond
Birthmark rt. arm
Spoke Russ on phone
Took keys phone notes comput purse
GOT GREEDY
SOS

The last 'S' is only partly formed, jagging sideways across the door to make the longest leg of the flattened red spider. That's when the door had been kicked open.

He sits uneasily on the edge of the tub. Extracts his phone. Calls the police. The dispatcher is slow to comprehend. She wants too much basic information. She wants information he does not have. Her incomprehension sharpens into suspicion. Desmond promises to wait.

He needs air. Exits the rectangle made of smaller rectangles. Sits on the top stone step looking out over the tiny squishy yard. Grips the top of the iron bell.

The sky is clearing. Bluer by the minute. A sunny day for the fair. A full moon for the Moon Garden Festival. Who'd have guessed?

Ridiculously, he remembers the pageant. Hears Cal Aronson in his head. *This is still Texas and the Chacha is still a Texas rag and nothin' sells newspapers in Texas like a beauty contest. ... And you tell Laurie Weaver that I personally want her to cover the beauty pageant at the...*

He assumes that Cal already knows about the fire. He should call him anyway. Talk about how all of this ends. Talk about the fact that the *Chacha* will not pursue any story ever again.

He looks down at his phone. *Fuck Cal Aronson.* He wants to throw the thing out into the street. It reads his mind, trilling in his hand.

"Dez. Rick. Heard from Laurie?"

"Hey Rick. No. I have not. Guess you haven't either."

There is too much to tell. Between the building where Laurie worked and the building in which she lives, there are too many places to start. The police will soon be asking the kind of questions journalists don't like to answer. Media lawyers will need to start circling the wagons to protect the story and its sources. These are things Rick Stoddard and CBS need to know.

And then there is the other reason he needs to know. The thing he keeps pushing away. Rick, too, has tipped open this bell.

But he can't get the bathroom door out of his head.

The splintered wood. The cosmetic blood spider. The words will not come without a flood of terror and panic.

So the words don't come.

Doesn't matter. Rick will not take a breath.

"Look. I'm up to the requisite six messages now and still no call. I told her to cancel her Indiana trip. I told her I've got info about Chris Dawson. But now I'm startin' to get a little pissed. I'm startin' to wonder if you told Laurie to keep me out of the loop. Yeah, okay, I over-reached on the FOIA requests. That was... you should have known about that ahead of time. My bad. I'm sorry, okay? But I had my reasons. I'm tryin' my best over here to get ahold of this story, Dez. And I'm tryin' my best not to jump to stupid conclusions about whether you are on board or tryin' to freeze me out."

Rick is finally quiet. Waiting. It is time to tell him about not-so-stupid conclusions. Time to tell him about burning buildings and lipstick spiders. But he doesn't. He can't.

"What Indiana trip?"

"What?"

"You said you told her to cancel an Indiana trip."

"She wanted to go to the pen over in Terra Haute to interview Vasily Dudnik. We're tryin' to connect…"

"Oh. Yeah. She told me about that. I told her to go interview him. Why…"

"'Cause he ain't there."

"What do you mean?"

"Released two years ago."

"Transferred?"

"Released."

"You said they locked him up on a twelve-year sentence."

"They did. Fourteen years ago. He'd already served two years by the time the Connecticut Bar finally disciplined his lawyer for withholding evidence. I was counting twelve years from the wrong date. We'll just have to see if we can find him."

"Like he's ever gonna talk to you. To CBS."

"Maybe not. Probably not. But maybe he'll talk to Laurie. Or the people he hangs with will talk to Laurie. Hookers. Bartenders. Cellmates. Whoever. Worth a shot anyway."

A Crockett County Sheriff's cruiser makes a slow turn onto the street at the end of the block. Desmond watches it roll to a stop in front of the house. The officer appraises. Talks into his radio.

"Gotta go, Rick. I…"

"It's worth the effort, Dez. Vasily's lawyer is a partner in the firm that serves as the registered agent for Quinco International in the United States. Okay? You get that? If we can connect Vasily in any way to the Corbin Development… Well. Look. My point is we need to find this piece of shit. And dollars to donuts he ain't hangin' 'round Terra Haute."

Desmond knows. Without knowing anything, somehow, he knows.

He knows exactly where Vasily Dudnik has been *hangin' 'round*.

Chapter 82

Mable and Libby

Uprooting was not difficult. Libby Holder did not have any roots.

Not any more. Not without Mama Mable.

So Texas was as good as anyplace else.

They had lost themselves in Dallas and Fort Worth for a month until Antoine decided they would get more land for his money further south. From the stories he picked up here and there, Fort Stockton had seemed like a good idea.

But they never made it to Fort Stockton. They pulled off I-67 and stopped in little Corbin to stretch their legs. Libby walked off for an ice cream. Antoine went the other direction. He met a Marlboro man propped up on the back legs of a chair outside the *Coahuiltecan Trading Post*. Antoine went in and bought a new pack for himself. He sat in the chair on the other side of the door to the Trading Post. Lit up. Waited for Libby.

One thing led to another. Turned out the Marlboro man knew a guy looking to sell a house and a small pecan orchard. Hargrove was his name. Cale Hargrove's kid, Raimey.

And that was that.

"Pecan farmers!" Antoine had imagined the idea aloud, slapping the steering wheel. "Just how'd *that* be, Lib? Goddamned orchard-ownin' nut farmers. I'd say it beats the livin' hell outta harvestin' shit from septic tanks."

Antoine insisted that Libby own the place outright. She had shown just enough incredulity and confusion to elicit a half-assed explanation.

"Jus' tryin' to show you that I love you, honey. Tryin' to show that I trust you and that we always gon' be together. What's mine is yours and vice versa. Ain't no reason my name needs to be on the damn thing."

She might have been flattered. Might have decided that she was loved. That here was a man opening his heart to her. Exposing. Declaring. Putting his money where his mouth was

But Mable Holder had not raised a fool for a daughter. Spider was under a

686

glass. Or soon to be. Spider had information to trade. So Antoine was looking to disappear. He no longer owned property. No longer lived in any particular place. Not on paper. Made no sense for the light that had suddenly winked out in Louisiana to wink back on someplace else. Why make it easy?

She had understood, too, that it was important to Antoine that she not be just sitting around Gretna, available to anyone of a mind to ask questions about him. Or about Mable. She understood that Antoine's love was equal parts holding her close, controlling her associations and, in the event anyone ever found them, deflecting suspicion: if *Libby* loved him, if *Libby* trusted him, well then.

But the ABC Man had the same innate sense of value that all of the other boys had. You had to give a little to get a little. Give a little more, get a little more. Little Libby Ching-Chang-Chop had learned that lesson well enough. Life was a transaction. Love was a dime store costume –a nylon cape and a hard plastic mask with a slit for a mouth and an elastic cord that lasted for a couple of hours. Just long enough to get some candy in the bag.

Maternal love was the only true thing in the universe. A mama's love for her baby. Everything else was for shit.

She understood. Wasn't about love.

So she purchased a small house and a pecan farm with money not her own. Overnight, little Ching-Chang-Chop Libby Holder owned a tiny slice of south Texas.

Antoine's interest in marriage was no less transparent. She figured he wanted to keep what was his in the family. Accidents do happen. Didn't want Janeese showing up as next of kin. Or even the State of Texas stepping in to take it all back. Wasn't about love.

Not that it wasn't a risk. A marriage license was as much of a paper breadcrumb as a property deed. But it was as important to him as it was repellent to her. She had resisted.

"Don't see why it so all-fired important, baby," she'd said.

"'Cause a fresh start mean we ain't livin' in sin, Libby. I wanna do this right. I wanna do right by you. High time you become Libby Cherish."

"You never saw fit to marry mama."

"I didn't love your mama, rest her soul. Not like I love you. She'd want this for you and you know it."

And she had known it. Down in the place where we already know everything there is to know, Libby had felt Mable pushing her forward. Pushing her to do the unthinkable. *Keep goin', baby. Don't stop now. You see this through.*

They were married within the four cracked, yellowing walls of the Crockett County Clerk's Office. The whole thing took forty-five minutes, including the twenty minute cigarette break it took to convince the intake clerk that three hundred dollars would help resolve any concerns about when Antoine's hapless part-Asian bride-to-be was actually born.

"I'm just sayin', sir, this girl… woman… this *woman* was adopted as a little girl right outta that rice paddy hellhole our boys are fightin' in right now. So if you are any kind of patriotic American then you got to know that this here date on this here piece of paper is a fucked up guess. Goddamned gooks celebratin' the year of the monkey and rat and whatnot. Her mama never even knew the birthdate. She'd be right here with us to tell you so herself but she turned up murdered just about a year ago. I ain't expectin' you t'understand for free, brother."

Libby had aged two full years in the space of a single Marlboro.

Changing her name to Libby Cherish, they learned, was a separate deal that would take a lot of paperwork. Libby had voiced a practical optimism.

"We jus' gon' haft put that shit on the list, baby."

He'd kept her close, his wife. He'd been clear about what a husband expects. Her job was to fully occupy the house he had given her. The name he would be giving her. She did as she was told. Cooked. Cleaned. Made herself available. Tried her best not to make him angry. Forgave easily. Waited.

Antoine's job was to learn how to be a nut farmer. He knew nothing. First thing he learned was that his *harvesting-is-harvesting* preconception was naive. Hauling traps out of the water and emptying the catch into a bucket had its own challenges, especially in the dark of night when the traps belonged to others. But that kind of harvesting had not required any ladder work. Or cutting up his arms reaching into dagger-sharp branches to force a stubborn pecan tree to let go of its children.

Raimey Hargrove had been in a bad way. He sold off the machinery –the tree shaker, the pruning tower, the sweeper –long before he found a buyer for the property. That had left Antoine with forty-eight trees, a couple of rickety wooden ladders and his own two hands.

Did not take him long to see that he needed another pair of hands. Desperate, young and illegal, Basilio Gomez was willing to work for almost nothing. He was paid a few dollars an hour and a free lunch that he never actually ate. Basilio usually stayed up on his ladder while Antoine ate, asking Libby in timid, broken English if she would wrap the food up in foil so that he could take it back home to share with his wife, Clarinda. Antoine tended to shrug at this. Adjust his floppy straw hat. Keep eating.

"Suit yourself, boy, but you can take a damn break if you want to. Pay's gon' be the same one way or t'other. She may be hungry but she ain't up in the damn tree workin' in the sun. I'd keep my strength up if I was you."

Basilio usually just nodded and kept picking.

Two or three times a month Basilio's wife Clarinda would drop Basilio off so that she could use the car to drive into San Angelo to visit her sister. Over Antoine's objections, Libby made sure to make dinner for four on those days. Libby would loiter out front, watching for Clarinda to come back in the late afternoon to take Basilio home. Before the tire dust had settled, Libby would walk out to the station wagon parked in the shade of the large, sprawling pecan in the front of the house. She'd lean forward, hands out, like she was trying to assure a frightened child.

"You want you some fried chicken, baby? I made so much today I don't know what to do with all of it. And corn bread. Got me enough of that shit to make a damn corn bread house. Come on inside."

Clarinda's eyes were large and brown and unsettled, never still for long, always looking away, resting in unoccupied spaces, like birds flitting off to distant branches. She didn't look hungry. She was plump as a ripe fruit, dimples like little stars when she smiled, which was most of the time. She was playfully ashamed of her poor English. The words made her blush and cringe and look away.

Fashion, of all things, fabric and color, played ambassador. Libby wore skirts on the Clarinda days. Because Clarinda wore skirts. Might have been the only thing they could ever have in common. But it was something. Libby had once extended a hand. Carefully fingered the hem.

"Tell me you did not make this skirt? *You* done this? You did not. You *did?* *Really?* Clarinda, baby, you need to go into business."

Libby made lemonade. They shared the swing out back. Watched Antoine and Basilio up on their ladders conducting a hailstorm of pecans. Watched the quotidian celestial collision, the sun steadily plowing itself down below the tree line into the desert horizon beyond. Watched the slow, soundless suffocation of light.

Swing up. Swing back. Swing up. Legs out, like fingers slowly strumming against the belly of late afternoon.

Libby had always done the talking for both of them. Clarinda had nodded and laughed and looked away and sipped her lemonade. The swing, four ropes suspending a repurposed bench from the eve of the house, was made for two but with little room to spare. They sat. Sipped. Glided to and fro.

Yearning flooded the left side of Libby's body like a stream diverted out into desert soil. It pooled up along the entire length of her left thigh. In her left knee. Her left calf. Her left ankle. Along the outer edge of her left foot. Any place of contact with Clarinda's body, skin to skin, caused her heart to alternately thrill and ache in a kind of labored rhythm. She'd swung her bare left foot up into the air. Wiggled her dainty toes.

"You like that color, Clarinda? Call that *Hot Cherry Blossom.* You believe that shit? Got it on my fingers too. See? What you got on them toes, Clarinda? You want you some *Hot Cherry Blossom*? I let you use some. Want to get out of them shoes? How you say *shoes* in Mexican?"

Clarinda had blushed. Laughed. Cast her eyes away, brown birds flying.

But, then, Clarinda always blushed. Always looked away. No telling what she was feeling. Didn't really matter. It was the moment itself that mattered. It meant whatever Libby wanted it to mean. Every time the swing had reached its apex, backward or forward, in the split second before it reversed direction, Libby had felt the tiny, pillowed pocket of flesh between her bare legs humming and buzzing, an electric charge carried on the lips of secret waves that swelled into to her extremities and then receded.

And then returned. Receded. Returned.

In the swinging arc to the next apex, Libby's entire body seemed to exhale and to fall backward into cloud. She felt alive. She felt the desire of a new baby-green shoot, pushing its way up through the soil toward the light. In those moments, apex to apex to apex, strung together like twinkle lights in the arms of an enormous tree, she had felt normal.

Antoine ached every night from the life of a pecan farmer. Libby added muscle massage to her repertoire of wifely talents. She learned to isolate each muscle. Relax it. Lengthen it. Antoine quickly ritualized the relief. It started with a stiff drink and hot bath, drawn while he was finishing dinner. Then the massage, first to calm and soften, but eventually, inevitably, to arouse. Every evening started the same and ended the same.

Each night, as her husband floated away on a tide of satisfied exhaustion, Libby had put her clothes back on and descended the long wooden staircase of Cale Hargrove's old house to clean up the table and the kitchen. Clarinda's visits aside, the time cleaning dishes after Antoine's final shudder was Libby's favorite part of the day. She hummed to herself and sang all the old songs under her breath. Usually the cleaning ended before the old songs. So she started baking something. Messed everything up again.

On their way through San Angelo they had stopped into a record store. It had been like flipping through an old family photo album. *Bessie. Ma. Hattie. Sister Rosetta. Sippie.* Seeing those albums had stirred the sediment, clouding the water with the past. She'd remembered her mother heaving herself up and down that flight of stairs, hauling that record player, and then stack after stack of vinyl, as the worst storm she had ever seen took savage bites out of the house. There is no better measure of a person than what they try to keep dry in a hurricane. Mable had seen to Libby first, as always, until the day she died. But then, ahead of everything else, Mable had tried to save the music.

Back in the car Libby had told Antoine that she wanted to buy a record player. He'd laughed as he rolled down the window and lit a cigarette. Shook his head like she'd asked to buy a dolphin. But twenty miles down the road, rolling toward Corbin as they talked about how it was time she became Libby Cherish, Antoine had said he might just be inclined to buy her a record player and all the records she could ever want. They'd just have to see.

Most nights Libby could feel Mable down there in the kitchen with her. Drying her big hands on a tea towel. Shaking her head like she was keeping time to whatever Libby was singing. Humming along side. Waiting with her daughter. Counseling patience just like Bessie Smith might have with her daughter.

Whoa, Tillie, take your time.

Whoa, Tillie, take your time.

This could be a long night, Tillie. You take your time with it.

An accident was bound to happen eventually. The ladders were old. The wood was weathered and there was too much play around the rusted metal fittings. Raimey Hargrove had advised throwing the things out and buying new ones. Antoine had agreed. Impossible not to agree. But then one day had led to the next. The ladders had kept doing what ladders were designed to do and the job kept getting done amid so many other things to worry about.

Basilio had shown up early one day and had taken the better of the two ladders for a change, leaving the taller, older ladder for Antoine. When the second-to-top step split open, Antoine fell backward, twenty feet to the ground, grasping at branches that seemed to pull away from him, in towards the trunk.

He had landed hard. Right elbow shattered against the bottom rung. Left shoulder fractured against the end of a metal nut rake. He was lucky the rake did not puncture vital organs. Lucky he did not snap his spine. But Antoine had failed to appreciate his good fortune.

The hospital in San Angelo sent him home braced and slung. He could walk fine. He could bend and twist at the waist. But the left shoulder and the right elbow needed to remain immobilized. It meant, among other things, that Antoine was no use in the orchard except for barking orders. When Basilio threatened to leave unless he got some help, Antoine hired one of Basilio's friends for half the pay and consented to the purchase of two new ladders. He walked around kicking nuts and slinging abuse up into the branches.

Antoine's pain was constant and excruciating. The muscle relaxants and the opioids were unsung heroes. They surely helped, but there was so much pain left over that their contribution was near invisible. Sleeping was difficult without alcohol. Semi-consciousness became his resting state, interrupted by fits of impotent rage just to circulate the blood.

Without functioning arms, it had fallen to Libby to be his nurse. His second self. She put his straw hat on his head every day so he could go outside and yell up at Basilio and Óscar without getting sunburned. She cut up his food and fed it to him. Held a bottle to his lips. Bathed him. Wiped him. Suffered for his emasculation.

The evenings were long and hateful. Antoine railed at her from the bed upstairs, cataloging his pains and discomforts. Shouted down to her to bring him things. To service him. To make it all better.

She kept to the kitchen, the farthest corner of the house and the only place where she could plausibly claim not to hear him. She turned to baking. Cakes. Pies. Biscuits. Cookies. She filled the house with old-school aromatherapy. Rising, buttered dough. Caramelizing sugar. Melting chocolate. Bubbling fruits. Roasting pecans. Every morning Basilio and Óscar feasted before the yelling started. She sent Basilio home every afternoon with something extra for Clarinda.

In the hours after midnight, when Antoine was awake and yelling about the pain, she'd bring him a new trio of pills on a plate next to slice of something warm and gooey. Just like Mable had always served her up aspirin and antibiotics when she was ailing. Libby sat on the bed next to him and forked it in, humming as she did, like he was three years old. Waited until he quieted down. Waited until sleep reasserted custody, taking him back for another two or three hours.

She was always awake for a while after. Listening to him breath next to her. Listening to the coyotes confessing in the moonlight. Feeling the earth turning under the bed, sloshing the dark water of *Lac des Allemands,* hundreds of miles away.

Thinking. Humming to her mother's memory of Memphis Minnie.

…baby wants some bread, oh baby got to stay late as you can.
My bread gonna rise, gonna make you a man.
I'm gonna bake my biscuits
I'm gonna bake my biscuits
I'm gonna …

She waited until the full moon, for no other reason than that was when Mable's presence always seemed to be the strongest. Three chocolate pecan cookies would have been enough. But Antoine had started on them early. By the time Libby was easing him into the tub, he had eaten six. She pulled off pieces of the seventh cookie and one-by-one placed them on his tongue. He chewed slowly, eyes closed, head lolled back against the foot of the tub. When number seven was down and away she washed him gently with a cloth, cleaning all the places that were safe to touch. He made sounds that he must have thought were words.

She spoke like it was a conversation.

"I never took me a bath when I was young. Mama an' me was always shower people. Mama hated takin' her a bath. Prob'ly 'cause she so afraid of water."

Antoine had mumbled agreement.

"Only two things in this world would make Mama climb into a boat. Either

her life depended on it, like when you pulled us outta that hurricane, or she believed my life depended on it."

She had wrung out the washcloth. Dropped it over the faucet.

"What I want to know, baby, is if you forced her into that boat… or if you tol' her you was gon' take her someplace to see me."

A beat. Two.

Three.

Four.

Antoine had fluttered his eyelids. Tried to hold them open to see her. They pulled back like heavy stumps rooted into his face. His forehead furrowed. Ripples on the surface of a lake. He made a sound in the shape of a question. The warm water around his body sloshed.

Libby stood. Took off all of her clothes. Looked down at him. Spoke.

"Tired of waitin', Antoine. Tired of waitin' for Spider to get snatched up and flip on you; to say what he got to say. Tired of waitin' for the knock on the door. Mama say we got to do for our own self in this world. Mama always right."

She had stepped carefully into the tub, one foot, then the other, straddling his body. Ten perfect drops of *Pink Cherry Blossom*, five on each side, against the white porcelain.

The palm of his hand found her calf. Then, for a moment, calm. Stillness. A slow lapping of water.

She stood, one foot, then the other, squarely on the center of his chest, slipping him back and under. The back of his head thumped against the bottom of the tub.

Antoine's eyes flew open. Saw her. Knew. Understood. Limbs, previously immobilized with pain, suddenly thrashed. Sounds, soggy shouting sounds, he must have thought were words.

Libby kneeled down into the chaos. Slowly. Carefully. One on the broken shoulder. One on the shattered elbow. Focusing her weight. Just enough to hold half a man. A quarter of a man. She stretched forward. Pressed her palms against his forehead.

Closed her eyes. Heard her mother's voice humming from deep and far away. She wept until the water grew still and cold.

Outside, from every direction, the coyotes sang up into the ghostly blue light of the moon. That face of their creation. That memory of their abandonment.

Chapter 83

"What... *happened*?"

Second time he has asked the question. She hears him, somewhere through the rubble of her cognition.

But it is just another sound.

Another wall collapsing. Another slab of ceiling letting go.

"Olivia?"

Darrell Lewis reaches out. Touches her shoulder. She flinches violently. Stepping back. Darrell pulls both hands up into the air, surrendering.

"Hey, hey. I'm just... it's okay. I'm just ... your face... you've got blood..."

His dirty fingers touch his own face. His own neck. His own shirt.

"What happened to you, sweetheart? Who did this to you?"

She looks away. Breathes. Speaks.

"You're sure she's okay? I mean... you're not just tryin'..."

"I promise. She'da been..." Darrell looks over at the black pile of timber, still smoking in a lake of sooty water. Shakes his head. "*Man.* Olivia, she'da been burnt to a crisp if that guy hadn't gone in and pulled her out."

Another bit of relief comes first. The rest takes a second.

"That... what guy?"

"Hell, I don't know what guy. Some guy. Goddamned hero is who. Customer maybe, so I didn't ask his name. You know. Seen him around a few times before. Surprised they ain't both dead. But I'm tellin' you..." He stoops a little so he can look up into her swollen, bloodstained face. "She's gon' be fine, Olivia. Whole lot of smoke in her lungs. And a bad knock on the head. Concussed maybe. I bet they keep her over night at least. But she was sittin' up. Talkin'. Carryin' on like she does."

Olivia nods once. Feels the tears on her skin for the first time. She wipes her face. Cringes at the touch of her own fingers. Everything about her hurts. Leg. Back. Neck. But especially her face. Her left eye is a purple mess, nearly swollen shut. Her lower lip feels like a sausage that has expanded over a flame.

"I have to go see her," she says, turning. "Thanks."

"Is there anything I can do? You want me... to take you? Olivia?"

She doesn't answer. Leaves him. Limps off past the fire truck. Past the flashing cruisers. Moves on up the road. She aims for where she had abandoned Jesús Batista's shit-brown Ford Falcon. She hadn't even closed the door. She'd run for the pale, thin column of ashen smoke rising up above Ol' Faithful and her home. Not feeling the pain of her ruined leg. Not feeling the blood pounding inside her face. Just running. Crying. Shouting out Libby's name like a lost, terrified child.

She climbs in. Slams the door. Drives, rooster-tailing loose gravel and dust.

It had been a long night. Curled up in the raggedy back seat of a 1986 Falcon, parked out in the desert scrublands. Wet. Cold. Hurting.

But alone. Not another human to see or hear or feel. A saguaro or two. A green *palo verde*. That was all. No hearts.

That was the one thing she had needed. No hearts. The thought of Libby's reaction, the energy it would have taken to manage it, had kept her from returning home.

So she'd sunk like a stone to the bottom of her private ocean. Curled up into a ball. Breathed in and out. Hurt.

It was not until daybreak that she had finally fallen asleep. A cattle truck rattling up the access road had woken her late morning. In the course of her slow, painful relocation from the back seat to the front seat, she'd resolved to go home. Take a long, hot shower. Clean up. Pack a bag. Pack up the cash. Tell Libby she needed to get out. Tell Libby that she hurt a little but that she was fine. Tell Libby she had already reported an attack by some San Angelo stranger. Tell Libby that she would be back in a few days.

And then never come back again. Get in Jesús Batista's Falcon and just keep driving.

She would stop by the fairgrounds on her way out. Meet up with Sheldon Davis as planned. Give him back every last dollar of his money. Tell him the truth. Tell him that she had not exactly yanked the wheel to avoid his car. He had hemmed her in, true. Had he not been in the passing lane she would have had some better options. Options other than either hitting his car or running over the coyote, which had appeared suddenly out of the scrub on the side of the road, a pup wedged carefully in her mouth. She had yanked the wheel hard for the non-existent third option. That is what had flipped her car.

She would tell him that she had been using him to keep from drowning in her own life. Using him to fund a dream that was never meant to be. Tell him that he is a good man living a fucked-up life in a fucked-up world. Tell him that she is sorry.

And then go. Leave everything. Drive and keep driving until she runs out of gas.

That had been the plan. In relocating from the back seat into the front seat, beneath a brightening morning sky, that had been the plan. The desert spies could see the new resolve. The saguaro. The *palo verde*. The sea of scrub. It was the way she moved. Pushing through the pain. After a long, still night, she had a plan.

But the world, once more, had changed. Had become unknowable all over again. Libby was in the hospital. There was no more home. Nothing to pack. No cash to return. Smoke and ash. Nothing else. All she can do is drive.

The staff members at Shannon Medical Center are only responding to professional instinct. They want to disinfect her. Swab her clean. Bandage her. Why is she swollen, cut, bleeding, limping? What happened? Who did this? She has to promise she will admit herself after she has seen Libby Holder. The nurse scowls at here computer, muttering.

"*Holder…. Holder… Holder.* Are you family?"

"Yes, I'm family goddamnit. She's my mother."

So they escort her back. Through the show of sterility. The parade of casual competence on rolling silver stools. Carts of equipment, gliding quietly from curtain to curtain, room to room. Like large, white animals, heads down, sniffing.

Libby is propped up on three pillows, flipping through a *People Magazine*. Bandage on her head. Tube in her arm.

"Your daughter's here," announces the nurse as she pulls back the curtain. "You two catch up. I'll be back to get you a room, Hon. Then we'll get someone to have a look."

For the first time in Libby Holder's life, she cannot summon a single sound to express herself. *People Magazine* drops limply back onto the wrinkled sheet. Libby's mouth opens and closes silently, like she's a fish on a beach.

Baby. Baby. Baby.

But there is no sound. Just lips. Shaping the air.

Crying next. Embracing. Sobbing into each other's shoulder. Neither has any explanation for what has happened to the other. Doesn't matter. Not just yet.

But eventually.

Olivia is first.

She sticks with the vicious mugging. She'd put the drive to San Angelo to good use, cobbling together details. What the man looked like. Sounded like. Smelled like. What the police told her. How they'd even given her money for a hotel room. Why she hadn't called.

She had never considered telling Libby the truth. Not about Manny Soto. That would only lead to vengeance and prison for Libby. And that was if Libby was lucky. She wasn't a sniper. She'd make it personal. She'd want to see Manny's eyes as the blade went in and the lights went out. Or she'd want to watch *The Diamondback* burn.

"You listen good, baby."

Libby coughs violently. Her face closes in around the effort, like a catcher's mitt absorbing a fastball. She tries to breath slowly. Points.

"That no 'count muthafuck monsta got to die. You unastan? Handcuffs an' a plea bargain an' a few months in jail is too good. If you evah', an' I mean *evah,* see this piece a shit again, you come to me an' I gon' take care a *business.* Unastan' me? Fuck the police. 'Cause he…" She breaks. Swallows. "He… beat… my baby. He *beat* …"

Libby weeps again. Reaches out to touch Olivia's face, but knows enough to only pat the air around it. Olivia takes hold of her wrists. Clasps Libby's hands in her own. Waits until she has regained composure.

"What happened, Libby? Tell me."

Libby tells the story she has already told the police three times, adding the details that she had left out of those accounts. The man she had never seen before, foreign accent, dark eyes, paying extra up front for an extra good time.

"Muthafuck do his business but he don't want to leave. He jus' waitin' round fo' somethin' I don't know. Drinks him a whole bottle of my Rio Lobo an' a plate of cookies. A fuckin' *plate.* Then he start to lose his shit a little, talkin' in an' out of whatevah' kinda gibb'rish he speakin'. Kept askin' me when the fuck you comin' home. Man know yo' *name,* baby. He waitin' fo' *you.*

"I pretend I don't know what he talkin' about. He pull out a phone and start talkin' his foreign shit and walk out the house, well, *stumble* out the house 'cause he so fucked up by then he can't walk a straight line. An' I spy on the muthafuck, watch him diggin' 'round his backseat. Then he gone. I figure he passed out but then I can hear him 'round back, talkin' gibb'rish on the phone. Then he back again diggin' in his ride. An' I don't know what the fuck. So I go upstairs to get *my* phone. Only thing on my mind is callin' you to tell you not to come home 'cause I'm startin' to get a bad feelin' he someone who seen you at *The Diamondback* an' found out where you live and maybe he jus' gon' wait fo' you out in the dark. Man could give a fuck 'bout me. I weren't worried 'bout me a bit. I jus' wanted to keep you away. But you don't answer 'cause you already busy gettin' the shit beat outta you right here in San Angelo. So I go back down to the parlor an' there he is. Muthafuck out like a light on my couch. I mean *out,* baby. He out for three hours." Libby juts out a hand with three fingers in a *W,* stretching taut the tube in her arm. "Three. Fuckin'. Hours. I pat the man on the face. Pull on his leg. Jiggle his thang. Ain't nothin' doin' for this snorin' muthafuck."

"What'd you do?"

"I listen to Bessie is what I did. *Loud,* too. And still nothin'. Muthafuck like a dead tree on my couch. I go upstairs, call you again. Wait. Wait some more. Come back down and he *still* out. So I think *enough of this shit* and I get the key out his pocket an' go out to have me a looksee in the man's ride. Clean as a whistle, 'cept for four gas cans in the back."

"Gas?"

"Mmm Hmm. Mostly empty too. So I sit behind the wheel an' smoke me a jay. Wait for you to come rollin' up so I can tell you what goin' on an' keep you out of it. Next thing I know I'm wakin' up, looking at fuckin' flames in my bedroom window."

There is another gush of crying when she gets to the part about her mother. Mama Mable. About running to the kitchen for a pot of water. About taking a butcher knife upstairs to put out a fire.

"Mama still up there, baby. Still lookin' out for my no good, whorin' ass … she *still* lookin' out. Hell. Maybe yo' mama up there too. They up there lookin' out together. Tellin' me to grab that knife. I don't know. I don't know. I don't know. That some powerful shit though, 'Livia. I nevah felt like that before in my *en*-tire life."

"Darrell said a man pulled you out."

Libby's eyes widen. She snaps back into the present.

"*Fuck-all-day-face-no-kinda-priest!* My lil' ponytail writer friend! *Davis.* I be dead fo' *sho'*, baby. He comin' through the smoke an' flame like some kinda' fuckin' superhero. Lookin' for *you.* Drag my ass outside. An' guess who he brung with him?" She doesn't wait. "Fuck that. You nevah guess this shit. Dallas fuckin' Letti is who. Now look at me an' tell me that make any fuckin' sense. You even be-*lieve* that? Dallas Letti show up at *my* house? At *my* fire? *Damn!* I look up at her an' I think well, Libby 'ol girl, you really are fuckin' concussed 'cause here's Dallas Letti –*Mama's Girl* Dallas Letti and *My Man for a Dime* Dallas Letti and *Letti Blue* Dallas Letti –puttin' her arm 'round yo' shoulder. You believe that shit, 'Livia?"

Olivia does not believe that shit. Cannot wrap her battered head around it. All she can do is stare, mouth open. Her entire body is numb. Dallas… Letti. Libby keeps talking.

"An' she all fucked up too. She been through hell her own self. We both like concussed twinsies. Me an' Dallas. She holdin' my hand all the way in the am'blance, singin' spirituals the whole way, singin' go tell it on the fuckin' mountain, 'til they put us in wheel chairs an' roll her one way an' me t'other way. She somewhere in this place. Trust me, it help to be Dallas Letti when it come to gettin' a hospital room. Wonder what her room look like. Fresh flowers an' shit, no doubt. Signin' autographs. *No-kinda-priest* prob'ly up there with her right now. I told him I was scared to death for you 'cause you ain't come home and this dead badass muthafuck lookin' for you. Him an' whoever the foreign-fuck he talking to on his phone."

That is when the thought first occurs on her. It alights on the edge of her conscious understanding like a small bird, just long enough to be noticed before flitting away.

Manny Soto saved her life.

There is no room for this thought. Gone like a bird.

Libby is still talking.

"I ask Davis to go find you but he didn't even know where to start lookin' and I didn't neither. I'm just glad you safe, baby."

"And I'm glad you're safe," Olivia says. She is dizzy. Dallas Letti. In one of these rooms. It is all too much. She tries to focus on something real. Something practical.

"Think they'll keep you over night?"

"They say so." Libby sighs. "Dallas Letti can afford this medical shit. Not me. I got some money in the bank. But not much. Not much. An' now I got no home. No clothes. No records. All my music is gone, baby. Up in smoke. All my blues like a black-n-blue cloud up in the air."

A long, heavy absence of words. They squeeze each other's hands. Listen to the hospital beep and murmur and wheeze and clatter around them.

"Guess I should stop bitchin'," says Libby at last. "I ain't dead. You ain't dead. *No-kinda-priest* ain't dead. An' Dallas say I can come live with her if need be." Libby laughs a little to herself. "If you can even believe *that* shit. Who needs records when you livin' with Letti Blue?"

Libby points to the chair in the corner. The one with the blood-smeared pillowcase.

"An' I save yo' 'lil babies."

"My what?"

"Yo' 'lil cactus babies that yo' mama give you. Only thing I had time to grab. But I got all of 'em. Even that lil' dog. He fall off the nightstand. Under the bed, like he tryin' to run away. Fire every which way. Shit. I got to reach all around on the floor under that dead muthafuck's legs, but I got him. They all safe 'an sound in that pillacase."

The flood does not hit her until she is back out in the parking lot.

She sits behind the wheel of the Falcon, bloody pillowcase in the seat next to her, sobbing in the crook of her arm until her swollen face hurts so much from the new congestion that she has to force herself to stop.

So she breathes. Blinks. Tries to climb up out of herself. Tries to climb high enough to look back down on her life. Everything hurts.

So she focuses on that. The physical pain. The leg. The back. The neck. Face. Lip. Nose. Eye. These are rungs on a ladder. She climbs. Pushing down against the pain. Climbs. She looks down. Sees the lighter lying in the notch of rubber foam where Dashboard Jesus used to be. She grabs it. Finds a cigarette. Lights. Inhales. Closes her eyes. Exhales.

Climbs.

Eventually she is high enough up to see Sheldon Davis. High enough up to see the money. Bundles of cash that are now a soggy paste of ash beneath charred timber and sheetrock.

The plan this morning, as she had relocated from the back seat to the front seat, had been to give it all back. To come clean with Sheldon. Apologize. The plan had been to refuse the *heavier-than-normal* bundle he has for her. To give him a hug. A kiss on the forehead. And to never see him again.

But now.

Now she has nothing. Now Libby has nothing. What now? She blows smoke out into the afternoon. Waits for an answer. Something. Anything.

But there is nothing. In the mirror, Manny's fingers are angry, mottled bruises across her throat. Her front teeth are outlined in pink.

The sun has escaped, heading west, incinerating the thin, gauzy cloud cover. It seems a campaign of vengeance. Or salvation. Resurrecting all of the water from the miles of soggy earth. The air is heavy and humid with a kind of atmospheric reckoning.

Olivia starts the car. Drives.

The absence of any concrete plan leaves the old plan in place. It helps that she does not have anywhere to go. By the time she is twenty minutes outside of Corbin the traffic takes her into custody. It escorts her the rest of the way. A burly man in a neon orange vest looms in sharp relief against a darkening sky. His swinging arms show her where to park.

She limps her way through the throngs, looking for him in every face. But every face belongs to someone else. Every face looks back. Every face is embarrassed for her. Then horrified. She sees herself again and again.

There are two walking thoroughfares that lead to the acres of rides. Each route is packed with humanity. She hobbles past *Moon Gardener Way*. Turns up *Día de los Muertos Avenida*.

Happy, shrieking little skeletons are everywhere. They run from one booth to another, pulling larger skeletons behind. Walking bones clad in black tuxedos and vibrant Mexican dresses. Painted skulls beneath top hats and wide-brimmed *sombreros*. Women of all ages, black tresses threaded with ribbon and bound up in arrangements of roses and marigolds. The makeshift avenue is strung with colored lights and lined with vendors selling and celebrating. Pyramids of colored sugar skulls. Painted masks. Fruits. Breads. Flowers. Candies. Incense. Jarred candles. Painted skulls and figurines by the thousands. *Calaveras. Calacas.* On every table at every booth. Skulls. Eye sockets. Lining the avenue so that the dead might look on and approve. So that the dead might see that the living have not forgotten.

Mariachi everywhere. *Flamenco* everywhere. Some celebrants carry sleek black buckets, roving through the crowds handing out single carnations and marigolds to anyone who seems to be in the spirit. Six men cluster together in the middle of *Día de los Muertos Avenida* with trumpets and guitars, red socks showing beneath the cuffs of tuxedo pants. Red bow ties. Beaded *sombreros*. Strumming, singing, whistling. People are dancing in all directions.

Olivia weaves forward in her uneven steps. Passes. Pushes.

People look. Slow down. Puzzle over her choice of make-up. Then they look with muted scorn, eyes lecturing that Halloween was two days ago. Then realize that there is no make-up. A man with a bucket of flowers adjusts his course, turning away. The *Mariachi* band slips into an almost unrecognizable Mexican cover of *Highway to Hell*.

The line at the Ferris wheel almost completely encircles the ride. The wheel is lit at every weld. Every gondola is a flower of glowing color, burning away at the dusk. She hobbles two complete revolutions, looking. Looking. Suffering the return stares.

He is not here, of course. Why would he be here? Hours after the appointed time? No. It is a senseless mission. It is not even a mission. Missions are defined by a purpose. She has no purpose. And no phone.

She finds a bench. Sits. Extends her aching leg.

For a half hour she watches the tide of people. She is outside of it all, looking in as always. Hands flattened up against the glass of an aquarium. Bubbles of color. Bubbles of sound. Bubbles pushing the big wheel around on its axis.

She tries to take stock. Put things together. Imagine her next step.

She can't do any of those things.

Now and again Manny Soto is in her head. Trying to get her attention. Trying to rip off her clothes. Strangling her. Saving her.

She stands abruptly. Looks around. Walks. All she wants is to leave.

Problem is that leaving always means going someplace else. There is no such thing as leaving without going someplace else. Except for that one last time, when you are ready to leave everything and everyone. Forever.

Jesús Batista's Ford Falcon is now covering all the bases. Transportation. Shelter. Friend. It is a strangely welcome sight, waiting where she left it, only now it sits under the pale gold spray of sodium vapor streetlights. She climbs in. Slams the door. Relishes the quiet.

That's when it occurs to her. She knows exactly where to find him.

She starts the car. Drives.

She should have known that she would not be able to park anywhere close to the town square. By the time she can see the lights of the *Fuente de la Luna* she is so tired of walking that she wants to sit down in the middle of the street and make people navigate around her. Step over her.

The fountain burbles in a ghostly pale blue beneath a lattice of vine, lights and flowers. Globes of soft blue light hang over the milling crowd, evoking an assemblage of moons. A lunar harvest, plucked from vines like celestial grapes. A school of silver fish, hoisted high on wooden poles, swims through the crowd from the fountain to the rows of chairs in front of the stage and back again. These are angry, chanting fish. There is no rhyme for *Pecos Bluntnose Shiner*. They make up for it in volume.

"Madre Luna! Mother Moon! Save the desert! Make it soon!"

One of the Bluntnose Shiners is blunter than the rest, improvising a saltier verse. *"Cocksuckers go home! Cocksuckers go home! Cocksuck..."*

The profane fish drops away sharply from the school. A hole opens. Two men in black t-shirts and black baseball hats with golden bull logos. They wrestle with the protester at the other end of the pole. It takes both of them. Shouting. Pointing. They confiscate the fish on its pole. Frog march the man away from the fountain, through the parting crowd, toward the back of the square. Disappear in waves of people. The school of silver fish reassembles. Continues.

"Madre Luna! Mother Moon! Save the desert! Make it soon!"

But the fish on sticks are no match for electronic amplification. They are a trickle of human voices lost in an ocean of sound. On the far side of the square, a ginger-haired girl in a blue one-piece swimsuit nimbly clogs her way from one side of the stage to the other. Her naked legs are a blur. Above the waist she is nearly still. Except for her arms, which are busy playing a fiddle, and her ecstatic lips, which are yodeling into a headset. The audience is wildly enthusiastic. Clapping. Stomping. The fish are undeterred.

"Keep your money! Screw your need! Save the desert! Stop the greed!"

Olivia keeps moving. Parting people. Skirting fish. She passes the fountain, tracing the perimeter of the town square until she is among those who are standing and watching the spectacle from the left of the stage.

She turns to look at the small blue-lit sea of folding chairs, each of them occupied, fanned out in front of the stage. It is hard to isolate individuals from the writhing blue mass. To separate out the drops. Nothing matters but the front row. She starts on the left.

He is almost dead center. The only one not enjoying himself. Olivia takes one step forward, out of the crowd around her. Stares. Waits.

The sound of clogging thunders down around her like hoof beats from a stampeding herd of yodeling, fiddling centaurs.

Stands. Stares. Waits.

Eventually Sheldon looks up. Sees. Doesn't see. Looks away. Looks back. Stares.

Sees.

Olivia nods at him. Turns. Slowly walks away. She traces the outline of the shape defined by the sea of folding chairs like she is walking a shoreline. She stops directly behind the last row. Waits.

The clogger crescendos to raucous approval. People are on their feet. A voice for radio rams its way through the sound.

"Stacey Kimball! All the way from Abilene! Make some noise, folks!"

And they do. Stacey Kimball takes a trio of curtsies, bow in one hand, fiddle in the other. The emcee tries to introduce the next contestant as stagehands assemble a six-piece drum set in the center of the yellow spotlight.

A cluster of people in front of her retake their seats, clearing her view of the aisle cutting through the assemblage of chairs. Not thirty feet away, Yvonne Lawry is standing in the aisle. Skirt. Heels. At the goddamned *Moon Garden Festival* like it's a Cotillion dance.

Miguel is next to her, both hands on Kevin's wheelchair. Kevin, in his wool hat and wrapped in a blanket, twists and writhes and rocks in his seat. Yvonne secures Miguel's jacket over her shoulders. She points up the aisle towards the stage where four people appear to be exiting the second row.

Olivia is relieved they are in front of her. That she has seen them first. It is not a conversation –with either of them –that she wants to have.

She wonders to herself what Yvonne thinks she's doing. Whether she thinks of Miguel as a ship she can sail or a slab of wreckage to which she can cling. She wonders if Yvonne has any inkling that Miguel's good heart will make him a liar and a cheat; will make him pretend his affections, to avoid hurting her, long after he has moved on. She wonders if he is gone already.

Miguel's younger brother, Eladio is suddenly there. Talking. Pointing. They are all craning their necks, looking toward the fountain. Except Kevin, of course. He has his own inimitable rhythm.

He wrenches himself to the side and back. Again. Again.

Then he sees. *Sees.* Stops.

Not a full stop. There is no such thing for Kevin. But a discernable pause.

His body careens away again, a carnival ride all his own. But he is back soon enough. Again. Again. Each time he elongates the pause. Looks. Sees. His eyes, beneath their fluttering lids, shout to her.

Olivia. Play. Again. *Olivia. Sing.* Again. *Olivia. Love.*

Olivia raises both hands, palms out, over the people seated between them. Higher. Wider. A long-distance hug. She smiles. Big. Open-mouthed. Her face will not allow smiles. She does it anyway. Silently mouths his name. *KEV-IN!* Miguel begins pushing him away. *Kev-in. I love you.*

It should not be possible to discern a change in his expression. Or to give it meaning. But she does. It should not be possible for either of them to find a way inside the other. But they do. In that instant, they do. Love works that way. It all works that way. Everything. Water. Light. Darkness. Time. It all finds its way in to the same place.

We are porous, temporary vessels. We are made to be dissolved.

She is full, suddenly, of his incomprehensible heart. Full and streaming tears. Her battered face hurts. She lets it hurt. Watches the four of them infiltrate the second row, directly in front of the emcee. Kevin continues his rhythm. Away and back. Away and back. He finds her one last time. Holds. Holds. His face, suddenly, a kind of stone. Eyes like shafts of light through a cave.

Not love this time. Fear. Terror. Something in the lightning storm he carries around in his head has scared him.

There is a pressure on her shoulder. A hand. Like Kevin has somehow reached backward across that distance with his mind.

A volley of drumbeats, like rapid cannon fire, shoots out across the square from the stage. The emcee introduces *"Ruthann Meyers from College Station!"* Crowd goes wild.

The hand squeezes. She carefully wipes her eyes. Sniffs. Turns.

Chapter 84
Abby and Davis

"There is something in the wax."

I had thought this was just more of Abby's nonsense. I had no idea what it meant so I had just let it go. That last call was so soaked in my own adrenaline I wasn't paying that kind of attention.

But there was something in the wax after all.

Abby, for starters, was in the wax. Or, at least, she was surrounded by pounds and pounds of it, along with two tanks of propane. The investigation showed that on the Friday before the fire Abby visited a hobby shop in south Dallas and picked up fifteen slabs of paraffin each weighing twenty pounds. Turns out Abby was a regular customer.

But there was more in the wax than just Abby.

While I was headed off to the hospital in handcuffs, the police were busy combing through Fat Jack's truck. They were looking for information about who I was, why I had stolen the truck, why I had fled a hit and run incident not far from my school, why I had fled my own arrest at the gas station, and what connection I had to the death of the unidentifiable person in a burning trailer all the way out in Fairfield.

The Troopers paid very close attention to the box of candles in the back of Jack's truck. Those were the candles that Abby and I were never able to deliver. She'd forgotten to take them with her the night Simon had slapped me in the face and told me to run home to the mother I don't have. One of the detectives had obviously seen the candles before. I watched him saw it open right there at the scene.

There were four tins inside each candle. Unlike the tin Abby had shown me in her kitchen, these tins were not holding essential oil lip balm. They were holding heroin. When you put all of the candles we delivered that day together, and when you multiply that by the number of deliveries Abby and Simon had made that year, it turned out to be more heroin than Dallas County and Harris

County had seen from any other single supplier. That's what the papers said anyway. You've read them. My lawyer said it was even more than that.

I was convicted in the press of murdering Abby before I was ever formally indicted by the legal system. We have talked enough about that and what it has done to my life. I'm not laying all of that out again. It won't help any.

Once word of the drugs got out, which was almost instantly, the newspapers and the television news went berserk. It was too sordid for them to wait for the facts. At first I was the lone killer. People had seen Abby and me together. At the fair. At the motocross. Here and there in Fairfield. All of those witnesses said that we were hanging on each other and were clearly involved sexually, which, given my age, added fuel to the fire. So to speak.

Then, when the police eventually caught Simon Dory in a cheap motel over in Georgia, the media decided to make the story about a sex and drug feud between the three of us; me, Simon and Abby.

Then the media started to get bits and pieces of the gruesome details. The neighbors had heard terrible screaming fights in the week leading up to the fire. The trailer door had been nailed shut from the outside. Abby's arms and legs had been wired to the frame of her cot.

What the evidence actually showed was that both of Abby's legs had been wired to the cot, along with only one of her wrists. Her right wrist was free. Police investigators and then prosecutors argued from the bits of copper wire found at the scene that Abby had managed to free her right wrist. But I knew better. I had seen firsthand how Abby liked to use that copper wire.

Unfortunately, I did not learn about Abby's free wrist until many weeks after my arrest. Until my lawyer finally got his hands on the actual forensics report, we were operating on the assumption that Simon had wired her to the bed and nailed her inside the trailer.

But one free wrist. That was when I really started to wonder.

My lawyer wanted to keep the focus on Simon Dory. The press needed a killer. The prosecutors needed a killer. I hung in there for a while. But with every passing day avoiding the truth became more and more difficult.

I cooperated fully with the investigation. I told the police everything I could remember about my time with Abby. Every conversation. All of the sex. Everything. I took them on a driving tour of every place we had been on our candle delivery route. They used that information to make six other arrests, all members of the heroin distribution ring.

But none of my cooperation seemed to matter to them. They had a witness to the scene between Simon and me in the front of the house. They had my fingerprints on the door to the trailer, blown two hundred feet into the neighboring lot by the explosion. They had my prints on the hammer lying on the kitchen floor.

It did not help matters that on my way to the scene of the crime I had escaped custody in a stolen truck; a stolen truck that had previously nearly killed a kindergarten teacher. The police interviewed Jack's Uncle Zeke who said the truck had been stolen out of his driveway and that he had reported the theft the very next morning. Police records verified that explanation.

Fat Jack said nothing to contradict his uncle. He insisted that I was his friend and that I couldn't have stolen the truck or had anything to do with the hit and run. But when asked how he could be so sure, Jack did not have anything to tell them. He denied ever having seen me in possession of the truck. He probably thought he was helping.

Fortunately, the police got to Skinny Kenny before Jack did. Kenny confirmed my story of leaving the house in Jack's truck the day of the fire. They took their sweet time doing it, but the police eventually put some direct pressure on Jack without his uncle around. He confessed to accidentally clipping the kindergarten teacher when she was crossing the street in a neighborhood near our high school. He panicked. He thought she was okay. He didn't have any clue about the brain swelling or that she had almost died. He thought it would all die down in a few months. He was planning on a friend of a friend "finding" the truck vandalized in a field somewhere. He did not expect his uncle to report the truck stolen since Zeke had himself stolen the truck ten years earlier from a man that owed him money. The police tracked down the registered owner in Houston. He actually pressed charges.

My vindication on the charges relating to Jack's truck never got a drop of ink in the newspapers. No one was interested in *unbelieving* what they already believed, which was that I was rotten through and through. Grand theft auto. Hit and run. The works. But I was vindicated by the facts and that made some of the police investigators start to scratch their heads. If that much of my story checked out, why not the rest?

Once they captured Simon Dory, things began to turn around. I could tell the case against me was loosening up. But it wasn't until much later, when I got the chance to read all of the police interview transcripts, that I understood why.

Simon confessed to all of the drug related charges and rolled over on his suppliers. Fishmongers, Abby had called Simon's bosses. They probably all used to be. But somewhere along the line they started meeting other boats out in the Gulf and taking in vacuum-packed heroin that they inserted into fresh-caught fish. They flash froze the fish on board and then brought it in to Galveston. Simon and others took it from there. I still don't know if the fishmongers knew about the candles. There was nothing in the papers about that. Simon was probably keeping a little bit for himself from every delivery run. I know they found a chest freezer full of fish in a basement I never saw.

Makes more sense that Abby hated fish so much. She'd said fish had come to represent a kind of death. That she could never trust what was inside. Because she had known what was inside. She also probably smelled them in her sleep. Each one had to be thawed enough to excavate the drugs and then refrozen. Abby's aromatherapy candles were not only a way of distributing the heroin, they were also a way of packing her brain with a different scent.

The police pressured Simon to help build a case against me. But Simon insisted that I was never involved except to deliver the candles on that one day. He said that had been Abby's idea, not his, and that Abby had insisted that I knew nothing about any drugs. That she had asked me along just for the company. They asked Simon whether Abby and I had a sexual relationship. He told them that Abby had always referred to me as just a friend but that he never believed it. He assumed that we were having sex. He didn't like it. He tried to stop it. They did a lot of fighting over me.

They asked him why he was so upset about me. They were trying to build a case of motive. They were trying to suggest that Simon had killed Abby in a jealous rage because she was cheating on him with me. But Simon disappointed them. He did not like me seeing Abby because I was too young. Because Abby was distributing narcotics. Because Abby was mentally ill. There was no jealousy. The police found that hard to believe.

But it was true. Because Abby Palmer was not her name. Imogen Dory was her name. She was Simon Dory's sister.

Imogen Dory.

They have the dental records.

She will always be Abby Palmer to me.

Imogen and her older brother Simon grew up in London. They were raised by their mother and abandoned by their father. The father was an alcoholic seaman who was lost in the North Atlantic before he turned forty. According to Simon, the schizophrenia came from his father's side. His mother had the cancer genes.

Simon left home when he turned eighteen, before his mother got sick. He came to the United States to live with his father's brother in Illinois. Marcus Dory owned a car dealership and Simon was good with cars. They had some pipe dream that Simon might become a part of that business and make enough to send money home. Marcus Dory stayed alive just long enough to help Simon become a U.S. citizen. He died of something. I don't know what.

After that, Simon fell in with a bad crowd. He got arrested for possession, served a few months, and then moved to Texas to stay out of trouble. But he obviously found trouble all over again.

Most of what I know about Imogen Dory I learned from reading the *Dallas Herald* articles that came out after everything was over. As much as I don't want to give any part of the media credit for getting anything right about me, the

Herald did their homework on Abby. Imogen.

Imogen worked for a London-based cosmetics company called *Guinevere's*. She lived with her mother. Abby only mentioned her mother a couple of times. She always referred to her in the past tense. So I should have known she was dead. I guess I did know. I think I just didn't want to talk about dead mothers. Abby was kind of my escape from all of that. Or she was supposed to be. So I never asked about her mother. I knew she had yellow hair and that some people called her *Goldie*. I knew that she loved her mom. Must have: she gave her mom's name to a stuffed bull. But that's all I knew.

I should have asked. It was the most important thing we had in common.

Simon claimed that Imogen was already showing signs of a problem before he left for the States. She did not have many friends. She was a suspicious child who liked to accuse others of things they clearly had not done. She alternated between believing that their father had been murdered and that he was still alive but in hiding.

Pancreatic cancer took their mother very quickly. Imogen found a way to blame herself. Something spoiled in the food she cooked. Or there was something wrong about the yellowish tint of the water that Imogen had chosen to ignore. Or she had allowed the television antenna to angle towards her mother's bedroom. She was sure it was all her fault. Imogen took leave from work and holed up in the empty house for days. Neighbors and her mother's friends came every so often to check on her. Imogen would never answer the door. And she never returned to work.

Guinevere's eventually fired her but, out of sympathy for what she was going through, encouraged her to apply for a company program to spend six months working for the new *Guinevere's* outlet in New York. They thought the change of scenery would do her some good. They helped with the visa paperwork. *Guinevere's* told the *Herald* that Imogen seemed very interested in the idea of seeing her brother again. They all thought he lived in Illinois.

Simon flew from Dallas to New York twice to see her. He said he could tell that even though she seemed happy, she was kind of unraveling. Mentally, I mean. I don't know what you shrinks would call it. But *going crazy* is what Simon meant. Each time he left to return to Texas, Imogen threw a screaming tantrum. Simon told the police that she was on the phone with him constantly. She was desperate not to go back to England. There was nothing for her there. She threatened to kill herself if she had to go back. Simon held firm. Taking care of his sister did not fit into his life.

He changed his mind when she called him after her release from the hospital. A neighbor had found her front door ajar and had gone inside to make sure everything was okay. Imogen was bleeding out on the kitchen floor. She had done a bad job on her wrist. Simon believes she wanted to be found; that she was trying to send him a message about her level of desperation. He said he confronted her about it but that Imogen denied she was manipulating him. She told him that she had been trying to keep some secret information in her head from falling into the wrong hands. Killing herself, she told him, had been the only way.

Either way, Simon got the message. Imogen needed him to look after her.

The two of them conspired on how they could make Imogen drop off the radar. Simon drove all the way up to New York, picked her up and brought her all the way back to avoid any sort of airline paper trail. But the person he brought back with him was not Imogen Dory. It was Abby Palmer.

He set her up in the house out in Fairfield, about two hours driving time from where he lived in Fort Worth. It was close enough that he could check on her or even live with her without completely changing his life, but still far enough away that if Immigration showed up looking for her at his place they would be disappointed.

But ICE never showed. As far as the feds knew, Imogen had a brother in Illinois.

The Fairfield house was not in Simon's name. It belonged to a friend of Simon's who had previously done time for stealing cars. Charlie Shake was his name. You've read about him. One badass redneck. It was his trailer Abby died in. Abby mentioned him once. She told me he was a friend of Simon's. Maybe they're cellmates now. Anyway, Charlie's free house came at a cost. Simon paid Charlie in fish. He claimed he had always intended the house to be just a temporary solution for Abby. Turned out to be permanent.

He also claimed that he had tried to keep Abby out of the business at first. She got involved in palmistry and astrology readings, which he encouraged. He gave her a monthly stipend so she could have some independence. He came by to check on her at least once every couple of weeks.

But if Abby was crazy, she wasn't stupid. Over time the secret of how Simon made his living became impossible to keep. He said it never really mattered to her. Abby wanted to stay in Fairfield. She knew that meant proving her loyalty to Simon. The candles with heroin inside, he said, had been her idea.

They kept her illness under loose control with a supply of anti-psychotics that one of Charlie Shake's crew stole from a pharmacy. I don't know the name of the drug. It starts with a 'T' I think. I'm sure you'd know it. You probably prescribe it every day. Simon told the police that Abby was pretty normal as long as she was taking the medication. But if she went without it, the paranoia really started to take control and she became hysterical. He said every now and then Abby would get hold of some marijuana or some other drug and that would really set her off.

Simon told police that on the day of the fire, he showed up to check on Abby and she was in bad shape. She was screaming and flailing at him. Trying to hit him. He discovered that she had flushed her medicine down the toilet days earlier and was having a full-on panic attack. He needed to go out and get her some more medication, but he could not take her with him and he did not feel good about leaving her alone. He said he actually thought about calling me to come be with her but then decided against it. He had successfully gotten me out of the picture. He did not want to take a step backwards.

So instead, Simon force-fed her enough downers to knock her out for several hours, he put her to bed in the trailer, and he nailed the door closed from the outside. When he was sure she was asleep, he headed off to meet Charlie Shake and whoever it was could get him the meds. While he was gone, Abby must have crawled out of the bottom of the trailer and come inside the house to call me. In the middle of that call, she must have seen him drive up and run back to the trailer. The police asked Simon about the hole in the floor of the trailer. He said he never knew about a hole. He thought it was probably something Charlie had made in case he needed to escape people who either wanted to put him in jail or kill him. Simon said had he known there was a hole, he'd have made other plans to keep her locked up while he was gone.

Simon told them that when he returned between three and four hours later all was quiet. He put the medicine in the bedroom and then went back out to the store for some food since the cupboards were empty and it was clear that he would be staying with Abby for a few days. When he got back, Simon saw the smoke as he was getting out of his car. He said he ran around back and tried to break into the trailer but it was already too hot. He needed tools to pry open the door. The hammer he had used to nail the trailer door closed was in the house. Then he remembered the tanks of propane. He knew he probably only had seconds. So he ran.

Then he saw me. Coming across the lot. Ready for anything.

He was trying to save me. I get that now. Simon was trying to save me. Save me from myself. He always had been. That's why he had slapped me out on the driveway. Insulted me. Allowed Abby to kiss him the way she did. He was trying to save me. He told me that he loved Abby more than I ever could. Maybe because he knew who she really was. She was Imogen Dory. She was his sister. She was crazy and he knew that too. He knew more about her being crazy than anyone. And he loved her anyway.

I think he meant that I couldn't love someone I didn't understand. I never knew Imogen Dory. I knew only the part of Imogen that was Abby Palmer. I didn't understand the rest because it was more convenient for me to not understand. I understood only the parts of her I *wanted* to understand. The parts that felt good. And those were the only parts of her that I loved.

But it was still love, Dr. Bees. It was still real. For me it was.

And it was for Abby too. It wasn't just something she told me on the phone.

She meant it. She loved me. Like I always wanted her to.

That was the problem.

When he had me pinned down on the ground, and bits of flaming trailer were dropping all around us, Simon said Abby thought she was trying to save me.

She ... was trying to save ... *me*.

I had always thought that it would be the other way around; that it was my job to save her. She made me promise. She said I'd know what to do when the time came. Save her from what, exactly, I never really knew. But I think maybe she thought I could save her from the voices in her own head. That I could make her normal and that we could exist together in my universe rather than hers.

But that meant she loved me. And loving me is what killed her. Like it killed mom. Because loving someone means wanting to save them. There's no getting around that. Abby was afraid of what she would do to me. What she would ask of me. What I would do for her. What I would sacrifice. Abby saw that I wasn't a man making my own decisions. I was a boy under the influence. That's why she allowed the humiliation on the driveway. Why she kissed her own brother that way. Why she told me not to call her. Why she called me up and said goodbye and then wired herself to the cot and lit the match before I could get there.

Abby had made a decision. She was trying to save me. From *her*.

I know what you are thinking. I know what you would say if I was suffering another hour with you in your office listening to that damned clock. You'd say that Abby has nothing to do with mom. You'd say it's not my fault. You'd say that Abby was mentally ill and under the influence of impulses she couldn't control.

But what is love if not an impulse we can't control? An urgent voice in the dark of our own head?

I hate you, Fredrick. I hate you for asking me to live through all of this again and again and again. I hate you for asking me to write it all down.

You have only succeeded in convincing me that I am a dangerous person to love. You have rubbed my face in the fact that that when called upon to show my love –I mean to really step up and take responsibility for my feelings and prove my love when that is the only thing left that matters –I will fail.

Do whatever you want to with this letter. Do not contact me. You were my mother's friend. You are not mine. We will never talk again.

Davis

Chapter 85

The gondolas lift up and away from him. They arc backwards over an invisible cliff. A waterfall flowing in reverse, carrying little barrels back in time. People look down. Point. Speak backwards.

It's like the wheel on a giant, old-fashioned paddlewheel boat. His mother's words are still in his back pocket. The gondolas do not look like the little rowboats of his mother's dream. But he imagines they do, draining water as they surface.

He pushes the image away. But there is another waiting to take its place. Abby on a much larger Ferris wheel. The *Texas Star*.

It is impossible for him not to remember. Skirt hiked up to her thigh. The sensation of her mouth on his like some warm, wet fruit.

Memory is not something to be denied. It is water flowing beneath the locked door. It does not ask for permission. Or announce itself. It just takes over. And there is no option to cherry pick; to separate this part of the water from that part of the water, letting only the good parts under the door.

It's all one thing. It's all coming in.

So he also can't help but also remember the copper wire, wrapped around Abby's naked ankle and wrist. Copper wire wrapped around his own ankle and wrist. Three boys spellbound on the other side of the gondola getting a free view of pink panties.

She had wanted to better hear the voices. Higher up was better, she'd said.

"I'm too low. There's too much noise at ground level. That's why I'm afraid of heights! They want me to be bloody afraid!"

The rest is coming. There is no way to stay dry.

But he tries anyway. Turns his back on the Ferris wheel. On Abby. Walks.

He is not sure why he is here in the first place.

He knows, of course. He is here to find Olivia DeLuna. He knows.

But he has no reason to think that she is here. It's the very place she absolutely did not want to be. Let alone riding the Ferris wheel. But he promised Libby he would come. Look around. Tell Olivia about her house. Warn her about bad men out looking. He'd left the hospital on a mission.

He clears the carnival rides. The phalanx of food vendors. Heads back down *Moon Gardener Way*. Mission or no, he cannot see past the goal of making it back to Dallas' truck. Any purpose beyond starting the engine is beyond him.

Going home. There's a purpose. Getting out of clothes that have endured both flood and fire in a single day. Sleep for a week. All of that sounded right.

Except that he can't go home. His own words are there, waiting for him, tucked into an unsent, unstamped letter that sits on the kitchen table. Deadly, life-ending words, for never having been spoken or read.

I have ordered a copy of your book. I will read it. I will meet you someplace that neither of us like and I will tell you what I think of it. I can't promise a pleasant conversation, but I promise to be civil. Then maybe we can take things from there and just see where it leads. I'm willing to try that if you are.

So he cannot go home. Not yet. Home is a jagged shard of broken porcelain. He is much too sober now to endure that pain.

Beneath the square of gauze on the side of his face are four stitches holding together the gash made by a blade of scorched mirror. The gauze is like a square of hurt that throbs with every step. He tries to focus on that fleshly pain. It is the least of all others.

But it is never so easy to slip the past. His senses betray him. History is in the air, riding the breeze. Roasted meats. Manure and the distant, large-animal smell of a Texas rodeo. Deep fried cheese. Spun confection. Thin currents of perfume diffusing in the air. Machine grease. Flowers in buckets and pots. Flowers hanging from wire. Flowers tucked in hair. The sound of frolic. Of youthful abandon. Softballs toppling bowling pins. Rings over bottlenecks. *Mariachi* from one direction, classic country from another.

And, everywhere, colored light. Tiny balls of it. Long strings of it. Spinning wheels of it. Children wearing tubes of it around their wrists and squishing it out through holes in the heels of their sneakers. It is a kind of starlight we collect. Glowing filaments of memory and time that tangle up in our hair and clothing and that snag on the things we have built as we hurtle through space.

That's what it feels like. To be young at the Texas State Fair after dark. That's how he remembers it.

True, the Corbin Moon Garden Festival is hardly the Texas State Fair.

But it may as well be. He tries his best to seal off the past. To consider the incredible story Dallas had told him in the belly of the fake boat. *Her* story. Tries to think of her almost drowning; of almost being *unable* to do what she needs to do. He even thinks of writing her story without permission. Imagines her reaction. Anything to distract from the tide of memory gushing across a desert of time. Funneling under the door.

But it is a pointless effort. It's all coming in. It's all one thing.

The aging palmist is still there. Like she is waiting for him. She sits in a folding chair outside her little tented booth, legs crossed, wooden sandals, hot pink toenails, chewing gum beneath her big black pile of Texas hair.

She had beckoned to him on his way in. Two bejeweled fingers up in the air like she was hailing a cab. "*Lemme give you a quick read, son. Best five bucks you'll ever spend.*" He'd nodded an acknowledgement that she existed. Kept moving.

But they both knew she'd have another chance at him on the way back out.

"Change your mind, did'ja?" It is almost a shout. Her smoker's voice is a low, thin reed. "Figured you for a smart man. Come sit a spell. Lemme take a look at that palm. Oh, come on now, son. Don't you trust me?"

Davis' attention snags momentarily on the word *son*. He repeats the nod as he approaches. He does not slow. She calls out to him.

"Suit yourself, then. If you ask me, you can't trust the bobbies."

It takes two full steps and half of a third. He stops. A cold electric charge climbs his spine like a large, hairy insect. He turns slowly. Looks at her.

"What did you say?"

The woman pulls in her chin, yellowing green eyes uncertain. Looking left then right.

"What. *Suit yourself?*"

"No. After that."

"I don't know, son. Come give me your…"

"What…" He stops. Takes a breath. Calmer. "Did you say?"

He watches her play it back in her head, deep under the mountain of hair. A boy with an inflatable sword passes between them. Davis does not move. The palmist clears the phlegm in her throat. Speaks.

"I said, if you can't trust me you can't trust nobody. Now come sit…"

He stares, suspended in the moment. Two. Three. Four.

"Sorry," he says finally. "I can't. Sorry. Sorry."

He turns. Walks. The words will not stop throbbing in his head. *You can't trust the bobbies.* Abby. The smell of her. The sound of her voice. Every inch of her nakedness wrapped around his young body out in the gleaming silver trailer behind her house. *Don't trust the bobbies.* It takes everything in him not to run.

The palmist calls after him. "*It's not your fault,*" he thinks she says. Maybe. Or maybe not. He can't trust his own ears. He wonders if he is losing his sanity. Wonders if fatigue and adrenal exhaustion and a freshly pickled brain have conspired to create audible hallucinations. Wonders if this is how Imogen Dory felt when she started to lose her sanity.

He navigates clots of people. *Truck. Truck. Truck.* It's all he can think. *Just get me to the truck.*

"Davis!" It is not just one voice. It's a small chorus. He looks.

Ernesto. Marcela. Eladio. Matching yellow t-shirts. Waving wildly from behind the Desert Ark Foundation booth. He takes a deep breath. Changes course.

"You look like shit, man," says Eladio, wagging a *DAF* key fob at him.

"*Eladio!*" Marcela scolds. "*¿Es así como saludar a un amigo?* Davis, *nene*, what have you done to your face?"

He comes to a deceptively slow, casual stop. Tries to force the calm. Slips his hands into his back pockets. He feels paper. His mother's letter to Tallulah. After the events of last night there can't be much left of it. He imagines an indecipherable cloud of blue ink seeping across the paper, like something from a frightened squid. But his mother's words come without reading.

> *The great mouth closes over me and then I am inside, surrounded by stars and looking out through its enormous eye. Watching Davis drown.*

Marcela Rivera's expression is frozen in maternal concern. He considers what it will take to fully answer her question about his injured face.

"Short version? Broken mirror." He takes his hands out of his pockets. Points at the square of gauze. "Part of it ended up here."

"*Ohhh...*" she starts, face wincing empathetically.

"I'm fine. I'm fine. Really. How are you guys? Where's Miguel? He was..."

He breaks off as a woman steps up to the table. Heavy-set. Dirty-blonde. Sheepskin vest over a turquoise button-down. Jeans. Boots. Rawhide purse with tassels. Whatever it is she wants, she has forgotten to take the red, white and blue button off her vest. '*So you want to live in the USA? AmeriCAN. MexiCAN'T.*'

"What ya'll charge to take in a horse? Or ya'll just dogs and cats?"

Ernesto smiles broadly. Tips his hat.

"No. I am sorry. We do not take animals. SPCA has a booth." He points.

"Oh." She looks. Looks back. "Well what y'all do then?"

"The Desert Ark Foundation raises money for a consortium of organizations that provide resources to orphaned children. Drugs. Alcohol. Deportation. Abuse. You see? They need families. And the families need resources. Clothing. Food. Good jobs. That is why we are here." He picks a brochure up off the table. Offers it to her. She declines in a smoker's laugh.

"No. Nope. Don't got no orphans. Just a cantankerous mustang with a bad leg. My daughter and son-in-law say they got to put her down. Thought I'd try."

"I am sorry." Ernesto shrugs.

"Sad about the orphans though. Chil'ren need a mama."

"*Sí. Sí.* We try to find good homes. Good families."

"No, I mean *real* mothers. Real fathers. Y'all do your best, I'm sure."

Eladio. Loud. Clear. Offended.

"I have a *real* mother. I have a *real* father."

"*Eladio…*" Ernesto starts.

"My birth mother? She died with a needle in her arm when I was two. My birth father? Deported before I was born."

"*Eladio…*"

"And my brother? Dumped at a church when he was six weeks old. My *real* parents are standing in front of you, lady. My parents are as *real* as they get."

"*Eladio. Es suficiente. Es suficiente.*" Marcela pats him on the shoulder. "I'm sorry. Our son has strong feelings."

"Well." The woman looks from one to the other, eyes turning to glass. "I surely didn't mean no offense. Y'all have a good night."

They all watch her go.

"*Pendeja,*" spits Eladio under his breath. "Daughter should save the horse and put *her* down."

"*Eladio, détente. Por favor. Es suficiente.* You are a loyal son," says Marcela. "But one day that tongue will get you into trouble." She looks back to Davis. "Will you please take him with you? He has been stuck with us all day. Miguel is at the fountain watching the pageant with… with his… *his new friend.* Maybe the bathing suits will improve Eladio's mood."

"She wants us to spy for her," says Eladio. Marcela pretends to look offended. Looks to her husband for support. Ernesto nods gravely.

"*Sí. Sí.* She wants you to spy."

Davis laughs with the rest of them. But it is the last thing he wants. Company. Responsibility. He can't fence with Eladio about girls and sex and dancing. Not tonight. It takes too much energy. He wants to go home. He can't go home. He wants to curl up in the back of Dallas Letti's truck in the middle of the desert and sleep.

Marcela's face is waiting. Davis smiles a little.

"Sure." Jerks his head. "Let's go, Romeo."

"Oh, you are a good boy too, Davis. *Gracias. Gracias.* Such good boys."

The short trip through festival traffic to Corbin proper takes a long time. Walking would almost have been faster. Eladio is preoccupied with questions about the owner of the truck. He wants to know what Dallas Letti is like. Whether she is as mean as a snake like everyone says. Whether he has ever heard her sing. Someone he knows says Dallas Letti shoots coyotes for food.

"Pretty sure that's just talk," says Davis.

"Could be. José likes to lie. But his sister? Louisa? *Ooooo-wee!* Girl is beautiful.

Ella es una diosa. I mean, she melts men like little bits of butter on a hot tortilla."

"You have a shot at that you think?"

"Me? You know it, man! Only a matter of time. I mean, she's like, I don't know, maybe twenty-two. Twenty-three. So, you know. But age is just a number, Davis. Love conquers all, brother. Am I right?"

Davis smiles. Nods. They trundle forward in silence, stopping for groups of people. A skeleton on stilts.

"Didn't know that about you," Davis says, instinctively looking for that thread, that story, in spite of himself. "What you told that lady about you and Miguel. Back at the booth."

Eladio shrugs. Looks out his window. The towering skeleton wobbles. Recovers. Stretches forward.

"Don't talk about that much. Miguel never talks about it. I mean *never*. He just, you know…"

Davis knows better than to look. He drives. Waits. Eladio slices his hand through the air, drawing a line or severing an invisible rope. His voices quavers.

"*Abandoned* is not who we are, man. *Found* is who we are. *Loved* is who we are. That's all that ever matters." Eladio casts a sideways look. Beatific in his way. Untouched. He smiles. "And dancing. And girls."

The town square is full. Heads and shoulders wash back and forth, circling the falling water, bathing in a pale-blue glimmer. As if all of Corbin has congregated in a tidal pool beneath a full moon.

But it does not *sound* anything like a moonlit tidal pool. It sounds like chaos.

"Damn," shouts Eladio. He is up on his toes looking all directions. "*Este lugar es salvaje!* We're never gonna find him."

"Oh, shut up, Romeo. We both know why you're here and it has nothing to do with Miguel."

Davis points to the far corner of the square, over the heads of maybe four hundred seated on-lookers, to the stage. A pale redhead in a blue swimsuit is standing at a microphone with a man in a black suit and hat pumping her for information. "*Stacey Kimball. All the way from Abilene!*" The redhead holds up a fiddle. The emcee puts his hands on his hips. Works the moment.

"Well now I'm confused, Ms. Stacey. Are ya' gonna clog? Or are ya' gonna fiddle?"

Closer to where they stand, just on the far side of the fountain, people are chanting. Marching. Waving signs.

No. Not signs. *Fish.* Creatures made from *papier-mâché* and cardboard, each about the size of a loaf of bread, hoisted in the air on broom handles. Silver paint aside, they bear no resemblance to an actual Blunt-Nose Shiner. Their protesting handlers make sure the point comes across anyway.

Madre Luna! Mother Moon! Save the desert! Make it soon!

One voice spikes above the rest.

Cocksuckers go home! Cocksuckers go home!

The audience laughs at something in Stacey Kimball's explanation.

Cocksuckers go home! Cocksuckers go home! Cocksuck…

Madre Luna! Mother Moon! Save the…

A scuffle stops the chant. Two men in black t-shirts and hats: a bull, horns down, charges over the letters *"EBSecurity."* The men plow through the crowd, each seizing an arm of one of the protesters. He is an older, muscular contrast to the college kids hoisting silver fish on poles. He has his own pole, this man. And his own fish, though it is larger and fatter than any of the others. Larger than a loaf of bread, and more yellow than silver. None of the others step in to protect his right to shout profanity in the public square. The men wrestle away the pole as people fall back to give them a space.

The emcee, suddenly, from everywhere.

"Take it away, Stacey Kimball!"

Fiddling. Clogging. Alternating. Then together. The audience starts to clap in time. The protesters resume over the shouting match between security and their detainee.

Madre Luna! Mother Moon! Save the desert! Make it soon!
Sir!
Get your hands off of me, cocksuckers!
Sir! We will escort you out…
Keep your money! Screw your need! Save the desert! Stop the greed!

Eladio swats him on the arm. Points to the chairs.

"You take the fountain. I'll go see if they're sitting."

Davis watches him go, nimbly dancing through the small, shifting, blue-lit spaces winking between the passing bodies. People around the fountain cheer as the man overly concerned about cocksuckers is hauled through the crowd toward the front of the square, his wrists bound in a plastic zip-tie. A third agent follows, carrying the skewered yellowish fish like a flag. People part. They cheer, as if at a vanquished enemy.

The fish-on-a-stick pauses at the gap between the front row of seats and the stage. Swims through the air in front of poor Stacey Kimball from Abilene, trying mightily to fiddle-clog her way into stardom.

In the front row, a trim man in a silver mustache and a Stetson stands, laughing. He stops the security guard, takes custody of the passing fish. He turns to face the crowd, jabbing the pole up in the air with one hand as his other becomes a triumphant fist. The crowd erupts with approval as a blonde sitting next to the man yanks him sharply back down into his seat. The fish and its pole disappear with him as the man in custody, still shouting non-rhyming profanity, is hustled away from the stage.

The crowd cheers the protester's defeat.

Stacy Kimball clogs. Fiddles. Thinks the raucous sound is all for her.

Davis wanders. Looks for Miguel. Wants to hand off responsibility for Eladio's transportation. He completes a full orbit of the fountain. Overhead, the strands of lit blue globes hang almost within reach, like vines of glowing lunar fruit against a clear black sky. In the east, a ghostly gold nimbus is slowly inching up over the roof of the stage. A mother peeking in on her playing children.

"Thought you weren't coming."

The voice comes from behind. He turns. Smiles at seeing her so unexpectedly. Even more unexpected are the feelings. He can't account for them. He doesn't want to account. He just wants to feel.

"I wasn't coming. But how could I miss it? Happy *Day of the Dead*."

"*Sí,*" says Lucela with a smile. She is wearing a white, embroidered Mexican dress disappearing at the shoulders beneath a smooth black cascade of hair. She has a tamale plate in one hand and a taco plate in the other. She nods approvingly. "*Sí. Feliz Día de los Muertos,* Davis. Isn't all of this just so beautiful?"

"Yes." He nods. Looks around at the lights and flowers. "And so are you. You look… I'm guessin' your grandmother made that dress. Am I right?"

Lucela blushes. Her velvet eyes well up, holding their water in clear pools. One of them spills. Her hands are full, useless. His hands are empty, but timid.

"*Sí.*" She laughs in her embarrassment, teeth flashing. "You are right. *Mi abuela.* She wore this when she was my age." She sighs happily. "I know she is here tonight. I wore this for her."

"You more than do it justice, Lucela."

"Gracias, Davis."

The pause is just long enough to be awkward. Lucela looks down at her hands, mortified.

"Oh… you must think I am a pig!"

"Well, I was wondering." He laughs.

"*Oh Dios mío!* This is not all for me! I am with my mother. We've been walking all day. She needed to sit. Come sit with us." She gestures with the tamale plate. "Third row. There is an empty seat."

Part of him says *yes*. Part of him helps her with one of the plates and begins walking with her toward the stage.

Part of him wants to tell her everything that has ever happened to him. To press his wounded cheek in the soft curve of flesh between her neck and shoulder.

"Thanks. It's not the best night for me, Lucela. I need to go home. I need to sleep."

Her face begins a slow collapse. "Is everything okay? You look... What happened to your face?"

"Nothing. Everything's fine. I just need to sleep. I'm fine."

"You're sure?"

"Yeah, yeah. Enjoy yourself. I'll see you later."

"Tomorrow?" she asks. "At the store?"

"Yeah. Maybe tomorrow." He cannot conceive of tomorrow. "Tomorrow at the store."

She turns. Takes a step. Pulls the plates of food away from certain collision. Turns back. Looks at him.

"Davis? Sometime... would..."

"Yes," he says. Nods. "Yes I would."

He watches her go, making her way carefully toward the stage. Stacey Kimball thunders to a climax. The crowd erupts in sustained approval, as if to make up for its earlier distraction in vanquishing the profane fish. Eventually it ends. Stagehands hurriedly assemble a drum set. The emcee bids farewell and good luck to Stacey Kimball, tipping his hat.

"Now, as the judges scratch their heads over Stacey, I want to bring up RuthAnn Meyers from College Station. Y'all thought she was a geography whiz in that last round, I know, but wait 'til you see what she can do with a couple of drumsticks. And I ain't talkin' about chicken either. Come on up here, RuthAnn!"

A flash of light. Davis turns. Very back of the crowd. A man with a camera, pointed at the stage.

Ten feet away, to the left of the flash, she is there. Olivia DeLuna. Turning. Talking to a man. His hand is on her shoulder.

At first he doubts himself. Thinks he is seeing only what he wants to see. But then they start moving. The limp is hard to mistake.

He charts a path. Cuts through the line of protesting fish, keeping an eye on the couple. They stop at the back of the square, speaking closely. Then they turn up *Broken River Road*.

Three men pass them going the other way, just coming into the town square. One of them is vaguely familiar. The shape of him. Then the face.

It does not become clear until the man's hat comes into focus.

Fuck U Athletics.

Chapter 86

Olivia follows Sheldon to a corner of the square, just where it stops being the town square and becomes *Broken River Road*. Sheldon stops. Turns. Slips a red backpack from his shoulder. Opens his mouth.

Whatever he was going to say dies on his lips.

"Oh... *Oh my god.* Olivia..."

"I know. Stop. I'm fine. I..."

"Fine?" He has to shout. It's like he is yelling at the violence on her face. "You're not fine. You're ... you're... what the hell..."

"Don't make me explain. I got somethin' to tell you, Shel. I need you to listen. I almost didn't come. Probably shouldn't have. But I'm here. So you need to listen."

He stares. Taking her in. Wincing. Withholding his consent to listen. The drumming is too much. He looks around. Grabs her hand.

They walk up *Broken River Road,* all the way to the slatted wooden bench outside the *Coahuiltecan Trading Post.* Sit. Look at each other.

"My god, Olivia. What..."

"Shel. Please don't."

"Okay. Sorry. I won't. I'm listening."

She tells him almost everything. The coyote with the pup in its teeth. The dream of *Papi's* that is no more. Her intent to return it all, every last dollar, which she now does not expect him to believe. The fire. The currency of ash.

She leaves out any mention of Manny Soto. Leaves out any explanation, real or fabricated, for the carnage of her face.

"I'm sorry, Sheldon," she says. "I have been using you from the beginning. Lyin' to you from the beginning. You're not responsible for me. For this."

He grabs her hand again.

"You're wrong, Olivia. You're ... I was angry. I..."

"No. Your car never touched me. The coyote..."

"I know, but I was chasing you. Trying to force you to pull over. You were driving seventy miles an hour for a reason. Your injuries are *real*. The medical expenses you can't pay are *real*. I am responsible and I wanted to help. I still want to help. And I don't care what you use the money for, Olivia. I…"

He pulls the backpack up into his lap.

"I don't want your money." Cold. Defiant. "Keep your goddamned money."

"But you need it now more than ever. You got no home. No clothes. You need medical attention all over again. Libby can't help you. Hell, *she* needs *your* help. I can help *you* help *Libby*. Can't really believe I'm even saying that. If Libby hadn't stolen my things, I wouldn't have…" He stops himself. Takes a breath. Squeezes her hand. "Never mind. I can help. Whatever you need."

"I need to be alone. I need to be away. From everyone. From everything. From here. From you, Sheldon. I'm sorry for everything."

"Take the money," he says, putting the pack in her lap. "There is enough here to help. It's a start."

"No. I won't do that."

"Then take the music."

A beat. The bruising, the scars, the growing escarpment of swollen cheekbone flesh, elongate in confusion.

"What music?"

"Every song I have ever written. Well. Every *good* song. It's all in here."

She looks down at the pack.

"What? I don't… I don't understand. You write music?"

"I don't understand either," he says. "I… I asked you once what you and I were all about." He flips his fingers back and forth between them. "This. You and me. This thing I feel for you and that you feel for me."

She shakes her head.

"I don't feel…"

"Nope. I'm not buyin' it, Olivia. You can sit there and say that you haven't felt anything except a need for cash, but I don't believe that. You *do* feel something for me. That's why you're here right now. This isn't all about guilt."

She lets it sit. Feels him watching her. Searches for words. Echoes of amplified drumming from the town square bowl down the street. Sheldon resumes.

"I asked you that question up at the lake because I don't know what any of… any of *this* means. I'm not the sharpest tool in the shed, but I'm not a fool, Olivia. I'm twice your age. I get that. I don't expect anything like that. Not askin' for that. And I don't believe that it has just been all about the money. So I confess it's a mystery to me too. All I know is that I will do anything for you. Suffer anything. Give you everything. Everything of me. Of who I am. My life is about to change in a radical way. And I mean, like, *day after tomorrow*. The marriage, over. The business, gone. The career, empty. You are holding the last bit of money I can steal from myself to give you, so you may as well take it. And the only thing I *am?* The only thing meaningful to me that I can give you now? Is in that bag." He lets go of her hand. Points. "You remember your answer to my question? At the lake? Do you?"

She sighs. Nods. Doesn't speak.

"Damn right. You told me that you and I should be about the blues. I can do that, Olivia. Whatever in the hell that means, let's start there. Let's share that. And eating lunches outside. And talking about all the old greats. Concerts. Whatever. I just want to be in your life."

She looks away for a moment at the river of people coursing up and down *Broken River Road.* And it *is* a river. Of color. Of celebration. Of secret longing and heartbreak. Of desperation and hope. The emcee is bellowing. He looks back at her.

"I used to be that person. I used to feel things. Intensely. So intensely that it was like squeezing diamonds out of coal. I could shape those feelings. Write them down. Play them. Sing them. I used to feel love like a poet feels love. Like a poet suffers love. I used to give myself over to it. Let it destroy me and then resurrect me. I want to be that person again. You inspire me, Olivia." He stops. Shakes his head. "What a terrible thing to say to someone. So selfish to make someone a tool. But it's true. It's like you've come for me. Like you've come to bring me back across the river."

Olivia looks down at the Cavaliers backpack. Lifts it a little. Lets it drop.

"Sheldon... I'm not sure what... what you're proposing. I..."

"Just read them. You like music. Blues. You more than just like it. It's in you somehow. So just read them. Hear them in your head. Let me play them for you. Tell me what you think. Let's start there. See where it goes. Wherever it wants to go. Whatever it is."

"You're asking me... to be your muse for songs of suffering and misery?"

He smiles. Nods. "I guess so. Yeah. I 'spose that's as close to anything I understand about any of these feelings. Yes."

He stands. Kneels. Takes her hand. People are watching.

"Olivia DeLuna, beautiful, hobbled, scarred, beaten, bereft, lonely, homeless, battered soul that you are, will you please take my money and be my muse of misery?"

It hurts to laugh. It's excruciating. She laughs anyway. He laughs back at her. It is its own kind of music. Laughing through pain. Laughing at it. Pushing it hard in the chest. Laughing. She stands so that he will stand. So people will stop looking.

"I will not take your money," she says, extracting her hand from his. "I will think about the rest."

"And I'll settle for that."

"I have to go."

"Where?"

"I don't know. Someplace still. Quiet."

"I'll come with you. Let's just… go. I'll get you a hotel room someplace. How about a hospital room? A police station."

"No."

"Christ you're stubborn. Then let me walk you to your car. We can unload the sheet music and I'll keep the backpack and the cash. Deal?"

She hesitates. Starts walking.

They move slowly. She asks. He obliges. Tells her what has happened to push him off the cliff. Tells her about Grayson on the flight over and what all of it means. She is silent. Listens. Her leg ratchets up the pain. She puts her arm through his, pulling against his weight.

It is her answer to him. She knows this. They both do. It is not a conscious signal. But there it is anyway. He is smart enough not to acknowledge it. No sudden movements in the presence of timid wildlife. She remembers Kevin's remarkable stillness in the presence of the fawn. Sheldon just keeps telling his story.

A long walk to the car. Away from the ball field. The Falcon is parked on the street, behind *Corbin First Methodist*. Olivia fishes for the keys. Sheldon unslings the backpack. Each is focused on what is ahead. On what comes next.

So neither of them is thinking behind.

It is like being attacked by their own shadows, rising up off the pavement with a slight shifting of light. Silent. Synchronous. Dropping down over their shoulders like an iron blanket.

A thick strip of tape is over her mouth, blocking the exit for sound still too far down in her throat. There is a short, violent struggle next to her. The keys in her hand are pried loose. Gone. She wrenches sideways. Searches wildly with her eyes. Sheldon's mouth is a silver rectangle. His eyes are wide, burning fear.

The man holding him is a tall, blond specimen. Perfect pale skin. Something red and angry is up near his right eye. He zip-ties Sheldon's hands behind his back. Olivia's shadow does the same to her hands. It happens too fast. She is already in too much pain. She can see Sheldon struggling. Panicking. The blond shadow elbows him hard in the head. It's like stunning a large fish with a club. Sheldon goes still. It costs him a zip-tie around the ankles.

Olivia kicks. Shuffles. Writhes. Does her best to keep her ankles apart. A plastic noose tightens around her wrists, cutting into the flesh. She keeps kicking. She is beyond pain now. She just keeps moving.

Whoever is behind her aborts the effort to capture her ankles. She is yanked backwards by her wrists toward the car. A white hand jabs the key into the lock. Twists. Opens the trunk.

Sheldon goes in first. The bottom third of his bound legs hangs outside until the blond shadow forces them in like he is stuffing garbage into a sack. Then he turns, grabs her around the shoulders, spins her backwards. The other one, the one with the key, lowers himself. He pulls her legs out from under her and she sags between them. Gravity pulls at every bone. Claws at every joint as she rises above the street.

She drops down hard, backwards, on top of Sheldon. He muffles a scream beneath her.

Sight. Sound. Smell.

Singular sensations come to her. Imprinting just as the bottom edge of the trunk rapidly severs the outside world.

The smell. Oily. Rubber and grease and gasoline.

The sight. Blackness closing around the last lit image in her head. A face. A fleshy square. Sweaty. Dirty pores. Matted, reddish hair. Black baseball hat. A charging bull. *EBSecurity.*

The sound. A large, tooth-rattling explosion. Distant. And yet like a detonation somewhere deep in the center of her own chest. Something that was here and of the world a second ago, is now gone.

Darkness.

Sound. A door opens. Slams. The other, opens, slams. The engine. They are moving. Bald tires translate the street braille. Blind white fear in the dark. She cannot breathe. Manny Soto's fist has swollen her nasal passages. Her nose does not work like it should. It's getting worse. She works her tongue furiously, jabbing through her split lips at the inside of the tape. A speed bump. Her swollen face hits metal. She keeps working. The only pain she feels now is in her lungs.

As though she was in deep water.

The darkness around her begins to thin, lightening around the edges. The Falcon takes a sharp left. Her perception sloshes like soup in a bowl.

She is in bed. She looks up and they are there. All of them. Looking down. The cactus people. The little dog, a coyote pup, with the flower ears.

A different sound. No. Not sound. Feeling.

Vibration. For the first time in what feels like a very long time. Clear. Strong. No tuning-cigarette necessary. As though the trunk of Jesús Batista's shit-brown Ford Falcon was the perfect shape. An antennae dish. A cosmic catchers mitt.

Mother Ocean. Mother Ocean. Your sorrow so deep.
Your children have floated astray.
Down in green coffers such mem'ries you keep
Are you sorry you sent them away?

Sheldon groans through the duct tape. His body shifts sideways beneath her. She drops another inch. There is another deep explosion outside the car from places unknown.

Suddenly her mother is with her. The essence of her. The memory of her. Like a scent. A breath on the gooseflesh of her skin.

No. Not her mother.

Motherness. Maternity itself. The timeless embrace. The universal wrap. The trunk of Jesús Batista's Ford Falcon is not a cosmic catcher's mitt. It's a kind of womb. The vibration in her head is a heartbeat. It speaks, this vibration. It speaks. It answers.

Yes. Yes, I am sorry. Forever and always, yes. You are loved.
There is nothing else. Just love.

Chapter 87

Fuck U Athletics.

There has to be more than just one of those hats in the world. Whoever made it did not make just one of them.

So it could be anybody.

Could be. But it's not. It's not just anybody.

So much has happened since then. So many more important things. He shouldn't be so sure. But he is. Because it's not just the hat he remembers. It's the shape of the person under the hat. The height. The build. The way he walks.

So he's sure. Remembers the man straddling the Harley as the other one stood off to the side, reading the letter from his mother. The name comes soon enough. Travis something.

Shumaker. Travis Shumaker.

But recognition has come too late. Because the recognition is mutual now.

Travis Shumaker stops. The others with him stop. Travis speaks to them without looking away. Resumes.

Davis does his best to pretend he has not seen them. Has not recognized them. He angles off toward the rows of chairs. Stopping. Looking. Starting again. Arcing in towards the center of the square, then back again toward the stage. He looks back every so often, but cannot find any of them. Only nameless people in every direction.

To the best of his knowledge, the last time Travis Shumaker was in Corbin was the day Miguel Rivera's *Louisville Slugger* broke his elbow. Same day Travis was told never to come back to Corbin. He considers the odds that Travis has come back to Corbin unprepared for another encounter with Miguel. Unprepared for violence. They aren't good odds. The part of his face under the patch of gauze begins to throb in pain.

Like maybe it knows the odds too.

He stands near the southwest corner of the stage without any memory of getting there. RuthAnn Meyers –all the way from College Station –sits on a stool in a yellow two-piece and high heels, beating the hell out of the drums. The crowd fanned out in front of her is clapping along. RuthAnn loses them every so often with a barrage of non-rhythmic cannon fire but then snaps quickly back into a fat bass beat groove and the crowd falls in behind.

In the front row sits the mustachioed man. The vanquished silver fish, never resembling a Pecos Bluntnose Shiner in the first place, has suffered the humiliation of detachment from its pole and has been stuffed like luggage beneath folding chairs. One painted eye stares out forlornly from between the stomping boots.

Almost directly behind sits Miguel Rivera, sandwiched between a woman on his left and a boy in a wheelchair on his right.

Directly behind them is Eladio. Clapping. Talking animatedly to Lucela Flores. Trying his best to charm her. To seduce her against her own better judgment.

Lucela's mother is finishing her tamale, keeping time with her head. Lucela laughs at Eladio, who seems now to be telling a story with his entire body.

She throws her head back. Laughs. Laughs.

He has never seen anything less complicated. Or more true.

Paranoia returns. Somehow he knows. He knows when to look and where. Fifty yards away, cutting through people. Travis is alone but not alone. The others are somewhere. Coming from different directions.

He thinks of staying where he is. Surrounded by people. They won't assault him in public. But they will stick to him like a second skin until the time is right. They will wait. Eluding them now would be better.

The audience blocks him from the south. Travis is coming from the west. He moves east, around the back of the stage. He hopes to swing around the other side, reinsert himself into the throngs. Disappear.

But Travis has already thought of that. Or at least his friends have. They walk with purpose. He does not pause long enough to know if they have seen him. He moves quickly, ducking around an enormously proportioned family pulling a rolling cooler, in the only direction he has left: northeast, toward the array of blue toilets.

The idea of hiding inside one of the plastic outhouses occurs to him. Slip in, close the door and wait. Might work if no one sees him go in. But if they do see him go in, or if he has to try two or three of them to find an empty, it would be a disaster.

He realizes now his mistake. If disappearing was not possible, then he should have stayed put. Should have gotten Miguel's attention. Forced a public confrontation. He breaches the line of toilets, slipping between two Porta-Potties on the end.

On the other side of the toilet phalanx is the large dirt lot that used to hold the old *Corbin Public Library* before its relocation across from *Corbin Christ Presbyterian*. Now the lot holds a dozen service vehicles and two generators noisily pumping extra electricity into the town square. The two State Trooper cruisers are of immediate interest, at least until he is close enough to see that they are empty.

He hears movement from the direction he has come. People. He turns to look, but not long enough to assess whether the sounds are from indifferent Moon Garden revelers or from people who want to remove all of his teeth. Or stick a knife in his ribs. He keeps walking. Not liking the lack of illumination or the absence of people. Keeps walking. Movement for the sake of movement.

Stops.

Blinks. Stares.

Blinks.

Time collapses.

Along the farthest, darkest side of the lot is a trailer.

Like a silver boot box. A small forest of antennae on top.

Blue door.

It is not the same, of course. There are differences. Not as long. Not as tall. No curtain over the window. Sign on the door. He can see all of that. Even now.

But it is close enough.

His legs weaken beneath his weight. As if he has been walking for days. He looks over his shoulder. Back. The pain in his face throbs. Like it is shouting at him. He moves forward.

The sign on the door is an eleven-by-fourteen sheet of laminated paper. It starts with the name and logo. *EBSecurity*. Angry charging bull. Horns lowered.

Beneath that is the warning. *No Trespassing. Restricted Space. Eli Ball Security. 1900 South Glen, Fort Worth, Texas.* And then a phone number, web address, and a business license number.

He knocks just above the sign. Listens. Waits.

Standing at the door of this silver trailer, heart racing, he waits. Feels the past coming for him from behind. Closing that distance.

The throbbing in his face wants to call out. Wants to articulate the thoughts he is trying to suppress. Wants to say her name. Wants her to answer the knock.

"Davis, love! Knew you'd finally come 'round!"

No sound. No movement. He tries the knob. Locked. Again. Still locked.

He looks at the sign. The *EBSecurity* bull looks back.

Angry red eyes. Yellow horns.

No. Not yellow. Gold.

Goldie.

Sound. He turns in time to see Travis Shumaker emerge onto the lot, stepping through the line of blue toilets. Travis' face is turned away as he talks to others behind. There are four of them now.

There is no thought in his head except to drop. He does. Lies in the dirt. Rolls under the trailer. Breathes in the dark. Listens to the sound of walking. Boots over loose ground. Low laughter.

Possibility hardens into shapes of certainty. Dissolves again. Hardens into another. They saw him. They are surrounding the trailer. They did not see him. They are no longer looking for him. They are just passing through. Back again.

The boots stop, still some distance away. There are no voices. No laughter. They are looking. Waiting. They have not given up. He breathes. Stops breathing. Breathes.

He had dropped and rolled into the darkness almost without thinking at all. So there had not been any time to consider snakes.

But now. Now the thought occurs to him. Never a good idea to roll beneath a trailer in Texas without eliminating that possibility.

Time and place were in his favor. November in Town Square. But still. He listens in a different way. With a new focus of attention, closer to the ground. He would have heard a rattle.

Wouldn't he? Over the pounding of his heart? Wouldn't he?

His eyes have adjusted enough to see around him. He lifts his face an inch or two until he can feel with his forehead small metal protrusions from the bottom of the trailer. Looks.

He does not see any snakes. At least not in front of him or on either side of his body. Only dirt. Small rocks. Loose trash. He listens to the lot around him. Hears nothing. They are waiting. They are listening.

He lowers his head back to the dirt. Listens.

An awareness of something behind him. Behind and to the right. Just a few inches away.

And in the thin sliver of that second, he knows.

Instinct. Adrenaline. Forces he cannot control persuade him to sit up. Fast and hard. To stand. To run. As if he is in the middle of an open field.

His head connects mightily with the steel trailer like a hammer to a nail. Something hard and small inserts itself into his scalp. There is a sound. Surely there is a sound. Flesh and bone so hard and fast against a plate of steel? But it is not a sound he can hear over the pain behind his eyes as he collapses back to the dirt.

He lies dazed for a second.

Two.

Three.

A thin warm trickle on his forehead. The bridge of his nose. Then stars, white and shifting, begin to coalesce around the periphery of his vision. More and more of them, drifting, spinning in from all sides, merging into white. Bleeding into bleached brilliance.

He is floating. On his back in a boat. Rocking. A man kneels over him, terrified. Panting. Dripping. Weeping. Unaware his knee is burrowing into Davis' left arm, pinning it to the deck. The man's head passes back and forth in front of the sun. His bearded face, lips parting, descends like a blanket. Rises again as the light returns around it. His mother is in the water. He can't move. Can't blink. His chest is like concrete.

But he can remember. Can remember her thrashing forward. Coming for him. Trying. The sun goes away again. Fingers over his nose. The face descends. Rises again. Crying. Yelling. The bone knob of kneecap like an anchor pushing into Davis' arm.

Behind the face, on a bench along the side of the boat, is a buoy. White. Oblong. A coil of yellow rope tied to one end. Someone has painted a fish mouth on the other end. Little teeth. And an eye. Large, black, glassy. Ever-seeing. The eye cannot blink. Like he cannot blink. It can only stare. *Throw the buoy*, he thinks up at the man. *She can't swim. Throw the buoy.* The sun disappears.

Four.

He opens his eyes. Is able to think around the pain in his head.

Five.

Remembers what caused the pain. Remembers the jolt of fear.

Six.

Another release of adrenaline. He rolls sideways and back several inches to keep the snake in view.

But the thing behind him is not a snake. Not even close.

It's a fish. Made out of cardboard and paper. Shellacked and painted. The eye is a fat blue almond. It stares at him through the dark. It has been staring this whole time.

Davis inches up. Looks. The blood on his face redirects with the shift in gravity. She comes to him, as always, unbidden. Like a scent. A sound. A memory.

"I finally got a rake and dragged a big bit of grouper out from under the trailer. Wriggling with maggots."

The bottom of the fish has been cut open. Slit from head to tail. He spreads the slit with two fingers. Inside are guts made from shredded newspaper. Nested inside the newspaper is a block of waxy-brown putty.

Davis spreads his fingers. See it is not one block, but two.

Two blocks. Two wires. One cell phone.

Abby, again, like she is right next to him.

"Davis. My love. My lover. My brilliant boy. Everything is not going to be okay. Not ever again. Because there is something in the wax. Understand? There's something in the wax, love."

The flow from the hole in his forehead increases. He can smell it now, trickling into his eye. It feels like his heart is pumping through a raw nerve. Opening. Widening. Abby. Again.

"I call her Goldie. 'Cause of the horns, I suppose."

Again.

"Not ball like a soccer ball. Baal! B-A-A-L! He's going to kill everyone."

"Don't trust the bobbies."

Again.

"You'll know what to do when the time comes. Save me, Davis."

Again.

"Blew the bloody thing into disgusting chunks. They had so much fun the first time, they kept doing it. Blew up more fish than they ate. Fish-bangers they called them."

Again.

"That was finally it for me and fish. Between daddy and the fish bombs and the maggots, they all look like a kind of death to me."

It is looking at him, this thing, with its lifeless, painted, paper eye. Its body is not like a loaf of bread. It's larger. Fatter. And it is not silver. It's a dingy yellow.

Large and yellow. Like the fish confiscated by security. The fish now tucked beneath the audience. *Don't trust the bobbies.*

Abby's voice. Again. Shrill. Screaming through years of history. Over and over in his head.

"It's not a fish! It's not a fish! It's not a fish!"

Abby's voice, yes. But not Abby's face. It is his mother's face he sees. His mother's eyes, just above the water line.

"Save me, Davis."

There is no thinking involved. Not now. Thinking is useless. Processing, useless. Understanding, useless. There is only feeling. Dissolving into a larger consciousness in which everything there is to know has always been known. Always.

He tries to wipe the blood from his eye. Succeeds only in smearing it. He rolls from beneath the trailer. Does not look for Travis, the others. No longer cares about any of them. He stands.

And he *runs*.

He hears the sound of them from behind, from the very back of the lot. Words. Boots over dirt. A bottle.

But the sounds do not register. He is in his own head now. His father's novel, read in his mother's voice, all compacted into a single thought.

> *For the first time, Spencer saw it for what it was. Not a soapstone whale; but a warning. A comeuppance. A promise. A confession. An apology. A forgiveness. All in advance.*

There is no God to worship because there is nothing but God in the first place. Boats are made to carry an illusion. We are all made of water… That's why she drowned herself in that lake. She believed she could move on. Escape the prison of this plane. This limited vibration.

Simon Dory. Suddenly in his head. Simon. Red-faced with rage. Abby's trailer behind him belching flame and smoke. Simon bending over him as his face bleeds.

"You stupid bloody fuck! She was saving you!"

By the time he clears the barrier of blue toilets, the fastest of them, whoever was quickest off the mark, whoever grunts as he runs, is almost on top of him. He does not look. He plows through three teenage boys and sends them sprawling. Soda. Food. Outrage.

The blood is too much now. He can only see through one eye. He feels light-headed. Running. Making that heart pump faster. *Faster.*

He aims for the space between the stage and the front row of seats. Someone is singing. Playing the banjo. The grunting at his heels disappears. He feels the person chasing him stop abruptly at the shoreline of the audience.

He runs alone now. Four hundred people watching. Two steps ahead of a wave of surprise and exclamation.

The man in the silver mustache tries to stand. Davis pushes him hard in the chest, tipping his chair backward into Miguel's lap. The tip of the man's boot, flinging skyward, catches Davis in the chin. The blonde woman in the next chair exclaims with authority. Beyond her, it is Eladio's voice he hears, like a bell.

"Davis! What… Davis!"

He bends for the fish beneath the upended chair.

"It's not a fish. There's something in the wax. Save me, Davis."

As he stands he can see Lucela in her grandmother's white, embroidered dress, holding her mother protectively. Eyes wide. Innocent. Beautiful.

"Davis? Sometime … would…"

"Yes. I would."

He seizes the cardboard fish, freezing momentarily in place as the wooden pole falls easily away to the ground. He holds the thing at arms length, away from his body. Runs.

People shouting. Cowering as he passes, blood streaming off his face. The singing has stopped. Banjoing has stopped. He keeps moving. Sprints up the aisle. Turns west. Aims himself for the fountain. Aims himself for the town hall building, festooned with lights and flowers.

Two blocks from town hall is I-67. On the other side of that, like the distant shore of a river that divides one world from another, hundreds of acres of empty scrub. Thousands.

A white pickup slams on the brakes. Someone lays on a horn. Then another. He is focused on where he wants to be, not where he is. The reflective pavement marker catches his foot and he goes down hard on his head, sprawling forward off the road and into the ditch, re-opening the bandaged side of his face on a rock.

He lies still. Breathing. Bleeding. Pain, hot wires of lightning, scorches his skull.

Then darkness. Just the gentle rocking of a boat beneath him.

And then there is no boat. Just floating. Sinking.

Sinking.

Sinking.

It is the sound of a horn that brings him back to the surface. Clear and clean, slicing up through the deep. Pure vibration hammered into the shape of a sword.

He opens his eyes. Only one of them can see through the blood.

The cardboard fish stares back at him from the middle of the road. One eye, disappearing behind slowly-rolling tires. And then it is back again. Seeing him.

His mother's voice. Rising from the ink in her letter to Aunt Tallulah. Soft. Calm.

"I feel like I'm in two worlds at the same time. Like I'm a zombie. The walking dead. Like I'm a fish in the desert. Except that I'm alive. And I can see everything through that eye."

The fish disappears behind another obstructive tire. A small, blue Hyundai, immersed in the shadow of something much larger, like tiny swimming prey being pulled back into the maw of a predator a hundred times its size. Not just tall, this looming thing, but long, with a smooth cylindrical body that glides behind its fearsome head. All a glowing white.

The Hyundai tire rolls past the fish, revealing the slit along the length of its belly. Then the eye. Abby.

"Davis, love. It's not a fish. There's something… "

He is up in a wave of resurgent panic, scrabbling forward on all fours for the pavement. Twenty feet separate the rear bumper of the Hyundai and the grill of the long, white fuel truck. Half of that distance is gone by the time he lunges out onto the road, reaching desperately for the thing that is not a fish. He braces with his left arm, thrusting his right hand outward, in front of the double tires and the rolling shadow that paints another three feet of the highway black in as many seconds. He grabs the fish, pulling it to him, out of the path.

But all of his weight is still on his left arm, pinning him to the road.

There is no stopping a forty-ton tanker carrying nine thousand gallons of fuel. Not on a dime. It takes all three sets of tires and another fifty feet before the driver has a clue.

The sound of air brakes comes like a breathy scream. It is the last thing Davis hears as the world bleaches white.

He floats beneath a summer sky. The sun disappears again behind the weeping ranger's head. The man's kneecap, like it is made of iron, pins his left arm to the deck. The man lifts away again and the sun reappears in a watery nimbus.

To his left, the white buoy that has been made to look like a fish sits atop the pile of yellow rope. One eye. Looking at him. His mother's voice.

"Throw the buoy. Throw the buoy. Save me. Throw the buoy, Davis."

And he does. Rolls away from the pain. Struggles up from the deck of the boat. Stretches down for the buoy with his right hand. Gathers up the yellow rope. Horns, everywhere horns. He turns to face the open expanse of water, the ranger's boat wobbling beneath him.

Imagines the place he saw her last. Sees her face in the quieting ripples.

He winds his young body backward upon itself, coiling it as far back as it will go.

Uncoils. Lets it fly. Sends the buoy sailing out over the water.

The whole world moves. Suddenly. Violently.

He is propelled up into the air, flying backwards, falling, expecting water and finding hard-baked dirt.

There is no boat. No water. Just a desert that was once an ocean.

And yet, he feels as if he is floating. Suspended. Immersed.

Davis closes his eyes to the sky. He feels something immense and inexplicable and timeless glide beneath him. Through him.

Swimming. Devouring stars.

Chapter 88

She dreamt stars. Or thinks she did. Everything before that moment, before actually being conscious of consciousness, presents as dream. Like it is for anyone waking back into the world. Back into the here and now.

Until you really think about it.

Then you realize that part of you has always been paying attention. Listening. Seeing from inside the dark. While the rest of you sleeps.

The only thing that moves is her left eye. Open now. Blinking. Looking. Seeing. Faint stars shiver over the desert. They are clearer off at the horizon. Shimmering blue pinpricks. Directly above they threaten to disappear beneath a whisper-thin sheet of light spraying in from behind her. From the east.

The other eye, the other side of her face, swollen, battered, a fleshy fossilized imprint of Manny Soto's fist, presses down into the dirt. Her arms, joined at the wrists. She cannot feel them. Cannot identify them as arms. Her mouth, raw and burning. Her tongue feels granular earth. No more tape. She breathes in desert dust.

Sound. Howling. Distant and thin. Singing through the night. Searching.

No. Not howling. Not *just* howling. A siren. Sirens.

She remembers. Explosions.

A voice. Calm. Quiet.

Another. Not calm. Not quiet. Terrified.

She had dreamt those voices. Talking stars. Talking waves. Hadn't she?

"I don't know. I'm sorry, but I just don't. You made a mistake. And she's hurt. She's... she's not moving. She's..."

"No. Sheldon. I don't make mistakes. I pay very close attention. You see? You are the one who made the mistake. The two of you. You and your whore. You think you know what you are doing. But you don't. You have been greedy and stupid. We are prepared to stay out here all night. We're prepared to make it hurt. You. Her. Doesn't matter to me. But I want some answers."

Spitting. Something thick. Tenacious. Something that will not let go of lips and tongue. Again. Again.

"I don't have answers." Again. "I don't…"

Spitting. Again.

"Here. Use this. Wipe his mouth. I'm sure he wants to speak clearly. So that we will understand."

Movement. Muffled pain.

"Good. Now. Sheldon. Answers."

"Nicki… I never. Told anybody. About."

"No, no, no. Okay. Stop. Don't make it harder than it has to be. You're making a mistake. You're assuming that I know nothing. You're assuming that you can lie to me and that I will not know the difference. But… I already know so much."

Quiet now. Just the sirens, thin threads of lament unspooling in the distance. Coyotes too. Answering. Nowhere. Everywhere. Like a sound desert air makes as a part of its darkness or its temperature.

Mostly there is the sound of looking. The sound of two people staring at each other. The sound of eyes.

"So let me start the story for you. Okay? It starts like this. You came out to Corbin, asking questions. Property sales. None of your business. Not your job. But you were curious. Because you had come across some… information. *Old* information. *Bad* information. You were concerned. Or maybe you were down here for some other reason. No matter. You decided to ask questions. And your questions brought you to a whorehouse. A Corbin, Texas whorehouse. And so you decided that, while you were asking your questions, you may as well buy yourself a whore. You could not resist the temptation. The convenience. Okay? I understand. We have different tastes in whores, you and I, but I understand. Except that I am a careful man. You are not a careful man, Sheldon. When you bought yourself a whore, you ended up buying yourself a blackmailer."

"No. That's not…"

"*Ah. Ah.* Don't interrupt. You'll get your chance. I promise. Soon I will be quiet and listen to everything you have to say. But let me just get you started."

Silence. Brief. Halting.

"So. You got yourself some blackmailing whores. They're going to ruin your marriage. Going to ruin your business. They want money, of course. That's what a whore is. But these are some truly enterprising whores. Because they also want… what? Ahhh… *information*. Documents. Property documents. *Ah. Ah.* Let me finish."

Spitting.

"All of your questions have convinced them that you work for people who are violating the law. And so these enterprising Corbin whores decide to go up to the top. Decide to blackmail Gregor Buchvarov."

It is a soft, airy sound he makes. The child of a laugh and a sigh.

"They are thinking big, these whores. Yes. I think so."

"What… Nicki, I don't…"

"Stop. Stop. No. They sent him a *letter*, Sheldon. Do you think I'm stupid? You didn't even know, did you? Of course you didn't know. How silly of me. But they did. They sent him a letter. Told him you were out spreading the word. You look… perplexed. You really did not know that, did you? Of course not. They had you by the balls, these whores. They told you they wanted money. They told you they wanted sales documents. CDC records."

"No."

"*Ah. Ah.* Not your turn yet."

Silence. Waiting.

"And so what do you do? Do you come to us? No. We might have been able to help. But no. Instead you decide to make up a pretend lawyer. Send yourself some pretend invoices. Send yourself a lot of money. Your money, yes, but really it was Grayson's money, wasn't it? And our money. Advertising money that we paid your business to do a job. And then you spend a lot of time on your computer. Looking at emails. Attachments. Looking through property files. Downloading. Copying. And then, every few weeks, you get in a car and you go out to meet with your whore blackmailer. And… *Ah. Ah.* Let me finish. Let me finish. And you give her the money. And you give her the information. And this is where… well."

The voice clears its throat. To keep from laughing. She can hear the smile sidewinding across the dirt.

"There really is no other word for it, Sheldon. This is where you got really stupid. You… fell in *love* with the whore blackmailer. You thought you could make her your girlfriend. Poor Christi. Sweet, stupid Christi. No. Don't deny it. I have the photos. She wrapped you around her little finger. Working you. Making you believe that you were the one making the decisions. Making you believe that she loved you. That you were a *team*. That you would run away together. Yes? Don't answer, Sheldon. Your turn is coming. Wipe his mouth again. Christ. What a mess."

Struggle. Body against body. Muffled pain.

"Good. Okay? So, you decided that you could work together. Drain all of the money out of the business. Money the CDC was paying this business to do a job. You decided you would create a distraction by blowing everything up. Not *actually* blowing everything up. Of course. But by going to a newspaper. A reporter. Telling a reporter that the CDC was a front. A scam. You knew the reporter would talk to Grayson. Grayson would start asking his own questions. You were right about that part. Stupid, Sheldon. Really very stupid. But right. Grayson did start asking questions. So between the reporter and Grayson you predicted that someone would want some answers. You predicted an investigation. And when the time was right? You would have information to sell. Yes? You would write another letter to Gregor? *Dear Gregor, guess what we have?* Lists. Documents. Information. Or maybe that part was all her idea. Did she keep you in the dark? Doesn't matter. Now you know. Now you know."

There is a pressure in her chest. Small. A tiny bubble of air pushing up against the top of her trachea, traversing a path just above the desert floor. She fights it as long as she can. Closes her one eye. Bears down.

Fights it. Fights.

Coughs.

"Ah. You see? She is fine. Good. Sit her up. Sit her up."

Boots. Hands. The desert falls away from her face. Gravity reorients. Blood redirects. Pain brightens, tracing muscle and bone in lines of flame. Her arms. Legs. Face. The eye that is not swollen shut blinks. Focuses. Sees.

The three-quarter moon is up in the east, washing the scrub in a dim, spectral blue. To the south, maybe five miles, I-67 is a sparse line of rolling balls of light. Red one way. White the other.

They are sitting in the dirt. Sheldon and the blond man he calls Nicki. There is enough space between them for a large campfire. But there is no campfire. The man sits with his legs crossed, drawing lines in the dirt with a short stick. Next to him, half beneath his inclined knee, is a small, black shape. Could be a rock. But it is not a rock. Too heavy to the eye. Like any gun.

Sheldon's legs are out in front of him, still bound. Arms behind, still bound. His face –nose, mouth, chin –is a slick mess. There is not enough light to see color. A hundred feet off in the gloom, beyond the non-existent campfire, is the dark shape of the Ford Falcon. Trunk still open.

Sheldon's eyes are wide and white and searching. Probing the dark space between them. The boots beside her move back to him. Kick him softly in the ribs. A new voice.

"Face forward. I said, face…"

Sheldon's eyes turn away from her. The boots move back to the midpoint between them.

"Olivia. Good morning. Sleep well?" Nicholas Voss waits for an answer. Continues. "You are just in time to help Sheldon answer some questions, yes? Good." He turns back to Sheldon. "Now. I would like to learn of everything that you have given to her." His head pivots. "And I would like to learn of where *you,* Olivia, have put each of those things." Pivots back. "And I would like to know who *else* you have told about those things. Understand? If I do not like the answer from one of you, my friend will take out my disappointment on the other. Understand? This will test your love. Understand? Good. So. Sheldon. Let's begin." Pivots. "Olivia, I want you to be quiet for now. Say something without permission and we will start breaking Sheldon's bones. Understand? Good."

Pivots back. "Now. Sheldon. What have you given her?"

Sheldon tries to clear his throat.

"I only… I only gave her money. Nothin' else. I swear to you."

Nicholas Voss lets out a long, disappointed sigh. Uses the stick to scratch out whatever he is drawing in the dirt. Rubs his face.

"You are not convinced that I am serious."

"No… no."

"That is not the way this should go. So let's…"

"No, no, no. Nicki. I'm convinced you're serious. I'm convinced. But I…"

Nicholas Voss points the stick at him.

"Stop."

And he does. Nicholas keeps his focus on Sheldon's face.

But the stick drifts slowly left. Towards her. Stops.

"Let's try again."

The man between them moves over behind her. Squats. Rolls up her hair around his hand. Tightens it. Breathes heavily from his nose. Waits. Nicholas speaks.

"What. Have. You. Given. To. Her."

There is a sound out in the dark.

A kind of growling. Moving low over the desert on the far side of the Falcon. Except that it is not a growl.

It's a motorcycle.

Nicholas clutches the gun. Stands. Speaks to the squatting man holding her hair.

"Car. Now. I'll stay with them." He looks down, as if a parent lecturing children. "Sheldon? Olivia? I will aim for the face. Do you understand?"

Her hair unwinds. Falls. The boots next to her move. They carry the man away in a deep and quiet crouch toward the car. She remembers him now. His shape. Matted red hair beneath the black hat as the trunk was closing. Charging bull. Yellow horns.

Growing, swelling sound. Alien. Unnatural. Serrated. I knife sawing through earth and air.

She does not know her motorcycles. There are too many and they all sound the same. But in her memory there is only one. That same low growl moving over the desert floor. Louder. Bass notes agitating the air around her. Grabbing her ribcage, shaking her as she had leaned back upon the windshield of the shit-brown Ford Falcon. Passing. Fading. Stopping. Coming back. Louder. Stopping. The rider's voice shooting out of the rumble.

"Everything okay?"

Davis. She imagines that he is out there. Riding the growl. Remembers Libby telling her that he had come to the house. Had come to see her. Had come to *not* take her to the festival. So that they could *not* go together. Remembers his bloody face in *Pepita's*. Remembers his eyes finding her across a room of crowded tables. Remembers their urgency. Remembers Libby's concern.

"That mean up inside his cute li'l writer head is a fighter. He a violent man."

Remembers again his voice in the dark.

"You sure you don't need any help?"

She closes her eyes. Hopes Libby is right. Hopes he is a violent man. Sends a message, directing it out across the scrub to the approaching growl.

Everything is not okay. I do need help. Help me, Davis.

The crouching man in the black security hat reaches the car. Moves carefully around the back. Stretches a hand up for the trunk. Closes it slowly.

Her mind expects a *click*. Or a soft *thump*. Not that she could have heard it over the swelling noise. But when you close a trunk, you expect a certain sound.

It is not a *click*. Not a latching sound. Not a soft *thump* sound.

Instead, the trunk makes a large, sharp *pop*. Or seems to. A one-syllable noise, quickly swallowed by the desert. The shape of the man in the hat crumples to the earth. Screaming. Writhing.

Sound. Louder. Fuller.

It takes a beat. But then she abandons the idea that the trunk of the Falcon has anything to do with anything. Another form emerges from the other side of the car. Steps over the writhing, screaming man. Stoops. Retrieves. Throws something far out into the dark. Stoops again. Goes through his pockets.

The growling is a full roar. It comes from everywhere. Surrounds her. She feels it in her chest.

It comes around the other side of the Falcon. The front end. No headlight. Just dark shape and thundering sound. Accelerating.

Nicholas moves. Running from something he does not understand. Running from something that none of them understand. His path out into the scrub brings him just close enough.

He should have bound her ankles.

He goes down face first into the dirt. She is searching for the fire in her leg even before he lands, searching for the metal pins connecting her bones, searching for the inner strength of her pain, finding it, pushing off, launching herself.

She lands on his back just as he is trying to stand. He goes down again.

But he is too strong. She is too light. She has no arms. She is a fish in the desert. He is up, easily, suddenly, in a storm of black, roaring sound and she is falling from his back. She lands hard, on her side, flesh of her upper arm wrapping itself over a rock in the dirt. Nicholas stoops, reaching for her, reaching under her, reaching for the rock.

It is not a rock.

She tries to make herself heavy. Tries to mold her body to the hard shape. But he is too strong. She has no arms. No hands. Her head is all she has. So she uses it.

She cannot hear it, of course. But she can feel it. Bone to cartilage. Second nose she has broken in twenty-four hours.

Nicholas cries out, equal parts anger and pain, still digging beneath her for the thing that is not a rock. She closes her eyes to the warm spattering from his face.

She feels him find the thing. Feels him grab it.

The gunshot is instantly a memory. A fading, concussive blast disappearing behind the sensation of deafness and then of a shrill, vibratory ringing in her ears. She hears the explosion now only in the hollow of her chest.

But it had not come from beneath her. It came from above. And from the side. It came out of the growling, roaring cloud of sound and dust billowing behind her.

Sheldon. His voice. Nearby. Calling out. Shouting. Saying her name through the ringing in her ears. "*Olivia!*"

Nicholas. Bloody. Screaming. Rolling away. Clutching his leg.

Shapes. Standing over her. Two shapes. Two guns. The taller shape drags the man in the black hat, writhing, whimpering through the dirt. Drops him in a quivering heap on top of Nicholas Voss.

He kneels. Grabs the wrist of one man. Then the ankle of the other. Zip-ties them together. Nicholas thrashes and howls. The man in the hat is sobbing.

A voice, behind her, far above the roaring cloud and its halo of ringing.

A voice that does not belong to Davis Payne.

"*¿De dónde sacaste eso?*"

"*En su bolsillo.*"

"In his pocket, eh? He came prepared, this one? To tie up everyone in Corbin."

"*Sí. Guardado el último para él mismo.*"

The man stands, looking down at the writhing bodies like two snakes tied together. Shakes his head. Comes back to the shape of the shorter man behind her. Pauses. Nods. Dangles a sliver of metal between his fingers. A car key. Her car key.

"*Gracias mi amigo*" says the man taking custody of the key. "*Nos encontraremos pronto. Pronto.*"

The taller one moves out of view. The motorcycle behind her revs up, sprays a wave of dirt. The roaring shrinks to a buzz. Disappears out into the desert like an insect down a deep well.

Behind the wailing and whimpering is a sea of quiet.

Breathing. Wind over an abandoned seabed waiting beneath a rising moon.

Even the sirens have stopped. Even the coyotes.

She wants to wipe Nicholas Voss' blood from her face. She has no arms. If she has hands, she cannot feel them.

Behind her, a voice.

"He wants to aim for the shoulder. I tell him no, no, no. Too close to the head, *amigo*. And too close to the heart."

The man steps over her like she is a log. He's wearing boots. Jeans. He walks over to the knotted snakes. More of him comes into view. Heavy black shirt. Dark bandana around his head. Dark, shoulder-length hair. Ponytail.

"Too risky, I tell him. Aim for the shoulder and miss? Not good. There will be no suffering that way."

He bends over Nicholas, who falls silent, free hand up, wet and sticky, waiting for the punch. His nose is still flowing. He cringes. Waits.

But there is no punch. So he speaks. Tries to.

"This is unnecessary," says Nicholas, forcing calm. "We have a lot of money at our disposal." The other snake thrashes in pain, jerking Voss' body. He shouts up at the man. Fear. Rage.

"Motherfucker! Fucking wetback motherfucker!"

The man's boot finds a knee. Steps gently. Slowly increases the pressure. The profanity from below gives way to shrieking. The man thrusts down a hand. Grabs the neck hole of the black *Security* t-shirt. He pulls up sharply against the weight of the red-haired man, yanking until the shirt rips, dropping him back to the ground.

He pulls a folding knife from his back pocket. Cuts the shirt free, exposing a white, fish flesh torso. Replaces the knife. Tears the shirt into two pieces. Rolls each piece into a rope. Speaks.

"So I say to him, Enrique, we must aim for the knees. If we miss? It is just another bullet or two in the desert. But if we aim true, if we have God in our hearts, then there will be suffering without death."

He kneels. Ties one fabric rope tightly around the thigh of the red-haired man in the security hat.

"And suffering without death? That is the same as life without love." He turns, looks briefly at Olivia. "*¿Si?*" Then Sheldon. "*¿Si?*" He is clean-shaven. Young. He turns back to his work. "It is the same."

He pivots to Nicholas Voss, who slowly lowers his bloody, defensive hand. The man secures the second tourniquet. He yanks it tight. Once. Twice. Nicholas cries out in pain. The man stands. Speaks.

"And if you must live a life without love? Like these two? Like these *pendejos?* Then you must expect to suffer. Physical pain. Prison. Loneliness. Bitterness. Envy. Hate. All of that is suffering. But not death. Death is the *end* of suffering. In death you are a baby again, back in the arms of *tu madre*. Back in the bosom of love, eh?"

He points down to one. Then the other.

"Too good for you. And too good for you. You are not ready. You cannot go *around* the suffering. A bullet to the heart? No, no. Death without love is failure. A waste. You must *feel* your way *through* the suffering. Experience it. Wade through the middle of the swamp. You must *earn* your death. You see? *Eh?* You must find the love. You must find the joy. When you can find love from the depth of your own suffering? When you can sing sweetly from the bottom of the well? Then you are back home, *mi amigos*. But no one will come to save you. No one. Certainly not me. Or Enrique." He laughs at the idea. Shakes his head. "No, you must save yourselves. So. As I say. We aim for the knees."

Sheldon spits. Speaks.

"Can I... will you cut us free? Is your friend coming back? Can you get us... out? Back to Corbin?"

The man shrugs.

"*Sí.* I can cut you free. But I cannot take you. You must wait I am afraid. Who has a phone?"

Olivia sees her phone, wet, abandoned, somewhere beneath Manny Soto's truck. She shakes her head. Looks at Sheldon. He is shaking his head too.

The man turns and looks down at the knotted snakes, twisting in the dirt.

"*Teléfono,*" he says.

Nothing but moans and grimaces. He places the toe of his boot gently on Nicholas' shattered knee. Screaming.

The man again, calmly.

"*Teléfono.*"

Nicholas contorts. Plunges his unbound hand down into his pants pocket. Tosses up the phone. The man opens it. Nods approvingly.

"*Sí.* Three bars. Even here."

He slips the phone in his back pocket. Trades it for the knife, which he unfolds with a click. Sheldon is first. Ankles, wrists. Groans of relief.

Then Olivia. He stands her up. Kicks at the gun mashed into the dirt. She sees him, feels him, take in the wreckage of her face, working his way back in time. Excavating layer by layer. Nicholas' blood. The bruising and clotting from Manny Soto's fist. Older than that, the scars cut by the blue metal of a broken car. Older than that, isolation. Distrust. Older than that, predation. Abandonment. The dry, ancient seabed of a face. All of this he sees. Somehow understands. He nods.

"They each have one good knee left," he says softly. "They will behave, I think."

Olivia looks at him. Sees him for the first time. He is beautiful. Gleaming. Clear brown eyes. Skin, teeth, eyebrows, lips. Like someone imagined more than real. She looks down at the gun. And then over at the Falcon.

745

He reads her mind. Smiles. Covers the gun with his boot. Shakes his head. Olivia sputters.

"So… then… you're just… you're gonna steal my car and leave us out here?"

He laughs.

"I am not stealing your car. *¿Cómo te llamas, chica?*"

"Olivia. Olivia DeLuna."

"I am not stealing your car, Olivia DeLuna. No, no. *Es mi carro.*"

"What?"

Jesús Batista thumps himself proudly in the chest with both hands.

"*Sí. Mi ranfla.* That is *my* car. Olivia DeLuna.*"

He smiles simply. Watches her. Waits.

"I don't… I don't…"

"Is no difficult." He shrugs dramatically. Shakes his head. "I have been away. I have come back. I see some old friends and we go to the festival. Like always. Every year, the Moon Garden Festival. Then *Dia de los Muertos*. Every year. And this year they are on the same day! I would not miss it!"

He can see there is too much enthusiasm in his voice. Can see the confusion. Lets the smile fade. Wrinkles the smooth skin of his brow. Serious now. Starts again.

"I am in Toluca. Working for my uncle. And *mi madre* comes to me when I am sleeping. In a dream, you see? She says to me *Jesús, it is time to go back now. Time to see your baby girl so she does not forget you.* So the next day I call my friends. Start working my way back. It took time, but I am here. As you see.*"

He spreads his arms for inspection, in case she has not yet seen him standing before her.

"And then? Tonight? I am riding past the church on the back of Enrique's bad ass Harley Davidson and I look up and there is my car. *¡Mi coche!* I cannot believe it. I love that car!"

He looks from one bloody face to the other. Waiting for something that never comes.

New movement from the snakes. Writhing. Sounds. He looks briefly. Looks back. Continues.

"We sit for an hour waiting to see who comes. Enrique tells me to just steal the car but I tell him I am not going to risk prison and deportation all over again for stealing my own car. *Puedo ser pobre, pero no soy estúpida. Eh?* And besides, how do I know who is driving my car? Maybe some nice little old lady who needs it. *Algunos abuelita.* Yes? So we wait. We wait. And guess who shows up? Eh?"

He looks at her with his endless eyes. Olivia. Then to Sheldon. Back again.

"*You* do." He nods his head toward the men in the dirt. "*They* do. They put *your* asses in the trunk of *my* car. And I say to Enrique, well… what else, eh? *Sigue ese coche.* And so he does. We follow that car all the way. See them leave the road and so we stop. Cut the light. Cut the engine. Push Enrique's bike out into the desert for maybe a quarter mile. We are so quiet. Then Enrique says we should split up. He goes one way and I keep pushing his bike another way. *Aim for the knees*, I tell Enrique. He did, too. We both did. No life without suffering. Not for these two. They are not yet ready for death, eh?"

Jesús bends. Picks up the gun. Wraps the handle in the fabric of his shirt. Ejects the clip down into the dirt. Pulls the phone from his pocket. Wipes it clean. Hands it to her. Points south.

"That is I-67. *Cuatro millas. Cinco.*" Points east. "A mile that way is *Rancho Rio Road*. When they come?" He swings his pointing arm a couple of degree south. "Maybe about half-way between here and *Rancho Rio?* There is a body. A woman. She is not suffering. Not any more. I am thinking this is where they come to do their dirty business, eh?"

Jesús Batista reaches out. Squeezes Olivia's shoulder. Smiles. Sweet. Wistful. Wise. Walks away.

When the Ford Falcon roars to life, all they can do is stand and stare. He keeps the lights off. Drives it in a long, slow arc through the scrub until it sits idling about where the Harley had been. He reaches through the window. Hands Sheldon the empty gun.

"*Pendejos* have ripped Christ from my dashboard." Big, mirthful smile. "As though God can be tossed out of a window. As though God is not the entire car. The road. The dirt under the road. The air in the lungs of the driver. The lungs. The driver. Everything. There are no differences. There are no borders to separate this from that. Here from there. It is all one thing. Perhaps they will learn. Perhaps not."

He reaches into the passenger seat. Hands Sheldon the open *Cavaliers* backpack.

"*Es mucha de dinero, mi amigo,*" he says with a smile. "Spend it wisely, yes?"

And then he is gone.

There is nothing to lean on. They do not want to lie down in the dirt. Like they are dead. Like the poor, unknown woman lying out there in the dark, waiting to be found. Waiting for a name.

They want to be upright to keep eyes on the knotted snakes, writhing and moaning fifty feet away. So they can't lie down on their backs. But they hurt too much to stand.

So they sit, leaning up against each other. Back to back. Sticky. Smelling of blood. Waiting. Talking. Trying to make sense of it all until they can't talk about it any more and they have to talk about something else.

Their words are vibrations, body to body, up one spine and down the other. Her ears still ring from the gunshot that hobbled Nicholas Voss. No matter. Everything is vibration. Her entire body hears now.

The gun, reassembled, sits on top of the *Cavaliers* backpack next to Nicholas Voss' phone. Just in case.

She marvels at what Sheldon has said. Laughs a little.

"I had no idea that song was *yours*. I remember that one. *Break It to Me Slowly*? Damn, Sheldon. Really? That got some play. And *Just a Half-Pint More*, too? You're like the real deal, man."

Sheldon is quiet. She can feel him nod. Can feel him wait.

"Maybe you can play them for me sometime."

"I'd like that," he says.

Silence, awkward and stubborn. It does not want to leave.

"I can play piano a little," she says finally. Her heart pounds in her chest. Like she has jumped from a cliff, down into deep water. But his confession deserves her own. "I can kinda sing. A little."

Sheldon laughs. "You don't say. Well, Olivia DeLuna... now why didn't I suspect that all along? You've got it in your bones, kid. Should'a known."

"Maybe we could duet," she says.

"Believe me. You don't want my voice messin' things up."

"Come on, now. Can't be that bad."

"Oh yes it can."

She sings. It comes without thinking. Just above a whisper.

"*Them that's got... shall have...*"

She waits. Stillness at her back. A catch of breath.

Stillness out in the dim desert where the knotted snakes hold their moans for a second. Listening. Trying to understand. Waiting.

She tries again. "*Them that's got...*" Elbows him in the back. "*... shall have.*" He clears his throat.

"*Them that's not... shall lose.*"

He was right. He is not a singer. Not without a guitar on his leg to keep him in tune. Doesn't matter.

Olivia –broken, cut, scarred, beaten, strangled, suffocated –falls in behind. Strong, clear, clean. Voice, soaring out over the desert, that old, abandoned seabed. The sound is something inexplicable. Something beautiful. Something enormous and pure, swimming out and away only because it can. Devouring stars.

Whatever mama has, whatever papa has, blessed be that child. So it says in the Bible. Olivia sings it like the blues it has always been. Because that blessed child first has to come through nothing, has to come through heartache and abandonment before she can know the fortune buried deep in her emptiness.

Olivia closes her eyes, opens her throat and sings. Sings like the sound inside of her is the only truth left in the desert. The sound of forgotten water, still flowing deep and clear.

He has stopped singing. He is quiet. Not even breathing. It is all her now. Soft, now, like moonlight through clouds of ocean sediment.

It is the only thing out there with them. That sound. That tuned vibration. Nothing else. It subsumes everything. Even them.

"My God," he says when she is done and the sound is gone.

Like that's all he can think of to say. Like that's all that's left.

The moon is fully up now. The desert stretches out around them in all directions a pale, watery blue. A breeze surges and dies away. Surges again. Dies away. A ghost tide as the world rolls heavily across midnight on *el Día de los Muertos*. They are quiet for a long time.

She thinks of the horn. Again. The sound that should not have been possible, exploding out of Manny Soto's truck into a black, airborne ocean. Pain and triumph and vengeance and hope and regret and despair and sorrow and hate.

And love. When you put it all together. One sound. Just love.

It's in everything, she thinks. That sound. A kind of song. In everything. Pierce the fabric in just the right way? Cut the skin of the universe? Out it comes. Always there, that song. That vibration. Around us. In us. Of us.

The backbeat. The vibration of existence.

It's not a song we hear. Not a vibration we feel.

We *are* that vibration. We *are* that song.

We live in four-four time.

Jesús Batista. His voice, still here in the desert. *When you can sing sweetly from the bottom of the well? Then you are back home.*

Her own voice. From someplace deeper than she can name. *Let's make this about the blues. Let's share that.*

Silence. Music. Something swimming.

"I'm sorry," she says at last. "For all of this."

Sheldon sighs.

"Don't be. Not your fault."

"What Nicki said? About the letter? To what's his name? Gregor something? Rattin' you out? That sure sounds like Libby. Prob'ly meant well. But she'd do somethin' like that." She gestures off toward the bodies in the dirt, moaning, rolling back and forth against the pain. "I'm guessin' that's what brought all of this here to Corbin."

Sheldon twists sideways. They are shoulder to shoulder.

"When I first saw you, Olivia, it was like… it was like seein' a ghost. Standing up on those stairs. Looking down at me. I don't know how to else to put it. I was eighteen all over again."

"I think I should remind you, Shel, that when you saw me for the first time you were stoned out of your ever-lovin' mind."

"Doesn't matter. I was stone-cold sober the next day and you were still in my head. And you never left. Can't explain it, but I just couldn't get enough of you. All the anger was just an excuse to keep seeing you. To keep throwing myself in your path. Then I practically drove myself *into* your path. Nearly killed you. I'm the one that owes the apology. Forever, I think."

Silence. Another spectral tide.

"So… what ghost? That first night. On the stairs."

"A girl. Never forget your first, I guess."

A beat.

Two. Three. He shakes his head.

"She was somethin' else, boy. And then all those decades later, there you were. In that same house. At the top of those same stairs. *Mmm-Mmm.* I told you I used to work for the man who lived in that house. Libby's house. Your house."

"Not any more," she says. "Nothin' but a pile of ashes in front of an orchard now."

"We'll find you something, Olivia. Libby too," he says. "It'll work out."

Silence. Just the moon. One of the white lights in the distance turns off of I-67. Rolls north. Another follows. There are lights on top of those lights. Red and blue.

"Cale Hargrove. Cale and his kid, Raimey. Always in trouble with the law. Raimey kept the sheriff busier than a one-armed paperhanger. Kid was always getting locked up for something. I was the son to Cale that Raimey refused to be. I used to harvest the pecans in Libby's orchard. Cale's orchard, I mean. I stayed there sometimes when Cale was gone, usually out someplace cleaning up after Raimey. I brought Rose out there a couple of times. She'd stay over and we'd have the run of the place."

His body moves in a slow, soft laugh.

"That was somethin' else. When I think of bein' young and bein' in love and havin' my whole life in front of me? I think of her. And then… well, you just kinda brought her to life there for a second. Don't even really know why, either."

"Didn't work out between you two, I guess?"

"First loves never do. Not supposed to. Supposed to make everything that comes later pale by comparison." He shakes his head. "It was intense, but not very realistic. That one was doomed from the beginning."

"Why?"

"Lots of reasons, I guess. I was a white boy, for one thing. And she got, like, big. *Real* big. Too big for me."

The desert brightens unevenly in the bouncing sweep of approaching headlights. No sirens. There is no one out here to get out of the way. Sheldon grabs the phone. Stands. Reaches down.

"Leave the gun," he says. "Let's not get shot."

He pulls her to her feet. They raise their hands in the air up over their heads. Waiting for the phone to ring. Waiting for sheriff's dispatch to call and share the obvious. Waiting for the harsh lights and bursting static. Olivia folds one of her hands over one of his. Together their arms make a big *W* in the air. She looks over at him. Speaks.

"She got big? What, you mean like... *fat* big?"

"No, no," Sheldon says. "I mean, like, *famous* big."

Chapter 89
Dallas and Etta

Can't sleep, Pablo. This lump in my brain is restless. Tumor keeps punching the walls like it wants the fuck out.

I'd let it out if I could. Can't really say that I want to die. That I'm done with the world even if it is more than likely done with me. Still got my garden. Who's going to look after my little babies? What about you, Pablo? Now that you and *Papi's* are about to part ways, maybe you'd be looking to fill some time tending garden. I suppose you want to spend your new time with your own family. Just a thought.

Anyway, it's the middle of the night and I'm up writing on this letter instead of in my bed staring up at the ceiling and listening to rain. Can't believe they going to put on that damn festival in a downpour. I hope you have better sense than to go. We're too old to get that kinda wet, Pablo.

Me and Dixianne Draper got through almost a whole pizza before either of us got up the guts to really start talking about Ronni and Etta. Her mother and my daughter. Guess we were both afraid to get into it for our own reasons so we spent our time reminiscing like it was just yesterday that her and Etta were scrabbling around in the dirt after those chickens. Eventually, I ask her how her mother is and Dixie looks at me with her big blue eyes and tells me that Ronni been dead for near twenty years. *Twenty years!* The news hit me in the center of my chest like a fist. I wanted to ask her what happened but I held myself together because I could see in Dixie's face that it was all coming out. And it did, too.

Ronni Brill's life came to a stop at the business end of a pipe, swung by her boyfriend Kelsey. They were living in Little Rock, which is where they lived before Ronni escaped with Dixie to Corbin. Kelsey tracked her down, just like

Ronni was always afraid he would. *Kelsey Brattle*. How I wished I'd known that last name. Maybe I could have found him back when I had the FBI looking. Useless fuck of a person. He's still serving life in prison someplace. Florida I think. Dixie spent the last part of her childhood in foster care then got herself the fuck out of Little Rock, met her man, moved to Chicago, had her a couple of babies and when I bumped into her at the *Windy City Liquors* she was working for a bank. Wanted to be an accountant if you can believe that. Little Dixie knows her numbers. No doubt from counting all them chickens.

So when Dixie gets to the part about being put in foster care and then keeps going on about her own life I stop her in mid-sentence and ask her what the fuck did they do with Etta. And do you know that Dixie looked at me like I had just turned into a goat? Looked at me hard, and her face said, *'Rosetta what in the hell?'*

Turns out the last time she saw Etta, Dixie was in the back seat of Kelsey's car crying and screaming through the back window because she didn't want to leave Etta behind. Ronni was in the front seat crying and screaming out the front window for the same reason. Dixie said that Ronni really *did* think of Etta as her own daughter. But Kelsey Brattle was having none of that shit. He was not spending one redneck cent to feed someone else's mexiblack child.

Kelsey's idea of a good time was to just leave Etta at the *Santiago Chicken Ranch* but Ronni convinced him to leave her with her preacher friend. Her hope was that a man of God would be able to talk some sense into Kelsey. She thought if he heard it from a preacher Kelsey might agree to be on his way and just leave them all be, or if he was hell bent on taking her and Dixie away then at least take Etta too and keep them all together. Fat chance of that. Dixie said Kelsey barely slowed the car down. Left Etta and the preacher and the preacher's wife in the dust. Dixie said Ronni went at Kelsey with everything she had in the front seat, but she was just a little bitty thing. Kelsey could beat Ronni up and drive the car back to Little Rock at the same time.

But Ronni fought for Etta like she was her own. I owe her memory at least that much, Pablo. Ronni loved Etta for real. She was a mother to her. A *real* mother too. Beginning to end.

They never saw Etta again. Dixie said Ronni tried to call me but by that time I was back from Europe rolling across the country in my shiny almost-new bus. A month or two later and Ronni was dead, Kelsey was locked up and Dixie was in the system. Dixie said she always assumed that Ronni had reached me and that I had come back to Corbin and picked up Etta at the church. She'd see me on TV or hear me on the radio and imagine that Etta was happy and spending her time by some swimming pool, living the rich life with a celebrity mama who loved her while Dixie was being raised by strangers.

Makes me want to cry as I write those words, Pablo. Thinking how Dixie must have felt and how terribly wrong she was. How terribly wrong I was. Etta was in Corbin the whole time, raised by strangers. I replay in my head everything my own daughter must have thought of me when *she* saw me on the TV. When *she* heard me on the radio. I replay all of those thoughts of hers on a loop in my brain. Doctors don't know one fuck about tumors.

That talk with Dixie near destroyed me, Pablo. I spent a year trying to kill the pain the best way I knew how. Mr. Flake showed up again, this time with all his pretty little pill friends. I was not a young woman any more and the shit near ended my sorry life. Maybe that was what I was hoping. I was hospitalized twice to pump my stomach. I had a few friends that came to the rescue. They cleaned me up. Put me in rehab prison. Only difference between rehab prison and real prison is that in rehab prison you don't need cellmates who want to kill you because you want to do that shit for yourself. Near every day, too. Could not tell you at the end of any day whether I had another day in me. Bessie Smith liked to say *"It's a long old road, but I know I'm gonna find the end."* Well I spent many a night thinking I'd found it.

When I got out I was sober but broken. I didn't want anything to do with anyone. I hated everything and everyone in my wreck of a life. I sold my house and moved back to Corbin. Started drinking again.

I can hear you, Pablo, from all the way out here in the desert. I can hear. *Why the hell did you move back to Corbin, Texas?* Don't know how to answer that question except to say that Corbin is where I should've been the whole time. I should've been wherever Etta was because I was Etta's mother. I say *'was'*. Ever since rehab I have forced myself to understand that I have forfeited any right to that title. *Mother.* I have done that child wrong just like my mama told me I would. Too late now for me to ever, ever, *ever* even pretend to be her mother. That is no longer my right.

But here I am in Corbin anyway. Going on near four years now. I come back from Chicago and start all over again asking my questions. After talking to Dixie, it was easy to pick up the trail this time. Preacher was long gone but the *Chacha* had some articles to tell me what happened. The *Chacha* did not exactly make any accusations, but I could see Etta's fingerprints all over what happened out there. She was one angry little girl. And for good reason too. No need to tell you. You get the news. And I know you have been in contact with Etta. So you already know everything she wants you to know about that night. That's her story, not mine. But I will say this: that lying preacher Garvin Cross is lucky he was gone by the time I came back because I would have pulled his lying heart right out of his chest.

I thought about tracking her down. Would have been easy enough from those articles. But I stopped myself. I had no right to track her down. I had no right to pop up out of the blue —*Mama's back!* No. I promised myself and my own dead mother that I would leave Etta be. I promised that...

Fuck. And there it is, Pablo. In *ink.* You see? You see how lying comes so easy to me that I don't even know when I'm doing it? Here I am explaining to you about keeping some bullshit promise to me and mama. Like I'm some noble person! Truth is I wanted to find Etta more than anything in the world. And I would have too. But I hated myself too much and I was too afraid to take the face-to-face hating I had coming. Truth is I am a coward who does not deserve to look her own daughter in the face. There's the truth.

No way I am sending this to you now. Least I wrote it down. Least I can read it for myself before I drown in shame.

My long success at not being any kind of mother has left me with plenty of money. I used a little bit of that money to purchase a fuckload of desert land off I-67. Built me a modest little house with a big stone wall around it. Had some contractors haul out about a bazillion tons of sand and replace it with a bazillion tons of Grade-A topsoil and fertilizer. I couldn't sing and I couldn't mother and I couldn't stop drinking and I couldn't face my demons, but ever since Hammy give me that little olive tree in Stuttgart I knew I could grow things. So I set to gardening and talking and singing the blues to my little green babies.

Near three-quarters a mile out into the desert from where I built my house is the place Etta used to live after Ronni and Dixie and Kelsey left Corbin in a cloud of dust. I can't see it from my garden wall, but I can feel it out there in the dark. I own all that land now. I walk out there every now and then. Just me and Dr. Johnny. Just to look at the place and remind myself of what I have done. Etta living out there was the last time it would have been halfway fair for me to come back and put her in the car and take her home and be her mother. But I didn't, did I Pablo? No, I didn't.

Ever since the dust from Kelsey Brattle's tires settled back to the ground, Etta has been making it on her own in the world. So I bought all of that dust. I own it. I own the land Etta walked around on the last time she was my child. Like that is where my daughter is buried. The house is all burnt to hell, but the ark is still in one piece. Just like the *Chacha* showed it. Still standing after all these years. I go up there every so often and walk around in the rubble of that burned, busted up house. Look for signs of the daughter I used to have.

That summer when Etta and I were up your way near every night at *Mother Blues*, like we were our own little family, I gave Etta these little cactus people that my mama had given me when I was about ten. I loved those little dolls. No pricklies in them. They were all smooth and worn. Called them my little cactus babies. Then I started keeping time with Corny Roop and everything started to change. Never looked at the cactus people much after that. I kept them tucked away in the dark. But every time I found them I couldn't throw them out. Don't ask me why. Paint was all faded and the little cactus dog had a sloppy glued on ear. Lord knows it's not like I have a lot of warm fuzzy feelings for my mama. But I couldn't throw them out. I kept them wrapped up in a shoe shine cloth inside a little silver cigar box that Otis had stolen from someone along the way. And that summer after I left Otis I found them all over again at the bottom of a bag of clothes. I decided to give them to Etta. And she loved them just like I had. You probably remember her setting them up once or twice on the table at the club. Lining them up next to her Shirley Temple like they were all watching me sing.

And in a strange way, Pablo, having those little cactus people lined up on the table like that, it was like my own mama was there listening to me sing, through their little glued on ears. Sitting in *Mother Blues*. Proud of her baby.

Sometimes me and Dr. Johnny walk up to that burnt up wreck of a house in the middle of the night and I imagine that silver cigar box buried somewhere down in the middle of the rubble. Abandoned. Like I abandoned Etta and she abandoned me. And when I'm really hooched off my ass and can't walk back to my own house until I sober up, I sit out there in the dirt and imagine that the box ain't there under the rubble. I imagine it's gone because Etta took it with her. I imagine Etta couldn't leave her cactus people behind, just like I couldn't leave them behind. And sometimes when I'm that way I fall back in the dirt and look up at the stars and I can feel just a little bit happy that she still keeps something of me with her.

I know she is still here, Pablo. Somewhere around Corbin. Or San Angelo. God knows why. But she stays the hell away from me and there is no mystery about that. Since I've been back I have had only two signs of her. Was not long after I got back that word got around. I had to become a crazy bitch in the desert to keep people the fuck away from me. But eventually it all settled down and people stayed away and I could count on being alone.

But then about a year after that there was a week or two when I could tell there was someone out in the dark, on the other side of the wall. Watching me. Couldn't see anything and I didn't try either. I just sat real still in my chair and listened. And I could tell it was Etta. Don't ask me how. Even bad mothers have their instincts. It was Etta. I'm sure of it. One of those nights I walked out into the garden, all casual about it even though I was shaking like a damn leaf. I started digging in the dirt and singing songs just like I did when Etta and me were driving back to Corbin from a night with you at *Mother Blues* and Etta had her head on my leg and the desert air was pouring in the window and I was stroking her hair. So there I am digging in the dirt singing *God Bless the Child* and I can feel her out there on the other side of that wall in the dark listening. Just like we were back in that car. Just like we were back at *Mother's*. And then at some point I could tell she was gone.

The other sign of Etta came in the damned *Chacha* again if you can believe it. Some jackass ran her off *Silo Road* and she nearly burnt up. She nearly died, Pablo. I know you know all of this. You know more than I do I'm sure. First thing come to my mind were those mama dreams in prison. Etta screaming on fire. Etta burning inside a cage. Etta all sliced up and bleeding. Like mama knew everything that was going to happen to Etta from the very beginning. Like it wasn't five babies in the dream, it was one baby. All just Etta. After I read that article I went to San Angelo, telling myself that my place was at the foot of her hospital bed. But the nurse would not let me in without knowing who the hell I was. I wanted to tell her that goddamnit I was Etta's one and only mother and that she needed me. I wanted to. I almost did. But those words would not come out of my mouth, Pablo. I did not feel worthy of those words. The only words that made it past my lips were that I was her friend. *A friend!* Some friend I am. The cowardly kind I suppose. The kind of friend afraid to be told to get the fuck out of a hospital room. The nurse looked at me and said Etta was not well enough to receive visitors and that I should come back another time. I never went back. Because that's the kind of friend I am, Pablo.

But now get this. I mentioned the good-looking writer kid I got up here tearing down that old house. He shows up on his motorcycle applying for the job and tells me his name. Goddamned if he ain't the very person who pulled Etta from the flames of that car accident. Think about that, Pablo. The man who saved

Etta's life, is suddenly at my house asking for the job of tearing down the place Etta used to live. Now that is just God fucking with my already fucked up head. Or he's poking me in my tumor saying, *'Rosetta, you need to pay attention'*. I didn't tell the kid anything, but I sure hired his ass on the spot. I call him *Hero* and he hates that.

Reminds me that I had a dream about him last night. Me and Hero sitting in a blue bathtub in the middle of Texas nowhere. Trying the get the water out as we sink into the sand. He's bailing with a little hollow whale and I'm bailing with a little silver box. But they won't hold the water and we just keep sinking. Don't you try to make any sense of it, Pablo. You'll hurt yourself. Leave it to the professionals. Dr. Johnny's the only one who can explain that one.

Hero keeps after me to tell him my story. Wants to write it down for other people. Well fuck that. Been writing it down my own self. Just for me. Or maybe for you too. *Padre Pablo*. Still thinking on that one.

I still don't know what you're going to do with yourself after *Papi's*. After *Mother Blues*. Something that makes you happy, I hope. You're a good man, Pablo. Best man I know. Etta always wished you were her daddy. I have always wished that too. I'd have been a better mother if you were her daddy. At least it wasn't Otis DeLuna. Lord have mercy. She'd be ugly as sin for one thing. And she'd have his badness in her veins. Truth is I barely knew her father. I was young and stupid and working my way through just about every able bodied man who had the blues in his blood. A few wild nights at the place he worked. A night on a boat under the stars. And then he was gone with all the rest of them.

All of them but you, Pablo. You have never been gone from me. You are the deepest, bluest note in my song. You are the ocean buried in the desert of my heart.

I decided that if I send you this letter, it will be after I have passed. I don't want you thinking this is all about me needing company or forgiveness or some other shit you may or may not want to give. And I don't want the disappointment of sending this out and then you not coming. I don't want to go out that way. Waiting at the window, shriveled and old and drunk. When I am alone, no one around to show me otherwise, I am better than that. Younger. Softer. And I can still sing and you are still out there in the dark listening. That's how I want it to be.

And if I do send you this letter, and if you ever see Etta, then I guess you can tell her whatever you think is best about what you have read. I trust you more than I trust myself when it comes to Etta.

I have tried to be honest, Pablo. Bless your sweet soul.

Your Friend, *Rosetta Letti*

Chapter 90

Thumb to porcelain. Tracing as he listens. One letter to the next. Forward. Backward. Again. *C.B.S.*

He lifts the mug. Tips. Still empty.

Desmond pretends to drink anyway. Too many people in the room. Too many still making up their minds about who he is and why he is here. Wouldn't want them to think he can't tell the difference between full and empty.

Rick Stoddard has slipped back into his relaxed, shit-shooting rhythm. He is no longer briefing. He's telling a story. He's holding court in the corner conference room thirty-eight floors above Manhattan like he's back in the bullpen at the *Chacha*. Like he's the only one wearing a tie, but with his sleeves rolled up because he works too hard to risk encumbering his wrists. Like he's back to embellishing the commonplace into something hard to believe. Something incredible. Something that you might not otherwise accept were it not the *Chacha's* own barrel-chested, chisel-chinned Rick Stoddard assuring you that every bit of it was true.

Rapt attention from every direction. Several at the table are taking notes. More than one of the women in the room, Desmond bets, has either already had sex with Rick Stoddard —the family man with a four-year old daughter —or is actively distracted by the possibility.

"So, basically, what we found was the Russian mob pretending to buy thousands of acres of South Texas desert and then pretending to sell that same land back to itself over and over and over again."

He remembers Rick's last day at the *Chacha*. One arm draped over the empty water cooler and telling anyone within earshot about a car accident on a spur off of I-67. One driver pulls another driver out of a burning car by the wrists. Car explodes seconds later. Miraculously, Rick pulls up on the scene just in time to watch it all happen. Dodges shrapnel. Calls the ambulance. Tends to the victim. He tore a pant leg. *See?* Her blood is on his shirt. *See? It was like a war zone.*

That was always the irony about Rick as an investigative reporter. He doesn't find the story. The story finds him. Fucks him with the lights on. Shares a cigarette.

"I give 'em some credit for ambition," says Rick. "They took a simple scam and aimed for the goddamned moon. They got as far as they did because it was so audacious. It makes hacking into a presidential election look like a lark."

His hands fly apart like this is a story about fishing.

"But still, I think no one was asking any questions because the scope of the scam was so damn big. We tend to be suspicious of the little stuff. Right? Did they over-charge me for my oil change? If I buy this sex toy off the Internet, am I handing my credit card over to identity thieves? We're getting savvy to that kind of threat. But the more audacious the con, the more vulnerable we are. Our guard actually drops."

Byron Winter, head of the table, clears his throat. Scratches his beard. Reaches into a wooden bowl of salted peanuts like he is at a bar. His face is weathered and sun damaged. Fawn brown hair to just below the collar of his midnight blue suit coat. No tie. Open collar white dress shirt. He is, Desmond concludes, the aging hippie now leading corporate minions in the network news business. Selling out one expensive blue suit at a time.

Not that Desmond was anyone to judge on that score. He'd sold out decades ago, and for low-grade poplin.

Byron had opened the meeting. Introduced Rick with a flourish of motivation. "*I smell a Peabody, people. I smell a Murrow. Lot of work ahead. There is a lot of paper on the way. But I assure you, this one's going on the CBS mantle.*" Not a word since. But now he tosses a couple of nuts into the beard. Chews in soft crunches. Speaks.

"Rick, anything with this much paper behind it cannot be called a *simple scam*. This was as sophisticated as it gets. And it was aimed at ... well... it was aimed at *Texas*, which doesn't strike me as particularly fair."

Laughter around the table at the expense of the Lone Star State.

"No offense, Rick," says Byron.

"Hey, I was born in Sacramento," says Rick. "You're all good, boss."

Bryon laughs. Looks down the table at Desmond. "Dez?"

All heads turn. Wait.

Desmond looks across the enormous polished table. Over shoulders. Through the corner windows and out into the morning. To the west, the Hudson slides from grey to blue carrying the sun in brilliant bits of glass. To the north, Central Park foams baby leaf green from its stone grey terrarium. It is an alien palette. Unsettling.

"Santa Fe," he says, looking back at Byron. Smiles. "Nothing but sophistication on my end."

"Fine, fine," says Byron, grabbing another handful of nuts. "I'm in the clear then. But seriously, this thing was a complicated, multi-layered…"

Rick reasserts himself. His show. His attention.

"Complicated in the execution, maybe. But the heart of the whole thing was really pretty simple." Rick holds up one finger. "Pretend to purchase a parcel of land." Two fingers. "Then pretend to sell it off again for more than you originally pretended to pay for it." Three. "Repeat. Repeat. Repeat. Okay? Dozens of parcels. Hundreds phony sales. And it all only exists on paper. No realtor signs. No moving trucks. No wrecking crews. Hell, most of it is just empty desert anyway. All that ever mattered was the paperwork documenting bullshit sales."

He unclips the memo in front of him. Holds two pieces of paper end-to-end. Marches them through the air.

"Because when you lay all that of paperwork out end-to-end it forms a clear path stretching from the New Mexico border directly to Corbin, Texas. Do people understand what that means? Of course they do. Because people have been hearing for years –here and there, gossip, newspaper articles, investment advisories, environmental protests –that there is a move afoot to divert some of the Pecos River. There is a push to green up the desert. To make a new Eden. A destination river walk. Just like in San Antonio only bigger. Better. Big commerce. Big tourism. At least by South Texas standards."

Byron Winter nods. Chews. Crosses his arms. The Hudson River flowing in the distance behind him is doing its part to make the point. Rick puts the papers down. Continues.

"And forget about the river walk as a finished destination product for a second. Just consider it as a construction project. That's a river of new money, new jobs, new investment all by itself. That desert is greening up with money before the first drop of water ever leaves the Pecos. And who doesn't want that? Who doesn't stand to benefit from that?"

"The Pecos Bluntnose Shiner," says the woman taking notes on a large computer tablet. She is camera ready and younger than Desmond's shoelaces.

"Right," says Rick. "The shiners. Little silver fish good for some big free publicity. Let's stir up the whole *ecosystem versus shit-loads of money* debate. No way the Bluntnose Shiner is ever going to win that fight. Not in Texas. Meanwhile, the controversy is like a flashing road sign: *Invest here! Look for the tree huggers! They're fighting the money. So then that's where the money is.*"

Rick puts his hands on his hips. His arms form parentheses around the exclamation point of his torso. He turns his back on the room to look out at Central Park. Turns back.

"So you've pretended to buy and sell. You've whispered in people's ears about a plan to green up the desert. Planted articles. Created a buzz. And then you sit back and let greed and self-interest run the scam for you. Because suddenly every sector of the economy wants a piece of this thing. Lending. Construction.

Utilities. Retail. Tourism. Government. Foreign investors looking for the next best place to park their money. Texas legislators want to make it their idea. Everyone wants to reserve a place at the trough and they are willing to pay good money to do it. Who wants to be left out wishing they too had forked over a guaranteed refundable deposit? Not *Niemen's*. Not *Saks*. Not *Apple*. So, if you are a self-respecting Russian mobster, what do you do?"

They all wait.

"You take the fucking money is what you do. Most of it you send back to Mother Russia. The remainder you reinvest in the scam. Money to make a phony corporation appear legitimate, well staffed, and successful. Money for advertising agencies and public relations firms. Money to purchase a second failing title company. Money for glossy project investment brochures in six different languages. Money to hire real lawyers to lobby state and federal legislatures and to help broker peace between Texas and New Mexico over a water-rights fight. Money under the table to politicians and regulatory agencies. Dollar by dollar, clearing the way for a massive undertaking that you will never actually undertake. Really? Never? Why?"

They all wait.

"Because all you want to do –all you *need* to do –is keep *talking* about it. Keep it in the news. Keep it buzzing. Self-interest is going to do all of the selling for you and the investment money is going to keep pouring in. And then? When the time is right? Before you actually have to do anything substantive to convince people that you are going to follow through on anything? Before you have to stick a single shovel in the dirt? You vanish into thin air. All of those refundable deposits, gone. You..."

Byron leans into the table. Grabs a small handful of peanuts from the bowl. Cuts him off.

"Okay. Let's just... Thanks Rick. I'm not interested in becoming a successful con artist. I'm interested in reporting the story. We're on borrowed time as it is and it's getting crowded out there. The *Post* and the *Times* certainly have *their* shovels in the dirt. But we're still out front on this. All of you are here because there is a flood of paper coming."

Rick, already missing the attention.

"Byron's Right. The corruption angle is going to be big. Texas legislators taking money. New Mexico too. And maybe their congressional delegations. Agency executives taking gifts. Army Corps of Engineers. EPA. Still sketchy right now but there is some potential for huge news. The Corbin Development Corporation and Quinco International were really spreading it around. If not actual cash and prizes, then promises to share in the coming bonanza. So we've now got a dozen or more FOIA requests all coming due at about the same time. There's going to be a couple hundred thousand pages for us to read and prioritize which is why we need some help. And the Justice Department is generating more leads for us, well, for everybody, every day."

Byron, chewing, looking slightly irritated. Impatient. He scratches his beard. Exhales through his nose. Speaks.

"Seems to me that the challenge here is telling a story that can't be told by any two-bit stringer following D.O.J. press releases. My sources are suggesting a new set of indictments will hit the headlines in the next few days. And then that will inevitably be the news focus for a cycle. But look, people, I don't want to *follow*. I want to *lead*. Are there bodies buried in this thing that the badges don't know about?" He resists looking up at Rick. Looks down the table. "Dez?"

Bodies buried. The phrase lands like something soft and heavy tossed down to his end of the table. Desmond looks up. Opens is mouth. Rick is having none of it.

"Well, hold on a second, Byron. I think you're giving the *badges* too much credit. We've gotten where we are on this thing with a lot of shoe leather. A lot of phone calls. A lot of documents. A lot of questions put to a lot of people who really did not want to answer questions. The FBI is doing its thing, as are the Attorneys General in Connecticut, New York and Texas. But the feds are still playing catch up to some top-shelf investigative journalism, none of which would have been possible without CBS throwing down for this story."

Rick pokes himself in the chest, but then refines the gesture to include everyone in the room.

"We were the ones who analyzed those property transfer records. We found the dead people supposedly buying and selling. The phony right-of-way conveyances. We were the ones who found that the Corbin Development Corporation was a sham subsidiary of a sham parent. *We* did that. *CBS News.* We were the ones who first connected Quinco International with the Russian mob. Why, I kept asking myself, would an international development company be renting empty glitzy office space in three different countries? Why, I asked myself, would an international development company use *Jones & Block* –a piss-ant criminal defense law firm in Connecticut –as its registered agent? Isn't it interesting, I asked myself, that attorney Block's actual name is Blokovich? And that his Connecticut law license had been suspended for withholding evidence in defending Vasily Dudnik in a fraud prosecution? Vasily's conviction back then, by the way, was for using a bogus real estate agency to falsify deeds to Connecticut lakefront properties and then selling and reselling what he never actually owned. Sound familiar?"

Heads are shaking slowly in amazement.

"Vasily made good use of his time in prison. They spent ten years putting this plan in place. It seems so obvious in retrospect, but none of it was obvious at the outset. None of it. This took some work to figure out. And *we* did all of that.

CBS News. Not the feds. And when Vasily is sprung from prison and shows up in Texas as Nicholas Voss working for the so-called Corbin Development Corporation? Guess who put that together? Because it sure as hell wasn't the feds."

"Laurie, that's who."

It is his own voice Desmond hears. Alien and sharp. Accusatory. As if from someone else. All heads turn.

"Laurie Weaver started putting most of this together before you had a fucking clue, Rick. Before CBS had a fucking clue. Before I had a fucking clue."

Silence.

"And Laurie's dead now. Vasily Dudnik… or Nicholas Voss or Chris Dawson or whatever the fuck you want to call him… took her out into the scrub and shot her in the face. And that was the capper of a long and brutal night. Laurie gave up her life for this story."

Silence. Someone clears a throat.

"They took two other people out to that same patch of desert. Beat the shit out of them and would surely have killed them had they not been interrupted. They burned down my newspaper. Two people trapped inside, cooked alive. They sent a man to kill one of our sources in her home just outside of Corbin. Burned her house down. Two people barely escaped *that* fire with their lives."

He wants to stop. Wants to leave. But the sound of him keeps coming.

"They purchased a security contract for the *Corbin Moon Garden Festival.* They did that for the calculated purpose of detonating a bomb that would kill and maim a whole lot of people. Two bombs, actually. One in the front row of the audience and another under their own security trailer. The objective…"

"Dez," says Rick from far away, "this isn't really the focus, man. I mean…"

"The objective was to eliminate a small handful of people. People who knew things. Or who *might* know things. They were killing a *lot* of people in order to kill a *few* people. The greater the carnage, the less likely it was to be about two or three individuals. The more likely it was to be about… fucking… what… *environmental terrorists* out to save a fish. They used a convenient boogieman that existed only as a figment of a Texas news media spoon-feeding from Russian misinformation."

The telegenic baby with the iPad makes a disbelieving noise. Speaks.

"You're saying the environmental concern was all a ploy? I find that…"

"No. The environmental concern was legitimate. Whatever its merits, the concern itself was legitimate. Half a dozen national and regional environmental non-profits and a bunch of college kids. Hand-made signs. Cardboard fish on sticks. All real. But the threat of environmental *terrorism*? That was a complete lie. That was meant to soften the ground. Help explain the carnage ahead of time. We were all so… *fucking* inured to Texan environmental politics. So hobbled by laziness. So in the tank for that damn river walk. No one bothered to question why the Corbin Development Corporation was suddenly so concerned about the possibility of sabotage by fish-hugging environmental do-gooders. So concerned that the CDC was willing to provide all of the security for the festival for free. A gift that the cash-strapped City of Corbin couldn't refuse."

He laughs to himself. Shakes his head.

"*We* were the fucking fish. The Texas media. We bit that hook hard. My paper too. Front page of the *Chacha*? The week before the festival?" He holds up his hands, framing an imaginary headline. "*Threat of Environmental Passions Calls for Tougher Security at Corbin Festival.*"

Desmond lowers one hand. Leaves the other hanging in the air. Confessing.

"I wrote that one. I did that." He lets the hand drop. "Vasily had his hand up my ass and was using me as a puppet before I even knew his name. Vasily Dudnik knew us better than we knew ourselves. He knew that after we had buried the dead, including anyone who could point a finger, the whole fucking state would rally around the river walk. We'd make it happen. We'd show those violent fish-loving bastards that no one will frighten Texas away from progress. No sir. *Our* goddamned desert. *Our* goddamned river. *Our* goddamned money. *Our* goddamned destiny. Don't mess with Texas."

Silence. Rick sighs. Looks to Byron to take control.

"But. Laurie Weaver. A tired reporter for a tired, nearly dead newspaper. She pulled a thread and just kept pulling. Because beneath all of that beat-down tiredness was an ocean of tenacity and fucking great instincts. Better than Rick. Better than me. I resisted her at almost every turn because I was protecting Cal Aronson's fucking bottom line. That's how short-sighted I was. And Rick," he gestures without looking. "Well. Rick's always got his eyes on the prize, doesn't he? At least he knows a good thing when it falls into his lap."

Silence. He looks down at his own hands against the polished wood. He is no longer talking to a room full of people.

"But Laurie." He shakes his head. "Shit-for-luck Laurie. She just had a nose for it. Like her ear for music. She liked the old, raw stuff. Lightnin' Hopkins. Little Walter. Bessie Smith. Robert Johnson. We shared records. Not digital files. Fucking twelve-inch vinyl. Old scotch and real goddamned thirty-three and a thirds. We'd be at her place or my place, listening to some old, scratched-to-hell record, laughing and telling lies and drinking, and Laurie'd shoot her hand up in the air and shut me up and close her eyes and whisper, '*Listen, Dez. Listen.*'"

Silence. Like now they are now all listening to Laurie.

"'*Listen to this riff.*' Or '*listen to this lyric.*' Or '*listen to him stick the knife in right at the end of this bridge.*' Or '*listen to her voice break around this last note. Hear it? Like it's a bone breaking? Or a heart breaking? Listen.*' And I would listen. And I'd look at her face. And it was like she was someplace else. Someplace true.

And I could hear what she could hear and she was always right. She could always find the dead-center heart of any song. She knew where to find water in the fuckin' desert."

Silence.

"Her great, great, great, great grandfather was John Calhoun Weaver. A riverboat captain who died scuttling confederate ships in the Battle of Memphis. Her father was a Mississippi prosecutor. Her mother was a Freedom Rider and a freelance journalist."

Silence.

"So Laurie had it in her blood. She wasn't afraid to fight. She knew how to dig. She knew how to write a lead. She protected her sources. To the death."

Silence. Rick Stoddard opens his mouth. Draws a breath to speak. Byron flicks at him with a hand. Speaks like it is just the two of them.

"Desmond. What's your point? What is it you think we're missing here?"

Desmond looks up from his hands.

Faces. Eyes.

He sighs. Rubs his own face. His own eyes.

"There is no point, Byron. I'm sorry. I just... Really. I haven't slept well. You all have a lot of work to do and I... This whole thing has just sort of... I guess it's all still a little personal." He looks up. Takes them all in. Too much. "Look, I'm gonna slip out for a little food-truck therapy. You folks keep at it."

He is up. Moving. Rick Stoddard seizes the reins, dividing people into teams, assigning issues. The conference room door closes, suffocating his voice.

Desmond navigates the corporate landscape of polished stone for the elevator. The ride down is like a protracted sigh of relief.

Across the street is a phalanx of silver trailers. He is too hungry to care. Shortest line wins. He orders a hotdog with everything and a Coke. Sits on a bench two hundred feet away that borders a large stone planter. A long, narrow rectangle of daffodils rises up behind him, a conflagration of green and yellow.

People. Traffic. Riots of sound and smell and rolling metal. The currents of 52nd Street Manhattan divert around him as he eats, elbows to knees. He is mostly oblivious. Still in his own head.

There is a spatter of old, dried catsup on the sidewalk.

He does not see catsup.

He sees the blood spider that keeps crawling through his dreams. Sees lipstick legs stretching out from beneath a towel hanging from the back of a broken bathroom door.

"Chris Dawson" = V.D.
6 ft. Blue eyes
Shlder length blond

Birthmark rt. arm
Spoke Russ on phone
Took keys phone notes comput purse
GOT GREEDY
SOS

He has never wanted those to be her last words to him. For three months now he has tried to substitute more personal exchanges. Something with her wry, throaty laugh. Something in person and intimate.

But he is stuck with these words. These were her last. *GOT GREEDY SOS.*

And while they are not laughing words or delivered in person, there *is* an intimacy to them. There is no escaping that they were meant for him.

Only for him.

There had been two splotches of lipstick before that second to last line on the door. Footprints made by the blood spider. Easily ignored. They meant nothing. That is, unless you had been deciphering Laurie Weaver's chicken scratch for a very long time. Reviewing her interview notes. Reviewing *her* marginalia written all over *your* marginalia. If you had done that year after year, then you knew that they were not just red splotches. Not spider footprints.

They were asterisks.

* * *GOT GREEDY. SOS*

Which he knew meant that Laurie had been changing subjects. It meant that what came next was something new. Something different. *Pay attention. New issue.*

That Laurie had decided to introduce this new issue on the back of a bathroom door in lipstick mere seconds before Vasily Dudnik kicked it in could only mean one thing.

It could only mean that Laurie knew she was going to die that night.

"Those things'll kill you, Dez."

Byron Winter towers next to him. One hand in his rich, blue pocket. The other jostles two peanuts into his mouth. He has shed his suit jacket. His sleeves are rolled up. Leather bracelet. Cheap plastic Timex. Everyman's working stiff reporter. The CBS monolith behind him is a black glass waterfall, emptying an ocean from space. He sits.

Desmond finishes the last bite of hotdog. Wads up the foil. Drinks. Nods.

"I know," he says. "Thought I'd trade in the nicotine for nitrates to mix it up a little. Healthy living exhausts me. So much to worry about. Death-by-hotdog ain't such a bad way to go."

Byron's turn to nod. He takes a long breath.

"You know… the news can be a callous business, Dez. We have to deconstruct everything before we put it all back together. We dehumanize before we humanize. Guess I don't have to tell you that." Byron looks at him directly. "I'm sorry about that up there. I'm sorry about your friend. Laurie."

They watch the traffic. Byron eats another nut. Desmond drops the foil ball into the empty soda cup.

"I was sleeping off a half a bottle of bourbon the night she died."

"And you think that makes you guilty of something?"

"Vasily Dudnik never came for me. I've been looking over my shoulder for a long time now. Ever since I learned what happened that night. Nobody has ever come looking for me."

Byron nods. Waits.

"It's not like Laurie didn't know where to find me. She knew exactly where I was. But nobody came looking. After they killed her, they burned the *Chacha* to the ground. The building I worked in every day. They were gettin' rid of evidence. Gettin' rid of people who knew things. That's what that night was all about for them. But they never came for me. I was only six fuckin' miles away. But no."

"Which means what, exactly?"

"Which means she never gave me up. Coroner says they made it hurt. Before they killed her they did what they could. She never gave them my name or where I lived. I'm not a tough man to find. Nobody in Corbin is hard to find. A little more time and they'd have found me and taken me out into the scrub too. Put a bullet in my head. But they didn't have more time. They ran out of time. Laurie ran out their clock."

Byron nods.

"I got two calls on my landline that night. I answered both calls. No one was on the other end. I just shrugged them off. Didn't give them another thought. They had her phone. They were going through her recent calls. So they knew I was home, they just didn't know where that was. Laurie was probably already dead by then. She never gave me up."

Byron thinks for a beat or two. Speaks.

"Does it really surprise you so much that she was protecting you? No one could have predicted this, Dez. Not her and not you."

A taxi stops at the corner in front of them to pick up a man pulling a rolling black bag and talking on a cellphone. It all takes too long and the light turns red. Desmond waits for the honking to stop.

"She loved to paint. She did these bizarre…" Hands in the air trying to help with the words. "Sort of… desert seascapes. Bright colors. Octopus on a stagecoach pulled by sea horses. Scorpion pirate ships. That kind of thing. Something kids would like. Completely at odds with the person Laurie showed to others. Even me. I never really experienced that person. Never drilled down deep enough to tap into any of that. The Laurie I knew was pretty damn tough.

Cynical. Beat down, you know? But it was down in there someplace. That humor. Tenderness."

Byron rakes his fingers through his hair. Leans back against the bench.

"I don't think we ever *really* know anybody. Mysteries and riddles bumping into each other. Getting married. Divorcing. We think we know, but we don't."

"She was dealt a shitty hand. Parents died young. She had a brother with issues. He eventually stepped off a bridge in Philly. She was married twice. The first husband beat on her a lot. Second one cheated on her eight days a week and donated most of her money to casinos. The rest of her money went to an ovarian cancer scare."

"Well. At least she had some friends."

"Yeah, she had some friends. Johnnie Walker was always a little too good of a friend. Captain Morgan. But they were loyal. Johnny and the Captain and the Marlboro Man. And all of her old, dead, true-blue musician friends."

"Jesus, Dez."

"No, Laurie and Jesus never really hit it off. No comfort there I'm afraid."

"Right. So you're saying for Laurie it was the work. That's what she had."

Desmond nods.

"It was the work. It was the fuckin' newspaper business."

"I take it she was good at what she did."

"Laurie could have been a brilliant investigative reporter. Tough to be brilliant working for a little South Texas desert shit rag that's been going out of business every day for the past twenty years. The *Chacha* never gave you much to work with. Not much inspiration out there. She kept coming to work anyway. Kept showing up. But what I realize…"

A courier skids abruptly three feet in front of them. Checks the phone strapped to his arm. Types. Pedals off. Byron gives a small laugh.

"Thought I was about to be served with process," he says.

"I'll just bet you make a lot of friends," says Desmond.

"You have no idea. Sorry. You were telling me what you realize."

"Right. What I realize now is that beneath that resentful, insubordinate, contemptuous attitude –always working for her next smoke break and seemingly not caring much about anyone or anything –Laurie was always payin' attention. Like she was listening and waiting. Listening and waiting. And I'll be goddamned if she didn't tap into the ocean right under our fucking feet."

Byron nods. Silence. Stillness.

Stillness. In the middle of so much noise.

"And when she found it, she came alive. Whenever we talked about this shit –the river walk, the property transfers, Vasily, the CDC, any of it –I had this sense of Laurie, half drunk in a smoky living room suddenly closing her eyes and shutting me up and whispering *Listen, Dez… Right there… That lyric…* Or *that note… That's the beating, broken heart of this song."*

"She'd found herself a story," says Byron.

"She'd found herself a real fuckin' story. A story for her tenacity. For her love of digging. For finding the beating, broken heart of things. And she made it her dying act. Bringing this story into the world was the last and only thing that mattered. Like she died in childbirth."

Desmond looks at Byron. Waits for their eyes to meet.

"So she didn't die for your fucking *Peabody*, Byron. Or your *Edward R. Murrow*. Or beating the *Times* or the *Post* or the Feds. It was never about that. She didn't die to protect me. She didn't die for her love of any person."

"I get it, Dez. You're saying she died for the story itself."

Desmond jerks a hand up toward the thirty-eighth floor.

"Well she sure as hell didn't die for Rick Stoddard's meteoric rise."

Byron nods. Chews.

"Rick's just hungry. We like 'em that way. He wants to be there when the shit is coming down so he can talk about it the next day. That's fine by us."

Traffic. People. A water delivery truck noses into a loading zone.

"How many times has he told you the exploding car story?" asks Desmond. Bryon smiles.

"Four. Five. Keeps getting better, too."

"I'll bet. You know the woman in that accident, over two years ago now, was the same woman that Vasily hauled out to the desert in the trunk of a car and nearly executed?"

"No shit?"

Desmond nods. "Olivia DeLuna."

"That is some seriously shitty luck," Byron says. Then he falls silent. Shakes his head in secret amusement.

"What."

"I don't know. Just funny. My mother was a newspaper editor in Philadelphia. 'Bout a billion years ago. I actually worked for her for a year before I moved to Chicago. And I was working on this cabby competition story that turned out to have a low-level, city hall corruption angle to it. The licensing was all hinky and it turned out a city clerk was taking home a little extra at the end of the day. And there I was, green as a new blade of grass, having trouble connecting all the dots. I was basically writing two different stories –cabby competition and corruption –and mom was bleeding all over them and making me rewrite them. To the point that, you know, I was about ready to quit. And she finally she sat me down and said *'Byron, honey, listen to me. It's all one story. Everything you will ever write in this business is all one story. It's all connected underneath.'*" Byron turns a little. Looks. "And now here you are talking about Olivia DeLuna."

Two more peanuts meet their fate. Byron pans the street corner. Chews. Continues.

"And I'll tell you, Dez, that's the God's honest truth. We float around in our little boats, coming ashore here and there. We climb this mountain peak and that mountain peak. We stick a flag in this island and that island. We report this story on Monday and that story on Tuesday. Exploding car on Wednesday. Desert execution on Thursday. But if you drain out all of the water, when you reach down and pull the fucking plug out and watch the oceans swirl away, you realize that it's all one thing. Everything is connected underneath. As my hippie friends and I used to say half stoned out of our minds," Byron cracks a wry smile and spreads out his arms, embracing the turmoil, "it's all one bittersweet song, brother."

"Wise woman, your mother," says Desmond.

Byron's arms collapse and he nods.

"Lung cancer. Occupational hazard. It was ugly. Thirty years ago. Still miss her."

Byron pauses. Sorts through the last few peanuts in his palm. Looks up again.

"We have an island in our imagination. That's where the dead go. That's where the dead live on. But the universe is just another ocean, Dez. Time is just a distance to be travelled. And it's all connected underneath. Laurie didn't die for the story. She died *in* the story. She *is* the story. Always has been. Just like you and me and Vasily and everybody who almost died one night watching a wannabe beauty queen in a bathing suit play the drums. The shit we report as journalists? The thing we get awards for like we've discovered a new fucking continent? That's all just a little tip of rock poking out of the water. Beneath our little boats it's all so much bigger than we'll ever know. Existence is one big conspiracy."

Stillness, silence in a bubble, submerged in an ocean of chaos. Everywhere colliding color and sound. Metal and flesh dissolving in sunlight and the aroma of roasting meats.

"There's a place for you here," says Byron finally, jerking his thumb to the black monolith behind him. "Up there with us. Carrying this thing forward. You do good work. Rick's a good bloodhound but the baying is getting a bit old. You're a lot easier on the ears. I can use you."

Desmond sighs. Shakes his head.

"I appreciate that, Byron. I do. But I'm a fish out of water out here. Different rhythm. Your team is too fast. Too young. Too *made-for-TV* perfect. Gleaming eyes and white teeth. Everyone laughs too much. Knows too much all the goddamned time. I tried my first *Appletini* this week. And my last."

Byron laughs. "No good?"

Desmond looks up. Shakes his head. "Jesus Christ."

"You really going to leave this story behind, Dez? After all of this?"

"Not my story to leave. Never was."

"So what are going to do?"

Desmond straightens. Leans back. Shrugs.

"I'm a small town newspaperman. Even if that makes me a pallbearer for the whole fucking industry."

"So?"

"*San Angelo Dispatch* needs a General Manager. Someone who knows how to do more with less. That's me, I guess. Owners are fighting over where to cut. Someone thinks I can keep investigations in the budget." He glances over at Bryon. Laughs. "And you clearly think I'm crazy."

"Want to know what I think, Dez? Here's what I think." Byron chews contemplatively. Long enough that Desmond thinks he might not finish the thought. "I think you're full of shit."

Desmond looks at him. Longer this time. Waits.

"I think you're not leaving this story at all. I think you want to scoop CBS and the rest of us city slickers. I think you've got a bead on the bribery corruption angle of this whole thing. Could be the Texas delegation to Congress. Maybe the Governor of Texas himself. But I'm guessing it's someone well up the food chain. A project that big needs a lot of political approval. Lot of money at stake. Vasily knew how to chum the water." Bryon smiles. "How am I doin'?"

"I think you just likened the Governor of Texas to a Great White."

"Well I think you've got an inside source. One of your own. Maybe one Laurie left to you. And I think you're going to show up at the *San Angelo Dispatch* with a story in your back pocket the likes of which they've never fucking seen before. I think you're going to quadruple their investigation budget and I think you know that's exactly what Laurie Weaver would have wanted you to do. I think you're atoning for drinking yourself to sleep the night she died. And I think you're just getting started."

"I see," says Desmond. "What makes you so sure?"

"Because I didn't get where I am without my own instincts. And because I started out as a newspaper guy. Workin' for mom in Philly and then fifteen years at the *Chicago Trib*. I know a thing or two about corruption stories. Enough to know when there's one in the room and it's not mine to write. Am I at least warm?"

Desmond looks away. "I think maybe you should have been a fiction writer."

Byron nods. Tosses in the last three peanuts. Chews with a smile. Salt grains glisten in his beard. He stands. Brushes his hands together. Sticks the right one out. Desmond looks up and takes it.

"Let me know if you change your mind. Until then, I'm gonna try to take your lunch money every goddamned day of the week."

"I know. Thanks, Byron."

"See you in the funny papers, Dez."

It is a long way to his hotel. Too long to walk.

He walks anyway, pushing into a slow yellow tide of sunlight, an invisible sea that floods the concrete basin around row upon row of glass and iron kelp stretching up towards the surface of a watery-blue sky. He pins his stride to the cracks in the sidewalk. Two steps for every crack. He can't help himself. His brain sprinkles in the piano. Big Maybelle pushes him from behind. She's got those *Ramblin' Blues,* moving hard for that blue highway. She sings about wanting to run. Walkin', moans Maybelle, is just too damn slow.

Desmond takes out his phone. Dials. Listens. Speaks.

"Hey, it's me. Okay, I guess. You? Good. Made up my mind. I know. Well, I'm old and slow. You're gonna need to get used to that. I'm on a plane tonight so let's hook up tomorrow afternoon. Pull everything we've got on the G.O.T.'s schedule over the past three years. Four years. Our Secretary of State too. How big is the conference room? Well, let's fill it up Monday morning. I want all hands on deck. Get some sleep, kiddo. Lot of work to do."

Chapter 91

She is not in the moment.

She is in a different moment. Roughly five hours earlier, sitting at the piano in Yvonne Lawry's living room. Kevin is next to her, wheelchair right up against the keyboard. She plays a slow, steady, twelve-bar walking blues. Stepping up from the sixth to the minor seventh, stepping back down again.

First *C*. Then *F*. Then back to *C*. Over. Again. Again. Fifteen minutes straight.

First blues she ever learned, that slow amble. If she lets herself, she can feel Garvin Cross standing behind her. His ragged lankiness bending over the top of her. Long fingers, smelling of that gritty powdered soap, resting lightly on her shoulders. Encouraging her to think of the rhythm as a slow walk with Jesus on the road to Galilee.

But she has become expert at beating back those memories. Expert at keeping those roots severed.

So she keeps playing. Walking up. Walking down. First *C*. Then *F*. Back. Again. Over. Again. Twenty minutes. Kevin hurls himself forward. Then back. A spasm curls his body in on itself, twisting his neck, balling his fingers and spreading his cracked lips, but then lets him go. Forward. Back. Forward.

And she knows that in his mind he is walking. Stepping up. Over a fallen log, maybe. Over a curb. Stepping down again. Moving forward. Hands in his pockets.

Free.

And in that moment, she too is free. She wants to stay there, in that moment. Wants Yvonne to not come back from the San Angelo, or wherever she really is. Wants to walk these blues with the only person who understands her.

Five hours ago and she is still trying to crawl back inside that moment. Zip it up over her head. Because in that moment she is free not to think about *this* moment. Free not to dread this display of accountability. This show of closure.

The metal pins holding her leg bones together moan. Sing their *standing-too-*

long-blues. She adjusts herself against the wall. Tries to take some of the weight off.

Libby, next to her, pats her forearm without looking. *Still here.* That's all she means by it. *Still right by yo' side, baby.*

Sheldon, in all his awkward alien newness to her, is on the other side. Supporting her in his own, quiet way. They are flanking her, as if she might lose balance and pitch over one direction or the other. They see this as their job. This is just what you do.

At a moment like this.

Olivia looks across her mother's garden. Looks at the people lining the wall. One direction, then the other. All of them listening to the current remembrance. The sun is low now, a deep dying red veiled in afternoon haze. Reminds her of the end of the cigarette she would almost kill for.

Papi is there. Worn, asymmetrical, punching bag face watching from between the perfect sunflowers. He is the only one who seems to know enough to leave her alone. To not try to prop her up or keep her from falling over sideways.

The service is too small, she thinks.

For someone so famous. For someone known all over the world. There should be thousands of people here, backed up from the garden wall and spreading out across the desert, come to pay respects, come to tip their hat and say thanks for the music. Thanks for the feeling.

But there are not thousands. There are forty-two. Almost enough garden wall space for everyone to lean against and rest their forearms. A kind of standing pew made of rock and mortar.

The service is too *large*, she thinks.

For someone so infamous. Someone with no friends. For a recluse that did her best to drive others away. For someone uniformly known as a cast-iron bitch and a drunk who cared more about her plants than other people. There should be maybe four or five people here. Arms crossed. Looking at their watches.

But there are not four or five people. There are forty-two.

Might not have been any service at all. But word gets around. Little articles here and there. Little blips on the radio when all of the other news is done. *And finally today, the woman the blues world knew as…*

Two of the singers that travelled the country on that bus of hers –two of the original *Letti Blue Rollers* that owed their careers to her –took it upon themselves to pay their respects by organizing a farewell. They reached out to others from that life and several of them made the trip to Corbin, Texas. There are a few locals. Still others from various parts of the state. Houston. San Antonio. All part of the music scene. All tipping their hat to a part of their own history.

They take turns leaving their places at the wall, walking through the open gate into the center of the garden, like they are taking the stage, and telling stories about Dallas Letti.

"I remember driving through Louisville one night on that bus."

The woman doesn't look like she's in the business any more. Too put together. Too uneasy in front of other people. She is remembering a different life.

"We were on our way to St. Louis. And we were all hungry enough to eat the seat cushions. And Dallas told the bus driver to pull over to the Colonel's for some chicken. But they were closed except for the drive through. And of course the bus ain't gon' fit through that little drive through. So Dallas gets out of the bus… walks across the parking lot… and stands in line behind three other cars. People lookin' in their rear views. And then another car gets in line behind Dallas and the whole line inches forward. And we all across the parking lot in the bus, hangin' out the windows and laughin' so hard we were cryin'. I took a picture that should be makin' its way around that I want back but that I wanted to share with y'all tonight. Anyway, when her time come, Dallas walks up to that little speaker and grabs it by the throat like it was a microphone, throws her head back and *sings* her order."

The used-to-be, back-in-the-day backup singer, black bangles on her wrists, rings on her fingers, long hair in an up-do, closes her eyes. Channels the dearly departed.

I wants me five buckets of chicken, baby.
Mashed potatoes on the side.
I said I wants me five buckets of chicken, baby.
Mashed potatoes on the side.
Twelve Co-Colas, big bag of biscuits
And betta' make it snappy baby
I say you best make it snappy baby
Now you got to make it snappy baby
'Cause it time for me to ride.

Most of the stories are in this vein. A woman full of heart and soul and humor and music. A woman who was tough but caring. "She cared so much for us," says one. "We were the closest of families." Another fights back tears. "I was just a lost soul from Tuscaloosa who knew how to sing. Dallas took me under her wing. I thought of her as the mother I never had."

She discounts it all. Tries to. These are the things you say at a time like this. Every dead woman was *like a mother*. Every dead man, *like a father*. The family gets bigger and bigger. Make up a story. Everyone will nod. Cry. Pass the baton.

Next to her there is new movement. Sheldon is laughing quietly to himself. He hands her a Polaroid. Dallas, the late great *Letti Blue*, mother to all but one, is standing in line at a KFC drive-thru.

Olivia cannot help but try to claim her. The woman in the photo. Cannot help but search for something distinctively maternal.

Mom. Mother. Mama. Mommy. Madre.

Mirage. Heat waves in a desert of hurt. There is no water there. Not for her.

She passes the photo to Libby, who laughs so loud the man now speaking in the garden pauses in mid-sentence. People look.

Olivia glances up in time to see Dixie's watery blue eyes looking at her from beyond the fire stick cacti burning up the east wall. It is the child-Dixie she sees watching her –dirty little face with an angry chicken in her arms –hiding inside the adult.

Before an hour ago, the last time she had seen little Dixie Brill they were separated by a car window and a cloud of red, tail-lit dust, both of them crying. Dixie screaming from the back seat as Garvin Cross' long, scoured fingers closed over Olivia's shoulder.

Dixie Brill. Now she is Dixie Draper. Husband. Two kids. Good job. It was awkward and alien to see her. Time collapsing in a stiff hug. Dixie near tears. Olivia numb to everything.

"Etta… we need to find some time," Dixie had said, clutching Olivia's hands. "We need to talk. I spent a day with your Mom. A few years ago. In Chicago. I just… like bumped into her in a liquor store. That *can't* be just a coincidence. You'll prob'ly think I'm crazy but I believe my mama set that up, Etta. I never go into that liquor store. I mean *never*. And there she was. I believe we were meant to find each other again. Me and her. *You and me.* There's so much…" Her voice had broken. She looked away. Pulled it back together. "Your mother had no idea. She thought we took you with us. She searched for years. I can't believe I'm back here, Etta. I can't believe I'm looking at you. We… *please…*" Dixie had squeezed her hands, "we have to sit down someplace quiet. Please."

Olivia had stayed non-committal. Accepted Dixie's business card. Extricated herself as politely as possible. Continued walking up to her mother's house. Libby, suddenly next to her, had wanted the low-down on *little-blondie-blue-eyes-wit'-the have-mercy-titties* but Olivia had curtly declined. "*Not now, Libby. Just. No. Okay?*"

Dixie smiles wanly from across the garden. Looks away. Libby passes the photo on down the wall. The gray-haired councilman in the middle of the garden –dark suit, tie, boots –is a baritone. He is almost too comfortable in this setting. The way he pauses. Looks. Projects. He picks up where he left off.

"So while I did not know Rosetta very well on a personal basis, the city thought it was important for you to know its gratitude for her regular and generous contributions to our community. She never tied our hands on how to use her donations. But her priorities were clear enough. Drug and alcohol abuse treatment and prevention. Education, especially at the primary school level. The arts. And horticulture. This was a side of Rosetta Letti that maybe many of you did not know about. But her donations came from a place of deep caring and concern that defined the person we are remembering today every bit as much as the music that made her famous.

"So I am pleased to say that Rosetta Letti's final bequest to the city, combined with some funds that are now no longer ear-marked for a Corbin River Walk, will be used for two things of which I think she would heartily approve.

"First. The addition of music appreciation to our primary school curriculum.

"And second. The construction and maintenance of the *Rosetta Letti Botanical Gardens* at a site yet to be determined."

Sounds of surprise and approval. A light applause that sounds like finger snaps in the quiet afternoon desert. Like the first drops of rain. He gestures at the land around him. At the carpeting of purple winecups at his feet.

"It's appropriate that Rosetta's ashes were scattered in this garden. Not just because she loved to garden. And she did love it, didn't she?"

A collective murmur, like a low breeze, pushing through the plants.

"Like she loved her music. But it is also appropriate because Rosetta left something for each of us that will continue to grow within us as long as we live. It is not for me to define that thing. You already know what it is. I suspect it may be different for each of us. But, whatever it may be for you, you will each take it home with you tonight. And you will remember her for it. And it will continue to grow within you."

He pauses. Looks from one to the next to the next.

"For those of you who are from out of town, you will be interested to know about some Corbin lore we like to keep alive. The legend is of Evangelina Huerta, the common law wife of this town's founding father, Corbin Draego. He was a Scottish railroad magnate. Sheepherder. Cattleman. Came out in the eighteen seventies when there was nothing out here. Not much, anyway. And he put us on the map as a profitable ranching town. Built himself a large estate about fifteen miles southwest of here."

He points. The out-of-towners turn and look. Like it might still be there.

"Having done that, Corbin Draego, that very wealthy but very lonely Scottish widower, suddenly disappeared for several years. Off into the desert to no one knew where.

"And then one day, Corbin Draego returned with a young Mexican woman on his arm. Evangelina. Stunning to behold. She was a quiet person. A still person. Painfully shy. I say she was a quiet person. She was mute from birth. What she said to others, she said with large brown eyes and a wide, kind, hesitant smile. The whole town quickly adored her and celebrated the return of its founding father.

"Evangelina Huerta loved three things above all else. She loved Corbin

Draego. She loved music. And she loved gardening. Every Sunday, Corbin and Evangelina made the trip into town together. They went to church to worship and then they went to the town market. Every Sunday, Evangelina brought baskets of vegetables and flowers that she had grown in her garden. As Corbin Draego circulated and conducted his business, Evangelina liked to find a shady spot near the town square and watch the people. Sometimes she brought her guitar and played the music she had learned from her father, a *mariachi* in *Chihuahua*. People said that she played beautifully and that she quickly became a feature of the Sunday market that they anticipated. That they looked forward to.

"Well. Corbin and Evangelina soon had a child. A beautiful daughter they named Rosa. Rosa not only had her mother's looks and her father's charm and humor. God had given Rosa a voice. Not only did she grow up bilingual, thanks to her devoted nanny, but Rosa, it turned out, could sing like a bird. *Pájaro bebé*, Corbin called her. *Baby bird.*

"By the age of ten, Rosa was singing to packed church services. On Sundays, Rosa would sing the most beautiful Mexican ballads to Evangelina's accompaniment in the Corbin Town Square as people bought and sold flowers and vegetables. And meats. And spices. And candies. And candles. And hand-made trinkets.

"Little Rosa, you see, had a gift. She *was* a gift. She was adored not just by her parents, but by the whole town.

"But these kinds of stories are never without heartbreak, of course. Tragedy struck just before Rosa's fifteenth birthday. Rosa and her father were riding along on a cattle drive out to Las Cruces. It was Rosa's first such excursion. She was excited, bubbling on about it for weeks in advance. But at the New Mexico border they came on some bad weather that just kept getting worse. In the middle of the night a flash flood rushed through their camp. Several drowned that night. Including young Rosa. Swept away into the desert. Corbin Draego died trying to save her."

Silence. A bird from somewhere behind the house. A wisp of sage. Penstemon. Columbine. Breath from the desert as the sun burns lower and lower in the sky like a dying candle. The councilman clears his throat. Waits. Resumes.

"Of course, that had left poor, quiet Evangelina Huerta alone. Devastated. Beyond the reach of any consolation. People tried, of course. The whole town tried. But some wells are just too deep. Am I right?"

The mourners at the garden wall agree in low murmurs, shaking their heads.

"Some wells are just too deep. People rarely saw Evangelina after that. She never again appeared at her church, or at the Sunday market. She kept to herself inside the walls of Corbin Draego's large estate, which steadily fell into disrepair. And after a time, the only sign of Evangelina was very late at night. Travellers crossing the desert outside the estate reported hearing the sound of guitar. Slow, sweet tunes, accompanying only mournful coyotes.

"More than a few of these same desert travellers also reported torchlight glowing from the garden. That, in the depth of her grief, was where Evangelina Huerta spent her waking hours. She slept when the sun was up. She spent the nights in the garden. Playing old music. Digging. Fertilizing. Growing things. Coaxing life out of the ground.

"And as the legend has it, for years after the tragedy, every first Sunday after a full moon, the people of Corbin showed up at the town square marketplace to a dozen baskets of the most beautiful flowers and the largest, healthiest vegetables they had ever seen in their lives. Every month. Flowers and vegetables completely out of season. Flowers and vegetables that utterly defied the desert habitat. Flowers and vegetables that should not have been possible. And yet."

He holds up a finger. Looks at each of them in turn.

"And yet. As the sun rose. As the vendors showed up to set up their tables. As the townspeople of Corbin emptied the church and came to the market. There they were. Twelve baskets in a circle. In the middle of the town square. Bursting."

Silence. Olivia can feel Sheldon next to her. Looking. Checking on her. She does not move. They all wait.

"Well. Imagination takes over, of course. That's what makes a good myth. A good legend. The explanation that finally took hold, long after Evangelina Huerta was finally discovered to have passed, literally absorbed by the very garden she tended, was that in her grief she had forsaken the living sun and had cultivated her garden with moonlight. Not the hot, harsh, dry light of the living. But the cool, wet, *reflected* light of life passed. The light of the dead."

The light of the dead.

He lets the phrase linger. Lets it stretch out. Lets it settle into the soil.

"The City of Corbin eventually installed that large, white stone fountain in the middle of Town Square. A circle squared. Right where the baskets had once appeared after every full moon. They named it after Evangelina Huerta. And it sits there today, all of these decades later, in her honor. *Fuente de la Luna.* Fountain of the Moon. It is the centerpiece of our annual *Moon Garden Festival.* It is a testament to love and grief. Life and loss. To flowers and food and music. It sits as a reminder that the people who leave us are with us forever. That they live on in the reflected light of remembrance. That's where they speak to us. Sing to us. And by that reflected light they continue to nurture us and guide us through all of our days."

He pauses. They all wait.

"And so I am now humbled to stand with all of you in and around the garden of Rosetta Letti, the great Dallas Letti Blue. I can tell you that we will all take our turn tilling in the moonlight. We will all be reaping her harvest for a long time to come."

When it is done, people drift away in two's and three's. Dixie appears for another hug. Another plea. Then she too drifts off. Sheldon stands off to the side, against the wall, hands in his pocket as Olivia says good-bye to Libby. It is a tenuous peace between them, Sheldon and Libby, even after all that has happened and everything that is new.

"You goin' off wit' *massage-massage-all-the-way-divorced* then, huh?"

"Libby, you've got to stop calling him that."

"Why? Jus' 'cause he yo' *daddy?* Make all that shit worse, if you ask me, baby."

"Libby." They stare at each other in the reddening light. Tires crunch the dirt behind them. "You're hopeless."

"I am, too, huh?"

"Yes. You are. You feel okay out here by yourself? Why don't you invite that nurse back out here? You two seem to get on okay."

Libby looks. Scrunches up her face in incomprehension. "Ruth? You mean *nice-enough-but-lawdy-I-gots-me-a-cute-little-'ol-house-on-the-island-of-Lesbos* Ruth? That one?"

"Yeah. That one. You know, Libby." She puts one hand on each shoulder. "Bessie Smith and Ma Rainy both preferred women."

Libby shakes her off. "Ain't havin' this conversation, baby."

"I just want to make sure you feel… comfortable. Here."

"I'm good, baby. I'm good. All them months I spent livin' with Dallas, this place like my home too now."

"Libby, it is literally, *legally*, your home."

Libby makes a face. Shakes her head uncomfortably.

"Shit ain't right, baby. I may need a roof but I don't need to *own* it. Should be your home. *You* her baby."

Olivia's turn to make a face, pushing back against the implication in that word. *Baby.*

"She knew I don't want nothin' to do with this place. Besides," she looks Libby in the eyes, "you more than earned it."

Libby shakes her head.

"Who'da thunk I'd be worth a damn as a nurse? Although I guess it was mostly cookin' an' cleanin' an' keepin' the music comin' an' keepin' the booze comin'. Doin' everything Ruth told me to when she come by and doin' everything I wasn't 'sposed to do after she'd gone. Tellin' stories in the dark. Singin' the good songs. Yo' mama sho' knew her music I tell you what. Ever since we was both concussed and she took me in after the muthafuck Russians burn down my damn house? We thick as thieves."

"You were a good friend when she needed it most."

"She loved you, baby," says Libby.

"Don't start, Libby. I know you tried. But you can't fix a whole lifetime in a couple of awkward... I don't even know what to call them..."

"I call that shit *talkin' over some delicious san'wiches and hand-squoze lemonade* is what I call it. And I should know too 'cause I did all the squozin'. Don't matter what you call it, baby. She tol' me... that she tol' you... that she *loved* you. That she been livin' in some kinda horrible shame for what she done to you."

Olivia cannot hold the look. Libby is too intense. Too powerful. She looks up and beyond. Cathedrals of dust in the air as the cars caravan away, down toward the highway. A cardinal, somewhere, everywhere, sings them away.

"If it the last thing I do on this earth, baby, you gon' find it in yo' heart to forgive y'own mama. 'Cause she up in the moonlight now, just like the man said. Waitin' to hear it. Waitin' to feel it."

Olivia looks back. Almost angry.

"Why... Why do you care so *fuckin'* much about this, Libby? This ain't..."

Libby, ferocious now. Almost frightening.

"Why? I tell you why goddamnit. 'Cause my *own* mama up in that moonlight. With *yo'* mama. An' 'cause one day I be up there with 'em both, shining our moonlight down on *all* the babies. And 'cause in all the bad an' evil things I done in this life, you my one good thing, Olivia. You the soul I found on the road. You my one good thing. I owe that to my mama, an' I intend to see it on through."

Libby nods sharply. Softens. Swats Olivia on the shoulder. Moves off.

Olivia watches her walk up to the garden wall. She pauses as she crosses the threshold to the garden. Libby and Sheldon look at each other. Libby jerks her head in Olivia's direction. Sheldon nods his understanding.

Libby turns. Strides through the garden and into the house of her mother, the late, great Dallas Letti Blue.

"Think that will ever not be awkward?" Sheldon asks as they walk to her car.

"No," she says. "She'll always wait for you to hurt me somehow."

"Right. Except that I'm not some stranger now. I'm..."

Olivia wheels on him. They both skid to a stop.

"Look. No offense? Sheldon? But I ain't ever callin' you *daddy*."

Sheldon, hands up. Surrendering.

"I know, I know. I wouldn't expect you to. Hey, it's not like I had any idea about any of this either. Last thing I ever thought was that I'm someone's daddy. Yours or anyone's. I loved your mother, in a puppy love way, but that was never a two-way street and I knew it. She was older than me. And both of her races were wrong..." He shakes his head and makes a sound. "I don't mean *wrong*. I mean… that kinda thing back in those days…"

"Christ." Agitated. Impatient. "I know what you mean, Shel."

"Right. Well. Rose was prettier than anyone I had any right to be with. And with a voice like that? Even if she'd been ready to give the slip to Otis, I knew she'd never be with me for more than ten hot minutes before she moved on or someone elbowed me out of the way. No way that was happening."

"Well, Hell's bells Shelly, it's a damn match. I mean DNA is DNA, ain't it? So you obviously did somethin' right."

Sheldon sighs. Hands on his hips. He looks out at the horizon.

"Thought I could write her some songs and win her over that way. And she was just… I think she was just lookin' to be with the last person on earth that she should be with. And that was me, this scrawny little young, white, pecan-pickin' song-writer. She was goin' with Otis at the time. He was some scary piece of work, Otis. And Rose wanted out from under his thumb. There I was. Right place, right time. She'd sneak away over to Cale Hargrove's place. Right where you'd end up livin' all these years later. *Damn.* That still gives me goose bumps. I'm tryin' hard to believe that is just a crazy coincidence, but I got to say, Olivia, I'm losin' that fight every single day."

Unbidden, she thinks of Dixie. *Little-blondie-blue-eyes-wit'-the-have-mercy-titties.* Sees her pleading face. "*I never go into that liquor store. I mean never. And there she was.*" Feels the squeeze of her hand. "*That can't be a coincidence.*"

In the very back of her head is the sound. The horn from Manny Soto's truck that should not have been possible, blasting through the dark. Still there in her head. It has never gone away. That sound. That vibration. Same as the ringing in her ears from Jesús Batista's gun blowing a hole in Nicholas Voss' kneecap. The same vibration. A finger step on the keyboard from the minor seventh down into the prolonged note of something dark and bottomless. Kevin is next to her. Rocking. Clenching. He hears it. Feels it. Holds it. Rides it. A sliver of sound taken from something infinitely larger, swimming, pushing through deep water.

"Cale'd stay out most of the evening," says Sheldon. "Let us have the place. But it was all innocent fun. Just drinkin' and singin' and carryin' on…"

"Not all innocent," she says.

"Yes it was, Olivia. It was. There was only one time… you know."

"Well, yeah, that's all it takes, Shel. One time."

"We went on a road trip. All the way out to Keller Bay off Port Lavaca. Cale had a friend who had a boat he never used. Rose had never been on a boat. So I made it my mission. She made up some excuse to Otis and off we went. Gone three days. Going out took most of a day and coming back took a day. Spent most of that middle day out on this old beat-to-hell houseboat. Perfect day for it, too. Clear, sunny sky. Sea like a soft blue bed sheet. Slept out under the stars. I'm guessin' that was the night. Well. No guessin' about it. Had to be."

Olivia looks up at him. Her father.

"You're saying I was conceived on a boat."

"I'm sayin' you were conceived on the Pacific Ocean, a stone's throw from the little bitty town of Olivia, Texas. I'm sayin' that she may not have loved me and I may have been some kinda fool for thinkin' she might, but that you were conceived in a magical moment. I'm sayin' that for all the shock of finding this out now, it doesn't have to be such a bad, shameful thing. It can be okay if we just let it be okay."

"She was Dallas fuckin' Letti, Sheldon. You never told anyone? All this time?"

"Come on. Who'd believe me? When she hit it big I almost didn't believe it myself. Easier to just let it go. Move on. But now. Shit, honey. Facts are facts."

They are silent. Still.

"That's not who you are to me," she says finally. "I'm just fine without a mama or a daddy thank you very much."

"I know, Olivia. But after never knowing each other?"

"After almost knowin' each other a little too well, you mean?"

"After almost dyin' together?"

She resumes walking. Turns to him at the car, a green Pontiac with a blue driver side front door. Sheldon tries another tack.

"Since the divorce settled, I got plenty of time. Since Grayson agreed to pay me what's right for the business, I got plenty of money. I can do better than this piece-of-shit car, Olivia."

"Car was all I needed."

"After what I did to you?" His words are little shards of pain. Bits of shrapnel he has extracted from himself.

"No," she says. "I already told you. There was a mama coyote in the road with a pup…"

"I know all that."

"Then you know it ain't on you, Shel. *I* flipped that car. Okay? For the last time? I did that."

She tries to conjure the memory. Tries to see the animal. Its gently swinging baby. The ears. Eyes. Fur. But she cannot. They are ghosts now. Tricks of the light. She cannot honestly say whether they were ever there at all.

"And you were driving seventy miles an hour for a reason, Olivia."

"Don't want your money or your pity. Last time I'm gonna say it. Thank you though." The words sound harsh and cold. Like she has slammed a door in his face. She tries to prop it open. Show him it's unlocked. "You figured out what you're gon' do with yourself?"

Sheldon nods.

"Think so. Open my own studio. Write music. Record. Produce. Got an old buddy that wants in."

Olivia reaches for the handle. He stops her.

"Look. Olivia. I won't try to be your father. But we can still share our lives. Can't we? I mean, *shouldn't* we?"

She looks away. Off towards her mother's house. Libby is in the garden window. Watching. Olivia looks back at Sheldon like it is for the first time. Sighs. Hurt. Exhaustion. Confusion. In her mind she is reaching for Kevin, walking that slow, twelve-bar freedom.

"And just how do you propose we share our lives?"

"Music," he says. "Let's make this about the blues. Let's share that."

Most of her does not want to drive out into the desert. Out to the old place.

But there is a small part that knows she has to. If there was ever a day, today is that day. So she does.

Lights a cigarette. Puts the thing in gear. Drives.

The ark, her old refuge, is on its side, a brooding, broken hulk beneath the gathering dusk. Further up is the demolished house, like an abandoned carcass, its lumber bones picked clean by vultures.

But in her head, in the sweep of her mind's eye, it is all as it was before. Nothing has changed. She inches the car to a stop. Cuts the engine. The fading sky is shot through with contrails like hot scars cooling from blood orange to gray

She closes her eyes.

And then, almost instantly, she is in a different car. Miss Celia's car. Celia clutching the steering wheel as Olivia's young body shakes violently in the passenger seat and the world burns outside the windows. The wind like some horrible laughter. Up ahead, in the heart of the fire, in a place she can only see in her head, lies Lyle Cross. Face down on a wet, flaming carpet. Scissors, like the stalks of an alien silver plant, sprout from the white soil of his nape. The old piano, just beyond his dead outstretched hand, creaks and pops as it burns.

"Don't you worry, now, Olivia," Celia had said, pulling her close, not thinking. *"Mama's here, baby. Mama's here."* And in her head Olivia had repeated that desperate, urgent assurance down through the lid of the narrow silver box in her lap to the little cactus family inside. *Mama's here. Don't be afraid. You're not alone. Mama's here.*

A sound. The memory dissipates. Olivia opens her eyes to movement.

An asymmetrical figure rising from the darkening ground up ahead. Walking into the headlights. She lowers her cigarette hand out the window. Exhales.

"Hero," she says.

"Yeah. Don't call me that," says Davis, leaning in, right hand on the roof. "Dallas always called me that. She knew I hated it."

"But you are. Whole lot of people out there walkin' around right now that shouldn't be walkin' around. And every last one of 'em agrees with me. So."

786

She shrugs. Smokes.

Davis smiles in defeat. His left arm swings. What remains of it. There is no hand. No forearm.

"Between us we've got one good body," she says. "I'll trade you a decent arm for a leg that works."

He points to the cigarette.

"Mind?"

She hands it up. Davis takes a long drag. Holds. Exhales.

"Thanks," he says, handing it back. "First one of those I've had in awhile."

"How's the wagon?" she asks.

"A bitch. Makes me want to smoke. Like my lungs and my liver have some sorta suicide pact."

She nods. "I hear that. Goin' to those meetings though, right?"

"Only every ten, fifteen minutes."

"Got to surrender to that higher power."

Sunny and bright. Big smile. *Golly-Gee* fist through the air. She regrets her own tone. Regrets the instinct to cheapen the hope and struggles of others. Compensation through sarcasm.

But Davis seems impervious.

"Well. Yeah. Got to *find* the higher power before I can surrender. Not so easy."

"News flash, Hero. Higher power stepped out for a drink. Ain't comin' back any time soon. Wants us to work it out for ourselves."

"Could be. Meantime, I'm going for the free coffee."

She offers the cigarette again. He takes it.

"Nice service," he says. Smokes. Hands it back. "She'd have hated it."

"Got that right," says Olivia. Then, "How's Lucela? You guys still…"

Davis nods. Smiles. "She's uh, she's good. Lucela's good. *We're* good, I mean. Yeah. Didn't really think anybody knew about that."

"Davis. Come on now. Be surprised if anybody *doesn't* know. No secrets in this town."

"Oh, there's *some* secrets," he says, his eyes connecting with hers. "There *were* anyway."

It draws her up short. She pulls at the cigarette again. Exhales. All of the color has bled out of the sky except the memory of something blue and vast.

"Yeah. Well. Not for long," she says. "Anyway, Lucela keeps to herself, which makes her good people in my book. You could do a lot worse. But her mama loves to talk. So I'd assume everybody knows everything if I were you. 'Cause they do."

"Okay," he says.

"So what're you doin' out here?"

"Oh." Davis rakes his fingers through his hair. Glances over the car at the piles of old debris. "Service ended and I... I don't know. Just walked up for the hell of it, I guess. Haven't been out here in awhile. Need to finish what I started. Haul all of this shit away. Promised her I would."

"Like she'll ever know, Davis. Ain't your problem now."

Davis laughs again. "She'll know. Trust me. Dallas could see right through me from the beginning. I can feel her eyes on my back as we speak. She's not waitin' for any moonlight either. Shit's twenty-four-seven with her. So I got to finish the job."

"You can't do all this by yourself..."

She doesn't finish. Doesn't say the words *with only one hand*. Doesn't have to.

"Miguel and Eladio said they'd pitch in." Davis leans down again, reframing his face in the window. "Speakin' of which."

"What."

He takes the cigarette. Takes the smallest of hits. Hands it back.

"Miguel." Straightens. Exhales. "Ain't my place and he'd take off my other arm if he ever found out I told you, but... the man's still carryin' a serious torch, Olivia. If you don't know that, well... then maybe you should."

"Got a real funny way of carryin' a torch, Davis."

"You talkin' about Yvonne? Really? Come on. You know better than that. She's got her hooks into some..." he points derisively out across the desert, "some roughneck out near San Angelo. Miguel hasn't seen her in a month and he's not one little bit upset about it. He's just..."

"Yeah. I know what *he's just*, Davis. He's just nothin'. And you were right the first time. Ain't your place. Last thing I need right now is managing Miguel Rivera. Managing any man. No offense."

"None taken. Look. Lucela doesn't know what the fuck she's getting' into with me. I'm gonna end up throwin' her some curve balls she'll never see comin'. But Miguel... his eyes are wide open about you. Well. None of my business. Just thought you'd want to know."

"His mother hates me anyway," she adds. "Could do without that too."

"Marcela? Nah. Marcela don't hate anyone far as I can tell. She's just protective. Once you're in, you're her child too."

"Right. Guess I'm just gonna have to take your word on that."

Enough. Anything but this. She sees the segue. Pushes.

"Hear you're workin' for them now."

Davis laughs. "Man. Really aren't any secrets are there?"

"Not a one."

"Yeah. Well. They put me to work managing *Pepita's*. So I'm Eladio's boss now. Which he *hates*. I'm also heading up the fund-raising for the DAF. They want me to work toward opening a chapter in San Angelo."

"*Muy bien, amigo.* And in all of your spare time?"

Davis shrugs. "Workin' on my shit. Goin' to meetings every ten minutes. Tryin' not to live in circles." He pauses. She sees him thinking. Considering whether to add something else. "Writin' a book."

"Ahh. There it is. Writin' a book. About what exactly?"

He looks away. And then back. Smiles a little.

"About Dallas. 'Bout your mom. About her music and what it meant to my mom. About Bessie Smith and Hurricane Harvey and the Cumberland River flood of 1926."

She feels him waiting for a reaction. She nods. Rolls her eyes. "Well. Good thing she's dead, I guess."

"Not sure what that's supposed to mean, exactly."

"Me neither," she says.

"With her blessing, Olivia. I wouldn't do it otherwise. We went through something in that fuckin' ark over there. She saved my life not a hundred yards from here. 'Cause I was surely drowning. I was goin' down the neck of a bottle for the last time. Sooner or later." Juts his head sharply toward the ark. "And she knew it."

Silence. Olivia lays her head back. Closes her eyes. Waits.

"And then, you know, after everything in this town either blew up or burned to the fuckin' ground, or washed away, we talked near every day. She opened up. About everything."

She doesn't move. Waits.

"She wanted to get everything out. Wanted to set it free. And I said I'd do that."

Olivia opens her eyes.

"I'll bet. You'll excuse me if I don't buy a copy when it's done."

"Oh, you get one for free, Olivia. 'Cause I'm gonna need to talk to you."

"Why?"

"Because you're at the center of just about every song Dallas ever wrote."

"Right. Says who?"

"Says her. That's who. Says Rosetta Letti."

"No," she says. "Forget it. You go on and do what you gotta do. But I'm not interested in that history."

She takes another drag. Blows it out in a long tight stream.

Headlights from behind. Swords slicing the darkening air, cutting pale curtains of dissipating smoke and dust like suspended plankton. Olivia adjusts the mirror.

"Now who in the hell…"

They watch the car pull up behind. She recognizes him through the windshield when the lights snuff out. She waits until he walks up to the window.

"Papi."

"Etta. Woman said I'd find you out here."

"This is my friend Hero. Hero, this is Pablo Brown. Goes by Papi."

They shake.

"Davis." He speaks his own name, pulling his left arm behind his back. Instinct now, whenever he meets new people.

"No introduction necessary," says Papi. "Have to be livin' under a rock not to know you. Good thing you did, boy. Saved a lot of people and paid the price too. Some goddamned mess in this little town."

"It was that, sir," says Davis. "If I don't ever have to talk to another cop in a suit it won't be long enough."

They fall silent, awkward as the sky thickens, swallowing the wreckage whole. Davis kicks at the dirt.

"Well, guess I'm gonna walk on back," he says. "Pablo, good to meet you. Olivia," he stoops. Looks at her. "You know I'm gon' keep workin' on you."

"Oh, I have no doubt."

She watches Davis slowly vanish in the rearview mirror. Papi comes around and sits in the seat next to her. Closes the door.

"Workin' on you," he says. "Mean, like, for a date?"

She looks at him like he's crazy. He nods. Looks out the window at nothing.

"Nice service," he says finally.

"I guess."

They sit in perfect silence for a minute. Two. Three. The desert pushes in against the car from every direction.

"I used to come out this way," she says. "Every now and then. Sit out in the scrub. Drinking. In the dark. Watch her walkin' around in that house. Watch her out in her... her fuckin' garden. Drunk off her ass. Diggin' in the dirt. I could never bring myself to just... to just... stand up and walk through that gate."

Silence.

"Too much hurt. Too much anger. Like there was an ocean between us and I can't fuckin' swim."

Silence.

"It was easier to keep hatin' her. I didn't want to understand. Still don't. Too much work. Too hard. I just wanted to keep... hating. Still do. Even when I realized she'd moved back to Corbin, I kept hangin' around and hangin' around and hangin' around and yeah I had a good deal with Libby and a free place to live but any normal person would'a just left. Would'a gone anyplace else. Any fuckin' place. You know?"

She wipes her nose with the back of her hand. Her eyes. Her cheeks. Wipes her hand on her pants.

"But I stayed. I stayed 'cause I wanted to keep hatin' her. I wanted to feel her right over here in the middle of nowhere, in her stupid little house, knowing I'm out there. Waiting to reconcile. Waiting for me to show up. And then I'd never fuckin' show. Wanting her to feel what I felt." She pounds her chest. "What I *still* feel. That's what kept me here. That's…"

Papi squeezes her shoulder. Pulls her into his chest. She sobs in the dark exactly like a lost and abandoned child. Like she is terrified. Like her fingers have been pried, one by one, from the only thing keeping her afloat. Like she is sinking into the depths.

Papi leans the seat back. Strokes her hair. Time loses all meaning. Night collapses around them.

At first it is the scent of him that slowly brings her back. Tobacco and bourbon and cologne and sweat and old wood and stale smoke and cotton and leather all rolled into one. Like she is a girl again sitting in his lap at the club. Sipping a Shirley Temple and watching her mother own that shaft of smoky blue light.

And then it is the sound of his heart beating against her ear.

It bumps her back up to the surface in four-four time.

Eventually she clears her throat. Speaks.

"Libby worked on me pretty hard. At the end. Her heart was in the right place, I guess, but… They got to know each other when the house burned down. Libby moved in when Dallas got out of the hospital. Took care of her to the end. She knew there wasn't much time left. So she pulled out all the stops. Libby is a force of nature when she needs to be. She finally got me to go over there for lunch. Left us alone so we could talk."

She reaches. Pulls against the steering wheel. Sits up in her seat. Wipes her face. Looks out at the dark.

"Well I didn't do any talkin.' Dallas did all the talkin.' Tried to account for all the lost time. But it was like I wasn't even there. She was weak and not very coherent for a lot of it. Lapsed into these memories of life on the road. This tour. That concert. Started singin' *Amazing Grace*. Then she'd get her focus back for a few minutes. And it was like… It…"

She stops. Silence.

"Tell me, Etta," he says.

"It was like I just… sat on the shore… like I sat there in my little fuckin' boat, and watched her flail around for me. I didn't swim out to meet her half way. Never tossed her a line. I just listened for what I wanted to hear. Looked for what I wanted to see. She wanted me to fish her out of the water, Papi. I didn't do that. I wanted her to feel how I fuckin' felt, year after year after year. Abandoned. With no one there who gave a shit. And so I just… I just let her drown in that feeling."

Another squall of emotion. Wet and merciless. She holds her scared face in her hands. Rocks in her seat. But this too passes.

"You okay?" asks Papi, cradling her neck with his palm.

She breathes. Cleans herself up. Nods. "Yeah. Fuck. I'm okay. I'm sorry."

"Don't be. I've got something I need to tell you, Etta. About the club."

She blinks. Looks at him in the dark. Rotates her back against the door.

"What. What are they gonna do with it? Fuckers are tearing it down, aren't they? Fuckin' fast food? Liquor store? Goddamnit, Papi."

"Stop. Just listen. The Houston outfit that bought it from me? *MLN Entertainment*?"

"Yeah?"

"Owned by *Dallas Commercial Property Management*?"

"Yeah?"

"It doesn't do anything."

"What do you mean?"

"I mean the only thing that company does in this world is own that piece of property. The only thing it has *ever* done in this world is buy that property and the business sitting on it from me. To take it off the market."

"Papi... I have no idea what..."

He reaches over. Puts his hand on hers.

"Honey. *M...L...N. Maybelline Louisa Nogales.* Those are your grandmother's initials. And the '*Dallas*' in *Dallas Commercial Property Management* is not a place north of Houston. It's *Dallas*. It's Rosetta. Your mother dummied up this business. Bought the club out from under me without me ever knowing. She owned MLN Entertainment one hundred percent. Her lawyer come by last week. Explained it all. Showed me the papers. Showed me that now *you* own *Dallas Commercial Property Management* dba *MLN Entertainment*. One. Hundred. Percent. I'm the one who's supposed to tell you. 'Cause I'm the only fool you'll listen to."

Silence. In the empty distance, far across the ancient, abandoned seabed, the horizon is silvering.

"She bought it for *you*, Etta. She saved it for you. This is your mother, this is Rosetta, doing her best to pull *you* out of the water. Tryin' to save *you*. She knew that if she threw you the line directly, you'd never take it."

He watches. Waits. All she can do is stare at him. He nods.

"I know. Lot to think about. One more thing before I go and prove to Willa that I'm not lying dead on the road." He pulls an envelope from his blazer pocket. Puts it in her hand. "The lawyer also gave me this."

She looks down at the thing. Doesn't move. Looks up.

"She wrote me a long letter. Left it up to me whether I thought you should read it." Papi smiles at her, smiles *through* her, like a kind of current, sad and sweet and wise, as only Papi can. "I think you should."

She does not move for a long time. Long enough for some of the dark to drain out of the sky. It drains to the east. Toward a soft glow the color of old bone that pulls at everything. And everyone. Somewhere Manny Soto is limping around, and he feels that pull in his marrow. Jesús Batista, too, stops whatever he is doing and looks up. Libby at the window. Dooley Simms with his friends. Kevin in his chair. The whole planet wants to drift that way; wants to offer up all of our weightless hope to the glowing hole in the sky.

And she feels it too. Feels it pulling against the metal pins in her leg. Pulling against pain itself. It is the astronomical manifestation of longing and loss.

She climbs out of the car. Closes the door. Hoists herself up onto the hood and leans back against the windshield. She holds the envelope up in front of her face. It is thick and heavy with paper. She can't help but think of Sheldon, her father, handing her envelopes of cash as they ate lunch on the concrete shore of the San Antonio River Walk. The two of them as oblivious to everything as the tourists floating by in their pretend gondolas.

She squints. One word in her mother's script. *Pablo.*

She opens the envelope. Pulls out the letter. The pages unfold from their confinement like wings.

Still too dark out to read. So she waits. Watches the moon climb out of a sea that is far beyond her vision. Watches it rise, slowly bleaching the desert. Slowly pulling back the sheet. Until she is at the bottom of that ancient spectral ocean and she can read by the light of the dead.

She might have started at the beginning. If the letter had been written to her. But it wasn't. So she doesn't. She opens it at random. Reads.

This is the memory. Mother Blues *at about nine o'clock. I'm up on that little wooden stage. Blue lights in my eyes. Place is packed. Like always. Smells like tobacco and weed and sweat and liquor. Barbeque tang coming in from out back. Candles on those six tables up front. Pool balls clicking off in the corner under the glow of that big ass Michelob lamp. Headlights passing to and fro in the dark out the window. Men leaning back against the brass rail of that raggedy bar, drinkin and talkin sideways at each other as they look at me on that stage. No doubt sayin things that would shock their wives and mothers.*

Place really held on to the sound, Pablo. Held the sound in its arms like it was a baby. Cradled it. Oh, I could rattle that room. Not saying I couldn't. I could shake it like a can of hot beer. I could blow the windows out into the street. You know I could. And I did too. But it's the slow, deep tunes I remember most at Mother's. *Like dropping into the ocean from the top of July. Make everybody heartsick. See all them heads shaking. People cryin. Make them all remember what they've lost. What they want from the world that the world won't give up. I'm not telling you anything you don't know.*

She flips. Flips. Flips. Reads.

My earliest memories are sitting on the floor of our little bitty house listening to the radio as Mama sewed. She said I always stopped my wailing when the music was on. So that meant it was on almost constantly. That's where I first heard the blues. Bessie Smith on the radio, fighting with the angry growl of that big black sewing machine. And Big Joe Turner and Big Mama Thornton. Billie. Ella. Odetta. Mississippi John. Blind Willie. Lightnin' Hopkins. Alberta Hunter. Victoria Spivey. All of the good ones, Pablo. They just came pouring out of that radio. Entertained me. Rocked me to sleep. Paid attention to me. Mama fed me; I'll give her that. She worked hard to feed me and keep me dry. But the blues mothered me, Pablo. Cared about me. Understood me. My real mama was the blues itself. Sounds silly. Sounds like I'm back doing that Billboard interview. But it's truer than anything I know.

She lets the pages fall together. Lays her head back. Listens to the coyotes remember. After awhile she rolls to one side. Holds the letter up. Reads.

She reads from the beginning this time. *Dear Pablo.*

Because she knows. Way down deep. Way down where we already know everything there is to know. Where we know everything that is and ever was and ever will be. She knows that the letter was not written to Pablo.

Knows it was written, from the beginning, to her.

Chapter 92

The server is well-inked. A delicate green vine curls up her left arm. It disappears beneath a short sleeve and reemerges on the side of her neck in a red bloom. She's barely twenty-one. Not old enough to judge anyone about anything. But she does it anyway.

"So let me get this straight." She squints her heavily made, racoonish eyes. Makes a skeptical appraisal of the entire booth, from Davis, to Lucela, to Buddy Lincoln, to Elvis Broussard. "Grand Opening. Friday night. Rainin' like I don't know what outside. And I'm puttin' in an order for two iced teas and two seltzer waters."

"And a plate of onion rings," says Buddy, concerned.

"*MmmHmm*. And a plate of onion rings." She juts out her hip. Holds the scowl for another second. "Well y'all *do* know how to party, I'm tellin' you what." Then she smiles, eyes flying, letting them all off the hook. "I'm just messin'. I'll be back in two shakes. Y'all sit tight."

She weaves away through a group of six just arriving and is gone.

"Well now I just feel old," says Elvis.

"Hey, now," booms Buddy. "Wait just a minute. I'm in for a long drive tonight. Iced tea is about as strong as it's gon' get for me." He points. "That leaves two alcoholics and a pregnant woman. Ain't no one at this table old. I'm *authentic*, damn it. Not old. I've a mind to beat her with my cane."

They all laugh. Even Davis, who is not in a particularly laughing mood.

He is inexplicably agitated. For as much as he has been looking forward to tonight, it has arrived without him. He is someplace else. Not a laughing place.

So he covers. Smiles. Laughs. Fakes his way through. And having to do that, tonight of all nights, irritates him. But not even Buddy Lincoln is the wiser.

When the drinks come it is Buddy who makes the first toast.

"To books, babies and the blues."

They reach, closing the circle. Clink. Drink.

"The blues always comes first," says Elvis. He looks with mock seriousness from Lucela to Davis and back again. "But what's comin' next, the baby or the book?"

Lucela laughs. Rests her hand on her only slightly protuberant belly. "I am not waiting for his book. He writes like he proposes: too slow! This baby will be in college before he is done."

Davis laughs likes he means it. Part of him does.

But another part feels that backward pull. The suction of history. There is something about that joking lament *–the book that is never done*. It comes back, hitting him all at once, like the scent of something baking, wafting through the open window of memory.

"Conrad, honey, that book must be about a million pages by now! When is it ever gon' be done?"

His father had laughed self-deprecatingly across the table as he reached over the ceramic blue whale planter, spouting its bright green sprigs of geranium, and spooned more casserole onto his plate. His mother had laughed at him laughing. And he, Davis, all of nine years old, had laughed too. In the background Pearl Baily was on the radio singing about Santa Clause. And everything had been okay. In that little bubble, rising for the surface light, everything had been wonderful.

Perfect.

The place around them is filling up. All kinds tonight. Boots and heels. Sneakers and flip-flops. Hats and umbrellas. They all come in dripping. Shaking off the weather. Mostly groups of two's and three's. A few solos, most of them at the long bar.

And then there is Miguel Rivera, who'd said he wasn't coming. He sits at a table in the back corner, nursing a Modelo. Waiting.

Davis has been here only once before, back when it was called *Papi's* and the floor was a black-and-white checkerboard. Back before they had gutted it all and started over. And yet, grand opening aside, there is nothing *new* about the place. Nothing scrubbed and antiseptic. Not the look or the feel or the smell. It's all old.

Not old. Authentic. Original.

He stands. Excuses himself to go over and acknowledge Miguel. It's an excuse. He just needs some room. Needs a reset.

"Invite him over," says Lucela.

"I will. But I suspect he's not lookin' for company tonight."

Lucela nods. Places her hand on the only hand he has left. Smiles.

"If you go outside? To smoke a cigarette? Davis? *Mi precioso esposo?* I will know about it."

He retreats, cringing comically as the rest of them laugh. Turns his back.

He charts a course to Miguel that takes him through the middle of the club.

He moves in an unchoreographed dance of avoidance, twisting shoulders to slip unnoticed between bodies, tracing tables, stepping over fallen umbrellas and around scraping chairs.

He stops in his tracks when he sees her. But for a half-eaten burger and something fizzy and pink with a straw, Celia Morales is alone.

He smiles a little, musing. They are here for the same reason, Celia and Miguel. They are alone, too, for the same reason. They are here because Olivia has invited them. They are alone because they have never been able to replace her. They are both still waiting for her to come back. To resume what she abandoned.

So they still don't know her.

He reconsiders. No, they know her all too well. They just don't care what it means to know her. Because we love who we love. Want what we want.

So he will let them wait, alone in a crowded club. He will allow the moment to be whatever it will be without unwanted small talk.

Across the club, just past the bar by the hallway to the restrooms, the side door is propped open to a curtain of silvery rain. He looks back at the booth.

Lucela and Elvis laughing over the plate of onion rings. Buddy on his phone.

Davis turns. Heads for the opening.

There is enough of an eave that he can stand without getting wet. He leans up against the building. Pats the shirt pocket for the cigarette he knows is there. Puts it in his mouth. Finds the lighter.

He tries four times. Nothing. A few sparks. The trace memory of butane. He grins. Shakes his head. *She got me again*, he thinks.

He puts the lighter back in his pocket. Makes a mental note to test for an actual flame before he goes out. Next time, he thinks. He feels his mood pushing away the fact that Lucela cares enough to sabotage his lighter. Pushing away that he likes it.

A kitchen worker edges past him with a bag of trash. He holds it over his head on his way into the parking lot to the dumpster, stepping over puddles of dimpled light. Davis watches. Waits for the man's return. Maybe *he* has a lighter that works. Maybe he's married to someone who doesn't give a shit about his lungs.

"Damn," says the man coming back, slicking water from his arms and face. "Almost drowned just takin' out the friggin' trash."

Davis gives him a commiserating laugh and nods.

Almost drowned. Like it is something that can be prevented. Something *to be* prevented. The phrase comes to him as a snippet of dialogue invented by his father. A police detective to a man once accused of murder.

"It took your own attempted suicide to put you in that lake. The only way you'd have ever found this whale. You had to almost drown."

Davis sees that the kitchen worker is not a man. Younger than Eladio. If he has a lighter at all, then it is in spite of his mother, not his wife.

He watches the kid dive back into the light and sound of *Mother Blues*. Puts the cigarette back in his shirt pocket. Feels the letter.

His mother. Still in his pocket. Papering his heart. Echoing endlessly in his head. Echoes repeating echoes. Not just sounds. Everything.

He looks out at the weather. Castles of water and light hang in the air, shaped by traffic and wind. On the far shore of the parking lot is a low brick building squatting beneath a lit rectangular sign on a tall black pole. *Flask's.* The cartoon wine bottle sports a Stetson and a broad smile. Two stick-arms, a left and a right, waving.

Taunting. *Look Ma, two hands.*

Davis pulls up his collar.

Steps out into the rain.

The book needs a title. He thinks maybe a title will help him finish.

It will bear her name, of course. *Dallas Letti Blue.* The only name people will recognize. But the rest of it, the part that represents the real Rosetta Letti, is still incomplete.

So many interviews. He'd started with the people who had shown up for the service. They had helped to find the others. Old forgotten friends. Doctors and lawyers. Club owners, chauffeurs, housekeepers, publicists, and retired record company executives. He had interviewed everyone from largely unknown musicians and back-up singers, to some of the greatest living blues musicians anyone could name. So many different stories coming together to account for a single person.

And yet, somehow, still falling pitifully short.

He had spent days with Pablo Brown, a goldmine of information about their relationship, the early years of Rosetta's career, and the Texas music scene in which it all happened.

Dixie Brill, too, had been able to provide valuable information about Rosetta's friendship with Ronni, their competition over Olivia's affections, and the Monte-Carlo-smoking devil in a dark suit they knew as Hammy Lewis.

He'd even tracked down Casey Zoot, who was halfway through a ten-year sentence for burglary in New Mexico. Casey remembered Rosetta as the love of his life, whom he claimed to have wrestled free from the clutches of her abusive husband, Otis DeLuna.

Casey's lies and embellishments were easy to spot. Anything romantic or heroic. It was only the dull sediment left in the bottom of the pan that interested Davis. Traveling up and down the gulf coast from one club to another. The way Rosetta attracted musicians. Captivated crowded barrooms. Tipped generously. Fought unfairly. Wrote songs as Casey drove them to the next gig.

The booze. The drugs.

And always Etta –Olivia –hating Casey Zoot. Hurting and brooding in the back seat.

He wishes he could have had more time with Rosetta. She had given him everything her strength permitted, even though she hated it. At the end it had taken Libby Holder sitting shoulder-to-shoulder with her on the sofa, patting her hand.

"C'mon now, baby. Can't be stoppin' in the middle of no story. You want fuck-all-day-face-no-kinda-priest to go home an' jus' make up some shit? 'Bout Letti Blue? Be like Tony Bennett singin' yo' songs. Fuckin' Neil Sedaka or some shit. Come on, Ms. Letti. Finish yo' story an' I put on a record an' then put you to bed."

Hours with Rosetta. Still. It wasn't enough. Not even close.

He'd spent more time with Olivia than anyone else. She'd hated the process of disclosure, of opening herself, even more than had her mother. Getting information out of Olivia had been much more difficult. And had taken a lot longer. He'd been able to approach Rosetta directly and she had told her story head-on. Like someone with no time left to lose. But Olivia still had lots of time left before feeling that kind of pressure. She had to be approached sideways. Lots of cigarettes and coffee and talking about anything *but* her mother.

So he was patient, knowing that all of Olivia's rivers would eventually lead back to that ocean.

Whether she liked it or not, Olivia had needed it. The opportunity to talk. To be heard. To let herself feel. The more she talked, the more she wanted to talk. They were not efficient discussions. Most of what she told him was not particularly useable in a biography about Rosetta Letti except as general background.

Still. It was all important.

Whenever he began to wonder whether his conversations with Olivia were actually worth his time, he thought of Rosetta up in the ark, talking to him in the darkness about the Cumberland River Flood of 1926. The night she had saved him from drowning in his own sad song. It seemed appropriate that after Rosetta's passing he should be sitting somewhere out in the desert with Olivia. Letting her talk for as long as it took.

It had not been a waste of his time. It had all made a difference. Gradually, Olivia had relaxed a little as the past grew weary of the attention and loosened its grip. However tentatively, Olivia seemed to be stepping into herself, as if inheriting a kind of birthright. He had sensed that she was slowly taking ownership. Her mother. Her father. Her astounding talent. Even her future, the nimbus of which was glowing on the horizon long before it arrived.

Most encouragingly, Olivia had gradually begun to disown the unwanted orphan in the mirror.

"Don't guess I've ever really been motherless," she had said one night as they passed a cigarette in Rosetta's garden. They were sitting in the dirt, backs against the wall, blowing smoke up at the rising desert moon. Libby had been inside baking muffins, singing along to Big Mama Thornton. They had retreated to the garden just to hear themselves talk. *"Not if I'm bein' fair about things."*
Then she had listed them. Counting them off on her fingers.
"Papi Brown. Ronni Brill. Celia Morales. Libby. Sheldon. Probably should throw Alice Kendricks and Judy Mills in there too, even though I hated them. They tried to foster me 'til they couldn't try any more. And I'll never count Maria Cross, but maybe Garvin. In his own twisted way. He took me in. Let me play a piano. Let me have the ark to myself. Tried to keep me safe. Hell, even Dallas after she found out about Ronni. She'd have stepped up if she thought I'd have let her. I didn't make it easy, I guess. Not on anyone."
"You did what you could," he'd said. *"Too hard on yourself."*
"Point is..."
Inside, Libby had let loose with an improvised, profanity-laden chorus to *Sometimes I have a Heartache*. Olivia had taken the cigarette and never finished the point.
But she didn't need to. He knew the point. Point was there had always been someone to claim her. Someone willing to step up and into that maternal role. Always someone watching and wanting. Caring. Whether she knew it or not.
It made him think of Ernesto and Marcela Rivera. Caring. Stepping forward. Not only for Miguel and then Eladio, but for so many others. He had remembered Marcela at the campfire, telling her version *La Llorona's* ghost.
"Once she died, La Llorona understood what she had done. What she had lost. Her guilt keeps her close. Her sadness keeps her close. She has not floated out to the great sea. She is here. Among us. She looks out after our children. Protects them. She uses the living. Whispers in our ears."
He had almost asked Olivia what she knew of the story of *La Llorona*. But Olivia had continued on her own. He dared not interrupt.
"When I hear someone like Etta James sing... Mahalia Jackson... Billie Holiday... Dallas... it's like..."
She had stopped, as if unable to find the right words. She'd passed him the cigarette. He had smoked. Waited.
"It's like this really complicated sound. Like hundreds or thousands of little, bitty different sounds packed into one sound. One voice. Like everything that ever happened to them, good and bad, every beating and every kiss and every baby and every dead body floating in the water, like each one of those feelings is in there as a separate sliver of a note. And when they open their mouths to the music... it's like it all comes out as one..." Her hands had searched in the air. *"One thing. One sound."*
He had mightily resisted metaphors borrowed from physics and nature. The

hidden wavelengths packed into a beam of visible light. The drops of water feeding tributaries that blend into rivers pushing for the sea.

He had kept quiet. Let her go.

"Makes me wonder sometimes what it would sound like if you took every voice... like, you know, every blues song ever sung by anyone, any time, anywhere... in a club, or in a record studio, or on a railroad chain gang, or out in the cotton fields," she had nodded backwards to Libby, *"or in the kitchen... and if you packed all of those voices into a single sound..."* her hands had gripped an invisible rope, twisting it tighter and tighter, *"just what that would sound like."*

"Hmm. Don't know," he had said, handing her the cigarette. *"What do you think that sounds like?"*

Olivia had continued to hold the invisible rope. Looked at him for a second. Then let her head rest back against the wall and she had looked up at the moon.

"A horn," she'd said finally. *"It'd sound like a horn."*

"A trumpet? Sax?"

"No."

Davis had turned and looked at her. Remembered the sound that had awakened him in the ditch. Nodded.

He has stopped trying to navigate the puddles. Stopped trying to stay dry. *"Ain't no way to go around the shit,"* Elvis liked to say. *"Got to go through it."* So he corrects his direction. Charts a straight course across the parking lot for the illusory shelter of the liquor store.

Illusory. Truth is that we're all drowned. Submerged in the same sea. Breathing the same cosmos. Everyone who is, and ever was, and ever will be. To see that –to *know* it, even if you don't understand it –is to see everything instantly. Everything. Instantly.

And somehow his mother had seen it. Felt it. Known it.

Going in after him. She had followed a mother's instinct. A grandmother's instinct. A great grandmother's instinct. A great, great, great grandmother's instinct. Endless. Radiating out in all directions. Permeating all dimensions. The mother of all motive forces. A mother's instinct to protect. To save.

And, somehow, that instinct had survived the body that did not survive. It had escaped in those last bubbles, out into the cosmos.

That maternal imperative to reach out. To connect.

To show the way.

He thinks of all the people still living after the festival who would not now exist except as scattered bits of bone and viscera. Thinks of all of the senseless death and misery radiating out, like a circular black wave, person to person, family to family, generation to generation, pushing out from the scorched epicenter of Corbin Town Square. All a certainty had his pain and guilt not exiled him to little Corbin Texas. Where nothing ever happens. Entire families reduced to stains on the backs of mangled folding chairs. Lucela obliterated. Olivia executed in the desert. Libby Holder burned into smoke in her home. Rosetta Letti, alone at the end with no one to know her story. Celia Morales, spiraling down into a bottle, drowning.

But none of that had happened.

A life of guilt and pain. A quarter of an arm.

And because of that, none of the rest had happened.

Flask's Liquors has its own eave. Davis presses his back against the dirty brick wall. Slicks the water off his face and head, just as the kitchen worker had done. *Damn. Almost drowned.* He looks back across the asphalt sea at *Mother Blues*, it's light and sound now in the shape of a distant, yellow rectangle.

A portal. Happiness.

Is he happy?

Yes. Yes he is happy. Lucela. The coming baby. The coming book. The calling to write many more books. Friends, so many of them now, who will do almost anything to keep him from falling.

Of course he is happy. Of course.

But at times like tonight the happiness can feel inconsequential. It floats him like a tiny boat upon the surface of something infinitely vast. Infinitely deep. It keeps him tucked inside an illusion. Safe. Dry. Insulated from a cosmic ocean that dissolves all boundaries, all differences, except those he chooses to imagine.

Happiness. Sadness. Triumph. Abandonment. Solitude. Success. Ruin.

We are a species of boat builders. Sailors one and all.

He thinks of the ark. Still sitting out there in the desert. He has long since cleared away every broken board and shard of glass and ceiling tile that had once been a church and a home and a school and a prison of pain. He had taken his time. Removing pieces of the whole, one by one. Artifacts in need of understanding. Elemental bits stamped with meaning, like Abby's bag of Runes, laid out on a table to be read.

And one-by-one he had tossed them into the back of Rosetta Letti's truck and made trip after trip to the dump until it was all gone. He had kept that much of his promise to Rosetta.

But the ark is still out there. Off it's foundation. Leaning dangerously.

A promise unkept.

He will get to it eventually.

He doesn't care which bottle. Doesn't really matter. He slides back the cooler door. Grabs the *Melville's* Forty-Ounce Malt Reserve. Walks up the aisle toward the counter, his only hand clutched around the cold, thick amber neck of the thing.

Friday night at the liquor store.

He waits in line behind a woman and three others in front of her. She's holding a six-pack in one hand and a bottle of wine in the other. Her purse keeps slipping off her shoulder. She keeps hiking it back up.

On her wrist is a wide copper bracelet.

It never takes much to bring Abby back to him. Doesn't have to be copper. Or a British accent. A Ferris wheel will do it every time. The smell of jasmine incense. Or that slapping sound a screen door makes when it closes behind you. Candles. Trailers with antennae.

Did his mother pick her? Abby. And if so, why?

Was it because Abby heard voices? Because she was rapidly losing the ability to screen out the frequencies —the voices —that would break any human mind? Was it because Abby's fractured consciousness had offered Elizabeth a way in?

"Can you hear that?"

"What?"

"In your mind. That voice."

"What voice, Abby?"

"More like a feeling. A feeling you can hear. Or a sound you can feel."

"No, Abby. I can't."

"It takes practice. You have to tune your mind, Davis. Find the frequency."

The cashier glances up once, and not again. Davis slides cash over the counter. Doesn't wait for change or a bag. Heads for the exit.

The bottle is under his partial arm. He is unscrewing the cap before the door closes behind him. He walks out into the airborne sea, water sluicing out of the dark from every direction. As though it comes not from some black cumulus over his head but through the invisible fissures, cracks in the hull, trillions of cracks per square millimeter of space, connecting this dimension with every other dimension.

"Elizabeth believed that the barrier between life and death is... porous. That was the word she always used. Porous."

Davis holds the bottle up. Closes his eyes to the rain. Offers a toast to all of the things we cannot understand.

Turns it upside down.

It sounds like drinking, that soft glugging. The sound of swallowing.

He does not open his eyes until the bottle is empty. Light in his hand. Harmless. He turns back towards the building to find a trashcan. Stops.

"Another test." Lucela is dripping wet. She wipes her face.

Davis nods. Considers the bottle. Holds it with two fingers.

"Been comin' on all day. The club is harder than I thought it'd be."

"It's not the club," she says. "You don't have to hide it. I know what day it is."

Davis stares down at the puddle at his feet. Rain with a sheen of malt liquor.

"Tired of this anniversary," he says.

Just the rain. The hissing of light traffic in a sweep of headlights.

"Did you ever stop to think, though, that we'd never have met? That our child would not exist? That *I* would not exist right now? My mother? All of those people..."

"Yeah," he says. "All the time. I wonder sometimes if..."

"If what?"

He looks away. Shakes his head.

"Davis."

"Nothing."

"You wonder if somehow she was... steering you. Leaving breadcrumbs. Talking to you."

Davis stirs the puddle with his shoe. Laughs.

"You married *un loco*."

"*Quizás*. But then I am just as *loco*, Davis."

"Your grandmother," he says.

"*Sí. Mi abuela*. Always. She has never left me. *Y cuando mi madre muere...*" She breaks off. Like she can't finish. Then she does. "When my mother passes, she will not stop being my mother. She will speak to me in ways I can hear."

Davis sighs. Looks at his wife. "Sorry for bringing you out here."

Lucela shrugs. Nods at his one hand clutching the neck of the bottle like something dead. "Least you passed the test."

He walks to the trashcan.

"Like Elvis always says. Ain't no running away from this beast. Got to turn and punch the fucker in the face."

He stuffs the bottle down into the hole. Turns back to her.

"Every time I can destroy myself and choose not to? I show who's boss."

Lucela musters the smile he loves. Holds out a hand.

"*Te amo*," she says.

Davis places his only hand on her belly. Imagines the child on the other side –his child, Elizabeth's grandchild, Conrad's grandchild –feeling the pressure of his hand. Feeling his pulse. Hearing his voice. He looks at Lucela.

"*Yo también te amo.*"

They are too wet now to rejoin the others. They stand inside the hallway door, Lucela leaning into his chest, pulling his good arm over and around her. The lights are low now. A single spot. Like moonlight.

And there she stands.

Wet with deep blue sequins. Like she has emerged from some secret sea, reflecting the light back in a million small drops.

She sees them in the doorway. Pauses in mid-sentence. Looks at Davis.

He can see she is uncertain. Nervous. Maybe it's all the people. The scars. The leg. The moment. Whatever the reason, it's not easy.

Davis inclines his chin to acknowledge the look. Raises his three-quarters arm. Saluting in solidarity.

Olivia smiles a little. Turns away. Continues.

They lower themselves. Lucela takes the chair that is propping open the door. Davis stretches his legs out across the pavement. He leans back against the building.

The sky pulses with shocks of yellow light. Once. Twice. The rain finds fresh force. Like the heavens have tilted. Davis closes his eyes.

Piano. Slow, sparing, from the shadows. Posing a question.

A string bass. Deep, sonorous, resonant. In timid response.

A voice full of voices.

She fills the room. Vibration not felt for many years. Vibration into the old walls. Into the old floorboards. Down into the old joists and pilings.

The place soaks it up. It remembers. Like we all do. Like the desert, that old abandoned seabed, takes the rain as a memory of itself.

The heavens tilt. She lets it all out. Sings.

Mother.
Mother Ocean.
Your sorrow
Soooo deep.
All your children,
Your children still sailing
A-way.

Down in green coffers
Such mem'ries you keep
Are you sorry?
Are you sorry?
I say are you sorry
'Cause you left them
That day?

Mothers.
Oh, Blue Mothers.
My sorrow

Soooo deep.
Oh my mothers,
These blues I'm still singing
To-day.

Down in blue mem'ries
Your oceans I keep
I'm so sorry
I'm so sorry
I say Mama, I'm so sorry
Oh, it's to your blues
That I pray.

Acknowledgements

"Any similarity to real persons, living or dead, is coincidental and not intended by the author." It is a time tested disclaimer intended to ward off hurt feelings and litigation. It sits right up in front to remind the reader before the very first word that this is a journey populated with fictional characters. Fictional events. Nothing real.

Which is all well and good except that any fictional journey unwinds upon the topography of real experience. The blank sheet on which all fiction is written is a bed sheet draped over a body. Or a family. Or a city. All fiction is inevitably inspired by real people struggling to stay alive and make sense of it all as they orbit the sun a few times. It all ultimately comes from something *real*. Presumably readers understand that the beating heart of all fiction is true experience, however derivative. Woe unto the fiction writer who does not understand that what we do is less pure creation than it is literary processing and poetical interpretation of real people experiencing real events. For failing to acknowledge the body under the bed sheet would obscure the importance of giving thanks to those actual people without whose experience and struggle any literary processing and poetical interpretation would not have been possible.

So. There are hurricanes and then there are hurricanes. Like Katrina and Sandy before him, and like Irma right on his heels, and Maria after her, Hurricane Harvey was a real thing. Dozens died. Thousands upon thousands lost everything. It is relatively easy to tally up the various numerical statistics. Lives. Homes. Dollars. But the weight of human suffering that accompanies such events is immeasurable. Though Houston is still waterlogged and the flood is still sloshing around as I type these acknowledgements, *Mother Blues* is not about Hurricane Harvey any more than it is about the Cumberland River Flood of 1926. But those natural cataclysms, and others like them, are certainly there in the background. Davis Payne, Dallas Letti, Libby Holder, Mable Holder, and Antoine Beaudraine Cherish, fictional though they may be, all derive to some extent from the very real suffering and displacement caused by such real events.

In a novel that explores mothers and children and the imagined maternal orientation of the universe, "Mother Nature" is here a character in her own right. There is no writing a novel set in modern day Texas without some heartfelt acknowledgement of Harvey's enduring, soggy thumbprint.

If I am to acknowledge the reality that lurks behind the fictional, then I should also give some mention to the aptly named Wolves. Well. *Wolfs* –Victor and Natalia Wolf –if those are their real names. You may recognize them if you have spent any time looking at Post Office bulletin boards. The FBI believes Victor and Natalia are German citizens with ties to Russia where, having fled this country in 2006, they are believed to be hiding. In 2004 the Wolfs moved into Sunny Isles Beach in Miami, a place reputed to be a favorite for Russian organized crime and affectionately called *Little Moscow*. The Wolfs started a real estate development company called *Sky Development* to market a swath of rural land in central Florida called *Citrus Springs*. They started a multitude of other companies to help in the effort, including an unregistered and unlicensed title company to close the land deals.

You can guess the rest. Eager investors, many of them Russian nationals, lined up to buy cheap land ripe for aggressive flipping, never knowing that they would, in many cases, be reselling the property to phony purchasers: Wolfs in sheep's clothing. Many others paid a lot of good money for new houses that the Wolf's phony construction companies never had any intention of building, on property never to be turned over, memorialized in phony deeds never to be recorded.

The Wolfs, reportedly, knew how to talk a good game, preaching a gospel of easy money and finding opportunities to flash expensive jewelry, show up to their investment seminars in gleaming new cars, and to tell stories of traveling the world on their private jet. They even threw investor yacht parties. To these bedazzled audiences the Wolfs painted a picture of *Citrus Springs* as a thriving community where soon everyone in and outside of Florida would want to live. Invest early and retire early; that was the message. Victor and Natalia sold the same properties –land they insisted was ideal for grocery stores and schools and quality neighborhoods –over and over and over again to different, but equally clueless investors. They sold land to themselves, to dead people, and to made-up people that never existed in the first place. Lot values skyrocketed. Eventually, after raking in between 50-70 million dollars in just twenty-four months of effort –and without a single new road or house to show for it –the Wolfs vanished. Natalia absconded to Germany with her daughter. Victor was later spotted in Moscow. No telling where they are now. Go to school on the seller and the realtor before you buy your next home. Start at the Post Office.

Sad as it is, that should be the end of the story. But long after the Wolfs escaped, federal authorities learned that they had been working a similar, and larger, scam in Texas. They set up a new company in a new location: *Sky Group of Texas,* perched up inside a sleek glass Aventura high-rise office building. The office was empty, of course, and the phones did not work, but that was not among the information given to frothing investors. The people invited to the yacht parties and to the make-a-quick-fortune seminars were much more interested in the correspondence Victor and Natalia waved around *proving* that high-end retailers like *Saks Fifth Avenue* and *Neiman Marcus* were buying in. *The Sky Group of Texas* was going to build a new and beautiful city: *Sky Station.* Thousands of buildable lots. Man-made lakes. Walking trails through new trees. Hundreds of stores, eating establishments and hotels. *Gucci, Cartier* and *Macy's,* all coming. Everyone wanted in on the ground floor. Dozens of investors. Eight separate lenders, including five banks. Government lenders pledged tens of millions of dollars in utilities. *Sky Station* was the next big thing in a state that always thinks big. Except that the whole thing was a scam. Tens of millions of dollars invested for not a single shovel full of dirt.

I owe my limited understanding of these affairs to some helpful reporting by Michael Sallah of the *Miami Herald* and Catherine Shoichet of the *Tampa Bay Times.* The fictional scheme I have cooked up for *Mother Blues* and placed in the hands of Vasily Dudnik was certainly more ambitious than anything the Wolfs were able to pull off, but the difference is intended to be only one of degree, not a difference in kind. True, Victor and Natalia Wolf are not known to have ever plotted mass murder. Perhaps I should be concerned that confusion between the real and the fictional will injure their reputations. I shall bear the risk.

It may also be important for you to know that there actually was once a nightclub called *Mother Blues* located on Lemmon Avenue in Dallas, Texas. Don't go looking; you will now find only a car wash and a strip mall. *Mother Blues* had a great run through the Seventies and early Eighties, home to some of the biggest music acts in rock-n-roll history. Springsteen. Zepplin. Steve Miller. Boz Skaggs. Jimmy Buffet. The Fabulous Thunderbirds. Freddy King. It is not an overstatement to call *Mother Blues* the wildest and most popular music club of its time in Dallas if not the entire state of Texas. Eventually its founders met their various ends or drifted off. The building was demolished in favor of clean cars and bored teenagers.

But here is the important bit: the little *Mother Blues* club imagined for the book in your hand has absolutely no connection with the *Mother Blues* club that has actually earned its place in music and nightclub history. I tripped over that particular bit of history in a *Google* search near the end of my first draft of this book. Having decided on a title, I was curious whether a novel called *Mother Blues* would encounter any significant confusion. A May 2012 article for *Buddy Magazine* by Kirby F. Warnock entitled *"The Original House of Blues"* provided my first exposure to the once real nightclub. I might have taken the discovery with a dose of chagrin, changed the title of the book and the name of my imagined club, and resolved to next time conduct more Internet research *before* I start writing. Instead I took the coincidence of a real Texas nightclub called *Mother Blues* as nothing short of divine confirmation that I had chosen the right name and written the right book. This is an enormously convenient form of self-justification that comes easily to writers of fiction and that more people really should try. In any event, whatever you think of what you have just read, there is no point in blaming the old *Mother Blues* gang on Lemmon Avenue. They had nothing to do with any of this.

A list of real songs sung or remembered by the fictional characters in this book, along with the chapters in which they appear, and the names of the performers and songwriters, is set forth in a table following this acknowledgement. Of course, that kind of hat tipping is not even remotely sufficient. But how does one even begin to do justice to the influence that an entire musical genre has had on any creative work, let along the miserable and triumphant richness of the generations of life experience from which that musical genre has grown and evolved? One doesn't. The individual contributions of those who created and propagated this distinctly American art form are mountains that cannot be scaled. Or, at least, not by me. The organizing focus of this novel has been skewed toward the voice of women blues artists, but only because it suited these particular characters. It is certainly not my intention to slight any of the men. The entire constellation of blues genres and subgenres has come from countless artists, both genders, young and old, of all races, all interpreting, musically and poetically, real life in all of its darkness and aspiration.

Singling out a handful of blues contributors –even the undisputed greats – seems a silly exercise. That noted, never being one to shy away from silly exercises, I am grateful beyond measure, specifically for purposes of this book, to Bessie Smith, Ma Rainey, Memphis Minnie, Billie Holiday, Victoria Spivey, Mahalia Jackson, Big Mama Thornton, Sister Rosetta Tharp, Beth Rowland, B.B. King, Bonnie Raitt, Robert Johnson, Big Maybelle, Blind Willie Johnson, Nina Simone, Ruth Brown ... I cannot continue. I have changed my mind. It is too ridiculous and a silly an exercise, even for me. For those interested in reading about transformational women blues artists, I can recommend *Lady Sings the Blues*, by Billie Holiday; *Black Pearls: Blues Queens of the 1920's*, by Daphne Duvall Harrison; and *Blues Legacies and Black Feminism,* by Angela Davis. These books proved enormously helpful to me in getting inside many of my characters and understanding better what frightens them, angers them, and what gets them up in the morning.

It should go without saying that there is no substitute for listening to these artists, or for audibly tracing the evolution of a blues standard like *Nobody's Fault but Mine* from its origins in 1927 by Blind Willie Johnson through many dozens of different covers over the decades (including by artists as diverse as Rosetta

Tharp, Van Morrison, The Grateful Dead, and Willie Nelson) to a young, modern blues talent like Beth Rowland, who for my money now all but owns that song. This is not to mention *God Bless the Child* and *Ain't Nobody's Business If I Do* and so many others now so thoroughly woven into the fabric of Americana that they have become a kind of cultural oxygen or a grounding memory that helps us define ourselves. There are innumerable collections of foundational blues music that are easy to find, each offering but a teaspoon of the ocean. There are far too many to fairly recommend just a couple. You are on your own.

I will not be the one to leave Herman Melville off a list of acknowledgements. I join the legions of writers and scholastic test-takers who, since 1851, have plundered *Moby Dick* for the treasure of serviceable metaphor and transcendent meaning. Melville's ghost is certainly keeping a list of writers and test-takers he intends to harpoon. I am now likely also on that list.

And yet how does one pass up the opportunity to read into Captain Ahab's railing against the White Whale as an unknowable presence motivated by an inscrutable malice. "*That inscrutable thing,*" inveighs Ahab, "*is chiefly what I hate; and be the white whale agent, or be the white whale principal, I will wreak that hate upon him.*" Ahab and almost all who follow him pay the price for such slavish devotion to this gospel of hate and vengeance, as if there was to be some divine reckoning for following the wrong path in interpreting the unknowable. Ahab's ethic is a kind of idolatry when you really think about it. One might recall the brief conversation in Chapter 19 of *Moby Dick* between Ishmael, Queequeg and a shabbily dressed stranger named Elijah. Elijah warns the sailors against following a captain like Ahab, suggesting in a darkly ironic sort of way that a voyage aboard the *Pequod* under Ahab's direction would go just fine as long as they did not care about their own souls.

It is not such a big step, then, from Melville's literary wharf to the ancient Israeli desert in the Bible's *Book of Kings* where we meet another Elijah, a prophet living under the angry iron rule of none other than *King* Ahab. King Ahab, married to Queen Jezebel, took to worshipping the false idol Baal, forsaking the God of the Israelites. Just as Elijah of the wharf prophesied doom for those who follow *Captain* Ahab on a mission of vengeance, Elijah of the desert warns *King* Ahab that he is doomed unless he follows the one true God. No one in literature, alas, ever listens to Elijah. And there is always a price to be paid: drought and pestilence in the desert, demon albino whales in the oceans. Terrible.

I will leave it to readers to decide what cosmic presence ended up exploiting the conflict between the forces of Elijah and the forces of Baal that increasingly raged in poor Imogen Dory's (Abby Palmer's) afflicted brain as she grew into middle adulthood. But something or someone sure took advantage of the chaos, harnessing those voices for a purpose. I have tried to imagine, here, that there is a non-deific, maternally oriented sensibility to the Universe and to existence. I would like to believe in Tallulah's *Motherverse*. Wouldn't it be great, if nothing else, if we could cultivate such a sensibility among the living? But, and this is really the salient point, I can only imagine the look on Herman Melville's face upon learning that I have harnessed his characters to help me make that entirely fictional case. He has both my admiration and my apology. I await the harpoon in all due humility.

Finally, while I am acknowledging the contributions of real people, I also feel strangely obliged to recall a presumably true story I read many years ago involving a newspaper that had inadvertently inserted the wrong names into the wrong articles. People were upset, reputations called into question, retractions (no doubt too small and too late) printed. I no longer remember the newspaper or the particulars of the fallout, but the idea lodged in my brain as an interesting plot device: what happens when the guy who pulls a woman from a burning car and the guy who gets busted for solicitation each show up in the other guy's newspaper coverage? Small town mayhem and life-changing revelation is what happens. Obviously. And now here, years later, all for the sake of entertainment fiction, I have shamelessly traded on the embarrassment and grievous inconvenience experienced by real people victimized by sloppy editing.

So, lest such newsprint victims be made to suffer the additional indignity of being exploited for entertainment without any acknowledgment, allow me to close with this heartfelt sentiment: *Thanks guys.*

Song List

Following is a list of songs referenced or alluded to in this book, along with the names of the song writers and the artist whose version or performance of the song was intended to be represented.

Chapter	Song	Artist	Song Writer(s)
5	*Ball and Chain*	Big Mama Thornton	Big Mama Thornton
8	*Sometimes I Have a Heartache*	Big Mama Thornton with Muddy Waters	Big Mama Thornton
18	*Foolish Man Blues*	Bessie Smith	Bessie Smith
18, 43	*Devil's Gonna Git You*	Bessie Smith	Bessie Smith
22	*Didn't It Rain*	Rosetta Tharp	Unknown
33	*Careless Love*	Bessie Smith	Unknown
37, 69	*T'aint Nobody's Business if I Do*	Bessie Smith	Porter Grainger Everett Robbins
41	*I Got to Make a Change Blues*	Memphis Minnie	Memphis Minnie
43	*Moan, You Moaners*	Bessie Smith	Spencer Williams
44	*Yonder Comes the Blues*	Ma Rainey	Ma Rainey
45, 58	*New Bumble Bee*	Memphis Minnie	Memphis Minnie
47	*Mama's Gone, Goodbye*	Sippie Wallace	Sippie Wallace
47, 72	*Backwater Blues*	Bessie Smith	Bessie Smith

50	*There'll Be Some Changes Made*	Ethel Waters	Benton Overstreet
			Billy Higgins
55	*Don't Trust Nobody Blues*	Victoria Spivey	Victoria Spivey
55	*Nobody Loves Me But My Mother*	B.B. King	Riley King
55	*Louise*	Bonnie Raitt	Paul Siebel
56	*Bleeding Hearted Blues*	Bessie Smith	Cora Lovie Austin
56	*Me and the Devil Blues*	Robert Johnson	Robert Johnson
59	*I Wished on the Moon*		Dorothy Parker
			Ralph Rainger
63	*My Rifle, My Pony and Me*	Rickie Nelson	Paul Francis Webster
		Dean Martin	Dimitri Tiomkine
65	*I'm Gonna Bake my Biscuits*	Memphis Minnie	Memphis Minnie
69	*Lost Your Head Blues*	Bessie Smith	Bessie Smith
69	*Nobody's Fault But Mine*	Beth Rowley	Blind Willie Johnson
69	*Revolution*	Nina Simone	Weldon Irvine
			Nina Simone
72	*Down by the Riverside*	Rosetta Tharp	Unknown
72	*Lost Your Head Blues*	Bessie Smith	Bessie Smith
72	*Blue Spirit Blues*	Bessie Smith	Spencer Williams
73	*Misty Blue*	Dorothy Moore	Bob Montgomery
		Etta James	
73	*Young Woman's Blues*	Bessie Smith	Bessie Smith
74	*Gloomy Monday*	Billie Holiday	Angi Marian
			Lloyd Leweery
78	*Between the Devil and the Deep Blue Sea*	Ella Fitzgerald	Harold Arlen
			Ted Koehler
78	*Lucky Old Sun*	Ray Charles	Louis Armstrong
		Aretha Franklin	
78	*Rain is a Bringdown*	Ruth Brown	Ruth Brown

79	*Royal Garden Blues*	Bessie Smith	Clarence Williams
			Spencer Williams
80	*Luna Lunera (Whimsical Moon)*	Eydie Gorme with Los Panchos	Unknown
82	*Whoa, Tillie, Take Your Time*	Bessie Smith	Turner Layton
			Henry Creamer
82	*I'm Gonna Bake my Biscuits*	Memphis Minnie	Memphis Minnie
88	*God Bless the Child*	Billie Holiday	Billie Holiday
			Arthur Herzog, Jr.
90	*Ramblin' Blues*	Big Maybelle	Unknown

For Your Consideration

Independent writers and publishers, deprived of the reach and resources of their gold-plated, establishment relations (by a difference that requires astronomical telescopes and laser technology to calculate), live and die by the reviews of their readers, or the lack of such reviews. The same astronomical tools and laser technology is necessary to measure the depth of gratitude the author feels for those who, having now finished this novel, are willing to leave a review on Amazon to either encourage other readers or warn them away. It takes just a moment and you will have made a tremendous, even if incremental, difference in the lives of those who read independently published books and those who write them. Also, Heaven. You'll go to Heaven. Eventually. Thank you.

Reviews at: https://amzn.to/3BnwDhe

Visit Owen Thomas at his author website for information on upcoming books, photos, videos, excerpts, interviews, purchase links and to register for updates: www.OwenThomasLiterary.com.

About the Author

Owen Thomas is a life-long Alaskan living on Maui because life is too short for long winters. He has written six books: *The Lion Trees* (which has garnered over sixteen international book awards, including the American Writing Awards, the Amazon Kindle Book Award, the Eric Hoffer Book Award, the Book and Author Book of the Year, the Beverly Hills International Book Award and, most recently, a finalist in the Book Excellence Awards); *Mother Blues*, (a novel of music and mystery set in post-Hurricane Harvey Texas, Finalist for the American Writing Awards and the Book Excellence Fiction Award, and collecting a Bronze in the Readers Views Reviewers' Choice Awards); *Message in a Bullet: A Raymond Mackey Mystery*, (the first in a series of detective novels, shortlisted for the Best Mystery Book of the Year by Forward INDIES Book of the Year Awards and collecting a Silver from the eLit Book Awards); *The Russian Doll: A Raymond Mackey Mystery* (the second book in that series); *Signs of Passing* (a book of interconnected short stories and novellas, and winner of fourteen book awards, including the 2014 Pacific Book Awards for Short Fiction, the Indie Reader Discovery Award, the Great Southwest Book Festival, has garnered placements at the Paris, London and Los Angeles Book Festivals and was also named one of the 100 Most Notable Books of 2015 by Shelf Unbound Magazine); and *This is the Dream*, (a collection of stories and novellas that explore that perplexing liminal distance between who we are and what we want; Finalist for the American Writing Awards and the International Book Award in short fiction, and collecting a Bronze in the Readers Views Reviewers' Choice Awards). Owen maintains an active fiction and photography blog on Facebook, Tumblr and on his author website at www.owenthomasliterary.com.

www.ingramcontent.com/pod-product-compliance
Lightning Source LLC
Chambersburg PA
CBHW050116030726
47505CB00007B/1896